Sexton Blake, Detective

With an introduction by Michael Moorcock

Edited by George Mann

© IPC Media
Introduction © Michael Moorcock

First edition

Proudly published in 2009 by
Snowbooks Ltd.
120 Pentonville Road
London
N1 9JN
www.snowbooks.com

ISBN: 978-1-906727-413

Jacket art incorporates originals by Eric Parker
A catalogue record for this book is available from the British Library.

Please visit www.sextonblake.co.uk
the most complete repository of Sexton Blake material on the internet

Printed and bound in the UK by J F Print Ltd, Sparkford, Somerset.

Contents

DEDICATION

To Mark Hodder, for keeping the spirit of Sexton Blake alive

Publisher's Note

These stories are very much products of their time and as such do occasionally reflect views and opinions that are no longer considered acceptable. As far as possible we have refrained from altering the original text of the stories to better preserve the historical nature of the work. However, in a small number of instances we have felt it necessary to change or remove words that readers may find particularly offensive.

Acknowledgements

Thanks must be extended to the many people who helped me to lay my hands on the increasingly rare stories that appear in this anthology, as well as the many others that I also read as I whittled down the contents list: Stan Donoghue, Henk Hopman, Michael Moorcock and the incomparable Mark Hodder. This book would not exist without you.

SEXTON BLAKE, DETECTIVE

By Michael Moorcock

'DOES SEXTON BLAKE EXIST? Almost every day I receive letters from my chums asking me this question. It serves to show the great enthusiasm which the great detective has aroused in the minds of the readers of our new serial, "Sexton Blake in the Congo," as well as of our weekly complete novels which appear in "The Union Jack." Well, then, the great detective does exist, and very much so, as members of the criminal profession know to their cost. He is occasionally to be seen in his office, the whereabouts of which I am not permitted to disclose, other than to say that it is situated less than five miles from Charing Cross. Another thing I am not permitted to state is his name, for obvious reasons, he does not practice professionally under the name of Sexton Blake.'

THE BOYS' FRIEND · New series · Vol. 6 Issue 301 · 12/3/1907

SEXTON BLAKE STILL exists, of course. In fact, it's impossible for him to die from natural causes, as readers will discover, if not from this collection, then from the next book of Blake stories, written by George Mann, Mark Hodder and myself, which hopes to offer readers a few more cases pinched from the famous Index and given a touch of extra melodrama. He and several of his contemporaries, among them Tinker, Inspector Coutts, Mrs Bardell and Pedro the Bloodhound, are as incapable of fading away as the likes of Biggles, Just William, Tarzan, Nancy Drew or Doctor Who. Blake's longevity is considerably greater than Bond's, though there are people I know who can prove conclusively from the records that not only is Bond merely Blake with a few minor details changed but that Blake is evidently a direct descendant of Sir Percy Blakeney (otherwise the infamous 'Scarlet Pimpernel') as Wold Newton followers will know. Moreover, there's plenty of evidence that since the 1970s and in spite of his disrespectful 'resurrection' via recent wireless broadcasts Blake has been living quietly in legal wedlock with a well-known retired adventuress whose feelings for him were often hinted at in the fictional versions of his adventures, also culled from the Index, which appeared in a host of publications including, of course, *The Union Jack* and *Sexton Blake Library* which ran most of the stories collected here. How his editors have presented him and the way in which his chroniclers depicted him has depended as much on his anticipated audience as the fashion of his day. George Mann has done a superb job in showing how Blake matured, in fiction at least, over the years.

The first writer to be commissioned to write Blake's memoirs, once Amalgamated Press had secured the rights to publish his adventures in fictional form, was Harry Blythe. Blythe received nine guineas for his trouble but my guess is that his work was found unsatisfactory by the real 'Blake' (who had received a considerable fee and signed a complicated contract with AP) and it would take a while before a good team of writers was assembled who could be relied upon to present him as something at least close to the truth, even if the long, boring aspects of detective work were often cut out in favour of an unlikely piece of action.

This early history can be read either online on Mark Hodder's Blakiana website (www.sextonblake.co.uk) or in the previous compilation published by Wordsworth (2009). On the website you will not only find information about all the main characters and authors but there is even a layout of Blake's house.

As well as the pleasure of reading these stories, many of which are superior to better known thrillers of their day, we also have our curiosity satisfied about the earliest years of popular modernism. Editors', authors' and readers' tastes were all reflected in those stories which help act as a barometer of the tastes, attitudes and popular feelings through the British Empire from the late 19th century to the late 20th and into our present period. They offer a flavour of the times and form a record of how public attitudes changed quite radically in some ways and scarcely changed at all in others and especially how attitudes of writers and public alike were transformed on many levels as the idea of Empire faded into the idea of Commonwealth and we became a very different people.

George Orwell predicted that everyone who grew up reading the 'story papers' would be a ripe candidate for fascism. As it happened, I was one of those candidates (perhaps a little later than most) and, while they might have called me a woolly-minded liberal (because I supported the Race Relations Act) or a pie-in-the-sky idealist because I like being a European, nobody has yet to accuse me of being a ranting member of the BNP. It's always hard to know what to do with the language one finds in popular fiction republished for the pleasure of the reader. It's true the language in some of those early Blakes makes them subject to modern editing without losing the flavour of the stories. To leave such language out altogether would be to give a distorted view of how Blake stories reflected their era. Popular fiction offers an unselfconscious record of public tastes and when it disappears, the barometer itself is lost

That through the 1890s and early 1900s the editorial staff of Amalgamated Press (now IPC) took quite a long time to decide how to present Blake and to what kind of public is evident from the early stories reprinted here. George Mann has done a superb job in selecting work which is not only a good reflection of what was being published but which was good in its own right. All so-called pulp fiction suffers from the speed at which it is written. You will sometimes find repeated words in sentences; slightly contradictory statements being made; a tendency to finish the plot in haste at breakneck speed. Yet pulp fiction's very rate of production, the work of editors and writers able to think (and write) literally on their feet is what gives it enduring vitality and remains an inspiration to those of us who believe that fiction should not only take chances and catch the mood of its time, it should also never be frightened of seeming (or indeed being) vulgar. Vulgarity is inclined to endure, especially when there are other sturdy elements in the mix. That is why we continue to find the adventures of Sexton Blake entertaining, invigorating and, I have to say it,

educational to those of us who want an insight into the popular thinking of the past.

In those years before AP were sure where to aim their Blake stories we saw him go from one of the many stiff-collared detecting gents aimed at audiences hungry for more Holmes-like cases and presented as they might appear in such respectable magazines as *The Strand*, *Pearson's* or *The London*, bought very much for fiction by the likes of Arthur Morrison, Baroness Orczy, Joseph Conrad, H.G.Wells, G.K.Chesterton or Jack London, accompanied by solid wash drawings of the protagonists. In Blake's case, his clash with the evil Marston Hume, first of his enemies with a notable personality, by the excellent and mysterious Michael Storm, were amongst the earliest to be presented in this way, but clearly he was found to be popular with the boys who bought the massive bedsheet size weeklies AP published, including *Boys Herald*, *Boys Realm* and *Boys Friend*, which ran long serials containing most of the hallmarks of the boys adventure fiction of the day, including a great deal of jocular badinage and slapstick between characters (much of it borrowed from Talbot Baines Reed, Kipling's Stalky stories and Wodehouse's Wrykyn tales) and a set of recurring stereotypes, such as brave captains of the cricket team, fat boys, evil bullies and various members of racial minorities who usually turned out to be 'white through and through' at the end of their story. Tinker, Blake's young assistant, frequently found himself at these schools in the early days as did poor Nipper, assistant to Nelson Lee (Blake's closest successful clone), who found himself and his boss pretty much permanently at St Frank's, Greyfriars' closest rival, written by perhaps the greatest survivor of the pre-war Blake era, Edwy Searles Brooks, whose revamped Blakes (with Waldo the Wonderman transformed into Norman Conquest) were still appearing in hardcover into the 1960s.

Authors who turned out probably as many school stories as Blake adventures were William Murray Graydon and Cecil Hayter. They belonged to what was essentially a different age. There is something deliciously crazed about their stories if you can get over the racialism. Hayter's Africa is populated by alligators, emus and the fauna and flora of at least two continents. There's a surreal atmosphere to his landscapes, while his 'natives' appear to come from similar territory.

I'm sure I'm not the first to note that the Inari, whose treasure is sought in the story reprinted here[1], seem to have a lot more in common with a lost tribe of Incas than Lobangu's Zulus.

After *Union Jack* became 'Sexton Blake's Own Paper' the juvenile aspects of the stories gradually disappeared, although a few of the characters who had hung over from the early days with cut-price copies of the likes of Quartermain and Umslopogaas (Losely and Lobangu) continued to stay on in somewhat more sophisticated versions. Andrew Murray's Hon. John Lawless[2] (the spelling changed after the first few stories) was one of the best of a long line of gentleman crooks/adventurers to pit their wits against Blake. Hornung's cricketing cracksman Raffles, taken over by Barry Perowne, would be one of the last to be written for the SBL in the late 30s, reprinted in the 1950s. But the imperial bluebloods would gradually give way to more plebian characters. Again, the pleasure of reading the stories is increased by the way in which they act as a literary barometer, giving us an excellent idea of changing patterns not only in entertainment but also in popular thinking. I find it fascinating to trace the change in public taste as Blake moves into more familiar versions of our times. The writers fall into roughly two groups – those who wrote in the manner of wholesome periodicals for healthy (imperial) boys and those who brought a modern sensibility to the likes of *Union Jack* as the First World War loomed. We can see the end of the old and the beginning of the new in these stories as a breed of younger writers began to emerge.

Andrew Murray had a knack for creating series characters and another of his best villains was the malevolent Professor Kew who, in *Tinker's Terrible Test,* plotted a dastardly revenge on Blake's assistant. One of Murray's few superiors as a writer was Edwy Searles Brooks (whom I knew and admired as a boy). Brooks also created a group of superb villains and adventuresses who populated Blake's golden age, which had its beginnings around 1910 and had faded away by the early 1940s.

Michael Storm, who created George Marsden Plummer, a villain with extraordinary longevity, passed the character on to George Hamilton Teed, a Canadian writer who allegedly met Storm's widow on a boat. She suggested he 'ghost' her dead husband's stories. *The Great Bank Fraud,* however, is by neither writer, but by Lewis Carlton, who wrote a good number of Blake stories featuring Plummer.[3]

Teed is represented here by two stories, the first of which is the splendid full length novel *The Sacred Sphere,* featuring, together with Wu Ling and Dr Huxton Rymer, perhaps his finest adventuress Mademoiselle Yvonne Cartier. These stories were written, as the title pages announced, to 'Appeal to All Tastes, All Ages – Either Sex'.

Better than any of the Blake regulars Teed could suggest sexual attraction and tension in a few lines and there's no doubt that readers of these stories understood exactly what was happening between Yvonne Cartier and Sexton Blake. This steamy stuff had little in common with the wholesome stories of manly comradeship written for clean-living young chaps advertised and serialised in *The Boys Friend.* I wonder how many readers of, say, *The Boys Friend Library* retired blushing to their beds with, instead of a Hayter *BFL,* a Teed *Sexton Blake Library.*

It was not long before Teed's real identity was revealed[4]. He worked as a Blake regular for

---

3 After the mysterious disappearance of Michael Storm (aka Ernest Sempill), a number of Blake's chroniclers continued to write tales of George Marsden Plummer, the corrupt ex-Scotland Yard man, including Lewis Carlton and JW Bobin, before Teed eventually reinvented the character in the 1920s after returning from his service during the war.

4 Legend has it that after a period 'ghosting' stories for the late Michael Storm, Teed fell out with Mrs. Storm and approached the editors at Amalgamated Press to declare himself as the true author of the works in question. The editor at the time did not believe Teed's apparently wild claims, and challenged him to prove his case. Teed then seated himself at a nearby typewriter and hammered out the first few chapters of a new Blake tale. The editor was astonished and consequently bought the piece, and Teed went on to become a staple writer for the press.

---

1 *The Mystery of the Inari Treasure*

2 Originally 'Lawliss'. See *The Boundary Raiders*

several years and then did a long spell of war service. He had become one of the most prolific (and arguably the best) Blake authors, giving us Prince Wu Ling, the intellectual blue blood with whose ambitions to reunite China Teed was clearly sympathetic, Huxton Rymer, the brilliant doctor who had set aside his work on cancer to pursue a life of crime, often in the company of the likes of Marie Galante, the Voodoo Queen, or Vali Mata Vali, the French songstress turned crook, and many more, including perhaps the finest, sexiest, bravest and most beautiful bunch of adventuresses in all of popular fiction, among them Yvonne Cartier, Roxane Harcourt and June Severance.

Already, in 1915, Teed was considered the best of the Blake chroniclers, chosen to write a Wu Ling adventure, *The Yellow Tiger*, for the very first issue of *Sexton Blake Library*. Wu Ling appeared in the same year as Fu Manchu and in my opinion is a far better, subtler and more interesting character than Rohmer's. What's more, Teed did far more with Wu Ling over the years than Rohmer, perhaps because Teed had sympathy for the Chinese cause. After Yvonne had sided so thoroughly with Blake that it might be suspected they were secretly married, another great femme fatale was required of him and Roxane Harcourt's determination to be avenged on those who had destroyed her father and mother might have seemed like a rerun of the Yvonne series in shorter skirts, but there are subtle differences between the women which reflect the times when they came into being.

Although not exactly a lefty, Teed wrote stories often in marked contrast, say, to Gwyn Evans's. Reading Evans sometimes makes me think of Rex Warner's *The Aerodrome*, for the undoubted sense of Merrie Englande he could conjure up. Equally, his racial views could be nasty. He spent some time as a reporter in Palestine, and I think revealed how the usual awful British tendency to partition caused quite a few of the conflicts still concerning us. I find that reading Evans in context gives me a strong idea of what it must have been like to have overheard the average British official after his fifth gin sling at almost every officer's bar around the Empire in, say, 1935. On the other hand, Evans was without doubt one of Blake's best story-tellers and his Christmas stories were much looked forward to. To some extent I think my boss Bill Howard Baker, last editor of the SBL, might have been a bit like Evans. An incredibly warm and likeable drunk with appalling political opinions. *Suspended from Duty*! shows Evans's virtues and pretty much none of his vices. It's also another of the stories reprinted here which shows that fraudulent financiers and bent coppers are by no means new to our own day. At his best Evans did much to humanise both Inspector George Coutts and Mrs. Martha Bardell and knew how to use the Blake regulars to their greatest advantage.

In the eyes of a number of Blake enthusiasts, neither Evans nor Teed wrote Blake's greatest adventures but Anthony Skene[5], a government surveyor who travelled the country dictating his stories to his secretary (also rumored to be his mistress). Skene's great character was one of the few to have an original hardback novel (sans Blake) devoted to him. After some 70 years, the novel was reprinted relatively recently in a superb edition by the enthusiastic non-profit house of Savoy, who only publish books that are obscure and which they love to read. The novel, originally published in 1936, was called simply *Monsieur Zenith* and recorded the adventures of a character I borrowed for my Elric stories, written when I still worked for *SBL*, who became one of my most influential characters.

Skene based Zenith on a somewhat less glamorous, rather slovenly character he'd spotted in an ABC Tea Rooms some time during the First World War. Adding several Demon Lover/Byronic extras to the man he'd seen, making him wear full evening dress on all occasions (when not say disguised as Mrs. Bardell), making him play the fiddle like Pagannini and giving him an anti-social attitude and a drug habit to rival Holmes's or James Dean's, Skene produced an enduring anti-hero in Monsieur Zenith when the Albino debuted in *Union Jack* with *A Duel to the Death*.

Like Tinker and more rarely Blake, Zenith occasionally told his stories in first person, as, in part he does in *A Mystery in Motley*, revealing a tortured, courageous, existential soul. In *A Mystery in Motley* Skene, as he often did, picks a title offering a clue into character as much as plot. Perhaps that's why this is one of my favourite Zenith adventures, where he also flirts

---

5   The pseudonym of George N. Phillips

wonderfully with Julia Fortune.

Zenith is at his best when there is clearly sexual attraction between himself and a member of the opposite sex, whether she be a poor crippled girl, an ethereal princess or a resourceful secret service agent. These Zenith stories remain perhaps the most popular of all and the first edition of *Monsieur Zenith* is almost impossible to find. I believe there are only four known copies, two in private hands. I'm glad incidentally to see in the first Zenith story, *A Duel to the Death*, that Blake's Grey Panther is still an aeroplane, no doubt close to making its transition into Blake's Rolls Royce, which takes part in so many of the detective's great car chases. Zenith was one of the first real moderns to appear in Sexton Blake stories and his fascination for all types of inventions, including TV, often has the exhilaration of a Futurist.

Another popular writer, creator of The Criminals' Confederation, The Bat (perhaps the first of many precursors to the 'Dark Knight'), Professor Reece, and several other major characters, was Robert Murray whose *Lord of the Ape Men* is actually a lot less like an Edgar Rice Burroughs Tarzan story than it sounds, though Dr Satira has more of the qualities of an American horror pulp antagonist than most Blake villains. The *UJ* or *SBL* contained a few jungle lords raised by various mammals, showing first Kipling's influence and later Burroughs's, but Murray's isn't one of them. The story has the Gothic atmosphere which ran in an unbroken direct line from the earliest penny dreadfuls to so many AP/Fleetway publications well into the 60s and, if you count *2000 AD,* beyond! Stories of macabre terror were reprinted as the only text pages in IPC comics. This brooding atmosphere also haunts *The Gnomid* the story announced originally as Gilbert Chester's[6] masterpiece.

Chester wrote Blakes into the 1950s and saw all the story papers turned into comics. Blake himself appeared in comic form more than once and for a long time was a regular in *Knockout,* drawn by Eric Parker, whose distinctive style, influenced perhaps by Fred Bennett, an earlier Blake artist and AP regular, came to be associated with all readers of *UJ, SBL* and *Detective Weekly* and whose last Blake covers

appeared in the early 1960s. I had suggested commissioning them and sat in awe as I watched Parker order up artboard, poster colours and inks from the Fleetway stationery department and proceed to paint the covers directly onto the boards without even preparing a sketch! His depictions of M.Zenith remain for me the only true portraits ever made of the great albino. While by no means the draughtsman Parker was, Valda, who illustrated many Blake stories in *Union Jack* from quite early days, continued to illustrate *Detective Weekly* and *The Thriller* until they were axed as paper shortages became tighter in the Second World War.

I find it depressing that attempts to introduce Blake to a more recent public via the radio have reduced the character to a risible cipher, without humour or character. It's the easiest thing in the world to make fun of attitudes and manners which have gone out of common currency and presenting characters like Blake in broad parody demeans, it seems to me, everyone concerned. If any reader believes that the great Blake writers were unaware of the humorous, generic aspects of their thrillers, *The Next Move* should dispel that impression. Four of the top authors – Evans, Robert Murray, Teed and Skene – were asked to write a 'round robin' story. Teed set up the first episode, challenging his fellow writers to explain, for instance, the mystery of a London underground river, a prisoner in a punt, a brightly dressed organ grinder's monkey (deceased) and Roxane's presence all in the same opening. Gwyn Evans's next episode has lines which might have come from a Carry On or Monty Python script.

There's little doubt that tongues were firmly in cheeks by the time we were reading lines like *'Anastasia's gone!' he burst out wildly. 'She's gone, and with her my combinations!'* nor that Evans was not exactly serious when he introduced in his second chapter a dead parrot (a close relative to the Norwegian Blue).

As well as being a very enjoyable and well told story, *The Next Move* gives us an idea what it might have been like to spend an evening in The George or The Punch or any of a score of Fleet Street pubs with a bunch of Blake regulars who, while probably not being quite the Jacobean characters Blakian apocrypha makes them out to be, were clearly great company who enjoyed their work, respected their readers and at the

6   The pseudonym of H H Clifford Gibbons

same time had a lot of fun earning what were for their day very substantial fees (most of which went over the counters of the Fleet Street drinkers).

I was lucky to be a teenage journalist at the very end of that era when certain writers, especially the great Jack Trevor Story *(The Trouble With Harry, Live Now, Pay Later)*, had to be watched fairly carefully to see what they tried to slip into their stories, but the tales told about them (and which they told, too) were never quite as good as the reality. I was there when Jack Story explained to an editor who accused him of exaggeration that it was the prosaic stuff which had to be invented and the stuff which seemed impossibly unlikely which was the flat truth. He was right. In his case at least. A week later Jack told a story about me which had only the faintest origins in reality. You can expect nothing else of professional liars.

How many times Gwyn Evans smuggled his tiny girl-friend in a suitcase past the suspicious eyes of hotel managers we don't know, any more than we know how often editors were fooled into paying for stories by manuscripts whose first top few pages were typed while the rest were blank, but we can be sure all the tricks you hear about were tried once. I know, because I tried several of them myself.

As a boy I would send off a weekly postal order to 'story paper' dealers for copies of magazines like *Union Jack,* which I would buy in the order they had originally appeared. My original interest had been in P.G. Wodehouse and then in a commercial circulating library I found Brooks, whose style and often his characters had much of Wodehouse's flair. From Brooks's hardbacks it was back to his Blakes. His best writing was crisp and snappy, and travelled well through the 20th century, as I'm sure it will continue to travel. Then I discovered Zenith and my loyalties wavered a little as I sent off for stories with titles like *Marked By The Leopard Men,* which depicted the activities of the Tyneside Leopard men, whose blood-leader Zenith now was, and showed Blake and the Albino duelling with rapiers in a Gateshead pit.

Throughout my boyhood I did my best to collect all the Waldo and Zenith stories I could come by. Then I extended my loyalties to include Teed's characters. I have yet to find some, in particular those offering the adventures of Mdlle

Yvonne and Huxton Rymer, and I dream of the day when all the great Blake characters are made available in their own reprinted anthologies of stories. Meanwhile we have this enthusiastically and carefully made collection to offer a taste of what helped influence writers like myself and others from Ian Fleming to Alan Moore who recognise the bedrock of the fiction which still plays daily on our screens. Who choose to tap in to a mythological cycle Dorothy Sayers believed to be the nearest thing to a national epic we could ever hope to find in modern times..

I know I shall probably never read all my favourite Blake writers as the magazines grow scarcer and scarcer. Some of the copies I own are already close to turning to dust as fast as enthusiasts can create electronic files of their copies. With luck there are still complete sets in some libraries or even private collections. Meanwhile, the best most of us can hope for are enlightened publishers and editors who will put as many of the stories back into print as possible.

I am sure with this book we shall find a few readers like me who develop a taste if not for Blake himself, then at least for certain of the best writers. It's true that tastes have changed and attitudes improved but at their best these stories remain great escapism. I'm sure, too, they'll continue to inform and influence those who take pleasure in learning how our immediate ancestors thought and what, instead of a good TV thriller (which so many of these stories resemble) would send them to bed happy.

George Mann has done us all a great service in assembling this collection. I have a feeling that when this book comes out it will not be long before there are a few more keen Blake fans out there. I wish you hours of enjoyable reading. And if you like this book, why not show it to a chum and suggest they order a copy for themselves? If the real Sexton Blake is making a come back, then the very least we can do is cheer him on! Pushing at least 150, you can only admire his stamina.

MICHAEL MOORCOCK
LOST PINES, TEXAS,
AUGUST 2009

An Amazing Character! **ZENITH, THE ALBINO!** (See Within.)

THE UNION JACK LIBRARY

1½d

A DUEL TO THE DEATH

No. 837.   EVERY THURSDAY.   October 25th, 1919.

A DUEL TO THE DEATH

A MAGNIFICENT LONG, COMPLETE DETECTIVE NOVEL, INTRODUCING
ZENITH, THE ALBINO, ONE OF THE MOST FASCINATING AND AMAZING
PERSONALITIES IN PRESENT-DAY FICTION.

THE FIRST CHAPTER
THE STARS OF OUDE.

IT was a wild night.

Wind, thunder, and rain made weird organ music around the New Caister Hotel.

Out there by the old castle, midway between the low and desolate flats and the turbulent North Sea, the few buildings that existed reeled and complained beneath the assault of the gale, while, out on the submerged sands, wave after wave fell with a sound awe-inspiring and sad.

Within the hotel was desolation of another kind.

Dust-sheets and closed doors proclaimed that it was a summer hotel, and that the few had been driven to take shelter there must expect little, and be thankful for what they received.

But one at least of these storm-driven unfortunates was well able lo look after himself, and accustomed to get what he wanted wherever he happened to be.

Within a hastily-prepared sitting-room upon the second floor was the great detective, Sexton Blake, and with him were his inseparable companions, Master Tinker and Pedro, the bloodhound.

They had just concluded one of Blake's less interesting cases, one of those episodes of sheer, dull graft from which the most careful selection did not always protect him.

A notorious profiteer had put himself within reach of the law, and the law, in the person of Sexton Blake, had rounded him up and sent him to a well-deserved retirement.

The final scene had taken place upon the sea, and the exigencies of his Majesty's Service had caused the hurried departure of a certain T.B.D., and the marooning of Blake and his companions off the place where they now were.

All these things considered, they had little reason to complain; an extravagant fire blazed upon the open grate, and the table bore witness to a not unattractive meal recently deposed of.

Despite the recurring thunder, and the searching wind which moved even the carpet, as it billowed beneath the floor, the three were comfortable enough.

Sexton Blake, with a favourite briar between his teeth, was indulging in a refreshing idleness; Tinker had seized upon his favourite spot in the mathematical centre of the hearthrug; while Pedro was discussing an unusually satisfactory bone.

Such was the state of things at nine p.m. upon a certain day in December.

The grandfather clock which stood within the room had hardly reached the ninth of its deep, deliberate strokes, when its tones were lost in a thunderclap louder than any that had gone before.

"My hat!" said Tinker, amazed at its nearness and intensity.

And even as he spoke, it increased in violence, rolling and resurging until it culminated in a staggering crash.

At the same instant every light went out.

"Relight the gas; it is escaping!"

Sexton Blake's cool order reassured Tinker instantly.

He sprang to obey; but was prevented by a voice which came out of the darkness close beside him—the voice of a stranger.

"Leave it to me!"

The rich, deep tones were cultured and commanding, yet bore such a burden of sadness that one longed to behold the being from whom it came.

One by one the gaslights were relit, and Tinker found himself gazing at a young and handsome man in full evening-dress.

The stranger turned to Sexton Blake.

"Ah, Mr. Blake," he said, "I must apologise for this intrusion." He removed his hat with a flourish and exposed the strange fact that he was a true albino, his hair being white as snow, while his eyes glowed like rubies in the incandescent light.

"I am afraid you have the advantage of me," said Sexton Blake.

"Alas!" said the beautiful voice of the stranger, "your fame is world-wide, while my name is unknown."

Then he added, with a bow:

"I call myself Zenith!"

Sexton Blake returned the bow, but he did not speak.

A deep line of perplexity appeared between his eyes, and, with a glance which missed nothing, he scrutinised the person of his strange visitor.

There was silence. The only sounds were the crackling of the fire and the crunching of Pedro's bone.

"And what is the purpose of this visit?" asked Sexton Blake, at length.

Tinker looked up with surprise. His master's voice held an incisive resonance that was usually associated with action and danger.

Nor was the albino deaf to this. He smiled, and began stroking his chin with long, powerful fingers that were as well-kept as those of a woman.

"You have discovered something already," he said. "I congratulate you, Mr. Blake!"

He took a curved cigarette-case of gold from his waistcoat pocket, and lighted a tiny cigarette.

Instantly the pungent incense of opium filled the room.

"You have not answered my question!"

Sexton Blake did not move, or even open his eyes from the lethargy into which he appeared to have fallen. Nevertheless, it was impossible to ignore him.

Even the man called Zenith, the adventurer who had thrust himself upon them with such melodramatic effect, did not dare to refuse an answer.

"You wish," he said, with studied insolence, "to know the purpose of this visit?

"The purpose of this visit, my dear detective, is twofold. Firstly, the satisfaction of a desire to make your acquaintance; and, secondly, as I must admit, to gratify a childish taste for the theatrical."

"Then it is to you that we owe the extinction of the gas?" asked Sexton Blake.

"Precisely!"

"And why did you wish to make my acquaintance?"

"One naturally wished to meet a man with whom one has—er—business relations!"

"We have business relations, then?"

"I fancy, my very dear sir, that you have already suspected as much."

Zenith nonchalantly flicked the ash away from his cigarette, while a vivid flash of lightning filled the room.

"You, sir," he continued, "have the good fortune to represent society, to uphold righteousness; with me it is otherwise."

He shrugged.

"I," he said sadly, "am what Nature has made me—an outcast—something that is neither man nor beast. As man has fought and dominated the beast kingdom, so I fight, and will perhaps dominate the world of men. For twenty years I have dwelt in the underworld, a creature of the night and storm, and in all that time no living being has thwarted my desires, except yourself.

"Hence my wish to meet you face to face.

"Mine was the brain at the back of the Peel Case; mine the hand that took the Cranmer pearls. I fought you for the Giles-Havington letters, and a month ago I created the C.A. Exploration Syndicate—which you finally smashed.

"In each of those four cases I defeated you; but each cost me dear.

"In each case your hand closed on the tool, the catspaw, and in each case the inventor, the brain behind, went scot-free.

"Tell me now, did you suspect my existence?"

"I did," said Sexton Blake.

"Ah, I guessed it! And now that you have seen me face to face, what do your boasted powers of observation and synthesis tell you?"

Sexton Blake turned to the white-haired man with a calmness as great as his own.

For a moment he scanned the pink eyes, the expressionless face, the manicured hands, and the immaculate dress of the stranger, noting a hundred little facts, and mentally arranging them side by side. Then he responded to the sarcastic challenge he had received.

"You entered this hotel," he said, "at about fifteen minutes to nine. You then wore an overcoat longer than the one you are carrying over your arm, and a green or grey woollen muffler. You came in a car, which you left some little way from the hotel, probably near the sea-sands, and which drove off at a great pace the moment you left it. Your intention was felonious, and you have recently opened, or attempted to open, a well constructed safe."

"Really, Mr. Blake, this is too clever of you!" gibed the stranger. "Let me see if I can follow your reasoning.

"There are splashes of mud on my trouser-legs. They were wet, and are now dry. Moreover, when I entered I threw the end of a cigarette into the hearth. The cigarette could not have been smoked outside, the wet mud could not have been got inside. That fixes the time of my stay at one cigarette—or, as you have noticed from the one I was smoking—about fifteen minutes.

"The length of the overcoat you deduce from where the splashes end, and the woolly muffler from some fluff which still adheres to my collar.

"You have keen eyes, Sexton Blake!

"Then from the direction of the mud-splashes you deduce the retreating car; and, from the quality of the mud, the sea-sand.

"Lastly, of course, there is the business of the safe. That, I confess, is rather disconcerting. If I may sit at the foot of Gamaliel for a moment, how did you deduce that?"

"You have sand-papered your finger-tips," said Blake. "There are scratches upon your finger-nails, which are otherwise highly polished. Ergo, you have been doing something which requires great delicacy of touch—I suggest the picking of a safe lock."

"The point is yours!"

Zenith bowed again, with the exaggerated politeness that he affected.

"I don't know whether you have observed it," he said, "but your assistant is covering me with a pistol, while your dog is watching you for the word to floor me."

Sexton Blake signed to Tinker to put the pistol away.

"Quite unnecessary," he said. "Here, if I mistake not, is Nemesis in the guise of a police-officer!"

At the same moment there came a loud knock upon the door.

"Open in the name of the Law!"

"Dear me," said the man called Zenith, "I have stayed rather long!"

"Open the door!" ordered Sexton Blake.

Tinker obeyed.

Upon the threshold stood two police-officers, not unknown to the great detective—Messrs. Harris and Kellaway, both of the C.I.D., Scotland Yard.

Both instantly recognised Zenith as the man they were seeking, and, although to them he was nothing more than a very smart thief, they stepped forward gleefully to secure the prize within their grasp.

Then, finding him calmly talking with Sexton Blake, they stopped dumbfounded.

"I would seem," said the albino, "to be in some danger of arrest."

He laughed musically.

"Good-evening, gentlemen!" he said to the police-officers. "I think you are looking for the famous jewels that they fancifully call the 'Stars of Oude'?"

"That is so," said Detective Harris, silently locking the door.

"Ah, I am not surprised to hear it! They are pretty stones—very pretty. Have you seen them?"

Zenith plunged his hand into his trousers-pocket, and withdrew it closed round some object.

For a moment he held it out before the expectant police-officer, who fully believed that he was about to surrender the jewels which they knew him to have.

Then, with a sudden turn of the wrist, he allowed the object that he held to fall on the floor.

It burst, and flared with a sudden vivid light. It was a magnesium bomb!

For a few seconds the white glare struck the four men with complete blindness.

They could only reel to the doors to cut off a possible dash for liberty.

Again the laugh of the stranger rang out, ending in a reckless and triumphant cry that seemed to drift away from them.

The curtains flew up, the gaslights flickered blue, a wet wind smote the faces of the detectives, and an instant later they were gathered about an open window, beyond which was nothing. Only thirty feet below the stone flags of the courtyard glistening in the rain!

"By Jove! Suicide!" exclaimed Kellaway.

Sexton Blake leaned far out.

To his ears came the faint pulsation of a starting car.

"No," he said; "I think not. We shall see."

He held Pedro's nose to the floor where the stranger had been standing.

"Seek, Pedro!" he commanded.

"Now," he said, "if you gentlemen are ready, we will go down the stairs."

They descended the stairs, and Blake led the big bloodhound to the spot immediately below the windows of the sitting-room.

"Seek, Pedro!" he commanded again.

The dog set to work with almost human understanding, and an instant later, with Tinker at the other end of the leash, he was following an invisible trail in the direction of the new road.

"Have you a good car?" asked Sexton Blake, turning to the men from Scotland Yard.

"Yes," answered Detective Harris. "A Rolls-Royce four-seater. Fast," he added.

"Good!" said Sexton Blake. "I think we shall need it. You might get it tuned up."

Detective Harris agreed instantly; but his colleague, a new man at the Yard, turned upon Blake with a show of wounded dignity.

"Look here, Mr. Sexton Blake," he exploded, "I've heard all about you, and I know you're an old hand at this game; but I'm blowed if I see any reason for placing myself under your orders, and running about like a dog at a fair to gratify your whims and theories. How do you mean we shall want a car? Where's the body of the man who threw himself out of that second-floor window?"

Before the great detective could reply—if he had had any such intention—a long whistle came from the distant road.

"That means," said Blake, "that my assistant has picked up the place where the white-haired man rejoined his car."

"How could he rejoin his car?" burst out Kellaway. "He had no means of escape but that window, and cobbles to fall on! If our man was intent on suicide, let's find the corpse!"

By this time Detective Harris was round with the car.

"Wait a bit, Cully!" ordered the irate Kellaway. "You may be fond of working in the dark, but I'm not. I want to know what this Mr. Sexton Blake is driving at. I want to know—"

The senior Scotland Yard man got slowly down, and took his protesting colleague by the arm.

Then he led him carefully out of earshot of Sexton Blake.

What was said upon that occasion will never be known. Suffice it to say that, when they returned Detective Kellaway was very quiet and deferential indeed.

Little as the general public knew the indebtedness of Scotland Yard to Sexton Blake, Scotland Yard knew it very well.

They found Tinker and Pedro waiting beside a barren and loose-made country road. The beam of Tinker's torch was upon its surface, and he was reading its message like the skilled tracker that he was.

"Five men, or more?" asked Sexton Blake.

"Seven in all, I think, guv'nor!" answered Tinker.

Blake looked attentively at the faint impressions of the wet, sandy earth.

"Yes, you are right," he said at length. "Zenith arrived last and entered the car first. Therefore he is the leader."

Kellaway looked from Sexton Blake to Tinker, and from Tinker back to Blake. He was devoured by curiosity, but afraid to give it expression.

Blake smiled good-naturedly.

"You're a bit in the dark—eh?" he asked of Kellaway.

Kellaway laughed awkwardly.

"Well, as a matter of fact—" he began.

"It was really obvious," said Blake, "that the man did not commit suicide. To begin with, he was not the sort to do it, and, further, his circumstances were not desperate enough to drive him that far.

"Now, since he hadn't wings, he clearly had to face a thirty-feet drop, and since he had contemplated that drop, he had probably arranged for something soft to fall on."

"Gee-whizz, a jumping-sheet!" exclaimed Tinker.

"Just so!" said Sexton Blake. "I deduced a jumping-sheet from the beginning, and verified the deduction by tracks upon the surface of the yard.

"It was a skilled job. The man saw that he would probably be unable to get away with the gems once he had opened the safe. Indeed, he doubtless foresaw that they would be guarded. Therefore, he provided a short cut to safety by means of a jumping-sheet held by six confederates. To wait, as he did, not knowing whether the sheet was in place or not, and then to leap into the darkness on the spur of the moment, was an act of superhuman recklessness."

"If he drives a car as recklessly—" suggested Tinker.

"We shall never catch him," finished Sexton Blake. "Perhaps not. We shall see.

There is a long score between us, and it will have to be settled soon. It just happens that there is no room on this planet for him and me. It is his life or mine—a duel. I don't mind admitting, gentlemen, that I am by no means certain as to the end of it."

"Surely," said Detective Kellaway, "he would not go as far as murder!"

Sexton Blake laughed.

"Monsieur Zenith," he said, "does not value his life, or my life, or yours, or anybody else's above a snap of the fingers. Let her rip!"

By this time the detectives were in the Rolls-Royce, and well started along the eight-mile run of straight, flat road which leads to Acle Bridge.

Detective Harris had not exaggerated the capabilities of his car. Half rising in his seat in the tonneau, Tinker was able to see the red pointer of the speed-gauge rise from the forty-five to fifty, and then, unit by unit, to something like sixty m.p.h.

The wind fortunately was blowing in from the sea, and the rain had almost ceased.

Nevertheless, the night was still wild, and the darkness so intense that the detectives heard their quarry before they could see it.

It was soon apparent that the car in front had not the speed of a Rolls-Royce, but the difference was so small that much might happen before it was run to earth.

A solitary clump of elm-trees, a patch of bad road and inky darkness, compelled both cars to slow down, and decreased the distance between them to some fifty yards.

As they again emerged into the cloudy moonlight Tinker was able to count the occupants of the retreating car. There were six in all.

Either one man had left the car while it was within the now distant clump of trees, or both he and his master had made an error in counting tracks or seven men.

He turned to apprise Sexton Blake of his discovery. Sexton Blake was no longer in the car!

Tinker said nothing, but he sized up the situation at once. One of the crooks—probably the leader—had left the outpaced car while darkness

shielded his movements; and Blake, perceiving the manoeuvre, had devoted himself to the pursuit of that individual, leaving Tinker and the men from Scotland Yard to secure his confederates.

If Scotland Yard has one outstanding quality, it is courage. That, at least, has never been questioned. Both Detective Harris and his colleague, Detective Kellaway, were fully aware that the six men whom they pursued were probably desperadoes of the most reckless kind; they could not ignore the fact that the road was lonely and the night dark.

It would go hard with them if the crooks showed fight.

Yet neither the men nor the lad who accompanied them had any thought of compromise. It was their duty and their intention to see the matter through.

In the distance arose the warm lights of the Acle Ferry Inn, and the retreating crooks, as though inspired by that landmark, managed to coax an extra turn of speed out of their car, and drew away again.

As, however, they reached the bridge which now replaced the ancient ferry, the detectives heard the brakes shut on, and saw the fugitive car swing off the road and disappear. Too late to follow, the detectives were compelled to keep to the road, pulling up some hundred yards beyond the bridge.

The two men instantly drew their automatics, and, followed by Tinker and Pedro, rushed back towards the river.

The inn lay bathed in the fitful moonlight. Of car or crooks there was nothing to be seen; only from the bosom of the misty River Bure came the receding chuff-chuff of a big motor-boat.

"They've run the car into the river and stolen a boat," explained Detective Harris briefly; and, before the slow Kellaway had as much as grasped the situation, he was down at the waterside, dragging the tarpaulin cover off a powerful skimming-boat belonging to some private owner who was a disciple of speed.

"Who can drive this thing?" he continued. "Here, Mr. Tinker, you understand aeroplanes. Try your fist at this thing!"

Without a second's delay, Tinker sprang into the driving-seat, and started the six cylinders. A few minutes later they were the nucleus of a tidal wave, spinning down the river at unconquerable speed.

Once more the stern chase had begun, and once more speed was with the pursuers and against the pursued.

For five minutes they followed the winding stream, and then, cutting a curved and phosphorescent furrow in the tossing waters, the Mercedes swerved into an almost invisible staithe.

Tinker jammed the helm over, and, risking a capsize, followed at top speed.

There was a moment of darkness and slashing, wet boughs, and then the two motor-boats were alone upon a miniature sea.

They were crossing Barton Broad.

Although never more than a few feet deep. Barton Broad is some two hundred acres in extent, and the recent tempest had raised considerable waves upon its surface.

As speed increased the prow lifted high in the air, the boat all but flying. The detectives, who had crawled forward for a chance shot at the flying crooks, were almost in a standing position.

The circumstances were strangely romantic. In the darkness and the mist the low shores were quite invisible, and the two boats appeared to be alone upon some unfrequented sea. Ahead the fugitive Mercedes bored into the tumbling waves, and set up two diverging walls of water which its pursuers had to override. The skimming-boat sang a deep song of speed, and surged forward tirelessly in its wake, making nothing of waves or wind, putting its forty-five knots with the ease of a dream.

The Second Chapter

The Battle of the Broad—The 10 p.m. Express—The Mystery of the Car.

IT was clear from the first that the overriding and probable capsize of the fugitive Mercedes occupied by the six crooks was only a matter of minutes.

Not only was the skimming-boat much the faster of the two vessels, but Sexton Blake's assistant, having been compelled to drive all kinds of vehicles, from traction-engines to aeroplanes, in his adventurous life, was much superior to the pilot of the boat which be pursued.

Nevertheless, the great speed of the skimming-boat was a danger in itself, and in the darkness and on those strange waters Tinker did not dare to go all out. Instead, he contented himself with closely following the Mercedes, throttling down the engine, and looking to the turn of events to give him the chance he wanted. Events move pretty rapidly when one is travelling at thirty miles an hour, and it was clear that the crooks would soon be compelled to show fight.

But although a fight was the crooks' one hope of getting clear, they had very little prospect of deciding where or when it was to take place. If they slowed down without turning, the skimming-boat would leap upon them like a battering-ram; while, if they turned, it was more than likely to cut them in half.

Suddenly both pilots became aware that they had reached the far side of the broad.

Away through the mist a low wall of reeds became visible, and the two boats surged around with so little to spare that a cloud of wildfowl which they had awakened flew screaming directly above their heads. Tinker had not dared to ram for fear of running his craft ashore in the reeds, and now both vessels were again ploughing their way towards the open broad. The crooks had won the first point!

Nevertheless, the end was certain. The Mercedes might dodge and side-track the skimming-boat a dozen times; but in the end seamanship and speed would be served. Both parties knew this, and now began a conflict in which cunning vied with cunning.

Allowing that it must come to a fight—a desperate fight where quarter would be neither asked nor given—the crooks set themselves to have this skirmish as far from human habitation as possible, so that the advantage of numbers should remain with them; Tinker, on the other hand, was striving with all his skill to fence the enemy towards a part of the shore where the warm light of some dwelling glowed between the trees.

By carefully nursing the engine, he managed lo leave the wake of the heavy-laden Mercedes and put the skimming-boat along-side.

The distance between the craft was too great for shooting, but as it proved that the skimming-

—❑—

E END OF
HE OHASE!
—

crooks allowed
boat to crash
the reeds, and
out hesitation,
ker drove the
ming-boat into
their track.

—❑—

boat had speed sufficient to ram them, the crooks thought it well to wear away a few points.

This was just what Tinker desired. The present course of the vessels would run them ashore close to the friendly lights; and, as the skimming-boat was now on the outside of the circle they were describing, the Mercedes could not possibly perform a second breakaway. On the contrary, the crooks had got to fight there and then.

"Well played, Mr. Tinker!" exclaimed Detective Harris.

The fact that he and his colleague, with the help of Tinker, were about to attack six men, obviously gave him nothing but pleasure. Detective Harris had never been known to hesitate in the course of duty. His mind was incapable of holding the fact that the forces of justice do not always prevail—that he might even be killed. Had he been alone he would certainly have attacked the crooks singlehanded.

His were the last words spoken for some time. The crooks allowed their boat to crash into the reeds, and, without hesitation, Tinker drove the skimming-boat into their track, hitting some sunken obstruction, bounding into the air, and finally piling up absolutely on top of them.

There was just time to see a dark figure standing upright in the Mercedes, and fumbling with

a pistol, when he disappeared between the converging bulks, and a scream and a splash betrayed that one, at least, of the crooks would go crooked no more.

Instinctively, the three in the flying-boat jumped clear as she struck, and it was well they did so.

A moment later the frail shell was riddled with bullets.

Tinker found himself beside Kellaway. Both of them were face downward in the wet grass.

"Mr. Tinker, sir," said Kellaway, "we're up against it, I reckon!"

He pulled out a service revolver, cocked it, and pushed it into the front loop of his braces. Then he began to crawl forward.

"My hat!" whispered Tinker to himself. He liked a spice of danger; but here was rather more than he cared about.

He watched the reeds moving where Kellaway had disappeared. To attack the enemy in front was undoubtedly brave; but he remembered two maxims of Sexton Blake's which led him to decide against it. One was, to take no unnecessary risks; and the other, never do the obvious thing.

With a whispered warning to Pedro, who crouched in the grass beside him, a warning which caused the intelligent animal to remain still and quiet until further orders, he began to make his way backwards into the reeds which fringed the broad. It went against the grain to desert his friends thus, but he saw clearly that a frontal attack could only end in failure, while if his plan went well, and he were able to make a flanking movement, there was more than a likelihood of the crooks being thrown into confusion.

The water was bitterly cold, and by the time his short swim was over, Tinker was trembling in every limb. Nevertheless, he dared not delay; but as soon as the warmth returned to his fingers he took his automatic out of his cap, where he had kept it clear of the water, and, with the friendly pistol-butt against his palm, begin to walk cautiously towards the spot where an occasional report proved the battle to be proceeding.

He had not gone ten paces before he received one of the greatest shocks of his life. He almost banged his face against the wrong end of a gun-barrel, while the owner's gruff voice told him what would happen if he moved any farther.

"Stan' you there, baw, or I'll blow your 'ead orf!"

The owner of the gun was a typical Norfolk marshman, lean, brown, and fearless. Tinker saw that he would be an invaluable ally, and told him the facts of the case in a brief whisper. One of Sexton Blake's visiting-cards was evidence enough for the marshman that he was on the side of the law, and he promptly proceeded to use his own methods for dealing with the situation.

Firing his gun with an ear-splitting report, he shouted to an imaginary party of friends to close in, and charged through the reeds like a rhinoceros. Tinker, sure that the fellow had gone to his death, could not be out of such a gallant fray; and, whistling to Pedro, he also dashed forward. There were a few confused moments, a dozen pistol-shots, and crashing reeds told of retreating men.

Risking everything, Tinker put on his electric torch and searched the clearing where the fight had taken place. Shortly after his whistle he had heard Pedro growl, and he knew that when Pedro growled it was somebody's death-knell. Sure enough he found the bloodhound pinning to earth a middle-aged man of particularly villainous appearance, who had only saved his throat by allowing the animal to fasten on his arm; and, passing a loop of whipcord—"raid handcuffs,"

as they call it—around the man's wrists, Tinker made him stand up, and called Pedro to heel.

Leaving the prisoner to the marshman—who seemed to be enjoying the affair greatly—Tinker called out the names of the detectives, but without result.

Again and again he called; but a silence as of death had settled down upon the waterside, and the mist was thickening over it like a pall. There was nothing to he heard or seen of the two men.

A word to Pedro set him also searching, and in a few minutes Tinker found that, as regarded Kellaway, at least, his worst fears were likely to be realised. Kellaway lay in the grass not far from where Tinker had left him, and his life-blood was welling from a bullet-hole below the left shoulder. This Tinker checked by a first-aid dressing; but the poor fellow was evidently a serious case. Harris, whom they found a minute later, was insensible, but not seriously hurt. He had exchanged shots with one of the crooks until both ran out of ammunition, and then fought with hands and feet in the darkness, finishing up across the body of his opponent—the detective insensible, and the crook dead. The latter, as it turned out, had stopped two bullets, and actually died fighting.

Harris was delighted to find Tinker alive.

"Thank Heaven, Mr. Tinker!" he exclaimed. "I thought they'd got you as well as poor Kellaway!"

He staggered to his feet, bruised, pale, and very shaky.

He turned to where their prisoner stood in the charge of the marshman.

He and the crook exchanged a long glance of hatred.

"I know you," said Detective Harris. "You're Mark the Faker, the man who paints all the spurious great masters in London. We've wanted you a long time."

The man spat contemptuously.

"Well," he said between his teeth, "you've got me now. It's your innings. You'd better make the best of it, Detective Harris. It isn't the first time we've been on different sides of the wall, and I'll see it isn't the last."

"No; but it's a prison wall this time, my boy," said the detective; and, twisting the whipcord handcuff more tightly around the prisoner's wrists, he followed the marshman along a footpath to the country road beyond.

An hour later Tinker and Pedro stood upon Norwich Thorpe railway-station, waiting for the mail train to London. Tinker had discovered, by means of the telephone, that Blake had not returned to the New Caister Hotel; but he was too well-accustomed to a life of hard work and unexpected happenings to worry much about that. He knew that Sexton Blake was as well able to look after himself as any man alive, and he had strong hopes of his arriving at Baker Street in time for breakfast, in the morning.

Harris had collapsed after handing his prisoner over to the local police; and Tinker, seeing no possibility of picking up the trail of the three remaining crooks, had decided to follow out Blake's original plan of returning to Baker Street that night. He had his clothes dried at the police-station, and managed to get a good meal. Now he was feeling pretty fit, although tired to the point of exhaustion. He realised now that it would have been wiser to put up at the Royal Hotel, Norwich, as someone had suggested, and travelled to town in the morning; but the desire to be where Blake could easily find him had proved irresistible.

The mail train came in, and he, in common with a fair number of others, passed through the barrier to seek a comfortable seat. As he was making his way among the people on the platform, his attention was attracted by two men walking immediately in front of him.

What it was that first caught his notice it is impossible to say. In his tired state he was not very observant, but once his suspicions were aroused he began to draw conclusions which were rather startling.

To begin with, the men had the air of being dressed above their condition in life. They did not carry their clothes as their clothes deserved to be carried. Then, again, they seemed to have no luggage and no interest in anybody else, seemed to desire to keep together and escape notice. But the most important thing that Tinker noticed was the state of their boots. Although these had been recently polished, it was quite obvious that they were soaked through. True, the evening had been wet; but even the wettest weather will not soak boots to the very tops, as these had been soaked.

Tinker deduced that they had been actually standing in shallow water, and with this theory came the suspicion that here were two of the three crooks who had survived the battle of the broad.

Half-way down the platform the two men stopped before a third, who was sitting on a seat. They put their hands under the arms of the sitting man and helped him into the train.

Tired as Tinker was, the spirit of adventure again seized him. Although not certain, he was almost convinced that he had stumbled upon the trail of the men whom they had fought with earlier in the evening.

He determined to keep an eye on their movements. He would enter a compartment near to theirs, and when he left the train he would follow, at least far enough to find out whether his suspicions were justified.

In order to be sure of them, he gave the guard a tip, and arranged to be warned of any movement made by his quarry. A similar deal with the ticket-collector got him the information that the three men were booked to Liverpool Street; and, wearily climbing into his own compartment, Tinker allowed himself to fall asleep.

He was awakened by a wild yell!

Some time must have passed, for the train was travelling at top speed, and Tinker had the feeling of awakening from a long sleep.

The door which opened to the corridor was wide open, and half-way through one of the suspected men was flat upon his back, with the bloodhound on top of him!

"Here," he shrieked again, "call your dog off! He's killing me!"

"Down, Pedro!" commanded Tinker.

The dog reluctantly obeyed, and the man arose, trying with trembling hands to rearrange his necktie.

"I'll put a bullet through that dog!" he growled savagely.

"You'd better not!" said Tinker. "What were you doing in here, anyway?"

"What's that got to do with you? It isn't a reserved compartment, is it? I can come in if I like. But," added the man, "after the way your hound's treated me I'll see you a sight further before I do."

Tinker laughed in his face.

"My hat!" he chuckled. "I'll bet the old dog bowled you over like a ninepin!" Then he added, with a threat the man could not ignore:

"Now you'd better get out, or he'll be at you again!"

Muttering curses, and still working at his necktie, the unwelcome visitor withdrew. With a frightened glance at Pedro, he closed the sliding door, and limped away down the corridor.

"Good dog!" said Tinker. "Good old Pedro! You saved me from something nasty this time. I didn't know they would recognise me, or I'd have been more careful. I might have been knocked on the head very easily!"

The lad had again begun to compose himself to sleep when his eye fell upon a suspicious object which had fallen, or been thrown underneath the seat on the side of the compartment.

He bent down and picked it up.

"Gee-whizz!" he muttered, paling. "It was something worse than a knock on the head this time!"

He held in his hand a long, pointed knife with a knuckleduster handle—the kind of weapon which is known as a "trench dagger."

"Pedro, my lad," he said whimsically, "but for you they'd have got me for keeps. I don't think I'll go to sleep again. I don't feel like it."

He saw clearly that any attempt to follow the three men must now be certain to fail, because, knowing of his presence on the train, they would keep careful watch against it. Therefore he regretfully abandoned the idea, and when the train reached Liverpool Street set about finding a taxicab without any regard to their movements.

But once again Fate played into his hands. Just as his cab turned out of the station premises a large car, in which, without being noticed, he recognised the man whom Pedro had knocked over, was driven past him, and turned in the opposite direction.

Doubtless the crooks had watched his departure, rightly concluding that he had given up the pursuit, and were even now going about their affairs without any fear of detection.

It was a great opportunity.

He dropped the window and reached a pound-note to the driver of his cab. He had always found John Bradbury's to have a persuasive effect.

"Follow that car," he said, "and find out its destination. If you succeed I'll give you another of these!"

It was a short journey. They dropped down to Billingsgate Market, and began to follow the course of the river. At a spot a short distance above the Pool the chauffeur stopped, and threw open the door of the cab.

"There you are, sir!" he said triumphantly. "The car went up there!"

He pointed to one of the many short, narrow, and pathless streets which run down to riverside wharves and warehouses.

"Wait a minute!" ordered Tinker; and, with the bloodhound at his heels, he walked on in the direction indicated.

At the end of fifty yards there was a blank wall, and beyond that, presumably the river. Each side was a continuous succession of high warehouses. There was no turning out of the street, no exit but the one by which his taxicab had entered. Yet it was empty and silent as the grave.

Tinker went back to the cab.

"You're making a mistake," he said; "the car couldn't have gone along here."

"What next?" asked the man angrily. "I saw it!"

"You couldn't have," said Tinker. "Look for yourself. There's no way out of the street. If the car entered it at all it would be there now."

The man scratched his head.

"That's a fact, sir. I dunno. I could have sworn it did!"

"Wait!"

Tinker had an idea. He switched on his electric light, and examined the cobbled surface of the road.

Sure enough, there were the tracks of armoured tyres on the new wet film of mud, and they turned into the street which the chauffeur had indicated.

"You're right," admitted Tinker. "Here's the other pound-note I promised you. Now we'll just take down the name of the road, and I'll get back to Baker Street. I'm tired."

THE THIRD CHAPTER

THE HOUSE AT BUCKINGHAM—A NARROW ESCAPE—THEBLUE LAMP AT LAST—THE RAID.

AS Tinker had supposed, Blake's departure from the car had been due to the fact that his keen, observant eyes had detected a similar movement on the part of the arch-enemy—the man who called himself Zenith.

For a full minute after leaving the tonneau Blake had remained in the shadow of the trees, trying to glimpse the whereabouts of his quarry, but without success. He was fully aware that a false step might mean death, that even then Zenith might be levelling a pistol at him, and only waiting for his slightest movement to make sure of hitting a vital spot. Nevertheless, Sexton Blake was accustomed to taking risks, and at the end of the minute he came out from the shadows and glanced to right and left.

The road on which he stood was laid over grazing lands, which, unbroken save by slow-moving rivers, stretched for many miles in every direction; and, far over to the left, he perceived the figure of a man walking rapidly away.

He broke through the hedge, and followed. It was almost impossible to remain unseen in doing so, but he was armed and ready for anything. If it suited the man he pursued to settle the affair there and then, he was ready. Sooner or later it must come to death-grips, so why not now? Yet, as it happened, Zenith did not turn, and mile after mile Sexton Blake followed him through the night.

A light rain had began to penetrate the detective's clothes, and his feet, which were covered with loose shoes which he had been wearing in the hotel, were soaked to the skin by the time the pursuit showed any sign of having an end.

Near Buckenham, a pretty little town on the banks of the Bure, they came to a cluster of small farms and houses, and shortly afterwards to the boundary walls of a big estate. Zenith followed this wall for some distance, then the big iron entrance gates came in view, and Blake guessed that their destination was at hand.

He allowed Zenith a few minutes to get well away from the gates, and then, climbing the wall, he himself began to make his way towards the house, which no doubt existed at the end of the carriage-way.

After half a mile he emerged upon a fine lawn, at the other side of which a large mansion, with hospitably lighted windows, challenged him to further risks and discoveries. He accepted the challenge without hesitation, and, keeping in the shadow of the trees, worked his way around until he was close against the walls. He was certain of nothing. It might be, as it seemed, a respect-able private house, where he stood a good chance of being handed over to the police for attempted burglary, or it might be a hotbed of crime.

After attempting without much success to get a glimpse of the interior by means of the windows, he came to one which, although, like the others, heavily curtained, was not tightly shut, and allowed the sound of voices to be audible,

Blake listened.

"I tell you, guv'nor," a voice was saying, "you didn't ought to do such fings. I know you got the sparklers all right, but look at the risk. What for did you want to go and talk to that chap Sexton Blake, instead of making your get-away like a sensible—"

The beautifully-modulated voice of Zenith broke in:

"Jones, my poor fool, don't meddle with what you don't understand! I am going to have Sexton Blake put out of the way, and I wanted to see him before that happened, He is the only law-agent I have ever feared, and I had a natural curiosity about him."

"Beg pardon, guv'nor!"

Evidently Zenith demanded, and received respect.

"That's all right, Jones," allowed the master-criminal. "You mean well, but you're a fool! Now go and tell the boys that I'll see them here in ten minutes' time."

The voices of the two men passed out of hearing, and were cut short by the closing of the door. Evidently Zenith and his man had gone out of the room, and, in all probability, it was now empty.

Sexton Blake, still smiling grimly at the compliments and threats that he had overheard, pressed the casement window inwards very slowly. It opened without a sound, and he carefully raised himself into the opening.

Having pulled back the curtain, and waited to be sure the room was empty, he dropped down upon the inside, and, automatic in hand, took a swift survey of his position.

He stood within a deep window-bay, divided from the room by heavy velvet curtains, and, peering between these, he could see a large, brilliantiy-lighted and empty room, furnished with an astonishing quantity of furniture.

So extraordinary indeed was the quantity of furniture that the room contained that Sexton Blake ran the risk of another long and critical glance. He could hardly believe that even the maddest millionaire would load his house with the treasures of antique furniture, bronzes, enamels, ivories, pictures, tapestries, and the rest, as this house appeared to be loaded. He could not believe that Zenith, who was obviously a man of artistic taste, could take pleasure in such profusion. The matter was part of the mystery which he hoped to clear up by attending the meeting of the gang which he had just heard was to take place in that room.

Concealed behind those heavy curtains he stood an excellent chance of remaining unobserved; and at the worst there was the open window behind him, and the dark night to hide his escape.

He took up a position close to the heavy curtain, and waited. Men began to move about in the room, and presently to seat themselves. Then began a kind of board meeting, and the detective found himself listening to the debate of an organisation which dealt in considerable sums of money and controlled a huge number of servants.

It transpired that there were ships in their possession, and a branch at Buenos Ayres. The cultivated voice of Monsieur Zenith passed from subject to subject, and while he was speaking there were no interruptions.

It was at one of the times when the lesser lights around the table were disputing among themselves that Sexton Blake noticed a curious thing. The conversation, which had been heated and rapid, suddenly dropped; there were some whispered words, and the business talk was resumed.

But Blake detected that now the speakers were merely talking at random, for the sake of talking, and his alert mind began to seek a reason. Could his presence have been detected?

He chanced to glance down at his feet, and was horrified to notice that the velvet curtain had blown inwards, unperceived by him, so as to uncover to the sight of the men within the room the toes of his shoes beneath.

Blake knew that to move was to die. The desperate men who were watching those telltale shoes would certainly shoot if they began to disappear. He was wearing a pair of loose, easy shoes, which he had put on for use in the hotel at Caister, and very carefully he stepped out of these, and in his stockinged-feet stepped across to the open window.

He acted none too soon. Before he could so much as get a leg across the sill, the curtain where he had been standing was riddled with bullets. The crooks had evidently waited a sign, and all fired together.

"Jove! They wanted to make sure of me!" muttered Sexton Blake.

He dropped on to soft earth, and cut away at a tangent. It was not the first time that he had been the subject of a man-hunt, and he knew it would be fatal to cross the lawn. If, however, he were right in thinking that a certain outbuilding was a garage, there was at least a chance of seizing a car and getting away at top speed,

Sheltered by a clump of bushes, he looked back at the house.

Out on the lawn there were at least a dozen men, all armed; but, so far as he could discover, none of them sufficiently accustomed to the darkness to divine which way he had taken.

He reached the outbuilding, a spacious place, white-walled and trellised with wide-open doors. Inside, as he had hoped, there were several cars, and against one of them a man was busy with an electric torch.

Blake, in his stockinged feet, approached without a sound, and it is quite likely that, when he recovered from Blake's right-handed uppercut ten minutes afterwards, he had not the least idea of what had hit him.

As soon as the man had fallen, the detective made a rapid survey of the cars. There were a luggage-car, several covered motor-vans, which he could not divine the use of, and a mixed assortment of touring and runabout vehicles. But what interested him most at that moment was a powerful motor-bicycle which was leaning against the wall.

To run it out and spring into the saddle was the work of a moment; yet the delay which had already occurred, slight as it was, had given the gang a chance to discover the detective's chosen road of escape, and a shower of pistol-shots proved that they were already closing round.

It was dark as a wolf's throat in the carriage-way, but Blake did not dare to light a lamp. As he pelted along at thirty-odd miles an hour, he prayed fervently that the gate might be open. As the entrance came in sight he shouted as loudly as he could, "Open the gate! Open the gate!" Then he slowed down, and found a newly-awakened gatekeeper who held the key in his hand,

and did not know whether to obey or not. There was no time for discussion, already the rhythmic sound of a high-power car came from the far end of the drive, and escape must be made now or never more. Blake, realising this, walked quietly up to the gatekeeper, knocked him out, seized the keys, and threw the iron gate wide open. Then he passed through and closed it behind him.

He had planned to lock the gate upon his pursuers; but by the time it was shut, their car was already at a standstill, and only the bad light saved Blake from the bullets which pelted after him.

After that he was safe, except for the probability of an accident. The car hustled along behind him at a pace approaching sixty miles per hour, and to hold that murderous speed on a strange road without head-lamps taxed the detective's nerve as much as any experience of his adventurous career. Nevertheless, it was the only thing to do, and he went all out, avoiding sudden death by a hair's-breadth twice in every mile.

Presently they began to go through the outskirts of Norwich. After the darkness of the country roads, it was a welcome relief, and one or two turnings increased the detective's start. At the same time he dared rot slacken speed. He could imagine that the crooks were desperate at the discovery of their secret headquarters, and would ride him down amid a crowd it necessary.

He had just begun to fear that it would be necessary to traverse the City and take to country roads again on the far side, when, far ahead, he saw a blue gleam of a police-station lamp. He pulled up sharp, dropped his bicycle in the middle of the road, and rushed into the station.

Someone in the car sent a couple of shots after him, the car itself jumped the bicycle and disappeared at high speed. And that was the end of the affair.

Inside the station Sexton Blake was busy putting through a police-telephone call to Scotland Yard. After a moment he called the inspector in charge to the instrument, and that officer received instructions which made him a very respectful man.

Shortly after dawn next morning ten large cars filled with men reached Buckenham, and from every direction they drew in upon the house which Sexton Blake had visited on the night before.

The gatekeeper's lodge was empty, and the carriage-way deeply scored with tyre-tracks. The birds had flown. Blake had half-expected that. His main object was to secure the wonderful furniture—stolen goods, there was no doubt—with which the place was probably filled to the roof. His car was leading, and he himself was one of the first to enter by the open front door.

He found the hall stark empty—even carpetless, and turning into the room of his adventure, found that in similar condition.

He rubbed his eyes, and the high police officials who had shared the foremost car looked as if they questioned his sanity.

"Excuse me, Mr. Blake!" said one. "We understand that a large room—this one, if I mistake not—was crammed with valuable furniture?"

"That is so," said Blake shortly.

"And further, that you gathered from a conversation which you overhead that the remainder of the house was similarly furnished?"

"Just so!"

"Well, for my part, I am willing to believe that the late inhabitants of this mansion were as wicked as you like, but I do not believe that they were magicians. If you ask me to believe that they have removed a houseful of furniture such as you describe in little more than eight hours, then I admit—with all respect to your reputation, Mr. Blake—that I cannot believe you."

"I do not ask you to believe just that," said Sexton Blake calmly.

"And your evidence?"

The detective led him out to the drive, where in the soft grouud were track after track of big tyres deep in the gravel.

"I forgot to tell you," he said, "that in that big garage which you see there, they had half a dozen motor pantechnicons. I did not recognise them for what they were at the time, as I was rather—er—preoccupied, but now I have no doubt whatever."

"Um!"

The official was not convinced, but was too polite to say so. Instead he asked:

"And what do you propose to do now?"

"Follow those pantechnicons. You'll find the end of their journey within fifty miles."

"What makes you so sure of that? It seems more likely to me—"

"Because," explained Blake patiently, "if I am right about the quantity of stuff there was in this house, they must have made two journeys at least, and fifty miles is the greatest distance which they could travel twice over in a single night. Therefore, I say, that you will find some trace of the furniture within fifty miles."

"I hope you are right, Mr. Blake. We will see what can be done."

The official gave a few orders, and the waiting cars turned back on the tracks of the pantechnicons.

There was no difficulty about finding the road they had taken. The drivers of the police-cars hardly needed to moke inquiries, the tracks were so plain. Just outside Nayland, a little place near Colchester, there was a travelling circus with—as the posters said—"a mammoth tent capable of seating a thousand people nightly." Here the tracks of the pantechnicons diverged into a field already churned into a quagmire by the passing and repassing of the numerous cattle, traction-engines, and patrons of "the Greatest Show on Earth," and it was impossible to say in what directions, if any, the motor-pantechnicons had crossed.

Seized by a sudden idea, Blake leaned out of the car and called a hanger-on of the circus.

"Who's the boss of this?" he asked, indicating the circus.

The man grunted.

"Well, if you don't know," he said, with contempt, "It's Mr. Jarsper Hallerton as is the boss 'ere. Want ter see 'im?"

"Yes, I do."

"Well, 'ere 'e comes, and you can see 'im free, which is more than a sight o' people do nowadays."

A well-preserved man, broad, red-faced, typically English and straightforward, came slowly over to the waiting cars.

"You want to see me?" he asked. "I'm Mr. Jasper Allerton, as I dare say my man's been telling you. What can I do for you?"

Blake chanced a long shot.

"What time did they get the last bit of furniture out of your tent?" he asked.

"Good heavens! You've heard about it, have you? Why, about a couple of hours before dawn this morning. What's the matter? Anything wrong? You look like police! I suppose it isn't—"

"Stolen property," said Blake. "Every stick of it!"

"Dear, dear!" Mr. Allerton was obviously shocked. "I assure you, gentlemen, I had not the least idea of that! The man who saw me said that his master was an eccentric millionaire who was making a lightning removal to his town house. He even gave me a visiting-card. I don't know whether it's any use."

The showman produced the slip of pasteboard from his waistcoat-pocket and handed it over. It bore the engraved name "M. Zenith." and nothing more.

"Looks like a French name to me," said Mr. Allerton.

Blake offered no comment.

"Now," he said, "tell us how many vans there were."

"Six," said the showman—"six pantechnicons and four ordinary cars. Coming and going all night they seemed to be, although I suppose they made only two journeys apiece. But work! I never saw chaps work like it! I wish my fellows would turn to half as well! Like lightning it was. One minute my big tent was full to the roof, as you might say, and the next they were gone. Give you my words, gents, I never earned a pony easier; but if I've helped any crooked work, you can take my word for it I did it unknowingly. If I'd known it was 'blue pigeon,' I'd never have touched it with a barge-pole! I—"

Blake stopped him with a wave of the hand.

"Which way did they go?" he asked sharply.

The showman pointed along the road towards London, and began another lengthy speech.

But before he had said ten words the police cars were on the move, and within one minute they had disappeared along the London Road.

"Well, I'm—" said Jasper Allerton.

Showman as he was, he felt that life was just a little too exciting.

The Fourth Chapter

The Warehouse—The Agony Column— Zenith Triumphs Again.

SEXTON BLAKE had just finished telling Tinker of his adventures at the lonely house, and in the pursuit of the furniture vans.

"And you didn't trace them?" asked Tinker, astonished.

"No; we followed them quite easily into the very heart of London, and there"—Sexton Blake frowned with annoyance—"there we lost them. They vanished as utterly, as completely as—"

"As the motor-car which I followed," supplemented Tinker.

"Eh?" Sexton Blake was struck by the coincidence.

"That's a very interesting comparison, my lad," he said thoughtfully. "I'd give a good deal to find that furniture, and the man who engineered its removal. I tell you, youngster, I mean to get this man Zenith. He is as dangerous, in his way, as Reece or Kestrel or Kew, and he is more reckless than either. Until he is laid by the heels—"

Blake left the sentence unfinished; but Tinker, looking up with surprise, saw an expression upon his master's lean, resolute face which he had rarely seen before, and then only in moments of terrible danger.

To remove the effect of his confession the detective laughed pleasantly, and began to fill his briar with the strong tobacco that he affected.

"Now," he said briskly, "we'll have a look at this street where motor-cars vanish into thin air. Ring up the factory inspector for the district—Missington, his name is—and say that I want to meet him in South Street at two o'clock."

Blake had many friends among the public servants of London, and they were always ready to do him a good turn.

Precisely as the hour was clattering out from the City clocks Sexton Blake and Tinker alighted from a taxicab and shook hands with a thin man, bearded and spectacled, whose function it was to see that each factory hand had a proper amount of floor to stand on, air to breathe, time for dinner, and leisure for recreation. Whether he succeeded or not, he was certainly armed with a considerable amount of authority, as they were destined to find out.

"What is it this time, Mr. Blake?" he asked. "Not a bomb factory, I hope! That last little affair of yours that I took a hand in has aged me ten years!"

"A bomb factory?" said Blake. "I wish it were. There's something far more dangerous than bombs in the place which I hope we shall be able to enter!"

The factory inspector lit a cigarette, and Tinker noticed that his hands were decidedly shaky. Evidently he and Sexton Blake had shared a trying experience.

"More dangerous than bombs!" he repeated. "And what is that, sir, if I may ask?"

"That," said Sexton Blake quietly, "is a man who calls himself Monsieur Zenith."

They walked slowly from end to end of the short street.

"I understand," said the detective, turning to his assistant. "that the tracks of the car you followed traversed the whole length of this roadway, ran up to the kerb here at the far end, where we are standing, and then disappeared?"

"Yes, guv'nor," said Tinker, "that is so."

"Ah!"

Sexton Blake slowly searched the high walls which hemmed them in.

"We know," he said, "that the car entered this street. We know that it travelled to the end. And we know that, on its own tyres at least, it travelled no further."

He offered his cigar-case to the factory inspector, deliberately cut and lighted a weed for himself, and appeared to forget for a moment the whole of the affair that they wore engaged upon.

"I think that is the situation," he suggested at length.

Tinker nodded.

"Excellent! Well, now, since the car ceased to travel backwards, forwards, or sideways, and could not have travelled downwards, it is quite clear to me that by some means it was lifted into the air. We don't know by what means that could have taken place, but since it happened immediately opposite the warehouse, which, I perceive is occupied by Field & Conrad, hide importers, I think we will ask to make a little inspection."

"Very good, Mr. Blake!" said the factory inspector. "Nothing easier; but I warn you you will find nothing. They're a most respectable firm. I often inspect their premises, and they always treat me very well. Everything quite above board, I assure you."

Blake smiled. It was his experience that the most dangerous men are often quite respectable and above board in everyday matters. That was one of the characteristics which made them dangerous.

The factory inspector made a move towards the entrance of the warehouse, where an elderly man mounted guard over a time-register, but Blake stopped him.

"Just a moment," he said. "There is a question we had better ask."

He led the way back to the main thoroughfare.

"I think," he said to the factory inspector, "that there is a coffee-stall hereabouts in the early hours of the morning?"

"I believe there is, now you mention it," said that gentleman. "How did you know?"

Blake kicked a few small white objects which lay in the gutter.

"Eggshells," he said briefly.

"Well, well!" The official was most interested. "Fancy you noticing a little thing like, that! Why, I—"

Blake called a lounger from the other side of the street.

"Has the coffee-stall keeper got a shop?" he asked, bringing a few coppers out of his pocket.

"What, old Johnnie Binkham? Course 'e 'as!" said the man with astonishment that anyone should be ignorant of such a simple fact. "Nice little place it is, too! Just round in the Minories."

"Thanks!" said the detective, transferring the small change to the expectant lounger. "Johnnie Binkham, I think you said?"

They crossed Tower Hill and entered the Minories. The coffee-stall keeper was a plump, brown man, most willing to gossip about anything or anybody.

"I want to know," said Blake, "whether you saw a number of covered vans turn into South Street yesterday morning early?"

"Not while I was there," said the man. "What's the trouble?"

Sexton allowed the man to catch sight of a police-badge which Scotland Yard, by special dispensation, had granted him the right to carry.

"All right!" said the coffee-stall keeper hurriedly. "I don't want to ask no questions. I'm going straight now. I'll tell you anything you like!"

"Well, about those vans?" suggested the detective.

"Six of 'em," said the man, "just after five o'clock. I didn't know there was any 'arm in keeping quiet about 'em. Bloke give me a quid to say nothing. It was a nasty morning, and very dark; not another soul about, as you might say. I can't make out how you got on to it."

"Well, my man," said Sexton Blake, "the best thing you can do is not to try to make out how I got on to it. And, another thing is—"

"Yes, sir?"

"Forget that you've told me anything."

Followed by the man's protestations, they turned back into South Street, and once more approached the warehouse of Field & Conrad, hide importers.

This time, under the wing of the privileged inspector of factories, they passed through the low doorway and began to ascend a long flight of stone steps.

It was a typical building of its class. On each landing of its five stories were a pair of swing-doors, through the glass panels of which could be seen a bare expanse of flooring broken by occasional columns which supported the ceiling.

Here and there, parties of men were busy stacking and indexing huge bundles of hides. A more innocent-looking commercial building it would be difficult to find.

Following the plan recommended by the factory inspector, they began at the fifth floor, and, carefully inspecting each storey, worked their way downwards.

Before very long a stout, talkative man who described himself as the manager had joined their party, and was at great pains to describe all the operations they saw.

Much of what he said was too technical to follow, being full of trade terms and examples, but it was quite clear that he knew his job, as a sorter and distributor, from beginning to end.

At the second floor Sexton Blake stopped his flow of explanations and asked a question.

"I see," he said, "that you have an overhead track in this room, and at those doors, which presumably open over the street, there is a complicated system of girders. Now, what do you use that for?"

"Oh, that!" said the manager. "Oh, we don't use that now! I fancy the previous tenants had that for unloading from carts down below. We use the hand-crane, which is fixed to the outer wall—don't we, Mr. Missington?"

He turned to the factory inspector.

That official nodded in confirmation.

"Yes," he said. "I presume that the hand-crane is all you need for those bundles, heavy as they are?"

"That's so, sir—that's so. They're not quite so heavy as they look," said the manager. "And now, if these gentlemen are ready, we'll get along to the—"

"Excuse me," pleaded Sexton Blake. "I'm something of an engineer, and rather interested in this. Where's the traveller which runs on that overhead track?"

The manager laughed pleasantly.

"Ah, now, sir," he said "you've asked me a question that I can't answer. I expect the previous tenants had it removed, it's impossible to say."

The manager again relapsed into his technical descriptions, but Blake continued to inspect the overhead track. Fixed to the ceiling-beams, it passed from end to end of the large room, from the loft-doors already referred to, to iron doors upon the inner wall. In the middle a switch-line ran from a turn-table to another pair of doors now open, through which could be seen the deep waters of the Pool above London Bridge.

"What is behind those iron doors?" persisted the detective, pointing to the doors upon the inner-wall, through which the track disappeared.

The manager turned to the factory inspector with a trace of annoyance.

"I'm afraid, Mr. Missington," he said, "that my time is rather limited. All these questions are—"

"If you could explain this little matter to my friend I should be much obliged," said the factory inspector appealingly.

"Oh, certainly—certainly!"

The man was all willingness in a moment, but still he made it uncomfortably plain that he was wasting time which was very valuable to him.

"Well, sir," he said, "the only reply I can give you is that I don't know. Those doors connect us with the adjoining property, and, so far as I am aware, have never been opened."

"H'm—that's curious!" said Blake thoughtfully.

"And why is it curious, if I may ask?"

"Because those iron doors look to me as if they were open now."

"They certainly are not! I'll show you!"

The man walked across and rattled at the handles. The doors were firmly fastened. There appeared no reason to expect otherwise. The factory inspector came to the conclusion that Sexton Blnko was not such a clever man as people made out, but Tinker had noticed that the moment the manager's back was turned, Blake

rubbed the ferrule of his walking-stick upon the overhead track and brought it down glistening with oil. The track had recently been lubricated!

Blake apologised for his mistake about the doors, and allowed their escort to hurry over the inspection of the remainder of the building. They wished the manager good day and passed out of the entrance-door.

A few paces down the street, however, Blake stopped his companions and turned back.

"We've forgotten to look at the basement."

"It's all right," said the factory inspector. "It's a cold storage for the furs. I've been down there once or twice."

"Mr. Missington," said Blake, "I am most anxious that my assistant should see the cold storage plant. It will be a piece of education for him. Can you not take him down without worrying the manager?"

"Yes, I suppose I could."

They turned back and entered the building once more.

Tinker guessed that this second inspection was only a ruse, and he was not surprised when, by the inspector's side, he had descended to a p!ace of desolating cold, to discover that his employer had given them the slip.

As they left for the second time, however, Blake reappeared, and, talking pleasantly about the "interesting visit" which they had had, said good-bye to their escort, and led Tinker back to the waiting taxi-cab.

When the vehicle was well on the way to Baker Street and he had lighted a cigar, he turned to Tinker and said:

"Well, my lad, I suppose you are wondering what I did while you were in the fur store. The fact is that I had a very keen desire to see the dustbin—the floor-sweepings of the night before. I knew that that manager chap would be in the way, so I let him think we had gone; and then followed you through out into the yard."

"And did you find anything?" asked Tinker.

"I did."

Blake puffed contentedly at his cigar.

"I found pieces of fibre-mat galore—the sort of fibre-mat which they used to protect furniture, and, in addition, several old newspapers."

"Old newspapers!" exclaimed Tinker. "There's nothing in that, guv'nor."

"Wait," said Sexton Blake. "These newspapers were all of the one kind, all of one date, and all opened at the same place. Moreover, they contained a very curious advertisement, which some careless member of the gang had been unwise enough to mark with a cross."

He pulled a copy of the "Daily Mail" from his pocket, and read an item from the "personal" column.

"Meet me at S. Street at ten-thirty.—Z."

"That's clear enough, isn't it?" he asked.

"Where they have put the furniture is a mystery, but that it has been in that factory, and that the place is frequently used as a clearing-house for stolen antiques, I have not the least doubt. In addition, that advertisement convinces me that it is used by the gang as a place of meeting."

"My hat!" exclaimed Tinker. "It looks to me as If we'd got 'em by the short hairs!"

"Precisely! We will insert a similar advertisement, and have the place raided. Provided we can assure the police that Zenith is there, that fact alone will provide a sufficient reason for such a step, and the chances are that they will discover enough to rope in the whole crowd."

"But Zenith would not be there," suggested Tinker. "Since the advertisements are dictated by him, he, at least, would know that our advertisement was a trap."

"I had thought of that," said Blake drily. "But I anticipated that the advertisement, which no doubt occurs somewhat frequently, will not always be dictated by him. We shall see."

On arriving at Baker Street, Blake ascertained by means of the telephone that the advertisement was—as he had supposed—of frequent appearance, and that it was occasionally initialled not "Z," but "J." He at once arranged for an exact repetition initialled "J." to be inserted in the edition of the following morning, and, lighting a cigar, strolled round to the "Yard" to see Sir Henry Fairfax.

At ten o'clock on the following evening Sexton Blake and Tinker occupied a dark and narrow passage-way exactly opposite to the factory of Messrs. Field & Conrad.

It was a moonless night, and they were perfectly safe from observation, while a neighbouring street-lamp would give them every opportunity to scrutinise arrivals if the trap were indeed successful.

Every preparation for a grand scoop had been made. Near by, in a riverside yard, a hundred policemen were waiting for the commands of Inspector Coutts, and farther alone the passage in which Blake and Tinker stood the receiver of an emergency telephone dangled at the end of its wires. As soon as the birds were in the trap Tinker would telephone Inspector Coutts, and the police would close in like a net.

But would the trap be successful?

At ten-twenty-five South Street was as silent and empty as if London were a city of the dead. Suppose the man "J," who had sometimes arranged these meetings, were in touch with Zenith? Suppose he were dead? Suppose—

A hundred questions—a hundred occurrences which might have defeated his plans passed through Blake's mind. And then a man entered the street.

As he approached the lamplight they saw that he was a typical City merchant, silk-hatted and well groomed. He carried a well-rolled umbrella under his arm, a bulky newspaper, which was undoubtedly the "Times."

Blake's doubts came to life again, he was well aware that criminals do not always look like criminals; but this wayfarer was so obviously quiet, respectable, and substantial, so plainly able to "look the whole world in the face," that it was impossible to suppose him anything but what he seemed.

He passed along sedately under the lamp-light, and then, at the door where the timekeeper had stood, now closed and unlighted, he gave a sharp turn, and disappeared, and the narrow door silently closed behind him.

"One!" said Blake softly.

Tinker gave a sharp breath of excitement.

Another was not long in coming. A Billingsgate Market fish-porter actually passed the end of their passage. His padded, misshapen leather hat was on his head, his legs were encased in knee-boots, and fish-scales clung to his clothes. He stank of fish so that the smell drifted over to the detective in the passage-way.

"Surely," said Tinker—"surely that's a genuine passer-by!"

"No," said Blake. "I think not. Our friends appear to be artists in this matter of disguise."

And even as he spoke, the fellow lurched across the road, and disappeared into the factory of Field & Conrad.

The next was a City clerk. Then came a plumber and his mate, carrying their tools. Then, in quick succession, came several groups of

City men, an engineer in the merchant service, two Thames watermen, and a coster. It was a strangely-mixed gathering, and everyone either a masterly character study, or, which was perhaps stranger, exactly what he seemed. However that may have been, the skill with which they entered the street and disappeared quickly, silently, and yet without appearing anxious to avoid observations, was worthy of the admiration which Blake and Tinker could not but feel.

Half-past ten chimed out from the City belfries, and the street returned to its wonted silence and emptiness. Blake paced the passage nervously, he had looked narrowly at each man who had entered the factory, and he was certain that Zenith was not among them. This meant that his whole plan was defeated. In the absence of Zenith, the only man whom they were certain of finding evidence, the police would not act. The invasion of private property is a serious matter, and could be justified only by an arrest.

Then suddenly his gaze became fixed, and he drew in a long breath between his teeth. Monsieur Zenith was descending the street.

He was absolutely undisguised, although he must have known that his description, singular as it was, must have been almost public property.

The crook was in full evening-dress. A silk-hat was tilted towards the back of his head, and his unbuttoned overcoat revealed a white vest and necktie. In one hand he carried an ebony stick, while between the fingers of the other he held one of those tiny opium-loaded cigarettes which it was his custom to smoke.

The man was of such elegant bearing, so perfectly master of himself, so absolutely devoid of fear, that to Tinker at least there came a momentary regret that he would so soon be crop-haired and dressed in convict grey.

But there was not time for sentiment. Zenith had hardly disappeared when Blake reached for the telephone which swung out of a half-closed window.

"Hallo!" he whispered. "Yes. Zenith's in. Come along!"

One minute, two minutes passed away. Then at the far end of the street a mass of men began to assemble. Presently they moved forward. One detached himself, and came on in advance. It was Inspector Coutts. He walked up to the door of the factor, just as the members of the gang had done, and pushed heavily against it.

Then he turned to his men.

"The door's fast," he said. "Spread yourselves, boys. You know what to do. Arrest every man whom you find here. If any resists, knock him on the head."

Inspector Coutts puffed importantly. His big red face was perspiring with satisfaction. This was to be one of the triumphs of his life. He was fairly certain that if he captured Zenith, which he intended to do, Sir Henry Fairfax might be counted upon to do the handsome thing.

As Tinker joined the group around the door he noticed a plainclothes man whose face wore an expression of cold hatred, while he waited like a terrier who sees the rat-trap about to be opened. It was Detective Harris, who had survived the battle of the broad.

"Hallo, Mr. Tinker," said the detective. "Just waiting my chance to have a go at 'em, you see!"

Tinker nodded with a grim smile. He remembered how Detective Harris had sworn revenge, and he saw that no cook would receive pity at his hands that night.

There was no time for pick-locks. A policeman advanced with an axe, and smashed the door down.

A moment later there was a torrent of men surging up the staircase of the factory and overflowing into every room.

Presently the rush ceased, and men began to call each other from floor to floor.

The place was empty.

A few minutes later Blake and Inspector Coutts were having a short but extremely unpleasant conversation in the lobby on the ground floor.

"I understand," said Inspector Coutts, who could scarcely articulate because of disappointment and fury, "that you saw fifteen men enter this building!"

"That is so," said Sexton Blake calmly.

"Well, hang it, Blake, where are they?"

"I'm afraid I can't tell you!"

"We've got the place surrounded on three sides. There is no communication with any other building, that, I'll swear, and yet—"

"What about the fourth side?"

"That's the river. I suppose they swam away? You'll tell me that next!"

"Coutts, old man," drawled Blake. "You are a very able officer, and we get on very well together, but you mustn't talk to me like that!"

"Sorry, Blake!" Inspector Coutts, who was a very good sort, instantly allowed that he had made a mistake. "But you will admit," he added, "that it's a pretty thin story I've got to tell my chief."

Sexton Blake, despite his own annoyance, could hardly help smiling at Coutts' despair.

"Since the river is the only means of escape," he said, "they must have escaped by the river."

"That's so. Blake—that's so!" agreed Coutts. And then, not daring to look the private detective in the face, he muttered: "I suppose you're certain you saw them?"

"What do you mean?" asked Blake sharply.

Inspector Coutts led him to the first of the flight of steps which formed the only means of entering the building from the lobby. It was a freshly-whitened expanse of stone, and bore the imprints of many booted feet.

"Now," said Inspector Coutts, "I admit my men have made a mess there with their hobnails, but can you point to a single imprint which does not belong to our party? There's only yourself and Tinker who aren't wearing police boots, and we can easily spot those belonging to you.

"Don't be so short-tempered and peppery, for Heaven's sake!" he added. "Just have a look at it!"

Sexton Blake made a long inspection, not only of the step indicated, but also of the remainder of the flight. It was quite true. He could not find a single imprint which did not belong to the raiders!

"I'll tell you another thing," said Coutts. "I was first to enter, and I have a distinct memory that these steps were as white as snow."

Sexton Blake and Talker walked home in preference to searching for a taxi-cab. Blake was annoyed with himself for the flaw in his arrangements which had allowed Zenith not only to win another trick of the game, but actually to deal a blow at his reputation.

It was quite clear that Zenith's cleverness was unusual, that he was an adversary whom none could afford to ignore.

If he needed further proof, it was supplied early the next morning.

He had hardly risen when Tinker, brandishing the "Daily Mail," rushed into his bedroom.

"Guv'nor," he shouted, "here's a message for you. Talk about a bit of cheek!"

He turned to the "Agony" column and read:

"I congratulate you! That was very clever, but not quite clever enough. The next move is mine.—Z."

"Events are moving!" chuckled Blake. "When was that advertisement put in?"

"I have just rung up the paper and asked," said Tinker, proud to have anticipated the question. "It was handed in last night, just after eleven, and the messenger paid a special rate to have it inserted this morning."

"Run down to Hendon and get the Grey Panther ready," said Sexton Blake. "Zenith is mistaken. The next move shall be mine!"

THE FIFTH CHAPTER

THE GREY AEROPLANE—ZENITH WINS ANOTHER TRICK—TINKER TAKES THE RISK.

"ALL ready! Stand by! Let her go!"

Sexton Blake, sitting in the pilot's seat of his aeroplane, the Grey Panther, rapped out those orders to a small group of mechanics who had been retaining the machine until it was ready to "taxi" forward for the rise.

As the last words were spoken, the mechanics flung themselves clear, and the machine, with gathering speed, darted forward across the grass. One minute it was bumping heavily, and the next it was scarcely bending the grass; then, with a beautiful sweep, it rose and "banked" towards the smoke, which is London.

Blake had reflected that the best means of defence is attack, and that the only way of attacking Zenith was to do the, unexpected thing. Therefore he and Tinker—who accompanied him—were about to land upon the flat roof of the factory. If detected, they would have a fair chance of getting safely away again; and if, on the other hand, the landing was unobserved on that misty morning, then they would have the advantage of reconnoitring in a manner which was very unlikely to be guarded against. The police raid had failed to prove that Messrs. Field & Conrad were anything but genuine merchants, and the firm in question were now taking action against the police for alleged damage done and defamatory statements made. The confidence of the police was of great use to Blake in his researches, and he was willing to risk much to retain it. The secret of the factory—how it devoured cars and men, and left as little trace of their passing us though they had never been—would prove Field & Conrad to be at least accessories before the fact, and would relieve the Home Office—which controls the Police Force—from a grave embarrassment.

Besides that, Blake was faced with the certainty that the only way for him to preserve his existence was to strike at Zenith, and strike soon, at any cost.

They had not been able to get away until the late afternoon, and already the mists of evening half concealed their objective; nevertheless, by following the course of the river, they were able to pick out the roof where they hoped to land, jutting out, almost like a pier, towards the deep waters of the Pool.

Blake circled once, twice, and then, at a great height, cut off the engine and volplaned.

It was magnificent airmanship. Tinker, who rather fancied himself with an aeroplane, was amazed and delighted at the accuracy with which they touched the very verge of the flat expanse and stopped a few yards short of the parapet. The landing had been made with as much ease as if it were upon a field.

"Rather usefully disguised in their padded clothes, the two leaped out, and by previous agreement, pushed the machine back to the point from which it could most easily be restarted. Then they separated, Tinker to descend fire-escape ladders, and get information by that means, if possible, Blake to prise open a trap-door and enter the premises.

Tinker began his investigations at the fifth floor. The windows were uncurtained, and by very gradually exposing his pocket-mirror around the edge of the sash, he was able to see the interior reflected in its surface. Room after room he inspected, but still without result. It was after knocking-off time, and no doubt the employees, who were not in the know, if there were any, had already departed. Every room was tidy, and, except for bundles of raw leather and sheepskins, empty in addition. In one was a group of men—typical factory hands—smoking cigarettes and playing nap with a pack of greasy cards; but, after watching them for half an hour, Tinker could not perceive that they were there for any reason more interesting than that it was a

good place to gamble and smoke without interruption. They did not even have the air of expecting anybody.

At length he left, their window and continued to descend, but no discovery rewarded him.

"My hat!" he said to himself. "This crowd are pretty fly, or else the guv'nor and I are dotty, and the place is what it seems to be."

Remembering Blake's discoveries at that spot, he even ventured to cross the yard at ground level and lift the lids of the galvanised bins which contained the floor sweepings and rubbish; but, beyond the fact that he found several copies of Blake's faked advertisement of the day before, that also was of no avail.

He had now been at work for nearly an hour, and darkness was already near, yet he had not received the prearranged signal to return—the cry of a seagull.

"It'll be risky work getting away off that roof in the darkness!" he muttered.

He began climbing up the iron staircases with as much speed as caution allowed. The room where he had seen the card-playing was dark and empty, and he became certain that once more they had drawn a blank.

At the fifth floor, however, he checked himself, with a renewed interest. A small window, not accessible from the ladder, had begun to glow with a subdued light.

"Five minutes, more or less, won't make any diff," he said, and, climbing over the handrail of the fire-ladder, he extended the hand containing his pocket hand-mirror at arm's length towards the window.

He gave one glance into its surface, and then he drew back with a long, quivering intake of breath.

Alone, or in the company of his master, he had faced death more times than he could remember. They had fought and were fighting criminals as powerful and pitiless as the law itself—great intellects perverted to crime, whom even Sexton Blake interfered with only at the risk of his life. Both he and Blake had been more than once in the power of Reece, of Kestrel, of other high priests of crime, but never had he feared as he feared now.

Once again, and a hundred times more carefully, he extended the mirror and looked into the room.

Sexton Blake was sitting in a chair, and Tinker guessed from the position of his arms that his hands were manacled around the back of it. The pleasant light of a shaded electric lamp shone on his keen, intellectual face, and clearly showed a broad, reddened patch where—as Tinker guessed—a sandbag had hit him. He was pale, but gave no other sign of discomposure.

Opposite to him, and leaning languidly against the edge of a table, was the slim young albino who called himself Zenith. While Tinker watched, Zenith asked a question. Blake nodded, and the former placed a cigarette between his prisoner's lips, lighting it by means of a small gold spirit-lamp which burnt upon the table.

The room—which, when Tinker had last seen it, had been bare of even a floor covering—was furnished in a manner to which only the adjective "perfect" could do justice, and its two occupants, although one was a prisoner, seemed quite at ease and on excellent terms. But Tinker was not deceived. He had seen enough of Zenith to know that that arch-criminal was always perfect-

mannered, always pleasant; and at the thought of Sexton Blake's danger he sickened with overpowering dread.

"I must get back to that aeroplane sharp," he said.

It would have pleased him to fight through to his master and die fighting by his side; but he knew that the only thing to do was to bring help, and that speedily.

He hurried back to the roof. Of course, the vibration of the aeroplane engine would bring Zenith's men on top of him; but he reckoned on being, by that time, in a position to glide away from them at a speed of sixty miles per hour. He came on to the asphalted space with a run, and then stopped dead in his tracks. The Grey Panther had disappeared. Its tyre tracks crossed the flat roof from edge to edge, and at the far end grew fainter and fainter until the eye could not follow them. It was clear that the aeroplane had been flown away by some member of the gang, while he, deep down the ladder on the far side,

Without the least warning, the whole stack collapsed, and Sexton Blake measured his length on the floor.

had been as ignorant of what was going on as the gang had been of his existence.

It took him less than a minute to come to these conclusions, and before the minute was over he had returned to the fire-ladder. Not daring to remain to witness what was happening in the lighted room—whether by now Blake had been carried, a dead man, to some water-trap at River Level, or whether, he and Zenith were still vieing with each other in politeness—he descended once more to the yard and looked in vain for a way of escape. There was none. The factory had been constructed to be inaccessible by any other means than its external doorways afforded, and Tinker soon saw that he was hardly less a prisoner than his master.

He returned to the roof, and took a long glance down into the black waters of the Pool.

"It's a big dive," he muttered, "even if there's water enough at the bottom—which I doubt. But it's the only chance, and I've got to take it."

He removed his boots and crept out along a heavy timber which overhung the stream. A mist already clothed the surface of the water, and made the seventy-odd feet of space between seem even greater than it was.

"I'll swallow-dive!" he muttered. "That'll carry me out a bit."

One by one he let his boots fall from the boom, and watched them while they turned over and over in mid-air, disappearing at last with a tiny "plop." As they had disappeared, so, in a minute, would he disappear. Whether he ever returned to the surface would depend on luck and the depth of the water.

He let his padded airman's jacket follow the boots, then, at the end of the long boom, he rose to his feet.

For a second or so he stood poised at that dizzy height, and then, heart in throat, he allowed himself to fall forward.

Chest well forward and arms outstretched like the wings of a bird, he rushed downward. The oily dark waters were nearer—nearer, then—

"Now!" he thought, and straightened out for the plunge.

For a long minute, as it seemed, the brown water rushed past him; then, with some force, his outstretched hands hit the bottom of the river.

Had it been mud, he could only have suffered a dreadful death; but, although contact with the hard gravel shook him through and through, it left him free to rise.

A moment later he was treading water and congratulating himself. Then, remembering his mission of life and death, he settled down to a steady crawl stroke which Blake had taught him, and began swimming with the tide round towards Custom House Quay.

THE SIXTH CHAPTER

THE CAPTURE OF SEXTON BLAKE—A CONSIGNMENT OF ANTIQUES—THE FREEZING PLANT.

The capture of Sexton Blake had been a piece of sheer luck for Zenith.

After leaving Tinker, the detective had cautiously prised open a trapdoor and descended an unsteady ladder into the top floor of the warehouse. There, always with the greatest care, he had prospected in every direction, until at last he had come to the room which had first caught the attention of Tinker—the room where the employees of the place were smoking and playing cards.

Here he remained for some minutes, hoping to overhear some clue as to Zenith's movements or statements which would clear up the mysterious disappearances with which the warehouse was associated.

He was concealed from the card-players and their friends by a stack of sheepskins; and seeing that, if he could but climb to the top, he might be in a capital position to see and hear everything that transpired, he hauled himself slowly from bundle to bundle until the low ceiling was only a few feet above him.

He was just congratulating himself upon this attainment when, without the least warning, the whole stack collapsed, and he measured his length on the floor.

Half-stunned as he was, he put up a grand fight. He had no time to get at his pistol, and the greater part of his opponents appeared to be unarmed. Nevertheless, when they recognised him, as undoubtedly they did, they rushed upon him as one man. For ten seconds it was left, right, left—every punch a sleeping-draught; and then he was smothered by numbers. As he reeled back for a final scrimmage, a man who had worked round behind him struck hard and suddenly with a sandbag. The blow took Blake on the side of the head, and for three minutes or so he was, to all intents and purposes, a dead man.

The first thing that he became aware of on recovering consciousness was the beautiful but mocking voice of Zenith.

"Tut, tut, Mr. Sexton Blake," it said. "A most regrettable accident, only fortunate in that it brings us the pleasure of your company.

"And how do you come to be here?" the master-crook went on. "Let me do a little deduction."

He put his daintily-manicured finger-tips together.

"It is really too easy. Add leather clothes and goggles—I hope they are not damaged, by the way—to a flat roof, and the answer is an aero-plane."

He uttered a name.

"De Maupas!"

"M'sieur!" said a short, dark man, obviously French.

"You'll find an aeroplane up there"—pointing in the direction of the roof. "Get into it and fly it away. I don't like aeroplanes."

"Oui, m'sieur!"

Zenith was evidently accustomed to instant obedience. The man disappeared, and, a minute later, the diminishing drone of an aeroplane came faintly to their ears.

Then the master-crook turned to Sexton Blake with a little bow.

"Pardon, my dear Blake, if I may call you so. One has so many little things to attend to. But now, if you would care for a little conversation, I am at your disposal.

"Here," he added, turning to his men, who stood in a compact group at a respectful distance, "one of you untie Mr. Blake's legs so that he can walk up to my sitting-room. Where's Bletsoe?"

The man who had advanced to do his bidding allowed himself to smile.

"He's taking the count, sir," he said, with a backward jerk of the thumb to where one of the gang lay insensible upon the floor.

Zenith shook his finger waggishly.

"Ah, Mr. Blake, Mr. Blake," he murmured, "I'm afraid you have been rough with my poor fellows. I perceive that two of them are still 'taking the count,' as this good man puts it. It is indeed a pity that you thwarted me. Such strength as yours might have insured a long life full of incident. As it is—"

He shrugged his shoulders.

"But why should we dwell on this unpleasant-ness?" he drawled on, in his heartless, bantering tone. "Precede me, if you will, to my sitting-room, and you shall enjoy at least one perfect cigarette before the inevitable."

Blake, who had already recovered from the blow of the sandbag, rose to his feet and allowed himself to be guided to the little room in which Tinker had seen him. He knew that Zenith, for all his elaborate manners and distinguished polite-ness, would murder him in cold blood, and had probably determined already how and when to do it. He suspected that his last hour had come. What hope he had lay in the fact that Tinker was free, and might guess what had happened. This, however, was not a great consolation. Before help could arrive, it was most probable that he, Sexton Blake, would be only a name—that his dead body would be drifting slowly down the Thames, or lying in some secret shallow grave whither Zenith's motor-cars had carried him.

Nevertheless, he watched every move and weighed, every chance. Even to die fighting would he worth much.

But Zenith read his thoughts with diabolical cleverness.

"My friend," he murmured, "I hate melodrama; but, in case you are tempted to rush me, I have a pistol. I am a certain shot, and I should shoot you instantly!"

Blake smiled.

"You had better do it while you have the chance," he said, "for I warn you that you will not always have this advantage of me."

Zenith could not believe that such indifference was genuine. He lookod the detective searching-ly in the face. Then, bending forward he placed his fingers upon his prisoner's wrist.

For ten seconds he counted the pulsation of the well-filled arteries. Then he said, almost with awe:

"You are brave, Mr. Sexton Blake. You know your danger—or, at least, I think you do—and yet your nerves are as steady as a rock. I admire you; I envy you. But," he added, "I also fear you; and you must die."

He clapped his hands, and two of his men entered.

"Mr. Blake," he said, "you will go with these men."

His face had paled, and his voice had become harsh with emotion.

Sexton Blake rose, his hands still bound behind him, and the end of his cigarette still between his lips. There was nothing to do but to obey.

As he turned to the door between the two men, who doubtless were to be his executioners, Zenith stopped him.

"One moment," said the crook. "Suppose I offered you freedom in return for your word of honour to let me and my affairs alone for ever?"

"I should be compelled to refuse."

"I was afraid so."

Zenith seemed genuinely grieved. Nevertheless he turned to his men, and, without hesitation, ordered:

"Take him away!"

Blake allowed himself to be led down the stone stairs. He moved like a man in a dream. He perceived that, like a sheep, he was being led to the slaughter; but, unlike a sheep, he knew his fate. The only hope which now remained to him was that somehow he should get in a last fight—die as he had lived, attacking the enemies of society.

His executioners were leading him across the first floor, now in almost complete darkness, when a shrill bell sounded once—twice—thrice—

"Good heavens," said one of the crooks, "that's the vans here already!"

The other replied:

"Yes; we're wanted up top. What are we going to do about this chap?"

"We'll have to take him downstairs. The boss said—"

"Can't 'elp what the boss said!"

The men were one on each side of Sexton Blake, their hands under his armpits. In the half-darkness he could just detect a movement of the last speaker. The man had tightened his grip of the one hand, while the other had disappeared behind him—obviously reaching for a weapon.

Instantly the detective made the effort for which he had been saving himself. He kicked the legs from under his guards, and, falling with them, rolled clear before rising to his feet.

One, as it turned out, had been half-stunned by contact with the concreted floor; but the other

whipped out a pistol and sent half a dozen bullets after the escaped prisoner.

To rush across the room in the darkness without the use of hands for protection was taking big chances; but the situation was desperate, and Blake had to risk it. He made for the door, but had got his bearings wrong, and cannoned into a stack of hides.

Bruised and shaken, and pursued by pistol-bullets, he tried twice again. And then the electrics sprang into radiance.

With one hand on the switches, and a heavy automatic in the other, Monsieur Zenith stood watching him, with a smile.

"Truly, Mr. Blake," he said, "you are a dangerous man! It were doubtless better if I myself gave you your quietus with a bullet here and now; but I am a reckless fellow, and very vain. You shall live a little longer. There is something which I want to show you.

"Only—"

He raised the pistol until, to Blake's eyes, it showed a small black ring.

"Only you must give me your parole—your promise not to move from that spot for fifteen minutes."

Blake saw that the alternative was instant death.

"I agree," he said.

He saw that the mystery of the warehouse was about to be explained to him—that he owed the postponement of his destruction to an inventor who had never before had an equal to admire his handiwork.

"We have some very clever devices here, I promise you," said the young man.

The doors which opened above the street were thrown back with silent speed. Then followed the iron doors on the inner wall which had aroused his curiosity at the first inspection of the premises. Each man appeared to have a place and a duty; there was no confusion, no orders were necessary.

A telescopic system of girders slowly extended above the street, and from behind the iron doors came a swift, silent traveller running upon the overhead track.

The traveller disappeared beyond the outer wall, its chains extended downwards, running smoothly over oiled pulleys; then, with the ease of a dream, it raised the whole body of a small furniture-van and set it down in the middle of the wide floor.

Six journeys it made in as many minutes. Then the doors above the street were closed again.

Already the van doors were open, and men were extracting piece after piece of priceless antique furniture, tapestries, carpets; wonderful pictures and bronzes; porcelain and glass, unique in its perfection.

Blake watched the operations of the crooks with quiet interest.

Already they had stripped the vans, and article after article of the precious contents was being covered with hides, or thrust into boxes faked up to represent bales of sheepskins. In an incredibly short, space of time all the stolen furniture had disappeared, and in its place was an innocent stack of hides and sheepskins ready for transport to the river.

Now that the danger of leaving finger-prints was at an end the crooks began to discard their gloves, and to light pipes and cigarettes.

One of the bales was labelled, and Blake took careful note of the address, which was that of a leather-merchant in Bombay. Zenith noted his interest, and gave a short, mirthless laugh.

"Hope dies hard, Mr. Blake!"

"There is one thing more I want you to see," he said, "and then—well, then we must make an end of you for ever."

He gave an order, and the doors on the water front were thrown open. Nearby Blake could see one of the masts of a tramp steamer, and the traveller was instantly put into use to serve this vessel with the faked bundle. Again the crooks began a period of arduous toil, and the stolen furniture left the warehouse en route for Bombay as expeditiously as it had entered.

The transfer was hardly completed when Blake staggered to the wall, failed to keep his feet, and slid down on to the floor in a limp heap.

Zenith turned.

"Ah!" he muttered, "I thought that doped cigarette would get him."

He kicked aside a cigarette which the detective had only smoked for a moment, and called two of his men.

"Pick him up," he said, "and follow me."

Followed by two men carrying the insensible detective, he made his way to the ground floor, and, after traversing a lone passage, began a further descent into the fur store.

As the men descended the cold became more and more intense, until, at the basement level, it made breathing painful and numbed the extremities.

The master-crook motioned his men to depart, and turned for a last look at the man he had learned to fear.

Sexton Blake was already reviving under the influence of the biting cold. As Zenith watched him, his eyes opened, and he turned his head.

"I was afraid the cold might awaken you," said Zenith. "It would have been better had you slept on. We are in the fur store, and I have increased the cold until it is death to remain here, which is what you are in the position of being compelled to do.

"I will not tell you not to be afraid," he added, "because I well know that you are fearless. But I tell you to be of good heart. It is an easy death. Presently—in five or ten minutes—you will feel the desire to sleep; you will close your eyes, and that will be the end. Good-bye, Mr. Blake; in happier circumstances we might have been comrades; as it it, I am compelled to kill you!"

Blake made no answer. The crook walked swiftly out, and the heavy doors swung to behind him.

§

Tinker had emerged from the Thames in a state of exhaustion. There had been a strong tide running at the time of his dive from the warehouse roof, and, strong swimmer as he was, he had had terrible difficulty in getting ashore. Nevertheless, his first act, bootless and soaking as he was, was to seek a telephone, and ring through to Inpector Coutts.

"Is that Inspector-Coutts?" he said. "I'm Tinker." Then he added: "The guv'nor's right up against it! Zenith's got him. There in the warehouse in South Street. Get some men—anybody—and come round there at once! Even now the guv'nor may be—may be—"

The lad's voice broke.

"Quick, Coutts—quick!" he finished, and dashed out to get back to the warehouse as quickly as possible.

As Tinker's taxicab turned into South Street it almost collided with a police car containing Inspector Coutts and half a dozen men. The glaring headlights of the police car made the dark roadway as bright as day, and, even before Tinker and his friends had tumbled out of their respective conveyance, it was possible to see that the warehouse was closed and in darkness.

The police had already been in trouble about their previous futile raid at the same place; but, ignoring that fact, Inspector Coutts gave instructions for the door to be forced.

"Blake's been a good pal to me," he explained.

One of the men brought a crowbar, the door was forced and thrown back, and the raiders rushed forward to begin a laborious search of the warehouse room by room.

Needless to say, it produced nothing which threw any light upon the fate of Sexton Blake or even upon the illicit character of the building. The place had been freshly cleaned and swept, and not a trace of its late occupants remained! It was not until Coutts had given orders to his men to return to the Yard that Tinker thought of the fur store.

"What about the fur store?" he suggested. "There's a fur store in the basement, you know."

Inspector Coutts shook his head.

"No good," he said. "Why should they drag the poor chap down there when they could just as easily—"

He checked himself, and patted Tinker clumsily upon the back.

"Come along, lad, we'd better be getting out of here!"

Tinker struck out his chin obstinately. His face was white; but it was quite clear that he had determined to leave no stone unturned to discover his employer, alive or dead.

"I'm going to have a look at that fur store," he said.

"Very well," agreed the Scotland Yard man, "But I suppose you know that it's half an hour since we entered this building? And half an hour in that ice-house would freeze a Polar bear, let alone a man!"

Tinker knew that be was speaking the truth, but still persisted in his determination. Accompanied by the unwilling Coutts, he forced open the door which led to the basement, and descended into the intense cold on the far side.

At the bottom of the staircase there were insulated doors; but this also they forced open. Tinker was in a mood to stop at nothing.

They entered the big room, and passed along between the white enamelled racks. Tinker's teeth were chattering, and the cold made his head swim; yet he grimly completed his self-imposed task of searching the whole of the store.

At length it was finished, and he turned away with a lump in his throat. The place was empty. The slight hope he had had of finding his master there disappeared for ever.

"No luck!" he called out to the inspector, who had been obliged to retreat beyond the door out of reach of the intense cold.

"Everything's the same as usual here, except that—"

He was checked by a sudden thought.

The one particular in which the fur store differed from his previous experience of it was that the furs, which obviously belonged to the white racking, were piled up altogether in one huge, untidy heap.

"I wonder—" he uttered, with growing excitement.

Forgetting the cold, from which be had begun to suffer severely, he seized the uppermost furs—wonderful things, worth hundreds of guineas apiece—and hurled them aside.

For a full minute he worked at top speed, then he bent down with a sob of joy. Wrapped in layer upon layer of warmth-conserving fur—which he had somehow dragged down from the racks, despite his manacled, hands—was the unconscious, but still living, body of Sexton Blake.

THE SEVENTH CHAPTER

THE HOUSE NEXT DOOR—ZENITH "MILKS" THE TELEPHONE—THE BOMB.

THE furnished house next door to Sexlon Blake in Baker Street had been to let for some time, when it was taken by an elderly student of languages. The student was a pale man with dark glasses, and seemed to have very little idea of business. His references, however, were excellent, and, as he made no objection to a fairly stiff rental, he was duly accepted as a tenant, and moved in.

He being a teacher of his special subject, it was not surprising that he should be visited by a large number of adult pupils, for coaching therein, and on the afternoon of the first day in the new house he rang the bell and interrogated one of them.

"Have you fixed up the switch-line?" he asked sharply.

"Yes, sir," replied the other. "Blake's telephone wires are fixed to insulators on his chimney-stacks, and we have had no difficulty in connecting up to his line and running his wires so that they are almost invisible. If you care to place your ear to our 'phone, I think they are speaking now."

"Very well!"

Zenith—for such was the real identity of the "elderly student"—approached and laid his land upon the receiver.

"Silence!" he cautioned. "Don't forget that if we can hear them they can also hear us!"

He listened for some minutes.

"Good!" he said, at length, replacing the instrument, "Blake is 'phoning for a man from the Electric Light Company. Something's wrong with his fuses. That gives me a chance I was wanting."

He issued a sharp order.

"Tell Somers to get himself up in a uniform like that of the electric company's inspectors, and report to me here in twenty minutes!"

The man disappeared, and Zenith walked over to the telephone.

"Now," said the crook to himself, "we'll see whether it was worth my while to belong to the same West End club as Sir Henry Fairfax, the Chief of Police."

In a voice which was certainly not his own be gave Sexton Blake's telephone number, and waited, placidly smoking his cigarette.

"Oh, is that you, Blake?" he asked, after a minute. "Well, look here, can you come round to the Yard at once? I'm Sir Henry Fairfax, and I'm in a deuced tight corner, 'pon my word I am. Personal favour if you could. Explain everything then. You will? Good!"

"And I say," he went on, "bring your assistant and the dog with you; they are nearly sure to be wanted. You're starting now? Excellent! Good-bye!"

He rang off with a laugh of triumph.

As he turned away from the instrument a man in the electric company's uniform entered the room.

"Good!" he said. "You have been quicker than I expected. I compliment you. Now for your instructions: You will walk out from here as if you had just finished a job, and go straight to the house next door. You will explain that you have come in response to a telephone message, and the good lady will let you in. You will follow her out to the back of the house, and put her to sleep with a little drop of choloroform on a handkerchief. When she is safe you must knock three times upon the wall, and wait till the door-bell rings."

Zenith paused.

"Repeat that part of your instructions," he said.

The man repeated it word for word.

Zenith nodded.

"And now for the second part."

Between his slender fingers the crook began to roll a cigarette of opium-charged tobacco.

"The old lady will be removed. Directly she is gone you will take up the flooring in Sexton Blake's hall and place this immediately behind the threshold."

He took a square brass box carefully out of a drawer, and laid it on the table.

"It is a time-bomb, and it is set to explode tomorrow morning at nine-thirty—a time when the lad will be giving the dog a run and the detective will be alone in the house. Having deposited the bomb and concealed the fact that the door has been disturbed, you will leave the house, walk away in the opposite direction, get rid of your uniform, and remain away.

"At nine-twenty-nine-and-a-half, Greenwich time, you will ascend Sexton Blake's steps, and make a furious noise at the door. Knock, ring, break the window—anything to insure his being there at nine-thirty precisely. When you are sure that this is certainty you may make your get-away, but not before. Now let me see that you have remembered the whole thing!"

Again, without a mistake, the man repeated the whole programme from beginning to end.

"That is satisfactory," said Zenith.

He walked over to the window, and, standing just behind the curtains, watched Blake, Tinker, and the dog get into a taxi-cab and drive away.

He waited exactly one minute after the cab had disappeared, then he turned to the uniformed man.

"You may go now," he said.

The ease with which Zenith's assistant carried out his instructions was a proof of the crook's thoroughness.

After he had chloroformed the house-keeper, and given the signal of three knocks upon the party wall, he answered the door to a very efficient-looking nurse.

Outside he could see the kind of conveyance which is known as a fever van, and a couple of hospital orderlies waiting with a stretcher.

The nurse gave him Zenith's private sign, and he immediately admitted her.

She said, with a grin, "Where's the patient?" And, taking a blanket from one of the beds for the purpose, she wrapped up the insensible Mrs. Bardell, and helped the stretcher-bearers to carry her out to the cart. A small group of idlers had collected, and she waved them aside.

"It's a small-pox case," she whispered, and then added: "Ah, here comes a policeman!" in a tone of great satisfaction.

She actually called the policeman, and set him to keep back the sightseers. Then, after seeing that her "patient" was quite comfortable, she followed the stretcher-bearers into the car, and was driven swiftly away.

The sham electrician, who had prudently remained out of sight during this episode, returned to the half door and completed the carrying out of his instructions. Then he, too, departed.

At nine-twenty-five on the following morning he again entered Baker Street.

With frequent reference to his watch, which he had taken the precaution to verify by a synchronised chronometer, he made his way along its length until he came in sight of the house occupied by Sexton Blake.

On one pretext and another he delayed his progress until his watch indicated a minute to the half-hour. Then he walked swiftly forward, ascended Blake's steps, and rang the bell.

He strained his ears to hear footsteps on the stairs inside, but without success. He stole a glance at his watch, observed that the hands stood at fifteen seconds to the half-hour, and, without hesitation, thrust his elbow through the glass panel of the door. Instantly there was a sound of approaching footsteps, and, conscious that he had done his part in the intended crime, the crook hurried down the steps and away.

As Zenith had anticipated, the door was opened by Sexton Blake himself.

The detective stood for a second or two upon the threshold, looking alternately at the splintered panels and the retreating man, whom he had somehow identified as the individual responsible for the damage. He did not make any attempt to pursue, probably divining that there was something of greater importance in the wind, but not knowing what it was. For a few seconds he stood there, and then, puzzled, turned back to re-enter the house.

The crook, watching from a safe distance, saw the door fall slowly outwards on its torn hinges, and a cloud of dust swirl into the street, while to his ears there came a thunderous crash, followed by the tinkle of broken glass.

He hurried away, glad of the success of his enterprise, but, crook though he was, sorry to see a good man go under.

§

When Tinker came back from his run with Pedro, he was surprised to see a crowd collected in front of the door.

As he got nearer, he perceived that something serious had happened. Several windows were broken, and the door itself was off its hinges and leaning against the wall.

There was a policeman on duty at the gate, and, in answer to Tinker's urgent inquiries, he said huskily:

"There's a reverend gentleman inside. You'd better ask him, Mr. Tinker."

A rush of warmth seemed to pass over the lad's body from the feet to his head. Without knowing how he had come there, he found himself in the dear old sitting-room, seated opposite a clergyman, who was telling him that his guv'nor was at that moment lying dead upstairs.

"Would you—ah—would you like to enter the death-chamber?" asked the clergyman.

Tinker nodded. He could not trust himself to speak.

Placing an arm across the lad's shoulders, the clergyman led him to Sexton Blake's familiar bed-room, and stretched out a hand to open the door.

"Wait a minute," Tinker jerked out. "I—I don't think I shall want you with me."

He knew he must be hurting the man's feelings, but words did not come to him very easily at that moment.

"Oh, my dear lad!" said the parson. "Certainly, certainly! I quite understand!"

He mumbled to himself, and walked slowly away down the corridor.

Tinker paused for a moment, then, drawing a deep breath, went into the room.

The bed-room was just as Blake had left it in the morning. His bath-gown still lay crumpled up on a chair, while his favourite briar pipe remained just where he had put it down upon the dressing-table. But it was to the bed which Tinker devoted his attention.

The bed-clothes had been thrown back, and on the mattress, covered by a sheet, lay a tall figure, hands crossed on breast, like a sculptured Crusader.

Tinker reverently turned back the sheet, and looked long and earnestly at the face of his master.

Then, for what reason he could not have said, a doubt struck him—a single ray of hope.

Despite the fact that Sexton Blake's hair was singed, and his forehead disfigured by a long graze, there was a look about him which spoke of continued life. Tinker had been compelled to see several dead men in the course of his adventurous career, and the one or two signs of death which he remembered in their faces were not present in the face of his master.

Calling himself a fool for doing so, he leaned over to see whether he could detect any sound of breathing.

Then he almost swooned. Sexton Blake had seized him around the neck, and, with a gentle but powerful hand, suppressed the cry of astonishment which had risen to his lips. The detective pulled his head down, and whispered in his ear:

"Get rid of that parson! He's a crook!"

Then the figure on the bed resumed its impassivity, eyes vaguely staring, hands crossed upon the breast.

Tinker paced the room a few turns to regain control of himself. He saw instantly that Blake's feigning death was an important part of the difficult and dangerous game that they were playing, but he had considerable doubt of his ability to maintain an expression of sorrow after his wonderful discovery.

Presently there was a discreet tap.

Tinker concealed his face in the crook of his arm, as though he had been weeping, and opened the door to the sham clergyman.

"Let's get out of here!" he said, in a muffled voice, while he led the clergyman out, and, pretending that the act was an absent-minded one, he locked the door behind them and put the key into his pocket.

The parson checked him.

"My lad—the—ah—key," he murmured. "It is necessary for so many things."

"No one shall have it but me," Tinker burst out, and, walking along the corridor, locked himself into his bed-room.

The supposed parson listened for some minutes, and then, not hearing anything to alarm him, set about carrying out orders which he had received from Zenith earlier in the day.

He passed into the consultation-room, and began to pack the note-books, case diary, and other records which might contain anything dangerous to Zenith or his friends into a professional-looking black attache-case.

Tinker, who had been anxiously watching his movements, so as to be able to warn his employer the moment the coast was clear, could not but be aware of what was going on.

He waited until the crook bad gone so far that he could not pretend to be doing anything more innocent than bare-faced robbery, then, not forgetting to maintain his expression of profound grief, he stepped into the room and asked the supposed clergyman what he was doing.

The man was quite unabashed.

"I was just packing the more important of your dear master's valuable records," he explained. "But perhaps you'd rather I left them until you were able to help me?"

The man was perfect. Never for a moment did he show any trace of alarm, or by a single word betray that his clerical accent was not natural to him.

Tinker had a difficult part to play. He saw instantly that he had failed to prove anything which would make it possible for him to evict the fellow.

He took a big risk.

Walking right up to the intruder, he thrust his hand between the clerical coat-tails and into the crook's hip-pocket.

He was in luck! As he had hoped would be the case, the pocket contained the very thing necessary to prove that at the man was no parson, but one acquainted with a life of danger. He stepped back with a magazine-pistol in his hand—a magazine-pistol with a Maxim silencer—a very nasty weapon.

"What's this?" asked the lad. "By Heaven, you're a crook; and if you don't get out of here—"

The man was only too anxious to take his chance.

"Aw, come off!" he gibed, dropping his parson's voice, and relapsing into the vernacular of Sing-Sing. "You're a clever guy; but if I'd got the gun I'd raise Cain, and then some! We done Blake in, anyway, and we'll sure do you if you're troublesome. Awright, don't get rattled! I'm goin'!"

Tinker dragged aside the makeshift front door, and saw his unwelcome visitor off the premises. Then he rushed back, with a subdued shout of joy, and tore open his employer's bed-room door.

"Well done!" said the detective. "I heard what was happening!"

Their hands met in a hard, close grip.

"Guv'nor," said Tinker, "I—I'll never forgive you!"

"Tut, tut!" grunted Blake. "It's all part of the game!"

Nevertheless, he grasped the boy's arm affectionately.

"I had to do it," he explained. "I know Zenith will never leave me alone, or, what is more important, venture to give himself to his criminal pursuits, while he thinks I'm alive. While I was a prisoner, he told me himself that on September 17th there was to be a meeting of the whole gang in a barge which is moored off the warehouse in South Street, and if I can only get him to suppose that he need fear nothing from me, we may be able to bag the lot.

"The idea of shamming dead," Blake went on, "was really given to me by the policeman. The explosion knocked me right out of time, and when I came round they were carrying me upstairs. I heard the policeman say that, in his opinion, I was a goner, and determined to be one as far as possible until our doubtful friend had departed. I managed to let the police-surgeon into the secret without giving myself away, and I have no doubt that he is even now advertising the sad news as much as is necessary for our purpose."

Sexton Blake thoughtfully pinched the upper part of his own right arm.

"And now," he said, wincing, "if you've got any first-aid bandages handy, I should like to have a look at this arm of mine."

THE EIGHTH CHAPTER

THE RIVER POLICE—SECOND-LIEUTENANT BELLING.

"SILENCE! Keep together. Wait until the signal is given!"

Such were the whispered commands of Sexton Blake to the six large police patrol-boats which lay off the Customs House Quay, waiting for the signal to raid Zenith's assembly barge on the Pool.

It was September 17th, and, so far as Blake knew, the fact of his continued existence had remained unknown to his enemies. The bomb outrage, and the events which followed, had been unreported by the newspapers, so as to spare his many friends the shock of his supposed death, and a very quiet funeral had been arranged, so as to dispel any lingering doubt on the part of his would-be murderers. Therefore the detective had the strongest reason to hope that the meeting of crooks would take place, in which event it was more than likely that the man against whom he had sworn retribution would be laid by the heels.

While they lay there, clustered together in the darkness, the men muttering together, and the sluggish river lap-lapping against the embankment, Sexton Blake was attentively watching a certain point up-river where Tinker was on sentry-go, armed with a flash-lamp. The lad had already flashed the message that the gang were entering the warehouse, and from there, as Blake knew well, they would enter a large motor-launch which their wonderful system of pulleys would raise to the first-floor level and lower to the river when all their members were aboard. Then, leaving the warehouse as empty and innocent as they found it, they would be transported to the barge and hold their meeting. Tinker was in a position to see the passing of the motor-launch, and would signal this also.

Blake watched for some moments. Then the expected twinkling of Tinker's flash-lamp came across the water, and he knew that the enterprise was on a fair way to success.

He looked at his watch. In ten minutes they would attack.

Inside the barge a curious scene was being enacted. The interior of the vessel, although absolutely bare of any furniture, save one chair and a handsome occasional-table, upon which stood a decanter and one tumbler, was superbly finished in polished oak. The walls and ceiling were wainscot, and the floor was of narrow battens, polished like the floor of a ball-room.

Some twenty men of all classes of society stood talking in undertones around the walls, but the middle of the floor, and the chair which stood there, remained unoccupied.

It was Zenith's habit to sit among his fellow-crooks as a man who has no equals, and, keeping them on their feet as though they were in the presence of Royalty, set forth his plans of criminal campaign, or administer what he called justice.

On this night there was one among the assembled crooks who was new to the council-chamber, and, seeing no reason why he should not make himself at home, he walked up to the central table and began to mix himself a drink.

Most of the councillors watched him in horrified silence; but one of them, who perhaps felt himself to be responsible in some way, stepped up and checked his colleague.

"Here," he said, with a slight smile, "do you know whose that is?"

The crook, a hard case like all the rest of them, turned with a snarl.

"No, I don't," he said; "and I don't care!"

"Well," said the first, "it belongs to Monsieur Zenith."

"I don't care who it belongs to! I'm going to have a drink!"

He mixed the drink, and, raising it, turned to his friends.

To his surprise, they were watching him with horrified fascination, as one might watch a man who was about to commit suicide.

He put the drink down untasted.

"Here," he said, "who is this Monsieur Zenith that you talk about?"

The man who had spoken to him before condescended to explain.

"You probably know him by another name," he said, smiling. "Sometimes he is known as 'The Boss'!"

The first man turned pale to the lips.

"Why the deuce didn't you say so at first?" he complained. "I didn't know—I swear I didn't! How could I? I ain't never heard him called that what you said. I call you to witness that I haven't touched that glass except to pour out the guzzle! I—"

He stopped, shrinking. Monsieur Zenith was descending the elegant staircase which led from the deck.

The crook, who was, as usual for that hour of the day, dressed in perfect evening-clothes, handed his hat, coat, stick, and gloves to a man who waited for them, and took his seat in the chair, with a pleasant "Good-evening, gentlemen!"

Then he turned to the trembling crook who stood beside the table.

"Fortunately for you, I was witness that you did not put that tumbler to your lips. You will know better next time. Get back to your place!"

He took his seat and rolled a cigarette.

"As I came past Customs House Quay in my little motor-boat," he murmured, "I noticed a rather large number of boats and men assembled there, does anybody know what the meaning of it is?"

There was no reply.

"Singular!" commented Zenith. "I don't think the late lamented Sexton Blake could have—" He stopped. "No. I was somewhat under the influence of opium at our last meeting, but I don't think that I gave anything away. Let us get on with our business."

Meanwhile, out in the darkness, the concourse of boats which had aroused Zenith's suspicions was slowly surrounding the barge. The launch by which the crooks had arrived was discovered and led away, and, with a jarring contact of fenders on the side of the barge, the foremost police-boat discharged its crew on to the tarpaulined deck.

The River Police, than which there are no braver body of men in the world, tumbled helter-skelter down the staircase which led to the council chamber, and very soon a scattering of pistol-shots showed that some at least of the councillors had found it not worth while to be taken alive.

Blake, with his arm in a sling, followed close upon the heels of the police.

There had been no organised resistance, and, with the exception of one who lay face-down upon the oaken floor, the whole gang were lined up against the wall. One or two of the police were badly hurt, and several more were already at work applying first-aid to their own minor injuries. The remainder stood, pistol in hand, before their captives, ready to shoot at the first sign of treachery. It was a great scoop.

The police-officer who had been in command of the first boat came towards the detective with right hand outstretched in congratulation.

"Splendid!" he exclaimed. "Mr. Blake, the Force owes you another debt of gratitude!"

Sexton Blake looked around.

"Thanks!" he said, smiling. "But have you got the man that calls himself Zenith?"

The officer chuckled.

"We sure have!" he boasted. "Come this way."

He led Sexton Blake to the far end of the barge, where, handcuffed, and dressed in the gibus hat and light overcoat which Zenith affected, a tall, slim young man was leaning against the paneling.

Sexton Blake laughed heartily.

"That is not the man!" he said. "It's the raven wearing the eagle's feathers."

"Not Zenith!" exclaimed the other. "Then where is he? There's very little doubt that he was aboard. What's the meaning of it?"

The detective smiled.

"You must give me a minute to answer that question," he said.

Half-closing his eyes, he concentrated his whole mind upon the question.

"Zenith was here," he reasoned. "That's his coat and hat, beyond doubt."

"Then how did he escape?"

"The staircase was impassable. He could not go through the door to the river, or through the ceiling to the deck. Therefore there is a trap-door in this panelled wall."

He began to run his left hand along the panelling.

"Ah! As I thought."

To the surprise of the police, one of the panels opened like a door, and the detective stepped through and disappeared.

In a moment he was back again and hurrying towards the staircase.

"We've lost him" he said. "There's a door in the side of the barge, and he must have slipped out of that into a small boat which we overlooked. Follow me! There's still a chance if we've got a fast boat."

Sexton Blake, followed by three or four of the police, tumbled into the fastest boat which their party possessed.

In a moment the detective was sweeping the waters with a large head-lamp which he used as a searchlight, and, far away down stream he had the luck to pick up a small boat travelling at high speed.

"That's Zenith!" he shouted excitedly.

"Give me the wheel. Full speed ahead, and we'll have him yet!"

With both head-lamps full on, and the engine putting out its last ounce of power, they tore down-stream like a tornado. As the detective gauged their speed, his face took on an expression of fierce satisfaction. He saw that the small-power boat which the crook was driving was very unlikely to have the heels of them, and that the hour of reckoning, when he and his arch-foe were to meet for the last time, must be near at hand.

Five, ten minutes passed, and they could see Zenith's boat by the light of their head-lamps. The master-crook, covered by a rug, was huddled up at the wheel, and took no notice of their summons to surrender. One of the police drew a revolver, and began to send bullets at the figure before the wheel; but either his shooting was bad, or Zenith wore some protective material under the rug which enveloped him, for the shooting had no effect.

Yard by yard the police-boat overhauled the fugitive, and at last the two boats were running thwart to thwart. Then, maimed as he was, Sexton Blake sprang aboard and threw himself upon the figure at the wheel. Zenith was his enemy and the enemy of society, and he wished to be the hand that brought him to reckoning.

But it was not to be. Not then, at all events.

A moment later the detective gave a rueful laugh, and stood up with a bundle of travelling rugs in his hand. Zenith, always resourceful, had made a dummy figure of himself, propped it up at the wheel, and taken to the water. The gang, handcuffed and sullen, were even then being helped into boats which would carry them, or most of them, to a well-earned imprisonment; but the brain behind their organisation, the man who was in himself more dangerous than the lot of them, had either sunk for ever in the turgid river, or else, with a plausible story to explain his plight, was dragging himself ashore on some riverside beach.

The following evening, when the detective was sitting alone—Tinker having betaken himself to some place of amusement—there came a knock on the repaired front door, and Mrs. Bardell, who had returned that morning with a story which defied examination, brought up to her master a visiting-card on which was engraved: "Lieut. G J Belling, R.E."

"What does he want to see me about?" asked the detective.

"I don't know, not posthumously," stated the good lady, "but I think it was something to do with demobilised soldiers. He's a very haffable young man, sir."

"What made you think that, Mrs. Bardell? The ten-shilling note which you are palming so successfully?"

Not knowing what to say, Mrs. Bardell confined herself to simpering and hugging herself with her plump arms.

"All right! Show him up."

Lieut. Belling turned out to be a pleasant young fellow with red hair.

"You must excuse my smoked glasses," he said in a high-pitched but cultured voice. "My eyes were injured at Cambrai, and are still very sensitive."

He accepted a chair on the other side of Blake's hearthrug, and at once plunged into the matters of demobilisation and unemployment, as to which he appeared to have a great amount of information.

Sexton Blake, who had been deeply interested in the questions, was very attentive, and soon the two men were bending over a sheet of statistics which the young officer had brought with him.

"You see," said the young man. "I saw by the newspapers that you had been chairman of a meeting to discuss this very question, and my friends deputed me to come and see you on the matter. Now, these men from the Eastern theatres of war—"

And they plunged into technicalities.

For a long time Blake listened and advised, under the impression that he was helping a deserving cause, and then, quite by accident, he happened to glance sideways at his visitor's face. The dark spectacles had slipped a little, and from that standpoint he could see that the man's eyes were pink.

Now that it was too late, he recognised Zenith. The crook's acting—his disguised voice, his bearing, his real knowledge of his subject—had been so perfect that until that moment he had had no idea that the man was other than he seemed.

Alone, and his right arm useless, he was truly in a desperate plight. The one thing he could rely upon was his nerve, and that stood him in good stead. Not by the drawing of a breath did he give expression to his surprise.

As they moved away from the table, he said:

"Have a cigarette, will you?" And then, after a moment's delay, "Ah, there is the box!"

As if to find his case, he had thrust his hand into his hip-pocket where he invariably carried an automatic. The pocket was empty. It had been picked by Zenith as they leaned together over the table, and he was defenceless!

Nevertheless, he did not change his voice, or allow his enemy to detect that he was aware of danger. He continued talking iinterestedly upon the subject of demobilisation, and, as he smoked a cigarette with his left hand, one could observe that his fingers were perfectly steady.

At the same time, however, his mind was in a turmoil.

"Why hasn't he killed me already?" he asked himself. "Ah, I suppose he's afraid to risk the noise unless driven to the last resource; he is trying to work out some more silent way of attaining his end.

"But I am a dead man," he thought, as he went on laughing and smoking. "Unless Tinker turns up, that is."

"I must admit," his visitor was saying, "that I was rather surprised to find you alive and well. I had heard a rumour that you had been killed by a bomb explosion."

"I was nearly," Blake admitted. "But, as it happened, I was soon revenged."

"Indeed! How was that?" asked his visitor, with polite interest.

"It's a long story," said Blake, laughing. "But, in point of fact, the man who caused the throwing of that bomb was soon afterwards drowned in an attempt to evade justice by swimming the Thames."

Zenith looked keenly at the detective, under cover of his tinted spectacles. Did Blake guess his identity? He decided that it was impossible.

"What sort of man was this bomb-thrower?" he asked. "Of course, one cannot help feeling an interest in these people."

Blake smiled and knocked the ash off his cigarette.

"He was a crook," he said, with contempt. "Just a crook, and that's all there is to it. One of the vermin of the earth."

He watched a faint crimson suffuse the blonde face, and wondered whether he had gone too far. He knew that he was very near death indeed.

"Ah, a crook!" said the young man calmly enough. "That's what you call them, is it?"

"Yes; that's what we call them."

All the time Sexton Blake was thinking, thinking, thinking. And at last the germ of an idea began to form in his brain.

The crook glanced at the tantalus.

"I know it's a horrible liberty, Mr. Blake," he said, "but I happen to be very thirsty and I see that you have some most interesting decanters. May I? Would you mind?"

"Certainly not!" Blake was all hospitality in a moment. He reached over a Moorish table with his uninjured hand, and looked inquiringly at his guest.

"Brandy, I think?"

"So poison is what he has decided upon," thought Blake.

He filled two glasses, and thoughtfully turned his back to allow Zenith a chance to empty a small test-tube into the one nearest the detective's chair.

Now, in very truth, he was near the crisis. If he drank his brandy he was a dead man; if he refused to drink, Zenith would know that his disguise had been penetrated, and—well, it came to the same thing.

Again taking his seat, he pressed his foot upon a certain part of the hearthrug.

There were times in Sexton Blake's business house when he found it necessary to be interrupted as if by accident, and to bring this about, he had had a secret bell-button fixed beside his chair and covered over by the carpet. By a natural, easy movement he now made the contact, and

from Tinker's room near by came the whir of an electric bell.

"That's my door-bell," he said to his visitor, with a look of annoyance. "Would it be too much trouble for you to answer it for me? My housekeeper is as deaf as a post, and I am still a little bit groggy as a result of the explosion of that bomb I was telling you about."

The crook rose instantly. No doubt he was as anxious as Blake could have been to know by whom they were likely to be interrupted.

"No trouble at all," he declared. "I will run down at once."

Blake listened until he heard the crook's footsteps upon the stairs, then, with one swift movement, he was at the 'phone and putting through an urgent call. Not speaking above a whisper, he used a form of words which is the official S O S of Scotland Yard. It had been communicated to him by Sir Henry Fairfax himself as a special concession, and he was the only man outside the higher dignitaries of the Police Force who knew the secret. He had merely used a single word, and added the number which had been assigned to him on their register; yet he knew that in ten minutes his house would be invested by armed police, ten, twenty, a hundred if necessary, he had only to play for time—to live out that fateful ten minutes—and, instead of being Zenith's victim, he might live to see the crook led away a prisoner.

But could he live out that ten minutes? There was one very simple method. Now that Zenith was out of the room, he might easily lock the door, roll up a chair against it, and defy the crook to do his worst.

That course, however, did not commend itself to him. It meant that he would lose his man— that he would have put the S O S through for nothing.

Instead, he reseated himself and waited the fortune of war.

It might be that Zenith, having found nobody at the door, would guess that his intended victim was aware of his identity, and take the extreme risk of shooting him on the spot. On the other hand, their bit of play-acting might go on indefinitely. True, the moment that the master-crook found out that he had been tricked, as find out he must when a string of cars loaded with men stopped outside the door, would be a moment of the gravest possible danger. But Sexton Blake had played the game long enough to know that the most gravely-threatened man may live out a half-minute against tremendous odds when luck and resources are with him.

Therefore, he contented himself with changing the glasses—putting the one which held the contents of Zenith's test-tube nearest the chair of his unwelcome guest—and relighting his cigarette which still remained between his lips.

To do these things was the work of perhaps ten seconds, and, by the time the crook had reascended the stairs, he was resettled in his chair, and had the air of not having moved therefrom.

What was it now? A pistol-bullet and the end of all things, or further play-acting and the hope of life?

Directly Zenith entered, the detective perceived that there was to be no hurry. If his enemy resorted to violent measures he would still still pose and deliberate. Probably, whether satisfied as to his disguise or the reverse, he would still try to bring off his contemplated crime by some means which could create no disturbance.

"False alarm!" announced the sham lieutenant.

"Ah," said Blake, "it's the boys of the neighbourhood, no doubt. I'm afraid Mrs. Bardell is too easy-going!"

"Very likely," said Zenith.

The two men resumed their old position, face to face, on either side of the hearthrug.

While they talked Blake made several attempts, on one pretext or another, to fence round and get his visitor within reach of a left-hook punch on the side of the jaw which might prove a very adequate sleeping-draught. But the crook, without appearing to avoid him, skilfully managed never to occupy such a position that the attempt might be made with a reasonable chance of success.

They talked and laughed, to all appearances quite at ease, while all the time Blake was saying over and over in his mind: "Why doesn't he kill me? He must know that every minute's delay is dangerous."

He sipped his drink, hoping that Zenith would follow his example, and so consume the stuff—undoubtedly a rapid poison—with which he had doped the tumbler which now stood in front of him. But the crook evidently suspected the possibility of what had happened, for he refrained from drinking, appearing to forget his thirst in conversation.

The hands of the clock crept round, and the ten minutes' grace was nearly over, when from downstairs, probably struck upon the panels of the front door, there came a strange, irregular tapping sound.

The effect upon Zenith was magical. His face turned white, and he half-started to his feet.

"So, Mr. Blake," he hissed, "you've sold me?"

He reached for his hip-pocket; but, Blake, who had been expecting the move, snatched the poker out of the grate and sent the crook's automatic clattering, across the polished floor.

A moment later the two men were slogging each other, in-fighting across the small room. Zenith was as quick as lightning, and extraordinary strong for his build; but he soon saw that his chance of getting Sexton Blake at his mercy was not worth fighting for. The detective was a superb heavyweight, and the fact that his right arm was out of commission did not appear to embarrass him.

As the combatants drew apart, breathing heavily, after two full minutes of fast hard hitting, in which the crook's spectacles had been smashed and both men had received heavy punishment, the strange tapping sound which had aroused the crook's suspicions was repeated.

"You win this trick!" panted Zenith, and, turning, rushed full speed down the stairs.

Blake snatched up the automatic and took a pot-shot at his flying figure. He missed, however, and a moment later the slamming of the front door told him that Zenith had made his escape. The police would be too late.

THE NINTH CHAPTER

THE FINAL ATTEMPT—THE STEAMSHIP GOLDEN DAWN.

"TO-NIGHT," said Zenith, "at ten o'clock precisely, I will remove Sexton Blake!"

He lay upon a divan of black velvet, with which his white hair and pink eyes contrasted strangely. His beautiful hands were trembling slightly, and his face, under the influence of some powerful drug, was almost inane.

Yet his accent was as perfect as ever, and his threat was not less dangerous because it was uttered with a sleepy smile.

"On two separate occasions," he went on, "I have had Sexton Blake in my power, and, like a fool, let him slip between my fingers. This time there shall be no mistake!"

He allowed himself to sink into reverie, and the man whom he had been addressing—one of his lieutenants awaiting orders—maintained a respectful silence.

Presently Zenith went on:

"Bring me the gramophone records containing the speech of the detective's house-keeper."

The man wheeled forward a fine talking-machine, and inserted a record which he took from a case labelled "B."

In response to a sign from his master he released the turn-table, and the shrill accents of Mrs. Bardell filled the room. It was quite clear from what was said that the record had been made during the good lady's captivity in Zenith's "hospital," that, for some purpose of his own, the master-crook had caused many of her remarks to he rendered permanent for reproduction.

Two large double-sided records were run off before Zenith appeared to be satisfied.

"That will do," he said at length. "I think I've got it all right now."

He repeated a number of sentences used by Mrs. Bardell, giving them exactly her voice and intonation. His listener, despite the fact that he already knew his master to be a very clever mimic, was astonished at the accuracy of the imitation.

Presently Zenith checked himself rather sharply.

"Go over to that screen," he said, "and see if that receiver's in position. I've had a man listening on Blake's switchline all the morning, and I've had to warn him already that, when that receiver's off, Blake's people can hear us as well as we can hear them."

His assistant removed the screen, and inspected the telephone by which the crooks had been "milking" the wires used by Sexton Blake. The instrument had been fixed by an electrician belonging to the gang, and the type was somewhat unusual; nevertheless, the receiver appeared to be in such a position as to destroy contact, and the man was satisfied.

"Yes, I think it's all right," he said.

Zenith was already sinking into that torpor which is a phase of drug-taking, and took but little interest.

"Now listen," he said, "and don't ask me to repeat anything, because I want to go to sleep."

He took a tiny cigarette from a tray by his side, and lighted it at a spirit-lamp.

"This afternoon," he said, "you will cause a hole to be cut between our cellar and the cellar of the house next door, which is occupied by Sexton Blake. To-night at ten o'clock Mrs. Bardell will be cooking the supper, and the bloodhound will be in the kitchen with her. I shall pass through the hole which you will have cut, and, ascending to the ground floor, I shall fix the kitchen door on the outside. You will follow far enough to observe when that is done, and you will then give the signal for the electric light to be cut off at the main switch."

He sent a spiral of grey smoke twirling into the air.

"I shall continue on to Blake's sitting-room, where, at that time of the evening, he and his assistant will be sitting before the fire. They will have lighted candles or an electric torch, and the probability is that Blake will be walking to the head of the stairs to ask Mrs. Bardell what has happened.

"That will be my opportunity. I have been studying Mrs. Bardell, and I shall be made up to represent her. In that bad light the one difference that cannot be altered—the colour of my eyes—will not be noticeable, and the chances are a thousand to one that he wlil not have the least suspicion."

Zenith dropped his cigarette, and, leaning back, allowed his eyes to close.

"That's all," he murmured. "I shall get very close, and I shall knife him. He was a fool to—to—to—"

The charming voice of the master-crook died away. After a moment, seeing that his master was asleep, the other crept silently from the room.

At nine-forty-five that evening a small group of men assembled in the cellar of the house next door to Sexton Blake. They were the only survivors of the council of the criminal association which the genius of Zenith had called into being, and each of them was willing and ready for the crime which Zenith had set apart for his own hand. They had discovered what had long been known to their leader, that there was not room on the face of the earth for themselves and the great criminologist. Either they must be dispersed, and their plans come to nothing, or Sexton Blake must die.

As usual, where Zenith was organising, each man was told off for a particular duty. Two of their number stood by to remove and replace a cleverly-painted screen which occupied the hole in the brick wall, another was at the switch, ready to cut out the current upon the given signal, a fourth stood by to observe the fastening of the kitchen door, and so on.

They stood muttering in the darkness, and from time to time consulted their luminous watch dials. It was a strange scene, and pregnant with danger for that oft-threatened man who sat musing by the fireside almost above their heads.

At one minute before ten o'clock a quaint figure descended the cellar stairs. Elastic-sided boots and flouncing petticoats, a black silk dress, half covered by a white apron, grey corkscrew curls, and a marvellous thing of beads and lace, which Mrs. Bardell called a cap—such was Blake's housekeeper as impersonated by Zenith.

With the exact carriage of his model, Zenith waddled across the cellar floor, and, but for the fact that he had a cigarette between his lips, the crooks could hardly have believed that it was their leader.

The false wall was withdrawn, and, concealing a long knife within the bosom of his apron, Zenith entered the residence of Sexton and began to climb the stairs.

The one thing that he feared at the moment was the bloodhound Pedro, and when he heard Mrs. Bardell, within the kitchen, telling the animal not to be "voracious," he felt assured that his intended crime could not miscarry.

Approaching the kitchen, so silently that not even the dog was aware of his presence, he pulled the door close, and passed a locking-bar over the handle. Mrs. Bardell and the dog were safe, anyway.

He had hardly done this when the lights failed.

Hampered, but not deterred by the darkness, he traversed the ground-floor passage, and began to climb the stairs.

To his surprise the door above, where Blake's sitting-room was situated, remained silent and dark. He had anticipated some slight commotion to follow the extinguishing of the lights, or, at any rate, the opening of a door by someone who

wondered what the reason was. But nothing of the sort happened.

For a moment this filled him with anxiety for the success of his plans. Then it occurred to him that the probable explanation was that the detective and his assistant were either using an oil-lamp or sitting in the firelight.

This was, from his point of view, an entirely satisfactory state of affairs. In either event he knew that his disguise was absolutely impenetrable.

He climbed slowly up the stairs, and in his character of Mrs. Bardell he breathed heavily as he went, saying to himself, "Ah, deary me, these steps will be the death of me!" just as the good lady herself was in the habit of doing.

But at the top he began to believe that the whole of his elaborate character study had been in vain. He had had careful watch kept on the movements of Blake and Tinker, and his spies had informed him that they were still in the house at the moment of his entry; yet, when he opened the sitting-room door, prepared for a mock hysterical outburst until the moment came for a death-thrust at his enemy, he found the room in complete darkness and silence. Surely his spies had for once made a mistake!

He walked slowly into the middle of the floor, silently cursing his misfortune. Then, to make quite sure that not only this room but also the remaining rooms used by the detective were un-tenanted, he ventured to call out.

"Mr. Blake!" he shouted, in the shrill voice of his model. "Mr. Blake!"

Instantly he felt himself grasped on either side. An electric torch flashed out, and he found himself between Sexton Blake and Tinker. The latter held a police-whistle between his teeth, and Zenith saw that his visit had been expected.

The man was certainly an arrant poseur, for he laughed musically, and addressed his captors in the bantering tone which he invariably used.

"Well, well, my dear detective, you seem to have sprung it upon me once again. Would you mind telling me how you do these things?"

"This time it was quite simple," said Sexton Blake grimly, as Tinker's police-whistle rang out. "My assistant had the good fortune to over-hear your conversation of this morning when he took off the receiver of my telephone in order to send a message. I should imagine that you had been "milking" my wires and forgotten to shut down at your end."

"You are right, my dear Blake," asserted the crook. "I thought that clumsy electrician of mine was making a mess of things. I shall have to be very cross with him when he reports for duty tomorrow morning."

Sexton Blake raised his eyebrows.

"And do you imagine that you will be in a position to talk with your electrician tomorrow morning?" he questioned.

Zenith laughed again.

"Most certainly! You will remember a maxim of Napoleon's that one should first lay plans for defeat? Just so! Well, I have prepared for defeat, that is all!"

With a lightning kick the master-crook sent the electric torch flying into the window curtains, and once more the room was in darkness.

Tinker convulsively gripped at the arm that he held, expecting a ferocious struggle; but none came. Instead, the room appeared suddenly to be filled with cold air, and, in the darkness beside him, he was surprised to hear Sexton Blake utter an exclamation of disappointment.

"Wait a minute," said the detective's voice. "I'll get the torch."

Surely this was lunacy, thought Tinker. To leave him in sole charge of a desperate and resourceful man like Zenith, even for a moment, seemed to him to be courting disaster.

He tightened his grip on the arm that he held, and, every minute expecting a blow or a knife-thrust which did not come, waited while his employer groped in the curtains.

Then the light went up again, and Tinker found himself grasping the wax model of a fat woman's arm which was attached to a black silk dress, now ridiculously empty.

"I might have guessed it," grunted Sexton Blake, "if I had not been a fool! The fellow could not make-up his hands as the podgy hands of Mrs. Bardell, so he contented himself with false arms, his real arms being at liberty within the bodice of his make-up."

The detective and his assistant exchanged a glance of dismay. The open window, with its curtains moving in the wind, was eloquent of the means by which the master-crook had escaped. They knew well that to follow him was useless. By now the house next door, to which the "milking" wires had been traced, would be invaded by an irresistible force of police; but Zenith, the albino, remained at large—elusive, ruthless, inscrutable, a menace which would endure while life was in him.

"What I can't make out," said Tinker, at length, "is how he came to spare you, guv'nor. He was within a yard of you, with his hands free, and yet he didn't bring off what he came for!"

"I think," said the detective, "that we have to thank his unfamiliar garments for that. In point of fact," he went on, "when first we seized him he dropped a very pretty plaything which he had been concealing in the bosom of his dress, and I took an opportunity to kick it under the Chesterfield."

Sexton Blake bent down, and picked up a slender Italian stiletto.

"Another exhibit for our museum, my lad."

"My hat!" exclaimed Tinker, in a hushed voice.

"Don't be upset," said his employer. "It's all part of the game."

§

A week later Tinker, accompanied by Detective Harris—who was about to be promoted for his part in what the papers were calling "The Motor Mystery"—were rowed from the ladder of one of H.M. torpedo-boat-destroyers to board a certain tramp steamboat, which some poetical owner had christened Golden Dawn—the steamboat which Blake had seen loaded from the warehouse in South Street.

Still later, the deep-shadowed alleys of Bombay witnessed a swift armed raid upon the premises of a once-respected firm of wholesale leather merchants, and the police were able to recover a large proportion of the many objects of art which had so mysteriously found their way out of this country.

M. Zenith gave a finishing touch to the affair by a characteristic advertisement in the "Times":

"S. B.—To our next meeting!—Z."

THE END.

WELL MATCHED!

SEXTON BLAKE
AND
MARSTON HUME
ENGAGE IN
A DUEL OF WITS.

MARSTON HUME—Criminal.

THERE is no denying the fact that everyone was astounded when the news leaked out that Marston Hume had suddenly, and for no ostensible reason, given up practising.

Still quite a young man, he was the most able criminal lawyer the Bar had known for a quarter of a century—mercilessly logical in attack, brilliantly resourceful in defence. He himself admitted, in his coldly cynical way, that by sheer weight of argument he had got off, scot-free, three of the most cold-blooded murderers he had ever known, simply and solely because they had been able to retain his services, and pay for them.

He could have taken silk had he chosen, or, had he selected the field of politics, there were many who prophesied that in time he would inevitably have become Chancellor of the Exchequer. The man's genius for finance and for abstruse calculation was almost uncanny.

He did none of these things; he simply threw up his practice, and not one of his acquaintances ventured to ask the reason why.

The word acquaintances is used advisedly, for friends he had none. He would not have known what to do with a friend had he possessed such a thing. Human sympathy he regarded with contempt. A power of nice calculation, a logical deduction, appealed to him in a negative kind of way. For the rest, he was always dressed with scrupulous neatness. He had a strong, dark, lean face, with a masterful nose, and a thin-lipped, mobile mouth which would have been worth a small fortune to an actor.

His forehead was well developed, and the dark hair, unusually thin for a man of his age, receding from the temples, and brushed straight back, made the forehead appear more prominent even than it was. The eyes were steady, cold, and introspective. When talking to him it was hard to tell whether he was listening, or whether his thoughts were far away, following channels of their own. When he spoke in his turn, however, a strange alteration came over them, and they seemed to bore into one like twin gimlets.

He was a member of the Baddeley—the smallest club of repute in London, probably. It is the boast of the members that there has never been a fool on the books, and that their chef is without an equal.

Marston Hume's favourite seat was in the small bow window which overlooks Piccadilly. He would frequently spend a whole afternoon there, pencil in hand, a sheet of club notepaper on his knee, staring vaguely out at the passing stream of traffic.

On the afternoon in question, however, he was taking a silent part in a discussion between a well-known actor-manager and a famous surgeon, both of whom had just returned from a brief holiday in Monte Carlo, and the subject of discussion was not unnaturally the chances of the tables.

"It's all very well, my dear fellow," the actor-manager was saying, "but, all the same, I don't give a fig for your mathematicians! Do you mean to tell me that if you saw a run of, say, six reds, you wouldn't begin plunging on black?"

The surgeon laughed.

"I should; I admit it. That's human nature; but I know that, logically, there is no earthly reason why red shouldn't turn up again. What do you say, Hume?"

"It is a mere matter of fact. If the red had turned up ten times, it is still an even chance that it will turn up again. A run of seventeen occurs about once a year, but every time you stake your louis or five-franc piece, you must do so with the knowledge that you may just happen to have stumbled across one of those abnormally long runs. There is no such thing as a sound system. Chances at roulette, just as chances in our every-day lives, are governed by certain well-defined and unalterable laws."

"Talking of the chances of everyday life," said Mansell, the actor, "has the murderer of Mrs. Knyvett been discovered yet? She was by way of being a connection of yours, wasn't she?"

"An aunt by marriage. No, nothing more has come to light."

Falconer, the third man, leant forward.

"What case was that? I haven't heard anything about it. I've been away longer than you others, you know."

"Most extraordinary thing I ever heard," said Mansell. "I read every line I could get about it. Mrs. Knyvett was an elderly lady, very well off, living in Curzon Street, one of the smaller houses on the south side. That's right, isn't it, Hume?"

Marston Hume nodded.

"She lived all alone, with a butler and three or four maids. Her bed-room was on the second floor, facing the street. It was a large room, apparently, running the whole width of the house. There were no other rooms on that floor.

"She was known to have some very valuable jewels, which she always kept in her bed-room; and it came out at the inquest that she had a horror of burglars—so much so, that she had one of those old-fashioned bobbin latches attached to her bed-room door—a great heavy brass affair, that it would have roused the whole street to break down.

"To this bobbin was attached a cord, which led through a pulley to the head of her bed, so that she could latch the thing at night and unlatch it again in the morning when her maid brought her tea, without having to get out of bed.

"On the night of the murder she had been to an At-home, from which she returned late, and, according to the maid who helped her to undress, the jewels she was wearing, including a very valuable necklace of pearls, were left lying on the dressing table. Before dismissing the maid, she asked for some sleeping drops she was in the habit of using. She took three of these, and remarking to the maid that she was very tired, ordered her not to come to the room with thee tea before ten o'clock the next morning, instead of eight, the usual hour.

"The maid states that when she left her she was reading a novel by the light of the bedside candle, and she further states that she distinctly heard the click of the bobbin dropping into place as she closed the door behind her.

"The maid then retired to her own room on the floor above, and hurried into bed, as she was very sleepy. The next morning at ten, having had her breakfast with the other servants, she took up the tea as ordered. After knocking once or twice, and getting no reply, she concluded that Mrs. Knyvett was still asleep. She mentioned the fact to the butler, and said that she was going to run round the corner to the post, but that she would be back in a few minutes.

"Shortly afterwards she was seen going out with what was described as a small box in her hand; the box was covered with brown paper, fastened with string, and sealed.

"She returned at a quarter-past ten; but Mrs. Knyvett hadn't rung during her absence, so she waited till eleven, and then took up some fresh tea.

"Again she got no answer, and, being slightly alarmed, she summoned the butler.

"They tried the door, but the bobbin was, of course, latched; and after repeated knockings and hammerings had failed to elicit any sort of response, the butler went and fetched a police-man.

"After some consultation and the fetching of another policeman—an inspector this time—it was decided to break the door open. The three men hurled themselves at it, and under their combined weight the door and its fastenings gave way.

"Mrs, Knyvette lay on her side on the bed, as is asleep. On the exposed side of her head was a terrific wound, such as might have been caused by a life-preserver. Death, the doctors said after-wards, must have been instantaneous.

"No trace of any weapon was found, but the object of the crime was clearly evident. A clean sweep had been made of all the jewels on the dressing-table, including the pearl necklace."

"But how on earth can the man have got in?" asked Falconer.

Mansell nodded significantly.

"That's just the question everyone asked. There are three windows to the bed-room, each facing on to the street. The centre one of the three was open about a third of the way for ventilation. Right under this, however, there is a street lamp. Even granting that a man was sufficiently active to gain the sill of this window it would have been beyond the limits of probability that he could

enter and leave by it unobserved in the full glare of the street lamp. This was a point dwelt on very fully at the Inquest. So fully, that the coroner, in his summing up, without putting the matter in definite words, gave more than one veiled hint that the criminal should be looked for inside rather than outside the house.

"The maid had admittedly been the last person to see her mistress alive. Subsequently to that, the room had been, so far as the evidence went, inaccessible, yet Mrs. Knyvett was found murdered. The jewels were missing, no trace of them had been discovered, and at a quarter-past ten the next morning—or, rather, between that time and ten—the maid had been seen to leave the house with a sealed packet. When questioned about the packet and its contents, she refused point-blank to answer. I think I have all the details correct, Hume?"

"Perfectly correct. The maid refused all information as to the packet; the natural inference was, therefore, that it contained the jewels."

"And that the maid herself committed the murder after seeing her mistress to bed the previous evening," interposed Falconer. "Of course, I have never seen either the maid, the wound, or the weapon," he continued thoughtfully, "but I can tell you this much—that to inflict such a blow as would cause death instantaneously argues abnormal strength on the part of the maid."

"Very neatly put, my dear Falconer," said a voice behind them.

Mansell and Falconer turned instinctively.

"Blake—by all that's wonderful!" exclaimed the former. "The very man! If it hadn't been for him, I think that maid would have had a narrow shave of hanging. What good wind blows you in here, man? You haven't been near the club for a month."

"Busy," said Blake, nodding to Hume, and drawing up a chair. "So you were talking about the Knyvette case, were you? That unfortunate maid did have a rough time of it, no doubt. The

point raised by Falconer was one which I myself put forward. As a matter of fact, Bennett, the maid was physically incapable of striking that blow; she was a slight woman of middle age, weight eight-stone-five, with the feeble muscular system of a person who lives an indoor life.

"But, of course, there were many other points which told against her, and they told heavily. There was the fact that, so far as was known, she was undoubtedly the last person to see her mistress alive. There was the damning fact of the mysterious parcel, which was of just such a size that it *might* have contained the jewels, combined with her incomprehensible attitude in refusing all information about it. There was the further fact that, by the evidence of the other servants, she had a notoriously quick temper, and was prone to brooding over entirely imaginary wrongs. There was also one very curious additional fact, which only appeared in one or two reports of the case.

"Mrs. Knyvette, when out late at night, invariably took with her the latchkey of the front door, knotted to a corner of her handkerchief for safety's sake. The butler, an old servant, was not supposed to sit up for her on those occasions. The maid Bennett sat up only when her mistress was expected home at, or about, one; if she was likely to be late, Mrs. Knyvette, who was very fond of going about, managed for herself.

"On the fatal night in question, Bennett sat up, as we know, and was in readiness to let her mistress in; she unlatched the front door for her, and latched it again behind her. But there there was a peculiarity about that front door. In addition to the ordinary latch, it had the usual two bolts, one at the top and one at the bottom. The top bolt was too high for either woman to reach; the lower one was so stiff and so much out of line that the butler himself was unable to work it; consequently the door was left simply on the latch.

"After the discovery of the murder, it was found that the key carried by Mrs. Knyvett was missing. The handkerchief, showing palpable signs of having been knotted, was found near the bed, but the key was gone.

"When I argued physical inability on the part of the maid to strike the blow, the police at once set up the theory that she must nave had a male accomplice; that they committed the murder between them; and that she gave the man the key to let himself out with, in order to avoid slamming the door. But that theory is ridiculous; she could have let him out herself, for instance, and most certainly she would have made use of this imaginary accomplice to dispose of the jewels."

Marston Hume nodded.

"I agree with you entirely, Mr. Blake; the idea of an accomplice was absurd. No clever criminal would be so clumsy as to work with an accomplice. That sort of thing belongs to safe-breaking gangs and warehouse burglaries. The murder of Mrs. Knyvette was a crime on a different level altogether."

"It was a clever crime, cleverly handled," asserted Blake; "and though I managed to instil into the heads of the authorities that there was no real case against Bennett, still I must confess that I regard the matter as one of my failures."

"Because of the impossibility of obtaining any definite proofs," said Marston Hume gravely.

"Precisely. The proofs are ungetable—although I know the criminal."

"You think you do?"

"I more than think so—I am *sure!*"

Marston Hume nodded his head vaguely, and stared out of the window.

"I must confess I have puzzled over the case more than a little myself," he said at last. "To begin with, the poor lady was a connection of my own, as I told you; incidentally, it cost me some six thousand pounds—I think that that is what they valued the jewels at."

"Cost you?" cried Mansell, "My dear fellow, how do you make that out?"

"The Knyvett property reverted to me, as, though a comparatively distant relative, it turned out that I was the only one. The jewels, I suppose, would in the ordinary course have come to me with the rest. I was down with a bad dose of influenza all the week of the murder or I should certainly have investigated matters personally. As it was, I was obliged to rely on the reports of Mr. Blake here, who was kind enough to come and see me several times."

A faint suspicion of a smile flickered across Blake's face.

"Your illness was an unlucky coincidence," he said. "Had it not been for that, I am convinced that, between us, we could have solved the problem."

"It is possible. But, unfortunately, as it was, I was compelled to confine myself to theorising—a dangerous practice, without sufficient first-hand knowledge of the facts, as Mr. Blake will tell you."

"Fire ahead, Hume; let's hear your version," said Falconer.

Marston Hume pulled out his case of cigarettes, selected one carefully, and lit it.

"The first obvious point, to my mind," he said slowly, "is that the murder was carefully thought out and premeditated. The maid Bennett, of course, was innocent. For reasons which our friend Blake here has mentioned, and also for another, on which I, had I been acting as counsel for her, should have laid great stress.

"In her examination it at the time of the inquest, she stated definitely and positively that on leaving her mistress's rooms on the night of the murder she heard the click of the bobbin slipping into place, as she closed the door behind her. This statement is borne out by the fact that on the following morning it took the butler and two policemen to burst the door open.

"Bennett's past history is easily accessible. In none of her situations had there ever been the slightest question of her honesty.

"Now, had she been guilty of the crime, it would have been, on the face of it, necessary for her—after committing a cold-blooded murder, mind you—to have fastened the bobbin from *outside* the door *after* she had left the room—a feat which would be none too easy for an accomplished criminal, and for her, a sheer impossibility. On that one argument alone, I would have got her acquitted had she employed me as her counsel, in the event of the case coming up for trial."

"Your own theory, then, is what?" asked Mansell.

"As I said before, the crime was carefully prepared, and beyond all doubt premeditated. The criminal, in my opinion, was someone who, from time to time, had access to the house, and was perfectly cognisant of the habits of the inmates.

"He must have been in a position to know of my aunt's habit of carrying her latchkey with her, when out late—of her other habit of using drugs to ensure sleep—of the fact that the butler didn't sit up for her—of the further fact that the front door on those occasions was merely latched. And he must also have been able to keep an eye on her social engagements. Last, but not least, he must have had an opportunity of personally inspecting the action of the bobbin fitted to her bed-room door."

"Why that?" said Falconer.

"Because the bobbin must have been tampered with previous to the commission of the crime. Any idea of a man entering by the window is, of course, a mere fancy. The man entered by the door after the maid had left.

"He had—*must* have had, in some way or an-other—a chance to loosen the fastenings of the bed-room door, so that they would yield silently to a good firm push. Also, he had undoubtedly provided himself with a duplicate of the front-door latchkey."

"The missing key having been taken merely to complicate the case," suggested Blake. "I arrived at that same conclusion from a line of reasoning of my own; but don't let me interrupt."

"As you say," continued Hume, "Mrs. Kny-vett's key was taken with the sole object of making the affair seem mysterious. Having taken it, the murderer would certainly have got rid of it as soon as possible. Probably he threw it away, together with the jewels."

"*What!*" Mansell almost shouted; and Falconer edged forward on his chair.

"I say that when he threw the jewels away, he almost certainly threw the key away, too." repeated Marston Hume coldly. "Surely that is clear enough?"

"But, man alive, you must be romancing. You argue that a man commits a deliberately-planned murder for the sake of some thousands of pounds worth of jewels, and, having committed it, throws them away."

Marston Hume shook his head.

"I beg your pardon; my argument was nothing of the sort. I never for an instant suggested that the jewels were the motive of the crime. You forget that we are not dealing with an ordinary vulgar criminal. The jewels and the key were, in my opinion, taken merely with the definite object of leading any inquiry astray. As to the real motive, we must search further afield—revenge, homicidal mania, personal hatred—I can offer no explanation on that point. I have little acquaintance either with my relative's past history, or the people amongst whom she moved. I am certain, however, that Blake will agree with me that the jewels were merely a secondary con-sideration?"

"Undoubtedly," Blake assented. "The man was far too clever to keep such incriminating evidence; therefore he sacrificed them unhesitat-ingly. It was the act of an artist in crime."

"But look here," interrupted Falconer: "even granting all your premises—and Heaven knows they seem wild and fantastic enough—there is still a point not cleared up. The man, you say, had, on some occasion previous to the crime, obtained access to the room, and loosened the screw-plates of the rings in which the bobbin worked, so that a good firm push would tear them away noiselessly. That sounds reasonable and conceivable; but if this had been done, how is it that it took three able-bodied men to burst in the door the next morning; and, above all, how did the man manage to refasten the door from the outside?"

"The explanation is fairly simple. He loos-ened the existing screws, as I pointed out; but he had provided himself with another set of brass screws, a trifle larger—large enough to bite well in the holes already made.

"With these he would have been able to make good the fastenings, so that they were to all intents and purposes as firm as before. The old screws, the weapon, the jewels, and the key, he was, of course, careful to remove. As to the latching of the bobbin from outside, that would be no difficult matter to an expert—and this man undoubtedly was an expert. A sufficient slacken-ing of the cord and the deft manipulation of a thin, stiff piece of wire through the crevice of the door would manage the rest.

"Having slid the bobbin into place with a jerk of the wire, he would pull out the wire from the outside, let himself out by the aid of the latch-key, to avoid slamming the front door, secure in the knowledge that the murdered woman lay up above in a room apparently inaccessible from without, and doubly secure in the certainty that the police, in breaking in, would destroy any evidence of his tampering with the door fasten-ings."

"Very graphically put," said Blake. "You might almost have been there yourself. The descrip-tions which I gave you of what occurred whilst you were laid up must have been very detailed. There is one mistake, however, which your theo-retical criminal made. The police did not destroy all evidence of the bobbin latch having been tampered with. You might care to examine these.

Please handle them very carefully, for one day they may be the means of helping to hang Mrs. Knyvett's murderer."

He drew up a small smoking-table as he spoke, and produced from an inner pocket a flat tin case.

"Here," he said, "are two of the screws which the murderer himself affixed, as Hume described. You will notice that, as he again correctly theorised, they are larger than this third screw, which I myself took from a plate that had not been tampered with. But that is not all. If you examine them very carefully, you will detect here and there in the spiral of the screws small fragments of wax. In other words, the criminal, when he loosened the original screws, had plugged the holes with wax to prevent their working too loose before he was ready to act. The wax, I should judge from the hardness of it, had been there for some days.

"The lack of proof," said Hume, as he sauntered away, "must be, as you say, a great inconvenience." Blake stood watching him. "That man is a born criminal," he said to himself. "But one day I think his way will be mine."

Falconer examined the screws carefully.

"Heaven grant that I am never tempted to commit a crime!" he said gravely. "I shouldn't stand a ghost of a chance with two such brains as yours and Hume's working up a case against me. You both seem to have every detail of what happened at your fingers' ends."

"But not an atom of proof," said Hume.

Blake shook his head.

"Not an atom beyond these. As to detail, I could even describe to you the kind of screwdriver the man used. It was a trifle too small to bite the screws completely, and was probably one of those found in a certain type of pocketknife."

He took a cigar from his pocket, and was about to bite off the end when Hume leant forward and offered him his penknife.

"Pity to spoil a good weed," he said carelessly. "Use this."

Blake took it. At the top end of it was a small turn-screw about a third of an inch long, of the ordinary commonplace pattern.

Blake cut off the end of his cigar and handed back the knife. The turn-screw had been recently reground.

"That is just the type of knife I meant, curiously enough," he said quietly.

Hume nodded, and slipped it into his pocket.

"I thought so. All this argument has made me thirsty; I'll ring for the waiter."

"But look here," said Mansell; "you've explained a lot of things after a fashion, but what about Bennett, the maid, and the mysterious package?"

Blake chuckled grimly.

"It is the one touch of humour in the whole story. You would never guess what it really did contain. I found out by the kindness of the authorities, who managed to turn up the address for me—she had registered the thing.

"The parcel was addressed to a small dentist, and contained a spare set of false teeth, sent to be repaired; and yet the vanity of that bilious-faced middle-aged little scrap of a woman was so great that I really believe she'd have let herself be tried for murder rather than own up."

Mansell laughed, and the waiter handed round whiskies-and-sodas on a salver. Blake quietly waved his aside, and picked up his box.

"Good-bye," he said, nodding. "I'm going to stroll home."

"I'll come, too," said Hume, rising leisurely. "I want some fresh air."

They went out into the hall together.

"I should wrap up carefully," said Blake acidly, as they gained the street, buttoning up their coats.

"Why?" said Hume tolerantly.

"Another attack of influenza might prove fatal, especially if you should happen to lose another relative during your illness. Mrs. Knyvett's will left you the richer by forty thousand pounds."

Marston Hume looked him straight in the eyes.

"If that man hadn't dropped the jewels into some convenient stream, shall we say, it might have been forty-six thousand," he said slowly.

"Yes," said Blake; "it might have been forty-six. I wonder where you *did* drop them?"

Marston Hume lit a fresh cigarette under the light of the street lamp.

"Good-night," he said curtly; "I'm going the other way. I enjoyed our little chat immensely. The lack of proof, as you say, must be a great inconvenience."

Blake stood watching him saunter away.

"That man," he said to himself, "is a born fighter, and a born criminal—a criminal genius! But one day I think his way will be mine. I wonder where he did get rid of those stones— and the key?"

THE UNION JACK LIBRARY.

1½ D

GRAND XMAS NUMBER.

WALDO, THE WONDER-MAN!

A Clever Story of Strange Yuletide Happenings, introducing SEXTON BLAKE, TINKER, NELSON LEE, NIPPER, and a Fascinating New Character. Specially written for the Christmas Number of the "Union Jack" by the Author of "The Case of the Hollow Dagger," "The Studded Footprints," "The Terror of Trevis Wold," "The Crooks of Rapid Hollow," etc., etc.

No. 794.   EVERY THURSDAY.   December 28th, 1918.

The UNION JACK LIBRARY

With Which is Incorporated the Pluck Library

No. 794.   THREE-HALFPENCE.   December 28th, 1918.

WALDO, THE WONDER-MAN!

A Fascinating and Seasonable Story of Clever Detective Adventure, Introducing SEXTON BLAKE, TINKER, NELSON LEE, and NIPPER.

By the Author of "The Case of the Hollow Dagger," "The Studded Footprints," "The Terror of Trevis Wold," "The Crooks of Rapid Hollow," etc

The First of a Brilliant New Series.

Taken from Tinker's Case-Diary.

THE FIRST CHAPTER.

THE TRAGEDY AT THE CIRCUS.

"CHRISTMAS looks like being a regular old-fashioned one this year, guv'nor," I remarked, beating my gloved hands together. "By jingo, the snow's coming down with a vengeance, and no mistake!"

"Only a short flurry, I think, Tinker," said Sexton Blake. "But if this bitter weather holds, Christmas will certainly be old-fashioned, as you say."

We were striding along through the slush in the old High Street of Helmford, in Sussex. The snow had only commenced that afternoon, and none of it was lying, for it turned to slush almost at once.

But with the night it was quite possible that a frost would set in, and then the country-side would soon assume a very different aspect. Personally, I'm rather fond of a snowy Christmas—it seems more like the real thing.

The festive season was near at hand, and even Helmford was showing signs of it. Most of the shops were decorated in some way or another, and Christmas wares were on sale on every hand.

The guv'nor and I were not in Helmford on pleasure bent. We had run down that morning with the object of making some inquiries in connection with a case which I don't intend to refer to here—or anywhere else, for that matter. It was one of those cases

which present no attractive aspects, and which simply wouldn't be worth recording.

Our business was already completed, and it was now close upon tea-time. We were on our way to the police-station in order to have a word with Superintendent Hollins, who had assisted us generously in our inquiry.

Sexton Blake glanced at his watch in the growing dusk.

"We shall have some time to waste, Tinker," he remarked. "There's no train until six-fifteen, and we may as well occupy the time by repairing to the most comfortable-looking hotel and partaking of a substantial tea."

"You do make some sensible suggestions now and again, guv'nor—and this is one of 'em!" I said heartily. "This kind of weather makes the grub fly, doesn't it? I've got an appetite as big as two!"

The prospect of sitting down to a cosy tea in front of a blazing fire was most alluring, but there was no certainty that it would be fulfilled. Hotel tea-rooms are not always cosy, neither are they provided with blazing fires. However, I hoped for the best.

We arrived at the police-station, and the superintendent greeted us with a wave of his hand and a smile. He was a man of fifty, grizzled, and inclined to stoutness. And he was genial to a degree.

"I was just wondering what had become of you, Mr. Blake!" he said heartily. "I want you to come home to tea with me. I can promise you plenty of comfort, and my wife will look after you well."

"That's very kind of you, Mr. Hollins!" said Sexton Blake.

"Yes, Tinker and I will certainly accept your invitation. We shall be quiet delighted."

"Rather, sir!" I agreed. "Thanks awfully!"

"It's an honour, Mr. Blake," said Hollins. "As a matter of fact, I was going to ask you to stay a couple of hours or more. You can easily catch the eight o'clock train. It's the fastest one of the evening."

"That will suit us admirably," said the guv'nor without hesitation, making no mention of the fact that we had already decided to go by the six-fifteen. "I am quite delighted at the prospect."

It suited me right enough, for I didn't particularly care what train we took, so long as we went back to London that night. The superintendent was just preparing to leave for home, and five minutes later we all took our departure from the police-station together.

"I was right, you see, Tinker," said Sexton Blake, glancing at the sky.

The stars were shining already, and the snow-shower had passed. There was practically no sign of snow anywhere, but plenty of mud. Hollins' comfortable residence was only a few hundred yards away, and the guv'nor and I were soon being introduced to Mrs. Hollins, a buxom lady with a large smile, Miss Hollins, and master Hollins.

The latter was a cheerful-looking individual of about fourteen, and Miss Hollins was two years his senior—quite a nice-looking girl, too. I was decidedly glad that we had accepted the superintendent's invitation.

For the society was not only genial, but comfort abounded, and the food was first-class. After tea Hollins drew me aside while the guv'nor was engaged with the younger members of the family.

"Look here, Tinker, I want you to do me a favour," grinned the superintendent, winking, and tapping my shoulder. "It's not often I get a chance of spending an evening with such a distinguished gentleman as Mr. Blake; and I want to keep him here as long as possible. There's a good train at ten thirty—"

"What! Another change?" I chuckled. "That's all right, sir—"

"I'm not so sure of it, Tinker," interrupted Hollins.

"NOW, MY youngster Jack made me promise to take him to the circus this evening—there's one in the town just at present. I can't go, of course; so I was wondering if you'd act as a deputy. I dare say Molly will go, too."

"Why, I shall be delighted, sir!" I said promptly. "I don't think I've been to a circus for years and years, and it'll be a bit of a novelty. Besides, you want to jaw and smoke with the guv'nor, don't you, without any of us young people bothering about?"

The superintendent grinned.

"You've hit it exactly, Tinker—although I shouldn't have put it so bluntly as all that," he replied. "It's good of you, young 'un. I hope you'll enjoy the evening. But I can't say that circuses appeal to me much."

It thus came about that, twenty minutes later, I set out with Miss and Master Hollins for Capelli's Grand International Circus. I dare say it will be wondered how all this fits in with the case I am about to record. But it does fit in, because the whole extraordinary affair was centred round that circus, and the guv'nor and I would have missed one of our most mysterious cases if I hadn't gone to the circus that evening.

Having whetted your appetite, I hope, I'll now proceed.

Capelli's Circus proved to be a much larger concern than I had pictured it in my mind. The tent was a colossal affair, and the whole circus occupied one huge meadow on the outskirts of the town. There were tents and caravans and traction-engines galore, and the whole place was bustling with activity and life.

It was evident, too, that Signor Capelli would be rubbing his hands with satisfaction, for there were several dense queues for the cheaper parts, and a good attendance was assured.

"Looks quite a colossal business," I remarked, as we made our way towards the swell entrance. "I was half afraid that it would be just a third-rate show, but this looks—promising."

"I've heard that it's splendid," remarked Miss Hollins.

"Let's hope you heard the truth, that's all!" I said cheerfully. "This is where we go in, I suppose?"

We obtained three excellent seats right next to the ring in the very best part of the "house." Inside, all was brilliant, for the auditorium was literally a blaze of electric-light.

A band was playing musically—which was something of a novelty for a circus. Signor Capelli evidently believed in doing things properly, and the seats in which we sat were no exception—the real thing, with plush cushions and arms.

I had been terribly afraid that I was in for a dull, miserable evening, but my spirits had now gone right up. It was evident that Capelli's Circus was a show worth patronizing—and the performance itself fulfilled all expectations.

The crowded tent, the brilliant lights, and the excellence of the show put me into a very good temper, and I was really glad that I had come. Of course, I'm not going to describe all the various turns, but there wasn't a single "dud" one.

The two clowns, known as Full-o'-Fun and Chuckles, were comedians of remarkable ability, and not merely a couple of painted wash-outs such as one usually finds at the average circus. And there was a conjurer fellow, billed as "Osiris, the Card Wizard," who ought to have been in the West End of London.

The guv'nor has told me sometimes that I possess a decent eye for beauty, and I must remark that one of the lady performers was an extraordinary pretty girl, and strikingly clever, too. I admired her greatly.

There were elephants and a host of other animal turns, but I lost interest somewhat when the turn before the last made his appearance. This generation, according to the programme, was Waldo, the Wonder-Man, and I seriously thought of suggesting that we should go home, because this chap was really the strong man of the circus, and I never care much for that sort of exhibition. But the last turn was Durand, the eccentric tramp cyclist, and I wanted to see him.

Furthermore, I soon found that Waldo was like everybody else in this first-class circus-quite above the average. He wasn't a brawny individual with huge muscles, and a chest like Hercules. When he first came into the ring I thought there was some mistake, for Waldo turned out to be quite slim and not an inch above the average height.

"Why, that chap can't do much!" I remarked critically. "I don't believe he's as strong as I am."

"What about those weights the attendants are carrying?" asked Jack Hollins? "It takes two men to left one of 'em, and then they can hardly manage it."

I grinned.

"You innocent!" I said. "Those weights are prepared ones, I expect, and the attendants are engaged in a little game of bluff. They always do that sort of thing in these exhibitions, you know."

But Waldo certainly appeared to be genuine. For he announced that anybody was free to enter the ring in order to test his weights, as on some former occasions doubt had been cast upon their genuineness. Waldo further offered the sum of 50 to anybody who could prove that his weights and crossbars were faked.

"What about that, Tinker?" asked Hollins junior?

"Oh, I suppose there's a catch somewhere!" I replied.

Three members of the audience entered the ring, and some amusement was caused when they tried to lift Waldo's various crossbars and weights. One man just succeeded in lifting a crossbar an inch from the floor, where upon Waldo picked it up with two fingers, and tossed it up into the air as though it weighed no more than a couple of pounds.

"Oh, I say, that's a bit too thick!" I protested. "You're not going to tell me that that bar is as heavy as it looks. Those men are paid to go in the ring, I expect."

"Well, I don't believe it," said Miss Hollins stoutly. "I think he's genuine."

"I'll tell you what, sis," grinned Jack. "Let's dare Tinker to go in the ring himself. Anybody's invited—"

I jumped up.

"Good enough!" I exclaimed promptly. "I'm jolly curious, as a matter of fact, and it'll be interesting to see what happens. I expect Waldo will politely tell me that he's got all the people he requires."

But again I was mistaken.

"That's right—you're all welcome!" exclaimed the strong man heartily, as I leapt into the ring. "I can see that you're sceptical, my lad. Well, if you can lift that weight a foot from the floor I'll give you ten pounds!"

I grinned as I looked at him. The weight was an enormous one, and Waldo picked it up with ease and raised it above his shoulder-with one hand, too. Then he set down and looked at me.

"One hand?" I asked.

"No; you can use all you've got," replied Waldo genially.

Five seconds later I began to feel somewhat silly. I tugged at that confounded weight with every ounce of strength, but I couldn't lift it an inch. It was as much as I could do to shift it a short distance in the sawdust.

"Try this one," said Waldo invitingly.

He handed me a crossbar, which I took. But a second later it was on the floor, for I couldn't possibly hold the thing. I stared at Waldo in real amazement. There was no "swank" about him whatever. His strength was simply staggering—

something more than I could possibly understand.

"I owe you an apology, Mr. Waldo," I said breathlessly. "I should be greatly obliged if you could tell me what you feed on."

Waldo laughed, and glanced at a wrist-watch which adorned his left wrist. Then he picked up the heavy weight and the crossbar and walked into the centre of the ring, carrying them with ease. I started after him, still wondering whether I was dreaming or not. This was no ordinary strong man. I had never believed it possible that any human being could life such weights.

He took the crossbar and tossed it high into the air, where it went whirling up towards the canvas. It seemed utterly impossible that Waldo could catch the thing when it came down, but he did so—on the back of his neck!

I nearly fainted. Of course, there's a knack about doing that sort of thing, and plenty of performers do it, but not with weights of that kind. I half expected to see Waldo collapse with a broken neck. But he faced the audience smiling and cheerful.

The other three spectators had cleared out of the ring, but I still stood there, comparatively near to the ring exit. Standing in the opening were two figures—those of Signor Capelli himself and the pretty girl I have already mentioned. She was still in her circus costume.

As a matter of fact, I was racking my brains for the explanation. Could there be any trickery about those weights? To tell the truth, there was none—they were perfectly genuine. But I was in just that frame of mind when I sought to discover a fake where none existed.

Waldo was doing his turn now, and I watched him with great interest. After about two minutes it suddenly struck me that I had no further right in the ring, and I noticed that the proprietor was eyeing me with a certain amount of disfavour. He didn't actually like to order me out, but plainly showed that my services were no longer required. Signor Capelli was possessed of a face which had a most forbidding expression, and he was evidently not to be trifled with.

And so I deemed it just as well to get back to my seat; there was no sense in waiting to be given the order of the boot. But just at that moment something occurred which brought me up with a jerk.

In short, the real drama commenced at that second.

One of the ring attendants—a man in a gorgeous uniform—came hurrying rapidly through the wide opening from the adjoining tent, where, I judged, the various turns were prepared for their entrance into the ring.

The man approached Capelli, and stood before him, talking rapidly, and gesticulating. He was in a state of extraordinary excitement, and his face was as pale as death. I saw Capelli pale, too, and a startled light leapt into his eyes.

"Good heavens!" he exclaimed hoarsely.

He said more than that, of course, but only that one exclamation reached my ears. And the proprietor rushed off with the attendant, without even making his excuses to the girl. This, I knew, was the result of his excitement.

There were no other attendants near by, for Waldo's turn was a one-man show, so to speak, and during his performance the attendants took the opportunity of having a short respite.

Now, I'm a curious beggar, and when I saw Capelli rush off in that startled manner I wondered what could be in the wind. As it happened, I wasn't to be in doubt for long. For something occurred which gave me an opportunity of hearing the startling truth.

The pretty girl who had been left standing alone had lost all her colour, and was staring straight before her almost dazily. Then she swayed, as though about to faint, and collapsed upon her knees.

She was just in the entrance, and I don't think anybody saw her except myself. It was plain to me that something was very drastically wrong, and it was out of the question to suppose that I should tamely return to my seat when that sweet girl was on the point of fainting before my eyes.

I rushed up and bent over her.

"Is anything the matter, miss?" I asked quickly. "Oh, I say!"

She suddenly burst into a flood of tears, and there was a hysterical ring about her sobbing.

I couldn't stand that, and I placed my arm around her shoulders and gently raised her to her feet.

"Hold up, miss!" I said earnestly. "I'll call for help if you like—"

"They—they say that Gerald is suspected!" exclaimed the girl, gazing at me with terrified eyes. "Oh, it's horrible—it can't be true!"

"But what has happened?" I demanded.

She looked at me with a kind of bewildered terror.

"Mr. Durand has just been found dead in his dressing-tent," the girl whispered. "And—and they say that he was murdered!"

THE SECOND CHAPTER

AN ARREST AND AN URGENT APPEAL

"MURDERED!" I ejaculated, aghast. This was an astounding surprise indeed. I had never anticipated such a dramatic turn of events. There had been a hazy idea in my mind that one of the performers had met with an accident.

But a murder!

I felt, somehow, that the girl had got hold of the thing wrong. She had partially recovered herself in my presence, and was now looking at me as though I were an intruder—which, indeed, was the truth.

The girl's distress worried me. She was neither painted nor powdered, as one might have expected, and was altogether charming—especially in her pretty circus costume. And I didn't like to see her in such trouble.

Just at that moment two other girls appeared, and these were attired in everyday clothing. I recognized them as two performers who had completed their turn earlier in the evening.

"Why, Miss Hanwell, what's the matter?" asked one of them.

"Is it true? Is it true?" said Miss Hanwell, her voice husky.

"I really don't know what is the matter," said the other girl. "Mr. Capelli is terribly excited, and there seems to be a commotion outside Mr. Durand's dressing-tent. Is this young gentleman a friend of yours?"

I thought I had better explain.

"No, I'm a member of the audience, that's all," I said. "I was in the ring when Mr. Capelli hurried away, and this young lady nearly fainted, so I came to her assistance. She told me that somebody had been murdered."

"Oh!" exclaimed both the girls, in one voice.

"It was good of you to come to help me," said Miss Hanwell, giving me a quick, forced smile. "Thank you so much; I am better now."

This I regarded as a dismissal, but I didn't take my departure. All three girls went off, Miss Hanwell being supported by others. I gathered that Mr. Durand was a great friend of hers, or she would scarcely have been so affected. But then, of course, there was the "Gerald" she had referred to.

"Hang it all, this is a murder case; I'm going to see what's doing," I muttered grimly. "I shall have to risk being pitched out on my neck."

I completely forgot Miss and Master Hollins at the moment, but I suppose they were wondering what on earth had happened to me. Waldo was still doing his turn, although he had nearly finished, and the audience knew nothing of the tragedy—if, indeed, a tragedy had occurred. A storm of applause came from the auditorium, and it was evident that Waldo was going well.

I moved forward through the short, wide canvas passage into the adjoining tent. And there, against the flap of a smaller tent which evidently opened out of this, several people were collected. In order to make myself quite clear, I must explain that these extra tents were not of the round variety, but ingeniously constructed canvas arections adjoining the main tent itself. The canvas of the main tent actually formed one side of the other tents, thus there was no open ground intervening.

As I appeared Signor Capelli caught sight of me. He was standing with one of the clowns. And they both advanced in my direction.

"Well, young man, what do you want?" asked the proprietor sharply.

"I heard that a murder had been committed, and I thought that I might possibly be useful," was my bold reply. "I don't want to intrude—"

"Well, you are intruding, and I don't know how in thunder you managed to get here!" said Capelli, half angrily, "I shall have to ask you to go back to your seat at once, or, better still, I'll take you outside; the show's just over."

"That's not your business!"

"Well, I thought I might do something to help, Mr. Capelli," I said, presenting him with one of my cards. "I'm not simply an inquisitive busy-body."

Capelli, who was greatly agitated, glanced at my card.

"What's this?" he exclaimed. "'Tinker, Assistant to Mr. Sexton Blake!' I seem to remember that name—"

"Of course you do, boss!" interrupted the clown. "Mr. Sexton Blake is the famous Baker Street detective, and Tinker is his assistant. I reckon we'd better let this young gentleman stop. He's the real goods, I've heard."

Signor Capelli nodded.

"All right, I don't care!" he exclaimed, passing a hand over his eyes, with a very worried expression. "I suppose I shall have to knuckle under, as I always do. Only I hope this young gentleman is genuine, and not bluffing us."

"You needn't be afraid of that," I put in.

"I came here with Superintendent Hollins' son and daughter, and Mr. Blake is at the superintendent's house now. If this case presents any mysterious points, my guv'nor might be inclined to investigate. Anything out of the ordinary always interests him."

"I don't know—I don't know, I'm sure," said Capelli helplessly. "I think I must be dreaming, or something. A murder in my show! It might be a good advertisement, but I wouldn't have had it happen for ten thousand pounds. Potty, old man, you'll have to do the talking when the police come; I don't feel up to it."

Capelli, in spite of his forbidding looks, had an extremely mild manner, and I guessed that he was a most genial individual under ordinary circumstances. Full-o'-Fun, the clown, whose real name proved to be Mr. Benjamin Pottles, was a long, lank individual, and a perpetual twinkle seemed to lurk in his eyes—even now, in spite of the tragedy which had occurred.

"You leave it to me, boss," he said confidently. "But I'll be dashed if I believe your yarn. You're a heap more capable than you try to make out. And there's no sense in getting worried. I never was a believer in worry. It upsets a fellow, and he can't think straight. You keep calm, boss; that's my advice."

"And good advice, too, old man; I'm quite aware of it," said Mr. Capelli.

The "signor" was, of course, a mere affectation, for Capelli was obviously a native-born Englishman, and I afterwards learned that his real name was plain Bob Capel, and he had started life in a penny show.

Mr. Pottles, it was quite apparent, was almost on equal terms with his employer. In point of fact, he was Signor Capelli's right hand, being his private secretary and most faithful confidant. The clown, indeed, was a shrewd business man, and a remarkable comedian into the bargain. He was a most charming individual.

"There goes the band—and thank goodness for that!" exclaimed Mr. Capelli suddenly. "Poor Durand was to have been the last turn, but he's given his final performance in this world, I'm afraid."

The band was playing the National Anthem, and the great tent was already emptying. We in this private section were undisturbed, and only heard the crowds as they passed out into the dark meadow. Of course, attendants were hurrying about in all directions, but we were not disturbed.

"Can you tell me exactly what happened?" I asked, addressing the clown.

He shook his head.

"I wish I knew myself, laddie," he replied. "All we know at present is that Durand, the Tramp Cyclist chap, is dead in his dressing-tent. At least, we think he's dead. And nobody's allowed inside until the police arrive."

"Haven't you sent for a doctor?" I asked.

"Well, we're not quite brainless," replied Mr. Pottles. "The doctor ought to have been here by now, bust him! Great Scotland! Talk of the Evil One and he appears—although you'd better not let the doctor know I said that, or he'll use some of his surgical instruments on me."

Pottles moved away quickly as he spoke. A stranger had suddenly appeared, carrying a small handbag, and he was undoubtedly a member of the medical profession. It was written all over him, so to speak.

I followed the proprietor to the door of the adjoining tent, where Pottles was already explaining the situation. The doctor nodded, and disappeared through the flap with Full-o'-Fun.

Capelli remained outside.

"My nerves ain't what they used to be," he said, dropping his polished manner in his agitation. "I don't want to go in there and see the doctor messing about with the poor chap's dead body. Doesn't look so scared, Fletcher," he

added, turning to a mysterious-looking gentleman who stood near by.

The latter was attired in a long gown and a turban, and his face was swarthy, and the name "Fletcher" didn't seem to fit him. I recognised him as Osiris, the Card Wizard, and the clever conjurer who had performed earlier.

"It's a terrible business, Mr. Capelli," he said huskily. "Poor Durand is quite dead, I understand. But what I don't like is being suspected by those two confounded fools here!"

The "confounded fools" exchanged grim glances. They were men connected with the circus—not performers, but workmen; men whose duty it was, no doubt, to help in the work of erecting and dismantling the tent, and to attend to the lighting and other matters when the circus was in full swing.

"It's all very well for Mr. Fletcher to talk like that, sir, but we're only doing our duty," said one of the men. "It was Mr. Fletcher who killed—"

"You infernal idiot!" shouted Fletcher fiercely.

"Steady, lad, steady!" interrupted Mr. Capelli, grasping the conjurer's shoulder.

"There's no need to get excited. I don't believe you touched Durand. You can rely on me. There's some mystery somewhere, but it'll be cleared up."

"Thank you, Mr. Capelli!" said Fletcher quietly.

"Perhaps you'd better get to your caravan, and change," went on the boss. "The police will be bothering about here presently, and you don't want to answer their questions dressed up in that rig."

Fletcher was about to go when Waldo appeared. The strong man was now wearing a long wrap, and he was smoking a cigarette. He was a man of about thirty-eight, I judged, and he was smiling good-humouredly.

"Anything wrong here?" he asked, looking round with some surprise.

"Wrong!" repeated Capelli. "Don't ask me, old man! It's an absolute disaster! Durand's dead—murdered in his own dressing-tent!"

Waldo dropped his cigarette.

"You're not serious, boss?" he asked, in amazement.

"I wish I wasn't; but I am," said Capelli worriedly.

"But who did it? Who killed the poor chap?" demanded Waldo, aghast. "Durand was all right just before I went into the ring. I was chatting with him. He can't be dead; it's impossible!"

The proprietor shook his head.

"It happened while you were doing your turn, Waldo," he said. "It's a shock to you, of course. You left Durand alive less than half an hour ago, and now you find that he's been killed."

"But how—how was he killed?"

"Heaven alone knows!" said Capelli wearily. "Somebody said that a poisoned arrow had been stuck into his back. But that seems mad. When I went into the tent I found Durand face upwards, with a horrible look on his face. It gave me a turn, I can tell you. I sent for a doctor and the police. The doctor's come, and he's making an examination—"

"Hallo!" I interrupted. "The doctor's just come out!"

The medical man approached his face grave.

"You are Signor Capelli, I believe?" he said, addressing the boss.

"Mr. Capelli is good enough for me," said Capelli. "Is he dead, doctor?"

"Quite," was the reply? "I'm Dr. Marshall. I am afraid it will be necessary for you to send for the police, Mr. Capelli. The deceased met with no ordinary death. He was undoubtedly murdered."

"I've sent to the police-station already," said the proprietor. "Good gracious! To think that poor Durand is really dead! I was hoping—but what's the good of talking? How was he killed, doctor?"

"The man was poisoned," replied Dr. Marshall quietly.

"Oh, then it might have been suicide—"

"No, my dear sir, the unfortunate man could, under no circumstances, have taken his own life," interrupted the doctor. "The poison was not taken internally, but injected into the blood by means of a poisoned spike. It is the most remarkable case I have ever examined, and there can be no doubt that the arrow containing the spike was deliberately thrust into the deceased's back."

"Shocking!" said the boss. "It's absolutely—"

He broke off abruptly as two men appeared in the entrance of the tent. One was a constable and the other Inspector Freeman, of the Helmford Police. They came in briskly, and the inspector spotted me at once.

"Hallo! You here, Mr. Tinker?" he exclaimed, in crisp tones. "I thought you'd gone back to London with Mr. Blake. I've heard that there's some big trouble here."

"Ay, and you heard right!" exclaimed Mr. Capelli. "One of my performers has been found dead, and it seems that he was murdered. I suppose you'll want to ask a lot of questions?"

"Exactly," said the inspector, nodding. "I think I am talking to Mr. Capelli? Well, sir, I'm sorry this has happened. Has the body been disturbed since the crime was committed?"

"Nobody touched it expect the doctor."

"That's all right, then," said Freeman.

"Was the murderer caught, or—"

"Yes, sir, he's here!" put in one of the hands.

The inspector twirled round on his heel.

"Eh!" he exclaimed. "Here?"

"It was Mr. Fletcher who killed Mr. Durand, sir," said the man respectfully.

"Don't take any notice of the fool!" shouted Fletcher, boiling with anger. "I don't know anything about it! I didn't touch Durand! It's absolute madness to accuse me of this horrible business!"

Out came the inspector's notebook.

"It seems that we shall have to straighten things out a bit," he said. "What's your name, my man?" he added, pointing his pencil at the accuser.

"Bentley, sir."

"Well, Bentley, if you have any statement to make, you had better lose no time over it," said Freeman, glancing significantly at the constable.

The latter took his stand by the side of Fletcher, who was under no apprehension as to the meaning of the move. He clenched his fists, and his eyes flashed, but said nothing.

I was watching him closely, and I must admit that he struck me as being a very decent fellow. And he was acting exactly as one would suppose a falsely-accused man to act. His indignation and anger almost choked him.

Inspector Freeman, before taking Bentley's statement, entered the dead man's tent with Mr. Pottles. He was only absent a few minutes; and when he returned he was gingerly wrapping some object in his handkerchief, and he was looking very grim. It did not entail a large effort of imagination to guess that the inspector had taken possession of the poisoned arrow.

"See here, inspector; is it allowable for this man to make an accusation against Mr. Fletcher?" asked the proprietor, in a worried voice. "I'm willing to stake my life that Fletcher didn't have any hand in the affair!"

"That's quite likely, Mr. Capelli; but it is my duty to gather all the facts together," said Freeman grimly. "I can't make an arrest until I have sufficient evidence, and you can be sure that Mr. Fletcher will come to no harm if he is innocent."

"Keep your pecker up, old man!" said Mr. Pottles confidently.

This was addressed to Fletcher, and the latter smiled slightly, but with an obvious effort. It was my own private opinion that Bentley's accusation wouldn't amount to anything of value.

"Who made the discovery, and when was the murder committed?" asked Freeman.

"I was the first to enter Durand's tent," said Fletcher defiantly. "The time, I think, was just about five-past nine. I heard a cry, and entered the tent, to find Durand writhing on the floor—"

"If you don't mind, Mr. Fletcher. I will take your statement afterwards," interrupted the inspector, who was evidently bent upon conducting the inquiry in his own particular way. "I should like to have a few facts about the dead man, Mr. Capelli."

The boss shrugged his shoulders.

"I can't tell you much," he said. "Durand joined my show about six months ago, and he's always been quiet and well-behaved. He used to be on the music-halls, but I offered him better terms than he was getting. I always believe in paying my artistes well. Durand had no enemies that I know of, and I'll stake my bank balance that Fletcher didn't touch him, although the pair weren't quite friendly—"

"Oh, they had quarrelled—eh?" said Freeman keenly.

"No, of course, not!" snapped Mr. Pottles.

"Nobody could call it a quarrel—"

"I don't know who are you, sir, but at present I am talking to Mr. Capelli!" said the inspector, regarding the painted clown severely. "I may want you later on."

"Told off!" murmured Pottles sadly. "Properly told off!"

Freeman made a note in this book, and turned to Bentley.

"Now, my man, what have you got to say?" he demanded.

"Well, I believe that Mr. Fletcher killed—"

"I don't want to hear your private opinions," interjected the inspector. "What you believe is of no importance whatever. If you have any information to offer, however, I want to hear it."

"All right, sir," said Bentley. "Payne and I were standing—"

"One moment. Who's Payne?"

"I'm Payne, sir," said the man who had been with Bentley all the time.

"Very well! You can go ahead, Bentley."

"Payne and I were standing just outside, sir," said Bentley. "It was just after nine, and Mr. Waldo had commenced his turn. There wasn't much to do for a minute or two, and Payne and I were having a smoke. A minute or two later I noticed Mr. Fletcher go into Mr. Durand's dressing-tent—"

"But I came out again at once!" interrupted Fletcher hotly.

"Keep cool, sir, please!" said the inspector.

"Now, Bentley, did you see Mr. Fletcher leave the tent?"

"No, sir, I did not!" said Bentley decidedly.

"Did you?" asked the inspector, indicating Payne.

"I didn't see Mr. Fletcher at all, sir," replied the man. "My back was towards the tent, you see, sir."

"H'm!" grunted Freeman, making a note. "All this isn't very satisfactory. Well, go on Bentley! You saw Mr. Fletcher enter the tent. What happened after that?"

"I heard Mr. Durand speaking angrily, in a high voice, sir."

"Did you hear that, Payne?"

"Oh, yes, sir! Mr. Durand seemed to be in a fine temper."

"Did you hear Mr. Fletcher's voice, too?"

"I can't swear to that, sir," said Bentley, shaking his head. "But Mr. Fletcher was inside the tent."

"This evidence is very skimpy," remarked the inspector. "I can't—"

"But I haven't finished yet, sir," put in Bentley. "Two or three minutes after Mr. Fletcher had entered the tent Payne and I heard a kind of scream—a sort of gasp and a scream rolled into one, in a manner of speaking. We knew that it was Mr. Durand, because we recognised his voice."

"Well, and what did you do?" demanded Freeman sharply.

"That cry gave us a bit of a turn, sir," continued Bentley. "There was nobody else just near at the time, and so Payne and I rushed to Mr. Durand's tent, thinking that he had hurt himself in some way. And when we got inside we found Mr. Durand on the floor, near his chair, with Mr. Fletcher bending over him."

"Oh, indeed!" said the inspector, "Indeed!"

He made another note, and everybody present seemed to feel that a certain tenseness had suddenly come into the air. I glanced at Fletcher, and saw that he was biting his lips rather nervously. This was scarcely to be wondered at.

"I was the first to reach Mr. Durand, sir," went on Bentley. "Mr. Fletcher looked regular terrified, and I asked him what was the matter. He said he didn't know. He said that Mr. Durand must have hurt himself while making-up before the mirror. And just then Mr. Durand gave a kind of gasp and opened his eyes. I could see that he was nearly at his last gasp."

"Did he say anything?" asked the inspector quickly.

"He did, sir!" was Bentley's grim reply.

"Mr. Durand clutched at my coat and said these exact words, in a gasping voice: 'Fletcher has killed me—Fletcher has murdered me—I am going fast—' And then the poor old gentleman collapsed, sir, and died as we looked at him."

"Good gracious me!" muttered Mr. Capelli, aghast. "This is terrible—terrible!"

I was rather startled myself, for Bentley's statement was absolutely concise. The dead man himself had actually accused Fletcher with his last dying words! And Fletcher had been alone with him in the tent just before Bentley and Payne entered. The inspector was greatly impressed.

"Do you agree with what Bentley has said?" he asked, turning to Payne.

"Yes, sir; every word of it!" said Payne.

"Nobody else but Mr. Fletcher could have killed the poor gentleman. There wasn't another soul anywhere near, and hadn't been for five or six minutes."

"What about the tent?" I asked. "Couldn't a man have crawled underneath it from the outside?"

"Impossible, laddie!" declared Pottles. "The tent's pegged down as tightly as a brick wall. The only exit is by this flap here."

Inspector Freeman nodded gravely.

"Have you anything further to say, Bentley?" he asked.

"Nothing, sir, except that Mr. Fletcher and Mr. Durand were on bad terms," replied the man. "I dare to say that's why the murder was committed."

"What do you mean— bad terms?"

"Look here, Bentley, you'd better hold your tongue!" put in Mr. Capelli angrily. "It's none of your business whether Mr. Durand wasn't exactly friendly—"

"I'm sorry, Mr. Capelli, but I must insist upon this man finishing the statement!" put in the inspector firmly. "Go on Bentley."

"Why, sir, the two gentlemen didn't seem to hit it off together. As I might say," said the man. "Mr. Fletcher is engaged to Miss Hanwell, and only last week he had some angry words with Mr. Durand. It was the talk of the whole circus, sir, Mr. Durand had shown Miss Hanwell unwelcome attention, and Mr. Fletcher didn't like it. So he and Mr. Durand had an angry talk and nearly came to blows. They didn't speak to one another at all during the last two or three days, and everybody expected that it would end up in a real quarrel, or a fight. Then, of course, they were quarrelling just before the murder took place, as I told you sir."

Freeman, having made several rapid entries in his note book, turns to Fletcher.

"I can't ignore this evidence, Mr. Fletcher," he said quietly. "Of course you'll understand that nothing has been proved against you so far, but the statements of these two men can't be set aside. I'm afraid I shall to ask you to come with me to the police-station."

"Does that mean that I am arrested?" asked Fletcher between his teeth.

"You force me to be blunt. Yes."

There was a moments tends silence. Mr. Pottles was tapping his foot impatiently on the floor and the eyes were grave; Capelli breathed hard, and everybody else looked thoroughly startled.

"It's a shame!" declared the boss at last. "Fletcher's innocent!"

"But Mr. Durand accused him, sir," remarked Waldo gravely.

"I don't care what Durand said!" snapped Capelli. "Hang it all, that sounds heartless but I don't mean to be. Can't you realize that Durand was hardly responsible for his words? He was almost dead. He saw Fletcher, and thought Fletcher had done it. That's all it amounts to."

Inspector Freeman shook his head.

"That won't do, Mr. Capelli!" he exclaimed. "By what I can understand, the dead man was quite rational during his last moments. It is my duty to arrest Mr. Fletcher. I must—"

"Hold on, inspector!" I interrupted, "You've got no warrant, you know."

"I'm acting upon my own responsibility!" snapped Freeman. "And I don't need any teaching from you, Mr. Tinker. I shall be greatly obliged if you will look after your own affairs."

I shrugged my shoulders. And wasn't offended. The inspector considered that he was doing his duty, and, in a way, I had butted in when I oughtn't to have done. Fletcher, it seemed, was to be taken to the police-station on suspicion, and the warrant would follow later, should the evidence be conclusive enough.

But Mr. Gerald Fletcher had a word to say.

"Look here, inspector, I'm not going to get into a panic," he said quietly." I suppose you're simply doing your duty, but I have something to say."

"I should advise you to reserve it until later on."

"No; I'll say it now!" observed Fletcher grimly. "These men have told you the story from their point of view, and I mean to tell you mine. It will only take a few moments. At about nine o' clock I entered Durand's tent, in order to ask him a question concerning one of his trick-bicycles which had got damaged. He was sitting before his mirror, making-up, and ordered me that he'd kick me out if I didn't go quickly."

"That led to blows, no doubt," said the Inspector.

"No, it didn't!" retorted Fletcher. "I wasn't anxious to have a scene at that time, and so I swallowed my wrath and came outside. I stood just to calm myself while I smoked. Then I heard a strange screaming cry from Durand, and immediately re-entered the tent."

"Who was in there?" I asked curiously.

"Nobody but Durand," was the reply."He was lying on the floor, just against his chair, and as I bent over him Payne and Bentley rushed in.

You heard the rest from them. Durand certainly accused me, but why he did so is an absolute mystery unless he thought I had actually crept up behind him and driven the arrow home. I've got an idea that Durand really believed I killed him. But I'll swear that I'm innocent, and I know nothing further."

The inspector pursed his lips, and Bentley and Payne smiled between themselves in a manner which plainly told of their disbelief. And, to tell the truth, Fletcher's story did sound rather tall. It seemed to be a lame excuse.

There was a little commotion after that, for Freeman decided to take Fletcher away at once. He didn't even permit him to change his clothes, but bundled him straight on to the motor-car which had brought the inspector and the constable from the police station.

The constable, supported by two others of his kind, was send off, and an agitated consultation was held between signor Capelli, Mr. Pottles, Waldo and one or two others.

I stood by, listening with interest for the life of me I couldn't quite believe that Fletcher was guilty, although the evidence was so strong. His bewilderment and alarm had seemed perfectly genuine. But I was doubtful. Having heard the full story, I hardly knew what to think.

And then, quite abruptly, Miss Hanwell appeared. She had changed into a neat walking-costume, and really looked just as pretty as ever, in spite of her terrible distress. She was small and dainty, and her big eyes were almost feverish.

"Oh Mr. Capelli, is it true—is it true?" she exclaimed, clutching at his coat, "They tell me that Gerald his been taken away!"

The boss gave Pottles a despairing glance. "Poor lass, I'm Afraid it's really true!" he exclaimed, his voice astonishing gentle. "But you mustn't worry, Miss. Hanwell. Good gracious! Mr. Fletcher will be back again before long—"

"You're only saying it to soothe me," the girl interrupted, with terrible distress. "Oh, I don't know what to do! Isn't there somebody who'll prove Gerald's innocence? That inspector is a brute—a brute!"

The girl suddenly fixed her gaze upon me, and her eyes widened.

"Perhaps—perhaps you can help me?" she panted, rushing to my side. "Mr. Pottles told me that you are the assistant of Mr. Sexton Blake. Is he in Helmford? Do you think he will help me? Will you ask him—"

"Well, I don't know, Miss Harwell," I said uncomfortably.

"Oh, you will ask him, won't you", she pleaded, clutching at my coat-lapels, and looking up into my face with earnest appeal in her lovely eyes."You must ask him—you must! I can't offer to pay much money—"

"I say, hold on, miss !" I protested. "There's no need to talk about money. Of course I'll ask the guv'nor. I'll rush off at once."

"Thank you with all my heart!" said the girl, her eyes welling with tears.

"And, what's more," I declared, "I'll bring Mr. Blake back with me—if I have to drag him every inch of the way!"

"Good lad!" murmured Mr. Pottles. "Didn't I say he was the real goods, boss?"

It was an utter impossibility for me to ignore Miss Hanwell's appeal, and I resolved to bring the guv'nor back with me, by hook or by crook. I glanced at my watch, and then gasped.

The time was twenty-past ten.

And our train went at ten-thirty! Sexton Blake would be at the station, and there was scarcely time for me to catch him.

I should have to run like the wind.

THE THIRD
CHAPTER
SEXTON BLAKE INVESTIGATES.

SEXTON BLAKE waved wildly to me as I dashed on to the platform at the railway-station. The train was already in, and the guv'nor was leaning out of the window of a first-class compartment.

"I thought you'd turn up at the last moment, you young rascal!" he said sternly as I pelted up. "I was just on the point of getting out—"

"Then get out now, guv'nor!" I gasped. "Hurry up! The guard's just blowing his whistle! For goodness' sake jump out!"

"But, my good Tinker, this is the last train," protested Blake. "We don't want to be stranded here—"

I danced with alarm and impatience.

"There's been a murder, guv'nor," I panted, "and you've got to investigate!"

Sexton Blake hesitated for about a quarter of a second. Then he grabbed up our bags, hurled them at me, and jumped out on to the platform as the train was hunt commencing to move. I sighed with relief as I slammed the carriage door.

"Now, Tinker, I shall be obliged if you will tell me what all this means," said the guv'nor grimly."You quite understand that we have lost the last train, don't you? Unless you have a very good reason for this wild—"

"A good reason!" I interrupted breathlessly. "Inspector Freeman has carted off some poor chap to the police-station, on suspicion of murder, and a perfectly charming girl asked me to ask you—"

"Steady on, young 'un," said Sexton Blake, "You seem to be getting muddled. So a perfectly charming girl is responsible for this affair, eh? Dear me, I did not think that you were so susceptible to feminine charms."

I grinned weakly.

"When you see her, guv'nor, you'll understand," I said. "She's engaged to the poor chap who's been arrested. The evidence is pretty rotten against him, but I believe he's innocent. And Miss Hanwell was so terribly distressed that I hadn't the heart to say I wouldn't come to you. You simply must investigate the case; guv'nor—it's a regular corker!"

Sexton Blake eyed me rather amusedly.

"We wondered what had become of you," he remarked. "You deserted Miss Hollins and her brother at the circus, I understand, and they returned home alone. It must have been something very unusual to cause you to act in such a manner. Tinker. However, let me hear the yarn."

"I'll tell you as we walk along, guv'nor," I replied.

We grasped our bags, and left the station. There had been no more snow, and the night was now quite clear. A slight frost had set in, and the roads were not so slushy as before.

As we walked I told Sexton Blake briefly of the whole affair, and he was far more interested than I had anticipated. When I had finished he patted me on the shoulder reassuringly.

"There was no need for you to be in a state of uncertainty, my lad," he said. "Of course, I shall investigate this case. It presents many interesting points, and I shall be quite delighted to do everything in my power to help that girl. She seems to be very much attached to her fiancé, eh? With regard to fees, I shall accept none. It is not my custom to inquire into a problem just for the sake of financial gain. My income is quite sufficient without accepting payment from comparatively poor people."

"Guv'nor, you're a brick!" I said heartily.

"Nonsense, Tinker!" he growled. "Look here, we shall pass the police-station in a few moments, and I suggest that we look in. If possible, I want to have a word with Fletcher before going to the circus."

"That's a good idea, guv'nor," I declared.

When we arrived at the police-station we found some little animation. Inspector Freeman was evidently making his report to Superintendent Hollins, for the pair were in earnest conversation in the Superintendent's office.

"Why, this is a surprise, Blake!" exclaimed Hollins, when he appeared. "I thought you'd taken the ten-thirty to London."

"I was already on board, but Tinker dragged me off," explained the guv'nor. "I had an idea that I should find you here. There seems to have been some rather bad trouble in Capelli's Circus."

The superintendent nodded seriously.

"Yes, it looks ugly," he replied. "We don't often get murders down in this quite neighbourhood, you know. It's just possible that we shall have to get a Scotland Yard man down, but I'd prefer to handle it myself. I'm afraid Fletcher hasn't a leg to stand on."

"I'll bet he's innocent, sir!" I put it.

"No, Tinker, I can't agree with you," said Hollins. "'The circumstantial evidence alone is formidable, but Durand's last words were an accusation against Fletcher. Besides, there wasn't another soul who could have done it. The Inspector interviewed some other witnesses who came forward, and it has been firmly established that not a soul was near the tent at the time except Fletcher."

"What about Payne and Bentley;" I asked.

"Oh, of course, they were competitively near!" agreed Hollins. 'But they were outside, and a dozen witnesses are ready to swear that they didn't shift from their position until Durand's last cry was heard."

"Did you examine the tent, inspector?" asked Sexton Blake.

"Only briefly, sir," replied Freeman.

"Because there is just a chance that the murderer might have slipped in beneath the canvas—"

"No, that's impossible!" interrupted the superintendent. "Two men were within view of the rear of the tent all time. They were some distance off, it is true, making repairs to on brilliant lights on the spot, and no intruder could have escaped notice. It's no good, Blake. Fletcher is guilty—he must be. Consider the facts. He was actually bending over Durand; he was known to have entered the tent a few minutes earlier. There is nothing to corroborate his story that he left and stood outside. Bentley and Payne may have overlooked the incident, but I don't seem feasible. At all events, I shall obtain a warrant at the earliest moment."

"I scarcely expected anything else," said the guv'nor. "You're really left with no choice, Hollins. Until I have looked into the facts further. I shall keep an open mind. Is it possible for me to see Fletcher to-night?"

"Why, of course!" said Hollins readily.

"He's only detained on suspicion as yet, and you can interview him when you like. I hope he is innocent, because he seems quite a decent young fellow. But you know what love is, and this affair seems to have been brought about by a love-quarrel."

Five minutes later Sexton Blake and I were with Gerald Fletcher his cell. It wasn't really a cell, to be more exact, but a comfortably furnished apartment although the door and windows were secure.

The prisoner had been given an opportunity to clear his grease-paint off, and we now saw him as he really was. Furthermore, be had worn his ordinary suit beneath the long gown. He now stood revealed as a well-built, upright young fellow of about twenty-six, with features and honest, grey eyes. For the life of me I couldn't credit that he was guilty of a cold-blooded, premeditated murder—for that is exactly what the crime was.

He was very dejected, and there was a haggard expression upon his face. He regarded us rather dully as we faced him.

"I suppose you're a detective?" he inquired. "Well, it's no good questioning me—I told the inspector everything I know."

"I am a detective, Mr. Fletcher, but I am in no way connected with the official Force, " said the guv'nor, sitting down. "My name is Blake, and I am here at the request of Miss Ethel Hanwell."

Fletcher's eyes lit up, and his cheeks flushed.

"Do you mean to say that Ethel—I mean Miss Hanwell—asked you to come to me?" he asked eagerly. "And it's possible that you are the Mr. Blake, is it? Mr. Sexton Blake?"

"That is the case," said the guv'nor quietly. "It was only by chance that Tinker, my assistant, was at the circus. And it was to him that Miss Hartwell appealed. I have been requested to prove your innocence, Fletcher, but the facts that I have so far gleaned are very much against you."

Fletcher faced Sexton Blake squarely. "I appreciate your generous action in coming to my aid, Mr. Blake," he said. "If I were guilty I should be alarmed at your presence, because I know that a man has very little chance when you are on the scene. But I am filled with hope, for I swear before Heaven that I know absolutely nothing of. Durand's death. I am as innocent of killing him as you are yourself. Knowing all the facts, can you believe that statement? Do you believe it?"

"Upon my soul, Fletcher, I do!" said the guv'nor, gripping his hand. "Your attitude is that of an innocent man, and I am convinced that you are the victim of misfortune or a deliberate plot. You may rely upon me to do everything in my power to effect your release at the earliest movement."

"Thank you, Mr. Blake!" said Fletcher.

He gave no great display of emotion, but I liked him all the better for that. And I shared the guv'nor's opinion that he was a victim of circumstances. The police merely looked at the cold facts. It was not their business to be human. If the facts convicted Fletcher, that was sufficient. But we were quite different. Being unofficial, we regarded the case from a human point of view, so to speak, and formed our own opinions.

Fletcher repeated his whole story to Sexton Blake, who listed intently but made no notes. It was very seldom that the guv'nor made use of his note book. He preferred to store facts in his head.

Our companion could tell us very little about Durand. Nobody knew exactly where he had come from, except in the wide statement that he had been on the halls, and there was certainly no evidence that he had ever had any enemies.

"When you entered the tent, Fletcher, where was Durand lying?" asked Blake.

"Just against his chair, having fallen from it, I believe."

"Did you see anything of the arrow?"

"Not at the time. The poor fellow was face upwards, and the arrow had entered his back, so he was lying upon it."

"But that would have driven it right in," I remarked.

"I think it only entered about a quarter of an inch and when he fell over the point was probably dragged out," replied Fletcher. "It wasn't the wound which killed him but the poison. It's a most astounding thing, Mr. Blake. You might think there were some South American Indians about the place."

"I suppose there is no such thing in the circus?" asked the guv'nor keenly. "I have been considering that theory, Fletcher. It is just possible that Durand earned the hatred of some animal attendant, who took a drastic revenge. Are there many foreigners in the circus—semi-savages, I mean?"

The prisoner shook his head.

"Not one, Mr. Blake." he replied, "There are two or three negroes, but they are all honest, hard working fellows and are as civilized as any white man. Besides, Durand was on excellent terms with them. Mr. Capelli is always very careful about whom he engages— He won't have any riff-raff, I can assure you. He is an ideal circus proprietor in every way."

"Well, Fletcher, I'm afraid you can't give me much information," said Sexton Blake, rising to depart. "I shall go to the circus now and have a look round with my own eyes. You can rest content that I shall be working my hardest in your interests. And don't be despondent. We'll have you out of this fix before long."

"You've given me fresh hope, Mr. Blake," said Fletcher gratefully. "Ethel and I had planned to be married just after Christmas—"

"And so you shall be," declared Blake, smiling. "Christmas is very near, I know; but when that festive time arrives you will be a free man."

We left Fletcher in excellent spirits, and we were feeling confidant ourselves. I couldn't quite see how the guv'nor was to pursue his investigations, but he was brisk and alert, and meant to lose no time.

"Just after eleven, Tinker," he said, as we walked down the passage. "Why, it's quite early, considering we have the whole night before us, if necessary, and much can be done in a few hours. One of the most important points in a case of this sort is to get to work immediately. Delay is frequently fatal."

We left the police-station after Superintendent Hollins had assured us that he would come down to the circus himself later on. Nobody thought of going to bed on this dramatic night.

When we arrived at the circus field we found everything still and quiet. Lights were showing in many of the caravans, but the vast tent was dark. Only a few lights showed in some of the adjoining tents.

I led the way, being familiar with the place, and when we entered the tent next to that of the dead man we found several electric light burning, and the place was occupied by Signor Coppell, Miss Hanwell, Pottles, and Waldo. Tracy all turned curiously as we entered.

"It's all right, Miss Hanwell!" I called cheerily. "I've brought the guv'nor!"

The girl came forward eagerly.

"It's wonderfully good of you, Mr. Blake!" she exclaimed, her eyes shining. "I was terribly afraid that you would be too busy to give any attention to this terrible affair."

"I am never too busy to investigate a case which thoroughly interests me, Miss Hanwell," said Sexton Blake, taking her hand. "Moreover, your appeal was most earnest, and I have hastened to answer it. I have already seen Mr. Fletcher. And it may be some relief for you to know that I am entirely convinced of his innocence."

"Oh Mr., Blake! How splendid of you!" said the girl quickly? "I don't know how I'm going to thank you enough!"

"You must really wait until I have earned your thanks before tendering any," smiled the guv'nor. "But you needn't look so worried. Matters will soon right themselves."

"I hope so—oh, I do hope so."

Miss Hanwell was looking better already. It's a curious fact, but the guv'nor seems to instil confidence and hope into people as soon as he gets on the scene. His personality is amazingly inspiring.

Mr. Capelli bustled forward, and I had the honor of introducing Sexton Blake to company in general.

"This to a pleasure I never hoped to enjoy, Mr. Blake," declared the mam heartily. "I've had a few distinguished visitors in my circus at different times, but, by thunder, your presence here is the biggest honour of all! If it wasn't for poor Durand's death I'd be dancing with joy."

"You mustn't take any notice of the boss, Mr. Blake," said Pottles calmly. "He's the best guv'nor in the word, but he has his little ways. If you've come here to prove Fletcher's innocence, then I'm with you. I'll be dashed if I can believe that young fellow is guilty! I don't believe it!"

The clown had removed his paint, and was now an ordinary human being—a lanky man of about forty-five or fifty. His face was clean-shaven and lean, and there was some-thing about him which was immensely attractive.

Waldo had also changed and to look at him one would never imagine that he possessed the strength of four or five ordinary men rolled into one. He appeared to be very concerned over the whole affair.

"I'm afraid you've got rather a stiff task on hand, Mr. Blake," he said gravely. "Mind you, I'm staunchly by Fletcher. I've known him ever since he came into the show, and I'll stake my life that he's innocent. At the same time the evidence is so much against him that I'm hanged if I can see where you're going to start. The point which puzzles me is—Who stuck that arrow into Durand's back? It certainly didn't get there without hands."

"And yet that suggestion is not altogether impossible," smiled Sexton Blake. "One point has rather impressed me. Durand accused Fletcher, and that has seemed to open out a very interesting suggestion."

The guv'nor did not mention what this suggestion was, and I was rather curious, for I couldn't quite follow him. Waldo, I believe, was on the point of asking him what he meant, but refrained from doing so.

The guv'nor and I entered the dressing-tent, and found, as we had expected, a constable on guard. He wasn't looking very happy, and seemed quite cheered up by our arrival.

Seaton Blake examined the body carefully, and when he had finished there was a very thoughtful expression on his face.

"Well, guv'nor?" I asked curiously.

"The poison, Tinker, is undoubtedly one of a particularly virulent character from West Africa," he replied. "The point of the arrow was presumably coated with a dried solution, and a mere scratch would cause death within a minute or two. I have met with similar cases in the past."

"You've got no clue as to how it was done!"

"Not as yet, Tinker," replied Blake. "As I mentioned not long ago, Durand's accusation of Fletcher is most suggestive."

"Of what, guv'nor?"

"Well, consider the point, young 'un. Why, should Durand accuse Fletcher?"

"Because he thought Fletcher killed him, I suppose."

"But Durand would not have thought so had there been another man in the tent," said Sexton Blake shrewdly. "The inference, Tinker, is that there was nobody in the tent when the arrow struck Durand in the back. Fletcher came in a moment afterwards and the dying man at once assumed that Fletcher had flung the arrow. After all, it was quite a natural consequence. Do you follow my train of reasoning?"

"Quite easily, guv'nor," I said. "These things don't seem to be apparent until you make them clear. You suggest, then, that the tent war quite empty—except for Durand himself when the arrow struck him in the back?"

"Exactly!"

"But couldn't somebody have crept up behind the man's chair?"

"With a mirror immediately in front of him?" said Blake. "Come, come, Tinker, where are your wits? The mirror is a large one, and Durand had a view of the whole tent as he sat making-up. No intruder could have surprised him from the rear. That fact is established, furthermore, the only exit is by doorway. We are brought back to the one certain fact that Durand was alone at the actual moment of the murder."

"Perhaps I'm dull to-night, guv'nor; but I'm jiggered if I can understand!" I said frankly. "If Fletcher didn't throw the arrow, and if Durand was alone, where the dickens did the arrow comes from?"

Sexton Blake smiled.

"It is that point, Tinker, which we have to settle, and I don't think it will be very difficult one," he replied evenly, "But I think I can hear our friend the superintendent, and we had better join him."

We found Hollins in conversation with Mr. Capelli. Pottles was absent, being engaged in the task of escorting Miss Hanwell to her caravan. There was really no need for her to remain on the scene, for nothing definite could be done before the morning.

"I intend to have look in Fletcher's caravan, Blake," said the superintendent. "It is just a formality, but we may be able to get some information. There is no telling in a case like this. Fletcher must obtained that poisoned arrow from somewhere, and we may find a letter, or a receipt, or some other incriminating document."

"But you don't believe that Fletcher's guilty, sir?" I demanded warmly.

"I am compelled to do so, Tinker," replied Hollins grimly.

I felt rather incensed. The police, having got their man, set to work to prove him guilty. Their object was to fish up all the evidence they could against him. They didn't seem to consider the idea of establishing his innocence.

Since Fletcher's caravan was to be searched, I determined to be on the scene, if possible. The superintendent and Sexton Blake passed out into the night, guided by Mr. Capelli himself. I followed, and soon we arrived at a large, roomy caravan, sumptuously decorated within and without. Everything connected with this circus was magnificent, and the caravans in general were finer articles than I had ever seen before.

Hollins unlocked the door—having obtained the key from Fletcher—and entered. He proceeded to strike a match, but Capelli suggested that he should switch on the electric-light.

"Well, upon my soul!" said the superintendent, as the caravan became flooded with soft illumination. "How do you manage this, Mr. Capelli?"

"Each caravan has its allotted place wherever we stay, and there are branch wires from the main cable at different intervals," replied the boss. "Simply a matter of pushing in a plug I believe. But I'm no good when it comes to electricity. You'll have to ask Pottles if you want any further information. He knows all about these things."

I managed to get into the caravan behind the others; although Mr. Capelli himself remained outside. The interior was cosy and luxurious, the whole place being fitted up like a ship's cabin of

The UNION JACK Library ⁹

FOUR STIRRING INCIDENTS IN THIS MAGNIFICENT STORY.

1. Blake and Tinker saw a dark figure enter the tent. (See page 8.)
2. Waldo, in the goods-train, is confronted by Nelson Lee. (See page 15.)
3. Waldo escapes from the burning caravan. (See page 14.)
4. Tinker hailed Sexton Blake frantically as the train moved out. (See page 6.)

the first class. I felt that I'd like to live in that caravan myself.

The search was not a difficult one, and the only article of furniture which really held out any prospect was a small bureau affair, fitted flush against one of the walls. It was of the walls. It was of polished mahogany, and had several small drawers, with brass handles.

The superintendent drew blank in the first one, finding only some writing-paper, a safety ink-wells, pens, and so forth. The second drawer seemed to stick a trifle, and Hollins had to tug fairly hard. But when it came open he uttered a sharp exclamation and his set grimly.

"Look at this, Blake—look at this!" he ejaculated.

Very gingerly he held up a short arrow—an exact duplicate of the one which had caused Durand's death.

"Oh, my goodness!" I muttered, in dismay. "Mind the point, Hollins, whatever you do!" said the guv'nor sharply. "One scratch is enough to cause death, if this specimen is coated with poison, too. Let me glance at it; I'll soon make sure."

The superintendent was quite relieved to hand the arrow over to Sexton Blake. It was about four inches long, and was made of some exceptionally hard wood, dark in colour.

"Yes, this is prepared, just like other," said Blake, after a short silence. "There's a matchbox on that shelf—just pass it to me, Tinker. We'll put this point out of harm's way."

The guv'nor emptied the matches out of the box, thrust the arrow-head inside, and pulled the slide over it. Then he wrapped the whole thing in a sheet of newspaper, and handed it to the superintendent.

"And let me warn you to be most careful," he said. "If I were you, I should lock it away as soon as you get to the police-station. If any of your men get monkeying with it, they'll be dead within a minute."

"What an infernal object to carry about!" said the superintendent. "Stowing the parcel here, Blake, is absolutely damning for Fletcher. He'll be convicted, without the slightest doubt; and he deserves to be, too, the coldblooded scoundrel!"

Sexton Blake smiled.

"You must allow me to disagree with you, Hollins," he said, "I am by no means upset by this discovery. On the contrary, I am inclined to be elated; for it is a sure indication of Fletcher's innocence."

"Innocence?" The superintendent stared. "Innocence?"

"Precisely," said the guv'nor. "We both agree, Hollins, that this is a ease of premeditated murder, and the man who planned it was clever. Assuming that man to be Fletcher, would he be such an utter fool as to leave this arrow here—to be found by the first searchers? He overlooked it, you think? But that won't do, old man. No murderer would overlook a point of that sort."

"Then, how did the arrow get here?"

"It was obviously planted in that bureau after Fletcher had been taken away," replied the guv'nor. "The murderer has resorted to a somewhat clumsy subterfuge, and I am rather surprised. Let me suggest, Hollins, that you should make a point of ascertaining if any other caravan keys fit this door. The result of such an inquiry might be instructive."

Sexton Blake turned and went out. Hollins and I followed, and the door was relocked. And then the guv'nor performed a little operation which somewhat surprised the superintendent.

In short, he sealed the door top and bottom, and then repeated the performance on the window.

"Just a little precaution," he remarked "If those seals are broken in the morning, Hollins, we shall know that somebody else has access to this caravan—and by another key."

"It's my opinion, Blake, that you're wasting your time," said the police official. "It doesn't give me any pleasure, I can assure you, to gather all this fatal evidence against Fletcher. But the man's guilty, and I can't feel any pity for him. I'll wager that you don't prove his innocence!"

"We shall see, Hollins—we shall see," observed Blake calmly. "And now, may I make a suggestion?"

We had been joined by Mr. Capelli, Pottles, and Waldo, and they were all anxious to hear the results of the research. The superintendent briefly told them, and poor Capelli was nearly overcome.

"This is shocking, Pottles: it's getting worse and worse!" he said helplessly. "Before long I shall begin to believe that Fletcher—"

"Don't you believe anything of the sort, boss," interrupted the clown. "You will have observed that Mr. Blake is quiet. He doesn't agree with the superintendent, or I'll eat my buttons! Mr. Blake's deep, and I'll go all the way on him."

Hollins turned to the guv'nor.

"What's that suggestion you were going to make, Blake?" he asked.

"Oh, that we should quietly go home to bed, and leave all further investigation until the morning," replied the great detective smoothly. "We can do nothing further tonight, I am sure. Further, I should suggest that the body is removed from the tent at once, and taken straight to the mortuary. It will then be unnecessary to leave a policeman on guard here—which, I am sure, will be a relief to Mr. Capelli."

The superintendent was not inclined to adopt the suggestion with regard to the body; but Sexton Blake persisted, and at last got his way. A constable was dispatched to fetch the ambulance—a small affair of the usual type, propelled by two men. It arrived within twenty minutes, and Durand's remains were placed upon it, and conveyed to the mortuary. A past-mortem examination would be necessary of course, but that was a matter for the police.

We said good-night to Mr. Capelli and the others, and then took our departure.

But, on second-thoughts, the boss decided to accompany Hollins to the police-station, being anxious to settle a few points which were causing him some concern. The circus was due to move on to its next town in a day or two, and Capelli was afraid that complications would arise, and he wanted to settle the things at once.

"I can't sleep with all this worry on my mind," he declared, shaking his head, "I shall probably be keeping you out of bed for an hour, superintendent; but you don't mind, do you?"

Hollins assured him that be need not concern him, and we walked on, having now left the circus behind.

I was in a state of interested speculation. Never for a moment did I believe that Sexton Blake had been serious when he suggested that we should postpone the investigation until tomorrow. Such a thing was utterly against his system, and I wasn't hoodwinked.

The guv'nor had some plan in his mind—but what was it?

THE FOURTH CHAPTER

AN ASTOUNDING ADVENTURE.

SUPERINTENDENT HOLLINS turned to Sexton Blake as we strode along.

"By the way, Blake. You'll have a deuce of a job to find sleeping quarters at this time of night," he said. "I can give you and Tinker two excellent beds, and there'll be no charge for a wash and brush up in the morning."

"I shan't refuse your hospitality, Hollins," said Sexton Blake. "Tinker and I will take advantage of your very generous invitation."

"And, what's more, I'm going home straight away," said the superintendent. "I've given Freeman all the instructions he needs. We may as well have our little interviews in comfort, Mr. Capelli. And I shouldn't be surprised if Tinker is in need of some supper. I don't believe he's had any yet."

"And not likely to, sir," I replied ruefully.

"How's that, Tinker?"

"Ask the guv'nor, sir."

"Oh, so you are not quite so dull now, my lad?" said Sexton Blake. "You weren't deceived by my little manoeuvre? The truth is, Hollins, I want you to excuse Tinker and me for about an hour."

"What on earth for?"

"Well, we are somewhat eccentric individuals," said Blake vaguely. "I am anxious to go off on a little inquiry of which I will tell you later. All being well, Tinker and I will turn up at about one o'clock."

The superintendent was frankly astonished, but he assured us that he wouldn't lock the door before one o'clock. His threat that we should be bolted out after that hour had no effect upon us.

And so we branched off down a side road, while Hollins and Capelli pursued their way. The guv'nor and I strode on briskly, bound goodness knows where. I thought it about time to learn the truth.

"Now guv'nor, what's the game?" I asked pointedly.

Sexton Blake came to a halt.

"The game, Tinker, is quite a simple one," he replied. "We must retrace our steps to the circus with all speed. I have a mind to examine that dressing-tent in private—without any being present except our two selves. I succeeded to getting every-body neatly out of the way, and the coast is now clear."

"It's something deeper than that, guv'nor; you can't diddle me," I remarked, as we set off back to the circus. "Your idea was to throw somebody off the scent, wasn't it?"

"Perhaps!"

"Who?"

"If you can't guess, Tinker, I shall not enlighten you." was the guv'nor's exasperating reply. "But, my observations have somewhat more thorough than I have revealed. You have had the same opportunities as myself—"

"Oh, chuck it, guv'nor!" I growled. "I'm not you, am I? You can see things that I miss altogether. I don't know how it is, unless you've got second sight. I don't mind admitting that I'm in a horrid state of bewilderment."

"Let us hope that it won't last very long," chuckled Sexton Blake.

We arrived in the meadow where the circus was pitched, and found that everything was black and deserted. A somewhat blustery wind had sprung up during the last hour, and the sky was overcast, promising another fall of snow.

"We must be very cautious, Tinker," whispered the guv'nor. "Follow me, and don't speak unless you have a very strong reason."

"All right guv'nor; although I don't see that it matters much," I replied. "Those tents are flapping about pretty noisily, aren't they?"

This was actually the case, the canvas of the main tent booming up and down like the sails of a schooner at sea. Snow was again falling but only in fine flakes, and hardly sufficient to powder the ground after an all-night downfall.

We approached the tent we had entered earlier, it was in total darkness, and, indeed, the whole place looked utterly deserted. Durand's dressing-tent adjoined this one, but the entrance to it was not in the open; we had to make our way into the other tent first.

But before we had moved forward ten yards, Sexton Blake grasped my arm and held me back. I couldn't quite understand what the game was, until he pointed into the darkness ahead.

I peered forward intently.

And then I dimly saw the figure of a man against the tent entrance. His back, so far as I could edge, was towards us, and he evidently had no idea of our approach. It was impossible to see who the man was.

As I watched the man seemed to fade away; at all events I could see the dark figure no longer against the lighter surface of the canvas, And the guv'nor's grip relaxed.

"What an infernal nuisance, Tinker!" he breathed irritably.

"Who was it, guv'nor?"

"I can't say for certain, young 'un, but I have my suspicions," was Sexton Blake's reply. "My plan is somewhat upset. I did not think the man would risk entering the tent so soon as this. However, our only course now is to discover what the fellow is up to."

"No, no. Hollins gave instructions that the tent was not to be guarded in any way. This man is of far more interest to us than a constable, Tinker. His very presence here proven that my theory is not entirely wrong. Fletcher did not commit the murder, that much is certain."

We crept forward once more, and when we arrived at the entrance we found the flaps loose, and their interiors black and quiet, except for the continuous noise made by the uneasy canvas.

Sexton Blake did not pause for more than a few seconds. Then he entered the tent, and I followed hard at his heels. The entrance of Durand's dressing apartment was to the left, and we knew its approximate position. But, even without this, we did not find it necessary to flounder forward in a state of uncertainty. For a sudden streak of subdued light revealed itself in the smaller tent.

With catlike tread Blake moved across the sawdust, his footfalls making no sound whatever. Not that a few slight noises would have mattered, with all the creaking of ropes and booming of canvas going on. The wind was helping us considerably, for it drowned all sounds of our approach.

As we reached the doorway the light was extinguished, and when the guv'nor applied his eye to the narrow space between the two flaps he saw nothing but blackness. I bent down, kneeling in the sawdust, and looked, too. But I might have well have gazed into an inky pit for all that I saw.

We remained in those positions for fully three minutes, using our ears. And we heard several sounds which were certainly not caused by the wind. A sudden clatter was followed by a low, but unmistakable curse.

After that I could have sworn that I heard somebody mounting some steps or a ladder, although such a thing seemed impossible. Steps would be the most likely, I reflected, because this little tent wasn't high enough to accommodate a ladder. The roof at the sides was no more than ten feet from the ground.

And then the light appeared again, just for a flash. This time it came from above, and I caught one fleeting glimpse of a stepladder near the canvas wall which divided the tent from the main auditorium. A crouching figure, with its back towards us, stood on the top of the steps. But before I could visualize any details or form any opinion the light went out.

What was the man doing up there? Who was he? Had it been Sexton Blake's intention to pursue a similar investigation, near the roof? Personally, I couldn't for the life of me understand what the game was.

There was a sudden crack, as of splitting wood, and then a mutter of satisfaction. Sexton Blake touched my shoulder and moved silently backwards. I followed him until we stood well out of earshot.

"But who is he, guv'nor?" I asked.

"It is really impossible to say, for certain," replied Blake. "Therefore, Tinker, we will wait and watch. It will still be possible for us to obtain the evidence we require, I believe. At all events, hasty action at this juncture would have no satisfactory result. We must be patient."

We moved quietly out of the tent until we stood under the clouded sky once more. The cold wind blew into our faces, and I pulled my overcoat-collar up round my neck. The guv'nor was doing the same.

"Supposing the chap gets away by some other means, guv'nor?" I whispered. "We shall look a nice couple of idiots if we stand at this door for two or three hours!"

"My dear Tinker, you have my full permission to describe your own appearance as often as you please, but there is no necessity to drag me in," said Sexton Blake calmly. "The man will make his exit by this doorway, since it is the only handy one; moreover, he would not be so foolish as to leave the flaps unsecured during the whole night."

We retreated some little distance into the darkness, but kept our gaze carefully centred upon the tout. And our wait, as it turned out, was

not of long duration. Five minutes had scarcely passed before we saw the intruder emerge.

He laid something down on the ground, and then carefully secured the flaps. Having done this, he seized the object he had placed in the grass, and strode off across the circus meadow, but not in the direction of the caravans.

"Come, Tinker!" breathed Sexton Blake.

He led the way, and I followed at a distance of about twenty feet. We moved noiselessly through the soft grass, and our quarry walked on with no suspicion that he was being so closely attended.

The darkness was intense, and it was only by keeping our gaze fixed upon the dim figure ahead that we were able to keep him in view. I looked elsewhere for a second on one occasion, and fully half a minute elapsed before I again picked out the moving figure ahead.

Where he was bound for was something of a mystery for he seemed to be directing his steps towards the lower end of the big meadow which was utterly deserted. It was my private opinion—and the guv'nor's, too, I fancy—that the stranger was intent on burying the object he had brought out of the tent.

If so, nothing could have been better. We could watch him at work, wait, and then dig up the mysterious article, which, I had no doubt, was a valuable item of evidence. Otherwise, why this secret performance, in the dead of night?

Right ahead of us, at the lower end of the meadow, stood several willow-trees, and a profusion of other bushes. If the man broke his way through this barrier we should have some difficulty in finding him again.

But he halted before reaching the trees. For a moment he stood as though irresolute, and then flung his arm out.

Splash!

The sound came to us distinctly, and we understood. The marauder had flung his burden into the water. There was a river running through the lower part of the meadow. We had seen nothing of it, of course, and had not known of its existence.

Sexton Blake, even as the man flung up his hand, rushed forward like the wind, in an effort to avert the disaster; for it would be a very real disaster if that article of evidence was lost.

The stranger twirled round, uttering a low gasp.

The next moment Blake was upon him, but too late to save the situation. And then an amazing thing occurred. The guv'nor is a fighter of the first quality; he can generally tackle two ordinarily strong men with ease and comfort.

Yet this straggle lasted about five seconds only.

Our quarry grappled with his assailant, and I expected to see him—the stranger—go down at once. Instead of this, Sexton went up. That's the literal truth. The guv'nor was picked up like a feather, hurled high into the air, and dropped with a terrific splash into the river.

"Great Scott!" I gasped.

I rushed forward blindly, caring nothing for the odds. The guv'nor had been pitched into the river. Then I tripped over something, and nearly fell. It was a heavy piece of wood, like the branch of a tree. I grabbed it eagerly, and dashed to the attack.

The mysterious stranger turned even as I pelted up, becoming aware of my presence for the first time. I didn't wait to ask questions. Probably I was excited; certainly I was furious. And I whirled the wood round, and brought it down upon the bare head of my quarry.

Crash!

I was almost startled as the wood smashed in two over the man's skull; I thought I had brained him. To my utter amazement, however, he did not seem to notice the blow at all. He gripped me with frightful strength, and I went soaring into the air, all arms and legs.

Then I descended—into the icy waters of the river. By the time I came up, splashing and gasping, struggling against the swift current, the astounding man who had performed the miracle was no longer to be seen.

THE FIFTH
CHAPTER

SEXTON BLAKE RECONSTRUCTS THE CRIME—AND BRINGS A CLEVER SCHEME TO LIGHT.

SEXTON BLAKE was clutching at the bank when I found my bearings.

"You all right, Tinker?" he asked huskily.

"Yes; although this current's a bit swift!" I gasped, striking out. "Oh, my hat! Bathing's all right in the summer-time, but I jib at this, guv'nor!"

Within a minute we were both on the bank, dripping and shivering. The water, as I had intimated, was not exactly warm, and the icy wind did not improve matters. But the guv'nor and I are hardy customers.

"A fine mess we've made of it, Tinker!" snapped Blake, with chattering teeth. "A fine mess indeed! We have not only lost the man himself, but also the evidence he tossed into the water."

"There's plenty of evidence that he tossed us into the water, guv'nor," I said, jumping up and down, and beating my arms. "His strength must be staggering! The way he pitched me into— Great guns!"

"Well Tinker?"

"He—he must have been Waldo!" I gasped.

"Exactly."

"Did you know all along?"

"I did not know, but I suspected," replied Sexton Blake. "This incident leaves no doubt on the subject. No other man but Waldo could have exhibited such extraordinary muscular power. But he knows that we did not recognize him, and I have no fear of him running off."

"But—but his strength is nothing, guv'nor!" I panted. "He was bareheaded!"

"Is that anything remarkable? I knocked his cap off," said Blake. "But I fancy he recovered it before fleeing—"

"He was bareheaded!" I repeated, in a startled voice, "and I broke that chunk of wood over his skull! It was enough to brain him on the spot! Just look at the thickness of it, guv'nor!"

I picked up the piece of wood, and the guv'nor peered at it.

"The wood is rotten, no doubt," he remarked.

"It's not, guv'nor: it's as sound as a bell," I declared. "Just feel it!"

Sexton Blake did so,

"And you broke this over Waldo's head?" he asked doubtfully.

"Yes, guv'nor—positively!" I said. "I gave him a frightful whack!"

"Then his skull must be thick," commented Blake grimly, "But this is a waste of time, Tinker; and we shall catch dreadful colds if we stand about here—"

"To say nothing about pneumonia, or something just as bad," I said, shivering. "I vote we rush off to the superintendent's place."

Sexton Blake nodded.

"Presently, young 'un," he said briskly. "For the moment we have another task. We are both soaking, so another dive won't do us any harm. If you don't feel like it you can pelt away; I'll follow."

I stared wondering.

"Do you like diving in this liquid ice, guv'nor?" I asked.

"No, Tinker, I dislike it exceedingly;" he replied, "But I have a mind to see how deep the water is. If the bed of the stream is within diving distance, we might possibly succeed in recovering the article which Waldo threw in."

"Oh, I see," I said. "Well, I'm game."

Anything was better than standing still, and I dived straight into the river without further delay. Sexton Blake followed, and we found the muddy bed with ease, Incidentally, I found it with my head, and got a faceful of awful slime. After that I dived more cautiously.

For five solid minutes we kept up the game, and the exercise took some of the chill out of our bones. We were breathless, and unrewarded.

"It's no good, guv'nor!" I gasped. "We'd better give it up."

"Just one more dive, Tinker," said Blake.

He disappeared as he spoke, and came up a few moments later, And this time he held something in his hand.

"I think I've got it," he spluttered triumphantly, "It may be something far wide of the mark, but—No; it is the prize I was after."

We scrambled out, and hurried away without a pause. I was too uncomfortable to think about the thing which Sexton Blake held in his hand; all I wanted was to get to Hollins' place, tear my clothes off, wrap a blanket round me, and squat down in front of a roaring fire.

After we had covered about half the distance, however, I began to feel better and reflected upon the incident which had just occurred. Without a doubt the man who had thrown the guv'nor and I into the river was Waldo. But I couldn't quite get the hang of things.

"Look here, guv'nor," I said as we ran. "I'm not suggesting that the fellow wasn't Waldo; but he couldn't have committed the murder—he's positively innocent of that, anyhow."

"Why are you so sure, Tinker!"

"Well, guv'nor— Waldo's got a perfect alibi—a cast-iron one!" I declared. "I'd be willing to go into court at any time and swear that Waldo bad nothing to do with the crime—at least, with the actual killing of Durand. Because, don't you see, Waldo was doing his turn at the very moment the murder took place. He was in the ring, in full view of all the audience."

"Quite so, Tinker. But we will discuss this point at a more opportune moment," said Sexton Blake. "Presently I hope to demonstrate one or two facts which may prove of interest to our friend the superintendent."

Two or three minutes later we reached our destination, and Sexton Blake rutted thunderously upon the door. The hall light was a powerful one and the front door was provided with glass panels. Sexton Blake and I could see one another distinctly for the first time.

"Oh, my only hat!" I ejaculated.

"If my appearance is anything like yours, Tinker, I must indeed be a spectacle!" grinned Blake cheerfully. "However, we have done well, so we mustn't grumble at these little drawbacks."

We were both mud-streaked, and our faces were hardly recognisable. The door opened, and the superintendent stood before as, smiling.

"Not so late as you intimated— Great heavens!" gasped Rollins, starting back. "What in the world— Is—is that you, Blake?"

"I freely forgive you for being in doubt, Hollins," said the guv'nor, striding into the hall. "And I am afraid we shall cause you some little trouble. Ah, the warmth of this hall is most grateful!"

"But--but what's happened?" demanded Hollins, aghast.

"Oh, nothing much!" I replied, "We've been exploring the bed of the river—that's all. The guv'nor had a fancy for diving exercise."

Hollins was sensible enough not to ask question. He rushed us upstairs into the bedroom which had been prepared for us, and five minutes later we had stripped off every rag; and then Sexton Blake tumbled straight into a bath—of lukewarm water, by the way, no hot being available. I followed him, and after a brisk rubdown, attired myself in some overgrown pyjamas and several blankets, by this time I was feeling warmed and content.

Sexton Blake was similarly attired, and together we descended to the warm dining-room, where Mr. Capelli was still sitting. Mrs. Hollins and the family had retired to rest long since—which was just as well.

"Well Blake, I don't know what on earth you've been up to, but I think you're in serious danger of developing influenza tomorrow," said the superintendent, shaking his head. "You've caught a chill—"

"Nonsense!" laughed Sexton Blake. "Tinker and I are not the kind of people who catch chills, Hollins. We exercised ourselves well, and didn't allow the cold to get a grip on us. I observe that Tinker is eyeing the table hungrily—and that is not a very serious symptom."

The guv'nor wasn't far wrong, for, to tell the truth, I was famished, not having touched a morsel of food since tea-time, and a sharp wintry air has the effect of putting an edge on a fellow's appetite.

I was soon busy with the good things. But Sexton Blake did not join me. He, of course, had partaken of supper at the correct time, while I was in the midst of the excitement at the circus; Hollins prevailed upon him, however, to imbibe a steaming hot cup of beef-tea.

Between sips Sexton Blake explained what had occurred, and the superintendent listened with great interest and considerable astonishment. Mr. Capelli, also, was enthralled. The guv'nor did not lay particular stress upon the strength of our opponent, and thus gave his listeners no clue as to the identity of the marauder, Blake probably intended to spring that little surprise later.

"A most remarkable affair!" said Hollins, scratching his chin. "It seems to prove, though, that there's some hanky-panky about this business. Blake. Either the fellow is an accomplice of Fletcher's or somebody entirely unconnected with the crime."

"Which is an indication, Hollins, that you believe in Fletcher's guilt," smiled the guv'nor. "Well, I don't, and I shall make it my business to establish the young fellow's innocence."

Mr. Capelli slapped his thigh.

"That's the talk, Mr. Blake!" he exclaimed, "By gosh! I hope you succeed, that's all! Fletcher was my favorite—and is still, if it comes to that. I don't believe he did it—hang me if I do!"

"I'm afraid we shall have to hang Fletcher," said Hollis, with grim humour.

"Not while the guv'nor's alive!" I said cheerfully.

Sexton Blake smiled and bent down towards the fireplace. Just inside the fender was the article he had salved from the river-bed, drying. By now the outer wetness had vanished, and it was possible to handle the thing without becoming grimy.

"And this fellow obtained what you've got in your hands, Mr. Blake, from Durand's tent?" asked the superintendent.

"Yes. It was fixed up on one of the crossbars near the roof."

"Well. I'm hanged it I can understand it!" put in Mr. Capelli, "What is the affair, Mr. Blake, anyhow?"

"I am now about to ascertain," replied the guv'nor.

I watched him with interest while I demolished the last few mouthfuls of my supper. The thing which Sexton Blake was turning over his hands appeared to be a neatly-constructed contrivance of wood. There was something which looked like an extra stout piece of elastic, too, fixed between two prongs.

"Queer-looking arrangement, guv'nor," I remarked perplexedly.

"Yes, Tinker, you are quite right," agreed the guv'nor. "I can well understand why our energetic friend was so anxious to get rid of it—for here, superintendent, is the apparatus which was the direct cease of Durand's death. Fletcher did not throw that arrow, or oven handle it."

"I don't quite follow you, Blake," said Hollins.

"Do you see this elastic spring?" asked the guv'nor. "Do you see the cleverly-devised socket in the centre of it? Into the socket Hollins, the end of the arrow was fitted. At a given time the spring was released, and the arrow plunged into Durand's back."

"That's a bit tall, isn't it?" asked the superintendent doubtfully. "You're surely not suggesting, Blake, that some clockwork arrangement was fitted—like an infernal machine in a filmplay? My dear man, how could the fellow who fitted it up know that Durand would be sitting in his chair at the exact time of the release of the spring?"

"I am not suggesting that any clockwork was employed," replied Sexton Blake. "Indeed, it would have been impossible. Further-more, there is a short portion of string attached, which points in another direction. Can you tell me, Mr. Capelli, if Durand was in the habit of making up before his mirror at a set time every evening?"

The boss sat forward with a jerk.

"Well, that's queer!" he declared. "Poor Durand was a masterpiece for regularity. He was like an article of clockwork himself—always got up at the same hour, always practised his tricks at eleven to the minute, and always went into his dressing-room as Waldo was going into the ring. And during Waldo's turn he'd sit in front of his mirror making up. Hated being disturbed. A most particular fellow in every way—and not very good-tempered, either."

"It was well know, then, that Durand would almost certainly be sitting in his chair at the exact moment of the murder?" asked Blake. "I am not hinting that anybody could be positive on that point, but the chances were all in favour of Durand being in that position?"

"That's right, Mr. Blake—dead right!" said Capelli.

"Very well, then. We arrive at the fact that Durand was in a settled position at the time of the crime," went on the guv'nor. "Anybody releasing the spring of this contrivance would know almost to a certainty that the arrow would enter Durand's back— There was just a chance that something would go wrong but a very slim chance. The odds were all in favour of success."

"That is all very well, Blake!" put in Hollins, "But that confounded thing couldn't have been released without hands, could it?"

"Certainly!"

"But you're overlooking the fact that the only person within reasonable distance of Durand was Fletcher himself—"

"For the moment I have dismissed Fletcher altogether," interrupted Blake quietly. "Fletcher is not concerned in this case whatever—his presence in the tent was an unfortunate complication—which, however, the murderer immediately took advantage of, for he 'planted' a second arrow in Fletcher caravan."

"A very pretty theory of course," said Hollins. "But can't accept it, Blake. I must have proofs, you know—"

"I am quite prepared to supply them," interrupted Sexton Blake. "And, Hollins, I am not merely voicing a pretty theory, as you call it. I intend to reconstruct the crime, exactly as it happened, and I can do so in a very few words There is one question I should like to ask you, Mr. Capelli."

"Ask a hundred, if you want to, sir!" said the boss readily.

"Can you tell me if your strong man, Waldo, throws a crossbar or a weight into the air during the course of his exhibition?"

I jumped.

"Why, of course, he does, guv'nor!" I exclaimed excitedly. "He did this evening. Anyhow; I was in the ring when he did it!"

"The lad's right," said Mr. Capelli nodding. "It's one of Waldo's favourite tricks. The man's a wonder! Strongest fellow on earth, I should say! I wouldn't lose him for a thousand pounds!"

"I'm afraid you're going to," said the guv'nor calmly.

"Good gracious!" ejaculated Hollins, "Do you mean—are you hinting that Waldo is implicated in this murder?"

"I will go further, and say that Waldo is the actual murderer himself!" said Sexton Blake. "And what is more, I will prove it!"

The circus proprietor jumped up, "But this is terrible—terrible!" he exclaimed. "I've lost Durand—one of my best performers—but I'm hanged if I can afford to lose Waldo! From a personal point of view, I like Fletcher fifty times as much as Waldo, but Waldo's one of the main-stays of my show!"

"Really, Mr. Capelli, we can't consider your circus in a grave matter of this nature," put in the superintendent. "Mr. Blake has made a very positive statement, and I know him too well to suspect that he is talking without excellent reason. Now, Blake, I should like you to be a little more candid. How could Waldo have committed this crime while he was in the ring? Man alive, he's got a solid alibi! A clever defending counsel could tear that evidence to pieces in five minutes!"

"Not when it is complete," replied the guv'nor smoothly. "Durand died a few seconds after Waldo had thrown the crossbar into the air— because that crossbar severed an invisible string which was stretched from Durand's adjoining tent to one of the supports of the auditorium.

When that string was broken this apparatus was put into operation, and the arrow sped down on its mission of death. A highly ingenious arrangement, no doubt, but highly dangerous also. It was absolutely necessary to remove this affair, and destroy it as soon after the crime as possible. I suspected Waldo almost from the first, and I believed that he would visit the tent before morning. But it was my plan to get there first and to take this thing down before Waldo's arrival. However, I don't think we have much to grumble at, as things have turned out."

The superintendent scratched his chin again.

"But, according to what you say, you know that this contrivance was fixed up?" he asked. "You knew it before you saw the man removing it?"

"I did not know, but I had my own ideas," replied Blake. 'You see, Hollins, accepting the fact that Fletcher was innocent, it was quite obvious that no human hand had thrown the arrow. Therefore, a mechanical contrivance was employed. Such a contrivance was necessarily within the tent, and probably near the roof. I intended, therefore, to examine the place."

"Bless my soul, its marvellous—it's wonderful !" declared Mr. Capelli. "How you arrived at that conclusion, Mr. Blake, faily beats me! And it was right—dead, plumb right! Well, if Waldo's really guilty, it'll give me pleasure to read in a morning paper that he's been hanged. Show or no show, the man must be a cold-blooded brute!"

"You're beginning to convince me, Blake," said the superintendent. "In fact, I don't know that oughtn't to arrest Waldo straightaway on suspicion. But how can I? Where's the proof? You can't identify the man, who removed that thing from the tent, because you didn't see him properly. And there's no actual evidence that Waldo had a hand in the game. And what about motive? Where's your motive?"

Sexton Blake smiled.

"I am quite ready to admit that our case is very incomplete at this point." he said. "As you say, superintendent, you can't touch Waldo just now. You have no justification for doing so."

"But won't he bunk after what happened to-night?" I asked concernedly.

"I don't think so, Tinker," replied the guv'nor. "To bunk, as you expressively put it, would be the act of a panic—and I don't think Waldo is lacking in wits. If you disappeared, suspicion would instantly attach itself to him. He knows that as well as do. To stay in the circus, however, and to maintain a bold front, is an attitude likely to deceive the police."

"I am flattered!" remarked Hollins.

"Well, I think you will admit that you did not suspect Waldo," smiled Sexton Blake. "Tinker is afraid that the man will flee because of that little incident at the river. But Waldo knows that he was not recognised—it was impossible to identify anybody in such darkness—and although his exhibition of strength might lead us to suspect him, he is aware that we could not make any definite accusation, therefore, he will remain. Being a clever man, he will know that it is safer to remain than to flee. A game of bluff might succeed, whereas deliberate flight would set the hounds on his track In next to no time. I intend retiring as soon as possible, Hollins; but I want to be up in good time, for there are some careful investigations to be made in the morning."

The superintendent was impressed. He openly admitted that Sexton Blake's experience was fifty times wider than his own, and he expressed the belief that the guv'nor's deductions were correct. But it was evidence he wanted—something tangible to grasp at, something that would convince a jury.

Sexton Blake promised to supply it, and Mr. Capelli was carefully warned to keep quiet, and to give Waldo no hint of his peril. And so the boss went off with mixed feelings. He was relieved to know that Fletcher would soon get his freedom, but to lose Waldo would be a blow.

Nothing else happened that night, and in the morning both the guv'nor and I awoke, not in the shivers of approaching influenza, but fresh and bright and by no means harmed by our overnight adventure.

After an early breakfast, we set off to the circus with the superintendent. Sexton Blake had automatically taken charge of this case, although Hollins was the chief man so far as the public eye was concerned. Our first task was to make a more careful examination of Fletcher's caravan.

We entered before anybody knew of our presence—except, of course, the numerous circus workers who were already on the move. Mr. Capelli had not appeared, and we did not seek him.

The guv'nor was particularly interested in the polished front of the drawer which had contained the second poisoned arrow.

"As you'll notice, Hollins, this drawer goes in somewhat stiffly," he remarked. "That may have a special significance."

"How?"

"Well, the average man upon closing this draw would place his hand upon the surface, and push it steadily; he wouldn't carefully grasp the brass knob and ease it in. And fingers, my dear Hollins, are is the habit of leaving impressions, especially when those fingers happen to be sweaty. Waldo, I noted, has somewhat moist hand. We will just try a little experiment."

The guv'nor took from his pocket the little powder-blower. He operated it upon the surface of the drawer, blowing a fine grey powder over the polished woodwork. It settled quite evenly.

Blake gently blew the powder off, and the effect was immediate. There, standing out in clear relief against the dark blackground, were the distinct prints of four fingers, and a slight smudge probably caused by the thumb.

"Well, I'm hanged!' ejaculated the superintendent.

"You see how important it, is, Hollins, to think of these little details," said Sexton Blake. "It was just a chance whether the finger prints were here or not, and my reasoning proved sound. You will possibly say that these are the marks of Fletcher's hand. I fancy not, but it is a matter which we can soon settle. This drawer may well be the finger-post pointing to the scaffold—for Waldo. I should advise you to preserve that drawer as though it were worth a fortune."

"We shall have to take Waldo's finger prints, somehow; we must have them for comparison," said the superintendent. "At least, if Fletcher's fails to correspond. But there's another stumbling-block, Blake—and the biggest of all. Why should Waldo kill Durand? That's the question I want answered. So far as I can learn, there was no friction between the two men whatever."

"We know nothing of their relations, do we?" replied Sexton Blake. "I should suggest an examination of Durand's caravan. It may lead us nowhere, but, on the other hand, it may be highly instructive. In any case, it is a task which must be performed. We are not possibly to hope to settle this case unless we do get them."

Hollins agreed, and we emerged from the caravan, looking it very securely behind us. I forgot to mention that the guv'nor's seals were perfectly intact when we opened the door-proving that nobody had tampered with the caravan during the night.

Fortunately, we met Mr. Capelli outside, talking earnestly with the lean clown, Mr. Pottles. The boss readily agreed to hand the superintendent the key of Durand's caravan, and we proceeded there forthwith.

As Sexton Blake bad foreshadowed, the result was eminently satisfactory, for within five minutes the guv'nor turned up a most interesting document from a locker. It was a document, indeed, which spelt Waldo's doom.

It was in the form of a receipt in Durand's handwriting, and had evidently been written out in advance, all ready for pending the signature—undoubtedly the dead man's signature.

And this is how the document read

"I, James William Durand, hereby solemnly agree to remain absolutely silent regarding certain information concerning Rupert Waldo which is in my possession. I agree to accept the sum of £200 (two hundred pounds) in acknowledgment of my silence, this statement being a full and complete receipt.

"(Signed).........................."

The superintendent read the document eagerly.

"Phew!" he whistled. "This is important, Blake!"

"Important!" echoed the guv'nor. "Why, my dear Hollins, we need look no further for the motive. Durand obviously attempted the gentle art of blackmailing and obtained Waldo's promise to pay him two hundred pounds for his silence. The money perhaps was to have been paid last night. Bud Waldo killed the fellow rather than pay up. A pair of rascals, superintendent!"

"By George! You're right!"

"And it leads us further still," went on Blake. "Waldo knew very well that Durand was a menace to him. A blackmailer is a most unsatisfactory person to deal with. There is no guarantee that he will not make fresh demands, at any moment. To submit to one means that a victim must submit all along the line. And the secret concerning Waldo is obviously a black one, and his very safety is imperiled, otherwise he would never have gone to the length of murder. I have an idea that the Finger-print Department at Scotland Yard would have no difficulty in identifying those finger-prints."

"You think Waldo is a criminal?".

"That is my theory," replied Blake. "Do not the facts lead in that direction? We will suppose, for the sake of argument, that Waldo is an escaped convict. Durand recognized him as such, and threatened to expose him if he did not pay. Waldo either had to pay or rid himself of his persecutor. He chose the latter course. And I must remark that I do not feel particularly sorry for Durand. A blackmailer, Hollins, is a particularly vile kind of person."

"But there's a flaw in your theory. Blake,' protested the superintendent. "If Waldo is an escaped convict, he wouldn't be performing publicly in a circus. The thing is impossible."

"On the contrary, Waldo had sense enough to realise that safely lay in that very publicity," said Sexton Blake. "Who would dream of looking for an ex-convict in a circus, appearing boldly in the public eye twice daily? Bluff is a great thing, Rollins, and it frequently succeeds—more often than not, in fact. But we are not going to leave this matter to conjecture; we will apply tests. And the first one is to get Waldo's finger-prints."

"A difficult matter!" growled Hollins.

"You will pardon me—a simple matter," smiled the guv'nor.

And it was. Sexton Blake took a photograph from a drawer in Durand's caravan, and spent fully ten minutes upon it, preparing both surfaces most carefully with a little material of his own manufacture. Hollins, being careful to hold the photograph by its edges, sought Waldo out, and politely asked him if he could identify the likeness.

Waldo couldn't. But when that photograph was returned into the superintendent's possession the finger-prints of the strong man's right hand were beautifully impressed upon the surfaces. A careful comparison established the fact that they tallied in every respect with the prints on the drawer-front. Waldo suspected nothing, but the net was drawing very tight around him.

"And now, the next thing is to pay a visit to London," said Sexton Blake briskly as we walked towards the police-station. "I take it, Hollins, that you will keep Waldo under obser-vation until I return, although the fellow mustn't know it. Be very careful on that point."

"You can trust me!" declared the superintendent grimly.

And twenty minutes later Sexton Blake left for London, on a mission which was to mean a very great deal to Waldo, the Wonder Man.

THE SIXTH
CHAPTER

TINKER GIVES ST. FRANK'S A CALL—UN
–AVOIDABLY DETAINED—THE ESCAPE OF
WALDO

HELMFORD was a decent little town, but there wasn't much doing on this blustery winter's morning, with Christmas looming near. I found myself with time hanging somewhat heavily on my hands.

There was nothing to do, in fact, until Sexton Blake returned.

There would be no sense in my hanging about the circus, for we did not want to give Waldo any hint that he was suspected. Superintendent Hollins had taken steps to ensure that Waldo would be kept under observation. Not that this was a difficult task, for the man had obviously decided to boldly remain, believing that the evidence of his crime had been destroyed, and that he was safe.

Moreover, my presence near the circus would only have an effect which we didn't desire—Seaton Blake had gone to London, and it was far better that I should clear out, too. Waldo would then fondly kid himself that we had turned down the case, and had retired in confusion.

But what could I do with myself until half-past five, the time when the guv'nor's train would arrive from London? Helmford, as I hinted, was not exactly bristling with amusements. There was a picture-theatre, of course, but the enterprising manager of this concern did not throw open his doors to the public until the hour of six. There were no restaurants, no museums, and it seemed that I should have to stow myself away in the superintendent's residence.

Then I was struck by a brain-wave.

The queer thing is that it didn't come to me before. Helmford was only about twenty miles from Bannington—half an hour's train-ride—and St. Frank's College was quite close to Bannington. At St. Frank's was my old pal, Nipper, to say nothing of Mr. Nelson Lee, the well-known Gray's Ian Road criminologist. At present Nelson Lee and Nipper were at the great public school, Lee acting as House-master, and Nipper ornamenting a junior Form. They seemed to like the life, because there was no reason why they should remain there. And Nipper had confided to me that they found plenty of excitement down at St. Frank's—plenty of detective work upon which to expend their surplus energy.

Why not a flying visit to St. Frank's?

Why not, indeed ! It was the very thing, for I suddenly remembered that to-day, was a half-holiday at St, Frank's. The school would be practically on the point of breaking up for the Christmas holidays. I got rather a jar when I thought of that. What if everybody had already cleared out?

"Oh, well, I'll run over and see, anyhow!" I decided. "It'll be something to do, and that's better than hanging about aimlessly. And if Nipper isn't there I'll slaughter him when I see him next time!"

Accordingly I hurried to the station with all speed, and found that the next train for Benton—the station for St. Frank's—was due in thirty-five minutes, it would land met at Benton soon after three.

There was a train back at ten minutes to five, which would set me down at Helmford with ten minutes to spare before the guv'nor's train steamed in. Nothing could have been better, and I was feeling quite cheerful. I shouldn't have much time at St. Frank's, but it would be a little jaunt.

Well I arrived, and as I strolled through the quiet village of Benton a few fine flakes of snow were beginning to whirl down from the leaden mass of clouds overhead. The roads were hard with frost, and there were plenty of signs that Christmas was near at hand.

There were plenty of signs, also, that St. Franks was still occupied. Shouts and cheers, which floated over the hedge as I approached the school, assured me that a football match was in full swing. It was a senior game, however, and there was no sign of activity on Little Side, except for a wild confusion of fags, who tried to make themselves believe that they were playing football.

I turned in at the gateway, and found the Triangle almost deserted. Three juniors were engaged in a fierce argument near the gate, however, and I recognised them at once, having been to St. Frank's on other occasions.

"How goes it, my merry triplets?" I asked cheerfully.

The three juniors broke on their argument and stared at me.

"What the dickens do you want, you grinning ass?" demanded one of them, eyeing me suspiciously. "I seem to remember your face——"

"My dear chap, I couldn't forget yours!" I remarked sweetly. "It's been in my dreams—or, rather nightmares—ever since I paid my last visit to this august seat of learning. I believe I am addressing one Handforth?"

"Well, you're not addressing two!" snorted Handforth. "And what do you mean by saying that I've appeared in your rotten nightmares? If you ain't careful, my son, I'll punch your silly nose for you!"

"That would be unfortunate, because I should be under an obligation to commit acts of violence which are foreign to my gentle nature," I grinned, "No offence, Handforth; your uncle is only joking."

"Look here, you cheeky outsider——" began Handforth.

"Hold on!" interrupted one of the others. "I've must remembered who this chap is. He's Tinker!"

"I thought he was something of that sort," said Handforth tartly, "Well, we don't want ant pots mended today—"

"Ha, ha, ha!"

"I mean Tinker—Sexton Blake's Assistant!" roared the other junior.

"The one and only!" I agreed cheerfully. "At the same time I have no objection to mending a few pots if necessary. A chap with a name like mine must keep up appearance, you know. I'm an expert with the soldering-iron."

"Oh, Tinker!" he exclaimed. "Why, I knew you all the time! That is to say I recognised you, but couldn't quite remember where I'd seen your ugly—handsome dial before. Glad to see you again, old son!"

We all shook hands, and after that I spent a few moments in wiping mine on my hand-kerchief— Handforth having thoughtlessly held a caramel in his hand while arguing. It didn't improve the caramel; neither did it improve my hand.

"I should like to mention that I am pressed for time," I said, "This conversation is delightful, but I really came here to see Nipper. Don't tell me he's out, or I shall never forgive you."

"No; he's in the study—C, in the Remove passage," said Handforth. "He and his chums are getting ready for going away, I believe. We break up in a day or two, you know. And this year we're going to have a jolly fine Christmas—a peace Christmas, by George! No more puddings without any plums in 'em!"

I grinned, and strolled across the Triangle towards the Ancient House. I made my way to Study C and entered. Nipper was sitting in front of the fire with his two chums, Sir Montie Tregellis-West and Tommy Watson. They didn't look round as I entered.

"Don't come botherin' now, dear old boy!" remarked Tregellis-West, "We're just discussin' our program me for the holidays, begad!"

"Well you don't look very busy, I must say," I replied "Handforth told me you were packing but—"

"Tinker!" roared Nipper, leaping up.

He tore round the table and grabbed my fist. Tregellis-West and Watson followed suit, and brief explanations followed.

"You bounder!" said Nipper. "Fancy you and your guv'nor being in Helmford! You'll have to stop to tea, you know, and then we'll have a good old jaw afterwards."

"Impossible!" I declared. "I've got to go back by the four-fifty train or, I shall miss the guv'nor at Helmford; and there's going to be an interesting event this evening unless I'm mistaken. A murderer is to be arrested and if I'm not there he might escape!"

Nipper grinned. "Oh, rot!" he said. "But I can quite understand why you want to get back; I should be the same myself. You'll have to stop to tea, though. We'll have it especially early in your honour."

"Good!" I said heartily.

And so preparations for tea were soon in train, and we finally sat down to the meal—a royal spread—with comfortable time to demolish it. Several other fellows were invited in, including Jack Manson, Somerton, and De Valerie. The fact that I was at St. Frank seemed to be a

matter of interest to almost everybody, although I couldn't quite understand why it should.

Tea was over by half-past four and this left us plenty of time to stroll dove to the station—twenty minutes, in fact. Nipper was half inclined to ask his guv'nor if he could go over to Helmford with me, but decided not to do so, because there was no train back.

I spent a few minutes with Nelson Lee just before starting out. He looked the same as ever—brisk, alert and full of energy. He told me to prevail upon Sexton Blake to run over on the morrow, if it could be managed

Having promised, and having said good-bye, I started off briskly for the station with Nipper and his chums. What with the dusk, and the heavy clouds, the lane was almost pitch dark as we strode down it.

"Better hurry, dear fellows," remarked Sir Montie. "We've only got about ten minutes you know an' trains have a frightful habit of comin' in to time when you want them to be late—they have, really!"

"Yes; we'd better buck up," I agreed.

We hastened our footsteps, for, to tell the truth I was rather anxious. Under no circumstance did I want to miss the train, for it would be a disaster if I missed the denouement of our case at Helmford. I always like being in at the finish, and feel swindled if I am left out in the cold.

As we hurried along I gave Nipper a few details of the affair. And then I became aware of the fact that a number of dark forms had emerged from the hedges a few yards ahead. They closed in upon us as we approached.

"Begad!" murmured Tregellis-West. "An ambush!"

"Look here, you chaps, whoever you are!" shouted Nipper, "No larks! Tinker has got to catch his train in five minutes, and it's not quite the thing, anyhow, to play tricks on a visitor."

"Really?" came a drawling voice. "Well, opinions differ. I think it'll be a rippin' joke to make your detective pal lose his train. If you don't surrender, we'll do more than detain you!"

Nipper turned to me quickly.

"It's Fullwood & Co—in force," he whispered. "They're the biggest cads in the school, Tinker. Awfully sorry, but I couldn't prepare for this, could I? We shall have to use our fists I'm afraid.'

"No need to be afraid." I said grimly. "I'm feeling just in the mood for a scrap and I know you're game at any old time. I'm not going to lose that train, I give you my word!"

But I did.

Fullwood & Co., we found, were in far greater strength than we first imagined. They had obtained the support of a crowd of rotters from the River House School—a small establishment in the village. These fellows were led by a frightful outsider named Wellborne. And Nipper and I were overpowered, in spite of our game fight. Tregellis-West and Watson were also overpowered.

"You confounded rotters!" panted Nipper furiously. "Do you call it funny to make a visitor lose his train?"

"Rather, by gad" grinned Fullwood. "I'm half-inclined to roll you in the ditch, but I'll be kind an' let you off. It'll be good enough if we make our pal lose his silly train. It's due already."

I was raving, but couldn't do anything. And my feeling can be imagined when I heard the train in the distance. It stopped at the station, and then came the steady puff—puff as it re-started on its journey.

I was unable to get to Helmford in time.

Of course it didn't really matter—my presence wasn't at all necessary—but I felt thundering wild. Wellborne and his friends took themselves off as soon as the train had gone, chuckling hugely. And Fullwood & Co. tried to escape too. But Nipper and I and the other two had our revenge. We forced the cads to fight and whacked them thoroughly. Fullwood hadn't reckoned upon his support leaving him so early.

But this punishment, although swift and satisfactory, did not get me to Helmford, and I knew there was no other train until nearly eight o'clock. Nipper was full of sympathy, but he couldn't do anything.

"You've got a telephone at the school, haven't you?" I asked. "The best thing I can do, I think, is to ring up the superintendent at Helmford, and tell him what's happened. Then the guv'nor won't expect me."

"It's about the only thing to do," agreed Nipper.

And we strode somewhat savagely towards the School. Meanwhile, events were moving apace at Helmford. Sexton Blake had come down from London by an earlier train, which possibil-

ity I hadn't reckoned upon. He was in Helmford even as I was going down to the station to catch my train.

And with the guv'nor was an old friend of ours——Chief Detective-Inspector Lennard, of Scotland Yard. The inspector was extremely cheerful, and Sexton Blake himself was in a similar mood.

For his mission had been an entire success. The finger-prints had been identified at Scotland Yard within twenty minutes. The records brought to light a set of prints which had been taken at Dartmoor four or five years back. They were the finger-prints of a man who had then called himself William Waldron—undoubtedly Waldo.

He had been sentenced to a term of ten years' penal servitude for burglary with violence—an astoundingly clever crime which had been upset at the last moment by a mere fluke. The police had been rather startled at the ingenuity and cunning displayed by the burglar.

However he had been caught, and sent to penal servitude. He only served three years, however, having escaped from the convict settlement during an outbreak in a dense fog. That had happened three years ago, and Waldo still had four years to serve.

The simple truth was that Signor Capelli's amazing strong man was an escaped convict, badly wanted by the police. For this reason alone he was to be immediately arrested. But the evidence against him, in connection with the murder, was quite sufficient to send him to gallows.

The unsigned document found in Durand's caravan supplied the motive, and the spring apparatus which had been thrown into the river by Waldo would certainly condemn him utterly. That apparatus could have been fixed for only one purpose, and it could have been worked by only one method. Waldo was unconscious of the net which was closing tightly around him.

"I must say that you've been deucedly smart over this job Blake!" said Detective-inspector Lennard heartily, as they entered the police station. "That's nothing new, of course. You generally leave a pair folk behind—and I don't mind admitting it. Fletcher will free within an hour."

"That's splendid!" smiled Sexton Blake, thinking of the sweet-faced girl who was waiting so anxiously. "He never ought to have been arrested, although I can scarcely blame Hollins. He had an idea that the evidence was overwhelming, until I knocked the stuffing out of his facts."

"He's a countryman," said Lennard, grinning.

They found the superintendent in his office, and he jumped up at once, eager and anxious.

"Well?" he asked quickly. "Have you done anything, Mr. Blake?"

"Quite a lot," replied Sexton Blake.

"Waldo is an escaped convict, Hollins, and he is particularly wanted by this gentleman here, Mr. Lennard, of Scotland Yard. But I have seen nothing of Tinker since my arrival. Do you know where he is?"

"Yes," said Hollins. "He went to St. Frank's College this afternoon, to see some friends, and then managed to miss the train back. He rang up not five minutes ago, and asked me to tell you."

"I suppose we can manage without him," said Blake drily.

Ten minutes were spent in deep conversation, and the superintendent was greatly delighted to learn that Lennard carried a warrant for Waldo's arrest. Fletcher would be released as soon Waldo was brought in.

There was no delay now. The time was very favorable for the work in hand. The circus was quite, and there would be no activity until six or half-past. It was far better to get the arrest over.

Accordingly, Sexton Blake and Lennard set off accompanied by Superintendent Hollins. When they arrived at the circus-field they found everything dark; although numerous dim figures were moving about the great electric arcs and the myriad fairly lights had not yet been switched on.

"I supposed we'd better have a word with the proprietor, to begin with," remarked Lennard. "But we must be careful, you know. We mustn't let our man slip through our fingers at the last moment."

But they were saved the necessity of approaching Mr. Capelli's gorgeous caravan, for the boss himself came striding briskly over towards the main tent. He was intercepted, and heard the news with mingled feelings.

"Bless my soul!" he ejaculated. Good gracious me? And I've been harbouring an ex-convict for two years! Why, I shouldn't be surprised if you tell me that I'm going to be arrested too! I've committed a shocking offence, haven't I?"

"The chief inspector won't be hard on you, Mr. Capelli," chuckled Sexton Blake. "You need

have no fear that you will get into trouble. But we are determined to take Waldo away with us, although I'm sorry that you will lose him."

"Hang it all, I'm glad to be rid of the man, dashed if I'm not!" said the boss. "I don't want gaolbirds in my show. No, sir! And he seems to be a murderer, too! The scaffold's the place for such a brute!"

"Do you know where Waldo is at the moment?" asked Hollins.

"In his caravan, I think," said Capelli, turning. "Yes, all the lights are on. He's having tea, I suppose."

"Well, he'll have to finish his meal at the police-station—if he finishes it at all!" said Lennard grimly. "Let's get it over, superintendent."

They made their way to the strong man's caravan, Sexton Blake and Lennard leading. Hollins came behind with Mr.Capelli. There was nothing dramatic about the entry. Sexton Blake knocked at the door, and it was opened by Waldo.

"Oh, it's you, Mr. Blake!" he said genially. "Come in—come in!"

Sexton Blake entered, and Lennard immediately followed. The superintendent remained on the steps at the doorway, whilst Mr. Capelli was outside.

"Your name is Rupert Waldo?" asked the chief inspector quietly.

Waldo regarded him curiously.

"Yes; but what of it?" he asked.

"I have every reason to believe that you are William Waldron, and that you escaped from Dartmoor Prison three years ago!" said Lennard grimly. "I have here a warrant for your arrest, and let me advise you— Hold up, man!"

For Waldo had staggered back, his eyes wide with fear and dreadful alarm. He sank into a chair, pale-and trembling, the sudden shock of this dramatic arrest was too much for him. His great strength availed him of nothing now.

"How—how did you find out?" he muttered weakly. "By Heaven—it was you Blake!" I knew it was you ! I suppose you think I killed Durand, too? You fool! You'll never produce the evidence against me!"

Lennard and Blake exchanged a significant glance, Waldo's words, practically constituted a confession, and it was perfectly obvious that no mistake had been made. Sexton Blake had known what he was about. "I shall have to handcuff you,

Mr. Waldo." said the chief inspector briskly. "I hear that you are somewhat strong—and I can't afford to take chances. I'm glad you've got sense enough to take this quietly.

"I don't care what you do!" muttered Waldo listlessly.

Lennard produced the "bracelets," and neatly snapped them over his prisoner's wrists. Waldo gave a start as he heard that ominous' click, and he gazed at his wrists as though dazed. Then, full realization dawning upon him, he glared from the inspector to Sexton Blake with wild hatred blazing in his eyes.

"You may have got me, but you won't hold me for long!" he exclaimed, his voice quivering with fury. "I spent three years of perdition, and I'll never go back!"

"I'm afraid you won't have the chance," said Lennard grimly. "Quite a different sort of fate is awaiting—Now then—now then!"

Lennard's voice rose sharply as he uttered the last words. For Waldo had leapt to his feet, and stood facing his captors, with a dangerous light gleaming in his furious eyes. Then suddenly he laughed.

"Do you think I care for these?" he asked contemptuously.

He held out his hands, and, with a sudden swift movement, tore them apart, the steel snapping with a sharp crack. Waldo appeared to perform the feat with ease but it must have required an enormous effort. And the sudden jar of the handcuffs upon his wrists grazed his skin badly.

"Lend a hand, old man!" shouted the inspector.

But even as Sexton Blake and Lennard were about to spring forward, Waldo grabbed up a small oil heating-stove, which had been burning on a shelf. He did not wait a second.

Crash!

The stove was aimed straight at Sexton Blake's head, but the detective dodged in the nick of time. The thing struck the wall, fell to the floor, and a great sheet of flame rose up. The burning oil spread all over the floor, and in less than a second the tablecloth was flaming up, too.

"Good heavens !" gasped the inspector.

He backed out of the flames blindly, and tumbled out into the open, Sexton Blake following him. But they both saw Waldo blunder forward, trip, and fall headlong into the heart of the flames.

"Come outside, man—come outside!" yelled Lennard.

Smoke was rolling out of the doorway in clouds, but in a sudden burst of flame, which drove the smoke away; those at the doorway saw Waldo staggering to his feet. His coat was on fire, and he was beating at the flames desperately. Then, again he, fell, uttering a wild shriek. The smoke obscured the whole dreadful scene.

"He's done for!" gasped Hollins hoarsely.

"Well, he's only got himself to blame!" snapped the chief inspector.

Sexton Blake wrenched out his handkerchief.

"We can't leave him there, Lennard!" he said sharply. "Tie your handkerchief round your face, pull your gloves on. We'll make one swift attempt to get the fellow out, although I'm afraid he'll be beyond human aid."

The inspector was no coward, but he didn't care for the task. However, he was game, and instantly obeyed Blake's instructions. A few precious seconds were wasted, and when he and Blake charged into the burning caravan the smoke was rolling out in choking masses, and sparks were flying in myriads. Crowds had already collected outside.

Sexton Blake was first to and he groped blindly on the floor where Waldo had been seen to fail. The heat was overpowering, although the flames had now died down for a few seconds. Quite suddenly, however, a burst of fire drove the detective back, and the whole interior was revealed to him.

Waldo was not there!

He had gone—vanished! In spite of his dreadful burns, he had escaped! The thing was staggering, and Blake could hardly credit it. He felt that he was mistaken; but at that moment a great shout came from the superintendent at the door.

Blake and Lennard staggered out into the open, half-choked, scorched, but not actually burned. They found Hollins in a state of great excitement.

"He's gone! He's got away!" he panted.

"But how—how?" shouted the C.I.D man, "He was burnt to a cinder!"

"I don't know!" gasped Hollins. "Pottles was running up a minute ago; and he saw somebody leap from the window and streak across the meadow, leaving a trail of sparks behind him. That was before the crowd got here. The man must be like a demon from the pit! No human being could stand that fire!"

"Which way did he go?" demanded Blake. "Why didn't you follow, Hollins?"

"I thought you were overpowered," said the superintendent huskily. "Waldo went across to the road—"

But Sexton Blake and Detective-Inspector Lenard were already running. With very little difficulty they discovered that Waldo had rushed to the railway-station. Astounded people had been seen him dash past, and had started blankly.

As the pursuers approached the station they beard the steady puffing of a train and Lennard muttered something strong. But it turned out that the puffing had been made by the evening goods-train.

An excited porter was in the booking office.

"Looking for a lunatic?" he shouted, as Blake and Lennard appeared.

"Yes!" said Sexton Blake promptly.

"He's on that goods-train, then!" exclaimed the porter, "Never see such a thing in my life! He dashed across the up-line, and jumped into an empty truck like a flamed grasshopper!"

"Why didn't you stop the train, you idiot?" roared Lennard.

"It ain't none of my business!" growled the porter, glaring. "I did wave my arm; tryin' to attract the guard, but he must ha' been asleep. It's no good stoppin' the train up the line because the chap will nip off,"

"The man is talking sense," said Sexton Blake sharply. "He's right, Lennard. To stop the train would be to lose Waldo. On the other hand, our prisoner will remain on board until the train reaches its first legitimate stop. Where is that, my man?"

"Bannington, sir," said the porter.

"We shall have to phone the Bannington police," went on Blake. "The man in control there is Inspector Jameson, I believe—a particularly dull specimen, too. He'll muddle the thing thoroughly— By James!"

"Thought of something?" asked Lennard quickly.

"Yes; Tinker is at St. Frank's," said Blake.

"I'll ring him up instantly and tell him to persuade Mr. Nelson Lee to hurry to Bannington. Lee's a splendid man, and he won't make a mess of the affair. Where can I find a telephone?"

There was one at the station, and Sexton Blake was soon getting busy. For the moment he had ceased to wonder at Waldo's amazing flight, and all he thought of was securing the rascal.

And there was a distinct chance that the murderer would be captured.

The Seventh Chapter

An Exciting Finish—And A Surprise!

NELSON LEE looked round swiftly.

"You boys all right?" he asked.

"Yes, sir; drive away!" I replied promptly.

We were in the Triangle at St. Frank's. Nelson Lee's fast racing car was throbbing impatiently, and Nipper and I had just tumbled into the rear seats. As I spoke Nelson Lee slipped the clutch in, and the car glided off.

I had received the guv'nor's urgent 'phone message, and had got Nelson Lee on to the wire at once. We soon knew what was amiss, and Lee had decided to speed straight to Bannington by car. Needless to say, Nipper and I were to go with him. Nipper's chums would have come along, too, but every second was of value, and they were away to the village. If we met them we might take them on board, but we couldn't waste time in looking for them.

We roared through Bellton without seeing a sign of Tregelist-West and Watson, and continued our way to the local town of Bennington. I was rather staggered. Waldo had escaped, in spite of all the precautions. He had defeated both the guv'nor and Detective-Inspector Lennard. How? Something must have gone very badly wrong. Sexton Blake had given us no details except that Waldo would probably be skulking on the goods-train when it arrived in Bannington.

We reached our destination ten minutes before the train was due, and found a number of police already on the spot, with Inspector Jameson in charge. He was looking very important, and greeted Nelson Lee with a nod.

"Oh, have you come here in connection with this goods-train business, Mr. Lee?" he asked. 'I'm afraid you won't be able to help us much.

I have everything in train for the capture of the man."

"I was sure that such would be the ease, inspector," said Nelson Lee politely. "May I ask how you propose to effect Waldo's arrest?"

"The inspector smiled.

"The goods-train will come to a halt in the station very shortly," he replied.

"My men will be lining the platform, and I can assure you that the prisoner will have very little chance of getting away."

"But you will surely have some men on the other side of the line?"

"I was not thinking of doing so."

"I have no wish to interfere, but I should like to make the suggestion" went on Nelson Lee smoothly. "And you must allow me to point out, Inspector, that the station lights are rather bright, and a policeman can easily be recognised from quite a distance. Waldo will certainly see what is afoot, and I am afraid he will no longer be in the train when you search it."

Inspector Jameson tugged at his moustache.

"What do you propose then?" he growled.

"Why, that the train is pulled to a standstill outside the station, where all is dark," replied Lee. "You can have your men posted along both sides of the line, and if Waldo makes any attempt to escape he will be spotted immediately. It seems to me that method would be far more satisfactory."

"The other method would be a dismal failure!" Nipper murmured.

I grinned, and nodded.

"Well, I don't admit that there's much to choose between the two plans," said Jameson. "Still, I don't mind adopting your suggestion, Mr. Lee; perhaps it'll be just as well."

It was quite apparent that the inspector was a bit of an ass. Left to himself he would have allowed Waldo to get away without the slightest difficulty. Nelson Lee's plan was really the only sensible one possible. Indeed, there was quite a chance that Waldo wouldn't be on the train when it arrived. He would jump off at the first opportunity.

But the odds were against his doing so until the goods-train slowed down. Waldo would certainly never wait until the train drew up against the platform. His plan would be to escape in the darkness, and Nelson Lee's scheme was the only one which would frustrate this.

Fresh orders were soon given, and the constables hurried away along the line, Nelson Lee with them. Nipper and I followed, bringing up the rear. And when the men had got to their appointed places the rumble of the train was already audible.

There was a signal far out here, and it was still at danger. The headlights of the train came into view, and then the trucks commenced clanging together as the engine's brakes were applied. The great locomotive creaked and groaned.

There was not a sign of any man near the track; on both sides the country looked black and deserted. And before the train came to a standstill a dim figure rose from one of the trucks, and leapt lightly to the ground. He did not even stumble as he alighted.

Then three beams of light abruptly centred themselves upon him. And he stood stock-still. The man was Waldo, but in such a dreadful condition that I started at him with horror and amazement.

His clothing was in rags—burnt, apparently. There were terrible burns, too, on his hands and face, and he looked simply awful. A great shout came from his lips as he realized that he was ambushed.

Then he dashed away. The lights were supplied by the torches of Nelson Lee and Nipper and myself. We simply hurled ourselves forward to intercept the murder. We did so, and two constables arrived at the same moment. Waldo charged through the whole crowd of us like a mad bull. He hit out right and left, and Nipper and one policeman went down immediately.

Waldo's strength seemed to be as great as ever, and he tore on. Nelson Lee uttered a sharp exclamation, and whipped out his revolver. He had no intention of getting the rascal get away.

Crack!

The revolver spoke sharply, but Waldo did not pause for a second in his flight. Yet Nelson Lee's bullet had sped true. Waldo's left trouser leg was practically burnt off below the knee, and his bare calf was revealed. Even as he ran we saw the blood trickling down his leg.

"This is uncanny!" panted Nelson amazedly.

He ran forward at full speed, Nipper and I following. We left full speed, Nipper and I following. We left the lumbering constables far behind and even then we couldn't catch up with Nippon's gov'nor. Nipper himself was bruised, but not inclined to give up the game because of that.

I looked ahead anxiously as I ran. Was Nelson Lee gaining? He was an astounding runner, beating me hollow. But Waldo, in spite of his terrible injuries, was keeping his distance ahead. In all truth he was a wonder man!

Over fields and meadows we ran, with an occasional ploughed field by way of a change. But inch by inch Nelson Lee was gaining. And all the rest of us were stretched out in a line over the countryside. It was a stern chase, indeed. But the end was abrupt.

Nelson Lee at length succeeded in reaching his quarry. The detective knew well enough that an ordinary struggle with him would certainly led to disaster.

So Nelson Lee adopted other methods.

He caught Waldo's shoulder as he drew alongside, jerked the man around, and then obtained a grip which held the murderer absolutely helpless. It was just a little trick of ju-jitsu, and it had only succeeded because Waldo had not turned to face his pursuer.

"If you attempt to get away you'll break your back, remember that!" panted Nelson Lee. "Remain still, and you're safe."

Waldo had sense enough to realize that he was beaten. His strength was against him in such a position as this, for a sudden effort of exertion would unquestionably result in his breaking of his own spine.

And in this position we found that pair when we arrived. If Nelson Lee had not been on the scene there would have been no murderer to take to the police-station. All the credit belonged to Nipper's guv'nor.

When the constables came up Lee advised them to bind Waldo's ankles with extra stout bonds. Not until this was done did Lee release his grip. And then Waldo gave a short laugh.

"Well, I had a good run, so I mustn't grumble," he said smoothly. "I think you hit me with a bullet, didn't you? I felt a slight jar, I believe."

"A jar!" I gasped. "Oh, my hat!"

Lights were thrown upon Waldo. And it was then seen that he was bending round and rumbling the bullet wound—actually rubbing it! But this was not all. His forearms were blistered and burnt-scorched horribly! He ought to have been writhing with agony. But yet he picked at the burns, tearing the loose skin in the mostly

ghastly fashion. And he smiled all the time. And I suddenly realized that he was not at all exhausted.

"Don't do that!" I gasped. "Can't you feel and pain?"

Waldo laughed.

"This will show you!" he replied shortly.

And he rubbed the burns vigorously. Any ordinary human being would have shrieked aloud at that treatment, but Waldo merely chuckled. I realized why my blow on Waldo's head, delivered near the river, had had no effect.

It was an absolute fact that this astounding man felt no pain! His burns, his bruises, the revolver-shot wound, all meant nothing to him. It was the amazing thing I had ever be held. Any normal man would have been unconscious long since. The burns alone would have been sufficient to render him helpless.

But we had got him, and that was the main thing. He was conveyed to the police-station by the triumphant Jameson, although why the inspector should have been triumphant was rather a mystery. He had been right off the map when the actual capture was made.

Sexton Blake and Chief Detective-Inspector Lennard arrived shortly afterwards, and the guv'nor was high in his praise of Nelson Lee's fine effort. But Lee merely laughed, and said that he had quite enjoyed the adventure.

He and Nipper lost no time in getting off in their car, but not until he had made Sexton Blake promise that we should both run over to St. Frank's on the morrow. We were quite eager to go, as a matter of fact.

Having seen that Waldo was safely under lock and key, we left for Helmford again, Lennard remaining in Bannington. And when we arrived at our destination we found that Fletcher had already been released.

Needless to say, Miss Hanwell's gratitude was very great, and she thanked Sexton Blake for his wonderful services, in a flood of tears. The tension had been very great during the last day or two, and the girl had not been able to bear up now that all danger was over. She seemed to look upon the guv'nor as a kind of magician.

We spent a very pleasant time at St.Frank's, and then returned to London.

Our work was done; the police had to do the rest.

But Sexton Blake and I received a big surprise on the following morning paper that the murderer known as Waldo, the Wonder Man, had escaped during the night. He had burst open his cell with apparent ease, and had utterly vanished. No trace of him could be found.

Exactly five minutes later Mrs. Bardell entered with a letter which had just been delivered by a District Messenger. It was an astounding communication, and this is how it ran:

"Did you think that I would remain in custody? I have you to thanks for my present position, and I shall remember it. Now that I am up against the police—the enemy of all men—I intend to start a campaign of crime. I tell you this frankly, knowing that you cannot harm me in the least. But my first effort, Mr Sexton Blake, will be to get even with you. —Waldo, the Wonder Man."

Sexton Blake looked at me, and I looked at Sexton Blake.

"Hang it all, Tinker, the man's an audacious rascal! I can't help having a sneaking admiration for him," said the guv'nor. "But he's a cold-blooded scoundrel, and he will assuredly end his existence on the gallows!"

"But when, guv'nor?" I asked pointedly.

"Ah, I can't tell you that, Tinker!" Sexton Blake replied. "It seems as though we are to have some further adventures with the astounding Waldo. Is it merely a threat, or shall we really feel his sting in the near future?"

It was a question I couldn't answer, but time would answer it for me.

And, incidentally, time did. But before we had any further adventures with Waldo, Christmas came upon us, and one invitation we accepted was to spend a day with a newly-married couple who were not entirely unconnected with circus life. Their Christmas was the happiest in their whole lives, and ours was by no means gloomy. In fact, we spent a really joyous time, and I remember wondering, even as we sat round the lazing Yule log, how long it would be before we again met Waldo the Wonder Man!

THE END

The Bara Diamond.

SEXTON BLAKE
AND
MARSTON HUME
ENGAGE IN
A DUEL OF WITS.

MARSTON HUME—Criminal.

MARSTON HUME was sitting in his favourite window seat in the Baddeley Club, immaculately dressed, as usual; one of his customary button-holes of deep-red carnations in his coat. His eyeglass, severely plain, was firmly fixed in his eye; but, in spite of these creature comforts, and the fact that he was smoking an excellent cigar, he wore an air of abstraction.

An open newspaper lay across his knee, and for the third or fourth time he read a certain paragraph in it, and then stared vacantly at the passing traffic.

The paragraph in itself was of no vast interest to the general public.

"We understand," it ran, "that Messrs. Van Hyars, of Amsterdam, have successfully finished the cutting and polishing of the great Bara diamond. This remarkable stone, it will be remembered, was discovered in the new German West African fields. The competition to acquire it was unusually keen, owing to its peculiar colouring and its freedom from flaws. Many offers came from Eastern potentates through their agents. Eventually, however, it was purchased by a group of high officials of the Etat Privé du Congo, in order to present it to King Leopold in recognition of his wonderful foresight and ability in the development of the resources of the Congo area. The price paid, before cutting and polishing, was reported to have been eighty-five thousand pounds."

A grim smile had flickered over Marston Hume's face as he read the reference to King Leopold of Belgium, and the ostensible reason of the presentation; then he fell to thinking along other lines.

The finished stone was now in the care of the Van Hyars at their offices in Amsterdam. The presentation would naturally take place in Brussels. Though short in distance, the journey from one city to the other is of a cross-country nature.

Hume, staring out of the window, was mentally picturing to himself the various stages of the journey and possible contingencies.

Just before luncheon time, Sexton Blake and several other men came trooping into the quiet room, and Hume recalled himself to his present surroundings with an effort and a quickly suppressed sigh of impatience. Whenever Blake and he found themselves in the same room together, each was conscious of a sudden feeling of tension. It was a subtle, unexpressed feeling, quite unnoticed by others who were present; for both were men with extraordinary powers of self-restraint and repression.

Nevertheless, each tacitly acknowledged the force of the other's personality, and kept watchful guard over speech and action, realising that they were already embarked in a duel which, however prolonged, could have only one ending—the destruction of one or other of them.

This feeling was to Hume like strong, heady wine; it added zest to his life, and made him at times outspoken to a point bordering on rashness. On Blake it acted differently; his one object was to obtain tangible proof incriminating Marston Hume, and all other considerations were subordinated to that end.

"The man," he said to himself, "is a danger to society—a genius, a prince amongst criminals! But he must be stamped out, at any cost."

Several of the newcomers spoke to Hume; Blake contented himself with a nod, to which the former responded with a slow smile. Conversation became general as they moved off to the dining-room. Yet all the while Blake was watching Hume, and Hume was watching Blake. Each man knew instinctively that, however heartily the other was apparently laughing and chaffing, he was in reality waiting to seize on some unconscious self-betrayal. Marston Hume lost his air of abstraction, and talked lightly and brilliantly; Blake was comparatively silent.

That same afternoon Hume left London, and the Baddeley saw no more of him for a period of several days; nor did Blake catch a glimpse of him till the evening of the seventeenth of the month.

On that night Blake and Bathurst were having a bit of dinner early at a restaurant, prior to going on to a play. They had barely finished their fish, however, when who should stroll in but Marston Hume—button-hole, eyeglass, and all. He saw them at once, and strolled over to speak to them before going on to his own table.

After he had left them, Blake leant across the table.

"I'd give fifty pounds," he said in a low tone, "to know why that man has come here to-night. He never does anything, without a definite object. He meant us to see him here, of course; but why? Mark my words, Bathurst, we shall hear something startling within twenty-four hours. Well, it's no use wasting time in idle speculation. We shall know more about it by this time to-morrow."

Blake proved to be a true prophet, for very early the next morning he received a long cable message from Brussels, from a highly-placed official, imploring him to go over by the first available boat, on a matter of the greatest urgency and to keep his journey as secret as possible.

At first, having Marston Hume constantly in mind, he was on the point of refusing. Some instinct, however, made him change his mind, and he scribbled a hasty acceptance of the commission. Giving Bathurst hurried instructions to keep an eye on Hume's movements as far as possible, he packed a few things and hurried off via the Dover and Ostend route, and was in Brussels that same evening.

He had not been in his hotel half an hour, before two Belgian gentlemen were announced. One, the elder, was Count Wanderweide, the sender of the telegram; the other a M. Munster, one of the heads of the detective department, and an old acquaintance of Blake's. Both men were in a state of extreme agitation.

"Mr. Blake," said Count Wanderweide, hardly waiting for the formalities, "a terrible thing has happened; the Bara diamond has been stolen!"

"Let me have particulars, please?" said Blake. "I thought it was still in the hands of the Van Hyars, at Amsterdam?"

"So it was until the evening of the day before yesterday. Let me tell you the story. Nearly a fortnight ago Messrs. Van Hyars notified us that the stone was ready, and asked us to make arrangements for fetching it away—a responsibility we undertook. Some notice of this found its way into the newspapers, in consequence of which we delayed fetching the stone away at once, on account of the added risk owing to the publication of the news. During this short interval the diamond was placed in a small satin-lined brass-bound box in Messrs. Van Hyars' strong-rooms."

Blake nodded, and leant back in his chair. His ears were listening to every syllable and weighing it carefully; but inwardly he was haunted by a mental vision of Marston Hume sitting in the bow window of the Baddeley poring over a newspaper.

"Go on, please," he said curtly.

"Munster here, and I, meanwhile, laid our heads together as to the best means of getting the stone to Brussels without attracting the attention of the expert thieves who might very probably be on the look-out.

"Finally, we decided on a scheme which we thought excellent. Munster, as you know, speaks English like a native. We arranged that he should get himself up in the guise of the ordinary travelling Englishman, carrying, slung over his shoulder, an ordinary hand-camera. Inside the camera, carefully wrapped in cotton-wool, we proposed to place the diamond. I was to accompany him, though not ostensibly. I have the misfortune to be well-known to many people all over Belgium and Holland, and we thought that there was more than a possibility of my being shadowed, as my connection with the Etat Privé and the proposed presentation is also well-known. I was really to act as a decoy, whilst actually keeping an eye on Munster's safety. We both put up at the Poste, in Amsterdam."

"One moment, please," said Blake. "When and where were these plans discussed?"

"Here in Brussels, in the private rooms of the offices of the detective Bureau. No one but myself and Munster had any knowledge of them."

"You are sure that they were not talked over between you, either en route or at the Hotel de la Poste?"

"En route, although we travelled together, we did so as strangers, exchanging no word or glance. At the hotel, on the night of our arrival, we certainly talked over the final details late at night in the privacy of my room, after everyone had gone to bed."

"Humph! You have the number of that room?"

"Yes, No. 19; but I assure you no one saw Munster either leave or enter it—we took good care of that."

"Go on."

"After luncheon on the 16th, we went to Messrs. Van Hyars, separately, each provided with a special note of authorisation. We were received by the two brothers, and taken into the strong-room where the diamond was kept. The stone was taken out, carefully packed, and placed in the camera in their presence. At the suggestion of the elder Van Hyars, and as a further blind, it was arranged that I should carry the original brass-bound case, duly sealed, and securely locked into a formidable looking despatch-box. The idea being that should any attempt at robbery be made, I should be the victim, and Munster could get away in safety with the diamond.

"We waited by arrangement in the Van Hyars offices until we had just time to catch the Flushing train—we intended to return via Flushing, and so round to Brussels.

"A closed carriage with a specially-selected driver was waiting for us at a side-door, and we drove direct to the station.

"Here Munster and I became once more strangers—I walking a yard or two behind him, but keeping a sharp look-out. I had secured a carriage to myself in advance, and raised a certain amount of protest for appearances' sake when Munster got in, but finally backed down, and we travelled entirely by ourselves the whole way to Flushing, where we arrived early in the morning. We were wide awake all the time, both doors were locked, and no intrusion possible.

"At Flushing we had an hour or so to wait for the Brussels train, and we breakfasted at neighbouring tables in the café, in full sight of one another."

"This being the early morning of the 17th—yesterday," Blake interrupted.

"Quite so. We arrived at Flushing about a quarter to seven, the train was late, we got into the train for Brussels at 8.15. During that time we were never out of one another's sight, and from Flushing to Brussels we again had the carriage to ourselves. We were worn out with anxiety and fatigue, and during that part of the journey we took it in turns to doze; but, as before, the doors were locked, and no one could possibly have entered. At Brussels a private brougham was waiting for us, and we drove straight to the Bureau.

"In the presence of my colleagues Munster opened the case and took out the camera—for the first time since it had been put in in the Van Hyars' offices.

"He opened the camera, and there was a cry of amazement. The stone was gone. The camera was completely empty. I need not dwell on our feelings of shame and humiliation—it would be of little use. We recounted in detail every precaution we had taken, and an angry discussion at once took place as to what steps to take. It was unanimously agreed that secrecy was imperative, and at my suggestion it was agreed that I should wire for you the first thing this morning."

Blake sat for a long time in silence.

"Were you already provided with tickets from Flushing to Brussels?" he asked at last.

"No; we were returning by an alternative route."

"Which of you bought the tickets?"

Count Wanderweide shrugged his shoulders with the air of a man who is weary of futile questions.

"Munster did. There was rather a crush, and he was nearest the barrier. I stood by watching. We had left ourselves rather less time than we had intended. The time is altered at Flushing, as you know, and we had been relying on our watches."

"Then you must have glanced at the station clock to realise that you were late—possibly you even paused to re-set your watch by it."

"I believe I did, now you come to mention the fact."

Blake brought down his hand on the table with a thump.

"Then it is a hundred pounds to a penny-piece that that was when the exchange was made!" he cried.

Count Wanderweide stared. "The exchange? I fail to understand."

"The exchange of cameras, of course. Your idea of placing the stone in an ordinary hand-camera, such as are turned out by the thousand, immensely facilitated matters from the thief's point of view. But that is not the important fact. The real importance lies in the certainty that, somewhere or somehow, the man overheard you discussing your plans. If your account is accurate, it cannot have been in Brussels; it must, therefore, have been at the Hotel de la Poste, in Amsterdam, when you both thought yourselves so secure. Anyhow, he knew that a camera was to be the real hiding-place—and what is more, he must have had an opportunity of seeing the camera itself, for he was sufficiently well acquainted with it to supply himself with a duplicate. Have you the camera with you, by the way?"

"Yes," said Munster. "It is in the ante-room. I will fetch it."

He returned shortly, camera in hand, and Blake, opening the black leather case, drew out the camera—an ordinary box snapshot.

"If you can identify that as yours," he said grimly. "I will own myself in the wrong and apologise."

Munster turned it over doubtfully.

"It's the same size and pattern," he said; "but I must confess that I rarely use the thing, and have never paid much heed to it. One moment, though, I dropped it once, a long time ago, and it leaked a little. I repaired it inside with some gummed black paper. If this is mine, we shall find the paper still there. I admit that I was so flabbergasted by the loss of the stone that I never gave the camera a thought."

He opened the camera slowly, and peered into the interior. Then, in silence he passed it across to Blake. The interior was in perfect condition, and showed no signs of having been repaired at any time.

Blake nodded again.

"That proves my contention, as I expected. You, Munster, were taking the tickets, stooping with your head close to the little opening, and busied with your change and so forth; there must have been a period of close on two minutes, during which you were quite unconscious of anything going on behind you—except, perhaps, that you were being pressed by the other people waiting.

"During those two minutes, and taking advantage of Wanderweide's temporary lack of vigilance, the thing was done. The man had been waiting for just such an opportunity. He had his duplicate camera, without a case, held under a rug or an ulster, on his arm; he gets behind you, and presses close up, and the rest is the work of seconds. Any common pickpocket could have done it.

"You may take it for granted that he overheard you at Amsterdam, laid his plans accordingly, and returned direct to Flushing, arriving there on the evening of the 16th."

"And afterwards?"

"After taking a ticket to Brussels, or some intermediate station which he had no intention of using, his natural course would be to stroll out of the station to the quay, and get on board the Queenboro' and Flushing boat. Whilst you were speeding to Brussels, all unsuspecting, he and the diamond were being hurried towards England, with the certainty of a long start—even had it occurred to you to make sure of the security of your treasure in the train."

Count Wanderweide groaned.

"But what can we do?—something must be done!"

Blake looked grave.

"Undoubtedly—we can do many things; but I tell you frankly I have little hope of success. You, Munster, for instance, can ascertain through official channels whether a ticket was issued yesterday at Flushing for the 8.15 train, to any station between there and Brussels and not made use of. If that was the case let me know at once. Meanwhile, I will say good-night, for I shall be busy."

The first thing the next morning, Blake dispatched several telegrams, the replies to which came whilst he was at breakfast.

The first was from the manager of the Poste at Amsterdam, and was the reverse of hopeful.

"The rooms on either side of No. 19 were unoccupied on the night in question," it read. "No.

17, two rooms away, was occupied by a French gentleman, who left early the next morning."

Blake read the message over twice and laid it aside. The next was from the Station Hotel, at Flushing.

"In reply to your despatch, an Englishman, registering in the name of Hume, stayed here on the night of the 16th, and left early the following morning."

Blake rubbed his hands.

"A glimmer of light at last," he muttered.

Shortly after breakfast, Munster came hurrying in.

"Your surmises have proved correct so far, Mr. Blake," he said. "We have discovered that a through ticket to Brussels by the 8.15 was issued at Flushing that morning, which remains unaccounted for. It was not given up. The presumption is therefore that it has been destroyed. What do you propose to do next?"

"I shall return to England by the next boat," said Blake curtly. "I have a possible clue, which it is imperative that I should follow up without loss of time. If it comes to anything, I will cable you."

When Blake reached London he found Bathurst waiting for him at his rooms.

"Hume?" he asked sharply.

"Hasn't moved out of his rooms. I've got two men constantly on the watch. He is going out this evening, though."

"How do you know?"

"I met Falconer at the club, and, in the course of conversation, he happened to mention to me that Hume and another man were dining with him this evening."

Blake's eyes gleamed.

"A stroke of luck at last! Old man, there is a chance, just a chance, that we may catch him tripping at last. Has a small parcel come for me from Amsterdam; I wired for it?"

Bathurst nodded.

"Came by the last post."

"Good! I wish you'd turn over those papers in the corner there and see if you can find me the 'Telegraph' of the eleventh, whilst I get rid of my travel stains and have a change."

Bathurst rummaged about, and found the paper, and Blake pored over the columns eagerly.

At last he stopped with his finger on the paragraph relating to the finishing of the diamond.

"That settles it!" he said. "This was the paper Marston Hume was reading the day I told you of in the club. He has got the Bara stone right enough, and at present, so far as we know, he still has it. He stole it from Munster early on the morning of the seventeenth at Flushing, and he took special pains to prove to us that he was in London the same evening. Come along! If he's dining out, he must have started by now. It's illegal, but I am going to ransack his rooms."

In reply to the hall-porter's announcement that Mr. Hume was out, Blake explained that they would go up and wait on the chance of his returning, and as soon as they found themselves alone Blake set to work.

The rooms were small, but well furnished. Hume, amongst other things, was a fair amateur artist. An easel with an unfinished water-colour stood in one corner, and on a table near the window was a small modelling turntable, with the beginnings of a statuette in wax.

The search was a complete failure, so far as any signs of the missing stone went, but in the small cupboard in the hall Blake unearthed a gladstone. It bore the usual chalk scrawl of the Customs officials, partly rubbed out, a label of the Station Hotel at Flushing intact, and a small corner of another hotel label, obviously recent. The corner remaining was of a peculiar red colour, with a thin design in black line.

Blake pulled out the packet which had come from Amsterdam; it contained half a dozen fresh labels from the Hotel de la Poste, neatly packed between two sheets of cardboard. He compared one of them with the corner. Their identity was unmistakable.

"A trip at last!" said Blake. "We can prove now that he went to Amsterdam, and stayed at

the Poste, where Munster and Wanderweide put up. He stayed there under a French name, adopting some slight but clever disguise, and he managed to get a room next but one to Wanderweide's. You know those Continental hotels. Nearly all the rooms have communicating doors. To unfasten one of them would be mere child's play to him; and there is no doubt that he listened to Munster and Wanderweide talking over their plans.

"We can do no more good here now. To-morrow I shall take the only course open and confront him with my knowledge of his movements.

He'll be dangerous when cornered, but there's no other way."

It was with a very stern, set face that Blake made his way round to Marston Hume's the next morning early.

Hume was standing by his window table, with an elaborate smoking coat on, leisurely working at his wax model, his cuffs turned back for the purpose.

"Good-morning!" he said coolly, as Blake came in. "This is rather an unexpected honour."

"Intrusion would suit your purpose better," replied Blake. "I have come to have a little chat concerning the Bara diamond which you stole from Munster."

Hume's eyebrows went up.

"On the morning of the eleventh," said Blake grimly, "you read a paragraph in the paper relating to the stone. That same day you left town. You stayed at the Poste at Amsterdam under the name, as I have just ascertained by cable, of M. Abbeville. You left the hotel on the sixteenth for Flushing. The number of your room was seventeen. Before you left you had ascertained the details of Munster's plans. The night of the sixteenth you stayed at Flushing under your own name. You robbed Munster at the ticket-office the next morning, and took pains to show yourself to me in London that same evening. The Bara stone is still in your possession."

Hume's hand dropped idly to his coat pocket. Blake guessed the truth—that the pocket contained a revolver.

"Do you realise, Mr. Blake," said Hume slowly, "that you are in an extremely unpleasant position? Last night you entered my rooms without any authority and searched them."

Blake nodded. "Perfectly true, he said."

Hume glanced at the bell.

"If I were to ring that and send for a policeman, complaining that I had missed something of value, I could have you arrested on the evidence of the hall-porter."

"True again. But it would be rather absurd, and I should be released very shortly."

"There remains the other alternative. I warn you that if you attempt to hamper my movements I shall not hesitate to resort to it. That I went to Flushing is perfectly true, that I went there in my own name is surely natural: Why on earth should I use another? Whilst there I called on an old client of mine, a bookmaker whom I

once defended, and who lives at Middleburg—a very innocent action on my part, and one I can prove—but that I went near Amsterdam or your man—Munster, I think you said his name was—I defy you to prove."

"The proof is easily obtainable—your gladstone will be quite sufficient."

"My gladstone! Shall I ring for it?"

"Please; but if you attempt to tamper with it I shall shoot."

Hume rang the bell.

"The interview is becoming melodramatic," he said. "Bring my small gladstone to this gentleman," he added, as the servant opened the door; "he wishes to see it."

The bag was brought, and Blake, turned it over eagerly, only to give vent to an exclamation of disappointment. The tell-tale fragment had been carefully removed, and in its place was a label bearing Hume's name and address, neatly written in his own hand.

"I fail to see how my bag can assist you. It seems to me that you entertain the most ridiculous suspicions concerning me, and fail utterly to support them by a particle of proof.

"If you are not satisfied, there is an excellent likeness of me on the mantelpiece; why not send that to your friends in Amsterdam—they might be able to identify it?"

Blake shook his head.

"I should be the last to deny your cleverness in disguising yourself. But I know that you took the Bara stone, as surely as I know that you murdered your aunt for the sake of her money."

"Knowledge," said Marston Hume coldly, "and proof are two very different things. When I was practising, I have on more than one occasion known a man to be guilty, yet proved him innocent. In my case it would seem that you are making ineffectual efforts to reverse that situation."

"In my experience," retorted Blake, "a criminal invariably makes a fatal slip sooner or later. In this case you repaired yours in time, but the game is not played to a finish yet."

Hume politely stifled a yawn.

"In which case it resembles this little wax model I am working on. Good-morning!"

Some days later Blake received a small wooden case through the post. To the inside of the lid was fastened a newspaper cutting:

"The Maharajah of Pertola has just left Paris for India. He aroused considerable curiosity during the latter part of his visit by wearing a stone strangely resembling the missing Bara diamond. One of his suite, however, informed our representative that the stone in question had been in the possession of the Maharajah's family for generations."

In the case itself there was a cleverly executed bust in wax, and a note in Hume's neat writing.

"I send you the enclosed," he wrote, "modelled from a recent photograph of the Maharajah of Pertola, not because of its artistic merits, which are slight, but in the hope it may prove of personal interest to you.—Yours truly,

"F. MARSTON HUME."

"Good morning!" said Hume coolly, as Blake entered. "This is an unexpected honour." "Intrusion would suit your purpose better," replied Blake.

CHRISTMAS SPECIAL NUMBER
The UNION JACK. 2d.

THE
SACRED SPHERE

ILLUSTRATED BY VAL.   WRITTEN BY the AUTHOR of "The Yellow Sphinx"

"MIKE LANGTON'S VOW" starts on page 47.

No. 528. NEW SERIES.]   November 29th, 1913.   [EVERY THURSDAY.

No. 529. November 29th, 1913.

THE SACRED SPHERE

❦ *A Christmas Story with a Deeply Laid Plot* ❦

INTRODUCING

SEXTON BLAKE, YVONNE, DR. HUXTON RYMER, and WU LING, etc., etc.

PROLOGUE.

THE great Dominion of Canada was flinching under the lash of the blizzard. From east to west, from north to south, all the fiercest elements of December seemed to have combined to bury the face of the land beneath a weighty coat of white, and hide beneath towering drifts the roads and trails of plain and valley. For twenty-four hours it had been snowing—not the soft white flakes which fall against the face in delicate caress, but the blinding, cutting, sandy ice-flakes of the blizzard.

In the cities everything was dislocated; in the country travel was impossible. From Halifax to Winnipeg the railway service was in disorder. News filtered through slowly,

CHRISTMAS COMES BUT ONCE A YEAR,
AND WHEN IT COMES IT BRINGS GOOD CHEER
1913

for most of the telegraph wires were down. Meagre reports arrived, however, of trains being blocked by mountainous drifts through which even the rotary snow-ploughs failed to eat their way. In Nova Scotia a train had been half buried under an avalanche of snow; in Quebec another train had left the rails, and had gone rolling and tumbling into a snowy abyss, to be lost to sight in a deep drift.

But nowhere in that great expanse of country was the blast more fierce, or the drifts more mountainous, than in New Brunswick.

In summer, a green emerald is set in Canada's fair brow; in winter she is a cold white diamond—her great forests bent under the white blanket—her streams and rivers smooth paths of ice—her coasts desolate grey bulwarks against the winter's blast.

Three feet of snow already carpeted her forests before the present storm broke—three feet of white, softness which had come with December.

Then, all had been bustle in her great lumber camps. Gangs of men who had gone in at the approach of winter had been kept busy making the "tote road" along which the huge sleds of logs would go tearing to the river. Other gangs made the woods ring with the steady whirr of the axe in the frosty air.

From dawn to dark, horses and men toiled in the shelter of the woods, the steaming sides of the horses changing to white frost as the cold air condensed against their flanks; and the beards of the men became white fringes of icicles. The breaking of the blizzard had stopped all this, however, and now men and horses were under cover, the former whiling away the time by rough horse-play in the bunk-house, the latter contentedly munching oats in the rude but warm stables. For it was Christmas Eve and, storm or no storm, the morrow meant a free day.

Still the tempest showed no signs of abating. Even the great herds of moose and caribou and deer sought the retreat of the denser timber; the partridges whirred silently onward to seek the shelter of the wide spreading fir and spruce; the otter and the mink dived deep into the cold but untroubled waters and even the white furred rabbits disappeared into the deepest part of their runs.

King Blizzard reigned supreme.

In the far south-west corner of New Brunswick, where that British province breaks into the State of Maine, lies the town of St. Stephen, noted somewhat widely for the past glories of great timber industries, and its present advancing manufactures.

Between it and the American side runs the far-famed St. Croix, that deep blue river which De Monts sailed up over three hundred years ago. Then the high fertile hills which smile down upon it were covered by dense forests of timber, and the Indian was lord.

Now the white man holds it in his sway; the timber has disappeared; the hills have been changed to waving stretches of green; the red man has gone into the Great Unknown, and the habitations of civilisation edge its banks.

But one thing remains unchanged. Its great tides still rise and fall as they flow into or out of Passamaquoddy Bay with the same unbroken regularity which marked them in the time of De Monts and Champlain; of Columbus and Balboa; of the still earlier Norsemen; yea, of the dim unwritten past, before even the red man himself came from the distant shores of Asia.

From the water's edge to the distant height, where the hills became lost in the stormy sky, was all the land under white, for here, too, the blizzard had struck.

Far up the river, where the fresh water predominated, the wharves of the sister towns of the American Calais and the British St. Stephen were locked in ice; but far down, where its little island of St. Croix, where De Monts landed and where the salt spew of the bay defies the cold, the water was open, only a few rushing cakes of ice, like miniature Arctic floes, telling the conditions which prevailed higher up.

And the swift closing day of the blizzard was Christmas Eve here as everywhere else.

About two miles out of St. Stephen, on the road which leads to the timbered point which guards the entrance to Oak Bay, stands a dilapidated frame building which one might imagine deserted, did it not bear on its front in rude letters "Looey-Sing, Laundry and General Store."

Why a Chinese laundry should be established in such a desolate spot is a matter of mystery. One thing, however, was certain. The word in front was the only evidence there was of a laundry, for none came to Looey Sing with garments to be washed.

It made some pretence of being a general store, for on the shelves were a few rusty tins of vegetables and boxes of tea; a barrel of biscuits formed a convenient nesting-place for the mice which swarmed there; a cask, which was supposed to contain molasses, lay on its side against the wall, and another— presumably oil—butted against it.

A box of onions, a maggotty cheese, a few paper bags, and a show-case filled with a varied assortment of "candy" mouth organs, chewing gum, and ten cent watch chains, made up the balance of Looey Sing's stock.

At maximum inventory it might go to fifty dollars; at a bankrupt auction it would do well to bring five.

No customers had broken the musty silence of Looey Sing's shop that stormy day. As a matter of fact, the door had not even been unlocked since the preceding afternoon. The lack of custom seemed not to worry the Chinaman, however, for he sat hunched over the little stove in the back room which formed his abode, smoking yellow cigarettes, and gazing with imperturbable calm into the red coals.

From the small square of glass in the rear of the room could be seen a wild snow-covered stretch of woods running down to the river; then the ice-covered bosom of the river itself, clear and blackly sinister, where the howling blizzard whipped the snowflakes from the smooth surface and sent them whirling inwards to the bank; then came the American side of the river, now lost to view in the careering curtain of the storm.

Farther to the left, the unbroken expanse of ice reached its climax, and patches of open water, in which rode small floes, showed where Jack Frost lost his sway. In front of the shack was a rough, little travelled road, now hidden under the drifts, though here and there, where the wind found a spot unprotected, it swept it bare to the frozen mud. No houses could be seen, although several farms surrounded the abode of Looey Sing.

Not until the fading light of early afternoon made it impossible to see did the motionless Chinaman rouse himself from his position. He did so with a slow, cautious movement, and his slant-set eyes darted about as though the lonely spot were the centre of spies interested in his doings—an unconscious habit assumed by Looey

Sing during a long life of curious dealings, and had anyone been interested in the psychological wonder of a laundry in such a place, he might have found in the Celestial's manner a clue to the mystery.

He moved about with Oriental calm and noiselessness. His immediate object was harmless enough, consisting of the preparation of a cup of tea, which he drank after the fashion of the natives of the Shantung hinterland—thick and black. This done, he tidied up again in a scrupulous manner, and approached the pane of glass at the rear.

For some minutes he gazed out at the now invisible river, but the sharp staccato sound of the hail and snow on the window told him the storm still raged.

After a few minutes he turned back, muttering cryptically in pidgin English:

"Twenty mo' at two hunled dollals. Fo' tousand dollars fo' Looey Sing."

Then he replenished the fire and resumed his seat, once more attacking the yellow cigarettes. Not until it was past six did he move.

It was as dark now as it would be at midnight, and neither man nor beast was abroad in that lonely spot, though, in the town further up, a few intrepid spirits had braved the elements, determined to finish their Christmas shopping.

From a cupboard in the corner Looey Sing took out a long coon-skin coat and cap of similar fur. When he had donned the coat and had drawn the cap well down on his head, his deep, yellowish eyes peeped out with all the cunning of the little beast from which the fur originally came.

After that he did a surprising thing. He went into the front shop and dropped a bar over the door; that finished, he returned to the rear room and unlocked a door which led out to the back of the shack. It seemed strange that any

man should have business outside on such a night, but undoubtedly Looey Sing had.

Throwing open the door, he braced himself and clung to it, for the blast which swept in threatened to tear it from his grasp. With a last glance around the room, he took a long breath and, bending low, stepped out, closing the door after him.

For a moment the force of the wind seemed as though it would press the breath from his lungs; the hail cut into his face like gunpowder, and his legs sank to the knees in drifted snow.

These things did not deter Looey Sing from his purpose, for he began scrambling and fighting his way along towards the near-by woods.

Once he gained their shelter it felt as though he had come out of a world of chaos into one of calm. True, the driving storm found its way

there, too, but the wind was tempered, and the hail was filtered by the heavily laden branches. The roar of the wind reached him from high up, but compared with the unprotected stretch of road, it was a haven of silence.

The lack of big drifts made it easier to get along in the woods. Looey Sing picked his course with the certainty born of intimate knowledge through the dark aisles between the trees. Always he was descending, until twenty minutes after he had entered the shelter of the trees he came out at the river's edge.

Even now he did not pause but, turning to the left, began to walk more quickly. His heavy gum shoes gripped the ice without slipping and, close in as he was, the overhanging trees broke the force of the storm.

For another ten minutes he kept along on the ice until he came to a small wood-girdled cove.

Had he been able to see distinctly he would have perceived that the darker patch directly ahead was open water; but its proximity held no terrors for the Celestial.

Too often had his eyes rested on that spot during the day. Swinging along the edge of the little cove the Chinaman came to a pause before a small shed, the door of which took up almost the whole end of the building.

He fumbled in the pocket of his coat for a few minutes, and when his hand emerged it held a long electric flash tube and a key. Taking the tube

A PERILOUS DASH THROUGH THE STORM-SWEPT NIGHT
For an hour Looey Sing sat rigid, his eyes peering ahead, his whole attitude one of disregard for storm and ice and darkness until, dead ahead, a single light appeared. Then he bent forward and shut off the engine. (*Page 4.*)

in his left hand he pressed the switch, revealing a strong hasp on the door, secured by a heavy padlock. Into this he fitted the key.

A moment later the double doors swung open, and before him was a long, heavily-built motor-boat.

Its bow was towards him, and between it and the sides of the shed was barely room to walk. It rested on a small framework of wood set on four rimmed, tramway wheels, and these in turn on two rails which passed out under the door, and disappeared in the depths of the black water.

Keeping his light going, Looey Sing made his way along one side of the boat until he reached the stern. In the rear end of the building had been set a tiny winch, the chain of which held boat and wheeled frame in the shed.

The Chinaman crawled in over the stern and, bending, released the iron clasp which held the winch. Almost at once there was the low ramble of the wheels as they moved along the track, the louder rattle of the chain as it unwound from the winch. Each moment the boat gathered speed.

Already the bow was outside, nose pointed towards the water; then the cockpit shot past the door, and the whole affair went rapidly down the incline to the water.

A splash in front, an uplifting of the bow, a few icy drops of water in his face, and Looey Sing was afloat with the framework continuing down the submerged track until it should reach the limit of the chain.

Still grasping his light, the Chinaman moved forward to the engine and bent over it. A moment later there was a series of sharp coughs as he swung the fly-wheel. Again he turned it, and the rhythmic hum of the engine followed. Leaping to the tiller, he sat down and bent low.

As the boat gathered speed and sprang onwards through the black stretch of open water, the full force of the wind hit him; the boat struck floe after floe and drove them before her or sheered off quivering; but Looey Sing sat rigid, his eyes peering straight ahead, his whole attitude one of disregard for storm and ice and darkness.

He headed the boat straight down river and, helped by the onrushing tide, he was soon far out in mid-channel. The exhaust of the motor, muffled even on ordinary occasions, was totally lost in the greater roar of the gale. From the shore he was invisible and unheard, though it

was unlikely that any other human being was abroad that gale-swept night.

For fully half an hour the motor throbbed unchecked while the boat drove on through the night. He had passed through the Narrows now, and was well down in the wider part of the river.

The red light at Bog Brook had flashed by like a fleeting spark from the devil's engine; the dilapidated old breakwater which lies at the entrance to the Narrows had been invisible, so thick were the snow and sleet.

Still the motionless Celestial bent low, and still his eyes searched the dark stretch of the river ahead. To his left he saw the light of the first lighthouse.

No sooner did he leave it behind than the second on the Canadian side appeared; then suddenly far, far ahead a tiny spark pierced the storm, winked, was gone, only to reappear and disappear again and again.

It was the revolving light on St. Croix Island— the little island where De Monts and Champlain spent the terrible winter of 1604.

Now to his left, with the shore lighthouse behind, a dim black line marked the timbered bank. This, too, was soon lost to view, and there took its place a wider expanse of dark water. He had reached Oak Point, where the narrower part of the river ends, and sweeps abruptly up into the bay of the same name. Then, and only then, did Looey Sing change his course.

Putting the tiller hard over to starboard, he swept on in a great curve around the point, and kept on in his present course until the timber on the shore loomed startlingly close to him; then he set her head straight.

It was quieter in the bay. The storm was now behind him, and in close to the shore the point to his left formed a wind break. The sleet still flung itself at his face, however, and his mittens had been frozen stiff by the flying spray.

For ten minutes he kept on his present course, following the line of the shore until, dead ahead, a single light 'appeared. It came out of the storm as though careering along on the wings of the wind, but even as the Celestial looked, a darker, bulk appeared beneath it.

Holding the tiller with one hand, Looey Sing bent forward and shut off the engine. The boat, driven onwards by its own impetus, gave more to the tossing waves as its speed lessened; then slower and slower it went until the black bulk

THE SACRED SPHERE

ahead grew close, and the nose of the motor-launch gently struck the side of a schooner.

She was anchored in under the lee of the shore, with every sail clewed up and hatches battened down. Certainly she would have created no comment had she been seen, for it was a night to make any ship run for shelter. The only suspicious circumstance was the fact that she should be so far up the river at that time of the year, but that detail had been attended to, if one judged her purpose by her cargo, which was coal, to be discharged at the little town of Red Beech almost across the river on the American side.

Evidently those on the schooner had been on the look-out for the Celestial. Barely had the motor-boat struck the side, when a rope was thrown over, to fall across the gunwales. Looey Sing grasped it, and tied the end to his boat, then, leaping upwards, he caught the side of the schooner, and drew himself over.

Two men were standing on the deck, and without a word they conducted him aft to the small, dingy saloon. A smoky oil lamp lit up the place, and showed them to be white men.

One was tall and gaunt, with smooth-shaven face, and sharp, pointed features—a typical American skipper of the coasting type. The other was short and of a stocky build. What the first lacked in hirsute adornment he made up for.

His face was almost covered by a flaming red beard and moustache, his small eyes peeping forth like those of a weasel. His arms were extraordinarily long, and even under the thick blue serge of his coat showed big and powerful. His legs were short and bowed. Had his beard been black he would have looked not unlike a gorilla.

They both waited until the Celestial had divested himself of his mittens, coat, and cap. While redbeard pushed forward a bottle of whisky and glasses, the taller one spoke.

"Jehoshaphat! Looey Sing, you are sure some Chink! I didn't think you'd get here to-night."

"Me say me come—allee light, me come," answered the Chinaman, pouring out and gulping down about four fingers of the neat spirit.

Then redbeard broke in, and though he addressed his companion as captain, it was evident from his tones that the title was a mere matter of form. Undoubtedly he dominated the other.

"Believe me, captain, we ain't got no time for talk. If Looey Sing wants to get back with

his cargo, he will have to hump himself. If this gale gets any worse, he will find himself piled up on the island, and then there will be the devil to pay. I'm gettin' nervous, I am, and the sooner we makes the beach with our legitimate cargo, the better pleased yours truly will be."

"Oh, close your trap before you fall in!" grunted the individual addressed as captain. "The Chink has kept word, and wants a blow before he goes back. If he had been piled up on the shore before he reached here, we might have had a chance to kick."

"Believe me, if he had, yours truly would have been ploughing the drifts on the Canadian side by morning," rumbled the mate.

Looey Sing had sat as impassive as ever all this time, moving only once, and that in order to pour out another drink. Now he looked up.

"You bling them all light?" he asked, looking at the captain.

"Sure as anything you know, Looey," answered the other. "We hit the Bay of Fundy two days ago. Hung about for a bit until nightfall. The motor-launch from St. John turned up sharp on time, and passed over the cargo to us." Gave us a little matter of five hundred tins of opium, too. Then we clamped on all sail, and tried to get up the river before the storm broke, but it caught us from behind this side of Lubec.

"Believe me, all the winds in the Atlantic have sure come to this old river to celebrate Christmas. We were off Red Beech about noon, but beat up and down the river. Signalled we couldn't make the wharf to-night, and would anchor up here. So there you are, Looey, my boy. If you are ready, we will get the cargo out and into your boat."

"I all leady," answered the Celestial. "You bling money?"

"Sure thing," said the captain, "Get the dough out, Reddy," he added, turning to the mate. "Looey wants to see the colour of it before he moves. Thinks we might skin him."

"No, me not tink that," said the Chinaman imperturbably. "Business is business, and Looey Sing allee samee business man."

The mate had opened a big sea-chest while the Celestial had been speaking, and taking out a large canvas bag, tossed it on the table.

"There you are," he rumbled. "Four thousand plunks of the best Canadian greenbacks."

Looey Sing undid the string which held the mouth of the bag together, and took out the contents. They proved be a thick wad of banknotes of all denominations, from five dollars to a hundred dollars. Some were dirty, greasy, and microbe-laden, others new and crisp.

But their condition mattered not to Looey Sing, for the oldest notes received the same caressing attention as his yellow fingers ran through them as did the newer ones. All was grist which came to the Chinaman's mill.

When he had counted them, and verified the amount, he replaced them in the bag, and stuffed it in turn beneath the blue laundryman's jacket which he wore.

"You bling five hundred tins opium?" he said, look up at the Captain.

"Yes. How much do you want for putting that through, you old heathen?"

"Two dollals tin—one tousand dollars."

"Caesar's ghost! Why don't you make it a little more?"

For answer, Looey Sing spread out his hands.

"Two. dollals," he said, in a sing-song tone. "No mo', no less. Allee samee last time."

The captain shrugged, knowing the futility of arguing with the Celestial, for Looey Sing's position was unique. He constituted the main link in a long and complicated system of law evasion, and, knowing the full strength of his position, acted accordingly.

The mysterious cargo of which the captain spoke might be passed through many hands until it reached Looey Sing, and after entering American territory, it might pass through many more, but did the Chinaman in the ship's cabin that night refuse to do his part the whole vast system of "underground" commerce would be held up. Consequently, another thousand dollars was counted out to Looey Sing, and these followed the canvas bag beneath his jacket. Then he stood up.

"Now me leady," he said calmly.

"Wait a minute," said the captain, motioning him back to his seat. "We have a special package this time."

"Jehoshaphat! You are sure some Chink, Looey Sing. I didn't think you'd get here to-night," said the captain, as Looey Sing entered.

He glanced at the mate as he spoke, and that individual departed surlily, presumably on some unspoken order.

Looey Sing subsided, and waited.

"It ain't like the others, neither," went on the captain, biting the end off a stogie.

Still the Celestial waited, his face as impassive as ever, though perhaps his eyes had narrowed the barest trifle.

"For Heaven's sake, don't sit there lookin' like a hanged yellow sphinx!" exclaimed the captain, pouring out a drink.

It was very evident that the special package, whatever it might be, was of a different nature from any he had carried before.

"Me wait," was all Looey Sing said.

"I didn't know about it myself," went on the captain hurriedly, "until it was put aboard from the boat which met us in the Bay of Fundy. I refused it at first, for this class of stuff is not to my liking; but Higgins, the mate, persuaded me to take it. The agent for St. John says the New York channels for this class of goods is closed—too risky now—and if we handle the regular cargoes, we must take a certain number of these.

"This one, in particular, is very special stuff, and before I hand it over, let me tell you it's a case clear through to China. It is meant for a mandarin of the Purple Button there, and if any harm comes to it—well"—and the captain sank his voice to a hoarse whisper—"the Brotherhood of the Yellow Beetle will take vengeance; and I guess you know what that means, though I've only got a vague idea myself."

"You talk much, much," said the Celestial, twirling a cigarette in his fingers. "If Blothelhood Yellow Beetle say clear thlough, you bet Looey Sing obey. What is the package?"

"I guess you had better see it," answered the captain, and at that moment the door opened.

Both he and Looey Sing looked up. At first it seemed as though the bearded mate was the only one to enter, but as he came within the penumbra of the hanging oil lamp, it was seen that he was dragging someone behind him. As he drew close he stood aside, and revealed the slim form of a girl.

Her face was concealed by a heavy veil, and her body was wrapped in a long, capacious coat of squirrel skin; but an intangible something in her pose told of youth, and the tangled masses of fair hair made it seem impossible that aught but beauty could be stamped upon the features beneath the veil.

She was relaxed in attitude, and the support of the mate's arm told the experienced Celestial that she was in a condition of semi-consciousness only, as she had been and would be while in the hands of the underground system. For, be it understood, that a victim in a continual condition of semi-consciousness through drugs is a victim without cognisance of time or place or distance; and with that complicated system this is as it should be.

The mate looked at his chief.

"Did you tell him?"

The captain nodded, and took another drink.

"Yes; but, hang it! I don't like it. She's white, and no wife for any purple-buttoned mandarin—whatever in blazes that may be—he's yellow."

"Oh, dry up!" growled the mate disrespectfully. "Do you think the rake off we make out of this is to be picked up every day? Will he take her?"

The captain turned to the Chinaman.

"Will you?" he asked a trifle thickly, for the spirit was beginning to tangle his tongue a trifle.

Looey Sing nodded slowly.

"Yes, me take he'. Put he' in the boat."

The mate withdrew with the girl, presumably to do so, and involuntarily the captain heaved a sigh of relief, for he was glad in the first place to get the girl off his hands, and, in the second place, Looey Sing had not, as he expected, asked for extra money for taking her.

The Chinaman rose at that moment, and the captain followed suit. Together they made their way to the deck and across to the side-beneath which the motor-boat swung.

The gale had now eased a little, and already patches of star-studded purple were showing overhead as the clouds broke and scudded-along at hurricane speed. The snow and sleet had let up, and the black line of the timbered shore now stood out clear cut and distinct in the frosty night air.

They paused at the side and peered over into the boat below. A solitary figure sat in the stern, though its lines were blurred. They both knew, however, that it was the girl.

Then the trample of feet sounded along the deck, and two sailors appeared, each bearing a small wooden case in their arms. These they lowered into the boat, and returned for more and more, until ten cases in all had been put aboard. It was the opium.

Again the sound of trampling feet came along the deck, this time much louder. A body of men next appeared, marching in single file. They drew up in line before the captain and Looey Sing, and the latter, taking a lantern from the hand of a sailor, walked slowly along the line, inspecting them one by one. There were nineteen in all, and their faces were yellow, their eyes slanted.

They were countrymen of Looey Sing's, bound by the great underground route from England through Canada to the United States—that country which forbids unconditionally the entry of Chinese.

Girl, opium, and Celestials, be it noted, were alike referred to collectively as "cargo," and individually as "packages." Such was another detail of the System. Satisfied with his scrutiny, Looey Sing passed the lantern back with a grunt.

"All light," he said briefly. "Go on!"

The line of men needed no further order. One by one they went over the side and dropped into the boat below. When the last had disappeared, Looey Sing went back to the cabin and donned his fur coat and cap; then, stuffing his hands into his mittens, he passed out and over the side.

A moment later, the rhythmic hum of the motor came upwards, the boat swung and headed for the point. Ten minutes later it had gone, not even the muffled sound of the exhaust reaching the schooner. When it had quite disappeared, the captain and mate returned to the saloon, and began an attack on the whisky-bottle.

They had done a pretty stroke of business—in fact, it was only one of many strokes which they had done. Five hundred tins of opium and nineteen Chinamen had gone through, not to speak of the slim girl, who had completed that stage of her long journey through to China, there to become the wife of a yellow mandarin whom she had never seen.

Yes, all things considered, the captain, the mate, and the crew of the schooner looked forward to a happy Christmas Day on the morrow.

All during that cold, spray-flying trip Looey Sing's "cargo" sat hunched up in the bow and amidships, shivering and silent. As for the fur-clad girl who sat beside him in the stern, she gave not the slightest sign that she was aware of her change of quarters. Only a low, muffled moan issued at intervals from behind the thick veil. Undoubtedly, though in a semi-comatose condition, some subconscious feeling was causing her to suffer.

Looey Sing himself neither spoke nor shifted his position, except to move the tiller as occasion demanded it. What might be behind those inscrutable eyes no man might tell. Not even his own countrymen had the temerity to address him. To them he was for the time being as a sovereign lord, holding their destinies in his wrinkled yellow hands.

Back along the course he had come went the Celestial. A jutting point on the American side of the river shut off the view of the revolving light on the island, now far behind. One lighthouse had been passed, and soon the steady flame of the other was dead ahead.

As the boat swept onwards, nosing the still outrushing tide, the old breakwater which before had been invisible, came into view.

It, on the one side, and the lighthouse on the other, sped past; then they struck the Narrows where still burned the red light of Bog Brook. A few moments only, and they were in the wide river, again heading for the wooded cove where stood the boat-shed.

On reaching the entrance, Looey Sing cut off the motor and let the boat drive in under its own impetus, until it gently nosed the slip, quivered slightly, and lay quiet, rising and falling gently on the little waves of its own making. A low, guttural command sent the nineteen Celestials over the bow, and another order set them at work pulling on the rope.

While they held the boat steady, Looey Sing picked up the girl as though she were a child, and carrying her along to the bow, passed her over. Leaping over himself, he entered the shed and began winding up the winch. Slowly the wheeled frame came out of the depths, until its grooved cross-pieces received the keel of the boat; then frame and boat together began to move upwards along the tracks.

Five minutes, and they were back in their original place in the shed, the doors had been closed and locked, and Looey Sing stood on the slip outside surveying his "cargo." A moment only, and he signed for the girl to be passed to him.

With her in his arms, he uttered a low grunt, and struck off along the ice edging the river's bank. He turned in at the point where he had before left the woods, and without pausing, walked swiftly along, leaving the others to scramble along after as best they could.

Before breaking from the cover of the woods into the open, he stopped and surveyed the snow-clad stretch between him and the shack. Not a sound of man or beast broke the silence of the cold, frosty night; but just as he was beginning to move forward again, a silvery note floated faintly to their ears from far up the river. It was the church bells in the town above, ringing out the summons to the Christmas Eve service.

Not until the last chime had died away did Looey Sing advance, and if the bells of the strange gods had struck any deep chord in his nature, he gave no sign.

The rear room of the shack was exactly as he had left it. The coals in the stove now burned red, and the Celestials crowded about it, glad of the welcome heat.

Poor wretches! What hardships and suffering they truly pass through in order to reach the forbidden land where every day will be a golden day—so they think—and in a short time they

Looey Sing found it a hard task feeding the subconscious girl, but at last he accomplished it. (*Page 6.*)

will be able to return to the land of their sacred ancestors with wealth and position, there to live the lazy days of the lotus eater.

Looey Sing gave them little time to thaw their stiff joints in the rear room. Placing the girl in a chair, he moved over to a corner and rolled away a barrel of flour which stood on end. A small trap-door was disclosed, and this he lifted up. Then he signed to the Celestials, who descended one by one. Looey Sing himself followed.

The cellar beneath proved to be a bare, stone-walled room formed by the foundations of the building. In the centre stood a small stove, and along the sides were ranged several rude benches. It was windowless, and how it received ventilation was a mystery.

Looey Sing pointed to a heap of wood and coal on the floor beside the stove, and then to the benches.

"Remain here until I come, unworthy pigs!" he said gutturally, in Chinese. "There is wood and coal for warmth. There are benches for rest. I will bring food when I come. And, by all your unworthy ancestors, let me hear no sound!"

With that he ascended the stairs again and closed the trapdoor, rolling the barrel of flour back into place. This done, he approached the girl, and drew her chair nearer the fire. Swiftly he moved to the cupboard in the wall and hung up his coat and cap.

After, he drew out several dishes and jars, and set to work to prepare food and drink for the girl. When he had finished, he went over to her and lifted the veil she wore until her features were visible.

The fair promise of her hair was not belied. Her features, were small and perfect, and though she was white as death, cold pallor lent to rather than detracted from the appealing sweetness of the face. Her eyes were closed, but one could imagine them deep blue wells containing all the promise and softness of the morning sky.

Looey Sing wasted no time in surveying her features. He had work to do, and it must be done. It was no easy matter feeding her, but after some time he accomplished it. Then he lifted her up and laid her on a couch, drawing a heavy rug over her.

With a last look around, he closed the door of the store, and departed for the outer shop. There he spread out several rugs on the rude counter, and soon dead silence reigned over the apparently deserted shack of Looey Sing, laundryman and general storekeeper.

§

Twenty-four hours later, when all the Christian world was celebrating the festivities of the Great Day, a long "double-runner" sled drew up in front of Looey Sing's.

Barely had it come to a stop when the door opened, a dark figure shot out and into the dark shelter of its covered top. Another and another followed, until nineteen in all had gone. Then came a twentieth, bearing a burden wrapped in fur.

The burden was placed in the sled, the figure which had borne it spoke a few words to the driver, and the four powerful horses which drew the sled started off on their roundabout journey by lonely country roads to the next stopping-place, which this time would be on the American side.

The door of Looey Sing's shop slammed behind him, and he returned to the rear room, there to sit hunched over the fire, smoking his eternal yellow cigarettes, gazing into the red coals—seeing what pictures, thinking what thoughts, Heaven only knows.

END OF PROLOGUE.

THE STORY.

THE FIRST CHAPTER

CHRISTMAS EVE AT BLAKE'S—KENNEDY FROM THE 'STATES—THE DUCHESS OF CARRISBROOKE—THE HAND OF WU LING.

THE usually austere appearance of Sexton Blake's consulting-room at Baker Street presented a distinctly gala appearance. The desk, the chairs, the table, and even the floor were littered with a varied array of books, leather articles, silver and gold cigarette and cigar-cases (some studded with glittering diamonds or sapphires), and all the thousand and one things which go to make up the Christmas tribute to that difficult individual—a bachelor.

It was Christmas Eve, and the presents had been arriving by post and messengers all day.

Tinker sat half buried under an avalanche in one corner, endeavouring to fit a heavily-studded collar on the disdainful Pedro, who eyed the blaze of the distant fire with a longing eye. Blake himself was seated at his desk, gazing about him with an air of helpless bewilderment.

Each year the same thing happened, and each year he became lost in his own rooms, futilely hoping that something would turn up to prevent the same thing the following year—a something which as yet seemed to successfully evade the harassed bachelor.

Mrs. Bardell boldly declared what he needed was a wife—a nice, homely body who would keep him in order, and with her sewing— But she never got farther than that. Blake always waved her away.

Though only four o'clock in the afternoon, it was already dark and cold outside. A few wet flakes of snow were trying to make a show in the midst of a drizzling rain. Served by the acoustic properties of the street, the constant bleat of motor-horns, and the heavy rumble of 'buses came to them through the fast-closed windows.

Wet or no wet, it was Christmas Eve in London, and Londoners must be served.

Certainly the cosy, though littered, consulting-room was a pleasant retreat on such a day.

Blake had been sunk in reverie, his eyes gazing unseeingly into the mounting flames of the fire. He was roused by Tinker giving up his attempts on the unreciprocative Pedro's neck, and as the lad rolled the dog over and over in a rough-and-tumble, Blake turned back to his desk with the faintest of sighs.

What had caused the touch of sadness in his thoughts it is hard to say. Perhaps he was thinking of the misery which must exist even at such a time when goodwill reigns supreme; perhaps he was thinking of the past, and of some happy moment now gone for ever; perhaps he was thinking that, with all his work and all his interests, even with Tinker and Pedro he was just a trifle lonely.

Whatever it was, he cast it from his mind, and an introspective smile crossed his face as he picked up the pile of cards which lay on the desk before him.

They were cards of good wishes and seasonable greetings from every part of the globe, and had Blake cared to speak, he could have told you that almost all of them had their inception in some past deed which he had performed for the sender.

What a volume of memoirs they would have made!

There were cards from Japan, China, and the mountain-girded Tibet; cards from Honolulu, Fiji, and Easter Island; cards from Australia, New Zealand, and one even from an expedition in the Antarctic; cards from South Africa, Mombassa, Khartoum, and Timbuctu; from South America, Mexico, and the West Indies; cards from the United States, Canada, and Labrador; an avalanche from the British Isles, and a towering pile from every country in Europe, most of which bore a coronet.

What stirring moments they recalled; what deep currents of plot and intrigue and crime; what potential forces brought clashing together in terrific collision and mortal combat; what depths of smiles and tears—of joy and of sorrow!

Tinker, having finished his impromptu struggle with Pedro, in which the bloodhound got the worst of it, for the simple reason that he was too lazy to struggle, looked up from where he sat on the prostrate animal.

"I say, guv'nor!" he said, "this is a bit of all right, isn't it? No case for two days, and it looks as though we would eat the old gobbler in peace to-morrow."

"I hope so," smiled Blake absently. "A little spell of idleness at this time of the year will do us both good. By the way, if you will go to your room and look on the table, you will find a trifling remembrance which I got for you."

Tinker grinned with a strange shyness.

"If you will make the same journey to your room, you will find something on the table, too," he said, as he rose.

Blake smiled and stood up.

"All right, my lad, we will both go and see what inspiration we received."

They departed, each his different way—Tinker along the corridor to his room, which was next to the laboratory, and Blake through the dressing-room, which led off from the consulting-room. Less than a minute later they both returned. Blake's smile had widened, and Tinker was in convulsions.

In their hands each held a large Morocco leather case containing a silver-mounted Colt's automatic revolver of exactly the same calibre.

"Well, if this isn't about the limit," stuttered Tinker, when he succeeded in getting his breath. "I got one for you and you got one for me. I gave you one because I heard you say the trigger, of your old one was wearing a bit."

"And I yours, my lad, because you lost your own the last time we were in South America, and I knew you hated that old six-shooter you carry. Never mind, as it happened, we both got what we needed and would put off buying through hating to break in a new gun."

Simultaneously they both took the revolvers from the cases, and worked the ejectors with experienced fingers. While they were so engaged, a knock came at the door, and Mrs. Bardell entered to announce a visitor. Blake frowned impatiently, and was on the point of telling her he could see no one, when the caller himself appeared in the door. The frown left Blake's face instantly, as he recognised who it was, and Tinker grinned in welcome.

"Well, well, Mr. Kennedy come in," said Blake cordially, as he advanced and held out his hand. "It is a surprise to see you in London at this time of the year."

The man addressed as Kennedy strode into the room, and shook hands first with Blake and then with Tinker. He was a man of medium size, a trifle stocky in build. His chin was clean-shaven, and a close-cropped sandy moustache hid his mouth. His nose was big and straight, his eyes keen and humorous. A pleasing personality altogether, and the last man one would pick as the most brilliant private detective in the United States.

"You can just bet I wouldn't be here if it wasn't necessary," he laughed, taking the seat Blake indicated. "Great Scott! You are upset here. All this array would make a tempting haul, Mr. Blake."

Blake opened a box of cigars and passed it over. "To tell you the truth, I don't know what to do with the stuff," he said. "I am seriously thinking of starting an anti-Christmas present league, with myself as president."

"Yes," put in Tinker, "and he's the worst of the lot himself. We have despatched enough merchandise from here this week to stock a good sized general store."

After a few more light remarks, in which the joke of the revolvers was explained to the appreciative American, Blake glanced at his visitor quizzically.

"Did you come to get any information?" he asked.

"Well, not exactly that," answered Kennedy. "To tell you the truth, I came for a bit more. I want your co-operation in a case on which I am working. I have been digging into a certain matter for well over six months now, and honestly, I am up against a brick wall as solid as the Gizeh pyramid."

Blake knit his brows.

"Six months," he said reminiscently. "I don't seem to recall any big crime which took place in New York six months ago."

"And you wouldn't, for the simple reason that everything has been kept mum," answered Kennedy." It isn't a crime, strictly speaking. It is a colossal fraud, and I have been retained by the Secret Service Department to ferret out matters. I have come over here, because I feel that the affair has its inception on this side. The finished perfection of its operation proves that."

"I am afraid I don't understand."

"You will in a few minutes, if you say you will join me."

"As a matter of fact, I had intended taking nothing on until the New Year. My own affairs have been sadly neglected of late, and coming on the end of the year, I should like to get everything fixed up. However, if it is a matter of exceptional interest professionally, I don't mind considering it."

"I guess you will find it interesting enough from a professional point of view," remarked Kennedy. "At any rate, I will run my chances and tell you the details. I will give them to you exactly as they were handed to me; then, if you are interested, I will give you an outline of everything I have done during the past six months."

Blake nodded.

"Very well," he said quietly. "I can at least promise you my closest attention."

Tinker drew closer in order to hear, and after deliberately knocking the ash from his cigar, Kennedy began:

"I was in Washington," he said, "just a little over six months ago, when I received a wire from the head of the Secret Service Department in New York to come on at once in order to take up a special case. I turned over the work I was on to an assistant, and caught the train that same night. I reached New York at ten o'clock, and at ten-fifteen was closeted with the chief.

"You will recall that just over a year ago, there was a big shake up in the Customs and Immigration services at New York and Boston, and as a result, the inspection became of a much more rigorous nature than it had been previously. Though the reason was not made public, the shake up occurred owing to the fact, that large numbers of Chinese were slipping into the country by way of those two ports.

"Of course, we know a good few get in over the Mexican and Western Canadian borders, but only bribery could get them in through ports like New York and Boston. After six months it was found that, regardless of the care taken at those two ports, the Chinese colony in each was increasing.

"A thorough investigation proved conclusively that they were not getting in by either of them. The question was how was it being worked? That was when they sent for me. Now, Mr. Blake, if you are interested in the subject, I will tell you what I have done."

"By all means proceed," said Blake. "I am always interested in matters Celestial."

"Well, as soon as I was in possession of all the facts the chief could give me, I went along to my hotel and got out a map. I guess I studied that in detail until daybreak, trying to put my finger on the weak spot. I couldn't seem to locate it, however, and the next day decided to try a bit of quiet detective work.

"I got myself appointed as Special Immigration Officer with unfettered authority and a roving commission.

"The first place I made for was New Orleans. I put in a fortnight there; then I moved on to Mobile. In that way I worked up along the coast, putting in a week or a fortnight at each port, as the case seemed to warrant. I hit on a few curious things, but had worked clear up to New York without hitting a single thing that said 'Chink.'

"I put in a solid month in New York, and from there went to Boston. Nothing doing. On to Portland, Bangor and Machias—still nothing doing. From Machias I moved on to Eastport, and from there up the St. Croix River to Calais. And though I know, as sure as I am sitting here,

that the game is being worked through some point at which I touched, I struck not the faintest sign of what I was after. I was in a quandary for fair.

"That was a month ago, and I then decided to try Canada. I got back into civilian clothes and crossed the border. I mixed with all classes, and must say the officials on that side gave me all the aid in their power. Finally, I decided that whether the Chinese were coming direct from the sea through one of our ports, or whether they were getting in via Canada, the starting point of the system was on this side. I wired the chief I was coming over, and here I am."

"How about the six months during which you have been working on the matter?" asked Blake. "Has the influx stopped at all?"

"Not on your life. Why hang it, it has increased if anything."

"H'm! They seem to have hit on a pretty clever system in order to defy the law, under your very nose."

"That is exactly what has put me on my mettle. I have shelved everything else, and I vow I will not touch another case until I unravel this riddle. At the same time, I want your help if you will give it to me."

"I must confess the affair interests me keenly," rejoined Blake slowly. "It just happens, that for some time past I have been up against a Chinese organisation myself, and although I had an intimate knowledge of that subtle race before, I have certainly learned a good many new facts concerning them. If you think my assistance will be of value to you—why I don't mind joining you."

"Put it there," cried the American, thrusting out his hand. "You have sure taken a big weight off my mind. You know all the wrinkles on this side of the pond, and if that yellow riddle has its inception here, between us we ought to hit it."

Blake smiled as he shook hands; then he grew grave again.

"Have you no clue of any description?"

"Absolutely none. I tell you, Mr. Blake, it is as though they dropped from the sky. In fact, I even went so deep into the matter as to seriously consider the theory that they might be coming over by aeroplane, but a thorough investigation made that end in smoke. They are getting in regularly, and once they reach the security of the big Chinese colony in any of the large cities, it is hopeless to dislodge them. That is all I know."

"It is certainly a matter which will require a good deal of thought before we make a move over here," remarked Blake. "I think, however, if there is anything like that having its genesis here, we will eventually discover it. I have a most intimate acquaintance with the haunts and habits of the Chinese in this metropolis. For my part, I hardly think we shall find what we seek in London, however.

"For one reason, my own investigations have taken me through Limehouse a good deal lately, and I must surely have discovered some trace of what you mention, had it existed. The biggest proof of such a thing is the crowd which patronises the different opium and gambling dens. If these crowds keep changing all the time, it is safe to assume that something is going on; but if one sees the same faces week after week, it is a safe bet that their operations are being carried on locally. And for some time past the latter has been the case here.

"No, Mr. Kennedy, in my opinion, if the beginning of the system is in England, we stand much more chance of striking something suspicious in places such as Cardiff or Liverpool than in London. Please understand that is purely a tentative theory, and is subject to correction."

The American had followed Blake's every word with the closest attention. When the latter had finished Kennedy spoke quickly.

"By ginger! Your argument is sound, Mr. Blake. Now I had the idea that the game started here in London, but the more I think of it the more I am inclined to agree with you. Cardiff and Liverpool both have big Chinese districts, I know, and from what I have heard, they are pretty tough, too."

"They are not as bad as the river front of Canton or the water stretches of Shanghai," answered Blake; "but I assure you they are quite odious enough for this country. I am sorry I cannot go into the matter further with you to-day, Mr. Kennedy, but I have an appointment for dinner this evening. However, I should be very glad to see you to-morrow morning, and then we can discuss things as well as arrange a plan of campaign. Besides, I should like to turn the matter over in my mind to-night. Something might occur to me."

"By all means do so, Mr. Blake," replied the other rising. "I myself am due to dine out to-night. How will ten o'clock in the morning suit you? I feel guilty, I assure you, breaking up your Christmas in this manner."

"Oh, that is all right!" smiled Blake, getting to his feet. "Ten o'clock in the morning will suit me excellently. Tinker, just jot that appointment down."

When Kennedy had departed, Blake returned to the desk, and was just about to sit down, when Mrs. Bardell again entered, and informed him that a lady wished to see him. The frown of irritation again furrowed Blake's brow, but he curtly bade the housekeeper to show her in.

He sat impatiently tapping the desk with the end of a pencil, and so silently did the visitor enter, that not until Tinker coughed, did Blake become aware that she was in the room.

As his eyes rested on her face, he rose at once, and bowed.

"Won't you sit down?" he said quietly.

As the woman inclined her head, and walked across the room, it was easy to see what had inspired the gentle quietude of Blake's tone. She was a tall, well proportioned woman, of middle age, or more. Her simple, though rich, costume of black, topped by a small delicately-turned hat, spoke of taste, and the means to gratify it.

Her carriage was perfect, and her clear-cut features were those of a woman who must have ranked as a noted beauty in her younger days. Her head was poised on her shoulders with a dignity almost akin to haughtiness; her whole bearing was proud and reserved.

In her eyes, however, Blake's keen gaze had read deep tragedy, and from his knowledge of human nature he knew only too well how serious it must be to make a woman of her stamp confide in an outsider, even though that outsider were Blake.

A glance sent Tinker out of the room, and when the door had closed softly behind him, Blake turned to his visitor.

"You wished to see me upon some matter?" he asked gravely.

His visitor bowed her head.

"You are Mr. Blake?"

"Yes."

"I will first tell you who I am," she went on.

As she spoke, she passed over a card to Blake, and his eyes widened the barest trifle as he read the name engraved upon it. It was: "The Duchess of Carrisbrooke."

It must indeed be a matter of urgency to send her Grace to see him on Christmas Eve of all times.

Blake laid the card on his desk, and glanced up. "I judge that you are in a difficulty of some description," he said quietly.

"If it is my advice you have come to seek, I am at your service."

The woman studied him for a few minutes in silence; then she leaned forward.

"Mr. Blake, I do not know you, but I come to you at the instigation of my husband. He has told me that not only are you an investigator of crimes and mysteries, but that you are a chivalrous gentleman as well."

Blake bowed, but made no reply.

"For that reason," continued the duchess, "I have come to confide in you, and tell you what has caused both the duke and myself the greatest anxiety during the past fortnight."

Blake held up his hand.

"Pardon me, your Grace. Before you confide in me, I should like to say something."

"By all means do so."

"It is this. What your trouble is I have not the faintest idea, but if I am to listen to you, and give you the benefit of any experience I may have, I must insist upon absolute frankness on your part. Only by receiving your full confidence, can I be of use to you."

"It is hard to tell you everything, Mr. Blake, but I promise you I shall reserve nothing."

"Then I am quite ready," responded Blake.

"To begin with, Mr. Blake," said the duchess, "You may know of the famous Carrisbrooke pride, and how it causes any member of the family to flinch from publicity. Two weeks ago something occurred which upset us dreadfully, but for a solid fortnight we have carried on the investigation ourselves, owing to our desire to keep it from the public. That occurrence happened while we were in Cardiff.

"At that time, my husband, my daughter, and myself went to Cardiff, where my husband was to attend a directors' meeting of which he was chairman. We stayed at the Hotel North, where we always put up when there. On our very first evening there, I had a frightful headache, and retired to my room about seven in the evening.

My husband and daughter went down to dinner alone.

"After dinner, my daughter ran up and kissed me good-bye, saying she was going to walk along with her father to the offices where he was to attend a meeting that evening. As it was less than three blocks from the hotel, I did not feel nervous about her returning alone, for she had done the same thing scores of times.

"As the evening passed on, and she did not return, I began to feel a trifle worried, but felt satisfied she had remained there, intending not to return until her father did.

"About half past nine I dozed off, and did not waken until I heard my husband in his room, which adjoined mine. I called to him, and he came in at once. I asked him why Sybil had not come in to see me before going to her room. He looked at me in surprise, and said he had no idea, that he hadn't seen her since she left him at the offices about a quarter past eight.

"It took us about ten minutes to discover the drift of each others remarks, but when we did, it began to dawn upon us that I had seen nothing of her since just before dinner, and that he had not since a little after eight. At my request, he rang for my daughter's maid. When she appeared, I questioned her, but she said positively she had not seen her mistress since she had dressed for dinner. She thought, as I did, that she was with her father.

"By then we were terribly anxious, but it seemed that she must be about the hotel. I sent the maid down to the office to search the lounge and writing-room, but there were no traces of her. I myself went to her room, but met with the same result there. My husband had also gone to the office, and as discreetly as possible was prosecuting further inquiries there. The commissionaire at the door stated positively that he remembered her going out with the duke, but that she had not come in since. He was on duty all the evening, and must have seen her had she done so. I was nearly frantic.

"My husband got on the 'phone, and called up his fellow directors. They came round at once, and after binding them to secrecy, he told them what had occurred. A search party was organised at once. All night until daybreak they scoured the city, but without result. It was only too evident now that something of a serious nature had happened.

"It was when they were returning at dawn that the first and only clue was found. It was between the offices and the hotel, that one of the search party found a soiled white, evening glove in the gutter. I recognised it instantly as one my daughter had worn. This proved she had come back that way after leaving her father, but she had never reached the hotel.

"Since then, we have been working day and night. Our most trusted friends have assisted us, and the search has been carried on, not only in Cardiff, but in Liverpool, London, and half-a-dozen other places. The police have been searching also with a full description of her, but they have discovered nothing. In addition we have advertised in every English and Continental paper offering a reward of fifty thousand pounds for her safe return. But each channel has led to a blank wall.

"From that day to this, we have seen nothing of her, and heard nothing of her, with the exception of the finding of her glove. My husband would have come, but he has broken down, and was compelled to take to his bed.

"That, Mr. Blake, is the story, without any reservations of any description whatever. It is needless for me to say if you can be of any assistance to me, you will find my gratitude of a deep nature."

Blake had listened to her story with the closest attention. It had been easy enough to see that each word was a stab of agony to the proud woman, but her mother-love had overcome her dread of the conventions, and now, even if publicity were demanded, in order to get back her daughter, she would face it with a brave face, though her heart might crumple up from the arrows of a harsh world, which is prone to revel in the troubles of their fellows.

For a matter of two minutes, Blake sat turning over in his mind the story she had told him; then he leaned back.

"I remember reading the advertisements which you placed in the papers," he said quietly. "Pardon me, but I suppose your daughter was in love with no one of whom you and your husband did not approve?"

"No—decidedly not. She had never been troubled by her affections. If she had, I must have known, for she was perfectly frank with me in every way."

"Of course," went on Blake, determined to probe each point to the bottom, "in a case of this kind, your Grace, we must not look for a clue only in the present, but examine past events as well. Therein we may discover some apparently trivial thing, which, on analysis, will prove to be the keynote of the mystery. I do not say this is invariably the case, but it is more often so than not. For that reason, I am going to ask you to give me in a very few words a resume of your daughter's life during, say, the past four years. By the way, how old is she?"

"She is just twenty. Four years ago when she was sixteen, she went to Paris, to the same school which I attended when a girl. Then she returned to London, and made her début, being presented at Court that year. That season we spent in town. From there we went to Cowes, and from Cowes to our Scottish estates for the shooting. The winter we spent at Nice, and in the spring spent a month in Paris before returning to London.

"On our return, my husband was given a diplomatic mission to China, and it was decided that my daughter and myself should go with him. That was a year ago. We went through to Hong Kong, and from there to Pekin. For three months we stayed in Pekin, and only reached England in July, as we had loitered in Ceylon on the way back. Then we went to Scotland, and from there to Cardiff, where she disappeared."

"And in all that period of time—think very carefully, please—there was nothing of any description whatever which brought your daughter before your immediate horizon more than usual?"

The duchess, knit her brows, and studied the carpet.

"I shall endeavour to think if there was," she said.

Blake did not hurry her, and not for several minutes did she look up.

"I have gone over the whole four years, Mr. Blake, and beyond one little thing which occurred, I can think of nothing. Moreover, this occurrence, in a way, had nothing to do with my daughter—that is to say, it was not of her making."

"Ah! I should be glad to hear what it was if you don't mind," said Blake imperturbably.

"It was while we were in Pekin. There, owing to the diplomatic nature of my husband's business, we had to entertain and be entertained by a good many of the native Chinese government officials.

"When we had been in Pekin about a month, my daughter complained that one of them—a Dr. Li-Fuang—had made himself obnoxious to her by attempting to pay her some attention. Not caring to have any unpleasantness, we simply arranged that she should attend no more dinners or entertainments. She spoke once afterwards of having met him in the gardens, and though he had been the model of politeness, she said she was frightened of him. After that, she did not mention the matter again for the reason, I imagine, that she did not meet him.

"That is the only occurrence during the past four years which could be classed as abnormal, and even that is a mere trifle. If you had not seemed to attach such importance to even a trivial matter, I do not know that I ever should have recalled it again."

Blake drew a pad of paper towards him without replying. Picking up a pencil, he jotted down a few notes over which he pondered for some time, while his visitor watched him anxiously.

Finally, he looked up.

"I must confess there seems little during the past four years upon which to build," he said briefly. "At the same time, every item is of value, and if that is all we can only govern ourselves accordingly. I don't mind saying, your Grace, that from a professional point of view, the case presents many difficulties, caused chiefly, by your delay in coming to me. You can rest assured that if your daughter was kidnapped by force, there is a daring brain behind it all, for the average man would think twice before striking so high.

"Of course, it may be that her kidnappers had no idea of her identity, but I do not think that is the case. Were it so, it would mean only another case of a young girl disappearing into the maw of those creatures who prey upon society, and not one of them exists, but would jump at the chances to return her for the enormous reward offered, particularly since you specified that no questions would be asked. No, it seems to point to a certain knowledge on the part of the abductors. At first, I was inclined to think the contrary, but we have had visible proof that even fifty thousand would not tempt them.

"That means it is your daughter whom they want—not money. That being so, there must be a powerful motive behind it all. Once we get our fingers on that it will not be hard to trace the perpetrators, for the motive of any given deed, if strong enough, inevitably points to the perpetrators of the deed, no matter how skilful they may be in covering their tracks.

"In a matter of this description the police are useless during the earlier stages of the investigation. Owing to the great lapse of time which has taken place between her disappearance and your coming to me many of the clues which then existed are certain to be obliterated by now. However, so strong is the evidence of great motive that something may still remain from which a start may be made.

"It just happens that I am entering upon a case which in a remote way runs parallel to this affair, for the points of investigation begin at the same places where your case must be taken up. Owing to that fact, I am prepared to accept your commission, and do what I can towards recovering your daughter, though, mind you, I do not want you to build too much on my ability to do so.

"That is all I can say at present, your Grace. Needless to say, you have my profound sympathy in your trouble, and I can promise you no pains shall be spared to return her to you safe and sound."

The duchess breathed deeply and held out her hand. The cold repression of the face had gone down before the swelling sorrow of the mother, and the fine eyes were drenched with unshed tears.

"How can I thank you, Mr. Blake?" she said chokingly. "She—Sybil—is every thing in the world to her father and me. Her strange disappearance has driven me nearly frantic, and my husband, though he tries to keep up before me, is slowly breaking under the suspense and anxiety."

Blake pressed her hand sympathetically. He made no reply, knowing silence under the circumstances was best.

As the duchess rose to depart she again held out her hand.

Facing as she was, her eyes rested on the desk, from which Blake had also risen. Grasping her fingers, he was about to make some sympathetic remark, when a wide look of utter incredulity in her eyes caused him to turn and follow her gaze to where it rested on the desk. Unconsciously, he was still holding her hand.

As for the duchess, she seemed utterly oblivious of the present, and in this fashion they both looked at the same object.

In itself the thing at which they gazed was not out of the ordinary. It was a small framed sketch of a head done in bold, heavy lines. As a work of art, it had perhaps no particular merit; but as a study in the utter impassivity of which the human mask is capable it was a masterpiece. Barely a dozen lines were there in all, but the bold, heavy sweep of the few which existed portrayed the full face of a Celestial.

His forehead was high and noble; the eyes, slant-set wells of inscrutable wisdom; the nose almost European in the thin, aristocratic turn of the nostrils; the mouth a paradoxical mixture of kindliness and cruelty, of decision and indulgence, the chin bold and obstinate; the head a masterpiece from a master mould.

It was the head of the thinker, the student, the leader, the unyielding dictator, and yet the head of the noble, the aristocrat, and the kindly homemaker.

To Blake it was the head of one of the strongest men against whom he had ever been pitted, the head of a fanatic to whom life was of no real value, and yet the head of a man honest in his purpose; the head of Wu Ling, Prince of the Royal blood of China, descendant of the ancient and noble Ming Dynasty, one time claimant to the Chinese throne, privileged wearer of the Royal saffron, and present head of that colossal organisation which was the greatest menace the white races had ever known—the Brotherhood of the Yellow Beetle.

Somewhat surprised at the interest of the duchess in the picture, he turned and faced her, only to find her eyes meeting his.

"Where—where did you get that picture, Mr. Blake?" she asked hesitatingly.

"That?" he returned lightly. "I sketched that myself from memory, your Grace. It is the face of a man against whom I have been pitted on several occasions, and, I might add, the face of one of the ablest men living to-day."

She nodded slowly.

"I—I know him, Mr. Blake."

"You know him?" he echoed, in surprise.

"Yes. It is Dr. Li-Fuang, whom we met in Pekin."

"Impossible!" exclaimed Blake, knitting his brows. "His name is Wu Ling—Prince Wu Ling. He is one of the few privileged wearers of the yellow."

"Then I am doubly sure, Mr. Blake, for once— only once— when my husband and I entertained a small party of Chinese of high rank, Dr. Li-Fuang wore a yellow tunic."

Blake bent forward suddenly.

"Tell me, your grace, did you notice his hands?"

"Yes."

"And on them did you see a large yellow topaz of a particularly deep colour?"

"I did, for the simple reason that it is so noticeable."

"Then it is, indeed, Wu Ling," muttered Blake, dropping her hand, and beginning to pace up and down the room. "This coincidence is more than important, your Grace. It has caused a seemingly trivial occurrence which happened to your daughter in Pekin to assume proportions of the greatest magnitude in reference to her disappearance. Is it possible—is it possible that he is the man? No—no, I can't believe it, and yet—"

Still muttering to himself, he swung sharply round, and came to a stop before her.

"This discovery, your Grace, has started an entirely fresh trend of thought in my mind. If, on consideration, it proves to be of the nature I think, then, indeed, is the case a difficult one. If Wu Ling and Dr. Li-Fuang are one and the same, and I must confess it seems so—then I shall need all my resources, physical and mental, to ferret out the truth of the problem. If he is, then the abduction of your daughter has some deeper purpose than mere possession. It would mean that she was intended as a hostage, or there—"

Blake paused, for he did not care to voice the thought which came to him—namely, that she might well be intended as the wife of one of Wu Ling's numerous lieutenants, who had seen her and admired her, and for whom Wu Ling had pulled one of the numerous strings he possessed in order to secure her.

His own obnoxious attentions to her in Pekin might have been only an attempt to worm himself into her confidence in order to pump her regarding the true nature of the duke's diplomatic mission, for Wu Ling was a man who believed in knowing the other man's hand before he laid any of his own cards on the table.

Of one thing Blake was certain. He knew Wu Ling, did not wish her for himself. The prince's nature was too cold and austere for that.

So exercised was Blake over the discovery, and so anxious was he to devote his mind to the contemplation and analysis of the different points presented, that he made his adieus to the duchess as brief as possible, promising her that he would communicate with her on the morrow.

When she was gone he called Tinker, and ordered the lad to get down the Index. That done, he sat down and rapped out:

"Get me also my tabular analysis of the 'Mysterious Disappearances of Young Girls' during the past twelve months. Turn up the section dealing with Continental and eastern traffic."

Tinker obeyed at once, and for a solid hour Blake pored over a mass of facts and figures which he had compiled from cases of his own, as well as from information furnished him by his friend Inspector Thomas, of Scotland Yard.

At the end of that time he pushed the book from him and rose.

"Seven o'clock, my lad. Just time to dress if we are to keep our appointment to dine with Mademoiselle Yvonne at eight."

THE SECOND CHAPTER

THE DINNER AT YVONNE'S—BILLIARDS—
BLAKE TELLS YVONNE ABOUT THE TWO
CASES—YVONNE DECIDES TO HELP—IN
CARDIFF.

BLAKE and Tinker, with Pedro at their heels, left the Baker Street apartments at ten minutes to eight sharp.

The chauffeur, who was rarely used by either of them, was at the kerb in the big grey car, and, in view of the rain and snow which still fell, the top had been drawn over and the side curtains lowered.

Blake ordered the man to drive to an address at Queen Anne's Gate, and sank back in silence, still pondering on the remarkable facts which had come to his notice that day.

Mademoiselle Yvonne had been living at Queen Anne's Gate ever since the memorable affair of "The Mystery of Walla-Walla."

How she met and yielded to Blake's conditions at that time will be recalled by those who followed the case. Since then she and her uncle (Graves) had been living quietly, and a pleasant intimacy had grown up between them and Baker Street.

True, she had more than once been on the wrong side of the strict demands of the law, and more than once Blake had been forced to stretch out a stern hand in order to curb her intentions.

From time to time he had attempted to impress ideas of conformity with the law upon the quixotic girl; but her laughing eyes had only met his with a provoking inattention which had routed all his well-marshalled arguments.

For the time being he rested content in the strangely happy moments he passed there, and, though he did not attempt to analyse the reason, he knew in his heart that did his visits

stop for any reason it would mean something big going out of his life.

Tinker had become almost as frequent a visitor as Blake, and as for Pedro—well, the heavily-studded collar, which in the afternoon he had pretended to hold in contempt, and which now he wore with every evidence of pride, had been Yvonne's Christmas gift to the big fellow.

Even in the early days of her remarkable career, when the world, not knowing of the deep motive which had inspired her outrages on society, called her an adventuress, Pedro and she had always been warm friends.

If she still entertained the same deep love for Blake she managed to conceal it from him; but at night, in the privacy of her own room, where the mask of convention was dropped, the sketch of the detective, which hung on the wall, looked down on many hours of suffering as she lay with wide eyes staring into the darkness, thinking of what she felt was a losing battle, the while she held close to her lips the little miniature of Blake, which always hung from her warm throat.

For Yvonne's nature was not that which changed or forgot, and, above all, it was not the nature which gave up hope. Had it been, she must long ere this have slipped quietly out of Blake's life never to reappear in it.

She met them in the hall as they were ushered in, and the warm clasp which passed between her and Blake told of the pure feeling which existed between them, in spite of the deeper things which were held in leash.

After greeting Blake, she turned to Tinker, and both astonished and caused to blush that usually self-possessed lad by placing her arm over his shoulder and wishing him a happy, happy Christmas.

Pedro was compelled to promenade before her with slow dignity, the while the collar was examined by her critical eyes.

At that moment Graves appeared, and the whole party moved on into the library, where the butler served cocktails for Blake, Graves, and Yvonne, and a syrup for Tinker.

Punctually on the minute they went in to dinner. The meal itself was not unlike any other Christmas Eve feast among intimate friends, though perhaps the undoubted force of the individuality of Blake and Yvonne lent an element to the occasion which was lacking in the average gathering.

Grave, sober, and almost curt in his profession, Blake was an admirable dinner companion. His repartee was pointed and brilliant, his fund of small talk inexhaustible, his change of subject sparkling, and as finished as the rapid play of a rapier.

Yvonne was particularly dazzling on this night. She was dressed in a delicate shade of green, with the unmistakable stamp of Paris about it, from the low-cut neck of which her white throat rose like a column of alabaster.

Her bronze-gold hair was dressed low on her head, and fashioned in heavy coils held together by two jewelled clasps. A thin gold chain about her neck guarded a great emerald, which gleamed startlingly deep against her white skin, and on her left hand she wore one ring—an emerald solitaire.

The big stone suspended from the chain at her throat had been Blake's gift to her in the stormy past, and a thin platinum chain, which disappeared beneath her corsage, was mute evidence of the invisible miniature from which she was never parted.

Course after course appeared, and was taken away. As a seasonable banquet it was a huge success, as a product of the culinary art it was a masterpiece.

When the servants had withdrawn, and the decanter was being eyed by Graves with a longing gaze, Yvonne rose and got a small gold cigarette-case filled with her own special brand of Russian cigarettes.

Blake accepted the case Graves pushed over, and for a short space of time they smoked and chatted quietly. Then Graves got to his feet and suggested that Tinker should play him a hundred up in the billiard-room. The lad jumped up with alacrity, and they passed out, leaving Blake and Yvonne alone.

For almost five minutes silence reigned between them; then Yvonne spoke.

"I have been wondering if you would be able to find the time to go for a very short cruise in the Fleur-de-Lys as far as Tunis and back," she said, with a tentative look at Blake.

"It is most awfully kind of you to invite me," answered Blake, warmly, "and I assure you I should like nothing better. If you had asked me last night, or even this morning, I think I should have said 'Yes' without hesitation; but since then I have accepted two commissions which promise to take all that time and resources I have."

"Are they of such a nature that they cannot be put off?"

"I am sorry to say they are. One of them is of a particularly urgent description."

"I am sorry. My uncle and I would have enjoyed having you and Tinker immensely."

"You will go yourself in any event, I presume?" remarked Blake.

Yvonne shrugged her white shoulders.

"It is indefinite as yet. This rain and snow are depressing, and I thought a change would be pleasant."

"I have been racking my brains over something for the past two hours," went on Blake, "and it has just occurred to me that perhaps you might help me out. It would not interfere with your proposed trip, but if you consented, I should like to keep in touch with you, in order to let you know if I needed your help."

"I should be only too delighted," answered Yvonne quickly. "What is the nature of it?"

"It is a case where I may need the presence of a woman in order to look after a young girl. The whole thing rests on whether I am successful or unsuccessful in my quest."

"If that is the case, then I am sure you will need me," said Yvonne softly.

"I am afraid you entertain too high an opinion of my abilities," laughed Blake, with a faint tinge of embarrassment.

"That is not very flattering to my own poor accomplishments," she smiled, with a reminiscent look in her eyes.

"Oh, I didn't mean it that way!" protested Blake. "But to return to the subject of which we were speaking, mademoiselle. Perhaps you would care to hear the facts, since you may be called upon to join in the affair."

"I should be very proud of the confidence."

"I suppose in reading the papers you have noticed the announcement of an exceptionally large reward in the 'Personal Columns'?"

"Fifty thousand, isn't it?"

"Yes."

"Oh, yes, I have seen it for several days running. The description follows of a young girl who is missing. It occurred to me as I read it that she must belong to a wealthy family. I put it down to an elopement with an undesirable suitor."

"That is the explanation which would naturally strike one," responded Blake. "It happens, however, that such is not the case. She has been missing for a matter of two weeks, but only to-day was the matter placed in my hands. It is on account of the great lapse of time that I feel dubious regarding the success of my investigations. But if you care to hear the facts, I will relate them. Needless to say, it is a case for the observance of strict secrecy."

Yvonne lighted a fresh cigarette, and leaned forward, her eyes resting on Blake's.

"Whether or not I can be of assistance in the matter, you know I will respect your confidence."

Blake lighted a cigar, and puffed for a few moments in silence. Then he began.

First he dealt with the visit of the duchess that afternoon, and with the very distinct signs of suffering she evinced. From that he went to the kernel of the subject, and related in detail all she had told him. After that he spoke of the startling coincidence of his sketch of Wu Ling with Dr. Li-Fuang, and of the suspicions such a coincidence had roused in his mind.

Yvonne knew only too well the calibre of Wu Ling, for she had been of no small help to Blake at the time Wu Ling had abducted John Strang, the American multi-millionaire, and she herself

had suffered at the hands of the prince. Consequently, she followed Blake's every word with an added interest, and when he finished her lids drooped over her eyes in concentration.

"It is your idea, then, that the daughter of the Duchess of Carrisbrooke has fallen into the hands of Wu Ling?"

"I wouldn't go as far as to say that," responded Blake. "At the same time, it strikes me that it is the girl herself who is wanted. No organisation or individual to whom she was simply worth the price of a human being would be able to resist the enormous reward offered. Of course, Wu Ling's likeness to Dr. Li-Fuang, and his possible identity with that individual, is little to build on at present.

"Most Chinamen look alike to the inexperienced European, as do Europeans to the untravelled Celestial, and it is just possible a certain similarity in the features of Wu Ling to those of Dr. Li-Fuang may have caused the duchess to think it was the doctor. I include those points in my deduction, but the whole structure is of the most unreliable nature so far."

"I judged from what you said that you will go on to Cardiff?"

"Yes. It happens that another case upon which I have entered will take me there and probably to Liverpool as well. Oddly enough it also deals with the Chinese, and even before I had heard the story of the duchess I had decided to go to those places. In any event the beginning of the trail lies in Cardiff.

"If the latter is the case it is more than likely that one of the numerous Chinese secret societies, or 'tongs' has been used as the instrument for her capture and to send her out of the country. They have many devious and secret ways, and who knows, the two roads, apparently so widely divergent, may lead to the same spot in the investigation."

"When will you leave?"

"I have an appointment at ten to-morrow with Kennedy, the American Secret Service man, who has sought my assistance."

After I have discussed the details with him, I may decide to go on to Cardiff in the afternoon. I shall leave in any event not later than the following morning. Too much valuable time has already been lost. So you see, mademoiselle, why I may need your assistance.

"I am sorry, mademoiselle, but I cannot permit it. You might fall into their clutches yourself, and—well, I——, I——" For once in his life, Blake was at a loss for words.

"Into whatsoever hands the Lady Sybil has fallen, she will be in a state of collapse, and will need a cool, sympathetic friend of her own sex to tide her over the reaction. Her own mother would be the worst person in the world for the case, for she would dwell on what had occurred, and that would be bad. Now, can I count on you?"

"You know you can, Mr. Blake," answered Yvonne quickly, "No matter where I am, or what I am doing, I will drop anything, and come out at once as soon as I hear from you. It makes no difference where you wish me to go, or what you wish me to do, I am ready."

"Thank you very much indeed," said Blake, holding out his hand. "I knew I could depend on you."

Yvonne looked at him with a hint of pleading in her eyes.

"Won't you let me help you, anyway? You know my feelings regarding these vampires who cause so much misery to my sex. In order to overcome them and sweep them out of existence one cannot overlook the bald facts or wear gloves in one's treatment of them. I should, do everything you said, and perhaps I, as a woman, could discover some of the channels along which so many young girls disappear, in

many cases to be kidnapped abroad and married against their wills to wealthy foreigners, where a man, no matter how clever he might be, would fail. Who knows this case might be the means of uncovering a gigantic system."

Blake shook his head and smiled.

"I am sorry, mademoiselle, but I cannot permit it. I have no misgivings as to the thoroughness with which you would do your work, and I would more than back your brains against those of the people we are after; but such a thing as you suggest is fraught with too much danger to you. You might fall into their clutches yourself, and—well, mademoiselle, I—I—"

And for once in his life Blake was at a loss for something to say. Yvonne's heart contracted with a wild, exquisite pain as Blake's halting words told her that her disappearance would mean a big thing to him, and her eyes grew very soft.

All unconsciously, Blake's reasons for not accepting the offer of her services had started a vague train of thought in Yvonne's mind, and had he only dreamed what it was he would then and there have exacted her solemn promise not to participate in the affair until he sent for her.

Unfortunately, he had no idea of this, and so a tiny idea was formed in Yvonne's mind which was to lead her into the jaws of the System, and to show her the hideous depths of misery which it caused. The same idea was to send Blake into an agony of self-reproach that he had not exacted the promise, and a deadly fear for the safety of the wilful, quixotic girl, who held a bigger place in his affections than he would acknowledge even to himself.

The silence which had fallen upon them was broken by the entrance of Graves and the jubilant Tinker, who had beaten the older man in three straight games.

"Tinker simply played rings around me," grumbled Graves, lighting a cigarette. "I couldn't seem to hit a ball."

"I am seriously considering giving up detective work, and becoming a billiard professional," said Tinker, with mock seriousness. "I will take on Gray first."

"You will, eh?" smiled Blake. "Well, just to take you down a peg, young man, I will give you twenty and play a hundred up."

"I wish I had kept quiet now," grinned the lad. "But come on, guv'nor—I'll take you on."

They all moved back to the billiard-room, where Graves proceeded to make a book with Yvonne on the result. She championed Blake, and Graves was highly pleased, for certainly Tinker had been in great form. But what a sad surprise was in store for the lad and his backer!

From the minute he picked up the cue Blake settled down to business, and it looked as though Tinker was not even going to have a shot. Using a break off the red as his play, Blake engineered the balls up to the top of the table. With them in that position he began to pot from the break into the side pocket, causing the red to cushion about until it struck the lower end of the table and rolled back—to stop within half an inch of where it had lain before.

"My lad, you played very badly," said Blake magnanimously. Before you take on Gray you want to learn that one off the red."

Then he turned to Mademoiselle Yvonne.

"And now, mademoiselle, I think we will be going. It was awfully kind of you to invite us out of our cave, and I assure you we have more than enjoyed it."

They moved back into the hall, where Tinker and Blake donned their coats. Just as they did so the door-bell rang. It proved to be the chauffeur, who had returned for them, and while Yvonne was speaking with him at the door Blake seized the opportunity to slip back into the library and lay a package on the table.

It was his Christmas present to Yvonne.

Yvonne and Graves looked on with keen enjoyment while Blake piled up a great lead. Poor Tinker was entirely out of it.

It was pretty work, and, moreover, not easy. Blake, however, played with deliberation and coolness, not hurrying his shot, and putting exactly the proper force into his stroke. It was a walk over for him from the start, and although Tinker played well when he did get a chance, Blake had chalked up too much against him.

It would be unfair to give the score the lad made, but had he really needed any taking down it was certainly sufficient to give it to him. He did not, however, and took his beating with a cheerful grin.

"I might stand a chance with you if you used one hand," he said ruefully, as he put away his cue.

Then they departed for Baker Street, though it had required stern measures to dislodge Pedro from his place in front of the fire in the library. And as the powerful car picked its way along the wet streets through which the Christmas crowds still thronged, how little did Blake dream of the decision and move Yvonne was to make before the night was over.

Back in her house Yvonne had wandered into the library, and there discovered the package Blake had left. She unwrapped it at once, and, as her eyes fell on what it contained, an involuntary cry of pleasure broke from her lips.

It was a perfect sphere of pure jade in an exquisite blending of green and pink and lavender shading to pearl. Every inch of its surface was decorated with a series of carvings portraying the descent to earth of the first "Son of Heaven" (the name given to the Chinese emperors) and His supposed formation of the great empire for His chosen people. As an example of ancient workmanship it represented months of the most skilled labour; as an objet d'art its value must have been enormous.

Yvonne knew Blake had picked up several splendid specimens of jade on his last trip to China, and judged the sphere before her to be one of them; but not until she read the note which accompanied it did she know that the piece before her was supposed to have been handed from the first "Son of Heaven" to His successor, and so on to each new emperor through all the untold ages of that mysterious country until it had reached the last ruler of the Ming Dynasty—that line which fell before the conquering Manchus just over two hundred and fifty years ago.

And by the same token it is worthy of note that it was at the same time the "pig-tail" first made its appearance in China, being the form of head-dress of the Manchus and imposed by them on the conquered Chinese.

With the last Emperor of the Ming Dynasty the Sacred Sphere of jade disappeared. Many wild tales regarding its fate were spread abroad.

Some said the fleeing "Son of Heaven" had cast it in the Lake of the Three Moons before the Manchu entered the city. The lake was emptied, and though many skeletons of bygone victims were found, there was no sign of the Sphere.

Others said that the High Mandarin had secreted it in order to present it to the Ming Emperor when he should return to the throne. He lost his head over it, but if he knew where the Sphere was he did not speak.

Again it was said that the first "Son of Heaven" had stretched down His hand from above and had snatched it away in anger that the Manchu should rule, and that now it reposed with him. Be that as it may, the Sphere was never found, and in the course of time, when all hope of its recovery was given up, the latter story became the one most generally accepted. And now after all these ages it had come to light.

In his rather bulky letter regarding it Blake mentioned all these facts, and added:

"I need not tell you, mademoiselle, that did the Chinese know of its existence each one would strain his every nerve in order to recover it. Above all, would Prince Wu Ling do so; for, remember, he is the only royal descendant of the ancient Ming Dynasty, and looks upon the later Manchu as an upstart and usurper, though in reality he himself is Manchu of an older generation.

"With the Sacred Sphere in his possession he would become even more powerful than at present. The sight of it would rally every Celestial in the country to his banner, and, in their excited fanaticism, they would sweep over the earth with all their millions in a flood no human dam could withstand. For that reason you will see the necessity for keeping its presence in your collection—to which I hope it will add an interest—a profound secret."

When she had read and re-read Blake's letter Yvonne excitedly called to her uncle, who was lazily knocking the balls about on the billiard-table. He came through at once and examined the Sphere with interest, the while Yvonne explained its history, and added for his benefit Blake's caution.

"What will you do with it?" he asked, when he had completed his examination of the cycle of pictures which formed the story on the Sphere.

Yvonne shrugged.

"Since Mr. Blake has so definitely expressed the need for secrecy regarding my possession of it I can only act accordingly. It is a great temptation to put it in the case with my other jades, but the very fact that he thought me worthy of receiving such a gift makes it incumbent upon me to prevent any publicity regarding it. It is not large, and since that is so I think I shall keep it where I keep the thing I value most highly."

Graves smiled.

"And that, I imagine, is the invisible something which hangs from the chain about your neck."

"Exactly," answered Yvonne coolly. "I shall put it in a chamois bag this very night and attach it."

She took it in her hand as she spoke and turned towards the door.

"You will not be going to bed for some time, I suppose?" she said, pausing and looking back over her shoulder.

"No. I shall be smoking and reading for at least an hour yet. Why?"

"It is just possible I may be down again. I have some thinking to do."

"Good heavens, you are not planning another coup, are you, Yvonne?"

"If I am it is not of the nature you think," she laughed. "If I am not down again within an hour you will know I have retired."

With that she was gone, and, with a shrug, the luxury-loving Graves settled down in an easy-chair before the fire and picked up a magazine.

"Heaven knows what is running in her mind," he muttered, as he lighted a cigarette. "I wonder if it has emanated from any remark of Blake's. They seemed to be talking very earnestly together after dinner. Heigho! I suppose I shall be dragged out again to go rampaging half over the globe and be kept busy dodging the law."

On reaching her room Yvonne closed and locked the door, then she crossed quickly to a small easy-chair which stood before a cheerful open fire. Sinking into it she propped her elbows on her knees and sank her chin in the cupped palms of her hands.

The ticking of the little gold clock on the mantel was the only sound which broke the silence of the next half hour. At the end of that time she stirred and lifted her head. As she did so her eyes rested on the Sphere, which she still clutched tightly.

"Yes," she murmured softly, though her eyes held the faintest touch of weariness in them, "I will do it—for him. He does care what becomes of me, and I—I will prove to him what I can and will do."

With that she rose abruptly and approached the dressing-table. Pulling out a drawer she took out a small morocco jewel-case. Opening this she searched about until, she found a small chamois bag containing a diamond-studded watch. The watch she returned to the jewel-case, after which she placed the Sphere in the chamois pocket.

It fitted perfectly, and it was not long before her nimble fingers had drawn out the miniature and fastened the bag on-the chain beside it. That done she pushed them both back beneath her corsage and passed out of the room.

Graves was still sitting in his comfortable position before the library fire when Yvonne entered.

"So you have decided," he said, laying down his magazine.

She nodded, and drew up a chair beside him.

"Yes, uncle, I have. I am sorry to spoil the trip we had planned to take, but after carefully thinking the matter over I have decided to leave for Cardiff to-night."

"Leave for Cardiff to-night!" echoed Graves, in astonishment. "What on earth for?"

"Listen, and I will tell you."

Then Yvonne began, and told him briefly what Blake had told her, though she kept all names to herself.

"He would not say so," she went on, "but I know that the assistance of a woman in this affair would be of great value to him. On thinking the matter over, however, I have struck what is in my opinion the best mode of procedure."

"And that is?"

"To reproduce as far as is possible the exact outrage which was perpetrated upon the girl, who is missing."

"I don't think I follow you."

"It is very simple. I shall put myself in a position where, if they so desire, the System will have every opportunity of kidnapping me."

"But, good heavens, Yvonne, that is madness! You put yourself in deadly peril. I refuse utterly to countenance any such idea."

"I have quite made up my mind, uncle, and I think my own brains will carry me through any immediate danger. The ultimate success of the move will depend upon the way in which you carry out what you have to do, and whether Mr. Blake succeeds in following up the lead I give. If you both fail, of course, I shall find myself in an unenviable position. But you must not fail—he will not fail."

"Perhaps you will deign to be a little more explicit," said Graves sarcastically.

"I will," she replied imperturbably. "While I am changing you will ring up the garage and have Alec bring around the big motor. He can drive, and we will get away by midnight for Cardiff.

"To-morrow we shall have an opportunity to spy out the land, and to-morrow night I shall begin to put into operation the plan I have thought out. If it fails, then I shall try the next and the next night until I succeed or see that it is useless."

"A nice way to spend Christmas Day," grumbled Graves.

" For the purpose I have in mind no day could be better," she replied, rising. "I shall be down in less than half an hour, so please get Alec on the 'phone at once."

While Yvonne hurried away to change and pack what she desired Graves proceeded to do her bidding. Punctually at the end of half an hour she was down again, carrying a small handbag.

She found her uncle eyeing the cosy fire regretfully, and had Yvonne only dreamed in the slightest degree what she was to go through before she again stood in that comfortable room even her intrepid soul would have quailed.

But it is the mercy of Nature that, in most of the big things of life, we are ignorant of the pitfalls and dangers surrounding them. Were it otherwise, man would have scratched the elate of achievement far less deeply than he has.

A few minutes later Alec arrived. He was too inured to the sudden whims of his mistress to show any surprise at the unusual summons, and had Yvonne calmly announced that she intended leaving for the middle of the Sahara, it is a safe bet that Alee would have made his preparations without the quiver of an eyelash.

For much of the success of Yvonne's daring coups in the past was due to the unswerving loyalty and frank worship of every member of her famous "circle."

Yvonne led the way to the waiting motor, and when most of London was wrapped in sleep— the adults with pleasant dreams of the restful morrow and the children with rosy mind pictures of the treat in store for them—the rhythmic hum of the engine purred a lullaby as the big car started on its long journey.

Yvonne curled herself up in the corner of the tonneau, and almost before the last lights of London had been left behind she was fast asleep. Graves smoked for some time in silence, then he, too, succumbed to the song of the engine, and only Alec remained awake, sitting motionless over his wheel, his goggled eyes fixed rigidly on the dark road ahead.

For all the world he might have been some relentless gargoyle steering a thundering Juggernaut through the wet mystery of the night.

"From the time they left London until they made the outskirts of Cardiff, the engine never changed the tone of its song, up hill and down hill, through muddy, narrow lanes and along lonely level stretches it had gone without a change of gear.

As they entered the first of the streets of that coal-begrimed city, however, Alec slowed down and turned his head the barest trifle.

"Where shall I drive, mademoiselle?"

His voice awoke Yvonne, and when he had repeated his question, she murmured sleepily:

"The Hotel North."

Through the silent streets they sped, past long lines of small tenements until they reached the better quarter; then came the technical schools, the museum, the public library, and, finally the Hotel North. There Yvonne and Graves alighted, their luggage being taken in by a yawning night porter.

Alec departed to put the car in the garage, and the others went at once to their rooms. It was still dark, and making an appointment to meet for lunch at twelve, Yvonne and Graves retired.

At that very moment Tinker and Blake were fast asleep at Baker Street, all unaware of the distance which Yvonne had put between herself and them since they had left Queen Anne's Gate the previous evening.

It was certainly a strange way in which Yvonne spent that Christmas afternoon. Immediately after lunch she had the car brought round, and before entering it, took care to heavily veil her features. She directed Alec to drive slowly through the streets by the docks where the Chinese quarter is situated, and certainly not even the dingy purlieu of Limehouse exceed in sinister suggestion the dock dens of Cardiff.

Like Liverpool, New York, Melbourne, and all seaport towns, it attracts to its meaner districts a horde of the lowest vampires in human form, spawn of vampires before them, and progenitors of other vampires to come.

Night born and night bred, their days are spent in idleness waiting for the hours of darkness, when their nefarious trades can be carried on and their pockets profit accordingly.

Since its marvellous leap into the position, of a great point of export and the prosperity given to it by the great South Wales coal mines which feed it, Cardiff has reached a rank of greatness in its business and a level of depravity in its dens.

There, the sailor arriving from a long voyage and with money in his pocket, falls an easy prey to the sharks which are ever on his track, but in this it is no better, no worse, than other placed of a similar nature.

But large or small, there is something in the Chinese atmosphere of such a place which deepens the sinister meaning of its purpose and creates an abyss of mysterious retreats into which many men and women disappear, never to come to the surface.

And it was into this type of nest which Yvonne went that afternoon.

Though her veil was heavy, enough to conceal her features, it was not too heavy to prevent her keen eyes from photographing on the retina of her mind an accurate impression of the district and the plan of its streets.

For two solid hours the motor turned up one street and down another; then Yvonne signified her wish to return to the hotel.

Over a cup of tea in the sitting-room of her suite, Yvonne gave Graves his final instructions.

"I shall leave here at half-past seven," she said. "I want you to follow me at a discreet distance. Be sure and keep far enough behind to attract no attention. It will be necessary for you to put on a rough suit, and as far as possible assume the appearance of a sailor ashore for Christmas Day. That will guard against suspicion being aroused. Have Alec do the same, and take him with you.

"As for me, I have brought a disguise. It will give me the appearance of a girl from the country, and I fancy I can carry off the part. Of course, nothing may happen at all, but one never knows. If any of the agents of the System are about, they are sure to remark my appearance in that district alone, and the unsophisticated nature of my appearance will lead them to think that I am a country girl in Cardiff for the day, who has lost her way—which is what I desire. If that does occur, I shall then look for some move on their part.

"It will have to be strategy, for I shall not give them the opportunity to take me by force. That is why I shall stick to the more frequented thoroughfares. I am hoping that one of them will approach me, and inquire if I have lost my way. When I say 'Yes,' they are bound to offer to show me how to go, and if they are of the System, that way will be into one of the retreats where they will keep me.

"That is where you and Alec come in. Do nothing if such a thing occurs; but follow cautiously, and watch where I am taken. From that moment it will be necessary for one of you to remain on watch every moment. They may keep me a day, they may keep me a week; but I fancy it will not be longer than that. It is their policy to get their captives out of the country as soon as possible. I shall probably be taken away with a batch of others, and it is bound to be at night.

"I have wired to Captain Vaughan at Plymouth to steam around here, at once with the Fleur-de-Lys. As I came in, this afternoon I received an answer saying he had left. He should be here to-night. Tell him what I have done, and watch carefully to which ship I am taken. Do nothing even then, but watch for her departure.

"By that time Mr. Blake should be here. Tell him all the facts, and have him join you. As soon as the ship on which I am taken departs, follow in the yacht. Then you must do the rest yourselves.

"It is certain that no harm will come to me until I reach my destination, wherever that may be. But you must move before then. I would suggest training the bow gun of the Fleur-de-Lys on her after she got to sea, and boarding her; but, of course, Mr. Blake may prefer to follow on in the yacht and make no move until she reaches port. That I leave to you.

"Only one thing, uncle, let me impress upon you. The whole success of my plan depends upon the ability of you and Alec to make sure first of the retreat to which I am taken, and, secondly, of the ship by which I shall be taken out of the country."

"I said back in London, and I say now, Yvonne, that the whole plan is madness. You will, however, do as you have made up your mind to do, and that being so, I can only second your efforts to the best of my ability. You may rest assured that both I and Alec will be on the job each minute and watch every move."

"I know you will," answered Yvonne. "Only"—and as she spoke there was a little catch in her voice—"it would be terrible if you missed me. And now I shall get ready. You had better do the same."

At half-past seven that evening, when the Christmas festivities were at their height all over the city Yvonne, dressed as a demure country girl, made her way from the hotel and turned in the direction leading to the congested, odious district by the docks.

And as she walked along she murmured softly:

"It is for him! Oh, if I can only succeed! But—but if I fail!"

THE THIRD CHAPTER

IN WHICH RYMER IS INTRODUCED—HE APPOINTS HIMSELF SECOND MATE—AND RECOGNISES YVONNE.

AMONGST all the vessels which were in the Port of Cardiff for over Christmas there was one moored at a lonely quay in the shadow of a great coal shed, which had as captain, mate, and crew as choice a collection of seaport scrapings as one could find in a world tour. Her name was Eastern Queen.

She was a brigantine of ancient build, and her patched sails from the mizzen sail forward to the flying jib and aloft to her topgallant sails told of a skimpy owner or a captain who stuffed his expense sheets.

It happened that in the present instance the former was the case, for Captain Jonas Pettigrew was both master and owner, and not a penny did he spend on the ship, which for many years had given him a nefarious living, beyond absolute necessaries.

Not that he hadn't the money. He had plenty, for he was one of the few individuals who had reduced the game of illegal gain to a fine art, and, unlike most of his ilk, hoarded his money.

Had Jonas Pettigrew lived two hundred years ago, he would have made a name for himself as a contemporary of Morgan, Kidd, and Black Peter of Spanish Main fame. But he was by no means discouraged at this unfortunate delay in his entry into this world.

Ever since the Eastern Queen had come into his possession twenty years before, by the simple expedient of knocking her captain and owner overboard whilst trading among the South Sea Islands, Captain Jo had done many things and had sailed on many strange cruises.

Of recent years he had been occupied in the profitable pursuit of smuggling arms into Morocco, and it was only during the past six months that he had taken on a new and even more profitable lay.

This was, so he deemed, a cinch, for it consisted of leading human cargo aboard at Cardiff, and sailing with it to different ports, but mostly to Canada.

As mate he had a man whom he had picked up years ago in Sydney, and a worthy understudy of his chief. The crew were a mixture of white, black, and yellow, and consisted of the port scrapings of New York, 'Frisco, Shanghai, Sydney, Melbourne, Alexandria, and Heaven knows where else.

The safe delivery of his previous cargo, plus a steady, fair wind, had enabled Captain Jonas Pettigrew to return to Cardiff, presumably from the successful delivery of a cargo of coal in Canada.

Most of the crew had gone ashore on the previous day, and had wasted little time seeking their favourite dens, there to spend the great day in drinking, gambling, or "hitting the pipe," whichever way their fancy took them. Be very sure their ideas of a happy Christmas did not rise above that level of depravity.

Dropped into this world from ancestors of a similar breed, kicked and beaten through a depraved childhood, sent with curses and blows before they grew up to steal a living in any way that offered, they are hardly to be blamed, considering that they knew nothing cleaner or better.

But what a field for education, instead of spending huge sums in trying to convert the Chinese and Moslems who do not wish to be converted.

As long as a man lives steeped in such an atmosphere his moral senses become more and more blunted until anything clean or straight or decent looks to him namby-pamby. And yet, in his heart—and he undoubtedly has some semblance of that organ—he must know that the cheap depravity of the lower levels is a losing game—not only from a moral, but from a physical, a mental and a financial point of view.

The youth who, in a spirit of unwise emulation attempts to fill his pockets by the get-rich-quick method of accumulation, has about as much chance of ultimate success as a snowball has of remaining intact in the middle of the Sahara desert.

And it is because the average well-intentioned individual works only upon the theory of moral downfall that the beginner in the crook game thrusts aside warnings with the disdainful optimism of ignorant and inexperienced youth.

Rymer writes his treatise "On the Emanations of Radium in Relation to their Action on Cancer, and the Curative Power Thereof."

If he understood straight from the shoulder that he was hitting the trail others had hit, and was travelling at an unbelievable pace towards the point where he would become a doddering old fool at forty, a physical mass of repulsion, or the inmate of a six by ten cell, he might begin to see that the game was a poor one from the start.

The odds in draw poker are pretty heavy against the player, but the odds against the punter in the crook game are stupendous.

All the crew had not gone ashore, however. The cook, a big negro from Martinique, had remained aboard, preferring the company of a bottle of Jamaica rum in the solitude of his galley rather than the more noisy—and expensive—hilarity of the dens.

Besides him, one of the sailors was loafing about the fo'castle, preferring to wait until the hours of darkness before venturing ashore and inevitably returning before daybreak.

The captain and mate were also aboard, but beyond that delightful quartette, the ship was deserted.

Had any of the others looked in upon the solitary sailor in the fo'castle during the afternoon, they would have found him occupied by an odd

form of recreation for a member of the crew of the Eastern Queen.

He was sitting against the end of a bulkhead near the door, which was half open in order to permit some light to enter the fo'castle. Though it was a cold, raw December day outside, he apparently felt it not, for he betrayed no sign.

Between his teeth was the stem of an old pipe, and rising from the bowl was the blue smoke spiral of heavy black jack. On his knees rested a small book of red leather, in which he was writing rapidly; and therein lay the wonder of his occupation, for had one examined the written words closely, it would have been seen that they were of a strangely technical nature, and had the examination been extended to include all that had been written, one would have been astonished to discover that it was the partially completed manuscript of a profound treatise "On the Emanations of Radium in Relation to their Action on Cancer, and the Curative Power Thereof."

It was a technical effort which would add lustre to the name of the most prominent scientist, but nothing more incongruous could well be found than such a work being conceived and written by a rough, bearded sailor in the filthy fo'-castle of one of the most disreputable ships afloat.

But so it was, and had some of the aforesaid scientists read the work, they would have shaken their heads, and said it was strangely like the language of that once famous surgeon, Dr. Huxton Rymer, who had suddenly dropped out of the exalted position in his profession which he once held, and had disappeared from the ken of his old associates. And, strangest of all, they would have been right, for it was Rymer, and no other.

Even the black scrubby beard of several weeks' growth failed to hide the heavy sweep of the powerful jaw; though cut and bruised and stained, the fingers still had the long, sensitive appearance which was an index to the man's nervous capacity with the knife; the face still possessed the marks of past refinement, though the eyes were beginning to have a brooding look which in the past a certain vein of optimism had kept at bay. How he came to be an ordinary seaman aboard the Eastern Queen is very soon told.

Some time previously Rymer had been in a fair way to clean up a big haul in Ecuador, and, in fact, had already clinched a hundred thousand pounds before Sexton Blake had stepped in and upset his nicely-planned little coup.

Unfortunately for Rymer, this interference on Blake's part plus the vengeance of a certain Indian whom he had betrayed, had made Ecuador too hot to hold him, and had necessitated his seeking a more salubrious climate.

Through Blake's magnanimity, prompted by the detective's own desire to keep certain diplomatic occurrences a secret from the general public, there had been no police information passed against Rymer, and, as a consequence, he found in New York the salubrious atmosphere of which he was in search.

There he got hold of the money which he had salted away, and for a time spared nothing in the gratifying of the most extravagant taste. Even a hundred thousand can be spent in time if nothing is being added to it, and when Rymer began hitting the faro table, it began to have some big holes made in it. A few weeks of this, and he awoke one morning to find his balance consisted of only ten thousand.

That day he drew every penny, and in the evening sought the gambling rooms. In a spirit of reckless bravado, he put the whole lot on the ace to win.

It lost, and on this one turn of the cards departed Rymer's hopes of recouping himself. Then he had wandered out, and with the loose notes which he found about his clothes, plus a hundred dollars which the house had loaned him on leaving, he made for the east side, and began to steep himself in spirits.

At the end of a week he woke up to find himself lying on a couch in the back room of some dingy den, and a conversation which he had overheard there had resulted in his offering his services to the speakers.

They turned out to be Captain Jonas Pettigrew and the mate of the Eastern Queen, and since then Rymer had been one of the most exemplary seamen aboard. A couple of fights in the fo'castle had achieved his standing there, and now none bothered him. That was just previous to the last voyage of the Eastern Queen from Cardiff.

When the dying light made it impossible for Rymer to follow the fine lines, he closed the book with a heavy sigh, and placed it carefully in the inside pocket of his waistcoat.

At times the true scientific nature of the man predominated, and it was during those moments that an outlet of some kind was necessary—an outlet which he found in the compilation of his treatise. No sooner had he put the book away, however, than the scientist gave place to the other element in him.

Rising softly to his feet, he took a careful look through the open door along the deserted deck; then he once more thrust his hand in his pocket.

It emerged, clutching the folded clipping from a newspaper which he carefully spread out. Only one complete announcement had escaped the rough cutting, and this he proceeded to read.

It was headed :

"FIFTY THOUSAND POUNDS REWARD OFFERED.

"The above reward will be paid, and no questions asked, for information leading to the immediate recovery of a young lady of the following description:

"About five feet six inches in height, fair hair and complexion, fine, regular features, blue eyes, a tiny mole under the left ear, and a barely perceptible dimple in the centre of the chin.

"At the time of her disappearance she was dressed in an evening gown of pale pink, was wearing black satin pumps, and over her gown a heavy fur coat of grey squirrel.

"Disappeared from Cardiff on the evening of the eleventh. All communications respecting the above to be addressed to Crick, Palmer & Martin, Solicitors, London and Liverpool. Strict secrecy guaranteed under all conditions."

When he had read it and re-read it, Rymer folded up the paper and thrust it back in his pocket then he leaned against the bulkhead, and smoked thoughtfully.

"We left left here two months ago," he muttered, "so there was no chance of her being in the cargo we took. Anyway, although I didn't get a squint at the Chinks we had, I would have heard something about it if there had been a woman aboard. Of course, since the Chinese, the Japs, the Turks and that breed don't dare come on and publicly marry English girls, they manage to get them as wives just the same, and with all due respect to Captain Jonas Pettigrew, I imagine he has been the means of bringing 'married bliss' (?) to more than one Celestial.

"The point is, from what den here was she taken, and by what route was she got out of the country? I have been in this cursed ship long enough to discover that there are many underground routes having their genesis in Cardiff; but what I can't figure out is whether she was taken East or by way of America. If I could only discover that, I should be a long way on my investigations.

The very fact that such a reward has been offered, and is still being offered, proves that she comes from a high family, and that she must be intended as the wife of some mighty exalted foreigner who knew his chances of receiving her consent to marry him in the ordinary way were jolly remote.

"But that fifty thousand gets my eye. If I can put my fingers on it, I will do so, and to blazes with Captain Jonas Pettigrew and his cursed ship! My first move is to hang about the dens, and see if I can find out what ships of this nature have left Cardiff during the past two weeks; then, with that information, I can perhaps trace which den supplied her cargo, and then drop on what I want. This is too big a thing to let slip through my fingers."

At that moment Captain Jonas Pettigrew himself came along the deck, and thrust his bearded face through the open doorway.

"When are you going ashore for your leave?" he asked, in a strangely mild tone.

He did not know to this day just what Rymer may have overheard in the New York joint, and, in addition to that, there was an intangible something about his newest recruit which caused him to use a less snarling tone than to his other seamen.

Rymer eyed him coolly.

"I had intended leaving the ship about seven, Captain Pettigrew. Have you any particular reason for asking?"

"Yes. If you want to put in much time, you had better leave earlier. We take on a cargo to-night, and, as the tide serves, we will get down channel at daybreak. The people ashore want to take advantage of the fact that it is Christmas night. A less strict watch will be kept."

Rymer was keenly disappointed to hear that they were sailing so soon, for he had little hopes of being able to complete his investigations in one evening. It would have bothered him not a whit to desert the ship, did such a move suit his purpose, but he felt that while aboard the Eastern Queen he was, in a way, in direct touch with the System he was endeavouring to

fathom, and that there, if any place, he would find what he sought.

Even if he failed to track the missing girl and swell his slender resources by the addition of the magnificent reward, he might drop on to something which would serve as a lever for causing the System to disgorge some of its ill-gotten gains. Not for nothing was Dr. Huxton Rymer content to remain an ordinary seaman. These reasons caused him to curb any disappointment he felt.

"All right, captain," he said briefly. "I have very little to do. I shall be aboard again before we sail."

"Very well. The mate and I are going ashore to beat up the crew. I suppose the blinking loafers are all drunk."

With that the bearded face withdrew, and his heels sounded heavily as he stamped back along the deck. Once he had gone, Rymer lost no time in preparing to go ashore.

In less than five minutes he had donned a heavy coat, stuck a soft slouch hat on his head, and drawn on a pair of gloves. This done, he opened the sea-chest under his bunk, and took out an automatic revolver, which he dropped in the outside pocket of his overcoat. Then he kicked open the fo'castle door, and made his way along the deck and over the side to the quay.

For several minutes he walked through a maze of narrow, silent streets lined with warehouses. Turning out of these, he came to a saloon on a corner which stood as the outpost to the illuminated district beyond. Along this street went Rymer until he came to a narrow side street, turning off to the right. A few yards up he paused, and knocked at a door.

It opened almost at once to admit him, and he found himself in a low-ceiled room containing a bar against the opposite wall. Against the other walls were rude benches, upon which sat a conglomeration of seamen representing almost every nationality imaginable.

The air was heavy with the fumes of beer, spirits, and tobacco, and a babel of talk ascended from all sides. The bar-tender was a Chinaman. It was the den where Rymer hoped to discover the names of any likely ships which had sailed within the past two weeks.

Strolling across to the bar, he ordered a whisky, and when he had received it, took it to a corner somewhat away from the crowd. Near him was a half-intoxicated seaman from the Eastern Queen, and from his own words Rymer knew this man was posted on most of the inside facts regarding the underground business of the port.

He made no attempt to get into conversation with the fellow, but waited for the other to make the first advance. They were not long in coming. As his bleary eyes recognised Rymer he shifted nearer.

"Hallo, ol' sport!" he said thickly. "Thought you were stayin' aboard."

Rymer smiled genially.

"I thought I would come away for an hour or two," he replied. "Did you know we were sailing at daybreak?"

"Is that right?"

"No doubt about it. The captain told me just before I came ashore."

Then Rymer sank his voice to a confidential pitch.

"He said the people ashore were taking advantage of the fact that it was Christmas night, and intended rushing a cargo aboard to-night."

The other nodded solemnly.

"Yesh," he said, "they think the United States have agents at every port watching for departures, but I don't think sho. I know every bloomin' bend in the game, and I ain't never seen no agents all the years I been mixed up in it. No, I haven't."

Rymer shrugged.

"I suppose they have to be cautious?" he said carelessly.

"Cautious!" snorted the other. "Le' me tell you, my friend, they're a lot of blamed fools, thash wha' they are. I could run five times as many out of thish 'ere port than they do. Yesh, I could."

"Oh, I agree with you there. At the same time, they ship a good many, I guess?"

The other nodded heavily.

"Yesh, a good many, but not ash many ash they could. Why they ain't sent none since the Belle of 'Frisco sailed two weeks ago. The cargo we take will be the first since. Though, min' you, ole sport, I only tell you this because you're a shipmate."

"Oh, you needn't worry," rejoined Rymer, with a yawn. "Have another drink?"

The inebriated one decided he would, and when it had disappeared, Rymer seized the op-

portunity of a diversion created by several new arrivals and slipped out.

"Got it first shot," he muttered, as he strode quickly down the street. "I might have guessed it. The Belle of 'Frisco, she is an old steam tramp, and ready to be piled on the rocks. If I remember rightly, she takes the underground cargo to Canada, and transfers it to a boat out of St. John. And it's Sam Loo who is agent. It is a good thing I kept my ears open aboard the old Eastern Queen."

So absorbed was Rymer in his thoughts, that he almost passed the street leading to Sam Loo's place. The necessity for recalling himself to his surroundings caused him to look up, and his brows knit slightly as he saw ahead of him a man whom he knew as an habitué of Sam Loo's, and a girl, who looked as out of place in that district as Rymer in his present garb would look at a Court function.

She was for all the world like a country maiden who had come into the city for Christmas, and in the confusion of its crowds and streets, had lost her way.

Unconsciously, Rymer slowed up in order not to overtake them, though after the first cursory glance, he gave the pair little attention. In that district one saw many queer sights, and certainly it was none of Rymer's business.

The pair ahead continued up the dark street, until Rymer saw the man pause. A second glance showed him that it was exactly in front of Sam Loo's door. Then that which followed happened so quickly, that it was all over in a moment.

The man turned like lightning on his companion and threw an arm about her shoulder. Well, Rymer knew what that meant, for in the hand would be a drug-soaked handkerchief which would soon cause the victim's senses to flee. Any stranger in the district would think it only an inebriated couple; any frequenter of the district would not give it a second glance.

Rymer saw the girl struggle for a few moments; then, as the drug overcame her, she relaxed and sank back in the man's arms. Picking her up as though she were a child, her assailant carried her to a side door leading into Sam Loo's, and disappeared through it. Like a shot Rymer was after him, and before the door clicked to, he was inside.

To his surprise he found himself in a well-furnished room, where Captain Jonas Pettigrew and the mate of the Eastern Queen sat drinking with Sam Loo himself.

The man who had entered before Rymer, was in the very act of laying his burden on a couch. Sam Loo had started to rise, but on seeing Rymer, he sank back with a snarl, for, though like the rest of the crew, Rymer was admitted to the outer rooms, only those on the inside, like Captain Pettigrew and the mate, were admitted to the heart of the den.

Rymer saw that only bluff would carry him through, though certainly the presence of the captain was an asset.

"What you want?" snapped the Chinaman. "You get to blazes out."

Rymer coolly drew out a cigar and lighted it before replying.

"There is no need to get nervous, Sam," he said, quietly. "Captain Pettigrew will tell you I am one of his men, and all right. Moreover, he has appointed me second mate of the Eastern Queen, and so you see, as I rather thought I would find him in here, I am not infringing any rules by coming."

The mate gasped in amazement, and with Sam Loo, turned to hear Rymer's extraordinary statement indignantly denied by the captain. The latter, however, was looking at Rymer.

To tell the truth, he was quite as surprised to hear Rymer say he had been appointed second mate as were the others, but had Sam Loo and the mate followed his gaze, they would have lead in Rymer's eyes an explanation of what followed.

In those compelling eyes, Captain Jonas Pettigrew for the first time saw he had met his master. Therein he read a nameless menace to himself did he deny the truth of Rymer's statement, and, had he any lingering doubts about the wisdom of agreeing with the seaman of whom he had always secretly stood in awe, the suggestive bulge in Rymer's outside coat pocket settled them. He took a big gulp of spirits, then laughed shortly.

"I didn't intend to announce it until we sailed," he said, turning first to Sam Loo and then to the mate, "but it makes no difference. Yes, I have appointed him second mate."

"But he ain't got no papers," exclaimed the mate, incredulously.

"Pardon me, but you are mistaken," put in Rymer. "I have master's papers." (which hap-

pened to be the truth, owing to the fact that among the many things collected in a long career, were the papers of a captain who had met a sudden end in Rio, and of whose effects Rymer had mysteriously become possessed).

No sooner did Sam Loo hear the captain's confirmation of Rymer's statement, than his manner changed like magic. He became once more the suave, smiling Celestial, for it paid to stand in with all those who were of such assistance to him in disposing of his peculiar cargoes.

Moreover, a more detailed look at the stranger's face told him there was indeed a man to be reckoned with.

He rose and bowed.

"My congratulations," he said in tolerable English. "We dlink your health in a few moments."

Turning to the captain he added:

"It is, then, all right to discuss matters before him?" Pettigrew, after another furtive glance at Rymer's eyes, nodded.

"Oh, yes. He is one of us now."

"In that case we will go over and see what Jerry has brought," said the Celestial.

The man who had captured the girl had disappeared almost at once on entering, but now reappeared, bringing in tow an old woman, who might have been of any nationality, so wizened and bent and yellow was she. Sam Loo waved them both aside, and the quartette drew close to inspect the unconscious girl.

Before them they saw a young woman with the bloom of health in her cheeks, and the curve of youth in her features. She was dressed simply as any country maid would dress, but even had she been garbed in rags, nothing could have concealed the pure beauty of her face. As Sam Loo saw it he breathed deeply.

"It is fine—fine," he said, betrayed out of his usual Oriental restraint. "His Excellency Fu Kan, Governor of the district of Hamai, has sought a wife for many months. She will do him, and it will be a fitting reward for her. She will become his wife, and the wife of the Governor of Hamai is a personage in China."

"How will you send her?" asked Captain Pettigrew.

All at once Sam Loo became the man of business.

"She might go by the Belle of 'Frisco," he said carelessly, "or by the Eastern Queen, if you care to handle the matter."

"I am quite willing," responded the captain. And the price?"

"The same as always—one hundred pounds."

"The governor of a district in China will pay many thousands for such a wife," broke in Rymer. "Since by your own words she will become a lady of such station, one hundred

pounds is not enough. It is worth five hundred, and five hundred you must pay."

The mate, who was always governed by Captain Pettigrew, said nothing, and strange to say it was to Rymer, and not to the captain, Sam Loo turned to begin the haggling.

To his surprise, Rymer had not named a high price with the intention of coming down, and when he stuck to the original sum without giving a trifle the Celestial, after half an hour of solid argument, spread out his hands in defeat.

"Have it if you will," he said. "It is robbery."

Rymer smiled and sat down, and the avaricious glint in the captain's eye told him he had established himself solidly in the latter's confidence; for the road to Captain Pettigrew's hatred or liking was through his pocket.

The old woman departed with her charge, followed by the man Jerry, and the quartette were left to drink the health of the new mate, which had been postponed.

And even as they raised their glasses were Graves and Alec planted outside watching the house into which the country girl had vanished, for it was Yvonne, and that had been the end to her daring plan.

To become the wife of a Chinese governor!

When the drinks had been disposed of, Captain Pettigrew rose, and the others followed suit.

"What time will you send the cargo aboard?" he asked, turning to Sam Loo.

"It is now nine. They will be at the ship by eleven."

"All right. We will go along and beat up the crew and be there to receive them."

After a few more words, the three seamen departed,

Looey Sing carried the intended wife of the Chinese mandarin to his lonely hut.

leaving Sam Loo to despatch his cargo. This he proceeded to do at once.

Going to an inner room he called to another Celestial. The latter, a short fat individual, appeared at once.

"Have you the full number ready?" asked Sam Loo curtly.

"Yes—forty," replied the other.

"Send only thirty-nine. Keep one back, I care not which. Send them through the underground passage to the next street. Let them start from there one by one at intervals of a minute, and make their way to the dock where the Eastern Queen lies. Have a taxi called and see that it is drawn up in that street. I will take the fortieth to the ship-myself."

The other turned at once to obey, and Sam Loo departed to get ready to take the intended wife of a Chinese governor to the ship which would start her on her long journey.

Captain Jonas Pettigrew drew up as soon as he reached the street outside Sam Loo's joint. Turning to the mate he said:

"Make tracks into Sam's front bar, Kelly, and dig up any of the crew who are there then hunt out the rest, and see that the drunken dogs get aboard in time. We will go along and get ready for the cargo."

As the mate swung and made off, Pettigrew turned to Rymer.

"You come along to the ship with me. You and I have one or two things to talk over."

Rymer made no reply, preferring to wait until he reached the Eastern Queen before having any explanation and possibly a row. If the latter became necessary, he wished the solitude of the captain's cabin, where he had no personal doubts about the outcome.

They lumbered along in silence, until the black bulk of the coal-shed on the quay loomed up, then appeared the tall spars of the vessel, looking strangely slender against the cold starlit sky. On going aboard, they discovered the negro cook was the only one there so far, and he was for the once out of commission in the solitude of his galley.

Pettigrew led the way aft, and on reaching the saloon, closed the door which opened into the companion-way.

"Now then, Hutton, or whatever your name is," he said, "perhaps you will favour me with an explanation as to why you have appointed yourself second mate of the Eastern Queen?"

"Why, you said in Sam Loo's that you yourself had done that," replied Rymer coolly, lighting another cigar.

"Cut out the hot air, and get to business," snapped the captain.

Rymer's jaws came together with a click, and he swung sharply:

"Look here, Captain Jonas Pettigrew," he said in low, curt tones. "I happened to overhear a certain conversation of yours in New York, which gave me a fair idea of the business upon which you were engaged. It just happened that I was looking for an opening where the profits would be rather more than the exact return for work done. If I had been a stool pigeon or a spy, I could have greened your game on the first call of the cards. I didn't, but I kept my eyes and ears open, and I know the ropes now.

"You know, as sure as you stand there, that I am no ordinary seaman, nor would I remain one for long. With me, it is a case of 'fifty fifty' at least, and that is why I have become your second mate. Use me square and you will find I will do the same by you. When I get tired of the Eastern Queen and her affairs, I will slip away quietly, and no one will ever be the wiser from anything I know. If you allow me a hand in the game, you will find your returns bigger, as they were to-night in Sam Loo's.

"Put me in charge of your cargoes; let me into the inside know of this system, and it will pay you. Now which is it to be, peace or war? And before you answer, let me tell you I am a bad enemy for any man to have."

Pettigrew bit the end off a cigar.

"I guess you have slipped one over on me this time," he grunted, "But let it be peace. You remain second mate."

"And you put me wise to the inside workings of the game?" persisted Rymer.

"Sure. To-morrow we will talk."

Rymer breathed a sigh of relief. As soon as Pettigrew told him how the cargoes were rushed through to their final destination he calculated it would not take him long to discover what had become of the missing girl, for whom the big reward was offered.

Then, the fifty thousand for him, and perdition to the Eastern Queen.

At that moment the trampling of feet on the deck overhead told them that either some of the crew or the first part of the cargo had arrived. Pettigrew jerked his thumb upwards.

"Go up and see who it is," he said. "If it is the crew, kick them into the fo'castle, and keep them there; if it is the cargo, take charge and put them away. Here are the keys."

He tossed over a bunch of keys to his new second mate, and picking them up, Rymer made his way up the companion to the deck.

At the very top he met Sam Loo himself, and leaning heavily against his arm was the figure of a woman. A few steps behind stood the old woman whom Rymer had seen back in the den.

"Quick!" said the Chinaman, as soon as he recognised Rymer. "Get her out of sight before anyone comes! The old woman goes with her to look after her."

"All right; come on," answered Rymer.

Turning, he led the way along the deck until he reached the forward hatchway. The hatch itself worked on a hinge, and this Rymer threw back. A ladder led downwards into the darkness of the hold, but the faint starlight disclosed the fact that a floor had been set in a few feet down.

Rymer put his leg over the edge, and descended a few rungs, then clinging on with his right hand he held up his left arm for the captive. Sam Loo picked her up and lowered her until Rymer caught her, and steadied her over his shoulder. In this fashion he descended the rest of the way, and stood away from the bottom of the ladder until first the old woman, and then Sam Loo, had descended.

With his burden still over his shoulder, Rymer led the way along the rough flooring until he came to a door. Into the lock of this he fitted several keys until he found the right one. When the door swung open it revealed a small cabin at the opposite end of which could be seen a half-open door leading into another cabin.

Evidently these were to be the quarters of the intended wife of the Governor of Hamai and her duenna.

The new second mate of the Eastern Queen moved on into the inner cabin. Then he laid his burden down on a couch. As her head went back on the pillow her eyes opened for a moment.

Although they met Rymer's fairly, there was no recognition in them nor, in fact any cogni-

sance of her surroundings, for the drug still held her in its grip.

It was more of a mechanical action of the lids as the change of posture was subconsciously felt. The fact that they had opened, however, had wrought a swift change in the appearance of her features.

Before, they had been coldly perfect, but without the finish of expression and touch of life which the open eye gives to the face.

Back in Sam Loo's place Rymer had gazed upon the still features with the others, but then they had stirred no chord of memory. Now, however, the eyes had lent a familiar touch to the face; but before he could be quite sure the lids had dropped, and it was again a cold mask.

He straightened up as Sam Loo's voice sounded. He was speaking in English to the old woman, who would accompany the captive.

"You look after her," he said curtly. "Keep beside her every minute until you reach China. Then hand over the letter to His Excellency the Governor of Hamai. He will reward you and give you money to return. If you fail in your duty you had better never been born."

"Oh! you rest easy, my child," croaked the old hag, with a shrill cackle. "Old Mother Peters knows her duty, that she does. The bonnie lass will be safe with me until she becomes the happy bride of his Excellency."

Rymer interrupted her garrulousness with a gesture.

"I think, in order that not too many of the crew know of her presence on board, I had better see after her needs personally," he said. "The old woman can occupy the outer cabin, and if any curious eyes are about they will only see her."

"A good idea!" nodded the Celestial. "I can see, Mr. Mate, that you are a big asset to Captain Jonas Pettigrew. With all due respect to that excellent man, he needed just such a hand as yours aboard the Eastern Queen."

"They need firmness, and they will get it from me," grunted Rymer, as he led the way out.

For the next hour he was busy getting the thirty-nine Celestials who composed the cargo settled in the narrow quarters which were to serve them during the journey. Kelly, the mate, had rounded up the crew, and from the lot had managed to find a number sufficiently sober to work the ship down the channel.

As soon as he got an opportunity, Rymer sought the cabin aft which was now to be his quarters, and locking himself in, sat down to think.

The vague familiarity of that face had stirred his thoughts so persistently that he knew it had suggested no trivial occurrence in the past. Consequently, he was determined to search his memory until he put his finger on the incident. In the game upon which he was engaged, no coincidence obtruding itself from the outside could be neglected.

It was a strange medley of pictures over which his mind went as it delved into the past. All countries, all peoples, moments of opulence and months of poverty, carnage, and the smoke of battle, dark retreats and brilliant mansions, jails and prisons, flight and hiding, hunger and thirst, and plenty.

And then away back in the time when crime was fresh, even to him, he raked up the incident he sought and fitted it to the lovely face which had started the search.

It was during his presence in the Republic of Ante Rita, in South America, when Mademoiselle Yvonne was startling the world by her daring coups. President Pearson, of that country, was to be her next victim when she had met Rymer and invited him to join forces with her. Then, because he had disobeyed her, she had dismissed him.

Again Fate had thrown them together, but only for a brief interval. That was at the time of the abduction of John Strang, the American multi-millionaire, by Wu Ling. Then, Rymer had had his hands full to preserve his own skin. Now Fate had again thrown them together, and as he realised the startling truth, he rose and began pacing up and down.

"Has she fallen a victim to the System?" he muttered, "or is her capture voluntary, and only part of some deep purpose she has in view? Mademoiselle Yvonne does not strike me as the type to fall a victim to any System, and yet she is helpless and alone.

"Rymer, my boy, it strikes me you are getting into deep water; but if you can't snatch something out of it, you deserve to be shot. In any event, I shall keep my eyes, open and see what her game is—if she has any. If not, and she is a victim, who knows, I may find her very useful."

With that he turned and sought the deck.

THE FOURTH CHAPTER

BLAKE IN CARDIFF—GRAVES' BAD NEWS— PREPARATIONS TO RESCUE YVONNE

KENNEDY, the American Secret Service man, arrived at Baker Street on Christmas morning sharp, at the hour Blake had named.

The consulting-room presented a more orderly appearance, due to the fact that Mrs. Bardell had taken advantage of the early morning hours to bring some sort of order out of the confusion the litter of presents had caused. Blake was toasting his feet before a cheerful fire, a pipe in his mouth, and a book on his knees.

He rose at once, as Kennedy entered, and while Tinker took the visitor's coat and hat, and passed them out to Mrs. Bardell, led the American over to a big easy chair beside his own.

"You are cosy here," smiled Kennedy, sitting down with an air of contentment and taking a cigar from the box Blake held out. "It's cold outside."

"I judge so, from the turned-up collars of the passers-by, said Blake, with an answering smile. "Anything new regarding the matter of which we were speaking yesterday afternoon?"

Kennedy shook his head.

"Not a blessed thing. I was in hopes that array of grey matter you possess would evolve some more brilliant, suggestion."

"I am afraid I have been doing a good deal of thinking regarding other things," laughed Blake. "My mind has been occupied with an incident which occurred soon after you left, yesterday. And, in a way, it is a bit of a coincidence."

"Indeed!" In what way?"

"In that it brings in an element—though to be sure but remotely—which yours contains, or I should say, which composes the main structure of yours."

"What—Celestial?"

"Exactly. It is a curious story in a way, and oddly enough the first point of investigation regarding it begins at one of the places we spoke of—Cardiff."

"Then you have accepted it as a case?"

"Yes, principally because it presents an interesting professional phase, and furthermore, because the investigation of it will not conflict at present with our problem. Then, if as I hope, we clear up the matters which are bothering you, I shall continue until I succeed—or fail. If you are interested, I will give you an outline of it, in so far as it has any bearing on matters Celestial."

"I should be very pleased to hear it."

Blake leaned back and began speaking in short, terse sentences. He sketched a rough description of the case up to the point where it brought in the journey of the Duke of Carrisbrooke and his family to Peking. Then he dwelt more in detail on the subject, and when he detailed the disappearance of the Lady Sybil, in Cardiff, it did not take much to see that Kennedy was highly interested.

"By ginger!" he exclaimed, when Blake had finished. "That is an interesting case, from a professional point of view. But what on earth possessed them to let two weeks go by before consulting you?"

"A misconceived notion that amateurish methods would locate her," answered Blake, with a shrug.

"It was a mistake—a big mistake. At the same time, I can tell you a little something about that game. It is this: the Chinese who are in California often take back wives on their return to China, and to my knowledge a good many of those wives have been imported for them from Europe.

"Now, as you say, the missing girl may have been taken direct to the East if this incident regarding Pekin is the explanation of her disappearance. On the other hand, your theory that she may have gone via America, strikes me as more probable. If she is gone that way, it is a safe bet that she has been taken by the same underground system by which the Chinese are finding their way into the States. In that case, the investigation will certainly run parallel for a certain distance.

"I have never been put on the investigation of matters Chinese in California, but I know this thing goes on, though by what route it is worked I haven't the faintest notion. In fact, as I told you when I came, the whole proposition is an absolute mystery to me."

"And it is a mystery which we must set ourselves to clear up without delay," said Blake quietly.

Then he turned to Tinker.

"Bring me the book of charts, my lad; also volume nine of the Index."

He drew a table between his chair and that of his visitor, and, when Tinker brought the articles he required, he laid the book on his knees and opened up the charts.

Kennedy bent forward, and for two solid hours those two giants of their profession pored over maps and notes from the Index, considering every possible route having advantages which might attract, an underground system which wished to evade the eagle eye of the law.

Certainly, it must be a route presenting many things strongly in favour of evasion, for no inspection is more rigid in every way than that of the Customs and Immigration officials of the United States.

At the end of two hours Mrs. Bardell announced dinner, for Blake had changed the hour of that meal to midday, in order that Tinker might realise his anticipations regarding the "gobbler," before they left for Cardiff. Kennedy yielded to Blake's insistence that he should remain, and the three moved in with Pedro coming along behind, sniffing the air with a pleasant anticipation.

The feast was fully up to the expectations of both the lad and the bloodhound, and when it became absolutely impossible to continue a further attack on the good things, Tinker leaned back with a happy, and at the same time regretful, sigh.

After dinner Blake and Kennedy renewed their discussion, and at three sharp Blake stood up.

"I think it will be the best plan to motor through to Cardiff instead of going by rail. How do you feel about it, Mr. Kennedy?"

"I am in your hands while I am here," replied the latter. "By all means let us motor if you think best," Blake turned to Tinker.

"Ring up the garage, my lad, and order the car to be sent round."

I think in that case I will get a taxi and go on to the hotel for my bag. I shall be back in twenty minutes," said Kennedy.

"All right," answered Blake. "In the meantime, I shall be getting a few things together myself."

True to his promise, Kennedy was back in twenty minutes exactly. While he had been gone,

Blake and Tinker had packed their bags, the former taking the precaution to put in a disguise he had used during the past five months a great deal.

It was the disguise of a Chinaman, and those who have followed the records of Sexton Blake's journeys into the different Chinese districts of the big cities of the world, as well as into the heart of China itself, will know how perfectly he carried it off.

It was just half-past three when Blake dismissed the chauffeur and himself took the driving-wheel. Tinker and Kennedy were in the tonneau, with Pedro at their feet. Blake occupied the front seat alone.

Then, throwing in the clutch, the detective turned the car and headed for the country on their long drive, totally unaware that only a few hours, before Yvonne had ridden over that same road, to put into operation her daring plan which was to have a far different ending from that which she herself had intended it should have.

They made better time on the journey than did Yvonne, for they had the last of the daylight during the first part of the journey and, though darkness, no rain on the latter part, as had the other car.

Consequently, they reached Cardiff a little after eight, having made not a single stop on the way. Like Yvonne, Blake drove to the Hotel North, for he had a desire to start his investigations regarding the disappearance of Lady Sybil from the place where she had been staying when it occurred.

When searching for the genesis of any crime, Blake almost invariably found inspiration for its reconstruction in the spot where it had its inception.

As the three of them descended from the car and started to enter, Tinker gave an exclamation of incredulity which caused Blake and Kennedy to swing sharply. There, coming along the street, was Graves—or, at least, the face was that of Graves.

His clothes were the clothes of a dock labourer, and looked oddly incongruous on the usually immaculate man who wore them. Tinker's exclamation caused him to glance up also, and a look of intense relief appeared in his eyes as he recognised Blake.

Hastening forward, he held out his hand.

"Thank heaven, you have arrived!" he said fervently. "I was just going to send you a wire."

Blake shook hands with him and presented him to Kennedy.

"It is a surprise to see you here," he said, knitting his brows. "I thought you and Mademoiselle Yvonne either at Queen Anne's Gate or on your way to the Mediterranean. But we can't talk here, and from your expression I judge something serious has happened. Come into the hotel."

"Yes, I can't tell you here," answered Graves. "I am staying at the North myself. Have you dined?"

"No, we are going direct to the dining-room."

"In that ease I will join you there shortly. It will take me only a few minutes to change."

They moved on into the hotel, and while Graves hurried up to his room the others made their way to the desk in order to register, and then on into the dining-room.

Needless to say, Blake was deeply puzzled over the unexpected discovery of the presence of Graves in Cardiff. His first thought was that it had some bearing on what he had told to Yvonne, and that therein he would find an explanation of the strange occurrence.

In that he was right.

Exercised as was his mind over the matter, he became silent, and neither of the others interrupted his chain of thought Kennedy was endeavouring to puzzle out who Graves was and what connection he might have with his own case; and as for Tinker, he knew the signs too well to interrupt.

Ten minutes after they sat down, a very different looking Graves appeared, though the expression of worry in his eyes had by no means departed. He gave his order jerkily, and turned to Blake.

"I am afraid something very serious has happened."

"I shall be glad to hear the details at once, if you don't mind," answered Blake quickly. "You can speak before Mr. Kennedy with perfect freedom."

"I'll begin at the moment when you and Tinker left Queen Anne's Gate on Christmas Eve," went on Graves, after taking a gulp of wine.

Without pausing, he went on to relate all that had happened from that moment until Yvonne, in the garb of a country girl, left the Hotel North earlier in the evening. He paused at that point to take another gulp of wine, then he resumed:

"Alec and I followed her as she wished. I hated the whole proposition, and was dead against it from the start; but she would do as she had planned, and you know how hopeless it is to oppose her when her mind is made up."

Blake nodded.

"I know. Go on."

"Well, she hadn't got very far into the district when a man approached her and, we judged, asked her if she had lost her way. We saw Yvonne nod her head, and after a few more words start off with him. We followed at a distance. They turned up a dark side street, and some way up, stopped before a house of some sort. At that moment we saw the man throw his arm about Yvonne's throat, and a moment later she collapsed. That meant drug, and as such a move wasn't in the programme, both Alec and I started forward to rescue her.

"As we did so, another man in seafaring costume hurried by, and before we reached the spot the whole three of them had disappeared into the house. We drew off, and debated what we should do. Alec was for entering and demanding her, for it looked to us as though she had got into a pretty tough joint, and the fact that she was drugged to get her there caused me to feel mighty nervous.

"She is clever, but in a condition of coma she is just as helpless as anyone else. I thought an entrance might do little good and only alarm them. That would mean the hastening of whatever fate was in store for her. Anyway, I decided to move cautiously, and then it occurred to me that I would send yon a wire telling you in detail what had happened. I left Alec on the watch, and came round to do so. Well—I met you at the very door of the hotel. That is all."

Blake had listened tensely to every word Graves had uttered. When he finished the detective leaned back with a strange look in his eye.

"It was cleverly thought out," he muttered, more to himself than for the benefit of the others. "If anything would show what channel was used for the kidnapping of the Lady Sybil, that would do so. But, my heavens, what deadly danger she is in!"

"It was foolish and reckless in the extreme. There is only one chance in a thousand of such a plan succeeding. The idea of having the yacht

sent here was good, and it may proven tremendous asset before we have finished with this affair. But Chinese, the Lady Sybil, everything, will have to be shelved for the moment. Yvonne must be saved. An entry by Graves and Alec would have precipitated matters at once. Force is useless in a case of this kind. Strategy must be employed if I am to succeed."

As he reached this point in his musings, Blake looked up.

"You do not know if the Fleur-de-Lys has yet arrived?" he asked curtly.

Graves shook his head.

"No, but I think not. Had it done so, Captain Vaughan would have come here at once to report. Yvonne said he would be here to-night, though."

"The wisest thing you ever did was to refrain from entering that place. As you say, it would have brought matters to a very unpleasant pass for Yvonne. The mistake you made, however, was in not communicating with me the moment she expressed her intention of doing such a thing."

"I didn't dare!" replied Graves. "By the way, you said in your note which accompanied that jade sphere that she should keep it in a safe place."

Blake leaned forward suddenly.

"Yes!" he snapped. "What about it?"

"Well, I am wondering if there is any chance of that being seen. She put it in a chamois bag and hung it for safety on the chain about her neck. It was concealed, though, by her bodice."

"My heavens!" gasped Blake hoarsely. "Yvonne in the hands of Celestials, and in possession of the Sacred Sphere of the Son of Heaven. It means either her death or, by a very long chance, her lifelong imprisonment, as something sacred herself, which would be worse than death. This is awful! I must do something without delay. If you have all finished we will go to my room."

As they had done so they rose and followed Blake, who was already half way towards the door. They almost had to break into a trot to catch him up, so swiftly did he walk, and, in fact, he had to hold the lift a moment until they came along. In his sitting-room Blake waved them to chairs, and kept on into his bed-room without any explanation.

Ten minutes later he came out again. When he did so Kennedy and Graves shot, up from their chairs in amazement, and serious though the affair was, a furtive grin passed over Tinker's features.

Well he knew the disguise in which Blake was attired.

It was the disguise of a Chinese coolie, coarse and simple. His face was a perfect reproduc-

tion of the Celestial type, and his eyes looked as slant-set and as heavy-lidded as those of any Chinaman out of Canton. His shuffle was perfect; his bearing superb.

He approached Kennedy and spoke briefly.

BLAKE SEES YVONNE.

Blake, disguised as a Chinese coolie, meets Yvonne during her morning exercise.

"I am sorry it has become necessary to put into operation the plan I had intended, before we had spied out the land," he said. "However, you will understand the necessity. The young woman who has gone into the jaws of that den is a very old friend of mine and, I may say, dear to me. I should never forgive myself if I did not do all in my power to rescue her."

A strange quiver entered Blake's voice for a moment, but when he next spoke it was gone. Even when a thing touched himself, he realised that for all practical purposes he must be the cold analytical machine. To be anything else would cause his better judgment to be in danger of becoming blurred by the dictates of his heart, which told him to gather together a force and raid the place without delay.

But Blake had too intimate an acquaintance with the Chinese and their ways not to know full well that there were probably half a dozen underground exits from the den by which the occupants would all escape were a raid made. They could easily enter, but the place would be empty, with probably a sleepy Celestial behind the bar and a seaman or two drinking beer. The wiles of the Celestial must be met and conquered by wiles. It remained to be seen if Sexton Blake could do it—in time !

"My plan is that I go on at once to the street where she disappeared," he said, after a moment's pause. "Graves will show me the way. I think you and Tinker had better remain here and be ready for any message; also you can be on the look-out for Captain Vaughan—Tinker knows him. I will leave Graves and Alec outside, and enter the place. I may be in there an hour, I may be until daylight, and, if my identity is discovered, I may never get out. However, do nothing until daylight. If I am all right, I shall have communicated with you before then."

"I shall, of course, follow your lead, Mr. Blake," said Kennedy, with a faint tinge of disappointment, though he was too experienced a detective himself not to realise the truth and force of the other's statements. "I should dearly love to take an active hand with you, but I daresay I shall be of more use outside. In any event, I can obey orders as well as give them. Tinker and I will remain here every moment until daylight. If you send word for any move to be made, you can depend on its being done to the best of our ability."

"You certainly can," exclaimed Tinker.

"Good!" said Blake. "With you and Tinker here, and Graves and Alec outside, I shall feel that I have something dependable behind me. By the way, Graves, you had better write a note to Captain Vaughan before we leave, instructing him to keep up full steam. It is impossible to tell where things are going to wind up, and in a case of this kind we need every aid we can lay our hands on. You, Tinker, send word to the garage to have the car made ready for immediate use. Have the lamps refilled, and petrol put in. We will neglect no precaution; then we shall have no regrets."

While he had been speaking, Graves had written a hasty note to Captain Vaughan, which he passed over to Tinker. A moment later he and Blake departed, leaving Kennedy and Tinker to carry out their part while he entered the den of the yellow tiger and pitted his wits against those of the wiliest race which has ever evolved from our ancient Simian ancestors.

Graves, spurred on by his anxiety regarding Yvonne, walked at a pace which satisfied even Blake. In less than a quarter of an hour he had turned up a dark street and indicated a house far along in the shadow.

"That is the place," he said, in a low tone.

Blake, who had been walking with head bowed, looked up.

"That," he said, in a soft tone which was almost icy with suggestion, "that is Sam Loo's place, and Sam Loo is one of the wiliest Celestials out of China. We indeed have our hands full to outpoint that gentleman. But one thing is proved. It is no common den into which Yvonne was taken. If anywhere we are apt to find traces of the secret underground system which we know exists, then at no more likely spot could we begin. It was at Sam Loo's I had intended making a start."

"On the other hand, if it is discovered that Yvonne is in possession of the Sacred Sphere, for which every Celestial has been on the watch for two hundred and fifty years, then no man can tell her fate. But here comes someone. Is it Alec?"

Graves peered ahead at a shadowy, figure which was looming up from in front.

"Yes," he answered, after a moment. It is Alec."

Blake draw up and laid a hand on the arm of the other.

"We will wait for him. It will be best not to be seen congregated outside Sam Loo's."

Owing to the fact that Blake was wearing a long, heavy coat, Alec did not see that he was apparently a Chinaman until he drew close; then he gazed in amazement. Graves cut short the question which sprang to his lips. "This is Mr. Blake," he said quickly. "Anything new?"

"Not a thing, Mr. Graves. After you left three men came out of the door through which Mademoiselle Yvonne disappeared. They looked like seamen from one of the ships, and after talking for a bit, one of them went one way, and the other two in a different direction. One of that pair looked like the man who entered the place immediately after Mademoiselle Yvonne, but I wasn't positive."

"It makes no difference," put in Blake. "The main point is that she has not been brought out of the door by which she entered. That means she is either in there yet, or that she had been got away by another exit. Tell Alec what I have planned to do, Mr. Graves, and be sure you keep the watch every minute. If I have any message to send to Kennedy I will communicate with you in some way. You had better keep this coat for me. It is of a better quality than a lower class Chinaman would wear, and little things like that must be taken into account."

He was slipping off the coat while he was speaking, and, after tossing it across to Graves, drew out a cigarette and lighted it. That done, he nodded briefly to the other two, and passed up the street at a shuffle, heading for the public room of Sam Loo's joint.

This part of the place was as innocent in appearance and reality as the public bar of any other place in Cardiff. It was cut up into three sections to which any man, habitué or stranger, had entrance. There spirits, wines, and beers were served, and were of as good a quality as the law intended they should be. Like most saloons, it did a good trade, and, being in a choice location, had a particularly large clientele from the ships in port, a clientele which spent well and was easily pleased.

It served Sam Loo as a regular place of business, and had the greed of that cunning Celestial not driven him on to devise ways of breaking international law, he would have done well enough just the same, for the bar paid a handsome profit.

Beyond the last section of the main bar ranged several small rooms, much patronised by mates and captains, particularly of the ilk which handled Sam Loo's cargoes. Into these the stranger or the police rarely penetrated, though they would have seen nothing of a compromising nature had they done so. It was at the end of the passage off which these rooms opened that the true inner life of Sam Loo's joint existed.

Locked on the inner side, the passage door defied entrance by the uninitiated did they by any chance wander that far—which was unlikely. Night and day a Celestial sat on the other side of the door, ready to open to any who gave the password; but having an electric button near his hand which he would press did anything of an alarming nature occur.

From where he sat he could look into the gambling-room, which was crowded day and night by sea captains and sailors of every nationality, and from every part of the globe, Chinese from the district, negroes, Portuguese, Spaniards, Dutch, Swedes, Americans, English, Irish, end even Scotch. The gambling-room might have been called the first step towards the inner sanctum of the den, but an entry to it by no means meant the privilege of proceeding further.

Beyond this room ran another passage which led to the opium room, a room closely guarded by two Celestials. Into that room many men passed in to hit the pipe, and spend the hours in fevered dreams of crimson hues, but to wake to the full cold reality.

It, like the gambling-room, was unusually full. Beyond it, again, was another passage, and this led to the private quarters of Sam Loo, where that gentleman transacted the multitudinous details of his extensive interests, received those with whom he had business of a particularly private nature, concealed his human cargoes, even made away with human beings did the necessity arise, and, in fact, lived the secret existence of a man whose wealth is gained by the despoiling of his fellows, whose ways are the ways of night, whose power is felt but seldom seen.

And it was into the web presided over by this watchful spider that Blake went. Little attention was paid to him in the outer bar. Such patrons were common there.

He shuffled along to the bar where a group of other Celestials stood, and barely lifted his heavy-lidded eyes as he asked for a drink. He spoke in the pure dialect of Southern China, and as most of the Celestials made it a custom to speak in English, no matter how broken, his use of the native tongue brought the attention of his immediate neighbours to Blake, which was exactly what he wished.

He gave not the slightest sign that he noticed their looks, however, but when he paid for his drink he pulled out a handful of gold from which he took a sovereign. The eyes of the other Celestials dropped to hide the avaricious gleam which had entered them as they saw the gold, but still the newcomer stood impassively sipping at his drink.

After a few moments one of them turned and spoke in Chinese.

"You come from the south?" he asked.

Blake nodded his head slowly.

"Canton," he said briefly, and returned to his drink.

"You just arrived?" persisted the other.

Then Blake lifted his head, and his sleepy eyes examined his neighbour before replying. His attitude was a perfect reproduction of the new arrival who was determined to be cautious with strangers, even though they were of his own nationality.

"You from the south?" he asked in his turn, ignoring the second question.

The other nodded.

"Yes. Canton."

"You been here long?" went on Blake.

"No. Six months. I come over from London."

Blake returned to his drink.

"I, too," he said briefly. "You know Han Wau in Canton?"

The other turned quickly.

"Han Wau I know well. He is the husband of my unworthy sister."

"In that case, you must be a particularly choice rascal," reflected Blake, "for Han Wau is one of the biggest sharks in the city of Canton."

Aloud he said:

"I know Han Wau very well. Been in his place plenty of times."

"What you come here for?"

The newly-arrived Cantonese shrugged, and then looked around carefully.

"I come from London to see Sam Loo. You know Sam Loo well?"

"Like a brother."

"You take me to see him?"

"How much?"

"One—two gold pieces?"

"Three."

"All right. You take me. I give you three."

"When, you want to see him?"

"To-night."

"All right. You wait here. I go to see if he speak with you."

Blake returned to his drink, while his new-found acquaintance made his way through the many devious passages until he reached the door leading into Sam Loo's private quarters. In about ten minutes he was back.

Blake still stood as impassive as ever, his eyes gazing at the counter before him as though he were oblivious of all that went on around him. His new acquaintance now announced that Sam Loo would see him.

"What your name?" he added.

"My name is Chen Foo," answered Blake. "And yours?"

"They call me Wou," answered the other. "Now you give me three gold pieces, I take you to Sam Loo."

Blake dug his hand into the pocket of his loose coolie trousers, and drew out the requisite number of sovereigns.

Wou snatched at them greedily; then turned.

"You follow me," he ordered.

And together they started through the bar towards the passage leading past the private rooms.

At the door which admitted them to the opium room Wou paused.

"If Sam Loo ask you, you say you know me well in Canton. I tell him you old friend of mine and Han Wau."

"All right," answered Chen Foo. "You old friend of mine."

He kept as close as possible to Wou whilst the latter rapped lightly on the door at the end of the passage. He was anxious to know what password admitted one to the inner sanctum of the joint, and from Wou's confident bearing he felt satisfied the latter was one of the best-informed habitués of the place. It began to look as if his carefully-made plan might work to some extent at least.

In answer to the knock a sliding panel, which Blake would almost have sworn did not exist had he not seen it, opened, and a yellow face filled the space like a hideous sketch in a cramped frame.

Wou uttered the one word "Cardiff" and Blake knew he had the password. The panel closed without the slightest noise, the door swung open with a barely perceptible click, and they passed through.

Along the dim perspective of the passage Blake saw the entrance to the gambling-room, and towards this Wou led the way. It was crowded as usual. Several different games were in progress, including poker, faro, fan-tan, and roulette, though perhaps the faro table claimed the largest number.

The air was heavy with the smoke of many pipes, cigars, and cigarettes; the smell of spirits and beer hung persistently over all; several boys hurried to and fro bringing drinks. It was a typical gambling joint.

Without pausing Won passed through to the pipe-room, with Blake at his heels. Passing along between the rows of devotees who lay in all stages of mental saturation from the drug, they entered the passage leading to Sam Loo's private quarters.

There Wou tapped lightly on the door. A guttural voice bade them enter, a soft click followed as the lock was released from the other side, and at last Blake stood before Sam Loo himself.

As he returned the look of the latter, he endeavoured to trace some indication in the face of the Celestial of the undoubted ability he possessed; but beyond a hint of capacity in the broad, high forehead, he saw nothing of a striking nature.

Sam Loo looked not unlike countless thousands of other Chinamen who had come to the Occident years before, made money and started for themselves, increasing their legitimate profits by dealing in illegal goods.

Most profitable of all is the transportation of their own countrymen into countries where their entry is prohibited; and not only into the United States do they manage to get, but it is beyond question that vast numbers of prohibited Chinese find their way into Australia, via the lonely and unguarded coast of the great northern territory.

The Celestial studied the man whom Wou had brought to see him; then he waved his hand.

"You go out, Wou!" he ordered. "I talk with your friend!"

Wou turned at once, and the door closed behind him. When the sound of his shuffling footsteps had died away, Sam Loo looked up again.

"What you want, Chen Foo?"

"I come to Cardiff because I hear I can get to America," answered Blake in Cantonese. "I hear the great Sam Loo get me through."

"Who tell you?"

"I hear about it," said Blake evasively. "Maybe Kan Wau in Canton tell me."

"Eh—eh? You know it will cost much money?"

"How much it cost me?"

"Much—much! You speak English?"

"I speak Chinese," answered Blake.

"You must learn English. All Chinese who live in America have to speak English. Otherwise they run great risk. What, you pay to go?"

"One hundred gold pieces," answered Blake, with a well-feigned air of caution.

"Not enough. It will cost you three hundred gold pieces."

"All right. I pay you three hundred gold pieces if you get me through. But I want to go at once."

"Impossible. If you had come in one day sooner I could have managed it. As it is, you must wait for one week, ten days, maybe two weeks."

"I pay more to go at once," said Blake, with Oriental calm, though inwardly his heart had quickened at Sam Loo's remark.

If he could have been sent one day sooner had he come in, it meant that Sam Loo must have disposed of a batch that very day—perhaps that very night. If he had, it was almost a certainty that Yvonne would have been included; for, safe though he might consider himself, Sam Loo would never make the mistake of keeping her in England longer than he could help.

Anyway, one thing was certain—Sam Loo was a participant in the great underground system; and though that was a very small discovery in comparison with the whole length of the channel used, still it was a beginning; and with even a small beginning, Sexton Blake felt he was on solid ground, and stood a fighting chance of ferreting out the rest of the affair.

His idea that the investigation of Kennedy's problem, and the search for the missing Lady Sybil would run parallel for a certain distance, had proved correct; and that being so, it pointed to a strong connection between the genesis of each.

Yvonne's daring plan had undoubtedly been a clever method of reproducing the disappearance of Lady Sybil—and, as it happened, had been Blake's own idea of what he should do.

It had struck him at the time that a woman would be a great asset, but he had never voiced his thought. It had presented too much danger to be considered for a moment. And now Yvonne's act had placed her in that very situation. Above all was her danger increased a thousandfold by her possession of the Sacred Sphere.

All things considered, it was not at all surprising that his endeavour to save Yvonne should form the index finger which pointed to the existing parallel of the other two cases. Altogether, it was a curious mixture of Chinese cunning and, if he were ever to reach the end of his quest, Blake knew he would need all his wits about him. But the question of Yvonne's safety was, to his mind, the most pressing matter of all.

If she had already left Sam Loo's place, and was now aboard some vessel which would take her out of England, and decrease the chances of helping her, then if he failed, it would mean her disappearance for ever. Of that he felt certain. And impelled, also, by the feeling that his search for her would lead him toward, rather than away from, the solution of the other two cases, he made up his mind to fight hard in order to induce Sam Loo to ship him that very night, cost what it might,

All this providing it was not already too late. In that case it would be a stern chase with the yacht as soon as he discovered the name of the ship; but if that course had to be followed, he swore he would, if necessary, scour every sea on the globe in his search.

Sam Loo had been sunk in thought for some time. Though Blake did not know it, he was wondering if the Eastern Queen had already sailed—and if not, could room be found for another man? This newcomer from Canton had money, and Sam Loo hated to let anything slip through his fingers. Besides, there was the extra freight he had paid on the girl to be made up.

"I tell you what I do," he said finally. "There is a batch going through to-night. Maybe they gone—maybe not. Anyway, I try to get you onboard; but it cost you five hundred gold pieces. If you pay that, I send for a taxi and me

try. If me fail, I pay you back two hundred, and you wait for next ship."

For answer, the man known as Chen Foo thrust his hand inside his blue jacket and drew out a wad of notes, which made Sam Loo curse himself, for not having asked a higher figure. Chen Foo counted out five hundred pounds and passed them over, then returned the balance to his pocket.

"There is the money. Now you get me away."

Sam Loo carefully counted over the notes, and put them safely away. As soon as that was over, he rose quickly.

"You wait here. I go and make arrangements."

Blake nodded and sank into a chair, while the other opened a door and disappeared.

As soon as he was gone, Blake jerked a pencil and piece of paper from his pocket, and wrote as follows:

Graves.—I think Y. has already been taken away. I am being shipped through as one of them. I may fail. If so I will be at the hotel later. If not, you will know I have succeeded. I dare not risk asking the name of the boat, and as soon as I am aboard, shall no doubt be kept closely confined. If I don't return, find out the names of all vessels which have sailed for America to-night. The number should be very few indeed—if more than this one. Then have the yacht leave as soon as it arrives. Take Kennedy, Tinker, and Pedro, and follow; but don't make any move on the high seas, and keep out of sight on the horizon. She may be a steam vessel, and she may be sail. If the latter, the chase will be a slow one. Make for the port where she is bound, and call at the post-office there for news. I will arrange to have some word there instructing you what to do. Tell Kennedy that I am also on a strong scent regarding his matter. Kennedy is to take command of the party in my absence, as in a matter of this kind he knows from long experience what I want done, and how to do it. Be sure to make no blunders.—S. B."

Barely had he folded his note around a sovereign when Sam Loo hustled in, and announced that the taxi was waiting. Blake rose at once and followed him. If Graves and Alec had obeyed his orders, he should have no trouble in conveying his note to one of them as he went past.

Sam Loo led the way down a flight of stairs into a rough cellar. From there he went along a long underground passage, which terminated in another flight of steps. At the top the door opened into a plain room, and that in turn into a passage which led to a street-door. Blake could understand now why, if Yvonne had been taken away, her departure had not been seen by Graves and Alec.

The taxi was at the kerb, and they entered at once. Evidently the driver already had his instructions, for he drove off as soon as the door slammed. As they tore around the first corner and went past the front of Sam Loo's place, Blake leaned his elbow on the edge of the opened window in the door of the taxi, his hand hanging out in a careless manner. Though his eyes wore half closed, he was searching the dark street carefully.

Suddenly a shadowy figure appealed on the kerb, less than two yards away from him. With a swift turn of the wrist Blake jerked the gold-weighted note from his hand, and as they sped by he heard the soft thud as it landed at the feet of the watcher.

Then they turned another corner, and the result lay in the lap of the gods.

§

It was the same moment in London.

In a luxuriously-furnished bed-room in a big City mansion, a white-bearded man turned restlessly in bed and opened his eyes. A woman, with white hair and proud features, sat in a low chair beside the table near by, on which stood a carefully shaded electric lamp. The sick man's trembling voice broke the silence as his eyes rested on the woman.

"Is there any news yet?" he asked, in a whisper.

The woman rose at once, and laid a cool hand on his forehead.

"Hush, dear!" she said soothingly, though her own voice trembled slightly, "No news yet; but Mr. Blake is on the case, and if anyone can find Sybil he can."

"Ah, Blake! I had forgotten. Yes, yes; if anyone can find her he can!"

And as the thought brought rest to his tortured mind, the Duke of Carrisbrooke little knew of the danger into which Blake was going at that moment, in his endeavour to save another girl as well as the Lady Sybil.

THE FIFTH CHAPTER

SEXTON BLAKE IS QUARTERED—RYMER
PROPOSES TO YVONNE—ON THE TRACK OF
THE EASTERN QUEEN.

WHEN Rymer left his cabin after his astounding discovery that it was Mademoiselle Yvonne's face and no other which was recalled to him by the eyes of the helpless girl below, his mind was in such a whirl of puzzled amazement over the reason of her presence there that, for the moment, he was deaf, dumb, and blind to every external happening.

The crew of the Eastern Queen were already preparing to cast off. Men, scarcely yet sober from their Christmas debauch, were up aloft unreefing the frozen, icy sails; others struggled with the hawsers, which had frozen stiff during the cold days the Eastern Queen had been in dock.

If nothing else, Captain Jonas Pettigrew was a thorough sailor, and his hoarse voice rent the frosty night air like the reports of a pistol as he snapped out bawling orders to his men. The first mate was nowhere to be seen.

Rymer lent a hand mechanically, and as he kicked a slacking seaman, but five seconds after he had done so, he would not have remembered it, so absorbed was he in his own thoughts.

Consequently, it is not surprising that he paid little attention to a taxi which raced recklessly along the slippery quay, and drew up perilously near the edge. As he had not seen the mate since the latter had left him and the captain in the city, he put it down to the tardy arrival of that individual, with perhaps the tail-end of the crew.

He proceeded with his task of directing the work forward, and paid no more heed to the matter, until he saw Captain Jonas Pettigrew and Sam Loo approaching him along the deck. For one awful moment he wondered if the wily Celestial had in some way spotted his game, had put the captain wise, and that now the reckoning was come. His hand drifted close to his hip, but his face showed no signs of what he was thinking.

Pettigrew spoke while yet several feet away.

"I have sent the mate below to stow away the cargo," he said. "There are thirty-nine of them. They came along while you were looking after the other affair. Now, they are too crowded down there as it is, and three of them have been put in a place where there isn't room to swing a cat. We want room for one more. Sam Loo is very keen on getting him away. Can yon fix up some place for him? Sam says he has money on him, and we might screw something out of him to let him come as a sort of favour."

Rymer knit his brows.

"The girl and the old woman occupy the only places," he said slowly. "There is a place near them containing spare sails. It could be dug out and would do, only one could overhear what was being said in the other place; and as the girl, when she becomes conscious, will speak to the old woman in English, it would be unwise. The less any outsiders know the better."

Sam Loo pushed forward.

"Then that is all right, Mr. Mate?" he said quickly. "The man I want to send doesn't speak a word of English. He's fresh from Canton and wants to get through to the States as quick as he can."

"In that case, I guess I can fix him up," rejoined Rymer. "You had better see him, captain, and tell him through Sam Loo that we will arrange, as a favour, for him to come if he coughs up fifty quid."

Pettigrew nodded.

"I'll attend to that. Will you have the place fixed up at once?"

It will be ready in ten minutes," answered Rymer. "I will do it myself."

He turned as he spoke, and made his way along to the forward hatch. Descending by the ladder, he went along past the place where he had put Yvonne, and kicked open a door, which opened into a rough sort of cabin, filled with a heterogeneous collection of sails, twine, and tools.

These Rymer dragged unceremoniously out, and, lighting a stump of candle left by the ship's carpenter, proceeded to fix up a rough sort of habitation for the last member of the human cargo.

A few old sails folded up and jumped on formed a makeshift bed, and, with the exception of putting in a bucket of water for drinking purposes, this was the extent of Rymer's preparation to receive the passenger.

Barely had he finished when footsteps sounded outside, and Captain Jonas Pettigrew appeared, leading a tall Celestial of impassive mien clad in coolie costume.

He stood silent by the door whilst Rymer kicked the last of his bedding into shape. Then he walked forward and surveyed his surroundings.

Whilst he was so occupied Rymer turned to the captain.

"Did you get his money?"

"Yes. He paid up like a lamb. He gave ten pounds extra, and got Sam Loo to make arrangements that he should have the same food we have aft. He is a particular cuss."

"I guess the richness of the food won't hurt him," retorted Rymer sarcastically. Then, to the new arrival, he said:

"Well, these are your quarters, Chink. If you don't like them don't kick, for in the first place it wouldn't do you any good, and, in the second place, it is all we have. You don't speak English, so you don't understand what I have said, but I guess you can grab what I mean."

The Chinaman never blinked an eye during Rymer's remarks, and, as far as one could tell, understood not a single word.

When Rymer had finished the Celestial uttered a few words in rapid Chinese, which neither Rymer nor the captain understood, though they both knew a little of the language.

A moment later they departed, leaving the Celestial alone.

He stood impassive as ever until the sound of their footsteps had died away; then he stepped softly to the door and turned the key. That done, he drew out a cigarette and lighted it, after which he sank down on the pile of sails which was to be his bed.

"So," he murmured softly, as the blue smoke curled upwards, "your passenger speaks no English, eh? Well, you have bled me freely between you; but if you don't repay me a thousand times over in more than money, then my name is not Sexton Blake.

"Undoubtedly, I have come aboard the ship which holds the balance of the human cargo, but the question is am I aboard the ship which holds Yvonne ? That is the question which must be settled, and until I find the answer I shall not know whether my deductions have proved trustworthy, or whether I have come on a wild goose chase which will be the biggest farce on record. But I can't believe the different analyses which I have made are all wrong.

"It stands to reason that Sam Loo would rush Yvonne out of the country at the very first opportunity which offered, and even if she only fell into his hands this evening, why should that alter his procedure! He would certainly gain nothing by holding her there, and, by his own words, another ship is not leaving for at least a week.

"On the contrary, it seems to me that he would work doubly quickly, for she was a totally unexpected addition to his cargo, and, seizing her as he did, he will think a hue-and-cry will be raised by morning. The more I think of it the more certain I feel that she was shipped away.

"But—and there is the crux of the whole matter—is she on this vessel or on another? If Sam Loo had a very large consignment of men to send away, it is just possible that two vessels may be leaving. However, that is one of the unknown cards in the game which must be risked if I am to play a lead. It is, at least, a relief to find I am not herded with the others. Truly money does a lot, even with the underground system, the pulse of which I think I am beginning to feel.

"Now for the second, and, probably, most surprising element which has entered into this strange affair, and may yet cause serious complications. If that man who passes a mate of the Eastern Queen, and who has arranged these luxurious quarters for me, isn't someone I have met before I shall begin to have no confidence in my memory. If I could have seen him without his hat I should have known in a moment. His beard hides the true mould of his features, and the brim of his hat shades his eyes. But those hands, that voice—whose are they?"

For the space of ten minutes Blake—or Chen Foo, as he was known—sat smoking, delving into the past in much the same way as Rymer had delved, when he endeavoured to recall the suggestion conveyed to him by Yvonne's features.

Slowly Blake was searching the mental gallery of faces which he possessed, and, in truth, it was no small one. One by one he fitted them to the frame of the mate, and added the hands and the voice; but one by one he rejected them, until suddenly one face loomed out of the mists of the past, and remained focussed by his mind.

That face he saw with the beard stripped from it. The hat was removed, and the high, intelligent forehead rose white above keen grey eyes, below which a straight, powerful nose was placed. The hands were white, not cut and bruised, as were

those of the mate; but it was the hands beneath the marks of toil which Blake saw.

Lastly he fitted the voice to the picture he had woven from memory, the human voice, which is the greatest betrayer of him who would hide his identity.

And as the completed picture unfolded itself before him he saw that it was indeed the picture of one whom he knew well, one whom he had hounded and caught, one against whom he had been pitted, before—yea, and one to whom he had been lenient on more than one occasion.

It, was the face of Dr. Huxton Rymer!

As he realised the startling truth Blake rose, and, pulling off his Chinese slippers, began pacing up and down his narrow quarters with the stealthy tread of a panther, thinking, thinking, thinking.

The creaking of blocks overhead and the heavy trampling of feet told him they were at last getting under way. The distant sound of lapping water reached his ears as the Eastern. Queen slipped away from her moorings.

There was no port-hole in his quarters, but he knew it must be nearly dawn.

He had been pacing up and down for several hours, and the fresh candle which Rymer had put in the neck of a bottle was only half burned down. Glancing at his watch, he saw that it was just past six.

It seemed unbelievable that his thoughts had consumed so much time. But there it was. He had not had time to feel weary, so engrossed was he in attempting to read some meaning in the maze of bewildering facts which appeared before him.

Less than forty-eight hours had passed since the Duchess of Carrisbrooke had come to his apartments in Baker Street to ask his assistance. Since then developments had taken place with almost bewildering rapidity. .

Yvonne's aid had been sought and promised. Then she had exceeded the limits which Blake had mentally placed upon her participation in the affair, and now she was heaven only knew where.

Captain Vaughan, on board the Fleur-de-Lys, was steaming with all speed around from Plymouth to Cardiff—perhaps had already arrived at the latter port.

Kennedy, Graves, Tinker, and Pedro were in Cardiff. Bloke himself, disguised as a Chinaman, on his way, by an unknown route, to an unknown destination.

And, last of all, Dr. Huxton. Rymer had suddenly been thrust into the complicated problem.

Where it might all end, what might be the finish to it, Blake did not attempt to fathom at this stage of the game. Of one thing only was he certain, and that was the strong indication that he had indeed inserted the thin end of the wedge of solution, into the mysterious and complicated workings of the great underground system which trafficked in human beings and human souls.

That being so, it meant that as long as life lasted he would apply every faculty he possessed, as well as every material resource, to the clearing up of the affair, no matter what it cost in time, money, or mental strain, nor where it might eventually lead him, even though it might be into the jaws of the yellow tiger himself.

At that moment a sound caught his ear which caused him to bring up with a jerk and stand scarcely breathing. It seemed to come from the direction of the partition to his right, and, as a repetition of the sound proved this to be the case, he moved softly across and stood with his ear pressed close to the wall.

He could hear much more distinctly now, and it was evident that the sound, whatever it might be, came from the other side of the very partition against which he stood.

It was the sound of a human voice—nothing remarkable in itself, to be sure—but on-board a vessel like the Eastern Queen it was remarkable, for it was the silvery voice of a woman, and the language in which she spoke was English.

Blake held his breath, so intent was he on hearing.

At last the faint, high-toned murmur rose to a louder pitch, and as its tine cadences passed through the partition to the listening man, a strange dry glitter came into the heavy-lidded eyes, the only visible indication of the exultant tempest which was raging beneath the calm exterior.

Only one woman in the world had that delicious hesitancy of speech, and that woman was Mademoiselle Yvonne.

Although the voice came from the other side of the partition, it was not close enough for Blake to distinguish the exact words.

He judged—and rightly—that it emanated from an inner cabin, the door of which must be partly open. It was probable that Yvonne was talking with someone rather than speaking to herself, and as the sound of a faint, cracked treble reached him Blake knew this was the case.

He passed his hand across his forehead, and gaped stupidly when he found it came away wet. Only then did he realise how tense had been the strain of hope, and how utterly repressed had been his every feeling.

At that very moment a knock came at the door, and, stepping across, he turned the key. He imagined it was someone with food, and his thought proved correct.

He had hardly expected to see Rymer again for some days, at least, thinking the cook's boy would be sent with his food. But, to his surprise, it was Rymer, and no other.

He entered abruptly, and set a dish of food on the floor. Then he departed without a word.

Blake stood motionless until the door closed behind him. As it did so he heard Rymer walk along and knock at the door next to Blake's.

With a spring the detective was across the cabin, and had turned the key in the door.

A second time he heard voices, and just reached the partition in time to hear Rymer say in English:

"Good-morning, Mother Peters! How is your charge this morning?"

Then came the old woman's voice in reply.

"The bonnie lass is well, sir—very well—and hungry, too. She has been asking this last half-hour for her breakfast. Ah, me! She'll make a bonnie bride when—"

"All right! All right!" snapped the second mate testily. "Breakfast is being prepared now. When it comes, and you have finished, bring your charge on deck. I have arranged that you both exercise in the mornings. The others will exercise during the afternoons. I myself will come to fetch you."

With that he slammed the door, and a wave of disappointment passed over Blake, for he was racking his brains for some means of communicating with Yvonne. As long as the old woman was with her that would be well-nigh impossible. However, all he could do was to watch his chance and seize it if it came.

He judged from what he had heard Rymer say that he, in common with other Celestials, would only exercise during the afternoon. If Yvonne went on deck in the morning, that meant he would not even catch a glimpse of her; but he drew consolation from the thought that his deduction had led him to her unerringly, and time might provide an opening.

Judge of his surprise, therefore, when, after he had finished the plate of food Rymer appeared and jerked his hand towards the deck.

"You are to go up for exercise," he said, "and if you don't understand what I mean, you had better hurry up and do so."

Blake made a few gesticulations which were intended to convey the fact that he understood those of the other, and a moment later he was following in Rymer's wake, on his way to the deck. Evidently his extra payment had achieved him a certain amount of favour over the other Celestials.

On reaching the deck he walked at once to the side, and stood gazing across the stretch of water at the distant coast of Devon. A fair wind was carrying them down the Bristol Channel at a spanking pace, and Captain Jonas Pettigrew had taken advantage of it by clapping on every inch of sail.

Off to starboard could be seen the coast of South Wales, just emerging from the morning mist. All about them were several trawlers out of Bideford, Ilfracombe and Clovelly, little dreaming of the cargo the scudding Eastern Queen bore as she went past.

Straight ahead loomed the desolate Isle of Lundy, whose two brilliant lights had now gone out until another night should come.

Further, on was Hartland Point, stretching away from Gallantry Bower until it broke suddenly and swung south-west to merge in the rocky and dangerous coast to Land's End.

Behind them, on the port side, lay Bideford Bar, guarding the entrance to the Taw and Torridge, and further still, Morte Point, where many a ship has gone to destruction in the teeth of the northern gales which sweep the coast. Swansea was a faint cloud to starboard.

A great thoroughfare is the Bristol Channel, and a great watery thoroughfare has it been ever since man first navigated his rude dug-outs along the endless coast which bounds the British Isles.

There the Romans sailed their war galleys and built massive piers to receive the trade which they built up; there the Vikings and the Saxons fought and lost and conquered, to be conquered in turn by the implacable forces of Nature; there

the richly laden galleons from Virginia and the West Indies sailed to Bideford with cargoes of tobacco and gold and silver; there Drake and Grenville sailed in the glorious days of the Good Queen Bess and the Spanish Main; and there the same indomitable Drake harried the fleeing ships of Philip's Armada until they sank or ran but to sink further on.

There the great ships of every age have sailed, bringing their cargoes from every port in the world, and always from the dim, vague past has the sea taken its toll—an insatiable monster who demands and gets what he demands.

Until now, Blake had made no attempt to discover if Yvonne were on deck. He felt that caution was the keynote while he was on board the Eastern Queen, for full well did he realise the sharp eyes which would unceasingly watch every move of his, be he cargo or not; for in the business of trafficking in human beings one has to be careful.

Footsteps approaching along the deck caused him to straighten up and turn. As his eyes wandered over the deck in Oriental impassivity he saw, not ten feet away, the figures of two women.

One was short and old and wizened, the other was taller and slim. Her face was concealed by a heavy veil, and her hair was almost hidden by a soft, crush hat; but in one place a tiny wisp of bronze gold escaped to the morning air, and Blake knew that his ears had not betrayed him.

It was indeed Yvonne.

Not by the slightest flicker of an eyelash did he betray the emotion which surged over him at the actual sight of the daring, reckless, lovable girl. Though he could not see her eyes on account of the veil, it seemed to him that they rested on him in passing, for her head was turned in his direction.

In any event, even if they had, she would never have recognised in the coarsely clad Chinaman standing by the side, the clean cut figure of the vigorous detective whom she little thought so near her.

Shortly, after they passed him Blake saw Rymer approach and stop them. The detective shifted his position, and brought his ear into a line with the trio along the deck.

In the noise of the rushing water along the sides and the creak of spars and cordage overhead, it was difficult to catch what Rymer said.

Sexton Blake brings his wonderful
brain into play, probing and delving
for an explanation of Lady Sybil's
disappearance.

Had it not been for the carrying properties of the latter's bell-like tones and the acoustic properties given by a ball-ring sail, it would have been impossible.

He addressed the old woman curtly.

"You can stay on deck a while longer, Mother Peters," he said looking straight into the hag's eyes. "Your charge has been on deck long enough. I will take her below."

"But I will go, too," answered the old woman. "Sam Loo he say not to leave her a minute."

"You are under my orders now, not Sam Loo's," snapped Rymer. "You do as I say."

As he spoke he moved, until he stood close to her, and Blake could have sworn he saw the dull gleam of a piece of gold as it passed from Rymer's hand to hers.

When she spoke again her voice was fawning and cringing, as are the voices of her kind.

"If you say I must, then I must," she said. "Only not long, sir, not too long. The bonnie lassie would be lonely without me."

She finished with a harsh cackle which made Blake's blood run cold. As yet the veiled girl had stood motionless and apparently unheeding the talk which was going on between the two. Blake could not tell whether Rymer's voice had awakened any old memory or not; but of this he was now sure, that Rymer had in some way spotted Yvonne's identity. That being so, it meant an increase to the already sufficient peril which surrounded her.

She made not the slightest objection as Rymer took her arm and led her towards a narrow companion-way which was set about 'midships. It was obvious from this that the quarters where Blake and Yvonne had been placed contained two modes of ingress and egress, a fact worth noting for the future.

Barely had they disappeared from view when the sleepy-looking Celestial, who still leaned against the side turned and shuffled along forward. Reaching the forward hatch he stood and gazed for a moment over the bow.

Only a few of the crew were visible about the deck, and they were occupied in coiling ropes and slushing out the scuppers; the big Martinique negro sat in his galley on an upturned bucket, peeling potatoes, a man lounged over the wheel at the stern, and the first mate leaned over the rail of the poop deck.

Captain Jonas Pettigrew was evidently below, and Rymer had gone down the companion with Yvonne. The old woman still paced up and down the deck waiting for the permission of the second mate to return to her charge.

All this Blake saw as he slowly turned his heavy-lidded eyes, interested in nothing, as always; then he tossed away his cigarette and swung himself over the edge of the hatch. At any hazard, he intended being on hand when Rymer should interview Yvonne, and all signs pointed to the suggestion that such an interview was about to take place.

On his arrival at the foot of the ladder, Blake stood for a moment peering along in the direction of his quarters. The faint murmur of a deep voice reached him, and he knew Rymer had already reached Yvonne's quarters. There was no hint of the slushing shuffle in his walk as he moved noiselessly along.

Reaching the door leading into Yvonne's quarters he caught Rymer's voice more distinctly; a moment later he was past the danger zone and in the security of his own cabin. Swiftly he turned the key, and more swiftly still he hastened across to the partition.

There was a lull in the sound of Rymer's voice, but as Blake pressed his ear hard against the thin wood he heard Yvonne's voice, strangely weak.

"What is it you wish to say to me? Is it not enough that I am in your power, going I know not where? Why do you persecute me in this manner?"

A short pause followed, then Rymer's deep tones again sounded;

"There is no persecution intended, my dear young lady," he said suavely, "if you listen to reason. But since you ask me what I wish to say to you, Mademoiselle Yvonne Cartier, I will tell you."

Blake heard a startled exclamation as Yvonne's name dropped mockingly from Rymer's lips. Dead silence reigned for fully a minute. At the end of that time Yvonne's voice came calm and unruffled as of old.

"You seem to have the advantage of me, Mr. Mate. Perhaps you will be good enough to tell me who you are?"

"Then you do not deny that you are Mademoiselle Yvonne?"

"I admit nothing—I deny nothing."

"I am surprised that you haven't recognised me before this," went on Rymer. "We are really quite old friends, mademoiselle!"

"Indeed! I am afraid—oh! my memory serves me better now, Dr. Huxton Rymer. I had failed to notice your hands before. Now that we know on what footing we stand, perhaps you will explain your reason for coming here? From past experience I judge it is a proposition to sell some of your friends."

Blake's grim features broke into a fleeting smile as he heard Yvonne's sarcasm. It was very evident that that resourceful young lady was fast getting a grip on herself. Rymer's momentary silence proved the shot had told.

"It just happens that I am here to do nothing of the sort," he said at last. "What I am here for is to find out why you are aboard this ship bound for China to become the wife of a Celestial?"

"So I am bound for China, am I?" rejoined Yvonne. "Really, you are most obliging, Dr. Rymer. And I am to become the wife of a Celestial, am I? How delightful!"

""I guess any information I give you won't do any harm," said Rymer grimly. "You can joke about it if it gives you any consolation, but believe me, mademoiselle, you were never in a tighter place than you are right now. Whether you got here through some scheme of your own, or whether you were caught as others have been caught, I don't know, but I propose finding out before this voyage is over. In any event, you can take it from me that all your ingenuity will not get you clear without my assistance. That is straight. Moreover, I am prepared to give you that assistance providing you agree to my terms."

"Indeed! Might I inquire why you are so willing to help me, Dr. Rymer? If I remember rightly, you have no reason to be so."

"I will tell you."

Blake leaned close as he caught the tense tone of Rymer's words.

"Listen, Mademoiselle Yvonne! Away back in South America, when with my assistance you landed Jim Pearson for two millions, I would have been a loyal partner of yours. You thought otherwise, and we parted."

"When you disobeyed my orders by trying to murder Sexton Blake's assistant," broke in Yvonne.

"I tried to make him walk the plank, and would have made his master, too, if I had had the chance, for I hated them."

"Perhaps I but that gave you no excuse for disobeying."

"The reason for my hatred did. That reason was because I loved you, mademoiselle. I loved you from the first moment I met you at the President's ball in Santa Rita. I loved you while I worked with you. I have loved you since, and I love you now. For you I would do anything, if it would bring me your love in return. I would even run straight. That is the reason why I would help you now."

"If a man's love be worth having it is not the love which promises to perform, on conditions. It is the love which gives all, asking nothing in return. That is a love which you never had nor ever could have, Dr. Rymer. Even if I needed your help I could not accept it for such a reason, for—I do not love you!"

"By heavens, let me tell you that whether you love me or not you will be my wife!" blazed Rymer. "I had a chance until Sexton Blake came on the scene. Why you should care for a man who had hounded you all over the globe, and even put you in prison, I can't see."

Then his voice changed to a curious note of pleading, and Blake felt almost guilty as he listened.

"Say you will marry me, Yvonne. I swear to you I will do everything you say. One word, and you make of me what you wish. You may theorise all you please about love, but I tell you I love you with every atom of my nature, and it is not a love to be baulked."

"And I have told you I do not love you, and never could love you," answered Yvonne. "If you meant half you say you would leave me alone. When I want your help I will ask for it."

"Then listen to me," said Rymer, in tones now deadly cold. "If you have come here on some scheme of your own you may think you have left traces which your confederates can follow. Let me undeceive you. When you were seized and taken into that joint in Cardiff I was immediately behind you. When you were taken out you were taken by a long underground passage which led into another street. Then you were put into a taxi and hurried down to this ship, which sailed the same night. So your friends could not trace you even were they as clever as Sexton Blake himself.

"When I tell you that, for once in your life you are helpless, and at the mercy of a system which never lets go its grip once they get a hold, I am not telling nonsense. Without my help you will go through to China as sure as the sun rises, and once there even I cannot help you. If you prefer to be the wife of a Celestial rather than be mine, that is a matter for your own taste. Only—and mark my words—either you marry me or you go to your fate."

"Even with all your boasted love you are not making me this offer without some private axe to grind," said Yvonne. "You must need my help in some plan of your own, and feel that it is a tremendous asset to you."

"I will be frank with you. I do need your help. I joined this ship for just one purpose. It is to locate a girl who has disappeared, for the reward is worth working for. With you helping me we could pull it off without a chance of failure, for now that you are started on the underground channel you are bound to go the same way she did. You could keep on until we were positive, then I would get you clear of it before you were taken out of 'Frisco."

"Your great love certainly doesn't prevent your permitting me to continue in the awful peril you have painted," remarked Yvonne cuttingly. "I am afraid I must refuse to entertain any such suggestion, Dr. Rymer. If I have got into this position of my own accord, rest assured I shall get out of it with the same success. On the other hand, if I am here as an unwilling captive, I think I shall be able to get free just the same. But be quite sure, Dr. Rymer, before anything forced me to become the wife, either of you or any Celestial, I should prefer to, and would, wed death.

"Now go, please. I am tired."

"All right," exclaimed Rymer furiously. "Have it your own way. We shall see if you get free."

The loud slamming of the door indicated that Rymer had gone off in high dudgeon, but still Blake stood with his ear against the partition.

Suddenly the sound of choking sobs broke, out in the next cabin, followed by the jerky cadence of Yvonne's voice.

"He is right—he is right," she said, over and over again. "If they took me away from the

place in Cardiff by another street, uncle would never know, and will think I am still there."

Her voice died away then, and Blake, with a silent step, drew away from the partition. Thrusting his hand in his pocket he drew out a lead pencil and again approached the wall. A moment later a soft, regular tapping sounded as he struck the end of the pencil lightly against the wood.

Had a Morse operator heard it he would have recognised it at once as the famous telegraphic code, and, moreover, he would have known that Blake was tapping over and over again the letters:

Y-v-o-n-n-e—Y-v-o-n-n-e—Y-v-o-n-n-e.

Without stopping for a moment he kept this up, with his ear pressed against the wall. Fully ten times had he tapped out the word before the sound of sobs in the next cabin ceased, and a dead silence followed. Once more Blake struck the letters:

Y-v-o-n-n-e.

A moment later a faint noise reached him from the other side. Bending his head he deciphered the message which was being tapped:

I-n—h-e-a-v-e-n-s—n-a-m-e—w-h-o—a-r-e—y-o-u?

As the sentence finished Blake again raised the pencil and tapped out:

B-l-a-k-e.

Even through the partition he heard Yvonne's incredulous gasp; then the sound of her door came to him, and the sharp tones of the old woman broke out demanding to know what Yvonne was doing on the floor.

He did not wait to hear her answer, but thrust his pencil away and drew out a cigarette. He had achieved one important thing, anyway, and that was the conveying of the knowledge to Yvonne of his presence on board. That in itself was a good deal, and, if nothing more, would be a tremendous comfort to her.

Knowing her well though he did, Blake would never know of the great stab of exquisite pain which had shot through Yvonne as she heard the almost unbelievable fact of Blake's presence tapped out to her.

Stepping quietly to the pile of sails, Blake closed his eyes in thought. He made an odd picture as he sat there on the rough pile of sails, the flickering light of the candle falling on his yellow face, and his heavy-lidded eyes drooped over an impassive Celestial countenance.

But even when alone he did not permit himself to forget his role. One never knew where a hidden spyhole might exist, and he knew what his life would be worth did the faintest hint get to Rymer of the man who really existed beneath that yellow exterior.

Now that the game had moved another step he had much pondering to do, not least of which was a deep consideration of Rymer's startling proposal to Yvonne and his feverish declaration of love for her.

It was odd what a peculiar feeling made itself evident in the region of Blake's heart as this thought occurred. He had experienced it before when Rymer had been speaking, but had anyone suggested it might emanate from his own unacknowledged regard for that young lady he would have regarded them with pitying contempt.

It is a well-known fact that the cleverest lawyer looks after his own affairs very imperfectly. Was it possible that the brilliant detective who was so keen in his analyses of others, and the motives which governed them, could not analyse himself?

Be that as it may, it was certainly a fact that Yvonne's danger had spurred him on as no professional case had ever done.

§

Back in Cardiff things had been moving swiftly. It was Alec at whose feet Blake's gold-weighted message had fallen as the latter sped past in the taxi with Sam Loo. Yvonne's faithful fellow had picked it up, not comprehending at first that it might be Blake's promised message. Graves, who was on guard some distance up the street, saw Alec approaching and went to meet him.

"What is it?" he asked quickly.

"I dunno, Mr. Graves," answered Alec. "I was standing down there when that taxi went past. As it did so this was thrown from it and landed at my feet."

Graves eagerly took the note and handed the sovereign to Alec. They moved across to the rays of a sickly light which shone from a ship-chandler's shop near by, and there Graves spread out the note. As he took in the meaning of Blake's hurried message he turned sharply.

"It is from Blake," he said, with an unaccustomed vigour in his usually drawling tones.

"He is on the trail. My heavens, what a man he is—what a genius! We must lose no time in getting back to the hotel."

They hurried off down the street, and, hailing a crawling four-wheeler, ordered the man to drive at once to the Hotel North. There they found Kennedy and Tinker waiting as had been arranged.

Graves passed the note at once to Kennedy, who read it, and in turn gave it to Tinker. When the lad had finished he looked up.

"Well, the guv'nor says he may not land what he is after," he said, "but I guess we might as well go ahead with what he suggests. If I am any judge he will land there with both feet."

Kennedy smiled at the lad's loyalty.

"I wish I could inspire such loyalty in my assistants," he said. "But you may be right. In any event we will be prepared. He says not to make any open move on any account, but to make it a stern chase. We will follow his instructions. He also suggests that I take command of matters in his absence. Are you all agreed?"

"I am," answered Tinker, "Anything the guv'nor says is good enough for me."

"I shall be very glad to have you do so," remarked Graves. "I can also answer for Alec."

"Then that is settled," said Kennedy. "Now to apportion out our work. Tinker will go to the docks and knock about picking up any gossip he can, regarding outgoing vessels. I will get into touch with one or two shipping men. It will be necessary to knock them up at their private houses, but I wish to get hold of a list of any vessels which are due to leave. I will endeavour to find a pilot. You, Mr. Graves, will remain here and await Captain Vaughan's arrival; then you can give him the necessary instructions. Perhaps it would be as well if Alec accompanied Tinker."

They all rose at once and began to prepare to carry out their different duties. Tinker departed with Alec, Kennedy sought his room for an overcoat, and Graves made his way to the lounge in order to meet Captain Vaughan when he came in.

The captain did not make his appearance until almost three in the morning, and looked extremely astonished to see Graves sitting waiting for him. Hard on his heels Kennedy came in, and the three talked over what was to be done. It seemed that Captain Vaughan had made port several hours before, but had not arrived at the hotel sooner owing to the fact that he had been attending to an injured sailor.

It was not until a little past six that Tinker and Alec returned. Kennedy glanced up eagerly as the lad approached.

"Well, Tinker, any news?"

"Very little, Mr. Kennedy," replied the lad, but I am not so sure that it isn't what we want. No vessel left the harbour between six last night and six this morning. The Grace K. Williams, tramp steamer, bound from Cardiff for Rio, and loaded with coal, cleared at six last night. The next vessel to clear was the Eastern Queen, brigantine, loaded with coal and bound for St. John, New Brunswick. Those are the only two."

"Good boy!" cried Kennedy. "I found out about the Grace K. Williams myself, but the hour at which she cleared puts her out of reckoning. In my opinion, gentlemen, the Eastern Queen is our quarry. If you are all agreeable we will move in and have breakfast, then for the Fleur-de-Lys and a slow chase across the Atlantic."

THE SIXTH CHAPTER

BLAKE REGAINS THE SACRED SPHERE— AND IS TRANSSHIPPED.

IF Blake thought he would have many opportunities of communicating with Yvonne he was disappointed. Whether the old woman had become suspicious in any way at finding Yvonne on the floor he could not tell.

This much he did know, however. The hag left Yvonne alone not the smallest fraction of a second. Had Blake been less experienced he might have tried to bribe her, as he had seen Rymer do, but his knowledge of the type told him that did he try such a proceeding it would be a colossal mistake.

She had taken Rymer's gold, it is true, but it had been only because she knew he would have his way in any event. The only individual to whom she would be loyal was the man who gave her her living—Sam Loo—and that not out of love, but from a wholesome desire to protect her own skin.

She had lived long enough in the Celestial atmosphere to know full well what exquisite torture would fall to her share did she betray Sam Loo. She had seen a little of such things, and had no desire to experience them herself, though she was ever ready to lend a hand when some helpless victim was the subject.

Did Blake reveal his knowledge of English— and such revelation would be necessary did he attempt to bribe her—he knew that she would make off post-haste to tell Rymer. While on board ship it was her policy to curry favour with the official who held her comfort in his hands. For these reasons Blake felt that a waiting game was the only thing.

This plan, he imagined, would be Rymer's as well. He had been turned down too hard by Yvonne to make another attempt without devising some fresh mode of attack, and the very fact that he felt he held her at his mercy would tend to make him more confident as to the ultimate success of his efforts.

In this way the days passed with monotonous regularity. Every night when he retired, and every morning when he rose Blake moved across the cabin and struck the partition one light blow.

It was a signal to Yvonne that he was near her and watching, and though she seldom dared to reply to it he knew it would tend to comfort her.

For as the days passed it was a foregone conclusion that black despondency would assail her when she realised to the full the dangers by which she was surrounded.

New Year's Day passed without incident, but on the following day Blake achieved another step in his efforts which caused him considerable satisfaction.

For some reason or other, which Blake was inclined to put down to the work of the old woman, he had never been allowed on deck in the morning since his first day out. He had been compelled to go up in the afternoon with the other Celestials, and as a consequence he had not caught a single glimpse of Yvonne since her interview with Rymer.

To be ready for any opportunity of communication which might occur Blake had spent some time in the solitude of his quarters writing a note on cigarette paper. Anything larger would be extremely difficult to pass, and as he had not a little to say it had been most difficult to get it all in the small space at his command. He had persevered, however, and the result was a fairly decipherable note.

This is what he had written:

"On no account make a move of any description. Your game's a passive one. Rymer did not exaggerate danger into which you have come. Foolish girl to do so. Rymer may make no move until just before landing—if then. If he does, hold him off in some way. I am planning day and night. Leave everything to me, and when it is time to move you will hear from me. Fleur-de-Lys following. Important: In some way must manage get Sacred Sphere to me. It will be tremendous danger to you if plans fail at present. Do this without fail, but be careful. Keep up your courage. Will rescue you eventually.—S. B."

This note he had carried with him day and night, ready, if the chance came, to pass it to Yvonne. And how that chance did come was owing to Rymer's over-indulgence in celebration of the New Year's festivities.

On the morning after, Blake's breakfast was brought by the big Martinique negro. So regularly had Rymer appeared with his meals that Blake imagined immediately something must be wrong.

As he ate the coarse food he began to reflect. He remembered that Rymer had always had a weakness for the rich things of life, and if Captain Jonas Pettigrew had by any chance put in a stock of spirits it was just possible the New Year had been ushered in by much hilarity in the after part of the ship.

It happened that Jonas Pettigrew was just enough of a New Englander to attach great importance to that day, and for the occasion he had brought to light, not only spirits, but wine, which on ordinary occasions his frugal nature would not permit him to dispense freely.

It had been exactly as Blake thought, and when the morning wore on without any signs of the second mate he decided to risk a journey to the deck.

With this idea in mind, he softly opened his door and looked out. Not a soul was about. He gave a glance at Yvonne's door, then turned and made his way, not towards the forward hatch, but in the direction of amidships, where the narrow companionway which Yvonne used was situated.

He had no idea if Yvonne and the old woman were yet gone on deck. Things had been quiet for some time in their quarters, and he thought it just possible they were. He reached the companion without seeing anybody, but as his head emerged above the level of the deck he saw Yvonne coming towards him, her features heavily veiled as usual, and with her was the old woman.

Naturally, she would have no idea which Celestial was Blake, and he dared not risk a meaning look under the eagle eyes of the old hag. Instead, he turned his head away indifferently, and stepped to one side as they approached. But the side to which he stepped was the side on which Yvonne walked, and as her hand swung past as she went by Blake's fingers touched it for the barest fraction of a moment.

When he did so his hand had held the tiny note; when it came away it was empty. Yvonne's quick wit had helped her in that moment, for the slightest hesitation or bungling on her part would have caused failure, if not exposure.

As they disappeared along the deck Blake made his way to the side, and stood gazing over for several minutes; then he turned and made his way back to his quarters. That was the step which he had achieved.

That afternoon he took his exercise as usual. He went up ate, and the short winter day was fast closing in when he started to descend. Before he did so he cast his eyes around the cold grey horizon, and far astern he saw a black cloud of smoke. He wondered if it might be the Fleur-de-Lys, and it happened that it was.

And Yvonne! What of her since the morning she had received the astounding intelligence that Blake himself was on board the Eastern Queen?

Ever since Mother Peters had entered and discovered her crouching on the floor by the wall she had been watched incessantly. Even in the privacy of her own cabin she seemed to feel the eagle eye of that old wretch upon her. She could not make out when her jailer slept, unless it were that she possessed the canine faculty of sleeping with one eye open.

But not fifty nor a thousand Mother Peters could see into her heart or hear the song of gladness which it sang. The deadly oppressiveness which had begun to assail her, and the plain facts of the danger which had confronted her, seemed to melt away in the rush of confidence and love which overwhelmed her when she thought of the silent, unyielding force of the man so near.

Never while he lived would Blake know how she awakened early in the morning, lying with closed-eyes and throbbing pulses, waiting for the one stroke which would tell her he was there. And at night when she had retired, regardless of the eye of Mother Peters, she would surreptitiously pull from her throat the miniature which hung there, and when his nightly signal came she would press her warm lips to it and breathe ever so gently "Good-night!"

And it was this love which Dr. Huston Rymer desired.

It was only by the slimmest margin that Yvonne succeeded in getting the note which Blake thrust into her hand. She had, as he thought, no idea that the Celestial whom she had seen on deck the first day was in reality Blake.

At the same time, she knew he would seize the first opportunity which came of communicating with her. Consequently, from the moment she left her quarters until she returned she was on the watch for anything which might occur.

No opportunity occurred of reading the note until she had retired that night. Even then she made no attempt to do so until after Blake's signal, and on this night, as she had done only once or twice before, she risked a reply. It would tell him that she had received the note, and no matter what it contained would do exactly as he said.

Then carefully concealing it by her arm from the prying eyes of the old woman should she chance to be spying, she opened it up, and began to read the almost microscopic writing which covered it. When she had finished, she lay back and blew out her candle.

For a solid hour she remained steeped in thought. At the end of that time she had come to a decision as to how she should convey the Sacred Sphere to Blake.

Though she had passed with it so far without discovery it was only because she had not been kept in a state of coma by drug. If that had been the case, the old hag's sharp eyes would have detected it long since.

But after she reached America it was another matter. Through the underground channels there no risks would be taken, and the chances were if she were not kept in a complete state of unconsciousness she would, at least, be kept partially

so, and in this condition her trinkets would be at the mercy of Mother Peters.

This conclusion arrived at, she rolled the cigarette paper up into a tiny ball and calmly swallowed it. That done she proceeded to do a curious thing. Slipping out of her bunk, she searched about the floor until she found one of the shoes she had worn during the day.

With that in her hand she returned to her bunk, and kneeling down rested the shoe, heel downwards, on the edge, then putting all her weight on the shoe she bore down heavily, until there was a sudden give. The shoe had come away in her hand, the heel had fallen into the bunk.

Yvonne laid the heel and the shoe on the floor, and slipping back into her bunk settled herself for sleep. The next part of her plan would not be put into operation until the morning.

It was before daybreak that she awoke, and lay as usual waiting for Blake's signal. Something must have stirred the detective earlier than usual this same morning, for his stroke sounded against the partition less than half an hour afterwards. Like lightning Yvonne was out of her bunk.

Picking up the shoe and heel, she bent down close to the wall and began to hammer boldly. At the second thump Mother Peters entered on the run, but Yvonne went on coolly, as though she did not exist. For once that cunning old hag was completely befooled.

She saw the slipper, the heel which had come off, and the kneeling girl hammering at them as though to fix them. What more natural? But she did not know that those same thumps were carefully calculated in the space of time between them, and that on the other side of the partition the Celestial Chen Foo was spelling out the words:

"M-y-p-i-l-l-o-w—"

Yvonne dared risk no more, and when Mother Peters approached and demanded the shoe she handed it over meekly. The old woman sent it to the carpenter to be fixed—proceeding which would naturally have occurred to anyone.

Two hours later, when Yvonne left her quarters for exercise on deck, she possessed one thing less than she had. That was the Sacred Sphere. It lay under the pillow on her bunk, and it remained to be seen if Blake would succeed in getting it.

In his cabin Blake had heard Yvonne's first tap. He was about to turn and light a cigarette, but when a second and then a third tap came he stood

SEXTON BLAKE, DETECTIVE

motionless. All he caught of the first word was the letter "y."

The word "pillow," however, he got perfectly, and it needed little deduction on his part to guess that the missing letter was "m." It meant that Yvonne had read the note, and had acted without loss of time.

It seemed an eternity before the listening detective heard the door of the adjoining cabins open and the swish swish of their skirts as Yvonne and Mother Peters passed on the way to the deck. Blake gave them time to reach the companion-way before he moved.

When he judged they had done so he noiselessly unlocked his door and looked out. There was nobody about. Stealthily he passed out and tiptoed along until he reached the next door. If Mother Peters had locked it all Yvonne's strategy and his caution would go for naught—for that day, at least. Unconsciously, he heaved a sigh of relief as the door yielded to his pressure. A moment later and he was inside.

Did chance bring Rymer or anyone else at that moment, his position would be as precarious as it had ever been in his long career. He touched the powerful automatic which was concealed beneath his jacket, and vowed grimly that if he were discovered he would get a few of the ship's company before they overcame him.

Instinct as well as the observations he had made told him Yvonne's cabin would be the inner one. To this he made his way at once, and pushed aside the half-open door. A familiar perfume met him as he did so, and even had he not known before he would have been certain now that Yvonne had lately occupied it.

Before him, against one wall, ranged her bunk, neatly made up. At the upper end was a large pillow, the smooth appearance of which gave no hint of what might be underneath. Two strides took Blake to it.

With a quick thrust, he pushed his hand under the pillow, and his fingers closed on something hard and round enclosed in a soft chamois covering. It was the Sacred Sphere of the ancient Ming Dynasty. He smoothed the slightly rumpled pillow, and turned to make for the door.

Just as he reached it, and was about to pass into the outer cabin, a knock came at the outer door, followed by the turning of the handle. Blake stiffened, and stood behind the shelter of the narrow door. Had he, after all, grasped

success only to have it snatched from his grasp? It certainly looked like it.

He heard the outer door open and a heavy step sound in the other cabin. Whoever it was, it was neither of the women. Then the footsteps approached the door behind which he was concealed.

Silently his hand slipped up under his jacket and gripped the butt of his revolver. As it did so, the hand and forearm of a man appeared around the edge of the door, the fingers gripping it as their owner stood and surveyed the cabin.

One glance showed the fingers and arm to be Rymer's. If he came six inches more nothing could avert discovery, and, from Blake's point of view, a premature settling of accounts between them. At that moment he heard a mutter.

"Must have gone up by the companion as I came down the ladder."

With that, Rymer's arm disappeared, and his footsteps sounded as he passed through the outer cabin and slammed the door. How little he dreamed how close he had been to Sexton Blake—and death! for had Blake and Rymer had a settling of accounts that day it would have been to the death.

Blake's fingers loosened their grip on his revolver, and he stole into the outer cabin.

"A close shave," he muttered. "He is sure to go up on deck to see if they are there, but he may return to see me, since he hasn't been about for a day. I'd better get into my cabin as soon as I can."

Softly he turned the handle of the door and slipped out. A moment later he was in his own cabin, and barely had he thrust the Sacred Sphere into an inner pocket, when there was a knock at the door.

It was Rymer.

From that day on Rymer's attentions to Yvonne and Blake were as unremitting as they had been during the first days of the journey. If he was weaving any new scheme in his mind which included Yvonne he kept it to himself, and beyond letting her feel how completely she lay at his mercy he left her alone.

As for Blake, he ate, exercised, and slept with maddening regularity. It was well he had communicated with Yvonne on the one slim chance which had offered, and that she in turn had lost no time in acting on his wishes; for from that day not a solitary chance presented itself for any communication between them.

Blake was kept to afternoon exercise, and beyond the morning and evening signal they neither heard nor saw anything of each other.

With that almost uncanny favour which Nature sometimes showers on evildoers, the Eastern Queen was given a fair wind clear across the Atlantic, and exactly nineteen days out of Cardiff, the blue coast of Nova Scotia appeared to the westward. That afternoon they rounded treacherous Cape Sable, and a little later lonely Seal Island was passed. Then they turned into the Bay of Fundy, and headed for the southern coast of New Brunswick.

Captain Jonas Pettigrew evidently had some reason for not laying his course direct for the port of St. John, for he made off a point to westward until first the Wolves and then the Island of Grand Manan appeared.

The latter, a crescent-shaped, lonely island inhabited by a handful of fishermen, came in sight just as night fell. The brilliant light on Southern Head, which rears itself at the very edge of gigantic cliffs against which the sea beats in wild fury, and about which the gulls wheel, shrieking with an almost human wail, shone out just as the waves grew leaden.

Far away at the other end twinkled the sister light on North Head, and a distant gleam showed where the outermost rampart of Campobello stood sentinel at the entrance to Passamaquoddy.

Little indeed had those barren coasts changed since the ancient red man stood and gazed in wonder at the unbelievable expanse of water with which the Great Spirit washed his doorstep.

With the lights of Grand Manan on her port bow, the Eastern Queen scudded along until she passed White Head; then the man at the wheel threw her over, and she headed up the Bay of Fundy, laying her course almost parallel with the near, but invisible, coast of New Brunswick.

All night she kept on this course; but as day broke over a grey, stormy sea, Rymer, who was on the poop, saw a black speck speeding towards them. It grew larger and larger, and through the flying spray, which curved outwards from her bow like lips of alabaster, he saw the slim, black shape of a powerful motor-boat.

Nearer and nearer she drew until within hailing distance. As a shout broke over the water, Captain Pettigrew and Kelly, the mate, appeared. Pettigrew waved his hand in reply, then turned to Rymer.

"We transship our cargo here. You had better have them brought on deck at once."

Rymer nodded curtly, and turned to go below. When Captain Jonas Pettigrew had explained to Rymer the workings of the underground system as far as he knew it, Rymer had seen a big complication ahead for him in the transshipping of the cargo in the Bay of Fundy.

It meant the removal of Yvonne from his immediate supervision, and though he had played a waiting game, he had by no means given up his intentions regarding her. Furthermore he was as determined as ever to get his fingers on the reward offered for the Lady Sybil, and though he might know all the theory of the underground system, he realised only too well that this would avail him not at all unless he personally could follow through the secret chambers in company with a cargo.

A wild idea entered his head to disguise himself as a Celestial and attempt to get through in this way, but second thoughts showed him the idea was ridiculous. His knowledge of the language—or lack of knowledge—was sufficient in itself to preclude any possibility of success on that score. And yet to make a false move now would be to spoil every one of his carefully laid plans.

During the long voyage he had given the matter very deep thought, and a plan had occurred to him which, could he carry it through, promised some meed of success. Consequently, he showed no signs of his inward perturbation as he went to do the captain's bidding.

In anticipation of soon landing, the main body of the Celestials had gathered together what bundles they possessed. As for Blake, he had not been on deck since the Island of Grand Manan had disappeared from view the previous evening, and though he could tell the vessel was "heaved to," he had no idea for what reason.

Things had been strangely silent in Yvonne's quarters, and a feeling of foreboding came over him as the silence continued. It was not until some time after Rymer had haled him on deck that he discovered the reason.

He joined the other Celestials who stood lined up against the side for inspection and count. A furtive smile, almost broke through Blake's impassive features at the humour of the situation.

With Dr. Huxton Rymer as second mate on a ship which smuggled Chinese, with Yvonne a captive on the same ship, and with Blake accepted as one of the Celestials, it was a situation which appealed to the sense of humour of the latter.

Rymer showed how little he realised the true condition of things as he walked along the line, counting and making a cursory examination of each man as he passed. Blake was the last in the line, but evidently Rymer thought his daily inspection of the fortieth man sufficed, for he barely glanced at him.

This finished, a rope ladder was thrown over the side, and as Blake stood nearest he was the first to descend. It was then he saw the motor-boat for the first time, and as he realised the meaning of it all he was for once in his life at a momentary loss what to do.

If Yvonne were still aboard the Eastern Queen it would indeed upset his plans to leave. Then he remembered the silence in her quarters and moved ahead. His deductions had led him correctly so far. He would not relinquish them now.

He leaped from the bottom of the ladder across to the deck of the motor-boat which swung alongside. A big cabin was placed forward, and into this a short, bearded individual motioned him. Blake descended the few steps which led into it, and as he gazed ahead through the semi-darkness of the place, he saw, stretched out on a couch at the far end, the relaxed figure of a girl. Beside her was the old woman.

Only too plain now was the meaning of the silence in Yvonne's cabin. She had already been forced into unconsciousness by a drug, and in this state she would undoubtedly be kept for many days. No matter how willing she might be, she was now powerless to assist Blake in any plan he might devise for her rescue. From now on it was a lone hand for him.

The rest of the Celestials followed hard on his heels, and when the last man had entered, the rope holding the motor-boat to the brigantine was let go. The purr of the motor sounded as she drew away, and a moment later she had swung round, heading Blake knew not where.

It began to look as if he would have his work cut out to succeed in getting a message to the Fleur-de-Lys. He realised, however, that the motor-boat could not cruise for long in the Bay of Fundy with a cargo of Celestials on board. They must land some place soon, and as he never crossed a bridge until he came to it, Blake closed bis eyes, and waited for the next step in the game.

So far, he had succeeded in taking two tricks. The third was now being played, but it remained to be seen whether Blake would win or lose it.

The day wore on, and about four in the afternoon another night began to shut in on them. It was deadly cold outside, for no more bleak stretch can well be found in the winter time than the storm-swept Bay of Fundy. A fire in the cabin made it fairly comfortable there, however, and thinly clad as were some of the Celestials, it was well this was so.

It was not until Blake judged it to be past six that the motor-boat showed any signs of slackening speed. First she slowed down to half speed, then the engine stopped altogether. A moment later a soft bump told Blake they had struck a mooring of some description.

Just then the man with the beard poked his head into the cabin, and said in fluent Chinese:

"Look here, you fellows, we have docked, and unless you want to be caught, let me tell you to do exactly as you are told. You will come out one by one and land. A man on the wharf will point out where you are to go, and as you value your lives go straight there. You will have to stay in the place two days. The vessel which takes you on the next part of your journey is two days late. Now then, old woman, give me your charge. I will go first, and take her."

He moved along as he spoke, and picked up Yvonne as though she were a child ; then he made his way out, and disappeared in the darkness, followed by Mother Peters. Blake was at the door in two strides, intercepting another man who had started to go out.

Pushing past, he gained the deck, and found they were moored beside an old wharf in a harbour of some sort. All around the shore were strings of lights, and behind ranged a city.

At first Blake was confused, but as he got his location more perfectly he recognised the sheet of water before him. They were moored in St. John Harbour, the great winter port of Canada.

This much he discovered, but no more. A gruff voice to his left caused him to turn and start in the direction from which it came. He found himself stepping from the motor-boat across the side to a landing at the foot of a flight of steps which led down from the top of the wharf.

A shadowy figure approached, and pointed upwards. Blake mounted at once, finding, as he did so, that the steps were treacherous and slippery from the frozen slime which covered them.

At the top another figure stepped forward, and pointed to a row of dark buildings at the head of the wharf. As Blake looked in that direction he saw a blotch some distance ahead also making in that direction. He knew it to be the man from the motor-boat with Yvonne in his arms, and old Mother Peters trotting along beside them.

Now, if at any time since he left Cardiff, was Blake free to escape. A few quick strides would have put him out of reach of the nearest of the agents of the System, and, as far as he could see, he was at liberty to traverse the full length of the dark wharf without being accompanied.

With a genuine parcel of "cargo" a guard is only necessary in order to protect them from their own mistakes, for the Celestial who is anxious to get into forbidden America is only too ready to trust himself to the care of the System until it finally lands him in the Chinese quarter of Boston, New York, or wherever he is booked to go.

Blake's hand insinuated itself up under his jacket, and his fingers closed on the butt of his revolver. For a fleeting moment the idea came to him to make a dash, knock on the back of the head the man who carried Yvonne, tear her from his grasp, and make his escape.

Had Yvonne been conscious, such a proceeding would have stood some chance of success; but he realised the old woman's cries would bring the rest of the agents down on him hot-foot.

If it had been nearer the city, where police and immigration officials might be about, even then he would have attempted it, but so lonely was the spot at which they had landed he knew full-well it was given over to the mercies of the night-prowlers of the harbour front.

By this time he was half way up the wharf, and the sudden disappearance of the party ahead through the open doorway of one of the buildings put an end to any thoughts of an attempt to escape.

He quickened his pace somewhat, for if they were to be hidden in the same house, he wished if possible to be near Yvonne. Then he stood some chance of knowing whether she would make one of the party which would leave in two days' time.

He found a man standing by the door, and as Blake approached the fellow scrutinised the detective's features. Satisfied that he was one of the cargo, he pressed a button. A moment later the door swung open, and Blake was pushed through into a dark passage-way.

A hand came out of the darkness and led him along to the foot of a flight of stairs. Up this he was conducted, until at the top a door was reached.

On being opened, it proved to be a big room containing no furniture, except a long table in the centre and about two score of mattresses ranged on the floor against the wall. The door closed behind him, and the sound of retreating footsteps told him his guide had departed to bring along the next man.

Blake made a quick examination of the room and windows, for he realised he must make a move soon in order to communicate with the party in the Flour-de-Lys. There were no doors beyond the one by which he had entered. A glance at the windows showed them to be closed on the outside by heavy shutters. A move to open one of them would soon attract attention, and moreover he doubted if it would be of any use, for from the location of the room he judged it to look out on the rear of the house itself.

As he heard footsteps again approaching up the stairs, he turned away and threw himself down on one of the mattresses, murmuring:

"Well, about the only thing I seem to have achieved to-day is to discover the name of the motor-boat—the 'Spitfire.' That is not much, but if she is the one which takes us away from here, it may be the card which will win the trick. Time will tell."

The door opened just then to admit another Celestial, and Blake nonchalantly lighted a cigarette. They began to arrive thick and fast now, and in less than half an hour the whole forty had been safely lodged in the big room.

The next day and night passed even more monotonously than those on board ship. During the day, Blake amused himself by writing a short code message to Tinker on cigarette paper, and from one of the other Celestials he got an envelope. Enclosing the note in the envelope, he sealed it, and wrote on the outside:

"Yacht Fleur-de-Lys. In Port. Urgent."

And underneath:

"Finder keep money, but please take note to above address at once. It is important."

Then taking a piece of paper from one of the bundles of another Celestial, he wrapped it about the envelope, at the same time enclosing two English sovereigns. That done he tucked it beneath his jacket to await a chance.

On the evening of the second day the bearded individual from the boat appeared, and spoke in Chinese to the "cargo."

"Half of you will have to remain here another two weeks," he said curtly. "Half will get ready to leave to-night. You will be taken aboard inside an hour; but we don't leave the harbour until daylight. I have brought forty slips of paper with me. In order that you may not squabble over who is to leave and who is to stay, I have left twenty-one slips blank and the other nineteen I have marked with a cross. Those who draw marked slips go; those who draw blanks remain. Now, then, look lively!"

Blake listened in consternation to this unexpected denouement. Since the party was to be divided up into two and sent at different times, it was obvious that they were to be sent directly into the channel which would carry them across the American border. The question was, would Yvonne be sent with the first party, or the second?

If with the first, it was essential that Blake should leave with it also; if the second, then to leave now would cause him to lose sight of her entirely, and Heaven only knew what developments, might take place before he again discovered her whereabouts. But something must be decided, and decided quickly.

Suddenly he remembered that instead of the "cargo" being halved, it had been divided into unequal parties, one of nineteen and the other of twenty-one. He argued from this that the smaller party, which was to go first, must be smaller for the reason that the extra facilities were required in another direction.

That being so, who more likely than Yvonne and the old woman? Besides, since she was being kept in a state of unconsciousness it was natural that they should dispose of her as quickly as possible.

This conclusion reached, Blake moved forward with the others to draw his slip, determined if he drew a blank to buy or, that failing, to take by force a marked slip from one of the lucky ones. He was determined, by hook or by crook, to go with the first party.

Thrusting his hand in amongst the forest of yellow fingers which stretched out eagerly for a slip, Blake grasped one and drew it out. A wave of disappointment swept over him as he saw the side towards him was blank. Quickly he turned it over, and heaved a sigh of relief as there before him he saw a rude pencilled cross.

Fortune was with him, so far. He was to go.

As soon as the draw was over, the man from the boat marshalled up the nineteen and started them for the wharf one by one. Blake squeezed into a middle place, for he judged those at the front and rear would be more closely guarded than those between, who would be trusted to follow the leaders. The bearded man himself would probably bring up the rear.

At intervals of a minute they were started off, and eight were gone before it was Blake's turn. As the man in charge signed to him he passed through the door and down the stairs. A man there let him out and pointed towards the wharf. Blake bent his head and started over the road.

Half way across his arm shot up under his jacket, and he drew out the note he had written. Without slackening his pace in the slightest degree he hurled it from him through the darkness. A soft thud somewhere behind told him it had landed on the pavement.

He realised to the full the risk he had run; but it was his only chance of communicating with the Fleur-de-Lys, and must be taken. The note might even now fall into the hands of one of the agents of the System, or into the possession of some unscrupulous dock loafer.

In either event, the money would be kept, but the note stood little chance of being delivered. However, that had to be risked.

Two minutes later Blake descended the steps and crossed to the motor-boat, which he saw was the same by which he had come. The other eight men were already in the cabin, and he took his place beside them.

A curtain now concealed the couch at the upper end of the cabin, but the bottom of a woman's skirt which could be seen sticking out told him old Mother Peters was there—and that meant Yvonne. Blake began to wonder if, after all, he might not swing the third trick in the game.

Hour after hour passed, and still they sat there silently waiting for day to appear. After what seemed an eternity of time, the first grey of dawn began to spread across the winter morning, and with it came the tramping of feet on deck. Low voices as though in argument followed, and Blake, who sat somewhat near the door, shifted his position in order to hear.

They were speaking in English, and evidently cared little whether they were overheard by the Celestials, or not. One voice Blake recognised as that of the bearded individual; the other was—Rymer's!

At last the latter had moved, and as he listened Blake knew he was lying to the other man.

"I tell you Pettigrew says I'm to go through with them," he said. "I have special business to put through at the other end, and besides, he thinks I should keep an eye on the cargo."

"Well," grunted the other, "this is the first time Captain Jonas Pettigrew has ever taken such a fatherly interest in the cargo after it has left his hands, but I suppose it is all right."

"If you have any doubts on the matter, send and ask him," bluffed Rymer boldly.

"By ginger! I would if I didn't want to get away at once," responded the other coolly. "However, stay if you want to."

They moved away at that point, and Blake heard no more. He had heard sufficient, however, to tell him that Rymer had by no means given up his intentions regarding Yvonne, nor his determination to trace through the channels of the underground system the whereabouts of the missing Lady Sybil.

He had deserted the Eastern Queen, and no doubt in a few hours Captain Jonas Pettigrew would be scouring the city for his missing second mate.

Five minutes later the purr of the motor sounded; the boat slipped away from the wharf, and they began moving through the icy water of the harbour on the outflowing tide, heading for the bay beyond.

§

Just before dawn appeared that same morning, a heavy brewer's cart drew up at the head of a broad quay farther up towards the city, at which a slim, graceful-looking yacht lay moored. The driver tied his reins about the whip stock and swinging over the wheel made his way along the quay. He drew up as he reached the gangway of the yacht and, opening his mouth, emitted a hoarse hail.

"Floor-du-Liz ahoy!" he shouted.

The bow watchman on the yacht came to the side and looked over.

"Ahoy, yourself!" he said.

"I've got a letter for you," called the carter. "Shall I bring it aboard?"

"Sure thing, old son! Just waltz up the gangway. I'll call the skipper."

The man on the quay lumbered up the gangway, and stood waiting. A moment later a sailor appeared and led him to the chart-room, where sat Captain Vaughan in pyjamas and dressing-gown.

The man handed the letter over.

"I was comin' along by the docks about an hour ago on my way to the stables," he said. "I kicked something on the pavement, and lookin' down I saw a packet. I opened it, and found that note and two gold pieces wrapped up. Well, I put the gold in my pocket. You can see on the envelope that it said to do so. As soon as I got my horses hitched up I drove along here with it."

While he had been speaking, Captain Vaughan tore open the envelope and glanced with knitted brows at the writing it contained. Suddenly he turned to the sailor.

"Have Master Tinker come here at once. Also call Mr. Kennedy and Mr. Graves."

The sailor hurried away, and in less than five minutes Tinker was there. Captain Vaughan thrust the paper over to him.

"I can't read this, my lad. Is it in code?"

Tinker took the paper and glanced at it eagerly.

"Yes, yes!" he said quickly. "It is from the guv'nor, and as plain to me as English. Who brought it?"

The captain jerked his hand in the direction of the carter.

Tinker turned to him:

"Where did you pick this up?"

"About half a mile down the docks, just opposite the old Colonial Wharf."

With a ringing cheer Blake led the sailors from the "Fleur-de-Lys" to the attack.

"Do you know a motor-boat here called the Spitfire?"

"I ought to, seein' as she lays at the Colonial Wharf, and I pass her every mornin' and evenin'."

"Good!"

As he spoke, Tinker thrust his hand in his pocket and drew out a sovereign.

"Here you are for your trouble. You needn't wait any longer."

The man took the gold, and tipping his cap awkwardly lumbered out, evidently more than pleased with his day's beginning.

As soon, as he was gone, Tinker spread the paper out on the table. At the moment Kennedy and Graves appeared, and stood just inside the door as they heard the lad's voice.

"This captain, is what it says :

"'Arrived and held in house opposite some old wharf. Transshipping in bay to motor-boat Spitfire, and brought here by her. Leave on Thursday or Friday by her. Imagine during hours of darkness or early dawn. Watch her and follow in Fleur-de-Lys. If we get into American waters, tell Kennedy to strike. We may be transshipped again. If so follow. And in any event move in

American waters, but not before. Don't know that this will reach you, but am taking a chance. If hear nothing from you will try to communicate later. Yvonne well so far. Dr. Huxton Rymer one of the gang. Tell Kennedy thirty-nine Celestials besides me in the cargo. We must bag the lot.—S. B.'"

Twenty minutes later the Fleur-de-Lys slipped her moorings and headed for the Bay of Fundy under full steam.

The Seventh Chapter

The Fleur-de-Lys Attacks—The Fight—Rymer Escapes with Yvonne.

THOUGH, it was well-nigh a month since the great Christmas Eve storm had swept across Canada, the surroundings of the little shack which bore the sign "Looey Sing, Laundry and General Stores" showed little change.

Perhaps the snow was a little deeper, and the drift-piled road had long ago been beaten into a hard, slippery track by the sleighs of the farmers.

Now it looked like a discoloured ribbon winding over a mantle of virgin white, the purity of which stood out startlingly against the emerald edging of fir and spruce.

Though the cold was not abated, and each night showed the thermometer down to twenty degrees or more below zero, the river was ice-bound no more. Great, powerful icebreakers had come up and ploughed a channel through it by which the small river steamers which supply the isolated fishing islands of Campobello and Deer Island could reach the wharves in the town above.

There they disgorged their cargoes of salt fish, frozen fish, and pickled herrings, which would soon go speeding north to Madawaska and Restigouche to the great lumber camps.

In return they loaded tier upon tier of flour in strong wooden barrels, cakes of tinned vegetables and meat, sacks of bran and shorts and middlings, molasses and pork and salt, not to mention the eternal barrels of pilot bread and cases of "candy," for the fisher children on those lonely islands have both a sweet tooth and a marvellous capacity for anything which pleases that quality of the palate.

Two miles below, in Looey Sing's shack, the same dingy stock still decorated—or encumbered—the front shop. The back room, where that uncommunicative Celestial passed his days and nights, showed not the slightest change, and, with Looey Sing himself sitting before the stove and smoking the eternal yellow cigarettes, it might have been back on Christmas Day, not nearly a month later.

As he had done on Christmas Eve, and, in fact, as he had done every day since, Looey Sing sat impassively until the short winter day drew to a close. But, unlike the days since that other one, he rose shortly after and proceeded to don his fur coat and cap. Replenishing the fire, he opened the rear door and stepped out into the clear, frosty air.

Up above in a cold silver sky a chill moon sailed, bathing the snow-covered country in rays of cobalt. The hard facets of the encrusted snow glittered in the light like myriads of diamonds, throwing back the rays in countless points of light. The emerald woods had deepened in tone to that of the black fastnesses of the boundless ocean.

Somewhere in the distance a telegraph-wire sang, as wires do in Canada in the winter. In the woods a sharp, pistol-like report sounded from time to time as a weighted branch cracked in the frosty air.

It was a true winter night in New Brunswick, and even the apparently unemotional Celestial must have felt it, for he stood a moment gazing about him at the cold virginal glory of it all.

Taking a long breath of the biting air, he turned and crunched along a well-beaten path until he disappeared in the woods. He followed identically the same course which he had taken on Christmas Eve.

In near the edge of the bank a wide fringe of ice still clung, though now its once glittering surface was coated with snow. Further out many startling reports sounded as great stretches of ice would split in two, the dividing line which appeared being the only sign that this had occurred. The channel itself where the water ran free was a black band on a vast carpet of brilliance.

Following the bank of the river, Looey Sing kept on until he reached the little wooded cove where stood the boat-shed. There he proceeded to unlock the doors and busy himself at the winch. A moment later the boat rolled down the tiny track on its wheeled framework, and as the latter kept on into the black depths, the boat floated free on an inky bosom.

The purr of the engine broke out almost at once, and, as Looey Sing took the tiller, the boat headed down river in a wide sweep which brought it well out in the middle.

Over the same course went Looey Sing until he came abreast of the point guarding the entrance to Oak Bay. There he swung the tiller hard over, and a moment later the boat was driving along close to the shore, headed up the small bay.

No driving storm of hail and sleet blinded him this night. The moon threw into clear outline the timber-bordered shore where it broke against the tossing waters of the bay, which, fed by the salt spew from Passamaquoddy, defied the frost. Helped by the moon, he could see along for some distance, and a close observer might have noticed a barely perceptible flicker of the heavy lids as he peered ahead over the bows.

Long ere this the masthead light of the schooner should have shown. Certainly there was no mistake on the part of the Celestial. He had in his pocket a code telegram telling him the day and the hour at which the schooner would be an-chored in the accustomed place. It had been sent from St. John just before the motor-boat Spitfire had left with the first batch of cargo.

Even in stormy weather connections had never been missed before; and certainly the elements could not be the reason on this occasion, for a fair up-river wind had been blowing for three days. At the very latest, the schooner should have made the rendezvous by dark. And yet it was now a certainty that she was not in the bay.

The motor-boat had now reached the spot, and passed over it at slackening speed. Soon the engine stopped, and as she went ahead under her own impetus Looey Sing sat contemplating the expanse before him.

"I no undelstand," he muttered, as he turned and gazed astern. "Teleglam say she be here. She not here allee samee. Someting happen. I go down river see what. Allee samee, Looey Sing no likee."

Once more he carefully scrutinised the bay, but not the remotest sign of a barque of any description could he make out. As far as could be seen, he was alone on the cold bosom of the bay. Starting the engine again, he sent the boat around, and went back the way he had come.

When the flashing light on St. Croix Island appeared he laid the boat's head for the American side of the river. Reaching there, he again altered his course, and in the black shadow cast by the tree-covered Devil's Head he started down river on his search for the missing schooner.

§

While Looey Sing was speeding along in his attempt to locate the schooner a startling de-nouement had taken place a few miles down, just off the lonely shore on the American side, in St. Andrew's Bay—the small basin of water which passes on the flow of the river to the gaping maw of Passamaquoddy.

It was, in fact, a culmination of the third trick of the game upon which Blake was engaged, and as yet the issue was not decided. Certain-ly, Blake little thought the deciding card was coming through the night in a motor-boat. But how the crisis came is only explained by going back to the moment when the Spitfire, with her illegal cargo on board, stole out of St. John Harbour on the wings of a misty dawn.

Though his note to the Fleur-de-Lys had been written before he had any idea as to what Rymer's next move was to be, on thinking things over, Blake felt satisfied that, even had he known, he would not have altered the wording of it.

On the contrary, he felt that Rymer's appear-ance on the scene was a satisfactory point, for it meant one more loose thread gathered in. And certainly the skein, was already sufficiently tangled.

Had he only known if his note was destined to reach the Fleur-de-Lys, he would have felt that his feet were on firmer ground than they were.

As it was, he had to go ahead as he would were the whole game to be played out by himself alone; and did the others turn up, then, if the issue by any chance hung in the balance, their arrival might turn the scale.

Reconstructing the line of thought he calculated Rymer would follow, and in view of the tenacity of purpose he knew that gentleman to possess, it was not hard for him to read the meaning of Rymer's coming.

Once she was clear of the harbour the Spit-fire tore on down the Bay of Fundy, keeping in sight of the coast. It was a rocky outline in the winter-time at best, though in summer no more glorious fancy of Nature can be found than the zephyr-kissed shores of New Brunswick. From the few glimpses he caught of the shore through the cabin window Blake judged they were doing about twelve knots, and he was not far wrong.

All day the boat kept up this pace, and all day the Celestials sat in the stuffy cabin, ignorant of the next step in their long underground journey, but confident in the power of the men in charge to eventually land them where they desired to go. It was not until late afternoon that the boat's speed showed signs of slacking, and all hands moved with an unconscious air of relief. Even the impassive Celestial can feel the deadly drag of monotony.

It was evident that the schooner to which the bearded man had said they would be trans-shipped was in sight, and had there been any doubt in the matter, a loud hail on the deck of the Spitfire put it to rout.

An answering hail from over the water sounded faintly, and the motor started again as the Spitfire was headed in that direction. Five minutes later the cabin window on the port side was overshad-owed, and a soft bump told Blake it was the side of the schooner. The man with the beard thrust his head into the cabin almost immediately.

"Look alive!" he ordered. "One at a time, and don't waste any time about it. There is smoke astern. It is probably a steamer coming up."

The Celestial nearest the door lost no time in acting, and the rest followed him hot-foot. Blake passed out last, and as he did so he saw Rymer behind him, bearing Yvonne in his arms. Evidently old Mother Peters had swallowed his bluff, as had the bearded individual.

Blake, being the last out, was still on the ladder which led over the side of the schooner when he heard Rymer's voice beneath him. Turning, he looked down, and saw the other was signing for him to take Yvonne and pass her over. Throwing one leg over the side, in order to steady himself, Blake leaned down, and held out his arms.

As Yvonne was placed in them and he felt the warmth of her relaxed body, a great wave of weakness swept over him, and for a moment he swayed; it was followed by a flood of rage at the whole cursed work of the System, and never in his life had Sexton Blake been nearer losing command of his temper than at that moment. He was beginning to realise that Yvonne's danger had struck a deeper chord than he imagined.

He held her very gently until Rymer reached the deck, though something at least of what he felt must have shown in his eyes, for as he took Yvonne, Rymer looked at Blake, and shivered slightly as he did so.

Had Blake been able to see his own eyes at that moment he would have understood the reason. He had veiled them so quickly, however, that Rymer began to feel uncertain whether or not the expression he had seen there was his own imagination. But, from time to time, he looked at the silent Celestial with a curious glance, and resolved that in future he would keep Chen Foo at a distance from Yvonne.

As soon as the "cargo" was all aboard and sent below, the Spitfire drew away and headed back for St. John. Then, as night closed down the schooner, which, by the way, was the same one which had borne a cargo to Looey Sing on Christmas Eve, took advantage of what breeze there was and laid her course for the mouth of the St. Croix River.

About an hour later a row of lights showed on the starboard side. It was the steamer, the smoke of which had been seen astern some time before,

and in the glow of the electric bulbs Blake, who was leaning over the side, thought he recognised the slim lines of the Fleur-de-Lys.

For a moment he was puzzled as to why she should pass them, supposing it was she. Then he remembered that in his note he had told Kennedy to strike if they got into American waters. To do that the yacht would have to be authorised by the Government officials on the American side.

This meant that before striking the Fleur-de-Lys must make an American port in order to get the necessary papers of authorisation. In that was explained her reason for passing them, and, if it were she, there was no doubt but she was running for Eastport, that coast city of fish warehouses and sardine factories, which is situated at the very mouth of the St. Croix and which the schooner herself must pass before entering the river.

About seven the following morning the schooner passed through the channel between Deer Island and Campobello, and, coming away in a wide track to windward, headed up the river. The wind, which was fair, began to ease, and the outrunning tide meeting the waters of the bay, combined to make her progress slower.

However, with a moderate run, she should make her rendezvous, and, from the suppressed air of relief which rested on the lantern-jawed captain, Blake judged he hoped to do so.

As they passed Eastport, off to the left, he scanned the long line of wharves with an eagle eye. There were small river steamers moored there as well as a couple of big outside boats which traded between Eastport, St. John, and the larger port of Boston. Intermixed was a medley of sardine boats, some auxiliaries, and a host of open motor-boats, to say nothing of several schooners whose bare spars looked like a naked forest.

At first he could see no signs of the graceful lines of the yacht; but as the schooner shifted her course he caught sight of a white yacht moored at a short wharf below the Custom House. It was the Fleur-de-Lys, and he knew now his note had been delivered.

Slowly the shore passed until the schooner nosed the waters of St. Andrew's Bay. It was past noon now, for a good deal of time had been consumed in tacking. As a matter of fact, if the wind held, the captain figured on making St. Croix Island about dark, and the rendezvous a little later. This he usually contrived to do unless the weather forbade, for he had no fancy to heave to around the point in Oak Bay in daylight.

It was just after they had entered the bay and were making a long tack to starboard which carried them well over into the Canadian side of the river, that a cloud of black smoke appeared astern. Beneath it a shape rapidly came into view.

It began to overhaul them quickly, and as the captain of the schooner saw his next tack would take him fairly close to her, he issued orders that all Celestials who were on deck should go below at once.

He had no desire for any curious eyes to see the countenance of a Chinaman peering over the side of his ship, though in truth, the rapidly-falling night practically precluded any such possibility. Little did he dream of the identity of those on board the yacht.

So far as his next tack was concerned he was right. It carried him across into American waters, and as he got within hailing distance the lantern-jawed captain received a shock.

On the bridge of the yacht stood two men in uniform. One of them had been leaning over the rail watching the schooner as she crept along over the imaginary line in the middle of the river which formed the boundary between the two countries. Then he curved his hands around his mouth, and shouted:

"Ahoy! What vessel is that?"

The captain of the schooner muttered a deep and fervent curse as he approached the side and spat into the water, then he raised his voice:

"Schooner Southern Cross. Who are you?"

"Out of where?" came the voice of the man on the yacht, ignoring the counter-question.

"Out of Boston—bound for Red Beech."

"What is your cargo?"

"Coal."

"Heave to. I wish to come aboard."

"I'll do nothing of the sort! Who in blazes do you think you are?"

"I tell you to heave to, or I'll put a shot into you!"

"When you show me any reason why I should, then I will—not before! I want to make port tonight, and ain't goin' to heave to for anyone!"

With a ringing cheer Blake led the sailors from the "Fleur-de-Lys" to the attack.

A silence followed, then the voice again came:

"This is the yacht Fleur-de-Lys, temporarily in the service of the United States Immigration Department. I propose going aboard to inspect you and examine your papers. Will you heave to?"

Before replying, the captain of the schooner turned and spoke to the red-bearded mate, who had come on deck in haste.

"Have her put over hard," he said, in a low tone. "We'll run for the Canadian side."

The mate jumped to obey, and a moment later the schooner heeled as the booms came over, and she went off on a new tack. Almost immediately, there was a dull report astern, and a four-inch shell crashed through the rigging, taking a quantity of cordage with it.

The foresail came down with a ripping, tearing sound, and the foretop-sail flapped wildly as her stays gave. The captain leaped to the wheel, cursing, and shrieking out orders to the crew to cut away the damaged rigging, tried to keep her on her course. The yacht was now coming up hand-over-hand.

Seeing that the schooner did not stop, the gun again crashed out, and this time the foremast itself came down. At that the captain brought her round, and calling to his men, ordered them to arm themselves. The bow gun of the Fleur-de-Lys had done sufficient damage.

Blake had gone below with the rest of the Celestials, and though he could hear voices, which told him the yacht had drawn up and Kennedy was striking, he made no move until the first guns boomed out, then he acted.

Leaping to his feet, from the dark corner where he sat, he made for the door of the rough quarters in which the "cargo" had been put, and before any of the others could grasp his intention, he was outside. A moment only, and he had turned the key in the door, effectually stopping the participation of the Celestials for some time at least.

He made for the deck on the run, looking little like the heavy-lidded Celestial, Chen Foo. At the foot of the companion-way he stopped, but only long enough to draw his automatic; then he began taking the steps two at a time. On reaching the deck, a strange sight met his eyes.

The dying light was just sufficient to enable one to distinguish what was going on. The spars and sails of the schooner hung helplessly from aloft, and on deck a confused litter of sails and ropes almost made the forward part impossible. Though a man still stuck to the wheel, she refused to answer her helm, and was drifting in slowly towards the American shore.

Almost the first person he saw was Rymer rushing forward, yelling like a madman, and brandishing a heavy Service revolver. The captain and mate were tossing over weapons of every description to the crew, who were massing behind the tumbled heap of cordage. In close was the yacht, drawing nearer every moment, and even as he looked she bumped. Then began a fight which, for swiftness of action, equals any tale out of the old stories of the Spanish Main.

Kennedy, Captain Vaughan, Tinker and Graves, leaped over the schooner's side, almost simultaneously. Hendricks, the mate, with Alec and the seasoned crew of the yacht, followed in a stream, armed with revolvers, cutlasses, and even belaying-pins. Almost ere their feet had touched the deck a heavy revolver fusillade met them from behind the heaped-up sails.

Blake made a running leap and hurled himself over a hatch to join the attacking party. His presence acted on them like a sharp spur, for as Tinker gave a hoarse cheer, the others took it up, and with Blake at their head, dashed forward. Two sailors had gone down under the first volley, and now a second volley came from behind the barricade. Some damage was done, and of the leaders, Hendricks was struck in the arm.

Until now the attacking party had held their fire, but at Blake's command they fired. It was a terrific volley which followed. Every revolver was one of heavy calibre, and seasoned as were the sailors, their aim was cool and steady.

A medley of shrieks and groans broke out on the other side of the barrier, but it was very evident that no surrender was intended, for several shots came zipping at the attacking party. That was the last volley from either side.

Blake and his followers were too close now for revolver work. With a sharp order he clubbed his revolver, and, followed by the others, stormed the barricade. He made an odd-looking figure as he mounted over the heap of sails and cordage, risking everything to get into a hand-to-hand struggle. His blue jacket fluttered loosely, and his queue flapped behind him like a long braid. The sleepy look had left the eyes, however, and the cold fury in them was distinctly Anglo-Saxon.

For Blake was seething with a rage which had been steadily growing in him ever since he left Cardiff. Circumstances had made it necessary to hold it in check, but now that the crisis had come he gave it full reign. And Tinker, who had seen his master under all sorts of conditions, said afterwards that never before had he seen Blake fight as he did that night.

He swept over the barrier in a furious rush which defied opposition. Striking hard and straight with the heavy butt end of his revolver, he drove a couple of sailors to the deck and kept on, not knowing nor caring whether he was alone or whether the others were behind him.

He had one object in view, and that was Rymer. Nothing mattered now but to come to grips with his old enemy, and exact in one final settling, the revenge he felt was due to him.

At that moment one of the men who had been left aboard the Fleur-de-Lys switched on the searchlight, and trained it on the scene of the conflict. It lit up a strange sight indeed.

The captain of the schooner was lying doubled up in the scuppers with a bullet in his leg. Reddy, the mate, was wielding a belaying-pin, in a deadly struggle with Kennedy, the American Secret Service man. Tinker was cutting viciously with a short sabre at a big negro, who wielded a huge meat chopper with deadly intent. Hendricks had stopped long enough to bandage up his wounded arm, and with a sabre in his free hand, was driving a couple of sailors forward.

Alec and Captain Vaughan were in a tough melee with half a dozen Swedes at them, and the balance of the yacht's crew were fighting grimly in single combat. Each had picked his man, and with joy of battle in his eye, was fighting with sabre, revolver, belaying-pin, or in some cases bare fists.

Blake was occupied with a third, but straining every effort to reach Rymer, who, since the captain's fall, had assumed command.

He was standing back a bit, directing the efforts of his men. And yet he had taken no active part in the struggle, not because ho feared to come to grips—for Rymer was never a coward—but because the attack had sent all his plans crashing to the ground, and his mind was working madly in an attempt to devise some means of averting the disaster which threatened.

It had been no small shock to him to see a Celestial leading the boarders, but not until the searchlight swept across the deck did he recognise the features of the man to whom he had handed Yvonne, and whose strange look on that occasion had caused him to shudder.

Even yet he had not realised the full truth, but as Blake's third man went down and be leaped towards Rymer, rapping:

"Come on, Rymer. You and I have a settling together!"

Then the light of recognition filled Rymer's eyes, and a soft curse broke from him.

Fool that he had been not to see through that disguise before.

It seemed that nothing could now prevent that long delayed clash; but something did, and that in the person of the wounded skipper, who, unseen by Blake, had rolled out of the scuppers and grasped his late passenger with all his strength about the ankles. Rushing as he was, Blake came down with a heavy crash, his head struck the deck with frightful force, his revolver flew into the scuppers, and for the time being he was non est.

Crawling forward, the skipper was about to deal him a further blow, when a great black shape shot through the night into the circle cast by the powerful searchlight, and before the terrified captain could help himself, he was rolling over and over in a death-struggle with Pedro's jaws at his throat.

The blow Blake had received had only partially stunned him, and in a few seconds he staggered to his feet. Well was it for the skipper that he did so, for only his command to Pedro prevented the great bloodhound from finishing his work.

He leaned against the side and passed his hand across his forehead. Before him the fight still raged, though with slackening vigour. Half of the schooner's crew lay about the deck, out of commission for the time being. The other half were being slowly driven forward to the fo'castle by the yacht's crew, though they stubbornly disputed every inch of the way. To all intents and purposes, however, it was a losing fight for them.

Of Rymer there was no sign. Even before Blake had fallen, Rymer had seen the day was lost, and, not even waiting to settle his old enemy, he had dashed below. A few minutes after he had regained consciousness, Blake saw the reason for Rymer's flight.

Coming out of the after hatch he saw a head, then a body, and finally a pair of legs. Another figure, and another, and another followed, until eighteen stood on the deck. Rymer had released the Celestials and turned them loose.

If the fight that had gone before was hot, that which followed beggars description. A few words from Rymer telling them they stood in danger of being captured after their long secret journey, had let loose a flood of savage rage which was deadly in its ferocity. Every one of them bore knives, and as the last reached the deck they tore along forward, shrieking like maniacs.

Only those who have witnessed the sight know the intense ferocity of a Celestial when, running amok. Now, not only was there one, but eighteen, every one of whom had a knife in his hand and murder in his heart. Had Blake needed anything to clear his dazed senses that sight was sufficient.

With a swift motion he bent and reached his revolver out of the scuppers; then, levelling it, he began to send a hail of lead into the onrushing Celestials which succeeded in sending three of them to the deck, but did not stop the rest.

He gave a loud shout to warn the others, and, clubbing his revolver, stood ready to receive the attack. In a moment it was upon him. To this day Blake could not tell you exactly what happened from that on.

From the moment he found himself in a sea of yellow faces, with a dozen knives flashing in the rays of the search-light, he lost all count of detail and time. The berserker rage again seized him, and he fought with the fury of a madman.

A fleeting glimpse of a white face close to him told him that at least some of the yacht's party had seen the rush and had turned to meet it. Blow after blow he sent crashing straight into the yellow faces before him.

Man after man had gone down, but if he himself was wounded he did not yet feel it. His blue jacket was slashed to ribbons where the knives had ripped it; both his arms were bare to the shoulders, and his sleeves lay on the deck, clean cut away by the knives. But Blake heeded it not. A red mist suffused his eyes, and he only knew that he was fighting for his life.

Suddenly the press before him eased as others came to his assistance. He was aware that Hendricks on one side of him and Tinker on the other were swinging their sabres with deadly effect. In the momentary breathing spell he had he stood motionless, listening to a sound which came across the cold, frosty night air.

It was the throb of a motor growing louder each moment. Was it reinforcements from Eastport, or merely someone from the shore who had been attracted by the boom of the gun earlier in the struggle. In a few moments he was to know.

Even as he once more pressed forward and turned aside a slashing blow, the sound of the motor grew more distinct, and finally approached close to the schooner's side. It was Looey Sing, though Blake knew him not.

At almost the same moment Blake saw Rymer stagger down from the poop deck bearing a burden in his arms. Behind him came the old woman. In a glance Rymer took in the features of the new-comer, and approaching him, spoke rapidly. Blake saw the Celestial nod and turn back to the side.

In a second he read the meaning of Rymer's words. He had divined the identity of the Celestial, and had told him he had a precious burden which at any cost must be got away. As he realised this, Blake pressed forward savagely; but though he fought like ten men, he could not overcome the row of knives which kept slashing at him.

In less time than it takes to tell, Rymer was over the side with his burden. The old woman followed with surprising agility, and as she disappeared, Looey Sing turned and shouted something in Chinese to the Celestials. There were only about ten of them left in the fight, but as Looey Sing's hail reached them they swung like lightning and raced towards him. Blake, knowing Chinese as he did, understood that hail only too well. Looey Sing had shouted:

"Come quickly, pigs, if you would escape!" And they lost no time in going.

Their fallen comrades or the crew of the schooner mattered not if they could save their own skins and reach the golden land in safety.

With a shout, Blake tore after, followed by Hendricks, Tinker, Kennedy, and Alec. Graves, Captain Vaughan, and the sailors were still occupied with the crew of the schooner.

Had it not been for Rymer's anxiety to further his own plans, and his utter indifference to the fate of the Celestials, they might even then have got clear, for once they gained the boat they stood a good chance of getting away.

No sooner had Looey Sing reached the boat, however, than Rymer pushed off, the result being that the Celestials who flung themselves over the side landed not in the boat but in the icy water of the river.

Then it was that Blake and his companions, who had followed to deal out punishment, perforce had to turn to and take active measures to save the floundering beings in the water, which had already chilled them to the bone, and at the same time driven all the fight out of them.

As for Looey Sing, when he saw what had happened, he bent without the slightest haste and started the motor. A moment later it shot away from the side and headed at full speed up river, its occupants utterly indifferent to the struggling men in the water.

Blake cursed silently and redoubled his energies in order to lose no time. One by one the dripping Celestials were dragged aboard and sent to find their way to the cook's galley, where a fire burned.

As soon as the last was safe, Blake hurried forward, to find that the desertion of the Celestials and the fall of the mate had broken the last thread of resistance of the crew of the schooner. Already Captain Vaughan had driven them into the fo'castle and locked them in.

As soon as he got within hearing, Blake spoke quickly:

"Captain Vaughan, we must cast off at once. A motor-boat has come alongside and taken off Rymer. With him is Yvonne."

The captain, swung quickly, and rapped out an order to Hendricks.

"Mr. Hendricks," he said, "take six men and keep them aboard as a prize crew. Lock the Celestials in the cook's galley, and keep the crew in the fo'castle. Have your men cut away the wreckage, and make back to Eastport as best you can."

Then he turned to Blake.

"All ready, Mr. Blake. We will board that yacht, and, if human power can accomplish it, we will overtake that motor-boat."

At that moment Kennedy and Tinker came rushing up, with Pedro loping along behind them. They asked no questions, for well they knew Blake's intention as he sprang over the side of the Fleur-de-Lys. They followed hot-foot with those of the yacht's crew who were to go after them also.

It took very few minutes for those skilled hands to throw off the grappling-ropes and let the yacht drift away, from the schooner. A moment later Captain Vaughan, who, with Blake, had gained the bridge, rang the engine-room telegraph, and the yacht began to gather way.

They were none too soon, either, for the American shore loomed perilously close. It was evident to those on the yacht that Hendricks would have his work cut out to get the wreckage, cut away and make what sail he could, before the schooner grounded. And once aground, the outrushing tide would soon leave her high and dry, though not before the drifting ice-floes had done considerable damage to her sides.

The searchlight had been left trained on the schooner's deck in order that those left on board might have her light to work by. Now, however, Blake swung it around and sent its long, sword-like rays shooting along the bosom of the river.

Up, up, up they went, until they passed off the water and rested against a black point which stood out lonely and grim in the night. It was Joe's Point, which hides the bar at St. Andrew's from the view of navigators coming down the river. Not once had Blake picked out the motor-boat.

Again he brought the light back to within a few hundred yards of the yacht, and again it went travelling over the water. Suddenly a black blotch appeared in the path of silver. It was moving at a rapid pace, and Blake needed no more to tell him it was the fleeing motor-boat containing Rymer, Yvonne, Mother Peters, and the unknown Chinaman who had come to their rescue so opportunely.

The schooner had now been left well behind, and the yacht was beginning to reach the full power of her engines. Swiftly though the motor-boat was travelling, it could not escape the white rays which Blake held steadily on it.

In this fashion the chase went on for some little time, until at last the extreme end of Joe's Point entered the penumbra of the searchlight, and almost simultaneously the motor-boat disappeared behind it. For a time at least it must be a blind chase. The yacht forged on, keeping well out in the channel, for the St. Croix at night is a difficult passage for those who are familiar with every foot of it, let alone those to whom it is strange.

Captain Vaughan had been up it twice, many years before; but in the lapse of time one's memory dulls on many trivial points of a tidal river, and at night, with an outrushing tide, it is these trivial points which may crop up and dislocate one's plans. They drew steadily nearer the point, and finally swept past at top speed.

Once more Blake sent the light forth, and far ahead, sticking to mid-channel, he picked up the motor-boat. Robbinston flashed by on the left, and in a few minutes they caught the gleam of the revolving light on St Croix Island. It was there that they again lost sight of their quarry, as the island hid it from view.

Captain Vaughan veered off to the American side in order to pass the island, and once again they picked up the motor-boat. It was flying straight up river, and had already left behind the point at the entrance to Oak Bay where the rendezvous was, at which the ill-fated schooner had failed to appear.

From that on it was an open chase until the old breakwater appeared. No sooner had it done so than Blake heard Captain Vaughan utter a low exclamation. He turned sharply.

"What is it, captain?"

"It has just occurred to me that with the tide more than half-ebb it is going to be mighty tricky getting through the Narrows just beyond the breakwater. There! With the light as it is now, you can see how the point on the Canadian side juts out and appears almost to touch the American shore."

"And there goes the motor-boat through," muttered Blake, as he held the light steady and followed with his eyes the configuration which the captain had pointed out.

Then aloud he said:

"Our quarry is gone through, Captain Vaughan. If it is a possibility, the Flour-de-Lys must follow. Remember your mistress is aboard that boat and at the mercy of Dr. Huxton Rymer if we fail to overtake it."

"You can count on my putting the yacht through if there is water enough to float her," returned the captain grimly. "Above the Narrows the river is wider and deeper, though in a hundred years the sawdust from the mills higher up has choked the channel considerably."

Both men turned in silence and stared ahead over the lit-up waters. The motor-boat was just disappearing behind the point which jutted out at the entrance to the Narrows, and a moment later she was lost to view.

Though it tried him sorely, Captain Vaughan rang half-speed as they passed the breakwater and entered the harrow water ahead. Through that cramped channel the tide rushed wickedly, carrying with it huge blocks of sharp-pointed ice which had broken off higher up. The Fleur-de-Lys nosed them unflinchingly, and a sigh of relief went up as she passed the first point in safety.

Slowly, with the dainty hesitation of a timid though determined maiden, she pushed on until the second bulge of the bank appeared. Now she hugged the curved bank on the American side, for there the water ran deepest. Ahead could be seen the red light of Bog Brook, telling of the danger, and behind them glimmered the Canadian lighthouse opposite the breakwater.

Every man on board leaned over and watched tensely the while the yacht forged ahead; then suddenly a deep, unconscious gasp ran over her from stem to stern its they felt a faint jar.

The Fleur-de-Lys had grounded in the Narrows, and not until the returning tide floated her could she hope to complete the passage.

For a single moment Blake raised his clenched hand and let it drop savagely on the rail of the bridge, the while he cursed silently. For one fleeting moment he contemplated taking a boat and, with half a dozen sailors at the oars, rowing after the motor-boat.

Then reason showed him how futile such a proceeding would be. No. For the moment he acknowledged himself beaten, and, with brooding eyes, he turned and went below, none attempting to speak to him.

With swift step Blake entered a cabin and shut the door. Drawing out a cigarette, he sat down and began to give his mind to the unfortunate denouement which had occurred. Certainly Rymer had so far played the winning card of that night's trick.

Not until the returning tide floated the Fleur-de-Lys did Sexton Blake move. It was now well past two, and the others, weary from the long fight, had turned in without undressing, to snatch a few hours' sleep. Simultaneously with the floating of the yacht they all appeared.

Blake was already on the bridge, and as Captain Vaughan came up he said curtly:

"Captain, we will go on through the Narrows until we reach the wider part ahead. Then we will turn and go back. I want you to break the record to Boston."

The captain looked at Blake in wonderment for a moment, for it was not like the detective to abandon a chase once he had set out upon it. He was too well-trained, however, to make any comment, and replied:

"All right, Mr. Blake. As soon as I get out of these treacherous Narrows yon will see what she can do."

THE EIGHTH
CHAPTER

RYMER TELLS THE TALE SUCCESSFULLY—
ON THE WAY TO BOSTON.

WHEN Rymer had turned loose the cargo of Celestials, and with a few words had spurred them on to join in the slaughter on deck, he had sped along with no definite purpose in view to the cabin where Yvonne was kept.

His one idea, so far, was to create a scene of confusion on deck, under cover of which he might have an opportunity to turn events to his own advantage.

It was ever Rymer's policy to use a man or a system as long as it served his purpose, and when it had ceased to be useful to cast it aside as one does a dilapidated hat. It mattered not a jot to him that the captain and crew of the schooner might be overpowered and in the parlance of the country caught "with the goods on." They had served their purpose as far as he was concerned, and now he would, if possible, get clear.

For a bare moment he wondered if it would not be wiser to leave Yvonne and make use of the precious moments for his own protection. Then the dogged greed of the man came to the fore, and with it his undoubted love for Yvonne.

It was a strange combination of good and bad which contributed to the making of his decision; but had he needed anything to clinch it, the memory of the look in Blake's eyes as he called to his old enemy was sufficient.

He found Yvonne on a couch, unconscious, with old Mother Peters in maudlin terror on the floor. Rymer picked Yvonne up bodily and roughly kicked aside the old hag, who clutched his knees, begging him to save her.

"Get up, you old fool!" he snapped. "Nobody will trouble to hurt you. If you want to come with me follow close, but let me tell you I won't wait."

With that he hurried out, the old woman trotting along at his heels, muttering a wonderful mixture of prayers and curses and forebodings.

On his way to the deck Rymer formed his plans. Under cover of the fight he would lower a boat and get away, if possible. Before he could be overtaken he might reach the Canadian shore, and on that side of the line the yacht had no authority to carry on the fight.

He knew that Blake would follow, regardless of boundary lines, but he vowed grimly that once he gained the shelter of the timber on the shore it would take a strong force to land under the hail of lead with which he would meet them.

At that moment he had reached the deck, and there met Looey Sing, whose timely arrival had served as a marvellously fortunate occurrence for Rymer. The reader has seen what followed then, and how the chase progressed from the time Looey Sing sent the motor boat flying up the river until they passed safely through the Narrows, where the Fleur-de-Lys grounded.

It was only a short distance now to the wooded cove where Looey Sing kept his boat, and with unerring skill the Chinaman drove her in until she gently nosed the slip. Rymer lent a hand, and together the two worked the winch in silence until the boat rested on her wheeled framework in the shelter of the shed.

When Looey Sing had jerked the old woman out of the boat, and Rymer had taken Yvonne, the Celestial turned to the white man.

"You follow me," he said curtly. "We talkee when we get to my place."

He set off at a swift pace on the way to his shack followed by Rymer and the whimpering old woman. Once within its safety he bolted the door, and waved his companions to chairs. Rymer laid Yvonne on a couch, and turned to the fire with a sigh of relief.

For the moment, anyway, he was safe, and if he was any judge of the Celestial capacity for cunning, he thought he stood a good chance of getting entirely free, though to be sure, the Celestial must not be told all.

What had become of the yacht he had no idea. All he knew was that her searchlight had suddenly failed to follow their course, and on looking back just before entering the wooded cove, he had seen nothing of her.

As soon as he had divested himself of his fur coat and cap, Looey Sing lighted a yellow, cigarette, and turned to Rymer.

"Now, then, we talkee!" he said.

Rymer nodded his head.

"Yes, I will tell you how everything happened."

Slowly he related to the Celestial how, as mate of the Eastern Queen, he had been in charge of the cargo of Celestials leaving Cardiff for St. John.

"After we transferred them," he went on, lying cheerfully, "Captain Pettigrew thought it best that one of us should personally accompany the girl. Sam Loo valued her highly, and as she is intended to be the wife of his Excellency Fu Kan, the Governor of Hamai, we could afford to take no risks. In fact, Mother Peters here bears a letter from Sam Loo to the governor himself."

Looey Sing turned quickly.

"Is that light?"

The old woman felt the safest course was the truth, and nodded.

"Yes, I have the letter. See!"

As she spoke she drew it out, and held it up. Looey Sing took it, and closely scanned the Chinese characters.

"It is the writing of Sam Loo," he said, handing it back. "Go on!"

Rymer did not answer for a moment. Now, if ever, was his opportunity to discover if the Lady Sybil had been shipped through the underground route; but he realised he was treading on very dangerous ground. A bold lie would be necessary to draw the truth from Looey Sing, but if his lie was clumsy, the Celestial would, at once become suspicious. However, he decided to risk it. He lighted a cigarette with an air of nonchalance, and went on.

"The reason we thought this the wisest plan was because another special bit of cargo which was sent through some time ago has not been heard from since."

Only Rymer knew how his heart hammered while he waited for Looey Sing's reply. At last it came.

"What bit of cargo you speak of?"

"It was sent from Cardiff about ten days before Christmas," answered Rymer. "The tramp

Wu Ling recognises Yvonne and Rymer.

steamer, Belle of 'Frisco, brought it out with a consignment of Chinese."

"That cargo went through my hands," rejoined Looey Sing curtly. "Nineteen men and a girl. The girl was sent through from here Christmas night with the others, and arrived safely in Boston. She may be there now, she may be in 'Frisco. I don't know."

Rymer breathed more easily as he realised his lie had gone down. Now he knew he was on the right track, and that the Lady Sybil had indeed gone by this route. If he could only play his cards rightly he would win out yet.

"Everything passed as usual," he said, returning to the explanation Looey Sing sought. "I joined the Spitfire the morning she left harbour. We had nineteen Celestials besides myself, the girl, and Mother Peters, here. We picked up the schooner in the bay, and transferred safely. The Spitfire then returned to St. John, and we made for the river.

"Nothing of a suspicious nature occurred until we got well into the river, and then the yacht you saw hailed us. When we refused to heave to she sent a couple of shots into us, and came alongside. You saw pretty well what followed."

"Then someone betray us," said Looey Sing.

Rymer nodded.

"Yes, and I happen to be the only man who knows who it was."

"How that?"

"I will tell you. Just before we left Cardiff Sam Loo came aboard, and asked us to take one man extra, though we were full up then, and getting ready to leave. Well, we took him, and saw nothing suspicious about him. Sam Loo said he had just landed in England from Canton. He was one of the nineteen who left St. John in the Spitfire, and in some way he let the cat out of the bag to his friends, who must have followed us the whole of the way from England in the yacht. He is no more Celestial than I am, but is an Englishman, and his name is Sexton Blake. Did you ever hear of him?"

Looey Sing took one step across, and grasped Rymer by the arm.

"Is that the tluth?"

"Of course it's the truth."

"Then we move quick. I hear of Sexton Blake. I know of him velly well. He dangelous man."

"I know him, too," rejoined Rymer gloomily. He might have added: "I know the yacht, and all

aboard her as well; and let me tell you, my friend, that the yacht and everything on her belongs to that girl lying on the couch."

He did not add this, however, for he had no intention of letting anyone but himself become aware of Yvonne's identity. All this time old Mother Peters had remained silent, her eyes darting from one to the other.

Looey Sing she accepted unquestioningly as part of the System to which Sam Loo belonged. Not yet, however, did she understand Rymer. From the very first she had mistrusted him, and yet not one solitary occurrence stuck out which by any chance she could call suspicious.

He had done as any other member of the System would have done while on the Eastern Queen, and in the escape from the schooner he had done more, for not many of the members of the System would have risked a delay in order that she might come, too.

This generosity on Rymer's part awoke no gratitude in the breast of the old woman. She felt certain that he had some game of his own to further, and that had she have been in the way she would have been left behind. Which, as it happened, was the literal truth.

Confident though he was that he would eventually bend Yvonne to his will, Rymer had no fancy that her awakening should find that resourceful young woman without the old woman to care for her.

He felt he knew Yvonne well enough to be certain that no matter whether she had fallen into the hands of the System voluntarily, or accidentally—though since the fight he knew the former to be the case—and no matter how she might feel towards him, she was bound to be a little grateful that he had run some risk in order to bring the old woman, regardless of the fact that she owed her present position to him. And he was right, as later events were to prove.

Looey Sing had been in deep thought over since Rymer had finished his explanation. Finally, he tossed away his cigarette, and turned to the other.

"You wait hele," he said. "I go to see if I get something to take us away to-night. If Sexton Blake on the tlail, the System she bust up. Anothel way must be found. It just happen the 'gleat head' is in Boston. I go thlough, too, and see him. Looey Sing, live hele no more. I must send teleglam to St. John, too. They bound to sealch thele pletty soon."

He shuffled away as he spoke, and entered the front shop. A moment later Rymer heard the tinkle of a telephone-bell, and Looey Sing's voice followed asking for a number. As soon as he got it, he asked who was speaking, and, evidently satisfied, said:

"You come now—to-night—instead to-mollow night?"

Evidently the person at the other end said he would, for Looey Sing said "All light!" and rang off.

Then, he came back to the rear room, and began writing out a code message to warn the St. John agents.

"Me give that to deliver to send," he said as he folded it up. "He be hele in half an hour. You wait. Looey Sing go to pack up."

He disappeared into the front shop again, and Rymer drew up a chair before the fire, determined to let things take their course.

From the little Looey Sing had said, it was evident they were going through to Boston. If that turned out to be the case, it would suit him down to the ground, for he knew Boston thoroughly, and trusted to devise the next step in his own game when he reached there.

If he had only known the identity of the man to whom Looey Sing referred as the "gleat head," and who the Celestial said was now in Boston, Rymer would not have sat so confidently before the fire in the back room of Looey Sing's shop.

Instead, he would have taken Yvonne, and trusted himself to Fate, and risked Blake's vengeance rather than walk into the very jaws of the yellow dragon, as he was destined to do.

For the "gleat head" was none other than Prince Wu Ling, autocratic ruler of the powerful Brotherhood of the Yellow Beetle, prince of the royal blood of China, and one time claimant to the throne through his being the direct descendant of the last ruler of the Ming Dynasty.

Looey Sing returned to the room at intervals in order to get one or two things which he proposed to take with him. It was marvellous when he finished how little he really intended to take, and had Rymer only known it, almost half of his bundle was composed of banknotes of every denomination and condition. Looey Sing had profited exceedingly cut of the "cargoes" handled by the underground system.

A few minutes after the Celestial had finished a knock came at the front door. It was the driver of the covered sleigh which was to take them over the border. Rymer, at a sign from Looey Sing, picked up Yvonne, and made his way out.

The sleigh was a big, roomy affair, piled up inside with heavy fur rugs, and on the bottom wore several foot-warmers. It was hardly less warm than Looey Sing's back-room, and when they were all in, a curtain at the back kept out prying eyes, and kept in the warmth.

Then a creak followed as the runners moved over the frosty road, and the shop of "Looey Sing, Laundryman and General Storekeeper" was left to the solitude of the winter night. Never again would the silent Celestial return, and until someone entered, the mice could hold high carnival in peace.

Up towards the town of St. Stephen went the driver. When he reached its outskirts he made a wide detour, which took them through a wooded road to a point beyond Milltown, the cotton town which adjoins St. Stephen. From there his course took him over a road, heavily lined with snow, and banked on either side by the tall spruce and fir, the cheerful birch and the lonely pine.

Almost at the very moment when Sexton Blake on board the Fleur-de-Lys made his way to the bridge to instruct Captain Vaughan to make for Boston, the sleigh containing Rymer and Yvonne crossed the line by way of the frozen river several miles up. At last they were in the States.

When the first grey of dawn appeared, the driver pulled into a lonely road leading to a more lonely looking farmhouse. There his passengers alighted, while the driver turned and started back for the Canadian side.

At the farmhouse the fugitives spent the day until night fell, when the farmer, who was one of the agents of the System, hitched up, and again they started.

In this fashion they continued their journey for over a week—driving all night and resting during the day, and thus was it that the cargoes of the underground system were put through to their destination.

Through the vast solitude of the Maine woods their course took them. They went by the loneliest roads in order to avoid the settlements and towns; and be it known that in Maine and New Brunswick such a proceeding is not difficult to accomplish. On from Maine through the snow-covered State of New Hampshire they passed until on the tenth day they reached Massachusetts.

At last they were on the final leg of their long journey, and soon, very soon, Rymer would need to play his next card.

If he had only known whom he was to find at his destination!

THE NINTH CHAPTER

LADY SYBIL'S ORDEAL—RYMER WALKS INTO THE LION'S DEN AND IS SENTENCED.

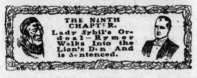

THE city of Boston, in the State of Massachusetts, is the industrial centre of New England. Its population exceeds the half-million mark, and it is indisputably one of the greatest points of imports and exports in the United States.

If you ask a Bostonian what is Boston, he will gaze at you with a blank stare, and placidly inform you that Boston is the centre of culture in the United States and the hub of the universe.

Although the casual visitor would doubtless make some reservations regarding the latter statement, at least he would freely grant that the city was a marvellous hive of industry.

In itself, it is one of the most important railway centres in America, being the converging point of a myriad lines. Its woollen imports and exports are the largest of any port in the United States. Its manufactures are world renowned, for from it come boots and shoes, cotton goods of every description, confectionery, furs, hats, and a list of the needs and luxuries of man too numerous to mention.

All about it, like satellites about the mother planets, circle a host of smaller cities and towns, having their great woollen, cotton, and shoe factories, and making together one of the greatest manufacturing and industrial centres of the world.

Not only is Boston a great business port, but it is also the home of culture and education. Harvard, one of the greatest universities in the world, has its home there, and draws within its classic portals students from every part of the globe. Its museum of fine arts, its world-famed library, its technical school and medical colleges, all tend to contribute to the atmosphere of culture, and its public buildings are masterpieces of the builder's art.

There the first spark of the American Revolution was struck, and there was cradled the protest against slavery which gave rise to the American Civil War, dividing thousands of homes against themselves, and saturating the green fields of the South with the blood of her sons.

It is the birthplace of many eminent literary men and painters, statesmen and orators. The works of its poets are read in every home in the land, and its writers have by no means remained in the lower ranks of their craft.

And not only has Boston achieved distinction on these lines, but it has seen the springing into fame and power of many captains of industry, for more and more is commerce spreading out over the city.

The once aristocratic and exclusive residences of Beacon Hill and Back Bay in many cases now stand cheek by jowl with great retail shops. Their occupants, who find the proximity of trade an offence to their sense of the fitness of things, have sought refuge in Beacon Street and Commonwealth Avenue.

But if it is the city of industry and education, it is also a city of narrow streets and hidden vices, as is every other city in the world.

There, as in New York, Chicago, 'Frisco, and Montreal, is the inevitable Chinese quarter, and certainly the man who knows his way about can at times see things as unspeakable in the neighbourhood of Harrison Avenue and Kneeland Street, as he can see in the famous Mott Street district in New York, or in Little Lonsdale Street in Melbourne.

In a heavily-curtained, upstairs room, not a hundred miles from Kneeland-Street, one cold, sleet-driven night in the early part of February, sat two men. Plainly furnished though it was, the room was a welcome retreat on such a night, for with the north-east wind whipping in off the bay in the winter time, no more cheerless place can well be found.

A table, a couch, three or four chairs, and a few really fine rugs, made up the furniture of the room. On the table was a nickel-plated oil-lamp, and sitting before some papers spread out beneath its glare were two Celestials.

One was stout and deliberate in his movements, though each gesture carried an air of deference in its train. Sexton Blake could have told you it was San, the faithful and indispensable lieutenant of Wu Ling. The other was the prince himself.

At present his eyes were bent on a telegraph form which lay on the top of several others. San's attitude was one awaiting his chief's pleasure. When he had read and re-read the telegram Wu Ling looked up, his deep, inscrutable eyes searching those of his lieutenant.

"It seems that destiny sports with us, San," he said slowly.

"Excellency, it is, as you see, the work of the man Blake."

"True, San, true. He it is who has thwarted many moves of mine. Never before has any man dared to pit himself against Wu Ling. And yet he still lives. San, the man Blake must go!"

"It is also the opinion of your most unworthy servant, Excellency."

"It was a mistake to take the Lady Sybil," went on Wu Ling, musingly. "I should have taken other means to gain the information regarding her father's purpose in China, and what report he made to his own Government when he returned. She has been a complication, and, if I mistake not, it is her disappearance which put the man Blake on the track of the System I have so carefully organised. But since we have taken her, she will tell us what we wish, or pay the penalty.

"Looey Sing's message says he arrives to-night. He also says the old route is no more a secret to the authorities, and that he has been compelled to leave. Well, if the pig wishes to save his own skin what matters it? He has been faithful, and will prove valuable elsewhere. But the girl he says he is bringing—who is she? And the other man? He doesn't say. For that I must wait.

"He did well to send the warning to the agent in St. John, but he was too late. A thousand curses on the man Blake and his ancestors! Eight of

my countrymen wounded in the fight, the captain and crew of the schooner beaten on their own ship, ten more captured, and twenty-one in St. John seized and deported. Thirty-nine men lost who would have gone to swell our forces here, and, worse than all, the secret route discovered! Pigs, dolts, fools! A thousand curses on them!

"To think that the man Blake came through as one of them, befooling even Sam Loo! He is getting old and careless. I will order him to China, and the price of his mistake, shall be his head. It is well, indeed, that I had the daughter of the English duke kept here until my arrival from 'Frisco."

For a few moments Wu Ling bent his head in thought; then again he spoke.

"San, have the girl brought in. I would speak with her. I shall then deal with her. Matters must be adjusted without delay before these stupid American pigs discover too much."

San rose at once, and, with a low bow, went out softly. Wu Ling sat perfectly motionless until he returned leading a girl garbed in English clothes.

Over her costume of pale pink, now soiled and crushed, was thrown a heavy coat of grey squirrel. Her features were now free from a veil, and though her eyes showed marks of the suffering through which she had passed, and her face showed a deadly pallor, she was still lovely to look upon. She seemed for all the world like some white flower which had been thrown into a choking bed of yellow poppies.

Wu Ling gazed at her with steady eyes, and as hers in turn rested on his, she made the first audible exclamation which had left her lips since she had awakened from drugged unconsciousness.

"Dr. Li-Fuang," she said, in low, vibrating tones. "So it is you whom I have to thank. Am I, then, in the city of Pekin? If you have the slightest vestige of feeling in you, tell me, I beg of you. Tell me where I am! Tell me what month, what week, what day it is! Tell me how long these creatures have kept me drugged, and tell me what is your purpose! Is it the custom, of Dr. Li-Fuang, the eminent Chinese statesman, to eat the salt of a foreign diplomat and return his hospitality by stealing his child?"

"Lady Sybil, you shall know all in good time, and rest assured no harm will come to you if you do as I demand. Then, and not before, you will know in what city you are. Then, and only then, will you know what month it is, what week, what day—yes, Lady Sybil, I will even tell you then what year it is!"

"Then it is the New Year!" she cried brokenly. "Oh, my father and mother will be mad with grief!"

"The sooner you do as you are asked, then the sooner will their grief be assuaged," replied Wu Ling suavely. "And, remember, Lady Sybil, your father is getting old!"

She swayed slightly upon her feet, and at a sign from Wu Ling, San gave her a chair.

"What is it you wish?" she asked in a whisper, her eyes wide with terror and suffering.

Wu Ling bent forward and fixed his eyes upon her.

"When you were in Pekin with your parents, you acted as secretary to your father, I think?"

She nodded, but made no audible reply.

"You also repulsed the attentions of Dr. Li-Fuang, or in other words, my attentions. Well, rest easy, my dear young lady, I never wanted to marry you; but I did want something else, and that is what you are going to give me to-night."

"What is it?"

"Information which you possess. Listen! Your father came to Pekin on a diplomatic mission which coincided with certain secret treaties which my Government made with Germany. He apparently came to make certain proposals regarding English trade with China, at least, so everyone thought but myself. I knew he came to investigate secretly our treaties with Germany. Not until he was gone without making any serious proposals did the others see that I had been right.

"While you were there, I made advances to you, thinking I might extract from you the information I needed. I saw I had made a mistake, and resolved to await my chance. That chance is come, and the price of your freedom is to tell me exactly what report your father made to the British Government on his return to England. If you tell me, I pledge you my word that you shall go free and unharmed. If you refuse—well, your fate will be more terrible than in your wildest dreams you could conceive."

"In other words, you have come like a thief in the night, have torn me from my home, have brought me to some strange city, and have made the price of my freedom the betrayal of my father. You have made one mistake, Dr. Li-Fuang. You forget that you have English honour to deal with. You may take my life, but you cannot force me to betray my father. I refuse utterly!"

"Your life will not be forfeit," rejoined Wu Ling, in a tone of quietude which was far more impressive than any heated remark. "The dead rabbit feels nothing. Your punishment will be to keep you alive, and leave you at the mercy of my creatures. It will be to you a thousand times worse than death. You will know neither the city nor the town where you are kept. Your past life will be but a memory. You will be dead to your family and your friends.

"Your father and your mother are old. You are an only child, the pride and joy of their present, and a comfort for their declining years. All that will be over. To them you will be dead. To you the memory of them will be a spur of torture which alone will be sufficient to break your will and sear your soul.

"Think well what it means before you refuse, Lady Sybil. Think well of what you have left, and what the future will be. Now go! Think to-night, and in the morning let me have your answer. By it I shall be governed, and I tell you with all meaning that, if you refuse, your fate will be exactly what I have painted. Take her back. San."

San had to support the sobbing girl from the room, for the deadly menace in Wu Ling's tones had told her even more than the words themselves into what a living hell she would be thrust did she refuse to do his bidding.

But it meant betraying—perhaps politically ruining—her father, and she had too much of the ingrained English notion of honour in her to sacrifice another in order to save herself. And yet what a price!

Certainly, as she was led back to the charge of the woman who guarded her, she had a problem to settle that night which was as torturing to decide as any young girl torn from a sheltered home had ever grappled with.

How little we really grasp the idea of the thousands of miserable problems which are settled for good or ill every night all over the world in similar fashion.

It is a putrid condition in the plague spots of the earth, and every man should make it his creed to help to restrain or stamp out, as he would any deadly disease, the vultures who thrive on it.

And when the young men—for with them lies the remedy—who are too lackadaisical to bother, realise that the best men of the country are banding together for this very purpose, it behoves them to join the ranks, as every British man, who is a man, is doing, either actually or in spirit.

When San departed with the Lady Sybil, Wu Ling turned back to the pile of papers before him. So far as any outward signs were concerned, he showed no trace of being affected by the sentence he had just passed. Nor was he.

Prince Wu Ling was a man with just one purpose in life, and he was all the more dangerous to humanity because he was honest in that purpose, and, according to his lights, honourable in his methods.

That these did not coincide with the Anglo-Saxon idea of how things should be done is no reason why Wu Ling should be condemned, and on that very point had Sexton Blake shown the deep insight into human nature, and the complicated motives governing its actions, which he possessed.

That purpose was one which was a creed with Wu Ling. Descendant of a dynasty which could trace its history back to a time when the Anglo-Saxon race was unheard of, bred in the mystic lore of generations of ancient scholars, steeped in the pure philosophy of Confucius, and with an inborn reverence for Taoism, he felt to the uttermost depths of his nature that the Celestial race and no other was the race destined to be the rulers of the earth. To him the Anglo-Saxons were as flies of yesterday. In his heart he looked upon them as an accident of civilisation, and the thieves of credit; thieves, because they made use of inventions ancient for centuries in China, and presented them to a credulous world as children of their own intelligence.

The utter indifference to human suffering and the apparent savagery of the Celestial caused the Anglo-Saxon to shudder with horror. To Wu Ling, the very sensitiveness which caused them to shudder was the token of an effeminate nature. He was the product of a school which believed in drastic measures where punishment was necessary, and would never have countenanced the more humane—to him the more effeminate—notions of the Anglo-Saxon.

It was his one dream to sow in their midst the seeds of discontent and terror, to play off one against the other, to pit white against white, and from the sowing to reap a crop of victory for his own kind; to feel the heel of the East on the West, to carve a path of saffron through a field of white, to raise on high Confucius, Buddha, and Taoism. That was his hope, his aim, and his ambition.

As a knock came at the door Wu Ling raised his eyes. As he thought, it was San, but, contrary to his expectations, his faithful lieutenant had not come to resume the work upon which they had been occupied. Instead, he stood just within the door, and bowing low, said:

"Excellency, the pig Looey Sing has arrived. He sends his unworthy homage to you, and begs your Excellency will grant him audience. He brings with him the man and girl of whom he spoke in his telegram, and also an old woman who looks after the girl."

"Is the girl conscious?" asked Wu Ling curtly.

"Yes, Excellency. The dog Looey Sing tells me he stopped the drug yesterday."

"Then I will grant audience. Let them all be brought before me."

San again bowed and departed. In a few minutes he returned. Behind him came Looey Sing, and following him Yvonne, leaning on the arm of an old woman, with Rymer bringing up the rear.

Wu Ling had turned his attention back to the papers before him, and probably it was because his head was bent over them that at first Rymer failed to recognise him.

Had he done so it is certain that his ideas of getting possession of the reward offered for the Lady Sybil, as well as his intentions regarding Yvonne, would have been thrust aside in one mad dash for safety, for Dr. Huxton Rymer and Prince Wu Ling had scores of old standing to settle.

Not recognising the prince, he followed the others across the room until they all stood before the desk. Then Wu Ling looked up. In one all-seeing glance his eyes swept the quartette before him until they came to rest on Rymer. Without the flicker of an eyelash he said curtly:

"San, lock the door. Put the key in your pocket."

With a surprising agility for one of his bulk, San obeyed, and Rymer, who had uttered one startled gasp of recognition, controlled his features, realising that if ever in his life, bluff and nerve were to serve him now was the time.

When San had returned to the side of his master Wu Ling turned to Looey Sing.

"You tell me of failure, Looey Sing," he said slowly. "Is that what I ask of you?"

The Celestial spread out his hands.

"Excellency, I have served faithfully. By day I have planned, by night I have worked. It is not the fault of Looey Sing. The man Blake left from Cardiff. He never reached Looey Sing. Had he done so I would have killed him. Instead, I risked all to go to the succour of the cargo. Those I bring with me I saved. Anything more was impossible, Excellency."

"Blake, Blake, always the man Blake!" mused Wu Ling, never taking his eyes off Looey Sing's face. But had he done so he would have seen the half-closed eyes of the girl with the glorious bronze-gold hair light up suddenly as the name left his lips.

"You speak the truth, Looey Sing," went on Wu Ling. "You have done well. I have indeed no blame for you. The fault lies with Sam Loo, a fault for which he shall pay dearly. Go now! I have things for you to do, and will talk with you to-morrow."

"Your unworthy servant is grateful, Excellency. Always will he serve you with his life."

With that Looey Sing departed, no doubt congratulating himself warmly, at the outcome of the dreaded interview with his chief.

At the same time it was only a sample of Wu Ling's justice, for the prince never punished unless punishment were deserved. When San had again locked the door and returned, Wu Ling ignored Yvonne for the time being, and turned to Rymer.

"Dr. Huxton Rymer," he said, gazing inscrutably at Rymer, "is it because you have my interests at heart that you come here to-night?"

For a moment Rymer was silent. Then he looked up.

"Wu Ling, I knew not that you were the head of the System when I joined it. At the same time I have worked for its interests, and at a time when all appeared to be lost I saved the most important part of the cargo at the risk of my life. She stands here before you."

"You lie!"

As Wu Ling uttered the words with deadly calm he leaned forward.

"Listen to me, Doctor Huxton Rymer! Do you think Wu Ling organises a System without having the means at hand to know everything which affects that system? Fool! Do you take me for a babe?

"Before me I have a report which tells me how you gained admittance to the crew of the Eastern Queen. Another report tells how you proclaimed yourself second mate in the private room at Sam Loo's. A third how you deserted the Eastern Queen in St. John, and joined the motor-boat Spitfire by saying the captain of the Eastern Queen had sent you. Again, you leave the schooner as a rat leaves a sinking ship, but you still continue on through the channel of the System. And now you stand and lie to me—Wu Ling!

"Do you forget that I know you to your very depths? Do you forget the time, when I dragged you out of an opium den, a weak, doddering imbecile, and put you on your feet? Do you forget your treachery when the American, John Strang, was in my power? And again, when in Ecuador you first sold the secret of a dead man to Andrades, the Spaniard, and in turn to sell us to the president? Bah! You child, to pit your wits against Wu Ling.

"For days have I sat here, waiting to see who the white man was who came with Looey Sing. I dared to hope that it was the man Blake walking into my arms. But, at least, he is no infant. You joined the System for some purpose of your own. It matters not now what it was, for it has failed. In any case, you are a traitor to the System, and by the rules of the Brotherhood all traitors are punished by death.

"But death will not be your reward, Dr. Huxton Rymer. From you will be exacted the payment for past treachery as well. And your punishment will be lifelong slavery in the rice fields of China, with the raw hide lash when you shirk. San, take him away!"

As San advanced to do his bidding, Rymer made a move as though to resist. The sight of a shining revolver in the hands of the latter, however, caused him to think better of it. He threw one strange look at Yvonne, who had listened with horror to the sentence, then with bowed head he turned and passed out.

As Yvonne turned back to Wu Ling, her eyes were, swimming with tears, for though he had chosen the crooked path, Rymer had once been a gentleman. Moreover, he had expressed for Yvonne all the love his nature could feel, and it is hard for a woman to thoroughly hate the man who chooses her above all the world as the recipient of his love.

When Rymer was gone, Wu Ling looked at the old woman.

"Well, old hag, what have you to say?" he asked curtly. "You come from Sam Loo?"

Mother Peters almost grovelled on the floor as she bobbed forward, and began a long-winded tale.

Wu Ling cut her short.

"Answer my questions!" he ordered. "Are you in charge of this girl?"

"Oh, yes, your Excellency!"

"To where is she bound?"

"To China, Excellency, to become the wife of the Governor of Hamai. I bear a letter to him." "Give it to me!"

"Oh, yes, your Excellency!"

The cringing old woman drew out the letter and handed it to the prince, who, without looking at it, tore it to pieces and dropped it on the floor.

Then he turned to San.

"Take her out!" he ordered. "I will decide what is to be done with her!"

San obeyed, and was returning to take up his old position, when Wu Ling said:

"And, San, leave me for a bit."

With a murmured "Yes, Excellency," San passed out.

Then Wu Ling turned to Yvonne.

"And now, Mademoiselle Yvonne," he said softly, "we will talk."

The Tenth
Chapter

Sexton Blake's Demands—Wu Ling's Emotion—Homeward Bound—The End.

JUST about the time when Looey Sing, with Rymer and Yvonne, reached the end of their long drive, and entered the house near Kneeland Street which sheltered Wu Ling, the closely muffled figure of a Chinaman turned out of Harrison Avenue into Kneeland Street.

The hail and sleet were driving in off the bay with a terrific force, which sent all who could go into the warm protection of their homes.

The Chinaman who battled his way against it seemed utterly oblivious of the discomfort of it. In truth he was, for his thoughts were too absorbed in a certain problem to heed aught but the purpose on which he was bent.

Though he looked a Celestial in every particular, and though he had passed as one for many days, he was far from being one. Underneath that muffled exterior was the personality of Sexton Blake, and on this night he was on his way to put to the test the truth of information gained through many weary days.

When Blake astonished his companions on board the Fleur-de-Lys by deciding to give up the pursuit of those in the motor-boat and run for Boston, it had been no blind chance on which he was bent. Down in the solitude of his cabin he had marshalled before him all the facts which he possessed, and one by one had connected them up into a workable whole.

It seemed certain to him that, even did he succeed in tracing the trail taken by the occupants of the motor-boat, he would stand no chance of coming up with them before other developments had taken place, chief of which was the warning of the unshipped "cargo" which still waited in St. John.

Moreover, now that the cat was out of the bag, the smugglers along this particular underground route would abandon everything—at least, until the storm blew over. That being so, it meant that they would run for safety, and where more likely than to either the originating point of the System or the end of it.

As the originating point in Cardiff was known, and as the route through to the St. Croix River was also known, it left only the American side of which Blake and Kennedy were still ignorant.

It was certain that they would not double back, only to put their heads through the noose, but, instead, would scuttle for shelter at the other end. That might be Boston, New York, Chicago, or 'Frisco. Portland Blake discarded, for the reason that he considered it too small a city to be a final point in a system having such gigantic dimensions as the one upon which they had stumbled.

Boston being the nearest point, it was just possible they would make for there, and if so he might yet succeed in wresting success from apparent failure. It was at that point in his deductions that he rose and made his way to the bridge to give orders to make all speed for Boston.

A stop at Eastport on the way was necessary, in order that Kennedy might land. He was to go on to Boston by rail, and had arranged that, with a dozen Secret Service men, he would be on hand there night and day did Blake discover anything further. On that point Blake and Kennedy had their first difference of policy.

The American was all for gathering together a good-sized force, and making a clean sweep of the Chinese district in search for any Celestials without documents of authority proving they had a right to reside in the United States. Since half of the route had been discovered, it would not be difficult to discover the other half, once the ringleaders were in custody.

On that point Blake differed with him. He never for a moment forgot his promise to the Duchess of Carrisbrooke that if he succeeded in discovering the Lady Sybil all publicity would be rigorously suppressed. Now he had a further reason for desiring to work in secret, and that was Yvonne.

Did he adopt Kennedy's plan, and did a raid take place, every newspaper in the country would blazon forth the news on the following day. And if the two missing girls were discovered, then their names would come out. What a feast for the reporters to dwell upon! Mademoiselle Yvonne, the famous adventuress, and the Lady Sybil, daughter of the Duke and Duchess of Carrisbrooke, rescued from a Chinese den.

Blake squirmed when he thought of it. It was only by sticking doggedly to his point that he won out. He had pledged his word that, in return for Kennedy's guarantee of secrecy, he would not rest until he had placed in the hands of the American the exact route used from the time the "cargoes" crossed the American line.

From Eastport he sent a wire to the authorities in St, John, and had the satisfaction of receiving a reply saying the twenty-one Celestials had been gathered in, and would be deported at once. Then he sent a cable to the chief of the Cardiff police, asking him to arrest Sam Loo.

Not until he got to Boston did he receive a reply to that. It said:

"Sam Loo disappeared. It is stated he has returned to China."

And months later Blake discovered the Celestial had indeed gone to China, and had there paid the penalty which Wu Ling demanded.

At Boston Blake landed at night, and made his way towards Harrison Avenue.

No more was he disguised as the coolie Chen Foo, but now wore the richer robes of a Chinese merchant. Tinker, Pedro, and Graves had remained on board the yacht to await developments. If Blake had any success he was to let them know at once, and they, in turn, were to communicate with Kennedy. Then they would act.

From the moment the duchess had been startled by the sketch of Wu Ling, which stood on his desk, Blake had felt that in some way the prince was behind the whole system into which he had been so suddenly plunged.

If that were so, it was just possible that his search might eventually take him clear through to China, and if Wu Ling did chance to be at the head of it, Blake was inclined to hope it would, for not until he had tracked the nefarious business to the fountain head would he rest content.

Thus far had his deductions gone, when he made his way into the Chinese quarter of Boston for the first time. Five long days and nights did Blake spend there, and only the perfection of his disguise ever got him through with his life.

On the very first night he had sought lodgings behind a gambling-room, and had given out that he had come through by way of Mexico. As he knew the code greeting of the Brotherhood of the Yellow Beetle, it was not long before he was admitted freely to every place in the district.

Day and night he toiled, asking a careless question here, listening closely there. When alone in his room, he would jot down the information gained, and what an array of names he had gathered. Sixty-eight in all there were, every one of which was the name of a Celestial without the papers of residence which he should have possessed. Only on the fifth day did he discover that a suppressed air of excitement, which hung over the quarter, was due to the expected arrival of no less a personage than Wu Ling himself, who was coming through, incognito, to hold a conference of the Eastern section of the Brotherhood. A little judicious questioning on Blake's part, revealed the place where Wu Ling was to stay.

That afternoon he sent a long code message to the yacht, and when the evening was well advanced, he bundled up, and went out into the storm. He was on his way to play the final trick in the game, and none knew better than Blake the calibre of the opponent against whom he was to be pitted.

Anticipating every unexpected thing which was liable to occur, even Blake did not guess that, at that very moment, Yvonne was standing alone before Wu Ling.

It had been no small surprise to her to discover that Wu Ling had recognised her so promptly, for though, during her period of unconsciousness, any marks of disguise had been practically erased, her very pallor seemed to her to change her appearance to a wonderful extent.

She had possessed little notion that her daring plan was to lead her into the clutches of Wu Ling, and though his words still rang in her ears, she was silent, thinking desperately what line to take. She realised thoroughly that, unless succour reached her from some source within a very short time, she would be forced to drink to the dregs the bitter cup of suffering.

Wu Ling sat waiting patiently for her to speak, watching her as a cat does a mouse. Now that he had her in his hands he had no intention of hastening matters.

A low knock at the door at that moment brought a crease of irritation to his brow, and a sigh of relief from Yvonne. It meant that, at least, she would gain a few minutes respite, and could better decide what course to pursue.

Wu Ling curtly cried "Enter!" and, as the door opened, San appeared, bowing apologetically.

"Excellency," he said, "your unworthy servant prays your forgiveness, but one is below who insists upon seeing your Excellency."

"Who is it?" asked Wu Ling.

"He gives no name, Excellency, but bade me by the oath of the Brotherhood to seek you at once and crave from you an immediate interview. The unspeakable dog says his unworthy business is of an urgent nature, Excellency!"

"Since he is of the Brotherhood, and seeks by the oath, I can but see him," replied Wu Ling slowly. "Take this girl away, San. I will talk with her when he is gone. Send him up!"

San bowed, and taking Yvonne by the arm, disappeared through the door. Less than five minutes later, it opened to admit the muffled figure of a Celestial, from whose coat the melting snow still dripped.

He closed the door, and coolly locked it; then he tossed aside his coat, and bowed low to Wu Ling.

"Prince Wu Ling, it was somewhat of a surprise to know you were in Boston; but since you are here, I have sought you. We have business to discuss."

For the space of a full minute Wu Ling regarded the man who had dared to enter and speak in such terms to the autocratic head of the Brotherhood of the Yellow Beetle.

At the end of that time, his lids dropped with a barely perceptible motion, and one slim, sensitive yellow hand stretched out and rested palm down on the table.

"So," he said softly, "it is you, Sexton Blake. At last you have come!"

Blake bowed ironically.

"As you see, Wu Ling. I have come, but not as you hope."

"You talk bravely, my friend," rejoined the prince. "Do you think, then, you can walk into the lair of the tiger and escape unscathed?"

"Not only do I think so," responded Blake, stepping forward a pace, "but Wu Ling, I know so. Moreover, when I leave the lair of the tiger, I shall leave not only unscathed, but with that which I have come to get!"

"Indeed! Do you think, Sexton Blake, that Prince Wu Ling is the man to court defeat in a meeting for which he has been longing? Is the past nothing to me? Is it only to forget that under certain circumstances I was compelled to yield to you? Is it for nothing that I learn how you befooled Sam Loo in Cardiff, and betrayed to the authorities the system I took months to organise? Is Wu Ling the man to forget these things? No; a thousand times no, Sexton Blake!

"You and I have been ranged on opposite sides ever since the man Halliday escaped from China with the secret of the Yellow Beetle. Destiny, which up to now has been against me, has at last placed you in my hands. It has, indeed, been kind to me this night. From the wreckage of the System have come many whom I sought. The exposure was worth it. And now, if you have anything to say, say it, for soon you go to meet the fate in store for you."

"You talk with confidence, Wu Ling," replied Blake coldly. "It is not like you to boast without reason, and yet on this occasion you do so. Not yet has the time come when I go to meet what fate you choose to give me. Instead, I come tonight to make demands—demands which you will grant. Even as you sit there so confidently,

Prince Wu Ling, you are at my mercy. And now I will tell you why I have come."

"I have told you to speak."

"I have come to demand from you the person of the Lady Sybil Druce, daughter of the Duke and Duchess of Carrisbrooke, who has fallen into your power."

"Might I ask what makes you so positive?"

"Certainly. The fact that Wu Ling and Dr. Li-Fuang are one and the same is the reason. Secondly, I demand the person of the young woman who reached Boston this week. She was the last portion of cargo through the underground system, so no mistake will be made as to whom I mean. Thirdly, I demand the peaceful surrender of the following Celestials, at present residing in this district, and not possessing papers of residence!"

As he spoke, Blake drew out a long sheet of paper, and began reading out the list of names he had copied during the past few days. When he had finished, he looked up.

"That, Wu Ling, is what I demand!"

"Since you make your demands so boldly, perhaps you will enlighten me as to how you expect to enforce them."

"Certainly. My cards will all be laid on the table, Wu Ling. In the first place, I may say that at this very moment the place is surrounded by a large force of Secret Service men under Mr. Kennedy, of whom you will have heard. If I am in here longer than a certain period of time, they will at once raid the premises. In his possession is a sealed envelope containing a list of the sixty-eight men I have named.

"If I fail, he is to open it, and a clean sweep of the district will follow. Not only will those sixty-eight be captured, but every man who possesses no residence papers. Moreover, many of those who are legally entitled to reside here will be deported for conspiracy. I do not think for a moment that such a raid will touch the person of Prince Wu Ling, for you will, of course, be provided with diplomatic papers making you immune from the law of the land. Great publicity will follow, however, and I do not think, Wu Ling, that such a thing will fit in with your plans.

"I have also taken the precaution to send to my assistant a sealed envelope to pass on to the Duke of Carrisbrooke, should anything happen to me while I am in here. I leave you to judge what action will be taken by England if they discover you have abducted the daughter of a man who ranks as high as does the duke, and who went to your country on a special mission.

"In order to make my demands definite, Wu Ling, I have been compelled to consider many things. The demand for the sixty-eight men whose names I have given you is for Kennedy. This I was compelled to promise him in order to prevent him from raiding the district without delay and making a clean sweep. Since it was through my efforts that your System was broken up and your cargo captured, he was compelled to accept my terms, as you will have to do.

"My reason is simple. I wish no publicity any more than do you. Neither your country nor mine can tolerate a diplomatic complication of such a description at the present time. You know that is a fact. What duty I owed to the United States I have performed. It is now for me to bring to a completion the rest of my purpose, and for that reason I have made the foregoing demands and conditions. There is one more demand which I make."

"It is?"

"A description of the route by which your cargoes wore brought to Boston after crossing the line between the United States and Canada. And in regard to the two prisoners I have demanded, Wu Ling, an essential condition is that they be unharmed. Now your answer."

"Your demands are far from modest, Sexton Blake," answered Wu Ling slowly. "To-night there have come into any hands many whom I sought. I swore that the vengeance of the Brotherhood should be dealt out to each—you included. Is it now for me to alter my decision, and again yield to you? No."

"Listen, Wu Ling," said Blake curtly. "It is not a case of what you wish. It is a case in which you are helpless. You have much more to lose than you have to gain by refusing my demands. If that were not so, should I be fool enough to walk in here without a weapon of any description?

"In the past we have been opposed on many occasions. You know me well enough to be aware that I never strike unless I know where my blow will fall. The day must come when these struggles between us must end. It is not the law of Nature that they should continue."

"And for that day I pray," interrupted Wu Ling sombrely. "You are cunning with the cunning of the East, Sexton Blake. It is true that greater things are at stake than revenge on those whom I hold. The demands you make must be granted in order that other matters may be saved."

As Wu Ling made his dignified avowal of defeat, something inside Blake suddenly relaxed, and for the first time he realised the cold beads were standing out on his forehead. Simple though the words were, he knew what a depth of meaning they held, and what a crashing blow it must be to Wu Ling to see victory snatched from his very grasp. And yet, true to his nature, the Celestial betrayed not the slightest sign of the tumult raging inside him.

Blake took another step forward, and spoke very slowly:

"In that case, Wu Ling, I will ask you a favour."

"What is it?"

"That you have brought here at once the young woman who last arrived."

"You mean Mademoiselle Yvonne?"

"Then you know?" asked Blake quickly.

For the first time a smile broke across Wu Ling's features.

"Am I an infant?" he said curtly. "It shall be as you wish. Unlock the door. I will ring."

Blake turned to the door with an extraordinary feeling tugging at his heart. His pride would not permit him to ask if Yvonne were safe and well, but an unaccustomed frenzy of impatience filled him as he waited for Wu Ling's ring to be answered. And, throbbing in his brain, was the thought that he and he alone had saved her.

San answered the ring, and Wu Ling curtly bade him to bring Yvonne.

A moment later she came, looking strangely like a tired child, with the pallor of her face throwing into relief the big deep-blue eyes and the tangled bronze hair falling in distracting masses over the drooping neck. Little did she dream that she was coming to Blake. To her it was but a summons to hear what Wu Ling had not had time to say.

As she entered she glanced dully at Blake, who stood facing her, his eyes no longer those of the Chinese merchant, but keen and wide as usual, and yet filled with a wonderful tenderness.

Slowly the tremendous truth beat its way into Yvonne's mind. Her eyes grew misty, and her lips trembled as she drew in her breath sharply. Every feature of the man she loved with all her nature stood out clear and white, stripped of its disguise. A wayward hand brushed across her eyes, but the mist of happiness could only yield to the joy of realisation.

Blake took a step towards her, and as his movement told her he was no chimera of a distraught mind, but a glorious, living reality, she stumbled, blindly towards him, her arms outstretched, and he caught her just as she gave a low moan and collapsed.

Blake held her very tenderly, and pushed the heavy hair back from her head. He could feel her heart beating wildly with the throbbing relief of the bird who has reached the shelter of the nest before the hawk could strike.

She had not fainted, for she stirred slightly, and opened her eyes.

"You—you—you," she whispered, feeding her eyes on his, the while her hand beat aimlessly against his shoulder.

Blake bent his head until his lips were very close to her ear. The sweet perfume of her hair assailed him, and its soft masses brushed his eyes. For a moment he closed his lids, then he whispered:

"It is all right now, little girl. You are safe, and no harm shall come to you."

Yvonne's white arm crept up until it rested against his cheek, then her soft fingers fluttered lightly over his face.

"You; oh, it is you!" she whispered again. "I knew you would come."

Blake lifted his head, and, with his arm supporting her, led her gently across to a chair.

"We shall leave soon," he said, smiling. "There are one or two things yet to be attended to."

He turned to speak to Wu Ling, but discovered, with surprise, that he was no longer sitting at the table. As he turned back the door again opened, and the prince entered, followed by the Lady Sybil, who gazed in surprise at Yvonne.

How Wu Ling had departed so quickly Blake didn't know, but a panel in the wall near the table would have explained the mystery had he investigated it.

When the prince had once more taken his seat he turned to the Lady Sybil.

"When you were in here before," he said curtly, "I told you what I desired of you. Since then conditions have changed. You are free to go."

As the girl stared stupidly, Blake stepped forward, and in a few quiet words explained

"You- you—you!" whispered Yvonne, stumbling blindly towards Blake.

"It is Rymer," she whispered. "He has been condemned to lifelong slavery in the rice-fields. Won't you save him?"

"It is strange to hear you pleading for Rymer," answered Blake, with a touch of coldness in his tones.

"Oh, please do not misunderstand me!" she pleaded hurriedly. "He is a white man, and, no matter what he has done to you and me, it would be awful to let him go into that living hell."

"I will see what I can do," said Blake thoughtfully, turning back to Wu Ling.

The prince showed no signs as to whether or not he had heard Yvonne's request. He still sat as inscrutable as ever. Blake regarded him for a moment, then he spoke.

"Prince Wu Ling," he said slowly, "when I came here to-night I made certain demands and laid down certain conditions, to which you agreed."

"That is right," responded the other calmly.

"That being so, I can make no fresh demands," went on Blake. "And yet, Wu Ling, I would ask a favour."

"I listen."

"It is that you hand over to me the man Rymer."

"It is impossible," answered Wu Ling curtly. "Though we are on opposite sides, and though your race and mine must one day crash together in a final struggle, I have for you the love of a brother, Sexton Blake, though when I can sweep you from my path I shall do so. If you asked me anything material I would gladly give it to you as the recognition of man to man. And always you know that if you will join us, the East will receive you and place you second only to Wu Ling. But what you ask to-night I cannot grant. I

who he was. She listened in stupefaction at the unexpected news, and when he saw she was on the point of breaking down, Blake motioned to Yvonne. In her happiness, Yvonne yielded to the other all the sweet consolation of her nature, and as she led the Lady Sybil aside, Blake said, with a fleeting smile:

"I told you on Christmas Eve, I should need you to look after her."

And Yvonne flashed back softly:

"And I told you I should always be ready to do so."

Then Blake approached the table, and sat down beside Wu Ling.

"Now, prince," he said quietly, "if you will kindly give me the route of the System, we will make arrangements for the handing over of the sixty-eight men to Kennedy."

For fully a quarter of an hour Blake was bent in concentrated attention while Wu Ling sketched out on a map a detailed outline of the way the cargoes were brought after leaving the Canadian side. When the prince had finished Blake folded up the map and thrust it in his pocket.

As he rose a soft swish sounded behind him, and he felt a small hand on his arm. Turning, he gazed up into Yvonne's eyes.

"What is it?" he asked, with a smile.

have waited long to got my hands on the traitor Rymer, and now that I have him I shall not let him go."

Blake's eyes dropped in thought as Wu Ling finished. He realised the truth and justice of the reply from Wu Ling's point of view, but, if he could, he would grant Yvonne's plea.

Ever so slowly his hand went beneath his jacket, and emerged a moment later bearing a chamois bag containing something round. He paid no heed to Yvonne's smothered exclamation as she saw what it was, but began methodically to undo the string which held it together.

A moment later the light gleamed on an exquisite jade sphere as it slipped into his hand, and he held it out to Wu Ling.

"Will you give me Rymer for this?" he said softly. "You, Wu Ling, are the representative of the ancient Ming Dynasty. It is unnecessary to tell you what it is which I hold in my hand."

Not even Wu Ling's inborn capacity of repression could withstand the shock as his eyes rested on the Sacred Sphere which for two hundred and fifty years had been lost. His eyes closed as a sharp pain assailed him, and his long fingers curled up in a paroxysm of emotion.

Blake sat motionless, waiting.

Finally the prince got slowly to his feet and held out his hand,

"How you came to possess the Sacred Sphere of the Son of Heaven I do not ask," he said in a voice utterly unlike his own. "You ask me will I give you the man Rymer for it? I would give a thousand such dogs! I would give life, honour, wealth! I would give a kingdom!"

"Then take it, Wu Ling," said Blake quietly. "It is yours."

Slowly the hand of the prince stretched out until his fingers hovered over the sacred symbol of his line. So tense was the silence that Blake could hear the two girls breathing in suspense. Probably never in the annals of history had such a priceless treasure returned to its own in a more dramatic manner. In that moment Blake confessed to himself that Wu Ling was the true prince and worthy representative of the Ming Dynasty.

As Wu Ling's fingers closed on the sphere, and found it no mad dream but a reality, a shudder went through him, and he sank back into his chair.

Blake rose at once.

"If you will give orders to one of your men, Wu Ling, I shall be going."

The prince touched a bell, and as San appeared he said:

"Conduct Mr. Blake outside. Hand over to him the man Rymer and the men whose names he will give you. If he desires anything else give it to him."

The faithful San gazed stupidly at his master, wondering what had come over him; but at a gesture from the prince he turned and started out. As the others followed, Blake and Yvonne looked back.

There sat Wu Ling, with the sphere before him. In his hand was the golden god Mo which he always carried before him. His eyes were closed. He was praying.

"I am glad now you gave it to him," whispered Yvonne, laying her fingers on Blake's arm.

"And I," he said, as he slipped his hand over hers.

And so they went out together, leaving the prince to his golden god, his prayers, and the Sacred Sphere.

§

When Rymer came stumbling out of the room where he had been confined, not knowing what Fate held in store for him, Blake stepped forward and looked him in the eyes.

"Rymer," he said curtly, "you were condemned to slavery in the rice-fields of China. Knowing nothing of it, I would have done nothing to save you from it. Mademoiselle Yvonne, however, has seen fit to plead for you, and her plea has been granted. You belong to her, and what she says shall be done."

Then he turned, to Yvonne.

"Mademoiselle," he said, "what is your wish?"

Yvonne looked up at Rymer.

"You deserve little from me, Dr. Rymer," she said, "and if we meet again on an equal footing I shall exact payment for every moment of suffering you have caused me. At the same time, I do not wish to strike you when you are helpless. My desire is that you go, and I hope I shall never see you again!"

Rymer listened with bowed head to Yvonne's words. All the decency in the man's nature had risen to suffer the shame of his position. When she had finished he lifted his head as though to speak; then he thought better of it, and turning, passed slowly out of the room.

Ten minutes later Yvonne and the Lady Sybil had been handed over to the care of Graves and Alec, who lost no time in getting them to the yacht. Tinker remained with Blake, and the two were soon busy checking over the list of names as San produced the men Blake called for and handed them over into the custody of Kennedy and his deputies.

How Blake had managed it the latter couldn't begin to guess, but when the list finished, Blake drew out the map and gave it to the American. Kennedy held out his hand.

"You have made it possible for me to make the biggest scoop on record, Blake," he said huskily. "I shall never forget this as long as I live!"

Blake gripped his hand warmly.

"And secrecy is the watchword," he said, with a smile.

"I pledge you my word none but my chief shall know the true facts," replied Kennedy.

Then, after shaking hands with Tinker, he went off with his men, and Blake, with a look of deep weariness in his eyes, started with Tinker for the yacht.

Whether he was thinking of Yvonne or whether he was thinking of Wu Ling it is hard to say, nor would any but himself know the reason of any weariness of soul which assailed him.

Such was the man Sexton Blake.

§

It may seem strange to think of Christmas festivities being held after that great day is past, but so it was on board the yacht Fleur-de-Lys as she steamed on her way from Boston to London.

A cable had been sent telling the duke and duchess of Blake's success, and under Yvonne's care the Lady Sybil had entirely recovered. Most of the members of that party had passed through too much not to feel the relief.

It was on the first night out that the Christmas banquet was held. Captain Vaughan was at one end of the table, with the Lady Sybil on his right. Yvonne was at the other end, with Blake beside her. Tinker was on Yvonne's left, and across from him was Graves.

For once in his life Blake blushed as Graves gave a rousing toast to the man who had brought to others the happiness they felt that night, and for the moment his weariness passed as Yvonne lifted her glass and gazed at him ever so softly with a look of sweet challenge in her misty eyes.

THE END.

PARRIED!

BEING THE STORY OF ANOTHER
DUEL OF WITS BETWEEN

SEXTON BLAKE
AND
MARSTON HUME

MARSTON HUME—Criminal.

"MY dear Bathurst," said Blake, "I have always told you that, sooner or later, Hume would make a slip. This time he has—a bad one—so bad that it must inevitably hang him.

"A man—a clever man—may commit one crime in his life with impunity; two, perhaps, if he has nerves of steel and no conscience. But he cannot take to crime as a profession without coming to grief in the long run.

"Marston Hume, who might have become famous in almost any of the professions, chose to cast his opportunities aside and take to crime. The excitement of his new life, or some strange, little understood, instinct has driven him to a third crime, and this time we have proof—ample proof—and his new career automatically comes to an end."

"Do you mean you have really got him this time?"

"Beyond all shadow of doubt. I have proof of motive—proof of his presence on the scene at the time of the crime—a witness who can swear to his identity, and in a few hours I shall have the man himself."

"What is this new case, then? Remember, I have been away, and am completely in the dark," said Bathurst.

Blake lit a cigarette before replying.

"It is rather complex, in a way," he said; "and, but for my solitary witness, I confess I should have despaired of proving Hume guilty. There is—or, rather there was—a certain Mr. Maxwell, a middle-aged man, of considerable wealth, who lived at Triton Mansions. He was a man who dabbled considerably in financial matters, and was, from what I could hear, rather of the type which delights in getting up rows at general meetings, and asking awkward questions at inopportune moments.

"Some days ago, Mr. Maxwell was found dead at the bottom of the lift shaft at Triton Mansions. His flat was at the top of the building, and he had evidently fallen nearly the whole height of the house. His body was discovered early the next morning by the hall porter when he came on duty.

"I should explain that the porter goes off duty at nine at night, and returns to work at half-past six in the morning. Neither he nor his wife sleeps on the premises. After his departure, the residents are accustomed to work the lift for themselves, each flat-holder having a small gun-metal key to unfasten the grill gates guarding the shaft.

"At first it was somewhat naturally thought that Maxwell had been the victim of a piece of carelessness on his own part. His flat was on the top floor, as I told you, but the well-shaft rises higher than the rest of the building, and the lift itself was found to have been raised to the highest possible limit, the bottom of it being some three feet above the top of the grill-door used by Maxwell.

"It was concluded that he had come out of his rooms on to the dark landing, opened the grill, and pulled on the rope to shoot the lift up—its usual position was on a level with the entrance hall. He would have heard it rumbling on its upward way; then, it was supposed, he must have hurried back into the flat for something he had forgotten. On his return, oblivious of the fact that it was possible for the lift to go higher than his floor, and being in a hurry, he stepped, as he thought, into the lift. In reality he stepped into space.

"The occupants of the ground floor were away—the basement is used merely for storing purposes—so no one heard the crash of his fall.

"That was the whole story, so far as it went, at the moment. No one dreamt of questioning it. The newspapers gave it a short paragraph under the headings of 'Deplorable Lift Accident,' and 'Sudden Death of a Well-known Financier,' and there the matter would undoubtedly have ended, had it not been for the fact that a young mining engineer—Snelling by name—called on me on the evening of the discovery. He had just seen the case in the papers, and he was in a great state of excitement.

"It appears that Maxwell had employed him privately to go out and report to him on the true condition of a certain group of mines, run by a company known as the 'Ardua Development Syndicate.' Maxwell was a large shareholder, and, though the shares stood at an inflated price, for some reason best known to himself, Maxwell was suspicious.

"Snelling had returned only the previous day with his report. In this he condemned the whole group as a barefaced swindle; the mines were, for all practical purposes, non-existent, and, for two years, dividends had been paid out of capital.

"Snelling took his report straight to Maxwell—he had obtained his information by working as an ordinary miner—and Maxwell was furious at the state of affairs revealed in the report.

"The two men had another meeting on the afternoon of the day of the accident, when Maxwell announced his intention of showing up the whole fraud at the next board meeting. Meanwhile, he swore that the report itself—which was typewritten—should not on any account leave his person, night or day.

"In view of these facts, and the desperate efforts the founders of the syndicate would make to prevent the report being made public, should they get a hint of its existence, Snelling was convinced that his employer had been the victim of foul play.

"This, in spite of the fact that it had been ascertained that Mr. Maxwell had an invitation for that evening, which accounted for his leaving his rooms at a late hour.

"Thinking that there might possibly be something in Snelling's story, after all, I went down with him to Triton Mansions.

"The hall-porter knew Snelling well, and made no difficulty as to admitting us to the flat, which we searched thoroughly. There was no doubt about it. The report was missing, and it could be proved that Maxwell had not left his rooms between the time of Snelling's going away and the hall porter's going off duty for the night, for the latter called on Maxwell to ask if there were any letters for the post. He was answered in the negative by Maxwell in person, who was at that time in dressing-gown and slippers. I should add that he kept no servant of his own, relying entirely on the porter and his wife for attendance.

"Whether he had had a visitor subsequently to the porter's departure, was another matter, however. The main front door is left on the latch all the night through, and half a dozen people might have come and gone.

"There were no signs or suggestions of a struggle in the flat; all was neat and orderly. The one definite fact that we could ascertain was that the report was missing.

"My notion is that Maxwell's unknown visitor was a man whom he had no reason to suspect, but who was in some way cognisant of the existence of the report, and that, taking advantage of an unguarded moment, he deliberately pushed or threw Maxwell down the shaft, and then went down and searched the body for the report. With this idea in view, Snelling and I thoroughly examined the well at the bottom of the shaft.

"Whilst doing so, I found this." And fumbling in his waistcoat-pocket, Blake produced a curiously-shaped sleeve-link, which he tossed on to the table. Bathurst bent over it, and gave a start.

"Humes'," he said. "I'd know it anywhere."

"It was lying in a litter of dust, at the extreme corner of the well," said Blake. "And to me, at any rate, it told a story all its own."

"What was your next move?"

"I ascertained without any difficulty that Marston Hume and the dead man had been acquainted. In fact, I was able to prove that they had dined together at a restaurant on the evening preceding the crime. There, however, I found myself momentarily at a standstill, and it was not till the evening of the third day after my visit that I ascertained any more. Then my information came through the columns of the evening papers; and it came as a bomb, which not only puzzled me for the moment, but created a veritable panic on the Stock Exchange.

"The missing report, with all its, condemnatory details was found.

"It appears that a junior clerk was strolling down one of the passages of Warnford Court—there were few people about at the time—when he saw a big official-looking bulky envelope lying squarely in the passageway.

"He picked it up—the top had been opened—and read the name Maxwell on the cover—no address was given. With pardonable curiosity—or it may be with the idea of finding the owner's address—he drew out the contents. Being a shrewd youth, a few sentences were sufficient to show what he had got hold of, and he took it to the head of his firm.

"They happened to have a grievance against the Ardua Company, and the news of the report of its contents spread like wildfire. At 11.45, according to the market reports, Arduas stood at £3 15s. a share; when the house closed, they were down to ten shillings, and frantic sellers reduced the price subsequently to rock-bottom.

"To anyone holding the threads of the story as I did, it was, of course, obvious that the missing report had been placed deliberately where it was found. Snelling, to whom I had made no mention of Hume, though I had shown him the link, to enable him to identify it, was astounded. Of course, the publication of the report was just the very last thing he had been expecting. However, he had little time to reflect, for irate shareholders were pursuing him every where, to get at the truth.

"I spent the next two days in dingy brokers' offices, and I can assure you that the result was most interesting.

"In the few days between Maxwell's murder and the finding of the report, Marston Hume, in half a dozen different names, had sold no less than twelve thousand Arduas, at an average price of £3 12s. 6d. per share. Of course, he did not possess a single one. During the ensuing panic he had bought at prices varying from five shillings to a sovereign, mostly below half, however; in other words, he had made for himself a profit of close on three pounds per share on twelve thousand shares, and so far as his dealings with his brokers went, he had made his profits perfectly legitimately.

"Still, however, my hands were tied. I could prove that he knew Maxwell; that he called at Triton Mansions on the evening of the crime; that he had netted, as a result of the disappearance and subsequent timely finding of the report, a fortune of, roughly, thirty-six thousand pounds; but all my proofs would have gone for nothing. He is a man of almost European repute, you must remember; no suspicion has ever touched him. He would have replied that Maxwell was a friend of his, and had given him the straight tip about Arduas; that he was certainly with Maxwell early on the night of the crime, and broke his link in opening the door of the lift; and that, not only did the finding of the report come near upsetting his calculations, but that he was ignorant of its loss.

"In the face of such a declaration, on his part, I should have been helpless, unless I could prove that the time of his visit coincided with the hour of Maxwell's death.

"Maxwell's body was found by the hall porter a few minutes after half-past six. The man went at once for a doctor living nearby. The doctor viewed the body a little before seven. In his opinion Maxwell had then been dead not less than seven hours, possibly he had met his end an hour earlier. That death had occurred not later than midnight he was positive.

"Now, it so happens that Maxwell's invitation, which was found on his mantelpiece, was for 11.30. It was an 'At-home,' so he would aim at getting there about midnight; a taxi would have taken him to the address in a quarter of an hour. Presumably, therefore, he wished to start at a quarter to twelve. At three minutes after the quarter Hume was seen to leave Triton Mansions, and I can prove it."

Bathurst sat up with a jerk.

"If you can prove that, he's done."

"Precisely; he's done; and I'll tell you how I managed it. I put in a carefully worded advertisement in several of the papers—not mentioning Triton Mansions, of course, but a block of flats on the opposite side further down—offering a reward for the answer to some purely fictitious inquiry.

"I was afraid it was going to be a failure, when a funny little cockney man, named Simmons, answered it. I cross-examined him, and he answered truthfully, though desperately eager to win the five-pound reward. He had been in the street at the time, he said, but had seen nothing of the imaginary accident I had invented.

"I asked him if he had noticed anyone in the street at that hour, and he at once admitted, having

seen 'a bloke—reg'lar toff,' come out of Triton Mansions, which he was in the act of passing. I asked him why he remembered the fact, and his own words were, 'Becos 'e stared at me so 'ard, I felt as though 'e was lookin' through me. I arst 'im for a light, and 'e give me one 'imself—starin' at me all the time. And arterwards I kept on thinkin' 'e was follerin' me.'

"I asked him to describe the man, and he had got Hume to the last detail—eyeglass, carnation, and all—even to the fur on his overcoat.

"I picked out a batch of a couple of dozen photographs, three of which were of Hume in different costumes. He spotted these at once, without an instant's hesitation. So I gave him his fiver, and took his address. I have it here in my pocket-book. I am going round there now to rout him out, I want him to see Hume, and recognise him in the flesh in my presence. That done, I shall apply for a warrant at once. You can come along, too, if you like."

"You bet I will," said Bathurst. And, putting on their hats and coats, they sent for a taxi.

The drive to the small house in which Simmons occupied a single back room only occupied a few minutes.

"Better tell the man to wait," said Blake. "You may as well wait, too; I sha'n't be a second. Mr. Simmons in?" he asked of the woman who answered the door.

"Yes, sir; came in a few minutes back—first landing, door on your left."

"Thanks," said Blake, and ran lightly up the stairs. The next instant the woman and Bathurst heard him give a shout of mingled horror and rage, and he called frantically to the latter to come up.

Bathurst rushed up, the woman following more slowly behind. The door of Simmons' room stood wide open, and Blake was standing on the threshold. Inside, lying face downwards, asprawl on the bed, was Simmons—strangled.

Bathurst cried out, and the landlady shrieked. Blake turned the body over. A glance was quite sufficient—the man was as dead as a doornail.

Blake looked at his watch, it was nineteen minutes past four.

"What time did you say Simmons returned home?" he asked.

"On the stroke of four, sir; that was 'is usual hour. I see 'im come in myself."

"Seen anyone come in since, or leave?"

"No, sir; after 'e come in I went down to the kitchen, the front door was open then; after a bit I 'eard the wind bang it to with a slam; and shut it must have stopped till I opened it for you gents. None of my lodgers came home till late, exceptin' poor Simmons there, he always came back at four and 'ad a rest; then 'e'd go out again later, and come in at closin' time—very reg'lar 'e was."

Blake glanced at the figure on the bed.

"You'd better lock this room till I can send the police to you. Here's my card, in case of trouble. Come, Bathurst, we must be off at once. Jump in."

"You don't mean," said Bathurst, as the taxi sped along, "that this is—"

"Hume's handiwork? That's exactly what I do mean; and, in a way, it's my fault the poor wretch was murdered. You remember Simmons' words about Hume staring at him, and his fancy later on that he was followed. Hume had just committed one crime, he was conscious that he had left a clue in the shape of a broken sleeve-link, which he dare not stay to search for.

"This man he realised at once as an additional danger, and he took the boldest conceivable course. He studied the man's face, and impressed it indelibly on his memory; also, without a doubt, he found out where the man lived by shadowing him home. Afterwards he must have watched him to find out his customary movements, ascertaining that he was in the habit of returning home at four every afternoon. Carefully though I worded my advertisements, he must have seen through them. Simmons alive, he would realise at once, could hang him; therefore Simmons must die. He must have watched his chance and slipped into the house unobserved, and into Simmons' room a few minutes before four. Probably the poor wretch didn't even have time to cry out, taken by surprise as he crossed his own threshold. When it was over, Hume went out and banged the front door after him, safer by far than trying to close it cautiously.

"Now, everything depends on your finding Hume as quickly as possible. He can't have more than a quarter of an hour's start of us, and he is sure to head direct for some place where he is well known. We'll try the club first."

But at the club they drew blank; in fact, whilst they were still hurrying there, Marston Hume, spotlessly immaculate as ever, was walking swiftly down a theatre corridor leading to the private sanctum of Mansell, the actor-manager, and a fellow-member of the Baddeley Club.

The room, luxuriously furnished, was unoccupied. Hume closed the door softly, took one swift glance around him, and strode to the mantelpiece. On it was an old brass Dutch clock, the hands pointed to four-thirty; with a deft twirl of the forefinger Hume slid the minute-hand back till it marked ten minutes to four.

Then he seated himself in the most comfortable armchair, and thoughtfully polished his nail on his sleeve.

The door behind him opened once more, and Mansell came in.

"Sorry to have kept you, my dear chap!" he exclaimed.

"Not a bit; I've scarcely been here a moment, but I was at a loose end, and wanted someone to chat to. Turn me out, if I'm in the way. I know your rule about not seeing interlopers before four, and I see I'm a few minutes ahead of time."

"Not a bit; not a bit!" said Mansell. "Bless my soul, I'd no idea it was so early—must have got through quicker than usual to-day. We're arranging to commence rehearsals for the new play. Have a drink and something to smoke?"

Mansell, as Hume well knew, was a most absent-minded man in some ways, and if once he got started on any favourite topic he would hold forth for hours, quite oblivious of all else. Owing to this same trick of absent-mindedness, too, it was well-known that he never carried either a watch, a walking-stick, or an umbrella, because he invariably left them about and lost, them.

"Thanks," said Hume. "I'll have a whisky-and-soda if I may; try one of these cigars of mine— they're a new sort. How's the play coming on?"

"Capital, my dear chap; capital! We shall make a hit."

Hume nodded; no man knew better than he how to lure Mansell into one of his discursive moods.

After a long explanation ending in a discussion as to the best reading of a certain passage, Hume glanced furtively at his watch. He had kept Mansell chatting over the hour; it was now five thirty—the clock on the mantelpiece made the time ten minutes to five.

Marston Hume offered his host another cigar, and took one himself, strolling over to the fireplace to throw away the old stump. Having lit the fresh cigar, he stood leaning with his back to the mantelpiece in such a position as to conceal the clock-face, and continued the conversation.

Mansell was no longer in a position to see the time, even had he given it a passing thought.

"By the way," said Hume, blowing out a cloud of smoke, "have you got any sketches of the costumes in that portfolio there? I should like to have a look at them, if you have."

"Certainly. Wait a minute; I'll switch on this light and bring them over to the table; we shall see better there."

"Let me give you a hand," said Hume, and moved away from the mantelpiece. Mansell's back was towards him, as he had calculated, and with a single quick movement he put forward the clock hands again to thirty-three minutes past five. Before Mansell could turn, Hume was beside him, helping him with the drawings. It was a quarter to six before they had gone through them, and Hume, who had accomplished his object, had difficulty in suppressing a yawn. At last he looked at his watch again—ostentatiously, this time.

"Good heavens!" he exclaimed. "I'd no idea how late it was; do you know I've been wasting close on a couple of hours of your time? I must be off at once!"

"Eh?" said Mansell. "Good gracious, how the time has flown; it's your fault—you mounted me on one of my hobbies, and this is the result"

Hume's quick ear had caught the sound of hurried footsteps in the corridor. He raised his eyebrows slightly, and with a slight sardonic smile bent once more over the portfolio.

"Quick work!" he muttered to himself. "My friend the enemy is becoming a nuisance."

The door was hastily flung open, and Blake stood on the threshold; his face lighted up momentarily as he caught sight of Hume.

"Ah, Hume! there you are at last!" he said sharply. "Excuse me, Mansell, but I've been hunting for him everywhere; I've news of the utmost importance for him. Would you mind leaving us for a moment? Bathurst is outside; we sha'n't be more than a few moments at longest."

"Use the room as your own," said Mansell. "I have to go round to the front of the house to see to one or two things."

He nodded and left them.

Hume seated himself in an arm-chair; Blake remained standing.

"You seem in a great hurry, Mr. Blake; what is it you want?" he said, smiling.

"I want you for the murder of Maxwell," was the grim answer. "When you pushed him down the lift-shaft your sleeve-link was torn out in the momentary struggle—as you know. You dared not stop and look for it. I looked and found it. I have it in my pocket. You robbed him of a private report by which you subsequently made close on thirty-six thousand pounds, using different names."

Marston Hume smiled again.

"It's a thousand pities that Mansell doesn't go in for melodrama," he said slowly. "You could write such splendid plays for him, my dear

Blake. After all your lurid imaginings, a plain statement must sound dull; yet here it is:

"The late Mr. Maxwell was a friend of mine. From time to time he gave me good tips for mining and other speculations. On this occasion, he told me that he had just got a private report about Arduas, confirming his idea that they were worthless. In gambling, I claim no higher morality than my neighbour. I sold a large number of shares in small blocks under different names, to avoid spoiling the market, and waited for the publication of Maxwell's report. His sudden death and the unexpected way in which the report was made public came to me quite as a surprise."

"Quite so," said Blake gravely. "Only, I happen to have a witness who can identify you and prove that you left Triton Mansions on the night of the murder at three minutes after the quarter to twelve."

"In that case," said Hume, "looking at things impartially, and regarding myself for the moment as Counsel for the Prosecution, I should proceed to call the witness. The evidence, if it stood cross-examination, would be very incriminating, Where is your witness?"

"You fiend!" said Blake. "You know as well as I do that you strangled the poor wretch a few minutes after four this afternoon. He entered his house at four; five minutes afterwards the front door was heard to slam. Bathurst and I arrived less than a quarter of an hour later, and found him dead. We have been hunting for you ever since; and now, by Heaven, I've got you!"

"Ah!" said Hume, thoughtfully, puffing out another cloud of smoke. "If you can prove that I murdered your witness this afternoon I might as well chuck up the sponge, mightn't I?"

Blake nodded.

"Where did you say the poor wretch lived?"

"Simmons was his name, and he lived in Portsmouth Street, Fulham."

"Fulham, eh! That's twenty minutes in a taxi from here, I should say, and you narrowed the time of the murder down to between four and, say, ten minutes past?"

"Quite so."

"Well, as you can no longer call your witness, I must call mine, and put an end to this melodramatic nonsense. Be so kind as to telephone yourself and ask Mansell to come here."

Mansell's back was turned towards him, as he had calculated, and with a single quick movement Hume put forward the clock-hands again to thirty-three minutes past five.

Blake did so, and in a minute or two Mansell returned.

"Well?" he asked.

"So sorry to bother you," said Hume, "but Blake here is trying to make out that I can be in two places at once. I am willing to bet him half a sovereign he is wrong. Just to oblige him, tell him, will you, at what time I came to see you?"

"At ten minutes to four. Why?"

"You are positive?" said Blake.

"Quite, my dear chap, and we've been sitting here talking ever since, till you turned up on the scene."

"In that case, you see, Blake," Hume said suavely. "It was utterly impossible for me to have been in the purlieus of Fulham at the time you mentioned, wasn't it? I'll trouble you for

half-a-sovereign, please, and we really mustn't take up more of Mansell's time."

Blake glanced at his watch, the clock, and Hume.

"Quite so," he said, "We must be off; here's your ten shillings."

Mansell let them out, and closed the door thoughtfully.

"There's a good deal more behind that than I understand," he said to himself, slowly.

There was.

ANOTHER PLUMMER YARN

The UNION JACK. 1d.

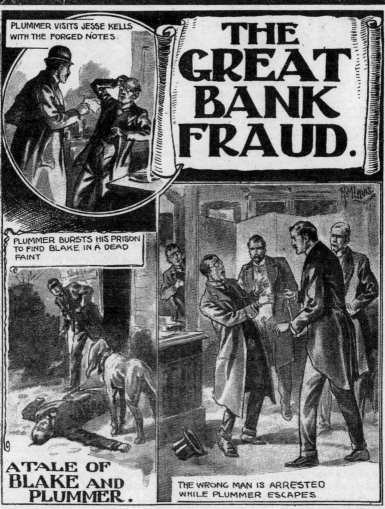

PLUMMER VISITS JESSE KELLS WITH THE FORGED NOTES.

THE GREAT BANK FRAUD.

PLUMMER BURSTS HIS PRISON TO FIND BLAKE IN A DEAD FAINT

A TALE OF BLAKE AND PLUMMER.

THE WRONG MAN IS ARRESTED WHILE PLUMMER ESCAPES.

NO. 473. NEW SERIES.] November 2nd, 1912. [EVERY THURSDAY.

THE GREAT BANK FRAUD.

Being the Account of yet Another Struggle for Victory between Sexton Blake and George Marsden Plummer.

THE FIRST CHAPTER

THE LIFE LUXURIOUS—THE FORGED NOTES—JESSE KELLS.

THE large red motor-car that dashed along the road from London to Lingfield was one of many other vehicles taking their occupants to the race-meeting at Lingfield Park, but certainly there was not one of them larger, of more modern design, or more elaborately fitted. It was the type of car in which one might have expected to see a party of men and women, but only one man occupied the spacious back of the car, and he was sunk down into a corner so that it was hard to see much of him.

Practically all that was visible of this man was a rather hard, lined face, the upper lip adorned by a grey moustache, and a fringe of almost white hair that showed beneath the brim of his Homburg hat. A monocle was in his right eye, lending it a rather vacant look, but the left one was not lacking in expression.

The eye stared straight ahead as the car dashed on, obviously seeing something far more im-portant to its owner than the stream of traffic or the scenery of Surrey. It was a strange eye, too, of a colour decidedly unusual, and its possessor had known times when he had wished fervently that Nature should not have made him so uncommon in this respect, for it had been his agate-coloured eyes that had given the identity of George Marsden Plummer away, and led to his defeats at the hands of Sexton Blake. There were few greater masters of make-up living than this disgraced ex-detective-sergeant of Scotland Yard, but it was beyond him to change the eyes to any great extent.

Smoked glasses would have done much to hide the agate-colour. True, but it has to be remembered that deep down in the master-criminal's soul was a great conceit, and only now and again had he forced himself to disfigure his appearance in that manner.

George Marsden Plummer was now on his way to the races, and the expression of anxiety on his face was caused by the knowledge that in his pockets reposed something less than five hundred pounds.

Five hundred pounds! To the luxury-loving ex-convict it was penury, a sum that hie would easily spend in a month or less, and now he was searching for a plan of campaign that would improve his resources. He had been back in England some little time, willing enough to be idle on the money that he had forced from Luke O. Zitmann and others, and feeling secure even from Sexton Blake so long as he did not have to work. He knew that the great detective, always full of cases, was not likely to waste his energies in a long search until he found a clue, and that would not be possible until Plummer came out of his idleness to stretch out his greedy hands for wealth.

The great red car entered the enclosure at Lingfield Park, took up its place with the others, and Plummer roused himself and strolled across to the stands. By nature he was a gambler, as most of the great criminals must be—gambling with liberty, and sometimes even with life and death.

For the time-being Plummer put his future away from him and turned his attention to the matter in hand. It was possible that with luck in betting he might increase the five hundred pounds in his pockets, and so give himself longer time to think out schemes for the future.

It was a fine day, and even in the fall of the year Lingfield was pretty enough, the lawn, dotted by its well-dressed crowd, looking more as if a garden-party were in progress than anything else.

Plummer strolled about as unconcernedly as anyone, quite at his ease. He never forgot that by birth he was an aristocrat, with bluer blood in his veins than many of those present could boast of. It was at those times that he almost forgot what his life had been, the crimes with which he had stained his hands, and now—with money short—of the future that would mean more crime.

The course was cleared, the numbers of the runners were up in the frame, and the loud voices of the bookmakers broke out above everything else.

"Four to one the field! Seven to one bar three! Five to one Gipsy!" one of the biggest bookmakers in the "ring" cried, and Plummer crossed to him.

"Fives Gipsy?" he asked.

"Yes, sir," the man answered. "What's it to be?"

"Five hundred to one hundred," Plummer said, producing one hundred pounds in notes, and the bet was booked to him.

The master-criminal took up a good position for watching the race, for if luck were with him he might still be able to postpone his return to the path that might lead him to prison.

Now the ten starters came cantering past to go to the five-furlong starting-post, and Plummer looked after them with eager eyes through a pair of field-glasses. Gipsy, the horse he had backed, was going well, he told himself, and if his luck only held—Ah!

The horses had reached the gate, and for once in a while there was little delay. The rubber tapes of the "gate" had scarcely been lowered a couple of minutes before the horses were in line, a moment of hesitation followed, then the usual cry:

"They're off!"

The horses had broken away from the gate almost in a straight line, and were coming with a dash down the slight slope of the first part of the five-furlong course. Then they were stringing out a bit, the favourite leading in the middle, a bunch of three horses close behind him and Gipsy on the rails, her jockey riding with obvious confidence.

"She'll win!" Plummer muttered, his fingers gripping harder on his glasses.

The partisans of various horses began to shout their favourites home. Above all rang out the name of Wild Fly, who was still in the lead, but suddenly, with less than a furlong to go, the great cry went up on all sides:

"Gipsy wins! The favourite's beaten!"

Gipsy had suddenly shot out along the rails with a clear lead, her jockey riding hard now, and Plummer, with a sigh of relief, allowed his stiff body to relax. The luck was with him after all, and on the first race of the day he was to be a winner of five hundred pounds. It was one of his fortunate days, and by the end—

"Favourite wins!"

The cry of "Gipsy wins!" had been too premature. The favourite was making another game effort, and though there was only a short way to go it was possible that she would get up and win on the post.

"Favourite—Gipsy—fav-our-ite!"

It seemed to Plummer that the horses passed him dead level, and he looked sharply across to the number-board. Either he was a richer man by five hundred pounds, or his slender stock of money had been badly decreased.

"Curse!" he muttered, as the favourite's number went up in the frame above that of Gipsy, the board at the side stating that the former had won by a short head.

With a savage look in his eyes, Plummer went to the refreshment-room and fortified himself with a bottle of champagne. The wine drove away something of his gloom, and there was a sneer on his lips as he looked at the men about him, wondering how much they were worth, and why they had been favoured by Fate, instead of her lavishing her gifts upon such a worthy person as himself. That, with his intellect, he could long since have made fortune honourably did not so much as occur to him. The criminal kink in his brain made but one kind of career possible.

The time for the second race arrived, and a second hundred pounds left Plummer's pocket, so that even he felt a touch of apprehension as he turned away after paying the money. If the horse did not win he would have less than three hundred pounds left.

Plummer stood there watching curiously the various people who made bets, but there was only one who really interested him out of the ordinary. This was a little man, who could not have been less than sixty, but whose deeply-bowed shoulders gave the impression of greater age. He was dressed in a frock-coat of a bygone fashion, and his hat would have horrified a self-respecting hatter.

This man looked up with mild eyes through a pair of glasses at the bookmaker, but Plummer did not fail to notice the curious, little nervous jerkings that his head gave, something in the manner of a bird who fears danger.

Plummer watched to see what bet the old man would make, and was surprised to see him hand over a note for twenty pounds, for from his appearance it was hard to believe that he had many notes of such value in the world. Perhaps he was one of those born gamblers who cannot stop so long as a coin was left, and who meet with the inevitable end in the gutter.

It was time to watch the second race, and until it was over, and Plummer had again lost, he paid no attention to the strange little man in the old-fashioned clothes. The latter had apparently lost, too, for he did not go up to the bookmaker for payment, though he was there almost the second that the betting started on the next race, Plummer waiting impatiently behind him.

"Twenty pounds Carway, to win, please," the little man said, drawing a pocket-book out, and it was all that Plummer could do to repress an exclamation of astonishment as he saw how well it was filled. The next moment his eyes were full of greed, for as the thin, bony fingers of the man turned the notes over in search of one for twenty pounds the master-criminal saw that nearly all of them were for a hundred pounds apiece, and he would almost have sworn that there were two there of a thousand. "Would you mind giving me change for a fifty," the little man asked.

"Right, sir," the bookmaker answered, crumpling the note in his hand, while he produced the change. "There you are. And what can I do for you, sir? Your luck's out at present."

The bookmaker waited with the crumpled note still in his hand, apparently having forgotten it for the moment.

"I shall have to be careful," Plummer answered, a touch of harshness in his voice, "I'll have fifty on Accumulator."

"Very good, sir," the bookmaker said, taking the note that Plummer held out to him. "For a hundred? Here's the fifty change, and thank you."

The note that changed hands was the identical one that the little old man had given the bookmaker, and Plummer thrust it into his note-case with the others already there, and strolled away. Instinctively he made his way to the refreshment-room to buck himself up after his second loss.

As the master-criminal gulped the wine down, he cursed inwardly as he thought of the notes that were disappearing from his case, and he drew the book out to make sure exactly how much was left to him.

First there were his own notes, amounting to two hundred and twenty-five pounds, then he came to the crumpled one that he had received as change from the bookmaker. Mechanically he began to smooth it out, then his face set hard, and he stared down at the note.

"Nothing wrong with it, sir, I hope?" the waiter behind the bar remarked, noticing his customer's expression.

"No," Plummer answered quickly, forcing a smile to his lips, and thrust the note back with the others. Then, he finished the champagne, and walked out.

Going to the paddock, Plummer found a quiet corner by the horse-boxes, and there, for the second time, he looked at the fifty-pound note. And as he did so his face went harsh again, and his agate-coloured eyes were very ugly.

The master-criminal would not have hesitated to rob his nearest friend—had he possessed one—in the meanest possible way, but his brain was so curiously formed that he practically regarded fraud as his own peculiar privilege. He should by rights have been in society, he told himself, and so he preyed upon those people who were there.

There was no doubt about it. The banknote was a forgery, though a remarkably clever one. In such matters, Plummer was one of the greatest experts living, and it is probable that not one other man in a thousand would have detected anything wrong with the note. There was only one little trivial detail incorrect, and it was chance that had caused even the criminal to notice.

Plummer sat there with the note back in his pocket, planning what he should do. If he gave the little man in charge of the police, he might find it hard to prove that the note came from him, and it was also possible that he had acted innocently in the matter. Besides, Plummer was not fond of the police, even though he believed himself to be able to beat them at any time.

With his mind still uncertain as to a course of action, Plummer made his way back to the stand, and his agate-coloured eyes, ugly as they well could be now, quickly discovered the little man in the ancient clothes. He was seated there quite unconcernedly, his eyes looking dully towards the courses plainly suggesting that he took little interest in the actual racing.

For once Plummer scarcely watched the racing either, and when his horse scrambled home by a head, he did not hurry to go away and draw his money. Instead, he stopped and watched the old man, who at last rose from his seat, and walked once more to the bookmaker, with Plummer close behind him.

Again a bet was made by the little man, and again the master-criminal saw that he received change. Quickly as possible he took his place before the bookmaker, and asked lor his winnings.

"Glad the luck's turned, sir," the man said cheerily, with the knowledge that too many losses may wean even the wealthiest man from the game. "How much is it?"

"Two hundred and fifty."

Plummer had been quick enough, which had been his intention, to prevent the bookmaker putting the little man's note into his satchel, and now he received it with others in settlement of his winnings.

The master-criminal made no journey to the bar this time, but hurried straight away to the paddock, and a quick inspection showed him that the second note was a forgery, too.

Then Plummer sat with his chin resting on one hand, thinking as hard as ever he had done in his life. The loss that the forgeries meant to him, if he did not in turn "plant" the notes, was considerable, and he had no intention of letting it pass. He was sure now that the little man had acted deliberately, and that probably all the remainder of the notes he possessed, saving those he had received as change, were the same.

They were beautifully-designed notes, too, so good, indeed, that Plummer realised what might be made out of them in the hands of a capable man—himself for example.

And why should he not make use of them? If there were enough he could plan one gigantic coup, and go on with his luxurious mode of living. There would be risk, but not nearly so great a one as some of his schemes had involved.

Was this little man one of a gang, or did he work alone? If there was a gang to deal with there might be difficulties.

From the course and the stands came the cries that told Plummer that a race was in progress; but still he remained seated, his eyes fixed on the ground, and the few people who noticed him thought casually that he had been hard hit. Possibly they would have changed their minds if they could have seen the expression in the master-criminal's eyes when he rose to his feet and walked swiftly back to the stands.

Plummer's mind was made up,

The little old man was in his accustomed place, and after one glance at him, Plummer made his way from the stands and across to where his car was waiting.

"I shall not need you," he said to the chauffeur. "I have met some friends, and will return to London with them."

"Yes, sir," the man answered without interest, and Plummer returned to the stand and his watching of the little old man.

There was only one race remaining to be run; but, despite Plummer's love of gambling, he neither betted on the result or took the slightest interest in it. His eyes were continually glancing to where the little old man sat, and when the latter rose to leave, Plummer was close enough behind not to lose sight of him.

THE SECOND CHAPTER

TRACKED—THE HOUSE AT BECKENHAM— THE FORGED FORTUNE.

THE little old man alighted with a number of other racegoers at Croydon Station shortly before seven o'clock in the evening, and pushed, and was pushed, to the exit. But for all the crush, Plummer contrived to keep him well in sight, and he emerged from the station no more than a score of yards behind his quarry. It was usually he who had been the hunted, and somehow the knowledge that he was the tracker, and possibly the champagne that he had drunk during the course of the afternoon, filled him with a sense of triumph. If he was right in his surmise, the little old man had unintentionally made a coup easy for him.

The old man did not hurry, but strolled along the crowded streets, busy with their Saturday night shopping, and even paused from time to time to glance into windows. Certainly, he did not look like a 'guilty' man, but Plummer had no doubts on the matter.

At present the plan that he had formed was vague, but there would be time enough for him to complete it when he had got the notes into his possession.

In the main street the old man hesitated before a dairy, then went in, and when Plummer strolled by, a glance showed him the old man sipping a glass of milk, and he grinned at the thought of the type of refreshment that he would have when his coup had been accomplished. He even glanced at a public-house, although he had had plenty to drink that afternoon; but prudence held him back from it, though he cursed under his breath when he had been compelled to wait for ten minutes or so.

Then Plummer was on the track again, and it led him to a tram labelled, "Penge." The old man went inside, and the master-criminal mounted to the roof. Around him were other men returned from the races, men of the cheaper class, discussing the events of the gambler's day; but he took no heed of them.

It was not until the Penge police-station was reached that the old man alighted, turned to his right, and walked slowly along the road that leads to Beckenham. How far it was before the man turned up a side street, Plummer did not know, but inwardly he cursed at the distance, and thought of the gorgeous night that he had promised himself in town if he were successful at the races. Then he remembered his depleted pocket-book and the chance that Fate seemed to have thrown in his way.

The road into which the old man had turned was a narrow one, and none too well-lighted. The houses on either side were little more than cottages of a uniform pattern, of the uninteresting type that is to be found in every suburb of London.

The old man turned into the strip of garden of the fifth on the left, and as he drew a key from his pocket, Plummer saw that the place was in pitch-darkness. Did that mean that the man lived alone there?

Plummer walked on, turning after covering a hundred yards or so, and returned to the cottage. Without hesitation he went up the path, noting that there was a glimmer of light in the hall now, and knocked boldly on the door. There was a big game of bluff before him, but he felt quite equal to carrying it through successfully.

There was no answer for a time, then the door slowly opened, and the little old man stood there, as mild-looking and innocent in appearance as ever. He had removed his ancient frock-coat, and wore an equally old coat of the lounge variety. For a moment it seemed impossible to the master-criminal that his suspicions of the man could be correct, then he noticed certain chemical stains on the wrists of the garment, and knew that he was not wrong.

"Yes?" the little man queried, and it seemed to Plummer that his low voice was not altogether steady.

"I wish to see you, Mr.—er—"

"Jesse Kells," the old man put in slowly, "I do not think that I know you."

"At present—no," Plummer agreed. "You will soon—quite well."

The innocent eyes of Jesse Kells met the agate-coloured ones of the master-criminal, and were held by them.

"It would be better to go in," Plummer said, with a shrug of his shoulders, and there was no doubt left in him. He held this little forger in the hollows of his hands, and when he closed his fingers upon him it would be to squeeze him dry enough.

"It would be better to go in," he repeated, and like a hypnotised bird Jesse Kells drew aside. With a big man Plummer might have hesitated to walk in front; but there was no fear about him now, and he led the way to the room at the end of the passage, to look round with an air of disgust when he had entered. Then the little man had followed him, and was standing helplessly by the common deal table in the centre of the kitchen, on which was laid bread-and-butter and a glass of water.

Plummer did not hurry to speak. Before all else he wished to have his victim in a state of alarm, and there was nothing like delay for accomplishing that. In fact in the end it was the old man who broke the silence.

"You wish to see me?" he said faintly. "I do not desire to be discourteous, but I have work to do to-night."

"Of this kind?" Plummer asked meaningly, taking his notecase from his pocket and drawing from it the forged notes. "They are clever, though I could suggest one improvement."

Jesse Kells reeled back against the table, only the edge of it seeming to keep him from falling.

"Where—where did you get them?" he gasped.

"Lingfield," Plummer answered calmly. "I regret to say that they were in exchange for some good ones of my own."

Jesse Kells moved from the table and collapsed into a chair. If he had previously looked old, he looked now like a corpse, save for the wide, appealing eyes.

"Who are you?" he whispered. "Is it—Scotland Yard?"

Plummer realised the advantage of being mistaken for a detective, and nodded.

"Own up!" he said sternly. "What is the face value of the notes that you have made?"

The old man passed his tongue across his lips, and his eyes wandered about furtively until they came back to Plummer's, and the hard menace that the latter held appeared to pull him together.

"A hundred thousand pounds," he answered slowly.

"What!" Plummer ejaculated.

"That is the amount," Jesse Kells persisted doggedly. "I have been at work on them ever since I—I—"

"Left prison," Plummer prompted, with a sneer.

"Yes," the old man said, lifting his head; "but, before Heaven, I was an innocent man!"

"They always are," Plummer put in drily.

"I was," Jesse Kells insisted, "It was because I was such an expert engraver that I was accused, and because the real criminal was my friend. He got away, and I suffered for both. Ten years' of misery, to come out to find my wife dead!"

The old man buried his face in his hands, and the tears sprang from between his fingers. Plummer looked at him savagely, angry at the halt, caring nothing for a man's grief or sorrow.

"Oh, get on!" he snarled. "You are a forger—that is enough! How did you come to do this if you were honest, and how is it that the police have not kept an eye on you?"

"Why?" Jesse Kells raised his head, and his face was harsh. "Because, when left prison I was a man with the stain of crime upon him, and no one would employ an engraver who had been convicted of forgery. I had money that my wife had hoarded up for me, so that I was not in want, and I had it on me when I died."

"When you what?" Plummer cried, believing the man to be insane.

"Officially died," the old man answered drearily, and Plummer shuddered as he thought of the time when he had officially died, too, in Bleakmoor Prison.

"It was a train smash up North," Jesse Kells continued, "and there was one body that could not be identified after the fire. I was known to be on the train, and it was decided that the charred remains were all that was left of a wretched forger. So I got away, and no one has troubled me since."

"But the notes?" Plummer urged. "You could have started afresh as an honest man."

"I know," the old man admitted; "but I have had the fancy to prove the innocence of my other self, who is dead."

"But how—"

"In this way," Jesse Kells interrupted: and a little colour came back to his cheeks as enthusiasm gripped him. "With just enough to live on—my wants are small—I decided upon this plan: I would make the notes, to show how capable I am of swindling honest people. Were I really a criminal I would make a large number, as I have done; even change a few of them, in which I have also succeeded; then take the rest boldly to Scotland Yard and tell the truth. Would that not be proof enough of my innocence?"

The little old man paused, and looked appealingly at the man he believed to be from Scotland Yard.

"You will spare me?" he pleaded. "Perhaps I have been wrong."

"Where are the notes," Plummer demanded—"all of them?"

Jesse Kells dragged his notecase from his pocket, then from various parts of the room he produced forgeries from hiding-places—from a tea-caddy, from a hollowed-out loaf of bread, and from other strange places, until the table was fairly littered over with them.

"That is all," he said dully.

Plummer did not seem to hear him. With eager hands he was taking up the notes one after another and examining them carefully, a great greed in his agate-coloured eyes. They were certainly remarkably good forgeries, and very few people beyond Plummer and Sexton Blake—if any happened to fall into the detective's hands—would be likely to detect them for some time.

Jesse Kells stood looking on, for a time almost without understanding; then his attitude changed. He saw the expression of Plummer's face—the awful greed of it—and drew a little nearer, though he stopped as the criminal commenced to stow the forgeries away in his pockets. Possibly he asked himself why he had not been formally arrested at present, and why—

"I shall take no action in the matter," Plummer observed, buttoning up his coat; "though in future I should advise you—"

"You are not a detective!" burst from Jesse Kells. "Give me those notes back! I'll take them to Scotland Yard, for fear that they fall into the hands of a rogue. Give them to me!"

Plummer's face set hard, and he backed towards the door. Once he got away he did not think that the little man would attempt to interfere with him, as his story would be likely to send him back to prison, though, strangely enough, Plummer believed it.

"Don't be a fool!" he said shortly. "Thank your lucky stars that—"

But, desperate, forgetting his age and smallness, Jesse Kells had snatched up the poker and leapt at the criminal, striking him hard on the shoulder before he had time to defend himself.

In a moment Plummer's vile temper was at fever-heat. He only knew that he had been struck, and that was enough for him. He raised the arm that tingled from the blow, and his fist crashed into the other's teeth, sending him to the floor. But the unequal fight was not yet over.

Jesse Kells, the old man who had taken such strange steps to prove his innocence, in a dazed way knew that he had been duped, and that the man who had accomplished it was a scoundrel who would not hesitate to make use of the forged notes. Half stunned though he was, he flung himself at Plummer's feet and gripped him by the ankles.

"You sha'n't go!" he panted. "The notes!"

Plummer tried to kick himself free, but the little man held on with surprising strength.

"Let go, you fool!" Plummer snarled.

But all that the other did was to hang on and gasp out—"The notes—the notes!"

With an oath, the master-criminal snatched down for the poker that had fallen from the other's hand, and there was a hideous thud as it struck the side of the little man's temple. Twice after that he struck in his anger, though the fingers no longer gripped his ankles, and Jesse Kells lay still, with his head in a growing pool of blood.

Then the mania to hurt vanished, and breathing hard, his face white, Plummer looked down at the quiet body and the suggestive stain by the head.

Had he killed him? Had his rage driven him beyond the line of crime that, so far, he had tried to avoid?

He stooped down and reached out a shaking hand, but only to draw it back before it could touch the body. He went towards the door, but stopped and glanced back over his shoulder.

"He's—he's shamming!" he stammered, but his eyes were fearful as he stood there in the doorway. "Ah!"

Plummer crouched back against the wall as a knock sounded on the front door; then he heard the click of the metal flap of the post-box, and heaved a great sigh of relief. He might have known, he told himself, that old Jesse Kells would not have visitors.

But still the master-criminal stood in the doorway, his agate-coloured eyes always on the form of Jesse Kells although he knew that he must get away as quickly as possible, whether or not the man he had struck down were dead.

There were steps in the street, sounding harshly on the gravel of the side-walk, and somehow Plummer forced himself into the narrow hall, and, with damp fingers, pulled the door of the kitchen fast behind him. And now that he could see the still thing no longer, his wits returned to him, and he crept to the front door and listened.

All was still, not a sound in the street, and Plummer hurried along it with the air of a man who has just escaped some awful fate, going to the left instead of to the right, where the main road lay. Three side-turnings swallowed him up before his roundabout course brought him back into Penge, and he went straight into the nearest bar and ordered brandy, gulping it down at a draught.

"Another!" he said shortly. But that he left unfinished, the idea entering his brain that old Jesse Kells might have already come round and given the alarm.

It was only when London was reached an hour later, that Plummer felt that he could breathe easily, for he was in the great city that he had always found to be the easiest hiding-place for a wanted man.

§

The waiter who was attending upon Plummer at breakfast, eyed the distinguished visitor at the hotel, who was known as Stephen Neilson doubtfully and anxiously. The master-criminal had been staying there for more than a fortnight in his disguise, and during that period he had displayed a love of luxury in the matter of eating and drinking that had filled the waiter who attended upon him with amazement, if not with admiration. Moreover, the guest had shown a tendency to tip lavishly, and therefore, the waiter was anxious that on this morning he should be eating practically nothing.

As a matter of fact, Plummer did not look well. His face was deadly pale, and the lines about it were now largely natural instead of being due entirely to the art of disguise. His fingers moved restlessly among the knives and forks, and dish after dish he sent away untasted.

It was no bodily illness that was upsetting Plummer, however, and drawing him away from the habits of a lifetime. But all through the night he had remained awake, not even removing his clothes, and wondering, always wondering whether the body he had left so still had stirred yet, or whether it would never move again.

"Is there anything else you would like, sir?" the waiter asked solicitously.

"No," Plummer answered sharply. "Yes, take the food away, and bring me a brandy-and-soda—a large one."

It was by no means an early hour of the morning for breakfast, for somehow the ex-convict had discovered one habit that even in his fear he could not break, and that was to do anything in a hurry. Save under the greatest necessity, he was not to be seen early in the morning, and at present that necessity—so far as he was aware—had not arisen.

Upstairs, in a carefully-locked portmanteau, was the pile of forged banknotes that had been stolen at Beckenham—the notes with the face value of a hundred thousand pounds, which were to have been sacrificed by Jesse Kells to clear his character.

Through the night Plummer had wondered whether it would not be best to leave the hotel, change his disguise, and then quietly destroy the notes. Other plans were sure to bring themselves to his active brain before long. That was the great point. How long might it be before he could replenish his stock of money?

Two morning papers lay on the table beside Plummer, but though he had more than once

BLAKE DISCOVERS TEEN BOUND AND GAGGED

THE RING CAME AWAY AND BLAKE FELL TO THE GROUND.

PLUMMER THREW TINKER INTO THE RIVER.

H. M. Hewitt

THE FIGHT BETWEEN BLAKE AND PLUMMER IN THE BARN.

picked them up, he had not at present dared to look at them. He was afraid that his worst fears would be confirmed, and that by now Scotland Yard would be looking for the murderer of the man at Beckenham.

The brandy was brought, and the criminal drank it down thirstily, causing the waiter to murmur, as he walked away: "Must have had a thick night."

Plummer sat back in his chair, waiting for the spirit to take effect, and it was not long before the glow of it crept up from his body to his brain, soothing out the imaginings that had obsessed it all night. After all, why should the old man be dead? He himself had received worse blows and recovered.

The criminal's hand went up instinctively to his head, where under the iron-grey wig was the trepan-plate that he had worn for years.

Yes, he thought that had been a far harder blow, but, for all that, he was still alive—a strong man.

Plummer picked up the nearest of the papers with the quick movement of a man who has made up his mind to an unwelcome act, like the gulping down of medicine, or the quick killing of an injured pet. Then the sheet was open before him, and a glance showed him that Jesse Kells had not lain long alone in his cottage.

There it was in the centre column, the heavy black type of the heading and sub-headings screaming out for attention, and the master-criminal forced himself to read.

He was the chief actor in the tragedy—excepting the poor old man who had been struck down—yet he was probably one of the last in London to know of the full extent of the affair.

"SUBURBAN TRAGEDY.
"MYSTERY MAN STRUCK DOWN.
"WHAT THE POLICE FOUND.

"In the early hours of this morning there came to light in a cottage in a quiet street in Beckenham, what promises to be one of the most sensational cases of the times.

"Tayville Road is a sheltered place given over to cottages suitable to the lower middle-class, and No. 13, at which the victim of the strange affair lived, is much the same as the others, save in certain respects. For years it has been occupied by a Mr. Jesse Kells, an old man who

has for a considerable period been regarded as the mystery of the neighbourhood, and which is likely to have a remarkable conclusion. Until to-day the mystery consisted merely in the fact that the old man lived there quite alone, doing his own housework, taking no interest in his neighbours, and asking for none. Hie patch of garden in front has been neglected, most of the paint has long since vanished from the door and window-frames, but as Mr. Jesse Kells was his own landlord, nothing was thought of that.

"The tragedy, if that is to be its end, is simply as follows:

"P.-c. Tooks was making his way through Tayville Road this morning, when he noticed that there was a light burning in the hall of No. 13, which has never been the case on any other occasion when he has passed the cottage. His suspicions were aroused, as the old man had the reputation of being a miser, and he thought it possible that burglars, believing this, had broken in.

"With great promptitude the constable tried the door, to find it locked, and after repeatedly knocking without receiving a response, he called up a neighbour, was let through the house, and in that manner reached the small garden at the back of the cottage. A light shone from the crack of the shutters over the kitchen window, and through the slit the constable could dimly see a form lying on the ground. The door was immediately forced, and Mr. Kells was found lying insensible in a pool of blood, his head terribly injured. The weapon with which the wounds were inflicted was evidently a heavy poker, blood-stained, that lay close to the body.

"Police and medical aid were sent for, and then it was that the most sensational aspect of the affair was brought to light. The police refuse to say much concerning the matter, but two neighbours who were present at the time have been able to inform us that a complete forging apparatus was discovered, with plates that leave no doubt that a large number of Bank of England notes must have been forged. So far as our informants know, however, none of the notes were found.

"The injured man was at once taken to hospital, but he only recovered consciousness for a few seconds, when he murmured what is believed to have been: 'Tail man—eyeglass— Lingfield races.'

"What this signifies it is impossible to at present surmise; but the police will probably search the neighbourhood this morning for any information of a man answering that description having been seen in the neighbourhood last night. It is to be hoped that the clue will be productive of results.

"For the present it is useless to discuss the possibilities of the situation, and the police are anxiously waiting for the injured man to fully recover consciousness. The only theory that we can advance at present is that the man had a partner, that there was a quarrel, and that the climax was an attempt to murder."

Plummer laid the paper down, and there was a troubled expression in his eyes. He almost wished that he had killed Jesse Kells. Then there would have been no description of any kind. True, the man might not recover now, but the chance was enough to make the criminal uneasy.

The thought of the forged notes in his portmanteau chilled him, and it was by sheer strength of will that he prevented himself going to his room and destroying them at once. But the apartment was heated by an electric apparatus, which would prevent his burning them.

He must get rid of the notes, Plummer decided. But how was it to be done?

The master-criminal sat in gloomy silence. Now that the necessity had arisen for him to destroy the forgeries, it went badly against the grain. More than ever it seemed to him that he should have made a fortune out of them, and now it was slipping from his grasp as others had done.

Presently Plummer signalled to the hovering waiter.

"I shall want my luggage brought down from my room in half an hour," he said. "I am leaving here to-day."

The Third Chapter

The Next Move—Plummer Robbed— The Only Way—Sexton Blake Called In.

IT was evening, verging upon night, as Plummer left the Hotel Imperial. In the morning he had taken his bags to London Bridge, and placed them in the cloak-room, for somehow throughout the day he had not seen the possibility of removing the incriminating evidence that one of them held. Besides, he still had qualms with regard to letting the notes slip from him, and also Jesse Kells might die without being able to tell his story. A change of disguise had not been difficult to bring about, for it had simply meant the removal of the grey moustache and the monocle, so that Plummer had no fear of being discovered.

The master-criminal had dined well, but on this occasion the influence of food and drink failed to cheer him as he walked moodily along the Strand. Where he intended to go to with his bags, he had not the faintest idea for the present, and he was half inclined to forsake them, though there were reasons against that.

In one of the bags was a complete make-up outfit that Plummer regarded as a necessity, and which he would have found it hard to replace, not to mention a small but very complete set of burgling tools that the criminal had obtained in Paris while on his way to London.

It was not often that Plummer chose to walk, but to-night his mind was so full of the present— and the future—that he scarcely knew that he was doing so. He went mechanically from the Strand to Fleet Street, and round to his right, and over Blackfriars Bridge. It was there that he turned to the left to reach London Bridge.

As usual, the master-criminal was dressed in a manner that suggested money, and if he had not been so preoccupied he might have noticed three men at the corner of the bridge whisper together, then follow in his wake. At the same time it would have occurred to him that the night was dark, though even then it would have seemed unlikely that the most daring of roughs would venture to attack him in the broad thoroughfare. He did not know, however, that further along the road was entirely stopped, and that he would have to make a detour. Needless to say, that the roughs were aware of the fact.

Plummer walked on until he came to the obstruction, noted it mechanically, and as mechanically turned to his left into a narrow street, the darkness of which would have warned a cautious man. The roughs grinned and followed, or, rather, two did, and the third disappeared up some mysterious alley.

When Plummer raised his head at last, his mind made up to his course of action, the fact that he was followed had not come to him. He had decided that the forged notes would have to go, and that he must live quietly on the genuine money remaining to him until a fresh scheme of fraud entered his criminal brain.

With his mind free for the moment of his plans, Plummer caught the sound of the footfalls behind him, and there was something in their stealthy tread to make him turn his head sharply, a fear gripping at his heart that in some manner the police had got on his track. For an instant he saw with relief that these ragged men were not officials, and he was so sure of his own strength that an attempted attack by them did not worry him. But as he turned his head back again the whole of the danger that awaited him flashed upon him, and he was too late to resist.

The rough who had slipped away through the alley leapt from the shelter of a dark doorway. He threw his arm up in defence, but almost before it was shoulder high the world had grown black for him, and he dropped to the ground, stunned by a blow on the temple,

"Bash 'im another," one of the roughs suggested.

"Gawn, get away," the other objected, already on his knees beside the prostrate man, "'Ad all 'e wants, matey."

With the fingers of experts, the thieves set to work, something between amazement and awe in their expressions as they realised the extent of their haul.

"S'pose it's all right," one of them said doubtfully. "'Ow we goin' ter plant it, anyway?"

"By gettin' lagged if we don't look slippy," another man growled. "Lor, a chap would think as you was in your own drorin'-room. I 'ave seed perlice 'ere."

"All right, we'll 'op it," the first agreed. "We'll fix it when we're safe. Got the 'ole lot?"

"Not 'arf," the other answered sarcastically. "If it 'adn't 'ave been fer me low pals I'd 'ave been made chief searcher at the Yard by now."

Three roughs hurried away into the darkness, and Plummer lay still, much as Jesse Kells had on the previous evening, such are the weird turnings of the wheels of Fate.

Ten minutes passed before a passer-by stumbled upon Plummer, hesitated nervously, then bent over him. Fortunately for him, the insensible man was coming round, and it was with profound relief that he found himself able to get him to his feet.

"Hurt much?" the newcomer asked anxiously. "I see that you've had a crack on the head."

The criminal looked about him dimly, hardly as yet realising what had happened, but knowing that he was not anxious to attract undue attention.

"Ought to be a policeman along soon," the newcomer ventured. "You could complain to him. Would you know the man again?"

"No," Plummer answered dully. "There must have been three of them."

"Pity, I should have a brandy if I were you. There's a public-house a hundred yards away."

Plummer nodded, making the pain in his head worse, so that he could scarcely walk, but he made the effort, pushed open the swing-door of the public-house and staggered in. The other man had helped him there, but he hurried away as soon as Plummer was inside. He had no wish to be mixed up in an affair that might end in the police-court.

"Brandy!" the master-criminal said hoarsely, gripping the edge of the bar for support. "Been knocked down—faint."

There were three or four roughish-looking men in the bar, but they evinced no particular interest as the barman poured out the drink.

"Fourpence," the latter said; and the tone of his voice implied that matters of this kind were not new to him.

Plummer swallowed the drink off, and dived his hand into his pocket. Then his already pale face went ghastly, and he snatched up at the pocket in which his notecase had been, to discover it had gone.

"Robbed!" he gasped, his wandering faculties returning to him with the shock, as his groping fingers assured him that not so much as a penny remained on him.

"'Ere, you weigh out!" the barman said truculently. "I've had your type before, pretending to have been knocked down and robbed, so as to get a free drink."

Then Plummer's anger, starting with the pain in his head, and roused almost to madness by his loss, blazed out. He gripped a heavy decanter that stood on the bar, but before he could use it his wrist had been snatched, and another man had gripped him from behind. The next moment the barman was in the public part, and, struggling and kicking, Plummer was thrown out on to the pavement. He swung round, staggering so that he nearly fell, but the blow that he had received made him feel sick and weak. If he struggled, the police might be sent for, a surgeon would examine his head, and it would be discovered that he wore a wig.

Plummer leant against the wall, at a few yards from the public-house, from the doorway of which the barman still watched him vindictively. For the time being he was not himself, and even the fact that he had been robbed of all his genuine money had become a dim, intangible thing. Soon he would realise it once more.

A policeman went heavily by, half stopped as if to speak to the well-dressed man who stood with his hand pressed to his head, and went on, probably putting him down as a common "drunk."

The sight of the man in blue roused Plummer a little, and he managed to leave the wall, and walk on with a stagger. Slowly his weakness grew less, and the terrible state of his affairs was plain to him—he was penniless. He wanted to go somewhere to think, to steady himself for the future that had suddenly turned so dark, but there was no shelter open to him without money.

With a despairing feeling the master-criminal went through his pockets again, and cursed as he found how completely the criminals had done their work, and beyond that his inordinate pride in his own ability was wounded. He, a prince of crime, had been set upon and robbed by mere roughs.

Plummer reached the main road, and from there reached the little hill leading up to London Bridge Station. Scarcely knowing that he did so, he walked up to the entrance, but only to stop outside the booking-offices, and make a great effort to collect his wits.

"Why had he meant to come there in the first place?" he asked himself. "There must have been an object, but what was it?"

Plummer inserted his fingers into the pocket where his watch should have been, but all that he drew out was a small scrap of paper—a cloak-room ticket. A small thing, but sufficient to bring his memory with a rush.

Of course, his two bags were lying there, the one with his clothes and make-up, and the other with the forged notes, and as he thought of them his mind was made up. After all, he would have to use the notes, and take the risks that the passing of them would entail. He would only change a few, just enough to get him away, There would be no danger in that.

But in his heart of hearts Plummer knew that he intended to go on with the greater scheme, and lay his hands upon the hundred thousand pounds that was the face value of the notes.

Pulling himself together the master-criminal examined himself in a handy mirror, to find that he showed practically no sign of his recent encounter with the roughs, and assuming a jaunty air, he walked to the cloak-room. In a minute or so his bags were handed over to him, and, declining the aid of a porter, he carried them into the waiting-room. Luckily for him it was empty, and with nervous haste he unlocked the bag that held the forged notes, and drew out several of the value of five and ten pounds. The larger ones would have to be negotiated in a more roundabout and elaborate manner.

After that Plummer hesitated for a brief space, then, with all the swagger at his command, he walked up to the booking-office.

"First return to Brighton," he said, in authoritative tones. "I hope that you won't mind a fiver as I am out of smaller change?"

The clerk in charge took the forged note proffered to him, looked at it, and glanced from it to the commanding face of Plummer, little guessing that it was all that the latter could do to keep his limbs from palpably shaking.

"Certainly, sir," the man answered, and though the criminal's sigh of relief was inaudible, it was there all right.

With the ticket for Brighton, and the change in his pocket, Plummer carried his bags away, but hesitated close to the platforms. Then the saloon on his left attracted his attention, and he went hastily into it.

It was half an hour later that Plummer, a trifle flushed about the cheeks, and with his eyes exceptionally bright, marched behind his bags, carried by a porter, to the express train for Brighton. The spirits that he had drunk had brought back all his old confidence, and he had decided that he might as well go to the coast as anywhere else. He wanted time to think out his scheme, and in his present condition he had no fear about it being a success.

§

Sexton Blake was plainly in the best of spirits, and he laughed softly as he walked up and down his sitting-room. His clothes, too, suggested something of a holiday spirit, and the bags lying ready on the floor also pointed to the fact that the famous detective was about to take one of his rare holidays.

Tinker had much the same air as he hurried into the room in a brand-new tweed suit, dragging a large bundle of golf clubs with him.

"Here we are, sir!" he cried. "Ready to face the stormy ocean, cross the Alps, or watch the minstrels at Margate, according to orders."

"Right you are, my lad," Sexton Blake answered. "You had better run along with this cheque to the bank, I have some gold, so you had better bring the fifty pounds in notes."

Tinker almost sprinted off with the cheque, for it was not often that he or his master took a holiday. So far as he himself was concerned, he would just as soon have been busy at the work he loved, but he knew that of late Sexton Blake had shown unusual signs of fatigue, and that a rest was necessary to him.

The detective continued to stroll up and down the room, humming a tune between draws from his pipe, his face looking years younger now that it was not set in hard thought, and at the end of ten minutes Tinker returned.

"Here you are, sir," he announced, handing over the notes that he had drawn from his pocket. "Four tens and two fives."

Sexton Blake took the notes, and with the instinct of a man accustomed to allow nothing to escape him, looked at them closely. Then slowly the smile faded from his lips, and from his pocket he drew the magnifying-glass that even on a holiday never left him, while Tinker looked on in surprise.

The detective lowered the glass after examining every one of the notes, and his face once more wore the hard, set-look that was always there when there was business on hand.

"As I thought—forged," he said, in a low voice.

"What?" Tinker gasped. "But I brought them from the bank, sir."

Sexton Blake shrugged his shoulders, and his narrowed eyes were upon the notes.

"Even banks may make mistakes, my lad,'" he answered drily; "and these are exceptionally good forgeries."

The detective dropped into a chair, crossed his legs, and pressed the tips of his fingers together.

"We—we shall go on the holiday?" Tinker ventured hesitatingly.

"I think not," Sexton Blake answered, rousing himself. "Ring up the manager of the bank, and tell him that I must see him at once."

"Suppose he can't come, sir?"

"He must," the detective repeated. "This affair may be more serious than the few notes passed upon you—far more."

Tinker went to the 'phone, and in a very short time he was through to the manager of the bank.

"That you, Mr. Bronson?" he asked. "Mr. Blake wants to see you at once. You can't come?"

Tinker looked inquiringly at his master.

"Ask him whether he would rather have an affair of forged notes placed in my hands, or in those of Scotland Yard?" he said impatiently. "Then ring off; it'll fetch him."

Tinker obeyed, the receiver was back on its stand, and Sexton Blake lay back in his chair with his eyes almost closed. After a brief hesitation, his assistant carried the packed bags from the room, and returned to remain quietly by the window for the events that were to happen.

It was no more than ten minutes later that there was a violent ringing and knocking at the front door, and Tinker went off to answer it. Then the door of the consulting-room was opened.

"Mr. Bronson—from the bank," Tinker said, a half-suppressed grin on his face, and retired.

The Fourth Chapter

Startling News—Getting to Work—A Large Coup.

WHY Mr. Bronson had ever risen to be the manager of an important branch of a very important bank, it is hard to say, unless sheer luck or influence had placed him in that position. Anyway, there he was, quite satisfied with himself, and abundantly assertive with regard to his own abilities and the wisdom of those who had placed him in command.

Beyond that, he was a little man with a white waistcoat, a frock-coat that looked as if it would burst if he attempted to button it, and a pair of lavender trousers, which on his short legs aggravated the perky little walk that in his own select suburb had earned him the nickname of the "cock-sparrow," a fact of which practically every inhabitant of the suburb, was aware of barring himself.

It should be mentioned, perhaps, that Mr. Bronson's face was pink and white, was edged in on either side by a small whisker, and that his mouth was puckered up in the thoughtful expression to be seen in the statues of famous statesmen, but scarcely anywhere else. Only one further fact is, more or less, necessary, and that is that up to the present, despite middle-age having been left some considerable distance behind, the bank-manager's work had not been arduous enough to appreciably thin out his hair.

Now Mr. Bronson stood just inside the doorway, his mouth more compressed than ever, his left leg slightly advanced, and his right hand upon his watch-chain. It was an effective, attitude for him.

"This is unusual, Mr. Blake," he said, in his pompous voice, though his eyes strayed a little uneasily to the notes lying on the table.

"Most," the famous detective agreed. "Most."

Mr. Bronson lost something of the dignity of his attitude, and though he reversed feet he kept his eyes on the notes.

"I—er—fail to understand," he said. "What is the matter?"

"That I don't like being paid forged notes from a bank," Sexton Blake replied. "You will find them on the table."

"Im-impossible!" Mr. Bronson stammered, but for all that he hurried to the table and took up the notes.

"I see nothing wrong with them," he said slowly.

"Possibly not," Sexton Blake answered impatiently; "but you may take it from me that they are forgeries. You had best apply to the Bank of England, and, in the meantime, pay out no more of the series."

"But—I have," Mr. Bronson said hesitatingly. "I don't know why, but there has been a large demand for notes to-day, and we must have paid fully a thousand pounds from that series, which came from our head-office yesterday."

The detective whistled softly, and sat up in his chair.

"The head office would have got them straight from the Bank of England?" he asked sharply.

"Yes," Mr. Bronson admitted, adding dejectedly: "But you must have made a mistake."

Sexton Blake rose to his feet, and nodded at the notes.

"You may as well take them," he said coldly; "they are of no use to me."

Then it was plain that the bank-manager was convinced, and the last fragment of pomposity left him.

"What—what do you intend to do?" he asked.

"See if I can pick up a clue, if you wish it, and—"

"Yes, yes," Mr. Bronson agreed quickly. "There must be as little publicity as possible. Terrible! Terrible!"

"In the meantime," Sexton Blake went on, "get back all the notes of this series that you possibly can from your clients, and if they have already parted with any, find out who they have been paid to, otherwise there will be complaints to the police, and inevitably they will be traced back to you. You must advise the head-office, and they will be able to make inquiries at the Bank of England. That is all."

Mr. Bronson hastily picked up his hat, which he had laid down while examining the forged notes, and there was nothing of swagger about him as he left the room. Before he could reach the front door, however, there was a wild knocking on it, and when Tinker opened it, Detective-inspector Lurgan, of Scotland Yard, almost fell in in his haste, recovered himself, and stared at Mr.

Bronson, whom he had met on business before, in a far from friendly manner.

"Another of you!" he snapped angrily. "If you knew your business better, it'd save us no end of trouble."

The poor little bank-manager was already practically in a state of collapse, or he would undoubtedly have resented the tone of the Scotland Yard man's voice.

"What—what do you mean?" he stammered.

"That there are complaints of forgeries from five of the branches of your bank to-day, and I reckon that you're the sixth!" the inspector growled. "Isn't it enough to make us savage to know that your men haven't sense enough to discover them?"

"Re-really, inspector," Mr. Bronson quavered. "I think that you are going too far."

"Do you!" Inspector Lurgan sneered. "Well, I don't, seeing that we warned you after that affair at Beckenham that there was likely to be a flood of forged notes in circulation."

And poor Mr. Bronson, even his lavender-coloured trousers looking wilted, drifted out into Baker Street, while the detective hurried through into Sexton Blake's consulting-room.

"Nice affair this, Mr. Blake!" the Scotland Yard man said without preliminary greetings.

"Forged notes?" the Baker Street detective queried.

"Yes, and Heaven alone knows how many!" Inspector Lurgan answered, flopping into a chair, and instantly bounding up again. "It's the worst thing that we've struck for a long time. By to-day we have already had complaints of more than twenty thousand pounds' worth of notes that have been passed, and more complaints were arriving when I came to see you."

"Then you wish me to help you?"

"Of course, if you can spare the time."

"I am yours to command," Sexton Blake answered, with a dry smile and a shrug of the shoulders. "I should have thought that you would have known that by now."

"And we appreciate it," the inspector said, with a graciousness that he was not always in the habit of showing. "Shall I tell you what we have done at present?"

"By all means."

Sexton Blake relit his pipe, and settled back in his chair, his eyes closed, every line of his face drawn with thought.

"Go on," he prompted; "minutes may count in this case."

"We have feared something of this kind ever since the discovery at Beckenham," Inspector Lurgan explained. "It was an easy theory that the old man who was injured had been making notes practically since taking up his residence at the cottage, and that meant that a very considerable number must have been produced. I need not remind you that there have been remarkably few cases of really skilful forgery for some years, which suggested that the notes made at Beckenham had been hoarded up to be used in one great coup when all was ready. The risk of detection would be practically the same. You follow me so far?"

Sexton Blake nodded, and his eyes remained closed.

"Our inquiries in Penge and Beckenham failed," the inspector continued; "and all that we could do was to warn the banks and wait for the man Jesse Kells to recover consciousness, which so far he has not done; in fact, the doctors still say that his condition is critical."

"What else?" Sexton Blake queried. "What have been your steps in the matter?"

"Practically nothing at present," Inspector Lurgan answered lamely. "Only one thing is certain, and that is that the forged notes must actually have been issued from the Bank of England. There can be little doubt that there is one man there who is guilty, for how could the notes have been changed in so many instances while being sent to the branch banks? In one case, at least, it is practically certain that there would have been some hitch, but there has been absolutely none. In consequence, we intended to arrest the cashier who issued the notes, to find that he left last night for his holidays. He had stated what his destination was to be, but it is most probably a false trail. That is all."

Sexton Blake lay back in his chair, and for a short time did not speak.

"The cashier was a trusted man?" he asked at last.

"He had been at the bank since a boy, and would have retired next year on a good pension."

"Had he a family, or was he likely to be a man to live over his income?" Sexton Blake asked.

"Our inquiries say 'no' to both those questions," the inspector answered. "In fact, it can easily be proved that the cashier has been saving for many years, and has quite a comfortable nest-egg in Government stock.

"I tell you, the affair is an absolute mystery, one of the hardest that it has ever been our lot to have brought to us. We can only imagine that the cashier succumbed to a sudden temptation—"

"Oh, nonsense!" Sexton Blake interrupted impatiently. "If it had been a sudden temptation how did he contrive to have the forged notes ready? The only other possible suggestion is that he was working with this Jesse Kells—unless he is innocent."

The inspector shrugged his shoulders despairingly.

"What do you propose to do, Mr. Blake?" he queried.

"Go down to Beckenham," Sexton Blake replied. "By the way, I suppose it is not known yet whether genuine notes were taken for the forged ones?"

"There can be no doubt about that, but it will take a short time to ascertain the numbers of them as the entry has been removed from the books; probably they will have been changed by then."

"Right! I shall be ready for you in five minutes."

Sexton Blake passed into his dressing-room, and Inspector Lurgan frowned as he heard the famous detective humming a tune. It was a serious business to him, and his was not the nature that could understand a man like Sexton Blake, and that his great happiness was in his work; and the more difficult it was the better.

§

A policeman guarded the entrance to the cottage at Beckenham, for though the tragedy was a week old there were still idle people to come and stare at the place, and with the modern craze for souvenir hunting so prevalent—even the scraps of an aeroplane that has dashed its brave pilot to death not being sacred from the clutches of these human vultures—it was as well to be careful.

The constable on duty touched his helmet to Inspector Lurgan, eyed Sexton Blake curiously, then proceeded to be very important in the matter of moving on two gaping children and an old woman. The two detectives had come straight to Beckenham, save for a call at Scotland Yard

where they had learnt that more complaints had been received, the total of forged notes known to be in existence totalling the face value of close upon thirty-five thousand pounds.

Inspector Lurgan unfastened the door with a key, and led the way into the narrow passage.

"Every article is in the position in which we found it," he said; "though some have been moved and replaced with the greatest care."

"No notes at all were found?" Sexton Blake asked.

"Not one," the inspector answered gloomily. "That's the worst of it."

"I'm not so sure," Sexton Blake murmured. "If all the notes have already been disposed of you may be right, but if there are any left the utterer of the rest may make a slip."

"I doubt it," the inspector said hopelessly, as they went into the kitchen where the tragedy had occurred.

Sexton Blake stood in the doorway, looking about him closely, his keen eyes noting the poker on the floor, the end of it close to the suggestive stain on the boards, something of the hideousness of which had by now been covered by a layer of dust. After that he crossed to the cupboard, and examined the contents of it.

"Whether Jesse Kells worked alone he certainly lived alone," he said, with conviction. "You will see that there is only one cup; in fact, one of everything. The injured man had not expensive tastes. Where is the apparatus?"

Inspector Lurgan turned to the right, and pushed open a door in the wall.

"Mind the steps as you come down into the cellar," he said warningly.

A match flickered in the detective's fingers and the next moment he had turned on a powerful light. It revealed a very small cellar, which had in the first instance probably been intended for the storage of coals, but there was not so much as a grain of that useful mineral about now. Instead, was about as complete an apparatus for forging and engraving as any man could have desired, and Sexton Blake moved about it with the greatest interest, his eyes narrowed, his finely-cut nostrils moving like those of a sensitive dog.

"It's a one-man outfit," he said at last; "there can be no doubt about that. Again—as in the case of the kitchen utensils—there is only one of everything. If the missing cashier was an accomplice he could not have been a working one."

TINKER IN DISGUISE ON THE LOOK OUT FOR PLUMMER.

BLAKE VISITS AUGUSTUS MELTON IN PRISON.

BLAKE WATCHED THE SHADOWS ON THE BLIND.

THE DOOR OPENED SUDDENLY AND PLUMMER APPEARED WITH AN EVIL GRIN.

"Seen everything?"

"Wait."

Sexton Blake made another tour of the cellar, then he shook his head and straightened his back,

"There is nothing to be learnt here," he said. "Was there anything of importance found in any of the other rooms?"

"Absolutely nothing!"

"Then we may as well be going."

Detective-inspector Lurgan looked more than a little disappointed as he left the cottage. Although he never cared to admit it openly, he had a great admiration for the powers of the famous detective of Baker Street. At times he had known him accomplish things that appeared to verge on the miraculous, and possibly he had expected something of the kind in this instance.

"What do you make of it?" he asked, as they turned into the main road.

"Nothing," Sexton Blake answered readily.

"Oh," the inspector murmured, still more gloomily,

A paper-boy came hurrying down the road, yelling at the top of his voice, a streaming placard flying out beside him.

"Errest o' Benk o' Englind official!" he shouted. "'Orrible sensation!"

The boy stopped at a gesture from Inspector Lurgan, and hurried on again as soon as he had sold his paper.

"They've got the cashier, Augustus Melton," the inspector observed grimly, after glancing at the front sheet of the paper.

"Where?" Sexton Blake queried.

The inspector looked at the paper again, and an expression of surprise crossed his face.

"Hanged if they haven't arrested him at the lodgings at Brighton that he said he was going to," he said slowly.

"I thought as much," Sexton Blake murmured. "He is not the guilty man."

"Unless he reckoned on a colossal bluff," the inspector said, trying apparently to hope that something would come of the arrest.

But Sexton Blake shook his head, and paused to light a cigar.

"There are few criminals living with the nerve for it," he answered.

"How about Plummer?"

Sexton Blake examined his cigar to make sure that it was burning evenly.

"So it is your turn to see that man's hand in everything big," he remarked. "Well, I admit that he is capable of it, and such a daring scoop would appeal to his vanity. Now we had better get along to Scotland Yard. I am rather interested in the people who have had the forged notes passed upon them, and after that we must see this Augustus Melton."

"If possible," the inspector said. "In such a big case the chiefs may consider it inadvisable for the present."

"If so they can reckon me out of the hunt except on my own account, my friend," Sexton Blake answered drily. "I must have a free hand or nothing."

"Oh, I dare say that it can be managed," the inspector admitted, and they made their way to the station.

THE FIFTH CHAPTER

A CLUE AT LAST—THE STRANGE STORY OF AUGUSTUS MELTON.

SIR HENRY FAIRFAX, Commissioner of Police, looked even more than usually serious as he faced Sexton Blake and Inspector Lurgan. At all times his position was no sinecure, and of late there had been an uncommonly large number of involved cases, with a great outcrying of the public when certain of them had not been cleared up satisfactorily.

"There is a list of the present complaints, Mr. Blake," he said. "You will see that they total over the forty thousand, and there is no knowing what others may be made."

"Exactly," the Baker Street detective agreed. "Has any statement been made by Augustus Melton?"

"No," the Commissioner answered. "I thought that you would like to be present. When he was arrested he appeared to be too dazed to do anything but protest his innocence; in fact, he was in a state of collapse."

"An innocent man would be," Sexton Blake said.

"You think that?"

"It is unwise to think too much at present," the detective answered, and turned to the list on the table.

For ten minutes Sexton Blake examined the paper carefully, and against two of the entries he made ticks.

"I see that there is a complaint from the Brighton Railways that a forged five-pound note was changed with them on the evening of the seventh day ago, and there is also another one from Brighton dating the next day. How is it that the complaints were not lodged sooner?"

"They were only detected when every bank in England was warned by us," the Commissioner replied. "It was then possible for the banks who had received the two notes to trace them to their source. There possibly is no connection between the two paltry affairs and this colossal fraud. Is it likely that a man with such a scheme in hand would risk arrest for such small sums?"

"It depends upon his circumstances," Sexton Blake said, "and remember this—eight days ago Jesse Kells was injured at Beckenham. If the forged notes were stolen from his cottage—we ought to be able to assume that to be the case— the thief may have been hard up, and needed money to carry out his greater scheme. Whether he had known all along what Kells was, and waited his opportunity to strike, we shall proba- bly never learn, unless the injured man recovers. I think that we had better see Augustus Melton at once."

"Certainly," Sir Henry agreed. "I will ring for the car."

It was only a few minutes later that the Com- missioner, Inspector Lurgan, an official short- hand-writer, and Sexton Blake, were ushered into the cell at Bow Street, where the bank cashier had been imprisoned.

He sat there on the wooden bench, a thin man. Grey-haired, his clothes dishevelled, his face between his hands, and did not attempt to look up until the clang of the door roused him. He looked at the callers with a dazed expression on his face, his eyes sunken with fatigue, his lips a little apart. For only an hour or so had he been in the cell, but anyone who knew him would have told you that that brief incarceration had turned him from a well-preserved man of late middle- age to an old one.

"I warn you," Sir Henry said sternly, though not unkindly, "that any statement you may make will be taken down in writing, and may be used at your trial in evidence against you. You are not compelled to make a statement, but are at liberty to reserve your defence until you have consulted a lawyer."

Melton looked dully at the Commissioner, and his slack lips moved.

"I am innocent," he muttered, like a frightened child repeating a lesson.

"That remains to be proved, Mr. Melton," Sexton Blake put in quietly, and he could not believe that the man was guilty of so big a fraud. He was plainly one of those machine-made crea- tures, good at their work, but who have been in a groove for so long that they are utterly inca- pable of getting out of it. "I may tell you that I am Sexton Blake, the detective, and I am equally anxious to prove either your innocence or your guilt. If you are really innocent you may be able to help me to establish it."

The accused man passed a shaking hand across his face, and slowly a look of understanding came into his eyes.

"I am innocent," he said again. "I never thought that when I went on Thursday for my holiday that such a thing as this could happen to me."

"You mean on Friday night," Inspector Lurgan corrected sharply, while the shorthand writer made notes.

"No, Thursday," Melton persisted. "It was to have been Friday, but when I returned home on the previous evening there was a letter from my chief at the bank saying that I could start then. I was surprised."

Sexton Blake, the Commissioner, and Inspec- tor Lurgan looked at one another questioningly.

"You have the letter?" Sexton Blake asked.

The colour rose into the cashier's face, and died away again.

"No," he answered plaintively. "I tore it up. I did not think to keep it."

"Perhaps it does not matter," Sexton Blake said kindly. "You can prove that you arrived at Brighton on Thursday night?"

A groan broke from the accused man, and he buried his face in his hands.

"It is all against me," he moaned. "After all these years of faithful service."

"Bunkum," Inspector Lurgan said angrily, heedless of the frowns of the others. "You must be able to prove where you were. What did you do?"

Melton raised his head slowly, and his lips were trembling.

"Believe me, I will tell you all, gentlemen," he said huskily, "though I am ashamed of what happened. I—I have always been an abstemious man, and, being single, have lived in two rooms, having most of my meals out. Well, on the Thursday night a friend I met recently called for me, and suggested that we should go out, and as all my luggage was ready, in fact, sent on in advance, I saw no harm in it. After that I—I am afraid that I must have taken too much, though I do not remember having more than two glasses of wine."

"Go on," Inspector Lurgan prompted grimly.

"I seem to remember dining, though I don't know where," Melton continued. "I woke up with my head aching and feeling ill, and I could not imagine where I was until I found that I was lying in a barn. I left that, and reached the road. An inquiry informed me to my surprise that I was close to Brighton, and scarcely knowing what I was doing I walked there."

The man made a little despairing gesture with his hands.

"It was Friday night—late!" he whispered.

Inspector Lurgan laughed, but checked himself under a look from Sir Henry.

"I didn't want my disgrace to be known—that somehow in the—the state I was in I must have tried to walk to Brighton, and I told the landlady of the lodgings that I had taken that I had arrived by train. This morning I was arrested."

The man pressed a hand to his head, and collapsed on to a seat, and in a moment Sexton Blake was bending over him, for he had fainted.

"About the weakest story I ever heard," Inspector Lurgan sneered. "What do you think of it, Sir Henry?"

The Commissioner hesitated. He was a just man, unwilling to commit himself without proof, but in this case there really seemed to be no doubt that his subordinate was right.

"It seems like it," he admitted.

Sexton Blake, strange to say, was making no attempt to bring the fainting man round, but was examining him closely, trying his pulse, his heart, and lifting the lids of his eyes. When he looked up from the examination there was a slight smile on his lips.

"In one matter at least this man has spoken the truth, Sir Henry," he said. "There is every indication that he has recently been drugged."

"Might have done it to substantiate his story," Inspector Lurgan growled, and it was then that Sexton Blake showed a touch of temper unnatural with him.

"Really, inspector," he said, "I always believed that according to law a man was innocent until proved guilty."

Then the famous detective turned to Sir Henry.

"You might send for a doctor," he added. "There are several important questions I must ask the accused without delay, and he will confirm what I have told you, unless I have forgotten all my knowledge of medicine."

Sir Henry motioned to Inspector Lurgan to go for the doctor, and in a short time the divisional surgeon arrived, having been called up on the telephone. He was about as unlike a surgeon as one could have expected to find a man, though his skill was fully equal to his reputation, for he was considerably more like a police-sergeant in plain clothes.

"That you, Blake?" he said cheerily. "Thought you'd be in this case, somehow—just the touch of unusualness. Let me have a look at the patient."

"Mr. Blake thinks that the prisoner has been—" the Commissioner began, but the detective interrupted him quickly.

"I would rather have an unbiassed opinion," he said quietly.

The surgeon bent over the man lying on the bench, and his examination did not take him long.

"It's a faint now," he said. "I can soon bring him round, but he has been suffering from the effect of a drug."

"Given recently?" Sexton Blake queried.

"I should say that it was at least twenty-four hours ago—certainly not less," the surgeon answered, without hesitation.

Even Inspector Lurgan permitted something of the expression of doubt to leave his face, but Sexton Blake betrayed no sign of his triumph. He was a man who never spoke without reason, so that it was nothing new for his statements to be verified.

The surgeon set to work quickly upon Melton, and in a few minutes he had opened his eyes, while colour had come back into his cheeks.

"I'll leave some stuff, in case he has another attack," the surgeon said briskly. "I don't suppose you want me now?"

"No, thanks," Sir Henry answered.

"Then good-bye, Sir Henry. See you soon, Blake. Afternoon, inspector."

Then the door closed upon the bustling surgeon, and the officials and Sexton Blake were left once more with the accused.

The latter looked stronger as he rose to his feet, and his expression was not one of such great timidity or fear.

"I am sorry, gentlemen," he said quietly, the stimulant that the surgeon had given him having steadied his nerves. "Is there any more that I can tell you?"

"You will please answer one or two questions," Sexton Blake answered, taking the initiative in his usual manner. "In the first place, who was the friend you were out with on Thursday?"

"A Mr. Weirson, sir."

"You know his address?"

"No, the fact is that I met him less than a week ago."

"Where and when?"

"Going in the train to Brighton to look for lodgings for my holiday. It was a chance meeting, and I have cause enough now to be sorry for it."

Even Sexton Blake started at this information, remembering the forged note that had been changed at London Bridge on that identical night, and the other that had been cashed at Brighton. As for Inspector Lurgan, he stared in a manner that there was no concealing.

"And you told him who you were, and what your business was?"

"To some extent, yes, sir," Melton answered reluctantly; "but it was not until the next day, when I dined with him, the Sunday, that I really spoke to him at all openly. He appeared to take such an interest in everything."

"He would," Sexton Blake murmured. "Can you give me a description of the man?"

"Tall and grey-headed," Melton answered thoughtfully, "and with very keen eyes—curious coloured eyes. That is all that I can remember of him."

For the second time Sexton Blake started, then he addressed Sir Henry.

"We may as well be going," he said. "I have no more questions to ask, and it is scarcely nec-essary to wait while the statement is transcribed. I doubt whether there will ever be need for it to be signed."

A sharp cry broke from Melton, and he took a step forward, his right hand outstretched.

"You think that I—that I shall be proved in-nocent?" he stammered.

Sexton Blake smiled, willing enough to put the man out of his suspense, for he no longer doubted his innocence, and that he had been made the foolish tool of one of the greatest scoundrels in the world.

"It is very unprofessional, but as I am not of-ficially attached to Scotland Yard, I will say yes," the detective answered.

"Oh, thank Heaven!" Melton murmured, and dropped to the bench, and once more covered his face with his hands.

Then the door had closed upon the man to whom Sexton Blake had given his ray of light, and Inspector Lurgan turned angrily to the famous detective.

"Most imprudent!" he snapped. "We are a long way yet from proving the prisoner innocent."

Sexton Blake shrugged his shoulders, and did not appear to be troubled by the other's annoy-ance.

"At least, you will never prove him guilty," he answered, "though we shall have to wait for the full proof of his innocence until we have laid our hands upon the real criminal."

"And you think that it is Plummer come back to England?" Sir Henry asked, in a low voice.

Sexton Blake's jaw set hard and became prom-inent, and his whole bearing was that of a man who faces great things and means to see them through to a successful issue.

"Yes," he answered simply. "I never imagined that he would keep away, and I know of no one else who could have carried out this coup. Then there is the description of the eyes. If only Jesse Kells recovered consciousness we might be sure!"

"What will you do next?"

"Go back to my rooms," Sexton Blake an-swered, "I want to think. By the way, did I not notice that one of the complaints was from the manager of the Vaudeville Hotel, in London—a forged fiver, I think?"

"Yes," Sir Henry said.

"Then you had better go there and make inquir-ies, inspector," Sexton Blake ordered. "It is possible that that is the trail that will tell us where Melton dined and was drugged. Get a photo of Melton, and take it with you. Let me know the result by 'phone at Baker Street. We may at least get a better description of the friend."

"Yes, that is right," Sir Henry agreed; "but I am afraid that the man—if it is Plummer—has had time to get clean away."

"That depends entirely upon one thing," the detective remarked—"whether or not Plummer has parted with every one of the flash notes. From what I know of the man, he will run any risk in his greed to make his haul as great as possible. I will be going now, and you may be sure to find me at Baker Street."

§

Evening had drawn in, and Sexton Blake sat in his favourite chair, a cold pipe between his teeth and his coat snowed over with ash, as it always was when he was thinking. Tinker was in the room too, but he had effaced himself as completely as possible, though his limbs were stiff with keeping still. He might have gone out for a walk with Pedro, but he feared that in that case news might arrive during his absence, and his master leave without him. Not that he had been able to help as yet, but there was the hope that the great pleasure of his life might be realised soon.

On the return of Sexton Blake the lad had scarcely dared to ask questions, but when he had ventured one as to how the case was going, his master had answered briefly:

"Plummer!"

A simple answer, just the mention of a man's name, but to Tinker it offered boundless possibilities. He remembered the duels that he and his master had fought with the master-criminal, of the successes and the partial failures, and he longed once more to be in the thick of it.

As for Sexton Blake, his thoughts can be analysed clearly enough. Now that he was certain that it was Plummer who had brought off the coup with the forged notes he did not find it difficult to fill in most of the details.

Either by knowledge or chance, the criminal had discovered the hoard of notes that Jesse Kells had made, and to get them he had struck the old man down. After that luck had favoured him—presuming Augustus Melton to he per-

fectly innocent—when he had met the man in the train, at once seen his chance, and pumped him for the information that he required to perfect his scheme.

How Plummer had obtained the paper to write to Melton it was hard to say, but it was easy enough to take that as an accomplished fact; and then he had got him out of the way by drugging him and taking his place at the bank, paying out the forged notes and placing the real ones in his pocket. That he had also planned to be able to change them safely Sexton Blake was sure.

Now the one question that remained was, had Plummer finished his coup, or had it only been an anti-climax, with the end still to come? The detective hoped that the latter was the case, and—

The telephone-bell rang, and Sexton Blake half started up in his chair.

"See who it is, lad," he said. "I take no fresh case, of course."

"Hallo!" Tinker cried. "Yes, I'm Tinker. You must speak to the guv'nor."

The lad turned from the instrument.

"It's Inspector Lurgan, sir," he said, "and he's got news for you."

Sexton Blake rose abruptly, every sense alert, and took the receiver from Tinker.

"Hallo?" he said. "Yes, I'm Sexton Blake. What have you discovered?"

"A man answering to the description of Melton did dine at the Vaudeville on Thursday," the inspector's voice answered, "and there was a man with him such as he described. The waiter says that Melton appeared to be ill, and that his friend took him away in a car.

"By the way, you might like to know that Jesse Kells has recovered consciousness, and he states that the forged notes were to the face value of a hundred thousand pounds."

"Anything else?" Sexton Blake asked sharply; and there was a faint smile on his lips.

"There's a rambling story that doesn't count for much," the inspector answered. "No time to tell you all now. I'm trying to get on the trail from the Vaudeville. Goodbye!"

"Here! Wait a minute!" Sexton Blake cried. "See that the papers don't get hold of the fact that Kells is conscious."

"All right!"

Sexton Blake hung up the receiver, and started pacing the floor, an expression of excitement on his face. So far as was known, scarcely half of the forged notes had already been changed, and he knew that Plummer would not be content with that.

But how would the master-criminal act to change the notes that he had left? The tale of the colossal forgeries had become public property in some mysterious way, with the consequence that every money-changer, banker, hotel owner, and even shopkeeper, would be on the look-out for flash paper. For a time at least it would be the hardest possible task for anyone to utter a forgery. By now, too, the news would have been flashed to the Continent and published there, closing that convenient market for the swindler with notes to change.

There was just the chance that Plummer had gone straight to the Continent after leaving the Bank with his spoil on the Friday; but, again, Sexton Blake did not think it probable. With a smaller amount of money to negotiate he might have done it, but not with fifty thousand pounds or more. No, he was still in England, either arranging or prepared to carry out his fresh coup.

What was the most unlikely thing that Plummer could be expected to do? It was that of which Sexton Blake was trying to think, knowing that it would be the master-criminal's most probable move. He was not like the ordinary swindler, but a man of far keener brain, who reasoned much in the same manner as his great enemy of Baker Street, and the latter did not hide that fact from himself.

Sexton Blake threw himself into a chair, and tried to place himself in Plummer's shoes, and suddenly a possible solution came to him.

It was the Bank of England that had been swindled out of the real notes, for they would have to refund them to the other banks, and it would appear natural that the criminal would have done with them for good, which was precisely the reason why it should be that institution that would have to suffer the second time, unless it were prevented.

Fortunately, too, Plummer had no reason to believe that his identity was suspected, and that would make him all the bolder. True, he might have discovered that Sexton Blake had called in connection with the case, but with Jesse Kells still unconscious, he was likely to feel sure that he had left no clue behind. Also, so far as he knew, there was nothing to show that there

were more forged notes to be changed. He would know that the view to be taken would be that the coup had been made and was done with.

"Tinker," Sexton Blake said sharply. "Get into a disguise and go down to Beckenham. You know the hospital that Jesse Kells is at. With the papers silent as to the old man's condition, Plummer may try to find out for himself, for his plans would all depend upon that. Do you think that you'd be able to see through a disguise of his, or would you rather that I went?"

Tinker looked indignant, and drew himself up with a great assumption of dignity.

"I've not often failed you, sir," he answered; adding hurriedly: "You've been taken in by him, so far as that goes."

"Quits, my lad!" Sexton Blake laughed. "If you see a man you think resembles him, follow everywhere."

"And what are you going to do, sir?"

"Inquisitive as ever!" Sexton Blake murmured, with a reproving shake of his head. "But if you want to know, I am going to try and hunt up the Governor of the Bank of England."

THE SIXTH
CHAPTER

TINKER WATCHES—THE BLIND BEGGAR—TRACKED HOME.

THE cottage-hospital that is situated near Beckenham, and to which Jesse Kells had been taken, is not a large one. From the outside it looks like a rather rambling private house, and there is nothing save the usual board asking for donations to suggest that it is anything else. In the ordinary way few people passed it directly at night, save only courting couples and the large number of motor-cars that have of recent years done much to detract from the quietness of the place.

On this evening, however, there was quite a crowd assembled on the pavement staring up vacantly at the lighted windows, and occasionally uttering a whispered question as to which room it was in which the injured man lay, as if fearing that their voices might penetrate to him and disturb him.

There were some who in low tones said that they had often seen old Jesse Kells, and went so far as to hint that they had been clever enough to guess all along that he was a forger. A postman, who had finished his rounds, was most emphatic on the subject, nearly getting into a fight with a navvy, who would say "Hush!" every time that he spoke, and all the efforts of the one policeman present failed to keep the people moving. They would split up, as if with a firm determination to go their various ways, suffer from a common change of mind, and drift back again, as is the manner of a crowd.

Close by the kerb stood a ragged beggar with a shade over his eyes, and a tin can with a placard above it that announced him to be "Totally Blind." It was a strange kind of sympathy that had led the crowd to assemble there, and likely as not he lived in hopes that a little of the sympathy extended to the injured man would splash over in his direction.

Not far away was an insipid-looking young man, who, when anyone drew near to him, made a habit of inquiring how the patient was progressing. His clothes were of the type that his class consider fashionable, being weird in cut about the collars and cuffs, and his turned-up trousers revealed a pair of passionately-coloured socks. For the rest, he continually smoked cigarettes.

Yet behind this insipid exterior, with its pale face and slight moustache, was the tough young body and ready brain of Tinker, who had lost no time in disguising himself and hurrying down to Beckenham. He had been outside the hospital for half an hour now, and his incessant questions had not been without their reason. They gave him a chance of looking into the eyes of the men he addressed, looking for the agate-coloured ones of Plummer.

So far, Tinker had seen no one who in the least resembled the man; but he remembered the criminal's marvellous powers of disguise, and was afraid that he might miss him.

Fresh people joined the crowd, while a few of those who had been there a long time drifted away; but still, there was no one who in the least resembled the criminal. The one suspicious person, in Tinker's mind, was the blind beggar, but even in that case his suspicions were very slight—in fact, they only amounted to a suspicion.

Time went by until ten o'clock struck, and a large motor-car pulled up, causing the beggar to move, grumbling, and at once the crowd pushed towards it.

"The car of the specialist from London," someone said confidently; and when a brisk man of between fifty and sixty came from the hospital, it was only by the aid of the policeman that he was able to make his way to the car.

A dozen questions were thrown at him from all sides, but all of the same import—how was Jesse Kells, the man of mystery?

"The same," the doctor answered shortly. "There is not likely to be a change for some time."

Tinker chuckled inwardly as he heard the words, knowing the instructions that Sexton Blake had given to Scotland Yard, and obviously they had impressed the necessity for silence upon the surgeon. Then his eyes were upon the blind beggar, and he saw that the man was moving away with the rest of the crowd. Tinker prepared to follow, especially as he noticed with what apparent ease the man walked, but a question asked close to him caused him to turn his head casually, though it was a simple enough one.

"Can you tell me the way to Beckenham Junction?" an elderly man with stooping shoulders asked, and Tinker remembered having seen him as one of the waiting crowd.

"I believe that the next train to London is from there."

"Straight along the road that bends to the left, and you'll run slap into it," the questioned man answered.

"Thanks, very much!"

The elderly man moved away, and Tinker looked after him thoughtfully. Apparently the questioner had come all the way from London to stare at the hospital, which seemed strange conduct in a man of his age. Was it possible that it could be Plummer in disguise? He might easily have come to one of the other stations that serve Beckenham, and therefore had to ask his way.

Tinker looked at the blind beggar disappearing in the distance, and then at the back of the retreating man, and of a sudden he saw a thing that caused him to make his mind up.

The elderly man raised his right hand to his lips, but drew it away with a sharp, nervous gesture.

It was only a small thing that anyone might have done, but it held a great significance for Sexton Blake's young assistant. For years Plummer had been addicted to biting his nails down to the quick—a habit that on one occasion at least had helped to cost him his freedom—and the man in front, plainly intending to do that, had hastily checked himself. That and asking the way to the station convinced Tinker that the grey-haired man was the master-criminal in disguise.

The latter walked briskly along the pavement, past the old-fashioned houses and shops that hang together in a small space, as if shrinking to each other away from their modern brethren which have sprung up year by year.

For the second time the man in front made the gesture towards his mouth and the swift checking of it, then he was passing the old parish church with the new steeple, and before him was the slope leading down to the station.

But on the right, very large and impressive, stood the station hotel, a couple of traps and a motor-car outside, and the lights from the windows suggesting all sorts of comforts on this rather chilly night.

The thing that happened next was exactly the one that Tinker had expected. The man with the grey hair turned through the hotel entrance instead of going straight to the station, and that was precisely what Plummer would have done, with the consequence that Tinker waited with added cheerfulness, though taking care not to let his keenness peep through his disguise of flabbiness.

Rather more than ten minutes later the grey-haired man emerged, and it seemed to Sexton Blake's young assistant that he now walked more uprightly and with a swing in his stride—in fact, a slight return towards the swagger of Plummer. The latter made straight for the station, followed by Tinker, and live minutes later a train for Victoria pulled in there.   The grey-haired man at once stepped into an empty first-class compartment, and Tinker, after a slight feint of looking for another compartment, followed him.

The man with the grey hair looked at the newcomer with ill-concealed annoyance, if not positive anger; and as Tinker looked innocently back at him, he could have cried aloud in triumph, for the agate-coloured eyes were those of Plummer.

He was sure that there could not be another pair like them in the world.

"This is a first!" the man snapped,

"I know," Tinker answered mildly. "Father always lets me travel first—it's so respectable."

The grey-haired man glared, but Tinker looked back at him innocently, smiled, then drew out an evening paper and began to read it, afraid that with too close a scrutiny the man opposite might see through his disguise.

Kent House Station was stopped at, and the grey-haired man fidgeted. Next came Penge, and he rose sharply to his feet, and left the carriage, slamming the door with unnecessary force behind him. Tinker glanced round the corner of his paper, then thrust his head out of the window in time to see the grey-bearded man step into a compartment three doors away.

"Got you!" the lad chuckled. "You won't get away this time!"

Then the train had swung into the long, evil-smelling Penge tunnel, and Tinker guessed that if Plummer intended to make any change in his disguise that it would be there. That it was probable he was certain, for why, otherwise, had Plummer taken the trouble to change carriages?

Through the tunnel, went the train, passed through Sydenham and Dulwich without stopping, and pulled up at Herne Hill. If Plummer had the faintest suspicion that he was following, this was the most likely place where he would attempt to throw his pursuers off the track; but when the train started again, Tinker was certain that the man had not left it. From here it ran fast to Victoria, so that Tinker was able to settle back in his corner with a sigh of relief—Victoria! Tinker was one of the first out on the platform, but once he was there he did not hurry himself. He seemed to be hesitating in which direction he should go, until the door of the third compartment away opened, and a well-dressed man, with dark hair and a slight moustache, and of somewhat military appearance, emerged. Tinker glanced at the face, then at the clothes, and he saw that they were the same that the grey-haired man had worn.

Oh, it was Plummer right enough, and he would never lose sight of him now until he was in the hands of the police.

The criminal walked briskly from the station, with an air of self-possession and confidence, and apparently without a fear in the world. Tinker followed through the crowd, at a sufficient distance to avoid detection, but close enough to be certain of not losing sight of his quarry. He wondered to where Plummer meant to go, and whether he would drive. He hoped that the latter would not be the case, for the chances of a block in the street letting the leading vehicle through always added to the danger of losing the trail.

To Tinker's relief, Plummer walked from the station, paused to light a cigar, and stepped briskly along Victoria Street. There was plenty of swagger in his walk now, and the lad who followed knew that he was thoroughly pleased with himself, and guessed the reason. It was the faked information that Jesse Kells, the actual forger of the notes, was likely to remain unconscious for some time. That was the one thing that Plummer desired. That he still had the remainder of the notes to change was proved by his visit to Beckenham, for otherwise he would have been better employed in making sure of his safety.

The end of Victoria Street was reached, and Plummer passed across Trafalgar Square. Then to Leicester Square, and at last into a small turning off Rupert Street, where may be found many small but quiet, comfortable, foreign restaurants, one of which was known as the Boulevard, and it was into that that Plummer turned. For a moment as he did so, Tinker caught the light from the doorway upon his face, and saw the look of contemptuous disgust there.

The restaurant was one with a big reputation for giving a good dinner at a small price, but it was not likely to appeal to the aristocratic tastes of Plummer. Possibly he would be able to manage, the food, but the crowd around him, which at the Boulevard is of a most varied description, would fill him with disgust. Yet he was a man who had worn the drab uniform of a convict, sweated and toiled, and broken his hands in the stone quarries of Bleakmoor, and lived on the meagre food that had been his well-deserved lot.

But that was the character of the master-criminal. Never for a moment could he forget his birth, or his belief that his real position in life should mean a house in Park Lane and every pleasure or vice that he cared to indulge in.

Tinker watched the man enter, and through the door contrived to follow his movements until he was seated. He saw Plummer look round hesitatingly, then walk straight to a table where a man sat alone. That was enough for Tinker, and he at once set out in search of the nearest telephone. If Sexton Blake was at Baker Street he must know at once, and if not, Tinker meant to follow Plummer until he had a chance of communicating with his master and bringing him on to the track.

The telephone was not hard to find, and Tinker was relieved at once to get through to Sexton Blake. In a few seconds he had told his news, and had received a word of commendation, which was quite reward enough for him. Then he hurried back and took up a position not far from the Boulevard Restaurant, for fear that by chance Plummer might not stop there as long as expected.

§

Plummer's face was full of disgust as he ate the small portions of various dishes that were set before him after the waiter in attendance had come near to having a fit at the manner in which the criminal had set to work on the hors d'oeuvres, which he had sadly diminished.

Opposite to Plummer sat a man of medium height, whose age might have been anything, between forty and fifty, with a rather long, clean-shaven face, and eyes that stared from behind a pair of high-power spectacles. He was dressed with a neatness and plainness that was almost painful to see, but for all that he evinced a keen enjoyment in his food, and the fact that he nodded to several of the fresh arrivals, and addressed the waiter by his Christian name, showed that he was familiar with the place.

What he was by profession—there was no possibility that he could be in trade—it was hard to say. Possibly a respectable lawyer's clerk, even a solicitor on his own account, or an undertaker of the very highest class who found relaxation from his gruesome business in this brightly lit French café.

Whoever he was, it was plain that Plummer took some interest in him, for from time to time he glanced at him quickly, as if measuring him up, and apparently his scrutiny satisfied him, for a smile dawned on his lips.

A fresh customer arrived—a man with clothes distinctly American, and whose face, with the high cheekbones, and hair cut round and long over the ears added to that impression.

After a short hesitation the new-comer took a seat on the other side of the room, opposite to where Plummer sat, and was quickly engrossed in a meal. Apparently he took no interest in anything but his food, and certainly no one took any interest in him, though Plummer had glanced at him, as it was his habit to look at the face of any fresh arrival.

The very respectable man opposite to Plummer had finished his meal, and, with a very tolerable cigar between his lips, was leaning back in his chair, and idly gazing around him.

"May I trouble you for a light, sir?" Plummer asked, helping himself to a cigar that the waiter had brought him, and ignoring the fact that the waiter was offering him a box of matches.

The respectable gentleman frowned, removed his cigar from his lips, and nodded towards the waiter.

"Alphonse has one," he answered, in a hard-cut voice.

The American, who was no other than Sexton Blake, had not failed to notice the incident, and, without being able to hear the words, he could be certain of what had happened. He saw, too, the expression of annoyance on the face of the man opposite Plummer, and the quick, angry look, quickly suppressed, that leapt into the latter's eyes.

Both of the men sat back smoking for a few seconds before Plummer tried for a second time to open the conversation.

"Beautiful weather," he murmured carelessly.

"Yes!" the other snapped, glaring through the smoke of his cigar and wriggling on his chair.

"So fortunate after the wretched summer," Plummer continued. "It must have hit places like this hard, don't you think so?"

"Yes!" the other man snapped again, and his fidgeting became more pronounced.

Sexton Blake was still watching the expressions of their faces, though he had no appearance of doing so, and he could see that Plummer was trying to force his attentions upon the other man, and was being repulsed.

Why was the criminal so anxious to know the man? For the present that was a question that the detective could not answer.

He had come to the restaurant with one intention only, and that was to take on the tracking of Plummer where Tinker had left off; but he was more than a little puzzled as to whom the other

man could be. It was strange, in fact, that the ex-convict did not keep himself to himself.

It may seem strange that Blake had not taken immediate steps to have Plummer arrested, but one circumstance against that must be remembered.

The master-criminal might have been arrested as an escaped convict; but, on the other hand, that would not bring home to him the charge of having nearly killed Jesse Kells, and stolen from him the forged notes. True, it was possible that they might be found in his possession; but Sexton Blake, knowing his man, considered it far from likely. However confident he might feel, he was not likely to take the smallest unnecessary risk, and it was probable that the rest of the forged notes were hidden in such a manner that if he were imprisoned they would never be discovered.

Then Plummer made one more attempt to open up a conversation, and on this occasion he met with a snub that there was no mistaking.

"You must pardon me, sir," he said, "but, I fancy that I have seen you at the Bank of England—the Law Courts Branch."

"Perhaps you have!" the other answered sourly. "I shall be obliged if you will confine your conversation with me to when you are at the Bank—if you have an account there!"

With which the highly-respectable gentleman called for his bill, paid it, and walked out haughtily. Curiously enough, at the same time Sexton Blake paid his, and he was close behind the other as he emerged.

As for Plummer, he sat back in his chair and grinned. He knew now that the other was engaged at the Bank of England, and that was precisely all that he required to know. Among other information that he had obtained from the unsuspecting Augustus Melton was that while he was away his place at the Bank was taken by a certain Charles Teen from the Law Courts Branch. It had also come out that the two men were in the habit of occasionally having supper on a Saturday at the Boulevard Restaurant. Plummer had not dared to ask for a description of the other, though he had been more than a little anxious to obtain it.

Then he had come to the restaurant on the off-chance of finding the man there, and spotting him, and his quick powers of perception had not failed him. He had been certain from the first that the man was Charles Teen.

In the meantime, Sexton Blake had followed Teen from the restaurant, and Tinker had at once strolled up to him casually, and asked him the time. The detective had pulled out his watch, and as he looked at it he whispered:

"Follow the man who came out before me, and find out his name. It may lead to nothing, but I have hopes."

"Right, sir!" Tinker answered; and was off on the track of the unsuspecting Charles Teen.

As for Sexton Blake, he hung about in the pretence of looking into jewellers and bookshops, and it was not long before Plummer emerged.

He made straight through to Leicester Square and back into the Strand. As he passed the Tivoli Music Hall he hesitated as if uncertain whether to turn in there, decided not to, and went on, Sexton Blake keeping him in sight.

It was a small but exclusive hotel that Plummer eventually entered, and Sexton Blake knew that he could not possibly have done so without being challenged by the hall-porter unless he were stopping there. In a moment his mind was made up how to act, and after a short space he entered the lobby, and walked up to the clerk's office.

"Say, can I have a room?" he inquired. "If you have I'll 'phone through for my luggage; it's at the station."

"I think there is one vacant, sir," the clerk answered, with all the indifference of the really well-trained clerk in an important hotel. "Yes; there is Number Fifteen, on the second floor."

"That'll do me," Sexton Blake agreed. "Is there a 'phone in the room?"

"There is a telephone in every room in this hotel," the clerk answered cuttingly. "I will have you shown to your room."

A minute or so later Sexton Blake had entered the room, and, after carefully closing the door, rang up Mrs. Bardell at Baker Street. His orders to her were concise and to the point, simply that certain bags with American labels on them were to be sent to the hotel in the name of Ford, and that the moment Tinker returned he was to ring up and ask for the same name.

That accomplished, Sexton Blake strolled down to the smoking-room, where he was not surprised to see the disguised Plummer busy with a cigar and a drink. He contented himself with a cigar, and glanced casually through the papers that lay on the table before him. Despite

that, however, he had no trouble in watching Plummer, who was seated only a short distance away, and the expression of content on that worthy's face showed that he was quite satisfied with the manner in which things were progressing.

It was just after eleven that Plummer yawned and left the room, and out of the corner of his eye Sexton Blake saw that he took the lift to one of the upper floors, which meant that he was retiring for the night.

The detective followed almost immediately, but not before requesting the man in charge of the hotel exchange to call him up as soon as anyone asked for him.

Sexton Blake found his luggage already in his room—two of the bags that he always kept packed in case of emergencies—but he made no attempt to go to bed, lighting a fresh cigar and settling himself down comfortably in a chair to wait for the message from Tinker.

To his surprise, however, twelve o'clock arrived without a call, and it was not until half an hour later that the bell tinkled, and the detective hurried eagerly to the 'phone.

"Yes, I'm Ford," he answered, then lowered his voice. "That you, Tinker? Good! Followed the man—went to a music-hall then to Kingston. His name's what?"

The detective could not help raising his voice sharply, for over the wire had come the answer:

"Charles Teen."

"Good lad!" Sexton Blake said hurriedly. "Go down to Kingston first thing in the morning, and watch the house. If Teen goes out do not lose sight of him; he may be in danger. But see that Plummer is not following, too. You will see me somewhere, though at present I cannot say where. Good-night!"

Sexton Blake replaced the receiver and seated himself in his chair again. The news that Tinker had sent him had confirmed his suspicions with regard to the changing of the rest of the forged notes; they were to be sent through the Bank of England, right enough. The detective had had an interview with the perturbed governor of that institution, and had learnt that the man who had taken, Augustus Melton's place was Charles Teen.

And Plummer had tried to scrape acquaintance in the restaurant with that identical man.

It was the great clue that Sexton Blake had wanted. As he rose to his feet and threw away the butt of his cigar, he felt that success was very near to him indeed, and that his only trouble would be to catch Plummer absolutely red-handed.

THE SEVENTH CHAPTER

PLUMMER'S NEXT MOVE—BLAKE'S DISCOVERY

CHARLES TEEN, being a single man and the possessor of quite a good salary, was a believer in mild enjoyment when the week's work was done, so it was that on Sundays it was his practice to leave his small but compact house in the hands of his aged housekeeper, and go out for the day.

In the summer months he might have been seen punting up from Kingston with the same painstaking care that he displayed in his work, taking no risks, and knowing to a nicety of a fraction the depths of the water in certain parts as he knew to the nicety every fraction in figures.

But now that the summer had passed Charles Teen's Sunday recreation had changed to a walk up the river bank, lunch at a comfortable hotel that he knew, another walk, dinner, and a journey home by train. Even in these solitary trips he found amusement, though often as not Augustus Melton had been in the habit of going with him. If it were in the punt, Augustus Melton, owing to his seniority, lay back on the cushions, and gave advice that his junior did not follow, though he received it gravely.

Anyway, Charles Teen would have been alone on this Sunday as his friend had gone to Brighton; but as he returned in the train after his walk, homeward bound to Kingston, he sighed as he thought of the change that had so swiftly and terribly come over the life of his friend. Of course, he was innocent and would soon be released, he told himself, but in the meantime it was most distressing—most.

It was in this frame of mind that Charles Teen alighted at Kingston. Possibly it was because of that he did not notice a lad in a tweed suit who alighted just after him, and even if he had there would have been no reason for the idea that he

was being followed to have entered his ordinary everyday mind.

Very moodily Teen entered his little house, letting himself in with a latchkey, and going straight through to his study at the back, turning on the electric light as he went. The house was one of several old-fashioned buildings of the same stamp, detached, and hidden away in a small side road which the casual visitor to Kingston would not have found in a day. Each possessed quite a good garden, and that of Charles Teen had been his pride and joy ever since he had taken possession.

Tinker—the lad in the tweed suit—passed the house, looked about him, and slipped into the garden of an empty house on the other side of the road. He had had a trying day keeping Teen in sight without attracting attention, and he was troubled that so far he had seen nothing of his master. What the latter's plans were, the lad had not the faintest idea, and he felt that in an emergency he would find it hard to act.

Charles Teen seated himself in his usual chair, but instead of taking up a book or paper, sat dismally with his chin in the palm of his hand. It was really time for him to have the mild whisky-and-soda that he allowed himself before going to bed, but to-night it remained untouched on the table.

There was a knock on the door, and Mrs. Chard, the ancient housekeeper entered. It was her invariable custom to be draped—it could not be called dressed—in severe black, and to-night it looked severer than ever to her master, as if she had gone into mourning for his imprisoned friend.

"Is there anything you require, sir?" she asked.

"No," Charles Teen answered drearily.

Mrs. Chard sighed and shook her head.

"It is very sad, sir," she said. "And to think as we believed him respectable all these years. Well sir, it only shows that it ain't always a black coat that covers a white heart."

Then, for the first time in the knowledge of Mrs. Chard, Charles Teen lost his temper. "Oh, get out!" he shouted.

Mrs. Chard departed with an alacrity that was a credit to her aged limbs, and Charles Teen sat back moodily into his chair again. In a semi-conscious way, he heard his caretaker go shuffling up the stairs to bed, and he roused himself and mixed the mild whisky-and-soda.

"Here's luck to you, Augustus," he said miserably, and took a sip of the drink. It was a long time before he took another one, however, and as he decided to finish the drink and go to bed, his hand stopped with the glass half-way to his mouth.

Surely he had heard a distinct click in the hall, just as if the front door had been unfastened. It was latched, he knew, but not bolted yet, as he never trusted anyone but himself to do that.

"Fancy," he said, with the glass still poised. "Poor Augustus's affair has made me nervous. I'd better get to bed at once. What—what was that?"

Certainly there had been a click this time, as if the front door was being fastened, and with a queer feeling at his knees and spine, Charles Teen looked about him for a weapon. There was not even a poker, however, as the fire was a gas one.

"F-fancy," Charles Teen stammered, though he knew that he was lying to himself to try and keep up his courage; then the door opened, and he started back with a gasping cry.

In the doorway stood the man who had tried to get into conversation with him on the previous night, an ugly grin on his thin lips, and a wicked look in his eyes.

"I—I have not the pleasure of knowing you," he stammered helplessly, then tried to pull himself together. "How did you get in? I shall shout for help. I—"

"You won't," Plummer snarled, stepping into the room, and closing the door behind him. "If you do, you are a dead man."

Charles Teen found himself looking down the barrel of a very nasty-sized repeating pistol, and with the last atom of pluck knocked out of him, he dropped back into his chair, and stared at the intruder.

"I'm not going to hurt you," Plummer sneered, "but you have got to answer one or two questions. Keep your voice low, and don't try games unless you want a bullet through you. To show you that I am usually in earnest, I don't mind telling you that I am the man who injured Jesse Kells."

Charles Teen's fingers gripped hard on the arms of his chair, and his face was livid. If his life had been different, he might have had pluck

enough; but there had been nothing in his existence to develop it. Besides, as far as that goes, it was a position to have shaken the nerve of the bravest of men.

"I'll—I'll answer," he quavered.

"I thought you would," Plummer said, with a low, evil laugh. "It won't take you long.

"First of all, aren't you the man—you will pardon the exaggeration in my description of you—who took Melton's place on Saturday?"

"Yes."

"And you will do so again on Monday?"

"Yes."

Plummer looked at the man keenly, to make sure that he was not lying, and he assured himself that he was too frightened for that.

"I presume that there will on Monday be a large amount in notes ready to be paid out?"

For a moment Charles Teen's jaw almost suggested firmness, but as the automatic pistol was raised so that it covered him steadily between the eyes, he answered hurriedly:

"Yes."

"Fully fifty thousand pounds?"

Charles Teen licked his dry lips, and nodded.

"Good," Plummer said, with another smile, and there was greed in his agate-coloured eyes. "This is the first time that I have found the Bank of England to be so convenient."

For all that, it was by no means the ex-criminal's first experience of the Bank. When attached to Scotland Yard, he had been detailed for duty there, and in consequence was quite familiar with most of its methods and work.

Plummer stood looking at Charles Teen rather thoughtfully, the pistol lowered; but presently he smiled again.

"It seems a pity to spoil my natural beauty," he remarked, "but at least it will be in a good cause. Kindly look at that picture straight in front of you, and remember that if you turn round, you will get a bullet through your head."

"Charles Teen answered nothing, but fixed his eyes on the picture, a not remarkably interesting photograph of a long-deceased aunt, with marked attention.

"I am sorry that it is nothing better," Plummer sneered, "but I dare say that it suites your taste—or you have got used to it."

The master-criminal walked slowly past the chair, always keeping his eyes on Teen; but he need have had no fear of him moving. He sat with his eyes glued on the photo, as if trying to hypnotise his aunt back to life.

Plummer reached the back of the chair, carefully laid his pistol down on the table, and drew a pad of linen and a bottle from his pocket. The next moment the room was full of the pungent odour of chloroform. Apparently the scent of it told Charles Teen what was coming, and the thought made him desperate.

He started to rise to his feet, but almost before he had started to bend his knees, the pad was over his mouth and nostrils, and he was being forced down with a grip that few living men could surpass. In less than a minute he lay back perfectly still, his head forced to the limit of the capacity of his neck, but still Plummer kept the pad there.

"That'll do," he muttered at last. "I can gag him later; but I must have his face uncovered until I have finished the first part of my task."

Plummer turned Teen's chair so that the lights fell full upon the white face and nodding head, and surveyed it critically.

"Ugly devil," he mused. "Bah! I shall have to put up with looking like that for a bit. It's fifty thousand more, my boy, a hundred thousand in all, and with that you'll make some of these so-called aristocrats sit up. Capital shall make capital, and in the end I'll—"

He checked himself abruptly, and pulled various articles from his pocket. There was a small hand-glass on a telescopic stand, a wig, and a small but very complete outfit of grease-paints.

Pulling a chair up to the table, Plummer set to work, and there is many a big actor who could have taken a lesson from him then. First the make-up that he had been wearing vanished, leaving bare the hard, cruel face of the master-criminal. Then his complexion took on the rather doughy tint that was Charles Teen's in the ordinary way, and piece by piece he built up the double of the bank cashier as surely as the finest portrait-painter could have done it on canvas.

Plummer examined himself with anxious eyes after he had slipped the wig on and clipped it here and there to make it correspond with the other's hair, and at last he was satisfied.

"The infernal glasses make it awkward," he muttered, "but I must try them, too."

From his pocket he drew a pair of spectacles similar to those that Teen wore, though the lenses in them were not so powerful. Natural glass with power to magnify the criminal dared not use, for the difference would have been, detected immediately by anyone who had ever seen the real glasses.

Plummer stared at himself again, long and intently, then removed the glasses and placed them in his pocket.

"It'll do," he said, with conviction. "Now to truss this thing up and put him in a safe place."

Plummer produced a coil of thin but stout cord from beneath his waistcoat, and had very soon made a workmanlike job of binding his victim, and that accomplished, he placed a gag between the teeth and secured it firmly behind the head, until Charles Teen was so securely fixed that a far more powerful man than he would not have had the least chance of breaking loose.

"Now where shall I put him?" he mused. "There's only that old woman to think of, but there mustn't be the smallest risk of his being found. In a house like this there should be an attic, and as there's only this man and the woman in the house, she isn't likely to sleep there, as there'd be plenty of rooms to spare. Shall I take him up now and risk it, or explore first?"

Plummer stood pondering for a few moments. Then he went out into the small hall, and listened. He saw that there was a light on the first landing, but beyond that he could see nothing.

"I'll do it," he decided. "If the worst comes to the worst, I can give her a dose to keep her quiet."

Going back to the room, Plummer picked up Charles Teen with the greatest of ease, and, carrying him like a baby, proceeded carefully up the first flight of stairs, fearing every moment that one would creak under him. There were two floors, and probably an attic floor, to the house, and the criminal calculated that Mrs. Chard's room would be on the second floor, in which surmise he was actually right.

Plummer paused on the first landing, panting a little for breath, for the life that he had led while squandering the money that he had made in America had not tended to increase his stamina. Then he went on again, treading more carefully than ever, certain that he had to pass the room occupied by Mrs. Chard.

The second landing was in darkness, adding considerably to the master-criminal's difficulties, and he had to press his body against the bal-

PLUMMER EAGERLY READS THE ACCOUNT OF HIS OWN CRIME.

JESSE KELLS ATTACKED PLUMMER WITH A HEAVY POKER.

PLUMMER IS ATTACKED AND ROBBED BY ROUGHS

PLUMMER IS THROWN OUT

ustrades to make sure of his direction. All that he could see through the gloom was a post that suggested a third flight of stairs, and the attic that he was counting upon. Then he stumbled, his foot catching heavily against a hole in the oilcloth, and almost immediately a scream came from close at hand.

For a second Plummer thought of trying to bolt down the stairs with his burden, but realised in time that it would be useless, and the next he had snatched away the unconscious man's spectacles and thrust them on to his own nose. A couple of steps took him to the bottom of the third flight of steps, but before he had the chance of ascending them, he heard a door opening.

With fast beating heart Plummer dropped Teen on to the stairs and waited. He saw that he had got to face the matter out, and his hand felt for the bottle of chloroform, that he had replaced in his pocket. If the worst came to the worst, he would—

The flickering light of a candle appeared, showing up the form of Mrs. Chard, swathed in something that looked uncommonly like a blanket.

"What—what is it?" she quavered.

"It's only me, Mrs. Chard," Plummer answered, assuming remarkably well the voice of Charles Teen. "I wanted an old box from the attic."

"Oh, is that all, sir?" Mrs. Chard sniffed. "Well, I don't call it nice to frighten the wits out of people at this time of night."

With which the caretaker slammed her door, and Plummer stood leaning against the cornerpost of the staircase, breathing hard, with his heart beating like a sledge-hammer.

Not for long was the master-criminal idle. He turned and picked up Teen, and went up the staircase with a good deal less caution than he had exercised before—in fact, there was no need for any. He had been discovered by Mrs. Chard, and had succeeded in bluffing her, and she was not likely to be inquisitive again.

On the top landing Plummer laid down his burden and struck a match, the light of which showed him that there was only one door. This he pushed open, to find, as he had expected, that it contained an assortment of old boxes and other rubbish. He laid Teen down in the middle of it, and with a sigh of relief left the room and closed the door behind him.

Going back to the sitting-room on the ground-floor, Plummer helped himself liberally to whisky, in a manner that would have shocked the real Charles Teen, and, feeling better after it, he turned out the light, coolly fastened up the hall-door, just as if in reality it were his own house, and went up to the first landing. The bed-room usually occupied by Teen was easy enough to locate, as the door stood partly open, and he went in at once.

"Tired," he muttered, seating himself on the edge of the bed, and starting to take off his boots. "No more of this for you after to-morrow, George."

And five minutes later Plummer was sleeping as peacefully as Charles Teen might have done, and to all outward appearances that man himself.

§

While all this was taking place, a figure had crouched in the garden at the back of the house, and it is hardly necessary to say that he was Sexton Blake. Throughout the day the detective had tracked Plummer, as his assistant had tracked Charles Teen, until eventually he had seen the criminal enter the house with a skeleton key.

Once the door had closed upon Plummer, Sexton Blake, knowing that Tinker would not be far away, had given a low, peculiar whistle, and he had instantly been joined by his excited assistant.

"You saw?" the detective whispered.

"Was that Plummer who went in, sir?" the lad asked in the same tone.

"Yes."

"Then I'm sorry for Charles Teen, sir."

"I don't think that you need be, my lad," Sexton Blake answered. "Plummer wants money, not the hangman's rope."

"I am going into the garden to watch the back of the house, for there is no light in the front. You will keep guard over the entrance, and if Plummer emerges give a bird-call—the hoot of an owl—then follow him."

"Right, sir. But if you tackle Plummer, you send for me!" the lad said earnestly.

"That's all right, Tinker," Sexton Blake answered, with a smile. "There will be no fighting to-night—so far as I am concerned."

Sexton Blake slipped away into the darkness, and it was not very long before he had clambered over the wall into the garden of Charles Teen's house, and was crouching in a clump of bushes that gave him a full command of the windows.

At present only two of these were illuminated, one on the ground-floor and one on the second, which the detective guessed meant that Teen was still up but that the servant or servants had retired for the night. It was on the bottom window, therefore, that he concentrated his attention, and it was not long before his vigil was rewarded.

The light was at the further end of the room, so that almost anyone moving about the room was bound to cast a shadow upon the linen blind across the window.

Suddenly the light grew stronger, which was caused by Plummer opening the door and letting in the added light from the hall. A figure at once showed up, and the next moment a second had put in its appearance, Sexton Blake read the proceedings like a book. He knew as clearly as if he had seen it that Plummer had stepped into the room, and that Teen had at once risen to his feet.

Cautiously the detective drew closer to the window, remembering the case of Jesse Kells, ready to interfere should matters grow desperate, but not even the faint sound of voices reached him. Reflected on the blind he saw a single figure draw nearer, the other having disappeared, as if dropping into a chair, then stoop, and remain in that position for a little time.

After that the shadows on the blind puzzled even Sexton Blake, for there was no reading the quick little movements that Plummer made as he disguised himself. Then the figure stood up again, bent, and disappeared.

Sexton Blake drew back further into the garden, his eyes upon the other windows, and at last a faint, flickering light shone in the top one of all, which was evidently uncurtained.

"Attic," the detective muttered. "Things are developing. I wonder what Plummer or Teen is doing up there."

In the darkness the detective's face set harshly as the terrible thought entered his brain that Teen might have been murdered. He was half inclined to break in, which he could have accomplished as easily as the criminal had. There was the discovery of the forged notes to be considered, and if the crime had been committed, it would make no difference whether the murderer was arrested now or later.

The light in the attic went out quickly, and a little later a figure reappeared in the bottom room, but only one, and the detective's face set more grimly than ever. He was certain now that the attic held a secret, and at the first possible moment he intended to investigate it.

For a short time the solitary figure showed against the blind of the lower room, then the light was turned off. Sexton Blake was at once ready to move, trusting to Tinker to follow Plummer while he investigated the secret of the attic, but to his amazement a light leapt up in a window on the first-floor, and the detective had to admit himself puzzled.

What if Plummer and this man Teen were partners? he asked himself, but put the notion away from him. If that had been the case, why should Plummer have troubled to get information out of Melton when Teen would have been able to give him all that he required ?

For ten minutes the light shone from the window on the first-floor, then the whole of the house was in darkness, and Sexton Blake was prepared to act.

Was there any way of reaching the attic from the outside? It did not seem likely to Sexton Blake, but for all that he moved close to the house and carefully examined the wall. It was blank enough, save where a new rain-pipe ran up right beside the attic window. To climb it would mean enormous exertion, even for a man of Sexton Blake's great strength, apart from the risk of a slip, followed by an ugly fall to the ground, but nevertheless the detective tested it, until he was sure that it was at least capable of bearing the weight of a man.

What was the secret that the attic held? Was there a dead man there? Were the notes that had not yet been changed hidden there?

Neither of the questions could Sexton Blake answer, and that was quite enough to make him take the risk of the climb, if he ever thought of the danger, which is not likely.

Removing his boots—for it would be easier to climb in socks—Sexton Blake started on his task. Many a man would have found it hard to get that distance up a pole, which allows a grip right round it, and in this case the grip was very different. But for all that the detective had no fear of failure, though by the time that he had got half-way he was breathing harder than usual. With set teeth he kept on, winning his way inch by inch, until his head was level with the sill of the window, though, of course, beside it, and he had to struggle on further, until it was possible for him to get a foot upon it.

Sexton Blake was on the window-sill now, a pretty precarious position, when the slightest loss of nerve would have sent him hurtling down to the ground beneath. For a few seconds he remained still, pressed close to the glass, waiting to recover his breath. At the end of that time he drew his electric-lantern from his pocket, and the beam of it flashed through the glass of the curtainless window.

From box to box the light went, picking out the lumber, and for the moment nothing more. But suddenly it stopped upon something that showed between the boxes, and Sexton Blake caught his breath as he saw it was a deadly-white face.

Was it that of Charles Teen—dead? Had Plummer for some reason put him out of the way?

Then Sexton Blake caught sight of the gag in the man's mouth, and a sigh of relief escaped him. Then he crouched on the window-sill, probably the strangest position in which a detective had ever to work out his plans for the future, and wondered what was best to be done.

Should he release Charles Teen? Why, anyway, had the man been made a prisoner?

The answer came to Sexton Blake very quickly. He remembered how Melton had been put out of the way so that Plummer could take his place and pass the forged notes; and now it was Charles Teen's place that he intended to take so as to get rid of the rest of the notes. It was a daring plan, but one most likely to succeed. Sexton Blake had suspected something of the kind—in fact, already planned his course of action with the officials at the bank, though he had not bargained that it would be quite like this.

No; if Plummer were to be caught red-handed, Teen would have to be allowed to remain in his present unpleasant position; there was no help for it. If Sexton Blake freed him, he would be compelled to arrest Plummer at once, or, anyway, before he had attempted to go to the bank, for at the first alarm he would guess that his prisoner had escaped.

Sexton Blake swung himself cautiously back on to the pipe and began his climb downwards, to find that the ascent had bruised his hands so much that every time he gripped, it was all that he could do to hold on for pain. The descent was almost as slow as the climb in consequence, and, as luck would have it, it was not to be accomplished without a mishap, which might have led to the most serious consequences.

When within ten feet of the ground, Sexton Blake's hands gripped at one of the bands of the pipe, and before he could get a fresh hold it had slipped and broken away. Backwards went the detective, in a fall that seemed likely to break his neck, but with the skill of a gymnast he turned a half-somersault, and landed feet first into a clump of bushes. The next moment he was sprinting back into the shadow of the bushes further off, and as he crouched behind them he realised that he was none too soon.

A light went up in the window on the first-floor, and there was the sound of the sash being raised.

"Who is there?" a voice snarled, and Sexton Blake knew it for that of Plummer. Also, on account of the light in the room, he could see that the man held a pistol in his hand.

"Come out, or I'll shoot!" the criminal snapped, as angry as if he were defending his own house; but the detective crouched behind the bushes and waited. So long as Plummer did not guess correctly how the noise had been made, he was not likely to take alarm.

For fully a minute the criminal must have remained in the open window; then Sexton Blake heard him mutter:

"Must have been cats—curse 'em!" And the window was closed and the light vanished.

"Sometimes it is even good to be mistaken for a cat," Sexton Blake chuckled, as he clambered back carefully over the wall and on to the pavement; "though I think that I should prefer some larger animal."

The detective walked quickly down the road, and his face was serious enough as Tinker joined him.

"What luck, sir?" the latter asked eagerly.

Sexton Blake's head went up, and his shoulders squared.

"To-morrow, my lad," he answered, "we shall make up for our failure in America. George Marsden Plummer will meet his Waterloo."

"Hooray!" Tinker cheered softly, but his master did not hear him. Just for a moment he was seized with the dread that he might fail yet; that Plummer's luck would stand him in good stead, and that he would be free to go on preying upon society again, with funds for the elaborate working out of his plans.

"Oh, impossible!" Sexton Blake muttered, with a shake of his head. "Come on, my lad, we'll get on home. I can do with a rest after the last day or so."

"I don't know that I can, sir," his assistant answered. "I sha'n't sleep for thinking of to-morrow; and I don't believe you will either."

"I wonder?" Sexton Blake murmured.

THE EIGHTH CHAPTER

AT THE BANK OF ENGLAND—THE EYE TEST—BAULKED BY FATE.

HALF-PAST eight, and the Bank of England—the very heart of Great Britain's wealth and commerce—had not as yet opened its doors; but, although there was yet half an hour to pass before that happened, there was still plenty going on behind the portals. Money was being brought up for tills—positively sacks of it—and beautiful white banknotes of values up to a thousand pounds, all of which would shortly start out on their tours, some to return in a short time, comparatively clean; others to knock about the world for years, and come back wearily in a dilapidated state; while some—and there are more cases of this than people imagine—never to return at all.

On this particular morning the scene inside the Bank was much as usual, save for one difference. Men made more frequent remarks as they passed one another, even stopping to exchange a few words, and on the face of the lowest employee to the highest there was a suggestion of tension, of an unnatural strain.

But then Augustus Melton, one of the Bank's formerly most trusted cashiers, lay in prison, accused of being guilty of passing nearly fifty thousand pounds' worth of forged notes, prac-

tically the biggest loss that the Bank had ever sustained. True, in its way, it was quite small to them, but it showed how even the best regulated machine can go wrong.

There was also in the Bank the feeling that there must have been at least one accomplice of the forger employed there, if Melton should prove to be innocent, and men who had known each other for years eyed one another suspiciously.

Punctually at a few minutes before nine the cashiers and other more or less important persons began to arrive, and it was noted by a few that Charles Teen, usually the first to be there, was this morning the last. It seemed, too, that he was a trifle pale and nervous, but that might have been accounted for by the fact that the imprisoned cashier had been his closest friend. Moreover, he must have been responsible for at least the paying out of some of the forged notes that were drawn on the Saturday.

Next came the managers of departments, grey-haired men of austere mien, among them Mr. Fildes, the head of the department for which Augustus Melton had worked. It was plain that he wished to discuss the stolen notes with none of his colleagues, for he hurried straight through to his room.

And the man who watched him most closely was Plummer, as, in Charles Teen's frock-coat, and in outward appearance the man himself, he waited to finish his great fraud.

Plummer was a man with nerves of steel—or they were as near that as any man's could be—but he could not forget the magnitude of the stake for which he was playing, and that the slightest slip would probably send him back to Bleakmoor.

Business started; but so early in the morning it was of quite a paltry nature, and Plummer found himself idle. At moments he was sorry that he had not cleared out already; then his greed got the better of that feeling, and also the desire to outwit Sexton Blake.

In his last affair in America he had out-manoeuvred the famous detective, although the latter had succeeded in breaking up the gang with which he had been connected, and that thought gave him confidence that he could do it again.

Business brisked up a bit, and as time passed Plummer fully recovered his nerve, though sometimes he glanced apprehensively at the men who entered the Bank, on the look-out for Sexton

Blake in disguise, or any of the Scotland Yard men; but it was not until he was preparing to go to lunch that anything happened.

"Mr. Fildes would like to see you, sir," a messenger announced.

Plummer started, but not so badly for it to be noticed, and under his paint his face went deadly pale. He already had his hat in his hand, ready to leave the building, and he was tempted to make a bolt for it. He scented danger in his manager sending for him, yet there might not be anything in it. The messenger had gone away, no one else had heard the message brought to him, so that there was nothing to prevent his escaping.

Plummer stood quite still and mopped the sweat from his forehead, unable to make up his mind, but then his fears cleared away. If he were suspected they would have sent for him earlier; and, besides, he would swear that no detectives, especially Sexton Blake, had gone through to Mr. Fildes's room.

Yes, he would go; there could be no danger, save in his imagination.

With his hat in his hand, Plummer went down the passage that led to his manager's private office.

§

In the manager's office were three men—the manager himself, Sexton Blake, and Inspector Lurgan—though it would have been impossible to recognise any one of them. The manager himself was disguised, much against his wishes, with a brown wig and beard that made him look very much younger than he really was; Inspector Lurgan sat at a table close by, dressed as a clerk, and sufficiently altered not to be recognised; and the man at the principal desk, Sexton Blake, was made up to the exact image of the real manager.

"I can't say that I like it, Mr. Blake," Mr. Fildes observed, with a shake of his head, and running his hand nervously down his false beard. "I suppose I am old-fashioned; but this appears theatrical to me—unsuited to the dignity of the officials of a great institution like this."

"There are times when dignity is not everything," the detective answered quietly. "I have no fear of failure; but, on the other hand, I prefer to be absolutely sure before I act."

"Right!" Inspector Lurgan growled from his table.

"Still, you will understand that I am doing it under protest," Mr. Fildes persisted.

"It is with the permission of the governor," Sexton Blake remarked. "Anyway, we waste time, sir. I believe that I am correct in saying that this supposed Charles Teen is due to go for lunch now."

"Yes," the manager admitted.

"Then I shall be obliged if you will send a messenger for him," Sexton Blake said, and his hand went to the revolver in his pocket. He did not see how Plummer could hope to make a dash and get away through the crowded streets; but, knowing the desperate nature of the man, he reckoned that it was as well to be on the right side.

As for Inspector Lurgan, he unostentatiously slipped a pair of handcuffs under a sheet of paper, and went on pretending to write.

Sexton Blake, in his disguise as manager, touched the bell, and a messenger entered.

"Tell Mr. Teen that I should like to speak to him," he said sharply.

"Yes, sir!"

The messenger departed, and Mr. Fildes stood wiping his brow, while Inspector Lurgan shifted in his chair. The only cool man in the room was Sexton Blake. He felt that the hour of his triumph had come.

Five minutes passed—ten minutes—and still the man who had been sent for did not enter. Inspector Lurgan looked round uneasily at Sexton Blake.

"I hope that you haven't left it too long," he said, and there was no sneer in his voice, for he was as anxious as the famous detective of Baker Street to once more have Plummer in his hands. "He may have suspected that—"

There was the sound of footsteps in the passage, a hurried knocking on the door, and it was burst open, to admit Charles Teen, hat in hand. His face was white, and behind his gold-rimmed glasses there was an expression of something very like terror.

"I have come to explain, sir," he said huskily, his words falling over each other, "that I—"

"One moment, Mr. Teen!" Sexton Blake interrupted, with so good an imitation of the manager's manner and voice that the latter started. "You will please hear me first. Since the recent regrettable incidents, which may involve a great loss to the Bank—"

"I—" Teen interrupted. "I can explain—"

"Wait!" the detective ordered sternly. "It is a very simple matter that I have sent for you for. I was about to say that since the affair of the forged cheques it has been decided to test the sight of every man in the department that handles them. This gentleman is a specialist." He waved his hand to the real manager. "Will you kindly remove your glasses? It will not take long."

Charles Teen had been standing there trembling, but he made no attempt to do as he was bid; and a smile crossed Sexton Blake's face.

"You are arrested, George Marsden Plummer!" he cried, springing to his feet and levelling his revolver at the other's head. "The handcuffs, inspector!"

Inspector Lurgan had been waiting for his signal, and he lost no time. With one bound he crossed the space between his table and the man he had to arrest, and the handcuffs clicked on to a pair of limp wrists.

"Easier than I expected!" Sexton Blake said coolly, lowering his weapon.

"There's—there's some mistake!" the arrested man gasped.

"Oh, don't fool, George!" the inspector growled, and snatched at the man's hair and gave it a vicious tug.

But the result was a strange one.

No wig came away, but, instead, the prisoner gave vent to a wild yell of pain and tried to shake himself free; and it was at that moment that the door opened, while every eye was upon the handcuffed man.

A man looked in, and, though it was only for a second, if the others had observed him they would have seen the living double of the prisoner, a look of amazement on his face. Then he had drawn back, and the door had closed softly.

Inspector Lurgan gave another wrench, with the same result; and it was then that Sexton Blake stepped forward, an expression of consternation on his face, and lifted the glasses that covered the man's eyes.

They were dull with tears of pain, and their colour was an uncertain grey.

"The wrong man!" the detective gasped, staggering back. "This is not Plummer!"

For a few moments there was inaction, the one man standing there handcuffed, the other three staring at him; but Sexton Blake was the first to recover himself.

"Quick!" he ordered, taking the real Charles Teen by the arm and shaking him in his excitement. "When did you get here?"

"Only just now," Teen faltered. "I was attacked last night—"

But Sexton Blake, waiting for no more, rushed to the table and rang the manager's bell furiously, and a messenger entered.

"Run!" the detective cried, and never before had he lost control of himself to such an extent. "Find out whether Mr. Teen has left the Bank!"

Mr. Fildes snatched off his disguise with an air of disgust, Sexton Blake leant back against the desk with the air of a beaten man, and the inspector stared doubtfully at the handcuffs on the arrested man.

Then the door opened and the messenger returned.

"Mr. Teen left the Bank about two minutes ago, sir," he announced.

"You may go," Sexton Blake said in a dull voice, as the messenger looked with amazement from the real manager to his double.

With the door closed, the detective raised his head wearily.

"Take off the handcuffs," he said.

Inspector Lurgan obeyed mechanically, and with the steel free from his wrists, Charles Teen recovered something of his nerve.

"I do not understand this outrage," he said coldly. "I came in here to explain why I was late. Last night I met with an accident."

Sexton Blake stood with lowered head, then slowly removed his disguise, while Charles Teen, gaining nerve with every word, related his strange story.

"Then I come here," he concluded indignantly, "only after having been rescued by chance by my housekeeper, and meet with this outrage! I do not know which of you gentlemen intends to explain, but that at least is due to me."

"Mr. Blake will," Mr. Fildes said, with a sneer.

Sexton Blake raised his head, slowly, and his eyes looked dully into the short-sighted ones of Charles Teen. He had hoped for so much, believed success certain, only to have it snatched from his hands at the last moment. Somehow, Plummer had discovered the escape and return of the real cashier, and had probably bolted into the streets of London that would swallow him up in a few minutes. Even pursuit was hopeless.

"Yes, I will explain," he said slowly, and in a tired voice related all that had happened, adding: "I can only regret the inconvenience that this has put you to. You will understand that it was in a good cause."

"I was against it all the time!" the manager snapped. "You have blundered, and that is all that there is to be said about it. I need not ask you to waste any more of your time or mine, Mr. Blake."

Mr. Fildes' voice was sneering, if not actually insulting, in tone, and as he heard it Sexton Blake raised his head with a jerk, the colour rushing into his face as if he had been struck a blow with a whip.

"Certainly I will go, Mr. Fildes," he said in a level voice, that showed the effort that it cost him to master himself. "The next time we meet will be when I have given Plummer into charge and restored the stolen money to you."

"Then," the manager answered, with emphasis on the word, "I shall be delighted to meet you! Good-morning! Please stay, Mr. Teen. I wish to apologise on my own account."

Sexton Blake walked from the office and the Bank with his head held high, Inspector Lurgan, looking positively savage, beside him. They halted outside as if by mutual consent, and it was the Scotland Yard man who spoke:

"A nice mess you've made of it, Mr. Blake!" he growled. "You'll have to admit to failure this time! Hanged if I don't think I could have made a better job of it myself!"

"You may try on your next cases," Sexton Blake answered.

"Very nice, too!" the inspector sneered. "That doesn't wipe this disgrace out."

Sexton Blake flushed again, and there was an angry look in his eyes.

"Always the same!" he said bitterly. "A man may have a hundred successes and one failure, but it is the failure that counts."

Then he turned on his heel and walked away, his head still held high, but with a great misery in his heart. A taxi was passing, and he hailed it, and got in with the weary gait of an old man.

"Baker Street!" he ordered.

As the cab started off, the famous detective's head fell forward on to his breast, and he brushed a hand across his eyes. He had failed! The others had spoken truly enough, though they might not have spoken so cruelly. He had told them that he would succeed yet, but now he felt that it was nothing but an idle boast that he had been stung to in his anger. The only thing that he had done was to lift the suspicion from Melton. But what was that when Plummer had escaped?

The cab moved on briskly, but Sexton Blake saw nothing of the traffic or the people. His brain was just a dull, aching thing that kept repeating "failure" until the word almost maddened him.

There was a tap on the glass, and the taxi-driver looked round.

"Baker Street, sir," he said. "What number?"

Sexton Blake gave it mechanically, and when the cab pulled up, stepped out, and paid the man. Nothing mattered now—absolutely nothing!

The detective turned to his door, and as he did so Pedro leapt up at him. He looked about for Tinker, but the lad was not there.

"Why was Pedro loose?" he asked himself dully. "It was careless of Tinker— Still, nothing mattered!"

He opened the door and walked through to his consulting-room, the great bloodhound going with him, and sank into a chair, but Pedro still pleaded for his attentions, laying his muzzle on his master's knee and whimpering.

"What is it, old boy?" Sexton Blake asked huskily, his hand fondling the hound's neck; and suddenly, as his fingers touched the collar, a vague hope dawned in him. Tinker was not there, yet Pedro had come to him, had been outside.

The detective snatched at the little pocket that was under the hound's collar—it had been used for the purpose of carrying messages before— and a cry escaped him as he pulled out a scrap of paper. He raised it to his eyes, but his hands shook so that he could scarcely read.

"Saw Plummer come out—no time warn you—am on track."

That was all, scrawled hastily in pencil; but as Sexton Blake read it a great cry broke from him:

"Heaven bless you, Tinker!" he said hoarsely. "We may win yet!"

THE NINTH
CHAPTER

TINKER ON THE TRACK—THE MESSAGE TO
SEXTON BLAKE.

SEXTON BLAKE had not given Tinker permission to go to the Bank of England when he himself had left the place, confident that he had finally cornered Plummer at last. He had not seen his way in having him in the building, especially as he knew that in his rage at being arrested, if he had the merest chance of success, the criminal might try to take vengeance upon the detective by injuring the boy he loved. On the other hand, he had given the lad no instructions at all, and after trying to occupy himself in the house, but all the time thinking of the "fun" that he was missing, he had put Pedro on the lead and made his way down to the Bank. At least, it was possible that he would see the prisoner brought out, and that would be something, he decided.

It was twelve o'clock when Tinker reached the neighbourhood of the Bank, Sexton Blake having admitted that the capture was not likely to be attempted before one o'clock; and though the great bloodhound with him attracted some attention, he was able to keep an eye on the entrance to the great building—or, rather, the one through which he hoped that the prisoner would be brought. As luck would have it, he chose the one used by the staff, and he haunted the pavement opposite without scarcely moving his eyes from the gateway.

It was shortly before one o'clock that he was to receive a surprise, and it was no small one.

A taxi drew up at the entrance, and a man fairly tumbled out of it. Tinker recognised in him Charles Teen, the man he had followed on the previous day, and knowing how the cashier had been left bound, he wondered what could have brought him there. Did it mean that the arrest had taken place, and the genuine man released?

Tinker hung on for a few minutes, feeling particularly dejected, but at the end of that time he was to be glad that he had done so.

Through the gateway came Charles Teen—or a man who looked uncommonly like him, at such a pace that he nearly ran into the porter

standing there, who looked after him in surprise as he scurried across the road, regardless of the traffic, making in the direction of London Bridge. Hardly knowing why he did so, Tinker followed, but very shortly he knew that instinct had led him right. He saw the man in front of him lift his hand and remove his glasses furtively, and he remembered how short-sighted Teen was.

Then the truth flashed into the lad's keen brain. He had seen the real Charles Teen enter the building, and somehow Plummer had managed to escape. For one wild moment Tinker thought of calling a policeman and giving the man in charge, but realised in time that as likely as not he would only be laughed at for his pains, while the man escaped. Besides, it was his master who had done all the work, and in his loyal young heart he meant to see that he should get it.

But with Pedro beside him, Tinker knew that he could not long go undiscovered, and with that thought an idea came to him. From his pocket he took pencil and paper, scrawled his brief message to Sexton Blake, and thrust it into the hound's collar.

"Home!" he ordered.

For a second Pedro hesitated, then he was bounding away through the crowded street, as safe a messenger as anyone could have wished for. He would not stop until he reached Baker Street.

Tinker was free now to follow Plummer, but a want of disguise hampered him considerably, for he dared not draw near to the man he was tracking. More than once the criminal had looked sharply over his shoulder, as if fearing pursuit, and once Tinker had been so near that he had caught the gleam of fear in the agate-coloured eyes. Oh, it was Plummer right enough. Tinker could understand why he did not take a cab, for there is always the chance that it will form a clue, and the criminal was too cute to risk that.

Over London Bridge Tinker followed Plummer, but had to dodge suddenly as the latter swung round and retraced his footsteps, the lad only saving being seen by abruptly putting his handkerchief over his face to check a violent fit of sneezing.

What did Plummer intend to do?

Tinker hesitated as the criminal hurried down the steps by which the Old Swan Pier can be reached, fearing detection in the quiet street below; but he saw that the risk would have to be taken. Ahead was Plummer, and the lad saw him turn along the lane, at the end of which was the stage from which the steamers ran. The summer service between Greenwich and Kew had stopped, but there was still one boat a day, at two in the afternoon, which ran up to Richmond.

For a moment it occurred to Tinker that Plummer might be contemplating suicide; but he quickly put that idea away from him, knowing the man's character too well. He was the type who clung to life all through.

Tinker paused and watched, and saw Plummer make an inquiry from an attendant, shrug his shoulders impatiently, and hurry forward on to the stage.

It was plain that the master-criminal had guessed that a few minutes after his escape every railway-station in London would be watched for him, and had seen a way out by this unusual route.

Tinker chuckled, and looked at his watch. There was still half an hour before the boat was due to start, and much could be accomplished in that time. First he could obtain some sort of disguise, and secondly he could wire to Sexton Blake. He had no fear that Plummer would change his mind and leave the landing-stage, for under those circumstances he would risk running into the police.

Tinker hurried up again to the main road, and in a few minutes had possessed himself of a coat with a high collar, and from an astonished hairdresser had bought several sticks of grease-paint and a box of brown powder. With those in his pocket he hurried to a post-office, and the following message was quickly flashing over the wires:

"Go to steamer landing-stage at Richmond. If not there, will leave message. Wear two carnations, one red, one white. Bring Pedro.—Tinker."

With only a few minutes to spare, the lad bolted back for the steps leading down to Old Swan Pier, and, by chance, when half-way down, he found himself alone. In an instant the brown powder was out, and he was smearing it rapidly over his face by the aid of a small glass that he always carried, and as he had learnt much of the art of quick disguise from his master, the effect was by no means discreditable. Two touches of an eyebrow pencil finished his disguise, and

with his coat collar turned up high over his chin, it was not probable that he would be recognised.

So far, Tinker flattered himself that he had done well, and he made at a run for the alley leading to the landing-stage. Then he slackened his pace to a walk, although the officials were already calling out: "Any more for Richmond?"

"One teeket, Reechmoud," he said, with a broken accent.

"Right, hurry up," the man at the box ordered, and Tinker was on the steamer, the gangways being pulled in immediately afterwards.

Tinker strolled along the deck, apparently interested in nothing in particular, but for all that, looking out keenly for Plummer, and his heart sank as he failed to find the man. Had he at the last moment changed his mind and chosen some other way of escape? If so, Tinker had failed, and he had hoped for so much in the way of helping his master.

Twice the lad promenaded the deck from end to end without success, and only one hope was left to him. Had Plummer gone below for a dual reason, the obtaining of liquid refreshment which he probably needed pretty badly, and also to keep out of the way as much as possible?

Tinker clung on to his hope, but when Blackfriars Bridge, Waterloo, and Westminster had been passed, and the steamer was on her non-stop run for Richmond, he began to feel distinctly downhearted. If Plummer had slipped him, he was not only on a wild-goose chase, but had sent his master on one, too.

A clear hour passed, and the lad sat dejectedly by the paddle-box, longing to go below to either confirm or dash away his hope; but he dared not risk the chance of being recognised if Plummer were there. His disguise was not bad, but the criminal had keener eyes than the ordinary for such matters, and with the knowledge that he was a hunted man, it was probable that his nerves were at the highest stretch, and he would take notice of every little thing about him.

Tinker could have cried out with relief as a man emerged from the forward saloon, for in spite of the partial disguise that Plummer still wore, his eyes alone would have been enough to make the lad certain of his identity.

Plummer was flushed, and a trifle unsteady on his feet, a proof that he must have been drinking exceptionally hard, for he was a man with a strong head for liquor, and he sprawled down on

to a seat after casting a suspicious glance about him. Very soon the nodding of his head showed that he was asleep, and Tinker quietly moved to another seat so as not to be at hand when the criminal awoke.

The boat went on steadily up the river, but Tinker did not take much interest in the scenery. At that time he was thinking of what would happen when the end of the journey was reached, and of only one thing could he be certain, and that was that he would stick to Plummer like a leach unless something remarkable happened to him.

As the journey wore on, Tinker began to be aware that he had had no lunch, but that was soon remedied by going below into the cabin, where he obtained a very good-meal, only to have a shock as he rose after finishing. Someone was coming down the gangway with uncertain steps, and Tinker drew aside to let him descend.

The next moment he was face to face with Plummer.

In a flash Tinker remembered the collar of his overcoat was down; but he was thankful that he gave no start of recognition. For a second he looked into the agate-coloured eyes of the criminal, then he had gone up to the deck.

"My aunt," he muttered, "I wonder if the beast recognised? Let's hope that he's had too much drink to see straight. Wish to goodness that these blessed boats had wireless on board."

Tinker moved away to the other end of the boat, a prey to very uneasy feelings, wondering whether it was possible that Sexton Blake would reach Richmond before the boat. By rights he ought to do so if he went in his car.

Once more, however, Tinker was to find that the work of capturing Plummer was not to be as easy as he had hoped, for for some reason or another, the steamer stopped at Kew, and positively the first man to step ashore was the master-criminal. He walked past Tinker without taking the slightest notice of him, and that made it at least hopeful that he had not recognised the boy.

Tinker had to follow, but it was with a feeling of uneasiness that he did so, and the feeling grew more intense when Plummer stepped on to a Richmond tramcar. True, it would take him to the place where Tinker hoped that his master would be waiting, but it might rouse the criminal's suspicions, if that had not already happened, if he recognised the brown-faced boy as the one who had been on the steamer with him.

Well, there was nothing to do but mount the car, Tinker decided, and as Plummer had gone on top, he promptly stepped inside, The new state of affairs did not please him, but for all that he did not intend to let his brain remain idle, and when half the journey to Richmond had been covered, an inspiration seized him. Several taxis had passed, and it was those that gave him the idea.

In a few seconds he had scribbled a message on a piece of paper, merely saying that he was on his way to Richmond with Plummer; then he had swung off the car, and stopped a taxi that was coming along.

"Where to?" the man asked doubtfully, as he looked at the brown-faced boy.

"I want you to take this to the steamer landing-stage at Richmond, as fast as you can," Tinker answered, "with this handkerchief. You will see a man there with two carnations in his buttonhole, one red, the other white; give them to him."

"Oh, gammon!" the man growled, making ready to start off again; but as Tinker thrust two half-crowns into his hand, he changed his mind.

"Right-ho!" he said. "But it's the rummiest fare I've ever had."

The taxi shot off, and Tinker looked for another, and was fortunate enough to obtain one with little delay.

"Catch the third tram ahead," he said quickly, "then keep it in sight."

"What are you, Scotland Yard?" the man sniggered.

"Never mind what I am," answered Tinker sharply. "It's five bob for you if you do it. Here, take the money."

The driver lost no time now, and the car, a new make, fortunately, leapt off in pursuit. In a very short time the first of the trams was passed, but it seemed an eternity to Tinker before the second was overhauled, and he feared that the one that was his objective would have reached its destination and discharged Plummer before they gained upon it.

No, there it was ahead, and Tinker felt the car quicken its pace as the driver pressed on the accelerator. They would do it yet.

Tinker sat well back in a corner, for though it was growing dusk now, his training had taught him to be as careful as possible even when everything seemed safe. Ahead the tramcar slowed down at the corner of Richmond Bridge, and Tinker signalled to his driver to slacken, then to stop as he saw Plummer alight.

"Done it all right," the chauffeur remarked. "Easy dollar, too."

But Sexton Blake's assistant scarcely heard him, for already he was hurrying off in pursuit of Plummer, wishing all the time that he had another simple disguise with him, for even now he did not know whether he had been recognised.

Plummer stood hesitating by the corner of the bridge, lighting a cigar, and Tinker had drawn to within thirty yards of him before he moved away and turned down the steps to the towing-path. It was a curious place for the criminal to make for at that time, when the dusk had already fallen, but there was no fear about Tinker as he prepared to follow. He was on the track, and meant to keep it whatever happened. Still, he wished that Sexton Blake had had time to reach the corner of the bridge.

As for Plummer, he walked on a little unsteadily, not once turning his head; but there was something in his eyes that showed that he was not merely making good his escape. If ever murder shone out of a man's soul, it did so then,

for the master-criminal had no intention of allowing a boy to stand in the way of a fortune that he had already made safe.

THE TENTH CHAPTER

A DANGEROUS TRAIL—A FOUL DEED—THE FLIGHT.

THE towpath was lonely. It seemed impossible that Plummer could help seeing the boy behind him—in fact, take notice of anyone who travelled along that lonely place in the dusk. It was cold even for lovers, who were, as a rule, the only people there after darkness had set in. It was desolate.

A petrol launch sounded its siren insistently; there was the throb of its engine, and the water lapped up against the towpath. And those were the only sounds that broke the stillness of the evening.

Every minute the dusk was drawing into darkness, as it will when the autumn comes, and as Tinker followed Plummer along the towpath, all that he had to guide him was the sound of the man's footfalls, for he dared not draw nearer. It was not fear that held him back, but the caution that Sexton Blake had taught him to exercise, and he hoped against hope that the detective, having received his message, was on his track. He would know the meaning of the handkerchief, that it was to be used for the purpose of putting Pedro on the scent, and in that lay the lad's great hope.

Still Tinker could hear the footfalls ahead, sometimes very faint, at other times loud, as Plummer's boots pressed on to loose stones, and he knew well enough that if the criminal had recognised him, and knew that he was following, serious injury, it not death, would be his portion. It was his duty, however, the carrying out of his loyalty to Sexton Blake, the man who had been both friend and father to him for years. What else mattered ?

Over on the left showed the lights of an hotel, standing close to the bank, and even so late in the season the sound of a string orchestra told that business was not yet done with. But Tinker scarcely noticed it in his anxiety to keep in touch with the man ahead.

The thought that Plummer had deliberately taken the towpath so as to lure him on occurred to Tinker, for what other reason could he have for going that way, unless drink had muddled his brain more than usual? Well, if that was the case, the risk would have to be taken, the lad decided pluckily, and step by step he followed in the wake of the man he knew would kill him rather than lose a fortune. It was just the life of a boy against nearly fifty thousand pounds, and there could be no doubt which Plummer would choose.

A gate clanged ahead, and Tinker knew that the master-criminal had passed to the loneliest part of the towpath, where the grass slopes down sharply to the river, and on the other side there are fields and clumps of trees—places in which a quick blow could be struck, and the body of the victim not be found for many days.

Tinker glanced over his shoulder, as if hoping to see Sexton Blake or hear the whimper of Pedro, but there was nothing in sight, and no sound save the footfalls ahead and the swish of the fast-running stream against the weeds close to the bank. Then the footfalls stopped.

Tinker paused hesitatingly, wondering what to do. Possibly Plummer had taken to the fields, meaning to cut across them, and so reach a road. On the other hand, he might be waiting, with all the evil in him roused, to stop for good the lad who was following him.

Tinker listened, but not a sound came to him, and again he looked back hopelessly over his shoulder for Sexton Blake. Why did he not come? Had Pedro failed to pick up a trail from the corner of Richmond Bridge, or was it that through some mischance the detective had not been in when the wire had been received?

Anyway, there was nothing for it but to go on. Tinker decided pluckily; but when he did so, it was with the utmost caution—on hands and knees. Fear made no part of his composition, but caution was a far different thing.

Somewhere ahead was the one criminal in the world who had ever defied Sexton Blake successfully, and Tinker meant that, if it were in his power, the man should not be the winner on this occasion.

Yard by yard the lad crept forward, but now it was quite dark, and at any moment he might run straight into the arms of the desperate man he was tracking. Any of the deeper shadows by the fence might hold him, and when he struck, it would be—

A dark form, like a great shadow, leapt out of the night, and fell upon Tinker before he could rise to his feet, and perhaps it was lucky for him that he could not do so, for Plummer's fingers would have been on his throat at once.

"You whelp!" the master-criminal snarled. "You and your cursed master—robbed me—kept fortunes from me—but, by Heaven, I'll put one of you out of the way now!"

Plummer's arms went round Tinker, lifting him and forcing him on to his back, although the lad struggled furiously against it, striving at the same time to get a ju-jitsu hold upon the man. There, however, he was powerless, for the swiftness of the attack had given him no chance, and he realised that all his struggling was futile.

Plummer's fingers snatched down at the lad's throat, and gripped it in a throttling hold, but for all that Tinker kept his head. Against the strength of Plummer, half-maddened with drink and fear, he could do nothing, and it seemed that the end had come for him. Yet, for all that, with the breath being choked out of him, he managed to think. How could he deceive the man who was trying to kill him, and—

"It's your finish!" Plummer snarled, and his face was so close to Tinker's that even in the darkness the latter could see the gleam in the agate-coloured eyes. "And Sexton Blake shall come next!"

Tinker felt the life being choked out of him, knew that unless something remarkable happened, he would be dead in a minute or so, and with quick instinct he closed his eyes, and let his head drop back. Even then, however, the master-criminal continued the pressure on his throat, and through the darkness he saw strange lights and shooting fires behind the lowered lids of his eyes.

In a strangely resigned way he told himself that he had done his best, and that if he died it would be in the service of the master who had always been so good to him. There was comfort in that.

Then Tinker, semi-conscious, felt himself lifted, a curse sounded dimly in his ears, and he had the sensation of falling through space until something cold struck him.

Of course, he was in the river, he knew that; but even the shock of the water could not bring his senses back to him at once. With feeble strokes he rose to the surface, neither knowing nor caring whether Plummer could see him, and, more by instinct than anything else, turned on his back, and let the stream carry him along, his strength so far gone that he could not make the effort to reach the bank.

As for Plummer, he stood on the bank, staring at the dark water, but his agate-coloured eyes, full of hate, could not make out anything of the boy.

"Dead!" he muttered, and laughed brutally, swaying a little as the drink that he had consumed took a grip on him. "Dead! Curse him!"

The master-criminal laughed again, but suddenly he checked himself, and looked fearfully about in the darkness. He was a murderer, and he had got to get away at once. But to where?

Plummer started back along the towing-path, but stopped, shivering. That way there were lights and people—even Sexton Blake. Tinker had been on his track, and did that mean that the detective was close at hand, too?

A kind of madness seized upon the master-criminal, and for the time being nothing but liberty mattered to him. He forgot the fortune that he had made safe, forgot to think clearly, and saw in his mind's eye nothing but the condemned cell. He felt the leather straps about him, saw the white-robed chaplain walking beside him as he went to the scaffold, and, with a cry of terror, he scrambled over the fence and started at a run across the fields.

§

Sexton Blake paced up and down the steamer landing-stage at Richmond, Pedro behind him. The message that Tinker had sent him had filled him with hope, but against that was set a fear for the lad's safety. He knew the nature of Plummer well enough, and the desperate character that he was when cornered, and Tinker's safety meant almost more to him than the capture of the master-criminal. The famous detective had left for Richmond in his motor-car as soon as he had received the telegram, with the consequence that he had arrived long before the steamer could do so, and the period that he had already had

to wait had shaken his nerves after the events of the day.

It was then that a man in the livery of a taxi-driver came quickly on to the landing-stage and looked about him. For a few moments he hesitated, then crossed to Sexton Blake.

"For you, sir," he said, holding out the scrawled message and the handkerchief. "A bit of a lad gave it to me—told me about your buttonhole."

Sexton Blake took the paper and handkerchief eagerly, and by holding the former close to his eyes he was just able to read it.

"I'd have been here sooner," the taxi-driver explained, "but I had a tyre burst, and had to wait to put on the spare. Hope it didn't matter?"

"No," Sexton Blake answered mechanically; then in a second he was the man of action again. He wanted to capture Plummer, but, above all else, he desired to see to the safety of Tinker.

"Cab waiting?" he asked sharply.

"Yes, sir."

"Then take me over the bridge."

A little later the taxi was speeding away from the landing-stage, was swung on to the bridge, and pulled up with a skidding of wheels on the other side.

"Shall I wait, sir?" the driver asked, as the detective got out.

"No," the latter answered, thrusting half-a-crown into the man's hand and walking to the corner of the pavement.

"Well, if this ain't a beanfeast!" the taxi-driver murmured. "Either this yere world's goin' potty or I'm dreamin'. Seven-and-a-buck for a bob fare! If they'd make it every day, I'd chuck the game in a year, an' keep race-'orses!"

With every nerve alert, Sexton Blake took from his pocket the handkerchief that Tinker had sent him, knowing full well the reason he had done so. It was to put Pedro on the trail. He held it to the great hound's muzzle, and as he sniffed at it he whined in understanding.

"Find!" the detective ordered, in a low tone, and, without a moment's hesitation, Pedro's head had dropped, and he was nosing for the scent of his young master.

The bloodhound was eager enough, but Sexton Blake, heedless of the people who looked on curiously, was quivering with nervous excitement. A strange presentiment gripped him that the worst had happened, and that, either to get away, or purely out of vengeance, Plummer had struck a blow at Tinker.

The corner of the pavement did not give Pedro the scent, and Sexton Blake led him a little further back. There was a whimper, a hard tug at the lead, and the detective knew that the bloodhound had found.

In what direction would the scent lead?

Still straining at his leash, Pedro made straight for the steps leading to the towpath, and as Sexton Blake realised what that meant his heart sank within him. For what other purpose than foul play could Plummer have led Tinker down to such a place? Of course, he had seen that he was being followed, and then—

"It can't be that!" the detective muttered.

But he broke into a run once the towpath was reached and he was out of sight of the people who had until then watched him curiously.

Pedro made no mistake about the scent, tugging away with a strength that showed how fresh it was; and as he hurried after the hound Sexton Blake hoped that he might still be in time.

Not a soul was passed, and the swish of the water made the detective shudder, though he was not an imaginative man outside his profession, He could picture Tinker lying among the weeds, his bright, young life cut off in its prime.

Pedro checked at the iron gate, but Sexton Blake quickly opened it, and they passed through and kept on along the trail without a hitch. Then, with dramatic suddenness, the bloodhound stopped, looked up into his master's face, and whimpered.

"Find!" Sexton Blake ordered.

And again Pedro went on, though it was not for long.

It was close to the edge of the grass that sloped down to the water that Pedro halted, muzzled round twice in a circle, then raised his head with defeat plainly expressed by the action.

The detective looked about him sharply, and his face had gone very white. Why should the trail end here so abruptly, and, if it did, what was the meaning of it?

Sexton Blake drew his breath in sharply between his teeth, and the sweat stood out on his brow as he realised the truth. If the trail of Tinker ended there, there could only be one way in which it had been cut short—the river.

With something like a sob, the detective slid down the sloping grass at the risk of a plunge into the cold water, his eyes peering down among the weeds, though he might have known that he was not likely to find Tinker there, while Pedro looked on wistfully, whimpering as if he understood.

Slowly Sexton Blake clambered back up the bank, and stood on the towpath like a man dazed. Mechanically he made one further effort to pick up the trail that had stopped so abruptly; but there was no life or hope in his voice when he gave his order to Pedro, and there was no change of expression when the bloodhound failed.

For at least a minute Sexton Blake must have stood there motionless, all the pain of his sorrow in his grey face. He told himself that Tinker, the one person he loved in all the world, was dead, and he blamed himself for having allowed the lad to take up such perilous work.

And it was George Marsden Plummer who had killed him—the master-criminal, the callous robber, the—

Sexton Blake's head went up, and on to his grey face came an expression of deadly determination. Tinker was dead, but at least he might be avenged, and his murderer sent to his proper fate—the gallows.

The detective drew from his pocket the electric lantern that he always carried, and there was hate and vengeance in his heart as he dropped to his knees and examined the ground, his eyes strained, his face suddenly haggard with the sorrow that had come into his life.

Tinker was dead !

The words drummed through Sexton Blake's brain as he moved slowly on his knees, the circle of light from his lantern revealing to him the movements of Tinker and Plummer as if he had seen them.

There were marks where Tinker had crawled on hands and knees, and there was the cut-up path where lad and man had come to grips. It was all too ghastly plain to the detective, and as he crawled towards the fence there was not a vestige of hope left in him. With that grew his desire for vengeance, though justice would be a better word for it.

The beam of light moved upwards, trailed along the top of the wooden rail fence; and there, sure enough, was a spot where a splinter had recently been broken away, the wood showing fresh and new. The next moment the detective was in the field beyond, Pedro clambering through, after him; and the man bent over the bloodhound, his face working, something like a sob in his voice when he spoke.

"Find," he ordered hoarsely, laying his hand upon the ground at a spot that Plummer must have crossed—"find, lad! It's a murderer we're after, Pedro—after the blackguard who has killed Tinker!"

The bloodhound looked up curiously at his master, as if he understood the words, then his muzzle was to the ground and he was at work.

Pedro whimpered, showing that there was a trail there right enough, but from it he looked up curiously at his master. Previously he had been following Tinker's scent, and he did not appear to understand why he should suddenly be on a fresh trail, for once a bloodhound is upon a scent he will not leave it for another if fifty cross it.

"Find; for Heaven's sake, find!" the detective pleaded, his voice broken with emotion. "It's Tinker we're out to avenge, lad—Tinker!"

Once more Pedro nosed the ground, and now he seemed to understand that he was to get on to the fresh scent, for after a few seconds he started off with a jump, dragging at the lead that Sexton Blake held.

The famous detective raised his head sharply, and his face was so hard that it might have been cut out of stone.

"I swear," he whispered between his teeth, and there was something almost terrible in his determination; "I swear that I will not rest until Tinker is avenged!"

Then Pedro was leading the way across the field, following the trail of Plummer, as sure a fate as death itself.

THE ELEVENTH CHAPTER

PLUMMER IN DIFFICULTIES—THE GREAT FIGHT—ESCAPE—THE END OF ALL.

PLUMMER left the fields, scrambling over a fence, and finding himself in a quiet road, where here and there showed the lights of fine houses standing well back in their own grounds. He stood there, looking over his shoulder, and

shuddering as he thought of the splash that Tinker's body had made when it had hit the water.

There had been no other way of escape from Sexton Blake's young assistant, and it was not entirely remorse or blood-guiltiness that filled the master-criminal with fear. It was the knowledge that Sexton Blake had loved Tinker passionately, and that he was not likely to rest until his slayer had been brought to the gallows.

Plummer caught his breath in with a choking cry as he thought of the gallows, and just then a clock struck eight and set him shivering. True it was eight o'clock at night, but there would be the same number of beats on the morning that they hung him. He reeled with fear and the spirits that he had drunk, then in sheer desperation he took to his heels and ran unsteadily away from Richmond, keeping to the lonely road.

How far Plummer went he did not know, but instinctively he slackened his pace as he reached a village, where light still burned in the shop windows. He was panting badly for breath, the sweat glistening on his face, and his black frock-coat was sprinkled with dust. He stopped, realising in a dim kind of way that his appearance was likely to cause comment, and with shaking hands did what he could to readjust his dishevelled clothes.

He must disguise himself. Yes, that was it, and when he felt recovered make his way back to London, obtain possession of the "bearer-bonds" that he had bought, and go away as quickly as possible. To where? Oh, a long, long way, to some country where Sexton Blake would not think of following him, and where perhaps he might lose the haunting fear of the gallows, and forget the white face of Tinker as he had thrown him into the swiftly-running river.

In Plummer's pocket was his small make-up case, with which he ought to be able to change his facial expression in a very short time—but where?

The master-criminal stood still, thinking deeply, his eyes peering to where the lights showed in the shops, and it was not long before he had made up his mind. He would get lights, and then in some secluded place he would alter his appearance.

Trembling inwardly, fearing the glance of the two or three people whom he passed, Plummer made his way to a little general shop and bought a packet of candles, but he did not leave the village with them at once. On his left was a comfortable-looking inn, and the sight of it sent the criminal half mad with a craving for strong drink to drown his fear in. For a short time he hesitated, then he was in the bar and ordering brandy in a voice that was strangely unlike his own.

Three times Plummer drank, until the spirit coursed up into his brain and brought him back something of confidence. A fourth time he ordered brandy, and though the landlord hesitated he served him, and the drink was gulped down as the others had been.

"Brandy," he ordered, swaying so that he had to grip the edge of the counter for support, but the landlord shook his head with determination.

"Sorry; you've had enough, sir," he answered.

Plummer's face went dark with fury at being thwarted by a mere publican, and his agate-coloured eyes flashed savage!

"You won't serve me?" he snarled, and his hand went out towards a decanter. "By Heaven, I'll—"

The landlord leapt back, and snatched up a whistle that hung on a nail behind him, and Plummer pulled himself together with a jerk, remembering that he dared not face the police. They would only be able to charge him with being drunk, but that would mean detention until the morning, and by then he wanted to be in London, ready to regain his fortune and contrive to get abroad with it.

"Sorry," he said hoarsely, and went staggering out of the bar, the door closing with a crash behind him.

"A nice lot," the landlord of the inn muttered. "I reckon I'd better call the police up on the 'phone, and let them know the kind of man who's about. Looks half a madman."

Plummer stood in the open air, swaying on his feet, one hand pressed to his head, his brain dulled with the brandy, He knew that there was something that he had meant to do, but for the life of him he could not think what it was. He was escaping; yes, he knew that. But how, and in what manner?

The criminal's brain cleared a little, and he moved off unsteadily down the road. Of course, he had meant to disguise himself, and he had the candles that were to give him light, safely in his pocket. He must lose no time, but where could he find a place in which to carry out his object?

Plummer passed beyond the line of shops to where the road was bordered by no more than dark hedges for a short distance, then, with dim eyes, he found the place he was searching for. On his left was a wooden building, which had at some time probably been a cowshed, and as the criminal touched the rusty key that had been left in the lock the door opened under his hand.

In the darkness Plummer swayed and almost fell, only keeping his feet by a great effort of will. He drew the packet of candles from his pocket, and tore the paper open, dropping the whole of the contents clumsily on to the ground.

Cursing, Plummer managed to strike a light, dropped to his knees, and contrived to thrust two of the candles into the loose earth, and light them.

"I'll beat you all!" he chuckled. "Great—greatest make-up in world!"

The man laughed with drunken triumph, but controlled himself as once more the fear of the thing that he had done returned to him. He was a murderer, and he could not tell how soon Sexton Blake might be on his track. If it was Jesse Kells who had died they would, of course, look for him, but now that it was Tinker, Plummer knew that his great enemy would never rest so long as there was the smallest hope of vengeance.

The master-criminal sat on the floor, and drew from his pockets his make-up outfit, which included a small looking-glass. After several efforts he contrived to make the last article balance, then he opened the case of paints and prepared to get to work.

"Curse the place!" he muttered dazedly. "Walls keep comin' in, an' in—want to get me—I know—ah!"

The man rose to his feet by an effort, and looked about him madly, thrusting out his hands as if the walls were really closing in upon him and trying to make him captive.

"Don' try it!" he muttered savagely. "Tell you goin' to get away—can't stop me—not you, or Sex'on Blake—no one—too clever for all of you!"

Then Plummer had squatted on the ground again, and was surveying his face in the little glass. He still wore the make-up that had rendered him the double of Charles Teen, but now beneath the paint the lines of his face showed in hard haggardness, and his eyes were bloodshot.

"What's make-up?" he mumbled. "Beastly ugly now— anyway. Goo' lookin' chap really— shame spoil you."

Plummer made an effort to pull himself together, and stared solemnly into the glass.

"Whiskers!" he muttered. "That's it—first of all—whiskers."

From his make-up case the master-criminal drew a plait of crape-hair, and clumsily began to draw strands from it, but his fingers almost refused to obey his will, and the small side-whiskers that he manufactured were far from being perfect. Next he uncorked a bottle of spirit-gum, dabbing his face with it beside the ears, and then sticking the false hair to it, the whisker on the left being considerably higher than the one on the right.

"Don' like it," he mumbled, in maudlin tones; "don' seem right—looks un-uneven!"

He made a second attempt to put it right, but with little success, and with an oath he took an eyebrow pencil from his case to alter the angle of his brows—one of the most effectual methods of disguise. His fingers moved waveringly, the pencil missed its mark, and a long smudge of black appeared on his forehead an inch above his right eyebrow.

Plummer was drunk, there could be no doubt about that. He wanted to lie down and sleep, but stronger than that desire was the knowledge that he was a murderer, and that Sexton Blake was still alive. He did not know that the detective had been waiting at Richmond, and that already he was on his track, and in a dim kind of way he did not believe that his enemy would know the truth until the morning at least. But, for all that, the fear of the man gripped him so that he dared not rest.

Swaying towards the light, Plummer rubbed out the mark that he had made, leaving a dirty smudge on his forehead, and tried again, with slightly better results, though it was only by a great effort of will that he kept his hands comparatively steady. Next, he turned his attention to the manufacture of a moustache, fumbling with fingers that were dead with drink and half refused to obey him. Somehow he finished his task, however, and gummed the moustache on crooked.

"Have to do!" he muttered, rising to his feet, carrying the glass with him. "All ri' until mornin'; make it better then."

Plummer swayed forward, his eyes closing, the sleep of drunkenness in his brain, and lurched himself back to consciousness.

"Got to get away," he said thickly, "Sex'on Blake—curse him!"

Leaving the lights, he stumbled towards the door and opened it, and as the night air swept against his face the whimper of a hound reached his ears. He staggered back, the truth entering his numbed brain, but he was too late. Out of the darkness leapt Sexton Blake, the light of the candles upon his white, haggard lace, and in his eyes the craving for vengeance.

"Murderer!" Sexton Blake said, between his teeth; then he was at the grotesquely made-up criminal. A heavy blow in the face sent Plummer reeling back, but he was not to be done for easily. The drink that gripped him took a new effect upon him when combined with his fear of capture, and suddenly he was a madman possessed of a madman's strength. His fist lunged out in return, and grazed the detective's jaw. If it had been an inch further forward it would have knocked the latter out.

"It's a fight!" he yelled savagely. "And I'll kill you as I've killed that cursed brat!"

The two men faced each other, breathing hard, as different types as could be found in the world, yet both the same in one respect—the hate that shone from their eyes. It was Plummer who restarted the fight, his left fist lunging out at the detective, but the blow was countered, and in return he received a swinging right in the jaw that started the blood running. Only for a second however, was his balance shaken; then, with the snarl of a wild beast, he rushed in and aimed a shower of blows at the detective.

A blow got home between Blake's eyes that made him stagger, and it was only by dropping to one knee and upper-cutting Plummer that he saved himself from being knocked out.

Sexton Blake fought his way to his feet, receiving more than one nasty blow as he did so, but the thought of Tinker made his strength equal to this man who had gone mad with drink and hate.

Sexton Blake swung hard, and sent Plummer down, but the man was on his feet again like a cat, his swollen lips letting out a string of curses. Then he stopped, as if he had suddenly become sober, and started to fight with deadly resolution.

The detective was dazed by the punishment that he had received, but for all that his brain kept its fixed determination. For a short time he practically contented himself with warding off the blows aimed at him, while he got his wind and strength back, and they came to him none too soon.

Under a body blow Plummer reeled back, and before he could recover himself Sexton Blake had crossed him and sent him down. He lay in a still heap, and though the detective stood above him, waiting for him to rise, he did not move. He was knocked out.

Sexton Blake staggered back against the wall, reeling, his breath coming thickly, but he was not inactive for long. A deadly faintness possessed him, but for all that his brain cleared, and he knelt beside the prostrate man. With shaking fingers he searched Plummer's pockets.

There was a roll of notes there that he must have taken at the Bank that day, but it was in the man's trouser-pocket that the detective found the thing that he was searching for. It was a small key, which he knew to be one of those issued by the Safe Deposit Company, and in a second he realised where the criminal had hidden his stolen fortune.

With the key and the notes in his pocket, Sexton Blake reeled through the doorway, and by instinct more than anything else closed the door behind him, and turned the rusty key in the lock.

"Hallo!" a gruff voice said, "What's the matter?"

In a dim way the detective saw the figure of a labourer before him, and he clutched at his arms.

"I'm a detective!" he panted. "Dangerous criminal in there. Go for the police!"

The man hesitated, but even in his dazed state, Sexton Blake still kept his manner of authority, and the labourer hurried away towards the village, the darkness swallowing him up.

"Tinker!" Sexton Blake gasped; then he had collapsed on to the ground in a dead faint.

For five minutes the detective lay there, his ears deaf to the sounds that came from the shed, or he would have known that Plummer had recovered consciousness.

There was the sound of snarling curses, followed by blows on the door, but Sexton Blake lay still, heedless of the efforts that his great enemy was making to escape, with Pedro licking his face, not understanding why his master did not rise and speak to him. Throughout the fight the great hound had stood helplessly by, and now he whimpered at the blood that touched his tongue.

Crash!

The door of the shed flew open, and Plummer, bloodstained and dishevelled, staggered out, and made straight for the body of the detective. He knew that he had been robbed of the key that guarded his stolen fortune, and he meant to get it back, whatever the cost.

Pedro, however, could understand one thing—that his master lay helpless, and as Plummer advanced upon him the hair along his spine bristled, and his eyes were wicked.

Plummer looked about him for a weapon with which to drive Pedro off, for afraid though he was of the animal, he could think of nothing but that Sexton Blake had the key of the locker at the Safe Deposit, in which lay nearly fifty thousand pounds' worth of bonds—the fortune for which he had risked so much.

The master-criminal saw a great stone, and plucked it up, but the gallant brute who was guarding his master was not to meet his end in that way.

There was the sound of voices, the quick fall of running feet, and with an oath Plummer turned and leapt away into the darkness. At that moment liberty was even more to him than a fortune.

Four men—the labourer Sexton Blake had sent for help, another man, and two policemen—came hurrying forward, and one of the constables knelt beside the insensible man.

"'Knocked about bad," he observed. "Best get him to the station as soon as we can."

The other men had hurried to the shed, but only to find it empty.

"That's the only thing to do," the other constable agreed. "You chaps lend a hand."

Ten minutes later Sexton Blake had been carried to the police-station, but it was half an hour later before he recovered consciousness. He opened his eyes weakly, looking about him in dazed fashion, but suddenly a spasm of pain crossed his face.

"You got the man?" he whispered. "Threw the lad into the river—murdered him."

"Sorry to say that he got away, sir," the sergeant in charge answered respectfully, for an examination of the injured man's papers had told him who he was. "The boy's all right, though. A boatman picked him up by Richmond Bridge."

"Thank Heaven!" Sexton Blake said, with a sob; then his eyes closed, as he fainted away again.

§

Sexton Blake looked very white and worn as he sat in his consulting-room. The fight with Plummer had injured him more than he had imagined, so that now, a month later, he was only convalescent.

"Is there any news, lad?" he asked, in a low voice, as Tinker entered the room, and looked at him anxiously. "Of course, there can be no doubt that Plummer has got away, though, thank Heaven, we robbed him of his stolen fortune."

"I'm afraid that is so, sir," the lad answered. "Inspector Lurgan says there isn't a clue, but I shouldn't let that worry you; you're not strong enough yet."

"And Jesse Kells?" the detective asked.

"He's out of the hospital, sir, and, on your advice, he's going to be allowed to go quietly abroad."

Sexton Blake nodded.

"All the others have been here asking about you, sir—Mr, Melton, Mr. Teen, and Mr. Fildes," Tinker observed. "You got them out of a nasty mess."

"Yes, I suppose so," Sexton Blake said wearily; "but I would have rather let the money go if I could have laid hands on Plummer—for good!"

The detective sat brooding for a minute, then he held out his hand to Tinker, and held the lad's fingers hard.

"Thank Heaven you were spared to me," he said huskily.

The End.

QUITS!

A SPLENDID TALE OF

SEXTON BLAKE

VERSUS

MARSTON HUME

MARSTON HUME—Criminal.

"MY dear Blake," said Sir Richard Courtland, "I am more pleased to see you than I can say. I was informed, semi-officially, that you were out of town, and when I sent my note round to you this morning, I almost despaired of getting an answer. However, here you are, so now let's get to business. Take that chair by the fire over there. My secretary, young Stretton, is out, and Thompson, the typist, I have sent off to lunch, so we have the whole place to ourselves."

Blake settled himself comfortably in the large, red-leather, official armchair, and prepared to listen.

Sir Richard Courtland is the permanent Secretary to the head of the Design Department of the Admiralty. A precise, genial, unimaginative man of eight-and-forty, scrupulously neat, with a smack of the Service in his manner, and in his own mild way a bit of a disciplinarian.

The rooms he occupied officially were two in number. The first, that in which Blake was sitting, was a large, airy apartment, with two big windows looking out over the street. It was furnished simply but comfortably.

In the centre of the room was a massive leather-covered writing-table, with a padded chair. On the window side of this was a large red morocco sofa. Two big armchairs to match were placed on either side of the fire. In a corner was another writing-table of a less obtrusive order; this belonged to Mr. Maurice Gower-Stretton, Sir Richard's private secretary. Between the two windows stood a big safe. Several rolls of plans and designs were fastened to the walls like maps, and on the left, as one faced the window, a second door led into a small ante-room, possessing only one window. This was the room of Thompson, the typist.

Blake took in these details mechanically, whilst Sir Richard was still coming to an anchor in the chair opposite.

"I can't exaggerate the seriousness of the situation," said Sir Richard at last; "but I must give you the details. First of all, for the past three weeks, at indefinite periods, the papers in this office have been tampered with after hours.

"The first case happened, to be exact, precisely seventeen days ago. I had been going through a series of rather complicated plans and designs. They were of no great importance, and, as I was still only part of the way through them when it became time to shut up for the day, I left them on my table there, with strict instructions that they were not to be disturbed.

"The next morning, however, on returning to the office, I found unmistakable signs that someone had been tampering with them. Of course I made a row about it, and held a full inquiry; but for the life of me I couldn't find out who the culprit was. Certainly neither of my own men was responsible.

"These offices, as you may have noticed, are rather curiously situated as regards the rest of the building, being isolated, as it were, in a little promontory quite by themselves. As a matter of fact, we are perched over one of the main entrances, and are quite cut off from all the rest of the buildings in the block. The passage outside this door is a mere cul-de-sac; no other door gives on to it, and the only access to it is by the single flight of stairs by which you ascended. This, as you know, commences near the porter's lodge, just inside the entrance, and terminates here.

"There is, I believe, only one key to this door. At the end of the day, either I myself, or young Gower-Stretton, locks the door—it just depends which of us is the last to leave—and the key is given to Jarvis, the porter, who hangs it up in his lodge.

"Jarvis is, of course, quite above suspicion; he has charge of all the keys in this section of the building, and has held his present position for years. The cleaners come in in the usual way in the morning, and each office, or set of offices, is unlocked for them in turn; but one of the strictest rules is that no cleaner is allowed to touch any paper or papers, under pain of instant dismissal.

"Yet, in spite of all this, the fact remains that someone has been obtaining access to these offices out of hours, and has been tampering with the papers from time to time."

"Are any papers missing?"

"So far, none. To tell the truth, the papers themselves have been of no importance, dealing merely with technical detail. But that isn't the point. The point, as I see it, is the horrible feeling of insecurity these night visits entail; and not only that—"

"Well?"

Sir Richard hesitated.

"What I am about to tell you is in the strictest confidence. To-morrow the detailed plans for the mines and defences of the new North Sea base will be handed over to me to file a précis of. That means that I shall be obliged to keep them here in this office, in the safe there, for at least three days. Think of it. Those plans, for which one nation, at any rate, would cheerfully give forty or fifty thousand, will have to be here for three days and three nights; and all the while I know that some unauthorised person has access to the rooms during the night."

"Have you taken any steps in the matter?"

"I spoke of it to my chief; but the only satisfaction I got was to be told that I was dreaming, and that the thing was impossible."

"Why impossible?"

"Well, you see, the whole of the outside of the building is constantly patrolled by police, right through the night. There are other police on duty in the inner courtyard, and at each entrance there is a porter's lodge."

"You mean that anyone trying to obtain access to these rooms would, besides having to force an entrance, be compelled to slip through the police patrol outside, evade those in the inner courtyard, and also pass close to Jarvis's box."

"Precisely. That is what makes it seem so impossible."

"And yet, supposing you are right, your anonymous visitor has done all those things over and over again with impunity. What do you imagine was his object in running such risks? Surely not the turning over of a few unimportant documents."

"I am horribly afraid he was searching for those very plans I mentioned just now."

"And which will be handed to you to-morrow. That argues that the man, whoever he is, is practically certain that sooner or later those plans must pass through your hands."

Sir Richard nodded.

"I am afraid so. That is why I sent round to you. I cannot make anyone believe in the danger. Yet I am as certain that it exists as that I sit here; and, from a purely selfish point of view, if the details of those plans once reach a foreign intelligence department, I'm a ruined man."

Blake rose, and strolling to the window, stood staring out across the wide, glistening street. Opposite to him there was a row of tall, narrow-frontaged houses. One was a bank, the others were mostly shops below and offices above. The street itself was thronged with traffic, and the dull roar of it came to him muffled through the thick, plate-glass, windows. A sickly gleam of sunshine came out, and as it did so Blake's sharp eyes noticed a curious twinkling flash from just above one of the window-screens in a third floor office directly opposite.

It vanished instantly; it was just an instantaneous flash, no more; but it left him frowning thoughtfully; tracing out the pattern of the carpet with the toe of his boot, as he stood half hidden by the window-curtain.

"Sir Richard," he said quietly, without turning round.

"Eh? Yes."

"You have already seen the plans in question, of course? You have a fair idea of their size and shape and general appearance?"

"Certainly, certainly."

"Then oblige me by selecting from any papers you have handy some that resemble the plans as nearly as possible. Spread them out well, and take them to the other window—as though you wanted to study them close to the light."

Sir Richard did so in a bewildered fashion.

"That will do, thanks," said Blake, after two or three minutes. "You are quite right in your suspicions—and what is more, you are being closely watched by a man in one of those offices over the way. I think I will be off now. I will look in again some time to-morrow, without fail."

Blake went down the stairs past the lodge of Jarvis the porter; but instead of turning out by the adjacent entrance, he turned inwards, across the enclosed courtyard, and left by another gate.

The problem which chiefly baffled him was how the watcher obtained access to the buildings. The Design Offices are a big block of buildings, standing practically by themselves. A regular rabbit-warren to the uninitiated; but, in common with other Government offices, they have one good point in their favour. Ugly they may be, ill-ventilated and badly-designed—in spite of it all, however, they are uncommonly hard to effect an entrance into without attracting undue attention. The windows are of heavy plate-glass, defying a diamond. The outer doors are clumsy and massive as those of an embryo fortress, and the outer stone parapet running all round adds yet further difficulties—to say nothing of the police.

After a brief survey on all four sides, Blake felt satisfied that any direct attack from without was hopeless. Wishing to avoid being observed from the windows opposite, he slipped down a side alley, and re-entered the street further along, where there were some small dilapidated, tumble-down shops, relics of a bygone era. Across the windows of these were plastered notices of compulsory sales, and others to the effect that the buildings were shortly coming down. Two of the shops already stood empty and tenantless, a picture of desolation.

The door of one stood ajar, and, acting on the impulse of the moment, he slipped inside and up the stairs. He had a feeling, an intuition, that he was on the right track.

At the head of the stairs was a skylight, and a trapdoor, with a movable ladder hooked to the wall close by.

He clambered up and opened the trap. It gave on to a rain-sodden grimy stretch of leads. The level of these varied considerably, some roofs being eight to ten feet higher than their neighbours. But all were negotiable for an active man, except the final rise, to the level of the flat top of the Design Office. This was quite twelve foot above any of the other roofs. Moreover, there was a gap eight foot broad to be bridged as well.

For a moment Blake was nonplussed, until he espied projecting from behind a cluster of chimney-stacks one of those small light emergency bridges, which at one time were by no means uncommon and were kept handy in case of fire, a single stout iron-bolted plank, fifteen or sixteen feet long, with a hand-rail on one side of it, the whole moving easily on two small metal wheels placed near the centre.

The thing was black with grime, and rusted and sodden, but it was sufficient, and Blake returned to the street well satisfied.

Sir Richard's office hours were from ten till five, and it still wanted some minutes of the latter hour when Blake called on him next day.

"You have the plans?" asked Blake.

Sir Richard pointed to a roll of papers on the table before him, and shrugged his shoulders.

"I have, and I'd give half a year's salary willingly if someone else had the charge of them. I spoke to the chief again this morning about my suspicions, and he practically laughed at me. All I can say is that I've taken ordinary precautions, and I can do no more."

Blake glanced at the roll casually.

"Look here, Sir Richard," he said at last. "Of course, you can't engage me officially, and equally of course I have no right to be on these premises out of hours. Still, if you like to stretch a point, and arrange with Jarvis that I shall be admitted into these rooms at say half-past ten to-night, there is a chance that I may catch your man red-handed. I have already a tolerably shrewd idea as to how he obtains access to the place, and as to unlocking this door, that would be a simple matter for an expert provided with the necessary implements, even supposing that he has not taken the trouble to make himself a duplicate key."

"My dear fellow, if you would," began Sir Richard.

"I will do my best," Blake interposed; "but mind, I can promise nothing. The whole thing maybe a failure. The man may not even turn up."

"We're bound to risk something," said Sir Richard. "And now, as you are here, you may, as well witness me putting these precious documents in the safe."

He opened the heavy door of the safe between the two main windows, pushed the plans well to the back of a lower shelf, and closed the thing again with a slam.

"Anyone else got a key to that?" asked Blake, "Your secretary, for instance, Mr. Gower-Stretton?"

"No, no one but myself. And mine never leaves my watch chain."

"So much the better. Now, if you will give Jarvis orders to admit me at half-past-ten sharp, I'll see what I can do, and will report to you some time to-morrow."

At half-past ten to the minute Blake was admitted by the small wicket gate, which opened out of the big iron-studded double doors, and, after a good deal of unbolting and unbarring, found himself standing beside Jarvis in the corridor outside Sir Richard's room. This, Jarvis unlocked with the key which he had brought with him in readiness.

"Thanks!" said Blake. "That will do for the present. I don't want you to make any difference in your usual routine. To do so might upset my plans. But if you hear me call, then come at once."

"Very good, sir," said Jarvis, saluting stiffly, and left Blake to his own devices.

Blake slipped quietly into the room, and, locking the door behind him, put the key in his pocket. Blinds there were none, and the heavy curtains were undrawn, consequently the whole place was dimly but sufficiently lighted by the reflection from the street lamps outside.

A faint aroma of tobacco still pervaded the place. Sir Richard always allowed himself one cigar during office hours after luncheon.

Blake, feeling sure that nothing of any importance would happen till the small hours, having inspected the typist's room beyond, flung himself on the big sofa, and enjoyed a couple of cigarettes in a leisurely fashion, being careful to drop all the tell-tale ashes into a newspaper spread out for the purpose.

As Big Ben close by boomed out midnight he threw paper, ashes, cigarette-ends, and all into the waste-paper basket, and began to make his preparations.

He was careful to keep away from the direct line of the big, blank, staring windows, though as he crossed the room he noticed that the house was still sitting, and he gave vent to an exclamation of annoyance, for that meant that there would be a certain amount of traffic passing to and fro in Whitehall for some time to come, and that his period of waiting would be necessarily prolonged in consequence.

Skirting along the back wall of the room, he slipped into the smaller apartment used by the typist. This was a mere narrow box of a place, the whole of the outer end being taken up by one large window; and the only door was that communicating with Sir Richard's room. There was no other means of exit.

This door opened inwards on to the smaller room, and Blake left it an inch or two ajar. Having done so, and after loosening his revolver in his coat pocket, he awaited developments.

Now and again a hansom went rattling past outside, or a homeward-bound taxi-cab droned by like a tired bee, and the sickly glare of the street lamps flickered uncertainly on the high ceiling.

Two o'clock, and a faint, almost imperceptible click brought Blake noiselessly to his feet, every sense on the alert.

He was close behind the communicating door now, so placed that were the door thrust suddenly open he himself would remain concealed behind it.

Click again. No louder than the clicking of a man's two finger-nails. The outer door swung open, showing an uncertain black, yawning gap beyond.

The next instant it was closed again, and there was a dark blur dimly visible against its polished panels.

The blur detached itself, and solidified into a human form, as it crossed to the better lit portion of the room—a man in an ulster and a soft cap. And then the light from the street lamps below, such as it was, fell full on the man's face.

Blake started, and bit his lip, till the blood came freely, lest he should make a sound. The face was the clear-cut, pale, imperturbable face of Marston Hume.

Blake slipped his hand into his pocket, and drew out his revolver in readiness, watching the other's every movement keenly.

Hume seemed quite oblivious of any possibility of his being watched. His movements were as quiet and deliberate as though he were in the smoking-room of the Baddeley Club.

He had let himself in with a duplicate key, nicely fitted and carefully oiled. His sense of hearing alone was enough to satisfy Blake on that point. Blake was quite convinced that he would be equally well supplied, as regards the safe.

He was quite right.

Marston Hume didn't even waste a glance on the papers on Sir Richard's writing-table. He passed straight to the safe; took a key from his waistcoat-pocket, and opened it as easily as if it had been his own despatch-box.

Blake half raised his revolver hand, and then changed his mind: He wanted, if possible, to catch his man in actual possession of the plans; then he could corner him, and summon Jarvis as a witness.

Hume took a packet out of the safe at random, and carried it to the window to examine it more closely.

Blake chuckled grimly to himself. It was the wrong shape and the wrong size; evidently Hume's knowledge was not so perfect as it should be, otherwise he would have known the precise appearance of the plans. Having satisfied himself that the packet he had taken was the wrong one; he placed it on one side and selected another.

He dared not strike a light, of course, lest it should be seen by a passing policeman outside; and was therefore compelled to take each batch of papers to the window.

The third lot, though not the plans, as Blake could see, occupied him longer. He pored over them, and then, to get a better light, passed to the window on the near side of the room, which was immediately over a lamp outside.

Here he was just beyond Blake's limited range of vision, and the latter waited impatiently for him to reappear and continue his investigations.

Two minutes passed—three, and Blake began to get uneasy. Suddenly he stiffened expectantly. He could have sworn that he heard a very faint rustle just the other side of the door.

He raised his revolver hand in readiness, and as he did so the door was suddenly and sharply swung to and locked on the far side.

He heard Hume chuckle quietly, and the soft thud of his weight on the carpet as he sprang back across the room; then there came another quick rustling of papers, and the muffled thud of the closing safe.

Blake hurled himself at the door frantically. Too late he realised how cleverly he had been tricked, But the door was strong and stoutly built, and he could do nothing with it.

He understood exactly what had happened, and the understanding made him none the less bitter. Hume must have recognised him through the field-glasses from the office window opposite on the occasion of his first visit to Sir Richard. Blake, for his part, had detected a man using glasses, obviously for spying purposes, but had been unable to distinguish the user. Moreover, the thought of Hume never crossed his mind, for he had heard that the latter was ill and confined to his rooms.

Hume, forewarned and on his guard, must have known perfectly well that Blake was in the inner room all the time, and had taken the wrong packages merely as a blind and an excuse to move out of Blake's line of sight. This successfully achieved, to glide swiftly along the near wall, slam the door to, and lock it, was mere child's play.

Meanwhile, Blake continued to hammer frantically, haunted by a terribly vivid mental picture of Hume making his way swiftly over the roofs with the plans.

It must have been quite half an hour before he succeeded in making Jarvis hear. He would have taken a chair and smashed the heavy plate-glass window but for the fear of involving Sir Richard; and even after making the old man hear, there was a further maddening delay owing to something having gone wrong with the outer lock, another delicate piece of attention on Hume's part.

He got free at last, however, and dashing down the stairs, was lucky enough to secure a belated cab. He drove straight to Bathurst's and roused him without ceremony, telling him briefly exactly what had occurred.

"But, great Scott, man, you must be wrong!" said Bathurst. "I was told only yesterday afternoon that he had been laid up for a fortnight or more."

"So was I," answered Blake grimly, "and, like a fool, I believed it, as he meant I should.

Meanwhile, we've got just one chance—a fighting chance—and it is this: Hume, as we know, always works by himself, and trusts no one. It is now past four in the morning. We can safely assume, therefore that he won't be able to take any definite steps for the disposal of the plans till, say, after breakfast-time, however anxious he may be to do so. We must take no more risks, though. I want you to get off at once and keep a watch on his place in case of accidents. I will be round about half-past eight."

True to his word, Blake turned up on the stroke of the half hour. Bathurst met him some fifty yards down the street, and signified that

there was nothing to report, and together they turned back to the house. Blake's ring was promptly answered by the manservant.

"Beggin' your pardon, sir, Mr. Hume is—" began the man.

"Exactly so," said Blake, and, sweeping him aside for Bathurst to deal with, he ran upstairs.

Breakfast was already laid on the table, and for an invalid Marston Hume seemed to be doing himself uncommonly well.

As Blake burst into the room, Hume was carefully adjusting his first buttonhole of the day, and studying the effect in the glass over the mantelpiece.

Quick as thought Blake turned his revolver hand slightly. There was a shattering explosion and a tinkle of glass as the bullet ploughed its way through the camera. "Curse you!" cried Hume, "you shall pay for that dearly."

He turned round with an expression of ill-concealed annoyance.

"You here?" he said curtly, staring through his eyeglass. "I told my man I specially did not want to be disturbed this morning."

"Tired after your last night's excursion?" asked Blake grimly.

"My last night's— Oh, no, no; not in the least, thanks! I quite enjoyed myself. Beastly pokey little holes, though, some of those smaller rooms, especially if you happen to be kept waiting about in them, eh?"

Blake bit his lip and said nothing. He was looking about him on all sides for a likely hiding-place for the plans.

Hume took a step forward from the mantel-piece.

"Don't let me detain you, Mr. Blake. You may go," he said.

Blake leant forward across the breakfast-table. He had just caught a glimpse of a corner of pale blue translucent paper protruding from the folds of the newspaper. He knew where the plans were at last. Hume had evidently been studying them, and had only just had time to conceal them as he entered.

"I will go," he said, "but I will take these with me, please." At the same instant he made a snatch for the papers.

He was quick, but Hume was nearer, and a shade the quicker, for he tore the papers away, leaving only a small fragment in Blake's grasp, and sprang back to the fireplace.

In an instant he found himself staring straight down the barrel of Blake's revolver.

"Put those back on the table or I fire," said Blake quietly.

Hume held the papers behind his back with one hand, with the other he straightened his buttonhole.

"You must see, my dear Blake, that your request is absurd," he said slowly. "You know that I have the plans, and, of course, I know; but if I once allowed them to pass into your pos-session, then everyone would know—a quite impossible situation. On the whole I think that this is the simplest solution."

Very deliberately, and with his eyes fixed steadily on Blake's revolver all the while, he dropped the plans into the heart of the fire and drove them home with his boot-heel.

"I thought you wouldn't be able to bring yourself up to the shooting point," he said pleasantly, nodding at the revolver.

Blake eyed him steadily and curiously. Hume had unflinchingly destroyed all proofs against himself, but incidentally he had destroyed papers worth to him many thousands of pounds, and that was not like Hume.

Ever since he had been in the room Blake had been vaguely conscious of a curious stale smell, which puzzled him. He let his eyes wander from Hume to different objects in the room, and suddenly he started, for the whole trick had become clear. On the corner of the writing-table there were a few powdery white flakes, and in a dark corner beyond the curtains stood a half-plate camera with a changing box attached.

The smell was of burnt magnesium ribbon. Hume, as a precautionary measure, had spent the small hours of the morning photographing the plans. The destruction of the originals was therefore a mere ruse.

Quick as thought Blake turned his revolver hand slightly. There was a spurt of flame, a shattering explosion, and a tinkle of glass as the bullet ploughed its way through lens and plates, completely wrecking the machine.

Hume, who saw Blake's intention too late, gave a hoarse cry of rage and leapt forward.

"Curse you!" he said furiously. "Curse you, you meddlesome idiot! You shall pay dearly for that one of these days soon!"

Blake smiled grimly.

"Till just now I fancied it was I who had a score against you. I think we will call this deal 'Quits,' Mr. Hume. Good-morning."

LISS—GENTLEMAN CROOK!

THE UNION JACK

THE BOUNDARY RAIDERS
FEATURING SEXTON BLAKE DETECTIVE

No. 554. NEW SERIES]   May 23rd, 1914,   [EVERY THURSDAY

The Boundary Raiders

Introducing SEXTON BLAKE and
The Hon. JOHN LAWLISS
—Gentleman Adventurer.

THE FIRST CHAPTER

THE EVE OF A TREMENDOUS ENTERPRISE

At nine-thirty on the twenty-third of April two men were seated in the library of a quiet house in Gardney Square, Mayfair. The taller man of the two, a lithe, muscular giant, had drawn his chair up to a small table, on which were spread out a number of important documents.

They were maps and plans, and a compass and a foot-rule, and from the scribblings on a sheet of paper close to the map it was evident that some calculations had been going on.

There was a certain air of distinction about the taller man. He was young, not much more than twenty-five of twenty-six. His face was that of a Greek god—clean-cut and intelligent. A pair of steel-blue eyes looked out from under the firm brown, and the chin and lips were strongly moulded.

The dark, clustering curls were gathered on his forehead, which was tanned, and the small ears and shapely neck stamped him as an aristocrat.

He was the Honourable John Lawliss, and the house was that of his mother, Countess Warlowe,

The man opposite him was of quite a different type. He was small, lean, and virile. His face bore traces of fever, and was tanned to a deep mahogany shade. His hands as they rested on the table were also burnt black, suggesting much exposure to hot suns.

They were evidently very much absorbed in their conver-

The Hon. John Lawliss disguised
as Sir Godfrey.

May 23rd, 1914.

sation, for their cigars, placed in the tray on the table, had been allowed to go out.

"I have accepted your every statement, Mavering," said the Honourable John Lawliss.

He had a very clear voice, and there was a strong, vibrating tone in it which hinted at great mental determination and a purpose behind the clean-shaven face.

"And, as you know, I am going to take the risk."

"That's just the point I want to be clear on, Lawliss," Mavering returned. "You know I came to you a week ago, and told you what had happened out there in distant Tatua. I came to you because—well, you had fagged for me at Eton, and I knew you then to be a dare-devil chap. I have been away from Europe for ten years, and have lost sight of most of my friends. When I came back to London, hardly anyone recognized me, and I found that my story was only pooh-poohed when I told it."

The broad-shouldered giant leaned back in his chair, and nodded his head.

"That's quite likely," he returned. "You forget that London is a very humdrum place, and a story such as yours borders on the romantic. We are a matter-of-fact people here."

"Oh, and there are exceptions," said Mavering, "and you yourself are one of them. You are the only man who listened to me, who believed my story about this great theft that Britain suffered."

"Yes, I believed you," said the Honourable John Lawliss, "and you will have proofs of that by to-morrow morning."

"You really mean to do it?"

The well-shaped lips of the younger man slipped back in a smile.

"I do," he returned. "It's just the sort of enterprise that appeals to me."

He arose to his feet, and stretched his supple body. "You know, Mavering," Lawliss went on, "I ought to have been born two hundred years ago; this commonplace world of ours has no room in it for me. I want to be doing things. All my ancestors were of the freebooter type. It was an Admiral Lawliss, you remember, who sacked the great cities along the Pacific slopes in the old, bloodthirsty days. Well, I am a descendant of that man, and the freebooting spirit is in my blood."

He leaned forward, his eyes shining, his whole attitude suggesting turbulent strength and power.

"I am going to see this thing through," said John Lawliss, "I suppose to the world it will be a crime."

"There is no doubt about that," said Mavering hastily, "and that's why I think that you are rather foolish. After all, you know, I simply told you about the affair. It was not I who suggested how it should be rectified."

The Honourable John Lawliss laughed.

"That's quite true," he returned. "I will not put any of the blame on you, Mavering. The whole of the enterprise is on my shoulders, and I will carry it out."

He began to gather the maps and plans together, folding them into a neat bundle.

"And you are quite prepared for your journey?" Mavering asked.

The Honourable John Lawliss nodded.

"Yes," he returned. "Sambo, my valet, is even at this moment packing my kit. I travel very light, you know, as a free-lancer should."

"He is a fine fellow, that Sambo of yours," said Mavering. "I suppose you are taking him with you?"

The Honourable John Lawliss nodded his head.

"Rather!" he returned. "He's black, but he's comely. I wouldn't part with him for all the gold in the world. He has been my valet now for five years, and he is more than a valet to me—he is a staunch companion. I picked him up first in Central Africa; he was one of a party of Masai hunters who followed my hunting-party. He has

been with me ever since, and civilization has not quite tamed him yet."

"He will be jolly useful to you in Tatua," said Mavering earnestly. "You will want a stout companion out there."

Lawliss glanced at his watch.

"It's ten o'clock now, old chap," he said, "and the first part of my task begins about midnight. I am afraid you will have to go."

Mavering arose to his feet, and held out a lean hand.

"I hate to leave you, Lawliss," he said, "but, as you say, this thing must be carried out by one man."

"I certainly would not drag you into it, old chap," Lawliss returned. "You see, to-night is really one of the most crucial moments of the whole affair, if I carry this through successfully, I will take it as a good augury for the rest of the trip. But if I fail"—here the broad shoulders were shrugged—"well, you will probably read of me as figuring in a Bow Street case to-morrow morning!"

"I sincerely hope that I won't read that," said Mavering.

They shook hands, these two men who had spent their boyhood together in the great school; then the Honourable John Lawliss saw his guest out of the study, and waved good-bye to him from the front door of the quiet house.

When he closed the door behind his companion, Lawliss turned and stood for a moment in thought. He was on the eve of a tremendous enterprise, it was only to be the first on many similar, but he realized that a new path was opening in front of him.

"I suppose that what I am about to do is almost criminal," he decided. "In the eyes of the world, my act to-night brands me as a felon. Well, what does it matter? I am sick of dallying about London, of going off on meaningless big-game shooting expeditions. I have always hungered to see life, to meet things face to face. My opportunity has come at last, and I will not turn away from it!"

His jaw set up in a grim line, and he returned to the study to pick up the folded papers, and slip them into his pocket. He switched the light out as he left the room, then, passing up the stairs, entered his own bed-room.

There were signs of packing in the chamber, for a couple of big canvas bags stood in the centre of the floor, and the bulging sides testified to them being well filled.

The Honourable John Lawliss pressed a bell close to the bedside, and a few moments later there entered the compartment a thick-set black man. He was dressed in blue serge, and his clothes were well cut.

"Got everything ready, Pete?"

"Yes, sah!"

Pete has laboriously acquired English, but his efforts to subdue the "ahs" of that language had been a failure, just as so many others of his race find it.

"And you have done everything else that I told you?"

"Yes, sah. De car will be round here at eleben o'clock, and Thomson knows what to do."

"Good!"

Lawliss strode across to the servant, and put his hand on Pete's shoulder.

"We are in for a real hot time to-night, Pete," he said. "It's going to be a bit different to your old hunting games. You're not afraid?"

The shining black eyes of the man gleamed as they looked at the handsome face.

"I ain't afraid ob anything so long as I am wid you, baas," said Pete.

"And I can say ditto to that, Pete," Lawliss returned. "Now, where are those things I brought this afternoon?"

Pete crossed the room and, opening a drawer in the wardrobe, he produced a parcel. The parcel was opened on the bed and revealed the fact that it contained two long dominoes—black cloaks which enveloped the wearer from head to foot—and also two masks.

The masks were of the large fringing type that covers the whole face, allowing only a portion of the lower jaw to be visible. There were slits in them through which the wearer could see, and, with a grin, the valet lifted one of the masks and held it in front of his broad countenance.

Lawliss glanced at his servant, and smiled.

"You look blacker than ever, Pete," he said. "It is certainly a splendid disguise so far as you are concerned. Anyone might think that the featured behind that mask were white."

"I think I am going to scare someone with dis on," said Pete.

A small leather suit-case was then produced, and the dominoes and masks slipped into it. Then the packing was completed and the last

strap was fastened. Pete helped his master to change his attire.

It was a blue reefer suit that he Honourable John Lawliss dressed himself in, and the silver buttons on the jacket were those of a famous yachting club. He slipped into a heavy cloak, and thrust his yachting cap into one of the pockets. When the cloak was buttoned, and an ordinary soft hat pulled on his head, no one could have guessed at the garb that lay beneath the coat.

"Thomson ought to have the car round by now, Pete," the broad-shouldered man said, glancing at his watch. "You had better go and see."

Pete slipped off, and returned presently with the news that the car was at the door. The black servant swung one of the heavy bags on to his shoulder. The ease and grace with which he preformed this task told of the tremendous strength in the dusky frame, and went off down the stairs with his burden.

Lawliss stepped to the door, and followed his valet with his eyes. As Pete turned the corner of the stairs, the rustle if a dress came to his master's ears. Lawliss tried to step back, but he was too late.

A slender figure in black appeared at the foot of the stairs and beckoned to him.

"Jack!"

The young man's brows contracted for a moment, then he stepped out of the room.

"All right, mother, I'm coming."

He was now to face the hardest ordeal of all. He went down the stairs slowly. His mother had already stepped back into her quiet boudoir; she was standing beside the fireplace, her arm resting on the mantelshelf, her head supported by her slender hand.

Beneath the subdued light her silvered hair and thin, fragile figure made a touching, pathetic figure. The tall young man hurried forward and wrapped his arms around the slender woman.

"I wish you would not worry, mother," he said, in a voice that shook slightly. "I am all right."

The woman turned to him, and put one of her arms around his neck.

"Of course, you are all right, my dear son," she returned. "But you see, I am a mother, and must worry about you. We foolish women have always to worry about someone. You are so big and strong you cannot realise what the word worry means."

He stooped to kiss her. Reckless, dare-devil though he was, there was one person in the world whom this man, who was born centuries after his time, did love, and that was his mother.

"I am a brute, dear," he said, "but I cannot help it. There is something in my blood that makes it impossible for me to remain at home; and, besides, I have been with you for a whole year this time, haven't I?"

The mother smiled.

"Yes, you have been with me a whole year, that is quite true. And I know what a sacrifice it has been to you. Why, my dear boy, I have seen you fighting against it. You have been wanting to get away heaps and heaps of times, but it was only your love for me that kept you in check. It is I who am unkind to you, but I cannot help it."

She ran her hands through the thick, clustering curls, and drew his head down and kissed it.

"You see, dear," the mother went on, "you are all that I have left, and you are so like your father. He was just as mad, and brave, and reckless as you are, and I loved him very dearly."

"Dear old dad!" said Jack Lawliss. "I am sorry that I never saw him. He must have been a real man."

"He was," said the mother, "and that is what makes me so content even when you go away. For you are so like your father."

"Yes, but he did things," said Jack Lawliss; "he had a better chance than I have. He lost his life away out in the Arctic wastes, searching for the Pole; but he did leave a name behind him, mother, and Lawliss's trail is still the track that other explorers follow in that great white waste. I have done nothing like that; there is no chance for me to do anything."

"And where are you going now?"

She saw the hesitancy in face. It was the first time that she had asked him that question, although it had been hovering on her lips for days.

The Honourable John Lawliss could not lie, it was beyond him; yet he dared not to tell his mother the truth.

"I cannot tell you, mother," he said; "it is a different expedition to any that I have ever undertaken before. I will let you know all about it when I come back."

"Is it dangerous?"

Again the wide blue eyes avoided hers.

"A little! Only just as dangerous as these expeditions always are."

"And you cannot even tell me what part of the world?"

"No."

She gave a gentle sigh.

"All right, my son," the mother returned. "I know that I can trust you. But, oh; be careful of yourself!"

Her thin arms tightened around him, and she strained him to her for a moment.

"You are all that I have," she went on, "although I don't suppose you will remember that. You are just a big boy, always facing danger for the love of it. But, oh, if you don't come back to me, you will break my heart!"

The Honourable Jack's arms went around the slender frame, and he held it tight for a moment, while he stooped and kissed the upturned face.

"Dear old mother," he said, "I wish I were not such a wild rascal. I'd love to be able to stay here at home with you always. But it's not in me to do that; there is the call of the wild in me, and I must go, or I believe I would die."

He was glad to get out of that room, and he halted outside on the threshold to draw a deep breath, much as a man might do who had some through a terrible ordeal.

Those partings had always been difficult, and this one, knowing what he was going to face, was the most difficult of all.

"Dear old mother," he thought, "it would break her heart if she knew what I was going to do. She is so honest and upright, and to think that her son was contemplating something that is almost criminal would terrify her."

The creak of the stairs behind him warned him that Pete was descending again. The servant had the second bag on his shoulder, and he was carrying the leather suit-case in his hand.

The sight of that case brought the Honourable Jack Lawliss's thought round on another track, and when Pete had passed him he went on down the stairs following the servant.

A big closed limousine stood at the door of the quiet house. The boxes were already placed in the roof, and Thomson, the driver, was strapping them into their places.

Lawliss stepped into the vehicle, and Pete slipped into the seat beside the driver.

"You know where to go, I suppose?" said the valet.

"Morberry Chambers, first turnin' off Dalvery Street, St. James's?" said the driver.

Pete leaned back in his seat.

"Dat's right," he returned. Only you hab to got to stop in de courtyard behind de chambers, and you ain't got to see nothing dat happens dere!"

"I'll be as blind as a bat," was Thomson's reply.

THE SECOND CHAPTER

WHAT HAPPENED AT MORBERRY CHAMBERS

"Good-night, Sir Godfrey, and bon voyage!"

A tall man in evening dress had just alighted from a taxi, and he turned and held out his hand to the man who had spoken.

"Good-night, old chap," Sir Godfrey Haverleigh said, "and thanks very much for the lift."

The taxi moved on, and the baronet, crossing the pavement, entered the dimly-lighted hall of Morberry Chambers. He passed up the stairs to the first floor, and let himself into his flat.

As he entered the study he switched on the light and glanced at the clock. It was exactly twenty minutes to twelve. There was a calendar under the clock, and the baronet smiled as he looked at it.

"The twenty-third of April," he said. "Well, I'll leave you as you are. It will be a long time before I require to use you again!"

There was a certain triumphant look in the man's face, and he dropped into a chair and drew out a cigar case, lighting a weed.

"It is the last night in my bachelor chambers for three years at the least," he muttered. "I wonder how this appointment of mine will turn out; Governor of Tatua! It sounds quite good, and I was certainly surprised to be appointed."

He leaned back in his chair and stroked his short, crisp beard.

He was by no means an uninteresting person to look at, and there was a certain virile strength in his face which suggested that he was used to command.

"The Colonial Office has a strange way of doing things," Sir Godfrey thought, "but I hardly think that they have ever made an appointment with such secrecy as they have made mine, I wonder what is the matter with Tatua, and why they should send me over there empowered to take over the office from General Rudolph Mantley? Perhaps it is as well for me that I am armed with all necessary papers, or Mantley might cut up rough about the matter, and refuse to acknowledge me as his successor."

He heard the sound of a key in the door of his flat, and turned his head. A dapper man entered, and bowed. It was Perkins, Sir Godfrey's valet, and he was carrying a heavy travelling coat.

"Got everything ready, Perkins?"

"Yes, Sir Godfrey," the man returned.

"We make an early start in the morning," the baronet went on. "I suppose you have settled up everything here?"

"Everything," Perkins replied. "I paid the bill to-night."

"And the heavy baggage?"

"Has gone to Marseilles to be called for," said the valet.

Sir Godfrey nodded his head.

"That's good!" he said. "I won't keep you any longer to-night, Perkins. Only be sure and turn up early to-morrow. You are my only travelling companion this time, and we have a long journey to undertake."

He pointed towards the sideboard.

"Have a drink," he said, "and I'll also have one. Brandy-and-soda."

The valet deftly poured out the drinks, and his master accepted a glass.

"Here's luck to us, Perkins!" he said, and the two men drank.

A few moments later Perkins, after glancing into the bedroom to see that all was right, walked down the passage and let himself out through the door.

Sir Godfrey heard the click of the door as it closed behind the servant, then the baronet sank into his chair again.

On the dark landing outside Perkins stretched out his hand to feel for the banister that ran down the stairs. As he did so he heard a swift breath beside him. He turned, but before he could make a movement there descended on him a heavy muffling cloak, and a strong knee was pressed in his back, and he was dragged down on the floor of the landing.

Before Perkins could move, a heavy cloak was thrown over his head and a knee was pressed in his back.

dinary ease, worming his way past the door without making a sound.

A puff of blue smoke came up from the man seated in the chair, and hung for a moment in the air. Nearer and nearer the figure moved, and at last it was close enough to the chair to raise itself on its feet.

Silently though the movement was performed, it did not quite escape notice. Sir Godfrey sensed the presence of that black-robed figure, and with a bound he was on his feet.

He had a vision of a tall figure in a mask and domino, and a white, firm chin beneath the fringe. A pair of luminous eyes were staring at him between the slits in the mask.

"Who the de—"

The baronet never completed his remark. With a spring the figure was on him. Sir Godfrey swung back a pace, aiming a blow at the man as he came. But the baronet's foot caught against a cushion, and as he reeled backwards the intruder was on him.

The men went down on the floor together, and for a moment a fierce fight took place. Sir Godfrey was by no means a weakling, but the figure in the black robe seemed to be endowed with more than ordinary strength.

A powerful hand, in which a wad lay hidden in the palm, was thrust suddenly out and settled on the baronet's lips and nostrils.

Realising what was about to happen, Sir Godfrey struggled desperately, but the grip of the fingers was relentless in its strength and at last the struggling man had to draw breath.

The strong narcotic did its work swiftly, and a second later the baronet lay a limp mass on the floor. With a quick movement the figure in the cloak was on its feet and, darting across the room, he reached the open door in the flat.

"All right, Pete, go on; I'll follow you."

Shuffling footfalls came to his ears, and he turned and stepped back down the passage, to re-emerge a moment later bearing the limp body of the baronet in his arms. Passing down the staircase he turned along the hall.

The valet, taken by surprise though he was, began to struggle. But mighty arms were round his body, and beneath their grip he was absolutely powerless. A moist wad came beneath the folds of the cloak, and dropped over his mouth and nostrils.

A convulsive movement ran through the fellow's body, then his head fell limply, and his limbs relaxed.

"The keys, Pete!"

It was a whisper in the darkness, and a second later a faint jangle sounded. The tall figure in a black domino stepped up to the door from whence Perkins emerged, and with a hand that was as steady as a rock thrust the key into the lock and began to turn it.

There was no noise, and the door opened presently, allowing the tall, dark-robed figure to enter. The light from the study sent a shaft across the passage, and, moving stealthily onward, the figure in the black cloak dropped on its hands and knees.

Through the crack of the door the intruder was able to see the chair, and the back of Sir Godfrey's head as it leaned against it.

The tall figure in the domino went prone, and then, inch by inch, began to creep into the room. For a man of his size, he moved with extraor-

Nearer and nearer the figure moved, and at last it was close enough to the chair to raise itself on its feet.

It was towards the back door that he made his way, a back door which gave access to a small courtyard.

Crossing this he emerged into a narrow lane, where a big limousine blocked the way. The door of the limousine was open, and the tall figure on the domino thrust his burden into a pair of arms outstretched to receive it. "I'll be back in a moment. Wait!"

Hurrying across the courtyard, the tall man darted up the stairs again and entered the flat. He made his way into the bed-room, where he found two bulky valises. He glanced around the room, and crossing over to the bed, disarranged the sheets and blankets, thrust a big fist into the centre of the pillow just at the spot where a man's head might have rested.

A suit of pyjamas had been left lying on one side of the bed, and these the tall man thrust into his pocket.

Darting across to the dressing-table next, he hastily gathered together a few toilet articles— razor, shaving-brush, strop, etc.

"Bath-room next," was his comment, as he hurried out of the bed-room.

In the bath-room he turned on the water first, then, taking a piece of soap, made a hasty lather and smeared it round the edges of the bath. A towel was next drawn from its rack and dipped into the bath, and then wrung out, to be thrown on the floor. "That look realistic enough," the man muttered; "I think I have seen to everything, and can leave it now."

As he passed the study, however, he paused to glance into it for a moment, the cushion which had tripped up Sir Godfrey Haverleigh had been upset, and stepping into the room, the man replaced it in position beside the chair.

"I think that will do," he muttered, as he turned away and extinguished the light.

He had worked speedily and well, carrying out his various tasks with a thoroughness which suggested a cool, clever brain.

From the bed-room he carried out the two valises, then, with the flat in darkness, he pulled the door behind him, and went down the staircase again.

His arrival at the limousine was received by a deep sigh of relief from the man in the interior.

"Straight ahead now, baas?" came the question, as the tall man dropped into his seat.

"Yes, Pete. Straight ahead."

The second figure whipped into its seat beside the driver and, at a whisper, the limousine moved off.

And so, speedily and well, the first act of a moving drama had been carried out.

The car was a 40-h.p. Demon, and one of the most modern type. It swung down Whitehall, across Westminster Bridge, and went roaring up Kennington Park Road, heading for distant Brighton.

It was the best part of sixty miles from the place where it had started to the famous seaside resort, and proof of the speed at which the car moved lay in the fact that it was only a few minutes past one o'clock when it took the last

rise, and came to a halt for a moment on the London Road.

Ahead of it glimmered the lights of Brighton, and the road on which it had come to a halt was lined with electric-car standards. But at that time of the morning the clanging vehicles no longer pled for hire and the road was deserted.

"This is about the place, baas?"

The figure beside the driver had dropped into the roadway, and he addressed his remark to the individual inside.

"Yes, this will do, Pete."

From beneath the driver's seat a long stick was produced, and to it was attached a thick tube of stout paper. The stick was then carried across the road to where a small circular railing guarded a young tree.

In this circle the stick was placed, then its bearer, striking a match, held the flame to the bottom of the tubular package for a second.

It was at a half run that he returned across the road, and he leaped into the vehicle at once.

"I suppose you have changed the numbers?" a voice from the interior asked.

"Oh, yes, sah! That was done while you went back to the flat the second time."

"All right, then go ahead."

The car moved off up the wide road, and went on into Brighton. It had just vanished below the rise when, suddenly, from the little enclosed railing there came a roar, and up into the air shot a streak of yellow fire.

A policeman, pacing calmly along a side-street, heard that hissing report, and saw the golden shower of sparks as they fell from the rushing rocket.

The constable tilted his head and watched the rocket as it soared. It was ovidently a powerful affair, for it climbed high into the heavens before it burst.

And, when it did burst, there came out from it a green ball of fire, which hung in the soft night air, casting an emerald tinge over the world beneath.

"I wonder what jackass let that off?" was the constable's comment. "Maybe he was practising for the fifth of November."

He paced along his beat again and turned into the main road, half expecting to see the belated individual who had been responsible for the rocket's flight. But the roadway was quite deserted and, after scratching his chin for a moment, the constable returned and resumed his duty.

Very few people had noted the green light, and certainly only one solitary individual knew what it meant.

About two miles from Brighton the long, slender shape of a private yacht was riding. On the bridge a sturdy figure had been pacing to and fro. He had gone up there at midnight, and had been watching the heights above the town.

He saw that green light flash like a wandering star for a moment in the quiet heavens, and reaching out, he touched a bell, and there came to his ears the dim clang of the gong in the engine-room.

The propeller began to turn, and the yacht, wheeling slowly, came moving shoreward.

It had no lights showing, and its progress was a cautious one. It took up a position between the two piers, and with noiseless rapidity there dropped from its side a little electric launch.

It was the man who had steered the yacht that too charge of the launch, and he headed for the shore. As he drew nearer he was able to make out the line of bathing-machines that dotted the beach, and he headed for the left-hand side of them.

Above the bathing machines he could see the lighted promenade, and presently there came slowly along the wide front a big car.

It halted at the end of the line of machines, and there emerged from it two figures. The man in the launch sent his little craft forward until its nose touched the beach, then he leapt ashore.

He was a bluff, sunburnt individual, bearded and thick-shouldered. He turned his head to right and left, eyeing the wide front. There was no one in sight, and presently the scrunching of feet on the beach told him that the men he was expecting had come.

"That you, Darrel?"

"Yes, sir."

A tall figure came out from the darkness. He was bearing a burden on his shoulder, and the man addressed as Darrel, stepping back into the launch, received the burden and deposited it carefully in the thwarts.

Behind the tall figure came a shorter one, who was also carrying something. The objects were wrapped in long, black coverings, but Darrel seemed to find it difficult to handle them, for there was a certain limpness about the burdens which made their transferring a difficult matter.

"Now the luggage!"

Again the two figures vanished, and this time there were three returned, bearing a quantity of boxes and straps.

Two of the new-comers stepped on board the launch, and the third man took his cap off.

"Good-bye, Thomson!"

"Good-bye, sir, and good-luck!"

"Thanks."

The figure on the beach turned and slipped back to where the car was waiting. He took his seat behind the steering-wheel, and the big vehicle began to move.

It formed a circle, then swung back along the promenade towards the London Road. But before it reached there the car came to a halt for a moment, and the driver, leaning out, looked seaward.

The darkness of the night baffled him, but presently, far from the shore, he saw a white light gleam for a moment. It shone and vanished here times.

Thomson leaned back in his seat, and the car glided forward again.

"That's the last I'll see of the guv'ner for a bit," was the man's comment. "I wonder what his game is, and what her ladyship will say if ever she learns the truth?"

Thomson little dreamed that just about that moment the stately lady to whom he was referring was already making a momentous discovery.

The Duchess of Warlowe had listened to her son as he left the house, and had watched the car glide away, then, passing into her own bed-room, she had spent an hour in the quietness there.

She loved the tall, reckless boy with the hungry passion that only a widowed mother knows. To her boy represented all that was good in life for her.

"I wonder what is taking him away this time?" she thought. "I know there is some mystery behind it; he has always been so open before. Elephant hunting or pearl-diving, he has always told me. But this time I am sure there is a secret somewhere."

About one o'clock in the morning she left her room and, hardly knowing what she was doing, made her way to her son's study. It was in its usual disorder. The desk was covered with papers, and on one of the tables lay a half-emptied briar pipe, while tobacco ash was everywhere.

The indulgent woman smiled as she looked around the room.

"Always careless," she said, "and yet I would not have him any other way."

She crossed to the desk and glanced at its disorder. Scraps of paper, torn envelopes, incitation cards lay in a confused heap, and from one of the pigeon-holes a leather-bound diary was projecting. The mother stretched out her hand and withdrew it.

It was one of her son's hunting diaries, and was well filled. She turned the leaves over until she came close to the end, and noted then that several new entries had been scrawled. The entries continued right to the end of the book, and it was obvious that her son had found the space insufficient for him, for he had evidently discarded the notebook and had got another one.

But the notes, brief and uncompleted though they were, attracted the mother's attention, and she began to read.

At first she hardly realized their import. They were simply scrawled paragraphs. Here and there the name "Mavering" was mentioned, and also that of "Tatua." There was also mention of boundaries and certain geographical observations, but as she read on the notes became more clear, and the last one, longer and more detailed than the others, made the woman drop into a chair suddenly, while over her face a veil of growing horror spread.

"Jack! Jack! Can it be possible? Oh, no, I won't believe it!"

She read the longer note again slowly, and her doubts vanished,

"That was why he left to-night so abruptly. He has gone to do this thing—he must have done it by now. Oh, my boy, my boy!"

The notebook fell from her fingers and, leaning back in the chair, the aged woman covered her face with her hands.

"What have you done? What have you done?" the anguished mother murmured.

THE THIRD CHAPTER

SEXTON BLAKE VISITS THE COLONIAL OFFICE

"Mr. Ramford McLaren's compliments, and he will be glad if Mr. Sexton Blake will be kind enough to call at the Colonial Office at twelve noon on April 30th."

"That means to-day, guv'nor," said Tinker.

He and Blake had been spending a few days in the country, and had only just returned to the chambers in Baker Street. The usual assortment of correspondence had been awaiting them, and the important letter from the Colonial Office was amongst them.

"I wonder what he wants with me?" Blake said. "I don't know of anything unusual happening lately."

"Bound to be something, guv'nor," the lad returned. "Those government officials are usually high-falutin and are not likely to trouble us unless they want to make use of us."

His master smiled.

"Seems to me you haven't got a very good opinion of the average Government official, Tinker," Blake returned. "Still, I think you are about right. Mr. McLaren, however, is quite a decent sort, and I don't mind keeping the appointment."

"Any objection to me coming with you?"

"I don't think so," the detective said. "You might as well come."

They had just time to change from their country clothes to a more suitable attire for town. Then the detective and his assistant strolled into the busy, sun-lighted street, and made their way towards the Colonial Office on foot.

Now and again a policeman would raise his hand and exchange a salute with the detective, but for the greater part of the journey they passed unobserved through the throngs of people.

London never takes much interest in its inhabitants, and the keen-eyed, clever-faced detective, with his alert, dapper assistant, was allowed to pass quietly along.

When they reached the Colonial Office, however, the door-keeper recognised them at once. Blake and his assistant were led up the wide staircase and into a cosily-furnished wait-ing-room.

A few minutes later a well-dressed clerk entered the room and conducted them into the presence of the great man himself.

Ramford McLaren, the Colonial Secretary, was a man of about forty. He was just the average, well-groomed politician, slightly bald, and with a certain air of nervousness which gave him the appearance of a man always perplexed.

"Good-morning, Mr. Blake," McLaren said, holding out his hand. "Up to time, as usual. It's very good of you to come."

He glanced for a moment at Blake's compan-ion, and the detective introduced him.

"I thought I would bring Tinker along with me, Mr. McLaren," Blake said. "He is my assist-ant, and although I don't know what you require of me, I thought that it might be advisable to have him with me."

"Pleased to meet you Mr. Tinker," said McLaren, with a quick, kindly smile.

He indicated a chair close to the desk, and Blake dropped into it, while Tinker, crossing to the other side of the room, seated himself on the settee.

McLaren, after fumbling with a bundle of papers on his desk, glanced at Blake.

"As a matter of fact, Mr. Blake," he said, "I really dint' know that I shall require you at all, and your visit here has been brought about by me alone, and much against the wishes of my colleagues."

"What has happened?" asked Blake.

"Nothing," said the Colonial Secretary, with a slight shrug of his shoulders; "that's the trouble."

He withdrew a slip of paper and, adjusting his eyeglass, which had been dangling on a black cord, spoke again.

"The affair is just a personal matter," he said. "On the twenty-second of this month my depart-ment agreed to a certain thing. We appointed a man as successor to another man in a rather good position. The new man was told of the appoint-ment, and was asked when he could proceed to take it over. His reply was that he was ready to go at that moment, and, finally, it was arranged that he should leave London on the morning of the twenty-fourth. All the necessary papers were handed to him, and myself and two other men intimately connected with the affair, dined with

the man on the evening of the twenty-third. I, personally, saw him to the door of his chambers and bade him good-night there."

"Yes, go on!"

"Well, that's all," said McLaren, rather sheep-ishly. "We knew he was going to start early on the following morning, and, just to make sure that he had done so, I telephoned to the porter in charge of the chambers and received the reply that Sir Godfrey Haverleigh had gone."

He tapped on the desk with a gold pencil-case for a moment.

"Of course, it is only a week ago," said McLaren. "I told Sir Godfrey that his movements had to be secret. As a matter of fact, I might as well tell you that he was going to supersede the Governor of Tatua. Now Tatua, as you know, is part of a big island that lies north of Australia. It is partly German and partly British, and even by the fastest steamer it would take Sir Godfrey the better part of five weeks to reach it."

"And what do you fear?"

"I don't know," said the Colonial Secretary. "I must say that I rather expected to receive a telegram of some sort, say from Marseilles, of some place like that. But, after all, Sir Godfrey is quite capable of looking after himself, and no doubt he might think it is best to keep his move-ments entirely secret."

The Colonial Secretary rose to his feet and stretched himself.

"It may be rather foolish of me," he went on, "but I have had an uncomfortable feeling about the matter. Even a Colonial Secretary you know, Mr. Blake, has his human feelings, and somehow or other I have a foreboding that this matter has gone wrong. Three days ago I received a curious postcard. Perhaps you would like to read it?"

He pulled out a drawer in the desk and pro-duced a card. It was an ordinary yellow type, as issued by the Government at any post-office. It was simply addressed to the Colonial Secretary, and the message was a very brief one—"Watch Tatua!"

The words were scrawled in big type along the back of the card. Blake noted that the postmark was "W." and that the card had been posted about midnight.

"Not a very big clue," said McLaren, with a laugh, "and yet, combined with the curious doubts I have had on the subject, it urged me to write to you. I telephoned to the porter at

Morberry Chambers , and he told me that Sir Godfrey Haverleigh's flat was just as he left it. For, by some oversight, the baronet's valet had taken away the key with him. As a rule, the valet left the key on a hook in the porter's office, but that morning, when the porter came on duty, there was no key there, so the flat has been un-touched."

"There is nothing very extraordinary about that," said Blake. "No doubt the early-morn-ing move made the servant forget that small matter."

"Quite so," said McLaren. "Only I think—well, if you had an hour to spare, Mr. Blake, you might go up to that flat and just have a look around."

He nodded towards the clean-shave, alert-eyed man.

"If there is anything doubtful about the affair I feel quite sure that you will find it out," he added. "There would be no good of a man such as myself going there, but I rely much on your keen observation. Just look round and let me know what you think. Will you do that for me?"

"With pleasure," said the detective.

McLaren turned to the telephone.

"I will ring up the porter now and advise him that you will be coming round. I think that my word will be sufficient authority to allow you to gain admittance to the flat."

"It might be better to communicate with the agents," said Blake. "There is just a chance of them having a spare key."

It was a good suggestion, and McLaren acted on it, and before Blake and his assistant left the Colonial Office the detective was assured that a messenger from the agents would be waiting for him at Morberry Chambers with a number of keys.

Blake and Tinker made their way to the quiet chambers and found the messenger, a pert-looking youngster, awaiting them. The boy had a big bunch of keys with him, and, after trying several, Blake found one which opened the door of Sir Godfrey's flat, and the two men entered.

It was curious to see the change that came over the detective as soon as he entered the flat. His luminous eyes darkened slightly, and his whole air became more eager and energetic.

"The flat has certainly not been occupied for at least a week," was his comment to Tinker, "You will note there is a thick film of dust on the hall-stand, and, see, a spider has been working!"

He pointed to a silver strand that hung across from wall to wall of the passage.

Tinker nodded.

"If anyone had come along here lately they would have broken that," he returned,

Blake broke the strand and went on down the hall. It was the study he entered first. The blind was still down, and he went across to the window and pulled it up, allowing the pale, spring sun-shine to flood the room. It was stuffy, and the rank fumes of cigar smoke still clung in the at-mosphere.

On the sideboard, dust-covered, stood two glasses, each with a little liquid left in the bottom of them.

The chair and footstool next attracted Blake's attention. Then, suddenly, his keen eye caught sight of something a little distance from the chair.

He took a quick pace across the room and knelt down on the soft carpet. It was a heap of tobacco leaves, crushed and broken, that lay on the carpet, the fragments of a cigar, and as Blake brushed away the stuff carefully he noted that there was a round, black mark on the carpet where the red end of the cigar had burnt a hole.

A few inched away from the cigar was another stain, and despite the fact that it was black and discoloured, Blake scraped a little up with his thumb-nail and placed it on the back of his hand.

Moistening his finger-tip, he rubbed it on the coagulated heap. A tinge of red appeared.

"Blood!" he said.

Tinker stood aside and watched his master with breathless interest. Blake's jaw was set and tight.

"I am afraid that Mr. McLaren's fears were not altogether unjustified," he said, in a grim tone. "Still, we will make quite sure first."

He pointed towards the heap of tobacco leaves.

"It must have been almost a whole cigar that," he said, "and no man would deliberately throw a lighted cigar on the carpet and crush it into a heap unless he was drunk or mad m and I don't think Sir Godfrey Haverleigh is likely to have been either of these two things."

"Then you think—"

"I think that there has been a struggle here, Tinker, and that cigar was probably in its smoker's hand when it was thrown to the ground."

Tinker looked round the room. The young assistant was cute enough, but the place, to him, seemed absolutely void of any sort of clue whatever. It had just that note of dusty orderliness which a deserted compartment would contain.

Blake smiled at the perplexity on his assistants face.

"You are not quite convinced, I see," the great detective said quietly. "All right; perhaps you will be convinced before we leave, Tinker."

He went across to the door of the study and examined the walls and woodwork carefully. A fragment of some black material wedged in the jamb of the door caught his eye. He withdrew it and held it up.

It was of some shining, black stuff, and the tight way in which it had been wedged in the crack of the woodwork indicated that some considerable force had been used.

"That's not the material of a man's attire," said Blake. "It's too light and shining for that. If it was a woman, what brought her into the flat? And certainly no woman could have thrown Sir Godfrey Haverleigh so heavily as to crush the cigar."

He stood for a moment, his brows drawn together in thought, then, dismissing the subject for a moment, he placed the scrap into his pocket and went on into the passage.

There was a door on the left, and he opened it and entered, to find himself in the bath-room. Here again, the blind was down, and he lifted it. Tinker, in the doorway, watched his master closely.

Blake was like a hound on the scent now. He knelt down and examined the floor, lifted the towel carefully and examined it, bent over the bath. The soapsuds had dried, and a movement of his finger scattered the dustlike residue.

There was a grim smile on his face as he straightened up.

"Very Clever," he said—"but not quite clever enough."

He glanced at his assistant.

"We are on the eve of a big mystery here, old man," said Blake. "There has been a deliberate attempt to conceal some sort of crime in this flat."

He pointed into the bath.

"This has been prepared carefully," he went on. "A man is supposed to have bathed himself here, yet there is no sign of any sort of dirt, and even the cleanest and healthiest of man must leave some trace behind him. Note: I rubbed the soap away from the side of the bath, but the place is quite clean and spotless! Had a man washed there, he is bound to have left some trace behind him."

"Yes, I see that, guv'nor."

Blake pointed to the floor.

"Then, again," he said, "there are no footprints. If Sir Godfrey had used his bath that morning, he would certainly have stepped out here to dry himself, and the marks of his feet would have been left. It is not likely that he would have cleaned up the bath-room after him, and it is also obvious that the valet did not perform this ceremony, or he would have lifted the towel and have left the place in order. A wet foot always leaves an imprint behind, and yet you see the floor is quite spotless, except for the dust."

"Yes, guv'nor, that is quite true."

The tall man in the domino had prepared his plans carefully enough, but he had not reckoned on them being searched by such a clear, clever brain as that of the famous detective.

From the bath-room Sexton Blake passed into the bed-room, and again his trained eye picked out the deceptions.

"This is even more crude than the other," he said. "That bed has not been slept on, despite the attempt of someone to make it appear so. He has ruffled the blankets and the top sheet, but he has omitted to make any impression on the bed itself. No, Tinker; whatever has happened it certainly is obvious that Sir Godfrey Haverleigh did not sleep in this flat on the night of April 25th."

Tinker was silent. Blake, with his arms crossed, paced up and down the room for a moment.

There were hundreds of theories that the detective could have built up, but Blake was not of that type of detective who jumped to conclusions. His way was to take a careful scrutiny and preserve an open mind.

He had established the fact to his own satisfaction that Sir Godfrey Haverleigh was either the victim of some trick, or had deliberately set himself the task of deceiving anyone who might have entered the flat after him.

The second conjecture, however, Blake quickly dismissed.

There was no earthly reason why Sir Godfrey should do that. He was on the eve of taking over a very important appointment, on which was, according to Mr. McLaren's own statement, an entirely unexpected one. There was no object in his vanishing, if he had vanished.

He made a careful search of the flat, but there was no other clue left behind indicating what had happened to the baronet.

Blake made his way down the stairs, and found the porter in his little office. A few questions elicited the information from the porter that Sir Godfrey Haverleigh had made it clear to everyone that he was leaving Morberry Chambers on April 24th.

"Perkins and I had a final drink together about nine o'clock, sir," the porter said. "He was a pretty close man was Perkins, and he wouldn't tell me where they were bound for. But I know it was fairly long journey, for he said he mightn't be back for a year or so. I hope there is nothing wrong?"

"I am not quite sure of that," said Blake, "but, of course, you will not be blamed for anything that has happened. You are quite sure that no one has entered that flat since the twenty-third?"

"I'll take my oath on that, sir," said the porter earnestly. "I'm on duty here almost all the time. Of course, I never used to go into the flat when Sir Godfrey was there; Perkins used to do all the work. But I promised Perkins before he went that I would see the place cleared up for him after they had gone, and he said he'd leave the key on the hook. I cannot understand why he didn't do it, for he was a methodical sort of person was Perkins."

He seemed aggrieved at this omission on the valet's part, and Blake smiled at the look on the man's face.

"Perhaps Perkins found it impossible to leave the key," the detective suggested.

"That might be so," said the porter. "But somehow or other I feel that he thought better of it. Couldn't trust me, like. I know there's wine and spirits and cigars there, but I'm an honest man and I wouldn't have touched a thing."

This was evidently a sore point so far as the porter was concerned.

"Oh, I don't think Perkins thought of that!" Blake went on. "You and he were rather good friends, weren't you?"

"Well, I did a lot for him on time or another," said the porter. "You see, they sent the heavy luggage on ahead to Marseilles—"

"What's that?"

"Two or three days before Sir Godfrey left, Perkins and I took a lot of heavy baggage down to Charing Cross. They were booked through to Marseilles, and had to be called for there."

It was quite an unexpected clue, but the majority of great cases often hinge on the chance word of a man.

"That's a rather good piece of information," said Blake. "I might be able to make use of it."

He and Tinker left Morberry Chambers and the detective headed at once for the Colonial Office, while Tinker went off to Baker Street.

When Blake entered his chambers again, the first thing he did was to cross the study and glance out of the window. Tinker, who had been sitting in a chair by the fireside, came forward at a signal from his master.

"Don't go in front of the curtains, Tinker," Blake said quietly. "I want you to look on the opposite side of the street."

Tinker followed his master's nod, and saw a shabby individual staring into the shop window on the pavement opposite.

The fellow seemed very interested in the contents of the window, but, after watching for two or three minutes, Tinker saw him turn round and cast a glance in their direction.

Blake drew back, with a quiet smile.

"I thought as much," he said. "That man saw you and I leave Morberry Chambers. He followed me down to the Colonial Office, and waited until I came out, then he followed me here."

Tinker smiled.

"That's rather quaint, isn't it, guv'nor?" he said. "It is not usual for a detective to follow a detective."

"I doubt if that individual knows who I am," Blake said slowly. "He certainly has no idea that I know he followed me. He is only a beginner at the game, however, and I soon tumbled to his ruse."

He thrust his hands into his pockets, and from the shelter of the curtain watched the shabby-looking man.

"There is something behind all of this," said Blake, "and I am going to find out just who that fellow is and what he is doing."

He turned to Tinker.

"It's not a very fair trick that I am going to carry out, but all's fair in matters of this kind. Have you any idea who is the sergeant on duty now in Baker Street?"

"I think it's Waldridge," said Tinker.

"Good! He's all right. I know he will do what I want him to do."

"What's the idea, guv'nor?"

Blake turned and strode across the study with Tinker at his heels. The detective entered his bed-room, and opening a cupboard, searched for a moment. It was a long, black overcoat that he produced at last, and crossing to the dressing table. He pulled out some of the drawers.

There were a number of beards and disguises of various kinds in the drawer, and in a few moments Blake had made himself up to represent a middle-aged individual.

He took a grey felt hat from the wardrobe and set it at rather a jaunty angle on his head, then with a gold-headed cane and a pair of light gloves, his preparations were complete.

"I am going to get out by the back way, Tinker," he said. "And I want you to follow me. Go and find Sergeant Waldridge, and tell him to come down to our street at once. I'll wait until I see you coming and as soon as you appear I'll grab that fellow and charge him with being a pickpocket."

Tinker grinned all over his alert face.

"I say, guv'nor, that's a bit thick!"

Blake smiled.

"We'll find out who and what that man is by it, anyhow," the detective returned.

Tinker slipped off, and succeeded in finding the police sergeant. A few words with Waldridge put him on the qui vive at once, and he turned and accompanied the youngster along Baker Street towards the scene of the little comedy.

They halted at the corner for a moment and Tinker glanced across at the shop. The man was still standing there, and a moment later Blake, in his disguise, came down the pavement, and halted to look in at the same window where the shabby individual was standing. He brushed against the man slightly, turned, stared indignantly at him, then, with a quick grab, caught the fellow by the shoulder.

"You—you confounded rascal!" cried Blake.

He had even changed his voice, and it was now a thick, angry one, and the way he shook the shabby fellow seemed to indicate that he was in a towering rage.

The man backed away from him, but could not release the grip of the strong fingers.

"Let me go! What have I done?"

"What have you done? Confound you, I'll show you what you've done! Police!"

Blake looked round and pretended to catch sight of the sergeant. He held up his gold-mounted stick and signaled to Waldridge.

The sergeant's face was as grave as a church-warden's as he crossed the street with ponderous tread.

"What's the matter here?" he asked.

Blake, in a furious rage, shook his fist at the face of his prisoner.

"This fellow is a thief and a pickpocket!" he roared. "I felt him trying to steal my watch!"

"It's a lie—it's a lie!" the man broke out, starting away. "You must be mad!"

The sergeant took a pace forward and caught the shabby individual by the arm.

"Mad or otherwise, a charge is a charge, my good fellow," he said. "And if this gentleman charges you with theft you will have to come with me."

Abject terror was written on the face of the man.

"Oh, no, no! It is impossible! Let me go! I can't come with you! I assure you it's a mistake! I—I am no thief!"

The sergeant tightened his grip on the arm.

"Then you can soon prove that," he said. "Come with me to the station."

"No, no! I can't go there! I dare not go to the station! I tell you it's a mistake!"

Sexton Blake felt sorry for the man, whose agony was fairly obvious, but the detective had a duty to perform, ad he hardened his heart.

If the man was innocent of any sinister motive, it would be easy to explain, and afterwards let him go.

"I assure you he's a dangerous ruffian, sergeant," Blake said in his assumed tones. "Don't let him go. I'll come to the station with you."

A taxi-cab chanced to come along at that moment, and it was signaled to, and a few moments later Blake and the sergeant and the cowering spy were seated together in the little vehicle.

As the taxi moved off the man's distress became absolutely pitiful. His lips trembled and he sweat poured down his face.

"I tell you it's a mistake!" he broke out. "I daren't go to the station!"

He looked appealingly at the sergeant.

"I can prove to you that I am a respectable man," he went on.

Waldridge gave an inquiring glance at Blake, and the detective nodded his head.

"If you can prove that, you had better do so. Who are you?" asked the sergeant.

"I—I am a butler. My name is James Drage. I—I am in service in London, and my mistress if the Duchess of Warlowe."

Blake leaned forward.

"A butler?" he said. "What do you mean by being dressed like that? More like a scarecrow than a butler!"

The man turned his head towards Blake.

"I don't know that it is against the law to dress shabby if one likes," he said in a surly tone. "Anyhow, you have made a mistake this time, sir, and if you like to drive to 17, Gardney Square, and ask about me you will find it's the truth."

Blake glanced at the sergeant again and nodded his head.

But there were reasons why the detective himself should not accompany the men, so he leaned out if the window and told the driver to halt for a moment.

"I leave this matter entirely in your hands, sergeant," he said. "If you think this fellow is as respectable as he says, then, of course, a mistake has been made, and you can let him go. But I advise you to see the lady who he says is his mistress, and find out all about him. I shall call at the police station later on and hear your report."

"Very good, sir," the sergeant returned, touching his helmet; and Blake, alighting from the vehicle, gave the driver the new address, and watched the taxi as it drove off.

The whole episode had not taken very long, but it had not carried Blake very far. He was convinced that the disguised butler had followed him from Morberry Chambers, but he had no idea why he should have done so.

"I'll get Waldridge's report when he comes back," Blake decided. "I must admit that it rather beats me. Why should a respectable butler take it into his head to follow me about London?"

He had heard of the Duchess of Warlowe, and knew her to be a woman of wide charity. Her very name on the shabby individual's lips had made an impression both on Blake and the police sergeant.

"If this man is working in the duchess's interests," Blake thought, "what on earth can it be for? Why should she be interested in visitors to Morberry Chambers?"

The thought perplexed him, and he walked back to Baker Street slowly.

It seemed to him that the case, that had appeared to him so simple at first, was now rapidly developing into a mystery worthy of his best efforts.

"My first duty is to find out what has happened to Sir Godfrey," he decided. "Unfortunately it would be no use calling to Tatua, because Sir Godfrey is not due to arrive there for at least five weeks. And, besides, I don't suppose McLaren would agree to that unless he was absolutely certain that foul play had taken place. For, by cabling to Tatua asking for information concerning Sir Godfrey Haverleigh, it would publish to the world the fact that the baronet was going out there as the new governor, and it is fairly evident from the Colonial Secretary's manner that that is just what he doesn't wish to reveal at the moment."

This phase of the business also rather perplexed Blake.

"Why should the Colonial Secretary be so averse to making this information public? It could only be something of vital importance that should make him hold his peace."

"The case grows on me." Said Blake, his stern chin tightening. "I'll get to the bottom of it, or know the reason why."

THE FOURTH
CHAPTER

AT MARSEILLES—THE YACHT MARGA

"The Duchess of Warlowe's action is certainly very strange," said the Colonial Secretary; "but I don't think I should worry about it if I were you, Blake. I think you are right when you say that your best plan is to go to Marseilles and make inquires about the heavy luggage. If it has been called for, then we may reassure ourselves, for it will mean that Sir Godfrey Haverleigh has been there and taked the heavy baggage away with him."

It was the morning following Blake's visit to Morberry Chambers, and the detective had just made his report to McLaren.

Sergeant Waldridge's account of his reception at the quiet house in Gardney Square had been rather an amazing one. The duchess had appeared terrified at first when she had caught sight of her servant with the police sergeant; but a moment later she had recovered her composure, and the official's inquiries had been met by an instant admission.

The butler had dressed himself in that shabby attire at the request of his mistress, and, although the duchess refused to reveal what the object of that curious proceeding was, there could be no doubt but what the servant had been doing was obeying orders.

"I have made a few inquiries about the Duchess of Warlowe," said Blake. "Of course, we all know her as a fine, benevolent woman. She has a son—the Honourable John Lawliss."

"Yes, yes," the Colonial Secretary interjected, "I have met him. He has played cricket at Lords several times. A fine, tall fellow, and a great athlete."

"But he is not in town now," Blake went on.

He was looking at McLaren quietly, and the Colonial Secretary returned his glance.

"That is nothing strange for Lawliss," he said. "He is a little bit of an adventurer in his way, just as his father was before him. He is always off big-game shooting somewhere or other, and I don't blame him, either. It's a much more healthy life for a young man to lead than knocking about town always."

Blake leaned forward.

"I find that he was in town on April 23rd," he said; "but since that date no one has seen him."

The Colonial Secretary leaned back in his chair and stared at the detective. The coincidence of the dates could not be set aside.

"Oh, but that's nonsense!" McLaren went on presently, "Lawliss is quite a fine fellow, and his mother fairly dotes on him. I am quite sure that he has nothing to do with Sir Godfrey's affair—if there is any affair."

"That's just the point," said Blake. "I find in cases of this kind it's the unexpected that usually happens, anyhow, I thought I'd let you know, for I intend to make for Marseilles. Only while I am away it might be worth your while to try and find out where this Honourable John Lawliss is. Of course, his absence might have quite an innocent explanation; but the fact of his mother being so keenly interested on Morberry Chambers, coupled with the fact that her servant followed me, first to here, then to my rooms in Baker Street, makes it appear to me that somehow or other there is a connection between the two. I may be mistaken, of course. But that is the assumption I have reached."

"Very well, Blake, I will do what I can," said McLaren. "As a matter of fact, I have been invited to attend a dinner to-morrow night, at which there is little doubt but what the duchess will appear. I will make it possible to meet her and have a few words with her."

"Good!" said Blake, rising to his feet. "If any developments should happen which it might be worth my while to know, you might send me a telegram. Just make it Poste Restante, Marseilles."

"I take it that you are travelling to Calais, and then by train?"

"Yes," the detective returned. "It's the quicker way."

The Secretary nodded his head.

"Of course," he went on, "our office stands all expenses. That is the only condition that I'll allow you to go on with this matter." He smiled. "After all," he added, "we might be only alarming ourselves for nothing. Even the fact that you found Sir Godfrey Haverleigh did not sleep in his flat that night does not prove anything. He may have arranged all these little things himself."

Blake was thoughtful for a moment.

"That's quite true," he returned; "but I hardly think he would go to the trouble of crushing a cigar into a heap, and leaving a stain of blood behind him that is pushing realism a little too far, Mr. McLaren."

"Yes, quite so," McLaren agreed.

He held out his hand.

"Well, I wish you bon voyage, Blake, and I feel sure that if there is anything to be found you will find it."

Blake and Tinker started for Calais by the afternoon boat-train, and began their long run through France late that evening. They went via Paris, carrying out that quick change from one station to another that the speeding traveler has to effect.

When they reached Marseilles, Blake, who knew the old seaport town very well, went at once to the place where luggage is kept for the ocean traveler, and began to make his inquiries.

The polite official in charge of the department, as soon as he knew the name of the famous questioner, became interested.

"The baggage has gone, monsieur," he said. "It was called for one—two—three days ago."

It was now May 3rd, and that meant that Sir Godfrey Haverleigh's baggage had been collected on the first.

"You are sure of the date?" Blake asked.

"Absolutely certain," the official returned. "As a matter of fact, I happened to be on duty at the time. It was at an unusual hour that they were called for. You see the Australian mail-boat left here on April 26th, and we rather thought here that that was the boat Sir Godfrey Haverleigh would catch. Of course, it was no business of ours, only we like to take an interest in the happenings of our department."

"Quite so," said Blake. "Then you say it was not a mail day when the luggage was collected?"

"No."

"Can you remember who it was who took the luggage away?"

"I would recognise one of them again, for he was coal black," said the official.

The man glanced at Blake.

"Of course, we had no idea that anything was wrong. All the vouchers were in order and correct, so we were obliged to give up the baggage."

"Yes, that's quite all right," said Blake. "There is no blame attached to you."

Another mystery had been added to the queer affair; for, if Sir Godfrey had left London on the twenty-fourth he ought to have reached Marseilles by the twenty-sixth at least, and in good time to catch the Australian mail. The fact of the baggage not being collected until the first made a big gap in the time, a gap which was hard to explain.

From the baggage department Blake went down to the world-famous quay of Marseilles, and continues his inquiries there.

For a long time he was unsuccessful, and at last he discovered one of the quay hands who remembered seeing a hand-trolley arrive with heavy baggage close to one of the flights of steps. The man remembered the incident chiefly on account of the fact that one of the men accompanying the trolley was black.

The man's report was certainly a brief one. He had witnessed the placing of the luggage on board a small boat, which had been rowed out to a grey-painted yacht. But there had been several yachts in Marseilles at the time, and he was hardly able to say which one it was.

The harbour-master, however, the individual to whom Blake next applied, was able to give the detective the names of every steam-yacht that had called there, and Blake, armed with the list of names, went to a telegraph office.

It was to Ramford McLaren, the Colonial Secretary, that he sent the following message:

"Can you inform me if any of the following yachts belong to Sir Godfrey Haverleigh or friends—Siren, Medivea, Sarsdale, Weatherly, Marga?"

He and Tinker then sought an hotel, and passed away the ensuing two or three hours.

It was late when the reply to his telegram came, but the answer brought a quick smile to Blake's lips.

"The yacht Marga is the property of the Duchess of Warlowe."

"Then that settles it," said Blake. "Rich or poor, I don't know what you are, John Lawliss, but you have got a hand in this strange affair."

The reader is aware that now, thanks to the modern system of exchanging information throughout the world, a vessel can be traced across the globe with unerring accuracy.

Within the next twenty-four hours Blake was able to locate the probable whereabouts of the yacht Marga. It had passed through the Suez Canal and was heading east.

The detective had to wait another couple of days before he could get a liner bound in that direction, and the yacht had had a long start.

"It's a long chase we are in for, Tinker," Blake said when, on the evening of the second day, he and his assistant stood on the boat deck of the big liner and watched the lights of Marseilles gradually die away in the distance; "but I think it's going to be a jolly interesting one. Even now we have nothing definite to go upon. After all, Sir Godfrey Haverleigh has the right to choose his own method of proceeding to Tatua, and there is just the possibility of his being a passenger on board the Marga. So, you see, this cruise of ours will be an eminently unofficial one, and I have really no authority to act."

He laughed quietly to himself.

"But there's one thing," he added, "and that is that those on board the Marga will hardly know that I am following them, and that is in our favour."

But, in that assumption, the great detective was mistaken. Blake had done all that was humanly possible to keep his movements secret, but he had a great force to reckon with.

Mother's love is perhaps one of the strongest passions in the world, and the detective little dreamed that within ten paces from him, seated quietly in a deck-chair, was the silver-haired mother of reckless John Lawliss.

It was only the strength of the passion for her son that had made that fragile woman hazard the journey.

She was dressed now in the quiet, sober garb of a nurse, and it was as Nurse Marsh that she had booked her passage on the liner, joining the ship at Marseilles just as Blake had done.

Nor did Blake know that when the yacht Marga touched at Port Said, a telegram was handed to the tall owner of it.

There was only one simple word on the telegram, "Beware," but it proved that the mother's love was strong and true.

There were stirring times ahead for Blake and his assistant, and the quiet woman sitting behind them, pretending to be interested in her book, was to play no small part in it.

THE FIFTH CHAPTER
A QUESTION OF BLUFF

Jallastown, the capital of the British portion of the great island of Tatua, lies at the entrance of a bay. Around the bay are wooded slopes, which rise steadily upwards to the great misty mountain.

Jallastown itself was a straggling collection of huts, built with that glorious irresponsibility that the native invariably adopts.

A stone jetty, of which the white inhabitants are inordinately proud, makes a convenient landing-place to the little capital, and on the level ground a little way from the jetty are a number of more pretentious buildings.

The white inhabitants of that town number in all about two hundred souls, and are mostly Government officials. There are perhaps, roughly, about a dozen fairly-well-built houses, the rest being native huts, and those corrugated-roofed bungalows which the white man finds the most convenient form of habitation.

In the centre of the town a square had been formed, and round this square the various Government buildings are grouped. The post-office, the hospital, the barracks for the police; and last, but not least, the Residency, the permanent abode of the Governor.

Jallastown takes itself very seriously, for it is the seat of Government.

The Colony consists of something like a million souls. It is quite true that the greater part of the population is black—fuzzy-headed, and very, very black.

The native of Tatua, in the not very remote past, was distinctly cannibal, and it is part of the Governor's duty to see to it that the native does not drop into his old vicious habits again.

Close to the jetty is a moored a big whale-boat, the property of the Governor. There is a special crew of natives, twenty lusty blacks, who are fed and clothed out of the revenues for the sole purpose of seeing that his Excellency travels in a state befitting his rank.

On the jetty stands an iron support, on which is fixed a great oil-lamp. There is always a policeman on duty on the jetty, and one if his tasks is to attend to the big lamp. On a clear night one can see the beacon eight or nine miles out to sea.

In the dusk of a tropical night a slender, grey-painted yacht, moving slowly over the peaceful ocean, was turning in the direction of that light. On the bridge stood John Lawliss, and by his side was the broad-shouldered figure of the captain, while Pete, the black servant, stood on his master's left.

"That's the light on the jetty of Jallastown, sir," Darrel, the captain said.

Lawliss peered through the dusk at the yellow star glimmering in the distance.

"Yes; I think you are right," he returned. "That's the end of your journey and the beginning of mine."

The captain gave the wheel a turn.

"We've had a very uneventful voyage so far," he said, with a glance at the tall figure by his side; "but I don't suppose the rest of your journey will be quite so smooth."

Lawliss laughed.

"I am not so sure about that," he returned. "It's all a question of bluff. Anyhow, I've put my hand to the wheel, and I'm certainly not going to turn back now."

He reached out and touched a knob, and the bell in the engine-room sounded. The yacht began to move forward at a swifter pace.

"You know what to do, Darrel?" he went on, turning towards the captain. "You drop the longboat and put my traps on board. Pete and I will go ashore. You will remain in the bay until morning, then you will make for the Tse River, and wait for me there. Go up the river as far as you can, but be careful, for there are a lot of shoals and silt about the mouth."

The captain of the Marga nodded his head.

"And when do you expect to—to join me, sir?" he asked.

There was a touch of anxiety in his voice and his eyes, as they rested on the tall figure beside him—had a worried expression in them.

"Oh, I am not sure!" Lawliss returned. "It all depends. A week—fortnight—month. Anyhow, you have plenty of provisions, and you can lie up in some quiet creek. All you have to do is to take care that you passengers don't escape."

"Oh, I'll see to that!" said Darrel grimly.

"And, coming to think of it," Lawliss went on, "I might as well go down now and bid them au revoir."

He turned and sauntered away, while Pete grinned at the captain through the haze.

"Dere hab been heaps ob trubble in day cabin," he said. "I 'speck dey will be jolly glad to see the last ob the baas."

"I shouldn't be surprised, Pete," was the captain's rejoinder.

The Marga was a sea-going yacht, and was of comfortable dimensions. The cabin into which John Lawliss stepped was a wide, spacious one. A big table ran down the centre of it, and along the sides were ranged cushioned seats. In one corner of the cabin two men were seated, chatting together. The taller of the two, a bearded man, dressed in a quiet lounge suit, looked up as Lawliss entered.

"Good-evening, Sir Godfrey!" Lawliss said.

The man who had been appointed Governor of Tatua shot an angry glare at the owner of the yacht.

"The comedy still goes on, I see," Sir Godfrey said. "I should like to know when it is going to end?"

He arose to his feet and stretched himself.

"Of course, you understand you will pay for this," he went on—"pay very dearly, too. The law does not allow you or any other man to interfere with the liberty of the subject. You will cool your heels in a British prison for many a long year as the result of this affair!"

Lawliss shrugged his shoulders.

"That's one of the contingencies," he returned, "and I agree with you for the most part. But still, these things have to be done now and again."

"What I would like to know is your object!" Sir Godfrey said, in a heated tone. "Is it ransom? For if that is your intention I can assure you that you have hit on the wrong man. I am by no means rich, and I certainly have no wealthy relations who would pay a large sum for my liberation."

The Honourable John Lawliss swept his captive a bow.

"You undervalue yourself, Sir Godfrey," the young man returned. "I am sure you have heaps of friends who esteem your worth at a big figure. But it's not ransom, nor do I expect to make a single penny out of this expedition."

"Then in Heaven's name, what do you intend to do?"

The wide blue eyes of Lawliss took on that curious, dreamy stare which sometimes came to them. It altered the whole expression of his face, softening it, making him less of an adventurer than a dreamer.

"My object?" said Lawliss. "Well, I don't think I will tell you now. It is such a mad, foolish one you would probably laugh at me, and no man likes to be laughed at."

He swung himself onto the table and, leaning back on his hands, looked fixedly at Sir Godfrey Haverleigh.

"As a matter of fact," said Lawliss, "to-night my real enterprise work starts. I am going to leave you, perhaps for a week or a fortnight. But I have arranged that you will be well looked after. Your troubles will only start if you try to escape."

"But this is insufferable, unbearable!" the baronet cried hotly. "You forget that I have a duty to take up. I can't afford to idle my days away on board this confounded yacht of yours!"

He brought his fist down upon the table with a crash.

"We have been here now for the better part of five weeks," he went on, "and during that time you haven't revealed to me a single word of what your intentions are. You can't go on like this, man. Mad though you may be, there must be some method in your madness."

Lawliss laughed.

"I am not quite sure that there is," he returned, in a gay tone. "Anyhow, method or no method, I am afraid that I must keep this thing quiet. But when I return—if I do return—I promise you that all that is mysterious and perhaps stupid to you now will be revealed."

He looked at Sir Godfrey steadily.

"In fact," he added, "I should not be at all surprised if, when I do return and tell you my story, you find me less of an enemy than—well, shall we call it friend?"

"No, by heavens, I won't!" the baronet roared. "You have held me a prisoner here, and you shall pay for it. The law has a long arm and will reach you some day, and it will be my turn then!"

The old reckless look returned to Lawliss's eyes, and with a slight shrug of his shoulders he slipped from the table.

"Oh, very well," he said—"have it your own way!"

He nodded towards a door in the saloon.

"I shall be sending down a sailor during the next half hour," he continued, "and I want you to hand over one of your travelling-cases. That big canvas one will do—the one on which your name is painted."

"What so you want it for?"

The master of the yacht smiled.

"That's another question that I can't answer," he returned; "but I can assure you that when I come back your case shall be returned to you intact. I will hold myself responsible for the entire contents."

Sir Godfrey Haverleigh was not by any means a patient man, and the veins of his forehead swelled.

"But what if I refuse?" he returned. "Why should I hand you over my belongings?"

John Lawliss's mouth was set like a trap.

"Then I shall be under the painful necessity of taking it from you," he returned, in a grim tone. "I don't want to do that, but remember, I have the right of might."

"You young hound!" the baronet roared, taking a couple of paces forward.

Perkins, who was the other occupant of the room, started to his feet and caught his master by the arm.

"What's the good, sir?"

Lawliss strode towards the door of the saloon and turned.

"Perkins is right, Sir Godfrey," he said in a cynical tone—"what's the good? I doubt very much if you would get the better of me single-handed; and anyhow, you forget that I have the whole of the crew behind me. Discretion if the better part of valour. Now, shall I send the man down for your kit, or must I take it by force?"

Their eyes met across the saloon; then, smothering an angry exclamation, Sir Godfrey gave a slight nod of his head.

"You take it by force, anyhow, remember," he returned, "as you have taken my most precious belongings—that is, my passports and papers."

Lawliss bowed.

"That is so," he returned; "and they are also my most precious belongings. But they will be returned to you, together with your kit, in good time."

He left the saloon, and Sir Godfrey, after whispering a few moments with Perkins, entered the cabin that had been allotted to them during the long voyage.

About half an hour later one of the sailors of the Marga descended into the saloon and Sir Godfrey indicated one of the heavy canvas kitbags. The name of the new Governor had been painted on it in large, black letters, and the sailor, swinging the bag on to his shoulder, carried it across the saloon and mounted the companion way.

Sir Godfrey Haverleigh, when the sailor had gone off, crossed the saloon, and tried to follow the man; but, to the baronet's chagrin, he found that the door of the saloon had been locked, and he was virtually a prisoner. The portholes which ran along the side of the saloon had been hooded with iron shutters fastened from the outside, and there was no possible chance of the baronet discovering the position of the vessel.

On the deck overhead he heard hurrying feet moving to and fro, and presently there came to his ears the rattling clang of the anchor-chain. A moment later the reverberating thresh of the engine ceased, and the anchor-chain roared as it was carried down into the quiet sea.

Then the steady rise and fall of the vessel told Sir Godfrey that it had come to a rest.

"Where can we be?" the baronet muttered, as he stroked his beard. "What is at the bottom of this curious affair? I am sure tat fellow is no ordinary criminal. I wonder what he has in his mind?"

His bewilderment might have been increased had he been able to enter the cabin if the deck which the Honourable John Lawliss occupied.

The young adventurer had dressed himself in a suit of white linen; there were epaulets on the shoulders, and the buttons were gilt and bore the Royal coat-of-arms. Around his waist was buckled a brown belt, to which a sword was attached.

A pair of white, tight-fitting riding-breeches, high, polished boots, and a white pith helmet on his head completed the attire, and he was ready to play his part.

He had already made himself up so far as his features were concerned, and at a first glance there was certainly a marked resemblance between this man and Sir Godfrey Haverleigh.

A beard of exactly the same hue as the natural one of the baronet had been affixed to the strong chin, and the goldbeater-skin by which the false beard was attached could not be seen.

John Lawliss's hair was much the same colour as Sir Godfrey's, and they were also like each other in build.

"Now for the papers," the young adventurer muttered, as he turned to a small locker in the cabin.

It was Sir Godfrey's pocket-book that he withdrew, and there were also a number of thick, official envelopes. During the voyage, John Lawliss had carefully gone through these documents, and, so far as he was concerned, he knew as much about the task that Sir Godfrey had to undertake as the baronet himself.

A knock in the door brought the tall figure rounds, and Pete's shining countenance appeared.

"Everything ready, baas?"

"Yes, Pete. But remember that in future I am Sir Godfrey Haverleigh to you."

Pete nodded his head.

"I won't forget dat, Sir Godfrey," he returned.

Pete had also arrayed himself in white attire, and his black face shining above the spotless uniform, gave him a rather curious appearance.

With a final glance around his cabin, the Honourable John Lawliss strode out of it, closing the door behind him. He made his way along the narrow deck of the yacht to the taffrail, where a portion of the rails had been removed, the long-boat of the yacht was already rising and falling on the water, and Pete had placed he canvas kitbag in the thwarts.

The captain of the Marga came forward and saluted.

John Lawliss held out his hand.

"Good-bye, Darrel," he said. "Don't forget to wait for me in the Tse River."

"Good-by, sir," the captain said, "and good-luck. Look after yourself, won't you?"

The fine white teeth of the young adventurer glimmered in the light of the ship's lantern.

"Oh, I'll look after myself all right!" he returned.

A few moments later he had landed lightly in the stern of the longboat, and the two men at the oars dropped into their places, and the boat began to move towards the lighted shore.

As they drew nearer to the light they noted that a figure in khaki was standing beneath the beacon, and presently a guttural voice hailed them.

"Boat ahoy!"

It was a native voice, but the words were English, and Lawliss answered them.

"Ahoy!" he returned.

The boat was now close to the jetty, and the native policeman made a signal with his staff indicating the landing-stage.

The longboat from the Marga scraped against the steps, and Pete was the first to alight, holding the boat steady for his master to step ashore.

John Lawliss made a fine figure as he strode up the steps, and the policeman, awed, no doubt, by the uniform, raised his hand to a quick salute.

It was a good omen, and the young adventurer chuckled inwardly as he returned the salute.

"You are on duty here, I suppose?" he said.

"Yes, sah!"

"My name is Sir Godfrey Haverleigh, and I want you to take me to the Government House. My servant will require some assistance to bring our traps ashore."

Pete carried the kitbag, and deposited it on the jetty, then returned for several smaller articles of baggage, consisting chiefly of gun-cases and hunting kit, making a respectable pile.

When the disembarkation was completed, Lawliss turned to his servant.

"You will wait here until someone comes to assist you, Perkins," he said.

There was not a vestige of a smile on Pete's face.

"All right, Sir Godfrey," he replied.

But as the black policeman turned and led the way along the jetty, Lawliss striding behind him, Pete's small black eyes glimmered like diamonds. To the black fellow the whole thing was one huge joke, and Pete had every confidence in the nerve and power of his master.

"This is where de fun starts," he thought to himself.

The oars in the longboat rattled as the boat began to make its way back to the yacht. Here and there in the town a light glimmered, and Lawliss, pacing quietly along behind his guide, found himself presently in the straggling square.

A two-storeyed building on the left attracted his attention. He saw a wide verandah beneath which a number of lights hung, revealing the fact that chairs and tables were placed along the boards. His guide turned towards the building, and presently Lawliss found himself mounting a couple of steps and approaching a wide doorway at which another policeman was posted.

"This must be the Residency," the young adventurer thought.

The policeman on duty at the door stepped forward as the tall figure of Lawliss appeared beneath the light of the lamp.

"Give his Excellency my compliments," said Lawliss, "and tell him I would like to see him."

He slipped his hand into his pocket, and pulled out a card—one of Sir Godfrey Haverleigh's cards. The policeman at the doorway stood aside, and allowed the tall figure to enter the hall.

The Governor's house was by no means a pretentious building, but it was certainly the largest in Tatua. The hall was roomy enough, and the walls were ornamented by various heads of game. There were a number of chairs all round, but Lawliss preferred to stand.

It was as though he was on the battleground, and he wanted all his energies for the coming encounter.

The policeman was gone for five or six minutes, but when he returned there was a doubtful expression in the dusky face.

"His Excellency will see you, sir," he said. "Come this way, please."

He spoke fairly good English did this dusky native, and, as a matter of fact, the Tatuans are noted for the rapid way in which they adopt the tongue of the protectors.

Lawliss strode down the passage with the policeman ahead of him. The uniformed man knocked on the door, and opened it.

As soon as Lawliss entered the room the powerful odour of alcohol came to his nostrils. The place fairly reeked of brandy. It was a small study that he found himself in, and at a desk was seated a stout man.

The man was dressed in a faded dressing-gown, and Lawliss looked at the face for a moment. There were pouches beneath the eyes, the chin was unshaven, and the whole appearance of the features were those of an inveterate drunkard.

"General Mantley?" said Lawliss.

The figure in the dressing-gown looked up. A feeling of nausea passed over Lawliss, and the chin beneath the false beard tightened.

His Excellency the Governor was more than half drunk then!

A fat hand was holding the card, and the heavy eyes were peering at it.

"Sir Godfrey Haverleigh!" said the Governor of Tatua, in a thick tone. "I am pleased to see you. Won't you sit down?"

Lawliss had expected many methods of welcome, but this humdrum one was certainly hardly anticipated. As a matter of fact, the old Governor was almost too drunk to be capable of coherent speech.

With a swift movement Lawliss withdrew a blue envelope from his pocket, and took out a document it contained. He strode across the room, and placed it in front of the half-dazed figure.

"I have been appointed by the Colonial Office to supersede you, General Mantley," he said in a harsh tone. "And here's my authority!"

"Supersede! Supersede!"

The dazed brain caught at that word, and with a half-movement the man straightened himself up slightly. The hands which were stretched out to take the documents from Lawliss's fingers trembled violently.

General Mantley made an ineffectual attempt to unfold the document and read it, but it was evident that he was much too intoxicated to understand its purport.

"Perhaps we had better wait until morning," said Lawliss. "I suppose you can find me a room?"

"Oh, yes, yes, with pleasure! Delighted, I am sure! I'm not quite myself to-night. I—I don't feel very well. This beastly climate!"

Lawliss turned on his heel. That slobbering, apologetic figure aroused all his ire.

"To think that a drunken rascal like you should represent Britain here among these natives!" he thought. "It's enough to make them revolt, and to bring disgrace to our flag."

When he had first entered that Residency he had felt a twinge of conscience, for he knew that he was there under false colours, and was going to turn a man out of his job. But all that had vanished now, and he felt his strength was equal to the task before him.

"It is time that someone came here," he muttered to himself. "It wanted a strong hand, and by heavens, I think I am capable of it!"

The Governor touched a bell close to the desk, and a moment later a native in butler's livery appeared.

"Show this gentleman into the guest chamber," said his Excellency, "and make him comfortable."

"Good-night, Sir Godfrey," he said. "I—I will see you in the morning."

"Good-night," said Lawliss, as he followed the servant out of the room.

When the door closed behind him the young man stood for a moment, glad to breathe the clearer air. The reek if brandy and the disheveled, unshaven occupant of the room had almost sickened him.

The butler led the way down the corridor and entered a room. Striking a match he lit the oil-lamp, revealing the fact that it was a bed-chamber. The place looked clean and comfortable, and was a welcome change from the study he had just left.

Feeling that it was necessary to begin work immediately Lawliss turned to the butler.

"My name is Sir Godfrey Haverleigh," he said, "and I have come here to take over the office of Governor of this colony. Have you been in the Residency long?"

The butler's eyes searched the bearded face.

"Yessah. I a very old servant. Bin here two-three years now."

Lawliss nodded his head towards the door.

"And does his Excellency usually spend his evenings like that?"

The butler pretended not to understand, and Lawliss stepped forward, placing his hand on the man's shoulder.

"Listen to me!" he said sternly. "I know there is something wrong here, and I am going to change it. General Mantley is more than half drunk, and you know it."

"Yessah, yessah!"

"Is he always like that?"

It was not Lawliss's usual plan to pump the servants, but in this particular instance he felt it was necessary.

"Sit down," he said. "I want to chat with you."

In less than half an hour he had pumped the butler dry, and had proved beyond a shadow of a doubt that, for the past year or so, the Governor of Tatua had been little else than a drunken figurehead.

It was only the white population, the Government clerks and officials, that had stood by the witless man and had saved him from open disgrace.

There is always a loyalty about a Britisher which, good though it is as a rule, is sometimes the cause of the unworthy being kept in a high place.

Not a breath of the truth had escaped to England, for Tatua, after all, is only a small corner of the great British Empire.

"And he drinks brandy, does he?" said Lawliss. "Where does he get it from? Where are the stores? Show me!"

He insisted on following the butler through the rambling house, and presently they were standing together on a big store-room. The butler indicated a number of cases in one corner of the chamber.

"They came last Tuesday, sah," he said. "they came from Clarkestown by the coasting steamer."

Lawliss stepped up to one of the cases. They were all labeled, "To his Excellency the Governor of Tatua, Jallastown," but on turning one of the cases up and examining the steel band Lawliss made a discovery.

On one of the bands a name had been embossed. There was the manufacturer's sign, and beside it was the word "Berlin."

"From Germany," said Lawliss, his eyes gleaming. "I thought so."

His face was like a mask as he turned and left the store to make his way back to his bed-room.

When he entered the chamber he found that Pete had arrived and was engaged in opening the small kitbags. The new Governor's canvas bag stood by a chair untouched. Lawliss closed the door behind him and Pete looked up.

"So far so good, baas?" he said.

"So far so bad," Lawliss put in. "Things are worse here than I thought. I'll have to get to work at once. The man in charge here is a drunken fellow, and I see now how the trick was accomplished."

He drew his figure up to its full height.

"Think of it, Pete!" he said. "The British Empire has been swindled out of two or three hundred miles of territory, and the price that the swindlers paid was a few bottles of brandy!"

He began to stride up and down the room, a splendid figure in the light of the lamp.

"But we will have it back, Pete; if we have got to fight for it we'll have it back. And we'll start to-morrow."

THE SIXTH CHAPTER
SEXTON BLAKE IN TATUA

"That is Jallastown, sir."

Sexton Blake and Tinker, who were leaning over the taffrail of the little coasting steamer, followed the squat finger of the mate as he pointed towards the mouth of the bay.

The morning sun had risen, and the rays were dancing on the galvanised roofs of the bungalows in Jallastown.

"Not a very pretentious-looking place for the capital of a big country," Blake said with a smile.

The mate grinned.

"It will be bigger some day," he said. "After all, Tatua only started to be civilised about twelve years ago, and we find it is doing pretty well, too. Our cargoes keep increasing every year."

Blake had lost no time on his journey, the traveler to Tatua must be a patient individual, for there is no regular service, though it is stated in the official guide-books that the steamer Wampun carried out a weekly passage to and fro.

In this case, however, the Wampun, thanks to a broken propeller blade, had delayed Blake four or five days. Both Tinker and the great detective were genuinely glad to see the end of their journey in sight at last.

The Wampun passed through the narrow entrance to the bay and let the echoes loose with a shrill blast of the whistle.

It was certainly the most important vessel that ever entered that quiet harbour, and it was quite justified in letting everyone know that it had arrived.

Shriek after shriek from the siren went rolling and reverberating up the wood-clad slopes, and about two hundred yards from the shore the squat-nosed little steamer came to a halt, and the anchor-chains rattled down into the sandy bed.

From the shore there came hurrying out a small squadron of boats and crafts of all types. The various traders who had their headquarters at Jallastown were evidently anxious to possess themselves of their new stores, and presently the steamer was surrounded by a yelling line of natives each in their crazy craft.

Presently from the jetty a big whaleboat came, the rowers moving with clockwork regularity that spoke volumes for their trainer.

The man at the head of the whaleboat was a European, and the big craft made its way through the smaller fry and came to a halt beside the companion-way that had been let down the vessel's side.

The white man in the stern clambered up the steep stairs and returned the salute of the broad-shouldered skipper.

"How do you do, McTaggert?"

"Quite well, Captain Orme," the skipper returned.

One of the stewards came forward bearing a mailbag, and Captain Orme took charge of it. There were also a number of other bags containing mails, but this particular bag represented the Government matter, and Captain Orme was personally responsible for the post-office arrangements in Tatua.

"Any news?" McTaggert asked presently. "Oh, by the way, let me introduce you!"

Blake and Tinker had sauntered up by then, and the captain of the coasting steamer turned towards them.

"Mr. Blake, Captain Orme; Mr. Tinker, Captain Orme."

Blake like the look of Orme and the man shook hands.

"Mr. Blake is going to stay in Jallastown a day or two," said McTaggert.

"Indeed!" the postmaster-general of Tatua remarked. "What brought you to our part of the world?"

"Oh, just a little curiosity!" Blake laughed. "It's about the only part of the British Empire that I haven't seen."

"You'll find it a very interesting part," Captain Orme returned, "although rather uncultivated in places yet."

By this time the steam winch had started to wheeze and the holds had been opened.

"If you like," said Orme, "I'll take you ashore in the whaleboat. There's heaps of room for you both, and your traps can follow on later."

"That's very kind of you," Blake returned; "only too glad to accept your offer."

Orme glanced at the captain of the Wampun.

"I suppose you sill be coming along later, McTaggert?" he said. "You will have to come and make your bow."

McTaggert raised his eyebrows, and Orme continued:

"Don't you know we've got a new Governor?"

"A new Governor?" McTaggert repeated. "That's news."

Orme smiled.

"But he's not in Jallastown at present," he said. "He left yesterday with a small army of carriers. By Jove, but he's an energetic fellow, and I for one am jolly glad he has come!"

It was on the tip of his tongue to say more, but the presence of Blake made that impossible. Only the significant glance which passed between the captain of the Wampun and the bright, alert figure in white, was not lost on the detective."

"How does General Mantley take it?" McTaggert asked.

The eyes of the official gleamed.

"Not very well, I am afraid," he returned. "We haven't seen anything of him. The new fellow only came here a couple of days ago. He just held a small reception, shook hands with us all, and then, on the following day, that was yesterday, started off as I told you. He has evidently made up his mind to see the whole of his territory, and he has got a jolly long job on."

Blake took a pace forward.

"I suppose you are alluding to Sir Godfrey Haverleigh?" he said.

Captain Orme turned.

"Yes, that's right," he replied "Do you know him?"

"Not personally," said Blake.

Orme's eyes were keen as they searched the face of the detective.

"Then how do you know that he is Sir Godfrey Haverleigh?" he asked, shrewdly enough.

Blake smiled.

"I am afraid I cannot answer that question now, Captain Orme," he said. "Perhaps later I may be able to do so."

He and Tinker passed down into the companion-way towards the whaleboat that was rising and falling on the waters, and Orme leaned forward towards McTaggert.

"Who is that chap?" he asked.

"Don't know," the captain of the coaster returned. "Seems a jolly decent sort, and is evidently a big pot in his way. They were all mighty civil to the Clarkestown, and they stayed at the Residency there."

"Blake! Blake! I seem to know the name," Orme went on.

There was no time, however, to puzzle his brain then, so presently he left the vessel and dropped into his place in the stern of the whale-boat.

At a word from him the lusty black crew set their backs to the work, and the big boat moved swiftly shoreward's.

"The correct thing for you to do, of course, would be to call on the Governor at once," said Orme, "but he is not here and I am afraid his predecessor is inaccessible."

"Why is that?" Blake asked.

There was something about the detective's face that inspired confidence. Tinker dropped behind, and Orme took Blake's arm while they sauntered along the deck together.

"As a matter of fact, old chap," Orme said, "our Governor was anything but a strong man. He was given to having too many pegs, and that's very fatal in this country."

"I see," said Blake.

"The new Governor dropped in here quite unexpected late one night. None of us knew anything about it until the following morning. But ever since he appeared General Mantley has sulked in some dark corner of the Residency. It has hit him rather badly, I'm afraid."

He smiled, revealing a set of whit teeth.

"As a matter of fact," he went on, "rumour has it that he and the new Governor had no end of a row the first morning. Of course, one can't believe all servants chatter, but they do say that the new Governor waded into that drunken old fool with his fists. We all know that General Mantley is a hot-tempered beggar, and I expect he started the fight first. Anyhow, from all accounts he got more than he bargained form and I think the real reason he has kept out of sight is because there would be too many marks of the conflict on his face."

Blake raised his eyebrows. It was a strange story that he had listened to.

"Of course I suppose what you people do in Tatua is very much different to what happens in town," the detective said. "Certainly the idea if a new Governor taking over office by giving a sound thrashing to his predecessor is not the usual way, is it?"

"Oh, we do strange things in the colonies," said Orme. "You see we are just a primitive

country, and have got to take the rough with the smooth. Anyhow, all the staff here agree that the new Governor is a mighty advance on the old one."

"What is he like?"

"Oh, a tall fellow with a beard. He looks as keen as mustard."

A tall fellow with a beard was something answering to the description of Sir Godfrey Haverleigh. Blake began to feel that, perhaps. After all he had come on a fool's errand.

"I think you had better come along to my bungalow," said Orme. "I can give you a room there, and you will be better off with me than in the Government house with a sulky old man."

Blake was only too glad to accept the offer, and presently he found himself installed in a cool chamber, while Captain Orme's servant prepared a hasty meal.

Tinker did not put in an appearance until the meal was almost ready, and as he sat down to the table, he glanced towards his master.

"We are not the only people who are going to stay at Jallastown, guv'nor."

Blake looked up.

"Indeed! Who are the others?"

"That nurse," said Tinker. "I saw her disembark a few minutes ago."

Orme looked up.

"A nurse?" he said. "That's interesting. The white population here is increasing rapidly. I wonder who she is?"

Tinker shook his head.

"We don't know," he returned. "She kept to herself very much during the voyage."

"Is she young?"

Blake smiled.

"Oh, no, on the contrary," he returned. "She is rather old."

"By Jove, I forgot," said Orme. "It's perhaps Nurse Marsh. I remember now that the matron of the hospital said she was expecting another nurse to join her staff. It had all been arranged in London. The hospital here is really run by a Church Mission, and its headquarters are in London. They send out nurses now and again to relieve others."

"Not the sort of place that I would like to send women to," said Blake.

"Oh, it's not so bad," Orme returned, jealous of the name of his young country. "It's really more healthy than most people think. One has only to be a bit careful in the sun, that's all."

It was quite a substantial meal that Orme placed in front of his guests. Most of the stuff was tinned, but there were several fresh vegetables of an unknown variety, which Blake and Tinker found most enjoyable.

The meal came to an end with strong coffee, and Orme handed Blake a choice cigar which the detective thoroughly relished.

"I'll stroll you round afterwards," said Orme. "And introduce you to the rest of the whites. There are not many of us here. We have a sort of club that we all gather at after dinner. It breaks the monotony of the day, you know."

He leaned back, and puffed at his cigar.

"As a matter of fact," he went on, "I was just a little bit upset yesterday. I rather expected that the new Governor would have asked me to go with him on his round. But he seems an independent sort of chap, and has gone off alone. That is to say, he is the only white man in the party."

"Then he has left his servant behind him?" said Blake.

"Oh, no," the captain returned. "He has taken his servant with him. I think he calls him Perkins, isn't it?"

"Yes, that's right," said Blake.

"Queer sort of name for a black man, anyhow," said Orme with a smile.

Blake took the cigar from his lips, and leaned forward.

"A black man?" he repeated.

Orme nodded.

"Yes," he went on. "Our new Governor's valet is not a native of these parts. I should think he is from somewhere round the Congo." Tinker and his master exchanged glances.

"One moment, Captain Orme," Blake said, speaking very slowly and distinctly. "Do I understand you to say that Sir Godfrey Haverleigh's valet, Perkins, is black?"

"Of course he is," the postmaster-general returned.

Blake controlled his features, but the doubts that had almost died in his heart awakened with increased intensity then.

Just before he had left London, he had taken the precaution of examining photographs of Sir Godfrey Haverleigh and his valet. It was the hall-porter of Morberry Chambers who had supplied him with the photograph of the servant and, ugly though Perkins undoubtedly was, he was certainly not black.

"How did the new Governor arrive?" the detective asked.

"Came in a yacht," said Orme. "It sailed on the following morning, and only one or two of us had a look at it. It went off down the coast. I suppose he must be a big pot to have a private yacht of his own."

"Did he bring much luggage?"

"No, only a couple of kitbags. I believe his heavier stuff is coming by ordinary mail; in fact, I rather expect that it is on board the Wampun."

Blake could have enlightened him on the subject, for the baggage was certainly not on board the Wampun.

Later in the evening, several of the other white members of the town dropped in, and Blake had little time to spare, but about nine o'clock, pleading fatigue, he retired to his room, and presently Tinker joined him.

"What do you make of it, guv'nor?" was the youngster's first query.

"There are only two answers to that," Blake said. "Either Sir Godfrey Haverleigh has gone mad, or else his place has been taken by some usurper, and I am rather inclined to the latter theory."

"You think someone is bluffing them here, pretending to be Sir Godfrey Haverleigh?"

"That's it," Blake returned. "The whole case points to something of that type. We know that Sir Godfrey's heavy baggage was taken on board the yacht; we know that Perkins, the valet, is a white man. Why should this new Governor be in such a hurry to start away immediately after he has arrived here? I tell you, Tinker, there is something at the bottom of this, and what it is baffles me."

"Then if it was another person who appeared here as Sir Godfrey that means that the real baronet is still on board the yacht?"

"Perhaps, but we cannot be sure. That is the first thing that I am going to work on."

Blake stretched his arms above his head.

"I am convinced of one thing," he said. "And that is that the yacht is not that far away. You see it represents to this false Sir Godfrey his only means of escape. It would be the act of a madman to send that away altogether."

"Yes, I follow that," said Tinker.

"Sooner or later that fellow will want to beat a retreat, and he must have a clear to him. I am going to find out which way the yacht went. There must be some natives all along the coast, and they must have caught sight of it here and there."

"And then, guv'nor?"

"Then I'll follow it," said Blake.

The whole case was beginning to enthrall him. There was a touch of adventure about it that appealed to hi spirit. He lay long into the night turning over the various problems, and when he did drop off to sleep, Blake was satisfied in his own mind that he had come near enough to the truth, so far as his theory of what had happened in Jallastown was concerned.

The man who had appeared as the new Governor was undoubtedly playing a deep game.

"I must find the yacht Marga," the detective decided. "I feel that it holds the key to the situation."

On the following morning he tackled Captain Orme, and, without exactly revealing what his object was, succeeded in getting the postmaster-general to send a few telegrams to the outlying stations along the coast.

By noon Blake had received the replies, and knew that the Marga had steered southward. He traced the movements of the yacht to a point about sixty miles down the coast where, according to the statement of the telegraphist, she had halted until nightfall, then had gone on.

"She has probably crept into some bay or cove," Blake said to Tinker. "Anyhow, that's good enough for us. I am going to follow her."

While he had been waiting for the replied, Blake had arranged matters with the master of a small tug, the only craft of its type in all Tatua. It was generally used for carrying the rafts of mahogany out to the cargo steamers that occasionally called there on charter.

The tug-master was only too glad to accept Blake's commission and promised to be ready to start off along the coast by the evening.

Captain Orme was obviously curious about the movements of this mysterious visitor, but he was too well bred to make many enquiries, and Blake kept silent.

In the evening, he and Tinker boarded the tug, and the little vessel began its journey. As they passed close to the broad bows of the Wampun,

McTaggert waved them a friendly adieu, a gesture which Blake and Tinker returned.

Then the little tug, dropping into its stride, snorted off out of the quiet bay, and, with its paddles thrashing at a lively gait, went off along the coast, leaving a wide, white mark behind it.

As soon as they were clear of land, Blake took the skipper of the tug into his confidence.

"I am searching for that yacht, the Marga. I think it is hiding somewhere along the coast. Did you happen to see it by any chance?"

"You mean the yacht that the new Governor came in?"

"Yes."

"I did get a squint at it," the skipper returned. "I was up early that morning, and was just in time to see it steering out of the bay."

"Good," said Blake. "Then you will be able to recognise it again."

The skipper, a lean, lanky Australian who had spent most of his life in the pearl-fishing ground, cocked his eye at the detective.

""What's the game?" he asked.

"I want to find the Marga," Blake returned, "I think there is something fishy about it, and that new Governor. Anyhow, I have come all the way out from England to make sure that Sir Godfrey Haverleigh really takes up his position here, and I am not going back until I am sure of that."

"This coast is like a honeycomb," said the Australian skipper. "You could hide an Atlantic liner in some of the coves."

"Well, we can go as far as Mamba Point," said Blake. Mamba Point was the name of the local telegraph station from whence the final report had come, and the detective knew that it was some place beyond that point that the missing yacht would be found. "And out search will start from there."

The lean skipper nodded his head.

"Well, that's narrowing the area down a bit," he returned. "The Tse River is only forty miles lower down, and it is German territory on the other side of the Tse River, So if the yacht is anywhere on our side it won't take us long to find it."

The sturdy tug drummed its way through the calm seas. The coast was absolutely dark, but the Australian skipper seemed to smell his way, for he held on at a good speed right through the night.

The little craft could steam its eight to ten knots, and somewhere in the grey dawn, Blake awakened from a doze, found that the tug was at rest. It was close to the shore, and on the spit of land jutting out into the sea was a collection of mud huts, and one white painted bungalow.

As the light grew stronger, Blake was able to see the telegraph wires stretched from the bungalow to the forest.

"That's Mamba Point," said the skipper.

Little thin blue pencils of smoke were rising from the collection of huts. The air was so still that the smoke formed itself in a blue veil just above the tops of the trees. A dog came leaping down the beach, and barked its challenge at the tug, while the clear reverberations came across the waters.

"Wouldn't mind spending a holiday there, guv'nor," said Tinker who, leaning over the wooden taffrail, was eyeing the scene with his chin in his palm.

Someone came bustling forward with hot coffee and warm rolls, and Blake and his companion did justice to the meal. Then the tug began its search along the coast.

Blake had been lucky in his choice of skippers, for the Australian seemed to know every shoal and shallow. Now and then the tug would come close to the shore that Tinker could almost touch the feathery branches of some overhanging palm. Then the little vessel would have to make a long slant out to sea again to avoid some treacherous sandbank.

Right through the day the tug worked its way along steadily, and cove after cove was searched without result. It was late in the afternoon, when the tireless skipper pointed ahead.

"D'you see where the water looks brown?" he said.

"Yes," Blake returned.

"Well, that's the mouth of the Tse River," the skipper went on. "It's pretty fast stream, and carried a big limp of Tatua away with it when it is in flood as it is now."

The tug steamed up to a headland, then wheeled round, and the wide banks of the Tse River opened out in front of them. They set a course mid-channel, and began to plug up against the stream. Gradually the banks of the river came closer, and the pace of the tug slackened.

"It's very shallow here," said the skipper. "I'm afraid we cannot go much further. I don't suppose I draw any more water that that yacht, and if there is no sign of her here, we might as well turn around and—hallo! What's that?"

It was rapidly getting dusk, and the tug was just creeping along on the left side of the river. Ahead of it was a sharp bend, thickly wooded. Above the wood was to be seen a little black cloud of smoke, smoke that was rising from some unseen object behind.

"If that ain't coal I'm a Chinaman," said the skipper of the tug.

They moved on slowly, and presently, through a gap in the trees, Blake was able to make out the slender outlines of a mast, and he felt sure that his search had come to an end.

After a brief consultation with the skipper, the tug was allowed to sag into the shore, and then, thanks to its shallow draught, was moored to one of the thick trees.

Blake and Tinker and the skipper, with a couple of hands, stepped ashore and began to move through the creeper-clad forest. The river took a sharp bend there, with the result that the ground over which they were passing was practically a peninsula, and the thin cloud of smoke guided them in the right direction.

The light held until they had all but cleared the forest, and ahead of them, some fifteen or twenty yards from the side of the river, lat the slender hull of the yacht Marga.

The Australian skipper hooded his eyes with his hands, and peered at the vessel for a moment. "That's it," he said, "no doubt about it. And now, what are you going to do?"

Blake smiled.

"Going to get on board," he said; "but as that might be a pretty tough job, I won't ask you to come with me."

He saw the lean, virile figure of the Australian skipper tauten, and the man turned on him.

"Look here," he said, "I knew that this wasn't any soft job when I started on it, and if you think that I am going to squat here in the forest while you get all the fun on board there you are mistaken. If there are any heads to be thumped I'm going to help."

Blake shot out his hand, and the Australian skipper closed his fingers around the strong palm.

"Right you are, old chap," the detective said, "and I'm jolly grateful to you. I can certainly do with some help."

The scene that followed then was quite contrary to all laws and customs of civilised countries. As a matter of fact, the Marga, being moored to the left bank of the Tse River, was really on German territory, and was entitled to such protection as that big Empire could afford her.

But Blake was not always trammeled by the laws and orders of countries and states, and presently the solitary sentry on the Marga, half-dozing over his post, was aware of a wet, shining figure rising up over the taffrail. The sailor leapt to his feet and made a rush, while his voice sounded in a quick, warning cry. The wet figure was now on the deck and, as the man tried to grab at it, it performed a quick and very effective trick.

It stooped slightly, so that the sailor went lurching over it, then the man found two strong hands gripping his ankles and, a moment later, he was jerked clean up in the air.

He gave a frightened yell as he found himself swung aloft, and then neatly and deftly thrown right over the side of the Marga into the shallow, muddy waters of the Tse River.

The splash with which his body took the water was heard by the captain of the yacht. The man came tumbling up the companion-way as hard as he could pelt, and behind him came a couple of his crew.

But by this time Blake, who was the man who had tackled the sentry, was now joined by Tinker and the lithe Australian.

The broad-shouldered captain of the Marga caught sight of the three figures darting towards him, and, unable to distinguish them as black or white in the darkness, he dropped his hand towards his pocket. But before he could reach the weapon the captain of the tugboat was on him.

The Australian's method was curiously effective. He simply cleared the last few yards at a bound and, rising well from the deck as he did so, his foot struck the stocky skipper fairly on the chest.

With a howl of rage Darrel was sent sprawling over the brass step of the companion-way and on down the steep well, dragging his companions with him.

"Quick, Tinker, follow him!" Blake cried, pelting down the stairs.

It was something like a dog fight that was going on at the bottom of the steps, for the growls and gasps seemed to come from every corner.

Tinker felt a stout arm close round him and, doubling his fist, the youngster struck out in the darkness, aiming at where the head would probably be.

The shot was fairly successful, and a round English oath proved that his blow had been a sound one.

The entire crew of the Marga numbered some fifteen of twenty hands, but fortunately for Blake, and unfortunately for John Lawliss, the captain had allowed eight or nine of the men to go off on a shooting expedition, and they were not due to come back until the following morning.

Darrel, the captain of the Marga, had not expected any attack of this sort, but his action in allowing so many of his crew to have shore leave resulted in his ultimate downfall.

For the Australian's attack had settled the matter so far as the captain was concerned, for the broad-shouldered fellow had been sent crashing down the stairs, and his head had struck against a projecting bolt, with the result that he was lying stunned now on the lower deck.

Blake and his companions soon mastered the other two, and then the opening of a door gave them the glimpse of a lighted saloon, and they bundled their captives into it.

The two sailors dropped on the cushioned seat of the saloon, and Tinker, with the revolver drawn, mounted guard.

Darrel was also lifted from the deck, and was propped up against one of the corners of the saloon. By the time the attacking party had collected their prisoners, another interruption took place, for a door on the opposite side of the room opened, and there stepped out into the space, a tall, bearded man.

He was followed by another shorter individual, and he glanced at the curious tableau in front of him in silence.

Blake wheeled as the men entered the room and looked at the taller one for a moment, then a sudden inspiration came to the detective, and he stepped forward.

"Sir Godfrey Haverleigh?" he asked.

The baronet nodded.

"That is my name," he returned, eyeing the lithe figure in front of him.

Blake was dripping wet, and the light from the lamp gleamed on his sodden clothes.

"What has happened?" the baronet asked.

Blake looked at him

"Before I answer you that question," he said, "I want to ask one; Are you here on your own desire, or are you a prisoner?"

The baronet shrugged his shoulders.

"A prisoner," he returned. "Not the slightest doubt about that." .

"Well, my name is Sexton Blake, and I have been employed by the Colonial Office to follow you and find out what has happened to you," the detective went on. "It has taken me a jolly long time to do that, but I think I have accomplished the task at last."

Sir Godfrey drew a deep breath.

"By heavens, you must have had a long chase!" he said, "and I am thundering glad to see you. This is the queerest business that I have ever heard of, and even now I can't make head or tail of it."

He pointed to the corner where the thick-set captain was seated, the broad-shouldered man had returned to consciousness now, and was lying back watching the scene in the saloon with half-closed eyes.

"That's the only man who can give you any information," said Sir Godfrey. "I have been trying to pump him, but he is as close as an oyster. I don't even know the name of the man who owns this yacht."

Blake smiled.

"Who the yacht used to belong to, you mean, Sir Godfrey," he returned grimly. "At the present it is ours."

Blake then told the baronet of what had happened at Jallastown, and the bearded man cursed softly to himself as he heard of the trick that the tall adventurer had played on the officials.

"By Jove! he must have a nerve," he broke out; "but what's at the back of it? What does he mean by it? Why should he tear off from Jallastown so quickly as he has done?"

"That is just what beats me," said Blake. "He must have an object behind it all. I expect he's just a swell thief or something."

He had raised his voice as he said this, and he shot a quick glance at the bronzed captain in the corner of the saloon. Blake had hoped that his

hard words would rouse the man, and he was not mistaken.

The thickset figure lumbered to his feet.

"You are wrong there, curse you!" said Darrel. "I don't know who you are, or what you may be after, but I can tell you this much, the gent who owns this vessel ain't no thief or rascal!"

He was swaying slightly to and fro, and his eyes beneath the shaggy brows were white and fierce.

"He's no thief," the deep voice thundered again. "I supposed the game is up, and you'll collar him and he'll pay. But the man that says that the Honourable John Lawliss is a thief lies, sir, and I'm ready to prove it!"

It was a battling speech, full of the grim fire that Blake loved to find in anyone. The short thickset man, swayed by his passion, was gripping at the corner of the table, while he flung his hot angry words at the silent listeners.

"Mr. Lawliss has a very faithful second in you," said Blake in a quiet tone, "but words do not prove anything. If your master has not carried out this trick for the sake of gain to himself, what is his reason?"

The skipper of the Marga drew a deep breath.

"I swore I'd tell no one," he said slowly, "but it seems to me as though you've got the winning hand."

He leaned forward slightly.

"If you want to find John Lawliss," he went on, "all you have to do is follow this river. It may be two or three days journey, I don't know, but sooner or later you will come to where he is, and you will find out what he is doing."

He dropped back on the seat and folded his arms.

"And that's all I'm going to tell you," he ended. "Find the rest out for yourselves."

THE SEVENTH
CHAPTER
LAWLISS WINS

"And you swear to this story?"

The Honourable John Lawliss, seated on a small camp-stool outside his little green canvas tent, looked hard into the face of the old native chief who was standing in front of him.

The Tatuan of name and account attains a certain dignity of countenance, and this old chief of a huge tribe had a certain air of command and importance about him.

His scanty locks were snow-white and the skin that he wore over his shoulders added to his proud bearing.

"What have I told you, O Excellency, is indeed the truth," the man returned.

He spoke in his native tongue, and Lawliss was able to understand him.

The little expedition that had started away from Jallastown had taken the best part of six days to reach the big native town on the banks of the river, and during that time John Lawliss had busied himself with learning the language from a capable interpreter.

The young adventurer looked little worse for his long trudge through the bush. His clothes were still as spick and span as ever, and the patent leather boots which he was wearing shone on the sun as he sat on the stool.

It was part of his plan to impress the natives, and certainly his white uniform and upright bearing carried a certain amount of weight.

It was a big game of bluff that this dare-devil man was playing and he carried it out with a superb aplomb.

"You say that ten years ago the Tse River ran in a different course, but that owing to a huge landslide, the course of the river was changed, and it set off on a new channel, cutting out a wedge of land?"

"That is so, O Excellency!" the native went on.

He pointed across the river to the right side, from whence Lawliss had come.

"Ten years ago," he said, "we were under the British flag, but the river came down in a single

night, and cut the channel that it now runs on, and lo! We found we were no longer British!"

It seemed as though the old chap had been nursing his grievance, and Lawliss smiled to himself.

This had been Mavering's story to him, and he was beginning to find that it was true.

"Then why did you not complain?" he asked.

The white-haired chief of the tribe made a gesture.

"We did complain," he went on. "Message after message we sent to Jallastown, telling them what had befallen, and urging your people to come and claim what was their own. But I am only a small man, O Excellency, and my words were unheeded."

"And what of the—the other nation? Did they ignore you?"

Chief Tao Pala smiled darkly.

"No they didn't ignore us," he returned. "There came through the bush a man, fat of face, and heavy of foot. Behind him he had a company of black soldiers, and they put up the flag-post you see in my village, and hoisted their flag with double eagles. Then they proclaimed that this village was now theirs, and a portion of the German Empire."

"And what has happened since then?"

"Very little except that they are trying to make us pay taxes. But we still send our taxes to Jallastown, for we are British and British we will remain."

There was something inspiring in the words of this uncultured savage, who, after all, was no small part of the British Empire.

John Lawliss felt his heart stir, and he arose to his feet,

"I salute you Tao Pala," he said, raising a hand to his helmet.

"Against many odds you have held true to the country that you care for. I will see to it that before I leave here you and your village will once again be British."

The chief took a pace forward.

"You mean that?" he cried.

The eyes of the young adventurer gleamed.

"That's what I have come here for. I know your story is true. I heard it weeks ago in far London. Did you ever meet a man Mavering?"

"Ma-vering!" the chief repeated. "A little man—was he a little man, keen of eye, and alert of bearing?"

"Yes, that's his description."

The white-headed chief clasped his hands together.

"I have indeed met him, and it was to him that I told my story. He promised that he would see my wrongs righted. And it was he who sent you to me? Ah, then he has not broken his word!"

He glanced again at the tall figure in the white uniform, then looked behind to the tent where the camp of carriers were seated. They were just ordinary carriers, and only two were in uniform.

The chief shook his head.

"To take back this territory, O Excellency," he said, "you will require the sword. By no other means can you do it."

Lawliss's teeth gleamed in a quick smile.

"That remains to be seen, Tao Pala," he returned. "If it comes to the sword, then sword it will be, but first of all I am going to try a more pacific method."

He pointed towards the river running along through its wide banks. To the uninitiated eye it might have seemed that the river had run over that course for ages. But the virgin countries have a way of adapting themselves to change which may easily convince a stranger.

"Where did the landslide take place?" asked Lawliss.

The chief extended a brown finger, and pointed towards the east.

"It is two days march from here, Excellency," he said, "where the river runs through a deep gully. One can see quite plainly where the old course was, although now it is overgrown with trees and only a few wells remain."

Lawliss nodded his head.

"To-morrow morning," he said, "we will start for this place. I want to see it."

He glanced at the big village.

"I want you to bring as many able-bodied men as you can spare," he went on. "You are coming with me, Tao Pala. For you and I must work this thing together."

He smiled at the brown man.

"You don't ask me what my plans are?" he went on.

Tao Pala shook his head.

"I know that his Excellency would tell me if he wanted me to know. I am content to trust his Excellency's judgment."

"That's well said, Tao Pala," Lawliss returned; "but I will let you into a certain portion of the secret. Look!"

He went to his tent, and drew back the flap revealing the fact that along one side of the tent were arranged a number of cases. There were, perhaps, nine or ten of them, each case was slung across a pole.

"I have brought those with me," said Lawliss, "for, as I told you before, Mavering gave me a pretty accurate account of what had taken place here."

"And what do the cases contain, Excellency?" Lawliss smiled again.

"They contain that which will bring your village and land around it back under the British flag," he said, "and will prove to the world that your story is a true one."

Tao Pala drew a deep breath; then, with a quick movement, he stepped forward, and, taking Lawliss's hand, raised it to his lips.

"I hail you as the saviour of my tribe," he said. "May your arm be as strong as your eye!"

At daybreak the following morning the loud beating of tom-toms awakened John Lawliss, and he arose and dressed himself. The faithful Pete brought his master a simple breakfast, and, as Lawliss sipped at his coffee, he saw the big gang of natives mustering on the outskirts of the village.

Each man was armed with a spear, bow and arrow, and shield. They made a splendid picture in the silver morning light.

"On the move again, baas?" said Pete.

"Yes," Lawliss replied. "You can get my tent struck. We are off on a two-days trek, Pete."

The carriers from Jallastown were well drilled by now, and in a few seconds the tent had been struck and rolled, and its carriers swung it aloft on the pole. Two hours after daybreak, the Honourable John Lawliss, with Chief Tao Pala by his side, started off from the village.

A great host of men, women and children followed the party, beating drums and chorusing some shrill war-song.

Lawliss, had he been at all doubtful about his enterprise before, must have felt then that what he was doing was right. For these people were hailing him as their saviour, as the bringer of peace and contentment.

For the first five or six miles there was a fair road through the jungle; then it became a question of single file, and the chief sent on ahead a couple of scouts.

The entire party must have stretched out for the better part of a mile or so, and the progress became slower. The end of the first day found them encamped at a water-bowl, and Tao Pala indicated to Lawliss the indisputable proofs that this water-bowl had once been a part of the old course of the river.

There was a distinct indication of the two banks where the stream had once flown, and the fact that the trees on either side of the banks were much older than the few stunted ones that grew between the banks pointed clearly to the fact that at a not very distant period the waters had covered that portion of the ground.

They started off early on the following morning, and John Lawliss and the chief, with a score or so of men, pushed on ahead, leaving the carriers and the rest of the party to follow on at a more leisurely pace.

Lawliss wanted to reach the gully where the landslide had taken place before nightfall, and he held on at a rapid pace, with the result that at about three or four in the afternoon he reached the spot he had started for.

The gully was a deep and narrow one, the river having evidently forced its way between the hills.

Chief Tao Pala pointed out the portion where the landslide had taken place, and he and Lawliss climbed the mound. It was overgrown with trees and creepers now, but when Lawliss reached the summit and looked about him, it was obvious that the chief's words were true.

For the great mound formed something like a dam, and the river turned sharply to the left at that spot, following a tortuous course westward.

The old bed of the river was plainly visible, and it ran up to the side of the mound. Had nature built a dam across a river, it could not have been more accurately placed.

There were also indications on the side of the mound where the landslide had taken place, for great masses of rock still jutted out from the brown earth.

"You see, Excellency?" said Tao Pala.

Lawliss nodded.

"And so would any man," he returned, in a stern voice. "Even a fool would realise what had taken place here."

He glanced at his companion.

"Chance threw down a handful of earth, and robbed my country of that territory which lies between the old course and the new," he said, "and, at the same time, Tao Pala, robbed you of the right to be called a British subject."

"That is so, O Excellency."

"And for ten years a drunken rascal has kept the truth away from England," John Lawliss went on. "Brandy had bought his silence, and this state of affairs might have gone on for many more years until out enemy would have had a good right to claim this slice of territory so opportunely handed to them by a mere slip of Nature."

"That's what we feared," said the chief. "And even now, Excellency, I don't see how you are going to change it."

The tall young adventurer seated himself on the top of the mound and watched the rover as it rushed past.

"We will change it," he said. "I tell you we will change it. Wait till my carriers come, and you will see how I will help Nature to right a wrong."

The words had hardly left his lips when a cry came from below and Chief Tao Pala turned. One of his native servants had climbed a tree, and was beckoning towards him, pointing eastward at the same time.

Turning in the required direction, Tao Pala shaded his eyes and looked. A moment later he had leaped to John Lawliss's side.

"See Excellency? White men and troops!"

Circling around the bottom of the mountain from which the great barrier of earth had fallen a few years before a line of human figures came nearer and nearer.

Lawliss arose to his feet suddenly. There were two white men leading the party, and one glance at the stout figures in uniform told Lawliss who they were.

"Germans," he said to himself.

The party swung on, and presently a harsh word of command sounded, and the black troops came to a halt, while the two white officers came forward.

Lawliss descended the mound slowly, and walked towards them at a leisurely pace. His lithe, handsome figure and the striking uniform made the two foreign officers stare for a moment.

"See, Excellency? White men and troop!"

Then, as he halted, they followed his example, and the three men saluted.

But there was no friendliness in that salute; it was rather the curt recognition that two adversaries give to each other previous to a duel.

"I am Captain Straboe, Assistant-Governor of German Tatua," the taller officer of the two announced. "Might I ask who you are?"

Quick as a flash, the young adventurer made up his mind.

"My name is Lawliss," he said—"John Lawliss."

"You are here on a hunting expedition, perhaps?"

"Not quite; I am prospecting."

The German officer's doubts slid out of his face, and he shrugged his shoulders slightly.

"Another fool Englishman," his thoughts ran.

"You should not have crossed the river, sir," he went on. "This is German territory, and you must first procure a license from our Governor before entering our ground."

Lawliss pointed towards the high mound which barred the mouth of the gully.

"I was only examining that land slide," he said.

He spoke in English, choosing his words slowly and deliberately, so that the others would follow him.

"It is a very curious formation of earth."

The two officers exchanged glances.

"A land slide you call it," the captain said. "No doubt it was; but it must have happened centuries ago, I suppose."

Lawliss knew that he was getting neat to the danger point, but his adventurous soul revelled in the fact.

"Hardly so long ago as a century, Herr Captain," he returned. "As a matter of fact, the guide who is with me says that it only took place some nine or ten years since. One can see quite plainly the old course of the river."

He pointed towards the left where, easily to be discerned, the old course ran through the gaps in the trees. The brow of the German officer darkened.

As a matter of fact, this little trick by which Germany had collared some two or three hundred miles of territory was well known to them, but they had held their peace on it, and had worked their best for the Fatherland.

To them it was simply a clever trick which allowed them to take a bite out of the British Empire.

"Oh, one cannot trust to the natives talk," Captain Straboe put in hastily. "They sat ten years, and mean one hundred; time is nothing to them."

He decided then that he would have to take stronger measures, and he nodded towards Lawliss.

"But I must ask you to go back to your own side of the river, sir," he went on. "This is German territory, and without a license you have no right to be here."

For a moment the hot blood of the young adventurer made the veins in his temple swell. But Lawliss, reckless though he was, was clever enough to govern his temper when it was necessary, and he did so now.

"If you will let me remain on this side in my camp until to-morrow, Herr Captain," he said, "I promise that I will be on the other side of the river by noon."

There was a meaning in his remark which escaped the notice of the stiff-necked German officer.

Lawliss saluted them, and turning on his heel, stepped along the bottom of the mound, to vanish in the trees.

The two German officers watched him until he had disappeared.

"A curse on him for a meddlesome fool!" one of the men said. "We have always expected that some time or other someone was bound to have noticed that mound, but I don't like the look of that man."

"Nor do I." the other officer returned; "but what can we do? We can only halt here and not move until he goes. It was a fortunate chance, Herr Captain, that brought us down here to-night."

They strode back to their party, which consisted of about fifty men and the natives, and presently the camp was formed. It was about five or six hundred yards away from the mound, and a sentry was posted on the left side of the camp to challenge anyone approaching.

At dusk the two German officers made their way down into the thick bush beyond the mound. They wanted to locate the camp of the Englishman, and presently they did so. It consisted of a solitary tent, and the fire gleaming in front of it revealed the fact that there were four or five black carriers sleeping peacefully round the glowing embers.

Satisfied that Lawliss's tale was correct, and that he was only a prospector travelling through the country with a handful of men, the officers retired.

They little dreamed that that camp was simply a blind, and hid the fact that a quarter of a mile away the real camp was situated, with its hundreds of natives and Chief Tao Pala and John Lawliss.

Somewhere about midnight the sentry on the German camp thought that he heard a sound coming from the direction of the river. It seemed to him as though it was the clicking of a spade on some hard surface.

The man listened, straining his ears, but the sound was not repeated, and, satisfied that he had been mistaken, he dropped back into his position.

As a matter of fact, German officers differ greatly from the British type. For they treat the dusky man beneath them as though they are dirt, and there is nothing of the comradeship that exists between white and black under the British flag.

Had that native sentry been a British soldier, he would probably have gone and reported the matter to the officers, but, under the stern, useless discipline that exists in the German Army, the man was afraid to go and awaken his superiors.

Yet that sound he had heard had not been an effort of his imagination.

On the mound a horde of shadowy figures were working with feverish haste. A tall, lithe figure was directing them on low-voiced commands. Spades and picks were being used, and pit after pit was dug in the heart of the mound, into which, one by one, the heavy cases that John Lawliss had carried with him were being placed.

The natives were working in batches, and it was Tao Pala who arranged the working parties. There was a vast amount of work to be done, but these brown-skinned fellows were working for something more than mere pay then. They were working for liberation from a hated rule, and they toiled like slaves in the darkness.

Within three hours the last of the heavy cases had been placed in position, and the earth carefully smoothed over the top of it. A rubber-covered wire was carried from the mound and sway through the trees. It was carefully hidden from sight, and it went on to the little solitary tent.

John Lawliss, with Pete and Tao Pala, complete the last item of work. He connected the two loose strands of the wire with a little electric battery.

"You understand now, Tao Pala?" John Lawliss said.

The chief drew a deep breath.

"I think I understand," he returned. "From that wizard-box will go a spark that will fire the mines you have laid?"

Lawliss nodded his head.

"That is so," he returned; "and, unless I am very much mistaken, we will blow that mound sky-high, and the waters of the Tse River will return again to their old course, and Britain will get her strip of territory back again."

The words had hardly left his lips when from the darkness beyond the tent there came a harsh challenge. Lawliss leapt into the entrance to the tent, his tall figure cutting a sharp silhouette in the yellow light from the lamp behind him.

Hurrying towards him was a little knot of men. He saw the familiar khaki; then suddenly he started, and drew himself up to his full height. For behind the leader of the party was a face he recognised—the face of Sir Godfrey Haverleigh.

The leader of the party came forward at a run, and Lawliss saw the glint of a revolver barrel as it was levelled at him.

"Stand still!" a clear, commanding voice cried. "Don't move, as you value your life!"

The tone was grim and threatening, and the hand that held the revolver did not waver. Lawliss looked into the clear-cut face, and saw a pair of hard, steely eyes fixed on him.

The young adventurer's hands dropped to his side, and he shrugged his shoulders slightly.

"All right," he returned; "I will not move."

A moment later the tent was surrounded by a circle of men, and Sir Godfrey Haverleigh stepped up to where Lawliss was standing.

"I told you that it would be my turn some day," the baronet said, in a grim voice, "and I have kept my word. I have got you, my masquerading friend, and you will have to pay now."

Lawliss's face was bloodless, but there was no fear in his wide eyes.

"It's a pity that you come so—so soon, Sir Godfrey," he said, in a clear tone. "I would have

been glad of your company here some two or three hours later."

"I doubt that," the baronet returned hotly.

The young adventurer's eyes flashed.

"I don't lie," he said. "I take chances, but that is a different matter. I tell you, Sir Godfrey, your arrival is just a little inopportune."

He turned away from the baronet, and looked at the clean-shaven man who had held him up.

"And who are you, might I ask?" John Lawliss went on.

They were curiously alike, these two men, although so different in character. Blake, with his strong chin and clear eyes, had the same virile personality. They looked at each other for a moment, and despite the fact that Blake had come half across the world to foil this man's schemes, the detective found a quick admiration coming into his heart.

Certainly the Honourable John Lawliss made a striking figure as he stood there in the entrance to the tent in his white uniform.

"My name is Blake," the detective returned, "and I have been authorized by the British Government to look into the affair of Sir Godfrey Haverleigh. You are my prisoner; I need not mention what your crimes are."

The white teeth of John Lawliss gleamed.

"I have interfered with the liberties of a subject," he said. "I suppose that is what you mean? Well, it's quite true; but I don't think Sir Godfrey Haverleigh has anything to complain about so far as his treatment on the Marga is concerned."

"I have everything to complain about," the hot-headed baronet returned. "Confound you, man, I was your prisoner, held under lock and key."

"Oh, I admit all that," said Lawliss. "It will make a fine story in the courts of justice in England."

He spoke a trifle bitterly, but there was no fear in his voice.

At that moment Tao Pala, with Pete behind him, came out of the tent. The dignified bearing of the native chief made an impression on the white men who had gathered around.

"Who are these men, Excellency?" Tao Pala asked, turning towards Lawliss.

The young adventurer laughed.

"I am no longer Excellency, Tao Pala," he said, in the native tongue. Then he stretched out his hand and pointed towards Sir Godfrey, "This is the real Excellency, this is Sir Godfrey Haverleigh, the new Governor of Tatua."

He turned towards Blake and explained.

"I am just telling this man, whose name is Tao Pala, and who is chief of the tribe here, that my little deception has come to an end. He accepted me as the new Governor, you see."

Tao Pala looked from one bearded face to another; then, with a quick movement, Lawliss stripped the false beard from his chin. The chief started back in amazement.

"But I don't understand," he said. "What does it all mean?"

The tall tugboat captain who had accompanied the party stepped forward then, the man was a past master in the Tatuan tongue, and it was he who took on the part of interpreter.

Tao Pala listened to his story, but the expression on the native's face was one of supreme discontent. It was not to Sir Godfrey, but to John Lawliss that he turned. "Then our plan, O Excellency?" he said.

Lawliss gave him a swift warning look, and the chief became silent.

"Plan! What does the man mean by plan?" Sir Godfrey asked when the Australian captain interpreted.

"That's more than I can tell you, Sir Godfrey," the captain returned.

Sir Godfrey Haverleigh turned to Blake.

"I will look to you to guard this rascal," he said, in a stiff tone; "he has given me sufficient trouble, and I don't want to let him slip through my hands now."

He and Tao Pala, together with the Australian walked away from the tent, and Lawliss, with a little nod to Blake, sat down on one of the canvas seats.

"It will be dawn in another hour or so," the adventurer said. "I don't suppose you want to take me back to durance vile before that time?"

Blake eyed the lithe figure keenly. There was no trace of the criminal about John Lawliss. Reckless he might be, to a fault, perhaps, but the wide eyes had nothing of the rogue about them.

"What was your game?"

"Eh!"

John Lawliss looked up. He had fallen into a half brooding fit.

"Why did you trap Sir Godfrey and come here?" Blake went on. "Was it just a foolish

prank, or was there something deeper behind it?"

They looked at each other, these two cool, courageous men. Then Lawliss leaned forward slightly, placing his powerful hands on his knees.

"I wonder if you will call me liar if I tell you?"

"I don't think so," said Blake.

Lawliss moved slightly, so that Blake might have a look into the interior of the tent. The little electric battery was standing in the centre of the floor.

"I came here chiefly to do that," he said.

Blake looked at the box with the wires running away beneath the wall of the tent.

"I am afraid I don't quite understand," he said. Lawliss laughed.

"You might have understood if you had come here perhaps an hour later," he said. "Oh, it was a mad scheme, but it was worth while. I have enjoyed every minute of it."

He lowered his voice and began to speak in a rapid whisper, and as Blake listened, his face changed.

"A mad enterprise!" he said at last; "perhaps the maddest I have ever heard of."

He glanced at the battery again. It seemed a very innocent affair and yet he knew that a touch of the switch which he saw on the top of the box would make history.

"I would have fired the mound at once," said Lawliss, "only Tao Pala had to send back to warn his people. You see, when the river is freed it will roar down the whole course like an avalanche, and there might be some unfortunate native in its track. We sent thirty or forty swift runners to warn the people what was going to happen. They started off at dusk, and by daybreak they would have been able to reach the tribe and warn them."

He rose to his feet and stretched his long arms above his head.

"I'd have given much to have seen the faces of those German officers after my mines had been fired," he said. "Their camp lies close to the mound now."

The crack of a twig sounded, and the Australian captain appeared.

"Sir Godfrey Haverleigh sends his compliments, Mr. Blake, and wants you to bring your prisoner along to the main camp. He has arranged for an escort for him."

Lawliss's face went ashen as Blake arose.

The young adventurer cast a longing glance back at the tent, then with a slight shrug of the shoulders, he turned and followed the lanky Australian, while Blake swung along behind.

When they reached the main camp they sound that Sir Godfrey had already taken command. The chief, Tao Pala, had arranged for an escort of forty or fifty men and Sir Godfrey was going to start off at once for Jallastown, through the bush.

"You had better tell Sir Godfrey your story," Blake whispered to Lawliss.

The young adventurer wheeled on him at once and shook his head.

"No fear!" he returned; "you forget that Sir Godfrey is a hide-bound official. What I was going to do was highly unofficial and would have no sort of appeal to him. What he will do when he gets back to Jallastown will be to write reams and reams of paper about this stolen territory. But paper will never bring back the Tse River into its proper course again. No! I have lost, and so have the British Empire."

There was a certain gloomy despair in the young face, and suddenly Blake felt a quick inspiration come to him.

"I don't know that you have lost," was his whispered reply.

Lawliss nodded his head in the direction of the cloud. "It means that what I came to do has been done, Sir Godfrey," he said.

He had no time to say more, for at that moment Sir Godfrey came up to them.

"We start for Jallastown at once, Blake," he said, turning to the detective, "and this—this gentleman has to accompany us. I have arranged for an escort for him, and I am sure that he will not escape." Lawliss looked at the bearded face of the man he had tricked so badly. Then, with a grim smile, he held out his hands.

"Better make sure of me, Sir Godfrey," he said.

There was a challenge in the voice, and the baronet was not slow to accept it.

"By heavens, I will!" he returned.

At a signal from him a piece of rope was produced, and the strong wrists of the adventurer were bound together. A roar came suddenly from the circle of watchers, and there flashed out a sturdy black figure. It was Pete, mad with rage.

The wild fellow from the Congo went at Sir Godfrey like a cat, and before anyone could realise what had happened, Pete had his fingers round Sir Godfrey's throat and the big baronet was on his back, half strangled beneath the fierce grip.

"Pete! Pete! Don't be a fool!" Lawliss cried.

But the devoted black was deaf to all cries, and it would have gone badly with Sir Godfrey had he been alone there. As it was, it took the Australian captain and two of his companions to drag the foaming, raging Pete away from his prostrate victim.

"He tied my baas up, and my baas is a man, the best man in the world!" Pete sobbed, shaking with rage.

Sir Godfrey scrambled to his feet from his undignified position, and a moment later Pete

had shared his master's fate, his arms being tied tightly behind him.

Sir Godfrey was obviously in an angry mood now, and he stared round with a frown on his face.

"Come, Blake!" he said, "we'll start at once."

But, to his astonishment, neither Blake nor Tinker moved.

"I'll follow you, Sir Godfrey," Blake said. "There is no immediate hurry for my return. I might even go down the river and come back to

"Mother!" cried Lawliss. "You here?" "I had to follow you, my son," the mother said.

Jallastown on board the tugboat."

He nodded towards the knot of armed blacks.

"Your escort is quite sufficient," he said, "and you will not require me now."

Sir Godfrey frowned for a moment, but, after all, Blake was a free agent, and could do as he pleased.

"Oh, very well, Mr. Bake," the new Governor of Tatua said swiftly. "I will see you when you return to Jallastown."

A few minutes later the party for the capital moved off, and Blake and Tinker were left alone in the main camp.

John Lawliss, with a double line of armed blacks on either side of him, and Sir Godfrey stalking along behind, paced on through the bush. Presently the dusk began to waver, and eastward there appeared the first grey fingers of dawn. They had been marching for the better part of an hour, and presently they found themselves wending their way up a sharp rise.

As John Lawliss topped the slope the morning sun rising out from the distance fell in a golden radiance on his face. He halted for a moment, then suddenly, from the bush behind them, far in the distance, there came a dull reverberating roar.

Over the face of the adventurer a look of sheer joy leaped, and he wheeled round.

Above the mists in the valley there was rising a great black cloud of smoke. It was vast and dense, and it hung in the still air like a veil. Sir Godfrey came up to the younger man's side and halted.

"What does it mean?" he asked.

Lawliss nodded his head in the direction of the cloud, and from his lips a joyous laugh broke.

"It means that what I came here to do has been done, Sir Godfrey," John Lawliss said; "and I think I know whose hand it is that has taken my place."

"What on earth do you mean? Why don't' you explain?"

Lawliss's fine eyes turned on the bearded baronet.

"I can explain now, Sir Godfrey," he said, "and even your hide-bound, red-taped, officious soul can do nothing to stop what has been done."

In rapid speech he outlined the story of the stolen territory.

"That explosion that you heard just now," Lawliss went on, "marked the blowing up of the mound, and by this time the brown waters of the Tse River are rushing back along the old course. It is going on towards the sea, a big brown wall, and every mile it leaps brings another mile back to England. By Heavens! I would like to see the faces of those German officers."

First bewilderment, then doubt, then admiration came into Sir Godfrey's face. The baronet was a commonplace type of man, but this extraordinary story that he had heard stirred even him.

"And you mean to tell me that you risked all that you have done just for the sake of coming out here to rearrange the boundaries?" he said.

Lawliss laughed.

"Why not? It was a little bit more exciting than pig-sticking or lion-hunting!"

A curious sound came from the new governor's lips, then, suddenly and swiftly, the baronet drew a clasp-like knife from his pocket, and with a quick slash of the blade severed the rope that bound the young adventurer's wrists.

"You are a mad fellow," he said, "but a dashed plucky one. And I am hanged if I am going to Jallastown until I find out whether that mound has gone or not."

He held out his hand, and Lawliss clasped it.

The governor's party had moved but slowly when leaving the camp, but when the order came to wheel about and go back, the pace at which the dusky fellows tore through the bush indicated where their hearts lay.

Presently they reached the banks of what had once been the river, and Lawliss came to a halt.

"Look!" he said. "Already!"

There was only a trickle of water in the centre of the channel now. Eagerly the party pressed on, climbing the opposite bank, and swinging forward through the bush. They reached the site of the main camp to find it deserted, but now to their ears came a medly of sounds.

Tom-toms were beating and long guttural choruses came to them through the bush. Discipline absolutely vanished then, and every dusky fellow in that party simply threw his arms down, and fled, helter-skelter, towards the sound.

Sir Godfrey slipped his arm beneath that of John Lawliss.

"We'd better hurry, old chap," he said, "or we'll miss the fun."

What his Majesty's Government would have said had they seen their representative tearing through the bush like a released schoolboy, need not be discussed here. But presently the little group of white men standing on the edge of a rushing, foaming torrent, found themselves greeted by two panting, breathless men.

Blake wheeled round and looked first at Sir Godfrey and then at Lawliss, then over the clean-shaven face a wide smile broke.

"I thought you would come back," said Sexton Blake. "It would have been a pity to miss a scene like this."

"I am sorry I even started," said Sir Godfrey.

He looked across the river which had now sought its old course, and in a tumbling, rustling fury was rushing seaward.

It swept the young growth of trees from its path, and it seemed as though the old Tse River was rioting with joy because it had come back to its old home again.

From where they stood, the little group of white men could see the camp of the Germans.

"There are your friends, I believe," said Blake, pointing across the stream.

Two figures in uniform were standing on the edge of what had once been the mound. There was very little left of that now, and the attitude of the two officers was expressive.

They seemed lost and bewildered, and one of them, raising his head at last, caught sight of the group standing on the knoll on the other side of the stream. He so far forgot his Teutonic dignity as to raise his clenched fist and shake it at the group.

Blake felt a hand pressed on his shoulder, and turning round found Lawliss close to his side.

"You found the switch easy to work, I suppose?" said the younger man.

Blake nodded.

"Quite easy," he returned.

"I knew you were going to do it," the adventurer returned—"I saw it in your eyes. That was why you remained behind?"

Blake bowed.

"Quite so," he said. "I thought that I might as well finish what was, after all, a very praiseworthy enterprise, even although it was carried out in a rather unlawful manner."

Lawliss laughed.

"Unlawful!" he repeated. "But you shared in it, anyhow. Hang it all, old man, if I laid the mine you fired it, and if there are to be any criminal proceedings about this, I am afraid you will have to take your place with me in the box!"

His last words were overheard by Sir Godfrey Haverleigh, and the baronet looked from the detective to Lawliss.

"I am surprised at Blake," he said, and there was a distinct change in his voice now, for it was full of a quiet humour. "It would look well for a great detective such as he is to figure in a cause celebre."

Blake laughed.

"It is not often that I help a desperate criminal such as this gentleman to achieve his object," he said in his quiet way, "but I think, on this occasion, I was justified."

Sir Godfrey nodded.

"Yes," he said. "I think that our friends the Germans will have a distinct difficulty in proving that the old course of the Tse River was not the real boundary of their colony. But that all remains for the future to decide. And now, gentleman, I really think that we might start back for Jallastown."

And later in the day they did start back, but it was a joyful going now. For the entire tribe, with Tao Pala at their head, insisted on accompanying the little hand of white men back to the outskirts of Jallastown itself.

Sir Godfrey went straight to the Residency and had a brief interview with the old governor. General Mantley was no longer under the influence of brandy and, as many weak-minded men do, he tried to have his revenge on the young adventurer who had tricked him so well.

"Consequences or no consequences," he roared, "I'll have him exposed. I have heard enough about it now to know that you were kept a prisoner by him, while he took your place."

Almost all the officials of Jallastown had gathered in the Residency, and heard this angry speech. Sir Godfrey Haverleigh waited until the ex-governor had completed his remarks, then he rose to his feet.

"I am very sorry to have to contradict you, General Mantley," the baronet said, "but you are quite mistaken. Mr. Lawliss was my host, I was his guest on board the Marga, and what he did was done with my full authority and permission."

Outside the window a guttural throat raised what was a swiftly-stifled cheer Pete, with Tinker's hand clasped over his dusky lips, staggered back beneath the window.

"Shut up, you fool!" said Blake's assistant. "It's all right, but you needn't make a song about it!"

When the scene at the Residency was over, there came out from the hospital a slender, graceful figure, dressed in nurse's garb. It came across the square, and John Lawliss, standing in the porch of the Residency, stared for a moment, then, with a great cry, he leaped across the verandah with outstretched arms.

"Mother!" he said. "You here?"

And Nurse March allowed herself to be folded in strong arms, and just for a moment the brave head rested against the broad chest. And if she shed a few tears—well, that was only natural.

"I had to follow you, my son," the mother said. "I see that you are all right, but I have lived in terror ever since you left London. Promise me that you won't go out on such a mad enterprise again!"

The wide blue eyes of her son darkened for a moment.

"I won't promise, mother," said John Lawliss, "but I'll try not to."

And with that the mother heart had to be content.

What happened afterwards is purely newspaper history, and is always down in the Yearly report books of Tatua.

Captain Straboe and his lieutenant headed back to their base and sent a long-winded account of what had happened to Berlin.

Sir Godfrey Haverleigh, on his side, had also to make his report, but the commission which ultimately sat to settle the matter had no difficulty in arriving at the truth.

A special party of surveyors went to the Tse River, and was escorted over the disputed territory by Tao Pala. The place where the landslide had taken place was their chief object, and only one doubt remained.

For, while the Germans swore that the removal of the mound had been a base trick played by the perfidious British, Tao Pala swore by all his gods that it had been an act of Nature.

"There came a thunderbolt in the night," ran his account. "Out from the heavens it fell, and smote the mound, and lo! the mound vanished in a cloud of smoke, and the waters of the Tse River returned to their old course."

And as Tao Pala and half his tribe had haunted the river for days, carefully removing all broken pieces of wood and other tell-tale evidences of that sort, the search party could find nothing to prove otherwise.

And so ended the second enterprise of the Honourable John Lawliss.

THE END.

THE
REMOVAL
OF
MR. SOAMES.

✳ ✳ ✳

MARSTON HUME—Criminal.

A SPLENDID TALE
OF
SEXTON BLAKE
versus
MARSTON HUME.

"MARSTON HUME'S given up his rooms," said Blake abruptly.

"You gave him a pretty good scare over those stolen plans; perhaps he thinks he'd better lie low for a while. It was touch-and-go that time," answered Bathurst.

Blake nodded gloomily. Hume was preying on his nerves more than he cared to own.

"There's more in it than that. He knows to an inch how far he can go. It isn't from fear of me that he has altered his mode of living—at least, not directly. I am as sure as that I am sitting here that he is planning some new piece of devilment. I have, as you know, been watching all his movements closely.

"Three weeks ago—that is, long before he mentioned any idea of leaving his rooms—he took an unfurnished studio in Fulham. Now, what on earth can a man like Hume want with a studio? He knows as much about pictures as I do about playing the 'cello.

"It is a very isolated place he has taken, standing in a neglected patch of garden, and contains a large studio, very lofty, with a top light, and no windows which can be overlooked, a small bed-room, and a bath-room. It stands well back in a slummy little bye-street. There is a piece of waste ground at the back of it. In short, for a man of Hume's rather sybaritic tastes, I can imagine no more uncomfortable spot in all London."

"What's his reason? You tell me that he never does anything without a reason."

Blake lit a cigarette and stared moodily into the fire.

"That is just what I'd give a great deal to know. He took the place as long ago as the fifth of the month. I've searched all the newspaper files through and through to see if there was any announcement or any message about that date which could conceivably affect him; but I found nothing. The intelligence he received must have come through some private channel. Meanwhile, here am I compelled to sit idle, whilst he is carefully planning and plotting one of his diabolical schemes."

For the next three days Bathurst saw little or nothing of Blake, for the latter was out at all sorts of extraordinary hours; sometimes returning at five or six in the morning, worn out with long, futile watching; at others, refusing to stir out of his bed-room till the afternoon, and then vanishing till luncheon time on the next day.

It was patent enough to the most casual observer that the strain was telling on him badly; he grew irritable and his health suffered, from substituting endless cigarettes for good square meals.

On the fourth day he came hurrying in in a state of great excitement.

"We are nearing the crisis at last," he said, flinging himself into a chair. "For whatever reason that studio was taken, we shall know more in the next forty-eight hours."

"Why, what has happened?"

"Hume has taken a through ticket to Constantinople on Saturday's Orient Express. Look here, my dear chap. I don't want to bother you, but the truth is, if I am to keep my wits about me, I must have a spell off. I want you to take my place for a few hours. Hume has just driven to the studio; I heard him give the address to the driver outside Cook's office. He is pretty certain to be there for some little time. I want you to go down at once and keep watch. If he comes out

As Blake ripped up the floor-boards, Bathurst and Harrison rushed in. "That man's the fiend himself, sir!" said the latter shakily.

don't lose sight of him for an instant, no matter where he goes you must follow him, by hook or by crook, even at the risk of his seeing you. For, if the worst comes to the worst, and he does spot you, the mere fact that he finds that he is being followed may scare him. Do you think you can manage it?"

"I'll do my best," said Bathurst.

"Good man; but be careful. He's a slippery customer. I'll be ready to relieve you when you come back."

Bathurst took himself off, and Blake settled himself down for a much-needed rest. He was still sleeping when Bathurst returned about two in the morning, but he woke instantly, freshened and alert.

"Well?" he asked sharply.

Bathurst shook his head.

"It is by no means well, I'm afraid. He was too clever for me. I lost track of him altogether for

close on three hours, but I traced him home right enough in the end."

"How did he give you the slip?"

"First of all, I had a long, dreary wait outside his studio. It had struck six before he came out. He had on a fur overcoat, and a soft felt hat, and he passed quite close to me without seeing me. That much I'm sure of.

"Turning into the Fulham Road he walked a little way and then hailed a taxi. I jumped into another one and followed him. He drove to the Café Royal, and dismissed the cab. I followed him into the Café. He took a seat at a table at the upper end, and ordered a sherry-and-bitters. I noticed that he seemed to be expecting somebody, or to be anxious about the time, for he kept glancing at the clock over the top of his evening paper."

"And at your reflection in the mirrors on the opposite wall, I expect," said Blake grimly. "Never mind, go on."

"I was skimming through the pages of 'Gil Blas' to kill time," continued Bathurst, "and all of a sudden I looked up and he had gone! How I came to miss him I can't tell. Of course, I realised at once that he had slipped out by the back entrance, and hurried after him. He couldn't have had more than a couple of minutes' start but when I got outside he was nowhere in sight."

"What time was it when you missed him?"

"Ten to seven exactly."

"Go on. What did you do next?"

"I hunted up all the most likely places I could think of—dining places, and so on—and then I tried the club, but I drew blank. At last I thought my best plan was to head back for the studio. I got back there about half-past nine, and sure enough the place was all lighted up. I could see the lights shining through the cracks of the blinds. Hume had left it in darkness, so I knew he was back all right.

"There was a man standing at the door of one of the slummy little houses opposite, and I questioned him.

"As luck would have it, the fellow had seen Hume come back; but I couldn't quite make his story out, for, according to him Hume must either have been hurt or uncommonly drunk,"

Blake sat forward in his chair, his eyes gleaming with sudden excitement.

"What's that?" he cried. "Tell me exactly what the man said."

"Well, according to his own account, he had just been round the corner for a jug of beer for supper when a motor came hurrying down the turning, and made him jump for the pavement. The street, as you know, is a cul-de-sac, and he wasn't expecting the car to come that way, so he naturally watched it with some curiosity. It pulled up opposite the studio garden door, and the chauffeur jumped down quickly. He opened the door of the closed tonneau, and helped out the occupant—another man, who, to use his own words, seemed as 'drunk as a lord.' One of them—he couldn't see which—unlocked the garden door, and the chauffeur helped his fare down the path. After a minute or so the lights were lighted in the studio, and the chauffeur came back alone, slammed the door of the garden and drove off."

"What time was that?"

"About half-past eight"

"The man spoke of the chauffeur's fare. I suppose the car was a taxi, then?"

"He said it looked like a taxi, but he hadn't noticed the car so much, it was the inebriated condition of 'the gent what owned the studio' that impressed him most. After seeing the last of him he went in and had his supper."

"And you?"

"I waited on and on till the studio lights went out. I wasn't going to let Hume give me the slip again—hurt, drunk, or sober—so I wouldn't leave until I was practically sure he had turned in for the night."

Blake nodded and smoked silently for a while.

"I wonder where Hume was between seven and half-past eight," he said at last. "If your man's word is to be relied on, he was either drugged or badly hurt in that hour and a half, or else—" He checked himself abruptly.

"We can do no more to-night, anyhow. As soon as it's light I'll send for a reliable man I know to mount guard over the studio, and to watch that end of the matter, leaving us with our hands free in case of emergencies."

This was done very early in the morning, and Bathurst arranged to look round two or three times during the day.

It was close on five o'clock on the Friday afternoon—a very foggy afternoon at that—when there came a hurried ring at Blake's bell. He had spent the greater part of the day pacing restlessly to and fro, fuming at his forced inaction, and more convinced than ever that Hume was busy planning come more than usually daring coup.

He rushed down to answer the the bell in person, but instead of being confronted with Bathurst, or the man he had placed on watch, he found himself face to face with a shabby-looking, faded little woman, with a sallow complexion and a pair of hard, bead-like eyes. She was evidently in a slate of great excitement and distress, and Blake checked his momentary impulse to say that he was too busy to listen to her.

"If you wish to see me, will you come upstairs, please," he said quickly, without waiting for her to speak. I can only spare you a few moments, so please explain your business as briefly as possible."

"You're Mr. Blake?" said the woman, following him into the room. "I've come to ask you to help me to find my husband. I'm Mrs. Soames and my husband was the man who got into trouble over the Margison will case."

Blake frowned, and, stretching up a long arm, pulled down a reference hook labelled M.

"They gave him seven years," continued the woman, "and he was no more guilty than I am. Then they reduced his sentence because he was quiet and well-behaved, and the end of it he was released yesterday morning. We had arranged it all between us, last time I saw him in the prison. He was to come up to London by a tram which reaches Waterloo at 7.30 in the evening—not before, because we didn't want him to reach home till after dark, on account of the neighbours; and I was to wait for him in the little house I've kept going. The folk round about all believed that he'd had an appointment abroad.

"He was to travel up with one of the prison officials who'd been kind to him. to keep Jim company like, lest he should feel strange; the man was coming up to London on his own account.

"Well, I waited and waited, and Jim—that's my husband's name—never came. I waited till past midnight, and the first thing this morning I went round to see the man from the prison, whose address Jim had given me.

"They'd come up by the train right enough, got to Waterloo at 7.30, and no sooner had they got out of the train than one of those chauffeur men come up to Jim and, touching his arm, asked him if his name was Soames.

"Jim says 'Yes,' and the man shows him into a motor standing by, saying he'd been sent to meet him and drive him home, because I'd moved since Jim was put away, and Jim was a stranger to Hammersmith, where I'm living now.

"Jim's warder friend laughed, and said something about my taking good care of him, and there they parted, and nothing's been heard or seen of Jim since."

Blake sat forward a little in his chair, and regarded the woman closely.

Do you think that he may possibly have absented himself voluntarily for a little while. There may have been reasons which you do not know of that—"

The woman shook her head violently.

"Don't you get any ideas of that sort into your head. There is a reason—the best of reasons— why Jim would have come straight to me, if something hadn't happened to him. We'd work to do, and I can tell you we shouldn't have been living in a small house for long, when once he was free. We would have been rich, and I should have been driving in my carriage like any lady."

Blake's eyebrows contracted.

"The work you proposed doing must have been peculiarly remunerative." he said drily.

The woman's bead-like eyes hardened, and a dull flush crept into her sallow cheeks.

"You're right. It would have paid—and paid well, and no trouble for getting it, either. I told you Jim was innocent, didn't I?—and that's the gospel truth. He was clerk to a solicitor, and just before old Margison died he sent for Jim's boss to draw up a new will, which was properly signed and witnessed. Jim was one of the witnesses. It left all the money but a few hundreds to charity, and cut out old Margison's nephew, who was a bad lot. That will was put in the office safe.

"But when the old man died, and they went to get the will, it was gone. Jim was the only person who had the keys besides the solicitor himself, and they accused him of having destroyed it for a bribe and, as bad luck would have it, they proved that Jim had close on a hundred pounds just then, which he couldn't account for. All he could say was that it had been given him as a loan by a man he knew called Masters. But this Masters couldn't be found anywhere, and the address Jim swore the man lived at didn't even exist. The prosecution mode a deal of that, and in the end Jim was found guilty."

Blakc, who had been glancing through the pages of his book, nodded.

"Quite so; and as the text of the later will could not be proved, a compromise was effected by which the charities took a third, and the nephew two-thirds. Still, I confess that I hardly see how the fact is liable to assist you in making a fortune.'"

Mrs. Soames looked more malignant than ever.

"Jim had a lot of time to think things over after he was put away, and whilst he was thinking he suddenly realised that he knew who this Masters was, all the while. Masters used to wear a curious sort of ring—a big, flat, blue stone, pretty near half an inch square, in a plain gold setting—lapis lazuli, they call it. When the prosecuting counsel was winding up his long speech, he stretched out his hand and pointed at Jim—his left hand it was—and on it there was Masters' ring, sure enough.

"Jim was that flabbergasted and dazed, he couldn't say anything at the time, and when they sentenced him he fainted. But afterwards he remembered—and he thought and thought, and kept his tongue between his teeth, till I was allowed to go and visit him the first time. Then he managed to tell me without being overheard.

"Masters, as he knew him, had a bit of a moustache, and walked with a curious stoop; did a bit of betting, too, and led Jim on to a bet. That's where the loan of a hundred came in. Jim was a bit behind, and Masters let him have the money to prevent Jim's boss finding out, as he said, but really because he wanted to be sure Jim was kept on at the office till the matter of the will was finished. Jim never saw Masters except after dark, too, which was another, Harry" cried Blake. "Good Heavens, what a blind fool I've been. There's not a moment to be lost!"

Mrs. Soames nodded complacently.

"Marston Hume—that's him! And Jim can prove it. Amongst that hundred there were two notes—ten-pound notes. Jim knew the numbers; those notes were given to Hume in part payment of a cheque he cashed at his own bank, yet Masters gave them to Jim!"

"You are sure?"

"Jim is; and I helped him to find out. I let lodgings to young gentlemen that worked at the bank, and I let 'em do much as they pleased, so long as they told me what was happening at the bank. And what's more, Margison's nephew drew out five thousand in cash and small notes a week after he got his money. Masters, or Marston Hume, got that, you may be sure, and he's got plenty more besides now.

"That's why I want you to help me find my Jim, so that we can make him pay—pay through the nose. Jim has all the proofs ready, and will make it hot for him!"

"Does Hume suspect—did you give him any reason to suspect that your husband had guessed who Masters really was?"

Mrs. Soames' sallow face took on a venomous expression.

"I gave him a bit of a jump once. I wanted to let him know there was trouble ahead, and keep him awake at nights, so I sent him a postcard with the word 'Masters' printed on it, and underneath a 'J' and an 'S'"

Blake threw up his hand.

"Then, as sure as fate, when you did so, I believe you signed your husband's death-warrant!"

Mrs. Soames went white.

"You mean he's got Jim?" she said weakly.

"I mean just that, unless I can prevent it. Now, go. If I'm to do anything I must act at once. Write your address down there and go. I will wire you as soon as possible."

Mrs. Soames, looking scared and shaken, went, and hardly had she left the room when Bathurst came in.

"Nothing to report," he said. "Hume is still there, and no one has been near the place but the dustman and a couple of tradesmen calling for orders, and— Good heavens, man, what's up?"

"Murder, probably!" said Blake hoarsely, "Get a taxi at once. I'll talk as we go."

As they flew along Blake gave him a brief outline of Mrs. Soames' visit.

"Hume must have known as early as the beginning of the month that Soames was coming out. He made it his business to find out his proposed arrangements down to the last-detail, and laid his plans with his usual diabolical coolness. He must have seen you right enough in the Café Royal, and given you the slip. I feel positive now that what your man at the cottages saw was not the chauffeur helping Hume down the studio garden, as he thought, but Hume, acting as a chauffeur, helping, or rather dragging along the man Soames in a drugged or semi-conscious condition.

"Hume, as you told me yourself, was wearing a fur coat and a soft felt hat. He must have ordered a car to be waiting for him at the back entrance of the café at, say, half-past six, or a quarter to seven.

"He slipped quietly out of the door when he saw you engrossed in your paper for the moment, jumped into the car, dismissing the chauffeur, and drove straight to Waterloo.

"To stuff his felt hat into his pocket and put on a chauffeur's cap and goggles would be the work of an instant, and form a sufficiently effectual disguise. He waited for Soames' arrival, gave him a bogus message mentioning Mrs. Soames' address, probably—and lured him, all unsuspecting, into the car. In the closed, cab-like body, chloroform or any ordinary anaesthetic could have been applied gradually through the speaking-tube, producing first drowsiness and then lethargy. He left Waterloo, as we know, a few minutes after half-past seven, and he must have driven about for some time to allow the anaesthetic to gain its full effect, for he only reached the studio at eight-thirty.

"Having disposed of Soames there and assured himself that the man was incapable, he drove the car back to the garage, returning on foot whilst your informant was enjoying his supper. After that—we shall see."

He leant out of the window and spoke a few words to the driver.

"Told him to go the round of the garages nearest the studio," he explained. "If we can find the car he used, it will be an important point."

They drew blank at the first three places they tried, but at the fourth Hume's name was known at once.

"Regular customer of ours, sir," explained the man in charge. "Yes, that's right; he had one of our cars last night—that green-bodied one over there. It was ordered to meet him at the back entrance of the Café Royal at half-past six. He drove himself, as he usually does, and brought her back a little before nine. Hope nothing's happened, sir? Nice, civil-spoken gentleman, Mr. Hume."

"I should like to examine the inside of the car for a moment, please," said Blake curtly; and striding across, he opened the door. A faint, sweet, rather sickly perfume was still perceptible, especially round the inner opening of the speaking-tube, to which a small fragment of cotton-wool was adhering.

Blake pointed this out to Bathurst silently, and then, striking a match, he searched the interior. Wedged in one corner of the seat was a small, crumpled scrap of paper, which he picked up and smoothed out; on it was an address scrawled in pencil—Mrs. Soames' address in Hammersmith.

Bathurst looked at it over Blake's shoulder and nodded.

"That settles it," said he.

"Yes, that settles it," replied Blake gravely. "And now for the studio."

They dismissed the taxi at the corner, not wishing to give the alarm by driving straight up to the door, and walked down the short turning.

They were still some thirty yards from the studio when Blake checked suddenly. No light

showed, and the man whom Blake had stationed there to shadow Hume was gone.

With a stifled exclamation Blake hurried forward, reached the top of the garden-door with a spring, and clambered over. Bathurst followed close at his heels, and side by side they dashed up the narrow path. Blake's face showed grey with anxiety. Without an instant's hesitation he flung himself at the studio-door; it creaked but held, and he drove at the lock with his boot-heel. The fastenings tore away, and they found themselves in the darkness of the small entrance-hall.

The door beyond was open, and they rushed into the studio itself. A faint light from without flickered through the crevices of the blinds— enough to enable them to distinguish their surroundings. Blake crossed to a gas-bracket and laid his palm against the glass globe. It was still warm.

"Missed by a matter of minutes," he said, and turned on the gas and lit it.

The studio was plainly but comfortably furnished. A glance, however, was sufficient to show that no one could be concealed there, dead or alive. Blake dashed into the bed-room; it contained merely a camp bed and a chest of drawers. The bath-room contained a fitted porcelain bath and washhand-stand ; but in none of the three rooms was there the slightest trace of the missing man.

They turned on all the lights, and for a full hour they searched every nook and cranny for some clue. Blake worked with a feverish energy which positively startled Bathurst; his face was drawn and haggard, and there was a growing look of dumb horror in his eyes which Bathurst could not understand. In two or three places he even went to the length of ripping up the floor-boards, yet still without result.

At last they were both startled by the whirr of the garden-gate bell. Bathurst ran to answer it, and found Blake's man, Harrison, standing outside.

"Come in, man—come in!" he cried. "What's happened?"

"That man's the fiend himself, sir!" said Harrison, shakily, as they joined Blake. "A bit more than an hour ago, he came out of the gate there and beckoned to me. I'm rigged out like a cab-runner, as you can see—and told me to get him a taxi. I got two; one for him and one for myself, waiting round the corner. 'Victoria,' he said to me, and gave me sixpence. I followed him to the station, and hung about till I'd seen him take a ticket for Paris; and I was just going to wait and make sure that he really meant going when he comes up as cool as you please, and hands me this note. 'Give this to Mr. Blake with my compliments,' says he. 'You'll find him either at his rooms or my studio.'"

Blake snatched the note and tore it open.

"Dear Blake," it ran. "I found it convenient to alter my plans at the last moment, and have started for Paris to-day, instead of to-morrow. I am going, as you are aware, for a short trip to the East; but any letters addressed to the Chatham will find me in due course. I found your man most useful and attentive. I leave my studio at your disposal till my return."

Blake read it to the last word; and then, to Bathurst's horror, burst into a fit of hysterical laughter. It was as though those few simple sentences had brought about a nervous breakdown, for he sat on a couch, his face buried in his hands, muttering to himself brokenly.

Bathurst seized him by the shoulder and shook him violently; he felt that he himself was being infected by some nameless horror.

"What is it, man?" he cried. "What is it? Where's Soames? He came in here, and he has never come out. Where is he?" he repeated savagely.

Blake pulled himself together with an effort, and rose, looking infinitely tired.

"Come," he said. "I will show you why Soames never came out of this fiendish place, I have been fighting against the realisation of the truth all this while; but in my mind I knew, and Hume's note puts the matter beyond all doubt."

He led them into the bath-room, and pointed to the big porcelain bath.

"That was where the poor wretch was disposed of after Hume had killed him," he said. "Look at these!" From behind a towel-rack he dragged out two empty carboys, which Bathurst had not noticed before. A drop or two of oily liquid remained in one of them. He tilted it on to the floor. "Concentrated acid," he said hoarsely; and pulling up a board he touched the leaden waste-pipe with his foot—it crumpled up like tinder.

Bathurst turned white.

"Merciful heavens, but it's too ghastly! And the—the clothes?"

"There is a big tortoise stove in the studio," said Blake dully that would reduce anything to ashes—anything, you understand; and the stove is cleaned out and the dustman came this morning—Harrison there, saw him. Hume leaves nothing to chance. His note shows that he knows the security of his position."

"But we could prove that Soames came here, and that—"

"You cannot prove murder without a body. Soames came here—and now there is no Soames, and there is no law that can touch Marston Hume. Let us go."

"The 'Union Jack' is to be seen in all the canteens, and is a great favourite with the boys out here."

(Extract from an Officer's Letter, "Somewhere in France.")

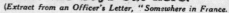

THE Union Jack 1^d LIBRARY

THE MYSTERY OF THE INARI TREASURE

Introducing Sir Richard Losely and Lobangu the Zulu!

No. 672.   EVERY THURSDAY.   August 26th. 1916.

The UNION JACK LIBRARY

With Which is Incorporated the 'Pluck Library

No. 672.]   ONE PENNY.   [August 26th, 1916.

THE MYSTERY OF THE INARI TREASURE

A Story of Thrilling Adventure and Detective Work,
introducing those Popular Characters
SEXTON BLAKE, TINKER, SIR RICHARD LOSELY,
and LOBANGU, the Zulu.

THE FIRST CHAPTER

IN WHICH SEXTON BLAKE BECOMES ACQUAINTED WITH MR. EUSTACE MERTON, AND HEARS THAT GENTLEMAN'S STORY.

The two Inari had heard nothing until Blake and Lobangu were almost on top of them. Then they charged!

IT was one of those close, warm evenings, with a hint of thunder in the air. The clock had just struck half-past nine, and Sexton Blake, who had been hard at work on a difficult case till after five that morning, was yawning over a book. It was a light novel of sorts—of a type he frequently read when he wished to distract his mind from more serious and practical things. The illogical absurdities of them irritated him just sufficiently to keep him awake and amused.

He had just come to the point where the hero was doing something which was pathetically and practically impossible, and had absently reached out his hand to the box for a fresh cigarette, chuckling quietly to himself, when the "buzzer" of the table-telephone at his elbow whirred.

He gave an exclamation of impatience, and lighted his cigarette before picking up the receiver. "What is it?" he asked testily.

"Man named Merton wants to see you," answered Tinker's voice from below; "says it's urgent, and looks as if it was. He's a gentleman—wears gold-rimmed pince-nez, is narrow-shouldered, and weak-chested.

"There's a big car waiting for him outside. Says he must see you, and won't speak a word about his business to anyone else, and won't go away till he has seen you. I've put him in the ante-room. Shall I say you're in China, or show him up? He seems as if he might be interesting."

Blake yawned again.

"All right, show him up," he said curtly, and tossed his book aside.

A minute or so later Tinker announced "Mr. Eustace Merton!" closed the door again, and went down to give Pedro his supper.

Blake gave his visitor one swift, comprehensive glance, and moved an armchair forward.

"Good-evening, Mr. Merton! I am told that your business is urgent. Please sit down, and let me help you off with your driving-coat. There are cigarettes and cigars beside you. You've had a longish drive, I see; that white dust suggests Surrey, and, at a rough guess, the Chobham ridges, or thereabouts. What is the trouble, and how did you happen to hear of me, by the way?"

His visitor thanked him, slipped off his coat, and helped himself to a cigarette, gratefully accepting the long tumbler which Blake handed him as he sank down into the chair.

"It's very good of you, Mr. Blake," he said, in rather a tired voice. "As to how I heard your name, I don't want to be fulsome, but it is almost a household word, I should imagine, and I had no difficulty in finding your address. To be perfectly truthful, I got it from a local policeman, to whom you had shown a kindness, and who appears to regard you as something superhuman. Incidentally I did come across the Chobham ridges. Though how you knew I can't say."

Mr. Merton, as Tinker had reported, was by no means a typical athlete. Blake placed his age at roughly thirty, short-sighted, narrowly-framed, though long of limb, and gaunt almost to the point of emaciation, also he had a cough which racked him from time to time. His saving features were a strong jaw, an intellectual forehead, and lips set in a thin, hard line, which, taken together, betokened a spirit of dogged determination. He was a quick observer, too, for though Blake was sitting in the shadow, and had merely shot a sharp glance or two at him, he turned to him with a rather sour smile.

"Sizing me up, eh? Well, I won't ask you for your verdict. I'll merely tell you that a few years ago I almost got my International Rugby cap, and was only a fraction of a second behind the record University time for the half-mile. Then a chill after overexertion, which developed into that infernal thing called consumption, and here

I am, as you see me—more or less of a wreck. That's one of the reasons why I live amongst the pine-trees as much as possible."

"I quite understand," said Blake. "I should have diagnosed it pretty much that way myself. The symptom, however, which I do not understand, is the bulge in your right-hand coat-pocket. A short-barrelled revolver, of course, which, I presume has some connection with your visit to me to-night."

"You've sharp eyes, Mr. Blake, and you are quite right. But, you see, when three separate attempts have been made to murder a man, he feels more comfortable with something in his pocket which gives him a chance of getting a bit of his own back. As a matter of fact, it's a beast of a gun; throws high, and kicks like a Texas mule. I was out there, once, and I know; but it carries a heavy bullet, and at three yards, or thereabouts, is positively deadly. I believe it would stop pretty well anything but a 'must' elephant, so it's sort of homely, and that brings me to the point of why I'm disturbing you at this time of night.

"As you know, my name is Eustace Merton, and I am living at a place called Elmsley Manor, which really belongs to my elder brother Jack. Jack was always a bit of an adventurer and a wanderer, and never could stick at home, in England for long at a time.

"He left home several years ago quite unexpectedly, after sending me a wire to go down and care-take the manor in his absence.

"A letter, which followed later, told me that he would be away for a considerable period, and that I should find a sealed envelope in the top right-hand corner of his desk, with instructions in a separate cover.

"In the meantime he left me the use of his car, a couple of servants, and an odd job boy, and power to draw on his bank for anything that was necessary in the way of expenses. In fact, I felt that I was rather in clover, for being a younger son, and a briefless barrister at that, I was none too well-off, as you can imagine. He made no mention of where he was going in the letter, and for a matter of that, I don't suppose—or I didn't at the time—that he was over certain himself. It was a habit of his to start off on one of his jaunts, say to Quebec, with a notion of going to Labrador, and ending up in Yucatan or the Brazils instead.

"As soon as I settled down, I opened the letter of instructions, and I must confess the contents rather startled me. Briefly they were as follows. If at the end of three years I had heard no word of him, I was to go through all his papers, and especially the contents of the big sealed envelope. If at the end of seven years I still had not heard, I was to consider the whole estate as my own absolutely. He went on to say that he had left a will and instructions with his lawyers to that effect.

"At the end of the third year I opened the sealed envelope. Here it is. I'll leave it with you to go through at your leisure, and I will ask you to be kind enough to keep it, for safety's sake, for it is since opening that, and gaining knowledge of its contents, that my own troubles began.

"I had not opened it more than a week when the house was broken into, and the room, the library in which it was usually kept, ransacked. As a matter of fact, I had, by mere chance, taken the papers up to my bed-room to go through them again that night. I heard the noise the man made in breaking in, however, and in playing cat's cradle with the furniture—at least, it sounded like that. So I slipped downstairs, half-dressed as I was, and went to see what the row was about.

"I had barely swung the library door open when a man loosed off a couple of shots at me before I had time even to see what he was like. Neither of them hit, though they came near enough to make me good and angry. I am still pretty nimble on my feet, and can box a bit, in spite of this." And he tapped his chest.

"I caught the fellow under the jaw, and he went down flop, knocking over the light by which he had been working as he did so. I grabbed for his revolver which he had dropped, and by the time I had found the candlestick and the candle, and got a light once more, the brute had recovered, or else he had been shamming half the time, and was off through the window like greased lightning. I hadn't hit hard enough, you see.

"At the time I thought it was just a common or garden burglary, but afterwards I changed my mind. Well, there was peace and quietness for a time after that, and I had almost forgotten the incident, when I had a second visitor. He burgled my bed-room this time. It is a room on the first floor, and I always sleep with my windows open. He had apparently noted this

fact. Anyway, he came in through the window about two in the morning.

"Very quiet he was about it, too. But I am a light sleeper, and heard him before he had taken a couple of steps inside the room. Again there was no light, and we had as pretty a rough and tumble as you can imagine. In the end, however, he winged me in the arm, and I had to loose my hold, so he got away.

"The irony of the situation was that on this occasion the paper which he was after—and I am convinced it was the paper—was reposing peacefully in the library drawer.

"The third attempt was last night. My cough had been very bad for a day or so, and I hadn't been able to sleep at nights, I had got so sick of tossing and turning about, that last night I made up my mind not to go to bed at all, but to put on a smoking-jacket and sit up in front of the library fire with a pipe and a book, and doze off when I felt able to. I should say that, after the second attempt, I had bought this revolver I am carrying, and had slipped it into my coat-pocket that particular night. Premonition, I suppose.

"It can't have been much past twelve, and I was reading away steadily, when all of a sudden the curtain over the window on my left was partly drawn aside, and before I knew what was up there was a bang, and a bullet whizzed close past my ear—so close that I could feel the wind of it. I was up and out of that chair in a flash, and it was a lucky move for me, for the next second another bullet had crashed into the back of the chair just where my head had been.

"It ripped the cover and knocked a lot of the stuffing out, and that made me really wild, for it was my favourite chair. I whipped out my revolver and blazed away at a bulge in the curtain. I fired on the rise, knowing the pernicious habits of my snub-nosed weapon, and I got home somewhere, because there was a squeal and a splintering of window-glass, and the bulge in the curtain collapsed.

"I raced across to the window and tore aside the curtains, forgetful of the risk I ran, showing up clear cut against the lamplight, and peered out of the window, which was partially open, and broken; but it was pitch black outside, and I could see nothing; though I could hear someone making off through the shrubbery at a shuffling run, and when I struck a match, there was a

"I whipped out my gun and blazed at a bulge in the curtain."

tidyish splash of blood on the floor behind the curtains, and more smears on the window-sill.

"The beggars, whoever they are—for I am certain there are two, if not more in it—had changed their tactics this time. Before, they had always tried to go for the papers first, and I butting in was merely an incident. This time, however, they had chosen to go for me first baldheaded, with the idea, of course, I suppose, that with me comfortably planted, they could search for the papers at their leisure.

"On none of the three occasions had the two servants heard anything, for they sleep at the top of the house at the back, and the odd job boy and the gardener both sleep out.

"On the previous occasion I had passed off the graze on my arm as the result of an accident; but this time there was no explaining away the bullet-ripped chair-back and the shattered glass,

though I could have managed to mop up the bloodstains, perhaps.

"I waited till morning, and then sent for James. James is my brother's manservant, and a treasure. I told him the whole story as I have told it to you. It seems he knew something about the papers my brother had left before. He recommended me to call in the police—a thing I had hitherto refrained from doing, and which I didn't want to do even then, much preferring to see the thing through off my own bat.

"However, in the end we arrived at a compromise. James was to consult a local policeman, a friend of his, in a purely private capacity, and ask his advice.

"The Manor House, by the way, is a secluded solitary sort of place far from anywhere, and, barring an occasional mounted patrol, the police have never come near it, so, of course, they were in ignorance of what had happened.

"James went off on his bicycle to consult his pal, and the policeman, who, as I say, regards you as something almost superhuman and uncanny; gave me, through James, the excellent advice to come to you without delay. And here I am. He also suggested that if I wasn't a fool, I should leave the papers in your hands for safety's sake. There they are, if you will be kind enough to go through them.

"But that is not the only point, Mr. Blake. I have a much greater favour to ask you. So far, I have dealt only with my own side of the question. Now I want to deal with the far more important one of my brother. If I seem to be in danger of a sort here, in peaceful England, on account of those infernal papers and the secrets they contain, how much greater must be the danger in which my brother stands, who has gone to ferret out those same secrets at the other end of the earth?

"For four years now I have not received a line or a word from him, nor have I been able to get any news, though I have cabled time and again.

"If he were killed, or, worse still, taken captive and perhaps kept in torture for years, I should feel myself to be his murderer if I left any stone unturned to try and save him or find him. I, as you can see, am too useless a kind of wreck to make the attempt myself. I've no particular objection to dying that I know of, but I have a very rooted objection to hampering an expedition travelling through difficult country by becoming a sick man, who at best would only be a clog on the wheel.

"Your policeman friend has told me, again through James, that you know more corners and corners and out-of-the-way places of the earth than most men. What I would most earnestly beg you to do is to endeavour to find, and bring home, my brother Jack.

"If you succeed, I can never be grateful enough to you. If you fail, at least I shall feel that I have done my best by coming to the best man know of.

"Amongst the other papers there, you will find a cheque dated to-day, and made out to you for a sum of ten thousand pounds.

"Wait, please. The sum may seem large, but so will your expenses be, by all I can gather. You will need bearers, equipment, expensive steamer journeys; possibly you may even need to charter a boat of your own at times. Shortly after my opening the papers, after the first attempt had been made to obtain them, I went to a friend of mine, a traveller and a member of the Geographical. He put down the cost of such an expedition at a minimum of five thousand, and laughed in my face when I suggested trying to undertake it.

"'My dear fellow,' he said, 'you'd be on the sick list before you'd got a quarter of the way; it would be madness.' And I know he spoke the truth.

"I must go now if I am to get back before midnight. No, please don't bother to come down. I can find my way, thanks. I will call for your answer in two days' time, when you have been through the papers and looked things over.

"Good-night, and many thanks for listening to my yarn.

"My great hope is that you will find the case sufficiently interesting to induce you to take it up after you have been through that bundle, and have read the whole story first hand.

"I have purposely refrained from giving you anything more than the vaguest outline, because I should like you to come at the core of the thing, as it were, with an open mind."

Blake nodded, and rang the bell.

"Goodnight, Mr. Merton!" he said. "Let me see, today is Monday. I shall expect to see you or hear from you, then, on Wednesday—is that right?"

"Yes. I will be here on Wednesday about luncheon time. If you would come round to the club, we might talk things over whilst we had a bit of something to eat. That suit you?"

"Capitally," said Blake. "I shall be delighted."

"That's settled, then," said Mr. Merton, as Blake helped him into his coat. "I'm awfully grateful to you. Good-night!"

A moment or two later Blake heard the big car give a preliminary hrrmph! and then go purring away into the night.

He was still fingering the big envelope curiously when Tinker and Pedro came in.

"Well," asked Tinker, "was it interesting?"

"It may be, or it may not. I haven't gone into things yet, but when a perfect stranger drifts in, and calmly hands you over a cheque for ten thousand pounds to undertake a job, and explains that he has nearly been murdered three times over, it certainly promises well.

"How would you like to go foreign again?"

"Tophole! I'm sick of this little village of London—so is Pedro."

"Humph! Well, that's the meaning of this cheque. I am to go through the papers and decide on Wednesday."

He pushed the papers aside as he spoke.

"It's too late now; we'll go into them to-morrow. It's a fairly bulky pile. Lock them up in the safe. There'll be plenty of time to run through them to-morrow."

THE SECOND CHAPTER

A STARTLING DEVELOPMENT

Blake was making cuttings from the newspapers the next morning over a late and dawdling breakfast. There was a fresh murder case, and several other items of interest, which caught his notice, and, it was a habit of his to cut these out with a pair of scissors and carefully file them away under different headings for future reference.

His library formed in this way was extensive. The cuttings were neatly stored away, and at a moment's notice he could pick out detailed paper accounts of a hundred or more interesting crimes—items dealing with new technical research work, special envelopes for toxicology, little known diseases and their symptoms, descriptions of historical jewels, and all sorts of out-of-the-way minor information.

It was really a very valuable collection from his point of view. When at home he invariably made his cuttings at breakfast-time, and equally invariably allowed his coffee and eggs and bacon, or sausages, to grow stone cold in the process.

If he was away—sometimes for a month—the papers were delivered just the same, and piled in an untidy heap till he returned, and was at leisure to go through them, then he would mark off a few hundred paragraphs and columns with a blue pencil and leave Tinker to do the rest— much to Tinker's disgust.

On this particular morning it was well past ten, and a fine sunny morning at that. Blake was in an old Norfolk jacket, scissors in one hand, a burnt-out cigarette in the other, poring over the precious papers, whilst the eggs and bacon on the dish before him had become transformed into a bad imitation of rough ice— the ice being the solidified bacon grease, when the telephone bang.

"Yes! Hallo!" he said, reaching out and picking up the receiver.

"What's that? Telegrams? All right, fire ahead!"

"Please be at home 11.30—very urgent— signed Merton."

"All right, thanks. Yes, I've got that," he said, and rang off.

"Wire from Merton," he added to Tinker, who came at that moment.

"The man who was here last night, you know. There must have been some fresh developments. He is coming here at half-past eleven, and says it's urgent."

"I'd better go and make myself respectable. Show him in here when he comes."

At 11.25 Blake emerged from his dressing-room fresh and immaculate in a blue serge suit.

He had barely lighted a fresh cigarette when he heard a car draw up, and, glancing out of the window, recognised it as Merton's, though he was unable to see anyone in it on account of the enclosed top.

He waited for a minute or two, puzzled that Tinker had not shown Mr. Merton up, and then, exactly as the clock on the mantelpiece struck the half hour, the door was flung open, and a small, dark, clean-shaven man was shown in, who was certainly not Eustace Merton.

Blake gave him one quick glance, and assured himself that he had never seen the man before. Simultaneously he dropped his right hand into his jacket-pocket, where an automatic lay alongside a box of matches.

He recalled Eustace Merton's story of the triple attempt on his life, and considered that it was by no means a bad idea to be prepared for similar accidents.

He made no attempt to draw the weapon, though his forefinger rested lightly on the trigger. It's just as easy to shoot, and shoot quickly, and with satisfactory accuracy, through a coat-pocket at short range as it is to waste time by drawing it out, and giving the other man a chance of firing first. The one disadvantage is that it spoils the coat.

The man was neatly dressed in dark tweeds, stood about five feet-six, slight, but wiry, and swarthy of complexion, with peculiarly pale grey eyes, and the mobile mouth of an actor. But his face and clothes were alike grey with the dust of the roads, and his eyes had a hard, strained expression in them, and a tinge of weariness.

"Mr. Blake, sir?" he said inquiringly, in the respectful manner of a well-trained manservant.

Blake nodded, removed his finger from the trigger, threw away his cigarette, and producing the matchbox from his pocket, lighted another.

"You, I take it, are James?" he said quietly. "Mr. Merton wired to me making an appointment at 11.30 this morning."

"Begging your pardon, sir," said James, "it was I who took the liberty of wiring in his name." "Oh!" said Blake.

The little man's face twitched as if with a sudden spasm or pain for an instant, but his voice was firm as he spoke again.

"Mr. Eustace was murdered—shot—at some time in the early hours of this morning, sir. I know that he had been to you, sir, about the previous attempts, and about some papers; so as soon as I learnt what had happened I sent off the wire, and drove the car here as quickly as I could."

"Shot this morning?" said Blake, springing up, and for once betraying his surprise. "Good heavens, man, tell me about it! Tell me everything you know, and be quick!"

"It was like this, sir. Mr. Eustace, as you know, took the car out last night and drove up here. He told me he was coming to see you—in fact, if I may say so, it was by my advice.

Blake nodded.

"He told me so."

"Well, sir, just as he was starting, he turned to me, and said: "I may be late, James. Don't wait up. Leave the front door on the latch, and a light in the hall. I'll put the car away.

"I did as he told me, sir, and left a bit of cold supper ready for him as well. Then I went to bed, sir, my room being at the back of the house in the far wing, but before I went I had a good look round to see that everything was safe.

"At a quarter to eight this morning, I took him up his tea, and was surprised to find the room empty, and that the bed had not been slept in. My first thought was that he must have made up his mind to stay in town for the night, after seeing you, though it was unlike him to do so.

However, I put down the tray, and started to open up the house and, tidy things up generally.

"The lamp in the big entrance hall had burnt out, and his supper lay there just as I had left it, untouched. The door, too, was still on the latch as he had told me to leave it. Yet something or another—I can't tell you what, sir—made me uneasy. It may have been that I had it at the back of my head that I had heard the car returning in the night. It's a very quiet place, sir, and one sort of notices sounds, especially at night. Anyway, I just stepped across the lawn to the garage to make sure, and there, right enough, was the car. That gave me a bit of a start, though, in a kind of way, I'd expected to see it there.

"It was all in order, a bit dusty after the run, but the lights were switched off and the rugs neatly folded in the tonneau, with Mr. Eustace's driving-coat, cap, and goggles on top of them; but of Mr. Eustace himself there wasn't a sign.

"He was never an early riser, being a bit of an invalid, and, as I said, his bed had not been slept in, nor had his supper been touched, and there was the fact that the lamp had burnt itself out."

"Sure it hadn't been turned out?" said Blake quickly.

"Quite, sir! I had a good look at it. It's a duplex, with a glass container. The wicks were still turned up, and badly charred, and the container was bone dry."

Blake smiled appreciatively. "You are a good observer. Go on!"

"Begging your pardon, sir, a friend of mine has talked to me about you and your ways, and I remembered that details like that might be important, and I was getting very anxious. I was puzzled, too. And then all of a sudden I remembered the library. I hadn't opened up that. And Mr. Eustace, when he was feeling bad, sometimes dozed there in a chair in front of the fire instead of going to bed. He had done that the night before he came to see you, sir."

Blake nodded.

"Well, I opened the door, sir, and I got the start of my life. The curtains were drawn back, so there was plenty of daylight to see by. One of the windows, the one that had been broken before, was open, and the place was a regular shambles.

"Mr. Eustace lay on the floor. He was quite dead. He had been shot in two places, one wound was right in the temple, sir, the other was in his chest, and he was still wearing the suit I had got ready for him to go to town in yesterday.

"The desk had been broken open and rifled. Its contents lay strewn on the floor, and some of the rest of the furniture. Anything that might contain papers, that is, sir, had been upset and splintered as though with a heavy chisel or an axe.

"Mr. Eustace himself was lying near the fireplace on the hearthrug. His revolver was gripped tightly in his hand, and four of the chambers were empty; but they hadn't been emptied to no purpose. One, it is true, probably the first, had gone high and smashed a picture. He may have been flurried, and he always said the revolver was too short in the barrel; but he had hit a man by the desk, for there was a great pool of blood there, and another man must have been hit about five feet from the same spot. The window sill, too, was literally smeared with blood, as the two crawled away.

"Begging your pardon, sir, but I should say that Mr. Eustace came back latish, put the car in the garage, and then, as he entered the house, heard a noise in the library, went straight there, and then what I have described might have happened, sir!"

Blake nodded.

"By your account, and the matter of the untouched supper and burnt-out light, I should say you were right. What did you do then?"

"I closed the window, sir, lest it should attract attention, locked the door, and put the key in my pocket, and came straight here as fast as the car would bring me, only stopping to send off the wire. I know you don't like things messed about, sir. I disturbed things as little as possible, and Mrs. Barnes, the housekeeper, won't go near the room. If she did, she couldn't get in. Except the men themselves, sir, no one but you and I know what has happened yet."

"Excellent!" said Blake.

"They must have watched Mr. Eustace pretty carefully, sir, seen him drive off to London, may have even heard him call out that he would be late—he said that to me just as he was starting—and taken their chance of working undisturbed. Then his return when they were in the middle of things surprised them."

Again Blake nodded.

"I'll come back with you at once," he said. "Start up the car whilst I get one or two things

that may be necessary, and I'll be with you in a couple of minutes."

"Very good, sir!" said James.

Blake stopped just long enough to give Tinker a few brief orders, and snatch up his pocket investigation case, and they were off, James driving, and Blake sitting back in the car smoking meditatively.

THE THIRD CHAPTER

BLAKE INVESTIGATES AT ELMSLEY MANOR—AND DEDUCES MANY THINGS.

THEY reached the house in a time that ought to have piled-up a big amount in fines for exceeding the speed limit.

It was a large house, and though the greater portion of it was shut up, of course, James and the housekeeper had evidently looked after everything with the greatest care.

Blake paused to examine the improvised supper-table, the meal untouched, the glasses clean and unused, and the full decanter and syphon. Then he glanced at the lamp.

"You are quite right, James," he said. "I think your reading of the matter is perfectly correct. The men were evidently making such a noise in their feverish search for the papers, knowing by experience that they wouldn't be heard by you or the housekeeper in the distant wing, that they themselves failed to hear the car come up the drive, and the opening and shutting of the garage door. Mr. Merton, however, heard them as soon as he opened the front door, and, as you suggest, went straight to the library without pausing to touch the supper on the table. Now let's go straight to the scene of the tragedy."

"This way, if you please, sir!" said James, and led him across the hall to a door on the right, and, taking a key from his pocket, turned it in the lock, and flung the door wide open.

It was a big room, with fine old furniture in it. Valuable pictures on the walls between the rows of bookcases, and more in the shape of big, leather-covered armchairs, made for added comfort. A pleasanter room under under ordinary circumstances it would have been hard to find. But now it was the scene of a ghastly tragedy, made all the more ghastly by the flood of sunshine pouring through the windows, showing up every detail with merciless clearness.

The wrecked and splintered furniture, the scattered papers, some of them blood-splattered, the ominous dark stains and smears on the carpet, and last, but by no means least, the gaunt, still figure on the hearthrug. To emphasise matters even more, and make the contrast still more vivid, through the windows there were views of orderly, sunlit flower-beds ablaze with colour, and there came faintly the twittering of songbirds and the lazy drone of bumble-bees.

Little flecks of dust danced and grew brilliant in the sun-beams pouring through the windows. Yet the room reeked with the acrid smell of burnt powder, and a bluebottle or two buzzed noisily against the window-panes.

Inured as he was to scenes of tragedy, even Blake felt a sort of physical revulsion at the picture before him. Outside everything was alive in the warmth and the sun-light.

Inside lay a murdered man, his face distorted and the upper lip drawn back, showing the teeth in a sort of defiant snarl.

Blake stood on the threshold for a full three minutes taking in every detail bit by bit, and focussing them on his memory, until at last James ventured to give a discreet cough.

"The door, sir, is still open, and Mrs.—the housekeeper that, is, might be passing through the hall at any moment. As yet she knows nothing of this, sir."

Sexton Blake nodded, and moved a step or two into the room, whilst James softly locked the door on the inside.

"Stay where you are, or sit in that chair, if you prefer it, said Blake. "I don't want more confusing impressions than can be helped, and in this light the carpet shows marks very distinctly. For instance, even from here I can see tracks which must be yours leading to the body and on towards the window there."

"Very good, sir," said James obediently, and sat down.

After another pause for a final look round, Blake went straight up to where the dead man lay. The wound in the temple was a ghastly one, a piece of the bone having been flicked clean out by the bullet. That in the chest was merely visible as a dark blotch on the waistcoat.

Neither of the shots had fired at point-blank range, for there was no scorching or powder-pitting. They had probably been fired from nearer the window at the far end of the room as the men tried to make their escape.

Blake left the body without disturbing it in any way, beyond taking a clean handkerchief from the dead man's pocket, and carefully covering his face. The fingers were so tightly clenched round the revolver-butt that he made no attempt to remove them, merely satisfying himself that James' version of the number of shots fired was correct.

Then he went down on his hands and knees, pulled out his magnifying-glass and examined the carpet here and there, moving very carefully. That done, he examined the broken desk and other pieces of furniture which had been smashed or tampered with.

Now and again he took from his pocket a small packet of very fine lycopodium powder, sprinkled some here and there, and blew the surplus away carefully.

James noticed that on each occasion what looked like a series of yellow-white blotches remained.

The papers strewn round the desk he paid no heed to what-ever. But to the footmarks and the window he paid attention. Only once did he speak during the whole of his examination, and that was when he was to close the window.

"James, James," he said reproachfully over his shoulder, "why did you close this? It might have taught us a lot, and saved us a lot of trouble. Never mind," he added quickly, seeing the little man's face drop, "we shall manage all right without it, and you have done splendidly. I've finished in here. Lock the door again behind us, and put the key in your pocket. Then show me the nearest way to the flower-bed under the window – the window with the new pane in it. I mean, through which the men escaped."

"Yes, sir," said James. "By the front door will be the quickest."

Blake examined the flower-bed, which was badly trodden down, made some measurements with a pair of pocket callipers, compared them with some notes he had jotted down, and walked a little way across the lawn beyond until he came to some bushes.

He studied these, went on a little further, and then returned slowly to James.

"There is a chalk road, or a chalk pit of some sort beyond those trees which border the grounds there, isn't there?" he asked absently.

"Why, of course there is, sir!" said James, in surprise. "You know the old chalk workings which were dug when they were making the road round the park, and for repairing the wall in places, and the—"

"I don't know anything of the sort!" said Blake sharply. "I have never been in this part of the country before – not within ten or twenty miles of it, anyhow, to my knowledge."

James stared.

"Quite so, sir. I remember you telling me so as we drove down; but then, how could you tell— about the chalk, I mean? No human being can see through that clump of trees."

"Deduction, James—deduction and logic. And now, if you could get me something to drink, and some bread and cheese, or something to eat, I should be grateful. I'll just amplify my notes in the hall, and have a cigarette whilst you are doing it."

"It shall be ready in ten minutes, sir," said James; and they went back to the house.

Blake busied himself with a notebook, and indelible pencil, and a cigarette, until James returned with the tray.

"Sandwiches—three sorts, sir," he said— "chicken, cheese, and mustard and cress—and some of Mr. Eustace's favourite claret."

"Excellent!" said Blake. "Don't stand there; sit down. Smoke, if you like, and I'll explain whilst I'm eating. You'd better have a glass of claret yourself, you look fagged out.

"You see these papers here? They are notes and diagrams. I shall leave them with you, and you can take them to your policeman friend when you report this business to the police officials. They may do him a bit of good. I dare say he'll get a promotion. For my own part, I must get back to town as quick as I can.

"The men concerned in the case – this particular phase of the case – are two. One man, whom we will call A, was short-height about five feet six – to judge from the length of his stride, slight of build, has a slender foot, wears well-made boots, size six; was wearing a dark blue serge suit at the time – there are indications of a few stray strands of serge on the rough stone of the window-sill; and has, I think, coarse, dark hair. I say coarse, because he certainly used violet oil

to keep it smooth. I could detect the scent on the single stray hairs I found easily; but I haven't my pocket microscope with me, so I can't tell the degree of coarseness for certain.

"The other man – B – is a much bigger man, reddish haired, I believe, wears a cleven boot, such as a golf boot, with nails set in little triangles of three on the soles. He was, roughly six feet. Both were armed with small-bore weapons, 303's, probably automatics – they run about that size; and revolvers, unless of exceptional pattern, don't. In this little pillbox you will find one of the bullets, partially flattened, which I found close to the fireplace, the scented hairs, and the threads of blue serge.

"B, the big man – as you can show your friend the policeman, from the various finger-prints I dusted over – has an abnormal stretch from the ball of the little finger to the tip of the thumb, and a deep, irregular scar on the forefinger of the left hand. It was he who did most of the breaking-up of the desk and other possible hiding-places, though, on occasion, A – who has slender fingers, almost like a woman's – helped him.

"I can give you no more details of any importance, but I can reconstruct roughly what happened last night. The two men came across from somewhere in the direction of the chalk-pit and the road behind the trees, for there was minute grains of chalk here and there in their footprints on the carpet here, especially in B's who wore nails, in spite of the fact that they had crossed the grass. They hid in the shrubbery for a while, waiting and watching. Possibly they saw the car go off, or possibly they saw you lighting the lamp and getting supper ready.

"Anyhow, they waited long enough for one of them to smoke at least a couple of goldflake cigarettes – the ends are lying there now – the other smoked a pipe. I saw the dottle, but touched neither that nor the cigarette-ends.

"Then they came up, forced the window with a clasp-knife probably – the latch is old-fashioned and weak, and it would be child's play. After which they got to work until disturbed by Mr. Merton's return. They must have worked by electric torchlight, I fancy, for there are no stray matches about the place, and no signs of candle-grease anywhere.

"Mr. Merton must have hit the big man in the body somewhere, for though he bled profusely, he was able to move with comparative ease, in spite of the heavy bullet. The other man, however, must have been hit somewhere in the left leg, for there were signs of the left foot trailing, and in places the big man had to help him along.

"On the return journey they passed to the right of the shrubbery, and after that I can say no more, except that if your friend can't find two badly-wounded men such as I have described, who would obviously be unable to move far or fast in a sparsely populated piece of country like this, and where cars are presumably few and far between, except those privately owned, he is not the man I take him for.

"Of course, there is just the possibility that there may have been a third man in it, who waited outside the wall with a conveyance of some kind; but I doubt it. Anyway, an examination of the road where they climbed the wall, and where there are certain to be bloodstains, will show."

"Yes, sir," said James eagerly; "I've got that quite clear!"

"Good! But there's one thing that I haven't" said Blake drily, "and that is this. How did they even come to know of the existence of those papers? Much more, how did they come to know that there was possibly great value attached to them, unless Mr. Merton had talked about them openly – say, in some public place?"

"I don't quite follow you, sir."

"Well, to some friend in an hotel, say, when—"

"By gosh! You've got it, sir!" cried James excitedly.

"You've just brought it all back to me in a flash, as it were, sir! Mr. Eustace used to talk to me confidentially, as it were, sir – this being a lonely place for him in the evenings, as it were – and the night he opened the papers and read them he was quite excited. He didn't tell me much about their contents, of course, sir – just something about an enormous fortune to be picked up somewhere abroad, which his brother – the master – had gone to look for, and that I was to send off a wire the first thing in the morning to a friend of his in town to meet him at a little wayside hotel at Longford for luncheon.

"The next morning I drove him there. I remember he was busy, reading and re-reading the papers all the time in the back of the car. His friend Mr. Helen was there waiting for him, and

they went to luncheon. I put the car away in the yard, and was sitting on a bench in front of the hotel, when Mr. Eustace caught sight of me, and beckoned to me.

"He told me to come in and get some luncheon, and I was glad enough to do so. There was no chauffeur's room in the place, only the main coffee-room, so I went in and sat down at a table in the far corner.

"Mr. Eustace and Mr. Helen had the papers spread out on the table before them, and they both seemed too excited to bother much about their food, though Mr. Eustace ordered a bottle of champagne 'in honour of the occasion,' as he said. The coffee-room was a fairly large one, but there were few people in it.

"The place depended mostly on week-end motorists, I fancy. Apart from my own, there were only three tables occupied – one by a lady and gentleman, the second by Mr. Eustace and his friend, and the third, quite close to them, by two men; and they were the men you've just described, sir, or I'll eat my hat! One, the big man with the red head, was dressed in rather a loud golfing suit; the other was a dapper, little, dark-haired man.

"Mr. Eustace was too excited to take any heed of them. He was reading aloud extracts from the paper to Mr. Helen, long bits at a time, and he had before him a map or diagram of sorts, to which they both referred from time to time.

"I was too far away to hear what they were saying, and it wasn't my place to listen. But I did hear certain stray phrases, such as 'There's a fortune in it!' 'It will be a great trip!' 'Jack must have—' 'Hundreds of thousands at least, I tell you, man!' And then he and his friend would fall to arguing or studying the map if it was a map, all over again.

"Those were the sort of scraps I heard sir; but the two men at the table near them must have heard every word, and got a good sight of the map thing too; I remember now that they gave up all pretence of talking themselves, and were listening intently as they smoked in silence.

"At last Mr. Eustace rose, beckoned to me, and gathered up the papers.

" 'I shall lock these away safely in my desk,' I heard him say. 'You think it over, and let me know.'

"And at that I went out to get the car ready and bring it round.

"As we drove away I noticed the two men were leaning out of the window, and watching us curiously. When we had gone they could easily have got Mr. Eustace's name and address out of the waiter for a shilling tip. He was well-known there; and what's more, I remember seeing those two men – or their twin brothers – in the village a few days afterwards, just before the first attempt was made on Mr. Eustace!"

"That settles it, then," said Blake. "What would you put the two men down as being?"

"Well, sir, I didn't bother about them much at the time; but, after all that's happened, I should say they were a couple of swell crooks, with a bit of money behind them – the kind that go round marking down country houses, under pretence of fishing, or sketching in the neighbourhood."

Blake nodded.

"I should fancy you're about right. Now, if you'll get out the car, we'll just drive to the station, and stop and give your friend the police-man these notes and exhibits on the way. Then you'd better wire to Mr. Merton's solicitors, and arrange about things. I must go straight back to London, and have a look into those papers. The last time I saw him he handed me a large sum of money to take an expedition out to look for his brother. I was in doubt as to whether to accept. Last night's events have decided me. I shall certainly go, if the papers seem to me in any way reliable."

"Yes, sir," said James thoughtfully, and said no more.

Sexton Blake reached town late in the afternoon, and drove straight to his house.

"Get some dinner sent in from the restaurant, Tinker," he said. "Order something nice, and plenty of it. I'm famished. We've got to be busy with those papers to-night. I've practically decided to go. I've been through poor Eustace Merton's case. It had some points of interest. You paid in that cheque?"

"Yes."

"Anyone called?"

"No one called; but Sir Richard Losely rang up from his club to say that he was staying in town to-night, and wanted to see you."

"That's pure, unadulterated luck!" said Blake, springing up and seizing the instrument.

"That you, Spots?" he asked, as soon as he was put through. "Good! Come round here at once; it's important. What? Oh, hang your dinner! Put

the man off; you can grub here. Yes, all right. Good egg!"

"Dinner for two, Tinker," he said. "And get out some of Sir Richard's favourite wine."

"For two?" said Tinker.

"Yes, for two," said Blake, grinning. "You and Pedro can share a bone, or anything you fancy on the mat. If you're both good, you can come into dessert!"

"Oh, we can, can we?" said Tinker. "You'll be sorry for that. I'll order you some food. But Pedro and I will have plovers' eggs, and caviare, and—'

"Oh, get out!" said Blake, and heaved a cushion at him.

Tinker got.

THE FORTH CHAPTER

THE CURIOUS STORY OF THE ELEPHANT HUNTER.

A QUARTER of an hour later Sir Richard Losely turned up, bronzed and burly-looking as ever.

"Hallo, Blakcy!" he said. "What's up? When you say urgent, it generally means somethin' pretty hefty. Phew! But it's hot to-night! Find me a long, fizzy drink and a cigarette!"

"Find 'em yourself, and don't be lazy. You know where they are. Then settle down, and listen while I tell you opening part of the yarn, as far as I know it!"

"Funny sort of host!" commented Sir Richard. "Fire ahead! Don't mind me. I know how to make myself comfortable!"

Blake gave him a brief account of his meeting with Eustace Merton, of the murder, after the previous attempts, of the papers, and finally of his own deductions.

He had barely finished when the telephone-bell rang.

"Trunk call," said Blake, with the receiver at his ear. "Hallo! Yes. That you, James? Right!"

He listened for a while, then laid the receiver down.

"Quick work, that! It worked out exactly as I said. They got the two men an hour ago, not half a mile from the house. They were hiding by the edge of a pool. Gone there for water, I suppose. Both done up, and one delirious. There'll be a proud policeman in that section of the country to-night. I told him not to drag my name into the show. I'm glad to have given him a leg-up. He seemed a decent sort, and had the sense to appreciate my methods, which is more than many of his kind do. Hello! Here's dinner! They've got those men, Tinker. James has just 'phoned to say so. Here, what the deuce have you got on that third tray?"

He whipped off the napkin and stared.

"Look here, Spots, the young villain has ordered just the same grub for himself as for us, and a double portion at that."

"One for me and one for Pedro," said Tinker imperturbably; but as Pedro doesn't care for sweets or savouries, I can eat his share of both."

"Oh, go and eat till you bust – the pair of you," said Blake, grinning, "and roll in again when you're through, for you certainly won't be able to walk."

When the meal was over and the table cleared, Blake brought out the big envelope and pulled out the contents.

The outer sheet was written on the "Elmsley" paper, and in the elder Merton's hand – as Blake recognised from other documents he had seen.

It merely read as follows:

"Dear Old Man, —When you read this, according to the instructions I gave you in the other letter, as to time and dates – and I know you won't read it before – the mere fact of your reading it may make you take it pretty well for granted that I am done in—a dead egg, in fact. I shall have played for a big stake, and the fun of winning or losing, and I shall have lost.

"In which case I have told the lawyer people to behave pretty, and hand the whole show over to you unconditionally, and you can marry and live happy ever after, as they say in the story-books.

"I always loved a good gamble, as you know, in a mild sort of way – not a gamble for mere coin of the realm, but a game in which you pit you wits and life against another chap's. It beats poker and all those fool card games hollow.

"In this case I am staking the limit on the yarn of an old elephant hunter who had some absurd notion that I had tried to save his life. I

didn't save it, as a matter of fact, because though I stopped the bull all right, it had already got him for keeps.

"He pegged out three days later, poor chap, and we buried him in a coffin make of old food-boxes. I never knew his real name, so had to put up a rough cross with just R.I.P. on it, and leave it at that.

"That was on my last trip.

"Before he died he insisted on my taking the enclosed papers from him, and I gave him a sort of half-promise to follow the thing up some time or another. It's that trek I am on now, but how it will end I can't say. I may come back rich beyond the dreams of avarice, or I may strike the long 'one way trail along which no traveller returns,' as Shakespeare or one of the writing johnnies puts it.

"That's where the gamble of the thing comes in. I'll be a millionaire or as much use as a dead mouse. Roll, bowl, or pitch. Walk up, ladies and gents – this way for the milky ones. So long, old man. – Your affectionate brother, J.

"P.S. – The papers I leave are the originals; so is the map. I have taken copies with me."

Blake laid the letter down and picked up the bulkier package. The writing was old and faded, and the paper soiled and yellow-looking, and weather-worn, and the front page bore a date seven years old. The spelling was quaint in places, but the general style of the story bore the impress of truth as set down by a man who had no reason to embroider it – just a mere straightforward statement of facts as they were known to the writer.

"Just on eleven months ago," it began, "I was up in the Itara district after ivory. I made a fairly good trip of it. I had forty bearers, and had got some fine tusks – not an 'escribello' amongst the lot – in fact, I reckoned I had made a good pile of money for that season, when I heard a strange yarn from a small native chief at whose kraal I was staying for a few days' rest-up.

"This is what he told me, and it made me sit up and scratch a bit, and think.

" 'Twenty years ago or thereabouts, a big Arab caravan had been up country on a slave raiding and looting expedition. They numbered, including the slaves, who did the portage, seventeen to eighteen hundred strong. They were known to have left Imbibi, which is at the back of the hinterland, laden with ivory, gold-dust, and emeralds, on their way back to the coast. The value of the loot, as far as I could gather, must have been nearing a hundred and fifty thousand real gold British sovereigns. Allowing for native exaggeration, call it a hundred thousand --- quite enough, anyhow, to buy a hen run with in the Old Country and some decent tobacco.

" 'They left Imbibi right enough, but they never hit the coast. They got held up in the swamp country Inari way, and not one of them came out alive – not only that, the loot was lost into the bargain.'

"Well, I listened to the yarn, and I cross-examined the chief. I made other inquiries too, without his knowledge. The more I inquired and the more I listened, the more the yarn seemed to hang together. So in the end I determined to go and look into things for myself.

"It seemed impossible to me that a young army of, roughly, eighteen hundred men, to say nothing of a dozen or more Arab chiefs of considerable importance, could have vanished like that without leaving a trace, to say nothing of the loot.

"I went up to Inari. It's a beast of a district – new to me, and, as far as I know, to any other white man. Swamps for miles and miles in all directions – saw-grass, snakes, and fever. There were bush paths through the swamps, but only the natives know them. They are as intricate and crooked as a dog's hind-leg, and a single false step means a dive into the swamp and an end of everything. The ooze in places is supposed to be a hundred feet deep and more. According to the native legends it is quite unfathomable.

"Naturally, I couldn't risk my bearers and their loads of valuable ivory in a death trap like that, so I made camp a little way from the edge of the swamp, and determined to push on with only my gun-bearer and one bag, trusting to luck to find a path; and, as a matter of fact, luck held good, for my men found and caught a stray Inari hunter who had come out across the swamps on to the plains after deer.

"They collared him. I don't say that they were over gentle in their methods either, but many things happen in out-of-the-way corners of Africa which wouldn't look nice in print. He put up a good fight, too, before they got him, and was using poison arrows, and blowpipe darts made out of inch-long thorns steeped in putrid deer's liver. The darts are stuck into the liver,

and the liver is sunk in a pool. By the time they're ripe, and have been covered over with some native gum, which is also probably poisoned, they're about ten times as deadly as a Mauser bullet. Two of my men died from scratches that you could have made with the point of a darning-needle, and which hardly drew blood.

"I did the best I could for them, but the medicine-chest was running low, and it was a toss-up between quinine and pain-killer. Neither did any good. A first-class surgeon with a hospital full of instruments might have done the trick, but I couldn't attempt anything of the sort with a worn-out old cave knife softened in the fire so as to make it easy to get an edge on it. They just swelled up and died.

"Personally speaking, I believe that the gum is kneaded up with snake virus of something of that sort.

"To get on with the yarn, however. I dashed the Inari boy half a pound of tobacco out of the stores, and told him that if he'd show me the trick of the paths across the swamps, I'd give him another pound. They're dead keen on tobacco thereabouts, though they grow their own - a course native stuff, vilely rank.

"He explained to me that we must start at moonrise, and aim to arrive before dawn, for if it was found that he had been guiding me, or was seen, his life wouldn't be worth a minute's purchase when once he got back to his own people.

"That sounded plain common-sense all right. So off we went as soon as the moon got up. I asked him how far it was, and he said about four hours' march, because, though the distance as the crow flies was only a matter of seven miles or thereabouts, the paths wound about and zigzagged so that the distance was more than doubled. Also, there were weak places in the paths which only one man at a time could cross, otherwise there was a danger of the whole path collapsing.

"As soon as the moon came up we were off. The Inari went first. I came next, and, as a matter of precaution, I had a rope round that Inari's neck, with the other end tied to my belt; my own two boys came afterwards.

At first our way lay through high saw-grass, so tall that we couldn't see anything of our surroundings – just the track for a few yards ahead at a time, no more; and the heat was stifling. But after about a quarter of a mile of this the grass thinned out, and finally dwindled to a low, stunted growth – mosses, and patches of vivid green grass. Wherever it is greenest it is most dangerous. Then when we got out into the open we could see.

"I've knocked about pretty well all over this corner of the earth, and I've seen more queer things than most people, I suppose, but that first sight of the Inari stronghold fairly licked anything else into a cocked hat as I saw it in the moonlight.

"Imagine miles and miles of swamp, seething and bubbling all round you, and making those weird, moaning noises which swamps do sometimes. Flamingoes, herons, and white ibis flitting about here and there, silent as hosts, and bang in the middle of it all a great big chunk of pure white marble standing about three hundred feet high.

"How it ever got there, I don't know. There's no other marble in the country for hundreds of miles. Still, there it was, a big plateau, level at the top, and, I suppose, roughly half a mile round, and nothing else but swamps for as far as you could see. I reckoned that at one time it must have been part of some big cliff barrier, the rest of which had crumbled away. Then one or two rivers had got lost, or, maybe, a lake, and made a swamp around it.

"All the time we were marching I was taking cross-bearings with my pocket compass, and jotting down distances in yards as the path turned and twisted. My tame Imari might be playing the square game, or, again, he might now, and I wanted to be able to find my way out of that swamp again on my own in case of emergencies.

"All the time we were marching I was taking cross-bearings with my pocket compass, and jotting down distances in yards."

"There may be other paths, or there may not. I was too busy just then to inquire, but I do know that without that map of mine no one, except and Inari, could make their way for a hundred yards or be alive at the end of it.

"As we drew nearer, I could see that the cliff was as full of holes as a rabbit warren – cave dwellings, in fact, connected here and there by outside passages.

"We got up to the rock in the end. The ground all round the base is firm. Then we dived into one of the burrows at the base of it, and began to ascend a series of niches – not stairs. I didn't fancy that part, for our guide had only to raise the long yell to bring down a thousand or so of his fellow-ruffians on top of us.

"However, the cold rim of my revolver-muzzle, pressed persuasively into the back of his neck, kept him good and sensible. As a matter of fact, I learnt afterwards that the Inari, relying on their swamps to safeguard the, never post any sentries, unless there's a row on with their nearest neighbours.

"In the end we came out on the top of the rock, and there, almost in the centre, was a great altar or sacrificial stone. On the west side of this is a low doorway, and that leads to the tribes' treasure-chamber down below. And it was a sight!

"The moonlight filtered in from some opening above, and gave plenty of light to see by. It was a huge, great, oblong room, with carvings on the walls, not that I was worrying my head about them just then.

"The whole place was chock-a-block with the hoardings of the tribes since the time Noah gave up yachting, I should think, and precious rubbish most of the stuff was; but the prize of the collection was the Arab loot, which was kept apart by itself.

"The tribes' loot was mainly stuffed heads, old weapons, and the 'mouti,' bags of a generation or so of witch-doctors and medicine-men. But the Arab loot was enough to make a man's mouth water.

"My trade has been hunting elephants all my life, since I was a four-foot-high pup, and what I don't know about elephants or ivory, there's not a man in this part of the country who can tell me. Well, those tusks were the most magnificent collection I had ever set eyes on – not a faulty one among 'em – none of your half-blackened, sun-cracked, rotten stuff.

"They must have been carefully stored, and they must have taken two or three generations to gather. Out here, a generation – or, rather, the average term of a man's life – isn't the proverbial threescore years and ten, especially if he's after elephants.

"The way I figure it out is that the Arabs, who were mainly on a slave-raiding expedition, collared all the ivory of the small tribes, which they 'stamped.' Some of those tribes' chief kraals are literally palisaded with tusks.

"As to the emeralds, I can't say much. I don't know anything about women's gew-gaws. But if those Arabs were as good a judge of stones as they certainly were of ivory, the stones ought to be worth a fortune in themselves. The gold dust was another matter. It was a good colour, with occasional large nuggets, done up in skin bags, weighing, maybe, forty pounds apiece or more, a fair bearer's load, anyway, if you're wanting to travel fast.

"As I said before, the whole caboodle was worth well over a hundred thousand pounds, after deducting the cost of an expedition to go and fetch it and trot it down to the coast. My notion was to get away back quick to the camp. It was getting near dawn, and apt to be unhealthy for strangers, by the time I had got through my inspection of that beehive of a place, so the Inari and I quit by the same way we had come, and went back across the swamps.

"The idea was this – to rest up behind the shelter of the saw-grass in camp. I had had no sleep for the best part of twenty hours. Then, as soon as it was dusk, start on a series of forced marches down to the coast, sell my own ivory, and start an expedition on a large scale to come and lift the loot with the Inari and my own sketch-map as a guide.

"It seemed quite a simple plan for the 'get-rich-quick' scheme, and I was so busy thinking it over and making notes that I forgot all about the sleep end of the business, which was sheer idiocy on my part, and got the Inari into my lean-to hut to make him talk instead.

"I dragged the yarn out of him bit by bit, and a pretty gruesome one it was. It seems that that big Arab caravan, not content with the loot they had already gathered, and the number of slaves, had planned a raid on the Inari to collect a few more captives.

"The Inari are only a small tribe, numbering about four or five thousand all told, women and children and all, their actual fighting force being somewhere round about a thousand, but they are cunning.

"A hunter who was out beyond the swamps brought them news of the approach of the Arabs, and the Inari chiefs knew that against such men, armed with modern rifles, they wouldn't stand a pig's chance in an open fight. They sent the hunter back with instructions to allow himself to get captured by the Arabs, who would certainly force him to act as a guide across the swamps.

confusion, and the whole caravan was panic-stricken.

"They tried to escape, and promptly plunged into the morass, where they began to sink quickly. The same fate overtook their bearers, who cast aside their loads, and fled in all directions into the sucking mud. Then, and not till then, the Inari showed themselves, heralding their approach with more showers of arrows, fired at short range.

"Then they stripped their helpless victims of their valuables – rings, bracelets, everything they could reach – and stamped them under the shiny mud, or thrust them down with spear-shafts and poles.

"We had got clear away, and had covered six marches without a single mishap, when the camp was rushed by a herd of stampeding elephants."

"He was to lead them truly along the secret paths up to a certain point where the paths are particularly puzzling, and then run for his life if he had the chance. All around that point, and for a quarter of a mile back, the rest of the Inari would be lying in ambush amongst the grasses on patches of firm ground known only to themselves, armed with their bows and poisoned arrows and darts, and at a given signal open fire from both sides, and throw the Arabs into confusion.

"The plan was carried out with complete success from the Inari point of view. The first couple of volleys cost the Arabs several of their leaders. The guide vanished in the general

"It was all over very quickly, and the entire booty of the caravan was in their hands. Their losses were only two men, whom and Arab shot at point-blank range, the recoil of his rifle sending him under before he could fire a third shot.

"That's the yarn just as the Inari told it me, and just as I have written it down. But my luck seemed to be dead out. We got clear away, and had covered six marches without a single mishap, when the camp was rushed by a herd of stampeding elephants. They must have been scared by something – many miles away probably – winded us, and charged down on the camp.

"The Inari was squashed as flat as a pancake by a big bull. You could literally have buried him between two shutters. Of my bearers, only three escaped. The camp was trampled out of existence, and I myself was hurled against a tree and stunned, whilst my favourite rifle was smashed to pieces.

"When we had pulled ourselves together more or less, and the storm of elephants had swept past, we began to take stock of the damage. It was obviously impossible that we four could tackle the ivory loads, a ration-box apiece, our guns, ammunition, and a few odd-and-end necessaries. So, in despair, I cached the whole of the ivory, and such of the stores as were still undamaged, and we set off for the coast. Instead of coming back with my pile, as I had hoped, I came back a poorer man by a long sight than I had started out. I was broke, in fact.

"I rested up, however, and raising some funds from men who knew me, started out with a small expedition to recover my own stock of buried ivory. When I have got that, and sold it, I shall organise a caravan on a big scale, and go after the Inari treasure.

"They got it, as the Arabs did before them, by murder and treachery. I mean to get it, if I can, by a fair and square stand-up fight. Then I shall quit Africa, and go home and rest-up in the Old Country."

There the manuscript ended, but there was a postscript in Jack Merton's handwriting.

"He was on this trek when I met him, and when the bull elephant got him. He told me where his cache lay, and how to find it before he died, and when he found himself going he gave me an outline of the story of the Inari treasure and these papers, telling me to deal with them as I liked. I believe that every word of his story is true, and now I am off to see for myself. His map of the swamp-path is enclosed on a separate sheet."

Blake detached the last sheet, flattened it out, and laid it on the table. It was a weird-looking affair, but had evidently been drawn with an eye to accuracy of detail.

"Humph!" grunted Sir Richard. "It looks to me more like a plan of the Hampton Court Maze torn in half than anything else, and even then it seems upside down."

They bent over it and studied it carefully.

It was drawn in indelible pencil, much smeared by damp in some places, on a sheet of paper evidently torn from a notebook. But if the drawing was childish, the compass directions and the distances in paces were evidently most carefully worked out.

The readings, for instance, would run something like this, to take a typical example:

"Acute angle turn, clump of reeds on right, green patch on left (very dangerous), direction N.N.E. forty-seven paces. Check, obtuse angle turn at thorn-bush scrub, North by West, one hundred and five paces, etc."

"By Jove," said Sir Richard, "the man was no artist, but he certainly was no fool! Dig out a big scale map, old man, and let's see whereabouts this Inari place is – if it's marked at all, which I doubt.

"Moko, the port we know, that's Dago country, and Imbibi we know – at least, we've been within a couple of days' march of it twice at least. The last time I nearly bagged an okapi, you remember, but the light was bad, and I got him too far aft."

Blake nodded, and Tinker got out a big, time-scarred map on which all sorts of annotations and corrections had been made in pencil and various coloured inks.

When you get to out-of-the-way corners of the world, maps are liable to be as full of fiction and errors as a housemaid's penny novelette. Not because of any fault with the map makers, but because of the inaccessible spaces which they are bound to fill in from hearsay or native information, which is generally grossly inaccurate, or so confusing as to be unintelligible, each tribe having a different name for its own pet trout-stream or range of ant-hills.

On their own particular map – the best that money could buy – the Inari country was simply represented by a plain blank space, a few dotted lines marking uncharted and doubtful rivers, and some faint lettering across the space spelling "Unexplored."

"That settles it!" said Sir Richard emphatically. "I'm on! A blank space on a map is as temptin' to me as a diamond tiara to a pretty woman. I'll wire down and get my kit packed. You can put me up whilst we rummage round for stores and cartridges and things. And we'll be off on Thursday. There's an East Coast boat of sorts sure to be sailing then. That gives us forty-eight hours to arrange things. That suit you?"

Sexton Blake nodded.

"I can't accept a ten thousand pound cheque without doing my utmost to earn it. I should have gone in any case. The s.s. Zanzibar sails on Thursday night or Friday morning. We know her. Comfortable old tub. No frills. And a decent skipper who will stretch a point or two in our favour. No other passengers to worry about, except, perhaps, a stray commercial traveller or two, and they won't be German these times, thank goodness!

"Now, I vote we turn in. We shall have a busy day tomorrow. You know your room, so hop it!"

Sir Richard hopped it, but just as Blake was yawning himself to sleep next door he heard Sir Richard give a deep bass chuckle to himself, as though he had suddenly hit on a huge joke.

THE FIFTH
CHAPTER
THE ARRIVAL AT MOKO-LOBANGU THE ZULU'S DRAMATIC APPEARANCE.

BLAKE had had a long and tiring day of it, and it was well past nine the next morning before he strolled into the breakfast-room, to find that Sir Richard had already been gone half an hour or so, and taken Tinker with him, as a hastily-scrawled note explained.

The breakfast – what there was left of it – was cold and clammy, so Blake, with the air of a philosopher, turned it over to Pedro, who equally philosophically did his best to save Mrs. Bardell the trouble of washing up. He had just about cleaned up the last, which had once contained scrambled eggs, when the front-door bell rang. Blake pulled the patent release which unlatched the door below, and yelled, "Come in!"

He heard footsteps on the stairs, and then there came a discreet tap on the sitting-room door, and, to Blake's surprise in walked James, in an immaculately creased pepper-and-salt suit, carrying his bowler in his hand, and wearing a crepe band on his left arm.

"Good gracious, James, what brings you here?" asked Sexton Blake, in surprise. "Any fresh developments?"

"No, sir; nothing, sir. But as you dropped me a hint that you were going in search of the master – Mr. Jack, that is, sir – I thought I'd be so bold as to ask you to take me with you, sir. Everything is in order at Elmsley, sir, and in good hands. It's all arranged for. And if I might come with you I'd be greatly obliged. I've got a bit saved, and would want no wages. I've been accustomed to camp life with Mr. Jack before, sir, and I think I may say I'm a good cook so far as roughing it goes. I can shoot, and I know a bit about natives, and can speak a smattering of dialects, enough to get along with sir."

"You can cook!" Great Scott, that's something great! Native cooking would kill an ostrich, as a rule. But, mind you, you won't get an Eagle range or gas-stoves and silver entree dishes where we're going."

"No, sir; but I can manage fairly well with a clay oven and some bits of wood. I've been with Jack before, sir, and he used to like the way I made a stew of alligator tail, if I may say so. It can be made to take very much like chicken, and —"

"By Jove, then, you shall come! We'll settle the matter of wages after. But you'll have to hurry up and get an outfit. I'll give you a list of necessaries, and you can have them put down to me."

"Begging your pardon, sir, I always travel like this, it feels more homely. Just a palm-leaf under my hat is all I want at times, and I've a change or two in my bag in the hall downstairs, sir. Shall I take away the breakfast things, and press your clothes, sir?"

Sexton Blake looked at the little man, who was as unmoved as though he were asking what time he should get luncheon ready, or order the car round, and burst into a fit of laughter.

"James, James, you'll be the death of me!" he chuckled.

"You talk as if we were going down to Brighton for the weekend. I can assure you we are not."

"No, sir; quite so, sir. Nasty, crowded place, Brighton, sir; trippers, and all that. Will you have the blue suit, sir, or the grey? I'll get them ready whilst you're having your bath, sir."

"Oh, confound you; give me either you like, and carry on! There's no arguing with you, and this is my busy day."

"Yes, sir. I'll have dinner ready at eight, if that is convenient – for two, I presume, sir. Your man will feed with me in the kitchen."

"My man? Oh lor'! Yes – poison him if you can," grinned Blake, and bolted for the bath-room.

That dinner, their last in England for a long time to come, was a huge success. James, having proclaimed himself a cook, proved himself one.

No restaurant chef could have turned them out a better meal, and Sir Richard chuckled appreciatively.

"We'll remember this in a month's time," he said, "when we're chewing canned horse and hard tack, with mosquito sauce, gratis and for nothing. The Zanzibar pulls out at dusk to-morrow, by the way, on account of the tide. So we'll have to leave here at eleven sharp. I've had all our gear, barring personal stuff, sent on ahead. Your lib for leave eleven one time?"

Blake nodded.

"I wanted the 'scears' of one of the rifles filing down a trifle, and the lock action of Tinker's revolver was suffering from signs of senile decay. He'll pick 'em both up on the way to the station, otherwise we're all right – 'en etat de partir,' as the French put it. The main trouble I foresee is to get bearers when we arrive at Moko, or whatever the name of the port is. It's a one-horsepower little river station, as far as I can remember, with a nasty surf on the bar outside, and we shall want a hundred and fifty to two hundred men at least, by all accounts, and good men, who aren't easily scared at that."

"Ah, yes," said Sir Richard non-committally, and yawned. "I suppose we shall." But when he had turned in, Blake heard him chuckling to himself. "Bearers! Oh, yes; we shall want bearers – heaps of them – that's where the joke comes in."

They sailed at seven the next evening, and dropped the mud pilot at an hour after mid-night.

The Zanzibar was ugly, the Zanzibar was old, and her very Sunday best pace was barely four-teen knots; but for sheer comfort and liberty of doing as you pleased, she beat a crack Trans-atlantic liner hollow. A Scotch engineer had the care of her engines. You could dine in your shirt-sleeves or a pair of pyjamas, if it pleased you.

There was no smoking-room, for the simple reason that you could smoke anywhere and everywhere from the bridge – where you were welcome, if you were a privileged passenger

and didn't ask fool questions – to the carpenter's private sanctum. Also, she was really seaworthy and well formed, and not a mixture of puttied-up plates and gaudy paint.

The small party had her entirely to themselves, to their undisguised delight, and they had their own provisions to supplement the ordinary ship's rations, so they did themselves most un-commonly well.

The old tub lounged down the Spanish coast and through the Straits into the Mediterranean quite unmolested, in spite of wars and rumours of wars. No one made rude remarks about her house-flag, nobody threw torpedoes or mines at her, and her cargo consisted mostly of harmless Brummagem notions, gaudy calicoes, and coast gin of a very inferior and deadly quality. The only lethal weapons on board were those that the small party had brought with them, and a brace of antiquated revolvers belonging to the captain.

Blake's chief concern as he lounged about on deck smoking and poring over maps was the question of bearers.

"It may delay us and hold us for weeks," he grumbled. "We ought to have a couple hundred at least; three would be better, and none too many, and at a place like Moko we shall be lucky if we can find a couple of dozen really reliable men. In other words, we shall have to sit on our tails and stew in that stuffy, reeking little mudhole of a place, whilst we send out some runners to try and bring men in. Worse still, the delay may just prevent our dodging the rainy season, and you know what that's like in these regions. The big rains will make the country impassable for months."

"True for you, my son, they will," said Sir Richard, and chuckled again.

"What are you giggling at, you ass?" said Blake irritably, and heaved a book at him.

All through the Red Sea it was just the same. Sir Richard definitely refused to bother his head about the bearer question, and took no interest in it further than to chuckle quietly whenever the subject cropped up. A man who can chuckle in the Red Sea in the hot season must either be enjoying a joke as deep as the Yellow Sea or he must be mad. Certainly he makes his neigh-bours feel that way. Yet Sir Richard seemed sane enough, ate enormously, praised James' cooking, and consumed vast quantities of iced lager.

Blake consulted Tinker on the matter.

"Look here, young 'un," he said, "what's the joke Spots has got up his sleeve? He's rapidly developing into a bad imitation of a laughing jackass."

Tinker shook his head.

"Give it up. He isn't dotty, and that's all I can say."

The Zanzibar put in at sunbaked Perim on business of her own. Blake and Tinker refused to budge. Perim is about as dreary as any place on earth. Sir Richard shrugged his shoulders and went ashore. He knew a couple of officers quartered there, stayed to dinner with them, and came aboard again in the cool of the evening. He had a broad smile on his face, as Tinker noticed that just as he came aboard he crumpled up a sheaf of cablegrams in his hand and dropped them overside.

Sir Richard, as a matter of fact, had been spending a very busy and expensive day at the wireless station, despatching and receiving messages.

"The joke's on us, whatever it is," Tinker reported privately to Blake a few minutes later. "He's just come up the accommodation-ladder, grinning like a Cheshire cat with the mumps, and he's been spending a young fortune on cables and wireless."

"Humph!" said Blake. "He has, has he? Well, we shall see."

They left Perim at dawn, and steamed east, past Socotra, then south and by west, down the coast. The low-lying African coast, broken occasionally by a high, bluff cliff, showing up to westward of them, was monotonous in the extreme.

On the six day after leaving Perim they reached Moko.

There was a bad sea on the bar, and the steamer had to lie off and wait for the surf-boats to come out.

Blake and the others took the first four for themselves and their equipment, though there was nearly a riot amongst Tinker's crew when they saw Pedro being lowered down in a sling.

Sir Richard's boat got away ahead of the others, "to fix things up," as he said, and the captain, chief officer, and engineer promised to come and dine with them at the local hotel, such as it was, in an hour or so. Moko is Portuguese territory, and a taste for rancid oil and doubtful eggs has to be acquired.

James, however, rose to the occasion, by gently kicking out the local chef and taking complete control.

Dinner was arranged for seven o'clock as the Zanzibar was due to sail at ten.

Sir Richard, who had mysteriously disappeared in the meantime, didn't show up until the meal was all ready, and the others waiting for him. When they had at last said good-bye to the captain and their other guests, they sat smoking on the veranda in the moonlight.

"About those bearers again," said Blake, blowing out a cloud of cigarette-smoke. "We must wade in early tomorrow and see what can be done."

"Sure thing," said Sir Richard lazily, and glanced at his wrist-watch. Then he clapped a whistle to his mouth and blew shrilly two shorts and a long.

Barring the tinkling of a mandoline from the back of a neighbouring store the night was perfectly still, and the sound of the whistle carried far, and was succeeded by a long silence.

Suddenly there came a faint, drumming sound, as of bare feet on hard earth, which grew louder and louder until it rose to a roar, and from out of the shadows of the palms before them a whole host of figures came leaping into the moonlight.

So sudden and unexpected was their appearance that Blake's hand dropped to his belt, and James, who was smoking a pipe at a respectful distance, closed in and gripped something in his coat-pocket.

Tinker stared, and Pedro rose to his feet with a warning rumble, hackles half erect.

Straight across the moonlit belt of sand, straight for the edge of the veranda, dashed some three hundred men – big men, with chocolate-coloured skins, whose broad spears flashed in the moonlight.

Within a yard of the balcony rail they came to a dead halt, in ranks four deep. The ranks parted in the centre, and a great figure of a man, with black ostrich plumes for a head-dress, and carrying and enormous spear, came stalking through the opening.

He raised his great spear aloft, and, as at a given signal, there rang out a shout:

"Inkosi kaas! N'kose. Bayete! Bayete! Bayete!

Blake sprang to his feet, and scared Portuguese waiters flew in all directions.

"Lobangu, you dear old villain, how did you get here?" he cried.

"Wow! Untwana, my father!" growled Lobangu, the old Zulu, who had been through many adventures with Blake, Tinker, and Sir Richard. "Did not Lukuna, the Inkoos Losely, send me word over the little wire that talks that thou hadst need of me and three hundred of my best young men? And, see, we are here! Three hundred men, all picked, trained to the spear, and trained to the chatter guns!"

"Oh, come up here, you old scoundrel, and shake a paw! Tell your young men to dismiss, and that they shall have a tophole feed. Tinker, see to that. You know what they will want!"

"Wow! Slippery one!" said Lobangu. "Thou art still M'lolo; and there is my lord Lukuna, and the king of all the beasts" – pointing to Pedro. "But the small, dark Inkoos I know not!"

"James," said Blake, rising, "let me present you to his Highness the Prince of Etbaia, one of the biggest old rascals yet unhung! I forget exactly how many times he has saved my life, and Sir Richard's, and Tinker's, or how many times we have tried to save his. But he means well!"

"Yes, sir," said James imperturbably. "I should be delighted to know his Highness!"

"Mr. James – Lobangu! Lobangu – Mr. James!" said Blake grinning.

Lobangu shook James by the hand European fashion, and gazed steadily into his eyes.

"A great little man," he said to Blake, over his shoulder. "A man who is unafraid, small of stature, but a great fighter, for he is of those who fights with his head!"

"Pass, James, and all is well," said Blake. Incidentally, trot inside and see if you can get the 'patroni' to produce some 'bubbly water' – in other words, cheap, sweet, coast champagne. It would kill a dog at forty yards', but Lobangu likes it!"

"Yes, sir," said James, and vanished.

"Now, then, you old villain," continued Blake to Lobangu, "kindly explain how you happen to turn up here, and what Lukuna had to do with it!"

Sir Richard chortled.

"Oh, say it's my fault!" he said. "Didn't you tell me that we should want a lot of men – not merely bearers, but men who could fight? Well, I didn't see why old Lobangu should be left

out of the picnic, so I spent a young fortune in cables, talking Ellington, who used to be one of my subs out there, to send runners up with messages and instructions.

"I did that from town whilst we were foraging round for equipment. At Perim, where you and Tinker were too lazy to come ashore, I spent a happy day at the wireless station, trying to ascertain whether everything was all right. Ellington sent back word that he himself had stolen some Government launches, and escorted old Lobangu and three hundred of his fellow-ruffians down to the sea, and put them on board a cargo boat due to arrive here three days before the Zanzibar – just about the time limit margin I had reckoned on.

"I got ashore first, as you remember, and went for a stroll until dinner was ready. In the course of that stroll I went in search of old Lobangu, who had camped his men about a mile outside the town, as I had told him in my message, and we arranged the little signal of a whistle for a dramatic surprise for you. I always had a weakness for stage effects. I think it came off rather well."

"It certainly did," said Blake. "So that is what you were chuckling over all to yourself, was it? Tinker and I had serious thoughts of putting you into a strait-waistcoat! Lobangu, you scoundrel, don't drink that fizzy gooseberry stuff out of the bottle. If you do, you'll blow up and bust. Besides, the best people don't do it!"

"Wow, Inkoos!" said Lobangu, grinning. "But this is great 'mouti' this bubbly water. It tickles the insides, and makes one want to laugh!"

"Humph! If you drink any more, you'll get maudlin and weep over your past sins, or talk about your rich relations, which is worse. Now listen to me whilst I explain what we're after, and what our plans are!"

He explained briefly, and Lobangu listened with deep attention.

"Wow, Untwana!" he said, taking a huge pinch of snuff, as Blake finished. "A strange tale truly – a strange tale, and a good one. I, too, have heard somewhat of these Inari, and of a great treasure lost in the swamps. Nay, how I heard is no matter. Thou knowest how such tales spread from tribe to tribe, and from camp-fire to camp-fire.

"Now it is a prisoner brought in, who hopes by the telling of it to save his life. Now it is spread about by the witch doctors for reasons of their own, and each teller of the tale adds a little, or lies a little, to make the tale greater, and himself more important. Of a score of such tales, the half of one may be true.

"Yet this one I have heard from several different men of different tribes, and a different times, and it always has the same tale in the main. Some five years back I had it in my mind to take certain of my young men – a regiment – and go and see for myself; but the journey is far and hard from the Etbaia country, and there was trouble on the Askari borders at the time, so I put the matter aside.

"But you – you have the story written down on paper, and a plan of the swamp paths; also you tell me that the white elephant hunter who wrote it down has seen the treasures with his own eyes. That is good talk. We will go and see. Now let us sleep, and to-morrow at dawn we will start!"

"One moment! Do you or any of your young men know this Inari country?"

"Nay, Inkoos – save by hearsay only. I know that it is a small country – a place of swamps, as you say; that the Inari are poison-folk, and held to be treacherous; and that their 'Great Place,' a big cliff, lies some thirty marches from here. More than that I cannot say!"

"Well, that tallies pretty closely with the written yarn," said Sir Richard. "We'll know more about it soon. And now, as old Lobangu says, we'll turn in!"

The Sixth Chapter

The Journey Through the Forest.

AT dawn the next morning they were off. It took them a good hour to get properly started. A first march is always the most tiresome. Loads have to be sorted out and adjusted, and a hundred-and-one odd-and-end details seen to.

In this case they were got through quickly, and without a hitch. Moreover, as there were bearers and to spare, the loads were cut down to twenty pounds apiece – a mere nothing – and the lost time was soon made up, for the men swung along at a fine pace. Also, as they were all picked men of Lobangu's own regiment of

guards, they were highly disciplined. There was no quarrelling over loads, and no straggling, as is usually the case, and their captains had little to do beyond giving occasional short, sharp words of command. These were left in sole charge, the white men and Lobangu going on ahead.

The first few marches, as they knew, lay along well-defined trails, used by the natives passing to and fro from the tobacco plantations and the cultivated fields; but after that they would have to make their final plunge into the unknown – a no man's land, about which no one could tell them anything, for the simple reason that no one ventured there.

The Portuguese were not daring enough. They were traders pure and simple, and they stuck to their plantations and waterways, like wise men, and the natives dreaded and shunned the unknown as they would the plague.

There were gruesome stories amongst the community, more-over, of an occasional outcast or pariah, who, gathering courage from desperation, had adventured off into the back of beyond, in the hopes of finding a new country and fabulous wealth; and of these, in recent years, only two had returned.

One – a white man, a wandering Swede, by all accounts – had gone "inside," and had been picked up by some rubber-gatherers five months later at the extreme limit of that part of the forest in which they worked.

He was more dead than alive, stark naked, and as mad as a hatter. He had the bush madness, which frequently impels a man who is lost to throw away everything – boots, clothes, even his water-bottle – under the delusion that he will be able to travel faster.

He was terribly scarred and emaciated, and had evidently been caught by the Inari and tortured. He lingered on for some time at the port hospital; but he never recovered his senses, and one fine day he vanished – no one could say where.

The second man was picked up dead and horribly swollen from poisoned wounds. From certain signs it was clear that he had only died an hour or so before he was found.

The most careful questioning of the natives, however, both by Blake and Sir Richard, failed to elicit the slightest information about the man they were going to seek for – Jack Merton – and this was the more strange because he must inevitably have had a large number of bearers with him. The only conclusion they could come to was that at the last moment, for reasons of his own, he had selected a different route, and not passed through Moko at all.

Blake's own party was quite a formidable young army, what with the white contingent, Lobangu and his three hundred men, and the half-dozen or so of guides, local rubber gatherers who had agreed to lead them into the forest to the furthest point which they knew. Beyond that, neither bribes nor threats would induce them to budge. The forest was haunted, they said – bewitched. There were no bush-paths beyond, no villages, nothing at all, not even drinkable water, and, in any case, they couldn't act as guides in a country where they had never been.

They were a chicken-hearted lot, and in the end Blake paid them off at the end of the seventh march, and sent them home, heartily glad to get rid of them.

The expedition now pushed on at an increased pace. Blake and Sir Richard taking it in turns to lay a course by compass.

The virgin forest was very dense and stiflingly hot, but it was amazingly rich in game and untouched rubber, and there was plenty of water of sorts, in spite of what the guides had predicted. It was tepid and muddy, and a white man drinking it unfiltered would probably have gone down with dysentery in a few hours.

But James boiled sufficient for their own use each day, and also passed it through their pocket pressure-filters. Lobangu's men, however, seemed to prefer it full-flavoured and unboiled, and it did them no harm. In fact, they thrived on it.

To economise stores, too, a dozen or so young men would go out at each camp with light throwing-spears, and bring in birds and meat, especially a small type of deer, which was very delicately flavoured. They could have got more, and got it quicker with guns or their rifles, of which they had a score or so between them; but Sir Richard and Blake sternly forbade the use of these. Nor did they shoot anything themselves, though sorely tempted sometimes.

For the sound of a rifle-shot carries an incredible distance in those solitudes, especially to the keen ears of a trained native hunter.

There were indications that they were nearing the far edge of the forest belt, and beyond that, if the old elephant-hunter's diary was to be relied on, lay a vast stretch of tall grass-country, in which the Inari hunters roamed after game.

The sound of a few rifle-shots, however faint and distant, might send some of the outermost of these racing back to report, and so at one swoop do away with the element of surprise on which Blake and Sir Richard were relying for success.

From the latest accounts they had been able to gather, and from hearsay evidence, the Inari fighting force was placed at the lowest estimate at two thousand, whilst some rose to as high as five thousand, or more. Moreover, they held a well-night impregnable position, surrounded in its turn by almost impassable swamps. A successful surprise seemed to be the one chance of avoiding heavy losses. The trees thinned out with each of the next two marches, and then, just before sundown, they emerged from the tree-belt, and saw in front of them a vast sea of high grass stretching away up to the skyline, and even as they looked the grass was dyed and stained with the everchanging colours of the afterglow.

Far, far away – it was impossible to judge the distances in that deceptive light – there appeared on the skyline what looked at the first glance like a rose-pink cloud of curiously regular shape.

Blake gripped Sir Richard's shoulder and pointed to it.

"The Great Place of the Inari," he said, "with the pink and gold of the afterglow playing on the white marble of the cliff. We go no further to-night. We'll camp here, and this will be our last cooked meal for a long time. The smoke of the fires won't be seen against the trees here, and it will be dark in another ten minutes, anyhow. But once we are down there amongst that saw-grass we sha'nt dare strike a match to smoke with. A little puff of wind, a spark, and – Pouf! The whole thing would be off like a train of gunpowder. That grass is as dry as tinder on the surface, anyway, swamps or no swamps. Ten minutes would make it a roaring sea of fire from skyline to skyline, and all that would ever be found of us would be a few charred bones and some burst cartridge-cases.

Sir Richard nodded grimly.

"I wish I took snuff like old Lobangu, or didn't smoke at all, like Tinker and Pedro!"

"You'll have to take to chewing, old man," said Blake, grinning, "so smoke enough to-night to last you for a week or so.

"James," he said, turning to the little man who was squatting on his haunches near by, roasting a couple of birds, his pot-hat firmly wedged on the back of his head – "James, after this you are dismissed from your post as chef."

"Me, sir?" said James. "I hoped I was giving satisfaction, sir! Sir Richard was good enough to say that he liked those roast pigeons and the native spinach last night, sir, and to-night I've got a special dish of cold doves' eggs, sir, by way of a side dish. They're almost as good as plovers' eggs, sir!"

"You're a prince of cooks, James," said Blake gloomily, "and I'm as appreciative and as fond of my tummy as the next man; but after to-night we must abjure the flesh-pots for a time, at any rate, and content ourselves with canned horse and dog biscuits. If you were to try and cook anything down there in that dried grass, the first dish on the menu would probably be yourself, roast or fried, but certainly quite useless for further cooking, and probably tough. Sir Richard might do for a joint, and the rest of us, including Pedro, could turn up as a mixed grill of sorts, I suppose. The only trouble is that there'd be no one left to tell us whether we tasted all right or not."

"I see, sir," said James, brightening up. "I'll put on one or two extra courses to-night, and cook half a dozen more birds or so, to do cold for to-morrow; and if I may say so, sir, I'd like the bearers to carry along several of those big seven-pound biscuit-tins, which are empty. I've got a sort of idea, sir, that I could find a use for them."

"Have it your own way, James. You're running this end of the show. Now I must go and roust out old Lobangu, and see if his ruffians have been making a supply of biltong, as I ordered them to do. They won't like that after browsing on the fat of the land, but they'll have to put up with it."

The mists came down over that sea of grass, and the ibis came out and flitted silently about, with flocks of the green heron and the grey for company, and now and again a string of flamingos shot wheeling noiselessly across the sky like a family of pale pink ghosts. The whole scene was unutterably sad and lonely, but unmistakably majestic.

After this meal, Blake, Sir Richard, and James sat and smoked. They sat for the most part in silence, staring out across the swamps. Lobangu took huge pinches of snuff, and Tinker scratched Pedro's ears. From the Etbaia, seated round their fires near by, came the sound of low, guttural talking in undertones, and now and again the soft clink of iron on stone as a man here and there put an edge to his throwing-spears or his broad stabbing blade.

The Great Place of the Inari had vanished out of sight with the afterglow, but in little more than an hour it shone out again, pure silver in the light of a low-hung moon.

"Begging your pardon, sir," said James, suddenly pointing with the stem of his pipe towards a little south of west, "but those birds over there aren't behaving natural. They ought, by rights, to be in their rookeries amongst those mangrove islands by this time – those little heaps of dark foliage amongst the grasses, sir. I mean; but they're flitting round and round. It seems to me that something or someone is disturbing them."

Blake nodded.

"I was thinking the same myself, James. Hallo! What's old Lobangu up to?"

Lobangu had suddenly risen, thrown away a precious pinch of snuff, and seizing his big spear, had beckoned to his men, who had also evidently been watching James' birds.

Quite silently Lobangu flung up and lowered his hand four times, fingers and thumbs slayed out against the night sky.

Instantly twenty of his young men rose and stepped forward.

"Untwana," he said, "something moves down there, a mile and a half, or it may be two miles, away. I go to see what, and will leave certain of these children of mine as out-posts. Do thou and Lukuna and M'lolo hold in readiness, and also the James man, so'as to come up with the rest if we need help. But the king of all the beasts must stay behind and guard the camp, for down there it will be a snake country.

"Rattlesnakes and moccasin, the black one, and possibly the green mamba also, and the king is no match for a snake in the darkness amongst the grasses. If it is merely a thing of cold steel, a small affair, then you will hear nothing. But if these Inari folk are out in force, then, see, I carry the short chatter-gun thou gavest me at my belt. If thou hearest two shots quickly – so, come as soon as maybe with every man available."

"I see," said Blake. "Fire ahead, and good luck to you! It may only be a hunting-party on the loose."

"Wow, inkoos," said Lobangu. "A hunting-party it may be. But, if so, the Inari are no hunters. See how they disturb the bird-folk yonder. So now for a little while farewell, Hialha Gahle N'Kose. We may be gone an hour, or if the evening breeze blows from us to them, the double of an hour. I cannot say."

At that he signed to his small band once more, and they set off down the slope, for the plateau on which the last of the trees grew was a good fifty feet above the saw-grass level.

If the Inari people were bad hunters, Lobangu and his men were as near perfection as possible.

From the moment they entered the outer fringe of the grass they were quite invisible from above, or, indeed, from anywhere at more than a spear's length away. No startled animal betrayed their presence by a sudden rush for safety, no bird when fluttering wildly away to give the alarm.

They were quite unable to see one another, for the grass was a good nine feet high, yet instinctively they kept perfect station, as Lobangu had ordered.

They assumed the favourite Etbaia formation – the crescent with the two horns pointing towards the enemy.

Lobangu himself was in the centre of the hollow crescent, a young officer was at the point of either horn, the men between being strung out at intervals of four paces.

The ground underfoot was marshy, with small pools here and there, but they were far away from the region of the dangerous swamps of which the elephant hunter had spoken.

Swiftly and silently they moved forward, the horns automatically stretching forward so that at the right moment they could close in on the enemy from behind, encircling him, and cutting off the escape of any fugitives.

At the end of half an hour the faint hiss of a snake was passed along the line, and each man stopped instantly, rooted to the spot on which he stood.

Then Lobangu, the master scout of them all, crept forward by himself, trailing his big spear after him. Right up to the Inari camp he crawled, warned of their exact position by the sound of

their voices talking in undertones. Then, lying flat, he cautiously parted the grass stems near the roots, and peered through.

The Inari, fifty-four strong, were lying or sitting close together in a small open space – a sort of island in that sea of grass. They were evidently a war-party of sorts apparently returning from a raid, and they had in their midst five captives – men of a different tribe – tightly bound together with grass ropes.

The Inari themselves were a strange-looking race, pale brown in colour, so pale as to be hardly darker than the sun-scorched grasses around them. In fact, in certain lights, especially in the light of the tropical moon, they blended so closely with the background as to be scarcely distinguishable at a short distance unless they moved.

They were short, squat men, averaging about five-foot four – an advantage in such a grass country – but they were stocky and tough-looking, all sinew and muscle, with no spare flesh.

They were armed with strong-looking bows, and carried a sheaf of arrows and two or three light throwing-spears with barbed heads. A few had blowpipes for darts as well, and each man carried a small skin pouch at his waist on the right side, which Lobangu guessed to be a spare supply of poison.

Their faces were almost as high cheek-boned as a Chinaman's, and they had cruel-looking little, upslanting eyes, which, combined with their light colouring and dank, dark hair, made them look more Mongolian than ever. The general impression they gave was one of cold-blooded treachery and cunning.

Two or three of them, whom Lobangu took to be chiefs, wore elaborate headdresses, and capes of birds' feathers; the others were naked, save for a sort of short kilt of feathers round the waist.

Having seen all he could, Lobangu crept back to his own line, and, beckoning to the two men nearest him, explained to them in a whisper the numbers of the Inari, how they were armed, and how disposed, illustrating this last part and the proposed plan of attack by drawing diagrams with his finger on the palm of his hand.

Then he sent them off in opposite directions down his own line to explain the situation to each man in turn, with explicit orders that on no account were the Inaris' prisoners to be harmed. On the contrary, they were to be protected at all costs. For, cunning old warrior that he was, he knew the value of the information that can be gleaned from a rescued prisoner, and the eagerness with which it is often given.

He waited until his two messengers returned, and then gave the agreed signal for the advance of the wings to begin – the croak of a bull-frog.

After that he waited patiently for the return signal, the repetition of the croak from the far side, telling him that the fatal circle had closed round the Inari camp.

As soon as he heard it, he and those nearest him also began to close in, creeping through the long grasses as silently as ghosts. Now but a thin screen of grass lay between them and the open space, and now they could see the Inari and their captives plainly.

Lobangu was just about to repeat the signal for the third time when there came a muffled sound and a rustling of grasses away on his left front. Instantly half a dozen of the Inari hunters sprang into sudden wakefulness, and let loose a shower of arrows at random. Two came whistling past Lobangu's head, but none did any damage.

Any hope of further concealment was useless, for the Inari were now thoroughly aroused.

Lobangu, quick to seize on the critical moment, yelled out the order to charge in a voice which rang high above the general din and confusion.

The Inari, locating the sound, fired in a volley of darts, arrows, and throwing-spears. But the Etbaia were all armed with light, strong shields, which could turn anything but a bullet, or a stabbing-spear, and which they were marvellously quick in using. Lobangu alone disdained a shield of any kind, relying, as was his custom, solely on his ability to parry either arrows or throwing-spears with his own great weapon.

Only one of his men had been hit so far, the one next to him on the right, who had received a deep graze from an arrow in his spear arm.

Lobangu and the rest swept into the open with their hoarse, guttural cry of "S'gee! S'gee!"

The Inari, seeing themselves attacked by a mere handful of men, some eight or ten apparently, less than a fifth of their own number, leapt forward eagerly to give battle, and feeling already assured of victory, Lobangu, a couple of strides ahead of the rest of his men, headed straight for the Inari whom he took to be the chief, a squat, broad-shouldered man, wearing a cape and headdress of parrot feathers.

Two spears the man flung at him; but Lobangu, bending low, dodged them both, and before the man could cast a third. Lobangu's broad blade had thrust upwards and forwards with the quickness of lightening.

The Inari's breastbone crushed in before the strength of the blow, his own spear fell from his hand, and as he toppled backwards the weight of his body slid off Lobangu's point and freed itself. He was practically dead before he touched the ground.

"S'gee!" roared Lobangu, and swept forward to meet the next man. But by this time the horns of the Etbaia were leaping forward and taking the Inari by surprise in the rear. They had expected no attack from that quarter, thinking that they had only to deal with the mere handful in front of them.

They tried to wheel, so as to face outwards in all directions, but the Etbaia gave them no time. In a trice they were all amongst them, the broad, stabbing-spears rising and falling with rhythmical rapidity, whilst the five helpless captives looked on in bewildered dismay.

The Inari fought well. They had the advantage of numbers, but they could do nothing against the rush of the Etbaia, who caught the blows of their lighter weapons on their shields, laughed, and then drove home with the stabbing-spear.

Though to those concerned it seemed as though the fight was prolonged for hours, it was really all over in under five minutes. At the end of that time a few of the remaining Inari, all slightly wounded, made a desperate dash to break a way through to safety, but the young men of the Etbaia hedged them in or bounded after them, and a single stroke made an end. The Etbaia had done their work thoroughly. Not a single one of their adversaries was left to creep away through the swamps and carry the tale home.

Their bodies were brought in and ranged in rows, and Lobangu, smeared with blood, which was certainly not his own lawful property, leaned on the haft of his great spear, and took toll of the dead – for all were dead, or would be in the passing of a few minutes. When an Etbaia spear strikes an enemy body fair and square, that enemy has little, if any time left in which to make his will.

"Fifty and four," he said, in his deep voice. "That was well done, my children."

And he took and extra large pinch of snuff.

Then he walked along the lines slowly, inspecting the dead men's weapons, and especially the parrot-feathered capes of the chiefs. Two of these he directed to be taken off, together with the head-dresses, not because he wanted them as trophies of war, but because in guerrilla warfare in wild countries it is always well to have a complete set of your enemy's uniform in case of emergencies. By the aid of it you can do scouting work which would be otherwise impossible. This is especially true at dusk or in the early dawn, when minor discrepancies may pass muster. Lobangu, skilled old warrior that he was, always had an eye ready for possible emergencies ahead.

Just as he was taking one of the capes from the hands of a young Etbaia to examine it, the latter staggered and fell back, tearing the cape from his grasp. Lobangu sprang forward and bent over him. The man had a deep-jagged wound in his shoulder, caused by a chance throwing-spear which he had torn out and cast aside; but the shoulder was already terribly puffed and swollen, and great beads of perspiration stood out on the man's forehead, though until he fell he had given no sign of being hurt.

Lobangu glanced at the wound, probed it roughly with his finger, and then went swiftly to the body of the nearest Inari chief.

Long experience had taught him that tribes who fight with poisoned weapons usually carry some sort of salve as an antidote in case of an accidental wound or scratch, or possibly because a neighbouring tribe with whom they may happen to be at war uses a similar virus.

Sure enough, now that the cloak had been removed from the body, it was easy to see that the man carried two skin pouches at his waist. Lobangu examined them both. The moon made it as clear as daylight. The first contained a greenish paste with a sickly fetid odour. A glance at the heads of some unused arrows which were smeared with the same stuff assured him that it was the poison used.

The second pouch was full of a whitish, cream-like substance, not unlike ordinary embrocation to look at, only thicker, and with a very strong aromatic smell.

He took some of this on his finger and dabbed it deeply but not urgently into the wounded man's shoulder. The latter winced and bit his lip to prevent crying out with the burning pain;

but his eyes, firmed fixed on Lobangu's never flickered.

For five minutes Lobangu watched him whilst others of his followers crowded round at a respectful distance. Then the man gave a deep sigh, rolled over on one side, and began breathing easily and regularly.

Lobangu touched his shoulder lightly; it was already cooler, and the swelling had visibly diminished, though the man himself was either fast asleep or under the influence of some narcotic.

Lobangu signed to two of his followers to pick the man up and carry him away, and told off half a dozen more to collect all the pouches they could find containing the white cream, but on no account to touch the green stuff. Then he looked round.

"One of my young men forgot himself as I was about to give the order to charge," he said sternly. "He cried out, and threshed about in the grasses like a wounded buck. Who of you was it?"

A man – a young man of barely twenty-five – came forward, supported by two others.

"It was I, Great One," he said.

"Thou, Undulu!" said Lobangu. "And hast thou not left the women's kraals long enough to learn to rule thy tongue, or to learn that we of the Etbaia know how to die silently if need be?"

The young man raised his head and thrust forward his chest.

"Thou hast thy spear, Great One. I am ready, and this time I will make no sound."

Lobangu half raised his spear and looked at him keenly. Undulu's eyes met his fearlessly.

"Why didst thou cry out?" Lobangu asked slowly.

The young man with an effort thrust forward his foot, which from toes to knee was swollen and puffed till his leg was nearly the same size from the thigh downwards.

"My father, as I lay in the grasses, a snake crawled over me and struck me unawares. See, there his fangs entered above the ankle joint, and already the world swims before mine eyes, and there is sound of rushing winds in my ears."

Lobangu reached out and took the young man's spear, which was clean.

"Let him be seated," he said curtly. "Now hearken to me, Undulu, son of Ungoloo. Thy life is mine by right, to take or not, as I choose. For Ungoloo's sake I choose not to do so on this condition. Take thy spear and this bag of white mouti. Cut three shallow gashes in thy legs, and rub in the mouti: Should you flinch, you die. It is understood!"

"It is understood, Great One. Give me the spear and the mouti bag."

Lobangu passed them over.

The young man fixed his eyes on his chief, and forced himself to smile whilst he cut three deep gashes in his leg. Then seizing the white cream, he rubbed it hard into the wounds.

His expression never altered till he had finished, though he must have been suffering terrible pain. At the end he held out his empty palm to show it, raised his hand half way in a salute, and rolled over in a dead faint.

"It is good," said Lobangu, and turned to one of his indunas. "Let two men carry him carefully," he ordered, "and see that he is well tended to. I did but wish to prove him, and punish him a little, for that outcry of his might have cost ten or more lives. Now we go back to camp swiftly. As for these" – pointing to the Inari – "by the time the sun is high to-morrow the vultures will have picked them clean. See to it that the prisoners are released, but well guarded on the march."

In ten minutes less than his stipulated two hours he was back on the fringe of the tree-belt with his two wounded and his prisoners.

Blake and Sir Richard and Tinker examined the feathered capes and the other spoils, for some of the Etbaia had brought back a collection of throwing-spears and other weapons, with interest.

"Begging your pardon, sir," said James, who had joined the group, "but Mr. Jack had some like those at home at Elmsley. He told me that they were given to him by the gentleman who used to hunt elephants, and whom he mentioned in his diary. He also told me that they were poisoned, and ordered me to boil them first, and then put on a thick pair of gloves before cleaning them up."

"Well, that shows we're on the right track, anyhow," said Blake. "Let's go and have a talk to Lobangu's prisoners. Give 'em a good feed, James. Nothing like grub to make a native talk."

The men's story was rather difficult to follow, for they spoke in a strange dialect. But, put briefly, it was this. They belonged to a tribe living on the edge of the grass country. The name of the tribe was Lava, or Lavu. They were a hunting tribe, not, strictly speaking, a warlike tribe, and occasionally they did some fishing in the forest streams. Game, however, was scarce in their section of the forest at certain seasons, and hunting parties used to go down into the grass country to get supplies. The Inari scouts and outposts knew of this, and were always trying to waylay some of their small parties.

This game of catch-as-catch-can had been going on for several generations, and though the Lavu generally won enough meat to live by, in anything like a fight they were invariably trapped or overpowered by the Inari and their poison weapons. They knew little or nothing of the inner swamps, but they knew a great deal of the Inari customs from prisoners who had occasionally made their escape.

Once a month, it seemed, the Inari medicine-men, or witch-doctors, held a festival, at which human sacrifices were made. The prisoners were laid on an altar at the summit of the Great Place, and at the full of the moon, the victims were mutilated, after certain rites, by the witch-doctor priests, and then hurled, still living, from a high point of the cliff into the swamps below as an offering to the gods or devils of the swamps, whom the Inari, with some reason, looked on as their natural protectors.

For many years, as far as the history of the Lavu went back with any degree of accuracy, these offerings had been made to a great stone image, which had towered up on one side of the altar – a hideous and repulsive thing in a squatting attitude, according to the accounts of the few prisoners that had escaped; but there had been a terrific thunderstorm during one of the heavy rain seasons, and the image had been struck by lightning and shattered.

After that the Inari had fallen on evil times; their ranks had been devastated by sickness, and as a race they had begun to dwindle and lose power, until some four and a half or five years ago they had set up a new god in place of the shattered image.

This was a white god – no larger than a man – who had stayed the sickness evil amongst them by the aid of strange drugs and "mouti." But they – the Inari – instead of escorting him back to his own Great Place, and loading him with offerings, had kept him a close prisoner, and loaded him with chains, fearing that one day he would vanish, and leave them unaided should the sickness return, and it was he who now presided at the sacrificial ceremonies, but with his face veiled, and chained to his throne and heavily guarded.

More than this they could not say, except that there was a rumour that now and again volumes of smoke and flame were seen issuing from his mouth, and that he went about always tended by guards, who watched his every movement.

Blake glanced significantly at Sir Richard, who nodded.

The Lavu spokesman went on to say that he and his men would willingly act as guides through the outer grasses and swamps in return for their lives having been saved, for otherwise they would certainly have been sacrificed at the coming full moon; but of the inner and dangerous swamps they knew nothing, except by hearsay from an occasional escaped prisoner of their tribe.

Sir Richard ordered them to be taken away and well cared for.

"What do you make of it?" he asked, turning to the others. "It seems to me that that yarn about the white god no larger than a man, and who is kept in chains in case he should try and do a bolt, spells in plain English Jack Merton. If so, we're in the nick of time, for it wants three days to the full of the moon."

"Begging your pardon, sir, I feel sure it's the master," said James.

Blake nodded assent.

"I'm willing to bet on James' instinct, and my own. We've tried our hardest to find trace of any other white man who knows the country round here, and we couldn't find one who had been within several hundred miles of it. So far as we know, only the elephant-hunter man and Merton have ever attempted it. If any others have, they've left no traces or records. We're in time if we can get there in three days from now – earlier, if possible, so as to be able to choose our own hour of attack."

Tinker glanced at Lobangu.

"What do you say, old man?" he asked.

"Wow, M'lolo!" growled Lobangu. "I say sleep, and start with to-morrow's sun. Nay, and hour before that, for one cannot travel fast in that grass country; and when we come to the real swamps, we shall go slowly indeed, and we must be able to choose our time of attack!"

"Same notion here," said Tinker. "Pedro and I are going to get some beauty-sleep, for I fancy that we've a particularly hefty time before us!"

Sir Richard regretfully knocked out his pipe. Sexton Blake flung away the fag end of a cigarette. Lobangu issued a few curt orders to one of his indunas as to posting and relieving sentries; and in a quarter of an hour the whole camp, except those on guard, were fast asleep.

THE SEVENTH CHAPTER

At the Base of the Cliff – A Brush with the Inari Sentries.

TINKER was awakened an hour before dawn by a prod in the ribs from Blake. He sat up, rubbed his eyes, and shivered, for there was a chill feeling in the air, and when he looked outwards and downwards over the grass country he gazed into a white sea of swirling mist clouds.

The whole camp was already astir. James, with beads of mist on his now somewhat dilapidated pot-hat, was cooking tins of sausages, and preparing coffee at a fire close by. Some twenty other camp-fires all around showed where the Etbaia were preparing their last cooked meal for some days to come.

Sir Richard was smoking a cigarette, and pacing up and down. Pedro was placidly gnawing a bit of deer haunch which had been given him, or which he had commandeered; and Lobangu was directing some of his men on some mysterious work of his own device.

By the time they had finished their meal, and Blake and Sir Richard were enjoying a final smoke before the start, an Etbaia runner came in to report. He saluted them, and turned to Lobangu, who had joined them.

"Great One," he said, "I have been down yonder, as my father ordered, and for seven miles through the grass country I have found no sign of any man alive!"

"It is good!" said Lobangu. "Inkoos Untwana! Lukuna N'kose, it were well to make a start. Shall I order the manner of our going?"

"Do as you like, old man," said Sir Richard; "and the sooner the better!"

"Wise words, Lukuna. Then thus shall it be ordered. Two of the Lavu guides shall pass on first, and behind them thou, Untwana and Lukuna, shall walk with the chatter-guns and the little guns which speak many times. Then there shall be three more Lavu guides, and behind them M'lolo, the slippery one, and the little man James, also fully armed. If the guides are in doubt at any point, they can take counsel one with another, and it is well. If they try and lead us astray, or act in any way which seems treacherous, then they can be shot down. Behind will come my young men, bearing our stores and such like. But why the little man James insists on the carrying of empty tins I know not.

"On either flank I will throw out a screen of ten of my best scouts, who will move abreast of us, and I myself will pass up and down the line from time to time to see that all is well. Should you or I or the scouts on either hand see anything amiss, the signal will be as before – the croak of the big frog of the swamps; and on that each man will keep his station, save the scouts, who will go forward and see what may be amiss!"

"Wise talk, old friend," said Blake. "See, even now we are ready! But where is the king of all beasts?"

"Here, Untwana," said Lobangu, stepping aside.

Blake and Tinker and Sir Richard stared, and then burst into a roar of laughter, whilst even the sedate James allowed himself to smile.

Six stalwart Etbaia warriors sprang into view, carrying three litters of plaited grass, slung on poles, two men to each.

The litters, or hammocks, were skilfully made, cool, and comfortable, with a mat awning above each. In two of them were the two wounded Etbaia, who already seemed in a fair way to recovery, thanks to the ointment; but in the third sprawled Pedro, in dignified ease, his splodgy paws hanging over one side, and slung beside him, within easy reach of his silly old nose, hung a tin can full of water, in case he should be thirsty.

"Well, I'm hanged!" chuckled Sir Richard. "That beats the band! Confound you, Pedro, you lazy old ruffian, you've got four legs, and I've only got two! Get out of it, and pad the hoof of weariness! If those two fellows are so keen on carrying somethin' in that travellin' boudoir of theirs, they can jolly well carry me! It only

wants some pink ribbons on the curtains to make it complete. Pink's my most becomin' colour, I've been told!"

"Nay; but N'kose," said Lobangu quickly, "thou would'st not have the king of all beasts walk through a snake country such as this! He is over-daring, and perchance, in the hunting, a snake might lash out suddenly, and bite him on the nose, which would swell up and cause him great pain, or worse!"

"Oh, lor'!" said Sir Richard. "Lead on, Macduff! Tinker, wire at once for some violet scent, or attar of roses, in case that rat-tailed lump of laziness should feel faint!"

Pedro turned his head lazily, and grinned – positively grinned, as though enjoying the joke. Then he stretched himself lazily, and pretended to go to sleep.

Tinker caught him a sound thump in the ribs, and the caravan fell into order as Lobangu had planned, and moved off.

They descended the slope, and entered the tall grass. Within a minute they were as wet as if they had been swimming in a river, and a cold river at that. For, what with the mist and the dew, and the rapid evaporation caused by the hotter air above as the sun rose, they were shivering before they had covered a couple of hundred yards.

At first their track lay along the route which Lobangu and his scouting party had taken, and in twenty minutes or so they came to the opening where the fight with the Inari had taken place.

The ways of the Tropics are strange, and at times ruthlessly savage. It was only a matter of hours since Lobangu and his men had ended the fight and left a pile of Inari dead lying where they had fallen; but even in that short space of time the carrion birds, the small animals of the grass country, and the myriads of insects had been at work.

What had-been men were now so many skeletons picked clean after that gruesome feast of the wild things of the air and ground. Nothing but the bones were left, which would lie and bleach there in that day's sun and the sun of to-morrow, and many to-morrows after that, till they became ivory white and grew brittle and finally crumbled away. A few spears and arrow-heads would remain to tell the tale of the fight, and that was all.

The Lavu guides saw and turned aside and shuddered. Lobangu, who happened at the moment to be alongside the head of the column, noticed this, and pointed.

"But for the grace of the great white lords, even so would you have been before the moon had risen and waned thrice. Therefore guide us well and truly, lest we let you fall once more into the hands of the Inari."

"True words, great Great One," said the leading guide. "So far as we know, we will lead you truly. If we fail, you can surely kill us."

"True words," said Lobangu grimly, and dropped back to the tail of the column.

As the sun rose and the mists cleared, the heat became intense, and it was a damp heat – the most enervating of all. As Sir Richard said, as he mopped the perspiration from his face and out of his eyes for the hundredth time, it was like marching in a super-heated hothouse at midday with a broiling August sun overhead.

With the clearing of the mists, too, came an added misery in the shape of myriads of mosquitoes and horse-flies, and a thousand other insect pests. Lobangu and his men seemed scarcely to feel these, nor did the Lavu, who were inured to a fly country; but the whites suffered terribly, all the more so because they were unable to smoke.

Blake and Tinker came off a bad best, though they were driven half mad. At the end of a couple of hours Sir Richard's face was so puffed up that he could hardly see out of this eyes, his hands were like boxing-gloves, and his fore-arm was as thick as his thigh.

James' head looked like a large mottled pink football with two little slits for eyes, whilst his bowler, now at least three sizes too small, perched on the top of his hair with a sort of Charlie Chaplin effect. But the worst sufferer of all was poor old Pedro in his hammock. He was suffering intensely from the heat, and though the mosquitoes had no direct effect on his tough hide, whenever he opened his mouth and lolled his tongue out, panting, he was compelled to close it again with a snap, and at each snap he swallowed about a pint of mosquitoes.

The Lavu men had told them that the great place of the Inari was not more than thirty miles distant as the crow flies, from their last forest camp, but that, owing to the winding nature of the paths, it was actually a good fifty to the edge of the dangerous swamps. Travelling was necessarily slow along those narrow winding tracks, and a march of twenty-five miles was good going.

Just about midday the leading Lavu guide checked and pointed. There was, he explained, a good water-hole with a spring of clear water a hundred yards or so further on on the right-hand side of the track, which was used as a camping-ground both by his own tribe and the Inari hunters.

"Then let's get to it," growled Sir Richard. "I'm parched with thirst, and I've as many of these infernal flies and insects on me as a travelling monkey-house."

The man led the way, and they came to a curious little lagoon-like lake of crystal-clear water, with a clump of mangrove trees in the centre. It was perhaps an acre and a half in extent, and from the trails many deer and other animals used it as a watering-place. The place was a natural hunting-ground. The lake itself was roughly divided into two.

Loads were thrown down. Twenty of the Etbaia were thrown out as a screen in case there might be another hunting-party of the Inari in the neighbourhood. The rest, with the Lavu guides, went to the lower pool to drink and fill their water-skins and prepare a meal.

Sir Richard and the others retained the upper pool for themselves. The water was pleasantly cool, and they drank greedily. Then, whilst James began to set out the meal of cold birds on the top of two food-boxes, Sir Richard, un-observed by the others, carefully placed his cigarette-case and a box of matches in his hat, clapped the lot firmly on his head, waded into the pool, and sat down with the water nearly up to his chin. Then, reaching up, carefully lit a cigarette and puffed away luxuriously. He was half-way through it before the others noticed him.

"What on earth are you up to, Spots?" asked Blake.

Sir Richard turned with a grin and blew out a great cloud of smoke.

"Enjoyin' myself," he said. "I can't set fire to the lake, can I? And I'm getting a bit of my own back. I reckon that by now I must have drowned several million of the mosquitoes and flies which have been makin' a meal off my Sunday best blood supply."

"What about moccasins and alligators? I say the trail of two large ones a little way back," asked Blake.

"Moccasins be hanged! They're all right unless you start knocking them about. Besides, they'll all be having a siesta in the mangroves there, and as for a 'gator, you're only got to be rude to him, and he'll bolt for dear life. He's not like a beastly crocodile with a pain in his hunger. He's real vicious."

Blake laughed.

"I think I'll come and have a smoke myself," he said; and wading in, he joined Sir Richard. That settled it. Inside a minute Tinker, James, and Lobangu were all in, and Pedro swam lazily round them, lapping furiously to try and wash the last pint of mosquitoes out of his mouth.

After that they had a good square meal, and rested up in stolid contentment, till one of Lobangu's indunas came up, and, saluting, said that the Lavu guides were anxious to be off if they were to reach the next water-hole for the night camp.

"Right-ho!" said Blake. "Tell 'em we'll start at once. Lobangu, you lazy old ruffian, get your scarecrows ready. We lib for march one time."

"N'kose!" grunted Lobangu, and strolled off.

In a quarter of an hour or so they hit the trail again in the same order as before, but following a slightly different direction. Their clothes had long since dried on them, but the rest, and the food, and, above all, the long draughts of water, had freshened them up tremendously.

They kept up a fine pace till just on sundown, and by the time they reached the second water-hole, which, like the first, lay a little way off the main track, the mist was swirling thickly all about them, and the air, after the baking heat of the day, struck dank and chill.

"Humph!" said Sir Richard, as they made camp. "As a specimen of a typical fever country, I give this first prize. There's only one bit of consolation – when the mists come on, those infernal mosquitoes go off duty. James, my son, hurry up with that grub. I'm hungry."

"Just ready, sir," said James, who had been performing mysterious rites of his own with his tin biscuit-boxes, and improvising a dinner-table a few yards away. "There's soup, sir, roast bush pheasant, and a savoury."

"Good egg!" said Sir Richard, and squatted himself on the ground by the table. He picked up his tin mug of soup, took a long gulp, and gave a yelp.

"Jumping frogs! It's hot!" he spluttered. "It's nearly boiling! Confound you, James, I've scalded my tongue! Why the deuce didn't you tell me? And how on earth did you manage to get hot soup? For I'll swear you've had no fire!"

Blake and Tinker, who quickly guessed the secret, chuckled, and old Lobangu's eyes bulged. He half suspected Tagati work on the part of James, for he had also swallowed a mouthful, and was making faces.

"Begging your pardon, Sir Richard," said James, with dignity. "It's them biscuit-tins, and a little contraption of my own which I used to cook for Mr. Jack with. You told me that I shouldn't be able to light a fire down here, Sir Richard, and, knowing swamp countries and the danger of catching fever and chills, I thought a hot meal would be preferred. So I cooked the meal last night, sir, and whilst everything was still hot I placed the saucepans, carefully covered up, in the tins, packed them round tight with grass, which of itself gives out quite a lot of heat, and there you are, sir, with plenty of hot soup.

"I intended to take out a patent for it, sir, just after my last trip abroad with the master. 'James' Intensive Cooking' I was going to call it. But before we got back one of those ladies who write the cooking articles for the fashion papers had got hold of the same idea, though she used wooden boxes and hay. So the patent idea was no use, sir. Still, I didn't forget it, and thought it might come in handy here. If I hadn't opened the box, sir, the soup would have been just as hot this time to-morrow."

"Great Scott!" said Sir Richard. "Give me half another mugful. You're a genius, and I'll take back all I said. Canned soup, and a 'donkey's breakfast,' and there you are. All done by kindness. James," he added severely, "you ought to join an Antarctic expedition. You'd be a treasure."

"Yes, sir," said James. "But I'm afraid they don't grow the right kind of grass there, sir, and seals are so messy, I am told. The next course, sir, is bush pheasant and desiccated potato, with hard-boiled stuffed eggs to follow. I had to use a little of the anchovy paste for them, sir. After that, sir, if you'll excuse me, I'll go and see to the coffee. It should be ready by now."

"Oh, my aunt!" said Sir Richard. "Find me a liqueur, and I shall fancy I am dining at the Savoy, with a string band playing 'Love Me for

Ever' or 'I Can't Get Anything Else,' or some fool nonsense like that. Here, waiter, get me a cigar!"

"Yes, sir; certainly, sir!" said James, and to everyone's amazement, produced a large, fat case. "Larranagas, Sir. Some of the master's best. I brought a box of fifty in a tin case in the hopes we may find the master. He was always very fond of his after-dinner cigar."

"James," said Sir Richard gravely, "you deserve to go to heaven."

"I hope not quite yet, sir," said James, with equal gravity. "If you'll excuse me, I'll go and see to the coffee." And he vanished.

"No harm in lighting up here in this infernal mist, is there, Blakey?" he said.

Blake pulled out a cigarette.

"If you can set fire to this mist, with anything short of a waggon-load of petrol, all I say is, do it!" replied Blake.

"Tinker, cut along quietly, and see how James does the coffee stunt."

Tinker nodded, and slid off down to the edge of the lake.

James, pot-hat and all, was ensconced in his kitchen – otherwise a small islet ten yards or so from the main shore, and in shallow water. The moon was just beginning to pierce through the mists, and Tinker could see him plainly as he bent over his tin with some enamel cups ranged beside him.

He was in the act of pouring out the first cup when tragedy quickly took the stage. A large alligator, who dreaming had been amidst the rushes close by, suddenly woke, and took fright, either at James or the smell of the coffee, or the faint splashing that Tinker had made. Anyway, he was off in a hurry to keep a business appointment elsewhere, and with a swish of his tail to give him impetus, a splash, and a strong smell of musk, he was off to catch the last bus home as hard as he could lick.

Unfortunately, the sweep of his tail had flicked James on the side of the head, and knocked him clean out of his kitchen into the water, followed by the coffee apparatus and the tin.

Tinker unfeelingly gurgled with laughter, and fairly doubled himself up when James reappeared, dripping, covered with mud and weeds, and minus his precious bowler.

"Never mind, old man," said Tinker, wading in to give him a hand, for James was partially stunned as anyone who has fallen foul of the tail of a fifteen-foot 'gator can easily understand.

"But the coffee has gone," he said, in a dazed way, "and Sir Richard——"

"Hang Sir Richard!" said Tinker cheerfully. "He's over-eaten himself already, so have all of us. You come along and get between the blankets, or you'll have a dose of fever in the morning."

As on the previous day, they started an hour before dawn, whilst the grey-white mists were still swirling about them, and at dusk at the end of the third day they reached the edge of the dangerous swamps, where their Lavu guides owned frankly that they were of no further use, as the country beyond was unknown to them.

The Great Place of the Inari, the marble cliff, was no more than three miles away at this point – in a direct line, that is to say – and loomed ghost-like and large.

They halted, and made camp once more on the fringe of the long grass. Those last tricky three miles, which might easily stretch out into double the distance owing to the difficulties of the trail, had to be covered before the moon rose high. For, though treacherous and deadly in the extreme, the ground beyond offered little cover.

"Look here, old man," said Blake, as he and Sir Richard pored over the sketch map. "By all we can learn, our man – Jack Merton, this is to say – has been turned into a little tin god by these Inari people, possibly because he is the first 'pukka' – white man – they have come across. By what those Lavu fellows say, there's bound to be a grisly business up above there to-night. Half a dozen poor wretches or so will be tortured and flung over the cliff into a mud-hole afterwards. It's up to us to stop that if we can. Now, my idea is this. You know natives, and you know that when there's any particular kind of jamboree on, they've no thoughts for anything but the particular business in hand.

"I'll bet you ten to one that at this very moment, they are all indulging in a 'beer drink' 'twala beer' – newly fermented at that. After which they'll set no guards, but go up to the cliff top and chatter amongst themselves until the performance begins. That will be our chance. We've got this map and a compass to go by. We can get along the paths whilst they are busy enjoying themselves, and with any luck we can bring off a surprise attack."

"Easy as shellin' peas!" said Sir Richard sarcastically. "But, my dear chap, you've forgotten the main point. There is the cliff right enough. Here is the pestilential swamp, and all the mosquitoes and little mosquitoes, and so forth. Likewise, here is the defunct elephant hunter's map – quite a nice, healthy-lookin' map, if you like – showing all the main roads and where the local village smithy and church is, even if it doesn't give the name of the best pub. But it has one 'sma' fault in it,' as Sandy would say. It doesn't tell you where the blessed turnpike begins! It might be here, or it might be twenty odd miles away."

Blake reached out a hand, and grabbed Sir Richard's wrist, which he felt tenderly with the tips of his fingers.

"Malaria, swamp fever, that's what it must be," he said thoughtfully. "Mental aberration, or mumps. Serious case."

"What are you drivin' at, you old idiot?"

Blake tapped Sir Richard's forehead.

"Humph!" he said. "Sounds hollow. Brain gone phut! Or may be defective eyesight. If you had a memory, my dear Spots – which, of course, you haven't – you would recollect that, according to our friend the elephant hunter's diary, he cached all his own ivory close to the edge of the swamp here. No being a fool; that would mean that he would not risk his ivory rotting in the swamp, but would have had some kind of platform made to keep it dry, and then build a mound over it. Well, we passed that mound on our left hand not two hundred yards from here. A mound is an easy thing to spot in a swamp, even if you were only looking for one as a dry camping-place. You were yawning at the time, and so missed it, I suppose. Tinker and James are back there now investigating."

"Well?" grunted Sir Richard.

"Well, fathead!" mimicked Blake. "If they find the elephant hunter's ivory there, it shows that we have got our bearings right, because the cache is marked on the plan here, and shows the entrance to the hidden path."

"Humph!" said Sir Richard. "All right, fire ahead, and call me an ass if you like!"

"My dear Spots, I never waste words or time on the obvious!" retorted Blake gravely. "And, by the same token, here come Tinker and James and old Lobangu, so we'll hold a council of war."

"It's the cache right enough," said Tinker as he came up. "James has been doing a bit of ferreting on his own account, and caught a glimpse of some of the ivory. Why on earth those Inari beggars haven't looted it before now beats me. They must have known that the mound couldn't have grown there of its own accord, and that it wasn't built there for nothing."

"Superstition, probably," said Blake. "Someone started the idea that it was a grave, as likely as not, and you know what natives are, even the worst of them. They'll cheerfully cut your throat, or murder their own grandmother, but they wouldn't touch a grave, even if they knew it was stuffed with precious stones.

"Now listen, Spots, and you too, Lobangu. This is my plan. It's now just after seven by my watch. The moon rises late, and won't be at the full till one o'clock in the morning, or thereabouts. Also, when it rises, it will be behind that cliff there at first, so all the ground on this side will be in shadow for at least another hour – nearer two.

"We can't all move out yet, for the festivities won't have properly began, and there may be one or two johnnies on the look-out up there. Seeing that it's a gala night, though, as we know, they don't usually keep any watch. Still, two of us might go on ahead now, and nose out the path without much risk of being seen, and come back and report. I vote that Lobangu and I go, and that we start at once. It's safer for two than for one, because, if one of us gets into difficulties, the other can help him out."

"Wise talk, Untwana," said Lobangu. "I am ready, and do thou bring with thee the little mapthing, though, for my own part, I would rather trust to my own eyes, for where men have passed to and fro the trail, however intricate, should read like one of your printed books. Let us start whilst there is still light enough to read the spoor by."

"Come on, then," said Blake. "You other fellows had better get grub, and save a bit over for us when we get back, for goodness knows when we may have a chance of another meal."

He laid down his rifle as only likely to be in his way, and took Tinker's revolver and some spare cartridges in addition to his own.

Lobangu stuck to his spear, and the automatic which Blake had given him on a previous trip.

Blake glanced at his wrist-watch.

"Twenty to eight, Spots!" he said. "We should be back by ten at the very latest, probably long

before. If we're not back by ten, then you'll
know that something must have happened to us,
and you'd better send out a couple of Lobangu's
best trackers to 'make look see.' Our spoor will
be fresh, and they'll be able to follow our line
easily enough. Fire ahead, Lobangu, old man!"

"N'kose!" grunted Lobangu. And, signing to
one of his men, told him to fetch three bags of
dried beans. These were the large white, very
nourishing beans, which the Etbaia used as their
principal food when on long marches; when
stewed or boiled, a couple of handfuls would
keep a man going for four or five days.

"What on earth do you want those for, you old
ruffian?" asked Blake. "This isn't going to be
a picnic!"

"Nay, Untwana; but in all bush trails and
swamp trails, the makers, unless they are fools,
lay blind trails, having no ending, to deceive
their enemies, and lead them into danger or an
ambush. Perchance we shall come on such, and
then, having proved them fake, we will place a
handful of these beans at the point where they
branch off from the true trail so that we may
know them again."

"Good idea, old man! Fire ahead! You go
first; for though I may know something about
track-reading, you've forgotten more than I ever
knew, and I'm not fool enough to pretend otherwise."

"So be it, Untwana!" said Lobangu. And, after
casting one swift look round, and a backward
glance to assure himself of his bearings, he
started off.

For the first forty or fifty yards the trail was as
plain as a pikestaff. Suspiciously so, Lobangu
thought, for he went slowly, and, sure enough,
at the end of seventy yards, the trail ended suddenly in a shivering green quagmire, into which
Lobangu sank to his knees in a second. But he
was prepared for something of the sort, and
flung himself backwards instantly.

"Even so," he said, imperturbably picking
himself up. "I suspected a trap, Untwana, but I
wished to see in what manner these Inari folk
laid their traps, so that we might know them
again."

"Hang it! We shall have to start all over
afresh!" said Blake.

"Nay, Untwana, not so! The entrance to
the true trail lies but twenty short paces back,
though it is cleverly concealed."

They retraced their footsteps, and at the point
where the false trail left the true Lobangu placed
a handful of his beans.

After that, he lead the way easily and swiftly,
and, to Blake's astonishment, it seemed surprisingly simple. The path, though it zigzagged, was
in most places broad enough for two men abreast;
and Blake came to the conclusion that either the
old elephant-hunter must have been a bad tracker
of anything but his own particular quarry, or, as
seemed more probable, the Inari had widened and
strengthened the path in places of recent years. In
fact, at some spots, there were clear indications
of this. Probably they had grown more powerful
and their enemies weaker in the course of years,
and so they had less need of concealment. The
path had also been straightened and shortened at
many points compared with the map.

At half a dozen more places they struck blind
trails leading into the deadliest part of the
swamps, and each of these Lobangu marked with
his beans after following them up to the end.

"This is children's play, Untwana," he said,
after the last of these; "for, look you, whenever
they would lay a trap, they make the false path
overplain, and it is much trodden down more that
the true trail itself. From that alone one may tell
which is which."

Blake nodded, and followed on, till at last they
stood on the terrace of firm ground at the base
of the cliff, which towered up three hundred
feet above them, with its burrow-like openings.
All these were high up, a fifty feet stretch to the
lowest, barring in one case, a single opening on
their left was on ground level.

Lobangu pointed to it.

"By that way the hunter of elephants must have
gone," he said unhesitatingly.

Blake nodded and glanced at his watch. They
had been a trifle over an hour, and of that nearly
twenty minutes had been spent in the following
up and marking down the blind trails. Now that
they knew the road, and could move swiftly,
and with certainty, the whole distance could be
covered in half an hour.

They rested for a little space, staring up at the
great cliff above them. Not a living thing was
in sight, but once an unearthly, bloodcurdling
scream rang out from a cave above them.

Blake shuddered in spite of the warm air.

"Let's be going, old man," he said, in an undertone.

"Good words!" grunted Lobangu. "This is an evil place. I can feel it in my skin, which tingles. Much blood has been spilt here, and more will be spilt to-night! Wow! But the cliff's shall run red when my young men get amongst these yellow-skinned monkey-faced poison folk with the spear. You shall see them, and shall hear. S'gee, s'gee. Now, inkoos, let us go!

It took them just half an hour to reach camp again, and they made their report whilst eating.

"Now this is what I propose," said Blake. "Lobangu agrees, for we talked it over on the way back. We leave all our stores here by the cache, and we'll leave the Lavu in charge of them, and the Lavu themselves in charge of Pedro. They won't dare to try to pilfer anything then, and, as a matter of fact, the poor beggars are so grateful that they wouldn't try it on in any case. We take only our weapons, and a pocketful or so of spare shells apiece. Those of Lobangu's men who have rifles must also carry an extra pouch-load of cartridges.

"We will start now, at once, though it's a bit early, for two reasons. Firstly, there is still a bit of mist hanging about, which will conceal our movements, and we can rest up if need be right under the base of the cliff, and out of sight from above. Secondly, we shall be on the spot in case they choose to advance the hour of the performance, which is quite possible, and may be able to save some poor wretches of prisoners' lives, for I don't suppose our Lavus were destined to be the only victims."

"Right you are!" said Sir Richard "Anything for a quiet life!"

"The rest of the plan we must leave till the last moment," Blake went on, "and be guided by circumstances. Tinker, you tote Pedro along to the cache, and tell him to be good and guard the stores. Tell the Lavus that we are off to squash the Inari flat, and that they are to wait here till we come back. Also drop them a gentle hint that if they so much as lay a finger on one of our chop-boxes, Pedro will treat 'em worse than a tiger; but that if they behave they shall go back to their own country rich men, able to buy wives, and cattle, and gramophones, if they want the beastly things. Now, Lobangu, get a move on your young men. They've had a good square meal. I know the Etbaia always fight their best on a full tummy, and, if I'm not mistaken, they

have already sensed what is coming their way, and are beginning to 'see red.'

"That is so, Untwana. They are like young hounds in leash."

Within ten minutes everything was in readiness, and the whole caravan, except Pedro, who looked very disgruntled at being out of things, and the Lavu moved off, Blake and Lobangu leading and acting as guides. Wherever possible, they went forward two abreast, but where the path narrowed, or was inclined to be weak in places, they dropped back into single file. At the end of three-quarters of an hour the last man had reached the terrace at the cliff-foot in safety.

Blake and Lobangu at once started off to explore the passage, accompanied by two indunas and a messenger. Sir Richard would have gone with them, but he had a big thorn in his foot, which had to be got out before the time for real action came, and Tinker and James stayed to help him.

Already a change had come over the place since Blake was there last. Then everything has been darkness and silence. Now a sound like the buzzing of some gigantic beehive, broken occasionally by faint, shrill cries, floated down from above, and the sky overhead was already flooded with a silver radiance.

Blake and Lobangu and their three attendants hurried into the tunnel-like opening with a feeling that they had not much time to spare. Half a dozen more Etbaia were left on guard at the cave entrance to prevent a surprise attack on those below, or to rush to the assistance of the advance party if need be.

There were no stairs, merely a smooth incline, which turned and twisted in the heart of the rock as the path mounted upwards, and every now and again this was lighted by loopholes cut in the rock-face very much as the elephant-hunter's diary had described. There were no side passages, either, the path evidently leading direct to the summit.

Lobangu and Blake, in the lead, had just reached a point about midway up, as near as they could guess, when, rounding a corner, they literally blundered into two Inari, who were apparently stationed there as sentries. Unlike the hunting-parties, they were armed with big spears, on which they were leaning, and wore some sort of protecting armour, with headpieces of the old Chinese pattern, and big, curved swords.

They were jabbering to each other in high-pitched, sing-song voices, and so had heard nothing until Blake and Lobangu were right on top of them. Then they turned and charged like wild-cats.

Blake, who had nothing but his rifle and revolver, neither of which he dared use for fear of giving the alarm, was momentarily at a disadvantage. He parried a savage thrust of the big spear with his rifle-barrel as best he could, and then, dropping his rifle, closed with the man before he could lunge again.

The Inari, though short, was tremendously powerful; a good wrestler, too, and as difficult to hold as an eel. He also dropped his weapon, the big spear, which was useless for close-quarter fighting, and tried to get either at his sword or the dagger at his belt. But Blake bore him backwards and got him down, with one knee on his chest, and, with one hand on the side of the man's chin and the other on the back of his skull, he forced the fellow's head slowly round. The man gave a muffled, cat-like scream. Then there was a snapping click, and the Inari grew limp; his neck was broken.

So quickly had it all happened, and so closely had the two writhing bodies been interlocked, that the two Etbaia indunas, watch their opportunity as they might, had been unable to use their spears for fear of injuring Blake. But when they heard that fatal click, and saw the Inari collapse and grow limp, they gave a deep grunt of satisfaction and amazement, and as Blake rose, breathing heavily after his exertions, they saluted stiffly.

"Wow! But that was a great trick of thine, Inkoos!" said the senior indunas. "Such a little thing, seemingly – a click like the snapping of a small piece of firewood – and see he lies there dead, as though our stabbing spears had found him! Some day, my Lord Untwana, we would beg you show us the secret!"

"I will show thee now," said Blake grimly, for his blood was up, and he was feeling good and fit. "Nay, do not fear. I will do it but gently – so!"

He took the big induna's head in his hands in the same way in which he had taken the Inari's and pressed a little.

The Etbaia made no sound, but his mouth hardened and his eyes began to bulge.

Blake released him promptly.

"Twice the quickness, and an inch more of pressure, and thou wouldst have been even as he, with thy face looking out between thy shoulders," said Blake. "A good trick, true, but a dangerous one. So be careful how thou makest use of it."

"Inkoos," said the induna, rubbing his neck and flashing his white teeth, "it is a great mouti! I felt but as a little child in thy hands. When we get up above yonder I will try it on certain of those Inari dogs! So it goes, and then so! I shall remember."

Just then Lobangu came padding softly down the slope, the blade of his big spear a gruesome colour, whilst he himself was bleeding from a graze on the upper arm.

"It is finished, Untwana!" he said. For, whilst Blake had been busy with one sentry, Lobangu had dashed after the other, who had fled to give the alarm. "He knew the way and the tricks of it, whilst I was ignorant. But I caught him in the end, and, though he fought well for so small a man, I got him in the throat, so that he could not cry out before he died. Nay, there is no poison in this scratch of mine. Besides, I have sucked it clean, and it is barely skin deep. Come, Inkoos! Let us hasten, for there are great doings up yonder!"

They hurried after him passing the body of the second Inari, and finally reached the top of the incline which, barring a shallow step the height of a man's head, was on a level with the great plateau.

Crouching behind this step, they surveyed the scene, which amongst all Blake's various experiences was the most eerie he had ever witnessed. The surface was not flat, but concave, in the manner of an old Roman amphitheatre, except that there were no tiers of seats; the rock merely slanted inwards.

In the centre of the hollow was a large sacrificial altar of stone, elaborately carved, by which stood a group of priests, or medicine-men, all clothed in feather capes and headdresses. Outside these, again, stood a compact ring of guards, with their big spears and heavy, curved swords. Then came an open space, and all around were seated the Inari, tier upon tier, each man with his weapon by his side. There must have been nearer three thousand of them than two, and it was significant that no women or children were present.

But what held Blake's attention chiefly was the figure seated on a high throne near the altar of sacrifice. The throne itself, which was covered with plates of gold, was set on an archway some ten feet high, also covered in gold, with flights of steps leading up to it on either side.

It was the figure itself that riveted Blake's attention, for it was, as he had been told, the figure of a white god no larger than a man, and instinctively he knew that the white god was none other than Jack Merton, the man he had come so far to rescue.

He wore a great feather headdress like the priests, only far more ornate, and in it was fastened a magnificent table emerald. He had a feather cloak, too, much longer than those worn by the priests, for it completely enveloped him from the shoulders to the feet.

The face was covered to the eyes with what at that distance seemed to be a gold veil, from behind which came a thin puff of smoke from time to time.

Blake could also see that, though the forearms were left free from the elbows down, the legs and trunk of the body, including the upper arms, were bound with heavy gold chains. Every detail was clearly visible in the bright moonlight.

Blake touched Lobangu on the arm.

"The white Inkoos!" he whispered.

Just as he spoke there was a commotion amongst the priests, and a hideous sort of high-pitched, nasal, screeching song was started, to the accompaniment of tom-toms and some string instruments.

Blake nodded to himself. He had heard that same din in Chinese theatres.

Instantly silence fell on the crowd, and four men – apparently high priests – came forward, wearing hideous gilded masks representing demons. Each carried a large sacrificial knife of what appeared to be toughened glass.

Three times they circled the altar, and then they took up their position on the topmost step. Instantly the tom-toms stopped their infernal din, and, by contrast, there was a silence that could be felt. Blake could even hear the low, deep breathing of Lobangu beside him. Then there came a rush from through the archway beneath the throne, and half a dozen guards came hurrying forward with something which fought and struggled and screamed in their midst.

The screams of the poor wretch were ghastly. It was a man – a well-built man, who towered head and shoulders above his captors. He wore

no clothing of any sort, and they could see his powerful muscles ripple and bulge as he struggled.

He was evidently of an alien tribe, a prisoner from beyond the swamps, and equally evidently he knew – by hearsay, at any rate – what was in store for him.

Straight to the foot of the altar the guards rushed him, and then the priests took him from them, and dragged him on to the altar, where they held him stretched out face upwards, still writhing.

Sexton Blake raised his revolver hand, but Lobangu seized it and held it down.

"Nay, Inkoos, the time is not yet," he whispered. "Him thou canst not save, and to try now would be the death of us all, and the white Inkoos younder!"

Lobangu was right; but it went against the grain to see the poor wretch murdered in cold blood.

The high priests raised their knives, and slowly – very slowly – they began. The Chinese are acknowledged to be the most scientific torturers on earth, who can extract the utmost limit of pain from a victim without causing him to lose his senses quite.

The Inari were of Chinese extraction, and they outdid their forbears in point of sheer devilish cruelty. The poor thing on the altar screamed as a cat screams in mortal agony, and that is one of the most ghastly sounds.

For five minutes, ten minutes, that ghastly performance went on. Blake's face was dank with sweat, and his hand slipped and slithered on his revolver-butt. In the end the priests seized the thing, which still struggled feebly and screamed, but was no longer a man, or even a human, and carried it through the archway beneath the throne to a sort of promontory, which jutted out from the edge of the cliff, in the full view of all.

Three times they swung it to and fro, then it was sent hurtling outward and downward, a writhing black speck against the moonlit sky, until it struck the liquid swamp, three hundred feet below, and sent up a great squirting fountain of black mud, which had already subsided before the squelching sound of the falling body striking reached them.

Even Lobangu was caught by the horror of it all.

The tom-toms started again, and he turned to the two indunas and the messenger behind him

"Go swiftly," he said, "and bring the white chiefs and my young men, for I would make an end of this, and the red mist dances before our eyes. Go swiftly as you may, for time passes!"

The three saluted and vanished.

"Now, listen, Untwana," said Lobangu, "and hearken if my words by wise words! In the fight which is to come we shall be, roughly, one man to ten – long odds, even though we have a certain number of chatter-guns, and they are not wearing their poison-bags and throwing-spears[1], as did the hunting or raiding parties out yonder.

"Now, Inkoos, our first aim is to save the white N'kose there, for which reason we have travelled all this way!"

"True words, old friend," agreed Blake.

"And after that to save the prisoners, and stamp these poison folk flat. Good! Then this is my plan. One man singly cannot fight ten, for of the ten there will always be two or three ready to stab him in the back; but if the young men fight shoulder to shoulder in serried ranks, they can fight, not ten, but fifteen times their number, if need be.

"So when the young men arrive we will charge straight for the great throne there, where the white N'kose sits, taking these Inari dogs by surprise, and there form a triple semi-circle round the throne on this side, a score or more being detached to guard the archway from the rear. Thou and Lukuna and M'lolo, together with the James man and such of my own following who have rifles, will mount the steps on either side of the throne, and, firing over our heads, hold off a charge at any point where the pressure seems greatest, and so give my guards of the Etbaia room to use their spear arms freely.

"In this way none can come near the throne of the white N'kose to do him harm; and we –we shall be facing outwards on all sides. Are they wise words, my father?"

1   The Inari were forbidden by the priests to carry poisoned weapons at any public assembly, owning to the numerous accidents which had happened from time to time. Poison weapons, in fact, were only allowed to be carried on the far side of the swamps and in enemy country.

"Wise words, Lobangu. And, hearken, here they come!"

There was a dull pattering of feet behind them, a brief word of command to open ranks, making way for Sir Richard and the others to pass.

Sir Richard was still limping a little; but he and Tinker and James joined Blake, who explained the situation, and Lobangu's plan; whilst the latter, leaving them for the moment, did the same to his indunas and captains, till each man knew what his exact duties were.

Those of the Etbaia who carried firearms were sent to the rear, so that the spearmen could take the first brunt of the charge, and ensure that those with rifles could gain the steps of the throne unheeded.

James paid little attention to anything or anyone but his master, whom he could see by peering over the edge of the step, his whole face twinkling with nervous excitement.

"It's him, sir! It's him, beyond a doubt! I can recognise his eyes even from here!" he said huskily.

He was quivering all over like a terrier at a rat-hole.

"Steady, man – steady," said Blake warningly, "or you'll be shooting wild! We'll have him safe inside the next ten minutes, or we shall be done in ourselves! By Jove, those infernal tom-toms have shut up again! That means another poor wretch of a victim. Stand by, you chaps!"

The words were hardly out of his mouth before Blake himself was out of the tunnel-like entrance.

"A woman, by all that's infernal!" he yelled. "I can't stand that! They sha'nt get their beastly hands on her!"

It was, in fact, a woman – or, rather, a mere slip of a girl – whom the guards were dragging to the altar. Unlike the man, she didn't scream or fight. She seemed to be in a sort of dumb, horrified stupor as they dragged her along.

"The woman first, at all costs!" yelled Blake; and made a rush, with the others and the Etbaia at his heels, the latter giving their deep-throated roar of "S'gee! S'gee! Um ka la la! S'gee!"

The rush of the attack was so unexpected and so unlooked-for that it carried them to the very steps of the altar before the Inari could well realise what was happening.

Blake, a couple of lengths in the lead, shot down the two guards who were holding the girl, and a priest who made a grab for her. Then, swinging her up in his arms, and letting his revolver dangle loose from its lanyard, he made a dash for the steps of the throne, followed by the rest.

"All right, Merton – friends – sent by your brother!" he shouted above the din, and laid the girl down in shelter behind the throne.

The man on the throne gave something between a yell and a sob.

"Get me out of these infernal chains," he cried, "and lend me a gun! Oh, do lend me a gun, someone, and let me have a chance at those fiends down there!"

Blake and Sir Richard wrenched him free of the soft gold chains, and James thrust a heavy revolver into his hand. Merton gave a sigh, like a man who takes a deep breath after a long plunge, and began to shoot. He paid no attention to the main crowd, some of whom were trying to get at him with spears. He concentrated on the priests, firing with murderous accuracy and swiftness, and at each shot a man dropped.

"Another!" he said curtly; and James thrust his second revolver into his hand.

"It's good – oh, it's too good to be true, after all these years!" he muttered thickly. "I'll make 'em pay – pay to the uttermost farthing! That's for you, Ogo! You're head priest no longer; you've tortured your last victim this side of the pit!"

As he fired a big priest, with a sacrificial knife in his hand, went crashing down face foremost across the altar; but Merton, not satisfied, let him have another bullet.

Blake glanced at him curiously. The man for the time being was as mad as a hatter, his lips drawn back in a wolf-like snarl. He was intent on one thing only –to kill, and to keep on killing, and Blake guessed at the years of humiliation and torture he was taking toll for.

Meanwhile, the Inari, roused from their first shock of surprise, were surging forward, pressing the Etbaia hard. Their first rush bore Lobangu's men back by sheer weight of numbers, until the semicircle round the throne was one dense, surging mob, hacking and stabbing furiously.

For five minutes or so the Etbaia were so closely pressed together that they had not space to use their big-bladed spears freely.

Blake and Sir Richard saw the danger quickly, and so did the others.

"Weaken their centre, and give Lobangu breathing room!" shouted Sir Richard. "Concentrated fire – rapid!"

Blake nodded, and the four rifles – his, Sir Richard's, Tinker's, and James' – opened a literally venomous fire from their magazines, which created something like a panic amongst the Inari. At that short range the many bullets literally moved through the densely-packed mass as a machine-gun might have done, a single bullet in many cases putting three men out of action at a time.

The Inari wavered, and thinned out in the centre under that murderous hail.

Lobangu waited his chance patiently, and then he and his Etbaia literally hurled themselves at the opposing ranks, drove a deep wedge through them, and then, wheeling, so as to face outwards in two directions, the drove the Inari like sheep into two pack. Whilst those with rifles, and Merton with his two revolvers, splashed lead vigorously over the wings, leaving Lobangu to look after the centre.

The Inari fought bravely for a little space. They had faced rifle-fire – that of the Arab caravan – before. But that had been but as a mere pattering of dead leaves to a whirlwind hurricane – the old-patterned and semi-obsolete rifle against the most modern type of quick repeater.

Moreover, at bottom, the Inari had the yellow streak of the bully, and the love of torture in them. So long as things seemed to be coming their way, and they hugely outnumbered the enemy, as they could see for themselves, they fought savagely and well.

But when things began to go badly, and they found themselves caught under that hail of lead in their wings, and their centre broken, and with all their leaders, the priests, down, and most of the temple guards as well, a sudden panic rippled through their ranks, spread like wildfire, and they began to give.

"They're breaking," panted Sir Richard, coughing in the acrid powder reek, - "they're breaking!" Now's the time! Keep it going! I'm nearly down to my last cartridge!"

"Me, too!" spluttered Blake. "Tell James to kick open or smash open the spare ammunition-case if he gets a chance."

Lobangu and his men, feeling that it was the critical moment of the fight, executed another manoeuvre with lighting-like rapidity, and, with their hoarse, blood-curdling cry of "S'gee! S'gee!" – "Kill! Kill!" split into two parties, and charged headlong right and left.

That was enough for the Inari. Though they still numbered four or five to one, they literally crumpled up and bolted.

But not even Lobangu himself could hold his young men now, and, as a matter of fact, his voice would have been inaudible above the din.

The Etbaia had lost not a few of their number, and they were seeing scarlet. They drove the Inari to the edge of the great cliff and over it by the score. Some even leapt of their own accord rather than face those terrible spears. The luckiest were those who were able to scatter and make for their bolt-holes at the far edges of the rock, and not all of these, even, got off.

Lobangu, unable to hold his men, did the next best thing, he led them – at least, he led one section, whilst at the head of the other raced a weird figure – Jack Merton, ex-heathen idol. He had torn off his robes and his headdress, and fought gracefully attired in a loin-cloth and the torn remnants of his gold veil.

In his left hand he held, long since empty, a rifle, and used it effectively as a club. In his right he had a heavy sword snatched from a dead guard, and every Inari who came within his reach was a good Inari inside a couple of seconds. In other words he was dead, or as good as dead.

He himself, racing ahead of the Etbaia, seemed to bear a charmed life. Again and again, two or three men, plucking up heart, would turn to make a stand against them. He never seemed to bother even to parry their thrusts, but when he swept on once more they would all be down and mostly dead.

Meanwhile James had broken open the ammunition-box and Blake and the others, fearing possible reinforcements on the part of the Inari, refilled their magazines and waited.

But no reinforcements came, and in an incredibly short time there was not a live Inari left on the top of the rock, and Lobangu and Merton returned at the head of their men.

They were a ghastly sight, covered with blood, mostly other people's property. The Etbaia had lost twenty men killed, at least another twenty were more or less badly damaged, and there was not a man that hadn't a scratch of some sort. But the Inari losses must have run to well over a thousand, to say nothing of big numbers of wounded who had got away into their rabbit-warrens.

"A great fight, Untwana!" cried Lobangu, flinging up his spear in salute. "A fight after my own heart. And the new white Inkoos – the Panther, he shall be named, for he is very swift – is a great fighter."

Merton, now that it was all over, had flung himself down on a rock, and was sobbing with exhaustion and over-excitement. The unexpected rescue, and the sight of men – white men of his own race – after all those weary years, were momentarily too much for him. So, they left him to quieten down a bit, not daring to show him sympathy yet.

Lobangu set such of his young men as were only scratched to clear the cliff-top of the dead Inari, which they did by throwing them into that selfsame swamp below into which the Inari had thrown their victims for generations.

Meanwhile, the indunas organised small patrols to search for stragglers and to watch the numerous burrows through which the fugitives had escaped into the heart of the rock below.

This was still going on when James – a sadly battered and powder-blackened James – came up to where Blake and Sir Richard were sitting.

"Begging your pardon, sir, but I thought you and the master might like a little supper, sir. It's just ready on the other side of the rock, sir."

Sir Richard started.

"Supper, by Jove! Yes, I'm ravenous! But how on earth did you get it?"

Blake also looked at him and chuckled. James was hare-headed, his clothes were mostly in ribbons, one side of his face was scorched with powder and smeared with blood, the other side was adorned with a beautiful black eye. In fact, he looked anything but a respectable manservant.

"Thank the Lord Harry that beast of a hat's gone at last!" said Blake grinning. "Come on, where's the grub?"

"Yes, sir – this way, sir," said James, and let them round the rock. There there was a table-cloth neatly laid, knives, forks, and all complete, with cold birds, a native salad, biscuits, and half a tinned cheese. But, most miraculous of all, there was a box of Blake's cigarettes, four bottles of champagne, and a bottle of red wine.

"Great Scott!" said Blake.

"It's all cold, I'm afraid, sir," said James. "But there'll be hot coffee in the thermos flask to come after, sir. It was the best I could manage."

"The best you could manage! You're a blessed miracle! How did you do it?"

Well, sir, I cooked the things beforehand, sir, and as there were two cases of wine left amongst the stores, I ventured to break one open, sir. Then I got three of Lobangu's young men to carry the things, sir, and leave them at the top of the passage by which we came, sir. I've just been to fetch them. Shall I call the master, sir?"

"Yes, quick, and bring Lobangu and Tinker, too."

When Merton came up he had quite recovered himself, and shook hands warmly all round.

"Excuse my making an ass of myself, you chaps, but when a man has lived in an infernal region like this for years without ever seeing a white face, it comes as a bit of a jolt when things happen quickly, and I wanted to get back on those brutes of Inari."

They sat round in a circle and ate ravenously, and smoked, and over their wine – Lobangu was allowed a whole bottle of bubbly water to himself in honour of the occasion – Merton told his story.

"It isn't so much of a yarn as you might expect," he said, inhaling his cigarette, and you must know the earlier part of it, or you wouldn't be here, and dear old James with you. So you know all about the old elephant hunter's story, and how I came to have a shot at this beastly place.

"All went well till I reached the outer swamps. Then illness broke out amongst my boys –some sort of fever I couldn't tackle – and then, in the midst of it, the Inari came and caught us at dawn.

"I was worn out with two nights' sick-nursing, and had just dropped off into a dog-tired sleep. They were all over us, and had stamped the camp flat, and killed the bearers before I was really awake.

"Me they saved and brought here. I thought my number was up, but they didn't treat me badly. A white man was a curiosity, and the priests kept me in secret. Then small-pox caught the tribe badly, and they were scared. I know a bit about doctoring – I practised in a half-hearted way once – and I pulled a whole lot of the brutes through.

"I had my medicine-chest from the wreck of the camp, and a good supply of samples, and I dare say I saved scores of lives by methods I would never have risked on a European. They're half Chinks, these beggars, you know, and you can't kill a Chinaman with drugs.

"Of course, the priests were getting all the credit, for the patients were brought to me by them secretly, and I was masked. Then they got an infernal notion into their heads to run me as a 'god' for business purposes.

"Three times I tried to escape, and each time I was brought back and tortured. Look here." He pointed to old scars on his body. "But the worst row of all was over those infernal human sacrifices. I refused point-blank, and they nearly killed me – in fact, for six months I didn't care whether I lived or died. After that they used to bind me on that throne thing with gold chains, and I used to shut my eyes when the killing began.

"My one consolation is that for the last two years they've allowed me to smoke. The native tobacco isn't bad, though they only chew it. The priests soon found that my smoking – breathing fire, and smoke they call it – was immensely popular with the common folk, thought I was a sort of dragon, I suppose, so I was supplied with unlimited tobacco.

"And that's about all there was till you came, deadly monotony, barring an occasional row. No chance of escape. I was too closely guarded for that. And a hundred and fifty thousand pounds of loot which I couldn't carry away for me to play with.

"Oh yes! Knowing that I couldn't get away, the priests gave me the free run of the treasure-house, and grinned evilly when they saw me poring over the things. I'll show them to you soon, but this time we'll take 'em with us.

"What's the news of Eustace? You saw him, of course?"

They told him briefly and quietly, and he sat silent for a while.

"Poor chap! Poor old chap!" he said at last, in a low voice. "Maybe he would have chosen that way in the end, though, if he had known the truth. He was practically doomed when I left, poor chap! Consumption, you know. I had several men, big men, in to see him without his guessing it, and they all confirmed my opinion. Let him rest in peace, poor chap!

"Look there!" he said, rising suddenly, and pointing. The great red disc of the sun had risen above the horizon, burying the whole cliff summit in a flood of crimson. "Now, come. I will show you the treasure-house." And he led the way to the big altar.

There it lay, just as the elephant-hunter described the room beneath the altar itself.

"I've been through it bit by bit," said Merton, "and I think a hundred and fifty thousand is too little by a third, and now it's ours by right of conquest.

"What I propose is this. We'll leave a handful of your Etbaia here to guard the summit. The Inari won't have any stomach for any more fighting, but it's well to be on the safe side. The rest can carry the loot across the swamps to the hunter's old cache. It will take five or six trips.

"Once it's there, I'll go, or send, to the Lavu kraals, and ask for more bearers, plenty of them, so that we can travel fast, and then it's hey for the coast! I saved the son of the chief of the Lavu from the altar once, and they'll do anything for me in return."

"Capital!" said Blake. "And we can provide the runners, for we've five Lavus down below guarding our stores."

§

It took two days before the last of the treasure was removed across the swamps, and the Etbaia garrison were withdrawn from the cliff, by which time a runner, bearing wild news of the defeat of the Inari, had reached the Lavu Great Place, and returned with five hundred bearers and offerings of cattle.

The next day they headed for the coast, Merton having insisted on Blake and Sir Richard taking a large share of the spoil.

"Only on one condition," said Blake, giving in at last, "that out of my lot I may buy James the finest hat in London, in addition to his share. What do you want, Lobangu, you old ruffian?"

"Snuff, Inkoos!" said Lobangu. "See, the horn is nearly empty. Snuff such as you gave me before, and – and some bubbly water, with the gold tops to the bottles."

"It's a bet," said Blake, and grinned.

THE END.

THE CASE OF THE LOUIS QUINZE SNUFF-BOX.

A SPLENDID TALE OF SEXTON BLAKE *versus* MARSTON HUME.

Blake turned sharply as Hume closed the breach of his gun on a couple of cartridges. "I am contemplating a fatal shooting accident!" said the latter, smiling evilly.

IT is given to some hostesses to mix up their guests in the most incongruous, haphazard fashion, to the extreme annoyance and discomfort of the majority of the house-party.

They mean extremely well. Their one desire is that everybody should have a thoroughly good time whilst under their roof; but they are so content with the world as they find it that they forget that less fortunately placed people may have grievances. It is this type of hostess who sends an unfortunate, and possibly dyspeptic, youth, into dinner with the pretty girl who refused him twice in five days less than a month before. Naturally he has one course left open. He sends himself an urgent wire from town the next day, and loses the prospect of a week's good shooting, or hunting, to which he has been looking forward.

This does not come from lack of brain on the part of the hostess, so much as from exuberant spirits, and a healthy and robust constitution, which fails to recognise the secret sorrows of the dyspeptic youth.

At the same time it causes complications.

No sane person could deny that Lady Marjorie Maxwell, an old standing friend of Blake's, had brains of most remarkable shrewdness; nevertheless, she was a hostess of the type in question, for the simple reason that she was impulsiveness personified.

She asked Hume because he was a brilliant conversationalist when he chose to exert himself, and because on the few occasions on which they had met he interested her.

She asked Blake because she liked him more than all the men she knew. Neither man had a suspicion that the other had been invited till they found themselves seated side by side in the private omnibus sent to meet them.

She herself certainly had not even the vaguest notion that they were more than casual acquaintances, for she had seen little of Blake of late.

Hume greeted Blake with a friendly nod, polished his eyeglass on his handkerchief, and replaced it carefully.

"Charming place Constantinople," he said blandly. "Just been out there for a short holiday. Know it?"

There were three other people in the 'bus—a man and his wife, and a youngster in the Lancers—a distant relation of Lady Marjorie's. Blake checked the answer which rose to his lips.

"It is chiefly associated in my mind with the use of the bow-string and the refuse of European capitals. I am glad to hear you enjoyed yourself. There is nothing like feeling at home when one travels," he said acidly.

Hume waved a well-gloved hand, and smiled genially.

"You are cultivating the art of epigram, I see. A dangerous habit, my dear fellow. An epigram, to be amusing, should contain a truth, and the truth is so deucedly unpopular."

With another flash of his strong white teeth, he turned his back on Blake, and, for the rest of the drive to the house, devoted himself to amusing the other occupants of the carriage.

Not one of the twenty odd guests who made up the house-party—not even Lady Molly herself—had the remotest suspicion that between the two men in their midst a duel of wits was in progress—a duel of which the stakes were life or death.

Both men maintained a calm and smiling exterior, joining heartily in the varied round of amusements, and taking their full share in keeping things going.

Hume, it is true, took every opportunity of trying to outvie Blake in whatever was going forward, especially when Lady Molly happened to be a spectator, whether it was at a game of billiards, or piquet, or in shooting over the covers.

But Blake was his equal, if not more; and try as he would, Marston Hume could obtain no decisive advantage. At last he took it into his head to try to monopolise Lady Molly herself. He undoubtedly admired her, and he took pleasure in being in her company as much as possible.

Blake noticed this new move on his part, but for two or three days he said nothing. Others, however, also noticed it, and Blake overheard a word here, and a smiling hint there, which made him resolve to take action.

The following day there was a shoot over some outlying covers, and Hume, who had contrived to get Lady Molly near him, shot surprisingly well, even for him, beating all the records of the other guns, including Blake's, for Blake had been absent-minded, and shot only indifferently.

"Feeling off colour a bit?" asked Hume, as he and Lady Molly came strolling up after the last drive. "You weren't up to your usual form quite."

"Not quite," said Blake. "Still, one can't always do all one hopes to. Molly, you are driving back, of course? Hume and I will stroll home together."

They saw her into the wagonette with the other women folk, and started off for the house by a short cut across the fields.

"Talking of doing all one hopes," said Blake, as they tramped on. "You are forcing yourself too much on Lady Marjorie's leisure. It must stop!"

For a fleeting instant a dull flushed spot showed on Hume's pale cheek, but it vanished as quickly as it had come.

"Liver out of order?" he asked pleasantly. "Whenever I see a man missing easy shots and interfering with other people's business I always put it down to liver. Beastly complaint!"

"You will make an excuse to leave the house within three days from now," Blake went on imperturbably. "I give you that much grace because Lady Marjorie is shrewd, and a sudden departure would arouse her suspicions. I particularly wish to avoid letting her guess the contamination she has unwittingly had to put up with."

Again that dull flush crept up into Hume's pale face.

"You are going too far," he said in a low voice. "I have already warned you that I will stand no interference. You have twice already caused me serious inconvenience, and I am not a patient man. Let me tell you, Mr. Blake, once and for all, that you are running a very serious risk."

"Contamination is the word I used," said Blake coldly. "You best know how aptly. I give you three days from this evening—no longer."

"And then?" asked Hume sneeringly.

"If I find you still here I shall wait till the whole house-party is assembled, and I shall tell Colonel Maxwell, before them all, exactly the manner of man you are, giving them all the facts in my possession. After which they must judge for themselves. So long as your presence concerned men only, I refrained; but now that you have had the impertinence to try to get your name associated with Lady Marjorie's—your name that, sooner or later, will be pilloried and execrated by all civilised people—I dictate my terms, and, by Heaven, if you reject them I shall act!"

"I believe that there is a law concerning criminal libel," said Hume suavely. "You may make wild statements, but you can prove nothing—nothing at all. I should certainly prosecute. I think, on the whole, that the verdict would ruin you. I price my character at a high figure."

Blake shrugged his shoulders.

"The price and the value are two very different matters, and, in the meanwhile, Colonel Maxwell's servants would have had the pleasure of kicking you out. In his case my word would be considered proof enough. In the case of your bringing an action, I should have some most interesting evidence to bring forward in public. You have, as I said before, three days' grace, on Lady Marjorie's account; but for her I wouldn't give you an hour."

Both men's faces showed white and tense in the murky gloom. They were quite alone, and masks and foil-buttons had been discarded for the naked point.

An ugly look came over Marston Hume's face; they were just coming to a stile, and he stepped back as though to let Blake pass first.

Blake had one leg over the top bar when he heard a click, and turned sharply, just in time to see Hume close the breach of his gun on a couple of cartridges.

"Well," he said coldly, eyeing the other squarely, "our conversation seems to have made you lose your nerve."

"On the contrary," said Hume, smiling evilly. "I am contemplating a fatal shooting accident—under the circumstances, it seems the simplest solution." He half raised the gun as he spoke.

"You have lost your head as well as your nerve, then," Blake replied contemptuously.

"Shoot, if you please. I should then have the satisfaction of knowing that you would hang a little sooner than I anticipated. You are standing in a clay path, and leaving tracks from which even a rural policeman could deduce the truth. Knave you are, but this is my first meeting with you in the character of a fool! I should advise you to put those cartridges back into your pocket if you value your neck."

Hume paused for an instant, and then gave a short, hard laugh.

"Thanks for the hint. I will," he said; "but, upon my word, there are times when you annoy me past all bearing.

"I'll walk the rest of the way alone, in ease I should be tempted past my strength. See you later." And with a nod he turned on his heel.

Blake watched him go, and then walked moodily back by himself, lost in thought.

Hume failed to put in an appearance at dinner that night, sending down a graceful message to Lady Marjorie to excuse his non-appearance on account of a blinding attack of neuralgia.

He was present at luncheon-time next day, however, and seemed all the better for his rest; but beneath Hume's apparent good humour

Blake could detect signs of a lurking uneasiness, and he seemed to be, even more than usual, on his guard.

The uneasiness was especially noticeable when the post-bag came in—twice within half an hour of the time it was due Blake saw Hume glance surreptitiously at his watch, and when at last it did arrive, and Lady Molly unlocked it on the table in the big hall, calling out, "Letters, good people all!" Hume was one of those nearest to her, and a look of annoyance passed over his face as she poured out the contents.

Blake noted that look, and had reason to remember it afterwards.

By the midday post the next day Lady Molly received a small registered parcel, which she opened with some curiosity. Inside was a beautiful specimen of a Louis Quinze snuff-box, and a brief letter.

The box itself was of rich deep Sèvres blue enamel, mounted in delicately-chased gold. On the lid, and on each side were small oval miniatures, inset, and surrounded by seed pearls.

The letter accompanying it was brief and to the point.

"Dear Madam,—Having heard of your well-known collection of jewelled snuff-boxes, I venture to forward you the enclosed in the hope you may care to purchase it. It has been in the possession of my family for many years, but unfortunately circumstances compel me to part with it. I have no idea of its actual value, but should be glad to take five pounds for it, if it should prove worth that price to you.

"There is, I believe, some trick in the manner of opening it which I myself am not acquainted with, but to you it will, I have no doubt, be familiar. An early reply would oblige."

The letter was signed Mary Leslie, and was addressed from a block of cheap flats in Chelsea.

Lady Molly threw down the letter, and snatched up the box with an exclamation of delight.

"Five pounds! Poor thing! Why, it's worth five times that, and more. Lavine would have asked me fifty at least."

She tried to open it, but only hurt her fingers.

"Now then, some of you clever people," she cried. "Which of you can do this for me?"

Half a dozen of them tried, but without success.

"Mr. Hume, you try," she said, handing it to him. "Surely you won't confess yourself vanquished by a little simple problem like this? Mind you don't hurt the enamel, though."

Hume laughed, and tried in his turn, but with no better success.

"I must take it to the Court of Appeal, then," said Lady Molly. "Mr. Blake, you spend your life solving puzzles—surely you, at any rate, can solve the riddle of my poor little box?"

Blake took it, and examined it carefully, first with the naked eye, then with the aid of a pocket lens.

"The trick is simple enough," he said at last; "but it is one of the most exquisite pieces of workmanship I have ever seen. The principle is as old as the old Medici rings. To open the box, all you have to do is to press this central pearl here. But you want to press just the edge of it with your nail, otherwise a very small needle-point comes out of that minute hole there and pricks you. Watch."

With his thumbnail he pressed on the outer edge of the pearl, and for the fraction of an instant those looking on caught a glimpse of a fine steel point no more than a sixteenth of an inch long. Then the lid flew open, disclosing the plain gilt interior.

"Well done!" said Lady Molly. "But I don't quite understand. What is the reason for the needle thing there? I don't want to prick my fingers, nor anybody else's."

Blake showed her a slight depression on the under side of the lid immediately beneath the movable pearl.

"Originally," he said, "boxes and trinkets of this type were made use of to remove an inconvenient enemy. It was an Italian invention. This small receptacle was filled with a virulent poison. The needle made a small puncture in the hand of the unwary victim, who was asked to help himself to a pinch of snuff, and a few hours afterwards he was a dead man."

Lady Molly made a little grimace.

"It's rather shuddering, isn't it? Still, it adds to its value." And she put the box down on the silver table close by.

In the big hall that evening after dinner the majority of the party were playing bridge. Blake was smoking and strolling idly from table to table. He rarely played himself, bridge being a game in which he took little interest.

Marston Hume also was not playing, which for him was unusual. Instead, he was amusing himself by talking to a pretty girl, a Miss Palliser, in one of the big ingle nooks.

Blake happened to pass near them as he strolled about, and the girl beckoned him towards her.

"Oh, Mr. Blake," she said, "I am dying to see that box of Molly's with the gruesome history! I was out riding when it came, and Mr. Hume tells me that you know all about it, and showed them the trick of it."

"I don't know that it is particularly gruesome," replied Blake smiling; "but I'll go and fetch it for you. It's on one of those tables over there by the windows, I think."

He fetched it, and explained it to her briefly.

"This is the trick of it, you see," he said, and pressed the spring.

Just at that instant Hume dropped his handkerchief and, in stooping to recover it, jogged Blake's elbow.

The result was that instead of pressing the edge of the pearl, his thumb pressed on the whole stone, and he got a small scratch from the needle in consequence.

"Sorry," said Hume, and then, as Miss Palliser held out her hand for the box, he took it as Blake was handing it to her.

"Excuse me one moment," he broke in quickly. "I think one of the stones has fallen out," and, turning half round, he held it under the lamplight with his back towards them.

Blake, who was answering a question of the girl's, only noted the movement subconsciously, and by the time he had finished speaking Hume had turned towards them again with the box in his hand.

"My mistake," he said, smiling. "It must have been some trick of light. I was almost sure a stone was gone from the centre setting. A pretty thing, isn't it? and, as Blake says, it may have been designed to cause a tragedy, which adds to its interest."

Half an hour later, as Blake was making his way to the smoking-room, he felt a sudden spasm of pain shoot through him, leaving behind it a curious numb feeling. A cold perspiration broke out on his forehead, and he stood for a few minutes clinging to the door handle.

He was all alone in the corridor, and there was no one to see what had happened.

Near by was a small staircase, mostly used by the servants. He dragged himself to this, and stumbled his way up. Twice he was compelled to stop and clutch at the wall for support, and it took him a good five minutes to stagger and crawl to his room.

Though his muscles were numbed, his mind was working like lightning, and a suspicion of the truth brought the perspiration to his forehead again.

With an effort he reached the bell and rang it.

It was answered by a servant named Johnson, who always valeted him when he was staying there, and whom he knew he could trust.

"I'm not well, Johnson," he said, speaking slowly, and with difficulty. Go downstairs, get Colonel Maxwell aside on some pretext, and ask him to come here. No one else is to know, understand? Then bring me a jugful of the hottest and strongest black coffee you can find, and some ammonia, if you can get it. Be quick! It's life or death."

When Colonel Maxwell and Johnson came hurrying back, they found Blake on the floor, his spine curved upwards, and his muscles tense. He was breathing with difficulty.

"Shut the door," he gasped. "The coffee—quick!"

They gave him the scalding hot coffee, which he swallowed in great gulps, and it seemed to ease him a little.

"Get me on my feet, and drag me up and down the room. Make me keep moving somehow."

Bewilderedly, but silently, they obeyed.

After a little while he demanded ammonia, and this, too, he forced down his throat, though it burnt, and made him choke and gasp. Then followed another period of dragging up and down; but after a while, and more coffee, and another dose of ammonia, he could move with a certain amount of volition, and the cramped muscles grew less tense.

"Put me on the bed," he said at last. "The constriction of the chest muscles has passed. Pile all the rugs and wraps you can on to me. I'm as cold as ice."

Good heavens, man! What's the matter?" asked the colonel, opening his mouth for the first time and flinging an armful of rugs over the bed.

"The matter is that I nearly spoilt your house-party with a funeral," replied Blake, smiling faintly. "I'm all right now, though—you saved me in the nick of time between you.

"Colonel, I wish you would go downstairs again. Don't breathe a word about this, but fetch that snuff-box that Molly had sent to-day; let no one see you, and for Heaven's sake hold it only by the ends—so. Johnson, get me another jug of coffee to warm me up a bit."

Colonel Maxwell returned, holding the box gingerly; and found that Blake had contrived to prop himself on one elbow, and write out a long telegram on sheets of notepaper.

He handed this to his host. "This must go off to-night at all costs," he said. "Let Johnson take it. Now put the box there on that shelf, and I'll trouble you no more to-night. I'm played out and must rest. Come to me to-morrow after breakfast, and when the answer comes to the telegram be good enough to have it sent to me at once."

"Sure you're all right," said the colonel.

"Quite, thanks! Good-night!" answered Blake faintly, and they left him.

At breakfast time Blake failed to put in an appearance, but sent word to the colonel that he would be down later, and to let the fact be known.

At ten, Colonel Maxwell knocked at his door and found him reading a wire which had just come.

"Ah! that you, colonel; good morning," he said. "I am still a bit shaky, but there are things I must tell you; before I do so, though, you must give me your word to say nothing and do nothing without my permission."

"Word of honour," said the colonel promptly.

"Very good; then I'd better start by telling you that I was poisoned last night—that much you probably suspect—but you don't suspect the truth; and that is, that it was a clever and deliberate attempt on the part of one of your guests."

"Good heavens," cried the colonel.

"A fact," said Blake quietly, "and the man's name was Marston Hume. Sit still—you have given me your word, remember. Hume and I are bitter enemies—the reasons, which are many, I will not speak about—it is sufficient that I know him to be a man who would be thrown out of any respectable house. And more, I saw him making friends with Molly, and told him bluntly that it must stop. I gave him three days' grace to clear out. The poisoning was the outcome of it. Yesterday morning, as you know, a snuff-box—this one—was sent to Molly to buy, at an absurdly low price. It came, according to the letter, from a

Mrs. Mary Leslie and was sent from 21, Tollington Mansions, a block of cheap flats in Chelsea. I had at that time no reason to connect the box with Hume, and he showed no interest in it, affecting ignorance of the secret spring by which it opened. It was I who showed them all the mechanism of it. I had examined it previously with a strong lens, and the needle point was then dull and harmless. The box was left lying about for anyone to handle who chose.

"In the evening when you were all busy with bridge—a game, which as Hume knew, I rarely play—he contrived to get Miss Palliser to ask me to show her the trick. I did so, and as I was in the act of doing it, Hume jogged my elbow causing me to give myself a slight scratch. Half-an-hour later I was seized with a sudden spasm of pain, and only managed to get to my room with extreme difficulty. I could scarcely move, but I could think. I knew, of course, that I was poisoned, and I could name the poison used— one practically unknown in this country and very hard to procure, though well-known to some Indian tribes—*curari*; taken internally it is harmless, but taken into the blood through a wound or a scratch it produces a paralysing and constricting effect, and death ensues from suffocation and the cramping of the heart muscles; it is very hard to detect. There are few poisons which absorbed in such minute quantities act so swiftly and fatally; so, with my own symptoms as a guide, I had no difficulty in naming it, or in guessing to whom I was indebted; and from that it was only a step to deduce that Mary Leslie was probably a myth.

"On the evening of the day on which I spoke to Hume, he excused himself from dinner. What happened was this—he had that snuff-box in his possession—harmless, it is true—but he also had a small amount of *curari*. He went up to town that night, when he was supposed to be in his room, and arranged for the posting of the box to Molly, with a plausible letter, knowing her fondness for such things. Later, into the box—then harmless, having been left for anyone to handle—he introduced some of the *curari,* probably whilst you were all settling down to cards, and induced Miss Palliser quite innocently, to spring the trap. I remember distinctly now that after scratching my hand, when I was about to give her the box as she asked, he snatched it away on the excuse of examining it;

his back was turned to us for a moment or two, and in that time he wiped away all the remaining traces of the poison with the handkerchief he had in his hand before letting her touch the box. Luckily for me I was able to take an antidote almost immediately; and also, I fancy, the poison itself had deteriorated."

"But, good heavens, man; are you sure of this—it—"

"You sent a telegram for me—it was to my friend Bathurst. I am having Hume's rooms watched, you must know. Here is the reply: 'H. was seen near his new rooms at 11.30 on night in question. M. L. never seen at 21, Tollington Mansions, though letters addressed there in that name, and rent paid regularly in advance. Flat is furnished but unoccupied. M. L. supposed abroad. Flat taken in name of M. L. six months ago by man, description corresponding to H.' That proves my theory so far, now take this lens and examine the point of the needle, you will notice minute fragments of fluff from a white handkerchief. You see them? Well, that proves the rest.

"But there we end. I cannot prove that Hume either ever possessed any such rare drug as *curari,* or that he inserted it into the spring of the box. I know that he did, for I had examined it previously under a lens, but to prove it is impossible—at present, at any rate."

"I'll keep my promise," said the colonel; "but to go down and order the scoundrel to leave the house instantly is a thing I insist on!"

"Very well," said Blake, with a faint smile.

The colonel was back in three minutes. "The blackguard's bolted, packed and went on the 9.40, after speaking through the telephone."

"To Mary Leslie," suggested Blake drily. "I knew you'd find him gone—my message to you to say I'd be down later warned him that he had failed, and he dared not stop and brazen it out.

"The main thing is that we're well rid of him without a scandal. I gave him three days, and he has gone just before his time limit. Now if you'll send Johnson to me I will try to get up and out into the fresh air. Don't let Molly suspect anything, that's all."

THE UNION JACK · 1^D·

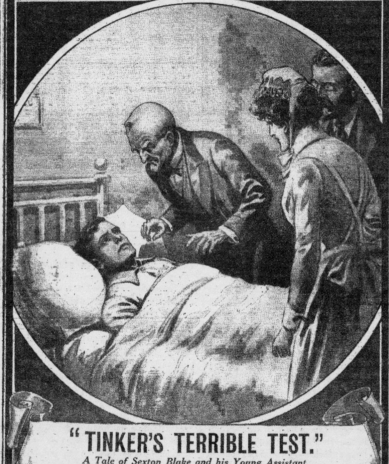

"TINKER'S TERRIBLE TEST."

A Tale of Sexton Blake and his Young Assistant.

Illustrations by H. M. Lewis

NO. 525. NEW SERIES.]   November 1st, 1913.   [EVERY THURSDAY.

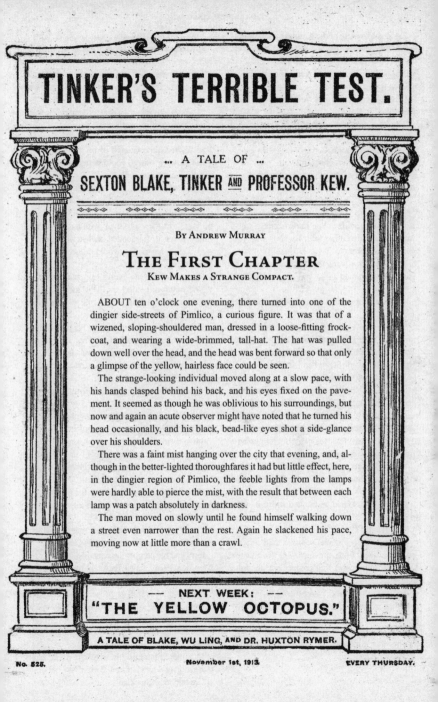

TINKER'S TERRIBLE TEST.

... A TALE OF ...

SEXTON BLAKE, TINKER AND PROFESSOR KEW.

By ANDREW MURRAY

THE FIRST CHAPTER
KEW MAKES A STRANGE COMPACT.

ABOUT ten o'clock one evening, there turned into one of the dingier side-streets of Pimlico, a curious figure. It was that of a wizened, sloping-shouldered man, dressed in a loose-fitting frock-coat, and wearing a wide-brimmed, tall-hat. The hat was pulled down well over the head, and the head was bent forward so that only a glimpse of the yellow, hairless face could be seen.

The strange-looking individual moved along at a slow pace, with his hands clasped behind his back, and his eyes fixed on the pavement. It seemed as though he was oblivious to his surroundings, but now and again an acute observer might have noted that he turned his head occasionally, and his black, bead-like eyes shot a side-glance over his shoulders.

There was a faint mist hanging over the city that evening, and, although in the better-lighted thoroughfares it had but little effect, here, in the dingier region of Pimlico, the feeble lights from the lamps were hardly able to pierce the mist, with the result that between each lamp was a patch absolutely in darkness.

The man moved on slowly until he found himself walking down a street even narrower than the rest. Again he slackened his pace, moving now at little more than a crawl.

-- NEXT WEEK: --
"THE YELLOW OCTOPUS."

A TALE OF BLAKE, WU LING, AND DR. HUXTON RYMER.

From somewhere in the darkness a scraping of a foot came to his ears, and he halted. A moment later, a burly, thick-shouldered man swung out of the mist, and a big hand was laid on the frock-coated figure's shoulder.

"Can I have a word with you, mister?" a harsh voice said.

The burly fellow was treated to a long, searching look.

"What do you want?"

"You—you're a doctor, ain't you?"

The thin lips of the wizened man lifted in a slow smile.

"Look here, my good fellow," he said. "There's no good of yon going on any further with this pantomime. You know exactly who I am. You and that other fellow who is with you, followed me from St. Cyr's Hospital!"

Dusk though it was, the blank dismay on the rough-looking man's face was plainly visible.

"I—I ain't—"

An impatient gesture came from the bird-like man.

"Don't waste my time," the shrill voice snapped. "You know well enough that I am Professor Kew of St. Cyr's. I saw you loafing about the gate of the hospital when I left it."

A faint chuckle sounded.

"I soon realised that you were following me," the cynical tones went on; "and I led you a long dance, didn't I? Right through the park, and on down Sloane Street. I made you step it out."

The burly man took his cap off, and passed a heavy hand across his brow.

"Right you are, professor," he said. "It strikes me my mate and I have been a pair of blinkin' fools!"

He turned his head and called softly into the darkness:

"Hi, Jerry!"

There was a moment's pause, and another man emerged from the mist. He was leaner and taller than the first-comer, but in dress and appearance they were very much similar. They were obviously "roughs" and their faces, looming in the dusk, were those of men of the lower type.

"Wot is it, Jem?" the newcomer asked.

The man addressed as Jem nodded towards Professor Kew.

"'E—'e knew orl abart us," he said, with a slight, uncomfortable laugh. "Knew we was follerin' Jim. That's why 'e led us all this way."

Jerry smothered an oath, for the chase had been a hot one, and the pace set by no means slow at times.

"I wished we'd known abart it sooner," he said. "'Ave you told 'im wot's on?"

"Not yet," said Francis Kew. "And, as I think I've wasted quite enough of my time in giving you fellows a lesson, you'd better hurry up and tell me what you want."

Jerry took a pace forward and lowered his breath.

"A pal of ours 'as been—as been badly 'urt," he said, "'E—'e was playin' with a revolver and didn't know it was loaded, and it went off. We was wondering if you would come and 'ave a look at 'im."

Kew glanced at the figures for a moment.

"Why did you select me?" he asked. "There are thousands of doctors in London who might have attended to our friend."

Jem jerked his fingers towards his companion.

"It was Jerry as picked on you, sir," he explained. "'E'd a friend who was in St. Cyr's once, and you operated on 'im and cured 'im. Jerry swears by you, sir!"

"That's very kind of Jerry," said Kew cynically.

But as he spoke he had not removed his eyes from the two men, and his quick brain was valuing them.

"Unless you are both criminals I am very much mistaken," Kew thought. "Criminals of the housebreaking type, I should think."

"We would pay yer very well for wot you did to our chum," the man went on eagerly. "How much?"

There was a lot behind that question, much more than either of the two roughs imagined.

Jerry and his companion consulted together for a moment in low tones, then Jem turned towards Kew.

"We wouldn't mind givin' yer a hundred quid in gold, so long, as you—you didn't tell anyone what was happening."

The vulture face of Professor Kew shone in the dusk.

"A hundred pounds!" he said. "It would have to be money down before I started."

The two men chuckled.

"If yer'll come wiv us now we'll put it into your hands at once," said Jem.

Kew had been making a swift mental calculation.

If those men were capable of paying a hundred pounds for a simple operation it meant that they were more than well supplied with money. There could be no doubt but what that money had been gained dishonestly. There was a suggestion of mystery about the affair which appealed to Kew, while his cupidity was also aroused.

"Very well," he said, "I will come with you. You say the bullet is still in the wound?"

"Must be, sir," said Jem. "The hole is there where it went in, but there ain't any 'ole to show that it's come out."

"I must get my instruments," said Kew. "I have chambers in Jermyn Street, and I keep them there. One of you had better come with me, and then he can take me to the injured man afterwards."

His brisk, business-like air seemed to satisfy the two rough-looking men.

Again they moved aside, and whispered for a moment, and then it was Jem who moved forward.

"I'll come along with you, sir," he said, "and Jerry'll go on and get everything ready for yer."

Kew wheeled round, and, accompanied by the tall, slouching figure, he plunged into the maze of streets until at last he reached a wider thoroughfare, and found a taxi. The vehicle took him swiftly up to Jermyn Street, and when he alighted from the taxi, Kew smiled to himself to find Jem at his heels.

"You're not taking any risks, my friend," said Kew quietly.

The big fellow grinned.

"Yer might 'ave a telephone," he said, "and I—I didn't want yer to—to talk to anyone."

Kew knew that the anyone Jem referred to was the police, and a faint stirring of humour came into the professor's brain as he went on up the narrow staircase.

Jem little dreamed that the police were just about the last people that Francis Kew would dream of holding communication with.

When he reached his chambers he switched the electric light on, then, while Jem stood in the doorway, Kew drew a small leather bag out of a cupboard and opened it. He selected a case of instruments from a long range of cases on

his desk, placed a bottle of disinfectant in the bag, and a few rolls of lint and antiseptic wool. Finally, a pair of rubber gloves were added to the contents of the bag, then Kew was ready.

The business-like way in which he had moved about his task had impressed Jem, and there was a certain air of deference, about the big fellow as he stood aside, allowing Kew to pass out of the room.

"There's only one thing I've got to ask yer, professor," he said. "We'll have to get into a taxi, 'cos it's a long way from 'ere. But when we gets out I'll 'ave ter blindfold yer."

"Why?"

They were passing down the staircase now, and Jem turned his head towards the figure behind him.

"'Cos you're gettin' a hundred pounds for the job, sir," he said, not without a touch of humour, "that's why. We don't want yer to find the place again."

Any doubts as to the nature of the task that Kew might have had vanished then, but he was quite content to agree to the stipulation.

It was a long journey that they took in the taxi-cab, and it was over the best part of an hour before they came to a halt at the end of an unlighted alley.

Kew had been watching every turn that the taxi gave, and his mind's eye took a quick photograph of the dark street down which they had passed. Half-way down the street Jem touched his companion on the arm, producing a thick handkerchief at the same time.

"We ain't got very far to go, sir," he said.

He did not know that Kew had been counting the lamp-posts. They had passed eight of them before they halted, and when the bandage had been adjusted over his eyes and Jem had taken his arm, Kew began to count his steps

First of all the thick-shouldered man led his blindfolded companion across the street, then they turned to the left when they reached the pavement.

Kew deliberately dropped into a little quick pace of about eighteen inches. He counted a hundred before Jem turned from his course, and Kew knew that he had gone fifty yards further down the street. He was turned towards the right then, and the hollow sound of their footfalls told him that they were passing under an archway. This time there were forty paces taken, then again he was turned to the left, and at the end of three paces Jem's voice sounded. "There's a step here, sir."

Kew cleared the obstruction, and found his feet on a wooden passage. He went down it about five or six paces still guided by his companion, then: "Stairs now, sir!" said Jem.

Kew felt the treads creak under him as he climbed, and the way in which the banisters ran told him that it was a circular type of staircase. There were twenty steps in the first flight and eighteen in the second, then he was led across a carpeted landing, and the change of temperature told him that he was in a lighted room.

"All right, sir," said the voice of Jerry, and the next moment the bandage was slipped from Kew's eyes, and he saw the interior of the chamber into which he had been led.

It was by no means a badly-furnished apartment. There was a mahogany wardrobe and a dressing-table, a big book-case well filled with volumes. In the centre of the apartment stood a wooden bedstead, and by its side was a small desk, on which a shaded lamp stood. There was a figure on the bed, and Kew noted a haggard face watching him from the pillow.

There was no need for Kew to ask if that was his patient. The face was drawn into a mask of pain, and the hands lying on the blankets were clenched and tight.

Jem and Jerry proved themselves efficient assistants in their rough way. Criminal though Kew was, he was a master in the art of surgery, and the grim operation was performed successfully, the bullet being discovered in the wound, the latter bathed and dressed, and the pallid-faced patient settled as comfortably as possible.

The wound was in the back of the shoulder-blade, but Kew did not comment on this, although a quick smile lifted the corners of his lips for a moment as he thought of the explanation that Jem had given him.

By no possibility could that wound have been self-inflicted.

It seemed to Jem and Jerry that Kew took an unnecessarily long, time over the completion of his task, for they noted that he sounded the man, tapping carefully on the chest, and listening. They did not realise what that meant, and Kew made no effort to enlighten them, but it seemed as though his patient understood, for there was a faint, half-mocking expression in the man's eyes as they met Kew's.

The whole operation had been carried out in silence, and it was only when it was over that Kew spoke to his iron-nerved patient.

"You have stood it very well," he said.

The man's face gleamed for a moment.

"I have stood more than that, my dear man," he replied in a faint voice.

It was a cultured, gentlemanly accent, very different to the rough tones of Jem and Jerry. There was a suggestion of refinement about the haggard face, and the mystery of it all came to Kew.

Yet he knew that it was useless to make any inquiries, for the men had evidently made up their minds to keep the matter a secret.

When he had first started his operation, Kew had placed his bag of instruments on the desk by the side of the bed, and the shade of the lamp had been tilted so that the light might fall full on the face of the patient.

After he had washed his hands in hot water, provided for him by Jem, Kew turned to replace his instruments in the bag. He poured a little of the disinfectant into the basin, and cleaned the polished steel probes of the the pincers. As he did so, his keen, black eyes wandered about him, and he saw on the edge of the desk a small bound volume.

It was one of the plays of Molière in French, and it looked as though it had been well-thumbed.

What followed then proved the cunning which Kew had as a second nature. The way in which he dropped the wide wad of cotton-wool over the volume seemed to be quite accidental, but when he picked the wad up again and placed it in the bag, the small volume was concealed in its folds.

He made no attempt to hurry his cleaning operations, and it was only when a growling word came from Jem that Kew hastened to complete his task.

"'Ere yer are, sir; I'm much obliged to yer," the big fellow said, holding out a small, weighty bag; "you'll find a 'undred o' the best there. Would yer like to count 'em?"

Kew simply weighed the bag in his hand, then dropped it into his pocket.

"No, that's all right," he said; "I don't think it would pay you to swindle me."

Jem grinned.

"I don't think it would," he agreed.

"And now, if you're ready, sir."

He lifted the folded handkerchief, with a suggestive movement. Kew nodded his head.

"Very well," he returned; "I'm quite ready."

Again the handkerchief was adjusted, and as Kew turned away a voice came to him.

"Thanks very much. Good-bye!"

"An revoir!" said Kew, with a meaning in his voice that did not escape the patient, for a faint laugh followed him out of the door and along the landing.

It was Jem who accompanied Kew, and he led the professor out through the hollow-sounding archway, turning this time in the opposite direction to which he had come. But if the big fellow hoped to deceive Francis Kew by that trick he was quite mistaken.

The professor did not even trouble to note the turnings now. He had memorised the way by which he had reached the place, and that was sufficient for him.

At the end of five minutes' doubling and turning, Jem came to a halt, and slipped the handkerchief from the bead-like eyes.

Kew found himself standing under a lamp-post, and at the end of the street he saw a lighted thoroughfare.

"You'll be able to find a taxi there, sir," Jem said; "and I think I'll leave you now."

He touched his forehead in a salute.

"I 'opes you'll keep yer word abart this affair," he added, a grimmer note sounding in his voice; "'cos if you were to break it—well, it mightn't be too good for yer."

The vulture face smiled.

"You need have no fear of my revealing anything of what has happened to the police, my friend" said Kew calmly; "I quite understand that they would be likely to ask some very awkward questions. Good-night!"

He strode off down the street, and Jem stood on the edge of the kerb watching him go. The curious shape of the surgeon made a distinct impression on the ruffian, and he shook his head doubtfully as he watched the vanishing form.

"You may be a professor,"' he thought; "and may be a big pot in yer way, but if yer ain't one of us now yer jolly soon will be, or yer face belies yer."

Slipping his hand into his pocket, Jem pulled out a packet of cheap cigarettes, lighted one, then turning on his heel began to stride back into the dusk.

Jem had neither seen nor heard the last of Professor Kew, and he was soon to discover that in many ways it would have been better for the man, rascal though he was, had he never set eyes on that vulture face.

For as Kew leaned back in the seat of his taxi, and was carried rapidly westward, one thought was running over and over in his mind. It was the result of a discovery he had made as he examined his patient.

"Absolutely in the last stage of it," he muttered to himself; "One of his lungs is completely gone. In less than three months that man will be dead—he is absolutely doomed to die."

The lean head was lowered on the breast, and the long, talon-like fingers were clasped together, while the small, beady eyes were clouded with thought.

"Dead in three months," Kew repeated; "nothing in this world can save him. I ought to be able to make use of a man like that, he is just the type of tool I require—someone who can carry out my plans and then obligingly vanish!"

A little cackle of laughter sounded.

"A dead man can neither give evidence nor suffer for any crime that he may have done," he mused on. "By heavens, this is an opportunity that I must not miss."

A quick thought came to him and, reaching out, he picked up his bag and opened it. The fold of wadding came beneath his groping fingers, and a few moments he had a small bound volume in his hand. There was an electric bulb in the roof of the taxi, and the switch was close to Kew's elbow. He turned the light on, then opened the volume.

On the inside leaf of the cover a name had been written in bold, clear writing:

"Gilbert Fordyce Dykes," he read slowly. "Quite a nice name."

The volume was closed with a snap, and again the bird-like figure leaned back.

"I must find a task for you, Gilbert," the beady-eyed surgeon muttered, half to himself; "there must be something that you can turn your hand to in the brief interval of time that is left to you on earth—something that will be of benefit to you, and most certainly to me."

But what that something was requires another chapter to reveal.

Out of that night's work, Francis Kew had to appear in a new and more sinister light, and a fresh departure in the annals of crime had to be recorded against him.

THE SECOND CHAPTER

AT LADY MARJORY'S HOUSE.

IN the spacious, well-appointed drawing-room of Lady Marjory Mountjoy's house, a party of people had gathered.

It was early in the afternoon, and the group seemed an animated one. In the centre of the party, with her regal figure drawn to its full height, Lady Marjory was speaking in her clear, crisp voice.

"I think it a splendid idea," she said; "I feel quite proud of it. I am quite sure that we will get heaps of money for the hospitals, and the idea will be such a novel one that everyone will feel inclined to contribute."

A murmur of approval marked her speech, and turning round slightly, Lady Marjory nodded towards a lean, stooping figure who was seated at the desk.

"What is your opinion, Professor Kew?" she asked.

Kew's bird-like features did not move. He had played a very small part in that discussion, contenting himself by sitting there and listening.

"I am quite sure that whatever Lady Marjory undertakes will be a success," he said, in that suave, half-cynical way of his.

Lady Marjory gave him a little arch bow in return for the compliment. Then the group broke up, and everyone began to chatter about what was going to take place.

It had been Lady Marjory's idea, and had certainly got the semblances of something new and original.

She was going to give a garden-party the latter part of the following week at which as many as possible would be invited to attend.

After tea had been served, it was the Lady Marjory's idea that a number of ladies, dressed in the garb of hospital nurses, should enter the spacious lawn with a miniature ambulance waggon behind them.

And into this ambulance waggon the guests were to be invited to put just whatever they pleased, either cash or jewels.

And as Lady Marjory was one of the wealthiest hostesses in London, it was not at all probable that her idea would meet with anything else but great success.

The general opinion of the guests gathered in the drawing-room was favourable; and as Kew listened it came to him that here was the very enterprise that he had been seeking. Into that tiny ambulance would be poured quite a considerable booty in the way of money, and even jewels, for it was Lady Marjory's determination that no one should escape.

Kew had been invited to attend the little reception in the drawing-room, and he had been one of the group of committee men and trustees who had come from the various hospitals

It was just about five o'clock in the evening when he found himself able to make his adieux, and leave the great house; and as he walked swiftly along through the wide streets his alert brain was turning over the matter that had just been put before him.

"There is not the slightest doubt but that there is something in it," he muttered. "These people will be forced to pay up, and lively, too. By Jove, what a haul that little ambulance will make if I can only get a hold of it!"

There was no thought in his callous mind of the needs of the hospitals for which the money was intended.

It was just the sort of reckless crime that appealed to Kew, and he felt that if he could carry it out, if he could make the treasure of the little ambulance his own, it would be a distinct move forward on the path of crime he had set himself.

And in his usual way, it was necessary that he should have a tool. It was then that Kew decided upon employing the man whom he had last seen stretched on the cot in the dingy bed-room in the East End.

A month had passed since that visit of Kew, and he had made no attempt to go near the man. But he had studied the papers carefully, and had an account of a robbery in which one of the men, in escaping, had been fired at; and it was stated by the man who fired the shot that he distinctly saw the fellow stagger and fall.

In his mind Kew was satisfied that the wounded man whom he had tended, was no one else than the man who had been fired at as he retired from his burglarious mission.

"I will look him up now," the little man muttered to himself; "he must have just about got over his wound, and it ought to be healed. I'll have to get him away from those two confederates of his, for they are no use to me. I recognised that the other man was a gentleman, and it is that type of man that I want to help me now."

Already the glimmerings of a plan by which he hoped to corner the little hoard that would result from Lady Marjory's subscription, had come to him. But it wanted elaborating, and Kew had first of all to find a tool capable of carrying out his instructions. He had also to find a tool who would not be likely to give him away in the event of failure, and the condition of the wounded man—the fact that he was deep in the toils of consumption, and from Kew's examination could only live a few months—seemed to point to him as an ideal person for the purpose.

"I don't suppose he knows he's so near to the grave," the cold-hearted criminal muttered; "and that is all the better for me. He might not be so ready to help me if he realised that the least shock, the least excess of rage, or fear or panic would give the final closing touch to that already, overburdened heart of his. Already, he is little else but a walking corpse. He might as well make himself useful before he goes."

It was on the Wednesday afternoon that Lady Marjory had called her guests together to make her announcement. On the following day, late in the evening, Kew, after leaving St. Cyrs, proceeded to his house in Maida Vale. He was only in the house about half an hour, but when he emerged there was a great difference in his appearance. He had discarded his usual frock coat and tall hat, and was now dressed in a soberlooking suit, over which he had slipped a singlebreasted coat that was obviously the worse for wear.

It was seldom that Francis Kew troubled to disguise himself, but he was going to a lowclass quarter of the great city, a quarter in which frock-coats and tall-hats are mainly conspicuous by their absence.

It was a proof of the wonderful memory of the arch-criminal that without halt or turn he made his way across London, and was dropped at last from the taxi at the street where he and Jem had alighted. As soon as the taxi had gone Kew

paced down the street until he reached the lamppost—the eighth lamp-post down the street—where Kew had been halted and blindfolded. The street was empty, and Kew was able to carry out his movements without being molested.

He crossed the street, then counted his hundred paces.

He came to a halt, and glanced towards the houses, and a quick smile crossed the thin lips, when he noted that he was only a few yards out of his reckoning; the archway standing just that distance further down the street.

Pulling the soft cap that he wore a trifle lower over his brow, Kew entered the archway, and once again took up his count.

He was more careful this time, making each pace methodically. The doorway, with its step, was gained, and a touch of Kew's hand found the door open.

With noiseless paces the thin, wizened figure went down the passage, turning finally as he reached the stairs. He climbed to the second landing, and made for the door opposite. It was pitch-dark on the landing, but there was a faint beam of light shining through the keyhole, and, dropping on one knee, Kew glanced into the room. He was able to make out the angle of the bed, and also a portion of the fireplace. There was a fire in the grate, and a chair was drawn up close to it. In the chair was seated a limp figure, and as Kew studied the face of the man he recognised it again.

It was that of the man on whom he had performed the operation. The man whom the fly-leaf of the book had told him was Gilbert Fordyce Dykes.

It was imperative for Kew's plans that he should see Dykes alone, and the rascally professor was not sure whether there was anyone else in the room, for his view from the keyhole was a circumscribed one.

Rising to his feet, Kew knocked twice on the door; then, in an alert attitude, drew himself back into the shadow and listened.

Had Jem or Jerry been there he would have heard their heavy footfalls making for the door, and he would at once have beat a hasty retreat. But for a moment there was silence, then he heard a voice call.

"Come in!"

There was a certain refinement about the tones, and Kew, turning the knob of the door, entered.

Gilbert Dykes had raised his head, and the black-shadowed eyes were fixed with a keen scrutiny on the wizened shape of the intruder.

When Kew had passed through the doorway he closed the door behind him, then turned towards the figure of the man in the chair.

"Come in, professor," the quiet voice said.

Kew, despite his assurance, was taken aback for a moment. He had not anticipated that Dykes would recognise him so easily.

"You know me, then, I see."

The thin, haggard face lifted in a quick smile.

"Recognition is not difficult," said Dykes. "I doubt if there's another man in England with the same type of countenance as yourself."

The vulture face went grim.

"Quite so," said Kew, sauntering across the room. "But I hardly thought that you were in a state to remember me again, when I saw you last. How is your wound?"

"Quite healed," said Dykes. "Only I'm just a little weak yet. Sit down!"

Kew dropped into the only other chair which the room contained, and for a moment the professor and his host eyed each other just as men do before engaging in a conflict.

"I do not put down your visit to anxiety on my behalf," said Dykes. "What have you come here for?"

Kew realised then the manner of man he had to deal with. Gilbert Fordyce Dykes might be a criminal, might even be wanted by the law, but there was no mistaking that he was a man of education, and it was more than likely that at one time he had moved in good circles.

"I might as well be frank with you," said Kew, in his cold tones; "and, in the first place, I believe that you are implicated in that Gower Street affair." He shot a searching glance at Dykes, and noted that the haggard face could not quite control itself. "The description that the porter gave tallies exactly with you," the professor went on; "and the position of your wound settles any doubt."

"Well," said Dykes, "that is all very interesting, but what are you getting at?"

"The robbery was a cool and carefully-planned affair," said Kew; "and I congratulate you on it. It was only a piece of bad luck that allowed you to be winged as you escaped. I want a man to help me with a plan that I have in view, and it appears to me that you are the right man."

"I don't quite understand you," said Dykes.

Kew leaned forward.

"I am also one of the type that prefers to help itself to other people's property," he said slowly. "The world's wealth is so badly distributed, that men such as you and I are entitled to try our hands at adding to our own stores."

It was a cynical and quite false statement, but it did not deceive Dykes.

"You mean that you are a thief?" he said bluntly.

Kew's thin cackle broke out.

"You can put it that way if you like," he put in.

"And you want me to help you in some scheme?

"I do."

"Why have you chosen me?" Dykes asked. "I can assure you that Jerry and Jem are both expert housebreakers—"

Kew made an impatient gesture.

"You quite mistake me," he said. "I am not of that ordinary burglar type. When I set to work on a thing it must be something worth while, and there is no safe-breaking or dark-lantern methods about my way. In this particular instance I want a gentleman, and you are the man for my purpose."

"What is your plan?" asked Dykes.

"Next Friday afternoon a big garden-party is going to be given at a certain well-known house in the West End. It is to be given in aid of the hospital charities, and the method of collecting subscriptions is going to be a novel one. Instead of the usual cheques and promises, the guests are going to be invited to place money in the shape of notes and gold, or money's worth in personal jewellery in a little toy ambulance that will be wheeled around the grounds. The contents of that ambulance is what I am after, for I know that it will be worth at least nine or ten thousand pounds."

"And your plan?"

Kew tilted his head on one side, and his bead-like eyes brightened.

"That must come later," he said. "I do not propose to make a confidant of you until you are out of here, and have agreed to help me."

The emaciated figure in the chair was silent for a moment.

"I suppose this is in the nature of a threat?" he said, "for if I refuse to help you, it means that you will probably give the police the necessary information?"

"I am glad we know each other so well," said Kew grimly. "That idea was, certainly in my mind; but, of course, you will not be such a fool as to refuse."

"Can you tell me the name of the people whose house we go to?"

"Well, there is no harm in doing that," said Kew. "It is Lady Marjory Mountjoy who is responsible for the party, and it will be at her town house."

Kew was not looking at Dykes as he spoke, and he failed to see the curious light which came into the dark eyes for a moment.

"Lady Marjory Mountjoy," Dykes repeated.

Kew looked up then.

"You know her?"

"I know Lady Marjory Mountjoy very slightly," said the man opposite him. And the meaning of his remark escaped Kew then.

"Here is my address in Jermyn Street," the professor went on. "I will expect you on Sunday evening. By that time I will have the whole of my plans ready, and—"

The creak of a board on the landing outside brought him on the alert. The man in the chair drew a quick breath.

"Look out for yourself," he said. "If it is either Jem or Jerry, I wash my hands of what may happen to you. They have been scared about you ever since they brought you here."

With a cat-like movement Kew had leaped from his chair; and a sudden dart carried him across the room. He had glanced round, but there was no place where he could hide, and, as he reached the opposite side of the room, the lock of the door creaked, and the door opened, allowing the burly, hard-jowled Jerry to appear.

There was no doubt but what the strain of the long hiding from justice had told on the fellow. His face was pallid, and a straggling beard had grown on his chin. His eyes had that quick, fox-like way of turning swiftly which tells of the brain-harassed.

"Are yer orlright?" he asked, striding towards Dykes. "I 'eard that someone came up the stairs just—"

Kew had pressed himself in the corner of the room, and Jerry had not noticed him. The professor began to move towards the door, but his foot chanced to strike against a stick resting on the

wall, and it fell. With a swift snarl Jerry wheeled round, and his eyes blazed as they alighted on the stooping figure in the shabby coat.

"'Allo, who are you?" Jerry cried in a thick voice.

The words had hardly left his lips before he had recognised the hooked nose and long, lean chin.

"The professor, by 'eavens!" the broad-shouldered burglar shouted, a quiver of rage running through his taut body.

He leaped across the room, his hands outstretched to grip at the lean, wizened form.

There was no mistaking his purpose. Fear and fury had maddened him and it was death that was leaping towards the arch-scoundrel crouching against the wall.

With a quick movement, Gilbert Dykes thrust his chair aside, and arose to his feet. The sallow face was intent and eager as it watched the bull-like rush that Jerry made, but no sound came from Dykes.

"I know'd you was a cursed spy!" Jerry roared, as he closed with his puny antagonist.

The thick fingers circled around Kew's wizened neck and tightened there.

But the very touch of the fingers, aroused the professor out of the momentary panic that had come to him. As Jerry's face, inflamed and livid, the hard eyes staring but from the low forehead, and the lips, with the straggling beard twitching convulsively, thrust itself forward into Kew's pallid one, the professor's lean fingers darted towards his breast. The hand slid in between the gap of the buttons, and fumbled in the pocket for a moment.

"Ye'll never git out o' this place alive!" Jerry hissed.

A convulsive shudder ran through Kew's body as he felt the breath almost choked from him. His face was growing black now, and the bead-like eyes began to protrude. With one last, desperate effort, the professor succeeded in withdrawing the little round steel tube that his talon-like fingers had been searching for.

From his position at the fireplace, Dykes saw the steel flash as Kew swung his hand back. Then, suddenly and swiftly, it was driven forward, and the shining point bit deeply into Jerry's thick throat.

The effect of that blow, not by any means a heavy one, was astounding. For, as Kew drew back his hand with the steel tube in it, Jerry seemed to stiffen suddenly, and his muttering voice died away in a whisper.

Breathless with interest now, Dykes came forward slowly across the room. He saw Kew raise his hand, and disengage the thick fingers that were around his throat. Then, with a quick stoop, the professor slid beneath the outstretched arm of the huge figure, and stepped aside.

Jerry still stood stiff and rigid, arms outstretched, and fingers still crooked as though they were holding the wizened neck.

"My heavens, what have you done to him?" Dykes breathed, staring aghast at the hulking, motionless form.

Kew, with heaving breast, rested against the wall for a moment, his eyes glittering, and his face, a mask of grim triumph.

"What have you done to him?" Dykes asked again.

He was close to Jerry now, and he leaned forward to stare at the man's face. It was set and motionless, but the eyes were wide and staring, and he could hear the breath coming and going through, the thick lips.

At the back of the neck, just where the backbone joins the bones of the skull, was a little bead of blood, which had oozed from the tiny puncture, and there was a little black, discoloured ring around it.

"I have prevented him from harming me or anyone else!" came the cold, cynical voice of Francis Kew.

"What is the matter with him?" Dykes asked.

Kew stepped up to the side of the wondering man, and balanced the steel tube between his fingers. Dykes saw then that at one end of the tube were a number of thin needles which ran into the hollow interior.

"Jerry is quite safe," said Kew. "I've only used a certain drug on him that has the peculiar property of numbing the brain-cells for a certain period. It is really a temporary-paralysis that he has now." He stepped to the side of the motionless figure, and nodded towards Dykes: "We might as well make him comfortable," he went on. "Help me to take him to the bed."

With Dykes at the other side of the man, Kew led the great figure across the chamber, Jerry moving his legs in a curiously stiff, jerky method, that was almost mechanical in its action.

When the hulking fellow was laid prone on the bed, Kew glanced across and met Dykes' eyes."

"I am rather glad that happened," he said. "It will be an object lesson to you."

The lean, stooping figure seemed a sinister, evil shadow as it loomed above the prostrate man.

"I have a short way of dealing with my enemies," said Francis Kew.

With an effort, Dykes removed his eyes from the vulture face, and looked down at the heavy, rigid countenance of the man on the bed.

"You have certainly settled Jerry all right," he said; "but, by heavens, I must admit that I thought he was going to settle you! How long will he be like this?"

"In four days' time the effect of the drug will have worn itself away," said Kew, "and until that time he is quite safe to be left as he is. Someone will have to feed him, of course."

He turned away from the bed as though to dismiss the subject.

With a clean handkerchief, Kew carefully wiped the needles on the deadly little weapon; then, pulling a sliding button up, the needles vanished through their small holes, and Kew replaced the steel tube in his pocket.

"It is safer than a revolver," he said, "and much less noisy." He glanced across at Dykes again. "Perhaps you are satisfied now that I am worthy of working for," he went on, "for I promise you that whatever I set out to do I accomplish, and there is no risk attached to it, either for myself or for those who work for me."

His cool, calm manner had its effect on the man opposite him.

Kew paced, across to the door, and flung it open.

"I shall expect you on Sunday evening, at seven o'clock," the harsh voice said, "and I will give you half an hour's grace. If you are not there by half-past seven. I will know that you do not intend to join me, and I will then, see to it that you never join anyone else!"

"Meaning Scotland Yard, I suppose?" said Dykes.

The vulture face glimmered at him from the doorway.

"Exactly," said Professor Kew.

The door closed, and for a long moment the tall figure of Fordyce Dykes stood rigid in the centre of the room.

"What a small place the world is," the man muttered to himself, with a half-cynical laugh. "Why should it be Lady Marjory Mountjoy's place that I should have to go to?"

He strode across to the window, and looked out into the grimy courtyard, and there was a curious expression in his sunken eyes.

"Marjory," he said, half to himself in a dreaming voice, "I thought I had seen the last of you! But, unless I am very much mistaken, Fate and Francis Kew will see to it that we cross each other's paths' again. I wonder what the outcome of it all will be?"

A sudden fit of coughing caught him, and for a long minute his thin frame shook with the fierce convulsions. When the paroxysm had passed, he raised the handkerchief to his lips.

There was a fleck of blood on the white surface, and Fordyce Dykes looked at it from out of his pain-racked eyes.

"I am going to help Kew on Sunday," he said, "I might well take the risk. It will give me some excitement; but I doubt if Francis Kew, or anyone else in his profession, can help me."

He turned away from the window, and the cold sweat that had come on his forehead was dried away.

"But I don't want to die in prison," the man murmured. "That would be a very unexciting finish to a life that has only been in existence for twenty-five years. No, if I am going to die, I'll die with my boots on."

THE THIRD CHAPTER

BLAKE AND TINKER ATTEND THE RECEPTION.

"WHAT'S the card, guv'nor?"

Sexton Blake and Tinker were seated at breakfast, and the great detective had been going through his usual morning correspondence, which, as a rule, consisted of letters from various organisations asking the wealthy and well-known detective for subscriptions.

Sexton Blake's charity was well-known in London, and no deserving case was ever neglected by him.

"Oh, a fete of some sort, Tinker," Blake said, handing the gold-edged card to the lad. "There's a letter with it."

The letter was written in a dainty hand, and Blake smiled as he read the name.

"I suppose we'd better go," he said. "You can come in this. Tinker. Here, read it!" Tinker read the note, which ran as follows:

"Dear Mr. Blake,—I have never had the pleasure of meeting you, but, my husband, who is in the War Office, knows you personally, and has given me your address. By the enclosed card you will see that I am having a garden-party next Friday, and there will be a subscription made in aid of the Hospital Charities. I want to make the thing a big success, and I have got rather a novel idea. I don't want cheques or things, but I would like you to bring along something of value in the way of jewellery of your own. The jewellery will be collected after tea, and afterwards it will be sold by auction. Whatever you give must bear your card, and something from such a famous man as yourself will, no doubt, bring quite a big price at the auction. Don't you think this is a cunning idea?

"Do, please come, and bring your assistant with you, whom, my husband says, is almost as famous as yourself. Am I mistaken, or is his name really Tinker?—Yours sincerely,

"Marjory Mountjoy."

There was a grin on Tinker's face as he returned the note. "That settles it, guv'nor!" he said. "Bang goes my new sleeve-links!"

Blake smiled.

"Yes; I'm afraid they'll have to go, Tinker," he went on. "But anyhow, it's in a good cause, and I know that every penny will go to the hospital."

It was on a Thursday morning that the letter arrived, and Blake promptly sent off an acceptance of the invitation. On the following afternoon, at about half-past three, he and Tinker left the unpretentious house in Baker Street, and, entering a taxi, were driven to the big house in the West End.

There was a crush of vehicles outside the wide gateway that told Blake the affair was going to be a pretty big one. He and Tinker found themselves at last on the spacious lawn where Lady Marjory was receiving her guests.

Blake's and Tinker's names were announced, and the regal-looking woman gave the detective a friendly pressure of the hand, while her splendid eyes rested with a certain amount of curiosity on the handsome face.

"Don't go far away, please, Mr. Blake," she said. "I have always wanted to know you. My husband has told me quite a lot about you."

The lawn outside the house presented an animated appearance, and Blake presently missed Tinker. The young assistant was evidently bent on enjoying himself, and Blake caught sight of the lad chatting away in a merry group.

Lady Marjory was glad when the reception was over, and she sought out a shady place on the lawn, seating herself at a little table, with Blake and a few other ladies and gentlemen around her.

The servants of the house were already beginning to serve tea, when Blake, who had been talking to Lady Marjory, saw the bright, animated face go suddenly pale. A shadow fell across the table, and Lady Marjory arose to her feet.

A tall, thin figure, with haggard face and hollow cheeks, was standing in front of her with outstretched hand. Blake stepped aside, but he could not help hearing the faintly-worded greeting that broke from the woman's lips.

"Gilbert—you!"

"And why not, Lady Marjory?" the new-comer replied in a quiet, cultured tone. "Aren't you pleased to see me?"

Lady Marjory had caught the thin hand, and was looking, with a rapt, almost anxious expression into the emaciated face.

"I hardly recognised you, Gilbert," she said. "What has happened to you? You have altered dreadfully."

"Four years makes a lot of difference to a man, Lady Marjory," came the quiet reply, "although it has made very little difference to you. You are lovelier than ever."

Sexton Blake moved further away then, for he realised that this meeting was not an ordinary one. It seemed as though for the moment Lady Marjory and her companion, had forgotten where they were.

A footman came forward bearing a tray with the tea things, and Blake accepted a cup.

As he raised the cup to his lips he heard the swish of a silken dress, and his host joined him again.

"Did you notice that man who spoke to me, Mr. Blake?" she said, glancing at the keen grey-blue eyes of the detective. "Don't you think that he is—is ill?"

Blake nodded his head.

"He certainly does not look very fit."

Lady Marjory was silent for a moment.

"He is a very old friend of mine, one whom I had lost sight of for years. His appearance just now disturbed me dreadfully. To me it looks as though he has one foot in the grave."

Blake himself had noted the sunken eyes and the thin, bloodless cheeks of the stranger. The great detective had seen too many men to be mistaken in his judgment.

"He is dying of consumption," Blake thought, "but I won't tell you that."

At that moment a little cheer rang out, and from a dense fringe of shrubbery a quaint little group appeared. Four beautiful girls, dressed in the demure costume of a nurse, each with a broad ribbon looped around her slender shoulder, came into view. Behind the quartette of nurses a little ambulance appeared. It was an accurately-made little vehicle. It stood about two feet high, and the body of it was about a foot high by a foot and a half long. The top was painted to represent a canvas cover of an Army Red Cross ambulance, but in the centre of the top a wide slot had been placed.

Behind the vehicle came other two demure-looking nurses, each with a ribbon in her hand. The ribbons were attached to the rear axles of the vehicle, and served to balance it as the little waggon trundled across the smooth turf.

Most of the guests were already aware of what the ambulance was there for, and a big crowd came behind it as it moved across to where Lady Marjory was standing

The sight of the ambulance seemed to banish Lady Marjory's depression for a moment. She placed her cup and saucer down on the table by her side and stepped forward.

"Pay, pay, pay! ladies and gentlemen!" she said in her clear, ringing tones. "And I will be the first."

With a quick, impulsive movement she drew her rings from her shapely fingers, and cast them, one after another, through the slot into the little vehicle.

There was a touch of personal sacrifice about the action which appealed to the guests, for as

DROPPING ON ONE KNEE KEW GLANCED INTO THE ROOM.

"MY HEAVENS! WHAT HAVE YOU DONE TO HIM?" DYKES BREATHED.

"PAY! PAY! PAY! LADIES AND GENTLEMEN," SHE SAID IN HER CLEAR RINGING VOICE.

"THE AMBULANCE," SAID SIR ARTHUR. "WE WE OPENED IT JUST NOW AND IT'S —IT'S EMPTY!"

"THERE IS A THIRD LINE OF FOOTPRINTS THERE."

IN "THE YELLOW OCTOPUS." DO NOT MISS IT!!

Lady Marjory stepped back the crowd closed around the little vehicle, and a perfect torrent of all kinds of jewellery, most of them extremely valuable, were slipped into the receptacle. It was a splendid ruby pin, the gift of an Indian prince, that Blake fastened to his card and dropped into the slot.

Around the lawn the smiling ladies went, drawing their rapidly increasing load. Standing by Lady Marjory's side, Blake watched their progress, and there was no doubt about the richness of the harvest they were getting.

The beautiful hostess clapped her hands together, and her face was alight with animation.

"Oh it's going to be such a success," she said, "and I am so pleased I It means so much for the poor sufferers in the hospitals."

"It was a very worthy thought, Lady Marjory," said Blake, "and deserves to succeed."

The ambulance had now reached the far end of the lawn, and Blake saw it wheel to make its way towards a path that ran around the edge of the shrubbery.

"They are going to take it to a marquee, and the little committee that I've got together will sort out the jewellery; then we're going to have an auction," Lady Marjory explained. "But, of course, we won't have the auction until after everybody's had tea."

A band that had been concealed in one of the outhouses began to play then, and Blake turned away. The huge party had broken up into a number of little groups, and the waiters and footmen were busy attending to their wants.

Blake moved through the throng, halting now and again to exchange a bow and a word with someone who recognised.

"I wonder where that young rascal has got to," the detective thought, "I didn't see him hand over those gold sleeve-links. Perhaps he's dodging that; but I'll take jolly good care that he pays up!"

Three or four minutes later the ladies who had drawn the ambulance returned to the lawn and joined their parties. Blake had sauntered close to the screen of shrubbery, and was just crossing the path, when he heard the sound of running feet, and, glancing down the path, he saw the portly figure of Sir Arthur Mountjoy running towards him.

The War Office official caught sight of Blake at the same moment, and into the heated face there leaped a flash of relief.

"Blake, Blake! The very man I want!" Sir Arthur broke out, darting up to Blake and catching the detective by the arm. "A terrible thing has happened! By heavens, I don't know what to do, or how I am to explain!"

His broad chest was rising and falling, and he was obviously in great distress.

"What is it, Sir Arthur?" Blake asked, drawing a little further down the path, so that they might be screened from the observation of the guests on the lawn.

"The ambulance!" said Sir Arthur. "We—we opened it just now, and it's—it's empty!"

He swept a hand across his face.

"Absolutely empty!" he said, with the air of a man too dazed to think. "But come, Blake Thank Heaven I have found you! Come and see for yourself!"

The excited man led the way down the path at a pace that was almost a run, and presently Blake found himself entering a small, striped marquee. There were four or five gentlemen inside, all of them obviously sharing Sir Arthur's feelings. In the centre of the marquee stood the little ambulance, but the top had been removed, and a glance into the interior revealed the fact that it was empty.

"All right, gentlemen," Sir Arthur broke out, running forward with his arm beneath that of Sexton Blake, "here as someone who can help us if such a thing is possible. This is Mr. Sexton Blake, the great detective!" It seemed as though every man there knew Blake, by repute at least, for they drew aside a little to allow the quiet-looking, alert man to approach the ambulance.

"You see for yourself, Blake," Sir Arthur said, "the thing is absolutely empty! These gentlemen were present here when I prised open the top, and they will bear me out when I say there was nothing inside it."

"That is so."

"Never was more astounded in my life!"

Blake's face became keen and set then.

"You say that you prised the top off, Sir Arthur?" Blake began. "Did you require much force to do so?"

Sir Arthur lifted the top and pointed to the marks where the steel chisel had been at work.

"It was meant to be difficult to remove," he said; "we were afraid of it tipping over, you see."

"Well, there's no doubt about its being empty," said Blake, with a smile; "and I am also sure that it was well-filled when it left the lawn."

Sir Arthur shrugged his shoulders in despair.

"Well-filled," he broke out. "Why hang it all, man, I dropped in a pair of diamond sleeve-links that were worth about ninety pounds!"

"My subscription was a diamond-studded cigarette case," another man observed; "and I saw it go through that very slot—"

Blake picked up the top of the ambulance and was examining the slot carefully. He did not say anything when he laid it down again, but he turned towards the entrance to the marquee.

"I'm afraid we'll have to make some inquiries," he said. "Do you think you could get one of the young ladies who drew the little vehicle to come here?"

One of the committee stepped forward.

"I can do that," he said. "My daughter Clarice was one of them. I'll go and fetch her."

He hurried away down the path and Blake turned towards Sir Arthur.

"Which way did the ambulance come, do you know?" he asked.

There were two-paths leading to the marquee, and Sir Arthur seemed to find it difficult to answer the question.

"I think it was the right-hand one," he said at last; "but I wouldn't be sure."

Blake ran his eyes along the gravel, and he noted the narrow lines such as might have been made by the little vehicle, but they led towards the path on the left.

"I suppose the right hand path is the most direct one to the lawn?" he said.

"Yes, that is so," said Sir Arthur. "Why do you ask?"

"Because it seems to me as if the ambulance came by the other path," said Blake, pointing to the lines.

The flutter of a dress on the right hand path heralded the arrival of one of the young ladies. She was still wearing the sash of blue ribbon, and there was a perplexed look on her fair young face as she halted in front of the group outside the marquee.

"The pater has just told me about what has happened," she said, in a little frightened voice; "but I cannot believe it. I don't understand."

Blake saw that the young girl was obviously frightened, and he set to work to calm her.

"Oh, I suppose we will find there is a very plausible explanation for it," he began; "and, anyhow, I'm sure that no blame can attach itself to you or your friends. But now, if you will help me, I would like you to show me the way that you came with the ambulance after you left the lawn."

The girl turned at once, and it was towards the left hand path that she headed, with Blake by her side, while Sir Arthur and his silent committee walked on behind her.

The left-hand path wound sharply and, about twenty yards down it Blake noted that there was another fork in the path. This was caused by what was practically a small island of bushes about ten feet in width, by about three times that distance in length.

The girl turned towards the left fork, but just as Blake wheeled to follow her he noted that the tracks of the ambulance ran right down the right branch.

"One moment," he said, coming to a halt; "are you sure that you brought the ambulance along this way?"

The girl stopped.

"Oh, no," she said; "only all the team came this way, but the gentleman who was sent to give us a hand made a mistake and took the other path."

"The gentleman who was sent to give you a hand!" Sir Arthur broke out.

Instantly the quick-witted girl realised that here was the partial solution to the mystery. She came to a halt.

"He met us just at the other end of this clump of trees," she said, "and pushed the ambulance for us. We all went on ahead, but not very far, and we could see him go down the other path. One of us called to him and he met us at the other end."

"Then," said Sexton Blake; "during the brief interval that this unknown gentleman helped you, the trick was accomplished."

"But that's impossible!" the girl cried. "We—we saw him nearly all the time. Look! you can see for yourself the bushes are not very thick."

It was certainly possible to get a glimpse of one path from the other, but the shrubbery was fairly thick, and, here and there, grew a trifle denser.

Blake saw that the red lips of the girl were beginning to tremble, and he placed his hand, with a little kindly touch, on her arm.

"I can assure you that you cannot be blamed for this," he said. "Whoever carried out the trick must have been an accomplished rascal, and must also have had confederates."

"Oh, it is dreadful! Dreadful! I will never forgive myself," the girl broke out, white to the lips.

The gentlemen closed round her and began to murmur their sympathy, and gradually the distracted little woman regained her nerve.

"I've only one more question to ask you," Blake said. "You say that the gentleman brought the ambulance round here, and you met him again?"

"Yes. He—he apologised for his stupidity, and we—we laughed at him. Oh, if I'd only known!"

The blue eyes flashed, and the little well-shaped fists were clenched.

"And he seemed a gentleman, too," the girl added. "In fact, he first stopped us to put something in the ambulance. It was a pearl tie-pin. I remember that quite distinctly."

Her father stepped forward.

"Would you recognise the rascal again, Clarice?" he asked.

"Oh, yes—yes!" his daughter returned. Sir Arthur glanced at Blake.

"Then it would be better if Clarice went at once and tried to find out if the man is still in the grounds," he said. "In fact, she might go down to the gates and watch anybody who leaves."

This suggestion was adopted at once, and the young lady in the nurse clothes and her father hurried off to take up their post.

Blake nodded to his companions.

"And now, gentlemen," he said. "I think we will just try to reconstruct the clever crime."

He led the way around the shrubbery, taking the path on the right. Half-way down he came to a halt and an exclamation broke from his lips.

"That door," he said, pointing to a small wicket gate let into the solid wall. "Where does it lead to?"

It was something like a groan that broke from Sir Arthur's lips.

"That settles it!" he broke out. "I'd forgotten all about that confounded doorway. It leads into a small lane that runs down behind our place. It hasn't been used for years, I believe."

There was a strip of turf, perhaps ten feet wide, dividing the path from the doorway. Sir Arthur made as though to step on the grass, but Blake touched him by the arm.

"Just a moment, Sir Arthur, please," he said.

The wealthy baronet and his companions halted and watched Blake interestedly. Stooping down, Blake searched about in the grass, then presently he moved off towards the doorway, halting and straightening himself up when he reached there.

"Two men have passed out through this doorway within the last hour," he said; "in fact, they may only have gone a few minutes ago. Look! their tracks are quite clear."

They had not been clear, but as the detective pointed them out, his companions were able to trace the distinct imprints of feet on the bruised grass. Blake knelt down and measured the tracks. One was that made by a foot not more than eight inches long, while the other was nearly twelve. The smaller footprint had made the deeper impression, a point which Blake remarked upon.

"It was probably the smaller man who carried away the ambulance," he said; "or rather, I should say, that portion of the ambulance which is portable."

"You—you really think that that is how it was worked?" Sir Arthur asked.

Blake nodded.

"It is the only way possible," he returned. "You must remember that the six young ladies were walking along the path on the other side of the clump of bushes. The man who was wheeling the ambulance had no time to stop, much less to break the thing open and take out the contents. Besides, you admit that you found it all you could do to open the thing yourself."

"Then you think that there was a duplicate ambulance made?"

"We will soon be sure about that when we get back to the marquee," Blake said. "I want to examine the door now."

He stepped up to the little wooden barrier and peered at the lock for a moment. It was of the ordinary type; the catch sliding back by means of a small knob. The lock and knob were covered, with rust, but as Blake pressed the knob, it yielded to the touch of his fingers and the door opened noiselessly.

"The hinges have been oiled and so has the lock," he said; "and quite recently too. Look! you will notice the oil-stains on the wood."

From the slot in which the catch moved in and out a trickle of oil was exhuming. Sir Arthur bent his head and examined the lock for a moment.

"You can see what has happened," he broke out. "That catch was screwed right through, but the screw that held it has been removed."

"Quite so," said Blake, stepping through the doorway.

Here he made another discovery. The keyhole, by which the lock could be operated on from the outside of the door, was filled in, and had evidently been painted over once, for the paint was still undisturbed.

"And all that took place was managed from the inside," Blake went on, pointing towards the sealed keyhole.

A murmur ran round the little knot of watchers.

"Which means that it was either some of our guests or the servants?" said Sir Arthur.

"So it would appear," Blake returned. "However, the main thing is that there is little chance of our finding the perpetrators now. There is no doubt but what they have escaped, the first man evidently making away with the booty, and the other—the rascal who tricked those innocent ladies so cleverly—coming back down the path as soon as he had handed over the ambulance, and following his confederate out through this door."

The terse versatility with which Sexton Blake built up the clever trick made a profound impression on his listeners.

"By Jove! That's splendid!" said Sir Arthur. "I think we must all agree, gentlemen, that Sexton Blake is right. He has made the whole thing appear like a picture in my eye. I can follow the whole rascally thing from beginning to end."

There was a murmur of assent from the group; then Blake, stepping in through the doorway again, closed the door.

"There is nothing more to be found out there," he said—"not for the present, at least. I think we might as well go back to the marquee and—"

His eyes had been resting on the grass as he spoke, and Sir Arthur noted him stiffen suddenly, as a well-bred pointer might have done.

"What is it, Blake?" the little baronet asked.

"Look!" said Blake, extending his finger towards the grass which ran along the side of the wall. "Unless I'm mistaken there is a third line of footprints there."

Thanks to the shadow cast by the wall, the grass there was damper than the rest, and, following Blake's extended hand, Sir Arthur and his companions were able to trace another line of footprints. But these did not come from the path, seemingly holding along close to the wall so far as they could be followed by the eye.

"It might be one of the two men," Sir Arthur suggested.

Blake stepped forward, and, finding a clear footprint, he measured it.

"It is quite distinct from either of them," he said. "It is just about nine inches. No; I'm afraid there is a third party—a third party who also passed out through that door."

"By heavens!" Sir Arthur rapped out. "It appears to me as if the place was swarming with thieves! Three of them, and one, at least, one of my guests! Good heavens, I'll never get over the disgrace!"

They turned then, and made their way back down the path towards the marquee, leaving the question of the third line, of footprints to be settled, Blake little dreaming of the real explanation of their presence, or he might have found a grain of comfort in them.

When they reached the marquee Blake went at once to the ambulance, and first of all picked up the loosened top.

"I had the first hint that the affair was a case of duplicating," he began, "by this." He pointed to the slot. The paint around it was unscratched and smooth. "I happened to know that there must be at least one scratch in the original ambulance," Blake said, "for the point of a ruby pin which I dropped in caught on the wood. And besides that, it was impossible for all those pieces of jewellery to be put in there without dulling the paint a little."

The matter seemed easy enough now that it was explained to them, and the loose top was handed round from man to man.

Blake leaned over the empty receptacle; then, placing one hand on either side of it, he gave it a sharp tug. The body of the thing came away in his hand, revealing the fact that the ambulance consisted of two separate pieces—the framework on which the wheels carried and the body which fitted into a square receptacle in the centre of the frame.

On each corner of the squared socket, clips had been placed to keep the body rigid, but, as Blake had proved, a sharp pull was sufficient to loosen them.

"That settles it," Sir Arthur groaned. "The fellow simply had a duplicate, and was waiting in readiness. As soon as his companion came along he snatched out the jewel-filled one and thrust the empty one back into the catches. The whole affair couldn't have been a matter of seconds."

A blank look passed round the group of perturbed gentlemen, for the neatness and cunning of the clever ruse hinted that it was the work of more than an ordinary brain.

"By Jove, Blake, I'm afraid that they've fairly got us!" said Sir Arthur. "And what a tremendous haul they must have made, too!"

They closed around Blake then, eyeing him anxiously, doubtfully.

"Do you think there is any possible chance of catching the brutes?" someone asked.

Blake's alert face set into a grim smile.

"There is always a chance of catching everyone, gentlemen," he said. "Even the cleverest criminal finds himself at the end of his tether one day or other."

"By Jove, I'd give a thousand pounds if we could catch them!" Sir Arthur broke out. "It's not so much for my own sake as for the sake of my wife. I don't know how the dickens I'm going to tell her—"

He never completed his remark, for suddenly the wide entrance of the marquee was darkened, and Lady Marjory, with Clarice behind her, hurried into the tent.

"Oh, Arthur!" she said. "I've heard all about it. What shall we do—what shall we do?"

She seemed to be in a state of feverish excitement—an excitement greater than the incident necessitated. Her face, was almost ghastly in its pallor.

Sir Arthur and the rest of the gentlemen tried to soothe her, and gradually Lady Marjory seemed to recover her nerve slightly.

It was decided then that the guests should be told as quietly as possible, and a general move from the marquee was made.

Sexton Blake had dropped behind, to exchange a word with one of the committee, and when he sauntered down the path he found himself alone for the moment.

On reaching the lawn, he noted that the guests were already making their departure, and presently he found himself in a little press of people, passing through the wide drawing-room.

He reached a big, high screen, and as he halted there for a moment, waiting his turn to pass out through the doorway, a low voice came to him:

"I assure you that it could not have been him, Clarice. Promise me that you will not say a word about it to anyone."

It was Lady Marjory's voice, and it was tense with emotion. Interested in spite of himself, Sexton Blake halted for a moment to listen.

"If you assure me, Lady Marjory, it is all right," Clarice's voice returned, "I will not say another word about it."

The surge of people caught Blake up then, and he was carried on through the wide doorway, across the hall, and on down the avenue to where the lines of vehicles were waiting. The scrap of conversation that be had heard, vague though it was, repeated itself again and again in Blake's mind.

"I wonder who it is that Lady Marjory is so anxious about?" he thought, "And why should she ask her friend to keep silent?"

He reached the pavement, and went on down the street for a little way. Sir Arthur had promised to look him up early on the following morning, with certain details which Blake had asked of him.

Blake stood quietly watching the groups of guests as they sauntered out of the wide gateway. He was waiting for Tinker, and presently the non-appearance of that youngster began to annoy Blake just a little.

"Hang the young beggar! I won't wait for him any longer!" he said to himself. "He knows the way to Baker Street all right, so he can follow me when he likes. I expect he's got interested with someone, and may have gone off with them."

Which, in its way, was true enough. Tinker had certainly got interested in someone, and had gone off with them. But the "going off" was not of the lad's own volition, and Blake's assistant was, at that very moment, in as tight a hole as ever he had been in his swift life.

THE FOURTH CHAPTER

TINKER IN TROUBLE.

THE beginning of Tinker's trouble was really caused by the fact of the youngster having forgotten the real object of the garden-party. He had met a youngster whom he knew, and they had got talking about matters sporting, with the result that neither of them noticed the ambulance making its tour of the grounds.

It was only when the little vehicle had been turned down the path by its grey-garbed team of beautiful girls that Tinker caught sight of it.

"My hat!" he said. "I forgot all about that thing. I've got a pair of sleeve-links to put in it. I won't be a moment." He nodded to his companion and hurried off across the lawn; but the branching pathways confused him, and he lost sight of the ambulance. His search for it brought him to the little island of bushes just as the lean figure of Dykes came darting back along the path.

There was a certain furtive haste about the man which brought Tinker's search to a halt for a moment. He saw Dykes dart across the lawn, open the door, and, after a quick glance to right and left, pass through it, pulling the door to behind him.

The way in which the man had made off was sufficient to tell Tinker that something out of the ordinary had happened, and, keeping close to the side of the wall, the lad hurried along it until he reached the doorway. A moment's examination enabled him to open the door, and he thrust his head out cautiously.

He was just in time to see a man wheeling a small hand-barrow on which a square object was placed, go round a bend in the lane. About twenty yards away from the man was the tall figure of Dykes in his correct morning-coat and tall hat.

Tinker had another glimpse at the barrow as it turned the corner, and he noticed that a big piece of sacking had been placed across the object on it. A few moments later the barrow and the man

following it had vanished. Then Tinker slipped out into the lane and followed.

The youngster had no idea of what had happened, but there was something suspicious about the affair, and Tinker's quick detective instincts were aroused at once.

"That fellow was evidently afraid of being seen," he thought, "and was jolly glad to get away. I wonder what the dickens it means?"

The only way to find that out was by following, and this Tinker did.

Any doubts that he might have had about the association of the man with the barrow and the well-dressed figure behind him were speedily disappearing as the chase went on.

The man trundling the barrow stuck to his task steadily, pushing the light structure on down the streets. He never looked around, but the figure in the morning-coat was always within sight of him, and, whichever direction the barrow turned in, the tall figure followed suit.

It was only when he crossed the traffic-filled thoroughfare beyond Hyde Park, and went on up Edgware Road, that Tinker began to appreciate the fact that he was in for a long chase.

"This is getting interesting," he thought, as he sauntered along, perhaps a hundred yards behind Dykes, "I wonder what the deuce is that fellow up to?"

Edgware Road is a long thoroughfare. Tinker was beginning to feel just a little tired before he reached the end of it. But the barrow was still moving on and presently it turned into a quieter street, vanishing from Tinker's view.

The youngster quickened his step, and reached the corner just in time to see the barrow disappearing down a narrow lane. The man in the morning-coat had now dropped all pretence of disinterestedness, and was walking along beside the individual pushing the barrow.

"It looks as if I'd come to the end of my chase at last," said Tinker, as he started off down the street.

He was sauntering along on the opposite side of the pavement, and as he reached the gap of the narrow lane he looked down it. He caught sight of a number of sheds, evidently used as storehouses. Outside one of them the barrow was standing, but its load and the men had vanished. The open door opposite the barrow indicated to Tinker where they had gone to; and the lad sauntered on, his mind busy with the new problem.

He had taken a careful mental note of the position of the shed, but he knew that it was too risky to go down that lane at the moment. There might have been another opening into the place, but Tinker was not going to risk a search.

He reached the other end of the street, and came to a halt. He was in something of a quandary, and, while his mind was still tackling the problem, it was solved for him by the appearance of the two figures of the men he had followed.

They both came out of the lane and turned up the street, moving off at a quick pace.

Tinker had slid into the corner, and it was well for him that he had done so, for he saw that the taller figure turned every now and again and looked back, as though, afraid of being followed.

"It would give the game away if I appeared now," Tinker muttered. "He has evidently got suspicious. I'll have to let them go."

Had Tinker been aware of what had really happened, it is very likely that he would have made an attempt to track the men; but, of course, he had no idea as to the valuable contents of the square-shaped package in its canvas covering.

So the lad waited until the two figures had vanished around the far end of the street; then, moving out from his hiding-place, Tinker went swiftly down the street, and turned into the lane. The barrow had also disappeared now; but the lad's memory was a good one, and he entered the cobble-paved lane, passing down it until he came to a halt at one of the stores. Two narrow tracks running up to the doorway indicated that his judgment was not at fault.

"They have put the barrow in here as well," he decided, approaching the wide double door. "I must have a look inside."

The doors were fastened by a hasp and padlock, and the padlock was a modern, well-constructed affair.

"There would be no chance of picking it with a bent nail," Tinker thought.

Above the wide doorway was a square opening, leading evidently into the loft. Above the gap hung a wooden arm, at the end of which a rusted block hung.

"I might be able to get in there if I could find a rope," said Tinker, glancing around him.

He went on down the lane, and presently, in a narrow passage, between two sheds, he found what is a common object in places of that type—a length of frayed rope.

It had evidently once been tied around a packing-case, for it was knotted and twisted together; but Tinker picked up the tangled heap, and set to work to unravel it.

At the end of ten minutes' work he had a length of rope, about twenty feet in all, which, although by no means very presentable, was strong enough to bear his weight.

All this had taken some time, and the first signs of dusk were settling as Tinker made his way back to the store again.

He had made a wide loop on one end of the rope, and, after half a dozen abortive efforts, the youngster succeeded in slinging the loop over the thick beam. Tinker worked it along the beam until it was close to the wall; then, after swinging on the rope to test its strength, the lad began to climb.

He climbed hand over hand, with his feet hanging limply beneath him, and the rope hardly moved as he swung upwards. A minute later his foot was on the ledge of the entrance to the loft, and a pressure against one of the wooden doors saw it give.

Slipping the noose from the wooden arm, Tinker gathered the rope into a neat coil, and deposited it on the floor of the loft close to the doors. Then he closed the gap behind him, and, moving cautiously now—for the loft was practically in darkness—he made his way across it to where a black square in the floor indicated the presence of a trapdoor.

The trapdoor was close to the back wall of the store, and to the wall itself a wooden ladder had been attached as a means of access to the loft. Tinker swung on to the wooden rungs and dropped swiftly through the trap, to find himself in the store.

Sufficient light was coming through the gap of the wide entrance to allow the youngster to make out the various objects in the narrow space. The barrow stood immediately inside the doorway, while on the left there ran a long bench. On the bench stood the square package, and the canvas wrapping was still adjusted on it. Beneath the bench stood several square, red-painted tins, which Tinker recognised at once as being the receptacles in which petrol is retailed. There was a tang of the volatile spirit in the air, and it was fairly evident that the store was used either as a garage or as a place for keeping motor-car accessories.

"Perhaps I've come on a wild-goose chase, after all," Tinker thought, for there was certainly nothing very suspicious about the look of the place.

He stepped up to the bench, and reached the canvas-covered package. He noticed now that the canvas was in reality a huge sack, such as forage is carried in, and the square-shaped object had evidently been dropped inside it.

Lifting one corner of the sack, Tinker pulled it back, revealing a glimpse of what it contained.

"Great Scott!" the youngster broke out. "It's the body of the ambulance!"

With quickened interest now, he tugged the light, square-shaped body out of its receptacle, and lifted it. In doing so he shook it slightly, and he felt its contents move.

Dropping it on the bench again, Tinker peered through the gap in the top, and, dark though it was, he was able to see the heap of glittering gems and jewellery.

"By Jingo! It's a case, after all!" he broke out. "These fellows have collared the whole of the jewellery, and taken the ambulance with them, too! I wonder how the deuce they managed that?"

So interested was he in his discovery that for the moment Tinker was oblivious to his surroundings. He lifted the box again, and turned towards the doorway, intending to carry it nearer to the light, so that he might make a close inspection. But as he turned away from the bench a faint creak came to his ears, and, with a quick start of alarm, the youngster whipped round.

In the back wall of the stores, close to where the ladder ran up through the trapdoor into the loft, a door, which Tinker had not noticed before, had opened, and framed in it was a wizened, stooping shape.

The whole scene leaped into Tinker's eyes like a flash. He heard a quick, angry exclamation; then the figure in the doorway leaped forward, and a long, thin arm was raised.

Tinker caught the flash of steel, and, realising his danger, the lad dropped his burden and made a lurch forward.

Phip!

The little, tense explosion of compressed air sounded, and something sharp and stinging buried itself in the youngster's cheek.

With a cry of pain, Tinker raised his hand and snatched the little, wool-tufted dart out of his flesh, casting it away from him; but even as he did so he felt a cold, numbing sensation run like an icy tide through his tense young limbs.

With a mad effort the plucky lad tried to reach the menacing, evil figure standing in front of the doorway. Tinker's tottering run carried him halfway in his journey; then the swift drug completed its task, and, with fingers that groped vainly for a hold, the lithe, active figure of the young assistant fell face forward almost at Francis Kew's feet.

"Jules! Quick!"

The sound of hurrying feet came, and then, in through the opened doorway, darted the stocky figure of the man who had been pushing the barrow. It was Professor Kew's chauffeur, and as his eyes alighted on the prostrate figure at his master's feet, a thin gasp of astonishment broke from Jules' lips.

Kew drew aside, and folded his arms across his narrow chest.

"You blundering fool!" he broke out. "Is this how you do your work? By heavens, it is well for me that I insisted on coming here at once!"

"But, monsieur—"

"What is the use of buts?" Kew blazed. "They will not explain the presence of this fellow. I tell you I only arrived here in the nick of time."

His anger was terrible to witness, and Jules cowered away from the rage in the cold, vulture-like face. After a moment Kew seemed to master his passion then, stooping down, he caught at Tinker's shoulder, and, with a quick pull, turned the youngster's unconscious body over.

The lad's white, stark face stared up at him, and Jules saw his master start, peer closer for a moment, then a thin breath came from the bloodless lips.

"Tinker!" Kew broke out. "By heavens! Can his master know what has happened?"

He straightened up sharply and glanced around him, with the sidelong glance of a bird of prey. There was just a trace of fear in the crouching figure as it turned its head from side to side.

"The loft!" Kew broke out, in a savage whisper. "Quick! Jules, see if anyone is there!"

With a bound the chauffeur reached the ladder and shinned up it, until his head was above the level of the floor.

"There is no one here, monsieur," he said.

"You are sure?"

"Yes, monsieur."

At that moment a double knock sounded on the wide doorway of the shed, bringing Kew round like a flash.

"That ought to be Dykes," he murmured; "but I must make sure."

A swift run saw him across the stores, and he applied his black, bead-like eyes to the narrow gap between the doors.

"All right, Dykes," he said, with a breath of relief; "come in!"

The tall man had gone round by the lane in order to assure himself that there was no one spying. As the door opened and Dykes entered, he caught sight of the figure of Tinker lying prone on the floor.

"Good Heavens! Who's that?" he asked.

Kew's face was a study of remorseless anger.

"That is someone who will have to pay dearly for his temerity," he said. "I have met him before, him and his master; but this is the first time that I have ever had a chance of getting him as he is now, helpless."

In a few words Kew explained to Dykes the discovery he had made, and just as he completed, Jules dropped down from the loft with the length of knotted rope over his shoulders.

In quick, voluble French the chauffeur told where he had found the rope, and what it implied.

"Yes, that's about it," said Kew, "he must have got in by way of the loft. But by what witchcraft did he find out that the ambulance was here, and how were his suspicions aroused?"

It was that question which tormented the keen brain of Kew; for in it he saw the implacable hand of his inveterate enemy, Sexton Blake.

"I haven't the slightest idea," said Dykes, glancing down at the pallid face of Tinker. "I never saw him before in my life. Is he dead?"

Kew shook his head.

"Not yet," he returned grimly; "but he is quite safe, and will remain so until I find a means of disposing of him."

His small eyes were full of a fierce satisfaction as he glanced up at Dykes.

"I must find out first how he came here, and who sent him," said Kew. "I want to know if his discovery was the result of an accident, or otherwise. If he was sent here by his master, Sexton

Blake, it means that our plans, by some way or other, have been found out."

"Oh, impossible!" Dykes broke out. "How could they be? Everything came off without a hitch."

His haggard face twitched for a moment.

"There wasn't even the slightest excitement in it," he said slowly; "it was just as though I was robbing an—an old friend. One who trusted me."

"Bah! You're getting sentimental, and this is not the time for that. I have first of all got to dispose of this fellow, and I dare not do that until I know how he came to find this place."

"I'm sure it was only an accident," Dykes said "in fact, he may have followed us. I told your man Jules, that I felt someone was tracking us. It was just an instinct I had, and I feel sure that I was right."

"Oh, we'll soon find out!" said Kew. "And, meanwhile, this young fool is quite safe here."

"You mean to leave him as he is?" Dykes asked, horrified.

A low chuckle broke from Kew's lips.

"Why not?" he returned. "He will not move hand or foot for the next forty-eight hours, and by that time I shall know the truth."

"And if you find that no one is aware of what has happened to him?" Dykes put in.

The cold, vulture-face nodded, and the small eyes took on a fiendish glare.

"If I find that out I will see to it that he never tells his story to anyone!" said Francis Kew.

He turned towards Jules and nodded.

"You can bring the swag along now," he said, "and leave everything else here just as it is."

The chauffeur picked up the little receptacle with its precious contents, and went off through the narrow doorway and beckoned to Dykes.

"Come along!" he said. "I am anxious to see what sort of haul we have made."

To reach the doorway Dykes had to pass the rigid figure of the lad, and suddenly, with a muttered word, the haggard-faced man came to a halt.

"No. I'm hanged if I can leave a chap like this!" he said swiftly. "I'm not quite such a merciless beast as all that. Just wait a moment, and I'll make the poor beggar a little more comfortable."

Kew had made an impatient step forward, but it came to him that it would be better for him to fall in with his confederate's suggestion, so, with a cold smile on his lips, the wizened, bird-like scoundrel leaned against the doorway and watched Dykes at work.

There were a heap of sacks in one corner of the store, and these Dykes gathered together, arranging them in a thick pad, and placing them along the centre of the barrow. On this rude support he placed Tinker, propping the lad's limp head upon a folded sack.

"Very pretty!" Kew sneered. "Are you quite finished?"

Dykes came across the store slowly.

"Yes," he said, "I'm quite finished, Kew. But there's one more thing I've got to say to you. I took a hand in this scheme of yours on the assurance that there would be no blood spilt."

The sunken face twitched for a moment.

"I have fallen low enough, Heaven knows," said Dykes, in a tense, bitter tone; "even to the extent of stealing from my own friend. But I have never been guilty of murder, and have never been associated with anyone guilty of it."

He glanced at Kew, and there was a meaning light in the deep eyes.

"The only being I have ever killed," he ended, "is—Gilbert Fordyce Dykes, and that is not so much murder as suicide!"

Francis Kew was sufficiently keen to see that the tall man, capable tool though he had proved himself, had a will of his own.

There was a moment's silence, then the professor shrugged his shoulders.

"Very well," he said, "I will tell you what I can promise. That young fool there has nothing to fear from me personally, and, whatever his fate may be, I will take no active part in it, and neither will you. Does that content your scruples?"

Dykes nodded.

"It does," he said, "so long as neither you nor I am guilty of harming this youngster, I am quite content."

He was soon to learn the subtle villainy of the lean, wizened rascal who had made his promise so glibly.

For in his heart of hearts Francis Kew had already sentenced Tinker, and was only awaiting to find out the truth about the lad's appearance, to carry the sentence out.

And the sentence was death.

THE FIFTH CHAPTER
THE NEXT MORNING.

AT ten o'clock on the morning following the garden party, Sexton Blake was seated in his quiet consulting-room in Baker Street. There was an unusually thoughtful expression on the clean-shaven face, and the steady eyes were just a little troubled. Sexton Blake had sat up late on the previous night waiting for Tinker to return. But the lad had not yet put in an appearance, and, knowing his young assistant's ways, Blake began to feel that something must have happened to the lad. It was very unusual for Tinker to stay away all night, and even when he did do so, he always made it a point to communicate with Blake, usually by telephone.

"I hope he hasn't got into any trouble," the detective muttered; "he always seems to be getting into some sort of scrape or other."

There was a deep and abiding bond of affection between the solitary detective and his young friend. They had been together so long, had been in so many tight corners, had shared in triumphs and failures, that Blake always felt uneasy and depressed when Tinker was absent.

The fertile young brain of the assistant had often been of great help to him, a fact which the great detective was the first to admit.

"I'll give him until lunch-time," Blake thought; "then I'll start in search for him."

There was an uneasy feeling at the back of his mind that all was not well with Tinker. It was just one of these premonitions that come to a man which he can neither explain nor define.

A knock at the door of the consulting-room aroused him from his musings, and he glanced up. The old landlady who attended to his and Tinker's wants, bustled into the room with a card in her hand.

"The gentleman says he has an appointment, Mr. Blake," she said, holding out the card.

It was Sir Arthur Mountjoy, and Blake asked the landlady to show him in.

The War Office official's healthy face was just a trifle pale, and there was a certain nervous excitement about his appearance that told Blake the baronet was still very much perturbed about what had happened.

"I—I suppose you haven't found out anything, Blake?" was Sir Arthur's first query.

Blake smiled quietly.

"I haven't had very much time, Sir Arthur," he said. "I'm afraid, however, that you will have to remove your objection to making it a Scotland Yard case. It seems to me that the rascals have collared the booty all right, and the only way of tracing it now is by the usual channels."

"And these?"

"You will first of all have to get a list of the various pieces of jewellery, or, at least, as many of them as you can. You can do that, of course, by communicating with the guests, and asking them to let you have a description of their personal gifts."

Sir Arthur flung up his well-shaped hands in a gesture of despair.

"But, my dear Blake, that would be a terribly long job," he protested; "and, as a matter of fact, I doubt if we'd ever get a complete list. You see, in a great many instances, people came along and brought friends with them whom neither Lady Marjory nor myself knew. It would be quite impossible for us to get into touch with these people."

"That is so," said Blake quietly; "and I quite appreciate your difficulty."

"As a matter of fact," Sir Arthur went on, "I would, rather do anything than allow it to get into the papers. I'm a fairly wealthy man, as you know, and Lady Marjory and I have been discussing it this morning. She suggested that I pay to the hospital charities a sum which we consider would cover the probable result of selling the jewellery."

Blake looked up swiftly.

"But that is a tremendous sacrifice, Sir Arthur," he said. "I don't think anybody could expect you to do that."

The baronet shrugged his shoulders.

"Well, it was really Lady Marjory's idea, and to tell you the truth, she has offered to stand the whole loss herself. She has a small income of her own, and it is realisable. In fact, she almost begged of me to allow her to do it; but, of course, I wouldn't listen to that."

Blake was silent for a moment. The information that he had just heard awakened a new train of thought in his mind, and the question formed in his brain: Why was Lady Marjory so anxious to shield the rascals who had tricked her?

"I think it is very foolish of Lady Marjory," Blake said aloud; "and it is practically conspiring to defeat the ends of justice, you know. You must not forget that these men are rascals, and have been guilty of a crime."

"That's exactly what I said to my wife," Sir Arthur broke out; "but then, you see, Blake, it is the publicity that she dreads. The idea of the collection was hers, and she feels in a sense responsible for it."

Blake leaned forward.

"I never care to advise a husband where his wife is concerned," he said slowly; "but in this case, Sir Arthur, I think I should be very chary of doing as you suggest,"

The baronet laughed.

"Of course, I don't want to throw away that huge sum of money," he admitted, "and I hope that you will do your best to find the brutes. But it is the Scotland Yard business that I am against. I don't want the thing in the papers, and everybody talking about it."

"Very well," said Blake. "If you refuse to put it into the hands of the police, of course, I cannot force you to do so."

"But I want you to go on with it, you know," the War Office official cried; "and, candidly, Blake, I feel that you can do more than any police. I have been congratulating myself about your presence at the party ever since."

He slipped his hand into his pocket, and brought out a silver-bound notebook, which he opened, turning the pages swiftly.

"By the way," Sir Arthur said, "I have brought the information you asked for. The firm who supplied us with the little ambulance is Thornton, Blere & Co. It is only a small place, and their offices and workshops are in Amaratz Street, Soho."

"You have not communicated with them in any way, I hope?" Blake said.

"Oh, no! As a matter of fact, I did not even know who they were until I asked my wife this morning."

He glanced at the list again.

"You also asked me to find out who the firm was who did the catering for us. It was Ligat's."

Blake had drawn a pad of paper forward, and taken the addresses down, then Sir Arthur arose to his feet.

"I'm going down to the War Office now," he went on, with a wry smile; "although I must admit that I don't feel very much like work. Please 'phone me as soon as you find out anything."

Blake pushed back his seat from the desk and arose.

As Sir Arthur held out his hand, he glanced into the detective's face.

"You seem rather troubled this morning, too, Blake," he said. "What's the matter? It's not my case, I hope?"

"Not quite," said Blake, "but, as a matter of fact, I am just a little worried. My assistant, Tinker, has not turned up yet."

"Oh, I remember Tinker!" said Sir Arthur quickly. "A bright-eyed, keen youngster. I shouldn't worry about him, he looks well able to take care of himself."

"He was at your party yesterday, with me," said Blake; "but we lost sight of each other just before tea, and I did not see him again."

"Did you wait for him?"

"Not very long," Blake admitted. "Under ordinary circumstances I wouldn't trouble about him, but Tinker has an uncanny knack of getting himself into tight corners, Sir Arthur, and I have a strong feeling that by some means or other he has got entangled again."

"By Jove!" the baronet broke out. "Do you think that he may have found out something about these thieving rascals?"

Blake shook his head.

"'I can hardly venture an opinion on that," he returned. "It would be pure guesswork. All I know is that he has not turned up yet, and knowing how regular he usually is, I am anxious about him."

"Well, you might let me know when he turns up," said Sir Arthur, as he turned away.

A few minutes after the baronet had left the quiet house, Blake also emerged, and turned in the direction of Soho. It was for the little toymakers' firm that he was heading, and after some difficulty he found it.

It proved to be a two-storeyed structure, standing in a yard stacked with timber. Blake made his way to the little office, and after he had stated his business to the clerk there, a stout, contented-looking man in his shirt sleeves, came out from the workshop, and approached Blake.

"Vot can I do for you, sir?" the little man said.

"I've called in connection with a certain order that you executed for Lady Marjory Mountjoy," said Blake. "It was a little ambulance, and I believe it was specially constructed for her."

Mr. Blere looked up.

"Dot ambulance again," he said; "you are the second person who has asked me about it to-day."

"Indeed! Who was the other?"

The jovial face set slightly.

"Dot's more dan I can tell you, Mr.—"

"My name is Blake," said the detective. "Sexton Blake. I have been employed by Sir Arthur Mountjoy to look into this matter."

"You mean you're a 'tec?"

Blake bowed.

"That's right!" he said.

The stout man came a step nearer.

"Vot's it all about?" he asked. "Is dere some mystery in it?"

"I'm afraid I can't explain that to you, Mr. Blere," Blake returned quietly; "not at present, at least. Still you can help me very much if you let me know just exactly what happened in connection with the ambulance."

"Vell, I don't mind doing dot," said Blere, "It has noding to do with me. I did the vork, and I've got her ladyship's written instructions, and dey'll haf to pay me!"

"Oh, I don't think there is much fear of that," Blake said, with a smile.

"Ain't dere?" said the guttural voice. "Vell, I'm not so sure about dot. I'll get paid for the first ambulance all right, but dey seem to vant to cry off for the second body vot I supplied."

Blake's eyes lighted up.

"The second body, eh?" he said. "Ah! That is the trouble, is it?"

"It ain't any trouble so far as I am concerned," Blere said. "My clerk can swear dot he got the telephone message ordering der duplicate body on the same day as the first one vos delivered. And ven the man came for the second body, ve made him sign for it."

Blake was on the scent of the affair now, and he began to question the toy-manufacturer closely.

"When was the original ambulance delivered?" he asked,

"Early in the veek," said Blere. "Lady Marjory asked me to send it up to her house. I believe dot dere vos a committee of gentlemen dere whom she vanted to show it to."

"And the second order—when did you receive it?"

"About two hours after the first one was delivered," replied the toy-maker. "My clerk took the order, and wrote it down in the telephone message-book. If you'll come into the office I vill show you der exact vords."

He hustled into the little office with Blake at his heels, and, lifting the message-pad from the 'phone, he turned the leaves until he came to the Monday section.

"Dere it is," he said, holding the pad out.

In a round, boyish hand was written a message as follows:

"Lady Marjory wants an exact duplicate made of the body of the ambulance supplied to her to-day. The body must be ready and complete by Friday morning, and Lady Marjory will send her own messenger down to receive it."

"Dot's plain enough, ain't it?" said the toy-manufacturer triumphantly.

Blake nodded his head.

"It seems so," he returned. "And you say that the messenger called on Friday?"

"Yes. And he signed for der second body before he took it avay vith him."

There was a long receipt-book lying on the desk, and Blere's fat thumb turned the leaves back.

"Dere it is," he said, indicating a line.

Blake glanced at the signature of the messenger, but could make neither head nor tail of it. It had been written in a cramped, indistinct scrawl.

"You are certainly in the right, Mr. Blere," Blake said; "there is no doubt that you did manufacture the two bodies." A grim smile crossed Blake's face. "We have had ample proof of that."

"Den vhy should her ladyship—" Blere stopped and looked confused.

"Her ladyship," Blake repeated; "does she know that you supplied two bodies?"

"She must do," Blere broke out. "It vos at her orders."

Blake saw that the stout man was trying to cover his mistake, and he did not pursue the matter. The little slip that Blere had made was quite sufficient for Blake's purpose.

"Lady Marjory has either been there," or has communicated with Blere," the detective mused as he found himself walking up the street again.

"And she has evidently asked him not to say anything about it."

There was a shadow of a frown on Blake's face, for Lady Marjory's movements were beginning to trouble him.

What purpose did she have in moving so mysteriously in the affair?

"Is she trying to shield someone?" Blake thought. "It seems to me as though it was very like it."

He made his way back to Baker Street, reaching there somewhere about twelve o'clock. There was no sign of Tinker, and Blake, after pacing up and down his study for half an hour, came to a swift decision.

"It is useless for me to go on with the case unless I can find out what Lady Marjory is doing," he said, aloud. "I will go and see her now."

It was not very far to the big house in the West End, and when Blake was ushered into the morning-room he found Lady Marjory and the girl whom he knew as Clarice seated together there.

Blake glanced keenly at his hostess as he approached, and he noted that the beautiful features were almost deathlike in their pallor, while a network of wrinkled lines had appeared on the usually smooth cheeks.

From her agitated way of greeting him, the detective saw that Lady Marjory was afraid—and it seemed to Blake as though her fear was chiefly centred on him.

Clarice also seemed to share the other's agitation in a minor way, and Blake felt the quick constraint that fell on the two ladies as he bowed to them.

"We were just talking about the dreadful affair as you came in, Mr. Blake," said Lady Marjory, in a hurried tone. "I suppose my husband called on you this morning?"

Her eyes were bright and feverish as they looked up at the detective, and Blake heard her catch her breath as she waited for his reply.

"Yes, Sir Arthur did call, Lady Marjory," said Blake.

"And—and did he tell you what we have decided to do?"

"I don't know how to answer that," Blake said. "I didn't know that you had come to any fixed decision."

"Oh, yes, we did!" Lady Marjory went on. "We—we don't want the publicity, and Arthur and I have agreed to pay the charities six thousand pounds, which we think would have been the probable result of the sale of the stolen property."

"Sir Arthur did mention that to me," said Blake coolly; "but I think I have persuaded him not to go on with it."

Fear leaped into the hazel eyes of the hostess.

"You persuaded him not to go on with it?" Lady Marjory broke out. "But I—I insist on going on with it. I will send the cheque myself this afternoon."

Blake's face was stern. He saw then that he would have to adopt a stronger attitude with the woman.

"You will be very foolish if you do that, Lady Marjory," he said; "for your action is simply encouraging crime. From what I have gathered to-day, I can assure you that the case has become very much more simple. I believe that we will be able to find the thieves."

"From what you have found out to-day?" Lady Marjory said, in a choked voice.

"Yes," Blake put in; "I have been to Thornton and Blere—"

"Ah!"

Lady Marjory sat down suddenly, and her slender fingers tightened over her handkerchief.

"And Mr. Blere has told me all about the duplicate body," Blake went on. "Of course, you did not order it, and, therefore, it proves that whoever did send that telephone message must have known the construction of the first ambulance. Must even have examined it, otherwise he would not have been sure that the second body was capable of being placed in the catches on the wheels."

There was a silence in the room, and Lady Marjory's eyes never left the clean-shaven, intelligent face.

"I'm afraid I'm very dense, Mr. Blake," she said, in a quavering voice; "and I don't quite understand. What is it that you really mean?"

"I mean that on Monday, when the ambulance was inspected by you and the committee of gentlemen, you must have shown to them the method by which the body of the little vehicle was held in its place. Isn't that so?"

"Yes, I did do that. But, as a matter of fact, it was first suggested by someone that the body should be made detachable."

" Who suggested it?" Blake asked.

Lady Marjory wrinkled her brows for a moment, then she shook her head with a little pathetic shrug of her shoulders.

"I can't remember now," she said. "I—I've had so many things to think about that my brain seems to be in a whirl. Perhaps I will remember later on."

"It does not matter very much," said Blake, little dreaming how much it really did matter. "The fact remains that it was someone who knew the construction of the ambulance that contrived the theft. He knew that the body was detachable, and could be removed easily and swiftly."

He looked at Lady Marjory for a moment.

"If we can find the person who took delivery of the second body from Blere, we can also find the thief," said Sexton Blake.

Lady Marjory arose to her feet.

"But why should you trouble any further, Mr. Blake?" she went on. "Both Sir Arthur and I have practically agreed to let the loss be ours. It—it is hardly fair of you to insist on continuing the matter."

Blake drew back a pace.

"Of course, if you are really bent on shielding the thief," he said stiffly, "there is nothing more for me to do. Do I understand that it is your wish that these criminals should not be brought to justice? That you deliberately want to allow them to escape scot-free?"

Lady Marjory's lips trembled, and her eyes glanced down to the floor. She could not meet the honest indignation in the blue ones in front of her.

"It—it is the publicity," she repeated, unable to find anything else to say.

At that moment there came a welcome interruption in the person of a footman who appeared in the doorway.

"Sir Arthur is on the telephone, and would like to speak to you, Lady Marjory," he said.

Lady Marjory looked at Blake and then at Clarice, and the detective fancied it was something of a warning, imploring glance that fell on the younger girl.

"I will not stay, Lady Marjory," said Blake. "I want to get back to my rooms. I may see you later, in the day."

It was impossible for Lady Marjory to say anything then, in front of the servant, and Blake left the house. But he went no further than the corner of the street, where, lighting a cigar, he puffed away slowly.

Half an hour later his vigil was rewarded, for he saw the slender, well-gowned figure of Clarice Tremaine come out through the high, arched gateway, and turn in his direction.

The girl did not recognise Blake until she was close to him, and as he raised his hat the detective noted a swift flush stain the lovely cheeks.

Blake had made up his mind now, and he went to the point at once.

"I have been waiting for you, Miss Tremaine," he said gravely. "I wonder if you know why?"

She looked up at him with the frightened eyes of a fawn. Blake's face was kindly, though stern.

"I want you to tell me the truth." he said. "I know that there is some secret weighing down on you. I can see that quite plainly. What is it that Lady Marjory has asked you to keep away from me?"

They were pacing down the pavement together, and Miss Tremaine had her head bent so that Blake could not see her face. But he saw the white-gloved fingers plucking at the edge of the leather bag she carried, and suddenly his patience was rewarded.

"I will tell you, Mr. Blake," Clarice Tremaine broke out, "I—I have tried so hard to be loyal to Lady Marjory. But I can't help it; the thing has been worrying me dreadfully. I did not sleep a wink last night for thinking of it."

"What is it?" Blake asked.

"The—the man who came after us to help us with the ambulance," said Clarice. "I did not tell you at the time, but I—I remembered seeing his face before. He was speaking to Lady Marjory just before tea." She glanced up at Blake's suddenly. "And, unless I am mistaken, you were quite close to them," she went on. "Don't you remember him? A tall, thin man he was."

Swift as a flash a memory came back to Blake of a haggard face with deep-set, sunken eyes. He remembered the little snatch of conversation which had taken place between him and Lady Marjory after the tall, thin stranger had gone off. Lady Marjory had been strangely disturbed.

"You are sure there is no mistake, Miss Tremaine?" Blake asked.

"Oh, no!" the girl returned. "His face was much too striking a one to forget!"

She came to a halt, and glanced up at Blake.

"As soon as I remembered where I had seen his face before I went to Lady Marjory," she said, "but she—she assured me that it could not have been the same. That there was some mistake."

Her voice took a stronger note.

"But in my heart I know that I was not mistaken," Clarice Tremaine went on. "The man who was speaking to Lady Marjory was the same man who took the ambulance round the path. I went to Lady Marjory this morning to get her to let me tell what I knew."

"And what did she say?"

"She told me that everything was going to be settled," Clarice said; "that there would be no need for me to trouble any further, as no one would lose anything, except—except her."

They looked at each other for a moment, then Blake shook his head.

"I hope you won't misunderstand me, Miss Tremaine," he murmured slowly. "I can assure you that I am Lady Marjory's sincere friend. I believe that she is a pure and noble woman. But I am also assured that she is making a sacrifice for someone that is not worthy of it. No doubt that very person has been relying on her clemency as rascals of that type often do. Only the most abject coward would shelter himself behind a woman's skirts."

Clarice Tremaine was silent for a moment.

"I wonder if you are right, Mr. Blake?" she said presently. "Lady Marjory told me the name of her friend. He is Gilbert Fordyce Dykes, and he is Lady Marjory's cousin. I believe they were once boy and girl sweethearts—at least, that is what she told me this, morning."

She held out her slim hand.

"And now," she said, "I have told you everything. But I hope that whatever you do you will try to avoid hurting Lady Marjory, whom I love very dearly."

Blake's smile was very gentle as he took the soft young palm.

"If you knew me better you would hardly need to ask that, Miss Tremaine," he said quietly.

"Still, I give you my promise. Lady Marjory will not be harmed by any act of mine."

It was a brighter, more contented girl who left the detective and went on down the street, with her light, graceful step.

"Gilbert Fordyce Dykes," Blake muttered. "Not a very common name. The web seems to be closing in now, slowly but surely. My next move, is to find this man."

How he accomplished that purpose another chapter must reveal.

THE SIXTH CHAPTER
TINKER'S DREADFUL ORDEAL.

"A MOST extraordinary thing, my dear Tremaine," said Kew, in his cool tones. "But, after all, I don't think there is anything that the committee can blame themselves for."

Tremaine—Clarice's father—was chatting to Kew in the smoke-room of his club. The professor had just arrived there, and the troubled committeeman had gone over the history of the case.

They had just finished lunch, and were having their after-dinner smoke, and Kew pumped the unconscious man until the whole details of the discovery at the garden party were in his possession.

"I only wish you had been there, Kew," Tremaine said. "You would have realised what an awful hole we felt in."

"Unfortunately, my duties at St. Cyr's kept me away," the cunning scoundrel said, "and, therefore, it was impossible for me to attend."

He leaned a trifle closer.

"And now," he went on, "I think that you said the—the detective who—who chanced to be in the grounds was named Sexton Blake. Is that right?"

"That's quite true," said Tremaine.

"And from his discoveries you came to the conclusion that there were at least two men in the affair?"

"Yes," the committeeman went on. "That fellow Blake is a wonderful man, and I have no doubt about it but what his theory of the case was absolutely correct."

Kew ventured to allow a sneer to cross his cold lips.

"Oh, theories are all very well, and those detectives are famous for that type of thing!" he said cynically. "But very often their theories prove to be anything but correct. Still, that is nothing

to do with me, and I am glad that someone is interested in the case."

"I saw Sir Arthur this morning," Tremaine said, "and he assured me that Sexton Blake was doing his best to discover the perpetrators."

"Has Sir Arthur seen Mr. Blake this morning?" Kew asked.

There was a touch of anxiety in his voice which escaped the notice of his host.

"He has," Tremaine returned, "but Blake had nothing new to report."

Kew then turned the conversation into other channels. He was quite content, for he realised that if Blake had known where Tinker was the detective would undoubtedly have made an effort, ere this, to have rescued his assistant.

And so the point which Kew required settling was no longer a difficulty.

When he left the spacious club premises about half an hour later the lean, stooping figure seemed to be very well satisfied with himself.

"I know now that Blake did not send Tinker on our track," Kew muttered, "and I don't care very much how he came to follow, and find the stores."

He was satisfied now that Tinker had worked off his own bat so far as the actual finding of the hiding place of the body of the ambulance was concerned. And that meant that neither Blake nor anyone else had any idea of what Tinker was up to.

The vulture face of the professor seemed to gleam like a death mask as he hurried along the streets.

He had made up his mind now that Tinker would have to be got out of the way. A memory of his promise to Dykes flashed into the lean scoundrel's mind, and his thin lips twitched for a moment.

"I promised that I, personally, would not be responsible for that young fool's death," he muttered, "and that promise I will keep. But he will have to die!"

It was towards the hospital that Kew turned his steps, and he remained in the great institution for the better part of three hours. It was almost five o'clock in the evening before he finally left his private room in the hospital, and when he did so he headed at once for the neighbourhood in which the stores were situated.

He did not take any particular care as he turned into the quiet side-street, and made his way towards the lane which gave access to the stores.

There was no one about in the street at that hour of the afternoon, and, it being Saturday, even the stores were untended and unoccupied.

It was down the narrow passage leading to the rear of the stores that Kew turned, and, crossing a courtyard and going on down another passage, he reached the small door let into the back wall of the store.

He withdrew a key, and thrusting it into the lock turned it and entered the half-lighted place.

It was his first visit since he had left Tinker on the previous day, and the first glance of his small eyes revealed the fact that the lad was still lying mute and motionless on the rude litter that the kindly hand of Fordyce Dykes had supplied for him.

Closing the door behind him, Kew stepped noiselessly across the floor of the small structure, and came to a halt beside the barrow.

Bending down, he looked at the white, motionless face of Tinker, and saw that the eyes were open. The eyes did not move, and yet, in their depths, Kew saw something of life dash, a shadow as it were of some inner feeling that crossed the dazed brain.

A cynical chuckle broke from the evil ruffian's lips.

"You can hear and see me," he said, in a low tense voice, "I know that. It is only your limbs and head and tongue and eyes that are paralysed, otherwise your brain is as clear and alert as ever."

Again the answering flash came into the wide eyes of the youngster.

"And as you can hear me," the voice of Kew hissed, "I might as well tell you what is going to happen to you."

He bent a little closer until his breath swept Tinker's rigid cheeks.

"You have deliberately placed yourself in deadly peril, you fool!" the scoundrel went on. "It is not the first time that you and I have crossed each other's tracks, and I warned you before that the day would come when you would bitterly repent it. And now that day has come, and, by heavens, I swear that you will never live to reveal what you have heard or seen here!"

The eyes into which he was looking so closely seemed to flash a mute defiance.

"Oh, yes, you're plucky enough!" Kew went on, knowing well enough that the lad could hear every word that was said, although his powerless tongue and inert body could not give any signal by way of reply. "I never doubted your pluck, but pluck is not everything, I have vowed that you shall die by my instrumentality, Tinker, and I mean to keep my word!"

Professor Kew was right when he said that Tinker could hear every word that broke from his thin lips. As a matter of fact, the lad had never lost consciousness. What manner of strange drug it was that Professor Kew had used on Tinker the lad was never able to discover, but as the dart struck him the lad felt his limbs give way beneath him, and he fell prone on the floor.

He heard every word that Dykes said to Kew, and he was aware of the kindly deed that the tall, haggard-faced man had done. He knew that Dykes had carried him on to the barrow, and had placed him there in as comfortable a position as possible, and Tinker had heard the door close behind the trio of thieves as they left the store with their booty.

And right through the long terrible night the lad had lain there in a state that was almost worse than death itself. He could neither move limb nor body, could not even turn his head and his lips and tongue seemed to have lost their power of movement.

Yet his brain, his clear, alert, quick brain was just as alive and potent as ever. There was a curious demoniacal torture about the effects of this deadly drug, for while it left its victim helpless it did not give a merciful oblivion.

It was a type of paralysis, similar to that which has sometimes seen a man laid in his coffin, though life and knowledge were still in the inert, body.

He had watched the grey dawn steal through the gap in the top of the wide doorway, had watched the shadows lengthen and then fade again, and at last he had heard the grind of the lock, and the quick, soft footfalls of Kew reached his ears, then he had seen the lean, evil face loom above, him.

The words which Professor Kew spoke sounded to Tinker like the breath of doom. He knew the implacable villain too well to hope that any feeling of mercy or remorse would soften him.

If Francis Kew said that he should die, it would not be the professor's fault if he did not carry that out.

Yet, helpless and in his enemy's power though he was, Tinker felt his brave young heart strengthen itself in readiness for whatever terrible trial lay before him.

"You will have to wait here for just a few hours longer, my friend," the voice of Kew whispered. "It is too light yet, for me to take you away, but as soon as the darkness comes I will return, and you will be taken somewhere where you will find the end of your existence!"

A thin, cackling laugh rang out, a mad, mocking sound in the quiet stores.

"You will die, you young fool," Kew breathed—"die, do you hear? And your master will not even know what has happened to you!"

The lean, evil face was withdrawn, and Tinker, listening eagerly, heard the soft footfalls pass across the store again and die away. Then the door closed, and silence reigned once more.

Dumb and helpless, the youngster lay on the barrow, his thoughts turning to a hundred things as he lay there.

"The guv'nor will never even know how I died," his thoughts ran. "By heavens, I wish I could send only one message to him! Oh, if I only had the will power to throw aside this deadly feeling that has come over me!"

But, strong-willed though he was, the drug had set its powerful bond on him, and he lay helpless and mute beneath its grim effects.

Hours must have passed before Tinker heard the crunching noise of wheels sound on the cobbled lane outside the stores. Then, a few moments later, there came the rasp of a lock, and the great doorway swung back, allowing a breath of the cool, night air to fall on the motionless figure of the lad on the barrow.

Hands were stretched out, and lifted Tinker from his rude litter, and he found himself being carried across the cobbled stones until at last he knew that he was in the interior of a vehicle.

His eyes, remaining in the same fixed position, were staring up at the root of the cab, and it was only his ears that could help him to realise where he was.

The boom of the two doors told him that his captors, whoever they were, were closing the stores again; then, a few moments later, he heard the sound of horses' hoofs, and the vehicle

began to turn slowly; then, at a more rapid pace, it passed out of the lane and turned into the smoother-paved street.

There was someone in the cab with Tinker. He sensed that, and he could hear the fellow's slow breathing.

But the custodian, whoever he was, made no attempt to get anywhere near to the lad; and, Tinker, lying half bent on the broad seat, was carried on and on through a maze of streets, until at last the vehicle passed through a wide gateway and came to a halt.

The man in the cab slipped out, and a few moments later Tinker heard voices close to him.

He was lifted from the vehicle, and placed on something which he recognised later as being a stretcher. Lying flat on the stretcher, his eyes first caught a glimpse of blue sky, then the top of a ceiling, as he was carried down a harrow passage.

Finally, he was carried into a long, wide, apartment, and, a moment later he found himself stretched out on what was undoubtedly, a hospital cot.

There was a light gleaming above his head, and presently there framed in the halo a nurse's face. The face seemed a kindly one, for the eyes were pitiful as they looked down at Tinker.

The lad heard her soft voice murmur something, and he strained his ears to catch what it was.

A moment later a deeper voice, that of a man, sounded, and this time he was able to understand the words.

"Yes, poor chap, he seems to be just about at the end of it, doesn't he?"

Almost unconsciously, Tinker felt someone raise his hand and hold it for a moment, then drop the limp arm back on the cot again.

"It's paralysis, isn't it?" the nurse whispered in a voice that was loud enough for Tinker to hear.

The reply did not reach him, but it was evidently an affirmative one, for he saw the nurse shake her head; then the head was withdrawn out of the little space which his eyes commanded, and the kindly hands began to attend to him.

He knew then that he was in a hospital, some quiet institution for the sick and ailing. Even then he hardly realised what it all meant, and just for a moment it came to him that, perhaps, someone else had found him in that store, and had shifted

THE PAPER FOR ALL CLASSES

TINKER'S DETECTIVE INSTINCTS WERE AROUSED.

FRAMED IN THE DOORWAY WAS A WIZENED STOOPING SHAPE

TINKER CLIMBING UP INTO THE LOFT.

"YOU ARE NOT FAR WRONG, KEW," SAID BLAKE: "I THINK I HAVE CORNERED YOU AT LAST."

THE DEATH OF GILBERT FORDYCE DYKES.

U.J.—No. 525.

him to this house of healing, as being the only place fit to receive him.

But he was soon to be undeceived so far as that was concerned.

As soon as he had been stripped and changed into the comfortable hospital garb, the attendant returned, then half an hour passed, and presently Tinker heard a well-known voice.

It was the cold, calculating tone of Professor Kew, and a few moments later, the little, stooping form, followed by another tall one, came to the side of the cot.

Tinker's eyes just picked out the malevolent face of Kew, and he saw the evil eyes-gleam for a moment into his own.

"Is this the case that you wanted me to give my opinion on, Doctor Randolff?" Kew's sibilant voice asked.

"It is, professor," came a deeper tone. "I feel sure that it is a case of paralysis; but I want your expert opinion on it as well, if you don't mind."

Kew bent over the motionless figure on the cot, and in his clever way he made his false examination.

The grave surgeon standing behind him could not see the evil, mocking look in the vulture face as it bent over the lad.

"You are quite right, doctor," Kew said, as he straightened up. "It is undoubtedly a case of brain paralysis. Some of the cells are affected, and I would suggest that there is some foreign substance pressing on them."

Tinker did not hear the other's reply, but Kew deliberately raised his voice so that his helpless victim might hear him.

"I suggest that you operate at once," the awful voice went on; "it is the only chance you have!"

Operate at once!

Horror surged into Tinker's heart then, and with all his will power he tried to make some sort of movement that would reveal his knowledge of what was taking place.

But it seemed as though every limb was bound in cold steel, and his effort was hopeless.

"No!" It was Kew's voice again. "I will not undertake the operation. I am too busy just now. But I am quite sure that you will be able to follow my theory, doctor, and, if you like, I will give you a rough outline of it."

Tinker heard the two men move away from the cot, and their voices died away into an indistinct murmur.

A faint, cold sweat, had gathered on the lad's brow, the only outward indication of the terrible, mental strain that he was undergoing. He saw now Kew's evil ruse. He had been taken to some hospital, and it was evidently one in which Kew was the consulting surgeon, for it was the evil professor who had been called to give an opinion on the case.

And Kew had deliberately lied to the house-surgeon, with the result, that soon, in a few moments, perhaps, Tinker would be carried away to the operating theatre, and laid on the cold slab, ready for the incision of the deadly knife.

In his young life, Tinker had been in many tight corners, but this ghastly experience was one that he had never undergone before. It was the dreadful torture of having to lie there, still and silent, thinking a thousand thoughts, but unable to raise even a hand to defend himself, that made the youngster's courage droop for a moment.

"Guv'nor! Guv'nor!" Tinker thought in his agony.

It was towards his great, kindly master that his mind turned now in his extremity. Often in the past, Blake had turned up just in the nick of time, and saved his young assistant and, even at the eleventh hour, now, Tinker did not quite despair.

"If I could only find some means of making them understand, of making them know what is happening to me," he thought, his brain reeling in his head.

He went through a very agony of doubt and despair then, and his staring eyes, fixed on the white ceiling above the light, shone with an unearthly radiance. Long moments passed, then at last another voice came to his ears.

"This is the patient."

It was the voice of the nurse, and Tinker felt kindly hands stretch out and lift him. A cold shudder ran through his young veins as he was lifted from the cot and placed on the stretcher.

Presently on its noiseless rubber wheels, it began to move down the ward, the attendants pushing it slowly down the wide gap between the cots.

There were many patients in that ward, some of them convalescent, and heads were raised, and hollow eyes followed the melancholy procession as it wended its way down the ward. The inmates realised that another human being was going to undergo a fierce ordeal—a necessary ordeal, no doubt, but one in which life and death would hang in the balance.

The doors at the end of the long ward were held apart, and the silent-wheeled stretcher passed out, while the doors closed behind it.

It went on down the waxed corridor, and the lad lying motionless on the stretcher, heard, afar off and dimly, the sound of a clock striking.

His alert ears caught each chime swiftly.

"Eleven o'clock," he thought.

He knew that he might never hear a clock chime again and suddenly, into his young heart there came a swift resolve.

If he had to die, at least he would die well.

He knew, or, at least, he could dimly judge of the agony that awaited him. It was not the first time that he had seen the interior of an operating theatre, and he knew just what manner of scene it was that he would take part in.

At the end of the waxed corridor, the ambulance was wheeled down a slight slope, and then Tinker found himself being moved, until at last he was placed on the operating-table in the centre of a great white apartment. He was immediately under a huge arc-lamp, and its light seemed to send a dazzling halo over every corner of the room.

Around him, dressed in white garb, there was gathered a little circle of quiet-eyed young men, whom Tinker knew were the students of the hospital.

They had assembled there specially to see this surgical operation performed by the house-surgeon. To them it was simply a feat of skill, and was specially devised for the purpose of saving the patient's life.

The great Professor Kew himself had advised the operation, and Kew was known to be one of the most skilful surgeons in London. Whatever his opinion was, stood, and not one of the quiet gentlemen standing there dreamed for a moment that he was taking part in what was little else than a dastardly crime.

The minutes passed slowly, and Tinker's heart began to throb so loudly that it seemed to him as though impossible that the quiet group around could not hear it.

A step sounded by his side, and above him there appeared the kindly visage of a bearded man.

It was the house-surgeon, and he was clad in a long, white, spotless robe that covered him from head to foot.

For a moment the bearded face looked into his own, keen yet kindly, with just a shadow of sympathy in the well-formed features.

"I don't think he will require an anaesthetic," the surgeon's voice said. "I think I can operate at once."

A chill, numbing cold crept like a tide into Tinker's heart.

His dreadful ordeal was about to commence.

Was there no hope for him? Had he to die there on that cold slab, in front of the eyes of those silent witnesses?

It seemed, indeed, as though he was beyond human aid.

With a slight scrape of his foot, the house-surgeon turned towards the little table on which the antiseptic kettle stood which contained his surgical instruments.

THE SEVENTH CHAPTER

SEXTON BLAKE WORKS HARD.

THE information which Sexton Blake had received from Miss Tremaine opened up a new track, on which the detective promptly set himself. He headed for Baker Street at once, and entered his study. The old landlady appeared, and informed him that Tinker had not yet returned—a point which began to trouble Blake more than a little now.

However, for the moment it was the missing jewellery that was his first object. He had undertaken the elucidation of the mystery, and, although Lady Marjory had almost begged him to give up his quest, Blake instinctively felt that it would be unfair to Lady Marjory herself if he were to do so.

"There is not the slightest doubt but what she is trying to shield that fellow Dykes," he thought, as he dropped into his chair by the desk. But Lady Marjory is of that warm-hearted, impulsive type who are capable of making many sacrifices, and very often for worthless causes!"

A quiet smile crossed the clean-shaven face.

"Oh, no, Mr. Fordyce Dykes," the great detective murmured grimly, "you are not going to shield yourself behind a woman! I want to find you and get to the root of this affair!"

From a small, drawerless desk, Blake pulled out a bulky notebook, the pages of which he turned over until he came to a certain section. There were three or four pages full of telephone numbers, and they ranged over all the exchanges in London.

Against each number was a certain mark, and Blake, after running his eye down one of the columns, lifted the receiver and gave a number. In a few moments a harsh voice replied.

"Is that you, Sam?" Blake asked.

"It's—it's Mr. Blake, ain't it?"

"That's right."

There was a slight pause, then: "Anything I can do for you, guv'nor?"

It was a marine stores in one of the worst streets around the Tilbury Docks from whence Blake's informant was speaking.

"Well, I'm not sure, but there might be," said Blake. "I want to find a certain man. His name is Gilbert Fordyce Dykes, and he is tall, rather sallow, hollow-eyed and hollow-cheeked. He dresses pretty well, and has been a gentleman. Have you chanced to see him anywhere about, Sam?"

"No, guv'nor. Ain't seen anybody of that description among the boys I know."

This conversation differed but slightly from the others that took place over the 'phone.

Patiently and methodically, for the best part of an hour, Sexton Blake waded slowly through his list of numbers. It was to all sorts and conditions of places that he 'phoned—shabby eating-houses, grimy-looking furniture shops, doubtful public-houses.

That list which Blake had in the book was worth more money than the detective cared to think about. It was the slow, painful harvesting of years, and Scotland Yard would have gone mad over it had it come into their possession.

They represented really the unregistered headquarters of half the criminal circles in London. They were mostly "fences," but each and every one of the speakers seemed to recognise Blake's voice, and were obviously only too eager to help him if they could.

And so, steadily, the detective gradually 'phoned his way through each district, until at last he received the information ha desired.

It was a guttural German voice that answered him, and it emanated from the person of a stout, greasy-waistcoated pawnbroker.

"I think I know your man, Mr. Blake. He's in tow with a couple of others dot go by the name of Jem and Jerry."

"What is their particular lay?"

"Dot vos more dan I could say," came the cautious reply. "But I know they are crooks all right. I can't say I haf ever seen the tall chap you vos talking about, but I heard the boys speaking about someone whom Jem and Jerry had vith them in their rooms."

"You know where they stay, then?" Blake asked.

"Yes. Second floor, No. 6, Doggel's Alley. Dot's a turning out of Marden Street, Vhitechapel."

Blake hastily scrawled the address on the corner of a blotting-pad.

"Right you are, Carl. I'm very much obliged to you."

"Of course, dis bit of vork is on der usual terms?" the stout pawnbroker remarked. "No names, no noding?"

Blake smiled at the receiver.

"Oh, yes, those are the terms, Carl." he said. "Good-bye!"

Pushing back his chair, the detective arose and stretched himself. He had been sitting so long at the same post that his muscles had become slightly stiffened; but there was a look of contentment on his face now.

"I'll get down to Doggel's Alley as quickly as I can," Blake decided; "for if Carl admits that he thinks it is the man, there is every chance of it being so."

Passing out of his study, the detective entered his bed-room, closing the door behind him. Ten minutes later the bed-room door opened to allow a square-shouldered, black-bearded man to emerge. There was a blue reefer jacket buttoned across the broad chest, and the brass buttons on the jacket were adorned with an anchor. A peaked cap was pulled down over the level brows, and it seemed as though, by some extraordinary means, Sexton Blake had actually made his body contract, for as he passed along the corridor he looked a man very little above the middle height.

Blake travelled by 'bus to Whitechapel, climbing to the top seats, and taking his place as though he was just an ordinary passenger. His make-up was just that perfection which long years of experience brings, and to anyone who chanced to look at him he was just a typical shell-back, dressed in his best, shore-going togs, enjoying a brief spell in London.

It was about five o'clock when Blake turned into Doggel's Alley, but in that narrow thoroughfare, between the high buildings, it was already almost dusk. At the various doorways were standing groups of shabby-looking men and frowsy, untidy women; while on the edge of the pavement sprawled little, dirty-faced children, enjoying themselves as only children can even in the most sordid surroundings.

Blake swung along with his rolling gait until he reached No. 6; then, after a glance round, as though in doubt whether that was the right number or not, he stepped into the dark passage, turning up the narrow staircase.

The stairs creaked to his tread as he ascended, and on the second landing he came to a halt.

There were two doors on the landing, and Blake went to the first one and opened it cautiously. He drew a blank there, for a glance into the dim interior told him that it was unfurnished and unoccupied.

Crossing to the other door, Blake listened for a moment. There was no sound, and, with one quiet breath, the detective thrust the door open and entered.

His eyes travelled around the chamber, and alighted at last on the bed. He saw a huge figure stretched out on it, with arms and legs rigid.

In the dim light it seemed as though the man was dead, and Blake, closing the door, hurried across the room. On the left of the bed there was a window, and, thanks to its elevated position, it was fairly light. Blake stepped to the other side of the bed, and, bending down, looked at the motionless man for a moment.

There was no mistaking what type of man it was that lay there. Jem's heavy, brutal face, white and rigid though it was, had not lost its criminal look.

Blake straightened up.

Just for a moment he had feelings that it must be Dykes who lay there; but there was no resemblance between this broad-shouldered, brawny ruffian and the tall, cadaverous-featured man whom the detective had seen speaking to Lady Marjory.

Blake's eyes were still resting on Jem's face, when suddenly he saw the head move slightly. Again he bent over the figure, and this time he placed his hand over the heart. It was beating slowly.

Raising his hand to the man's head, Blake turned the face slightly, and it was then that he noted that the eyes were open and staring straight at him. Despite the half-light, Blake saw that there was intelligence in the orbs. They had not the dull, vacant stare of the fevered.

"What's the matter with you, matey?" Blake asked, in a deep tone. "Ain't you well?"

Jem was just getting over the effects of the strange drug that Kew had administered. He was able to move his head, and even his body slightly; but, so far, he had not recovered the use of his tongue. Yet the big fellow tried his best, to speak, and the inarticulate muttering that came from his lips gave to Blake a clue of what was the matter with him.

"He seems to be half paralysed," Blake thought—"just as though he was recovering from the fever."

The detective felt instinctively that this was one of the two men whom he had come in search of, and he realised now that he would have to help this fellow to regain the use of his limbs if he wanted Jem to help him.

"Can't speak—eh, mate?" Blake said aloud. "Would yer like me to 'elp you? I've 'ad a bit o' experience with cases like yourn!"

Manner and voice and speech was exactly suited to the part that Blake was playing.

He looked down into Jem's eyes, and saw the hopeful gleam that leaped into them. The man even made an attempt to nod his head to indicate that he was only too ready for the experiment.

"Right!" said Blake. "I'll start now!"

A few moments later a dramatic scene began in that half-lighted chamber. Aided by his great strength, Blake had half-dragged, half-lifted Jem's partly-dressed figure out of the bed, and, with one of Jem's great arms over his shoulders, Blake was making the huge fellow move backwards and forwards across the room.

For the first few minutes all the movement was done by Blake, for Jem's feet refused to move, and he was simply dragged to and fro. But Blake presently began to feel a new warmth coming into the huge figure, the stagnant blood began to move more swiftly, and little by little, Jem began to feel the use of his limbs returning to him.

The sweat was pouring down Blake's face, but he stuck to his task, and for the best part of half an hour, the two figures paced up and down the chamber.

It was a hoarse murmur that first told Blake that he had been successful.

"I'm—I'm beat: let me rest a minute!"

They were the first articulate words that Jem had uttered for over a week, but Blake made no attempt to fall in with the fellow's suggestion.

"No! No! You've got to stick to it now. Come on! Stick to it—stick to it!"

And Jem, setting his teeth together, obeyed the commands of his companion, and presently his tottering footsteps gave place to a firmer, surer tread, until at last, with a great cry, the broad-shouldered fellow flung himself away from Blake, and standing in the centre of the room thrust his great arms above his head.

"I'm right—I'm right! Blow me, I'm right!"

It was a hoarse, tremulous voice that spoke, and Jem's ugly features were lighted up with a look of absolute triumph.

Lunging forward, he held out his hand.

"I—I don't know who yer are, mate," he said huskily, "but I'll never forgit yer for what yer've done for me. By 'eavens, I thought I was booked! For a week I've lain there 'arf dead!"

He passed his hand over his clammy brow, and a shudder ran through his thick frame.

"I feels as though it 'ad been a bad dream," said Jem; "the sort o' thing yer gits arter a 'eavy supper. But it ain't been no dream, it was real—real. And you was the man that's 'elped me out o' it."

He pressed Blake's hand in a fierce grip, then crossing the room, Jem, with fingers that shook slightly, struck a match and lighted the solitary gas-jet, then turned again to his visitor.

"I jest wanted to see yer face, mate," he said; "'cos I don't want ter fergit it, yer see!"

Blake saw that the man was genuinely grateful, and the detective's long experience of all classes of criminals had proved to him that very often the lowest type would sometimes rise to a fine level of human feeling.

Realising this, Sexton Blake took a bold step.

"You say you are grateful to me," he said, in his natural voice now. "I wonder if that was merely talk, or do you mean it?"

Jem stepped back to the mantelpiece, and was staring at the bearded figure.

"I—I did mean it!" he broke out. "Who are yer? Wot's brought yer here?"

Sexton Blake passed his hands over his face rapidly, and removed his black beard, the cap followed, and his clean-shaven face was revealed.

"My name is Sexton Blake," he said quietly; "I've no doubt you've heard of me."

Jem had leaped back to the bed now, and was clutching at the end rail of it.

"The 'tec?" he said. "Yer—yer've come for me, then, haven't yer?" Blake shook his head.

"Oh, no!" he returned; "I've not come for you! I was in search of a man named Gilbert Fordyce Dykes, and I understand that two men named Jem and Jerry were likely to know where he was."

"Is that the 'onest truth? Yer ain't after us?"

"I am only after Dykes," said Blake. "And now, who are you? Jem or Jerry?"

"I'm Jem, I am; but Jerry'll be 'ere presently, if yer wants to see 'im as well."

The big fellow had lumbered forward and dropped into one of the crazy chairs. He was evidently still weak from the effects of the drug, and his eyes were heavy as they stared at Sexton Blake.

"Oh, I don't know that I want to see, Jerry!" Blake said; "I've no doubt you'll be able to tell me all I want to know."

He came a couple of paces forward.

"Now then," he said, "where am I to find this man Dykes?"

Jem looked up at him.

"You're sure that you ain't going to go for Jerry an' me arterwards?" he said. "'Cos Jerry's my pal, 'e is." A sullen look came over his heavy features. "We've both done stretches in our time, but I ain't goin' to see 'im in chokey through any words o' mine."

Blake nodded. The very fact of Jem lying there helpless on the bed made it impossible for him to have taken any part in the robbery.

"I think you can make yourself easy on that point, Jem," he said; "the matter that I am investigating was something that took place yesterday, I don't know whether you know if Dykes took part in it, but I want to find out."

"Yesterday," Jem repeated with a note of delight in his voice; "then I can prove that neither Jerry or me had anyfink to do with it. 'E only went out for an hour yesterday, and that was to fetch a doctor—not that the doctor could do much good to me."

There was no reason for the fellow to lie, and Blake felt instinctively that he was telling the truth.

"All right, Jem," he said. "Then I can promise you that neither you nor your pal will appear in this at all. Now, what about Dykes? Has he been here to see you? Where will I find him?"

Blake had been watching the heavy face, and he saw a look of savage ferocity come over it. For six long days Jem had lain motionless, but his brain had been working all that time, and all his concentrated hate had been turned on one man.

"By 'eavens, I'll tell yer orl abart it," he said, leaping to his feet. "If yer wants to know where to find Dykes, I can put yer on the man who 'e's workin' with."

"You can?"

"Yus!"

Triumph gleamed in the burglar's features now, and his huge fists clenched and unclenched convulsively.

"It's the same man as laid me flat for a week—a 'uman vampire, that's wot I call 'im. Oh, 'eavens, wait till I gets a chance to lay my 'ands on 'im!"

"The name—the name! What is the name?"

"'E calls 'imself Professor Francis Kew!" Jem hissed.

Master of himself though he was, Blake could not repress the swift exclamation that came to his lips.

Jem leaned forward eagerly.

"Yer knows 'im, then, do yer?" he said.

Blake's blue-grey eyes flashed.

"By heavens, I do know him!" he returned. "He's the most cunning crook in all London. But how did he come to get in touch with Dykes?"

A savage oath broke from Jem's lips.

"Me an' Jerry was to blame for that," he said. "Dykes 'ad an—an accident, and we 'ad to git a doctor ter look arter 'im, an' we brought that skunk Kew 'ere."

Blake dropped into a chair, and nodded towards Jem.

"You interest me," he said. "Now, I want to hear the whole story."

The history did not suffer in the telling.

And when he finished his history Blake was content. He saw now that there was little doubt but what it was Kew's master-brain that lay behind the cunning crime that he had set himself to elucidate.

He arose to his fee, and nodded towards Jem.

"All right, Jem," he said. "I believe every word you have told me, and we'll call our little deal quits now: for if I was of assistance to you, you have been the same to me."

He turned towards the door, and Jem held out his hand.

"Where are yer goin', guv'nor?" he asked.

A grim smile flashed across Sexton Blake's lips.

"I'm going on the same errand as you went some time ago, Jem," he said. "I am going to look up Professor Kew!"

"I wish I could come with yer, guv'nor," Jem muttered. "I've got a score ag'in that 'ound that I'd like ter pay back!"

"I think all scores against Francis Kew will be settled before very long," the quiet, steady tones of the detective returned. "But you cannot come with me just now, Jem; this is a game that I must play alone."

He passed out of the chamber, closing the door behind him, and hurried down the stairs. A glance at his watch as he passed into a wider thoroughfare told Blake that it was now almost seven o'clock.

A taxi carried him back to Baker Street, and he reached there shortly before eight.

"No sign of Tinker yet?" he said to the landlady as he entered.

"No, drat the young scamp!" The landlady was never under any delusions so far as Tinker was concerned. They were both very good friends at heart, but the garrulous old dame always pretended to look upon Tinker as a creature born to trouble. "I should give 'im a good talkin' to, sir, when he comes back, if I was you."

Blake went into his bed-room, and as he changed, the fate of his young assistant began to obtrude itself.

"I shouldn't be a bit surprised if Tinker has got on to this matter," he thought; "it is just like him to stumble over something of the kind, and, by heavens, if he has crossed swords with Kew, his long absence suggests that he has had the worst of it!"

This, decision only strengthened Sexton Blake's determination to seek out Kew at once. There were several places where he knew he might find his man.

He telephoned first to St. Cyr's, and, without giving his name, received the information that Professor Kew had left there early in the evening, but was expected to return again.

It was, therefore, the flat in Jermyn Street that Blake made-up his mind to visit. Francis Kew in his bold way had never made any attempt to conceal his address.

From Baker Street to Jermyn Street is but a step, and as Blake halted on the opposite side of the pavement, he noted that the windows on the second floor—the floor in which Kew's chambers were situated—were lighted. A feeling of satisfaction came down on Sexton Blake as he crossed the street, and, entering the quiet doorway, made his way up the stairs.

His first knock on the door of the chambers was not answered; but he heard a rustle such as a newspaper might have made, as someone moved it.

He knocked a little louder, and then slow footfalls came to his ears, and a moment later the door was opened cautiously.

Blake had expected to see the little wizened shape of Professor Kew, but it was a tall, thin figure which stood in the gap of the door.

Stepping forward quickly Blake was inside the room before the man at the door was able to realise his intentions.

As he entered the detective glanced at the face, and with a quick thrill of satisfaction, recognised it at once.

It was the haggard, pallid features of Fordyce Dykes that he was looking into.

"Professor Kew is not here just now," Dykes began.

Blake sauntered into the chamber and coolly seated himself in a chair. Dykes did not notice that the chair which the detective occupied was so placed that Blake would be the first to reach the door, for the tall man had followed him into the room now, and was leaning against the desk.

"I wanted to see Professor Kew, but that can wait," said Blake quietly; "as a matter of fact, I also came to try and see you."

"To see me! Why?"

Blake's face was stern and set.

"Your name, I believe, is Gilbert Fordyce Dykes?" he began.

He saw the lean figure start and contract, while a furtive look leaped into the hollow eyes.

"It is hardly worth while for you to attempt to deny your identity," Blake went on; "for, as a matter of fact, I saw you on Friday, at Lady Marjory Mountjoy's garden party."

Dykes made a bold effort to recover his nerve, and partly succeeded.

"Admitting that I am whom you say I am," he said, "I quite fail to see why you have troubled yourself to come here in search of me."

He was doing his best to preserve a calm front, but Blake saw the thin fingers folding and unfolding, and he knew that the man was fighting hard to retain his composure.

"You may understand a little better, Mr. Dykes," he said, "when I tell you that my name is Sexton Blake, and I am a detective. I have been engaged by Lady Marjory to try and trace the whereabouts of the jewellery that was stolen from her garden party."

Dykes was leaning heavily against the desk now, and on his forehead, a couple of beads of sweat were standing.

"I—I did not know that anything had been stolen," he began.

Blake leaned forward.

"Oh, yes, you do!" he said, in an inflexible tone. "You know that you and your confederate carried out the trick with the duplicate ambulance. It was a cunning enough ruse in its way. But someone who saw you at work has identified you."

A sudden inspiration came to Blake. If Tinker was really in Kew's power, Dykes was certainly bound to know something about it.

A glance at the desk revealed the presence of a tray on which a little pile of tea-things stood. Blake also observed that Dykes was wearing a pair of slippers, and in an ash-tray were a number of cigarette ends, and these little clues, trivial though they appeared, were sufficient to tell Blake that Dykes had been in the chambers for some considerable time, perhaps three or four hours.

"Your informant has been rather rash in his statements," Dykes said, in a slow voice.

"I am quite prepared to trust him," Blake returned, taking advantage of the opening; "more particularly as he chances to be my own assistant, Tinker."

It was a shot in the dark. Just one of those tilts at fortune that one must take now and again if success is to be attained, and it had the desired result.

Dykes straightened up as though he had been shot, and a quick gasp of dismay broke from his lips.

"Tinker!" he repeated. "By heavens! Has he escaped then?"

Blake leaped forward, and his powerful hand closed on Dykes's arm.

"No!" he said. "Tinker has not escaped. But, by heavens, if you do not tell me where he is, you'll be in Vine Street before half an hour is passed!"

There was no mistaking the meaning in the detective's voice, and Dykes stood rigid and mute.

"Arrested!" he muttered. "But you cannot do that. What is the charge?"

"Theft, and—perhaps murder," said Blake, in his low voice. "And your accomplice, Francis Kew will soon be with you."

"You—you know that as well?"

It seemed as though Dykes had crumbled up now, for his clothes hung about him in loose folds, and his haggard face was ashen.

"I know much more than that," said Blake. "I know that you are simply a tool in the hands of the cleverest scoundrel in London; I know that whatever part you played was a minor one, and behind you was that bloodless vulture of a man."

He looked at Dykes for a moment.

"Francis Kew has always chosen his tools well," he said, "and has always taken care that he should have a loophole of escape. Can't you see that he has made an absolute tool of you, man? What part has he played? What risk has he taken?"

"None—none—" Dykes broke out, with a swift, indrawn breath. "I've known that all along. By heavens, I'm almost glad that you have come here to arrest, me, ever since yesterday afternoon I've lived in a perfect torment!"

He swung round, his face working convulsively.

"Kew had a hold on me," he said; "he knew that I—I was wanted by the police, and I only bought his silence by consenting to do what

he asked me to do. But, by heavens, Mr. Blake, when I—I met Lady Marjory—we used to go to school together, when we were little kiddies," he went on, his voice faltering—"I always knew that she was too good for me; but she knows that I have always loved her. I was never really fit to black her boots, and I knew it. But she—she always stood up for me, and was kind to me to the very end. Then yesterday, when I met her and knew what I was there for, to rob her and her guests, I tell you, sir, I felt the meanest cur that ever breathed!"

The sloping shoulders were squared suddenly, and the head lifted back.

"But, by heavens, I've done with it!" Dykes broke out, "If I am to die in a convict cell, then I will die there. But I'll be Francis Kew's tool no longer!"

He dropped into a chair, and, removing his slippers, began to lace up his boots. A paroxysm of coughing stopped the proceeding for a moment, and Blake saw the red stain on the white handkerchief as Dykes slid it into his pocket again.

The detective would have been more than human had he not felt a quick stir of compassion run through him, and his eyes were just a little softer as they glanced at the lean, thin figure.

He, of course, was already aware of how Kew had got into touch with Dykes, and now as he looked at the man on whom it seemed as though death had already placed its mark, a swift suspicion of the truth came to Blake.

In the past, Francis Kew had always chosen his accomplices cunningly, so cunningly, indeed, that Blake, despite the fact that he was aware of Kew's criminality, had never been able to bring evidence against the alert-brained rogue.

"By heavens, that man must be a cold-blooded fiend!" the detective thought. "For I know why he has chosen you now. His skill as a surgeon told him that you were practically

doomed to die. No doubt he hoped that death might intervene if ever it came about that you should have to give evidence against him."

He had moved away from the desk now, and a moment later Dykes arose to his feet.

"I am going to try to right a wrong that I have done, Mr. Blake," the tall man said, in a steady voice; "and if you came here to arrest me, I hope you will delay that until I have completed my task."

He stepped towards the door, lifting his hat and coat from a small stand that stood against the wall.

"I know where your assistant is lying," he went on, "and I want you to come with me to release him. After that, I will take you to Kew's house and make him deliver up the Jewellery."

The haggard eyes stared at Blake for a moment. "Can you trust me to do that?" he ended. "I know that I have forfeited all claims, but I— once was a gentleman, and I give you my word of honour, tattered and tarnished though that honour may be, that I will go with you to whatever police-station you choose to select, as soon as I have done these two things. Will you come, Mr. Blake?"

The detective inclined his head, and together the two men passed out of Kew's chambers and went down the stairs.

THE EIGHTH CHAPTER
KEW DRIVES A HARD BARGAIN.

IT was between nine and ten o'clock on Saturday evening that the vulture-faced professor, leaving the quiet hospital to which Tinker had been carried, made his way slowly back to the West End.

There was a grim smile on the lean, evil visage, and as the little wizened shape paced along with bird-like steps, Francis Kew had the aspect of one who is very well satisfied with himself.

He had arranged his scheme with the diabolical cunning characteristic of him. He was consulting-surgeon to that quiet hospital, and it was for that reason that he had selected it. He knew that the curious condition in which Tinker lay would baffle the house-surgeon of the institution, and he had relied on the fact of his calling him in to give his expert opinion.

Matters had panned out just exactly as he had hoped, and as the reader is already aware, Kew had given his opinion that an operation on the head was necessary. He had hinted that the paralysis, or coma, in which the lad lay was due to some internal factor, probably a bone pressing against the brain.

He knew, also, that such an operation is always attended with tremendous risk, and the odds were that Tinker would never recover from it.

"But I will have nothing to do with it," Kew muttered. "No one can point a finger at me, and even the susceptible Dykes, should he ever come to hear about it, will not be able to say that I took an active part in the affair."

His cold visage wrinkled into an evil smile.

"It is murder by proxy," said Francis Kew. "An unusual crime, I should think."

He did not hurry," for he knew that there was plenty of time for him to reach St. Cyr's. There would be at least an hour's delay in the other hospital before the operation began, and Kew only desired to be at St. Cyr's at the actual time that the operation in the other institution would take place.

It was just an additional alibi, an extra precaution in the event of any inquiries being made.

It was a quarter past ten when he turned into the quiet side-street in which the great hospital was situated, and he entered the wide hall, passing through it and making his way towards his own room.

He always walked with a noiseless pace, and his advent was not observed by the porter in his small office.

Kew reached the door of his room, and, in an absent-minded way, turned the knob and entered. It was only when he noted that the room was lighted, and two figures arose at his entry, that the stooping figure straightened up suddenly, and a low exclamation broke from his lips.

With a quick movement, one of the figures had slid across the room, and, a moment later, the man was between Kew and the doorway.

It was Dykes who had first caught the professor's eye. He was seated in the armchair close to Kew's small desk. The lean-jowled surgeon shot a quick, penetrating glance at Dykes; then, turning his head sharply, he glanced over his shoulder at the figure leaning against the closed door.

A thin, quick breath came from the professor's lips.

"Ah!"

It was only a monosyllable, but it suggested much.

Dykes saw the wizened figure tauten, as though Kew was calling on all his resources. For it was Sexton Blake who was facing the criminal, and the glance that these two ancient enemies exchanged was like the signal that marks the opening of a battle.

"I'm rather surprised to see Mr. Blake in the company of this gentleman," said Kew, his face dark with suspicion. "I take it that it means trouble for myself?"

"You're not far wrong, Kew," said Blake. "I think I have cornered you at last."

"Indeed!"

"Yes, I know the share you took in the robbery at Lady Marjory Mountjoy's garden-party. The man who was your tool has found it wiser to take himself out of your power."

It was an evil, malicious stare that Kew flashed in the direction of Dykes, but the haggard face of the tall, thin man did not change. Dykes was resting back in the chair, with his legs crossed and his arms folded over his chest. He made no attempt to enter into the conversation, evidently content to leave it in the hands of Blake.

"So you've cornered me, have you?" said Kew. "That sounds very pleasant!"

"Not so very pleasant for you," Blake returned, eyeing the cool villain calmly. "In a few minutes you'll be arrested, and Scotland Yard will deal with your case."

Kew glanced at the clock above the mantelpiece. It was exactly a quarter of eleven.

"Well, if you really mean to arrest me," he said, his face a mask that hid the sinister thought in his brain, "I don't suppose there's any immediate hurry, is there? I have one or two things to do—hospital work, you know—several diet-sheets to be prepared. You can spare me a quarter of an hour, I suppose?"

It was quick instinct that told Sexton Blake that there was something behind this coolly-voiced demand.

Francis Kew crossed the chamber, and Blake watched him like a cat watching a mouse. When the surgeon reached his desk Blake nodded towards Dykes.

"I want you to search that man," he said slowly. "See that he has no weapon about him."

Kew shrugged his shoulders and came to a halt, raising his hands above his head.

"Search away, my dear fellow!" he said; but his bead-like eyes blazed with a smouldering fury as Dykes, rising to his feet, obeyed Blake's request.

But Dykes's search was fruitless, beyond a few odds and ends. There was no weapon of any kind on Kew.

"You may sit at your desk now," said Blake, "but I want you to keep your hands above it. Anything you do you must do openly."

A sneer lifted Kew's thin lips as he seated himself.

"You don't think that I would attempt to kill either of you?" he said.

Blake's eyes hardened.

"Oh, no; it's not that I fear," he returned significantly.

Kew's curious cackling laugh broke out.

"Oh, I see!" he said. "You are afraid that I might commit suicide; but you need have no fear of that. I'm not nearly tired of life yet, and I assure you I find great pleasure in it."

His cool, easy bearing made a profound impression on Dykes. The tall man crossed to the mantelpiece, and, leaning on it, watched the wizened figure as it bent over the desk.

Kew drew a number of slips of paper towards him, and, dipping his pen into the ink, he began to mark out the various charts. Anyone watching him might have thought it was just an ordinary scene that was taking place, but it was really cloaking what was little else than an intense drama.

As a matter of fact, Kew had simply adopted the plan of marking the charts in order to gain time. He knew that he was in a tight corner—the tightest that he had ever been in—and his shrewd, lightning-like brain studied the problem over, trying to find the best way out of his difficulty.

Five minutes passed; then Kew, after a glance at the clock, leaned back.

"You are not of the type that one would care to make a bargain with, Blake," he said; "but still, I'm willing to make a proposal to you."

"I want no dealings with you!" Blake returned swiftly.

Kew shrugged his shoulders.

"That was the answer I expected," he returned. "Still, I think you might hear me out."

Dykes flashed a look at Blake and half inclined his head.

It was against Blake's wish to enter into any sort of conversation with the cunning criminal, yet something urged him to listen to what Kew had to say.

"I have no doubt you've got some plan at the back of your head," he said. What is it?"

Kew's thin fingers folded together on the palms as the hands lay on the desk. That was the only sign that the wizened man gave to indicate the tenseness of the moment. He was just hazarding a last throw with Fate, and his liberty depended on his success.

"The jewellery that Mr. Dykes and I collected," he began, "is quite safe, and I am prepared to return that." He nodded towards Fordyce Dykes. "And by doing so, of course, I clear this gentleman; for, unless I am very much mistaken, neither Lady Marjory nor Sir Arthur are very anxious to go on with the matter."

Blake did not know at the time that Francis Kew was a member of the committee, and it was through that that the vulture-faced surgeon had gained his information, so far as Lady Marjory was concerned.

"I cannot answer for what Lady Marjory may do," said Blake.

"Of course not," Kew returned. "I am quite content to let the decision rest with her."

He leaned forward slightly.

"As a matter of fact," he said, "I have foreseen something like this. I doubted my amiable accomplice here. Dykes is ready a criminal by accident, but not by instinct. I was afraid that he might turn at the last, and I have arranged that as soon as I am arrested the ambulance, with its contents, will be delivered by special messenger to Lady Marjory."

His sallow face twitched slightly.

"With all due deference to you, Blake," he said, "I doubt very much if you will be able to get Lady Marjory or her husband to make a charge against me—especially as I shall certainly see to it that Dykes takes his place along with me in the dock."

Blake hardly needed to be reminded of that fact, for his interview with Lady Marjory in the morning, and the information that he had subsequently received from Clarice Tremaine, had convinced him that, no matter what might happen, neither Lady Marjory nor her husband would appear to prosecute.

"It was very well thought out, Kew," he said; "but I think that I may be able to dispense with Lady Marjory's evidence. You see, I, personally, have an interest in the case." His voice took a grimmer note. "For among the booty that you stole was an article belonging to myself. I, therefore, alone, can appear in the part of a prosecutor."

It was a distinct hit, and it revealed itself in the quick twitching that came to the long, lean fingers on the desk.

"Very well," said Kew. "It is now my turn to bargain with you."

"You will find that a hard task," said Blake.

Kew's voice took a vibrating note.

"Have you any idea what has happened to Tinker?" he asked.

Dykes started, an action which did not escape the observation of Kew.

"I have no doubt but what my friend here took you to the empty stores," he said mockingly. "But you did not find Tinker there."

"Do you mean to say that you have removed him to somewhere else?" Dykes broke out. "I thought he had escaped."

Kew glanced up at the clock. It wanted five minutes to eleven!

With a dramatic gesture, the professor arose to his feet.

"I want to tell you something, Sexton Blake," he said, pointing at the clock. "In five minutes from now, unless you agree to my proposal, the boy whom you know as Tinker, will be as near to death as ever human being came!"

"Yon infernal scoundrel!" Dykes broke out, making a quick rush forward. "You promised me that there would be nothing of that, you promised that you would not injure him in any way!"

He was close to the thin, tense figure now, and for a moment the two men glared into each other's eyes.

"I have not broken my promise," Kew said sharply. "I said that I, personally, would not touch him, and neither will I! He is not in my hands, nor is he in the hands of any accomplice of mine, but I swear to you that in less than five minutes he will be close to the Valley of the Shadow!"

"There was no mistaking the intense earnestness in the terrible voice. Blake, despite his iron nerve, felt his heart contract suddenly.

There was no being in the world that the detective loved so well as that keen-eyed, merry-faced waif of the streets that he had made his assistant.

"Kew's vulture-face was set in a hard, grim expression, and it came to Blake that the man was speaking the truth.

"Five minutes!" said Francis Kew. "That is all the time you have left to decide in. You must either choose to let me go free or you can call in the police. But if you do the latter, remember that you are signing your assistant's death-warrant!"

"You unspeakable brute!" the tall, haggard-faced man broke out again. "Where is he? What have you done to the lad?"

"That has nothing to do with you, Dykes," Kew said. "The matter is not in your hands. It is Mr. Blake who has to decide."

He glanced again at the detective.

"I know that you have a big grudge against me," he went on calmly; "and so far as this case is concerned the odds of victory are distinctly with you." A spasm contracted the vulture-face for a moment. "You see already what I have to do; return the jewellery and even forgo my revenge on you and your assistant. If I do go free, it is ,with empty hands, and that is a very poor reward after all my work."

He certainly spoke the truth. Sexton Blake had the whip-hand, but there was always the case of Francis Kew himself to consider. Blake felt that he would have given all he possessed to corner the cunning-brained rogue. Yet—

"You have only four minutes now," said Kew.

A deep breath escaped from the detective's lips. He would have sacrificed anything, even his own life, but he felt that his own personal enmity against this man should not stand in the way of saving Tinker.

Many times and often had the youngster made great sacrifices for the sake of his beloved master. Tinker's devotion to Blake was the dearest thing that Blake had in life.

"I only want your word, Blake," said Kew; "and it will only cover this case. Should we cross swords again we will meet on level terms as usual."

Dykes turned to Blake. "For Heaven's sake agree, man!" he breathed. "Don't risk that, poor youngster's life for the sake of revenge on this dastard!"

"And I have one other offer to make to you," said Kew, in a slow, cynical tone. "If you do agree to my proposal, and you find out later that Tinker was not in danger, I am willing that you

should send the police here at once and have me arrested."

He waved his hand around the quietly-furnished room.

"I am not difficult to find," he said, "and I can assure you I'm not going to hide myself now. When we meet, Blake, we meet in the open, you on one side of the law and I on the other."

Dykes was close to Blake now, and he was looking into the grim, intent face of the detective.

"Don't hesitate for Heaven's sake," he breathed. "After all, that cur is right. He loses everything that he tried for, and you can give him his liberty for a little time longer."

"Time flies!" said Kew, in a thin, warning voice.

With an effort Blake, choked back the desire that had mastered him; and, striding up to the table, he looked into the vulture face.

"I agree to your terms, Francis Kew," he said. "Now, where is Tinker?"

Kew had been standing motionless during that momentous interview. But now, with a swift run, he crossed the room and reached a telephone fixed in the wall.

"Quick, put me on the exchange," he said.

There was a moment's pause, then Kew gave a number.

"Is that Margray Hospital?"

Dykes and Blake leaned forward to listen to the thin voice:

"I want you to go to Doctor Randolff at once. Yes—yes! I know he's in the operating theatre, but I'm Professor Kew, of St. Cyr's, and I find now that I made a mistake—"

"Heavens, what does it mean?" Dykes whispered.

"—the patient that I examined this evening, and who is now in the operating theatre must not be operated upon. Tell Dr. Randolff that I am coming up at once, and that he must not touch the patient until I arrive. Hurry up, now, and I will wait until you return!"

Unable any longer to contain himself Dykes flung himself across the room.

Kew had moved slightly away from the telephone now, but was still holding the receiver to his ear.

"What do you mean? Who is it that you are referring to?" Dykes broke out.

The vulture face turned to him.

"The patient I am referring to is Tinker," he said; "and when the porter of the hospital returns I shall know whether I have been too late or not!"

"You—you mean to say that it was Tinker who was going to be operated upon?" Dykes said, in a horrified tone.

The bead-like eyes of the professor glinted.

"That is so," he returned. "And, ss you see, I took no active part in it. Now stand back, and let me listen. I may have been too late."

At his words, Dykes staggered back a couple of paces, then a tense, grim silence fell on the room.

Suddenly a whirring noise was heard, and the silvery bell in the little clock on the mantelpiece chimed out the hour of eleven.

THE NINTH CHAPTER

THE END OF FORDYCE DYKES.

RIGID and motionless, yet with every nerve on the alert, Tinker lay on the operating-table, his eyes fixed on the glaring light above. There was a death-like silence in the quiet theatre, and the lad could hear the steady breathing of the little group of students gathered around the table.

The mental agony that the youngster went through then was such as he had never experienced before. He could not speak, could not move foot nor head, yet he knew all that was going on around him.

He could hear quite distinctly the hissing of the steam disinfecting kettle, and at last the shadow of the surgeon fell across him, and he saw the bearded face looming above him.

In an agony of despair the lad waited, and it seemed to him as though his heart was leaping convulsively in his breast.

A moment passed and then another, and Tinker's whirling brain which had now given way to the intense mental strain, began to clear slightly.

"Why didn't the man commence?"

The youngster felt as though he could not endure another moment of that awful agony. He felt as though his life was going out from under the terrible strain.

Something like a film had come over his eyes, as though from a great distance, he heard a voice.

The film cleared from his eyes and he noted then that the surgeon was no longer leaning over him.

"Go and see who that is!"

Tinker recognised the deep voice of Doctor Randolff. Someone moved from the side of the table and Tinker heard a door open.

A confused murmur of voices came to the youngster as he lay there beneath the glare of the light. Then, footfalls sounded close to the operating table, and a strange voice came to Tinker's ears.

"An urgent message from Professor Kew, sir," the voice said. "He—he does not want you to operate now—"

Tinker felt as though he was sinking into unconsciousness, and he strained his ears to hear the rest of the words.

"He—he is coming along."

A merciful oblivion came down on the youngster then, and he heard no more."

Tinker had fainted!

The message which Doctor Randolff had received sent a little sensation around the group of students. There was no attempt on the part of the surgeon, to gainsay the order. Francis Kew's reputation as a surgeon was too great for that, and professional etiquette prevented the lesser skilled surgeon from making any remark.

A couple of attendants came forward, and Tinker was wheeled back to the quiet ward where the nurse on duty took charge of him.

About half-past eleven a taxi-cab drove up to the hospital and from it two men emerged. They were Sexton Blake and Dykes and, after stating their business to the porter, they were led into the private room of Doctor Randolff.

What transpired there was never revealed, but some five or six minutes later, the surgeon with his two visitors behind him, entered the ward in which Tinker was lying.

Without a word to the nurse the surgeon went up to the young assistant's cot, and drawing a small sealed packet from his pocket, he loosened the wrappings and opened the box.

Lying snugly in a roll of antiseptic wool was a small hypodermic syringe. The plunger had been drawn, out to its full extent, and as the surgeon lifted the instrument its weight told him it was filled to its full extent.

He bent over the lad, and Blake and Dykes were not able to see what he did, but a few minutes later he straightened up and Blake caught sight of the syringe. The little knob of the plunger had been forced home now, and the injection, whatever it was, had been safely administered.

It was Francis Kew who had handed Blake that packet with a sealed note to deliver to Doctor Randolff.

Dykes came forward till he was close to the foot of the cot, and there was a strained, anxious look on the haggard face as it stared down at the motionless one of the lad stretched out on the cot.

For it seemed to Gilbert Fordyce Dykes as though Tinker was dead, so rigid and motionless was the figure.

The moments passed slowly, each of them seeming an eternity for the watchers. Then, suddenly, one arm of the youngster was raised.

An articulate sound came from Dykes' lips, but a quick motion from the surgeon made him control his feelings again.

Slowly the hand went up to the head, and was pressed against the lips and brow. Then, with an obviously painful effort, Tinker raised himself until he was resting on his left elbow.

His eyes travelled first to the lean figure at the foot of the cot, then to the bearded face of the surgeon. A spasm of pain seemed to run across the features for a moment, then Tinker's eyes went on and fell on the clean-shaven, intent face of his master.

"Guv'nor!" Tinker broke out, the dawnings of intelligence coming back to his face.

He stretched out his right arm, and a moment later Blake was by his side. The way in which the detective wrapped his arms around the youthful body, and hugged Tinker close to him was a revelation to Dykes.

He had always looked upon Sexton Blake as a curiously unemotional man, but it was evident that the detective had depths of feelings that he kept hidden from the outward view.

"It's all right, Tinker," Blake said, in a husky voice.

"Oh, guv'nor, I—I've had such a rotten dream!"

The lad had wrapped his arm around Blake's neck and was looking round the ward.

"And I ain't too sure that it was a dream," he went on, in a slow, uncertain voice. "Get me out of this, guv'nor, as quick as you can. I don't like the look of the place a bit."

The bearded surgeon came closer to Blake. "It is quite safe to remove him if you like, Mr. Blake," he said.

"Very well, then, we'll do it," Blake returned.

There was something pathetic in the way Tinker tried to help Blake and Dykes as they dressed him. The lad was obviously still weak and suffering from the terrible strain that had been placed upon him.

It was on Blake's arm that Tinker leaned as he left the hospital, and the trio entered the taxi cab to make their way down to Baker Street.

It was long after midnight before Tinker was tucked up in the sheets of his own bed and sleeping quietly. Blake and Dykes went into the detective's study, and when they found themselves alone a silence came down on them.

Blake had dropped into his easy chair, and had pulled out a briar pipe from its case.

"Help yourself to a smoke, Dykes," he said, indicating a box of cigars.

The face of Gilbert Fordyce Dykes was set in a grim, determined look.

"No, thanks, Blake," he returned. "I—I think if you have finished with me now, I—I'll go!"

Blake lighted his pipe before he replied.

"There's a spare bed," he said.

Dykes seemed to find if difficult to speak.

"No, I—By heavens, you're too good to me, Blake! I'm not worthy of it. You seem to forget that I am nothing else but a criminal, and that only the slenderest of chances prevented me from being in prison at this very minute."

"I never judge a man's character," Blake returned. "How anyone spends his life is nothing to me. It is quite true that you have been a criminal, and I do not even ask you how you came to seek the shady ways of life. But you did your best to help me, Dykes, and it is certain that had it not been for you, I should never have been able to find Tinker."

Dykes face went a shade paler.

"I will never forget that scene," he said. "It was the chancest moment that I have ever lived."

He looked at Blake suddenly.

"'You had to give your promise to Francis Kew," Dykes murmured, "and you cannot go back on that. But, by heavens, he extracted no promise from me!"

The tall, emaciated body was drawn to its full height.

"I feel that such a man moving about in London is a danger to the people," Dykes went on in a slow tone. "I feel that—" He came to a pause suddenly as though afraid of what he was going to say; then, striding across the room, he held out his hand to Blake. "Good-bye, Mr. Blake," said Gilbert Fordyce Dykes, "I don't suppose I shall ever meet you again, but I will never forget what you tried to do for me."

There was a certain grim determination in the tense tones that told Blake that it would be useless to attempt to argue with him.

Dykes had evidently made up his mind to do something, and Blake felt that he could almost make a shrewd guess as to what it was.

He arose to his feet and shook hands with Dykes. Then he escorted the tall figure to the front-door of the house, and stood on the step watching Dykes until the man had vanished.

"I wonder if I have done right?" Blake, thought, as he made his way back to his rooms again. "I think I know what is at the back of that man's mind. He does not mean to let Francis Kew get away so easily as he has done so far."

With his pipe between his teeth, and his hands clasped behind his back, Blake spent the better part of half an hour striding up and down his study.

"I believe I was right in sacrificing my hold on that rogue for the sake of Tinker," he decided, "although I don't believe I'd have done it for anybody else in the world. Kew will return the jewellery all right; he is too cunning to let me have a chance of going for him in that respect. It is a victory to me, as he says, but it is not a complete victory, and the personal feud between Kew and I has still to be settled."

He halted by the grate to knock the ashes out of his pipe.

"And it seems as though Dykes has also a grudge against Kew," Blake thought, half aloud, "I wonder how that is going to settle itself?"

He little-dreamed of the curious happening that was to mark the close of that memorable case.

For Blake was right when he had decided that Dykes was off in search of revenge. All the tall man's energy seemed to be centred on the one person, now, and that was the lean, wizened professor.

§

Through the empty streets of London Dykes strode like a shadow of doom.

On and on he paced until he reached the East End. He had walked the better part of six-miles, but the burning desire for revenge in his heart seemed to give a fictitious strength to his limbs.

Blake had told Dykes of the scene that had taken place in No. 6, Doggel's Alley, and it was towards that quarter that Dykes turned now. He wanted a man to help him, and he knew that he would have to seek no further than Jem.

The sparsely-furnished chamber on the second floor was in darkness when Dykes pushed the door aside and entered it, but the splutter of the match as he lighted it brought a bulky figure up in the bed, and the steel rim of a revolver-muzzle was thrust forward sharply.

"All right, Jem," Dykes said in his quiet voice, "I want a word with you!"

With easy nonchalance he crossed the room, paying no attention to the revolver, and lighted the gas.

"So yer 'ave come back, 'ave yer?" Jem broke out. "Mebbe yer found it didn't pay yer to git mixed up with that evil-faced skunk?"

"I never expected it would pay me, Jem. I was forced to do what he told me, and now, by heavens, I'm out for revenge!"

"Revenge?"

Jem's bulky figure was out of the bed at once, and his face was glaring into the haggard one of Dykes.

"Is that straight? Are yer goin' to 'ave a cut at Kew?"

"I am," said Dykes, "and I wanted someone to help me. I wanted a man who is a skilled housebreaker, and I couldn't think of anybody better than you. Besides, unless I'm very much mistaken, you'd like to get your own back on Kew yourself?"

The heavy jowl of the burglar thrust itself out suddenly, and his sullen features were suffused with a mottled rage.

"I should just think I do," Jem muttered in a savage undertone. "Wot's yer game, Dykes? I'm yer man whatever it is!"

"Oh, it's an easy game," said Dykes. "I'm going to Kew's house in Maida Vale, where he always lives, and then I'm going to get him to sign a confession admitting his robbery and the attempted murder. He'll sign that, or by heavens, I'll shoot him for the dog he is!"

"It'd be better if yer shot him first," said Jem.

Dykes wheeled on him sharply.

"I'll carry this out my own way," he said. "All I want is to get that confession and hand it to someone. I'll then give Francis Kew twenty-four hours to get out of England, and if ever he shows his face here again, he'll be arrested!"

"It ain't enough!" Jem said savagely. "It ain't half enough!"

"It's enough for my purpose," said Dykes. "I want to see him out of this country a ruined, known criminal. If I do that, I'll have done a little service in my life."

He arose to his feet.

"And now, Jem, what is it to be? Yes, or No?"

Jem began hurriedly to dress himself.

"It's 'yus!'" the hoarse murmur came.

A belated taxi had an unexpected fare in the shape of Dykes and his companion, and it was shortly after five o'clock in the morning that they stepped out of the vehicle and made their way to the quiet villa at the end of the little side-street where Francis Kew lived.

There was no sign of daylight yet, and presently, when they reached the little line of railings that divided the front garden of Kew's villa from the street, Dykes came to a halt and motioned to his companion.

Jem slid over the railings with a dexterous movement of his heavy body, and a moment later he was blotted out against the wall of the house.

Standing in the shadow thrown by one of the trees that stood at regular intervals along the edge of the pavement, Dykes kept watch.

The tall man was beginning to feel just a little weary now; there was a cold feeling about his limbs, and once as he stood there he had to clutch at the tree while the dark street swam around him. It was not by any means the first time that Dykes had had one of these fainting fits; it was the dread sign of a weakened heart.

"S-s-st!"

A faint hissing sound came from the garden, and with an effort Dykes recovered control of his weakened limbs again.

Peering into the garden he saw the shady figure of Jem beckoning to him. Leaving the shadow of the tree, the tall man slid over the rails of the garden, and, stepping noiselessly now, reached the bulky shadow of his companion.

"I've opened a winder at the side," said Jem. "I don't know wot room it lets inter, but I suppose you knows."

"At the side," Dykes repeated thoughtfully. "Yes, I think I know. That must be Kew's study. It leads out into a passage on the left of the stairs. All right, Jem, you can wait until I return."

Jem extended his arm, and Dykes felt something cold pressed into his fingers.

"Dunno if yer've got one or not, but this is a dandy," told Jem.

The cold fingers of Dykes closed around the butt of the revolver, then, wheeling round, the tall figure went round the angle of the wall and vanished.

His curiosity urged Jem into a course which he knew was against the wishes of his companion. The burglar did his best to stay where he was, but his feelings proved too strong for him, and presently he slid around the wall and darted down the side of it, reaching the opened window.

Dykes had already disappeared, and, kicking off his shoes, Jem drew himself through the window, dropping lightly into the dark room. He had to feel his way across the chamber, moving very cautiously step by step.

He followed the wall until he reached a doorway, and found that the door was open.

As he stepped into the passage Jem saw that the light from an outside lamp-post was shining through the coloured glass in the panels of the front hall. A movement ahead made Jem peer a little closer. As his eyes grew accustomed to the half light, he noted the tall figure of Dykes.

It was in a half-crouching position, with the hands clutching tightly at the top of the banisters of the stairs.

Jem heard a few quick breaths sound, then suddenly the tall figure slid away from its support, and with a faint thud it fell at full length on the tiled floor of the hall.

With an exclamation of horror Jem darted forward, and dropped on his knees by the side of the long figure. Stooping down, the burglar raised the head and listened.

There was no breath issuing from the lips, and the limp tilt of the head told Jem what had happened.

Gilbert Fordyce Dykes was dead.

At this sudden and terrible end to their adventure, Jem found himself kneeling for a moment unable to move.

"He's gorn!" the burglar muttered. "No doubt abart that."

Jem himself had been a witness of the death of Dykes, and he knew that it was no outside agency that had accomplished it. Both Jem and Jerry were aware that their gentleman companion had never been far from the borderland of death. His emaciated frame and the terrible cough that racked his body now and again were plain indications of that.

It was the tense excitement following the long exertion that had put an end to a wasted life.

There was a grim mockery in the fact that Dykes had died at the foot of the stairs that led to the bed-room of the man whom he meant to have his revenge upon.

It came to Jem presently that it would be madness for him to remain there, or even to allow his companion to do so. The burly fellow picked up the limp body, and its lightness was a revelation to Jem.

"Poor old Dykes!" he said. "He couldn't have been anything more than skin and bone."

How Jem escaped with his burden was only proof of the cleverness of that broad-shouldered burglar. But he did do so, and also succeeded in carrying Dykes back to Doggel's Alley.

§

It was weeks after before Sexton Blake learned the truth of what had happened, and then it was only an accident that sent Jem across his path.

By that time Lady Marjory and her husband had almost forgotten the incident of the robbery; but Blake, knowing that the woman would like to hear the story, visited Lady Marjory later on, and told her what Jem had said.

There were tears in the woman's eyes when he finished the tale, and she pressed her handkerchief to her eyes for a moment.

"Poor Gilbert!" she said. "You know, Mr. Blake, I think that he was always aware that death was going to come to him early in life, and that made him the mad, reckless man that he was. But he did do his best to make up for his transgressions, and I think that we can both pray for his peaceful rest."

THE END.

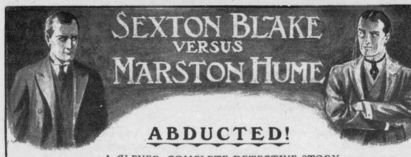

SEXTON BLAKE
VERSUS
MARSTON HUME

ABDUCTED!

A CLEVER, COMPLETE DETECTIVE STORY.

THERE is no doubt whatever that Hume was more than disconcerted by his failure to rid himself finally of Blake, in the case of the Louis Quinze snuffbox.

He had laid his plans carefully, and with great attention to detail, yet Blake had escaped, almost by a miracle, as it seemed; worse still, from Hume's point of view, Colonel Maxwell was undoubtedly in possession of at least some of the essential facts; and Hume knew very well that any chance of another invitation to Lady Molly's was out of the question.

He was far too clever to attempt to disguise to himself the plain truth, that the

One man heard Blake coming, and turned; but, before he could cry out, Blake caught him under the jaw, and he went over into the water with a splash.

miscarriage of his scheme had materially endangered the security of his position. His reputation as one of the leading lawyers of his time, and as a man of wealth and position, remained unassailed. True, any accusation brought against him, unless backed by irrefutable proof, would be laughed to scorn. Yet there were in existence three men who had seen beneath his mask—Bathurst, Colonel Maxwell, and Blake. Whenever he thought of those three he became conscious of a feeling of acute depression and irritation; but, above all, when he thought of Blake, he had a foretaste of a feeling to which hitherto he had been a stranger—and that feeling was fear.

There was no reason on earth for him to touch anything criminal again with so much as his fingertips—he had not even the excuse of lack of means, for he was a wealthy man. Yet he had the criminal instinct rooted deeply in him, and, as Blake had once foretold, having tasted blood, he could not stop. But for all that, his caution and his cunning never deserted him; he was in no way inclined to let Blake find him at a disadvantage, and when he made a move he made it warily, and after due deliberation.

So careful was he that for some little time Blake lost sight of him altogether. Once he saw him at the club for a few moments amongst a crowd of men, and once he got news that he had gone back to his old rooms to live; apart from that, their lives seemed to have diverged, and Blake busied himself with other matters.

It was during this period that John S. Rawn came to take up his abode in England, to escape the tyranny of the Yellow Press, and the belligerent attentions of the men he had ruined in Wall Street.

Rawn was a small-framed, old-young man, who had spent himself in making a colossal fortune. In actual years he was barely fifty; in nerves, appearance, and physical ability he was all of sixty, and had suffered wear and tear at that.

In the making of his fortune many less able men had gone under, and the methods he had used, when hard pressed, might have brought him within the pale of the law in a country less highly civilised than the States. He had managed, however, to escape the law's clutches, or to buy the law, lawyers, and judges, when escape seemed otherwise impossible—in fact, he had bought so extensively that he had made his native country too hot to hold him any longer.

It was this that induced him to come to England, to enjoy rest and peace, and carry on his business mostly by cable.

He bought a large country house, the largest he could find on the market at the moment. He purchased it—park, farms, shooting, and all complete; then he gave it a new name, and some very new furniture, and tried to settle down.

Before he had been there a month he began to receive blackmailing and anonymous letters from angry compatriots; and being of a nervous disposition, he tried to buy Sexton Blake.

Blake's reply was not sympathetic—to be exact, it was a point-blank refusal.

The wording of it caused Mr. Rawn considerable pain. In the first place, he completely failed to understand the reason of Blake's refusal; in the second place, he was convinced that the only man who could ensure his safety was Blake.

His need of protection at this time was particularly great. He was engaged in carrying through a more than usually nefarious deal, disguised as an amalgamation scheme, and he was well aware that there were a certain group of men who would go to pretty well any lengths to prevent the completion of the transaction. If they could once get him into their hands, he knew that he need expect no mercy—by fair means or foul they would compel him to disgorge; and, worse still, his cherished scheme would fall to the ground.

In his extremity he determined to make one final appeal to Blake.

"Dear Sir," he wrote, "In spite of your refusal, I am repeating my request for your services. What I require is very simple. Merely that you should come here and use your skill to ensure my personal safety for a period of seven days— viz., from the 19th to the 26th of December, inclusive. During that time I have to transact some delicate financial operations, and I have reason to know that every effort will be made to curtail my liberty and freedom of action, possibly to endanger my life.

"By the 26th the business referred to should be completed, and the danger will—temporarily, at any rate—cease to exist.

"Should you find yourself able to accede to my request, I shall be glad to agree to any terms you may think suitable."

This letter would in all probability have also found its way into the waste-paper basket, but for one small circumstance.

Glancing through his paper on the morning on which the letter arrived, Blake caught sight of a small advertisement, tucked away unobtrusively in a corner. It was brief and to the point, and read as follows:

"M. L.—Terms agreed to. Payment on delivery of goods. Punctuality imperative."

Blake read this over slowly two or three times, and each time the initials "M. L." attracted him more and more.

There might be thousands of "M. L.'s"— probably were—but he could not get it out of his mind that "M. L." also stood for Mary Leslie, the imaginary tenant of the flat in Tollington Mansions rented by Hume.

Furthermore, the wording of the advertisement itself, and the stress laid on the necessity for punctuality, seemed to him to dovetail in with certain phrases of the letter lying before him. "By the 26th the danger will—temporarily, at any rate— cease to exist," and "punctuality imperative," were by no means incompatible.

He sat back in his chair weighing over the pros and cons. Hume, in his own character, would never dream of appearing in such a matter; but if negotiations were being carried on through the mythical Mary Leslie, Hume, true to his methods, would be able to carry out any plan he had devised, without any of those with whom he was dealing being aware of his identity, and without accomplices, for his guiding rule was to work single-handed.

If there were any connection between the letter and the advertisement, the terms referred to were sure to be very high, and the difficulties big enough to hold out to Hume the prospect of that excitement which he craved for.

After careful consideration, Blake made up his mind to risk an acceptance of Rawn's proposition, and sent him a wire to say so.

That same evening he was ensconced at Burnham Park. He found Mr. Rawn crotchety and irritable, and firmly impressed with one central idea—that everything had its price.

On this point Blake soon undeceived him.

"We may as well understand one another from the first," he said. "Personally speaking, I tell you frankly that I am taking up this case for private reasons of my own, and not for any inducement that you have offered. On the other hand, I will do my best to safeguard you and your interests till midnight on the 26th; after that time our agreement ceases. But I undertake this on the sole condition that you place yourself entirely in my hands, and that I am free to give orders and make arrangements as I choose. If you go back on that, I wash my hands of the whole affair. Now, if you please, I want to see over the house—all over it; also I want to inspect your own private rooms and make any alterations I deem necessary."

Having made everything as secure as he could against a night attempt, he went on to lay down certain stringent rules for Mr. Rawn's movements during the day. Had it been an ordinary case of threats and blackmailing, Blake would have contented himself with a mere general supervision, but he had an instinctive feeling that Hume was the principal factor in the problem, and he mistrusted him more than all the secret societies put together; and, in consequence, took every precaution that seemed advisable.

John Rawn, he found, was an ardent, though rather nervous, motorist; an unathletic man even for his age, with a passion, in his unbusinesslike moments, for open air and English scenery. He drove his own car, a two-seated Zust.

Blake insisted strongly that, so long as his responsibility lasted, Rawn was on no account to go careering about the country without Blake himself as an escort.

In the ensuing five days he saw all that he wanted of the surrounding country, and more. They drove from soon after breakfast till long past dusk, through sleet and occasional snow flurries, and mud galore.

So far all had gone smoothly and uneventfully. Once or twice Blake found himself wondering whether or no the whole thing would prove a mare's-nest, but he never relaxed his precautions for an instant.

On the afternoon of the fifth day, dusk found them at a small village some ten miles from the Park. The Crown Inn, an old-fashioned, picturesque place, was a favourite halt of John Rawn's, and they stopped there to have tea and a warm up.

They were sitting over the big fire in the coffee-room, enjoying their tea and buttered toast, when the waiter came in and asked if one of the gentlemen was a Mr. Blake, because if so he was wanted on the telephone.

"Must be some of the folk up at the Park," said Mr. Rawn. "They know I often look in here about this time. I guess they must want you pretty bad, Blake, to try and rout you out here," he added, and glanced about him rather nervously.

Blake nodded, and went off to the private office where the telephone hung, frowning thoughtfully as he went.

Four or five minutes passed, and then the waiter put his head round the door again.

"Gentleman's compliments, sir," he said to Rawn, who was warming his toes at the fire, "and will you please to drive straight back home at once. He says he'll come on later, and it's urgent."

As has been explained, Rawn was a nervous man by nature, and the message, coming on top of the mysterious telephone call, made him as jumpy as a cat.

Flinging down a coin, and struggling into his coat, he hurried out to the car, and drove off as though all the rascals in the States were at his heels.

Two minutes later Blake re-entered the coffee-room.

"The weather's played the deuce with the wires," he said. "I can't get an intelligible sentence. It's all buzz—burr, and—Hallo!"

He had just reached a position which showed him that Rawn's high-backed chair was vacant.

He sprang to the bell and rang it violently.

"Where's Mr. Rawn, the gentleman who was here with me just now?" he asked the waiter impatiently.

"He's gawn, sir. I give him your message, and he was off like a shot. Seemed a bit upset, too."

"Gone! My message? Quick, man! What did I tell you to say?"

"That he was to go straight back 'ome at once, and that you'd follow 'im, sir."

"Where did I—Oh, never mind! Did he go alone, and how long ago?"

"Not more than two or three minutes, sir. He was quite alone, drivin' 'imself."

Blake dashed out of the place without even waiting to answer, and started running along the road as hard as he could go. That Rawn, by disobeying his explicit orders, and by being taken in by a bogus message, was in imminent danger, he hadn't a doubt. Moreover, Blake was running in a heavy motor-coat, and the car had had time to get a long start.

He had covered the better part of a mile when he fancied he saw a faint glimmer of light ahead, and put on a spurt. Soon the light became a certainty; it was the car's tail-light.

Another sharp spurt and he was abreast of it. The car was tilted over slightly to one side, and two of the tyres were flattened right down. It was pulled up at the extreme edge of the road, and a glance sufficed to show him that it was empty.

A big fur rug lay trailing half over the step, and that was all. Rawn had mysteriously vanished!

Blake snatched the tail-light from its socket, and flashed it round. There were no signs of a struggle visible. The road was quite deserted, and the big head-lights blazed steadily.

Bending down he examined the tyres.

One was ripped for a good three inches—a clean cut with sharp edges—right through inner and outer tubes.

The other had a jagged gash, in which something glistened and sparkled.

He pulled it out. It was a piece of a broken bottle.

The car had skidded before coming to a standstill, but not very badly, and, apart from the tyres, seemed to be uninjured.

He peered over the hedge in the faint hope that, after all, the affair might have been accidental, and that Rawn had been thrown clear; but there was no sign of him.

There remained the road itself to be examined, and, lantern in hand, he set to work to read the story from the tracks as best he could.

Retracing his steps for a hundred yards or so in the direction of the inn, and keeping carefully to the extreme edge of the road, so as not to confuse matters, he began to try to wrest the truth from the muddy, sleet-covered surface.

There were several tracks on the road, too, and he had to decipher them all by the uncertain light of the tail-lamp.

Rawn's car, where he first picked up the marks, was travelling easily and steadily, and the tracks ran smoothly until they came level with a blackthorn bush. At this point they swung erratically outwards into the centre of the road, left the ground altogether for three-quarters of the length of the car itself, and then curved inwards again, as though Rawn had made a desperate effort to right it, or to avoid something coming in the opposite direction. After that the deflated tyres had skidded wildly, and the car had come to a standstill.

Opposite the blackthorn, embedded in the mud on the near side of the road, were a lot of pieces of jagged glass. It was these that had done the damage.

Blake scanned them narrowly, picking up one here and one there.

"It was no accident that placed these here," he muttered to himself. "Humph! Three different types of bottles at least, and the piece of green glass in the tyre makes four. One broken bottle might have been chance; four, all in ugly-looking pieces, spread out, sharp side uppermost, across the near side of the road, are certainly not. The question is: How was Rawn removed from the car?"

He peered about him anxiously, a drizzle of sleet had begun again, and was already blurring the surface. There were footmarks—recent ones—beside the derelict, but a glance told him that they were his own. Another car had also gone by, in the opposite direction—a large car, so far as he could judge from the tracks. It had passed Rawn's, where it stood by the roadside, so closely that the mud-guards of the two must have almost touched, and the wheel-marks were as fresh, if not fresher. The ordinary common courtesy of a motorist should have made the driver of the larger car pull up to see what was wrong; but, so far as Blake could read the road, he had merely slowed down and then swerved outwards again without stopping.

"Proving," said he to himself, "that the beggar knew to a foot where the broken glass was."

Though there was desperate need for hurry, Blake pulled up the collar of his coat, lit a cigarette, and sat on the step of the derelict to marshal his facts in order.

The sequence of them was beginning to be painfully clear, and that the whole thing was Hume's work he felt positive.

Hume had studied Rawn's habits carefully. He would certainly have known that the inn a mile away was one of Rawn's favourite halting-places, and have laid his plans accordingly.

His chief difficulty lay in separating Rawn from Blake. To telephone from the local exchange and purposely render his voice indistinct, so as to cause delay, was a simple and obvious device. Ingenious, too; for Blake would naturally imagine that the call was because of something amiss at the Park. Had done so, in fact.

The next thing was to get Rawn away on some pretext. Going back over the matter, Blake realised how this had been done. Hume was driving a big car—from the Exchange to the inn would have taken him something under a minute. The waiter, though he certainly knew Rawn, was not familiar with either Blake's voice or appearance. Two men of approximate build look very similar to a casual observer when they are wrapped in motor-coats and wearing goggles. Hume, relying on the chance that Blake was still busy trying to get an answer over the telephone, must have stopped his car a few yards from the inn, given the waiter the message which sent Rawn flying out into the trap prepared for him, and instantly driven off again.

There was a branch road almost opposite the entrance, by taking which Hume could have gained the road to the Park half a mile above the trap.

The sight of his head-lights looming in the distance would have driven Rawn, who was somewhat nervous, over on to the side of the road, and, incidentally, over the glass already prepared. Feeling his tyres go, Rawn had naturally brought the car to a standstill as soon as possible; and, as soon as it was stationary, Hume had driven slowly by. He was a powerful man—the cars were within easy arm stretch—and to yank a puny little man out of one and into the other would have been a simple enough job.

After that a blow on the head, a threat even, or a whiff of chloroform, would have prevented Rawn from making any outcry.

So far it was plain sailing, and Blake, puffing at his cigarette, could picture every phase as clearly as if he had been present.

He was perfectly conscious that the minutes were flying by, and that with the passing of each minute Rawn was being taken another half-mile further away. But he realised that the shortest route to finding him again, and keeping his trust, was to sit there quietly and think, instead of rushing aimlessly about and questioning people to prove what he already knew in his heart was the truth.

"Now," he said to himself, lighting a fresh cigarette, "if I were Hume, and if I had Rawn by my side unconscious in the car, my first anxiety would be to get rid of him—to deliver the goods, in fact, with all the expedition possible. Having planned his capture, I should also have planned to hand him over to the people most interested in his whereabouts, at some convenient spot not too far from the scene of the capture itself. I should take care that the spot was isolated, and as far away from any villages or houses as possible, in order to avoid any risk of subsequent identification, and for my own skin's sake, I should have made reasonably sure that the men to whom I handed him over had a feasible scheme for getting him expeditiously out of the country. To get him away by any ordinary steamer route would be, naturally, out of the question. Rawn's enemies have no lack of money to attain their end.

"A small yachting harbour and a privately chartered yacht would be the most convenient type of place. I must get back to the inn."

He hurried back as fast as he could, telephoned to the Park for a big car to be sent down at once in charge of a reliable chauffeur, with another man to take charge of the derelict, and then demanded the largest scale map the inn could produce.

He studied this whilst waiting for the motor. The inn was roughly thirty miles from the nearest coast, and there were four possible places along the coast where a yacht might lie off, all about equally accessible.

The first two—St. Ermins and Seaholme—he ignored. They were watering places of some popularity, and, in his opinion, afforded too much publicity. There remained Wrexford, a

fishing village, and Bexingham, a favourite winter cruising ground, and a well-known place for "laying up." For some twenty miles the same main road served both places; but near the twentieth mile-stone a side road branched off to the right to Bexingham, across Brayton Heath.

The chances in favour of either place seemed about equal, and the whole thing was undeniably a gamble. On the whole, however, Blake thought Bexingham the more likely. There was only one village to pass through after leaving the main road, and the heath, a desolate stretch of country, appealed to him as just the sort of place he would have selected for the handing over of Mr. Rawn.

Just as he had come to this decision, he heard the car pull up outside.

"Bexingham," he said curtly to the chauffeur, as he climbed into the seat beside him. "Let her out all you can."

"The roads are—" began the chauffeur.

"We must risk that," interrupted Blake; and the man nodded.

For the next twenty miles they drove without exchanging a word, Blake leaning forward at intervals to clear the sleet from the glass windshield. Then they swung round to the right, along the heath road.

The big head-lights showed the surface clearly, and suddenly at a point a third of the way across the heath Blake yelled to the man to pull up.

The big car slithered and swerved dangerously, and finally came to rest, panting and throbbing.

Almost before it had stopped, Blake was out of it, and tearing back along the way they had come.

His keen eyes had detected something on the sleet-covered road in the glare of the lights.

He found it sixty or seventy yards in the rear of the car—a crumpled handkerchief, unmarked—and near by he could still just distinguish footprints and half-obliterated wheel marks.

He held the handkerchief to his face; a faint, sickly, sweet smell still clung to it.

The next minute they were off again. The chauffeur had caught the spirit of the chase, and he drove without any regard for speed limits. They rattled into the little main street, and pulled up at the small hotel most frequented by yachting men.

A pool of dirty oil in the roadway told him that he was not far behind.

"Where are the gentlemen who drove up a little while back?" he asked the landlord.

"There was one drove off, sir, after having a drink. T'other three are gone down to the hard." And he grinned. "One of 'em had got a pretty good skinful by the looks of him!"

"What was the man like who drove off ?" asked Blake suddenly.

"Dark, clean-shaven gentleman; same height as you, sir. 'Ad goggles on, and one o' them eye-glass things on a string under his coat. Come in by hisself in a mighty hurry. The others went straight down to the hard; I only glimpsed the backs of them."

Blake uttered an exclamation, and darted out of the place.

Clearly some part of the plan had miscarried, and Hume, instead of parting with his captive on the heath, as he had intended, had been obliged to drive the whole party on to Bexingham.

He raced down to the hard. A hundred yards away he could see a small boat's light dancing over the choppy water; and, at the water's edge, were three men—two standing, one in a huddled heap on the snow. Further out still he could just distinguish a yacht's riding light.

The small boat was travelling fast, and touched the edge of the hard just as Blake got within springing distance.

One man heard him coming, and turned; but, before he could cry out, Blake caught him under the jaw, and he went over into the water with a splash. The second instinctively stooped to rescue his comrade. Blake also stooped, snatched up the limp form of Mr. Rawn, and ran.

He heard the clatter of pursuit behind him; then someone shouted what sounded like an order, and the running feet stopped.

Mr. Rawn was not unconscious when Blake got him back to the inn, but he was deathly sick from fright and the effects of the chloroform combined.

Blake left him to the others to look after, and flew round to the telegraph office. The landlord, a more than usually observant man, had been able to give him a fair description of the car.

There was just a chance, Blake thought, of getting it stopped by wire; for that Hume would make for London he was positive. But the telegraph office was shut, and neither bribes nor threats could persuade anyone to send even a single message. So Blake returned in a very black humour, and as soon as Mr. Rawn had been partly revived, they drove back to Burnham Park, where they found a secretary impatiently awaiting their return with the announcement that a special message had just arrived from Liverpool by the boat train.

As far as Blake was concerned it was a drawn game. He had managed to frustrate the scheme, but Hume had slipped through his fingers just when success seemed within reach. For the rest, he thought Mr. Rawn a most unpleasant person, and felt very much inclined to tell him so.

UNION JACK 2ᴰ

Gilbert
Chester's
masterpiece—
the GNOMID

THRILLS—THRILLS—THRILLS—and SEXTON BLAKE!

No. 1,362.   EVERY THURSDAY.   November 23rd, 1929.

GILBERT CHESTER'S Latest, Greatest Sexton Blake Story.

The Gnomid
By Gilbert Chester

Chapter I
All for a Lady.

FROM the moment when Warrender entered Li Chun's dockside den, he knew his life hung by a thread.

If he had ever doubted, he harboured no illusions as, from a corner of the unsavoury haunt, he watched its patrons through a thick haze of tobacco smoke.

A dirty, ragged figure asprawl in his chair, Warrender lay back with half-closed eyes, apparently asleep and his lids leaden with drink. It was his sole safeguard, his seeming stupefac-

tion. He looked as degraded as the cut-throat crew before him.

Thieves, lascars, Chinks, flamboyant women, race gangsters—they grouped themselves into one big picture of sordid lawlessness.

Scourings of the underworld, all of them. And deadliest of the lot, Li Chun, the squint-eyed Celestial who glided about ministering to the needs of his patrons.

Now and again those oblique eyes of Li Chun's would seek him; and when they did so Warrender shivered. Once a C.I.D. man had penetrated to the interior of this joint—once, and only once. Next day his body had been found in the river.

If Li Chun *knew*—

Warrender shuddered afresh, beneath the dirt and rags. A breath of suspicion, and his fate was sealed.

Yet he stayed on. Feigning drunk, he dared not stir. That would be out of the picture. Then, too, he had his purpose for being here. And he was not a man lightly to be turned from his purpose.

Besides, the drunken young fool opposite interested him. Fuddled with whisky, he stood out from among the crowd, a bizarre figure from another world.

What was he doing here? A man whose grey lounge suit proclaimed Savile Row; whose Oxford accent emerged triumphant over his thick, alcoholic utterances while he argued to a counterblast of profanity!

Doing here? Well, that peroxide blonde at his side accounted for much. Her sort lured a man readily enough to his ultimate undoing. But why had she brought him here? Stranger still, how had Li Chun come to let him past those closely guarded doors? One got more easily into an arsenal.

Puzzled, yet intrigued, Warrender held his breath, while his gaze held the young fool, fascinated.

His every instinct told him that for him things worked rapidly up to a climax.

IT was not till the rat-faced man reached for a bottle that Warrender moved. Then he acted quickly.

As the bottle swung upwards, he lurched from his seat, a wide-chested giant, his sodden stupor flung off like a cloak.

"Hi!"

With a yell he leaped at Rat Face, spilling a lascar in his rush. The bottle missed, splintered on the farther wall. Simultaneously the young exquisite fell back across a table, the drink fumes jolted out of him.

"Oh, would you!"

Warrender's huge fist took the bottle-thrower's jaw as the man jerked a gun from his pocket. Rat Face backed snarling, flung to the wall by a terrific left hook.

For a second he stared at Warrender dazed, bewildered. Then, with an oath, he flipped his gun upwards, and a stab of orange-blue flame scorched Warrender's face.

In answer the giant caught up a chair, flung it full in the man's face.

The rat-faced man went down, shrieking. A second shot snapped out, and a little shower of plaster fell like snow from the ceiling. The bite of a red-hot needle had scored Warrender's ear. Then someone flicked the switch, and the room

went black but for the fierce red stabs of fire vomiting from the gunman's pistol.

Warrender sprang away, ducking as the lead sprayed. In the gloom, a babel of shouts muffled the shooting. Harsh yells—the screams of frenzied women—a tidal wave of humanity that bore over and past him as the foul crew fought frantically for the door and safety.

He went down on his knees, breathless, bruised, and the bullets whistling above him. Then he was up again, charging berserk at the last spurt of flame. Hemmed in, with the doors barred against him, his one hope was a smash through. Only across prostrate bodies was freedom to be won out of Li Chun's noisome den.

Someone got in the path of his onrush; but they fell away with a puffing gasp as he hit out. A final blast from the gun—the scurry of feet in the gloom—a cry of "Murder!"—a last wild stampede—silence. The panic-driven crowd had fled.

For an instant Warrender crouched, his fists clenched, his eyes boring the black void. Still quiet, except for a low whimpering in the corner. That, and the steady drip-drip of liquor from some overturned glass. Apparently he had the place to himself, except for the whimperer. Perhaps it was Li Chun.

Warrender straightened, found the wall, and groped along it for the switch. Light spelt danger, but the darkness was more perilous still. Better see what he was up against. Besides, he did not know the exits.

Snick! His fingers jerked the lever down, and the bar flooded with brilliance.

Barring a bowler-hatted figure, huddled in a corner, it was empty. About him was a litter of chairs and tables—flung down, overturned, and broken amidst a wreckage of splintered glass, all wreathed in a fast-thinning fog of gun smoke.

Warrender shot a glance at the frightened man with the bowler, another at an open doorway, a third at a gun close to his feet. With a grim smile he stooped for the weapon. As he pocketed it his foot touched something—a roll of canvas, partly unwound, and crushed in the late stampede.

One eye on the exit, he secured the roll. He had last seen it, he remembered, in the gunman's hand. The well-dressed young ass had clutched at it. H'm! Yes, that had been the start of the trouble.

With a quick frown, he wrenched it open.

It was the picture of a young woman, in queer, old-fashioned clothes. A beauty, her pale cheeks framed in a wealth of dark-brown ringlets, she smiled up at him mutely.

"By Jove! Cavalier period! Old, too, and marvellously executed!"

Entranced, he scanned the age-darkened pigments, and the fair face limned by some master brush of a long-dead hand. His own peril forgotten, he stood spellbound while he analysed the fine lace collar and its perfect reproduction, every thread faithfully depicted in minute detail.

"By Jove!" he reiterated, his eyes sparkling. "A genuine Van Dyck, or—"

As a shuffling of feet sounded behind him, he swung round, to find a small Jew at his elbow. It was the man from the corner, his bowler hat still forced down upon his spreading ears.

The Jew shrank away, his dark eyes wild with terror. Then, at sight of his diminutive companion, Warrender laughed. The Jew was unarmed, and he could have broken him with one hand.

"Well?" he queried sharply.

"Vat you got there, mister?" the other whispered, in the accents of Warsaw.

"A picture."

"Sure! I gif you a dollar for 'im! Yes?"

The Jew bent forward insinuatingly.

"I shouldn't wonder!" Warrender retorted contemptuously, his gaze on the canvas edges. They were jagged, as though slit by some knife.

"Ten bob, then?"

"Cut out of a frame, I'll bet!" Warrender shook his head. "Ten bob—your grandmother!"

"Vell, a quid?"

The dark eyes gleamed avariciously.

"Nothing doing, Ikey!"

"I gif you a fiver!"

Five bob to a fiver—in as many seconds! And this from one of a race world-renowned through the ages for business acumen!

Warrender's pulse quickened. There was something to this picture, and something to this Jew as well. Li Chun's patrons were gaolbirds—past or potential—to a man. And it was not Jews who filled the prisons.

What was this little Hebrew—shivering, yet for all his obvious fear, courageous— doing in this foul dive?

"My friend, I'm not selling—even for ten fivers!" he declared, rolling up the canvas. "Get that?"

The other shrugged.

"Vat! Ven you vill never get dat picture out of dis place?" Another shrug, with widely-spread hands for emphasis. "You fool! Because they do not come, do you think—" He gave an apprehensive glance at the door. "They vait for you outside—in the dark. You vill go down—so!"

Pantomime.

"And you?" Warrender queried.

The Jew put a finger to his nose.

"I know my own business, young man. Come—a fiver for the picture, and I vill show you some other vay out of here. A safe way—"

"I don't think!"

"But I tell you, fool, you do not know vat you haf dere—er—vat you are up against!" his companion urged, with bated breath. "In five minutes you vill be dead. But for me—"

"Oh, shut up!" Warrender propelled the Jew suddenly towards the doorway. "Hop it!"

He thrust the Jew violently out into the passage, slammed the door quickly, and locked it—then grabbed up an overturned table.

ABOVE was a skylight. He had already noted it while he sprawled in his corner. He dragged the table under it, mounted, and, with a few vigorous blows, beat at the glass. The fragments had hardly ceased falling as his heels disappeared through the opening. A minute later, scratched but triumphant, he had won his way across the slates, and dropped to a quiet alley beyond.

His trophy under his arm, he ran till he reached a main thoroughfare. Here he boarded a belated tram. Still nursing his loot, he got off at Stratford Broadway, and hailed a taxi.

"Golders Green!"

He lay back against the squab, his brows knit in thought as the cab jolted onwards. What was a picture like this doing in an East End dive? Why the Jew's eagerness to possess it? Why his hint of murder to regain it?

If genuine, it was worth big money. But by the same token, a white elephant. The unique is not negotiable in the underworld.

"Gad, but it's a puzzler! She's a beauty, though!" He smoothed the roll gently. "Pity she's dead, or I'd—"

He swerved towards the window as a high-powered car shot level. From it a man swung out towards the cab, one hand reaching for the door-handle. Behind him a second loomed, a gun in his fist.

The small hours—a lonely road—a car-load of crooks—a hold-up. Warrender sized the situation up neatly by the moment the first man had sprung on to the footboard. An instant later the door swung open.

For the second time that night Warrender acted. As the crook swayed in through the doorway something smashed home between his eyes. It was the empty gun from the floor of Li Chun's joint—thrown at short range with all the force of Warrender's powerful arm.

The man fell back into the road. There was a shout, a shot, the black shadow of another leap.

But Warrender was through the nearside door and on the stepboard. As the car slewed crazily to the kerb—the driver had clapped on his shrieking brakes—he jumped for the gutter, falling on hands and knees.

He saw the taxi skid wildly, crash into a lamp-post, and come to rest, with the big car beside it. The driver fell off his seat and took to his heels. As he vanished, the gang poured like a wolf pack over the stranded vehicle.

Stumbling up, Warrender gained a gateway with a single bound, won a back wall beyond, and gained the friendly shelter of a quiet side road, with the canvas roll still clutched beneath his arm.

His shoulder was seared with the hot sting of steel. Pulling up under a gas lamp, he clutched at his bicep, found something that protruded, and yanked it free. It was a knife of some kind.

Simultaneously he felt the thick, warm ooze of sticky liquid—blood. Still, a flesh wound, no more, fortunately. Stiffening himself, he stared down at the object in his hand. Yes, it was a knife, its haft carved curiously in the shape of a grotesque figure—part monkey, part crab.

Warrender stared at it blankly for a brief moment, then thrust it into his pocket. This was the third of the night's surprises—one which had narrowly missed being no surprise at all. Dead men are immune from such sensations, he reflected.

"Good enough!" he panted. And, the canvas roll still gripped under his arm, sprinted for safety and the distance, the night jazz-shaped and dimming to his reeling senses.

The Jew had been right enough after all. That girl in the picture had her admirers!"

CHAPTER 2
UNCOVERED!

ON the fringe of the West End of London lies Baker Street. A long thoroughfare, running northwards from Portman Square, it is a place of ghosts—half seen in the mind's eye amidst a parallel stretch of modern ferro-concrete buildings; blatant usurpers which flaunt their ornate fronts where structures of another era once had been.

Still, here and there an older house remains, drab yet dignified—pathetic survivors of an epoch past and gone. Almost one can hear the steady clop, clop of cab-horses' hoofs.

Such' impressions yet linger—phantoms of a yesterday never-to-be-recalled; the things of a London passed forever!

Passed—because Big Business has laid its greedy hand upon a street world-famous. Big Business—which retreats at six p.m., its clattering typewriters silenced, and its horde of silken-hosed young women tube-bound for the widening rim of London's suburbs.

The sun had dawned and set on the metropolis since Warrender's adventure. And the hour of six had struck some before. For the most, Baker Street and its buildings lay in darkness.

Yet in one of the few surviving old-fashioned houses a light still burned. It came from the first floor front, dimly seen through drawn blinds. Behind these blinds two men worked on, regardless of the clock.

Contrasting figures, one stood on the threshold of middle age, the other upon the starting line of life. The elder, a tall, lean figure, was known wherever Baker Street was known—Sexton Blake, the master criminologist. His companion, Tinker, though but a lad, was scarcely less famous.

His keen eyes focused on the bubbling liquid of a heated test tube, the detective bent forward, absorbed in his experiments. Behind him, the youngster's pen scratched monotonously to the compilation of some intricate data. Outside the hooting of passing traffic filtered through vaguely.

"Humph! Crystalline precipitate. Dull red. Yes, Mrs. Bardell, what is it?"

Blake raised his eyes as a discreet knocking sounded on the door.

A grey-haired woman thrust her head round the corner.

"A gentleman to see you, sir," she announced apologetically. It did not do to disturb Sexton Blake lightly when at his work.

"What name?"

Blake's eyes sought the test tube afresh.

"Ah, Mr. Blake sir, that's just it. Which the gentleman said, says 'e, as 'ow you'd know him."

"Huh! And you think—"

"Which my private and consequential opinion, Mr. Blake, is that he is one of them prize-fighters, sir. Shall I show him up to the insulting-room?"

"No, Show him in here; I can't leave this experiment."

And the detective continued studying the test tube as the door closed silently.

Mechanically, his fingers sought a drawer and drew it open. In the drawer lay an automatic, fully charged. At times the house received strange visitors—dangerous, too. Still intent on the chemical reaction, Blake could yet take his precautions. And, Heaven knew, he needed to.

He was still studying the crystals when he heard the door open. He straightened—one hand to the open drawer. On the threshold stood a young man—one of the biggest he had ever seen.

His housekeeper had been right. The visitor might well have been a heavy-weight boxer.

His huge frame masked by a well-cut suit, the newcomer came forward. As the saying is, he might have stepped out of a bandbox. Prognathous jawed, his rugged features—a marked contrast to his precise and immaculate attire—were familiar.

Sexton Blake withdrew his hand from the drawer and waved him to a seat.

"Good-evening, Mr. Warrender!" The detective viewed his flattened nose, broken in some bygone glove-fight. "I must ask you to excuse my receiving you in the laboratory here, but at the moment you arrived a chemical experiment was—"

"Ah, so you recognise me" the visitor murmured, dropping into a chair.

"To be sure. And so would any gallery girl," Blake answered, smiling. "It's my business to know people—especially people who stare out of every illustrated weekly. A star actor like Bertram Warrender doesn't easily hide his light under a bushel, my dear sir." He chuckled. "Well, I see you're just in from rehearsal!"

Warrender put a quick hand to his face, where a lurking smear of grease paint daubed his chin.

"Rehearsal?"

"Of course. Your show's going into production, isn't it? So what's that spot of make-up—Number Two, I observe—doing there, otherwise?" Blake smiled again. "It could only be rehearsals."

"You're right," Warrender announced briskly. "But for the fact I've been at it hard all day, I'd have been round here before. Barlow—that's our stage damager—is a slave-driver."

"And now he's let you go, Mr. Warrender, your trouble is—"

"This." The actor tossed a dagger on to the table. "What do you make of it?"

As became a man of action, he was terseness itself.

Blake picked the knife up and examined it closely while, behind him, his young assistant's pen went on scratching. For an instant he paused, his eyes on the carved handle.

"Humph! South American Indian work, I fancy. Peruvian, possibly, but South American certainly." He turned the hilt over. "Queer sort of gargoyle this, though. Can't say I've ever seen its like before. Some god perhaps. H'm. H'm." He shook his head, frowning at details of the grotesque figure. "Carved in ironwood."

He looked up.

"Where did you get it?"

"In the shoulder—fleshy part, luckily." Warrender tapped a slight bulge below his well-cut coat. "Last night. My taxi was followed—from Li Chun's, you know."

"Ah, Li Chun's—at Poplar?" Blake's eyes narrowed. "You've a nerve, my friend—if you were there."

"I wasn't recognised, I think. I went there pretty well disguised. Getting the atmosphere for my new part. It's a crook play, you know. Shan't do it again, though. Once bitten, twice shy. Still, I got the stuff I was after—and something else. This—"

He laid a roll of canvas on the table.

Blake spread out the roll, and, for a moment, inspected the picture. For an instant the girl's eyes laughed out at him from between the dark ringlets.

"A peach, eh?" Warrender commented. "What do you make of her?"

"More than I do of the knife, Mr. Warrender. She's a famous young lady—thanks to Mynheer Van Dyck, who painted her. You'd better not call her a peach, either. She's the present Lord Carham's property—or else I'm a Dutchman, like the artist."

"Gosh!" Warrender breathed, astonished.

He had not expected this lightning analysis.

"No—Lady Diana Carham, one of the ancestors, I fancy," Blake said, with another chuckle. "She was cut out of her frame, down at Murwood Manor, last week, by some intruder unknown. The police circularised her description, hence my recognition of her. One always recognises young women worth money. And she's worth—well, about fifty thousand pounds."

"Huh! Wish I was!" grunted Warrender.

"No doubt. So you got her at Li Chun's?"

"I did—this way." And Warrender described his adventure minutely. "What I can't fathom," he added, "is why they should go to so much trouble and risk to get back a picture that's naturally unsaleable."

"So you came to me?" Blake paused as the actor nodded. "Well, I'm obliged—even if, to be truthful, we're both in pretty much the same boat. I've been puzzling over the theft myself. And mysteries always intrigue me. I was half hoping that Scotland Yard would call me in. To date, they haven't."

"You're in now, though," Warrender declared. "And, since you're in, the next move's yours—if you care to make it."

"You're serious?"

"Never more so in my life."

""Then—" The detective turned to his assistant. "Tinker, my lad, see about getting the car round! We'll run down to Murwood. I feel in the mood for a motor run, and shall be finished with this chemical job in a minute."

A HIGH-SPEED run, lasting something over an hour, brought Blake and his companions to the lonely Fen-country, where lay the Carhams' ancestral home. The winding road that had led for long through mist-laden marshes emerged at length amongst a stretch of woods. Here, up a side road, marked on the detective's Ordnance map, the trio located a pair of wrought-iron gates, whence a hundred yards of tortuous drive-way brought them to the ancient house.

A long, low, three-quarter timbered building of the Tudor period, it lay like some intangible thing across the filmy night. Only here and there a light burned behind its leaded panes. But for the faint soughing of wind in leafless branches, all was silent.

"H'm! Pretty place for a burglary!" Blake muttered, as he rang the bell. "Miles from anywhere, and crammed with priceless antiques—or so they say. However—" As a white-haired butler appeared in the doorway. "Is Lord Carham in?"

"No, sir." The servant scanned him curiously. "He is out, sir."

"Then he'll be in presently?"

"Later, sir. I don't know when. He's out to dinner."

"Then when is the car ordered to fetch him?" Blake inquired, his lips pursed.

"The car is not fetching him, sir." Pausing, the butler focused narrowed eyes upon the visitor. "He preferred to walk."

He frowned slightly, as if to indicate that he thought the caller over-inquisitive.

"This is awkward." Blake half-turned to the actor. "It may mean hanging about for hours yet, or waiting till to-morrow."

"Which I can't. I've another 'call' at ten o'clock in the morning,W Warrender announced decisively.

"So I guessed." Blake gripped the roll of canvas, then eyed the butler again. "You had a robbery here last week, I fancy?"

The old man started. For an instant he glowered suspiciously at Blake from under his shaggy, iron-grey brows.

"Correct, sir!" he agreed, after perceptible hesitation. "Lady Diana's picture, sir. Cut clean out of its frame!"

"You'd recognise it?"

"Certainly, sir. But—"

"I think this is it," Blake said quietly, displaying the roll. "To save time, perhaps you'll be so good as to inspect it."

Excited out of his professional solemnity, the butler threw open the door.

"Come in, gentlemen—come in!" he exclaimed, beaming. "Perkins, another lamp! He beckoned a footman, in the background. "Bless my heart, sir, but this will be good news for his lordship!"

The three stepped into a large, square hall and an atmosphere of mullioned, leaded windows, old oak beams, and massive panelling. Here Blake spread the canvas out upon a table for the butler's inspection.

"The picture, right enough, sir!" he pronounced immediately. "Wonderful—wonderful! If I may make so bold, sir—where did you get it?"

"That's another story," Blake rejoined, smiling, "for Lord Carham's ear only. Meanwhile, you'd better have this!"

He produced his card.

"A detective, sir?" the old man murmured, peering closely at the little slip of pasteboard. "Perhaps, then, you will wait. His lordship will certainly wish to see you."

His manner regained a little of its former frigidity.

Detectives—mere policemen! Welcome visitors, of course … in the circumstances. Still, for all that, policemen. He drew himself up visibly.

"Yes, we'll wait," Blake said tersely. "Meantime, to make sure, I'd like to see the frame. If the canvas fits the jagged edges it's genuine."

"Very good, sir."

Their guide took them up the broad oak staircase to a gallery surrounding the hall, where portraits ringed the walls; old oil paintings of times gone by.

Here was a sea captain striking an attitude on his quarter-deck and housed in armour such as Drake or Raleigh might have donned. Beyond was a ringleted cavalier; yonder a man in flowing periwig, with an aristocrat of the Victorian era as neighbour.

To a man—and with some exceptions to a woman—they bore the same lineage.

Amongst them hung an empty frame, its inner edges fringed with ends of jagged canvas. At a sign from the butler, Perkins lowered it. When Blake tried the picture it fitted perfectly.

"Yes, it's the original, right enough." Blake announced. He glanced thoughtfully around the gallery. "Any other losses, Mr.—er—"

"My name's Calvert," the butler informed him. "No. The thieves got nothing else, though they did some damage."

"Forced a door or window, perhaps?"

"No, sir. They'd a key, evidently. There was no sign of anything forced. Barring that torn tapestry there, they left no traces."

The old man pointed to an ancient fabric, a curtain upon the wall. Taking the lamp from Perkins, Blake examined the tapestry, which, rotten from age, bore a jagged slit down the middle.

The slit had been newly tacked together with stout thread—evidently by some inexpert hand, and as if done in a great hurry. Curiously enough, though it hung from a rod, the sides and bottom of the curtain were secured to the wall panelling by little brass-headed nails.

A little puzzled, Blake inspected this arrangement closely. From their dinginess, the tack heads had been in place for many years—a sure sign that whatever hung behind the tapestry had been long covered up.

"What's this?" he queried, pressing his fingers to the fabric.

Old Calvert stretched out a detaining hand instantly, concern on his lined features.

"Be careful, sir, if you please! The tapestry's that rotten. Them stitches may give—"

Blake regarded him curiously. In his excitement, Calvert's meticulously precise grammar had gone to pieces. Why this panic lest this tattered curtain, already damaged, should be torn afresh?

"What's behind here?" the detective demanded.

Calvert gave a slight shudder, and for a perceptible moment hesitated.

"A picture, sir."

He spoke with apparent reluctance.

"What picture?"

"A mighty queer picture, sir. It—isn't lucky. It's—it's *devilish!*"

"What do you mean? Come, man"—as the butler hesitated—"what is the thing? And how can a picture be unlucky?"

Calvert shrugged.

"Luck's a funny thing, sir. There ain't—isn't—no rhyme or reason to it, in a manner of speaking. I'm no judge of such things. Still, they say it's unlucky. More than that, sir—downright disaster! And there's no disputing that it's brought misfortune to the Carhams whenever that curtain's been drawn aside."

"Nonsense, man!"

"What's behind this curtain?" demanded the detective. "A picture, sir."
"What picture?" "A mighty queer picture. It isn't lucky. It—it's devilish!"

"Well, the burglar tore that curtain, sir, and his Lordship lost this picture of Lady Diana. You can't deny that. That's misfortune, isn't it?"

"Temporary misfortune, Mr. Calvert," Blake corrected, smiling.

"You see, we've recovered the picture."

"Yes, sir, and all knocked about, if I may say so," Calvert commented, with a glance at the cracked surface. "It will never be the same picture it was." He shook his head gloomily. "Drat that burglar!"

"Well, he's left fingerprints on the curtain," Blake remarked, peering at some candle-grease marks on the tapestry. "Just bring that lamp a bit closer, will you, my man?"

He signed to the footman, who held the light to the fabric while Blake scrutinised some smudges through his pocket magnifying glass.

He was still intent on this when Warrender gave a sharp cry.

"Look out! The stuff's burning!"

Perkins whipped the lamp away, but too late. Like tinder with age, the tapestry was ablaze. A few seconds and it would be enveloped from top to bottom.

"The picture—picture!"

Calvert shrieked the words.

But the detective thrust him off.

"Mind out!" He tore the curtain from its fastenings, and stamped the flames out under his feet.

"No damage done, I think—"

He glanced up at the picture—and stared.

Glowering out from a vague, shadowy background was a Thing repulsive, hideous. It was a monstrosity—a squat beast whose dangling, scaly, enormous hands were a travesty of human hands, just as its lumpish, fanged, goggling face was a travesty of a human face.

Crouched, bunched together, the revolting, pinkish freak sat in thought—if such a grotesque, misshapen organism could think.

The first effect of the picture—apart altogether from any legends of misfortune connected with it—was distinctly disturbing, and yet, in some sinister, inexplicable manner, attracting. It was as if some magnetic spell of hypnosis held one's gaze to that brooding ugliness.

"My hat!" Tinker murmured in awe, regarding it open-mouthed.

"You blundering fool!" Calvert broke in with fury at the frightened footman. "Heaven knows what mischief you've done now! The accursed thing's uncovered a second time. Thanks to you and your—"

He shrank back, gasping, against the balustrade.

"*What's that?*"

From somewhere outside the house the air was cut by a wild, mortal scream. It was a scream of death agony!

CHAPTER 3
THE CURSE OF THE CARHAMS.

"Did you hear that?"

Warrender gripped Blake's arm.

For an instant the five men listened tensely. The air still seemed to quiver with the ring of that agonised scream, but there was no other sound.

"It—it came from the terrace," Calvert breathed, the sweat standing out on his forehead. He He glanced fearfully at the grotesque monster on the wall, and shook visibly.

"Never mind that gargoyle! The terrace, man—quickly!"

Blake, half-dragging him down the stairs, flung a door open and dashed across a lighted room and flung open some french windows on the farther wall.

From them a bright beam of light shot out into the night, flooding the terrace. It fell on a still figure, stretched out on the ground—a man fallen full length.

As one, the five raced to the spot. Blake dropped on one knee. It was a man in middle age, clad in evening clothes. Ghastly pale, the keen, aristocratic features looked skywards, terror writ large in their glassy eyes.

"His Lordship! Oh, my Heaven! Dead!"

Old Calvert stumbled down beside the body, wringing his aged hands. He began moaning to himself, like one distraught.

"Yes, I'm afraid—dead!" Blake thrust a hand inside the starched white shirt front, then rose slowly to his feet. He removed his hat.

"But how—how?" Calvert demanded.

"I'm wondering." The detective pointed to the dead man's chest.

The shirt front was pierced with eight small holes, widely spaced. From each welled slowly oozing blood.

Thunderstruck, his companions stared blankly down at the ghastly marks—disposed in the form of two crescents set back to back. It was as though two monstrous hands, armed with frightful talons, had bitten home into the dead man's chest—hands flung round him from behind in a grip, vice-like, terrific, irresistible.

"At least one of those claws penetrated the heart," Blake declared, peering down at the puncture-marks.

"Claws!" Warrender gave a stifled exclamation. "Why, heavens alive, they're more like tenpenny nails!"

"Claws or not, they did their business," the detective rejoined coolly. As he spoke, he drew aside the dead peer's shirt front. "See how the chest is lacerated."

The actor's lips met tightly. He gave a fitful shudder, then glanced anxiously round him.

"What was it—a tiger?" His gnarled fists clenched.

Blake shook his head decisively.

"No tiger has such claws." He paused deliberately while, the others held their breath. "No known beast has claws that would leave those marks, and in that position."

"Then"—Warrender mopped his sweating brow—"then what was it?"

Again he peered about him, his lips tensioned.

The detective had taken an electric torch from his pocket and was sweeping the ground in a wide radius about the body.

"Hallo! Stand still, everybody!" He halted, his torch ray steadied on something.

Then slowly he moved the beam onwards along the path of some queer footmarks on the damp earth.

Strange, indeed, they were—weird, bird-like impressions, yet set about a curious, bulbous indentation. They resembled nothing which the criminologist had ever encountered during the whole of his wide experience.

In a deviating line from the terrace steps they ended in a wide, trailing circle around Carham's body.

With his brows contracted Blake viewed first the spoor, then the dead peer, and next a half-finished cigar still glowing on the ground a few feet away, a cone of ash beside it.

Evidently Lord Carham had just ascended the terrace steps, smoking as he went. He had been taken from behind—silently and without warning. Of this Blake was certain.

Carham's footprints showed dimly. In unbroken sequence they evinced an evenness of impress that argued a steady stride. The peer had died in a second, and virtually without a struggle.

"Queer!" the detective muttered, turning again to Carham's blurred prints. "I wonder—"

"There! Quickly! Look!" Warrender's voice cut in through his musing.

He pointed down the terrace to the stone balustrade at its far end.

Wreathed in filmy mist, the balustrade showed faintly against the vagueness of a rising moon. Along it a shadow shuffled—swiftly, silently.

The four men held their breath, their eyes on the noiseless phantom. Squat, diminutive, it might have been a huge toad but for its gait. That, or some small bear, erect on its hind legs.

But the shape was neither toad nor bear. Bent stiffly forward at an angle, it sped down the coping as on castors—so fast it hardly seemed to touch the stonework. If it was anything at all, it was the very image of the repulsive thing in the curtained picture.

Warrender snatched an automatic pistol from his hip.

"Stop!"

As the gun spat Blake struck up the actor's wrist. The bullet whizzed skywards. Simultaneously the mysterious creature vanished.

"You ass!" the detective exclaimed in exasperation. "You've scared the thing now. And—"

"Gosh! Who's this?"

Tinker pointed past the balustrade where the drive swept in towards the house. From the trees about it burst a blaze of light—the headlamps of a car.

Straight on came the motor with a racer's speed. In the last few yards its driver brought it up, the brakes screaming. The engine stopped, and stumbling footfalls came noisily up the terrace steps past where the shape had been.

Still staring, the five men watched a lurching figure sway into sight. His heavy coat open, he staggered towards them, the gleam of a starched white shirt front half seen between the jerking lapels.

"'Sh'allo, you chaps—"

The newcomer stopped, his bloodshot eyes on the body. For a moment he stood swaying while he peered foolishly down at it, a hand to his forehead.

"Sh' ole man blotto, eh?" he queried thickly. "The ole-hic-hypocrite. T-tellin' me off, too, on'y lash week when I—when I—"

"Mr. Algy!" Old Calvert threw up a hand in protest. "You don't understand, sir. His Lordship's dead—murdered."

"Dead—murder?"

The other's jaw dropped stupidly. For a second he stood gazing at the butler, blinking.

"Yes, sir; dead!" Blake said sternly.

"Dead! My stars! But thash rich!"

The motorist threw back his head and burst into a maudlin peal of high-pitched laughter that echoed back from the ancient eaves in hollow mockery. His mirth ended in a raucous fit of coughing that brought him stumbling to the body. He would have fallen across it had not the detective caught and steadied him.

"Pull yourself together, you fool!" he ordered sharply, as a waft of whisky laden breath reached him.

But the drunkard threw him off irritably.

"Leggo, curse you! I—I've—hic—done nothin', I tell you! Lemme 'lone, will you!" He backed away, suppressed terror in his dilated pupils. "I—I've a right here, haven't I?" He swerved round on the butler. "You tell 'em, Calvert."

"A right, Mr. Algy? Why, of course—" The butler gave a deprecatory gesture. "Why not, when—" He stopped, then, with a sudden start, drew himself up stiffly. "I beg pardon, sir, I should have said 'My Lord.'"

"My Lord!" Warrender's voice broke from the background.

A flood light from the open french windows bathed the drunkard's pallid features. It was as though limelight had caught and thrown them into prominence.

It was the face of the young man at Li Chun's—the well-dressed inebriate round whom had started the fight.

WHAT had brought the fellow here? Warrender wondered, as, with Calvert's aid, he helped the drunkard into the salon, and there lowered him on to a Chesterfield.

But then—what had Carham's heir been doing at that Poplar dive? Why, too, had he laughed in that maniacal fashion when he found the peer was dead? The murder had brought him lands, wealth, a title. All the same, it was hardly a matter for such merriment.

Something of the same sort crossed Blake's mind as he got a rug and reverentially covered the body with it. Poor Carham could not be moved till the police had inspected his remains. In the meantime there was the new peer—

The latter had collapsed on the Chesterfield, seemingly exhausted after his crazy burst of laughter. His bead between his hands, he sat muttering to himself, his fingers twisting nervily.

Every now and then he looked anxiously towards the window, as if expecting something he did not wish to see. Between whiles he resumed his incoherent mumblings.

"Yes, sir—the next of kin. The new peer, you understand," Calvert murmured in Blake's ear. "I fear he'll play ducks and drakes with the estates, though. This is a sad day for Murwood. That infernal picture—the misfortune was sure to come. But this—"

"And his name?"

"Mr. Algernon Westerfield, sir. His Lordship's nephew. A most scatterbrained young gentleman, sir—if I may say so. In fact, my late master had forbidden him the house."

"Then what is he doing here now?" Blake demanded, his eyes narrowed on the wastrel. Westerfield's arrival had been breakneck, and timed almost to the minute as regards his uncle's death.

The coincidence was peculiar. Apparently its significance occurred also to Calvert. He shrank away, mute, unspoken query in his horrified eyes.

"I don't know, sir," he muttered, frowning. "Mr. Algy—my Lord—"

"Go 'way! Shut those rotten windows, will you?" the drunkard exploded fiercely from his place.

"Yes, certainly, my Lord—"

Calvert hurried to the french windows and closed them, while his new master watched him with fevered eyes.

As the lock snapped home the young wastrel drew a breath of relief. Falling back, he heaved a sigh, then broke forth afresh into a spasm of idiotic chuckling.

"Better get him to bed," Blake suggested. "We'll have nothing from him in his present state. He's in the way here, and there's work to do."

"Very good, sir," Calvert agreed, willing enough that this strong, lean-jawed man should take charge.

Going to his new master, he touched him diffidently on the shoulder, and murmured something apologetic in his ear. The young man muttered something inaudible, an apparent protest, then permitted the butler to help him to his feet. Steadied by Blake, he was helped painfully upstairs, still chuckling to himself at intervals en route.

"One moment—don't let him tread on that canvas!" Blake warned, with a sign for Calvert to halt his master.

The stolen portrait lay across the gallery, fallen where it had dropped when the dead peer's last cry of mortal agony rang in from the outer night.

Blake snatched the canvas up, and began to roll it carefully. A dull cry from the drunkard made him spin round. Westerfield, broken from Calvert's hold, was staring at the grotesque painting above the charred curtain.

"Wha—whash that?" he demanded, clutching the butler's elbow. "The curse, my Lord. The curse upon the house of Carham!"

"A-a-ah!"

The new peer let off an unearthly scream. His hands to his eyes, he staggered back against the gallery rail, trembling,

"Then I washn't canned, after all, the other night! It was real—*real!*"

"Pull yourself together, man! It's only a painting!" Blake said soothingly. "It's nothing, really—"

"Nothing!" The drunkard thrust him off wildly. "You're a liar! *I tell you I've seen it!*"

Between them Blake and the butler forced their distracted charge to a bed-room, where the detective left him in Calvert's care. Securing the canvas roll, Blake descended to the drawing-room.

Just how much lay behind Algy Carham's frenzied assertions he did not know. This might be but the delirious imaginings of an inebriate. On the other hand—

The detective frowned. He could not forget that sinister shadow speeding along the terrace wall. That, too, might have been a figment of minds overwrought by sudden tragedy—an illusion of the mists. And yet—

The shape had seemed real enough. And its very speed, its attitude, showed it was no ordinary animal.

He placed the portrait of Lady Diana on the table, where it promptly unrolled itself.

"We'll have a second look at those footmarks," he said curtly, turning to Warrender and his assistant.

"All right—" Tinker turned towards the window. But he never got there.

As he spoke, a frightful shriek rang out once more upon the mist-cloaked terrace. Something hurled itself against the window, and burst, with a rending crash, through the pane.

It was a young girl, panting with terror.

Gasping, she looked wildly around her, then collapsed on the floor, cut and bleeding, amidst a litter of splintered glass.

CHAPTER 4

THE GNOMID.

BLAKE sprang forward and raised the girl. She had fainted.

"Guard that window!" he ordered, and, as Warrender jumped to the broken pane, laid his burden on the chesterfield.

For an instant he examined her.

"Just superficial cuts," he announced tersely. "The glass missed her face, fortunately. Some water and a sponge will set things to rights! Tinker, see to it, will you?" He slewed round to the actor. "Well?"

"Can't see anything!" Warrender declared. "The mist's thickened. It's almost black. Still, there's no sound."

Blake went to the window and looked out. The actor was right. In that murk anything might prowl unseen. All was still, save for the faint whispering of distant trees. The very silence was charged with menace.

"Your gun, man!" he urged, and as Warrender handed him the automatic, strode out where the dead man lay.

Undisturbed, the body still lay under its rug. Returning to the drawing-room, he bent over the girl, in process of recovering.

After a little she sat up, staring about her in bewilderment. Then, as her eyes took in her surroundings, and she found herself amongst friendly faces, the fear died from her eyes.

"Where am ?" she breathed.

"Murwood Manor. Lord Carham's house," Blake told her.

But her beautiful features remained puzzled. It was clear the explanation meant nothing to her.

"Murwood Manor? Lord Carham?" She shook her blonde head. "Who's he?"

"A wealthy landowner, my dear young lady. But never mind. The chief point at present is, who are you, and why did you throw yourself through that window?"

She gave a shiver.

"I was forgetting." Her eyes moved apprehensively to the broken pane, much as the drunkard's had done. "It was that Thing—that Shape! It came up behind me without a sound. I thought it was going to clutch me. And—and—"

"Yes—yes?" the detective urged.

"I saw the light, and sprang. I didn't think—realise about the glass. But It—has it gone?"

"We've seen nothing, at all events," Blake said reassuringly. He looked meaningly at his companions. "But how came you on the terrace?"

"I'd been seeing a gentleman on business—Mr. Grifstein—at the Towers. That's near here. He wrote to me on a money matter. There was an appointment. But he was late, and I had to wait. That delayed me. I was taking a short cut to the station, but lost my way. I—I had an impression that something was following me, and the mists frightened me—"

"Naturally, Miss—Miss—"

"Anne Debroy. I'm an actress—a chorus girl," she murmured, her gaze shifting to Warrender.

"By Jove! I thought your face was familiar, somehow!" Warrender interjected. "We must have met in some show or other."

Anne Debroy shook her head.

"I recognise you, of course, Mr. Warrender. Everyone knows your photo, naturally. But"—she gave a wry little smile—"so far I've never had the good luck to get into the sort of play you appear in. I only wish I had!"

"Well, maybe you will," the actor remarked. His admiring glance suggested strongly that, if he had anything to do with it, her luck was about to turn. "But you were saying about the mist?"

"Oh, I just saw your lights, and made for here. I'd reached the terrace when that awful Shape pounced out on me from behind. And—and I hurled myself at the window." She looked down at her cut hands.

"Well, here are water and bandages at last," Blake said, as the door opened and Tinker appeared, followed by Calvert.

The butler bore a tray, on which were some strips of linen, a sponge, and a small basin of warm water. At the table he halted. It was already occupied by the Van Dyck canvas.

"Half a jiffy!"

Warrender sprang to move away the picture. As he caught it up, he gave vent to a startled cry, and looked towards Anne Debroy.

"What's the matter?" Blake queried, stepping to his side.

Warrender nodded at the portrait, then gazed once more at the girl. Like him, Blake started slightly in his turn. But for superficialities, the face of the girl in the picture was the image of Anne Debroy.

SKILFUL, expeditious, Sexton Blake began dressing Anne Debroy's wounds. In his younger days he had walked the hospitals, and, though most of his clients were ignorant of the fact, was entitled to subscribe the honourable letters, M.R.C.S., L.R.C.P., to his well-known name.

While he busied himself with Anne, Warrender took Calvert aside.

"Just what do you know about the history of that picture?" he asked.

"Well, sir, not a great deal. Only the family tradition, so to speak. It was Sir John Carham who painted it after he'd gone mad—"

"But, man, Mr. Blake has pronounced it a Van Dyck!" the actor protested.

"Can't help that, sir, begging the gentleman's pardon. But it was Sir John, right enough, who painted the hideous thing. Because he was crazy, I suppose."

"Hideous!" Warrender interrupted indignantly. "Why, it's beautiful! I've never seen anything so lovely, except—" He glanced at the actress. "Why, man, she's a beauty!"

Calvert stared at him in surprise for an instant, then at Anne. Warrender was holding the Van Dyck. As the butler eyed it, he, too, started.

"Lady Diana!" he breathed, with another glance at Blake's patient. "Why, they're as like as two peas—"

"Hush, man!" the star warned, as Anne glanced over towards them.

"Beg pardon, sir," The old man collected himself. In a louder tone, he added: "I thought you were talking about that queer picture, sir, up in the gallery."

"Quite right—quite right!" Warrender lied hastily. Anne's blue eyes were still regarding him suspiciously. "What about it?"

Calvert cleared his throat.

"Well, sir, as I was saying. Sir John painted it—way back in the reign of James the First, sir. That was before we had a peerage. It was Sir John, you see, who was really founder of the family fortunes."

"How was that?"

"Sailed off to the Ameriças, sir—as a gentleman adventurer, you understand. There were many of good birth who did that in them far-off times. Five years he was gone, sir, before he came back with a fortune, in gold and jewels."

"Plunder taken from the Spaniards?" Warrender suggested.

"I don't know, sir. Nobody knew exactly how or where he got his wealth. Except that it was somewhere on the Spanish Main. He told some tale of a long voyage up a mighty river—the Amazon, my poor late master always thought it was. Anyhow, he came back a changed man. He had grown morose and moody. And they say his face was the face of a man who had seen terrible things, and suffered."

"I don't doubt it, Calvert. And then?"

"Why, he just settled down to painting pictures, and that. He seemed to have no other interest in life. A patron of the arts, they called him. Finally, he went mad, as I've said. And the last thing he did was to paint that picture upstairs."

"But why?"

Calvert shrugged.

"I can't say, sir. I often wondered if he'd seen something of the sort while out in America."

"If so, I reckon his Lordship did well to come away," Warrender declared, grinning, "I've never seen anything to match it—outside a pantomime. But what's this curse?"

Calvert glanced round him nervously. He answered in a hushed voice.

"They reckon, sir, it was that brute—the Gnomid, they call it—that drove Sir John mad. Everyone's always been afraid of the picture ever since. It's an evil thing, and evil for the Carhams has always been wrapped up with it."

"Then why didn't they get rid of the beastly thing?"

"They daren't, sir. Sir John left a curse in his will on anyone who destroyed or disposed of anything he had painted. His pictures were to go down for ever as heirlooms in the family, he said. We've a lot of his daubs up in the lumber-room. But for that curse they'd have been made a bonfire of generations ago, I don't doubt."

"Humph! And the family really believed such rot?"

"They did, sir—and do. His heir tried to sell that Gnomid, and got stabbed in the back next day—before the sale was completed. Other things happened as time went on. Finally, one of the heirs had the picture curtained over, after which they say the trouble ceased. But there's always been ill luck whenever it's been uncovered. I don't know all the ins and outs of it, sir. But it's been a sort of tradition in the family for many generations—long before I came here," he added, with unconscious humour.

"And they've gone on cracking that comic gag ever since, eh!"

Calvert frowned.

"If you chose to put it that way, sir." He stiffened, with a taut little air of dignity. "As for comic—well, you've seen for yourself just how comic the thing is to-night. It always works, sir—always!"

"Er—maybe you're right."

The flippancy had gone out of Warrender. There was a point to Calvert's statement. Co-incidence or not, two such mischances had accompanied each recent unveiling of the picture—first robbery, and next murder.

"THERE, Miss Debroy—that's fixed you up, I think!"

Sexton Blake's voice came in welcome interruption to the actor's secret embarrassment. "But you're still looking faint. Mr. Calvert, if you could fetch some brandy—"

"Certainly, sir," the butler agreed, making for the door.

But before he could open it it burst inwards, and the new peer tottered into the room.

Lord Algernon's hair was dripping with water. Evidently he had been sousing his head in the washstand basin to work off the effects of the liquor he had taken. Partly sobered, he came forward into the room.

"Good heavens!"

Anne Debroy sprang to her feet. Her cheeks white as death, she stood staring at the young wastrel, who, in his turn, halted to peer at her in bewilderment.

"Goo'-night! Why, it's Anne!" His dissipated features broke into a grin of welcome. "Well, I'm bleshed! Pleashant shurprishe—what? How'sh yourself, dearie?"

"Thank you, Mr. Westerfield—that will do."

She backed away instinctively as he advanced towards her with outstretched hand.

"But, shweetie—"

"And I've already told you I don't want any of your beastly familiarity!" she cut in sharply. "You can keep it for those who like it. I don't, Mr. Westerfield."

"Aha!" The drunkard swayed forward, shaking his finger at her in mock gravity. "But you don't know—you don't know. Anne, my pet, I'm not a bloomin' mister—no, not me! I'm a lord, a peer of the jolly old realm, my dear—thatsh wha' I am—peer!"

"Since when?" she retorted contemptuously.

"Shince to-night—when my poor old uncle wash murdered—foully murdered. Shtill, they did me a good turn, the dirty dogsh! My dear, I'm Lord Carham!"

She gave a shudder.

"Is this true, what he says?" she asked, turning to Blake.

"Unfortunately, yes, Miss Debroy."

"All the same"—her red lips tightened—"I don't care if you're the Duke of Muck—I don't want anything to do with you, Lord Carham!"

"Ah, thash wha' you shay now. But wait!" Algy Carham laughed unpleasantly. "I'm a rich man now. And money talksh. Beshides, you should have sheen the way I fought for you sh'other night. They'd shtole your picture—Lady Di. Remindsh me of you, dearie. When I shaw they'd got you, why, I fought 'em all. Yesh—the whole lot of them, and—"

"Oh, pack it up, you fool!" Warrender seized him in his strong arms, swung him off his feet, and bore him like a child from the room. "You're going back to bed. Calvert!"

"Yes sir!"

The butler, went scurrying after them, concern on his aged features. Inwardly, no doubt, he sided with Warrender. But then the drunkard was his master now—and one calculated to give a deal of trouble.

Still, when a man grows old in service it is not so easy to find fresh posts. Of this, doubtless, the butler was thinking while in desperation he followed the hefty Warrender and his cursing, kicking burden, from the room.

Sexton Blake was thinking, too—though not of Calvert and his job. What was there between these two—Anne Debroy and Algernon, Lord Carham—that she stood there staring after him, disgust and fear on her exquisite white features?

CHAPTER 5
ONE THING AFTER ANOTHER!

"MISS DEBROY, you're looking tired and faint. Hadn't you better get to bed? One of the maids will arrange something, no doubt, for you if you speak to the butler."

Blake patted the girl sympathetically on the shoulder as the door closed behind Calvert.

"You're staying here—you and Mr. Warrender?" she queried quickly.

"No, we shall not be staying."

"Then neither shall I. Nothing—nothing—would induce me to stop in the same house as that man," she declared vehemently. "And if there's been a murder. Ugh! I hate horrors. No, I must go," she concluded resolutely.

"Very well, Miss Debroy—as you prefer," Blake said quietly. "Perhaps you're right. In any case, I must be going. It's essential the police should be notified at the earliest possible moment. Not that they can do anything in this mist—they can't. I'd have made a move before this otherwise. Only I realise the futility. Look—"

He threw the french windows open and stepped out on to the terrace, where a dense wall of fog greeted him. As he looked out a swift shadow seemed to melt into the murk—swift and silent, its going, like its very existence, doubtful and bewildering.

The detective took a step forward to give chase. Then, realising the abortiveness, he pulled up. After all, he was not sure there was anything there.

"What is it?" the girl asked, by his elbow.

"Nothing, I think," Blake returned, reclosing the windows.

"All the same, I shan't stop here. You understand? I won't—I won't!"

"And you shan't, either," Warrender announced from behind them. He had returned to the room unnoticed. "I've a cousin who's a little shack near here—a bungalow of sorts. He's abroad just now, but he won't mind if we force a window. Let's get out of this and put up there for the night."

"Very well," Blake agreed. "We've got to stay somewhere. The place you mentioned should be better than a local inn. We'll attract less attention. Strangers are always marked men in these remote districts. At the present juncture I'd prefer to go unnoticed."

The star shot a keen look at him.

"All right. I'll tell that butler chap. Let's be going."

A few minutes later the detective left the manor accompanied by his assistant, Warrender, and the girl. Algy Carham's bus still stood, its lamps burning, outside the old building. Pausing to switch off the lights, Blake drove away with his companions.

A short run took them at snail's pace to a small bungalow three miles away, and shadowed by high trees. Here Warrender forced a window catch, and, climbing in, opened the front door for them.

The place was empty, and to judge from appearances, had not been tenanted for many weeks. The shelves and table-tops were white with dust. In the hallway stood a push-bike, its nickel-plate red with rust.

"Old Jimmy—that's my cousin—comes here for a spot of fishing once in a while," Warrender announced. "Meanwhile, we've got the freedom of the city. Make yourselves at home, everybody."

"I suggest that you and Miss Debroy do that," Blake said promptly. "But Tinker and I ought to get a move on. The police ought to be notified of Carham's death. We must be off."

"You'll come back?"

"Certainly. In an hour or so, I expect. Meantime—" Blake slipped the automatic into Warrender's hand. "Here's your gun. Look after her." His voice dropped to a whisper.

"Then you think—" Warrender breathed.

"I think nothing—except that it's as well to be prepared," the detective answered curtly, but still in an undertone. "She's—well—too much like Lady Diana."

"I don't follow," Warrender said, frowning. "What do you mean?"

"Just what I say, my dear chap. Nothing more—nothing less. You'll understand later. I can't explain now. Anyway—keep you eye skinned. This game's not played out yet."

"If they come here to play it—whoever they are—they'll get the raw end of some tough melodrama," Warrender asserted, gripping the gun. "And it won't be a blank cartridge, either. I've fired off a heap of guns in my time. But it hasn't all been play-acting. I was in the War!"

"Then let's hope you haven't lost your marksmanship—" Blake checked himself as Anne, who had been exploring, came up to them.

"What are you men mumbling about?" she asked, with a glance at their stern faces.

"Oh, just a few simple arrangements," Blake replied, with a smile of amusement.

Womanlike, the little chorus girl had been busy with mirror and powder-puff during her brief absence. He concluded that Bertram Warrender had made a hit not entirely professional.

FOR a long time after the two detectives had gone Anne and the actor sat chatting. Their talk was casual, and interlarded with a quaint theatrical jargon which, in the circumstances, would have struck anyone but themselves as bizarre.

It concerned professional experiences, their hopes, ambitions, successes, failures. At no time did it touch on the events of the evening, or the grim shadow menacing misty Murwood. But that this latter was not forgotten manifested in constant glances, thrown by both, towards the fog-cloaked windows.

"Anne—" Warrender turned to her after one of several silences. "What's this between you and that Carham lad?" With the easy-going bonne camaraderie of their profession he used her Christian name.

"Oh, nothing—much." She gave a disdainful little moue. "We've just met. Hope we don't meet again, that's all. One bumps into all sorts of people in musical comedy."

"I've a mind to bump into that myself," Warrender commented seriously.

"Don't. It would be ridiculous—when you've made such a name in the legitimate." She shook her head wisely. "Wish I was in it myself."

"Dunno—I've a bit of a voice." Warrender went to the window as the wind stirred the curtains. "'When the night wind howls, in the chimney cowls, and the mist lies low on the fen—'"

He started singing in a voice like a foghorn as he raised the curtains to see the fog outside.

Anne put her fingers to her ears and laughed.

"That's Gilbert and Sullivan, isn't it? Only—don't. Suppose—they—" Then quickly—"someone heard. And, for goodness' sake draw those curtains."

"All right," he answered, with a jerk of the cretonne hangings. "Only I've ideas about my singing voice. What about us two in a duet, eh?"

"I'm afraid I'm not in good form, to-night," she smiled feebly. "It—it's been rather too like the real thing—your line—drama, you know."

"Sure, kid! You're looking all in. I'm an ass keeping you talking here!" he exclaimed contritely. "You must be—be—"

"Feeling tired? Well, yes." She rose. "I think I'll have a spot of shut-eye. There's a bed in the next room. If you don't mind—"

"Sure! You run along and get some beauty sleep. I'll sit up for old Blake and his lad. Give me a 'scream off' if you want anything; I'll be around." He held out his hand. "Well, so-long, Anne—"

"So-long, Bert!" Her slight fingers touched his momentarily, and the colour came into her pale cheeks. Their eyes met for an instant. Then hers fell, as did her hand. "So-long! I'll call if—if it's necessary."

Just that, and she was gone. As the door closed softly behind her, Warrender sat down abruptly, and began whistling to himself out of tune.

For a little he sat scowling heavily at the carpet. Then, finding a ukelele he tuned the strings after a fashion with his big, clumsy fingers, and fell to crooning over the tiny instrument in an execrable voice.

The sound would give her comfort, he felt—let her know he was on call in case of need. That neither voice nor instrument were on pitch did not worry him. Subconsciously, he played a serenade, his rugged features comically sentimental.

A bit of music helped a man to think. And this thing needed thinking over.

He was still deep in thought when a bell jarred stridently.

Warrender sprang up, gripping his ukelele. The bell was whirring, apparently in the heart of a blank wall.

"The devil!" His fragile uke raised like a club, he faced the wall fiercely, then flung the instrument into a corner.

Opposite was a cupboard door. From there the sounds were coming.

He ripped it open. On a shelf inside a telephone was ringing. With a testy oath he took up the receiver.

"Hallo?" he demanded, silently cursing "Jim" for his choice of location for a telephone.

He was mad with himself because it had startled him.

"That you, Warrender?" a husky voice demanded along the wire.

"Yes. Who is it?"

"Sexton Blake. I'm speaking from Murwood Manor."

"I say, what's up now?"

"Nothing much. Only we've cornered that brute. In a barn. It's locked in, but it's bashing itself against the door like a hurricane. I'm nervy in case the thing breaks loose again. If we'd only a gun! But there isn't one here. That's why I've rung through. I want you to bring that automatic of yours along and settle the brute's hash for it."

"Right-ho!" Warrender exclaimed. "I'll be right along. But; here, I say, what about Miss Debroy? She's asleep, I think."

"Never mind about her. She'll be all right now we've got the thing cornered. Don't disturb her. She might be scared being left alone. And you've no car, have you?"

"No; only a push-bike." Warrender hesitated. "All right, I'll be with you shortly. Toodle-oo!"

He rang off with a sigh of relief that the Horror was caged at last. One shrewd shot and its baleful life would be ended.

All the same, he hated to leave Anne. Tiptoeing, he went to the door and drew it open gently. She was stretched out on the bed, sleeping like a child, her pretty face beatific in repose.

Warrender shut the door hastily and seized on the push-bike. The sooner that infernal brute was scotched the better. Another moment and he was pedalling off down the road as if the devil were after him.

One shrewd shot—

But, then, he did not see the fitful shadow that loomed out on the lane behind him as the wreathing mist swallowed him up.

"SERGEANT, do you know if Lord Carham was up against anyone in this district—poachers, for instance?"

Sexton Blake's eyes left the moist windscreen for the face of the police-officer seated beside him. En route from the police-station back to Murwood Manor, the detective had been wrestling with this problem.

"Enemies-eh?" The sergeant shook his head. "Not that I know of, sir. His Lordship was always very popular in the district. A generous gentleman he was. Gave liberally to all the local charities, the cricket club, and so on. No, I don't think he'd any enemies."

"Then we must look farther afield for a motive," Blake muttered, his gaze returning to the road ahead. "As, for example, who stands to gain by his death. I—Hallo! What's that?"

He pointed through the windscreen as the car swung round a corner and a dull red glare burst through the thick vapours.

"By George, a fire!" the sergeant exclaimed, peering forward. "A pretty big one, too. And—Why, it looks like Mr. Murrell's place!"

"Murrell?"

"Yes, Mr. James Murrell. He's a cousin of that actor chap, Warrender. They're down here after the trout occasionally, and—Great Scott, sir, what's the matter?" This as the car shot forward like a bullet.

"Heaven knows!" Blake breathed as, bent over the steering wheel, he thrust the bus all out into the fog.

Regardless of danger, he took corners at top speed, racing for the glare ahead, his jaw set grimly and his thin lips tensioned. He had left Anne Debroy and the actor at Murrell's bungalow. The bungalow was now afire.

Brakes screaming, he pulled the powerful speedster up before the building. It was ablaze from end to end. From the windows great gusts of black smoke were belching. Round the eaves licked tongues of crimson flame.

Followed by his companions, the detective raced for the front door.

But it resisted his efforts. Leaving it, he found a window, and smashed in the pane with his naked fist.

A vast puff of acrid smoke burst forth. It sent him reeling backwards, coughing, choking. Recovering, he whipped off his coat, and, swathing it round his head, vaulted in over the sill.

A flash from his electric torch showed a bed, its covers crumpled. Someone had lain there, and—

His torch beam slewed to a chair, where, neatly piled, was a tiny heap of feminine garments—Anne Debroy's outer clothes.

"Miss Debroy—Warrender!" he shouted.

But the only result was the choking cough from his own smoke scorched lungs—that, and the fierce crackle of the flames.

A last swing of the torch proved the room untenanted. He groped for the door and flung it open. A hot blast of fire-streaked murk struck him. Still he pressed on, coughing, stifled, his torch-ray flung ahead of him.

Chairs, a lounge, stools—all empty! An overturned lamp—

Where were Warrender and the girl? Had they escaped, or—

He bent quickly. There was something on the floor—a black hump, wreathed in curling vapours.

It was a man—face downwards on the smouldering carpet, about him an oozing pool of dull red.

The detective stooped, turned the figure over quickly. A white face looked up glassily into his.

It was Algernon Carham—the new peer of the realm—dead!

On his chest were eight great blood-clots—the widely spaced puncture marks such as had bored his uncle's shirt front.

Again the thing! Again those frightful talons! But the fire?

Blake shuddered, then put the question from him. Seizing the body, he tottered with it to the door and burst it outwards with one mighty drive of his powerful shoulder.

The fresh air! His lungs filled gratefully. Dragging the corpse onwards, he lowered it to the ground.

"Sergeant! Tinker!" he shouted.

But his call died in the deafening blast of a gunshot. As he flung himself flat the air shrieked on high, with the whiz of hurtling lead. Someone was shooting at him.

The detective's hand touched something—a stout stake, the pale from some fencing. He gripped it, rose, and, with another shout, charged through the smoke at his unseen enemy.

"Here, guv'nor—coming!" Tinker's voice answered from somewhere in the murk.

Behind him boomed the sergeant's cheery bass. Ducking low, Blake dashed for the roadway. Another stab of flame greeted him. The phwitt of a singing bullet seemed almost to fan his ear. Then a rush of feet away from him. A scurry—a whir. The wrench of a buzzing self-starter; the roar of a racing motor-engine.

Then a red tail-lamp swiftly receded down the road. The gunman had seized his car!

For a few yards Blake followed. Then, realising the futility of running he walked slowly back to his companions.

As he reached them the bungalow roof crashed inwards, to a leaping cascade of high flung sparks. It was the end of Muddell's little dwelling.

Down the road something was coming from the direction of Murwood Manor. Another second and the swirling flames lit up a bent figure that swept up out of the mist.

It was Warrender, sweat streaming from his brow, his mighty form doubled up over the handlebars of a push-bike.

He was alone!

CHAPTER 6
ON THE MARSHES!

THE actor flung himself off his machine.

"Where's the girl?" Blake rapped.

"Isn't she with you, then?" Warrender gasped, collapsing over the bike. He was utterly exhausted. He had come hell-for-leather when he had seen the flames.

"No; she's missing," Blake said, steadying the actor. "Pull yourself together, old man. Every moment may be vital."

"Yes—I'm all—right. Just—winded!" Warrender forced himself to speak. "She's not in there, eh?" He glanced at the blazing building.

"No; I can swear to that, anyway. Wherever she is, she's not there," Blake told him.

"Thank Heaven for that, anyway!" The actor heaved a sigh of relief. "But what's happened?"

"I was going to ask the same question. Where have you been?"

"To the manor."

"But why?"

"Because I'm an infernal fool—that's why!" Warrender said savagely. "Someone rang through. They said they were you—that you'd got that horrible thing cornered in a barn. Would I bring my gun and finish it off? I fell for the yarn, and got to the manor only to find the whole business a washout. Just as as I might have guessed it was. I got the wind-up then, you bet! I—I pedalled back, puzzled at first, but when I saw the fire—well, I was too late."

"Yes, too late, I'm afraid." Blake muttered, biting his lip. "Look at this!" He drew Warrender over to where Algy Carham lay.

"Gosh!" The actor bent over him, slack-jawed. Then he straightened abruptly. I might have known. That husky, thickish voice! That was a trick of Carham's!"

"What was?"

"That bogus phone call, of course. The beggar wanted me out of the way. You saw how he leered at her, back there at the manor, earlier this evening. You saw, too, how she stood him off, bless her! The swine! This was his doing. I see it all now!"

Warrender gave a ferocious growl and shook his fist at the recumbent figure.

"You were meant to see it, Warrender."

"Eh?" the actor gasped.

"You wrong Carham."

"But how? He's here, isn't he?"

"Yes, he's here," Blake said slowly. "And dead, man—dead! Look at those talon-marks in his chest. He died as his uncle died."

"By Jove!" Warrender peered down at the dead man's chest, then straightened, frowning. "I thought he had fainted. But—but—"

"Would he come here deliberately—to his death? There's more to it than that." Blake shook his head. "Carham was just a pawn in the game—a greater game than either you or I have hitherto guessed at. You say someone rang you up—that they spoke thickly? Well, that, too, was a blind. Just as this wild-goose chase was they called you off on. It was probably hoped you would lay the thing at Carham's door."

"But"—Warrender glared down at the corpse—"look here! That thing killed him. Do you mean to tell me a brute like that could telephone? If so, I'm going mad."

"No," Blake smiled dryly. "Much as I'm growing to respect the power of that infernal creature, I'm reluctant to think it could telephone. But remember, brute beasts have done murder before to-day at the behest of human beings. It may be that this thing, whatever it is, is but a dumb tool."

"You're right." Warrender nodded. "I'm losing my grip—my sense of proportion. I see that now. Still—" He looked down, shuddering, at the frightful wounds. "What beast ever had such claws? Answer me that!"

"I cannot answer you, Warrender, my boy—at least, not now," Blake laid a kindly hand on the actor's shoulder. "But I shall one day. Perhaps sooner than you think. There's a solution to this problem somewhere, if only we can find it. And find it I shall, if I have to rake the whole world to do so."

"And meanwhile—Anne Debroy?" The actor breathed tensely. "Man, what are we to do?"

His voice throbbed with suppressed anguish.

"Our damnedest, old chap—we can do no more!"

"My heaven! If they harm that, girl—"

Warrender clenched his fists, with unconscious theatricality.

"We shall avenge her, have no fear," the detective said quietly. "In the meantime, 'there are more things in heaven and earth, Horatio, than are dreamed of in your philosophy'—or, come to that, in mine. And some of them, my dear Warrender, are mighty foul!"

THOUGH the detectives and Warrender searched throughout the night, there was no trace to be found of Anne Debroy. Next morning yielded results as negative. Tales, though, of the strange Shape proved rife throughout the district.

A belated cyclist, pedalling homeward through the mists of early morning, spoke incoherently of a fearsome object passed on the road. A county constable, also, had seen something of the sort—or thought he had. As confirmation,

the maudlin ravings of the village toper yielded yet further, if presumably unreliable, data.

At all events, dawn found this redoubtable worthy in a ditch, on the verge of collapse. High noon, and time for gossip, he had reduced the little community of Murwood to a state bordering on semi-terrorisation. It seemed the days of witchcraft were not yet departed.

All this Sexton Blake drank in for what it was worth—which was little or nothing. The footman, Perkins, from the manor, had been into the village early, and, the detective did not doubt, had talked. Stories of the picture, the family curse, and what not, were rife, to top which a ghastly murder, committed in the most weird of circumstances, might be deemed sufficient to start any ball of rumour a-rolling.

All the same, that sinister figure, flitting down the terrace parapet, had most certainly been glimpsed. Apart from this, the strange footprints remained. Then there were the extraordinary crescent-shaped wounds in the dead men's chests. There was no disputing the existence of two hands armed with talons unique in the criminologist's experience.

Still, none of this yielded up Anne Debroy, nor even a hint as to her whereabouts. She might have vanished into thin air, so thoroughly had she disappeared, leaving, incidentally, her street clothes behind her.

"That brute—whatever it is—broke into the bungalow and attacked her," Warrender declared. "With or without Westerfield's connivance—I don't care which. The beast overturned the lamp, which, of course, accounts for the fire. It's pretty clear Anne was disturbed without warning and that she just managed to bolt as she was, in her underclothes. She'll have just thrown off her outer garments to lie down. I think it's all pretty plain."

With sun up, the actor had regained his optimism. He clung to his newly-formed theory stoutly.

Sexton Blake, however, ventured no opinion. Beyond a non-committal grunt or so, he would say nothing. Only Tinker ventured to challenge Warrender's opinion.

"If she escaped only half-clad, she can't have got far without attracting attention," the lad pronounced. "That being so, why haven't reports come in of a girl found wandering—er—half-dressed? Well there are none, Mr. Warrender. How do you account for it?"

"All I can say is that Westerfield, whom she feared and hated, is dead," the star asserted. "Now that brute can't have carried her off, though he might have killed her. But there's no—body." Warrender forced himself to utter that final word with an effort. "No, my idea is that she's thoroughly well breezed, and fled the neighbourhood. She dropped me a hint of that last night, after you two had gone for the police."

"What hint?" Blake put in sharply.

"Said she'd a mind to make straight for Peterborough, where she'd come over from that day. Her show finished up there, it seems. I reckon she's got digs somewhere in the city. I've a mind to run over and see if that isn't just what's happened."

"I doubt it, old chap," the detective said, shaking his head.

All the same, Warrender, half-distracted, adhered resolutely to his plan. Afternoon found him en route for the famous cathedral town.

There was a clue to Anne's lodging in correspondence found in her vanity bag, left by accident at the manor. But a call at the address in question brought Warrender little comfort. Nothing had been seen of the chorus girl.

Baffled, the actor walked back towards the station, his former fears renewed—fears which, curiously enough, bulked out of all proportion to such anxiety as might reasonably be expected on behalf of so new an acquaintance.

The fact set him frowning. He was in the midst of an attempt to analyse the phenomenon to his own satisfaction, when engrossed in his thoughts, he came near to colliding with an oncoming pedestrian.

In the nick of time he side-stepped, to halt with a muttered apology. But he never finished the instant "Sorry." It was the rat-faced man from Li Chun's!

With a careless nod, Rat Face passed on, which was fortunate. The actor's face would have given him away otherwise. As it was, the fellow slouched off unconcernedly, his back turned to the staring Warrender. A moment later he stepped into the doorway of some shop.

The man who had dropped the Van Dyck! Rat Face, the originator of the melee at Li Chun's!

Facts flitted with lightning speed through Warrender's brain. Here at least was something!

As Rat Face vanished, Warrender strode back towards the shop the man had entered—a chemist's, as it transpired. Rat Face was busy inside, buying something.

For an instant Warrender hesitated; then recollected that he ran no risk of recognition. He had been well disguised that night, down in Poplar. Rat Face, would neither look for him nor remember him now.

Once on his guard, the star controlled his features. The actor in him won the upper hand. Not for nothing had Bertram Warrender gained his professional reputation. Poker-faced and nonchalant, he stepped into the shop, in time to see the salesman hand his quarry a small iron bottle.

"By Jove! Oxygen!" Warrender murmured. "Now, what the blazes does he want with that?"

Feigning interest in some photographic sidelines, the actor presented his broad back to the ruffian. Meanwhile, his quick wits were working overtime.

Oxygen was administered only to persons gravely ill—and Rat Face was hale enough. To be sure his ugly "clock," bore a brace of swollen blue marks—testimony to the wallop he had collected during that free fight at Li Chun's. But still, oxygen—

"No, my friend; there's something to this, I'll bet my shirt," Warrender muttered. "We're going to see—"

He waited till Rat Face quitted the shop, then, with praiseworthy caution, proceeded to trail him, as it turned out, to the station. Here Rat Face took a train on the Murwood branch, alighting, not at Murwood, but at a halt two miles previously. Lingering till the train began to move, Warrender sprang out on to the platform in time to see his man vanish through the exit.

With a cunning worthy of some Red Indian, the actor followed his suspect down a country road leading towards Murwood. Thanks to those fishing expeditions, he knew the locality well, and Rat Face had not gone far before his tracker knew he would have done better to get off the train at Murwood itself.

Then why not Murwood ? Obviously, since Rat Face had something to hide. Rat Face was not out to attract attention to himself or his gas bottle. Yes, there was something to all this.

Smiling grimly to himself, Warrender dodged down a woodland path in the wake of his quarry, to emerge at length on fen lands. These, Rat Face proceeded to cross with the cool assurance of one on familiar ground.

Warrender had now, perforce, to drop behind. In the open he dare not approach his man so closely as before. Ducking low in the shadow of dykes, he clung on obstinately, in his ears the dull, monotonous roar of some mighty motor, that grew ever louder and louder.

Still Rat Face crept on towards the spot whence the roaring came. Thanks to the dykes, Warrender could see little. When at last he ventured a peep, he was just in time to see his man vanish through a small door in a high range of fencing, from behind which the thunderous monotone seemed to come.

"Sounds mighty like an aeroplane engine," the actor said to himself, as, still sheltering in the dykes, he commenced a tedious detour of the ring fence which had received the ruffian.

But why the fence? What lay behind it? Again, why the noise? He was still considering this when he ran into a stolid-faced yokel, herding some cattle.

"That, sir?" the countryman exclaimed, when Warrender questioned him. "Dunno, 'zactly. They do say it's some airyoplane—a new sort, and very 'ush, 'ush, we useter say in the Army, time the War was on. Sorter Schneeder Trophy bus, us reckons, down at the George and Dragon. Anyways, they won't let no one near the place. There's a man with a shotgun on the lookout. Mebbe they're afeared someone'll pinch their patent, like. Lunnon folks, they is, I reckon from their lingo. Anyways, beggin' your pardon, sir, they be blamed furriners o' some sort."

A half-crown changed hands, and the yokel made off promptly, against the setting sun, intent on reaching the George and Dragon before the fat silver coin burned a hole in his pocket. Chuckling softly at his own acumen—after all, the successful actor must needs be a student of human psychology—Warrender possessed his soul in patience. Then, as the far-off figure faded out of sight, he slipped cautiously to the fence and hauled himself up.

The motor had stopped now. Inside the corrugated iron ring was a squat building, hangar-shaped. Its broad doors were closed. For the moment the yard fronting them was untenanted.

Straddling the fence-top, Warrender studied the premises. If a plane was housed inside, there was nothing to show how it could get out and take off from such cramped quarters. The ground, too, was damp and muddy, as witness a trail of footprints, criss-crossed and mazy, before the big doors.

Footprints! Surely there was also chain-work of bulbous indents, such as—

Bang!

A sawn-off shotgun went off with the blast of a thunderclap. There was a puff of grey smoke from the doorway, and the fence rang to a hail of pattering buckshot.

A shot—another—an answering yell. Then a third crash from the deadly weapon.

But Warrender swung of the fence like a monkey. Head down, he was speeding westward across the marshes.

He was unarmed, thanks to his Peterborough visit. One does not take guns to the cloister. Still, he trusted in his strength and speed of foot. It would be a stout man who overtook him.

But the guardians of the hangar had, too, their resources. Doubling through the dim light along his narrow and uncertain footway, Warrender heard behind him the deep baying of a hound. As he ran, groping, chancing his way in the all-but-darkness, he heard the fierce notes grow nearer and nearer.

They had set their dog upon him.

Gasping, panting, bewildered—for the rising white vapours and the night-cloaked fen baffled him, Warrender stumbled on. Then the swift pad-pad of racing feet behind him made him turn. The hound was close up now—one of the biggest he had ever seen.

He swerved despairingly, ran on a few yards, then, realising the uselessness of running, turned and stood his ground.

Like a cannon-ball the huge brute sprang.

Two forepaws struck his chest with the thud of a sledgehammer, two gaping jaws, two rows of bared white fangs, gaped for him. He felt the hot waft of fetid breath in his face, while two eyes, wolf-red, glared into his.

He reeled back, bracing his mighty frame to the impact. His hands found the quivering throat, and gripped it, his feet slid wildly in the mud. Then man and hound went down together, locked in a fierce embrace.

For a frenzied moment the pair rolled over and over, the frothing jaws thrusting, straining to get at him. But the actor hung on with the grip of desperation. Slowly but surely his steel strong fingers bit deeper into the Alsatian's neck.

An age-long span of agony, the mud scrunching beneath him, be-slavered, clawed, half blinded.

Deeper and deeper Warrender's thumbs drove into the creature's wind pipe. Deeper—deeper—

If only he could hold on! The pulsating throat stilled in his grip, but he went on gouging, gripping madly, teeth clenched, and his senses reeling. Then, spent at last he fell across the lifeless dog

HE raised himself presently, aware that the hound no longer stirred. Slowly, dimly, it came to him that it was dead. Laughing hysterically, he staggered up, brushing the mud

from his eyes.

"Gosh! That was a close 'un!"

"Hi! There he is!"

A harsh voice broke through the mists and a speeding figure burst through the veil of grey, To the left an answering hail went up. Then the grey went red with a flash of flame, and a bullet streaked past into the night.

Warrender spun round, sobered and himself again, and plunged off madly into the murk. Mud sprayed beneath his squelching boots. Behind him his pursuers fired, running as they aimed. Thanks to the gloom, their shots went wide; but because they were familiar with the path they pressed him hard.

Still, his feats on screen and stage were no mere fakes. Speed and muscle helped him now. As the race went on he began to wear down his opponents, who fell behind in the darkness.

"Good-bye-ee!"

He turned to wave a derisive hand, as, his own great strength maintained, he saw his pursuers failing,

"Good—" he began, and broke off, with a gasp.

The ground fell away suddenly from under him, and he plunged forward into a quagmire of mud. He floundered helplessly, sinking the more he struggled.

Vainly he tried to drag himself free. But his great weight proved his undoing. Higher and higher the mud rose about him. As it reached his armpits he heard his enemies circling about him.

"Where, is the blighter, Bill?" someone called through the mist.

A torch flashed out, searching the ground.

A dull chill of paralysis gripped Warrender. The mud was slowly rising. Now it was almost to his chin. Around him the searchers worked steadily, their torch beams flickering like monstrous glow-worms in the dark.

If he cried out it meant a bullet; and if he kept still ...

He shuddered as he felt the mud rising.

CHAPTER 7
AT GRIPS WITH THE GROTESQUE.

"HELP!"

Warrender gave a last despairing cry as the slime touched his lips. He waved an arm, hoping against hope, yet expecting nothing. How his ears buzzed! Was that one of the gunmen coming towards him?

"He's in there! Get your gun—"

A last futile struggle; then from outer night the rasp of a deep-throated growl. Another shout; the bark of a gun; the growl closer and fiercer. There was a scurry on the banks, a burst of firing above his head; the dull thud of racing footfalls coming and going; then—

"Man, where are you?"

It was the voice of Sexton Blake.

"Here!" Warrender called feebly; and a torch-ray caught his head and held there.

"Hold on, old chap; I'm coming!" the detective replied cheerily, and the beam swung away.

To the right it shone on some old fencing.

Blake sprang forward and with an effort tore a plank from its rusty nails.

"Here—catch!"

The plank splashed out alongside Warrender. Getting his chin on the edge of it, he worked one arm free and gripped it eagerly. Then another and another followed, to form a friendly raft as the actor got both arms about them.

Away in the distance the shots continued, still punctuated by ferocious growls. Cool, collected, and undismayed, the detective tore down more fencing. Flinging it near Warrender, he crawled out cautiously and reached him.

"You all right?" Blake asked, as he dragged the actor from the mud-hole.

"Yes—thanks to you!" Warrender sank down on the dyke, gasping. "But what good angel brought you here—just in the nick of time?"

"A canine one—my bloodhound, Pedro," Blake explained. "Tinker fetched him down from town this afternoon. We were out scouting, when we saw you trailing someone. We'd binoculars, and watched you from a distance. When the firing began we came out after you. Thanks to the dog, we got through quickly. Pedro and Tinker are chasing your pals. And the rest you know."

Warrender nodded. For a moment he stood regarding his own bedraggled figure disgustedly.

"By Jove! But I'd make a pretty sight in Piccadilly," he announced, grinning; then: "What do they want with oxygen at an aeroplane hangar?"

"Dope for atomization," Blake suggested, with a keen glance at the actor.

"Sure! But they'd need a big bottle for that. I mean a small one, from the chemist's—A Peterborough chemist's, by the way."

"H'm! That's different."

"It is—when a chap I bashed t'other night at Li Chun's has just fetched it."

"Well, he's had his own back with a vengeance, by the look of it," the detective remarked thoughtfully. "Incidentally, talking of back, here's Tinker with Pedro."

As he spoke the lad's slight figure bore in out of the mist, the bloodhound at his side.

"They've hopped it, guv'nor!" the youngster announced, pocketing his gun. "Old Pedro had the pants off one of 'em pretty well. He put the breeze up 'em, I reckon, properly! They've scattered for keeps, I think!"

"Then we'll be getting back to the manor," Blake declared. "There's nothing more to be done here now, with this mist. And the sooner Warrender gets changed the better. He's had enough excitement for one night."

Which was true enough; though, as it turned out, further dramatic incident was in store for the trio. Hardly had they reached Murwood Manor than a car came up the drive. Blake was still in the big hall, when the bell rang, and Calvert went to answer it.

"There's a Mr. Grifstein here, sir," the butler announced, coming back to the detective. "He wants to see Lord Carham's representative. He says it's important. Since you've—er—sort of taken charge here, sir, I was wondering if you'd see him?"

"All right. Who is he?" Blake inquired, inwardly rather startled at the truth of the butler's words. Strictly, he had no authority at the manor at all; but somehow—perhaps it was because the butler was only too glad to have someone to lean on—things seemed to have naturally drifted into his responsibility since the murder.

"The gentleman who bought Sir Abe Rodman's place yonder, sir—the eccentric millionaire who shot himself a year or so back. Maybe you'll have heard of him?"

Blake nodded.

"Yes, I remember seeing something about Rodman's suicide in the papers. If you'll show this Grifstein in I'll see what he wants."

He passed on into the study and sat down. A moment later Calvert appeared with the visitor.

Sexton Blake found himself face to face with the biggest and most obese man he had ever seen.

"Sit down, Mr. Grifstein."

The detective motioned the caller to a seat.

Mr. Grifstein smiled oilily, lowered his ponderous body with caution into an inadequate looking chair, then, his fleshy hands on his big paunch, paused to regard the detective while his finger's played with a massive gold Albert spanning his waistcoat.

"Ahem—you are Lord Carham's legal representative?" he began, his piggy eyes half closed. He spoke with an accent that was a mixture of foreign and North Country.

Blake inclined his head. "You may regard me as representing. Lord Carham's posthumous interests, sir—pending the discovery of an heir. Till then, you see, the estate is—er— somewhat in a state of flux."

"Ah, quite so, quite so." The visitor's thick lips twisted in another of his unpleasant smiles. "It is on that account I have come. To end this state of uncertainty, you might say."

"To end it—how?" Blake queried sharply. "Do you know of another heir, then, Mr. Grifstein?"

"An heir? Not exactly." Grifstein shook his head—it was a head that seemed too big for his body.

He sank back in his chair, still viewing the detective, his bulging collar hidden by his ponderous jowl. Then:

"The late Lord Carham—the old 'un, I mean—held this property in trust. It became *decouvert* by his death—a most regrettable affair, sir—most regrettable. But, to stick to the point, it became the absolute property of his heir, Mr. Westerfield."

"So I'm given to understand," Blake assented. "Well?"

"Mr. Westerfield wished to—er—anticipate his inheritance." Grifstein drove his great thumbs into the arm-holes of his waistcoat and, rocking back on the hind legs of his groaning chair, paused afresh to observe the effect of this announcement. As Blake's lean profile remained enigmatic, he continued: "In short, sir, I did business with him and bought the reversions."

"Which, I take it, means that you claim the Carham estate as your absolute property?" Blake demanded. No flicker of surprise crossed his calm features.

"You've said it, young feller!" Grifstein fished in his pocket. "Oh, here we are. Here's the papers, signed by the late Mr. Algernon Westerfield, and making everything over to me, in consideration of value received."

Blake took the papers and examined them. Subject to proper identification of Westerfield's signature, everything seemed in order. The document showed that Westerfield had parted in advance with his inheritance in exchange for a lump sum paid him by one Conrad Grifstein, described as "gentleman," and of the Towers, near Murwood.

While he perused the body of the instrument, Blake's mind worked swiftly. The arrangement was a common one, often resorted to by heirs pressed for money.

That Westerfield had been so pressed was more than probable, especially since, according to Calvert, Lord Carham had disowned him on account of his dissipated mode of living. It was just such fellows as Algernon Westerfield who as a rule resorted to moneylenders for advances on the security of trust moneys to come.

This being so, Blake hardly doubted that the document was genuine. Its existence in no way surprised him. Such a deal was characteristic of wastrels. And Westerfield was the sort who lived only for the moment.

It explained, too, his ill-timed but hysterical laughter as he viewed his uncle's body. Drunk as he had been, Westerfield realised that he had sold his birthright for a mess of pottage—sold it as the present papers proved, within a few months of Carham's death. Fate had played an ironic joke upon him. A man in the early fifties, his uncle's expectation of life had been one of many years. Instead, he had been struck down at once.

"Well, Mr. Grifstein, and what do you wish me to do about this?" the criminologist inquired presently.

"Make a note of them papers," Grifstein retorted truculently. "You understand? I've parted with my brass, and I claim the property, accordin' to justice and law. Get that?"

"To be sure, Mr. Grifstein—to be sure." Blake bowed his head politely as he returned the papers to their owner. "Your claim shall be duly noted, and, please, rest assured, it shall receive the attention it so plainly deserves."

AFTER the visitor had gone, Sexton Blake sat back in his chair, deep in thought. If Westerfield had sold his inheritance, then he had nothing to gain from his uncle's death. Only Grifstein could benefit through the catastrophe, since it would throw the property immediately into his lap instead of only after a presumable period of years.

But, since Westerfield had parted with his inheritance, it equally followed that no one had anything to gain from Westerfield's own demise. Grifstein could not possibly benefit from it. The property was his from the moment of Lord Carham's death.

Why then had Westerfield been murdered, as undoubtedly he had? Why, too, had his uncle been murdered—as was obvious, by the same agency as that which later destroyed his nephew? There was clearly a connecting link between the two outrages. What was it?

According to Calvert there was no other heir to the estate. Westerfield was the last of his line—the last simply because, by the patent of the barony, the peerage passed where requisite through the female branch. Apparently, no one had anything to gain by these deaths. There remained, then, the question of the family curse.

But Sexton Blake placed little credence in such legends, imagined or real. There was a key to the mystery somewhere, if only he could find it. But where—where?

His eyes half closed, he leant back, concentrating till the mirror before him grew misty. Out of the mist there slowly formed a mental picture—and at sight of it the detective's thin lips fashioned in a grim smile.

Yes, there was always a key, and—

He stiffened as, the imaginary mist dissolving, the surface of the mirror reflected actuality. In it was a clean, indubitable reflection.

It was that of a ghastly shape coming through the window behind him. Gorilla-headed, grotesquely clawed—it was the Gnomid, depicted in that old-time painting in the gallery upstairs!

Blake did not stir. The temptation to do so was maddening in its intensity, but he crushed it down. His eyes on the glass, he watched the brute behind him creep stealthily forward, its monstrous talons already spread to strike.

While he watched, one half of his brain kept him in amazement that the thing was, after all, an actually existing creature. Where it had come from he could not guess, in those moments of stupefied surprise; the fact that it was real swamped speculation about its country of origin.

Slowly, very slowly, the detective's right hand sought his pocket—sought it so cautiously that no movement showed. Nearer and nearer the shape approached. Closer and closer to his pocket did Blake's hand steal. When he found the butt of his automatic, the brute was within six feet of the chair-back.

The giant claws rose. The brute swung forward. And simultaneously the detective turned.

His chair shot backwards at his thrust. It caught the creature full in the legs. And as the claws smote the thing fell sideways, threshing the air with its frightful nails.

Without a pause in that sudden first movement, Blake spun round, his automatic raised. He had a glimpse of the Gnomid, big as a gorilla, crashing against the table. Then the lamp went over, and the room was dark. He was caged in with this frightful beast, helpless to see the swoop of its searching claws.

He leapt back to the wall, hugging his pistol. Somewhere in the gloom the thing lurked, hunting for him. He could hear the slithery drag of its feet, illusive on the thick pile carpet. But the sounds seemed ever shifting. Once—

twice—thrice raised his gun, yet held his hand. The brute was there and gone in a twinkling.

Now that creak by the table; again a faint sound to his right. The brute seemed to have eyes like a cat. Though Blake constantly changed his own position it followed him at every move.

It was between him and the door now; his way of escape was cut off! And to leave by the window meant exposing himself in silhouette against the faintness of the outer night. Besides, to leave this thing, inside the house, at liberty, and—

A dull scraping on the door startled him. Was it the Gnomid feeling for the handle, or— A low, angry growl followed. Then something thudded violently against the panels.

There was a gasp from the gloom—a hurried shuffle of feet across the floor. The Gnomid was going to investigate.

The interruption was Pedro, scenting an intruder!

Pedro, clawing at the obstacle which intervened between him and his quarry. Pedro, whose eyes could bore into the darkness—

Blake leapt for the door as, with a rush, his foul assailant whisked past in the dark. He seized the knob, his body half turned towards the window, and his gun on guard.

The knob stuck. And as he fumbled with it with his left, not daring to disengage his gun hand, the shape loomed at the casement. For a second it poised, forcing its grotesque figure out through the narrow opening, vaguely visible against the outer night.

In a flash Blake's weapon spat. There was a screech from the window—a tinkle of smashing glass.

Crash! The detective's gun belched fire for the second time. But the brute tore itself free and vanished. An instant later Blake got the door open.

The bloodhound dashed into the room, sniffed round him for a moment, and then, at Blake's gesture, plunged at the window, but could not force his mighty girth through it. Baffled and furious, he blocked the orifice—securely stuck there in his frantic efforts to win the garden beyond.

With a low cry of exasperation Blake found a second casement and wrenched it open. But by this time the shape was gone. And Pedro, jammed in the window-frame, was powerless to pursue.

So frantic was the dog that for a little it was impossible to quiet him. Then Tinker appeared, with Warrender and Calvert on his heels. Between them the four got Pedro loose. But by that time all hope of catching the creature had vanished.

Even so, Blake did not give up. With the aid of Pedro and a hurricane-lamp, he set out in pursuit, following a thin trail of blood dripped on the ground.

But the trail soon ended, as did the scent, at a small brook. Apparently the Gnomid had taken to the water.

"Well, the thing's vulnerable to lead," Blake muttered as, a thin cloud of sleet beating their faces, the four turned back towards the manor. "That's something, anyhow. Let's hope it's scotched for the time being. Meanwhile—"

"There's Anne," Warrender breathed despairingly.

"Yes, there's Anne Debroy," Blake agreed, nodding. Beneath his breath he added to himself: "Or was. We can only hope she is."

CHAPTER 8
LIGHT FILTERS THROUGH.

NEXT morning Tinker departed with the car on some mysterious errand. For a while Blake busied himself with some newspaper cuttings, fresh in by the early mail, with a covering letter from one of his agents.

The cuttings were of recent date, and apparently unrelated one to the other. The first concerned Anne Debroy; the second, Mordaunt Grifstein. One cutting was as follows:

COURT'S PRONOUNCEMENT. CHORUS-GIRL'S APPLICATION. LINEAL DESCENT PROVED AND ALLOWED BY JUDGE.

Miss Anne Debroy yesterday obtained from Mr. Justice MacIlroy an assent to the validity of her claim of descent from Ezra Bardon, a cloth manufacturer of the Seventeenth Century. Miss Debroy, who is a chorus girl, had occasion to prefer this claim in respect of a small legacy arising from the death of Mr. Charles Bardon, of Derby, who died last year intestate and ap-

parently without heirs. Miss Debroy, it appears, knew little or nothing of her family history till the late Mr. Bardon's solicitors traced her. Her romantic application to the Court was necessitated owing to some difficulty as to the marriage of an intermediate ancestor, the records not being wholly in order.

The second cutting ran:

AIRMAN EXPLORER'S RETURN.

Mr. Mordaunt Grifstein, who recently set out by flying-boat to find the source of the River Amazon in the heart of Brazil, reached London yesterday after what he stated to be a most successful trip. Not only is he satisfied, he told our representative, that he has definitely located the hitherto unknown source of the famous river, but, in addition, he has succeeded in securing a number of interesting specimens of the flora and fauna of those regions. Mr. Mordaunt Grifstein is the only son of Mr. Conrad Grifstein, the well-known financier of Jermyn Street, W., and the Towers, near Murwood.

"Well, that explains two things," Warrender declared, when Blake showed him the cuttings. "Firstly, I've a pretty shrewd idea what Anne's business was with Grifstein. From the fact of those reversions Westerfield pawned with him, I suppose he makes a business of advancing money on the security of inheritances."

"Yes, you may substitute 'moneylender' for 'financier,' I fancy, Warrender. The latter's just a newspaper euphemism."

"Then I take it Anne was negotiating an advance on that legacy of hers. Her shows had had a 'dry up' in Peterborough, she told me. And I know she was at her wits' end for the ready."

"I dare say you're right, old man," Blake murmured, still fingering the clippings.

"And then there's this explorer bloke," Warrender went on. "That explains that aeroplane lay-out on the fens. I've since heard that the land there belongs to old stick-in-the-mud—I mean, his nibs, Conrad Grifstein. If the son's a flier, it will explain a lot."

"But not a chase by gunmen, old son," the detective remarked, frowning. "They nearly had you last night."

"Yes, confound 'em!" the actor exclaimed. "I've a mind to drop in on those Grifsteins, and raise merry hades. In fact—"

"You're going to stay here with me, and let the Grifsteins alone for the present," Blake cut in firmly.

"But—"

"I don't want Mr. Grifstein offended by any hasty charges or recriminations," Blake said sternly. "Remember, we're hunting over his land, largely. Well, I don't wish to be hampered by any difficulties, which will undoubtedly be raised if we make an enemy of him."

"There's that that rat-faced tough, and the oxygen bottle!" Warrender growled, as, with visible reluctance, he resumed his place.

"Which reminds me—we've a little expedition to make," the detective went on coolly. "You let the Grifsteins be, my lad, and come along with me."

OUTSIDE a thick blizzard of snow was falling. Accompanied by Pedro, Blake and the actor set out into the storm, and, reaching the stream which last night had checked them, proceeded along its banks.

The brook led into some woods where, for a time, the two men and their canine searched the ground, intent on picking up the Gnomid's trail. But the latter seemed completely to have faded. Though they hunted systematically for three hours, no further signs of blood occurred.

"Curious!" Blake murmured. "From the red trail left last night, I must have wounded that brute pretty badly. He must have made a pretty quick get-away, too, or Pedro would have got him. A quick get-away means stress and strain, especially where wounds are concerned. Yet the injury seems to have healed up. Otherwise, why don't we find more blood?"

"That's just what I've been thinking, Blake, old man," the actor concurred. "Still, an animal like that couldn't very well apply a styptic

pencil to itself, could it? If it didn't, how did it stop bleeding?"

"You can rule the styptic pencil out," Blake said drily. "I—Hallo! What's the matter with old Pedro?"

Ahead, the hound was nosing into the snow, growling, and in obvious excitement. The two men hurried forward, to find Pedro pawing at a low, humpy object on the ground, half-buried by snow.

Blake thrust the dog aside, and, with the palm of his hand, swept away the newly-fallen snow. Stiff and stark lay the Gnomid, its grotesque, scaly hands clenched in an agony of death.

Blake knelt down beside it and inspected the squat monstrosity minutely.

It proved to be but a small creature after all. Barely three feet high, it followed the general outlines of Sir Carham's weird picture. In places the brute differed from its painted version in the gallery, but the differences were for the most part slight.

"That picture will have been painted from memory—perhaps after the passage of many years," Blake commented, running his hands over the body. "Allowing for that, there's no doubt this is the same sort of brute."

"Then you killed it, last night, with that shot of yours," Warrender said, eyeing the creature disgustedly. It was a gruesome sight.

"I think not." Blake shook his head abruptly. "I am quite satisfied, my dear chap, that the animal has perished from cold."

"Being wounded, and so unable to win shelter—eh?"

"You are a bit unobservant this morning," said the detective. "Surely you can see for yourself? The brute has never a mark on it."

"By Jove!" Warrender peered forward, inspecting the Gnomid closely. "Why, now you come to mention it, I can see you're right. But—" He scanned the criminologist curiously. "I thought you said you plugged the beggar as it got through the window? Besides, what about all that blood we found?"

"Well, it certainly didn't come from this thing, did it?"

Warrender paused, puzzled.

"Well—n-no. But—*You don't mean to say there's more than one of them?*"

"That is exactly what I do mean to say, my dear Warrender. You see, all else apart, that brute last night was much larger than this." Blake smiled curiously. "We are not yet finished with the Gnomid."

BLAKE got a hurdle, and between them the pair bore their grim find back to the manor, where Blake locked it in an outhouse. A little later the whir of an approaching plane brought them out on to the terrace in time to see a light machine land in a neighbouring field.

From the cockpit a slim figure descended. It was Tinker. The plane had formed the objective of his errand.

"Everything O.K.?" Blake asked, as his assistant came forward to meet them.

"All in order, guv'nor. I had her well-fuelled at Heston. And now—"

"Warrender will get our coats. We're going up, my boy. I want to have a look at that hush-hush hangar and its enclosure. They won't find it so easy to pot us in the air."

A little later the three set out, Blake in control of the machine. Rising easily, despite the thin blanket of snow, they circled into the air, then set out across the fens for the hanger.

As they approached it, several men came out to stare at them. But no shots were fired—the plane was too high for that. All the same, Tinker saw one of the fellows shake his fist at them as they passed over. Evidently the men below were ill-pleased at their proximity.

"Got your camera, young 'un?" Blake demanded of his assistant as they veered off into the blue.

"All correct, guv'nor!"

"Then get ready. I'm turning back. That telescopic lens will detect what the naked eye cannot spot. Only keep under cover. I'm flying low this time. I don't want any casualties."

Banking round, he flew back to the hangar, and swept over it, barely a hundred feet from the ground. This time bullets soared skywards at the plane. But, thanks to their precautions, no one was hit. Turning once more, the detective repeated his flight over the enclosure.

While the plane crossed it, Tinker's camera snicked busily, its lens focused through a hole in the floor of the cockpit. Finally, the men below

gave over firing. And, with the approach of nightfall, Sexton Blake packed up, satisfied that he had secured what he wanted.

Whatever the hangar's secret, the negatives exposed would have probed it—if, indeed, the secret was to be tapped from the open.

Swerving, he flew off towards the Towers, en route for the manor and the snow-clad field whence they had taken off. He did not want to have to make a landing in total darkness.

Below, the fens and the farther fields of the Towers estate streaked by in quick succession. Then the black blotch that was the house itself, and the shimmering surface of a lake beyond it.

Curious, Blake leaned outwards, his eyes on the panorama below. Wrapped in darkness, the big range of buildings lay like some monstrous slug, nestled amongst a setting of white-mantled trees.

"Grifstein's, eh?" Warrender muttered, watching the house in his turn. "Pretty mingy with his lights, isn't he? For a rich man—"

The actor got no further.

From below, beyond the house, a deep red glow burst suddenly as from the very ground.

Sexton Blake whistled softly. Dull and luminous, it came from the heart of the big lake. It was as though a fire were glowing beneath the water itself.

IN a room in the Towers two men were sitting. Face to face, they bent, glowering at one another across a flat-topped desk.

One—the elder—was Conrad Grifstein, his fleshy features aquiver with ill-suppressed rage. Opposite him sat a younger man—swarthy, thick-set, but of slighter build.

"I tell you, you fool, you're a dreamer!" The elder Grifstein spoke abruptly. "I've had enough of these senseless expeditions of yours. What's the use of meandering off into the far corners of the earth? There's no money in it—except you count spending. And you've spent a mint!"

"There's the cause of science, father," the younger man countered, controlling himself with an obvious effort.

"Science be bothered! I've no time for science unless it yields patents, or something you can exploit commercially. I'm a business man, I am. I want to see a dividend when I plug down my brass on the table. And curse me if I've seen the half of half per cent out of these crazy expeditions of yours, Mordaunt!"

"Meaning, you won't finance another?" the son snapped, his temper hot from years spent in tropical climates.

"You've got it; my lad! Not another cent will I put up for any such nonsense," the senior Grifstein said decisively. "I could have bought half Murwood with the money you've cost me. And for what result? You come home with a cageful of comic parrots and a clutter of other rubbish. I'm not interested in menageries."

"All the same, you've found some of my stuff mighty useful," Mordaunt Grifstein countered, his dark eyes malevolently on his father. "Don't forget that."

"I forget nothing, you fool. I'd be bankrupt tomorrow if I forgot anything."

"Then don't forget I lent myself to this precious scheme of yours, then, father—in exchange for a promise to finance another expedition. What about that?"

"I tell you I'm forgetting nothing. And I'm not forgetting, either, that the scheme hasn't panned out yet!" Conrad Grifstein said testily.

"You hold those reversions to the Carham estates, don't you?"

"Yes; but I haven't got the property, my lad—except on paper."

"You will, though."

"Huh! Perhaps. I don't know. Things aren't going at all to my liking. That fellow at Murwood Manor is called Sexton Blake, and he's a private detective. Bolshin's recognised him and—"

"Bolshin—that rat-faced burglar fellow you employed to get the Van Dyck picture?"

"Quite so. Bolshin's alive to everything. He knows all about this infernal detective. Bolshin's a tough chap. But, by gum, he's windy of Sexton Blake. Says the fellow's like a blessed bulldog. Never lets go once he's got his teeth in."

"I don't see what you want to go getting yourself mixed up with scum like that Bolshin for," the younger Grifstein grunted. "Or why you must go pinching Van Dyck pictures."

"That Yankee millionaire offered me a small fortune for the thing, Mordaunt. And, goodness knows, with this confounded new Moneylenders' Act on the Statute Book, a man has his work cut out to earn an honest penny. My expenses are enormous, especially with your capers to pay for, I've got to make money somehow."

"Well, you haven't got the Van Dyck—"

"No, thanks to that same accursed Blake and his actor pal. I went over to Murwood last evening and smelt out the land. Sized him up. Wish he was out of the way, I can tell you!"

"Only he isn't. The fellow has as many lives as a cat."

"Thanks to your bungling, yes!" Conrad Grifstein growled. "Don't talk to me about more money, Mordaunt, till I see some results. That's what I want—results!"

The moneylender brought his fat fist down heavily on the desk top.

"Another thing I want to see is obedience," he added. "D'you hear, my son? Obedience!"

"What do you mean?" Mordaunt Grifstein demanded, flushing.

"I gave you certain orders. You didn't carry 'em out. You thought you knew better. You did what you wanted—instead of what I instructed. That don't go with me, sonny."

"I've done enough of what you ordered," Mordaunt Grifstein answered, shuddering. "I'm taking no more risks, I tell you. I've done enough. I want to get out of this—back to the wilds. Give me the money you promised, and let me go!"

Conrad Grifstein laughed harshly.

"You've heard what I've said. I'm a man of my word. There'll be no money till you've completed my orders, Mordaunt."

"Is that so, eh?" Mordaunt Grifstein clenched his fists. "Is that so? Do you think—after what's happened, father—that you dare refuse me?"

"Sure—since you can't spill the beans, my son, without letting yourself in as well."

"You're an accessory before the fact—"

"Which won't help you, anyway, if you go sticking your head in a noose, fool. Besides, money talks. I'm top dog!"

"Yes, curse you!" Mordaunt Grifstein growled something inaudible under his breath.

He sat, clutching at the desk edge, his beetling black brows focused furiously on its polished surface, while the elder man sat gazing at him cynically.

Mordaunt's one desire was to be gone—to get out of the country. Yet for this he needed money—money to melt into the wild places of earth where the law and Sexton Blake did not run.

But this hard-faced, inflexible mountain of flesh opposite—the man he owned as father—was adamant. When he had done so much—and now had still further tasks to perform—still further risks to be run.

His black eyes fixed his parent coldly. There was no trace of affection in them. He had served his sire through fear. Now he served with a silent hatred—hatred because the wells of money he had so long enjoyed had dried up.

"Well, if I'm top dog—go do what I told you to do. Then we'll talk," Grifstein senior said bluntly.

"Do it yourself—"

"I'm an old man, Mordaunt. Too old."

"Too cowardly," Mordaunt Grifstein mumbled beneath his breath. Aloud he suggested: "Or let your stool-pigeons—this gang of yours—do it."

"Don't trust 'em. It must be you. Are you going?"

"Very well." Mordaunt rose suddenly, his big black pupils afire with purpose. "Yes, I'll go. I'll go—"

"Good! Glad to see you're coming to your senses at last. Every minute of delay spells danger, with that cursed tec hanging about. Hurry now—hurry—"

"Yes, I'll hurry—"

Mordaunt Grifstein smiled evilly and left the room. He knew what he was going to do now. It had come to him swiftly as he sat there facing his conscienceless parent.

MORDAUNT GRIFSTEIN reached a door situated below the staircase, and, descending a flight of steps to the cellars, found another door which he opened. It gave into a narrow passage, the floor of which gradually descended as he hurried along between its green, damp walls.

At the end was a third door, iron-bound and securely fastened. Taking a key from his pocket the junior Grifstein undid the lock, thrust the door open, and entered.

Beyond the threshold lay a species of rotunda, built like a conservatory, and spanned with glass mounted on steel members. Above the thick glazed dome aloft, the luminous green of deep waters showed curiously against the dazzling glare of electric light. It was the lake, seen from below through dense panes of glass roofing the rotunda.

In the centre of this strange, under-water room was a table with the remains of a meal half touched. Beyond, a slight form rose timidly as Mordaunt entered.

It was Anne Debroy, her slight figure swathed in a man's overcoat. As the explorer advanced she backed in a fright.

"What do you want now?" she gasped fearfully as Grifstein junior came forward.

"A word with you," he answered. "You are in deadly peril."

"I have known that these last two days," she returned, her lips tightened. "What else?"

"This. You need be in danger no longer if you will listen to me, and be sensible." As he spoke, young Grifstein paused to cast a cautious glance back towards the door through which he had just entered.

"How so?" Anne breathed, her eyes on him distrustfully.

"Because I have come to take you away, my dear. If you'll come away, that is."

"If—" She gave a little shudder. "Why, my one wish is to get free of this horrible place!"

"Then listen—" He gripped her arm tightly. "I will get you away—somehow. In spite of the danger."

"Then let us go—"

"Wait. There are conditions. I cannot run this risk for nothing. You do not realise what it means."

"And they are—" she began wearily.

"First, that you marry me once we're free."

"But why?"

"Because, Anne, I love you. Otherwise I would never dare attempt to save you. In attempting it I may lose my own life."

"Indeed?" her eyes sought him coldly. "Why this sudden affection, when you have played the gaoler so long?" She regarded him suspiciously.

"'I played the gaoler, Anne, because I needs must. Like you, I am in the power of others. You were brought here—"

"By that horrible brute—"

"Exactly." Grifstein junior smiled. "But he is dead. The way is open if you care to take it."

"On terms—"

"As you say—on terms. I dare not chance it otherwise. I can be sure of my wife. I cannot be sure of—well, one who is not my wife. If you were to testify against me I should be dragged into this thing—with the others—your real enemies."

"But if I swear not to incriminate you?"

"It would be useless. Listen, Anne. We will go away, you and I—to far places—warm lands where we can forget all this. Together we can demand—and secure—a vast sum of money. We need want for nothing. Why not throw up this life of penury? Surely you have had enough of want? Wealth, pleasure, freedom—life. That's what I'm offering you. And in exchange for what? Just a vow pledged between us!"

"A vow? When you're nothing to me! When I can be nothing to you!" She shook her head. "If you have a spark of manhood in you, you will free me without vows. You will prove first that you care—as you say."

He took a turn about the room, his black brows scowling. Then, as he saw she remained firm, he pulled up abruptly.

"Listen, Anne. There is no sense in talking this way. You are not in a position to bargain. I am your only hope. You do not understand. But for me you will perish, and soon."

"I think you are right. I have thought so for some time." She strove to repress a shudder. "But what is the good of life if it means—someone one cannot trust?"

Young Grifstein gave an impatient flick of his fingers. Her opposition infuriated him.

"Little fool—look at that pane up there!" He pointed to the ceiling. "It is a sliding panel, worked by a lever from the shore. One pull of that lever and the waters of the lake will rush in. You can guess your fate if that happens. Down here you are trapped like a rat. Do you realise that within an hour that panel will be pulled?"

"Have you no mercy?" she wailed appalled by this threat.

But the explorer shrugged callously.

"In the far places I have penetrated one does not bargain with women," he answered. " I have stated my terms. It is for you to choose. Do you wish life—on my terms? Or death? I can give you but half an hour."

"I must think—think—" Anne whimpered frenziedly.

"Then think, and well. In thirty minutes I shall return for your answer. You had better make sure of it, too. For if, then, I leave this room without you, your enemies will act."

She buried her face in her hands.

When she looked up he was gone, noiselessly. The door once again had fastened—the barrier that stood between her and the world of life.

She hated Grifstein, and before her the vision of another stronger man stood out.

What to do?

CHAPTER 9
Clearing Up!

"THIS way, sir. The tunnel lies beyond that door, there."

Calvert paused in the darkness, his quivering finger pointing towards the massive pile that was the Towers, half obscured in the driving snowstorm. As he paused, Sexton Blake gained his side silently.

Behind were Tinker and Warrender, guns gripped in their frozen hands. From the near-by lake the red luminosity they had first seen from the plane gleamed dully through the falling flakes.

"Very well, if you're sure," the detective muttered. "We can afford no mistakes, though."

"Indeed, sir, and I know I'm right," the butler answered. "Jarman himself—their butler—took me down the tunnel. It was in the old man's time. An eccentric, half-crazy cuss he was. Had this place built under the lake as a smoking-room. It was because he wasted so much money on such idiotic schemes that he got into difficulties and made an end of himself."

"All right." The detective stiffened. "Once that door is down we must rush the place!" He thrust a gun into Calvert's trembling hand. "Follow my assistant and hold up the servants—anyone who bars your passage. Mr, Warrender and I will take the tunnel. Whatever's in that under-water chamber we'll have it—or them!"

Stepping softly to the door, his feet noiseless in the thick snow, he took a jemmy from his pocket, and, with deft hands, prised the frame outwards. For an instant the woodwork hung on his implement. Then, with a sudden crash, the door flew inwards.

Quick as thought the detective plunged into an unlighted passage, Tinker and Warrender on his heels. The butler followed more slowly. He was old, and unused to such goings on.

At the end of a passage a hall showed dimly. Blake dashed in, standing off a scared footman with his revolver. As the flunkey backed, his hands above his head, Blake sprang to a door under the stairway.

"Hold that man off!" he ordered, and whipped the door open.

Calvert and Tinker covered the footman with their guns as the detective and Warrender plunged through the doorway and down some steep steps. At their base was a tunnel. Down this the two men raced full speed, till another door at the far end confronted them.

"The chamber!" Blake breathed, and hurled himself against the panels. But the iron-bound structure held.

"Hall there!" he yelled through the doorway.

And a girl's voice answered feebly:

""Hallo!"

"Stand away from the door, quickly!" the detective ordered. And, drawing the gun afresh, he placed its muzzle to the keyhole.

Bullet after bullet crashed into the lock. Beneath the hail of lead the lock broke up. Then, with a single kick, Blake burst the door and leapt into the room, the actor behind him.

"Thank Heaven!" Anne Debroy sprang towards them as they entered. "You've come—come! Take me away—take me away!"

"Sure, that's what we're here for!" the detective replied cheerily, when Warrender gave a shout:

"Look out! There—the roof!"

All three glanced upwards. In the glass dome a glazed panel was sliding noiselessly open. As it slid, a column of green water shot floorwards.

"By gosh, the door—quick!" Blake gasped, clutching at the girl.

But too late. The spouting wave of water caught them. With a roar of thunder the lake surged in, flinging the trio sideways like corks upon full flood tide.

Waist deep in a whirling, frothing maelstrom of water Blake fought madly for the tunnel mouth, his arm about the girl's waist. Higher and higher the foaming flood rose, so strong that it almost swept Anne Debroy from his grasp.

He thrust onwards, Warrender behind. The water was almost to their necks now. But the two men, strong as giants, battled through with their charge to the tunnel. Staggering forward, they gained the steps and dragged Anne Debroy up them, to stumble, gasping, out into the hall.

As they reached it a burst of gunfire smote their ears. Tinker and Calvert were firing at a group across the floor, half seen in the whirling gun smoke.

"Look out for the girl!"

Warrender squared his mighty shoulders and sprang out into the hall. A gunman, charging forward, met him.

It was Rat Face, his thin features twisted in fury. Seeing the actor, he swung his weapon upwards.

By Warrender stood a heavy oak table. As the crook fired, he ducked and gripped it. Then, as the Rat swept his gun around anew, he whirled the table off its feet and brought it crashing downwards, full at the face of his enemy.

The Rat went down, screaming, and his gun went off, plugging the oaken beams above. As he vanished beneath the splintering wreck Warrender sprang over him, and charged fiercely for the gang across the floor.

"Tinker, guard the girl!" Blake shouted, and leapt after a swarthy form in the act of darting for the window.

With a rending crash of riven glass the figure gained the garden, Blake vaulting out after him. It was Mordaunt Grifstein, bolting as if the devil were behind him.

Straight up the drive young Grifstein raced, then through some trees, where he paused to take a pot shot at the detective. But the latter hung on resolutely, and the explorer renewed his flight, this time for the fens.

When the fellow gained them Blake pulled up. He had no intention of being drawn into such a trap as a muddy morass which Grifstein knew far better than did he. Besides, he guessed the crook's intention. Wheeling back for Murwood Manor, he sprinted to the field where the aeroplane still stood, and, having buckled on his parachute, swung the propeller.

As the plane took off into the air another left the ground far out across the fens. It came from the hangar towards which Grifstein had made. Blake knew what this meant. The explorer had played his last card, and was breaking for the upper air and a safe getaway.

Up and up the two planes soared, circling desperately for the higher strata and the shelter of dense clouds racing along them. Higher and higher Grifstein's plane rose, till at last it melted into the white vapours. Then the detective's bus slid through the wreathing blanket, and the world vanished, lost in the moistness and the thunderous reverberations of the roaring engine.

Where was Grifstein and his plane? Which way had he cut and run for it the instant the clouds enveloped him?

Blake's keen eyes bored through the mists ahead, straining for tight of the fugitive. The clouds stretched everywhere. There was not a trace of him.

Swooping round, the detective drove on through the murk. What was that in front? A shadow, or—

His hand gripped the joystick as something like a monstrous bat swept towards him.

It was Grifstein and his plane doubling back cunningly through the clouds in an attempt to elude him. Grifstein caught and—

"Gosh!"

The detective thrust at the joystick, but too late. The other plane rushed to meet him. It drove down nose on, its spread of wings outstretched like monstrous hands to grip him.

For a second he glimpsed the white, twisted features of his enemy, and saw the pilot shrink. Then the two planes met head on with a frightful crash and, locked in a deadly embrace, plunged earthwards in a blazing ball of fire!

LIKE a stone from a catapult Sexton Blake shot out of the cockpit, flung far from the spinning holocaust that whizzed past towards the ground below. For a breathless moment he fell headlong, spinning over and over. Then a jolt at his armpits told the parachute had opened. His legs swung in beneath him, and the vast umbrella bellied above him, he sank sedately towards the earth at a speed of ten miles an hour.

Below—what? Trees, lake, buildings? He scanned the gloomy depths anxiously—their level marked by the blazing bonfire that rose from the twisted wreckage landed before him.

Then suddenly his feet touched something solid and he threw himself forward, struggling to free himself from his harness. His face and hands were buried in snow, but he struggled up to find himself in a field. A hundred yards away the burning planes writhed in a solid sheet of leaping fire. Away to the right lay a black shape—Grifstein, crumpled out of all recognition.

He was, of course, dead.

Blake went over and regarded him for a moment, then, throwing off the remains of the parachute, hurried back to the manor. He found Tinker and the actor in possession of the place, a group of frightened servants cowering before their twin automatics.

"Conrad?" the detective demanded as he entered.

Tinker jerked a thumb towards an open doorway.

"In there, guv'nor. We were too late."

Blake went in through the door and glanced about him. On a table a single lamp was burning. By it lay an empty medicine bottle, lying on its side. Beyond, collapsed across the table from his chair, was the monstrous shape of Conrad Grifstein.

He had taken poison; cheated justice.

For an instant Blake poised, his brows contracted. Then, sensing someone behind him, he swung round. It was Warrender.

"He'd done it before we found him," the actor said. "Though why—"

"This—"

Blake stepped to a half-open cupboard and pulled the door aside. Out fell a grotesque suit of painted canvas—a weird replica of the monstrous thing depicted by Sir John Carham's brush.

By it lay a pair of leather gauntlets, fitted with long steel talons worked on a strong spring.

"The Gnomid—the real Gnomid!" Blake breathed, frowning. "A spurious creature that camouflaged a man—"

"Conrad?" Warrender asked, with a glance at the dead moneylender.

"No; he's too big to get into that suit," Blake answered. "It was the son—dead, too, after a crash from the air."

"And the explanation?"

"We'll go into that later," Blake answered. "Let's get Anne Debroy out of this. She's already been through enough."

"AS a matter of fact, the whole thing was really very simple," the detective said as, with Warrender and his assistant, he sat in the study at Murwood Manor. "Though I did not see daylight at first, the links in the chain soon fashioned themselves before my eyes. From suspicions I came to certainties. My last doubts vanished when we found the dead Gnomid in the woods."

"Well, and from the beginning?" Warrender prompted.

"All right." Blake relit his pipe before proceeding. "Of course, you'll realise that a lot of what I am going to tell you I have only just discovered by inquiries at the manor and at Grifstein's place. And a lot of guess-work. However, we can begin with Westerfield—Lord Carham's wastrel heir—an heir he could not avoid owing to the deed of trust. Westerfield's profligacy drove the young fool to borrow money from Grifstein. This bloodsucker drove a hard bargain with him over the reversions—a bargain doubtless made easier by Westerfield's drunken habits.

"Anyway, Westerfield parted with the huge estate—or, rather, with his future rights to it, for a mere song. Hard up as he was, Grifstein could not resist the bargain. And how hard up he was we may well imagine since, by the confession of that wounded burglar whom you floored with that table, Warrender. Grifstein stooped to steal pictures for an American millionaire.

"This wealthy if not very honest person wanted Van Dyck's Lady Diana from Murwood Manor. So Grifstein commissioned this tool of his to break in and purloin it. While so doing, the burglar came upon the Gnomid picture.

"Now it so chanced that Grifstein's son was just back from Brazil and his expedition up the Amazon. Evidently there really exists such a creature out there, hidden deep in the heart of the impenetrable forests that ring in the river's source. I've no doubt that Sir John Carham really penetrated there, and that he did in fact see such a creature when on his travels long ago.

"However, to resume. Either young Grifstein accompanied the burglar, and so saw the Gnomid picture for himself, or else the burglar described what he had seen. One way or the other, young Grifstein recognised the beast in the painting as the same species as the specimen he had brought secretly back from the Amazon—perhaps with intent to spring a dramatic surprise on the Royal-Society.

"Then old man Grifstein intervened. He wanted money badly, and this picture stunt had failed, owing to his henchman taking it to that joint of Li Chun's, where it was recognised and recovered by Westerfield. You butted in when the fun started, and the picture was lost to them. Consequently, good-bye to the expected cheque from America.

"As an alternative, Grifstein hit on the dangerous expedient of encompassing the premature death of Lord Carham. This would naturally bring the reversions quickly into his hands. It was decided to use the Gnomid for this purpose. You see, such a creature could hardly be held responsible for its actions. There was this tale of the family curse, too. And, if superstition failed to cloak the deed, they could always assert that the brute broke loose and got out of hand.

"As you know, poor Carham paid the penalty of his nephew's folly. But, at the same time, unluckily for Grifstein, a second complication arose in the person of Anne Debroy. You noted how she resembles Lady Diana Carham?"

"Sure," Warrender agreed. "I've been puzzling why."

"Because, my dear man, she's a descendant. That little legacy she got from a distant relative necessitated her proving her own lineage. Circumstances compelled her to go to the Courts. Hence the matter got a certain amount of publicity. In this way Grifstein's attention was drawn to the matter. I gather he was constantly on the lookout to sweep heirs into his net.

"Now, I've procured a copy of the chart of descent pronounced valid by the Court, and I find Miss Debroy descended through a female Carham. She herself does not yet realise this. The chart is a complex one. But Grifstein spotted it at once. He saw a bad snag, moreover. Anne had a better title than Westerfield. Consequently, Westerfield, though he acted in good faith, was not the real heir. Grifstein unknowingly had bought a pup.

"Grifstein knew right away that his chances of recovering his advance from a ne'er-do-well like Westerfield were slim. So he got in touch with Anne, ostensibly to lend her money on the strength of her forthcoming legacy, but in reality to eliminate her. He dared not attempt to do so at his own house, but planned to murder her on her way back to the station. Thanks to us, this plot failed.

"All the same, Grifstein stuck tenaciously to his purpose. We were trailed to your cousin's bungalow, and the moment Tinker and I left to fetch the police the Grifsteins acted. Westerfield, intent on pestering Anne, butted in at the crucial moment and was killed. From what Anne says, he had evidently a spark of chivalry in him somewhere, and tried to protect her.

"Also, young Grifstein seems to have fancied the look of Anne Debroy. Instead of killing her, he removed her as a prisoner, evidently in hopes of her assenting to marry him. This would have secured her fortune to him, and he could have snapped his fingers at his father, with whom, as is evident, he had quarrelled. Naturally, Grifstein père could not expose his son without at the same time exposing himself.

"But, as you know, these plans failed, thanks to our interference. Though but for your spotting that crook over at Peterborough, Warrender, and that oxygen bottle—"

"And, by the way, what about that oxygen?" the actor cut in.

"The Gnomid was dying—of the climate, according to what I am told. They wanted the oxygen to keep it alive till their dirty murders were finished. Pneumonia, I fancy. At all events, they had the brute stowed at the hangar. No doubt that story of a hush-hush plane was deliberately put about to explain the close guard kept upon the place."

"But the thing was healthy enough to attack you, Blake, that very night," Warrender protested.

"My dear good chap, the Gnomid never attacked anyone. It was quite a harmless little brute. I saw that the minute I examined its body. Its muscular development showed that. The murders were done by young Grifstein, disguised to represent the thing, and by the use of a murderous gadget consisting of spring-operated steel claws. The Gnomid itself was so much camouflage— a harmless but fearful-looking creature let loose for the purposes of frightening superstitious village.

"The real murderer simply followed Lord Carham by treading on his tracks. Remember how blurred they were. The real Gnomid, of course, provided the necessary weird footprints—a red herring drawn across the trail. The conspirators were simply out to muddle the police. Well"—here the detective smiled complacently—"I dare say they'd have succeeded."

"But for you," Warrender murmured.

"But for all of us, my dear fellow," the detective replied generously. "You played your part in this, and an important one. Anne Debroy should be grateful. She's in the next room. Why not go in and see her?"

"What! When she's got this title and all this money?" the actor muttered, frowning.

"Pooh! Man, what about your reputation and your monster salary? Don't be a fool! Go in and win. Do you want her to have to ask you?"

"Heavens, no!"

Warrender made a hasty exit, and the door closed behind him.

Just what he said to Anne, and what she said to him, was a secret hidden behind its fine old oak panels.

But not a secret held for long, as the sequel—a marriage at St. Margaret's, Westminster—proved.

There, not many months later, Anne, Lady Carham, and baroness in her own right, was given away by Sexton Blake to Bertram Warrender, idol of the West End and champion of a hundred persecuted stage damsels. Most of those in the thronging crowds had seen the star's long sword flash as it leapt from its scabbard in defence of the heroine, a-gleam in the glare of limes and footlights. They had seen his pistol blaze, to the blast of blank cartridge, as he held a dozen gnashing foes at bay.

But few there realised that on one occasion that gun had cracked in real dead earnest, in face of odds even trimmer than those enacted on the boards.

There were rumours, to be sure—rumours that got into the Sunday papers. But only four there knew the real truth of the grim drama which had given him Anne for his bride.

Those four were himself and Anne; his best man, Tinker; and the tall, lean figure who bore the pretty bride to the altar, Sexton Blake.

And the Gnomid?

At the head of the fine, sweeping staircase of the Royal Biological Association's headquarters in Pall Mall there is an exhibit which is acknowledged to be one of the rarest treasures—the rarest treasure—of the institution.

It is the only specimen ever brought to Europe of that strange, monstrous, elusive beast known as the Gnomid. The unique rarity (about which the whole scientific world of biologists wrangled for months) has been presented by Sexton Blake, at whose expense it has been mounted and set up.

It has been referred to as an exhibit. Strictly speaking, it is not on exhibition. The thing stands in a niche at the head of the stairs; but so disturbing had its grotesque, terrifying appearance been to the members, that after a short time it was decided it should be covered with a curtain.

THE END

"MY dear fellow," said Blake one morning, in reply to a query of Bathurst's. "Your analogy—if you will pardon my saying so—is absurd. Marston Hume cannot be classified together with a batch of the more successful criminal of late years. He is a distinct specimen. Your ordinary expert in crime—your professed criminal—as apart from the animal who kicks his wife to death in a drunken frenzy—has only one object in view—money.

"He works for money—he plans for it—commits his crime for it, and in nine cases out of ten, having got it, the money in turn leads to his committal.

"He is unused to the possession of a comparatively large sum and spends it too freely on wine, or whatever his particular weakness may happen to be, and gets himself into trouble in consequence.

In the instance of Marston Hume the money element is altogether eliminated. If he chose to buy himself a fifteen-hundred guinea car, or to stock Savile Row with orders to-morrow no one would dream of suspecting him of having knocked an old man on the head for his money.

"He is a rich man—legitimately, and naturally rich in the eyes of the world—anyhow, provided with more than ample means; and, therefore, not only is the sordid aspect—the motive of the average crime—absent, but his wealth guarantees him a certain immunity.

"He murdered a relative for money, true; from the death of Maxwell, the financier, he reaped a small fortune; but in other cases his command of money has helped him enormously."

"Ready cash is better than a reputation, nowadays," said Bathurst nodding. Or rather it buys one. You may smile and smile, and so long as you are a millionaire in embryo, no man will venture to call you a villain."

"Precisely: Marston Hume, as a rich man, passes unquestioned and unsuspected; rob him of his most dangerous and effective weapon—his bank account—and you reduce him to the level of the ordinary criminal."

"Nothing I should like to do better," said Bathurst, laughing. "My own has galloping consumption; but how?"

Blake shrugged his shoulders. "That is a question I have been asking myself continually for the past month, and as yet I have found no answer. There seems to me to be just one small chance, and only one. Hume loves a gamble especially with the odds strong in his favour. One of these fine days he may make a stumble. Unless, of course, I can manage to bag him by the heels first."

By a curious coincidence, that very afternoon Blake received an urgent message from Sir Richard Lawley, a man he knew fairly well, asking him, if possible, to call on him at once at his office.

Blake, who had spent the day dawdling over his reference books, pushed them impatiently aside, and complied immediately. Sir Richard had sometime previously placed him under a slight obligation, and he was anxious to wipe out the score.

He found him sitting in his private sanctum—a small room opening off the board-room—awaiting him impatiently.

"My dear Blake," he cried, springing up to greet him. "this is very kind of you. I asked you to come round because we are in the deuce of a mess; and although the matter in question is quite out of your usual line, I am convinced that if any one can throw a light on things, you are the man.

"The trouble is this; I am, amongst other things, chairman of the "Tuxon and Islands Exploitation Co.," and between you and me and the gatepost, an uncommonly good company it is.

"Tuxon are its headquarters, and we own the entire rights over a group of something like a hundred small islands, round about—some of them mere waste sand bars. But the yield from the pearl fisheries, and from sponges, guano, and turtle—to mention only a few of the main products—is phenomenal. For the past five years our profits have been over thirty per cent, and we have recently made great improvements. The company, you may be sure, is absolutely sound and square, or I should not allow my name to be connected with it. At the end of last week the shares, the price of which has not varied for a month or more, stood at three; and the last cable advices from our general manager at Tuxon reported everything going satisfactorily, and the discovery of two new rich guano deposits on a cluster of outlying keys.

"During the whole of this week, however, some individual, or group of individuals, whose identity we have been unable to discover, has been selling big blocks of shares piecemeal. The company is only a small affair comparatively.

Yet ten thousand shares have already been sold, and we have been hard put to it to prevent the price of the shares from falling horribly as a result of so many being thrown on the market. We have snapped up the sales; but, in spite of it all,, the price has dropped by ten shillings, and is likely to drop another half-sovereign to-morrow—for some ugly rumours are getting about. You see, as bad luck would have it, cable communication has been cut off for the last three days owing to the eruption in Hayti and round about. All that is known is that the earthquake made havoc in Hayti itself, and we are unable to get word through to Tuxon on that account.

"We, ourselves, are not in the least concerned for the safety of our islands. They lie over three hundred miles to the south to begin with, they are not volcanic in origin, and they are outside the zone of influence; but rumour is already beginning to connect the sales and subsequent weakening of price with the Haytian disaster."

"There is no possibility of the individual, or individuals, having obtained more recent information?"

"Absolutely none. Whether to New York, the Continent, or ourselves, the cables or any news must come via Key West; and our agent there, a very smart fellow, would certainly have communicated with us at once."

"How far do you estimate the sales to be genuine? I mean how many shares do you consider the vendors actually hold!"

"Personally speaking, my belief is none. Of course there have been one or two small genuine sales, owing to the fall, but nothing of consequence."

"Ah!" said Blake, and began drawing meaningless figures on a piece of blotting-paper, with an air of abstraction.

"Then either the vendors must have more recent news—in spite of what you say—or—"

"Or what?"

"Or they mean to manufacture it."

"Good heavens!" said Sir Richard. "But in these days of wireless, and all that, such a thing is inconceivable."

"You forget that the position of your property and the earthquake have made it not only conceivable but possible, and that you are, for all practical purposes, back in pre-telegraphic days."

"Granting that, your suggestion argues that the whole thing must have been deliberately planned long ago. No, that can't be the case either—a man can't plan an earthquake, and if there had been no earthquake the cables would be working."

"I shrewdly suspect that it was planned, all the same. I can even vaguely realise how. The one necessary thing would be to get Tuxon temporarily isolated. You must bear in mind that in the last four years alone, the region immediately north of your property has been visited by more than half a dozen volcanic disturbances, and that an interruption of the cable service would be quite enough to cause serious uneasiness. That point would be the chief factor in any such scheme.

"Taking the situation as it is at present, and leaving out of consideration for the moment this mysterious seller of shares—imagine what would be the result on the market of a report through any reputable source, such as Lloyds', or Reuter's—that an upheaval and subsequent tidal wave had wiped out your company's group, or demolished it past recognition."

"I should say," replied Sir Richard slowly, "that 'Islands,' as we call them for short, would be worth about as much as the paper on which the certificates are printed."

"Exactly so; and before that report, transmitted in all good faith, had been contradicted—the unknown vendor would have bought up at waste-paper price, and netted a small fortune. I should say that that is precisely what will happen unless you are strong enough, as a company, to buy in every share offered—or unless a little idea which is simmering at the back of my head turns out to be a trump card."

Sir Richard sighed.

"It's the horrible uncertainty of it all," he began. "Hang it all, no one is infallible, and Nature plays strange tricks with us little humans. If I advise my people to buy and to go on buying and buying, and there should have been some sort of a catastrophe after all—that—supposing that after all this unknown man, or syndicate, has got hold of some private information which is true? What then—eh?"

"It is a possibility which certainly must be faced. If you ask me my opinion, however, I should say that such a contingency was most unlikely. I will go further—I will tell you, in confidence, that I am fairly sure I know the name of the vendor—the real man's, not the dummy's—which he has put forward to hide his identity. All I ask is a few days in which to lest my theory.

"And, to show you how much I believe in it—though, as you know, I am not a rich man—I will pay into your account five hundred pounds tomorrow, and commission you to have bought for me as many shares as that sum will cover when you receive a wire from me containing the one word, 'Purchase.' Good-bye."

Sir Richard had mentioned three days as the period during which cable communication had been interfered with beyond Key West. But in a small paragraph, containing a Router message in a seven-days' old paper, Blake read, shortly afterwards, that an alarming shock had been experienced twenty-four hours previously on the southern coast of Hayti.

That meant a gain of four days in point of time as regards knowledge of an eruption of some sort having taken place in that locality. Sir Richard and his colleague might very easily have overlooked the paragraph, which was slipped in at the bottom of a column, and only a few lines in length. On the other hand, a man, in search of any news of the kind, would not have failed to see it; and, if he were waiting to take advantage of it, the gain in time would have been of immense importance.

Later on, of course, the news had been given due prominence, but the paragraph which had been overlooked had heralded the coming of it.

All the next day, until Bathurst's return in the evening, Blake was a very busy man, and the result of nine hours' hard strain was exactly nil.

With Hume in his mind, he could surmise much, but could, as in former cases, where Hume was concerned, prove nothing.

He had not intended to say a word about the case he had in hand, but a well-cooked dinner has a wonderfully mellowing influence, and whilst they were enjoying cigars and some very excellent Chartreuse, Blake gave Bathurst a resumé of the case.

"Hume?" queried Bathurst. "He did a big gamble on a similar line in the Maxwell case."

Blake nodded.

"That's just it—Hume. Mind you, I haven't a shred of evidence. Everything I've tried has turned out a failure so far as getting even a hint of proof against the man concerned, and now I am going to take the law into my own hands—in short, I am going to kidnap Marston Hume. I am going to take possession of him and hold him in durance vile, as the melodrama has it, for the next few days.

"I am convinced in my own mind that he has planned a very clever swindle. My theory is that he has had his eye on this Tuxon Company for a long time. Its isolated situation is its vulnerable point. Given the cutting off of telegraphic communication, which from its position might—and, in fact, has—come about from natural causes— an event he was patiently waiting for—all he has to do is to send a pre-arranged message to an agent somewhere along the Floridan coast at Tampa, or Punta Garda—a man whom you may be sure he has paid well, and who is ignorant of his real identity. The man, with some extra days' grace—that is where the small paragraph comes in—sails a small chartered sloop down southerly, and, after the first scare is over, puts into Key West in a knocked-about condition, reporting that Tuxon and the neighbouring islets are clean swept out—demolished, in fact.

"Any man knowing those waters well could withstand a pretty exhaustive cross-examination, and the authorities at Key West will wire his report home pretty well verbatim."

"But the truth must come out later."

"Yes, and there lies the germ of the swindle. Hume buys when the market is knocked endways by his own man's bogus report; and clears something like twenty thousand—perhaps more."

"The spreading abroad of false intelligence, in order to influence the markets, is criminal."

"So is murder," said Blake curtly, "and of that we both know him to be doubly guilty. I don't care a snap of the fingers for the criminality of his action. I want to get hold of him, and keep hold of him, to ruin him financially, and for no other purpose. If I can keep him under lock and key until the false report is denied on reliable authority, I shall have scored my first great point against him."

"Suppose, for a moment, that he is not concerned in the deal at all."

"Then he can bring an action against me for assault, or on any other pretext he chooses—if he dares," said Blake grimly.

"When do you mean to go for him?"

"To-morrow. I daren't delay longer or it may be too late."

It was barely half-past nine when Blake knocked at Hume's small front door. The latter's manservant—who used to sleep out—he had dismissed when he left the rooms temporarily on a previous occasion, and he relied for his valeting on the caretaker in the basement. Hume answered the door in person, and gave a start of surprise when he saw who his early visitor was.

Blake took advantage of his momentary hesitation, slipped inside, and shut the door behind him, motioning to Hume to lead the way to the sitting-room.

The latter, recovering his usual cool, deliberate manner, did so.

"You are uncommonly early," he said, pushing forward a chair for Blake. "What is it this time— another mare's-nest?"

Blake shook his head.

"The truth is, Hume, it has struck me that you must have been a bit lonely of late—you are becoming misanthropic—so I have come to stay with you for a while."

Hume shook his head.

"In your company I should grow positively morbid. Also, I am afraid that I shall be very busy to-day; so, if you have nothing specially interesting to say, I might call your attention to the fact that the door is on your right."

"You are not looking well, Hume," said Blake imperturbably from the depths of the chair. "You want rest. The strain of getting rid of all those Tuxon shares—'Islands,' they call them, don't they?—has told on you."

It was a chance shot, but a tremendous issue depended on it, and Blake watched his adversary closely.

Not a muscle of Hume's face quivered, but he gripped a small ivory paper-knife, which he had picked up, so tightly that it broke with a snap.

Blake gathered himself together a little in his chair, his eyes still on Hume's, and laughed.

"Your nerves are certainly not what they were," he said. "That little exhibition of temper shows that my diagnosis of your case is correct."

Blake was watching, he was quite prepared for what was to follow; but even so, Marston Hume's catlike spring came a fraction of a second quicker than Blake had thought possible, and the weight of it carried him backwards off his feet.

They both went down, Hume on top, his hands groping for Blake's throat. At the first hint of action, the cool, suave, rather indolent man vanished, and in his place there was a primitive raging beast —a whirlwind of concentrated fury and hatred.

"I've got you now!" Hume panted in his ear. "I've got you now! Heavens, but it's good! I knew a time would come when I shouldn't be able to keep my hands off you! Man, how I've longed to feel my fingers work their way into your throat! Do you feel that—and that? I want you to feel all you can before the life goes out of you!"

The sentences literally shot out, with little jerky, breathless intervals, and there was madness in the convulsed face swaying and nodding just above Blake's own.

But just us the whirlwind fury of the man had gained him an advantage at the first, so now it proved his undoing by making him lose caution.

He was strong—stronger than most men—and his rage gave him added power. Moreover, he was utterly reckless and meant to kill—to kill with his naked hands, whatever the cost—but he was too eager. Blake was fighting for his life, and he knew it, and in such a fight there are no rules or etiquette. The opportunity came, and his right knee jerked upwards into the pit of Hume's stomach.

The latter groaned as the wind was knocked out of him, and the next instant Blake had wrenched himself free and had his man pinned in a locked grip.

"Lie still, or I'll break your leg!" he said huskily, for his throat had been badly mauled.

Hume tried to struggle, and involuntarily cried out as Blake pressed downwards. It was only a gentle pressure, but it wrenched the sinews badly, and for a moment he was compelled to lie still. That little respite served Blake's purpose.

There was a sharp click, click, and the handcuffs closed on Hume's wrists, which Blake had forced behind him.

Blake felt him quiver at the touch of the steel—not with fear, but with bitter, black rage—but he said no word. He bound his ankles with the strap of a field-glass case which hung just within reach; then he rose.

For a moment he seemed to hesitate, and at last, with a shrug of the shoulders, he took a table-napkin from the breakfast table, which had not yet been cleared, and deftly improvised a gag.

Hume glared at him sullenly, and Blake tied the gag.

"I'd spare you this if I could," he said; "but I can't trust you!"

Then, not without an effort, he lifted him and carried him into the bed-room, locking the door on him.

Quietly and methodically he set to work to tidy up and remove all traces of the struggle, occasionally going to the outer door to listen.

He had barely finished this when the caretaker came in to clear away. Blake was seated in a comfortable chair by the fire, smoking a cigarette and reading the paper. Incidentally the paper, hid his torn and crumpled collar.

"Beg pardon, sir," said the man civilly; "but can I take the things away?"

"Yes," said Blake. "Mr. Hume has finished. He's in the bed-room; he will ring when he wants you again."

The man finished his job and retired noiselessly, and Blake, left to his own devices, sat over the fire, lost in a brown study.

At three o'clock there came another knock at the door. This time it was Bathurst with Sir Richard Lawley, the latter looking very much perturbed, and carrying an early edition of an evening paper.

"You told me to bring him here if he wanted to see you," said Bathurst, indicating Sir Richard; "and here are the things you asked me for!"

And he planked on the table a good-sized packet of sandwiches, a flask, and some soda-water bottles.

"The news is out, Blake!" said Sir Richard excitedly; "and, so far as I can see, ' Islands' are done for. There is no doubt that, in spite of all I said, our property has been practically wiped out. Here, read it for yourself! Good heavens, what's happened to your collar?"

"I've been indulging in a little ju-jitsu on your behalf. Let's see the paper; this is better luck than I expected. I fancied we might have had to wait a day—probably two."

"Luck!" said Sir Richard bitterly. "Why, the company is done for—ruined!"

"Nonsense! This is only the manufactured news I warned you to expect! Get back as fast as you can, and set your brokers to work buying."

Hume glared at Blake suddenly after he had tied the gag.
"I'd spare you this if I could," said Blake, "but I can't
trust you!"

"But we have private advices from our own agent at Key West that—"

"Your own agent only got his information from the same source as this; so, of course, he seems to corroborate it. That was foreseen and calculated on. For goodness sake, go and buy every single share you can; and don't forget my five hundred! I'll look after this end of the business. Don't stop, man! I tell you I have proof positive that I am right, and the state of my collar bears witness to it."

"Very well," said Sir Richard; and he left them in no very convinced frame of mind.

"Now," said Blake, "pass those sandwiches, and let's see what the papers say.

"Humph! 'Terrific havoc caused by the recent earthquake! Islands devastated!' Humph! Ah, here we are!

"A small coasting schooner, bearing every sign of having encountered terrible weather, has just reached this port (Key West, that is, Bathurst.) Her owner, a man thoroughly at home in these waters, reports that the main Island of Tuxon has been practically submerged, only a small portion of the eastern coast being still visible; whilst the smaller islets, famous for their rich guano deposits, have vanished completely. Further north, the—humph! the rest doesn't concern us, except this last bit: 'the cables via Hayti are still unworkable.'

"I should say that 'Islands' would be selling at two a penny to-morrow, or thereabouts. By Jove, it was lucky I took the bull by the horns in time!"

"The bear would be more appropriate," suggested Bathurst, with a grin. "What have you done with him? Killed him, and hidden him in a cupboard?"

"No; but he paid me the compliment of doing his best to kill me—nearly did it, too! I shall have to send you out for some collars. He's in the bed-room across the passage, neatly trussed up; and there he will remain until the Hayti cable chooses to get into working order again. I must take him in some sandwiches soon; there's no point in starving the beggar."

For a day and a half Blake kept guard over his man, and browbeat the bewildered caretaker into a state of meek submissiveness.

On the afternoon of the second day, Sir Richard and Bathurst came flying up in a fast taxi, and burst into the flat.

"You were right, Blake!" cried the former excitedly. "We are saved! Read this; it's decoded from the message of our general manager at Tuxon. The line was clear this morning:

"'Don't understand your inquiries. All well here. Know nothing of any disturbance as mentioned. Cabled you four days ago re new deposits— very rich.'

"And yesterday you couldn't have sold a share for five shillings! They'll be above the normal again by this time to-morrow. I am afraid several of our smaller holders must have lost badly, though."

Blake nodded.

"They have to thank the man I am just going to fetch for that." he said grimly; "and I would have you remember the fact when you name the price which he must pay on settling day. I am asking nothing for my own services, but I stipulate that ten pounds a share shall be the minimum price."

"You—you have got him! That's why you've been installed hero for the last few days, then!"

"Yes. Ten pounds a share, remember!"

"That'll cost him at least a hundred thousand. Why do—"

"Why? Because I want to break him," said Blake curtly. "I will bring him to you."

The interview was brief, and it left Marston Hume face to face with the fact that the week-end would find him beggared and penniless.

"You clearly understand?" said Blake coldly. "I could have had you sent to prison. I prefer to leave you at liberty, a beggared, broken man! You will be less dangerous so!"

Hume stood by the table with a livid face, biting his lip, speaking no word; and, so standing, they left him.

"There was murder in that man's eyes!" said Sir Richard slowly, when they were outside. Blake looked at him and smiled. "Yes," he said quietly; "I noticed it myself."

Free Plate Within!

THE UNION JACK 2ᴰ

This Splendid
SEA-VICTORY PICTURE
IN FULL COLOUR

RULE, BRITANNIA!—The Surrendered German Fleet entering the Firth of Forth, led by H.M.S. "Cardiff" on November 21st, 1918.

Also
SEXTON BLAKE
in

"The Lord of the Ape-Men," introducing Dr. SATIRA,
also in this issue—
"The Three Just Men," by EDGAR WALLACE!

No. 1,206.   EVERY THURSDAY,   November 27th, 1926.

THE LORD OF THE APE-MEN!

The FIRST of a NEW SERIES, introducing Dr. SATIRA.

For old readers it is only necessary to say that the creator of the Confederation characters—Reece, Dirk Dolland, and the rest—is also the creator of Doctor Satira. Newcomers who have not known the glories of the Confederation series in the past may take it for granted that they are lucky in being present at the birth of what is destined to be an even greater attraction.

By ROBERT MURRAY
IN WHICH SEXTON BLAKE CHASES A ROBBER

THE FIRST CHAPTER

Two Howls.

IT was quite a chance meeting. Taking their usual evening stroll, Sexton Blake and Tinker, accompanied by Pedro, attached to a stout leash, had come upon Detective-Inspector Coutts in his favourite spot for meditation.

The C.I.D. man was leaning against the parapet of the Embankment, almost opposite to the pile of buildings known as New Scotland Yard. Coutts—a bulky, thick-set man, wearing a blue serge suit and a hard felt hat—had his elbows resting on the stone parapet, and he was frowning moodily down at the lapping river below.

His bristling, red moustache had a despondent droop to it, and he was champing his teeth on a particularly evil-looking, yellow cigar, that was spluttering and sparking like a damp firework,

The approach of Sexton Blake and his companions passed quite unnoticed, and the famous private detective of Baker Street halted, and there was a twinkle of amusement in his keen, grey eyes as he surveyed the drooping figure of his old friend from Scotland Yard.

"Another of life's little tragedies in the making, Tinker," he said quietly. "Here, evidently, is an unfortunate fellow, who, tired of battling for success in the great game of life, is contemplating the last resort of the failure and ne'er-do-well—suicide!"

"Humph! He'll make a mighty big hole in the water, won't he, guv'nor!" grinned Tinker, "Better give him a push-off, hadn't I, in case he changes his mind?"

These remarks fell upon deaf ears so far as Detective-Inspector Coutts was concerned. He rolled his cigar from one corner of his mouth to the other, and gave a jerk at the brim of his hat that tilted it at an aggressive angle over one eye—a sure sign that the C.I.D. man was seriously perturbed.

Suddenly recognising an old friend, Pedro, the great bloodhound, rushed forward, and, rearing up on his hind legs, planted his cold nose under Coutts' left ear.

It was an effective though somewhat drastic method of awakening the C.I.D. man from his reverie, and perhaps he could not be blamed for the wild yell of alarm that left his lips as he came upright with a jerk that almost jerked his hat from his head and sent the cigar into the river.

"What the blazes! Humph! So it's you and your confounded mongrel, is it?" he grunted sheepishly, unclenching his fists and straightening his hat, as he recognised Sexton Blake and Tinker.

"Exactly! I am pleased to see that your powers of discernment are as keen as ever, Coutts," replied the Baker Street detective gravely, as he produced a well-filled case and carefully selected a smoke. "Now that your piece of smouldering linoleum has gone to a watery grave, I suggest you have a cigar."

Coutts' taste in cigars was execrable; but it was a case of pocket rather than palate, and he readily availed himself of Sexton Blake's invitation.

"Nice thing to do—creep up behind a chap like a lot of blessed footpads!" he jerked irritably. "Young Tinker's idea, of course; sort of darn-fool trick he would suggest!"

"My dear Coutts, in the mood you were in I doubt if you would have heard a steam-roller approaching!" smiled Blake. "And a man of your profession is supposed to be always on the alert."

"Hear, hear, guv'nor!" agreed Tinker. "It would have been the easiest thing in the world to have lifted old Coutts by the heels and tipped him clean into the river!"

"You go and shovel coke!" snapped the C.I.D. man disrespectfully. "Little boys should be seen and not heard; and the sight of you's bad enough, without having to listen to your vapid babble. Why Blake hasn't been summoned for not sending you to school I'm hanged if I know!"

Tinker only grinned amiably. He and Coutts were the best of friends, though they often indulged in scathing personalities. If it came to the point either would willingly lay down his life for the other, and this risk had been taken by both many times in the past when Sexton Blake had been waging his stern, ruthless war of extermination against Professor Reece and the Confederation.

"Hang it all, Blake, I haven't set eyes on you lot for over a week!" went on the C.I.D. Man, suddenly changing the subject. "Called at your rooms last night, but couldn't get any answer."

"I dare say Mrs. Bardell had gone to visit her Aunt Sarah's cousin's uncle," replied Sexton Blake gravely. "Tinker and I only arrived back this morning. Been up North on Government work—weeding out some of these infernal Foreign agitators who have been living to stir up trouble amongst the British miners. I submitted a very satisfactory report to the Home Office this afternoon."

"Shouldn't be surprised if the guv'nor's name didn't figure in the next Honours list," added Tinker proudly. "Sir Sexton Blake! That sounds a bit of all-right, doesn't it, Coutts?"

"Never!" declared the Baker Street detective firmly. "I have no use for lilies. What's your trouble, Coutts? It's easy to see you've got something on your mind."

"It's these darned jewel robberies!" confided Coutts eagerly. "Surely you've read about them in the newspapers?"

"I haven't seen a newspaper for five days," replied Blake candidly. "They're all at home, and I dare say I shall find time to run through them this evening."

"Never mind about the newspaper. I can tell you all about the only matter of interest you will find in them," volunteered the C.I.D. man, pulling furiously at his cigar. "There's been a positive epidemic of jewel robberies in London during the past week. Without exaggeration, Blake, there's been nearly a million pounds' worth of jewels stolen from private houses and mansions in the West End."

"Phew! That's something like a rich haul!" exclaimed Sexton Blake, a glint of interest creeping into his grey eyes. "Do you suggest that these robberies are the work of an organised gang?"

"Either of an organised gang or of one individual," said Coutts. "But the scoundrel must be pretty active, for there have been three or four separate robberies during one night, and at considerable distances apart."

"And you have no clue to the perpetrator, or perpetrators?"

"Not the vaguest—until last night." Detective-Inspector Coutts was warming up to his narrative. His ruddy face had hardened, and he drew his cigar until the glowing end almost singed the fringe of his red moustache.

"Last night," he proceeded, "a constable in the Kensington Division was missing from his beat. A search was made, and he was discovered lying in the garden of the residence of Sir Alfred Austral. The man was unconscious, and had been crushed almost to death. He had no less than four ribs broken, and one of the bones had penetrated a lung. I may tell you that at the same time it was discovered that the house of Sir Alfred Austral had been entered, and jewels to the value of fifteen thousand pounds had been stolen.

"It was only this afternoon that the injured constable recovered sufficiently for the police to take a statement from him. It was not much that he had to tell. It appears that he was passing Sir Alfred's house—which was on his beat—when he heard a noise as though a piece of guttering had fallen from the roof.

Naturally, he entered the garden to satisfy himself. There was no moon, and it was pretty dark, but he caught sight of a dark figure swarming down one of the water-pipes that ran up the side of the house."

"Ah, a cat-burglar!" said Sexton Blake.

"A monkey, or an ape-burglar I should call it!" grunted Coutts. "I've never heard of cats climbing water pipes. Constable Rains was waiting at the bottom, and he grabbed the fellow as soon as he touched the ground. To use his own words, it was just as though he had tackled a 'human tornado and Samson rolled into one.' The burglar simple wrapped his arms around him and squeezed the senses out of him. It was just as if he had been caught in the claws of a gigantic crab. P.-c. Rains heard his ribs crack, and he knew nothing more until he woke up to find himself in hospital, nicely done up in bandages and plaster of Paris."

Sexton Blake stared thoughtfully at the ash of his cigar, and flicked it over the parapet into the river.

"Could the constable give no more detailed description of the burglar?" he queried.

"No. It was too dark, and it all happened so suddenly," replied Coutts. "He merely knows that the fellow was immensely broad, tremendously strong, and had remarkably long arms."

"My hat! Sounds more like a blessed ape than a man!" exclaimed Tinker.

"Apes don't steal jewels!" snapped Coutts scornfully.

Sexton Blake frowned, and blinked his eyes ruminatively.

"A somewhat remarkable combination," he said slowly. "A man who is broad, muscular, and weighty, and yet sufficiently active to climb up and down water-pipes. And a nasty customer to tackle, I should imagine."

"Well, yes, considering that P.-c. Rains is the present champion heavy-weight wrestler of the police," said Coutts meaningly. "He stands six feet three inches, and weighs sixteen stone, and yet this cat-burglar fellow handled him like a piece of putty, and almost broke him in halves. Oh, yes, I wouldn't mind tackling him—from a distance with a six-shooter!"

"Well, vague as it may be, you've got a pretty good description of the fellow," said Sexton Blake. "You can't call him particularly inconspicuous. You're bound to rope him in if he continues these jewel-raids."

"I've got to rope him in! The Chief has placed the whole case in my hands!" snapped Coutts grimly. "There's nothing gets his goat more than when one of his men is murderously assaulted in the execution of his duty. And the Press is making a big noise about the whole business. After all, a million pounds' worth of jewels stolen in one week is something to talk about. It's no secret that the Home Secretary himself is one of the victims. His own house was entered whilst he was entertaining a dinner-party, and the greater part of his wife's jewels lifted."

"At what time do these thefts generally lake place?" asked Sexton Blake, feeling for a fresh cigar.

"At any time after dark. Sometimes as early as eight o'clock."

Sexton Blake stared out across the black bosom of the river, where the reflected lights glimmered like rippling spears of flame, and an occasional tug-boat, with a string of barges lined behind, surged past, bellowing like a challenging bull in charge of a herd of kine.

"Well, it's obviously a case for the police. Coutts," said the Baker Street detective, at length.

"It's certainly not a one-man job. I don't see that I can help you, even if I wanted to."

Coutts grunted disappointedly. He had illimitable faith in Sexton Blake, and always expected him to come forward with some theory that would serve to simplify the elucidation of a knotty case.

Blake noted the C.I.D. man's fallen countenance, and turned and clapped him encouragingly on the shoulder.

"If you've an hour to spare, Coutts, I suggest you stroll back with me for a cigar and a whisky and soda, and we'll talk over those jewel robberies more fully."

The C.I.D man's face lit up again at once.

"There's nothing I should like better," he said gruffly. "An hour to spare! I've got all night. I'm on indefinite leave until I collar the brute who almost hugged the life out of poor Rains; but I'm hanged if I know how to start about the job!"

Many a person turned to stare curiously at the two men, the lad, and the bloodhound, as they strode briskly along. They presented a striking contrast. There was Sexton Blake—tall, lean, and hawk-featured, with keen, observant eyes that never missed a face that passed him by; Detective-Inspector Coutts—thickset, big headed, pompous, and with plain-clothes man written all over him; Tinker looked a normal, healthy type of young Britisher, well-built, ruddy skinned, and clear eyed.

Pedro was just a huge brown, solemn-eyed, hanging-jowled bloodhound, who loped along with his nose to the ground and his claws rattling on the pavement.

The trio and their canine companion did not pass unnoticed. A well-known Cabinet Minister, striding across from the direction of the House, waggled his umbrella in a jovial greeting, and many a sign passed between Coutts and the numerous plain-clothes men he encountered.

A burly ruffian, with a cap drawn down over his eyes, a muffler around his neck, and an unhealthy pallor to his surly countenance, stopped dead and cringed as he caught sight of Sexton

Blake, and then threw I back his shoulders and swaggered by with a feeble air of defiance.

"Jerry Gask, the coiner, who almost kicked his wife to death in Deptford," said Sexton Blake, at once, as his retentive memory flashed back over a gulf of years. "I believe he got a ten years' 'stretch,' so he can't have been out more than a week.

"And probably he'll be in again before another week passes," grunted Coutts, who believed in the dogma of "once a crook, always a crook."

It was then close on eight o'clock, and the streets were packed tight with traffic sweeping westwards towards Theatre-land, and the gaily illuminated restaurants and cabarets.

Sexton Blake chose his own particular way of reaching his rooms in Baker Street. It was not the shortest of routes, but it led him through the quiet, residential streets which were the haunts of the aristocracy—and the nouveau riche.

"There's something fascinating about this neighbourhood at this time of night," said the detective, as he strode along with the inevitable cigar clamped between his teeth. I always like to look at these big houses and try and imagine who the people are who live in them—and how they made the money that enables them to live here. There perhaps we have the residence of a retired soap-boiler, with a diamond-encrusted wife, and a pudding-faced daughter who hopes—vainly— to be presented at Court. And next door the scion of a noble family, who is so impoverished that he would unwillingly marry the soap-boiler's daughter, and—"

The detective broke of short, and coming to a halt, stared curiously down at Pedro. The big bloodhound had suddenly pulled up dead, and was behaving in a manner that was distinctly unusual under the circumstances.

His fur was bristling like the mane of a hyaena, and deep, menacing growl rumbled in his throat as he stood sniffing at the pavement, and then with a suddenness that almost jerked Tinker clean off his feet, made a dive for the farther side of the road.

"My hat, what sort of a scent's the lop-eared old idiot struck now?" gulped the lad, as he clung tenaciously to the leash, and endeavoured to hold the bloodhound in check. "Can't be a cat. He's no more interest in cats than he has in white mice!"

Pedro had evidently struck a trail of some kind, and it was a red hot one. Straight across the road he plunged towards a big, detached house that stood in its own grounds. Right up to the entrance-gates he went, and there he halted, and squatting down on his haunches, lifted his muzzle and let forth an eerie, mournful, blood-curdling howl that sent an unpleasant shudder rippling down Inspector Coutts' spine.

"Good heavens! What's the matter with the confounded animal?" gulped Detective-Inspector Coutts shakily. "Never heard such a ghastly row in my life. Can't you stop him, Blake?"

Sexton Blake spoke sternly to the bloodhound, but, contrary to habit, Pedro paid no attention to his master's voice. Again and again he bayed, like the mournful wail of a lost soul—a series of weird, nerve-racking, long drawn-out howls that sounded strangely out of place in this respectable West End thoroughfare. Only once before had Sexton Blake known him to give tone in such a manner, and that had been in the depths of an African jungle, when he had picked up the scent of some strange, unseen, and, perhaps, unknown animal of the wilds.

And then, as suddenly as he had started, the big bloodhound ceased his baying, and as the last tremulous echoes died away, the resultant silence seemed even more uncanny than that that had gone before.

And then the mute curtain of the night was rent by an answering cry of such a hideous character as seemed to freeze the very marrow in Sexton Blake' bones. It was a human voice this time, raised in a raucous screech of dire fear and agony. For several moments it hung on a long, quavering note, that suddenly merged into a coughing groan, and then silence again.

"A human death-cry, if ever I have heard one!" was the horrifying thought that flashed through Sexton Blake's mind!

The Second Chapter
The Burglar!

DETECTIVE-INSPECTOR COUTTS' normally-ruddy countenance was as white as a sheet as he took off his hat, and mopping the cold beads of perspiration from his forehead, stared nervously at his companions.

Tinker's knees were trembling beneath him; but Sexton Blake was as calm and imperturbable as over. Pedro was on his feet again, his fur still bristling like a scrubbing-brush, and his muscular body quivering from the tip of his nose to the end of his rigid tail.

It was hard to realise that they were standing in a quiet London street, within a stone's throw of the throbbing traffic and glaring lights of Piccadilly. The atmosphere was pregnant with tragedy and horror, that was not dispelled by the street-lamps and the lighted windows of some of the houses.

And then, in a flash, they were swept back to the prosaic modernity of their surroundings, and face to face with realities that they could understand.

The front door of the big house in front of them was suddenly flung wide open, and silhouetted in the oblong of light stood the figure of a man, his shirt-front gleaming white against the background of his black clothes. He raised one hand to his lips, and the shrill, imperative screech of a police-whistle awakened a hundred ear-splitting echoes.

Coutts was himself again in an instant. The sound of that whistle was a call to duty that could not be disobeyed, and, jamming his hat hard down on his head, he threw his weight against the closed gate.

"Come on, Blake—trouble of some kind in here!" he jerked. "This is where that ghastly cry came from. Seems Pedro wasn't far wrong after all."

Neither Sexton Blake or Tinker needed any urging. They were close behind Coutts as he flung the gate open and dashed up the path towards the front door. The man in evening-dress was still standing there, blowing his whistle for all he was worth. He was an elderly, white-moustached individual, and was evidently labouring under intense excitement.

"Hallo, what's the matter here? I'm a police-officer," jerked Coutts officially.

"What's all the trouble?"

"Murder—robbery!" gulped the man agitatedly; and he gave a start of surprise as he caught sight of Sexton Blake.

"Mr. Sexton Blake!" he went on gladly. "You seem to have arrived at the right moment. You remember me?"

"Sir Dicton Parsons, if I am not mistaken," replied the Baker Street detective, recognising a wealthy shipping-merchant whom he had met on more than one occasion. "This is Detective-Inspector Coutts, if you are in need of the service of the police. What has happened here?"

"I hardly know! A ghastly tragedy has occurred," replied the baronet shakily. "It happened whilst I was seated at dinner. I heard a ghastly cry, and rushed upstairs to find that my manservant had been murdered, and my wife's jewels stolen!"

Coutts started, and glanced meaningly at Sexton Blake. Another jewel robbery, following so close on top of the conversation they had had during the past half-hour! Was this another visitation of the mysterious cat-burglar who had been terrorising London for the past week, and who had already come near to murdering one policeman, and had succeeded in making a haul of close on a million pounds' worth of jewels and precious stones?

A couple of constables came tramping up the drive, attracted by the shrill summons of the police whistle, and they saluted smartly as they recognised the familiar countenance of Detective-Inspector Coutts.

The C.I.D. man gave orders for one of them to remain on guard outside the house, whilst the other fell in behind as Sir Dicton Parsons led the way into the hall of his palatially-furnished residence.

It was as much as Tinker could do to hold Pedro in check. The bloodhound's fur was still bristling fiercely, and he tugged at his leash with his muzzle held in the air, and deep, menacing growls rumbling in his throat.

They passed the open door of a dining-room, where a table was laid with snowy linen and gleaming silverware, and where a white-faced butler stood, holding a tray in one shaking hand.

"I was dining alone—Lady Parsons had gone to the theatre," volunteered the baronet. "And then it happened—that fearful cry of horror and anguish! By Heavens, it made my blood run cold. I recognised the voice of Barker, my manservant, and immediately rushed upstairs to my room. When I opened the door—"

Sir Dicton broke off with a shudder, and led the way up the broad staircase to the first floor.

"In here," he said huskily; and flung open a door on the right of the passage. Sexton Blake and Coutts entered the room together, with the others following nervously behind. The electric lights were switched on, revealing a handsomely-appointed bed-room, complete with a comfortable settee, and a writing-desk by the window. It was obviously a man's room, reserved for the use of Sir Dicton Parsons himself.

Sexton Blake's keen eyes swept the room in a flash, and finally crime to rest on an ugly spectacle that was presented in the centre of the room. It was the huddled figure of a man, who lay sprawling in an oddly crooked attitude. He was bent backwards at such an angle that his head almost touched his heels, and the sight of the man's face brought a gasp horror to Sexton Blake's lips.

The man bore the appearance of one who had been violently and brutally strangled. His cheeks were suffused with blood, so that they were purple rather than crimson, his glassy eyes were bulging almost out of their sockets, and his swollen tongue was protruding from his gaping mouth.

"By Heavens, it's murder right enough!" muttered Coutts, in an awed voice, recollecting the nerve-racking, strangled cry of anguish that they had heard from outside the house. Undoubtedly it had been the last sound that had been uttered by the unfortunate man who lay before them.

"Better remain outside, Tinker, and keep Pedro with you," said Sexton Blake gravely; and as the lad obeyed he knelt down and bent over the huddled figure on the carpet. It was that of a middle-aged, clean-shaven man attired in sober black. The detective needed no telling that the man was stone dead though he had not been dead for many moments. The strange angle at which his back was bent conveyed only too plainly that his spine was broken.

"He hasn't been strangled—there's not a mark on his neck," said Blake puzzledly, as he gently straightened the crooked form and laid it on its back, and struck with a sudden idea, he opened the dead man's waistcoat, and placed a hand firmly on either side of his body, just above his hips. As he moved his hands slowly up and down his eyes narrowed, and a gasp of consternation passed his lips.

The man had literally been crushed to death, as though a steam-roller had passed over the middle part of his body. There was not a sound rib in his body—every one was smashed to splinters, and driven into one another like a crushed match-box, and it was the same tremendous constriction as must have snapped the poor fellow's spine like a carrot.

Many years previously Sexton Blake had come across a native in Brazil who had been squeezed to death in the coils of a gigantic boa-constrictor, and the ghastly result had been much the same as this.

But there were no boa constrictors roaming about the streets of the West End of London, and Sexton Blake's eyes were blazing with excitement as he sprang to his feet and turned towards his companions.

"Coutts, this is another case of the long arm of coincidence," he said in a tense voice. "A short while ago you were telling me of the police-constable in Kensington who had been attacked by a cat burglar and almost crushed to death. This fellow has met with a similar experience, and he must be a victim of the same mysterious individual. Your cat burglar, or whatever you choose to call him, was in this very room not ten minutes ago!"

AN awed silence followed Sexton Blake's amazing assertion. Detective Inspector Coutts' jaw dropped in utter consternation. His florid cheeks paled, and he threw a nervous glance around the room, as though half-expecting to see some ghastly, fearsome figure spring out upon them. The constable, who had evidently heard of the terrible experience that had befallen his compatriot in Kensington, coughed uneasily.

"A cat burglar?" echoed Sir Dicton Parsons shakily, as he pointed towards a small wall-safe, the door of which had been wrenched open, and hung by one twisted hinge. "You're not far wrong, Mr. Blake. My wife's jewels have been stolen, including a diamond necklace valued at twenty thousand pounds. Poor Barker must have caught the thief in the act, and lost his life defending my property."

Sexton Blake strode quickly across the room, and, drawing the curtains, examined each of the windows in turn. There were three in all, and every one was closed and latched on the inside.

"The murdering scoundrel didn't gain admittance through these windows," he said grimly.

"And if he was here a few minutes ago, he can't be very far away now," declared Coutts in a queer, strained voice. "I—I suppose we'd better search the house. He may still be on the premises."

Sexton Blake nodded, but before he could speak there came a startling interruption. A loud yell of dismay sounded from outside the closed door, followed by the thud of a heavy fall, and then the savage baying of a dog, that gradually diminished in volume.

"By heavens, it's Tinker!" exclaimed Sexton Blake, his voice vibrant with alarm, and with one leap he gained the door and wrenched it open.

Outside, in the centre of the passage, sat Tinker, a dazed, bewildered expression on his face as he stared ruefully at one half of a broken leash that he held in his hand.

"What's the matter? What's happened, my boy?" queried Blake anxiously, as he assisted the lad to his feet. "Where's Pedro?"

Tinker pointed vaguely down the corridor.

"The silly beggar's gone crazy," he said irritable. "All of a sudden he made one dive, snapped the leash like a bit of cotton, and was off like a flash of lightning, he must have scented or heard something unusual. I think he's gone upstairs. Hark at him!"

From somewhere in the upper regions in the house the big bloodhound was barking in a manner that sent a queer shiver down Blake's spine. He knew the sound only too well—the note of a bloodhound closing in on its quarry.

"The murderer's still on the premises, and Pedro has scented him!" jerked the detective through his set teeth. "Come on, Coutts!"

Sexton Blake was first away. There were few things on earth that he feared, and he was filled with a fierce, relentless desire to come to close quarters with the cold-blooded villain who had broken into the house and brutally murdered the helpless manservant.

He could still hear Pedro baying in the distance as he sped down the passage and took the stairs four at a time. He halted on the second landing, and listened for a fraction of a moment. Pedro's savage baying came from still higher in the house, and, drawing a deep breath, he charged up the next flight of stairs, whilst his companions were still struggling up the first flight.

Even as he reached the topmost landing Pedro's eager, deep-throated barks, now close at hand, merged into a shrill, blood-chilling yelp of canine fear and anguish. It was a ghastly, unnerving sound, such as the detective had never known the bloodhound to give tongue to before, and it was follow by a heavy thud, and a low, snarling whine of utter terror.

The sound came from the farther end of a corridor that branched off to the left, and Sexton Blake swung round the corner like a racing motorist negotiating a hairpin bend. Everything was in darkness, but by a stroke of amazing good luck, his hand, as it slid along the wall for a support, encountered an electric light switch, and turned on a spray of bulbs that illuminated everything with a blinding glare.

The detective skidded to a standstill, panting, and wide-eyed with amazement and wonder. A few yards away Pedro, the bloodhound, lay crouching against the wall of the passage, his tail between his legs and his head sunk between his fore-paws. The big animal was trembling in every limb, and seemed utterly cowed and smitten with terror. There were flecks of foam on his jowls, and his bloodshot eyes were fixed fearfully on a closed door directly opposite where he lay.

The bloodhound paid no attention to his master—an extraordinary thing in itself—and when Sexton Blake spoke to him he only crouched lower and whined uneasily.

The detective cast one glance at the closed door, and, grasping the handle, threw his weight against the panels. Contrary to expectation, the door was unlocked and flew open, precipitating him headlong into the room beyond.

With an effort Sexton Blake managed to retain his balance, and stood swaying in the centre of the floor. The room was in darkness. Straight in front of him a greyish oblong marked the position of a window, and a draught of cold air blowing full in his face told him that the window was open.

Bang!

The door of the room suddenly slammed shut, and strong as Blake's nerves were, his heart was in his mouth as he swung round on his heels.

"Only the draught, of course," he muttered foolishly. And then something happened.

Out of the shadows a black, shapeless figure, with a dusky blob of a face, suddenly loomed, and before the detective could lift a finger to defend himself, two arms, like bands of steel, wrapped him in a terrible embrace, pinning his own arms to his sides, and rendering him as helpless as a child.

A hot, snarling breath gushed in Blake's face, and as the great, muscular arms gradually tightened, expelling every gasp of air from his lungs, and driving his ribs into his flesh, the detective realised, with frenzied horror and something akin to panic, that he was helpless in the grip of the mysterious cat-burglar, who had squeezed the life out of the unfortunate manservant who lay twisted and broken in the room below!

It was a dreadful moment and one that Sexton Blake never forgot. It was just as though he was gripped between the claws of a mammoth lobster. He could feel his ribs cracking beneath the strain; his heart was beating with laboured thuds, and his brain was commencing to reel, whilst brilliant lights flashed before his eyes. Every second he expected to hear his backbone snap like a dry twig, and he knew that he was in the first throes of suffocation.

But Sexton Blake never altogether lost his head, else he would have been doomed. With a gigantic mental effort he managed to grasp the situation, and immediately resorted to a trick that was not used in the best of circles, but which was usually effective against an unscrupulous opponent.

Deliberately, and with all the force and strength that he could command, he butted his head savagely into the dim indistinguishable face that loomed in front of him.

The force of the impact must have reduced his assailant's nose to a pulp—he distinctly sensed the crunch of the splintered bone—and, with a snarling gasp of pain, the man reeled back, and loosened his murderous grasp for a fraction of a second.

But it was sufficient time for Sexton Blake to get going. He slackened his knees, and, with an eel-like twist, wriggled clean out of the burglar's muscular arms, at the same time deftly tripping his opponent so that he was thrown off his balance and staggered backwards towards the open window.

One leap carried Sexton Blake backwards towards the doer, and his hand streaked towards the tiny automatic that he carried in a special pocket on his right thigh. The deliberate attempt to crush him to death had fanned his anger to a fierce flame, and he was taking no chances of a second attempt.

"Blake—Blake! Where are you, man?"

It was Coutts' voice ringing high above the stampeding of feet, and when Blake attempted to answer he could only manage a husky, breathless wheeze.

His gaze was fixed vigilantly on the shadowy, crouching figure of the mysterious cat burglar, and, with the quickness and agility of a cat, the latter suddenly swung round and leaped on to the sill of the open window.

A warning shout from below told that the constable who had been left on guard outside was not neglecting his duties, and had spotted the figure at the window, and, with a guttural snarl of fury and chagrin, the cat burglar stood upright, and, grasping the guttering above in his hand, drew himself upwards towards the roof.

It was not Sexton Blake's intention that the murderer should get away if he could help it, and he let fly with his automatic, aiming at one of the dangling legs just as it was drawn out of sight.

Whether he hit or missed was impossible to tell, for the man had vanished, and at the same instant the door was flung violently open, and Coutts came charging into the room, with Tinker and Sir Dicton Parsons close at his heels. It was the latter who knew where to find the switch and turn on the electric light, revealing the dishevelled figure of Sexton Blake, with his face unusually flushed and his pistol gripped in one hand.

"Thank Heaven you're safe, Blake!" gulped Coutts shakily. "What's happened? We heard a shot, and I thought—"

"It was I who fired!" panted the detective, jamming his automatic back into his pocket. "The cat burglar was here a moment ago. He did his best to crush the life out of me, but I got the better of him. He's clambered out on to the roof!"

"The roof!" echoed Sir Dicton excitedly. He can't get away from there unless he slides down one of the water-pipes, and you've got a constable on guard below. This way! There's a trapdoor at the other end of the passage, and a ladder we keep there in case of fire. I shall never forgive myself if we allow the murderer of poor Barker to get away scot-free."

A fraction of a second's thought convinced Sexton Blake that to gain the roof by means of the trapdoor would mean a waste of much valuable time. Where the burglar had gone he knew that he could follow, and without hesitation he clambered out on to the sill of the open window and stood upright with his back turned to the dizzying gulf of space that yawned beneath him.

By standing at full stretch he was just able to grasp the guttering of the roof above his head, and, without troubling to gauge whether it would support his weight or not, he drew himself upwards like a professional gymnast on a parallel bar, and with a sideways swing hoisted himself clean up on to the roof of the house.

In a trice he was on his feet again, peering searchingly in all directions. A grotesquely shaped stack of chimney-pots deceived him for a moment, and as he walked towards it he glimpsed the shadow of someone who was lurking in the shelter of the broad column of brickwork.

An instant later some bulky missile whizzed within an inch of Sexton Blake's ducking head, and shattered to fragments on the concrete behind him. It was one of the pots that had been wrenched clean from its setting, and two more followed in quick succession, but neither found their mark. Twenty yards away a trapdoor set in the roof shot open, revealing the head and shoulders of Detective-Inspector Coutts, and as though realising that he was in growing danger of capture, the murderer, who was crouching in the shadow of the chimney stack, emerged into the open and darted towards the farther end of the roof.

It was just the vague, dark shape of a man, who displayed a distinct limp as he ran, and Sexton Blake fell a fierce thrill of satisfaction at the thought that the shot he had fired had not gone astray.

"Halt! Hands up, you scoundrel! You can't get away now!" shouted the Baker Street detective warningly. "You might as well give in! The house is surrounded by police!"

It was a bold bluff, but it did not seem to have any effect on the fugitive. Though he was within a dozen yards of the edge of the roof he did not check in his limping stride. There was a sheer drop of sixty feet to the ground below, and Blake uttered a shout of consternation and dismay as he saw his quarry gain the end of the flat roof and launch himself into space.

He halted, waiting fearfully to hear the ugly, sickening thud that seemed bound to follow, but instead there came a tremendous rustle of disturbed foliage, and a cracking and splintering of broken branches.

He realised the truth as soon as he reached the edge of the roof. Some distance away—a far greater distance than he would have thought anyone could have spanned with one leap—reared a tall elm-tree, and it was into the top-most branches of this that the cat-burglar had hurled himself. Despite his injured leg, he had gained his objective. For a brief instant Blake caught a glimpse of the man, suspended like some great ape to one of the swaying branches of the tree, and then he drew himself into the midst of the foliage, and disappeared from view.

For a moment the detective could hear the sound of his progress as he lowered himself through the branches, and then there was nothing but silence, until Coutts came lumbering on the scene, panting and puffing with excitement.

"Where is the scoundrel, Blake?" he gulped. "Don't tell me he's managed to get away?"

"I'm afraid he has," replied Sexton Blake grimly, pointing meaningly towards the tree below. "He took a big risk, but his luck was in. But he hasn't got away scot free. I winged

him. I'm dead sure I put a bullet in his leg. Listen!"

The stuttering roar of a powerful motor-engine suddenly broke the silence, coming from no great distance away. It rose to a fierce, pulsing crescendo that gradually died away as the car started and moved off in direction of Piccadilly.

"There goes our man, if I'm not much mistaken!" jerked Sexton Blake in bitter chagrin. "He must have had a car waiting for him round in the next street. We've missed our chance, Coutts. Your mysterious, man-killing cat-burglar is still at large!"

THE THIRD
CHAPTER
THE BRASS MEDALLION.

PURSUIT was useless. Both Sexton Blake and Coutt's realised that at once, and in gloomy silence they left the roof by means of the trap-door, and re-entered the house.

Tinker and Pedro were waiting in the corridor below. The bloodhound seemed to have got over his recent fright, but he was still looking somewhat downcast, and he wagged his tail sheepishly as he caught sight of his master, and rubbed his head against his leg.

Sexton Blake stared puzzledly at the dog as he gave him an affectionate pat on the back. Pedro's extraordinary behaviour was inexplicable to him. Never before had he known the big bloodhound to be cowed or terrorised by any human being. He had the heart of a lion, and his courage had never as yet failed to withstand any test to which he had been subjected.

"Strange what put the wind up that dog!" grunted Coutts, as though divining the detective's thoughts. "In the ordinary way, he would have seized hold of that cold blooded murderer, and held on to him to his last breath."

"He seems to have had a terrific shock of some kind," agreed Tinker bewilderedly. "He absolutely refuses to enter the room where you had the scrap with the burglar, guv'nor. There must be something uncanny about the scoundrel to affect a dog in that manner."

"I don't know about uncanny; but there's something distinctly inhuman about the brute," said Sexton Blake slowly, as he felt his bruised and aching ribs. "I've never known such strength. I thought he was going to break me in halves. I only wish I could have had one good look at the fellow for future reference."

Detective-Inspector Coutts had already given instructions for one of the constables to telephone to the nearest police station, and by the time they had returned to the apartment where the body of the unfortunate man-servant lay stretched in the centre of the floor, a ring at the front door bell announced the arrival of the local divisional police-surgeon, accompanied by an inspector and a sergeant.

Whilst Coutts was giving the inspector all the details of what had occurred, the police-surgeon made a keen examination of the murdered man.

"Dead, of course—been dead for quite half an hour," he announced briefly. "Why, the man's crushed across the middle as though he'd been run through a mangle. He might have died either of a broken spine, suffocation, or severe internal injuries. I've never seen anything like it."

"Obviously murdered by the same scoundrel who nearly finished off P.-c. Rains, in the Kensington Division," remarked Inspector Pinner. "And you say you have been robbed, Sir Dicton? Anything of any considerable value?"

"My wife's diamonds—twenty or thirty thousand pounds' worth!" replied the baronet bitterly. "And by this time tomorrow they would have been secure in the Safe Deposit. I'd made up my mind to place them there after reading of all these jewel robberies."

Sexton Blake stood to one side, allowing the police to make their own investigations. It was not for him to offer an opinion until he was asked. Coutts had walked across the room, and was making a close examination of the empty wall-safe.

"Not a sign of a finger-print," he said disappointedly. "The scoundrel either wore gloves, or—What's the matter with you, Blake?"

Sexton Blake had suddenly uttered a sharp exclamation, and was staring surprised at his hands. Both were thickly smeared with moist paint, that certainly had not been there ten minutes previously.

"I was wondering how I got myself in this state!" muttered the private detective puzzledly.

"That's easily explained," volunteered Sir Dicton Parsons, with a faint smile. "You got your hands in that state when you hoisted yourself out of the window on to the roof. I have been having the house done up, and the guttering around the roof was repainted yesterday."

Sexton Blake rubbed his soiled hands ruefully together, and then a sudden gleam of excitement leaped into his grey eyes. After all, he had not been the only one who had handled the repainted guttering, and—

"If the murderer has left any finger-prints about I think I can find them for you, Coutts," he said confidently. "I wonder if you could supply me with a hammer and a screwdriver, Sir Dicton?"

Wonderingly the baronet procured these articles, and Sexton Blake led the way upstairs to the room where he had had his life and death struggle with the mysterious cat-burglar.

Coutts and Tinker watched him in blank amazement as he opened the window and clambered out on to the sill, with the hammer and screwdriver tucked in his breast-pocket.

"For the love of Mike what's the man up to now?" muttered the C.I.D. man under his breath. "If he wants to get on the roof again, why can't he go through the trapdoor?"

But Sexton Blake evidently didn't want to pay a second visit to the roof. Duly his feet and legs were visible, and there was a sound of hammering and wrenching, and then:

"Catch hold, Coutts, and be careful how you handle it."

Coutts' red face was a study in consternation and wonder, as he gingerly accepted the length of iron guttering that was passed through the window to him, and which was still moist with recently applied paint.

"What the blazes, Blake!" he spluttered irritably. "What's the idea of pulling half the house down?"

There was a quiet smile of satisfaction on the Baker Street detective's face as he swung himself back through the window, and bent keenly over the length of guttering.

"Just a thought," he said, pointing to a series of smudgy patches on the wet paint. "There is a first-class set of the finger-prints of your mysterious cat-burglar, Coutts. He left them—just as I did—when he climbed up on to the roof. You'd better take that guttering to the Yard, and have the prints photographed and examined as soon as possible. There is a remote chance that they may prove a valuable clue."

Coutts uttered an exclamation of excitement, and Inspector Pinner flashed a glance of ungrudging admiration at Sexton Blake.

"By Jove, that's a smart bit of work, Mr. Blake," he said candidly. "But those are the funniest finger-prints I have ever seen. There don't seem to be any of the usual loops and whorls that we use in classification."

"That's true," agreed the private detective thoughtfully. "Still, there's no doubt they are finger- prints, and that's the main thing."

Carefully Coutts picked up the length of guttering by the extreme ends, and carried it down the stairs. Just as Sexton Blake was in the act of leaving the room his attention was caught by something bright that lay on the floor just inside the door. He picked it up to find that it was a curiously carved brass medallion attached to a fine but strong brass chain. The latter was broken, as though it had been violently rent asunder. The light was poor, and Sexton Blake thrust the medallion into his pocket, intending to examine it more closely later on.

There was little more to be done in the house of death. Coutts and Inspector Pinner had filled several pages of their notebooks with facts and details, and an ambulance had been summoned to convey the murdered man to the nearest mortuary to await the coroner's inquest.

Coutts was anxious to get back to the Yard to make his report regarding the latest move of the mysterious cat-burglar, and Sexton Blake was not averse to returning to his cosy rooms in Baker Street.

Coutts dropped the detective and his young assistant there, though the journey carried him a bit out of his way, and departed, promising that he would not fail to let his friend know the result of the examination of the finger-prints and the piece of guttering as soon as they had been scrutinised by the Finger-print Department at Scotland Yard.

There was a bright fire burning in the sitting-room, and Sexton Blake heaved a sigh of relief when he had donned his faded, chemical-stained, tobacco-burned crimson dressing gown and well-worn slippers, and wedged himself in his favourite armchair.

"I thought my number was up to-night. Tinker," he said, as he thumbed a wad of tobacco into a blackened, charred briar pipe. "I've never felt such a grip in all my life. I thought my ribs were going to be stove in. I'll bet I'm black and blue where the brute wound his arms around me."

Tinker shuddered at recollection of the dead man-servant. But for his quickness and resource his guv'nor might have met with a similar fate.

"I'm glad you winged the beggar," he said heartily. "Pity you didn't smash his leg, so that he couldn't get away. Hallo! What's that you've got there?"

Sexton Blake had suddenly remembered the brass medallion that he had picked up in the top room of Sir Dicton Parson's house, and had dug it out of his pocket, and was examining it curiously. It was about the size of a half-crown, and on one side was crudely carved what looked like the figure of a hideous, grinning baboon, squatting on its haunches, with its hairy arms folded across its great chest.

On the the other side were engraved some strange hieroglyphics or symbols. It looked something like Hindustani, but the detective was unable to decipher the signs, though he was familiar with most of the Urdu dialects.

"I found this in the room where I got to grips with the cat-burglar," explained Blake. "It looks as though it had been wrenched from around somebody's neck."

"The burglar's, perhaps," suggested Tinker. "Though it's a funny thing for a fellow to wear, unless it's a kind of amulet, or lucky charm. Perhaps Pedro tore it away when he leaped at the man's throat, as no doubt he did in the first place."

The big bloodhound, who was lying on the mat, raised his great head as he heard his name mentioned, and casually Sexton Blake dangled the brass medallion in front of his nose. The effect was astonishing. One casual sniff, and Pedro leaped to his feet as though he had been shot, and with a deep, grumbling growl, and his fur standing on end, darted to the other end of the room, and flopped down in a dark corner.

"Well, I'll he hanged!" exclaimed Sexton Blake amazedly. "There's not the slightest doubt that this little article belongs to our friend the cat-burglar, but why on earth should Pedro be so frightened of the man? I've sever known anything like it. It's almost uncanny."

"Uncanny's the right word for it," agreed Tinker in a puzzled voice. "I didn't think Pedro was frightened of any living thing. This has got me guessing!"

"Well, we've got some sort of a clue, at any rate," muttered Blake, replacing the medallion carefully in his pocket. "I must get some expert on languages to decipher whatever is carved on the back of the charm."

Little did Sexton Blake realise the value of the clue that was now in his possession, or what amazing and sensational adventures into which it was to lead him and his young assistant.

A terrible peril and a deadly menace was creeping upon them like a black cloud across a clear sky—and the storm was soon to burst!

The Fourth Chapter

Pedro Goes Mad!

THE sensational experiences of the previous night were still fresh in Sexton Blake's mind when he arose the following morning, and after his usual cold bath and brief course of "physical jerks," sauntered into the sitting-room for his breakfast.

Grilled ham and eggs and steaming, fragrant coffee, such as only Mrs. Bardell could brew, combined well with the morning newspapers, which gave a full account of the latest exploit of the mysterious cat-burglar, and the foul murder that had been committed at the house of Sir Dicton Parsons.

"Detective-Inspector Coutts, of the special department of the C.I.D., New Scotland Yard, has the case in hand," read one paper, "and we have no doubt that this able officer will bring the career of the—cold-blooded murderer and jewel-thief to a speedy conclusion."

Naturally, there was no mention of Sexton Blake, or of the prominent part he had played in the events of the night before. Many and many a brilliant triumph had been recorded in the name of Coutts, when he had played only secondary role to the clever deduction and amazing skill of the world-famed "Wizard of Baker Street."

Pedro was himself again and seemed to have forgotten all about the uncanny criminal who had exercised such a terrorising influence over his canine mind when they had come to close quarters in the house of Sir Dicton Parsons.

Sexton Blake's morning work consisted in running through the stack of newspapers that had accumulated during the past week marking with a blue pencil those items of professional interest which were to be snipped out by Tinker and pasted in the ever-growing number of reference books which already filled several shelves of a bookcase in one corner of the room.

It was close on twelve o'clock when the noisy jangling of the telephone-bell jarred through the silence of the room. Tinker answered the call and turned towards his master, with the receiver still clamped to his ear.

"It's Coutts," he announced. "Obviously slightly perturbed and excitable, and wants to know if you can come round to the Yard at once."

"What about?" queried Sexton Blake vaguely, slashing away with his blue pencil like a bed-weary night editor.

"From what I can gather—you know how Coutts bawls, as though he was speaking from the other end of Europe?—it's something to do with fingerprints. Possibly the fingerprints on the piece of guttering he waltzed away with last night."

Sexton Blake's lean face registered a certain amount of interest as he tossed the pile of newspapers to one side and towered to his feet.

"Tell him I'm coming round now," he jerked, as he flung his dressing-gown over the back of a chair and vanished into his bed-room to make himself presentable for a visit to the headquarters of the C.I.D.

Five minutes later he and Tinker left the house together, and stood for a moment waiting for a stray taxicab to pass their way. Neither noticed the queer-looking individual in the long, black overcoat and blue turban swathed around his narrow head, who seemed to have been waiting outside the house, and who now came slouching past, and halted for a fraction of a minute opposite to where Sexton Blake and his assistant stood with their backs turned towards him.

He held some object in his hand that might, or might not, have been a metal syringe. Evidently it was, for as he pressed the plunger there was a faint, hissing sound, and an almost invisible jet of vapour sprayed itself generously over the suit that the famous detective was wearing.

Then the dark-skinned, beady-eyed man went shuffling unhurriedly on his way, looking no different from the numerous queer visitors from overseas who are always to be seen wandering about the streets of London.

A handy taxi came bowling along, and, having swallowed up Sexton Blake and Tinker in its interior, pursued a dead course for the big red-brick pile of buildings on the Embankment that housed the finest detective force in the whole of the world.

The Chief-Commissioner himself could not have secured easier access to Scotland Yard than did Sexton Blake, and with the manner of one treading a long-familiar path he made his way up the stairs and through a maze of corridors, and finally stalked into the barely-furnished room where Detective-Inspector Coutts sat, with his hard felt hat on the back of his head, and a glorified, rolled cabbage-leaf jutting from the corner of his mouth. He was engaged in conversation with a tall, clever looking man, whom Blake recognised as the chief of the Finger-print Department.

"Ah, here you are, Blake! Good man!" greeted Coutts bluffly. "Take a seat. Have a cigar?"

"Yes. No," replied the Baker Street detective, availing himself of the first invitation, and helping himself to one of his own woods. "Well, why this urgent summons, Coutts?"

The C.I.D. man slid a piece of cardboard plastered with small photographs, across the table toward his friend.

"Replicas of the finger-print of our friend the cat-burglar of last night," he said grimly."

"Well?"

Coutts nodded, and Inspector Boddam, of the finger-print department, obtruded himself into the conversation.

"Extraordinary prints, them, Mr. Blake," he said quietly. "There are nothing like them amongst our records. They are unique—at least, practically unique."

"In what way?" queried Blake keenly.

Inspector Boddam passed across another card bearing a row of small photographs.

"Those are the only finger-prints they resemble," he said, with a ghost of a smile.

"And whose prints are they?" challenged the Baker Street detective.

"They are the finger-prints of one of the big apes at present housed at the Zoological Gardens in Regent's Park. We took them for purposes of experimental comparison some time ago."

Sexton Blake was silent for a moment. His surprise was only noticeable by the manner in which the pupils of his eyes dwindled to mere pin-pricks.

"You're hinting," he said at length with slow deliberation, "that the cat-burglar who murdered Sir Dicton Parsons' manservant last night, and decamped with twenty-two pounds' worth of jewels, was not a human being, but an ape?"

"The finger-prints incline one to that theory. They are certainly not human."

Sexton Blake leaned back in his chair, and laughed quietly.

"This case is getting more interesting than ever," he said, a humorous twinkle in his grey eyes. "I never knew that apes were capable of violent language."

"What do you mean by that, Blake?" jerked Coutts, almost fiercely.

"I simply mean that the gentleman I butted in the face last night gave vent to some very fiery language," retorted Blake; "shocking language, in fact such language as I would not even repeat in front of you. Coutts, if he was an ape he must have mixed with very reprehensible company in his time."

Coutts' face fell, and he rubbed his nose bewilderedly as he stared at Inspector Boddam.

"That scotches your theory, Boddam," he grunted. "If it had been a parrot there might have been something in it. but apes certainly can't talk, let alone swear, no more than they can burst open safes and steal diamonds."

Inspector Boddam shrugged his shoulders, and ranged the two series of photographs side by side again.

"The fact remains," he said, "that those prints, are like no human finger-prints I have ever seen in all my years of experience, and yet they resemble in every way the imprints of the fingers of an ape."

Sexton Blake frowned thoughtfully at the glowing end of his cigar. He couldn't pretend to understand the extraordinary situation that had arisen. All the finger-prints in the world would not have served to convince him that the immensely-powerful individual he had grappled with the previous night was anything else but a human being. Apes didn't break open safes and steal jewels. Apes didn't as a rule wear clothes, and apes certainly didn't speak perfectly good English, and use language that was more forcible than polite.

"You will have to consider those finger-prints as negligible, Coutts," he said, rising from his chair. "They may comprise a cunning ruse to side-track us. There are such things as gloves with rubber-pads on the finger-tips, which can be made to leave any imprint you choose. Perhaps our friend, the cat-burglar, wishes to pose as an ape? Certainly he possesses the necessary strength and agility."

One thing Sexton Blake had forgotten. The strange brass medallion, with the figure of an ape engraved on one side, and the queer, undecipherable signs on the other!

The detective left Coutts groping helplessly amongst the shattered remains of his latest theory.

"The whole idea's utterly ridiculous, Tinker." Blake said, as he and his young assistant passed through Cannon Row into Parliament Street. "It only goes to show that the finger-print system of identification is not so infallible as many people appear to think. Apes are extraordinarily intelligent and receptive, and can be taught to do many things, but—"

Sexton Blake broke off short with a gasp of alarm, and gave a gigantic backward leap that carried him five feet away. Without the least warning a horse attached to a tradesman's cart that was standing phlegmatically by the kerb, had suddenly reared up, and with a shrill whinny made a ferocious dive at the detective, with bared, champing teeth, and wildly rolling eyes.

Desperately the driver of the van tugged at the reins, and shouted at the top of his voice. Right up on to the pavement the horse lunged, snapping in the direction of Sexton Blake like an infuriated camel, and decidedly more puzzled and alarmed the detective was compelled to take shelter in a tobacconist's shop, whilst a sturdy policeman grasped the animal by the head, and forced it back into the street.

"Better have that hoss muzzled, or shot," he said sternly to the driver. "What's wrong with the brute?"

"Hanged it I know," declared the driver bewilderedly. "Fifteen-year-old she is, and as quiet as a lamb in the ordinary way. Ain't nothing wrong with her now, is there."

There certainly wasn't. The horse was quite tractable again, and went ambling away as though it would have taken a dynamite explosion to disturb its equanimity.

"Humph! there's something about me the brute didn't approve of," muttered Sexton Blake puzzledly, as he resumed his way in the direction of Trafalgar Square. "First time I've ever known an animal to turn on me—and a horse especially."

"It's generally the other way round," agreed Tinker, for he knew full well that Sexton Blake possessed one of those personalities that endeared him to all dumb animals. A famous zoologist had once told him that he would have made an ideal animal-trainer, or a keeper at the Zoological Gardens.

The incident of the horse did not remain long in Blake's memory, though he was to be reminded of it in a most forcible manner before the day was much older.

Still pondering over the extraordinary situation that had arisen in connection with the finger-prints of the murderer of Sir Dicton Parsons' manservant, he paid a visit to his tobacconist's in Haymarket, and purchased a new pipe, and ordered a fresh supply of cigars, and the special mixture he had blended for his own personal consumption.

It was a clear, bright, spring day, and it was almost reluctantly that he and Tinker turned their footsteps in the direction of Baker Street.

"By James, I'd like to be in the country on a day like this," said Tinker wistfully. "What about ordering the car, and driving out for a round of golf, guv'nor?"

Sexton Blake's eyes lit up, and he hesitated, but then shook his head firmly.

"No, I'm afraid we've too much arrears of work to be wiped off, my boy," he said regretfully. "And I've several appointments this afternoon. Our trip up North has left us with a heap of neglected duty on our hands. We'll have a potter round the links on Saturday."

It was just after one o'clock, and Tinker's spirits revived perceptibly when he stepped into the house in Baker Street, and his nostrils were greeted by the pleasing aroma of grilled steak. The walk back from Scotland Yard had put a keen edge on his appetite, and even Sexton Blake—one of the sparest of eaters—rubbed his hands in approving anticipation as he ascended the stairs to his sitting-room.

Pedro was lying in the centre of the floor, basking in a patch of sunlight that streamed through the window, and he at once rose and came forward, wagging his tail in cheerful greeting.

"Hallo, you old son of a gun!" said Blake affectionately; and then, as he stretched out his hand to pat the bloodhound's head, an extraordinary change came over the great animal.

He came to a dead stop, every hair on his shaggy coat bristling on end, and his nose wrinkled in a manner that revealed all his gleaming, white fangs.

nary manner. He had reared him from a puppy, and Pedro had always shown the greatest devotion, sagacity, and implicit obedience.

Wild-eyed and shaking from head to foot with alarm and dismay, Tinker managed to dive in at last, and got a hold on the bloodhound's collar. By sheer force he managed to drag the dog away, and lugged him clean out of the room, closing the door behind him.

Sexton Blake drew a deep breath, and then uttered a low whistle of consternation as he surveyed himself in the mirror. His coat looked like a bundle of shredded rags, and he was amazed at the pallor of his face. It was not fear, but the tremendous shock of surprise that he had suffered.

He would never have believed that his own dog would have turned on him in such a manner. And yet it was only his clothes that had suffered. He himself had not sustained a single scratch.

Tinker came back into the room, his lips trembling, and a look of utter bewilderment on his face.

"He—he's as right as ninepence now, guv'nor!" he said huskily. "He was all right as soon as I got him out of the room. What on earth can it mean? Why did he spring at you in that manner?"

Sexton Blake shook his head gravely.

"I'm just as much befogged as you are, my boy," he replied. "I can't understand it at all. It's utterly inexplicable. Poor old fellow, he can't possibly have known what he was doing.

A menacing, snarling growl of hatred rumbled in his deep chest, and without further warning he suddenly launched himself straight at Sexton Blake.

Tinker uttered a shout of consternation and dismay, and instinctively Blake's hands flew up to protect his throat. There was a sound of rending cloth as Pedro's fangs sank deep into the breast of the coat he was wearing, and literally ripped it to ribbons.

Again the great animal sprang, growling and snarling like a fiend, and paying not the slightest attention to Tinker's fierce shouts of command:

"Down, Pedro—down!"

Sexton Blake's face was white and grim. It was one of the most disconcerting moments of his life, and his great fear was that the big bloodhound had suddenly gone mad, and would have to be destroyed.

In less than a minute his coat had been reduced to tatters, yet he himself was absolutely untouched. Never before had he known the blood hound to behave in such an extraordi-

I suppose we'd better send for the vet and have him examined."

Tinker gulped and dashed his hands across his eyes.

"But there's absolutely nothing wrong with him now," he muttered bewilderedly. "He's certainly not mad, else he'd have gone for me as well. I've left him in the kitchen with a bone, and he's as happy as a king. Perhaps—perhaps he mistook you for someone else."

"It's hardly likely," said the detective reluctantly. "Pedro would know me in the dark. There must be something wrong with the dog. Look at the extraordinary way he behaved yesterday. His encounter with that cat-burglar seems to have thrown him clean off his balance. He hasn't been the same dog since. He's all in nerves. We'll send for the vet as soon as we've had lunch."

It was in a none too happy frame of mind that Sexton Blake retired to his bed-room, and, stripping off his tattered garments, donned another suit. He did not dare dwell upon the possibility that Pedro had suddenly gone mad and would have to be destroyed. He knew that it would almost break his heart to have to part with the faithful animal that had been his devoted guardian and companion for so many years.

Mrs. Bardell had placed the lunch on the table by the time he returned to the sitting-room, but Sexton Blake and Tinker had completely lost their appetites. They sat in moody silence, merely picking at the succulent steak that their worthy housekeeper had been at such pains to prepare, and neither noticed the door slowly open, and inch by inch Pedro crept into the room, his tail between his legs, and a thoroughly chastened expression on his face.

Without a sound he walked straight up to where Sexton Blake was sitting, and laid his head across his knees, gazing up at him with a wealth of devotion in his eyes.

There was a lump in Sexton Blake's throat as he laid a kindly hand on the bloodhound's head. If ever a dumb animal was striving to express sorrow and regret and abject apology, it was Pedro at that moment.

"Well, I'll be hanged!" muttered the detective under his breath. "The dog's no more mad than I am, Tinker, and he realises that he's done something that he's ashamed of. I can't understand it at all."

"Perhaps he was dreaming when we came in," suggested Tinker hopefully. "Dogs do dream, you know. At any rate, it's pretty obvious that there's absolutely nothing wrong with him now."

A ring at the telephone distracted Sexton Blake's attention for a moment, and he walked across to answer the call.

"Some confounded idiot on the wrong number," he muttered irritably. "This dashed instrument's more trouble than it's worth, and—"

The detective's sentence remained unfinished as he whipped round on his heels and stared alarmingly in the direction of his bedroom. The door was ajar, and from within came a sound of fierce snarling and growling, and the rip and tear of rending cloth.

"For the love of Mike! It's Pedro again!" exclaimed Tinker uneasily. "What's he up to now?"

Sexton Blake strode quickly across and flung the bed-room door wide open. It was an extraordinary spectacle that met his gaze. In the centre of the floor lay the tweed suit that the big bloodhound had almost reduced to tatters when he had so inexplicably attacked him.

Pedro evidently was not satisfied with the damage he had already wrought. With bared fangs and savage snarls rumbling in his throat, he was ripping and tearing away at the discarded garments, and rapidly reducing them to a pile of rags. He turned as his master entered the room, and stood wagging his tail in a friendly manner, and there was a look in his eyes that conveyed as plainly as anything that he was quite satisfied in his own mind that he had been doing right by destroying the detective's suit.

"Well, I'll be blowed!" muttered Tinker wonderingly. "What's the matter with the silly old juggins? I've never known him to tear up anything before, except when he was a puppy, and didn't know any better."

Sexton Blake was silent for a moment, and a thoughtful frown creased his lean face as he patted the big bloodhound on the head, and kicked the tattered garments into a cupboard and closed the door.

"It seems to me that Pedro has taken an overwhelming dislike to that particular suit of mine," he said slowly. "It wasn't myself he attacked a little while ago, but my suit. There must be something about it that outrages his canine instincts, though I'm hanged if I know what it can be. I've worn that suit dozens of times before, and he's never behaved in such an extraordinary a manner."

"It certainly is a rum business," agreed Tinker puzzledly. "And what about that horse that made a dive at you and tried to savage you this morning? Perhaps it also took a dislike to your suit? It's just as well Pedro has torn the blessed thing to bits."

Sexton Blake nodded absently. It was certainly a peculiar coincidence that he had been attacked twice that day by a dumb animal, and he had been wearing the same suit on each occasion, and it seemed quite reasonable to believe that it was the garment in question that had infuriated both the horse and the bloodhound.

On second thoughts, the detective extracted the tattered remains from the cupboard and examined them closely. He even sniffed them, to see if he had come in contact with any disagreeable scent that would prove irritating to the dog's keen sense of smell, but he found nothing that brought him any nearer to a solution to the problem, and eventually dismissed the matter from his mind.

Sexton Blake found plenty to occupy his attention during the remainder of that day. His postbag was always a large one, and he had an accumulation of ten days' correspondence to deal with. Most of the letters found their way into the wastepaper-basket. Many were filed for future reference, and to the remainder the detective dictated replies, which Tinker took down in shorthand and typed out afterwards.

It was almost midnight by the time Sexton Blake had got up to date with his correspondence, and after a final pipe, and a much-needed whisky-and-soda, the detective sought his bed.

Nothing further had been heard from Detective-Inspector Coutts, and Blake's last waking thought was concerned with the mysterious cat-burglar, and he wondered if the latter would continue his depredations after his narrow escape from capture the previous night.

The detective had schooled himself to fall asleep almost as soon as his head touched the pillow, and he generally slumbered soundly for five or six hours straight off the reel. Therefore it was somewhat extraordinary for him to find himself lying wide awake within a very short time of his having slipped in between the sheets.

Annoyedly Blake glanced at the luminous dial of his wrist-watch that lay on the table beside his bed. The hands pointed to ten minutes to two, proving that he had not been asleep for much more than an hour and a half.

It was quite obvious to him that it must have been some unusual sound or disturbance that had penetrated to his subconscious mind and roused him to wakefulness. For several minutes he lay, listening intently, but nothing reached his ears save the far-away honk of a belated taxicab and the ticking of his watch.

And then the detective sensed that there was something, or someone, outside his bed-room window!

His every nerve was on the alert at once, and he scarcely dared to breathe as he turned over on his side and stared in the direction of the window, which lay to the right of his bed. He knew that the sashes were open top and bottom, but the curtains were drawn, and he could distinguish nothing.

Then his heart commenced to beat rapidly, and a queer, prickling sensation ran down his spine as a gradually widening band of grey light appeared in the centre of the window. He knew that it was no draught of air that had blown the curtains apart. It was someone crouching outside on the sill who had inserted a hand and was drawing them aside!

For several seconds Sexton Blake was too paralysed with astonishment to move a muscle. He fancied that he could discern a dark figure silhouetted against the night sky.

Lack of courage and resource was the last thing that could he levelled against the famous detective, and after the first shock of surprise he was as cool as an icicle again. With a silent, swift movement he groped beneath his pillow and slid forth the electric torch and automatic-pistol that he always kept there.

Creak!

Now the lower sash of the window was being pushed up to its fullest extent, and with the pistol gripped in his right hand and the torch in his left, Blake flung the coverings to one side and swung his legs out of bed.

Simultaneously he pressed the button of the electric-torch, and directed a beam of blinding, white light straight towards the window. The next instant a husky, strangled cry of horror and amazement burst from his lips,

Framed in the open window was the most hideous, evil face that he had ever set eyes on—a face the very sight of which seemed to chill the blood in his veins, and sent his pulsing heart rocketing up into his throat. It was not a human face, but a hairy, shaggy countenance, with a brutal, sloping forehead, and two tiny, unblinking eyes that gleamed red in the beam of the torch. A flat, wide nostrilled nose surmounted a vicious gash of a mouth that was over-filled with champing, yellow tusks of teeth.

In a flash Sexton Blake realised the amazing fact that it was no man, but an immense, hairy ape that was crouching on the sill of the open window. The hideous animal seemed rabid with fury and hatred as it stared straight into the heart of the powerful light that was directed upon it and poised itself for a leap into the room. A snarling growl bubbled from its slavering mouth,

and Blake could see the muscles of its long, shaggy arms tensen.

He had no time to think twice what action to take, and even as the ape was about to fling itself headlong towards where he sat on the edge of the bed, he raised his automatic pistol and pressed the trigger.

The weapon barked viciously, and he heard the thud thud of the bullets as they slapped home in the evil brute's broad, hairy chest. For a moment the great ape remained motionless, poised on the edge of the sill, and then, with a coughing grunt its muscles relaxed, and it toppled backwards out of the window.

THE FIFTH CHAPTER

WHO BROUGHT THE APE TO BAKER STREET?

ONE leap carried Sexton Blake right out into the centre of the room, and another stride brought him to the electric-light switch by the door. The ghastly horrors of the past few moments were relieved by the answering burst of light that flooded every corner of the room. The detective had no doubts that his shots had proved fatal, and that he had put a swift termination to the hideous ape's existence. Where the brute had come from, and why it had attempted to enter his room and attack him, was a problem that completely battled him.

He had scarcely time to throw on his dressing-gown and slip his feet into a pair of slippers when the door was flung open, and Tinker was precipitated into the room, his face white with alarm, and his eyes almost starling out of their sockets.

"Goodness, guv'nor, what's happened?" he gulped, heaving a sigh of intense relief as he saw that the detective was alive and unharmed. "What's the matter? I fancied I heard a shot!"

"It was no fancy—you did!" retorted Blake grimly. "I've had an uninvited visitor, and I was compelled to give him a dose of lead."

Tinker stared wildly around the room.

"A visitor? You mean a burglar?" he jerked bewilderedly. "Where is he? I suppose you fired to frighten him away?"

"No, I fired to kill," corrected Sexton Blake. "It was no man, but a gigantic ape that tried to break in through the window and attack me. If would have torn me to pieces if I hadn't plugged it with a couple of bullets."

"An ape!" Tinker's voice cracked with consternation, and he staggered back weakly against the wall. "Where did it come from? What was it doing here?"

"I've no more idea than you have, my boy; but if you think I'm romancing or have been suffering with nightmare I can soon set your doubts at rest."

With a few curt words, the detective related exactly what had happened, and, armed with his pistol and his torch, made his way towards the stairs, snapping on the lights as he went. There was no sign of Mrs. Bardell. Her room was right at the top of the house, and evidently the sound of the shots had left her undisturbed.

Even as Sexton Blake and his young assistant reached the ground floor there was a hearty, commanding rat-a-tat on the knocker, and, opening the front door, the detective was not surprised to find the burly figure of a police-constable standing at the top of the steps.

"Anything wrong here, Mr. Blake?" he asked, recognising the famous detective at once. "I thought I heard the sound of a shot as I was passing your house a few moments ago, and then I saw the lights go on in your sitting-room."

"Yes. It was a shot you heard, Briggs," replied Sexton Bloke, who knew all the constables on duty in that district. "I've had a particularly unpleasant caller tonight, and it was a question of shooting first and asking questions afterwards."

The constable glanced queerly at the detective. He knew that the latter was not the type of man to make use of a gun unless he had a very good reason. And no one had more deadly enemies amongst the criminal classes than did Sexton Blake, he was more hated and feared than the whole of Scotland Yard put together.

"If you'll come this way I fancy I can show you something interesting," went on Blake, inviting the policeman into the hall, and leading the way towards the back of the house. "My visitor has handed in his checks, but I don't think there will be any need for an inquest."

The little party of three passed through the kitchen and the scullery, and Sexton Blake unbolted the back door, and stepped out into the small garden at the rear of the premises. He turned into a recess directly beneath his bed-room window, and switched on his electric torch.

He was not mistaken. His bullets had not missed their mark. In a huddled heap lay the hairy carcase of the great ape, its eyes already glazed in death, and its cruel, tusked jaws set in a vicious snarl.

"Good—good gosh, it's a blessed monkey!" gasped the constable, starting back nervously, as though half fearing that the shaggy brute would hurl itself at his throat. "Why, it's almost as big as a man! Where did it come from, sir? Do you mean to say it tried to get in through your window?"

"Yes, and it was very nearly successful," replied the detective grimly. "If I hadn't awakened when I did, and had my gun handy, there's not much doubt that I should have had a painful passage into the next world. This brute could have torn me to pieces."

Tinker shuddered at the bare thought of the narrow escape his master had had, and the constable shook his head in blank bewilderment as he took a closer view at the dead animal.

"A bloomin' ape!" he repeated wonderingly. "Well, I've been some years in the Force, but I've never come across a case like this. It's a knock-out! How'd the ugly brute get here? D'you think it could have escaped from the Zoo?"

"That's not improbable. You could soon find out," said Blake. "I shouldn't think that there were many apes of this size, in England?"

"But why should the beast try to get in your window?" queried Tinker uneasily. "There's something funny about this, guv'nor. And how did it manage to reach the window?"

Sexton Blake pointed meaningly to a stout water pipe that ran up the side of the wall, and like a flash his mind went back to the events of the previous night. The robbery and murder at the house of Sir Dicton Parsons; the mysterious cat-burglar who had gained admittance by climbing up a water-pipe, and the unusual type of finger-prints that he had left behind!

Could there possibly be any connection between the previous night's affair and the unwelcome visit of the ape that now lay dead at his feet?

The detective stared at the hairy carcass with fresh interest. No, this animal was certainly not the mysterious cat burglar he had grappled with in the house of Sir Dicton Parsons. That was a theory that would not hold water at all, and yet he was convinced that there was some queer, uncanny link between the two events.

"I'd like to know how that there ape got here!" muttered the policeman. "He can't have come far, else he'd been spotted."

Sexton Blake wrapped his dressing-gown closer around his lean form, and turned to his young assistant.

"Fetch Pedro, Tinker," he said shortly. "Perhaps he can help in this mutter."

Tinker vanished in a flash, and was back almost at once, holding tightly to the stout leather leash that was attached to the bloodhound's collar.

Every hair on Pedro's coat bristled as he sniffed at the dead ape, and a series of deep, reverberating snarls gurgled in his throat. He needed no telling what was expected of him, and at once picked up the scent of the animal. With a shrill yelp of excitement, he laid his nose to the ground, and plunged across the garden, almost jerking Tinker off his feet.

"By James, that dog knows something!" exclaimed the policeman admiringly. "I've never believed in bloodhounds up to now."

Straight across the garden Pedro went until he was brought up short by the closed door that gave on to the passage-way used by tradesmen that ran at the back of the houses in Baker Street.

Sexton Blake drew the bolt, and flung the door open, and the bloodhound had no difficulty in picking up the scent again. He veered to the left, and bore straight away down the passage, dragging Tinker after him like a kite at the end of a piece of string, and with Sexton Blake and the constable bringing up the rear.

They passed the backs of a dozen or more houses before the passage made another sharp turn and led out into Baker Street. With his muzzle close to the ground Pedro held on straight to the edge of the pavement.

There he ranged round in a circle for a moment, sniffing fiercely, and then suddenly sank down on his launches, and, lifting his head in the air, uttered a long-drawn-out, dolorous howl, that Sexton Blake speedily quelled with a sharp word of command. He knew what it meant, and gave a disappointed shrug of his shoulders.

"He's lost the scent. The trail ends here," he said resignedly, and drawing out his electric torch flashed the beam on to the road.

Instantly his eyes lit up with a glint of satisfaction. He pointed to a moist patch of oil on the road, and the clearly-defined track of motor-tyres.

"There was a car standing here not so very long ago," he said meaningly. "Our friend the ape walked no farther than from this spot to the back of my house."

Tinker started, and the policeman rubbed his chin, and stared puzzledly at the detective.

"Do you mean that that ape drove up here in a car, Mr. Blake?" he exclaimed incredulously.

"He was driven up in a car," corrected Sexton Blake drily. "From what I can make of it someone brought the ape here in a car, and deliberately set it down at this very spot, where the scent begins, and ends beneath my bed-room window."

"Great Scott!" ejaculated Tinker incredulously. "Why should anyone bring an ape along and dump it down out of a car at this particular spot in Baker Street?"

Sexton Blake smiled queerly.

"You might just as well ask me why the ape should walk straight down that passage, turn to the right, clamber over the leading into our garden, and then climb up the water-pipe to the window of my bed-room."

Tinker's jaw dropped, and an eerie shiver rippled down his spine. There was something uncanny and beyond understanding about the mysterious visitation of the great ape. As Sexton Blake had remarked, why had it made straight for his house as soon as it had left the car, and with seeming deliberation scaled the water-pipe and endeavoured to enter the detective's bed-room?

"My hat, there—there's something dashed funny about this business!" muttered the lad in an awed voice. "Anyone would think that beastly ape had been instructed to break into your room and attack you."

"It may have been sheer coincidence," reassured Sexton Blake, though his voice did not carry much conviction. "I don't think anyone could train an ape to behave in such a sagacious manner."

"Then why in the name of sense was the brute dumped down just here, sir?" queried P.-c. Briggs. "My stars, I passed here not more'n half an hour ago. I might have run right into the confounded thing. This is a serious matter. We can't have people letting wild animals run loose in the streets. I'd like to find out who that ape belongs to"

At that moment the visiting sergeant of police arrived on the scene, and he was no less mystified and bewildered than the others when he was given an account of the strange affair that had happened during the past half-hour.

The sight of the dead ape left him more flabbergasted than ever, and it was at his suggestion that the little party made their way to Sexton Blake's sitting-room and made use of the tel-

ephone. First the sergeant rang up the nearest police-station, and then managed to get into communication with the head-keeper at the Zoological Gardens, and inquired if they happened to be short of one of their apes.

The reply was more expressive than polite, which was not surprising, considering that it was three o'clock in the morning, and the official had been summoned from his warm bed, and the sergeant was a trifle red in the face as he slammed the receiver back on its hook.

"Confounded idiot seemed to think I was trying to pull his leg," he grunted annoyedly. "Told me he had no vacancies for any more apes. I'd like to know what he meant by that!"

Sexton Blake suppressed a smile with difficulty.

"He evidently meant that there was none missing from the Zoo," he said soothingly. "I'm afraid we'll have to look farther a-field to try to find where the brute came from."

A few minutes later, reinforced by a generous whisky-and-soda, the sergeant and constable took their departure, and it was not long afterwards that Tinker returned to his bed.

The desire for sleep had temporarily deserted Sexton Blake, and though the fire was out, he plumped himself down in his favourite armchair, and filled and lit a pipe.

For almost the first time in his life he found himself completely baffled by the mystified events of the past forty-eight hours, and he found it difficult to rid his mind of the theory that there was some connection between the robbery and murder at Sir Dicton Parsons' residence and the visit of the ape to his own house that night.

"And yet how can there be?" he muttered irritably, tapping the stem of his pipe against his strong, white teeth. "The cat burglar certainly wasn't an ape, no more than the ape was a potential burglar. And yet—"

The detective broke off short, and drew a deep breath of bewilderment, as once again he recollected the brass medallion that he had found in Sir Dicton Parsons' house, and which, presumably, had been left behind by the cat-burglar when he had made his hurried escape.

Sexton Blake took it from the bowl on the mantelpiece, where he had placed it for safekeeping, and once again examined the circular, brass disc. Engraved on the one side was the figure of an ape, and it was an ape that had endeavoured to burst its way into his bed-room that night. The coincidence was a startling one. Surely it was something more than a mere coincidence?

The detective's high forehead was furrowed with deep lines of perplexity as he sat puffing at his pipe, and staring at the brass medallion until the figure of the ape seemed to assume gigantic proportions, and he almost imagined that it had suddenly become imbued with life, and was a counterpart of the hideous animal that had crouched on the window-sill of his bed-room, and glared at him with evil hatred and murderous intent in its red-rimmed eyes.

With a gesture of annoyance he tossed the medallion back on to the mantelpiece, and tapped the ashes from his pipe.

"This confounded ape business must be getting on my nerves," he muttered testily, as he rose to his feet and switched off the light in the sitting-room. "And yet I can't help thinking that that brass disc is the key to the whole mystery. At any rate, it's the only clue I've got, and I'll trot along to the British Museum the first thing in the morning, and ask Professor Haggerty if he can tell me what the thing is and what the letters on the other side mean."

Sexton Blake had scarcely risen and shaved the next morning when a furious ringing at the front door bell heralded the arrival of an early visitor. A stentorian voice in the next room a few moments later told him that it was Detective-Inspector Coutts who had called, and he strolled in to find the C.I.D. man standing in front of the fire place with his legs wide apart, his hard felt hat tilted ever his eyes, and his hands clasped behind his back.

"For the love of Mike, Blake, what's this extraordinary story I've heard?" he demanded brusquely. "Sergeant Bagnall tells me that a gigantic gorilla drove up to your house in a motor-bus last night, and, smashing the door in with one blow of his fist, made straight for your bed-room, and threw you out of the window into the back yard."

"I'm afraid you've got things a trifle mixed, Coutts," replied Sexton Blake, with a quiet smile. "I certainly received a visit from a member of the ape tribe, but not quite in such a sensational manner as you describe."

Briefly he related exactly what had occurred during the early hours of that morning, and Coutts listened intently, blinking his shrewd blue eyes, and puffing out his cheeks in a manner that was typical of him.

"Well, I'll be hanged!" he exclaimed at length, when the private detective had finished. "There's something dashed queer about the whole business, Blake. Where did the ape come from? Who dumped it out of a car in Baker Street, and why on earth did the infernal brute make a bee-line for your bed-room?"

"I should very much like to be able to answer all those questions," replied Sexton Blake, pouring himself out a cup of fragrant coffee. "I know that I have many enemies, but never yet has one of them succeeded in training an ape to find its way to my house and enter my bed-room and deliberately attack me. What of our friend the man-killing cat burglar? Was he also active last night?"

Coutts shook his head, and imparted a more acute tilt to his hat.

"No; there was no jewel robbery last night for the first time for the past ten days," he replied, with a hint of relief in his voice. "I reckon we put the wind up the scoundrel when we almost succeeded in capturing him at Sir Dicton Parsons' house."

"Perhaps he's not been able to get about?" suggested Blake. "I'm positive I shot him in the leg when he was clambering up on to the roof. He was limping when he ran across the slates, so it's quite probable that he's injured, and will have to lie up for a bit."

"Let's hope so, at any rate," grunted Coutts, helping himself to a cigar off the mantelpiece, and guillotining it with one snap of his powerful teeth. "A breathing spell might enable me to get on the brute's trail. But to get back to this ape business, Blake. Do you think there's any connection between the affair at Sir Dicton Parsons' and your visitor last night?"

Sexton Blake started sharply, and stared at the C. I.D. man.

"What makes you ask that question?" he queried.

Coutts smiled, and his chest measurement increased by quite a couple of inches,

"I've been putting two and two together,'" he jerked. "It struck me as strange that the finger-prints that the cat burglar left behind should resemble those of an ape, and on top of that it was an ape that broke into your room last night and endeavoured to attack you."

"Yes, I follow your line of reasoning," said Sexton Blake. "But you mustn't go beyond that, Coutts. There's no use thinking that the cat-burglar and the ape might have been one and the same. They weren't. I've met both of them at close quarters, and I can vouch for that. But there certainly is some connection between the two separate incidents, Coutts. Have a look at that."

The detective handed his companion the brass medallion engraved with the figure of an ape on the other side, and briefly narrated the manner in which it had fallen into his possession.

"Well, I'll be hanged!" exclaimed Coutts wonderingly. "So this thing was left behind by the cat-burglar when he made his get-away the night before last?"

"There's no doubt about it," declared Blake. "He was wearing it around his throat, and the chain must have snapped when Pedro made a leap at him."

"And what do you think it is? What does it mean?"

"I don't know, but I mean to find out. It may be a coin, an amulet, or a lucky charm. Professor Haggerty, at the British Museum, will be able to enlighten me."

"Well, we certainly seem to have stumbled on a dashed mysterious case," muttered Coutts, with a puzzled shake of his head. There'll be no rest for me until I've laid my hands on the cat-burglar, and found out where the dickens that confounded ape came from, and why it was set loose almost outside your house. I'm having in-quiries made all over London to endeavour to ascertain if the brute escaped from a private me-nagerie, a circus, or some animal dealer's."

"That's a good idea," approved Blake. "There can't be many apes of that size knocking about. But I don't think that this particular one escaped, else it wouldn't have been brought to Baker Street in a motorcar."

Coutts took his departure a few minutes later, anxious to get back to the Yard to see if there was any news for him, and Sexton Blake sat down to the breakfast table and helped himself to another cup of coffee. Tinker, who was seated opposite to him with his nose buried in a news-paper, suddenly glanced up with an exclamation of surprise.

"What do you think, guv'nor?" he said eagerly. "John Fade and Dirk Dolland are back

in London. They landed at Southampton yester-day, according to the 'Mail.'"

Sexton Blake's eyes lit up with interest as he stretched out a hand for the newspaper. It was well over a year since he had set eyes on either of the two men Tinker had mentioned.

John Fade was the well-known wealthy young explorer and globe-trotter, who had played such a prominent part in the long and fierce struggle against the late Professor Reece and the Confed-eration. Dirk Dolland—otherwise known as the Bat—was an ex-cracksman who had also ren-dered invaluable assistance towards capturing Reece and exterminating the all-powerful band of criminals that he had controlled.

Once this object had been achieved, after many years of savage, relentless warfare that had been waged in many parts of the world, John Fade had set forth on one of his spasmodic explorations and big-game hunting expeditions, and Dirk Dolland had accompanied him; for both were of a nature that demanded excitement and adven-ture, and they feared that the time would hang heavily on their hands now that Professor Reece was no longer alive.

That had been over a year ago, and the last Sexton Blake had heard of Fade and Dolland they were in India, and had been about to set forth on an expedition to the extreme north.

The brief paragraph in the newspaper verified this fact, and Blake scanned it with interest.

"Mr. John Fade, the well-known explorer, and his companion, Mr. Dirk Dolland, landed yes-terday at Southampton from the s.s. Berenga, after an eight months' tour and survey on certain almost inaccessible parts of Northern India, where they claim to have made many interesting discoveries. Mr. Fade will deliver a lecture at an early date."

"By James, I shall be glad to see Fade and the Bat again," cried Tinker enthusiastically. "It seems years since I set eyes on them. If they're in London they're sure to look us up some time to-day."

"There's not much doubt about that," agreed Sexton Blake, and finished his breakfast in thoughtful silence. The mention of John Fade and Dirk Dolland had taken his mind back to the stir-ring adventures and perils and horrors that they had shared together when they had been allied against the hosts of the Confederation. Life had certainly lost much of its zest since the infamous criminal organisation had ceased to exist, and Sexton Blake had had to settle down to the ordinary routine of his profession again.

Not that that did not contain enough thrills and excitement to satisfy the ordinary man, but Blake's palate had become jaded after years of active competition with some of the finest criminal brains on the face of the globe.

"I don't suppose Fade will remain long in London," he thought enviously. "The lucky beggar will be off again to some other part of the world as soon as the fit seizes him."

The detective had not lost sight of his determination to pay a visit to the British Museum that morning, and as soon as breakfast was over, he and Tinker left the house and stepped into a vacant taxi.

Their visit to the Museum proved a fruitless one. The man he wished to see, Professor Haggarty, was away in the country, and was not likely to be back for several days, and there was a frown of disappointment on Blake's face as he came striding down the steps, fingering the brass medallion that reposed in his waistcoat-pocket.

"Surely there must be somebody else who might be able to tell you what the thing is?" said Tinker. "Why, what about John Fade? He's been all over the world more than once, and there isn't a language that he doesn't know."

"Good lad!" said Sexton Blake approvingly. "I never thought of Fade, and as I intended to visit him in any case, we can kill two birds with one stone. He's just returned from India, and if I'm not much mistaken, this brass medallion comes from that part of the world."

Another brief ride in the taxi brought them to the big, gaunt house in the West End which was one of John Fade's several residences. The blinds were drawn, and the door was opened by an elderly manservant.

"Yes, Mr. Fade's back in England, sir, but he's not here at present," he was informed. "He went straight from Southampton to his house just outside Sutton. He rang me up from there last night. The Firs, that's the name of the place, sir."

Sexton Blake was not to be baulked of his objective. He had set out to see John Fade, and he did not intend to return until he had fulfilled this purpose. After all, it was no very far cry from London to Sutton, and he had no other claims on his time that morning.

The taxi-driver was not averse to making the journey, for he knew the identity of his fare, and he had no difficulty in finding John Fade's other house on the outskirts of Sutton. It was a somewhat gloomy-looking residence that stood in its own grounds, some distance from the road, and was half-concealed by a screen of fir-trees that had earned it the name that was painted on the gate.

"There's no need for you to wait; call back in about half an hour's time," instructed Blake, as he alighted from the cab, and he and Tinker made their way up the winding drive.

There did not seem to be much sign of life in the house. The blinds were drawn, and no smoke was coming from the chimneys, and Blake's lusty tug at the door-bell awakened a hundred hollow echoes.

But it brought no response. Again and again he pulled at the handle, and plied the heavy, brass knocker, but the door remained solidly closed.

"Looks as though we've drawn blank again," muttered the detective testily. "If Fade stayed here last night, he evidently left again pretty early this morning. It seems that— What's the matter, my boy?"

Tinker had suddenly laid a warning hand on his master's arm, and had his head cocked alertly on one side.

"Listen, guv'nor!" he jerked. "I thought I heard a noise inside. It sounds like someone hammering."

Sexton Blake bent down, and, lifting the flap of the letter-box, put his ear to the aperture. Tinker was right. From somewhere in the depths of the big house there came a dull, muffled, pounding noise, and then another sound that sent a thrill of excitement flashing through the detective's veins.

It was a man's voice, raised in a hoarse cry for help!

The Sixth Chapter

Reunion and Wreckage.

SEXTON BLAKE'S eyes were bright with excitement as he glanced at his young assistant.

"You're right, Tinker!" he said keenly. "It sounds as though someone's banging on a door, and shouting for assistance. There's something wrong inside this place. It strikes me that we've arrived at a timely moment."

"What are we going to do?" queried Tinker eagerly. "There's no use ringing the bell. If Fade or anyone else was able to open the door they'd have done so long ago."

"We'll have to force a way in," declared Blake, glancing speculatively al the door. It was a massive structure of solid oak, and it would have taken nothing less than a battering-ram to burst it off its hinges. "Perhaps we can find a window unlatched, and get in that way."

But every one of the windows in the front of the house was securely fastened with safety-catches and thumbscrews, and, reluctant to cause any damage unless it was absolutely necessary, the detective made his way round to the back of the house.

"Hallo, there! Is anybody outside?"

Tinker suddenly leaped a foot in the air, and Sexton Blake stopped short in startled surprise. A voice, hollow and sepulchral, seemed to have come from out of the ground beneath their feet. The detective bent down, and, pulling the long grass to one side, revealed a small metal ventilator set low in the wall, not more than a couple of inches from the ground. Undoubtedly, it was from here that the uncanny voice had sounded.

"Hallo! What's wrong? Is there anyone down there?" called Blake clearly.

A distinct gasp of relief reached his ears.

"Thank Heaven, it is somebody turned up at last, Dolland!" he heard a familiar voice exclaim. "Hallo, whoever you are! We've been cooped up in this infernal cellar for hours and hours and can't get out! Get into the house as best you can—I don't care if you smash every window in the house—and come and unlock the door! It's as cold as a refrigerator down here!"

"Is that John Fade speaking?" asked the detective.

A muffled gasp of surprise answered him.

"Yes. And who the dickens are you? Your voice sounds mighty familiar. Snakes alive, it surely isn't Sexton Blake?"

"You're right first time, Fade!" assured the detective cheerfully. "And Tinker's here as well. It strikes me we've called to see you at a propitious moment."

"Hallo, Blake!" hailed the languid, plaintive voice of Dirk Dolland, "For the love of Mike, get a move on, and come and let us out of this infernal cellar!"

"Smash the kitchen window and get in that way!" instructed John Fade. "You'll find the cellar steps on the right of the hall just outside the door."

With the handle of a spade that he found leaning against the wall Sexton Blake shattered one of the panes of the kitchen window, and, inserting an arm, pushed back the catch and lifted the sash.

Tinker was close behind him as he clambered into the room beyond and crossed to the door leading out into the passage. On the right was another door that stood ajar, revealing a steep flight of steps that led downwards into the darkness.

"Funny business this!" muttered the detective, as he drew his electric-torch from his pocket. "I wonder how on earth the silly beggars managed to get themselves locked up in the cellar? They travel half-way round the world and come back unharmed, and then land themselves in trouble the moment they set foot in England!"

Cautiously Blake made his way down the stairs, and found himself in a gloomy, stone-flagged cellar, which was empty save for some packing cases and stacks of flower-pots.

"Hallo! Where are you fellows?"

"Here!" came a voice from the farther end of the cellar; and the beam of the torch revealed a massive wooden door set in the brick wall.

Sexton Blake uttered a gasp of surprise as he realised that the door was locked and the key was on the outer side. It was not by accident that John Fade and Dirk Dolland found themselves imprisoned in the cellar. The position of the key showed that they had been deliberately locked in.

Blake's curiosity was thoroughly aroused as he turned the key in the rusty lock, and with a lunge of his shoulder flung the door crashing back on its hinges. Instantly two weird, ghastly looking apparitions came tottering out of the darkness beyond into the circle of light thrown by the torch,

Sexton Blake found a momentary difficulty in recognising either John Fade or the usually immaculate Dirk Dolland. Both were attired only in their pyjamas and slippers, and both were smeared from head to foot with grime, dust, and cobwebs. John Fade had a heavy calibre revolver gripped in one hand, and the Bat was armed with a massive steel poker.

"Dear old Blake! By James, you always seem to turn up at the right moment!" gasped John Fade, as he clutched the detective's hand and pumped it vigorously up and down. "'I could scarcely believe my ears when I recognised your voice. How did you know what had happened?"

"I don't know what you're talking about. I didn't know that anything had happened," replied the detective, as he greeted Dirk Dolland with a hearty grip of the palm. "It's quite by chance that Tinker and I are here. I only heard this morning that you two had arrived back in England! How on earth do you come to be in this state? Who locked you in your own cellar?"

"All in good time, old man! For goodness' sake, let's get to a warmer atmosphere!" jerked John Fade through his chattering teeth. "We have been cooped up in that rat hole for the past nine or ten hours, though it seems twice as long as that. And we might have been there for days if you hadn't put in an appearance."

John Fade led the way up the cellar stairs and along the passage into a handsomely furnished, oak-panelled apartment. But the place now looked as though it had been struck by a cyclone, and Fade uttered a low whistle of consternation as he surveyed the scene from the doorway.

Chairs and tables were overturned in hopeless confusion, and even the padded coverings had been ripped open. The carpet had been torn up from the floor, and a small safe in one corner lay on its side with the door gaping open. Even the pictures had been pulled from the walls, and the majority of the oak panels had been splintered and battered with some heavy instrument.

"Hum! Somebody's made a nice mess of my smoking-lounge!" said John Fade wryly. "What do you make of it, Blake?"

Sexton Blake swept the room with a single wondering glance.

"It looks to me," he replied promptly, "as though someone had been making an industrious search for something that I they were particularly anxious to find."

John Fade nodded, and glanced queerly across at Dirk Dolland.

"You're right, Blake!" he agreed. "If you'll wait five minutes while I slip into some clothes,

I'll spin you a yarn that will probably interest you."

The two men loft the room, and Sexton Blake calmly set one of the overturned armchairs on its legs, and plumping himself down, proceeded to help himself to a cigar from his well-filled case.

"Well, this is a knock-out, guv'nor," said Tinker, as he perched himself on the club fender in front of the fire-place. "Wherever we go we seem to run up against a bit of excitement. It looks as though this place had been raided by a gang of burglars. It's strange that it should happen the very first night Fade arrives back here."

Sexton Blake nodded absently as he pierced his cigar, and put a light to it. It was no use speculating as to what had occurred at the Firs during the previous night. He was quite content to wait until John Fade should return to give him first hand information.

Both men looked more like their normal selves when they re-entered the room a few minutes later, and it was easy to see that they had only recently returned from a tropical clime. Both were deeply tanned by the sun, and looked as fit as fiddles, despite their recent ordeal of being locked up for nine or ten hours in a cold, dark, damp collar.

It was evident that John Fade had a story to tell. His lean, hawk-like face was unusually grave and thoughtful as he picked up a table, and fetched a decanter, some tumblers, and a syphon of soda from an adjoining room.

"Salvage from the wreckage,'" he said dryly. "About the only articles in the house that appear to remain unbroken, for which Bacchus be praised."

The explorer poured out some drinks and passed them around before he seated himself, and took a hearty swig at his own glass before he spoke again.

"I've travelled to most parts of the world, Blake, as you know," he commenced slowly. "And I've seen some funny sights, and undergone some extraordinary experiences in my time. But in the majority of cases I've been prepared for them. For instance, if I ran up against a lion in Uganda, it would be no more uncommon than if I encountered a camel in Egypt."

"Exactly," agreed Sexton Blake, wondering what on earth the man was driving at.

"But," went on John Fade impressively, "what would you think, supposing you were to wake up in the night, in your own house in the heart of civilised, humdrum England, and find a gigantic ape bending over you?"

Sexton Blake craned forward in his chair, and stared amazedly at his companion. Then he uttered a short, discomfited laugh.

"I'm hanged if I can understand how you heard about the ape affair, Fade!" he jerked. It may be reported in some of the morning newspapers; but if you've been locked in your cellar for the past ten hours I don't see how you can have had an opportunity to read the newspapers."

It was John Fade's turn to look bewildered, and he stared at Sexton Blake with perplexity written all over his face.

"Newspapers?" he echoed. "Of course, there can't be anything about it in the newspapers. It was about twelve o'clock last night when I awoke to find a confounded ape standing in the centre of my bedroom."

Tinker's cry of amazement echoed through the room like a revolver-shot, and Sexton Blake fell back in his chair, and deliberately poured himself out a stiff whisky and soda.

"So you also had a visit from an ape last night?" he said quietly, though his nerves were tingling with excitement, for here was one of the most astounding coincidences that had ever come his way. "There has been a slight misunderstanding. Fade; I will explain later. In the meantime, let's hear your story."

"I've two stories to tell you," jerked Fade, with a meaning shake of his head. "The first one—which is really the second—won't take long; I'll condense it as much as possible. Briefly, Dolland and I landed at Southampton yesterday, and came straight here, instead of proceeding to London. In the normal way, I have a steward sleeping on the premises, but his wife is ill, and he went home after dishing us up a meal and seeing that we had everything we required."

John Fade took his cigar from his mouth and made a gulp at his drink.

"I suppose Dolland and I turned in about eleven," he went on. "I was reading a London newspaper—the first I had seen for many months—and I must have fallen asleep, leaving the light burning. The next thing I knew I woke up to find an enormous, hairy ape standing in the centre of the room glaring at me like a fiend.'"

Fade drew a deep breath, and his face twitched slightly at the bare recollection of the experience he had undergone.

"I thought I was dreaming at first," declared the young explorer. "But, thank goodness, I didn't lose my head. As the brute sprang at me I rolled over with the blankets wrapped round me, and slipped down between the edge of the bed and the wall. The bed is a heavy, low built, old fashioned one, and for the time being the ape was unable to get at me. I don't mind telling you that I yelled for all I was worth. There was a revolver under my pillow, but I couldn't get at it."

"I heard the row; it sounded as though someone was being murdered," intercepted Dirk Dolland, picking up the threads of the story. "I took jolly good care not to forget my pistol, and dashed along the passage into Fade's room.

"It gave me the shock of my life when I saw a dashed old man-monkey dancing about on Fade's bed, and ripping the mattress to tatters. It made one dive for me as soon as I entered the room, and I plugged it with a lead pill. I don't know where I hit the brute, but it gave a weird kind of cry, and scuttled out of the door and down the stairs.

"So long as we were armed we didn't care a hang about the beast. Fade collared his gun, and we proceeded to make a thorough search of the house. There was no sign of it on the ground floor; but we found the door leading to the cellars wide open, and charged down, thinking that we had the ape trapped."

"But it was the other way round," put in John Fade bitterly. "We'd no sooner entered the cellar where you found us than the door was slammed and the key turned in the lock; and we've been there ever since. There's no other way out of the cellar, and it would take a battering-ram to burst the door open."

Sexton Blake gripped his cigar until the crisp, firmly-rolled leaves crunched between his fingers.

"You're not telling me that it was the ape that slammed the door, and turned the key in the lock?" he said incredulously.

"No. There must have been someone else in the house besides the ape—several people, perhaps," declared John Fade.

"We could hear them moving about upstairs, overturning the furniture, and ripping open the safe."

"Burglars, eh, and accompanied by an ape?" muttered Sexton Blake, a gleam of perplexity and excitement in his eyes.

Coming so soon on top of his own amazing experience of the previous night, John Fade's astounding story knocked him sideways with bewilderment.

"There's more beyond all this than you've told me, Fade!" he challenged, wondering, and hoping that the young explorer held the key to the whole tangled, baffling mystery. "Why was your house broken into and searched from top to bottom last night? Your visitors were searching for something in particular. What was it? It wasn't an ordinary, common-place attempt at burglary!"

John Fade hesitated for a moment, and he and Dirk Dolland glanced queerly at one another.

"You're right, Blake," admitted Fade, at length; "I told you I had two stories to tell you, and you shall hear the second one in a few minutes. But first let me show you the cause of the whole trouble."

There was a distinctly nervous air about John Fade as he rose to his feet. First he drew the blinds at the windows, and then closed and locked the door. Finally, he walked across to a massive sideboard that stood to one side of the room, and swung open the door of the spacious recess beneath. The top shelf contained several bottles of wine, enclosed in straw jackets, and a variety of liqueurs, for Fade had the means and the palate for a well-stocked cellar.

On the lower shelf were three or four large biscuit-tins, and one of these Fade drew out and forced off the lid. At first sight the tin seemed to be filled to the brim with cheese-biscuits, but as Fade turned the tin on its side an oddly-shaped object, wrapped in a square of green baize, rolled out on to the carpet, accompanied by the layer of biscuits that had concealed it from view.

John Fade's hands were trembling slightly as he placed the bundle on a table, and proceeded to unwrap the enveloping cloth.

"The simpler hiding-places are always the safer," he jerked. "Who would think of looking in a biscuit-tin for this?"

A gasp of consternation burst from Sexton Blake's lips as the green baize was whipped away, and his eyes were momentarily dazzled as though he had gazed straight into the heart of a blinding searchlight, agleam with a dozen different coloured rays.

Yet it was nothing more than a queer idol, or image, that stood in the centre of the table. It was not more than nine or ten inches in height, yet it was thickly encrusted with precious stones that glowed and scintillated like liquid fire beneath the glare of the electric light.

It was evidently made of ebony, or some other hard wood, cunningly carved in the shape of a hideous, leering ape. The green, flickering eyes were comprised of two of the most magnificent emeralds Sexton Blake had ever seen. A double row of blood-red rubies formed the lips of the wide, snarling mouth, which was set with exquisitely-cut diamonds of the purest water, in lieu of teeth.

The thing looked almost alive as it stood quivering and shimmering in the centre of the table. Its value was fabulous. Sexton Blake had never seen such gems. A king's ransom would not have purchased the jewel-encrusted image.

"Gosh!" exploded Tinker, in an awed voice. "Are—are those stones real? Where did the thing come from? What is it supposed to be?"

"It is Darsha, the idol of the ape-men of Khurdan!" replied John Fade, in a grave, impressive voice

THE SEVENTH CHAPTER

INTRODUCES DR. SATIRA.

THERE was something evil and sinister and almost uncanny about the jewel-encrusted image of an ape that John Fade had produced from its hiding-place in the biscuit-tin, and Sexton Blake stared at it as though fascinated and unable to detach his gaze.

Here, obviously, was that for which the burglars who had broken into John Fade's house had been seeking, and there was small wonder that they had been so anxious and determined to gain possession of the jewelled ape. And they had been accompanied by an ape; and it was an ape that had entered Sexton Blake's rooms in Baker Street the night before, and attacked him in a frenzy of rage and hatred.

What possible connection could there be between these two separate incidents? The long arm of coincidence was being strained to breaking-point, and Sexton Blake's brain was in a whirl of utter bewilderment as he suddenly wrenched his gaze away from the leering, red-eyed figure of the ape, and turned interrogatively towards John Fade.

"Darsha, the idol of the ape-men of Khurdan!" he echoed wonderingly. "Where does it come from? How did it get into your possession?"

It was an amazing, astounding story that John Fade there and then related to Sexton Blake and his young assistant, who sat listening with a tense interest that forbade any interruption.

When they had left England months earlier, tired of the humdrum monotony of their existences, and lusting for fresh adventures after the extermination of the Criminals' Confederation, John Fade and Dirk Dolland had journeyed straight to India, intending to work their way north, penetrate the Himalayas, and visit the secret city of Lhassa.

But from a native guide they had heard an extraordinary story of a place called Khurdan, hidden away in the heart of the rugged range of mountains, where lived a race of ape-men, who as nearly as possible conformed to the "missing link" on which Darwin had based his theory of the evolution of man.

John Fade had scoffed at the idea, but his curiosity had been aroused, and, after much trouble and bribing, he managed to persuade the guide to consent to lead them to the borders of Khurdan. Beyond that point the native flatly refused to go.

"To be as brief as possible, the story the fellow told us was practically true," narrated Fade. "Dolland and I made some amazing discoveries, which will astound the whole of the civilised world when I publish my next book. The ape-men of Khurdan really and truly exist. They are immensely powerful fellows, speaking a distinct language of their own, and it is only by their hands and feet that they betray their original ancestry.

"They quite believe that they are descended from apes, and for that reason all apes are sacred in Khurdan, and the inhabitants worship a hideous, huge, carved statue of an ape that they call Darsha."

Sexton Blake stared incredulously at John Fade. He was half inclined to think that the young explorer was romancing and trying to pull his leg.

"How could you have learned all these facts if these ape-men, as you call them, speak a distinct language of their own?" he queried sharply.

"By bitter experience," replied Fade gravely. "Dolland was unfortunate enough to be compelled to shoot and kill an ape that attacked us soon after we had entered Khurdan. That same night we were attacked and overcome by the ape-men themselves. Now comes the most amazing part of my story. Having been made prisoners, Dolland and I were conducted to a vast cavern in the heart of the mountains and shown into the presence of the ruler of Khurdan."

"A super ape-man, I suppose," jerked Blake, with a slight note of sarcasm in his voice.

"No; a man as different from them as chalk from cheese!" retorted Fade sharply. "One of the most amazing men I have ever met; as civilised as you or I, cultured to his finger-tips, a brilliant scholar and savant—and yet one of the vilest, most cold-blooded scoundrels unhung! Dr. Satira—that is the name by which he introduced himself."

John Fade shuddered, and mopped at the cold beads of perspiration that had started out on his forehead.

"It is impossible to say what nationality the man is," proceeded Fade, checking the questions that Sexton Blake was about to unload. "He speaks perfect English, and he boasted that he was educated in Europe, and possesses degrees for practically every branch of science from medicine to mesmerism.

"And he is one of the most hideous men I have ever seen. I can't attempt to describe him. He has the eyes of a snake, the head of a vulture, the face of a fiend, and the voice of a cooing dove. He entertained us in lavish style one moment, and calmly informed us the next that we would be handed over to the ape-men the next morning to suffer the penalty of death for having killed one of the sacred apes of Khurdan."

"By gad, it makes my flesh creep when I think of what we went through," muttered Dirk Dolland, pouring himself out a fresh drink with a shaking hand. "Shades of Professor Reece! Dr. Satira has him beat to a frazzle!"

"That is perfectly true," agreed John Fade. "Reece was one of the most diabolical scoundrels unhung, but I should say that Dr. Satira exceeds him in every way. He calmly described to us the manner in which we should meet our death—I won't repeat it to you, Blake—and, being certain in his own mind that we were doomed, he waxed confidential, and took us to another cavern, where stood an enormous stone carved statue of Darsha, the ape-men's idol.

"Then he showed us that!" John Fade pointed to the blazing, jewel-encrusted figure on the table. "It is a smaller replica of the original statue of Darsha. Dr. Satira made it himself, and he boasted of the cunning motive that had inspired him. Apparently he had spent two years in Khurdan, slowly but surely gaining the confidence and subjection of the ape-men. One thing he could not learn from them—and that was how they had come into the possession of a skin-bag full of the most amazing diamonds, rubies, and emeralds he had ever seen.

"His cupidity was aroused at once; he knew that the stones must be worth quite million pounds; but the ape men resolutely refused to allow him to handle them, until Satira conceived the cunning idea of constructing a miniature statue of Darsha, the ape-god, and encrusting it with carefully selected jewels. I don't know what plausible yarn he spun the ape-men, but they allowed him to have his own way; and the jewelled ape was placed in a niche at the foot of the original statue of Darsha."

"Humph!" muttered Sexton Blake. "I take it it was this Dr. Satira's intention to ultimately steal the jewels and make his get-away from Khurdan?"

"Yes, he boasted that that was exactly what he intended to do," replied Fade. "All his plans were laid, and he was only awaiting his opportunity to put them into execution. He made a big mistake when he told us that near at hand was a swift torrent of a river that ran clear through Khurdan into Barachan, in Northern India. He had a boat concealed there, well stocked with provisions; and once he got aboard and cast off, the current would do the rest, and the ape-men would be helpless to pursue him.

"I'm getting long-winded. Let's get this story over as quickly as possible," said Fade, after another pull at his glass. "Without going into unnecessary details, Dolland and I managed to make our escape from the cavern that night. Thanks to all that Dr. Satira had boastfully told us, we were able to find our way down a passageway to the river, and, sure enough, there was the boat concealed, just as he had described. It was not until we had jumped in and allowed ourselves to be whisked away by the fierce current that I realised that Dolland had the jewelled ape tucked away under his coat."

Dirk Dolland grinned sheepishly, and threw a semi-apologetic glance at Sexton Blake.

"Old habit reasserting itself. I grabbed hold of the confounded thing as we were passing through the cavern," he admitted; and then, with a touch of defiance: "After all, I'm just as much entitled to it as that scoundrel Dr. Satira. But I'm beginning to wish I'd left it where it was."

Sexton Blake nodded. He was beginning to get a vague grasp of the situation.

"I shall never forget that journey down the river," went on John Fade. "We had only a crude paddle to steer with, and we were in danger of being dashed to pieces against the rocks at any moment. And that wasn't the only danger, Blake. It sounds deuced uncanny, and almost unbelievable, but thousands of apes appeared amid the trees on both banks of the river, and kept pace with us as we swept along, throwing sticks and stones and all manner of things at us. Some of them even jumped into the water and tried to swim out to as. They seemed to realise that we had committed some offence against the sacred ape-god of Khurdan."

Sexton Blake grunted scornfully, an expression of mind that, ultimately, he had cause to regret, and Fade gave a shrug of his broad shoulders.

"I don't blame you for being sceptical, Blake," he said quietly, "I was was at first, but subsequent events have caused me to alter my opinion. For example, let us consider what occurred here last night!"

Sexton Blake's eyes narrowed, and he toyed thoughtfully with the remains of his cigar.

"You actually believe, Fade," he said slowly, "that Dr. Satira, accompanied by a bodyguard of apes and ape-men, has followed you all the way back to England in order to recover the jewelled idol that Dolland stole from him?"

"I know it," declared Fade: "I have an uncanny feeling that Dr. Satira has not been very far away from us ever since we fled from Khurdan. There have been several attempts on our lives.

Whilst we were waiting for our boat at Bombay our room at the hotel was broken into and our luggage turned upside down. Someone was evidently looking for the jewelled idol, but I had deposited it in the manager's safe. A similar thing happened on board the boat itself, with no better result, but by this time it was beginning to get on our nerves, and Dolland and I deliberately went ashore at Port Said, taking the idol with us concealed in a camera-case, and didn't rejoin the boat when she sailed.

"I thought we had managed to throw Dr. Satira off the scent, but apparently he came straight on to England, and settled down to await our arrival. And he knew the moment we set foot on British soil at Southampton. And he knew that we came straight here to this place, instead of proceeding to my house in London. It was either Dr. Satira himself, or someone working on his behalf, who was responsible for what happened last night."

John Fade's voice had dropped to a husky whisper, and he stirred uneasily in his chair, and glanced round nervously as though half-expecting to see the dread figure of the mysterious Dr. Satira loom out of the shadows with a horde of ape-men snarling at his heels. It was the first time Blake had ever seen the daring, lion-hearted young explorer show the slightest sign of fear, and he marvelled—wondering what type of a man this Dr. Satira could be!

Struck with a sudden thought, he dived a hand into his pocket and drew out the brass medallion that had originally decided him on his visit to John Fade's house.

"Perhaps you can tell me what that is, Fade?" he said, handing it over to his companion.

John Fade threw one glance at the medallion, and a hoarse cry of amazement burst from his lips.

"By Heavens, where did you get this from, Blake?" he demanded excitedly. "It is a representation of Darsha, the sacred ape-god. That is the meaning of the inscription on the back. All the ape-men of Khurdan wear one of these as a kind of charm. You found it here, no doubt? It was left behind last night?"

Sexton Blake did not answer for a moment. His eyes were half-closed, and he sat with his chin sunk thoughtfully on his chest. The curtain of mystery was lifting at last, though there were many baffling points that still remained to be explained. John Fade's astounding story made it perfectly plain that the mysterious Dr. Satira was responsible for the epidemic of jewel robberies that had stirred all London during the past ten days.

The cat-burglar was one of the Khurdanese ape-men, who had already crushed one person to death in his powerful arms! Hence the extraordinary agility displayed by the uncanny burglar, and the fact that the finger-prints he had left behind differed from those of civilised human beings, and could be compared only with one of the apes at the Zoological Gardens!

Possibly, also, it explained why Pedro the bloodhound had behaved so extraordinarily on the night of the burglary and murder at Sir Dicton Parsons' house. The dog's instinct must have told him that he was dealing with something that was neither man nor animal, but something akin to both!

It did not take Sexton Blake long to relate the story he had to tell, and which coincided so closely with John Fade's narrative, and by the time he had finished Fade was striding agitatedly up and down the room with his hands jammed in his pockets, and his dark eyes blazing with excitement,

"By James, you did a nice thing when you stole that confounded jewelled monkey, Dolland," he said grimly.

"Who would have dreamed what the consequences would be? It is a far cry from Khurdan to London, but there is not the slightest doubt that Dr. Satira is here and he is not alone either. He appears to have embarked upon a career of crime in order to compensate himself for the loss of the jewelled idol."

Dirk Dolland bit his lip uneasily.

"How the dickens could the fellow have got into the country, accompanied by a gang of ape-men—and apes as well?" he muttered incredulously. "And where can he be hiding himself away? It must be somewhere near London, to judge by Blake's story."

"Now that we're on the right trail it oughtn't to take long to run the murderous brute to earth," said Sexton Blake, his jaw hardening ominously. "It'll be the gallows for him once the police get the handcuffs on him. I don't know how the law will be able to deal with the ape-man himself, who murdered Sir Dicton's manservant. It all depends if he is considered sufficiently intelligent to plead."

"First catch your hare!" remarked John Fade meaningly. "Scotland Yard will find Dr. Satira a slippery customer—and a desperate, unscrupulous one! He seems to have marked you down as a prospective victim, Blake. Possibly because you interfered with his plans the other night, and succeeding in wounding the brute he seems to have trained to commit his burglaries for him."

Sexton Blake nodded. He knew that Dr. Satira must be responsible for the ape that had clambered into his bed-room the previous night, and he was beginning to wonder if the scoundrel might not have had something to do with the peculiar behaviour of Pedro when he had leaped at him and torn his suit to shreds.

He remembered having heard several years back from a famous savant that a particular sect of natives in India possessed the secret of being able to antagonise animals against certain individuals, so that they attacked them without apparent reason. The savant had theorised that it was due to a certain scent, that was applied to the person of the prospective victim.

Such a scent previously laid as a trail would explain away the mystery as to how the ape had deliberately made straight for his bed-room when it had become released in Baker Street.

"I hope you soon lay Satira by the heels, Blake; but, all the same, I don't see how you're going to set about it," said Fade, with an uneasy shake of his head. "It may take weeks before you rout him out of his hiding place."

"I don't propose to rout him out," said the detective, rising and crossing to the leering, ruby-eyed ape on the table. "This is the bait that should catch Dr. Satira, and possibly within the next twenty-four hours. If he has come all the way from Khurdan to recover this idol, you may depend that he will stop at nothing to accomplish his objective."

Sexton Blake paused to light a fresh cigar and to put the finishing touches to a plan that had formed in his mind.

"Listen carefully to what I say, Fade, and follow my instructions to the letter," he went on gravely. "Tinker and I will drive straight back to town and put Coutts wise to all that we have discovered. Later on you and Dolland can follow. Take the idol with you, and go direct to your house in Bryan Square. If Dr. Satira is as cunning as you make him out to be he will be aware of all your movements. When you get to London, both of you wait indoors until I telephone you later in the evening. Perhaps it would be as well if you donned evening-clothes and prepared to dine out at about eight o'clock."

Beyond those enigmatic instructions Sexton Blake would say nothing further at the moment. the taxicab was waiting outside, and a few moments later the detective and his young assistant were bowling swiftly back into London. Straight to Scotland Yard they were driven, and Tinker was left to cool his heels in the cab whilst Blake sought an interview with Detective-Inspector Coutts that lasted for well over an hour.

THE EIGHTH CHAPTER
WHO IS THE MAN?

WHAT transpired at that lengthy confabulation Tinker had no idea, but there was a grim look of satisfaction on Blake's face when he finally emerged and completed his journey back to Baker Street.

"I hope we shall succeed in nabbing Dr. Satira and his cat-burglar to-night," was the only information he would vouchsafe his young assistant. "There is an outside chance that he will pay a visit to Fade's house in Bryan Square, and make another attempt to regain possession of the jewelled idol. If he does he will find everything prepared for him."

Over the telephone Sexton Blake did little more than repeat his previous instructions to John Fade and Dirk Dolland, who had arrived safely at the former's big house in Bryan Square.

"Be dressed to go out to dine at eight o'clock," he ordered quietly. "See that the back door is unlocked at that hour, so that Coutts and I can get in unobserved when we arrive."

It was almost half-past seven when Coutts put in an appearance at the detective's rooms in Baker Street.

"I've arranged everything according to your instructions, Blake," announced the C.I.D. man. "Twenty members of the Flying Squad will be concealed in a house not a hundred yards away from Bryan Square. The house is on the telephone, and the Post Office has been instructed to keep the line between there and Fade's house connected from eight o'clock onwards. You have only to lift the receiver of the telephone at Fade's residence, and that will be the signal for my men to rush along and surround the house. If this mysterious scoundrel, Dr. Satira, turns-up, as you think he may, we'll catch him red-handed."

A thrill of excitement ran through Tinker's veins. He was beginning to see the gist of Blake's carefully laid plans. Their success depended on whether the lure of the jewelled ape would prove sufficient inducement for Dr. Satira or his ape-man burglar to pay a visit to John Fade's London house that night.

Sexton Blake's face was grim and deter-mined as he dropped a loaded automatic into his pocket. Coutts had a taxi waiting outside, and by a devious route they drove to a quiet resi-dential street that ran at the back of one side of Bryan Square. Coutts had already made his ar-rangements with the occupant of the house that abutted on to the garden at the back of John Fade's residence, and by the aid of a ladder they scaled the dividing wall.

"There is a possibility that Fade's house is being watched from the front," Blake explained quietly to Tinker. "No one will see us enter, and when Fade and Dolland leave the place it will be thought that there is no one on the premises save the manservant, and we'll send him out as well."

They found the back door unlocked accord-ing to plan, and Fade and Dolland, faultlessly attired in evening-dress, met them at the top of the kitchen stairs, and conducted them into the handsome smoking-lounge on the first floor.

All the blinds were drawn and the electric tight switched on, and at Blake's behest Fade unlocked the safe that stood in one corner and placed the statue of the jewelled ape inside.

"Now you two can clear off," said the detec-tive calmly. "You will find a taxi waiting outside. Drive straight to any restaurant you choose in the West, but if you want to be in any fun that may be going you can return to No. 27, Naine Terrace, and join the crowd of plain-clothes men Coutts has waiting there."

"You can bet your life we will," declared John Fade. "If there's any chance of capturing Dr. Satira to-night I want to be in at the death!"

Jauntily, and with the air of two carefree young men, sallying forth for a night's enjoyment, Fade and Dolland left the house by the front door, and drove away in the taxi that was waiting for them.

A few moments later the manservant put on his hat and coat and followed suit, and Sexton Blake, Coutts, and Tinker found themselves alone in the house. They returned to the smoking-lounge, where Blake placed three chairs in a wide, cur-tained recess to one side of the fireplace.

"I shouldn't be surprised if we don't draw a blank, Blake," said Coutts pessimistically. "If this Dr. Satira fellow intends paying a visit here, what time do you expect him?"

"Any time between now and midnight," replied the detective, motioning to his compan-ions to seat themselves in the curtained recess. Then he switched off the electric light and joined them. "If it is known that Fade and Dolland have gone out, ostensibly to dine, they will be ex-pected back somewhere about twelve, therefore, if anything is going to happen it will be before that hour."

The telephone which was attached to a long extension of flex stood on the floor by Sexton Blake's side. He knew that he had only to lift the receiver to be in instant communication with the members of the Flying Squad who were se-creted in a house near by, and who would im-mediately swarm forth and surround John Fade's residence.

Ten o'clock struck, and Coutts yawned and stretched his legs. At the same instant Sexton Blake's warning hand fell heavily on his shoul-der, and Tinker felt the hair bristling on his scalp.

A distinct sound had come from beyond the hanging curtain—a scraping and fumbling, and then the faint squeak of a window-sash being raised. Someone was entering the room. A cold draught of air touched Sexton Blake's cheek like a grisly hand.

The next few seconds seemed like as many hours, until there was a sharp click, and a blaze of light sprang up, followed by an uncanny grunting sound.

Sexton Blake's hand dropped to the telephone by his side, and he applied one eye to the narrow crack between the curtains. What he saw sent a shiver of horror rippling down his spine, and his heart seemed to leap up into his throat.

Crouching in the centre of the room was a hideous, shaggy ape, similar to the one that had invaded his house the previous night. But the ape was not alone. Towering over the animal was the figure of a man with enormously-broad shoulders, a chest like a barrel, and long arms that hung down to below his knees. His face was repulsive in the extreme—flat-nosed, low-browed, and wide-mouthed, and set with ma-levolent little eyes that blinked and glimmered beneath shaggy brows.

Sexton Blake's throat went dry with horror. He realised that this must be the mysterious cat-burglar who had already murdered one man and half-killed another. Without a sound he lifted the telephone-receiver and placed it on the floor before he realised that a third person had slid stealthily through the open window.

He knew at once from John Fade's graphic description that this was Dr. Satira himself. The eyes of a snake, the head of a vulture, and the face of a fiend—it fitted the newcomer to a hair as he stood with his shoulders hunched and his hands concealed beneath the black cloak that shrouded his lean figure.

Tinker was trembling like a leaf, and cold beads of perspiration were coursing down Coutts' cheeks.

The ape had lifted its hideous jowl in the air, and was sniffing at the air, ere it suddenly turned and glared red-eyed straight at the hanging curtain that concealed Sexton Blake and his companions. Its hair seemed to bristle, and an ugly growl rumbled in its shaggy throat.

Sexton Blake knew that he must act at once. The signal had been given, and already the Flying Squad were on their way to the house. Quick as lightning the detective whipped out his automatic and flung the curtains to one side.

"Good-evening, Dr. Satira!" he said curtly. "I would advise you and your companion to put your hands up—quick!"

"Up with 'em!" added Coutts huskily, level-ling his own revolver in a hand that trembled perceptibly.

A hideous expression of malevolent fury flashed across the evil countenance of the mysterious Dr. Satira. and his snake-like eyes gleamed cold as steel.

"Ah, Mr. Sexton Blake," he said in a smooth, purring voice, and slowly he elevated his two arms above his head. In the nick of time Blake

caught sight of something that the man held gripped in his right hand. It looked like a round, glass ball, and even as Dr. Satira made to hurl it across the room Blake's pistol spoke.

His aim was true and accurate. There was a splinter of broken glass, and a guttural cry of fury and dismay. A shower of some liquid that had been contained in the glass receptacle show-ered Dr. Satira from head to foot, and the next instant a ghastly and terrible thing happened.

"By heavens, look at the ape!" screamed Coutts.

The huge brute seemed to have forgotten all about Sexton Blake and his companions. Its flat nostrils were dilated as it sniffed at the drops of liquid that had spattered the carpet, and then with no further warning than a harsh bellow of fury it flung itself at the figure of Dr. Satira, and, winding its long arms around him, buried its yellow tusks in his throat.

Dr. Satira attempted to scream, but the only result was a hideous, bubbling wheeze, and he went down on his back with the great ape tearing and ripping at him like a hyena with a chunk of meat.

Sexton Blake felt sick with horror as he lifted his pistol and crashed three bullets into the ape's shaggy back; and then there was a tremendous shattering of glass and woodwork as the third visitor—the towering ape-man—threw himself headlong at the half open window and crashed down into the garden below.

Police-whistles were screaming in all quarters, and shouts of alarm resounded from front and back of the house. Then there was a clatter of footsteps in the hall, and a crowd of plain-clothes men surged into the room, with John Fade and Dirk Dolland close at their heels.

All stopped short and stared aghast at the hideous sight in the centre of the room—Dr. Satira and the great ape locked together in a death-grip, the former's throat ripped open like a paper bag.

From the garden below the open window there came sounds of a terrific struggle—the grunting and gasping of men and the thrashing and floun-dering of heavy bodies. Then there was a sudden silence, broken by a stentorian shout of triumph:

"It's all right, sir! We've got him! But, by James, it was a tight thing! He's as strong as six men, and he's laid out three of us; but we've half a dozen pairs of handcuffs on him!"

Coutts heaved a sigh of satisfaction as he mopped at his pallid face. The mysterious cat-burglar had been caught at last!

John Fade uttered a gasp of recognition as he stared down at the man who was gripped in the arms of the dead ape.

"By heavens, it is Dr. Satira right enough!" he jerked, his voice husky with horror, and then broke off and bent lower, a puzzled look creeping into his eyes. Then, with a swift movement, he reached down and appeared to tear the dead man's face clean away amid a yell of horrified protest.

"It's all right," assured John Fade, pointing to the object he held in his hand. "It's a mask—the man was wearing a rubber mask! By heavens, it's not Dr. Satira at all!"

It was only too true. The shrivelled thing that John Fade held dangling between his fingers was a mask, cunningly made of thin, tinted rubber. The hooked nose was padded with cotton-wool, as was the semblance of high cheek bones. As a mask it was a marvellously life-like production, and would have deceived anybody, except from very close quarters.

It had been partially torn away by the gnashing fangs of the rabid ape, and the face revealed beneath was that of a swarthy-skinned native, who might have been a Hindu, or any one of the

many different sects in India. Sexton Blake took the mask, and examined it carefully.

"You're certain, Fade?" he asked. "You're certain that this man is not Dr. Satira?"

John Fade ran his fingers bewilderedly through his thick, dark hair.

"I—I can't be absolutely certain, of course," he admitted: "But I should say that it was a man made up to impersonate the original Satira. Yet, the man we met in Khurdan might have been wearing a mask, though I fail to see why he should have been."

"If you ask me," said Dirk Dolland slowly, "the real Dr. Satira is still at large. I guessed he would be too cunning to walk into the trap you set for him to-night. Still, you've got your cat-burglar, Coutts."

Coutts shrugged his shoulders.

"What I should like to know is, why did this ape suddenly turn round on this fellow, and tear the throat out of him?" he queried.

Sexton Blake knew, but kept his knowledge to himself for the time being, for he knew that it would only be discredited. There was no doubt in his mind that Dr. Satira—whether he be the dead man or not—was possessed of the secret lore of a certain tribe in India that was enabled, by the aid of a certain scent, to infuriate animals to such a degree that they recklessly and savagely attacked anyone to whom the scent had previously been applied.

"The glass ball that the man held in his hand contained a certain liquid, the scent of which would have sent the ape into a state of frenzy," thought Blake to himself. "He intended to throw it so that it would break and splash the contents over my clothes. Luckily my shot shattered the thing before it left his hand, and his villainy recoiled on his own head. Even his own trained ape was not proof against his own diabolical artifices!"

§

Handcuffed, and securely roped as he was, it took a dozen policemen to convey the powerful, ape-like cat-burglar to the nearest police-station.

"Hanged if I know how the law's going to deal with the brute!" muttered Detective-Inspector Coutts as he prepared to set off for Scotland Yard to hand in his report. "It'll take a clever lawyer to define his status, and determine whether he's fit to plead. He might be an animal, a human being, or a homicidal maniac. None the less he's committed about fifteen burglaries, one murder, and several attempted murders."

"That's not the main point," said Sexton Blake grimly as he lit a cigar and gazed thoughtfully up at the night sky. "What I should like to know is, have we got rid of the unscrupulous, diabolically cunning scoundrel who was the brains of the whole amazing business? Was the man in the mask the real Dr. Satira? Or is Dr. Satira still alive?"

John Fade shrugged his shoulders. He didn't know.

THE END

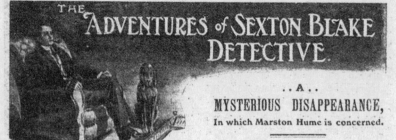

THE ADVENTURES of SEXTON BLAKE DETECTIVE.

..A..

MYSTERIOUS DISAPPEARANCE,

In which Marston Hume is concerned.

"YES, it's his work again, of that I'm convinced," said Blake to his friend Bathurst, as he poured himself out a stiff drink from the decanter on the study table near his elbow. Splashing some soda into it from a syphon, he looked at the golden bubbles rising in the glass with half-closed eyes.

"And although I have collected sufficient circumstantial evidence to satisfy myself that he is the author of this apparently motiveless crime in a fashionable country house in the Midlands, yet he must again go unpunished, solely for lack of legal proof."

"You mean—?" asked Bathurst.

"Marston Hume," said Blake grimly. "When I forced that man into the gutter two years ago, I thought he was done with crime; I thought he dared not reappear. He knows that I hold in my hand a chain of circumstantial evidence strong enough to hang him ten times over if only it could be proved. And any day," he mused as he blew a spiral of smoke towards the ceiling, "a trick of chance may bring that proof my way!

"It's the elusiveness of the beggar that worries me," he went on, after a pause. "It goes without saying that he has chosen London for his hiding-place—in better-class London, too, he should be found. Poverty—even its assumption—would hamper his plans. A disguised beggar would have no chance of reaching within miles of the high stakes for which Marston Hume is bound to play. Besides, he needed money—needed it desperately—and got it. The sale of the Lahore ruby—the ill-gotten gain of this latest fiendish crime of his—would put at least five thousand

pounds at his command. In funds, it is safe to assume he will spend that money carefully, scientifically—to spread his nets and lure victims worthy of his wits into his toils. Yet, where is he? What his method of living? His next contemplated crime? I've systematically searched for him in every likely spot in London, have laid traps for him, without result."

He broke off angrily impatient, and poked the fire into a steady blaze.

"I don't mind confessing," he added, with a half-whimsical smile, "that he's beginning to get on my nerves. I'm as jumpy as a cat— Come in!

Well, Morrison, what is it?"

"A lady to see you, sir," answered the servant, coming noiselessly into the room, and handing a visiting-card to Blake on a small salver.

"Bring her up," he said curtly, looking at the name before him with a curious interest leaping into his eyes. "It's Mrs. Sherringham," he went on, turning to Bathurst when the servant had retired. "You know—the mother of that youngster who disappeared so mysteriously some days ago. Thank Heaven for any diversion which will take my mind off that one hateful theme, if only for an hour or so— Good-evening, madam."

He crossed, the room and bowed to a tall, veiled woman who stood in the doorway.

He pulled up a comfortable chair near the fire for his visitor, and waited for her to be seated. She swept aside her veil and disclosed a beautiful, care-lined face framed in soft, greying hair—a half foreign face, with blazing dark eyes and a resolute, red-lipped mouth.

"You may speak quite freely before this gentleman," said Blake, as she gazed questioningly at Bathurst. "He is my confidential friend."

"Mr. Blake." She spoke, in a low, hurried voice, "It's about Emile. Since he disappeared, I've been half mad with fear. He is my only son—my only child," she added quickly, as if in extenuation her obvious distress. "I felt that I *must* come to you to-night. I cannot face the possibility that he is dead—yet that awful thought is always with me."

"Let me see," said Blake slowly, giving her time to compose herself. "It is just a week ago to-night since your son went away. Scotland Yard has the case in hand, I believe, Mrs. Sherringham?"

She tapped her foot impatiently on the brass fender-rail.

"And have done nothing. Today, when I saw one of the officials, he hinted to me that there might be serious reasons—of which even I, his mother, did not know—to account for his disappearance. Such a statement is an insult to Emile—an insult to me. We have travelled together over half the world. He is keen on sport—hunting, shooting, golf, fishing, fencing, were his recreations, and in these I shared. He does not drink, bet, gamble, play cards, nor go in for any of those so-called fashionable pastimes. He had plenty of money, and was not in love. He was in the best of health and spirits when he left me that day, and I have heard nothing from him since.

"I have visited hospitals, infirmaries, accident wards. I have telegraphed to every friend he knew, telephoned over half London. Scotland Yard has advertised—circulated his description broadcast throughout the country.

"I have offered a reward of five hundred pounds for any scrap of authentic information, yet nothing comes to hand. Until to-day I forced myself to believe that he would turn up, and that all this ghastly worry and uncertainty would be forgotten, but this afternoon—"

She paused, and looked huntedly around the room.

"What happened this afternoon to make you change your mind?" asked Blake slowly.

"He and I have a joint account at Wolverton's Bank," she said, dropping her voice to an uneasy whisper. "H drew on it what cheques he liked—a hundred pounds or so at a time, not more, just enough for his personal needs. To-day I received a visit from one of the bank officials, and what he told me frightened me. It seems that on the afternoon of Wednesday, the 3rd—the day Emile disappeared—a bearer cheque had been presented at the bank, just before closing time, for £3,000."

Blake looked up with sudden interest in his dark eyes.

"Who presented it?" he asked quickly.

"A man answering to Emile's description. The official—who, of course, had heard of the disappearance, and thought I ought to know of this unusual occurrence—brought with him the counter clerk who had received the cheque. That clerk described Emile to me accurately. He was wearing a long dark blue coat with an astrachan collar, and a bowler hat. My son is tall, clean shaven, wears an eyeglass, and is left-handed. The clerk distinctly remembered this last point, for the man who presented the cheque gathered up the notes and gold with his left hand, using his right arm awkwardly. There is no doubt in my mind that Emile went to the bank and cashed that cheque. But for what reason he could possibly require such a sum I cannot imagine."

"How was the money paid over?" asked Blake thoughtfully.

"Notes and gold. Six hundred pounds in sovereigns, which Emile put into a handbag, and the rest in notes—mostly for five and ten pounds apiece."

"Those should be easily traced." said Blake.

"They were presented at the Bank of England before midday on Thursday, the 4th—so the bank officials found out—and cashed. It was not until Thursday afternoon that I became really alarmed at my son's absence, and consulted Scotland Yard on the matter."

"At what time did you last see your son?" asked Blake, after a long pause.

"On Wednesday morning. He arranged to meet me at the Savoy for dinner, and he left the house about midday, telling his man, Dancey, that he would be back to dress at about seven o'clock.

"I waited at the Savoy until ten o'clock, then went to the theatre at which Emile had booked a box, feeling quite sure he would turn up before the play was over. It was just after eleven when I reached home, to find no sign of Emile. At last I went to bed, expecting a letter or wire would come in the morning to explain his absence. At midday I could endure the suspense no longer. I thought of motor accidents, and all sorts of horrors, and went with my story to Scotland Yard.

" I suppose," she went on, in a hopeless tone, "they have done their best, but it amounts to nothing. They have buoyed me up with hopes, suggestions, counsel, and advice—but they haven't found Emile. Mr. Blake, will you find him?"

The tragic mother-note in her voice was fierce almost in its intensity. It seemed for a moment to unnerve the two men who listened to its appeal. Blake looked at the strong, noble face and its deep lines compassionately.

"I will do my best, Mrs. Sherringham," he said simply.

She lowered her head, unable for the moment to control her voice. Her thin lips quivered, and her brilliant dark eyes grew dim with sudden tears.

"Did the bank officials show you that cheque?" asked Blake a second or two later.

Mrs. Sherringham took a small notebook from a gold bag-purse she was carrying, opened it, and took out a folded slip of paper.

"I brought it with me for you to see," she answered, passing the slip across to Blake's outstretched hand. "Genuine enough, without a doubt. It has, as you see, both my signature and Emile's. I always fill in my name when he gets a fresh book from the bank, so that he can use the cheques as he likes. It would take a very clever forger to imitate both these, for, as you see, our handwritings are peculiar and distinctive."

Blake held up the cheque to the light, and looked at it slowly through his powerful lens.

"By the way," he said, looking up sharply, "can you tell me what your son intended to do between midday, when he left the house, and seven o'clock or so, when he would presumably go home to dress for dinner?"

"He mentioned a fencing appointment," she answered. "He was a member of only two clubs. Beyton's and Harrison's, and was one of the most expert members of both, but Scotland Yard have been able to establish the fact that he had not been to either place for over a week."

Blake shot a sudden, incomprehensible look at Bathurst's face, and stood up suddenly, stretching up to his full height on the rug before the fire.

"You said your son was tall?" he said, a curious hard line growing round his mouth, and the pupils of his eyes narrowing to pinpoints. "Was he as tall—perhaps an inch taller than I?"

"Six feet one inch, exactly," answered Emile's mother, with a touch of maternal pride.

Bathurst opened his mouth as if stung into speech, then closed it again as Blake quietly sat down.

"And this is all you can tell me?" he queried. "I'll do my best, Mrs. Sherringham," he went on, without waiting for her to speak. "If your son Emile is to be found I'll find him—or the man who knows where he is." Almost it seemed to Bathurst he was registering a vow. "I will let you know the moment anything turns up." He rang the bell by his side for his servant to show her out as he spoke, turning abruptly away from the sudden look of hope which sprang up into dark, troubled eyes. "Good-night! Good-bye!"

When she had gone the two men faced each other, a question on the lips of each.

"Do you suspect Marston Hume?" said Bathurst.

"Can it be Marston Hume?" said Blake, both speaking together, half aloud.

Blake sat down by the fire and stared moodily into its cheery blaze.

"If it be he,"—he clenched his hands tightly till the veins on the back stood out like whipcord—"If it be he it will kill that woman. If Marston Hume has spread his net about that boy, it's murder! A double murder, Bathurst, for it will break the mother's heart. Heavens, think of it—for three thousand pounds! And once I held him in the hollow of my hand—and let him go."

He shook himself angrily, got up, and paced the floor.

"Hume is one of the finest fencers in the country, as I know to my cost. Can you imagine a surer bait held out to an enthusiastic young fellow who had mastered the art in schools like Beyton's and Harrison's? The teaching of a few new turns of arms and wrists the lure, a cheque for a few pounds enforced in payment, for the purpose of obtaining the youngster's signature, from which to forge a cheque fur a greater amount, a swift blow with a faulty foil, then death.

"The mother's signature is genuine enough. You remember she told us that she signed all the blank cheques in a new book," he went on, taking up the slip of paper from the table and holding it up to the light. "But the boy's, I think, we shall find to be an exceedingly clever forgery. Mind, Bathurst, we know the art and craft of the man to be almost without limitation. To him the thing is simple enough to be almost farcical."

"But you forget the bank clerk," interrupted Bathurst. "He knew Emile Sherringham and described him exactly, the clothes he was wearing, his trick of the left hand—"

"The simplest part of the whole thing!" snapped Blake. "Young Sherringham, you heard his mother say, was tall and clean-shaven—so is Marston Hume. The big overcoat with the thick astrachan collar turned up, the bowler hat pulled well down over the forehead, an eyeglass, the dominant left hand—who would know that better than a fencing master?—and the disguise is complete enough to pass muster in a crowded bank during the rush preceding closing time. Come on, let's get outside and breathe! Somewhere in London Marston Hume is hiding and playing his fiendish tricks. Let's find him."

"A tall order," said Bathurst. "Where shall we begin our search?"

Blake stood irresolute on his doorstep.

"Scotland Yard first," he said, in something like his ordinary quiet voice. "There may be fresh news there. Jones has charge of the case. We'll go to him."

That bluff official met Blake with a stolid face, but there was trouble behind his shrewd eyes.

"Body found," be said curtly, "an hour ago— Regent's Canal. Stripped of every vestige of clothing, but identity beyond doubt. Lying in the Marylebone mortuary. Like to see it?" He scribbled a few lines on his official card. "In the water some days," he added, as an afterthought. "Knife-wound in the neck, the evident cause of death. Good-night!"

Blake hailed a passing taxi in the quiet street outside and gave directions to the chauffeur.

"Think of that woman," said Bathurst, as they were whirled through the streets. "Her only son."

Blake nodded.

"I'm thinking of that—and something else," he said, and relapsed into silence till the journey's end was reached.

As the inspector had said, the cause of death was plain enough. A small hole, curiously shaped, at the side of the neck gaped badly. The sluggish water and the bumps and bruises of passing barges had not marred the pleasant, boyish face.

The official in charge gave gruesome details of the finding by the drags of the searchers, pointing out the exact spot on a chart of the canal.

"I was right," said Blake, almost bitterly, a few minutes later, as they plunged once more into the gas-lit streets. "That hole in the neck was not done by a knife-thrust. I've seen a wound like that before owing to the sudden breaking of a foil. It narrows our inquiry down, Bathurst. The man we want lives somewhere on the banks of the canal. Hume works alone. He would have to carry that body to the water and drop it quietly in out of sight— Here's a post-office," he broke off suddenly, dashing into an almost deserted building.

In ten minutes he was out again with the knowledge, that three houses in the area he suspected had recently changed ownership. The first he visited proved to be a small, select, girls' school in a side street just off the main road. The second, a gay, blue-tiled, freshly-painted house, the home of a stage favourite recently married to a stockbroker, and far enough away from the canal to be crossed off the list. The third, a big, deserted-looking house in the centre of a semi-circular sweep off the main road, the garden enclosed by a high wooden paling. Blake climbed over this, slipped across the neglected lawn, cautiously felt his way down a flight of uneven steps, and found himself in a quiet strip of garden, with the canal flowing sluggishly a few feet below the low stone wall.

When he joined Bathurst again, he was breathing hard, as though he had been running.

"Take this," he said, pushing a small revolver into his friend's hand. "And keep your wits about you—we've found Marston Hume."

He pushed open the high wooden gate, walked quickly up the flagged path to the hall door, and rang the bell loudly.

The door was opened by a neatly-capped maid.

"Is Mr. Hume at home?" asked Blake sharply, pushing her aside and stepping into the hall.

"Mr. Hume, sir?" repeated the girl dully. "He doesn't live here. This is Mr. Beyton's house. You've made a mistake, sir."

"If Mr. Beyton is at home," said Blake, "take him my card and ask him to see me at once."

At the far end of the hall, a door suddenly opened, and a fierce little Frenchman stood eyeing the group with angry impatience.

As he saw Blake his face lighted up with genuine pleasure and surprise.

"Ah, Monsieur Blake," he cried. "I am pleased that you should visit me. Come in!"

He bowed the two men into a big, fire-warmed room, Blake apologising for the late intrusion of Bathurst and himself.

"I understood," he went on, eyeing the walls, with their collection of foils, masks, and duelling-swords, keenly, "that a man I was seeking might be found here—a certain Marston Hume."

The little Frenchman shook his head.

"I do not know of such a man," he said, with emphatic gestures of his small white hands. "I have been in this house three months, perhaps he was here before I came."

"He was an expert with the foils. Monsieur Beyton, a past master of the art, your match and mine. Tall, lean—"

"Ah!" cried the old fencing master with enthusiasm. "Then it is of Monsieur Maton you speak. He—ah, he came here! Mon Dieu! His art, his cunning, his skill! Superb!"

"I know," admitted Blake sharply. "Where is he now? My business is urgent."

The little Frenchman flung out his hands wildly.

"He is gone. Where, I do not know. I met him one lucky day in the Saint Michael Salle d'Armes in Paris. You know that school, monsieur? And Maton, he was there, fencing. Mon Dieu! What wrists of steel! Tall, lithe, with constant threat of danger in his long arm. No one knew who he was, whence he came—and no one cared. I least of all. He and I became friends—and I am proud of his friendship. A little while ago, a month, perhaps, we came back here—he and I—to my home. It is here I live, my son has taken my place in my school and I live here alone."

"But Maton, as you call him," said Blake impatiently—"what of him?"

"I will tell you as quickly as I can. He fenced with me here in this room—once—twice—perhaps more. Always a one-sided bout, for I grow old. Then he asked me to send to my school for some of my pupils—three or four—and Monsieur Maton, always masked—a fad of his—

fenced with them. There was one—Monsieur Emile Sherringham almost a match for Maton. Those two together—mon Dieu, I can see them now! A worthy sight for my old eyes!"

"How often did Mr. Sherringham come?" asked Blake quietly.

"Several times—always in the afternoon."

"When was he here last?"

The old man shook his head.

"I do not know," he said slowly. "Two weeks ago I was called to Paris, and I left my friend Maton here to live in the home as long as he wished. Last evening, when I came back, he was gone."

The fire died out of the wrinkled face; the enthusiasm flickered from the quick, bright eyes.

"I am old," he went on in a duller tone. "All my life I have played with the foils. But Maton—ah, he played better than I! There was one trick—a trick worth knowing, which I shall show you, Monsieur Blake—you, who learnt your game in my school."

He sprang from his chair, crossed the slippery parquet floor with its thick skins and soft rugs to a case in the far corner, and selected a couple of finely-tempered foils.

Blake slipped off his heavy overcoat, took the buttoned foil from the old man's hand, and fell almost mechanically into position; and in a moment the two fell on guard.

Bathurst watched them fascinated. The brilliant lights from above threw soft shadows of their crouching bodies on the shining floor, where Blake had roughly kicked aside rugs and mats. The fire now and then gleamed dully on the thin whipping blades, grating and rasping together in thrust and parry.

The little Frenchman was shorter by a head or more than his tall combatant, but for several minutes neither gained on advantage. Suddenly, with a lightning-like movement, M. Beyton reached out low with his right arm, a quick turn of the wrist, and the flickering blade darted serpent-like beneath Blake's guard. The button touched his neck lightly at the side; and the old man laughed.

"With a duelling sword that touch on the neck, monsieur—and death," he said triumphantly.

"A good trick, eh?" he went on, replacing the foils in their case and locking it carefully. "Monsieur Maton promised to teach that trick to the young Sherringham—perhaps he will one day."

Blake's eyes were glued to a foil hanging on the wall, and answered absentmindedly:

"A good trick indeed! Where, Monsieur Beyton, is the companion foil to this?" he queried, with a sudden change of tone, pointing to a fine foil with a curiously engraved blade.

The old man looked up sharply.

"It is there on the wall. No! Then where is it? I would not lose that for anything in the world!" He was darting eagerly about the room, looking among the other foils with quick, nervous eagerness. "They were trophies won by my skill in Paris—when my arm was surer, and my eyes more steady—and one is gone! Perhaps," he said, slowly crossing again to Blake's side— "perhaps Monsieur Maton took it—as a souvenir. It was hanging on this nail when I left for Paris. He must have taken it—"

Blake curtly cut short the old man's garrulous explanation.

"Do you know what day he left your house?" he asked sharply.

The old man took from a drawer of an old carved writing-desk close at hand a folded sheet of paper, on which were written a few lines.

"Dated on the fourth of the month," said Blake half-aloud, after a tense pause, speaking to Bathurst slowly, and glancing at the graciously-worded thanks for the absent host's hospitality, and the regrets for the sudden termination of a most enjoyable visit, written in an obviously disguised hand.

"The little maid tells me that Monsieur Maton left at midday on Thursday after writing that note." explained the Frenchman, in his high-pitched voice. "But where he has gone I do not know. Perhaps he will come again, and then, if you wish to see him urgently, Monsieur Blake, I will let you know. Perhaps it is that trick you would like him to teach you?"

Suddenly the Frenchman, with a quick turn of the wrist, sent the flickering blade, serpent-like, beneath Blake's guard.

"I should like to find out if Maton was at home here on Wednesday last—the day before he went away. Could you ask the maids?" said Blake shortly.

"They would not be able to tell you, I think. Monsieur Maton came at will through that door there," pointing to a long French window, which Blake could see opened on to the garden. "The kitchens are down below in the front of the house; at the back here we are undisturbed all day."

Blake carefully replaced the rugs on the floor, eyeing one—so it seemed to Bathurst—unnecessarily long, bade his host an abrupt "Goodbye," a few seconds later, and went out once more into the night.

He and Bathurst had cleared the brightly-lighted thoroughfare of Marylebone Road and had turned into a quiet side street before Blake spoke.

"Plain enough to piece it together now," he said jerkily. "Old Beyton's sudden call to Paris give Marston Hume the opportunity he was looking for. He probably telephoned to Emile Sherringham, or in some way made an appointment with him to go to the house on Wednesday afternoon—the 3rd—to learn that trick, for which he demanded a cheque for three pounds; and so obtained the necessary signature.

I judge that £3 was the sum asked for, since on a cheque signed by Sherringham for that amount would obviously appear all the letters and numerals necessary for forging a cheque for three thousand.

Then, perhaps, after a short lesson, he managed to change his buttoned foil for that one which is missing from the wall, its point already broken off. A twist of the wrist, and it had gone home, leaving a triangular, jagged wound in a dead man's neck.

To secure a cheque from Sherringham's book, forge the signature, slip on his victim's clothes, and hurry to the bank, locking the door carefully behind him, would be all part, of the diabolical plot so simply carried out. Then at night an easy task to take the body out through the window and drop it over the wall of the garden into the water, his guilty secret safe for days perhaps—at any rate, hours. A visit to the Bank of England on the morning of the 4th, then flight, leaving nothing behind him but that note.

"I noticed," he went on, after a long pause, "that one of the rugs on the floor—a thick brown bearskin—was new. That, would he necessary if the one it was bought to replace was stained."

Bathurst shivered.

"Took that away in his luggage with the missing foil, or weighted it and flung it into the canal," he said, as if reading Blake's thoughts.

They had turned into Messenger Square at the end of their long walk before Blake spoke again.

"What use is it to know all this without a single shred of proof to support one's theories!" he said fiercely. "Marston Hume has scored once more—scored heavily—and once more has disappeared. But one of these days we shall meet face to face, Bathurst. One slip in his fiendishly cunning plan, and I've got him. Nothing will save him then."

His mouth closed like a trap.

DETECTIVE WORK—ADVENTURE—THRILLS!

THE UNION JACK 2ᴰ

Sexton Blake's Own Paper

A MYSTERY IN MOTLEY

SEXTON BLAKE and TINKER in the Best Complete Story of ZENITH the ALBINO ever Published.

No. 1,182. EVERY THURSDAY. June 12th, 1926.

A MYSTERY IN MOTLEY

All stories featuring Sexton Blake and Zenith the Albino are good, as readers of this paper have learned to know. The distinctive treatment of this one, however, puts it in a class by itself. A good story becomes a superlative story when the engaging Albino tells it in his own words.

PART ONE.

IN WHICH EVENTS ARE DESCRIBED BY, AND FROM THE VIEWPOINT OF, MONSIEUR ZENITH, THE ALBINO.

THE FIRST CHAPTER.

THE PRESERVE OF "SUDDEN-DEATH DAVID."

Of course it was dangerous of me to occupy a box at the Pallaseum; but then I am so used to danger that I am beginning to like it.

Most things that I do are dangerous— dangerous, I mean, to freedom. Danger to life does not touch me; for what is life to me that I should fear to lose it—to me, the albino? Pink-eyed! White-haired!

But for the fact that some perversity of fate has endowed me with a quick hand and with some measure of intelligence, mankind —normal law-abiding mankind—would long ago have robbed me in life, just as the lower animals will unite to destroy any individual who differs from the heard.

Were I forced to appeal from the arena as in the Roman games a defeated gladiator was permitted to appeal — the down turned thumb of the populace would doubtless be my answer; and I should die laughing ; because death is, after all, only a gateway to freedom.

More, much more that I fear death, do I fear life within a cage; and that why my greater enemy is he who would rob me, not of earthly life, but of earthly freedom.

Sexton Blake!

There is the man's name—Sexton Blake of Barker Street, investigator, criminologist, sportsman, gentleman; and my inveterate enemy.

Pitiable, is it not, that I—I, Zenith—should have for my enemy one whom I am obliged to describe in such terms? One of life's conundrums, to be solved, perhaps, by the coming of that right which is death.

I am thinking of that night which is death, now, when I sit at the back of my box and look fixedly, not at the stage, but all the stalls of the great theatre. For death is not far away, and it has a form which intrigues me.

To throw dice with death, that is, surely, a pastime which should bring forgetfulness; and I have only to whisper just above the tremor of the violins: "I am Zenith, I am here in the Royal Box," and behold the dice-box would ratter for a throw.

Death has come to me in many forms; and many men have come to me carrying in their hands the boon (or bane) of extinction ; but never in such guise as now.

Down in the stalls, four or five rows from the front, and well in the centre of the house, sits a short man with a full round, pinkish, babyish face.

He is enjoying the show; or, if he is not enjoying it, then his dissimulation is a miracle.

He has no eyes for anything but the stage, and his fat white hand is indolently tapping out the time of the music which is being played.

What a man!

I watch him for thirty minutes on end; and, during that time, not by a flicker of an eyelid, not by a momentary change of expression, does he betray himself for what he is.

What is his name? That I cannot tell you.

Something commonplace. That's a safe bet, anyhow; and of this, also, I am certain—whatever his name may be at this moment, as he sits there in the stalls, full-faced and fatuous like an overfed baby, that name, whatever it is, which he bears at this moment, appears on such correspondence as he may have in his pockets, upon his motor-driving license, upon his linen, upon every one of his belongings which normally should bear a name.

This, also I can tell you— he will answer to that name and to no other.

Piy him with strong drink, bat him over the head until his senses are practically gone, tear his naves to rages, if you can, with hours of third degree; and then try to jump him into showing any familiarity with his last name but one, and you will fail.

Paradoxically he does not act, does not impersonate. Merely changes his identity and becomes another man; and, when the identity has served its purpose, he sloughs it off, as a snake does an old skin, and is born anew with another name, another habitat, another character.

I know him as Rock, just because he called himself Rock when first I became aware of his existence.

The one or two of the underworld who know him by sight and the few who know him by reputations, refer to him as "Sudden-Death David."

That name, at any rate, will belong to him for ever.

It will be his until, perhaps, in a ripe old age, his grey hairs are borne to an honored grave.

I do not concern myself with ordinary men. If they stand in my way—well, that is a fitting epitaph. But this man is by no means ordinary. I am forced to treat him with respect. No, not with respect, with caution. If he stood in my way, the epitaph would perhaps be mine own. It depends upon the conjunction of trigger with finger.

And it seems probable that this matter of the epitaph will be settled soon. I am in the romantic and exciting condition of beings penniless; and, this night, I am going to poach upon his preserve.

This three-mile circle, the exact center of which is the Pallaseum Theatre, is the area which Rock has marked out for himself.

He has laid it down that not even a pockethandkerchief shall be taken within this area, but the taker shall furnish him, Rock, with a toll of the proceeds; and I —I am not going to snatch a handkerchief, or rob one of these pitiful bourgeoisie of a handful of paper money. I am going to take the prize which Rock has marked out for himself.

A trivial matter, a necklace worth a few tens of thousands; but a fortune to me, in my present state, and doubly worth getting, because I shall take it out of the hands of Sudden-Death David.

I can dispose of that necklace easily. Rock himself has prepared the machinery which I shall use. Of the money I have vital necessity.

True. I am sitting here, in the Royal Box, alone; and my clothes are, I think, adequate. But, when the footman has helped me into my overcoat and obtained for me a taxicab, I shall present him with half-a-crown for his pains; and that halfcrown will represent my entire fortune.

That is why I am driven to rob Rock the King of the Underworld.

There, as he sits in the stalls, pink and smiling, his great brain is busy with ways and means for committing this latest crime; and, when he has snatched the chestnut from the fire, I, Zenith, propose to eat it before his eyes.

That is amusing, is it not?

You laugh. I laugh with you.

To-night there will be a stir in the underworld. To-morrow that world which is not the underworld will be stirred also.

You will learn from your morning paper that the famous pink pendant, the pendant with matched pinkish diamonds, was stolen at the Countess Gulliver's reception.

You may learn with horror that else-where, in a taxicab, or on the Thames Embankment, or in sound quiet West End square, was found the body of a man.

It may be the body of one who has the ill-fortune to be an albino.

It may be the body of the highly respectable Mr. Jones, or Mr. Smith; or whatever he may be calling himself the pink-faced gentleman who sits just below my feet at this moment in the body of the theatre.

Neither you, nor your delightfully matter-of-fact police force, will associate the two events; but Mr. Sexton Blake will know.

At least, he will know if it is I against whom the dice are loaded.

If it should be the other-Sudden-Death David-he may know; or he may not.

Even to me Rock is a mystery. To Blake he may be unknown.What knowledge reposes in the great brain behind the sleepy eyes of Sexton Blake, even I cannot fathom.

Candidly, I wish I could.

We shall meet there to-night, Blake and myself, at the Countess Gulliver's reception; and Rock-he will be there also. I make no doubt that the card of invitation is in his breast-pocket at this moment.

The encounter should provide amusement for us all.

You will understand from this that there is dancing. That fancy costumes are being worn. That it is, in fact, a Bal asque.

It is I to whom this circumstance is necessary.

Blake has no reason to fear recognition.

Rock has no reason to fear recognition.

I fear nothing; but not yet am I baring my neck for the executioner's axe. Already the curtain may have been rung up on the last act of that tragic-comedy which for me is called life; but I have no wish to curtain the action. I must make arrangements to take a call when it is over, and, for that reason, I musts wear a mask.

You conclude that somewhere within a mile or two I have chambers, servants to wait upon me, and clothes to wear.

Yon are wrong. I have none of these things. Nothing but these clothes, hat, overcoat, and walking-stick, with the vestiare outside, and this half-crown for the footman.

Where shall I got file clothes that I need? How shall I find a couple of shillings which will be necessary to pay the driver of my taxicab? I do not know, I refuse to occupy myself with the question. I turn, if you will, a fatalist.The hour brings the event; and the event its exploitation. I shall direct the cabman to the first place that comes into my head, and I am sure-yes, somehow I am quite sure—that as I descend from the cab, or perhaps earlier, I shall see clearly by what means he is to get his two shillings, and I am to get the costume and the money which I require for immediate necessities.

I lean forward, rather incautiously, to see further back into the auditorium.

One or two late-comers have entered at the back rows; and people are turning to look at them.

I smile with genuine pleasure to see the vultures gathering. There will be a kill to-night.

Sexton Blake and his assistant have just taken their seats in the back row of the stalls.

Strange, is it not, that we three—Blake, Sudden-Death David, and myself—who are so linked together by invisible threads of Fate, should have elected independently to occupy the after-dinner hour at the Pallaseum, before going on to the Countess Gulliver's.

If Blake only knew, if he knew the true identity of that little fat man in the fifth row! If he knew what deeds he had done, is doing; and perhaps will do.

What a maelstrom of avenging justice would stagger that respectable theatre there and then! But Blake is laughing and chatting with his assistant, like the genial fellow that he is.

He does not know.

Or, is it that he does know, and is only biding his time?

Of that, I think, I shall learn something before the night is over.

The silent clock at, the back of my box tolls me that it is nearly ten.

I rise and ring for the attendant.

He brings me my overcoat, my stick, hat, and gloves; and I pass out towards the waiting taxicab, pressing the half crown into his willing hand.

For me, the night of adventure is beginning already.

THE SECOND CHAPTER.

THE NAME ON THE BOX.

I AM what you would call an unprincipled scoundrel; which means that my principles are not the same as yours. And how should they be?

You are normal; or, at least, I hope that you are, for the sake of your soul's repose.

I am an albino; and if I have no principles, I have at least a code. One, believe me, which I would not willingly depart from.

Some of it is illogical, the basis of fad and superstition; but still, to me, its integrity is a matter of vital importance.

One item of this ridiculous creed, based no doubt upon a childish vanity, is that I will not commit a crime for less than five pounds' and it occurred to me with considerable force as I was turning over the fancy costumes at Woolf's, whither I had travelled in the taxicab for which I could not yet pay the hire, that self-made laws are not less inconvenient than laws made by other people.

I had hoped that, during my short thrive in the taxicab, I should have been visited by some inspiration which should provide me with ample means for the expenses of the evening; but no such inspiration had come to me.

I had reached and entered the great shop without more exercise of my faculties than if I had been both blind and paralysed; and, now that they had received me with that excessive deference which I obtain everywhere, I was discussing costume after costume; and, also, idly wondering how on earth I should obtain one, in face of my code which does not permit me to commit a crime for less than five pounds.

The shop was a large one, and contained at that moment only one other customer, who, because of the tall system of shelving which partitioned itself, I could not see.

It would have been easy enough for me to cause a certain costume to be carried towards the window, away from the other persons in the shop; and then to incapacitate the fellow who was serving me; and, after that, to walk out jauntily to my taxicab.

Nothing easier. But the accursed fact which prevented any such action was that not one of the fancy costumes was priced above four pounds ten.

This price, of course, was for hire; and I might have compounded with my code by proposing to buy one.

This, however, would have been evasion, and my code does not permit of evasions. Ever then, even if I had followed the course of action which I have outlined, I should have had no money.

Certainly, I could have grabbed the salesman's pocket-book, which would have been likely to contain a pound or two; but then I do not do these things. I am a thief, but not a sneak-thief.

There is a difference.

I had come to the conclusion that here I could not serve the purpose which I had in mind. when I recognised tire voice of the other customer.

It was a man named James; and he had, and probably still has, the distinction of being body-servant, and I know not what, to the man whom I had just seen sitting in the centre of the stalls at the Pallaseum—to a man from whom others know as a Sudden-Death David.

Instantly, as a recompense for the hour of lethargy with which the gods had embarrassed me, there entered my head a perfect little drama in one act.

I saw, in a flash, the stage set and the entrances and the exits of the various characters set forth.

I saw, quite distinctly, who it was that should have the honour of paying for my fancy costume; and idea pleased me exceedingly.

Yes, it is a piece of delightful impertinence which leaps into my heart.

I listen for one minute longer, to make sure that James is nearing the end of his business in the shop; and then, telling the salesman that I had come to no decision, but will come back presently, I return to my taxicab and cause the man to drive slowly around the purlieus of Soho.

When I return to Woolf's, a large box is being packed with the costume, or costumes, which James has ordered.

I say to the salesman: "I have decided upon that costume of a harlequin which I was looking at. I want you to send it along with the things which Mr.James, has ordered. He asks you to include the charges upon his account."

The salesman bows. Evidently the credit of Rock is good.

"Certainly, sir."

And I return to the cab.

That is eminently satisfactory. So far, I have committed no crime. Rock will pay the bill; and his money, let me tell you, is as safe as the Bank of England.

Truly I have in prospect the trifling difficulty of securing my costume after it has reached Rock's present abode; but that difficulty supplies me with a thrill of excitement, and so is more than recompensed.

Of course, I know Rock's house in Upper Temple Street. Who doesn't? By those few who are in the know it is pointed at as it monument to criminal genius.

Perfectly appointed, of impeccable respectability, correct in every particular.

After making a call upon one of my fellows, a man from whom I could easily have borrowed ten pounds or so; but from whom I would borrow nothing; for that, also, is against my principles, I return to tiny friend the taxi-driver, whose bill against, me is rapidly increasing, and order him to drive to Upper Temple Street.

I ascend the steps to Rock's heavy front door-decorated in peacock blue and fitted with oxydised handles-and ask, of all things that a man will do, to see Rock himself.

His servant looks at me doubtfully.

He is one of the servants who belong to Rock's daylight existence.

"I do not think," he says, "that my master is at home."

I know, however, that he is lying.

"Toll your master," I order him, "that Monsieur Zenith is here."

He looks startled; but, not knowing what else to do, he shows me into a small room oil the hall, and departs to get his master's instructions.

The room has windows giving upon the, street, and, before I have been there thirty seconds, I see Woolf's small motor-van draw up in front of the house and one of their men descend with a large cardboard box.

Selecting the exact moment, I step into the hall, open the door, and receive the parcel.

The messenger only says: "For Mr. Park," and departs.

I close the door and return to the ante-room, carrying the cardboard box under my arm.

So Rock's new name is Park!

He has had so many— that it is not worth remembering.

I take an adhesive luggage label from an escritoire, slap it over the one bearing Park's name and address, and print my own name upon it, using one of Rock's quill pens for the purpose.

Audacity and good luck; and then again—audacity. That is the keynote of success.

The servant returns as I am in the act of laying down tine quill pen, to tell me that his master is at home and will be glad to see me.

He is evidently unaware of the arrival of the cardboard box, and I carry it out of the room in front of him and stand it down beside the door.

He must be puzzled at its presence, because it is of such a size that he could hardly have failed to notice it, had it been in my possession when I entered.

I know that, as soon as my back is turned, he will read the name upon the label.

That will, of course, allay his doubts almost completely.

"I wish," I said to myself, as I follow him up the staircase, "that I was as sure of getting out of this house alive, as I am sure of taking that box with me if I do so."

Sudden-Death David is standing before a roaring fire, a cigar is thrust in his face, and he looks so like the prosperous merchant that he is supposed to be that I—even I—am surprised.

He shows no sign of any emotion at my visit, neither pleasure nor the reverse: yet he must know who I am, or he would not have received me.

He must know that. I have penetrated his incognito: or how should I have been there. Yet these things do not perturb him.

"Monsieur Zenith," he says, with an hospitable accent. "Shall we shake hands."

"If you don't mind," I return, "I think not. It is a whim of mine only to give my hand in friendship."

"And between us," he queries, "there is not friendship?"

"Alas," I assured him, "we are at present strangers!"

"May I know why we have met at all?"

"Certainly!"

I light a cigarette—one of those little opium-soaked cigarettes which seem to bring me truly to life.

Never more necessary than now.

"To-night," I continue, playing this dangerous game for all it is worth, "you are going to the Countess Gulliver's reception. It is your intention to remove from that lady's possession a pendant of pink diamonds. I commend your taste. The object of my call is to suggest that, when you have secured them, you give then to me."

The man holds up a fat pink hand in protest.

"Pardon one, you have got this wrong in some particulars, Mr.—er—Monsieur Zenith. I am assuredly going to Countess Gulliver's reception: but I have no intention of stealing her jewellery. On the contrary, I should be the first to protect her against such loss. If, however, I were so unprincipled as to commit such a crime—this is only supposition, mind you—if I were, I think I should want to retain the proceeds of the crime for myself. Will you tell me what reason you have for thinking that I might present these stolen goods to you, in such an eventuality?"

I smile insolently, blandly. It is part of the game I am playing.

"Because," I tell him, "It would save me the trouble of taking them for myself."

The little man grins with pleasure at my effrontery.

"I don't think," he says, "that I can allow anybody to take the Countess Gulliver's diamond. Couldn't you content yourself with something easier—a watch, say, or a pocket-handkerchief? There will be plenty of such pickings at the ball to-night."

Instantly I am beside myself with anger. Is that not strange?

A calculated sneer would have passed me by. Cultured sarcasm would have left me cold; and yet this cheap gibe touches me just as the man meant it to.

He must see his danger in my face, because he says quickly:

"I hasten to inform you, Monsieur Zenith, that I am unarmed and quite at your mercy."

The man is clever. There is no doubt of that.

Nothing else that he could say would save him from my hands at that moment; but those words made it impossible for nine to attack, and the wonderful thing is that, although we had never met before, he knew that such was the fact.

I cannot hit a man who is incapable of hitting back.

Instead, I turn and walk out of the room.

"In order," I say to have the last word, "that there shall be no misunderstanding, I may as well inform you that at the bat masque to-night I shall be dressed as a harlequin."

He smiles and waves his cigar with a gesture of leave taking.

"And I," he informs me, "will be attired as Mephistopheles—a rather dumpy and rubicund Mephistopheles, I am afraid, but still it Mephistopheles."

This gives me an idea.

"I will wager," I say, "Countess Gulliver's diamonds to a bottle of champagne that you are not dressed in that costume at all."

He thinks I have insinuated that he intends deceit, and rises to the bait, just as I hope he will.

"I accept your wager," he says "with considerable doubt as to your ability to pay if you lose."

I shrug my shoulders.

"I am acquainted," I tell him, "with the machinery which you have prepared for the disposal of the Countess' diamonds; and that machinery I propose to use for myself, unless, of course, you succeed in winning the wager, and then it will be used by you. Au revoir!"

He waves his cigar again.

"Au revoir! Au revoir!" he chirps.

And as I descend the stairs I can hear him chuckling. He does not believe me. Well, that only shows that he is not acquainted with my history. I do not indulge in hot air.

Fortunately for me I always move silently; so that when half-way down the stairs, I am in full view of a visitor who stands upon the threshold, his attention is not called to my presence.

Quietly and swiftly I turn in my tracks and go back to the room where I have left Rock.

He is still standing just where I have left him, amid I am sure that by then he has dismissed me from his mind.

" You have won the wager," said the pantaloon, as Zenith turned. " . . . We will
drink a bottle of champagne together. Who
knows " —and he sniggered—" it may be your
last."

"Dog does not cat dog," I tell him.

"Sexton Blake is at your door."

"Sexton Blake," he ruminates calmly. "That is very interesting. Strangely enough, neither socially—er—nor otherwise, have I met the celebrated Sexton Blake. I shall certainly see him. It would be a very effective introduction if—"

"If," I complete, "you informed him that I was also in the house. Certainly that would be very agreeable to Mr. Blake and his friends the police; but I don't think you will do that."

"And why not?"

"Because, if you did, I should give certain information which would turn Mr. Blake's suspicions regarding your-self into certainties."

"Suspicions!" he exclaims, with the first trace of excitement he has betrayed during our interview. "No one has any suspicions concerning me—that is, no one who matters."

"Pardon!" I put in. Mr. Sexton Blake is at your door. What does that mean? Mr. Blake is a man who goes straight to the point—who likes to see for himself. He is at your door. That implies—or I think it implies—that he has divined something of this Jekyll Hyde personality which you have created with such astonishing skill. He wants to have a look at you. I know you are as clever as Mephistopheles himself, whom you intended to impersonate this night; but believe me Sexton Blake is as clever as you are. What a begins to suspect he will end by discovering."

The little fat man smiles.

He does not believe me.

His faith in himself is as great as my own in me.

"As regards your presence here," he murmurs imperturbably, "there is something to be said for your argument; and I shall not give you away. The door beside the fireplace leads to a smaller room. If you will remain there—"

To the manservant who has just announced the caller he says

"Please show Mr. Blake up. I shall be very interested to receive him."

I withdraw to the small room and almost close to the door behind me—almost but not quite.

As I do so I am laughing.

I, who seldom laugh, am laughing and at myself.

The cardboard box on which I have so incautiously written "Monsieur Zenith" —had I turned it so that the name was towards the wall, or had I left it with the name outwards so that it might be read by Sexton Blake, the man whose eyes miss nothing?

THE THIRD CHAPTER.

THE WAGER WON.

DECIDEDLY Rock is a master. The more I see of Rock the more I admire him.

He comes forward to receive Sexton Blake with a kind of simper.

I am certain although I cannot rise, that he looks a perfect fool as he stretches out his plump hand and tells Sexton Blake how honoured he is and how delighted he is, and what a wonderful experience it is to him to meet the famous detective.

He becomes quite lyrical in his admiration, and his encomiun is punctuated by Sexton Blake's quiet, crisp voice:

"Just so, Mr. Park!" And "That's very kind of you Mr. Park!"

And all the time—don't I know it—

Blake's blue-grey eyes are trying to read him.

But, by all the gods, he is a cipher which will take some solving! I, who know the man to be desperate and ruthless, and possessed of devilish cleverness—even I am half convinced, as I listen, that he is a fatuous fool; and Sexton Blake, surely, cannot know what I know.

And yet, what is Blake saying?

"I, Mr. Park, on my side, am as glad and as interested as you. I have suspected your existence for a long lime."

This was a facer for Rock. It mean if it meant anything—that Blake was on to him.

"Suspected my existence!"Rock is almost hysterical. "Really, Mr. Blake, you puzzle me. You do indeed. I am honoured that a, man of your eminence should trouble to make the acquaintance of a dilettante like myself; but when you say that you have suspected my existence, then, frankly, no, I really do not follow you."

"When I say," proceeded Sexton Blake, "that I had suspected your existence, I mean, really, that. I had deduced it. I have learnt in the hard school of experience that there are no effects without causes; and I have observed recently a considerable number of important effects which had no apparent cause. For that cause I have been looking; and I think that, Mr. Park, I have found it in yourself."

"I say, really. Mr. Blake—"

Rock was quite at his best in this sort of disclaimer.

"You know, I should be tremendously thrilled if I were able, only for a short time, to play the role of Rattles. But, I say, you are pulling my leg, aren't you?"

Sexton Blake proceeded just as if he had not heard the flow of protestation indulged in by the other.

"To take a concrete instance," he murmured, "I have discovered that preparations have been made to dispose of an expensive trinket, now in the possession of Countess Gulliver, whose house you and I and many others are visiting this evening. That is an effect of which, if I mistake not, you are the cause."

Splendid work!

In my hiding-place, I nearly betrayed Rock and myself by applauding.

So Sexton Blake had stumbled upon the same evidence as I had. He knew, as I did, something of the machinery which had been set in movement, to take those precious stones from a certain point to a foreign country, where ultimately they would be disposed of.

Rock had brought his criminal doings to such a fine art that he contracted to dispose of his spoils before he had obtained them.

He did not know what failure was; but, it seems, he was getting careless. For Blake knew, and I knew. Another thing, which, it may be, both of us were aware of, was that if Rock had made up his mind upon a course of action, that course of action would follow.

His face belied him.

I think that, years before, the true spirit which inhabited the body of Rock had died, and the spirit of some long-dead malefactor had taken its place; or else he had solved the secret of dual existence, and was able to contain the intellect of Hyde within the body of Jekyll.

Of course, he was frankly astonished and amused, and all sorts of things, at Blake's insinuation; but he charitably overlooked it—or so he said—in his pleasure at meeting the great man.

I laughed where I stood, not ten feet away from them behind the inner door.

I saw before me a night of sensation and event.

Rock had virtually accepted a challenge to relieve the Countess Gulliver of her diamonds; and I had made up my mind to relieve Rock of the Countess' diamonds when once he had them. That alone was an act almost tantamount to suicide; and, with Sexton Blake looking on, it promised to be a diversion of the most agreeable kind.

I was delighted, also, at the equivocal situation in which Rock found himself.

He longed, I don't doubt, to hand me over to the police; but he couldn't do that without giving himself away. To do that would not only occasion the question of what relations he, the respectable Mr. Park, had with a notorious criminal, but, also, he would be risking such revelations as to his activities as I was in a position to make.

"I wanted, above all," Blake was saying, "to have a look at you, Mr. Park, and I am glad that I have seen you. For the present, I will say good-night. Good-night! In all probability we shall meet again."

"Most certainly," burbled Rock. "And although you have hinted at some unkind things which I do not properly understand, permit me to say that I shall be delighted. It is a bal masque, as you are probably aware, so there is some probability, my dear sir, of our not, recognising each other. I must inform you that I shall be attired as a black Mephistopheles."

"And I," returned the private detective, "as a Crusader."

And now I guessed, although I could not see, that Blake had turned towards the door.

Our cards are upon the table and the game may begin.

Rock, so far as I could make out, followed the detective out of the door and down the staircase.

I could hear him saying as he went that he could not understand, but that he was most delighted, most charmed and most honoured—the most this and the most that, until the two were out of earshot.

I returned to the outer room—the room in which Rock had received me.

For a moment or two I had the room to myself, and I looked at it, interestedly.

Was it possible that in this intimate sanctum of Rock's there was no single thing which would give hint away? And I believed then, as I believe now, that there was no single thing.

Rock took leave of me with compliments and expressions of good will only less extravagant than those with which he had favoured Blake.

Even to me he acted a part.

That he was acting, and not his real self, I am well aware, and he must have known even then that he had no chance of deceiving me; yet, I suppose, the impersonation of a fool was to him almost second nature. He literally could not help it.

I was so far from being deceived that I heaved a sigh of relief when found myself, a living man, in the street out side his residence; and I was reassured, for Sudden-Death David had made two mistakes already in my experience—and for him to make mistakes was a new thing.

His star was waning.

One mistake was when he allowed his preparations for the disposal of the diamonds to become known to become known to the under world; and another mistake—one, to me, infinitely more amusing was his statement that he world appear at the bal masque as a black Mephistopheles; for in the box which I carried quite openly beneath my arts was the costume which he had intended to wear, and I knew that at that late hour he would probably be unable to obtain another.

Woolf's, the theatrical costumiers, had, as I knew, remained opened to a late hour for the convenience of those who were going to the Countess Gulliver's.

By now their door would he locked and their salesmen gone; and the same thing would doubtless apply to other of their faculty in the West End.

True, the costume of a black Mephistopheles is not uncommon. There might be hundreds in existence; but Rock had only an hour in which to find one, and I thought he would have difficulty.

My friend of the taxicab was waiting in the street outside.

By now I calculated he had an account against me for at least ten shillings; and as the reader knows, I was still in a condition of absolute penury.

Before the night was out it was mine intention to become possessed of jewels worth thousands; but, at that moment I was not possessed of so much as one penny-piece. Nevertheless, to a man who has the audacity of proposing to rob Rock, such minor difficulties are the salt of life.

I asked to be driven to the Wayfarers' Club—a useful institution, this Wayfarers' Club, because its members are scattered about the ends of the earth, and the officials do not know them.

I hall then, as the reader is aware, no possession beyond the contents of the cardboard box which I had misappropriated, and the very satisfactory evening gear in which I was attired.

It was necessary for me, not only to pay the taximan, but also to change in comfort into the costume of a harlequin.

I thought that for this purpose the Wayfarers' Club would be ideal, and so it was.

To the commissionaire, who hurried out to the kerb as soon as my taxicab had stopped outside the portals of that august institution, I said: "Pay this man, will you, and order me another cab in half an hour's time."

Taking his assent for granted, I passed into the club and desired to be in possession of its dressing-room. The attendant hesitated.

"You are a member, sir?"

The misfortune of my being an albino caused me to be remembered, and the man had very rightly come to the conclusion that he had never seen me before.

I looked at him, angry, astonished.

My hauteur was, although I say it. Impressive.

He apologised.

We have so many members," he explained. "Please come this way, sir." And I must say that he did his best to atone for his insolence.

Half an hour later, when, in the chequered finery of a harlequin, I entered a second taxicab, I had left behind me an evening suit which would certainly pay the club for my entertainment.

The costume of a black Mephistopheles, of which I had deprived Rock, I left there also; and in addition, two other costumes which the box contained —costumes of which I did not know the meaning.

It was the outfit appropriate to one of the King's musketeers, and implied either that Rock had intended to have a companion, or, what was more likely, that during the evening he had planed to change for his own purposes from one costume into another.

If that had been his intention, he was doubly thwarted, and I was doubly pleased.

Of Rock's personal gear I has taken only the rapier, which goes with the costume of a musketeer, and thrust it down the centre of the paper-covered lath which I carried, in my character of a harlequin.

I love the rapier. It was by chance a genuine weapon, and the possession of this yard of flexible steel gave me a feeling of security.

I carried a weapon which Rock would never suspect, and that was all to the good.

Again, at the Countess Gulliver's, I caused a servant to pay for the taxicab.

A trifle of audacity rendered this an easy matter, and the fellow no doubt recouped himself out of some reserve which the Countess provided for such eventualities.

Within the ball-room one of the two hired bands was hard at it; and, as I bowed over the Countess' hand, secure behind my mask, I could hear a foxtrot in progress in the recesses of her palatial house.

Countess Gulliver's was the place of which Queen Victoria was reputed to have said, "I have come from my house to your palace," and this elegant compliment had not lacked justification.

The wide, lofty rooms, with their ceilings, columns and plaster— of gilded acanthus leaves, seemed to be innumerable; and her hospitality was so lavish that her guests were conscious of no restraint.

By midnight over a hundred people were dancing; and the colour, and the music, and the perfume of flowers within the heated rooms created an atmosphere of exotic pleasure which entered the blood.

Blake, broad-shouldered and costumed as a Crusader, with his more lightly-built assistant in the garb of a man-at-arms, were easily recognisable: but Rock I had not identified.

The fumes of an opium cigarette—the accursed and beloved drug which transforms for me a sordid and shameful world into an elysium—was in my brain, and for an hour or more I allowed myself to forget.

The Countess herself, attired as a shepherdess, and wearing around her neck the pendant of pink diamonds which I had come to steal, moved freely among her guests, easily recognizable, despite the domino which covered the upper part of her face.

There were, of course, the usual attendant detectives costumed like revellers, but betrayed by their watchfulness and decorum; and, also, I noticed that Blake, the Crusader, watched the Countess wherever she went.

I could see that, like myself, he was ignorant of the time whoch Rock would shoose for his theft' and I abandoned myself—yes, I admit it—to the opium dreams which drifted in upon my consciousness, so that I moved like one in a dream. Knowing not which was fact and which was fact, which were living dancers and, which were the living dancers and which were the fictious created by the drug.

Happiness?Yes, of a sort.The only happiness I know save one, and that last is the happiness of mortal combat.

At the moment when the hour of one was chimed by a little silver clock in the alcove whither I had pursued a too beautiful naiad, who may, or may not, have been it creature of flesh and blood, I knew that my second happiness was to follow close upon the first, for l heard the voice of Sudden-Death David near to my ear.

"Yon have won the wager," he said as I turned. "I am not, as you see, a black Mephistopheles, but have accepted a costume appropriately resembling your own—being, in fact, a pantaloon. We will drink a bottle of champagne together. Who knows"—and he sniggered—"it may be your last."

THE FOURTH CHAPTER.

UNMASKED!

WHEN Park, or Rock, or Sudden-Death David, or whatever his name was, asked me to share with him a bottle of champagne, adding in his colourless voice, "that it might be my last," I was glad that, inside file paper lath, which I carried as part of my fancy costume, I had the rapier which I had annexed from among the other's belongings.

I have read of the villain who makesone turn cold at. a word—who hasn't? But never before or since have I met one, excepting Rock.

He could do just that, and he had the most vapid way of saying the most atrocious things.

What made it horrible was that one knew that, in the same careless, offhand way, he would do the most atrocious things.

Human life is nothing to me myself.

I am beyond the pale; how should I value life? But I snare, when I can, human happiness.

Rock neither spared nor cared for anything— life, happiness, nor decency.

Some freak of fate had given him the face of a pleasant fool and the brain of a malevolent scientist.

Had I not known hint, he would have moved me to laughter. As it was, he moved me to a most intense hatred.

Then and there, as I at opposite to him, drinking the champagne which a servant had brought, I hoped not only that I should succeed in robbing him, but that he would endeavour to stop me.

At the same time, now that I was opposed to this incalculable man, I felt nothing of that calm certitude which is mine as a rule, even in the most difficult circumstances.

I cannot say that I was afraid.

Fear is a sensation which I have not really experienced, but I was—how shall we put it?—uneasy; and by all the gods, I was right to e uneasy; and, by all the gods, I was right to be uneasy.

"A thousand pardons, good people, if the descent of a poor harlequin from Olympus has alarmed you," said Zenith, with an exaggerated bow. The lady laughed merrily. . . . " How, sir, did you mount to the roof of our car ? "

The unexpected—that was Rock's speciality. He sprang it on me now.

"I think," he said, in his mincing voice, "that your object in accepting the invitation of the Countess Gulliver was to rob that lady of her pink diamonds? How you obtained the invitation I don't know, and I don't want to know, and I don't want to know, nor how you reconcile it to your code to abuse hospitality; but, if you want the diamonds—"

He offered me his tortoiseshell cigarette case with the natural action of one offering a cigarette, and allowed me to glimpse, wrapped in cotton-wool, behind the elastic band which normally would have confined his cigarettes, at those half-dozen pink diamonds, which were excelled by no other jewels upon earth.

He closed the case again and passed it over to me.

"A very nice case," he said. "The 'cigarettes,' perhaps, are to your liking?"

This is too much for me.

I know there is a catch somewhere, but, whatever his bluff is, I buy it.

I take the raise with a short word of thanks, and drop it into the pocket which I have found in the hem of the loose cloak which is part of my costume.

"And now," he says, with a grimace of pretended sorrow, "we shall be losing the pleasure of your company."

I shake my head.

"No, I don't think I shall Leave you just yet."

The thought comes into my mind that here is it reason for the strange gift.

Rock wants a free hand for some super-villainy, and, in order to obtain this free hand, he is buying me off with a prince's ransom.

That is one theory.

Then there is another which crosses my mind.

Suppose Sexton Blake, the detective, is on to Rock? Suppose he knows that Rock has got the Countess's diamonds, then, in passing them to me, Rock has saved himself.

In touching the things at all, when Blake had, foreknowledge of his intention, he has been unspeakably rash.

Even he could not hope to leave the house with the jewel in his possession.

Yes, one of those two theories, I am certain, is at the hack of Rock's action.

Either he needs to be rid of me, or dreads a show-down. In any case, I determine to thwart him, and take pleasure in the determination.

Whatever the effect he desires to achieve by thus passing the jewels to me, that effect he shall fail to achieve. I will see to it.

"You had better go," says Rock, reading my intention as soon as I have half an hour from now, a. gong will be sounded, and, when the gong is sounded, all will unmask. Sexton Blake is here, and at least two Scotland Yard men. They will recognize you on the spot."

I get up from the table.

"Perhaps you are right," I tell him, and move away; but I have no intention of going right then.

He calls me back for a moment.

"One word." he whispers. "If, as you pass out, you think it necessary to bid adieu to your hostess, you will observe that, to all appearance, she is still wearing her diamond pendant. Be at case. Like most famous jewels, her pendant has it duplicate of paste. There has been a substitution. She I wearing the paste, but believes she is wearing the diamonds. One thing more—"

He pats me on the arm with offensive familiarity.

"As I did not pay for the champagne which we have just consumed, I have not settled my wager with you; but I will settle it—I will settle it, never fear,"

and. with a gust of windy laughter, the lean and skippered pantaloon hurried away to join the revels within the ball —room.

When I deal with nun » ho are my equals in intelligence, and something more than equal in intrigue—and to deal with such then is a real pleasure—I make the rule of always doing the un-expected thing.

I owe my life a hundred tinges over to this particular device— That of not doing what my enemies expect roe to do.

Now I did the last thin, which Pock would have imagined possible. He himself hat! put, the idea into to head whelk he said: "I don't know how you reconcile it with your cone to abuse hospitality."

It had not struck me in that way and I was grateful to hire—yea, even to hint —that he had saved me front a churlish act.

I had not, it is true, stolen the Countess' diamonds myself; but they had been stolen and as her guest, I was in honor bound to return them to her.

A further incentive to this, if I must be perfectly frank, was that such —an act would be un-expected by Rock, and might cause to go astray .sonic deeper, subtler scheme which he was, I did not doubt, about to put into operation.

I knew enough of .Rock to believe that, if the theft of the Countess' diamonds had been his objective on that night, he would have done anything rather than hand the diamonds to me .

He had undoubtedly intended to steal them all along, but when I had supposed that theft to be his final object. I had made a mistake—a mistake which Sexton Blake had shared with me.

I saw now that there was something else afoot and by returning the diamonds, and so cancelling out the first move of the grade he was playing, I might frustrate the whole.

With how I was to come out of if, except with an escort of police officers, I did not for the moment concern my-self.

I found the Countess in a corner of the ball-room, talking sedately to an old friend of her husband's.

She was still in the twenties, and an adorable girl, full to the brim with life and laughter, but for the moment she was quiet, and even anxious in her manner knew, as all the world I knew, that her husband was then at Geneva, and that, as the emissary of Great Britain, he bore a burden of responsibility almost unique in the annals of states-manship

It had been such a sudden call, this that had taken hint from the side of his young wife of the eve of their bag masque, and his wife had reason to be anxious for, according to the action which he took upon his mission would depend the repute with posterity of the name which was his and hers also.

I noticed that she was wearing around her neck a replica of the pendant which I carried in the cigarette-case within the pocket of my cloak, and I wondered, as I have wondered since, which was the original and which the paste imitation.

It would have been a device after Rock's own heart to send me away with the paste imitation and secure the real stones for himself.

"Your ladyship," I said, "will pardon the poor harlequin, bud: he pleads for a word apart with Your gracious self."

The girl flashed at me that frank, winsome smile which has won the hearts of all who have known her.

"The poor harlequin," she said—and she little knew how poor the harlequin really was— "the poor harlequin shall have with my 'gracious self the word that he craves."

She inclined her head in a gesture of dismissal to her cavalier, and he, after one curious glance, withdrew out of ear-shot and stood watching.

This bal masque had been made such a huge affair that it was almost as mixed as a subscrip-tion dance and the man was doubtless concerned for my behavior.

The harlequin wishes," I said, "to return to your ladyship a trinket which may, or may not, be of value." And unostentatiously as possible, I offered her the brilliant; which Rock had given me.

She uttered an exclamation of surprise.

"But how careless of my maid, that must be the pasts imitation of my penchant. Where, may I ask, did you find it, friend marquis?"

"It was given me," I told her, "by one who, like myself, has the honor to be your guest. He, like myself, was masked; and I — let us say that I have forgotten him."

Up till then the girl had been laughing at my ri-diculous pose, but suddenly she became grave—almost suspicious.

"There's a mystery here," she said slowly."May I know who you are, sir?"

I made her a bow and a fantastic flourish of my paper baton — that seeming harmless weapon which contained a flexible rapier blade.

"I pray your ladyship, of your clemency not to ask it. I have—alas that—I should put it—ren-dered you some very trifling service in returning this pendant, which resembles the one you wear. In return for that service may I ask permission to retain my in-cognito?"

In the hope that the episode would end in laugh-ter I sank on one knee and made her a gesture of mock submission. Countess Gulliver was not to be moved from her intention so easily.

"Sir," she returned, "you pique my curiosity and I demand—you, as your hostess—I demand that, you for one moment, remove your mask. See... I will be fair with you. I also will unmask." She whipped the domino from her brow and looked at me, laughing.

The beauty of the Countess Gulliver was re-markable. As a debutante she had set the Court raving. As it bride she had bereft the newspapers of superlatives; and I, Zenith, am not blind.

When she looked at me, face to face, with laughter in her eyes so astonishingly blue, I could not possibly have refused, had the act asked been my last act on earth. That it might indeed be my last act, or nearly, was not in doubt for not a hundred feet away I could see the Cru-sader, Sexton Blake, his white surcoat, and with crimson cross upon his breast, watching us.

Perhaps he had already begun to suspect; and when I removed the black cacique which covered both my head and my face he would know me.

It addition to himself and his assistant there were in that throng a round half dozen of Scotland Yard detectives, any of whom would recognize me on the instant.

Also, there were at least a hundred men, guests of the Countess, who would count it a virtuous act to help the police in bringing me down.

Nevertheless, I took the risk with both eyes open.

"When," said I, "her ladyship so far condescends it is not for the poor harlequin to refuse. Perhaps, however, he will be forgiven if he asks a boon in return."

"Methinks," returned the lady, "the poor harlequin doth stipulate too adroitly. Nevertheless I will hear what boon it is that he asks."

"He asks," I told her, "one dance—the dance which is just beginning," and without waiting for her answer I removed the casqued from my head meeting the eyes of Sexton Blake across the room.

A moment later I took the Countess— in my arms—I had sold my freedom.

Sexton Blake saw and understood.

Sportsman that he was, and is, he made no attempt to mar the rapture of those minutes which followed : only as I again met his eye, he pointed significantly towards the anteroom at this front of the house, and I nodded to show that I understood.

To be generous, to recognize— in a common thief, the same generosity and sportsmanship, that is something more.

Sexton Blake had paid me that compliment.

He was determined, of course, to effect my arrest, but he had desired that the Countess Gulliver's reception should not be scarred by any untoward incident; therefore he had made it clear to rendezvous at that distant ante-room, hung with blue brocade, knowing that when the dance was ended I should meet him there.

The girl had gasped with astonishment at the crimson eyes and the white hair: but after that I think the rhythm of the dance had taken hold of her senses and she forgot with whom she was dancing.

Such a dance! I have never met her like. That dancing which is the idealised interpretation of music—to such she lent herself with consummate understanding. I had sold my freedom, perhaps, for that dance: but I will not say that I had done ill to do so.

It was not until the first encore was half finished that she spoke.

"You," she said softly, gently, "you are an albino. There, is—forgive me—another albino they are talking about now named Monsieur Zenith."

I laughed, and for once, I believe, there was happiness in that laughter. "I am Monsieur Zenith, the mountebank, the adventurer, the thief: but madam, I am also your servant."

Some women would have stopped the dance, or at least have broken from the arms of such a man as I described my-self to be. But she, the Countess, had never such understanding.

Perhaps even she was thrilled a little by this momentary contact with a notorious man.

She danced, I think, even better after the revelation.

"And," she went on, "now that you have unmasked, others will recognize you just as I did."

I told her that that was of importance but she saw at once the implications of the fact.

"And it was I," she "said "who made you unmask! I have caused you to bury yourself."

Again I murmured some expostulation telling her the truth, that I did not care—that the moment was worth the price I might have to pay.

We danced in silence for a bar or so, and then some generous impulse made her stop against a small doorway used by the servants.

"Go through that doorway," she whispered hurriedly, "and you will find yourself upon an unfrequented staircase which leads to the street. Go. And—" the last words were almost in-audible—"good luck to you"

"Madam," I said, " with every moment that passes, the poor harlequin is losing a moment in Olympus. He cannot go because, for one thing, he is to dance with you; and, for another thing, he has an appointment which must be kept."

"With whom," she questioned, as we resumed the dance, "with whom is your appointment? With one of those charming nymphs or shepherdesses who are my guests to-night?"

"Alas, no, madam! My appointment—the appointment which I must keep—is with the private detective, Mr. Sexton Blake." She was surprised.

"Is he then a friend of yours?"

What was the reply to that?

"In a sense," I told her, "yes, he is."

But it was his life, or mine that night; and I knew it.

THE FIFTH CHAPTER.

JULIA FORTUNE.

When the music had stopped; and when, taking advantage of the masquerade, I had dared to kiss the hand of the Countess, I took leave of her and entered the large ante-room, now empty save for one man. That man was, as I knew it would be, Sexton Blake.

I locked the door behind me and threw the key upon the door, placing my foot upon it and looking Sexton Blake in the face.

"May I ask, my dear Blake, whether your counter of a Crusader incongruously includes an automatic pistol, because if it does, I am at a serious disadvantage?"

Blake smiled with the charm which always appealed even to mine.

"It does not."

So, when he might have had half a dozen companions, had he chosen, Sexton Blake had elected to wait there alone, unarmed save for the wooden property sword which hung at his girdle; and not knowing whether I carried a weapon or not.

I bowed my acknowledgment of his courage.

"I, too, am unprovided with a pistol, Sexton Blake; but, as I give you fair warning. I am not unarmed; and, if you stand between me and freedom, your life will be in danger. Between those heavy brocaded curtains: upon the front, wall, there is a window, and beyond that a balcony. It is my purpose to make my escape by means of that balcony; and, as I have to-night less than my usual desire to kill you, I hope you will not endeavour to prevent me."

It was useless; and I knew it would be useless.

His rush was as sudden as the striking of a snake. So sudden that I had to shorten the rapier to meet it and, but for the wooden sheath which concealed the blade, he would have died there and then.

As it was, the thing acted as a button to my weapon and the point barely touched him.

I put my foot upon the sheath and wrenched the flexible blade free then, bringing it above my head, I made him the fencer's salute: "A la mort!"—to the death!

He had nothing but his two hands and a wooden sword against the rapier; but, beyond the doors, he had a hundred allies: and I, so far as I knew, had not a friend in the world.

No; the odds were not so unequal as they seemed.

Before the locked door was discovered and the alarm given, I had, perhaps, two or three minutes.

During that time I had to kill my man and make an escape from a window the height and situation of which I did not know.

And then began the strangest duel in which it has been my lot to take part—wooden sword against rapier; and it was I who gave ground.

Yes, he knew something about sword-play, did Sexton Blake.

I am no stranger to the rapier and I have a wrist like steel; but he held his own. and more than held his own, across the full width of that wide floor. Although I was untouched, the point of his wooden sword threatened me every step of the way.

It must have been a strange sight, there in the blue brocaded room under the dim light of the shaded electrics and with the purple night there outside beyond the balcony.

Theatrical, I doubt not, except that no stage would feature so bizarre a combat.

Backwards and forwards we fought. There had come a knocking at the door; and now someone with a heavy weapon was battering there to break the door down.

When he succeeded, that would be the end.

Unless I could force my tray through the iron defence of that silent self-controlled Crusader I was doomed to an attack from all sides.

Up till then I had been fencing, confident that in the end, I could achieve my desire, which was to kill Sexton Blake without being touched myself.

I was, I suppose, anxious to assure myself, after the event, that, even had Sexton Blake possessed the rapier himself, the result would have been the same: but now I ignored the wooden sword, and set myself to break down Blake's defence by any means, however clumsy.

And I could not do it.

Twice he touched me, once upon the arm and once upon the breast.

Each time I gave him the fencer's acknowledgment; "Touché!" and the appropriate salute; and each time I returned with a fixed intention of sheathing my rigid weapon in his heart.

The combat ended in a way neither Blake nor myself could have foreseen.

A fierce lunge on my part, and a parry on his; and the point of my weapon embedded itself in the bill of the wooden sword.

At the same moment the lock of the door was burst, probably by means of some instrument like a jemmy: and a crowd of determined men rushed in.

I could see that they knew who I was; and were prepared to round me up with a minimum of delay.

It was Tinker, Sexton Blake's assistant, whom I had to thank for that, I doubt not.

I made a feint of using my fists, which, if it did nothing else, distracted Blake's attention; and then, not knowing the height of the balcony, nor what lay beyond, I rushed through the curtains and jumped into the darkness of the night outside.

It was not suicide.

At least, I fear death more than I fear life.

It was the result of that choice which any wild creature will make between captivity and a forlorn hope.

I jumped, as it happened, straight into the flexible branches—around the top of a tall tree—a birch-tree, as I discovered afterwards, which stood in the grounds which fronted the Countess' mansion.

As I clung to it, slipping downwards and seeking vainly to obtain foothold or handhold among its slender branches, the tree bent sideways and over, under the impact of my jump, and the strain my weight upon its summit, depositing me at last within the branches of a second and smaller tree some twenty feet beyond.

So, under the light of the stars and the glow of street electrics, the lissom and glittering form of the unfortunate harlequin travelled a wide arc through again the air ; then fell and travelled again, falling a second time—for the age

of miracles is not yet over—out to the roof of a passing car.

It was by no intention of mine, I can assure you, that I fell there instead of into the dust of the roadway, eight feet-below, not was I in a position to control the manner of my falling.

It is not pleasant to recall, but for ten seconds or more I must have lain there spread-eagled and glittering like a starfish dashed by the waves upon a rock where presently the sun will destroy both his colours and him.

In that ten seconds the car upon which I was an unintentional passenger had travelled some distance away from the scene of my acrobatic incident; and when, with a tremendous grinding of brakes, the vehicle was brought to a standstill, I was perfectly ready to deal with the situation—readier, perhaps, than the charming couple who left the vehicle at the sound of my fall, in order to stare at what, was for them, the most unexpected sight in the World—a harlequin in all his finery standing upright, with folded arms, upon the roof of their car.

They had more reason for surprise than had I, for I had some idea as to what was within the car—what was within any good make of car within the West End at that hour—and they had not the least idea what was upon the roof. So, rather nervous lest a bunch of detectives burst into sight, I hasten to reconcile these good people to the situation.

"A thousand pardons, good people," I intoned, with an exaggerated bow, "if the descent from Olympus of a poor harlequin has alarmed you!"

The lady laughs merrily.

She is a blonde, and I detest blondes, but she has a roguish face, which atones somewhat.

"I was not aware," she says, "that poor harlequins had any association with Olympus. How, sir, did you mount to the roof of our car?"

"Madam, my words are truer than you suppose. I did not mount to the roof of your car. I descended thereto from—up there!"

And I pointed at the stars paling in the dawn above my head.

"And now," pursues the lady, "that you have boarded it in this delightfully unconventional fashion, what do you propose we should do—drive on and use you as a mascot, or drop you somewhere where you can rid yourself of your motley?"

I see clearly that if they don't drive on, and that pretty soon, I am in for another flutter Sexton Blake, always supposing that that astute detective should credit the amazing fact that I had escaped with my life.

I need, above all things, that they shall drive on; but how to get down to it, that is the question.

"After three a.m.," I tell her, "and until the dawn, the world is topsy-turvy, and the poor harlequin is king. The commands of King Harlequin are that you drive on, and carry him with fitting Majesty whither you will."

She would have spoken again, but I ventured to cut her short.

"Drive on," I say. "It pleases me that you drive on instantly."

Childish nonsense, certainly, but it served its turn.

The lady curtseys gratefully. She has fallen in with my humour.

"Your commands, sire, shall be obeyed," she tells me. "Come Charles," this to her companion; and the two enter the car, which again moves in the direction it had taken before.

Who are they? I wonder. Who is the sullen man in evening clothes, who does not speak, and obeys his companion so unquestioningly? Who is this roguish blonde?

I think that somewhere I have seen her before.

It is a saloon car, and I sit cross-legged upon its domed body, meting the curious glances of the few people who are aboard with a careless indifference which is real enough.

Certainly my description must be known to every policeman in the country, and to a lot of people who have nothing to do with the police; but which of them would be mad enough to suppose that I, with a price on my head, should thus invite attention?

Just as there are two ways of saying nothing, talking too much and talking too little, so there are so there are two ways of avoiding recognition—hiding, or inviting inspection.

I do the latter.

The madness of motley, I think, burns through to the inner recesses of the brain.

More than that, it has an aura wide-spread and permeating.

I will swear that before we reached our journey's end—which turned out to be a night club—both the man Charles and his delightful companion were infected by the spirit of carnival; and, finding me still there upon the top of the car, the girl utters a cry of delight, and even her companion succeeds in smiling.

"Your Majesty," she says, "must come with us. The entertainment cannot but be unworthy of your regal pomp, but your subjects need you. I am waiting to see you leap high in the air and descend, like a ballerina, upon the point of your toes, here in the street beside us."

I laugh—I, to whom real mirth is unknown—and her companion shivers, as men do when I am moved to laughter; but the girl's expression remained unchanged.

She awaited the finish of the acrobatic leap with which I humoured her; and, then, placing her fingers upon my shimmering and skin-tight sleeve, she led me towards the portal of the building which had been her destination.

The man Charles stood there watching us, in his usual sulky silence, and then followed.

In the glow of the electric lights within the vestibule the girl saw the crimson-irises eyes, with their white lashes and the stone-white hair of the albino; but she accepted them as part of an agreeable madness.

She had, I think—indeed, she have had—the illusion that I was part of a fantastic dream from which she would presently awaken, but which, for the time being, she was determined to enjoy.

The establishment was a large private house in one of the streets between Piccadilly and Pall Mall, and was ideal, I should imagine, largely for gaming.

As was inevitable, seeing the role I had to sustain, I took the entertainment into my own hands and promoted plentiful libations of champagne.

I had lost the cloak which I had worn at the bal masque: and I did not have to explain that I had no money.

The fact, I think, must not have been obvious, nor was money expected of me.

I had brought to that depressing bourgeois company an unexpected hour of masquerade; and they showed their gratitude in the only way possible, by making me free of their cellar and of all that therein was.

By four o'clock the fun was riotous.

The girl had remained at my side.

We had supped together and danced together; and—yes, we drank champagne together; and I found in her a partner quick to exploit any wildest audacity which was my whim.

I was, indeed King Fool! and my subjects were fools without exception.

It must have been at about a quarter-past four when the man Charles obtruded upon our foolery.

"Julia," he said touching the girl upon her shoulder, "it's nearly time now."

"Julia!"

At that one word I knew who she was, where I had seen her.

Strangely enough, none had mentioned the name in my hearing during that mad hour; and I had forgotten my first self-questioning as to where we had met.

"Julia!" I exclaimed, turning to the girl. "Of course, you are Julia Fortune."

"And," she said unexpectedly, "you have only just discovered that, Monsieur Zenith. Assuredly your memory is not complimentary to me?"

I forgot to answer.

My whole mind was taken up with the discovery that I had made.

She was Julia Fortune, adventuress. Friend of Sexton Blake, and member of the British Secret Service; and she knew me!

Why had she not walked quietly to the telephone when she had first perceived my identity, and passed the word to Scotland Yard?

It would have been easy; and, if she had done so, that night would have been my last; yet I was sure that she had not.

Even had Blake himself, and the half-dozen Scotland Yard men who trot so obediently at his heels, entered the room at that moment, I should have been certain that it was not she who had informed them of where I was to be found.

And, within five minutes, I knew that my behalf was justified.

The girl had need of me. She had fallen in with my whims; she had exploited my delight in the masquerade, and remained at my side, against this moment.

She turned to me with quite another expression upon her fact—the expression which belonged to the Julia Fortune whom I had known of old.

"We must go now," she said. "Do your excessively close-fitting garments provide accommodation for an automatic pistol, because if not—" and she, the beautifully dressed, delicate seeming lady of fashion, produced, from Heaven knows where, a small but efficient automatic and smuggled it into my hand.

Ah, but it felt good to have within my grasp powers of life and death over enemies; and, if need be, over self; and the lilting laughter of Julia Fortune, and the charm of her, and the spell of this night of madness burnt into my blood until, blonde as she was, I would have died to do her bidding; and she knew it.

Yes, by all the gods, she had a brain, had Julia Fortune!

"Follow me," she said, turning towards the door, never doubting that I should follow.

The man Charles had disappeared.

Who he was, I had no idea.

Probably some other agent of her Secret Service who had done with the silent efficiency of that organization what he was instructed to do; and had then, with the same efficiency, vanished from the scene of action which he was not concerned.

"You," says Julia Fortune, turning to me, "are an ally—unexpected but doubly welcome. You shall smoke one of those odious opium cigarettes of yours: and then, if you will, you may sleep. I ant going to drive the car with you for passenger. We have a long way to go."

I obeyed her. Why not?

She was incapable of betrayal; and I knew it.

The opium gave me sleep—gave me Visions—wonderful, alluring.

So, as the new-born day came, to rob the London streets of mystery, I sank gratefully into the depths of unconsciousness—to dream—to forget.

Beautiful white poppy, I thank thee!

The Sixth Chapter.

"Where's my guv'nor?"

SEXTON BLAKE, broad-shouldered and despite the combat in which he had just taken part, unshaken, stood on the small balcony opening out of the ante-room, and looked with amazement through the haze of the summer night at the scintillating figure of the harlequin, flying in midair, to disappear through a screen of leaves forty feet away front, and twenty feet below, the balcony whence he had made his suicidal leap.

The nearer tree, to which the albino had first clung, switched back into place and rocked into stillness.

The screen of leaves and small branches which had engulfed him rustled; and in their turn were still.

The detective re-entered the ball-room and made his way— slowly—through the great house and out into the forecourt in the soil of which those trees had their roots, walking across the dewy grass as far as the high iron railings which edged the street.

The albino was a menace to society; and it was one of the dearest wishes in Blake's lead to render it impossible for the master-crook to continue his criminal activities.

At, the same time, the charming personality of Zenith, and his extraordinary vitality, made Blake reluctant to find that once so brilliant creature smashed and dying on the railings beneath the trees.

It was almost with relife that Blake realised that the forecourts and the street, which was visible there from, were alike empty.

As he returned to the house, he beckoned to one of the plain-clothes men, whose disguise his observant glance had easily penetrated; and sent him to make further investigations as to the fate of Zenith.

It was a matter to which at any other time Sexton Blake would have given personal attention; but at that hour he had something even more important to attend to.

It must not be supposed that the matter which occupied Blake's mind was the audaciously pre-announced threat to steal the Countess' pendant.

As he had already allowed Rock to become aware, he knew that arrangements had been made in advance for the disposal of that article of jewellery: but he did not under-estimate Rock as to suppose that the man's villainy ended there.

The operations of Rock were on such a scale that even the theft of that priceless pendant would not attract him.

Blake knew; or, at least, suspected, that if Rock had desired only the pendant he would have set some highly trusted subordinate to steal it, —remaining himself safe from any breath of suspicion until he could conveniently handle the proceeds of the crime.

No, if Rock himself were interested, then the matter must be both difficult and important.

Blake had little more than intuition to go upon.

He knew nothing against Rock. Who did? He quite believed that Rock's affairs might be fully investigated, and the man himself cross-examined, without any fact transpiring which would justify his arrest.

The leaking out of the fact that arrangements had been made to dispose of the pendant, and the association of Rock's name with those arrangements, had, perhaps, been the only important mistake which that past-master of crime had committed during twenty years of villainy.

The moment had come for the un-masking of the guests; and Blake, when he at length returned to the ball-room, found Rock, cherubic and bland as ever, unmasked, and enjoying an animated conversation with the Countess herself.

She, at least, had no suspicion of the man's honesty.

Indeed, as it afterwards transpired, she had met him abroad and cultivated his acquaintance because he amused her. She did not credit him with much intelligence, but his foolery was of the kind which the young matron found attractive, and, as she cultivated amusing people, she had made a special point of sending an invitation to Rock.

It was a perfectly natural mistake.

Many cleverer people than the Countess Gulliver had been deceived, but it was a mistake which was to cost her dear.

Blake joined his assistant, Tinker, and the two talked together gravely.

For the last hour Tinker had been having a hectic time, inventing elaborations of the foxtrot; but now he gained from his employer the impression that something crucial was in the wind, and sobered accordingly.

What it was, Blake knew no more than he; but Blake knew that Rock had gone out of his way to be present at the Countess' ball, and already her guests were beginning to take their leave.

The time was at hand when Rock must surely betray his reason for desiring to be present; and that he would betray it. Blake did not doubt.

He knew little about Rock, but one thing that he did know was that the man, once committed to a line of action, would on no account withdraw.

Undoubtedly Rock was there for a purpose, and the moment when he would reveal that purpose could not be far distant.

The door of the ante-room, with its lock-rail broken, had been thrown back, and the duel which had taken place within the ante-room had been represented as a rather extreme bit of ragging.

Few of the Countess' guests had any idea that one of their number during the progress of the ball had attacked another with intent to kill, and, failing his intention, had leapt from the balcony, twenty or thirty-feet above the level of the ground.

Still less did they know that that individual, whose harlequinade they had enjoyed, was the notorious Monsieur Zenith.

Even the Countess did not realize how near she had been to tragedy. She was laughing gaily with Rock, and when the first bars of a popular dance tune were played by the orchestra she began to dance with him.

The floor was filled with kaleidoscopic figures, and the two detectives, standing against the far wall, lost sight, for the moment, of the man they were there to watch.

"You'd better dance," said Blake quickly. "You'll be able to watch our man much easier dancing than still."

Tinker agreed, and a moment later the lad was skilfully steering a partner towards that part of the large room where he expected to find Rock.

Tinker, wholesome, good-humored lad that he was, had no difficulty in finding a partner, but his search for Rock was completely unavailing. Where could the man be?

The first break came in the music, and Tinker stood beside his partner, awaiting the inevitable encore.

He happened to be near a chair, and, with a word of apology, he sprang on to the chair and looked around him.

One glance was enough.

The white head of the pantaloon, with its nodding question-mark of hair, was not to be seen, nor was the gaily ornate costume of the shepherdess.

Both Rock and his partner had completely disappeared.

It is to be supposed that Tinker's dismissal of his charming partner was not unnecessarily polite. It is to be supposed, also, that she forgave him, for from any decent-mannered lad like Tinker discourtesy was so unbelievable that one naturally supposed a sound excuse. That excuse the lad certainly had.

He hurried across the ball-room to where he had found Blake, and then skirted the walls, looking in vain for the white surcoat and red cross of the Crusader.

He stopped a stout, red-faced buccaneer, who was one of the Scotland Yard contingent, and asked him excitedly for news of Seaton Blake.

"Here, Coutts, where is my guv'nor?"

"I don't know," exploded Inspector Coutts, for it was none other than that worthy, "and I'll trouble you not to call me 'Coutts.' Mr. Coutts to you, my lad!"

"Anything you like," said Tinker, good-naturedly. "But where's my guv'nor, Cou—Mr. Coutts—where's my guv'nor? I was with him a moment ago. We were watching a fellow named Rock, who was dancing with the countess, and now I can't find either of them."

Inspector Coutts grunted. He did not take the revelation very seriously.

"Have you looked in the supper-room?"

"No; but I will."

Tinker was off in a moment.

"I think," said Inspector Coutts to himself, "that I will make investigations in the same direction. The Countess has a very sound champagne."

He was destined, however, not to drink further of the Countess' champagne during that night, for at the door he was met by Tinker, who hustled him back to the ball-room at a pace so rapid as to be undignified.

"Got it from a couple coming into the supper-room," said Tinker. "They saw my guv'nor break open that door which leads to servants' staircase. There's some trouble about, Coutts— Mr. Coutts, I mean — and I want you to come with me."

The door leading to the servant's staircase was a double one, the outer portion being decorated to match the rest of the ball-room, and the inner part being covered with green baize to deaden the sound of its opening and shutting, and to keep from the ears of the dancers the sounds of domestic operations.

Inspector Coutts and Tinker found the first door standing half open and the second one torn and splintered, where the lock had been wrenched from its fastenings.

On the floor beside it lay a broken wooden sword, which Tinker recognized as having been part of Sexton Blake's costume.

"That," said the lad, "supports the story that I overheard, that my guv'nor broke in this door' with his sword. There's something doing here, Coutts, we'd better follow up without losing time."

Inspector Coutts and Tinker found the outer door, which gave access to the ballroom.

He was now far too interested to notice whether Tinker gave him his proper title or not. He nodded in agreement with the lad's remarks.

"Yes; you're right. It looks to me as if the Countess is involved in some trouble. What did you say, was the name of the man who was dancing with her?"

"Park," replied the lad. "'Mr. Gilbert Park, of Upper Temple Street. Do you know him?

"Yes, I know him."

The inspector knew almost everyone in London—almost everyone who had aroused the interest of Scotland Yard, at any rate.

"I don't think he can be involved. He's a perfectly straight man. There's no doubt of that," he added.

Tinker, as he hurried down the stairs towards the ground level in advance of the inspector, was guilty of a smile of derision.

Sexton Blake had informed his assistant earner in the day that Park was a very dangerous criminal; and Tinker would never admit that it was possible for his guv'nor to be wrong.

Nevertheless he did not stop to argue. He realized that this was a time for deeds, not words.

At the foot of the stairs they came upon the prostrate body of the Countess' butler. He was breathing heavily, and insensible, his open eyes showing only the whites.

"Black-jacked," said the inspector succinctly.

A black-jack is a short length of hosepipe drawn over an iron bar; and with such a weapon the unfortunate butler had been battered into unconsciousness.

A locked door dividing the servants' quarters front the kitchen offices was being heavily pounded from within; and, while Inspector Coutts proceeded to find the key and liberate the servants who had been imprisoned there, Tinker, acting upon intuition, threw open a heavy door leading to the street and ran at top speed towards a large touring-car which even then was moving away.

The driver was changing gears; and this fact enabled Tinker to lay a hand actually upon the back of the car.

He was not sure, of course, that this vehicle was in any way connected with the tragic occurrence which had evidently taken place at the house of the Countess; but he suspected that such was the case, and was very anxious to resolve his doubts by inspecting the interior of the car.

This, however, he could not do.

The speed accelerated rapidly; and although with one hand upon the spare tyre at the back he contrived to keep pace for a few yards, he was forced to let go and have the mortification of seeing the car disappear with its mystery in the maze of London streets where, among thousands of other cars, its identity would be lost.

In that few seconds when Tinker had been in touch with the car he had taken the only means which occurred to his ready wits of securing that it should be readily identified, by hanging the silver-painted casque, which had covered his head, upon the iron triangle which indicated that the car had four-wheel brakes.

He turned back to find Inspector Coutts standing at the still open door of the side entrance to the big house.

"Have you discovered anything of my guv'nor?" he asked. "Or the Countess; or Park?"

"Your guv'nor," Coutts told him sadly, "was set on by several men the moment he passed through the broken door. Some of the servants saw it. What has become of him now I don't know. My theory is that he was carried out to that car you just followed, and the Countess with him. Where Park is, I have not the least idea.

"That stunt," added the inspector, "of branding the car by means of your helmet, or whatever you call it, was not at all a bad one, young Tinker. I am going up to the phone; and I'm going to give orders that the number and direction of that car shall be noted by all police within the metropolitan area. It means a general warning; but I think the chief will stand for it. As the reports come in we shall get some idea of the direction which the car has taken".

"And now," he finished, "I am going over this ground again to see what we can discover. Up to the present the whole thing is a mystery."

Tinker was about to follow the inspector into the interior of the building when he noticed the motionless figure of a man leaning some fifty yards away against the high wall which surrounded the grounds of the estate.

This man, who was the only human being in the quiet street where they were, had the appearance of having been there for some time.

Tinker walked quickly in his direction.

"You saw just now," he said to the man, "a large car drive away from this house. You saw me run after it, I daresay. I am working with the police. I want you to tell me, if you can, exactly the description of the people who travelled in that car."

The man was of the kind who hangs about all the neighbourhood of important social functions in the hope of making a shilling by opening a door or running a message.

"I don't know anything," was his reply. "I only just come along, guv'nor. I don't know nothing at all about it."

The statement was a lie. That much was evident. It was evident, also, that the man did not care whether Tinker recognized it as the lie it was.

Tinker understood as well as if the man had uttered the words, that what he really said was: "Excuse me, I think it better not to be mixed up in this affair at all."

Tinker drew a ten-shilling note from his waistcoat pocket and allowed the man a glimpse of it.

"Think again!" he invited.

"I tell you," the man repeated, angrily this time, "I wasn't here, and so I don't know nothing."

Tinker turned away, disappointed and anxious.

He was beginning to have the feeling that the force to which his guv'nor was opposed in this matter was powerful and inscrutable beyond ordinary.

"'Ere, 'arf a mo', guv'nor!"

Tinker turned back to face the lounger.

"What I really want," said the man, "is to deliver a message. I've got to drop a parcel on a man somewhere around here and I can't read the address. Would you mind having a look at it?"

He fumbled in his coat-pocket and produced a fragment of paper which appeared to have been torn from a Memorandum book.

"These foreign names," the man continued, "don't 'arf puzzle me. You wouldn't mind 'aving a look at, it, would yer."

Tinker did mind.

He was in a desperate hurry and very anxious to find out additional facts concerning Sexton Blake's disappearance; but, being a decent youngster, and having come to the conclusion that he might have wronged the man by his suspicions he turned back, took the slip of paper and carried it to the light of a street lamp.

"Number of car, x15872, and colour navy, Six-seater, Five men and lady. The lady and one man apparently insensible. Danger. Say nothing."

Two ordinary domestic pins had been thrust into the bottom edge of the sheet so that the points just touched and their lengths made two sides of a triangle.

Tinker recognized what was, for the time being, that means of recognition between members of the British Secret Service which had been invented by the mysterious No. 2A, their leader and was changed by him almost from day to day.

Despite the fact that the message was ominous, it brought the lad a measure of comfort.

If the British Secret Service, silent, efficient, resourceful and immeasurably powerful, were interested in this matter then he possessed a powerful ally which could be relied upon.

"No," he returned, playing to perfection the part which had been indicated by the supposed lounger. "I'm afraid I can't read it any more than you can. You'd better go back to the man who sent you, and get him to repeat it.

"The number," he added, "is evidently twelve—number twelve."

"Well there," said the other, "that shows how bad the writing is. I thought it was twenty-seven."

The lounger slouched away into the darkness, and Tinker re-entered the house.

A casual observer would not have realized, first, that Tinker had obtained the information which he desired; and second, that two members of the British Secret Service, No. 12 and No. 27 respectively, had informed each other as to their identities.

The grey light of dawn was coming through the eastern sky, and the stars were paling when Tinker returned to the house.

The ball-room was almost empty; and, away in front of the mansion, car after car was departing with the last of the Countess' guests.

After a short interview with Inspector Coutts, front whom he obtained no additional information, the lad passed across the ball-room and went in search of the overcoat which he had worn over his fancy costume when, in their taxi-cab, he and Blake had travelled to the bal masque.

One other was even then taking a heavy cloak from the footman who had charge of such garments, and, to his astonishment, Tinker recognized Park—the last man whom he had expected to see there.

"I say," said Park, with his never-failing geniality, "do you happen to know what has become of our hostess? Everybody's asking. She seems to have disappeared."

Tinker watched him intently.

"Yon should know that," he said.

Park's astonishment was so perfectly done that the lad almost believed it.

"I—I assure you I have not the least idea. What makes you think that I might have?"

"Because you were dancing with her one minute before her disappearance."

"Was I? I had no idea of that. Do you mean to say—"

The man stopped, and a look of astonishment came into his face.

"Why, I remember now! She was dancing with me, and then, quite suddenly, she left me and went through the door towards the servants' quarters. Do you mean to say that she's not been seen since?"

"I do," replied Tinker. "I mean to say just that."

The other shrugged his shoulders.

"'Ah, well, it's very late. She may have been seized by a headache, and turned in. One cannot blame her. I'm hoping within the next few minutes to do the same. Good-night, young sir! Good-night!"

Tinker watched the man waiting within the vestibule until his car had drawn up at the porte-cochere.

The lad himself summoned the taxicab which he had retained, and, as Park's large car drove away, Tinker's taxicab followed it at the respectful distance of a hundred yards,

"Keep that car in sight," he ordered his driver. "Wherever he goes, follow him. I pay double fare all the time."

Park was a consummate actor, and, clever as Tinker was, his impersonation of a surprised and foolish gentleman completely deceived the lad; but, although Tinker's judgment in such matters was naturally inferior to the judgment of his employer, in affairs of minute observation he had little to learn.

He had noticed, without appearing to notice that Park's right sleeve was torn, and that two of the parti-coloured buttons which should have held it around his wrist were missing.

The man appeared to have been involved in a struggle.

This fact, coupled with Sexton Blake's warning that Park was a dangerous man, appeared to Tinker as sufficient warranty to follow Park, to find out whether he put into effect his expressed intention of going immediately to bed.

"If I don't succeed in tracing the touring-car," said Tinker to himself, "I may succeed in tracing Park; and one or both of those, things may lead me to the guv'nor. Here's hoping."

Fortunately the driver of his taxicab was an old employee of the detective's and the business of following another car was by no means new to him.

Through the heart of London, through the northern suburbs and out towards St. Albans, he kept the fugitive car in view, and yet without making it too evident that such was his object.

Within the taxicab Tinker slumbered peacefully.

He had had a tiring night, and calculated that he had a tiring day before him.

He had learnt from Sexton Blake the trick of snatching sleep when opportunity offered, and this was an opportunity.

It was a full hour before the cab came to a standstill, and, even before the driver had descended to open the door, Tinker was wide awake and ready for anything.

Rock must have approached the screen at his own end, for his face suddenly assumed proportions of a close-up, and for a moment it assumed a look of cold ferocity. " If you refuse," said his voice from the apparatus, " I shall take measures to make you change your mind, that is all ! "

THE SEVENTH CHAPTER.

TELEVISION.

LORD EUSTACE GULLIVER, emissary of Great Britain to the Extraordinary Convention of Nations Meeting at Geneva, worked hard and slept well.

He was accustomed to the intrusion of his private secretary during all hours of the day and night, and so received with equanimity the importunate summons which came to him just after half-past seven on the morning following the Countess' hall, he at that time, of course, being in Geneva.

"Awfully sorry, sir!" apologized the young man, "but there's a fellow out-side whom I think you ought to see."

"Tell him to wait," said Gulliver shortly. "I am—or was—engaged in having a most beautiful sleep."

"Sorry, sir," persisted the secretary, "but I gather front the little he will communicate that the matter is most urgent. It is, I think, a private matter —the Countess Gulliver—"

Lord Gulliver sat up in bed, now thoroughly awake and interested.

"My wife?" he said. "What do you mean? Is there anything wrong?"

"I don't think so, but I'm not sure. I suggest that you see this fellow."

"Very well, I'll see him. Take him into my sitting room. I'll be there in a minute."

Lord Gulliver slipped on dressing-gown and slippers and walked out through the door which led to the sitting-room of his suite.

It was already daylight; and the two young men who were his visitors had the appearance of having been awake for a long time.

"You are Lord Gulliver?" questioned one of them who seemed to be the leader.

"I am," replied the statesman. "What is your business with me? I trust that it is of such importance as to justify your disturbing my rest?"

"Whether you will consider it to be of such importance," replied the other, "I do not know — I am M. Charles du Maurine, and I have perfected an invention which makes television entirely practicable. I am paid a large sum of money to attend here and to demonstrate my invention to you at this hour."

Lord Gulliver became angry.

He was a zealous public servant, but this was not the hour at which his interest in science was greater than his interest in bed.

"Later in the day," he said, preserving with an effort the geniality for which he was famous, "I should be interested to see proof of your remarkable statement. At present—"

And he waved one of his well-kept hands, towards the door.

"In case you were disinclined to listen to me," pursued the other, "I was to tell you that my machine will be 'en rapport' with another machine in England, and will give you news of your wife, which you will be deeply interested to obtain. What that news is, I have no more idea than you have yourself; but, when I tell you that I am paid one thousand pounds sterling to give this demonstration, you will understand that the matter behind it must at least be important."

Lord Gulliver now perceived that an object of the size and shape of a cabinet gramophone had been brought into his sitting-room, and that it

was with reference to this object that the inventor was speaking.

"That, I take it." said the earl, "is the instrument which you are anxious to demonstrate?"

"It is. At seven-thirty precisely—that is to say in one minute from now—I am to tune in the duplicate instrument which is in the hands of my temporary employer. You will both see and hear to perfection, everything that is taking place before the duplicating instrument."

"Does that, concern my wife?"

"I am informed that such is the case. As to how it concerns the Countess Gulliver, I am not aware. My instructions are very explicit, but limited. May I take it that I have your permission?"

Lord Gulliver nodded.

"You have," he said. "Please go ahead and get this over as soon as possible."

With a word of apology the inventor drew the heavy satin curtains across the windows of the sitting-roost; and, when the room was almost completely dark, switched on a light somewhere within his instrument which made luminous a large plate-glass screen which had been covered by a door in the front.

At the same moment the voice of a man came from a loud speaker concealed in the mechanism.

"You are Lord Gulliver," it said.

"My instrument is already in operation, and I can see you and the men who are in the room with you. Also, I can hear every word which is spoken. As to who I am that need not concern you. I am using the precaution of a disguise; but it is a disguise so subtle that, when I have abandoned it, it will be impossible for anyone to recognize my new self by a memory of the old."

The voice was reedy and rather expressionless.

It belonged, one would imagine, to a person without much determination or intellect.

"Speaking to M. Charles du Maurer," continued the voice. "You will now place your instrument in operation."

The inventor walked forward and depressed the second switch.

Upon the ground-glass screen, with the effect of a cinema picture suddenly projected, and with almost the same definition, there suddenly appeared the representation of a large and rather dingy roost furnished with heavy, old-fashioned furniture, and lighted with two large bay windows, one on either side of a smoking fire.

Directly, in the middle of the floor, still clad in the contents of a shepherdess, and bound to a chair with ropes which passed around her body and legs, was the Countess Gulliver.

A few feet away was a man in the attire of a Crusader, who was similarly treated.

This man Lord Gulliver recognized as Sexton Blake.

In addition to this, there were two men dressed in white overalls and gauze masks; and another, fat, pink-faced and dapper, dressed as a pantaloon, whom the reader will recognize as Park, alias "Sudden Death David."

All these five individuals had their gaze turned to the front.

It was clear that they were looking into a screen similar to the one which now confronted Lord Gulliver and his companions.

"What devilment is this?" said Gulliver hoarsely.

"No devilment, my dear Lord Gulliver," the reedy voice ease out, "only an expedient to obtain your co-operation."

"My cooperation!" gasped the statesman. "In what, may I ask?"

"Send your secretary out of the room and I will tell you."

Gulliver turned to his secretary.

"Leave me, if you don't mind," he ordered. "I'll do anything to get to the bottom of this."

"Very wise of you," agreed the voice. "Now, sir, if your secretary is outside the room, of which, unfortunately, I cannot see the confines, and the door locked behind him, I will communicate to you my demands."

"My secretary is out of the room," responded Gulliver, "and the door locked behind him. Now, sir, whoever you are, let me know the meaning of this extraordinary affair."

"That is precisely what I was about to do. I represent a certain Balkan State which I need not mention; but which you will readily recognize when I continue. The State in question is seeking admission to the League of Nations. If the State obtains that admission, the position of the reigning monarch will be consolidated and his regime stabilized. It is necessary to my plans that this should not take place, therefore that State must be prevented from obtaining admission to the League."

"So," said Gulliver, "in order to obtain an assurance from me that I will betray my country, you have succeeded in abducting my wife and threaten to hold her as hostage? I warn you that your effort is futile, and that this outrage will be rapidly and efficiently punished. To begin with, you have made a serious mistake in supposing that I have sufficient power to prevent the inclusion of the nation you refer to even if I had the desire: and I may add that I have no such desire. I think there's nothing more to be said."

"As to that, I do not agree that there is nothing more to be said. If you oppose the inclusion of this nation, and the nation is still included, I shall be satisfied that you have done your best to pay the price which I demand, and your Countess, will be restored to you none the worse, save for the loss of a night's sleep, for her adventure.

"My terms are that you give me your word of honour as an English gentleman, which I know you will respect, to oppose by all the means in your power the inclusion of this certain nation among the parties of the league."

"And," said Gulliver, "if I refuse?"

The other must have approached the screen at his own end, for his face suddenly assumed the proportions of a close up.

The contrast of Rock's ridiculous costume, and his guileless face, with the words that he uttered and the role that he played, made his villainy seem incredible. Gulliver would not, could not, believe that the man was capable of criminal action.

For a moment Rock allowed to be visible behind the placid mask which he assumed a look of cold ferocity.

"If you refuse," he said, "I shall take measures to make you change your mind, that is all."

Lord Gulliver laughed.

This affair of faces upon a screen and hearing of a voice through a loud speaker, had no actuality. Although, if questioned, he would have admitted that the events now proceeding in that dingy room with bay windows, wherever it was, must be taking place, its actuality had not really convinced him.

"Well, I refuse," he said. "This is final and definite. Do you think—"

"I warn you," said the voice again, and the lips upon the picture moved in unison, "that I am a determined man. I mean every word that I say. I have no compunction. If you are recalcitrant for so long, you will see your wife done to death in that chair where she sits. Now that you know what my terms are I will proceed to convince you."

The possessor of the voice receded from the screen until again the remainder of the room behind him was visible, and picked up from a table a long surgical knife which had been lying there.

"First," he said, his voice coming as before from what seemed to be a great distance, "I shall cut away your wife's hair."

He walked over to his prisoner, and, holding her bobbed hair by the ends in a large handful, hacked it away close to the roots.

The girl screamed.

Her scream came from the loudspeaker to the ears of Gulliver and the inventor.

"Ah, Heaven!" gasped Gulliver. "If I could only get at you, you fiend!"

"But, you see," said the mocking voice, "you can't. You do not even know who I am. I am a hundred or so miles from you; and, although I fancy that my transmissions could be picked up, there is no likelihood that my situation will be discovered in time for an interruption. I speak, of course, subject to correction from our learned friend du Maurier."

"My lord," choked the young inventor, "I had no idea that my invention was to be used for purposes so detestable. I will do anything that you may command me. I will, if you order it, stop the transmission."

Gulliver wrung his hands and paced to and fro, and the mocking, foolish face of his tormentor again approached the screen, watching his every movement.

"In ten seconds," said Rock, with that disembodied voice which came so strangely, not from him, but from the instrument in a position where one would expect his feet to be, "I shall be compelled to take a further step. This time, reluctant as I am to may the undeniable beauty of your Countess. I shall be obliged, with this same knife, to cut off one of her ears!"

And, smiling, he rapped the glittering blade upon his finger-nails. The movement was quite plain on the ground glass.

"Not that!" said Gulliver. "Not that, I implore you! Look here, you brute, if you want money you can have it. Spare her, and you can have everything I possess."

"And yet," said Rock, "I want only half a dozen words—your assurance that upon your honour you will do what I desire."

"That," persisted the statesman, "I will not give. I cannot give it. Heaven help me!"

Again the voice of the Countess came to them.

"You are right, Eustace," said the brave girl. "If you give way— to this man I will never respect you again!"

Lord Gulliver turned away and hid his face in his hands, his outstretched thumbs pressed upon the cavities of his ears.

He was afraid to see or hear anything more.

Rock laughed, and his abominable laughter sickened the three men there in the Geneva hotel listening.

"Very well, then, we will talk to, I think, the left ear to begin with."

He walked slowly back to the chair in which the Countess was bound.

The man dressed as a Crusader, who sat in the chair by her side, strained at his bonds until the veins stood up like ropes upon his brow.

"You scoundrel!" he said. "If ever I get the use of my hands again —"

"But," Rock told him, "you will never get the use of your hands again, Sexton Blake. I am too busy to attend to you at present, but when I have finished with this lady—"

He seized the lobe of the Countess' ear and pressed the point downwards with cool delibera-tion, as of one about to carve a chicken; then he stopped, smiling.

Gulliver had removed his hands from his face, and, compelled by a horrible fascination, turned again to face the screen.

"Look here, you men," he cried out — "you men who are there— in the room with the Coun-tess Gulliver! You can hear what I say, I suppose. You know who I am. If that lady makes her escape unharmed there's a thousand pounds to each of you, if she escapes unharmed!"

Whether moved by pity, or tempted by the reward, one of the men stepped forward, seized Rock by the collar, and swung him aside.

"I am on to that. guv'nor," he said hoarsely. "I won't stand for it. Men who interfere in these matters have only got themselves to blame: but women—it's another matter. I won't stand for it. This ain't going any further!"

Rock had fallen to his knees. Now he rose slowly to his feet, dusted the knees of his silken breeches, with their ridiculous pendant tassels, and turned slowly towards the man who had attacked him.

As he turned there was a report, and the man fell to the floor in an attitude which betrayed that he was lifeless.

He had drawn an automatic, and with it covered Rock, yet Rock had fired so adroitly from some hidden place —in his loose garments that the other man did not even pull trigger.

The sound of the shot came from the speaker as clearly as if the pistol had been fired in the street outside.

The Countess Gulliver had fainted, falling forward upon the ropes which held her; and the second of Rock's confederates, thoroughly cowed, stood ready to abet any villainy which his master might dictate.

Rock had fired with his left hand from the hip, and in his right hand he still held the surgical knife, which, but for the intervention of his unfortunate confederate, he would by now have used to amputate the ear of the Countess.

Without troubling to find out whether his victim was dead or alive, although, in truth, the man's attitude left little or no doubt on the matter, Rock slipped his pistol back into the place from which he had drawn it, and walked again towards the insensible Countess, with the evident intention of proceeding to carry out the vile threat which he had uttered.

Blake, in his chair by the side of the Countess, had been straining every nerve, every muscle, in the hope of putting up a fight in her defence: but Rock's men had been trained to make no mistakes, and in binding Sexton Blake they had made none.

Since the moment when he followed Rock through the baize-covered door at the Countess' residence, and was efficiently batted into insensibility by a blow from one of Rock's men concealed in the darkness, he had not been allowed an instant of freedom, and, as he well knew, Rock's plans provided for his never regaining the freedom which he had lost. Indeed, he did not understand why his life had been spared until that moment.

Rock would allow no man to go on living who knew as much against him as did Sexton Blake, that much was certain; and, even if his struggles to release himself had been stopped by a bullet. Blake would not have hesitated to continue.

His life was of such little value now that he was in Rock's hands, that if, by throwing away his life, he could have gained for the unfortunate Countess ten seconds of respite, then he would have struggled, as indeed he did struggle, although now his struggling was in vain.

There was something in Rock's character which distinguished him from other human beings. Possibly it was that he did not know compassion. His manner in approaching the Countess for the purpose of exploiting her sufferings to extort from her husband a dishonourable contract was profoundly indifferent.

It was quite clear to all who witnessed the scene that his infamy would end either in the death of the lady whom he had abducted, or in the capitulation of her husband—that, in short, there was no alternative.

The husband was a man of considerable intelligence. He had seen Rock do murder, and he perceived that the man's statements were not bluff.

That being so, he had to choose—between dishonouring himself and his country, or witnessing a slow and brutal mutilation of the woman that he loved. He chose the former.

He was a man of the strictest honour and of great coinage, but he could not endure the torture which Rock had prepared.

The point of the delicate, razor-sharp blade had already drawn a red line of blood above the ear of the countess when he screamed the word "Stop!" Then, more calmly, he stated his own terms—the terms which he knew would mean the end of his career, perhaps even of life itself.

"If," he said, "the Countess Gulliver is uninjured, and in Geneva by the hour when the question of a certain nation's admission is brought up, then I will do my utmost to prevent the admission of that nation."

"That contract," said Rock, "is acceptable. I will point out, however that should you in the meantime commit suicide, or make arrangements for your own recall, you would not be abiding by its terms. Do you appreciate that?"

"I do. I give you my word of honour."

Gulliver's response was hardly louder than a whisper, but Rock heard him.

"In that case," continued the latter, "I will set about chartering an aeroplane to bring the Countess Gulliver to your side."

Taking no further notice of Gulliver who, together with the inventor and his assistant, must have appeared upon the screen which formed part of his own instrument, just as he and the occupants of his room appeared upon the screen of the instrument in Gulliver's hotel, Rock advanced with outstretched hand, obviously with the purpose of actuating the switch which put an end to the transmission both of telephony and television.

He was already portrayed at close-up proportions when he stopped, and a look of surprise came into his face.

"What's that?" he said, turning his head, and obviously addressing his second confederate. "Was that a knock at the door? Who could it be at this time in the morning?"

"I'll go and see," came the man's reply; and then came the sound of a closing door as he passed out of the room.

It was clear that Rock, his prisoners and his two confederates were alone in some building, and that the building was sufficiently remote to make any caller a matter of surprise.

So much was Rock perturbed that instead of switching off, he stood with outstretched hand, listening, not daring to make a sound, for fear that thereby he should lose information as to the meaning of that knocking upon a distant door.

"Go and see who that is," said Rock.

"I don't—"

What else he said, and what else occurred in that distant room, was lost to the diplomat, and to the others who waterbed beside him for the completion of Rock's sentence, and the occurrences which accompanied it. were blotted out by means of the lever at his hand.

He had switched off.

"Heaven, help me!" murmured the diplomat.

It was a prayer—as sincere a prayer as ever was uttered.

The Eighth Chapter

The Penalty of Miscalculation

THE morning stun was drawing a white mist from the dewy grass when Tinker skirted the lawn before a certain country house in the neighborhood of St. Albans, and. with considerable precautions against being seen, contrived to reach the front wall.

To this house he had succeeded in following the man whom he knew as Park.

As he possessed no exact information to the part which Park had played in the abduction of the Countess and the attack upon Sexton Blake, he thought it wiser to reconnoitre a little before coming out into the open. There-fore, taking advantage of every scrap of cover afforded by the architecture of the building and of the shrubs which surrounded it, he made a cautious inspection of the interior through window after window.

The downstairs rooms which he thus scrutinized were filled with old-fashioned furniture, but were all unoccupied, and had the appearance of having been so for a long time.

He had observed, however, that upon the weedy gravel outside the front door there were imprints of the feet of several men, some of these imprints being imprinted deeper than ordinary, as of men who carried a burden.

He felt sure that he was on the threshold of a discovery, and exercised caution accordingly.

It was well that he did so, for the first inhabited room that he came to—the room which contained the apparatus for television, the man Rock and his prisoners — was uncurtained; and, although he did not know it, if Rock had glimpsed sufficient of his head to contain a bullet-hole, the bullet would have been right there.

It is safe to suppose that Rock would have fired first and asked questions afterwards.

Inside the room, which was at the rear of the house, he had seen Sexton Blake, still in the garb of a Crusader, securely lashed to a chair; and by his side, similarly treated, and, similarly, still in her fancy costume, a lady whom Tinker correctly supposed to be the Countess Gulliver.

Rock was standing over the Countess and holding something against her head. But what it was Tinker could not see.

Fortunate it was for him that he did not see the knife which at that moment, Rock held against the ear of his unfortunate prisoner; for the lad, to his credit, could not have endured the situation, and would certainly have brought himself a fate which, even while he watched, befell one of Rock's assistants.

Rock himself was still attired in the flapping finery of a pantaloon and had not taken the trouble to cover his face; but his two assistants were attired in long white coats, which gave them the appearance of assistants in an operating theatre, and bags of black gauze which covered head and face completely.

Not having their master's facility for disguise, and having, doubtless, a very just fear that their description should agree with wine of the portraits in the Rogues Gallery at Scotland Yard, they had considered it discreet to adopt a complete disguise.

The windows to the room were formed of double sashes and double thicknesses of glass—a precaution against the weather occasioned by the exposed position of the house—so that Tinker could not hear the words that were spoken within the room.

The pistol-shot, when Rock fired at and killed his more humane assistant, was only just audible to the lad, so that again he was spared knowledge of events which would have harrowed his feelings.

The situation that Rock had made prisoners of his guv'nor and the Countess, and that one of his confederates, becoming mutinous, had been murdered by him was quite obvious to Tinker and the careless brutality with which the murder was carried out filled him with fear for his master's safety.

If Blake lived he was in a position to place the noose around the neck of Rock. Rock could not be blind to this fact; and, consequently, he would be inclined to add another murder to the one he had committed.

This much was evident; and it was also obvious to the lad that, since he could obtain no other help in time, to be of use, he must himself take action, however desperate it might be, to free Sexton Blake.

The message which he had received from the member of the British Secret Service, who was masquerading as a loafer outside the Countess Gulliver's residence, had told him that the car in which Sexton Blake had been carried away had contained four men in addition to the prisoners.

One of those four men had been murdered while Tinker watched, and another of them stood ready to do Rock's bidding within the room. What of the other two? Were they still in

the house? If so, the odds were heavy against him.

He returned to the front door and took the risk of very carefully measuring the footprints.

In this craft which he had learnt from Sexton Blake, himself a master of the game, Tinker possibly had no equal in the world; and after ten minutes of patient labour, he came to the conclusion that the persons whom he had seen were alone there, and that the odds against him were then only two to one.

But for the fact that he had witnessed Rock's cold ferocity and unerring pistol-work in shooting down his confederate, Tinker might have heaved a brick through the double window and attempted a hold-up.

As it was, his fear of Rock was so far increased that he set himself to discover a more subtle means of effecting his purpose.

After some thought he hit upon a plan, which, by reason of its audacity, held out a slender hope of success; and this plan, with characteristic promptitude, he proceeded to put into action.

Knowing now that his enemies were at the back of the house, he took no further pains to conceal himself, walked boldly up to the front door, and knocked.

It was this knocking which had so disturbed Rock that he had switched off the television apparatus and dispatched his, confederate to discover its cause.

The man threw the door wide open with a jerk, and stood there upon the threshold, feet wide apart, and a nasty look upon his face, waiting for the lad to explain his business.

He had removed the gauze from his face and thrown his white overall down—at the foot of the stairs just beyond where he stood. His hands were in his pockets, and one of them bulged in fashion which Tinker understood perfectly.

"Good-morning," said the lad cheerfully. "Awfully sorry to worry you with a call at this hour; but I'm afraid your house is on fire."

"What's that?" questioned the man, and then, reflecting that the place had long been disused, he added: "Impossible!'

Tinker grinned amiably.

It was his coolness, and that alone which enabled him to deceive the alert and nervous man with whom he dealt.

"If you will just stop out here," said Tinker "you will be able to see the smoke, coming from the roof. I caught sight of it as I was passing in my car."

The man was deceived.

Tinker's story was so plausible, and a deception seemed so purposeless, that the man thought it best to humour the lad by stepping out on to the lawn, and then to get rid of him as soon as possible.

As it happened, he did not care a snap of the fingers whether the house was on fire or not; and he knew that his master likewise would not care; but an expression of that point of view would not fail to create suspicion in the mind of this lad, and in the minds of any who had accompanied him in the car of which he had spoken, so that it was necessary to affect concern.

"I should think," he said, playing the part of a householder. "that you must be mistaken, young sir. You say you see smoke coming from the roof. Where is it? Let me have it look at it."

He walked forward by the lad's side across the lawn, and then, so suddenly that his pistol flew from his pocket, he found himself tripped, and crashed face downward upon the grass.

He had barely raised his head before Tinker snatched up his own heavy weapon and hit him behind the ear with the butt of it.

Twice the lad struck, and struck hard.

It went against the grain to strike that second blow against a man who was already half insensible; but Tinker was playing a dangerous game, and dared not take any chances.

By means of a device which is known as the "fireman's lift," the lad pulled the insensible body of the other across his shoulder, and heaved it into the midst of some grasslike plants which fringed the lawn; then he ran quickly into the house and slipped on the white coat and gauze mask which had disguised Rock's assistant.

He was, it is true, a trifle shorter than the man whom he now intended to impersonate but as regards breadth he would do well enough. And, for the rest, it was only necessary for his plans that he should impose upon Rock for ten seconds.

He uttered a few words of leave taking in a passable imitation of the voice of Rock's assistant; then, shutting the door, he walked confidently towards the rooms where Sexton Blake was a prisoner.

Had he known it, the chances were about nineteen in twenty that he was walking straight to his death.

Rock had an eye for details, and could draw and fire a pistol with extra ordinary quickness.

Tinker reckoned that when he entered the roots which he had seen, Rock would still be standing somewhere near the centre of the floor, and that he —Tinker—would get the drop upon him by means of the disguise.

It is extremely unlikely that this would have happened.

Tinker had been up against a gunman many tunes in his adventurous career, and was himself very quick with a weapon; but his natural aversion to kill would have given the other a fraction of a second; and, since the other had no such hesitation, it is probable that before that second was over Tinker would have been lying dead beside the other dead man whose sprawling body still lay where it had fallen behind the door.

It happened, however, that the fates were kind to Tinker.

Instead of events taking the course which he had expected, Rock opened the door from within at the very moment when Tinker reached it on the other side.

Rock opened the door with his right hand, and in his left hand he carried a pistol.

Having the advantage of surprise, Tinker was able to snatch the pistol out of his hand and throw it over his shoulder; and, further, before he had lost his advantage, he was able to trip Rock and pin him to the floor.

Like another before his time, however, he had underrated his adversary.

Rock was of slight build, and looked flabby.

His strength was not tremendous; but it was far greater than one would have expected.

He succeeded in thrusting the lad aside and staggering to his feet. His aim, of course, was to regain the pistol; but Tinker cross—buttocked him, and again the two of them came to the floor.

"Good lad," cheered Sexton Blake. "Keep at it and look out for tricks. I fancy he understands ju-jitsu."

The warning saved Tinker several times during the strenuous minute which followed.

Rock did, indeed, understand the Japanese art, of defence and offence; and fortunate it was that

Tinker at least knew enough to prevent the holds which Rock attempted.

As the two reeled, locked in each other's arms, the fatuous face of Rock, for once tense and frightened, close against his own, Tinker listened for Sexton Blake's advice, and acted upon it the minute it was given.

Blake, for his part, watched with the tense interest of one for whom life, and more than life, is at stake.

He shouted, just at the right moment, the order, "Back heel!" And while Rock was momentarily unbalanced Tinker kicked his feet from under him, causing the man to come down heavily upon the floor.

The concussion itself must have knocked Rock half silly, and the weight of Tinker coming on top of him knocked all the wind out of his body.

For a moment he was helpless,

"Now get your knife. Cut these infernal ropes. We've done it!"

Tinker sprang clear, and tore open the buttons of the long white coat which had hampered his every movement.

He was already opening his pocket knife when a blundering footstep sounded in the passage-way outside.

Before the lad could putt his pocket knife to the ropes which confined Sexton Blake, the door was torn open, and Tinker's late adversary—the man whom he had outwitted upon the lawn—burst into the room.

Apparently the fellow's head had been thicker than Tinker had supposed. He was to pay dearly for the miscalculation.

The man, as the reader knows, was unarmed, but reckless because of extreme range.

He ignored the threat of Tinker's automatic, and rushed forward. The bullet struck his ankle, and he came forward on his face. His outstretched hand, however, seized upon the lad's boots, and Tinker crashed just as Rock had succeeded in rising to a sitting position.

A moment later, his feet held by the man with the broken ankle and with Rock sitting upon his head, the lad lost what chance he possessed of bringing the affair to a successful conclusion.

His pistol-hand was pinned to the floor, and he knew that he was doomed.

The Ninth Chapter

Sexton Blake Forgets

"I SUPPOSE you wonder," said Rock, addressing Sexton Blake, "Why I have allowed your assistant, and yourself to live so long?"—

Tinker had been lashed to a third chair, and awaited, on the same terms as his employer, information of the fate which had been prepared for him.

Rock went on, smiling:

"I will tell you. This man here, who became troublesome and had to be shot, whom I shall bury very quietly in the garden outside this house—no one will worry about him. There will be no inconvenient questions asked as to where he may be; but you, Sexton Blake, and your assistant here, present a different proposition. You would be sought after: and, if I adopted such a clumsy device of putting bullets through your heads — a device which appeals to me strongly— I should sooner or later find the crime brought home to myself. That would never do. You must surely die; but you must die in such a way that no suspicion will attach to me.

"Therefore, it is my intention to arrange a motor accident. You will be dead all right when you are found. There is no fear that you will live long enough to lodge information against me. I will see to it. The car—in which you will appear to have been riding— will be found badly smashed up not far from here, and the broken speedometer will be registering sixty m.p.h."

Here he turned with a curse to the wounded man, who sat in one chair, with his injured limb extended over another, and punctuated his master's remarks by groans of pain.

"Confound you!" said Rock, "What are you making all that noise about? You had better be quiet, or I shall quieten you!"

He said the words softly, almost pleasantly.

The man knew enough of his master to understate the threat behind them; and although he was literally sweating with pain, he managed thereafter to remain quiet.

"Your demise," continued Rock, turning again to the detectives, "cannot, unfortunately, be arranged in daylight. Consequently you are reprieved until to-night. Until then you may keep the Countess company."

"Do you mean," choked Sexton Blake, "that it is your intention to keep this poor lady lashed to a chair the whole of the day? Can't you see that her fright has made her ill, and that the ropes are bruising her?"

Rock smiled, as at the capturing of a fool.

"Of course I can see that. What is to me? I do not even care if she dies, so long as her husband does not discover the fact in time to go back on his contract with me."

Again Blake struggled with all his strength to wrench himself free of the ropes which bound him although the reward of his success would have been a bullet in the brain.

"You cold fiend!"

Rock chuckled.

"Do not let us be melodramatic."

He tossed Tinker's pistol to his wounded confederate.

"You remain," he said, "on guard. If any of these persons makes a further attempt to escape, put a bullet through him!" And with this brief order he turned towards the door.

Then he backed slowly to the middle of the room and stood waiting, his pistol-hand concealed beneath the loose blouse which was part of his fancy costume.

Footsteps were sounding outside the door, and there sounded from the passage, of all things in that place, the joyous laugh of a woman.

The incongruity of Rock's ridiculous fancy costume, and of his vapid face, with the indomitable and ruthless will that looked out from his agate eyes, was so profound that the situation seemed impossible—part of a hideous dream.

The door opened, and Julia Fortune, in ultra-fashionable evening clothes, and accompanied by Monsieur Zenith, in his glittering, skin-tight garb of a harlequin, walked carelessly into the room.

Assuredly they were very close to death at the moment; and assuredly both of them knew it. Yet the voice of the girl as she impudently greeted Rock betrayed nothing of fear; and Zenith, to whom fear was unknown, seconded her without effort.

It is to be observed, however, that he was careful to demonstrate that his hands were empty.

"Oh," said the girl, "here is Mr. Park! You are Mr. Park, aren't you? Well, that is fortunate. We've been searching for you this last hour."

"Certainly," agreed Zenith, his rich, deep, effortless voice—that voice which would have made him a fortune on the stage—vibrating through the room, "this is Mr. Park. If you will permit me, Miss Julia, I will present the gentleman."

"Stop!" said Rock.

He said the one word very quietly; but both of his visitors knew, as he had intended them to know, that to continue meant death.

"Stop! I want a word with you. You came here—how I know not—to please yourselves. You leave here with your lives only if it pleases me!"

Why he did not press the trigger upon which his finger even then was whitening, is a mystery. Perhaps even Rock hesitated to take life again. Even to Rock it may be that the pathetic reminder of that prone figure behind the door had some dreadful significance.

"First," continued Rock, addressing the albino, "how did you find me?"

"I can answer that," said Julia Fortune. "I brought Monsieur Zenith here. I am an agent of the Secret Service, and our espionage system informed us some weeks ago that you had acquired this house. Our friend Mr. Sexton Blake informed us that you had contracted to dispose of certain jewels which the Countess only withdrew from her safe deposit upon special occasions. Therefore, knowing your interest in a certain country, we deduced that it was your intention to abduct the Countess and hold her as a hostage as a political advantage. Our deductions appear to be correct."

Rock showed a trace of disquietude.

"And have you," he queried, "a car-load or so of your confounded agents out there in the road beyond my gates?"

Julia Fortune laughed—a golden, full-throated laugh that held nothing of fear.

"Why, no. Save for Monsieur Zenith, I am unaccompanied. I drove the car myself. We of the Secret Service take into our confidence as few persons as possible."

"And what," said Rock, "is the purpose of your visit?"

"We have come," Julia Fortune told him, "to bring the Countess away."

Rock smiled again.

"And you," he said, turning to Monsieur Zenith, "do you indentify yourself with this lady's proposals?"

Zenith looked uncomfortable.

"I am afraid not. Any enemy of Sexton Blake is an ally of my own. I was unaware that Sexton Blake would be here."

Rock looked at him fixedly for a full minute.

"I believe you," he said "Your interest, then may be expressed—how shall we say it— in terms, of—er—finance? Eh? There is a whisper in the underworld that you are short of money. Suppose I offer you an—ah—honorarium to leave me alone, and to forget what you have seen here?"

"It would require." said Zenith, "to be an adequate sum."

"Certainly" said Rock. "We do not talk in hundreds. I will give you two thousand pounds here and now. Will that suffice?"

Zenith nodded.

"In notes of small denominations?"

"Precisely."

"Then I accept; but on one condition, the condition being that you allow me to put a bullet through the head of Sexton Blake."

Rock looked from Blake to the albino and back again.

"I don't know why I should object," he said. "But I will give you a warning. While your pistol is in your hand I shall be covering you also. If you attempt to use your weapon against anybody but the man whom you mention, you will drop dead in your tracks. I do hope that you appreciate the point?"

"I do," said Zenith.

It suited Rock's purpose, no doubt, that the guilt for the murder of Sexton Blake should be upon the head of another.

It gave him, anyway, a hold upon his, new ally such as he must have desired.

"Watch me," boasted the albino, "take the tip off his car as a sighter."

He walked back a few pace, drew his pistol, held it at arm's length above his head, slowly lowered it until the sights were upon his target, and then fired.

At the same time despite herself Julia Fortune uttered a cry and started forward.

Well it was for her in that moment that her fashionable clothes offered no concealment for a weapon.

Rock was taking no risks; and, had there been any chance of hostile action on her part, he wound have taken measures effectively to prevent such action.

In that confined space the report of the pistol almost deafened the singular company who were there.

Zenith hurled his pistol to the floor and uttered a cry of rage.

"A thousand curses!" he said. "I have missed. I ought not to be trusted with firearms if I can't shoot better than that. Give me the money and I'll get out."

''The money," said Rock, "you will find in that safe between the two windows. The, combination is 12675."

Zenith turned the numbered dials with rapid fingers; and then, with a cry of eagerness, threw the door wide open.

There was a muffled explosion, as some mechanical device exploded within the safe a cartridge of compressed gas.

The heavy fumes spurted full into the face of the albino, and he dropped limp and insensible beside the door.

For a moment suffocating fumes filled the room like a cloud of smoke; and then they cleared as rapidly as they had come.

Zenith lay spread-eagled upon the floor in front of the safe and beside him lay Rock as insensible as he.

The man with a broken ankle was looking, at point-blank range, into the muzzle of his own revolver; and clasped around the other end of that revolver were the steady muscular fingers of Sexton Blake.

"Keep still," warned the detective, "or I'll shoot the head off you."

He walked to the windows and threw them open, letting the clean, morning air of the, garden replace the heavy gas, which Rock had used as a weapon against a man who knew too much.

Half an hour later Julia Fortune had driven away in her car on the road back to London with the Countess as a passenger.

"Tinker, my lad," remarked Sexton Blake, as he helped the handcuffed Rock into the taxi-cab which had been brought to the door, "that was a very near thing. Rock's one mistake was that he was too sure of himself, and let us know too much. We shall thwart his plans by causing Lord Gulliver to be superseded at Geneva; and Rock himself—well, I hope meets the fate which he has deeply deserved."

They helped the wounded man out to the cab: and then Blake gave orders to the driver to get under way.

"But," objected Tinker, "you haven't forgotten the albino, have you, guv'nor?"

Tinker saw clearly that this was a chance for Sexton Blake to bring about the greatest coup of his career.

The arrest of the brilliant albino would be a triumph second to none among the many triumphs of Sexton Blake.

Again, since Blake seemed to be afflicted with deafness, he repeated:

"You haven't forgotten the albino?"

"I have," returned Sexton Blake blandly.

"Surely, guv'nor—"

The lad was about to object: but Sexton Blake stopped him with it stern order.

"You also," he told the lad, "have forgotten! We are paying a debt of gratitude. That is all!"

"What do you mean by that, guv'nor? Certainly the explosion of that gas gave you a chance to break your ropes."

"You think then." said Blake, smiling, "that I broke that rope by a muscular effort?"

"Of course I do, guv'nor. I saw you do it!"

Again Blake smiled.

"I did nothing of the kind, my lad, Zenith's pistol shot at me, instead of missing its mark, did exactly what he had intended it to do. He has often attempted my life in the past, and perhaps he will attempt it again: but he had pledged himself to obey Julia Fortune; and she demanded that he should obtain for me my liberty. With that bullet, for which he found such an ingenious pretext, he cut a section of the rope which bound me to the chair. We owe our lives to him; and that is why I have 'forgotten.'"

Tinker was astonished into a silence which lasted almost a minute.

"I wish," he said, at length, "that Zenith was on our side, guv'nor!"

Blake shook his head sadly.

"He never will be, my lad. By nature he is at war with the world, and must remain so. For the moment I forget him, because I choose to forget; but to-morrow, and the day after, and the day after that, I shall remember and go on remembering."

"Remembering," questioned Tinker, "a debt of gratitude.'"

"No," corrected Blake; "the debt is paid! He gave us life. I give him freedom. To-morrow we start again a duel to the death."

THE END.

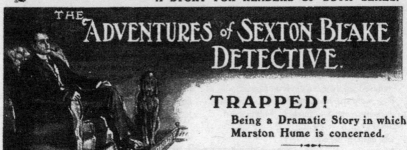

THE ADVENTURES of SEXTON BLAKE DETECTIVE.

TRAPPED!

Being a Dramatic Story in which Marston Hume is concerned.

SEXTON BLAKE was standing on the steps of the Baddley Club watching the press of theatre-going traffic with bored impatience. A small portion of the road just beyond the club was "up" for its annual repairs, and, in consequence, a blocked stream of taxis, motor-cars, hansoms, and four-wheelers flowing westwards occasioned considerable inconvenience and delay.

As Blake watched the slow, noisy procession a taxi, as if waiting for some given signal, shot out from a side street, squeezed in between a crawling hansom and a post-office van, darted with a swift turn of the wheel towards the pavement, recovered itself just in time to prevent a violent collision with a lamp-post, and swung into the line of traffic exactly opposite the club steps.

Seated far back in the corner of the cab Blake became idly conscious of the indistinct figure of a man – a vague impression merely, a blurred outline of a strong, impassive, clean-shaven face.

Even as he looked the figure bent forward a little to meet the sudden flare of a spluttering match, held by long, lean fingers, which directed the light a little uncertainly to the end of a cigarette clutched between the iron-hard lips.

Blake jerked forward down the steps as if impelled by a thrusting hand. Even as he moved the match was blown out, and the interior of the cab left in darkness as before.

But in that quick blaze of light the man on the steps realised that the one man in all the world who persistently defied and eluded him was within his reach at last. Altered, lined, aged, and curiously unfamiliar, the face was yet beyond doubt that of the greatest criminal of the age – Marsten Hume.

A few yards beyond, following in slow, halting line, was an empty taxi.

Blake nodded to the driver, opened the door, and slipped inside the moving vehicle, and looked around for the speaking-tube.

"Follow that yellow taxi just in front of the four-wheeler," he said curtly through it to the driver. "Don't, on any account, lose sight of it, and don't get near enough to be obviously on its track."

The man, scenting a generous fare, bent himself to the task, a comparatively easy one as long as the press of traffic kept the moving mass close together.

By degrees the yellow car forged ahead, the green one on its track. Over Blackfriars Bridge and south-east into Southwark Street raced the hunted and the hunter. Halfway down the leading car swerved at a left angle turn and plunged into dark, mean by-streets, deserted and forbidding.

"Pull up!" shouted Blake suddenly through the speaking-tube. They were now, he knew, in a cul-de-sac close to the river. The chase must be at an end.

He pushed a glittering yellow coin into the driver's hand, and slipped quietly into the narrow street – a row of dilapidated old buildings on each side, dark for the most part, and curiously silent; warehouses wedged in between dingy dwelling-houses, and dirty little gas-lit shops, all piled untidily together, and at the end a red tail-light shining upon a muddy yellow car. Just beyond this the sudden swirl of water could be seen splitting itself arrow-wise against the low hulks of barges and lighters moored clear of the fairway. The yellow car backed slowly down the roughly paved streets, the shadowy passenger no longer in the tonneau, and as it passed him Blake made a mental note of the number.

He walked with quiet, light steps up to the door of the house which the tall figure he was watching has entered. Blake pushed his whole weight against the door, and as it yielded suddenly he stumbled jerkily into a dimly-lit passage-way, a high, worn staircase at the far end. At the top of the stairs a man was fumbling with the latch of the door just on the left, his back towards Blake, who held his revolver in his right hand ready for emergencies. The door above grated slowly open, the grinding of a match on wooden paint-work rasped out, and a gas light flared up.

Blake stood irresolute, his quick eye searching nooks and corners suspiciously. He started towards the creaking stairs with cautious feet.

"Come on!" cried an impatient voice suddenly from above. "I'd know your footstep among ten thousand, Mr. Blake. Come straight up – you've got nothing to fear."

Blake started at the unexpected sound of the voice he knew so well. Then walked slowly up the worm-eaten steps and paused on the threshold of the open door at the top.

It was a comfortable half-dining, half-sitting-room, warmed by a glowing gas fire in the low grate, before it a supper-table drawn up, and in a low leather chair near it – Marsten Hume.

Blake's face was set in stern, hard lines, his eyes narrowed, his whole body held stiffly erect.

"Good evening," said Marsten Hume. "Your visit is not an altogether unexpected pleasure.

The whole top of the stairway, with a creaking of rusted chains, turned a complete somersault and took Blake down, down into the blackness below.

Have you dined? If so, you may smoke while I eat."

Blake closed the door, crossed the carpeted floor noiselessly, and looked at the man in the low armchair.

"One day," he said slowly, "I knew you would make a mistake, Marsten Hume. You've made it now in letting me track you here. Once before I held you in the hollow of my hand and I let you go. This time —"

He paused and walked across to a telephone instrument which his quick eye had noted on a wide window-ledge just opposite the door.

"This time?" queried Hume.

"Scotland Yard," said Blake grimly. "In ten minutes, Marsten Hume, I will have this place surrounded. I n the meantime, I've got you covered; the slightest movement on your part, and —"

"It all sounds very theatrical," interposed Hume, a trifle impatiently. "What's in the wind now? Explain, will you, while I eat my disgracefully late meal?"

Blake shot a quick glance at the cool, pale face, with the illusive smile flickering across the corners of the hard, determined mouth, and crossed back again to the table.

"I've changed my mind," he said suddenly, drawing up a chair and seating himself with the revolver balanced on his knee. "I've a few things to say to you before Scotland Yard turns up on the scene."

"As you like," Hume shrugged his shoulders. "By the way," he went on, in an almost lazy drawl, "this Scotland Yard business – on what charge am I to be arrested?"

"Any trumped-up charge will do for the moment," answered Blake, as cool as he. "Once you are safely lodged, pending inquiries, nothing can save you. The murder of Emile Sherringham will hang you, for instance. That can easily be proved now."

"I'm sorry," interrupted Hume. "But would you mind explaining more fully? Who is Emile Sherringham?"

"Also," went on Blake, heedless of the interruption, "there is strong circumstantial evidence to connect you with the murder of old Lady Lyne, and the theft of the Lahore ruby. Direct evidence that you attempted to kill me by setting a trap for me in my rooms – needle-points dipped in curare, wedged into the door of my study near the handle – the night you stunned my servant and stole an interesting collection of relics connected with some of your many crimes which I had gathered together – more than enough to hang you, Marston Hume," he finished grimly.

"You talk in riddles, " said Hume icily, his eyes glued on Blake's inscrutable face. "Contrary to your usual custom you've been reading newspapers, and, as a consequence, you accuse me of every undiscovered crime in the calendar. Now I," he added slowly, "haven't read a newspaper for over a year. When did these unpleasant thing you mention occur?" He leaned forward over the table, and with a curious, uncertain sweep of his hand took up a sandwich from a neatly-cut pile on a plate in the centre. "If you haven't dined," he went on, "try one of these – they're excellent."

The cool assurance of the man angered Blake. The long list of crimes deliberately planned, scientifically carried out, which reddened the hands of Marston Hume, flashed before him one by one – hideous crimes all of them – murder their ruthless end.

"The body of Emile Sherringham, with a triangular wound in the neck – obviously done with a broken fencing foil – was buried two days ago," he said, as if bringing a long train of thought to a sudden end. "And the boy's mother died to-day of a broken heart," he added, half reluctantly.

"Foolish woman," said Hume callously. "A boy killed by a broken foil, you say? Pity, but such accidents have happened before."

"It was no accident," snapped Blake. "A man answering closely to your description lured him to a house by the Regent's Canal to teach him a peculiar fencing trick at which you, Marston Hume, are adept. And, in teaching that trick, you killed the youngster. Forgery is one of your most artistic accomplishments, and, having killed the boy, you forged a cheque for three thousand pounds from one he had drawn out, and cashed it. Then you threw the body into the canal, and the next day disappeared from the house –but your host, the old fencing-master, will recognise you quickly enough when called upon to identify you."

"There was another unpleasant matter you mentioned," said Hume quietly – "something about a ruby."

"Stolen from Lyne House," went on Blake. "A little time ago you were able to get in there unobserved, steal the Lahore ruby, and substitute an impudent fraud, and, to silence the old lady who discovered you at your work, murder became a necessary part of the programme. There are people down there who will recall you easily enough - though you did pose as Sexton Blake."

"Anything else against me?" queried the cool, sneering voice.

Blake took a small notebook from his pocket and read out a list of crimes against which he had set the name of Marston Hume.

Marston Hume ticked them off on his fingers slowly one by one.

"A round dozen," he said evilly. "Quite a respectable record, though you must fail to prove a single one against me," he added, with a light laugh. "Let's leave those forgotten things alone," he went on, "and go to other things for the moment. I advise you Mr. Blake, to look elsewhere for the murderer of Emile Sherringham first – that was the man's name, I think? Also, for the thief of Lyne House. I can prove conclusively to you, and Scotland Yard, that I am innocent of either crime. Though I really don't see why I should take the trouble."

Blake got up from his chair, and, while covering the man with his revolver, backed across the room to the telephone.

"You see," went on the low, almost toneless voice, "it would be quite impossible for a man afflicted as I am to carry out those crimes you speak of. I am blind – stone blind – and have been for over a year. Quite melodramatic, isn't it?" The long fingers groped uncertainly to a jug of water, directed the lip carefully to the edge of a tumbler held aslant, and slowly filled it up.

Marston Hume took a long drink.

"Well, Mr. Blake," he said, in a pleasant voice, as he returned the empty tumbler to the table, pushing it carefully towards the centre away from the edge, "have you anything else to say? – if not, good-night! I'm tired."

Blake walked back to the table and looked at the man before him consideringly.

"I always gave you credit, Hume," he said, with slow deliberation, "for possessing brain-power above the average. This obvious lie is unworthy of even a lunatic."

"What? Don't you believe me?" queried Hume, raising his eyebrows. "If you have a few moments to spare and care to listen I will give you absolute proof – may I trouble you for a cigarette? The box should be on that stand near the door. Thanks."

Blake placed a cigarette within reach of the searching fingers, struck a match, then, suddenly leaning across the table, abruptly thrust the flaring end right into the pale, almost patient face – close up to the eyes within a hairbreadth of the black, dilated pupils. Not a muscle twitched, not even for a fraction of a second did the eyelids quiver. With an intake of his breath Marston Hume puffed slowly at the unlighted cigarette.

"Another match, please," he said apologetically. "Sorry to trouble you – it's gone out."

"By Jove, you're a cool hand!" said Blake, with unwilling admiration for the iron control of the man's nerves. "You've schooled yourself well, Marston Hume – but nerve won't save you."

As he was speaking he reached across and turned out the yellow gas jet, extinguished the glowing gas fire in the grate, plunging the room into absolute darkness. For some seconds – it seemed hours – he stood, scarcely breathing, within a foot or two of the quiet figure in the low armchair. Then, with a swift movement, he snapped on the vivid, concentrated light of his pocket electric lamp, and waved it within an inch of Hume's face, peering closely into the blankly fixed eyes.

Against his better conviction the truth was forced home that there was no reflection of light in the immovable pupils. The man was, as he had said, stone blind. Seeing eyes that could not possibly withstand that test and give no sign.

"I don't know what you are up to," said Hume, a little testily. "You've turned out the gas I know, because it no longer whistles, and the fire, for that went out with a bang. I wish you'd light both, will you? I hate the darkness, and the room already grows cold."

Blake complied with this grumbling request.

"It's a trick, of course," he said dully, sitting down again with the revolver once more on his knees.

"Trick? Nonsense! Over there on that desk near the window you will find a pile of letters. Turn up one under the name of Von Steiner – and you will see what that man, who is, as you know, the most eminent oculist living, has to say on the matter. I visited him in Dresden six months ago."

Blake turned up the letter and read its few, terse lines. Shorn of medical terms it gave forth the opinion of a world-famous specialist on eye diseases, that the patient, Marston Hume, was suffering from an obscure affliction of the optic nerve and incurably blind.

"A forgery, of course." Blake flung the letter down on the table almost contemptuously. "But difficult to prove at the moment, because Dresden happens to be some little way away from London."

"Still unconvinced?" queried Marston Hume, puffing away at his cigarette. "Von Steiner knows what he is talking about, even you must admit. He recommended me – just as a matter of form, of course – to place myself under Sir Duncan Wyllie's care, here in London. Like to hear what Sir Duncan has to say? His letter is also there, I think, in that pile."

Blake searched for and found the letter. It repeated the verdict of the German specialist, and bore the date of a few days ago.

"Still sceptical?" Asked Marston Hume, across the silence of the room.

Blake's face went suddenly white. Little drops of moisture beaded his forehead, and the angry, contemptuous light died out of his deep-set eyes.

The letter he held he knew was genuine enough. Sir Duncan Wyllie's curious handwriting was perfectly familiar to him.

"Blind men don't play with foils," went on Hume's voice tantalisingly. "Blind men cannot break into even familiar houses and steal gems.

Blind men do not set delicate traps in door handles – needle-points, I think you said, dipped in curare. What! Still intent on making a fool of yourself and calling up Scotland Yard?"

Blake had crossed over to the telephone once more and was ringing up the exchange.

"Oh!" Hume's voice was now a laughing sneer. "Sir Duncan's number! You prefer to get your news first hand. Well, I don't blame you. I'd do exactly the same thing were I in your place – under the circumstances. "

Sir Duncan – a friend of Blake's – happened to be at home. His unmistakable voice came clear across the wires. There was no possibility, he said gravely, of any mistake about the man Marston Hume, who had been to him a few days ago. It was a rare disease of the optic nerve, which frankly puzzled him, the only case on those exact lines he had yet met with, but none the less genuine – absolute, total, permanent blindness.

Blake put down the receiver and turned to the man in the chair, a network of puzzled lines gathering around his eyes.

"Convinced at last?" said Hume, with something like a smile of triumph. "It came on quite suddenly about a year ago," he continued reminiscently, leaning his elbows on his knees and propping his chin in the hollow of his hands. "I came here after that affair of the 'Island' shares, you remember? – you and Sir Richard Lawley crippled me over that. A hundred thousand pounds I lost – you ruined, beggared, finished me." He laughed harshly.

"This old house by the river has been my home ever since," he went on. "Instead of scheming dark plots of murders and thefts, I have lived here alone in darkness – painful darkness at times. An old woman comes in now and then to clean things up – for days at a time I don't see or hear anyone. I haven't spoken to anyone but yourself for Lord knows how long." He laughed again harshly. "So once again we have met, Mr. Blake, and once more I have baffled you. Good-night! Close the door after you – the hall door, I mean."

Blake paused with his hands on the knob.

"I feel convinced that your story is a lie from beginning to end," he said suddenly his eyes blazing. "And, what's more, I'll prove it."

He slammed the door behind him and walked towards the stairs. Halfway down a curious noise, coming from the room above, arrested his attention. Almost it seemed as if the man he had left were stumbling over the set of fire-irons in the grate.

Even as he stood and looked up sharply the rotten stairs seemed to split in two: a yawning chasm gaped beneath his feet. The whole top of the stairway, with a creaking of rusted chains, turned a complete somersault, and took him down, down into the blackness below.

At the same second a shot, deliberately aimed from above with deadly accuracy, rang out. Blake's hat was jerked clean off his head, and a trickle of something wet filled his eyes as he struck ice-cold water, which closed speedily over his face.

§

Fighting for breath, conscious of a red-hot pain across the top of his head, Sexton Blake came up from the bottom of the muddy river, and, treading water, felt his way cautiously about.

A few stokes this way and that brought him up against a slime-covered wall. Above, around, beneath, dank, mouldy darkness; and somewhere, not far away, a smiling, diabolical face, which had tricked him to his death.

The chill of the water numbed his hands and feet. Something must be done, and quickly, too, before it was too late. In a flash it struck him that there must be some way out of the deadly trap, else why that shot? At any rate, the thought stung him into action. Impossible to get out by the top, he knew; the walls must be high above his head, judging by the length of time before he struck the water when he pitched from the overturned stairs. If not above, then perhaps below. He listened intently to locate the sound of rushing water. It seemed to come from just outside the left-hand wall.

He made his way over to it, took a deep breath, and dived. Stretching out his hand as he reached the bottom, he felt for the wall, which should just be within arm's length. His fingers touched nothing but the resisting water. He struck out blindly ahead and upwards. As he came to the top, a soft moonlight took the place of darkness. Above, a twinkling, star-spangled sky; to the right and left moving lights, and just in front a moored barge.

In diving down he had cleared the depths of the outer wall and was free.

"Luck! Sheer, blatant chance!" he muttered. A few half-conscious strokes brought him up level with the barge. The red-hot pain at the top of his head was throbbing loud as a machine in his ears, and something warm dripped thickly into his eyes.

He clung on to the barge-side and shouted weakly, his voice trailing off. The answering shout from a couple of river police in an on-coming boat fell on deaf ears; for the first time in his life Sexton Blake had fainted.

A light was flashing into his eyes and a red-hot pain was searing into the top of his head when he recovered consciousness.

"Sooicide, o'course!" a gruff voice was saying. It seemed miles away. "Split 'is 'ead open, too, silly beggar! Best take 'im to the station."

Blake struggled into a sitting position on the floor-boards of the boat, and rubbed the mud and slime from his face.

"There's a flask of brandy in my pocket," he said jerkily. "For Heaven's sake, give me some!"

The two men started at the sound of command in the voice, and almost mechanically obeyed.

"Lor' love us, why, it's Mr. Blake! What on earth's happened?" ejaculated one of his res-cuers, bending forward and peering into the streaked face.

Blake laughed shortly.

"Hallo, Jackson; that you? An accident has happened," he said grimly. "I ought to be lying dead somewhere just about here, with a bullet in my brain. My hat saved me, I think. Not a bad shot, though, for a blind man."

He laughed again, a grim, mirthless chuckle.

"Pull for the shore, Jackson," he commanded sharply; "the Surrey side, as hard as you can go. Land me near those barges, if you can; I mean to find that blind man. You can take him in charge for attempted murder."

They obeyed him ponderingly, cowed into silence by the hard, low voice.

He shinned up the low wall as the boat slipped alongside – the tide was just at full flood – shook the water out of his clothes, and slipped off his sodden overcoat.

"Lend me that spare oilskin, will you? "he said; and took it from the men as they scrambled up after him, mooring the boat to an iron ring.

"Come on!" said Blake, his eyes ablaze. "Got a weapon about you? Mine's somewhere buried in the mud of the river. Ah, good! Yes, bring your lamp."

He darted towards the dark house he had quitted so unexpectedly such a short time before, mopping the top of his head with a wet handker-chief as he ran.

The door was closed when they reached it. Black burst it open with a thrust of his knee, and stepped into the dark passage. There was dead silence inside, save for the frightened scuttle of a rat across the rotting floor.

Blake crossed to the treacherous stairway, and climbed up on the outside of the stout oak bal-ustrade.

The door at the top was closed, the key on the outside. Blake turned it swiftly and locked it.

"Come up, you chaps!" he called out. "No, man, not by the stairs; by the rail outside, as I did! Now stand by for trouble!"

He unlocked the door and flung it open. The room was in darkness. From somewhere above there came a shrill, whistling draught, and a faint glimpse of star-bright sky.

Blake snatched the lamp from the man's hand and swung it round the empty room.

Marston Hume had gone, leaving an open sky-light and a thin iron ladder beneath to mark the manner of his going. On the discarded supper-table stood a small mahogany box, and near it a long, thin piece of rusted steel. The low, leather armchair in which he had sat was dragged from its place near the gas fire, leaving bare a rusty, rib-like lever projecting a few inches above the wooden floor.

Blake eyed it with a curious, puzzled frown; then pulled it slowly. Something creaked outside the door on the stairs with a noise of rusting chains. From where he stood Blake could see through the open door the stair-top turn over completely, and slowly reverse itself into place as the lever on the floor sank down.

"An old trap," he said to the astonished men. "Evidently built into the house ages ago as a ready means of getting rid of inconvenient people."

"That blind man you spoke about, sir," queried Jackson, after a horrified pause, "where's he gone to?"

Blake laughed bitterly, and pointed to the open skylight.

"Got away by that," he said shortly. "Blind!" he added contemptuously. "No more blind than you or I, though by some infernal cunning he has tricked two famous eye specialists into believing that he was stone-blind; and I put him through a couple of tests an hour or so ago, but was unable to trip him up. All part of a scheme, laid months ago, to guard against the day when he and I should meet to settle old scores; for he knew I should lay him by the heels sooner or later.

"He let me track him here to-night, so that he could get rid of me once and for all. Tipped me into the river by means of that staircase, and loosed off a revolver at me as I went down to make assurance doubly sure, missing my head only by a fraction of an inch. He was not blind, Jackson, when he fired that shot, not by a long chalk!"

As he finished speaking, Blake darted over to the fireplace and picked up some glittering fragments that lay there; sticky fragments of thick glass, which he rapidly pieced together into an oval eye-cup. It was stained deeply with a blue-black fluid, in which were a few half-dissolved greenish-silver crystals.

"This explains things a little," he said quietly. "It has been used recently, for the liquid on the glass is not yet dry. It is an easy matter to deduct that it contained a powerful narcotic which, acting on the optic nerve, induced total blindness for a certain space of time. When I made those test I spoke about, the man was undoubtedly blind from a recent application of the drug; as he sat and talked to me the effects gradually wore off, till, when I left the room, his sight had returned to normal conditions.

"A dangerous man, sir," said Jackson, taking a deep breath. "He ought to be found. Any use looking for him on the roof yonder?"

Blake shook his head.

"Not in the least. He had no intention of being found when he left these –"

He crossed over to the table and took up the rusted piece of steel.

"A broken fencing-foil," he explained, in reply to an unspoken question. "A piece of direct evidence in a certain crime of which I accused him. Then this box," he continued; "he stole it from my rooms some days ago. It should contain souvenirs of some of the most daring crimes of the century, of which I know him to be guilty, but cannot prove."

He opened the box as he spoke and glanced inside. It was empty save for a small piece of paper, neatly folded, lying on the bottom.

Blake took it up. It was addressed on the outside to himself in Hume's handwriting.

"Dear Mr. Blake, "it ran, "it gave me great pleasure to watch you from my window here taking your midnight dip. What a curious hour to select for a swim on a cold night like this! I would have saved you the trouble, if I could, but my recent eye treatment seems to have affected my sight. I fear my aim was none too good. Pray accept my apologies. – Marston Hume."

SEXTON BLAKE in a gripping, Human-Interest Story of the Downfall of Inspector Coutts, C.I.D., Extra long, and Complete.

UNION JACK 2ᴰ

—a *Gwyn Evans* story

SUSPENDED *from* DUTY!

No. 1,519.   EVERY THURSDAY.   November 26th, 1932.

SUSPENDED FROM DUTY!

A COMPLETE STORY OF DETECTIVE-INSPECTOR COUTTS, OF SCOTLAND YARD—AND SEXTON BLAKE.

FRAMED! AFTER YEARS OF DEVOTION TO DUTY AND STRAIGHT DEALING WITH FRIEND AND FOE ALIKE, INSPECTOR COUTTS, OF THE C.I.D., AND FRIEND OF SEXTON BLAKE, SEES HIS REPUTATION IN RUINS. SUSPENDED FROM DUTY! SMASHED! THERE'S JUST ONE PERSON WHO CAN SAVE HIM. YES, YOU'VE GUESSED WHO THAT IS. HE DOES NOT THRUST HIMSELF FORWARD, BUT ALL THE TIME HE IS WATCHING, READY TO AID. YOU'LL SEE HOW SEXTON BLAKE, ALMOST AT THE LAST MOMENT, EMERGES TO TURN INSPECTOR COUTTS' DOWNFALL INTO TRIUMPH.

CHAPTER I
CROSS-CURRENTS AT THE YARD.

"MORNIN', Coutts!"

Detective-Inspector Grimley smiled toothily, and with a trace of condescension, as his colleague Coutts entered the austerely furnished office at Scotland Yard.

He glanced significantly at the clock on the mantelpiece and rustled a sheaf of official documents.

"*Good*-morning, *inspector*!" replied Coutts, with ungenial emphasis.

The C.I.D. man had never liked Grimley. He was too suave and smiling. Until recently he had been a sergeant, but was promoted for rescuing a woman, the second cousin of an earl, from the Thames, and had the good fortune to have the act witnessed by a titled gossip writer.

As Coutts afterwards explained to his cronies at "The Place"—that discreet little public-house off Cannon Row where Scotland Yard men forgather, "If the woman hadn't had a title he wouldn't have wetted his uniform."

Coutts was a capable police officer and not "catty." Actually his somewhat acrid comment was justified.

The newly created Detective-Inspector Grimley was one of those large, smooth men with an expansive smile and expensive tastes. He was pertinacious, clever, but unscrupulous, and few of his colleagues could tolerate him.

Coutts, too, was pertinacious—but that is where the resemblance between the two Yard men began and ended.

Coutts was a bulldog. He never let anything go— except his chances of promotion. He was innately loyal; courageous, too. But had very little imagination, and less tact. He relied more on routine than ratiocination in his conduct of cases, and seldom acted contrary to the "Book of Words," as he called the Police Manual.

"Regarding this Ifield case, Coutts," said Grimley, ruffling the sheaf of documents. "Don't you think I'd better handle it? I mean to say—"

"I'll handle it," Coutts said curtly. "I know Izzy Ifield better than you—and besides, he's as artful as a lorry-load of monkeys."

Grimley smiled, but without mirth.

That engaging share pusher and con. man, Mr. Isaac Ifield, had recently clicked—one of the biggest clicks of his chequered career. It was a long and sordid swindle, and has little to do with this story of Sexton Blake's discovery of the curious behaviour of the green parsley on Gillie Carew's butter-dish; but some £50,000 was involved and Izzy, one of the cleverest planters who ever peddled scrip, had made a clean job of it.

He might have retired from the game and flaunted his winnings as a country gentleman but for the fact that Detective-Inspector Grimley had given him the tip that big trouble was brewing as soon as the police could pin him down to cases. Scotland Yard needed only another scrap of evidence, and the versatile Mr. Ifield would have qualified for a long holiday—in the country, certainly, but not on his own estate,

Izzy had thanked Inspector Grimley for his timely and considerate warning, and announced his early departure for abroad.

"As you like, my dear Coutts, but, as a matter of fact, Izzy isn't any longer with us."

"What do you mean? Is he dead?"

SUSPENDED

Something fell on the carpet with a slight thud. It might have been a thunderbolt, judging by the effect it had on Coutts. "Hand me those notes, Inspector!" snapped the Commissioner.

"No; Mr. Ifield left for the Continent by air yesterday."

Coutts clenched his fist.

"By heck! Somebody must have tipped him off," he growled. "Just when I'd got him where I wanted him!"

"It's most unfortunate," said Grimley sympathetically.

"I'm not satisfied, Grimley! There's been a good deal of leakage of information from this department lately. I'm mentioning no names, but one of these days there's going to be an unholy show-down, or my name's Crippen!

"What about the Puce Lobster?" queried Grimley suavely.

He was not referring to the hue of his colleague's face, however, though at that moment Coutts' florid features were almost purple with fury.

"Leave the Puce Lobster alone!" snapped Coutts. "That's my business, and don't you forget it!"

"H'm!" said his colleague meaningly, "I think I get you, my friend."

VERY quietly he withdrew, and as the door closed the fuming Coutts was left to ponder about the meaning of his last remark.

He jerked open a drawer and pulled out his private notebook, which he scanned closely. In it were recorded briefly details regarding the activities of the latest night clubs of the West End. Prominent among them was that fashionable Society rendezvous in Greek Street, Soho, the Puce Lobster.

That oddly named night club had interested Coutts professionally for some time. It was smart, exclusive, and popular among that section

From DUTY!

of Society known as the Bright Young People, many of whom were not so bright and not so young. Coutts had learned some strange stories regarding the frequenters of the place. Ostensibly it was a social and dancing club whose clientele consisted in the main of people loosely—very loosely—described as artists, literateurs and actors.

"Pah!" Coutts murmured aloud. "It's a bit thick! That's what it is—thick!"

The worthy man's remark was not meant to apply to the pungent cigar-smoke which presently enveloped him, but to the situation in general and Detective-Inspector Grimley in particular.

Grimley had been recently appointed by Sir Henry Fairfax, the Commissioner, to report on various notorious night clubs in the West End—and Grimley's reports worried Coutts,

whose knowledge of the dubious haunts of Soho was both extensive and peculiar.

The Puce Lobster had the distinction of being founded by Lady Melisande Norrie—nee Rosie Gluckman, a bright particular star of the Hilarity Theatre in the War years, whose photograph had brightened many a Flanders dugout and officers' mess, and whose song "When the War is over, Tommy, I'll be waiting in my glad rags," did so much to hearten our gallant troops.

Indeed, so much verve did she put into her singing that young Lord Norrie, a simple second-loot of nineteen, didn't wait till the War was over, but married her during his thirty-six hours leave from France. A sniper's bullet terminated his brief but hectic existence almost before his unblushing bride had finished dispatching postally the pieces of wedding-cake to her horde of relations.

The bereaved Lady Norrie was compelled by convention to wear sad rags for a suitable period, but she wore them with an air, and by virtue of her talent and newly acquired title became, one of the most popular young hostesses in Society,

Unfortunately, her husband left her little but an M.C. and an overdraft at Cox's, and if Gluckman pere had not succeeded in making a small fortune out of supplying insect powder to the War Office, her titled situation would have been anomalous.

Rumour linked the Lady Melisande's name with many people after the Armistice, but she still remained a widow—and a merry widow at that.

"And nearly as good as she looked!" the Hon. Ivor Trelawney, that brilliant and vicious dilettante once said of her. Trelawney was fond of Melisande, in his cold-blooded fashion. Indeed, it was he who inspired the idea of the Puce Lobster.

Melisande was delighted and thus her night club was founded, to the subsequent perturbation of the worthy Detective-Inspector Coutts.

The Yard man had long considered that many of the club's activities were illegal. He knew, of course, that illicit drinking took place, but that didn't worry him so much as its suspected connection with the alarming increase in drug trafficking in the West End.

The degenerate set of whom the Hon. Ivor was the acknowledged leader were a neurotic, fast-living crowd, among whom the dope peddler finds his readiest victims, and Coutts had a shrewd suspicion that the Puce Lobster was the headquarters of a dope gang.

Grimley, however, who had been specially detailed to keep the club under observation, maintained otherwise. His reports were invariably the same. The Puce Lobster was a decorous, law-abiding club, admirably managed by the Lady Melisande Norrie, frequented by people of the highest social standing, etc., etc.

Coutts was convinced that Grimley wilfully turned a blind eye to the true facts, and was possibly well paid for doing it. His moral astigmatism shocked Coutts, who, with all his faults, was as honest as the day, and, like practically every other officer, put the honour of the magnificent force to which he belonged before personal ambition and pecuniary gain.

"Curse me if I don't look into this business myself!" he announced. "And you watch out, Mr. Smarmy Grimley!"

CHAPTER 2
LOOKING ON AT THE LOBSTER.

"OLD man, I wouldn't have your job as a gift! Bright Young People! Oh, help!"

Derek Page, the star crime reporter of the "Daily Radio," surveyed the crowded dance floor of the Puce Lobster, and with an exaggerated shiver of revulsion, took a deep draught out of his tankard. His companion, Teddy Rampling, otherwise known as "The Spyman," one of the cleverest gossip writers in Fleet Street, shrugged his elegant shoulders.

"I'm thankful that my job deals with clean, honest crime!" added Splash. He was in his most cynical mood that night.

Known in Fleet Street as "Splash Page," because of his flair for securing sensational news stories for the "Radio," he had met young Rampling by accident in the West End, and had promptly accepted the latter's offer to share his table at the Puce Lobster.

"I'd like to know how you gossip writers live, work, and have your beans," he said.

"Give us the low down on some of these 'ere bright young sparks present. Who's this lot, for instance?"

He glanced significantly, towards the doorway, and his colleague swivelled slowly round in his seat. A party of people had just entered the swing door of the Puce Lobster, and were piloted to an alcove table by a deferential head waiter.

The newcomers were headed by a tall, somewhat stout man clad in an evening dress far too faultless to be gentlemanly.

He had a pinkish face, flabby, and a mouth that would have looked better on a woman. He had wispy side-whiskers, a lisp, and a monocle.

"That," said Teddie Rampling, "is the Hon. Ivor Trelawney, the celebrated poet and wit. Son of the Earl of Haverford, he toils not, neither does he spin—anything but 'yo-yo' at the moment."

"Who's the jane next to him? Her face seems familiar."

She was the epitome of femininity from her silver, high-heeled shoes, to her platinum blonde shingle.

"Lordy, Splash!" said Teddie. "That's the Hon. Monica Travers, and near her is Gillie Carew, the explorer. I wonder what brings 'em here to-night?"

"So that's Gillie Carew, is it?" murmured Splash, with a glance at the bronzed, handsome young man near that lovely girl. He knew, of course, being a newspaperman, of Gilbert Carew's romantic return to England after two years' trek through the wildest and most desolate region of the Amazon.

"They're engaged, aren't they, Ted?" asked Splash.

The gossip writer nodded,

"I believe so—" he began. Then, seizing Splash's arm, added: "Gosh! Look at our Rosie! The one and only Melisande, the Mayfair Mystery Woman. As a night club queen, she's got Texas Guinan licked to a frazzle!"

Splash Page's eyes narrowed as a woman entered from behind the dais and joined the party at the corner table. She was clad in a tight-fitting diamante frock, a one-piece dress of iridescent silk, which emphasised the contours of her figure attractively, and yet somehow combined modesty with sophisticated fashion.

The years had dealt gently with the Lady Melisande. Her eyes were dark and lustrous, her complexion flawless.

Idly Rampling turned and surveyed the rest of the ball-room.

"Queer lot here to-night. I don't know half of 'em," he murmured.

Splash glanced across the floor and stiffened suddenly,

"Hallo! Here's a bit of *my* meat!" he said in an undertone. "Take a look at the third table down by the palm"

Rampling sipped his drink, and observed a couple seated in earnest conversation at an adjacent table.

THE man was tall, swarthy, and handsome in a flashy, superficial fashion. He had dark, oily hair slicked back from a smooth forehead, and a thin moustache like a smear on his upper lip. His eyes were peculiarly penetrating, but too beady and quick-glancing to be prepossessing. He was clad in conventional evening kit, and wore a double collar and black tie, American fashion, with his frilled white shirt.

His companion was a slim, Eton-cropped girl, clad in a low-cut black-and-silver frock. Her eyes were oblique, the lids plentifully bedaubed with bistre, but she had a certain arresting barbaric beauty that carried off her outre clothes and exotic colouring.

"Who are they, Splash?" asked Rampling.

The crime reporter grinned.

"The gent in the tuxedo is Baltimore Smith, one of the slickest broadsmen and con tricksters that ever worked the Atlantic boats. His charming companion is Meg Brady. Take a look at her."

Meg Brady, alias Cardiff Meg, narrowed her slanting eyes, thus revealing her Mongolian origin, as she bent forward towards Baltimore. She was the daughter of a Welshwoman and a Chinese laundryman, and for ways that were dark and tricks that were vain Meg had the cunning of the proverbial Chinese and the wilyness of the proverbial Welshman—a combination happily rare.

"A well-matched pair, eh?" commented Splash Page. "We ought to see some fun in a minute, Ted. Wait till Baltimore spots a mug. His methods are a joy to watch, believe me."

At the near-by table Cardiff Meg's heavily hennaed fingernails dug into Baltimore's sleeve.

"Listen, Balty!" she hissed in a fierce whisper. "You think you've got this busy Grimley sweetened, but don't you believe it. He's a low, double-crossing skunk, and he'll do you dirt as sure as my name's Brady."

"It isn't. It's Feng Lee," drawled Baltimore Smith, with a chuckle.

"Think you're funny, do you, you big Yankee four-flusher!" the girl began venomously, then checked herself suddenly at the warning glance in Baltimore's beady, darting eyes.

Through her darkened lashes she gazed towards the entrance, then gave an involuntary gasp as she recognised the tall, well-built figure of Detective-Inspector Grimley himself.

Grimley was that phenomenon, a police officer who really looked well in evening dress. His hair was glossily brushed and parted, his batswing bow perfectly tied, his studs tasteful, his smile benign and all-embracing. Suddenly he spotted Baltimore, and his smile grew even more toothy.

"Gosh!" murmured Splash. "Here's where the fun starts, Ted. D'you know the chap at the door, with a grin like a dental ad.?"

She peeled ten of the notes off the wad and handed them to Grimley. "Coutts is a stubborn old ass, but I think he'll see reason," he said.

"Vaguely," said Teddie. "Seen him before somewhere."

"That," said Splash solemnly, "is our gallant sergeant—I beg his pardon, gallant Inspector Grimley, who rescued the Hon. Agnes Chomm from a watery grave. A nice man, they tell me. My pal Coutts loves him."

Teddie Rampling chuckled.

"This is where the drama begins, Splash," he remarked, jotting down a few names on his shirt-cuff. "Among those present during the spectacular raid on the notorious night 'aunt, the Puce Lobster, was Mr. Derek Page, the eminent tripehound; Mr. Baltimore Smiff—"

"Shut up, you ass!" cut in Splash. "There ain't gonna be no raid. 'Cos why? Fair Lady Melisande has got our friend Grimley sweetened. He'd do anything for a lady of title, Coutts says. Even get his nice uniform wet. Watch him!"

Detective-Inspector Grimley strolled nonchalantly towards Baltimore's table and bowed ironically to Meg.

"Good-evening, Miss Brady! Good-evening, Mr. Smith!" he said affably. "Do you mind if I join you for a little? I am—er—expecting a friend."

"Hallo, Grimley!" said Baltimore with civility but no cordiality in his tone. "Sit down."

"Thanks!"

Mr. Grimley sank elegantly into a chair and signalled a waiter.

"What's your poison?" he asked. Grimley shrugged.

"I don't touch alcohol, as you know. I'd like a cup of black coffee, please."

Baltimore grunted and gave the order.

"You're looking very charming to-night, Meg," said Grimley gallantly. "Quite a spot of colour."

"Miss Brady to you, *Mister* Grimley," retorted the girl tartly. "You man-hunting snoop-hounds forget your place. Too blamed fresh."

"Now, Meg!" warned Baltimore. "I'm sure we're very honoured to have Inspector Grimley's company with us."

Grimley laughed; he seemed to be amused.

"What are you doing these days, Balty?" he queried.

The crook shrugged.

"Me? Why, haven't you heard? I've swallowed the anchor. I'm starting a nice little business in the City."

Grimley smiled sceptically.

"You couldn't go straight, Balty; your backbone's a corkscrew. You're the original crooked man who walked a crooked mile and found a crooked six-pence against a crooked stile."

"I suppose you think that's funny!" snapped Meg indignantly. "Listen, Balty! I'm not sitting here to be insulted by this cheap skate of a jumped-up flatty!"

She seized her handbag, savagely crushed the half-smoked cigarette in the ashtray, and rose to her feet.

"Now, listen, Meg!" pleaded Baltimore. "Don't be silly. It's only Mr. Grimley's fun."

The girl tossed her head, and without another word crossed the dance floor towards the exit. Splash Page nudged his colleague.

"Exit the lady, registering hauteur. Meg's got the temper of a fiend when she's roused. I'd give a good deal to know what Grimley and Baltimore Smith are talking about," he added, with a sigh.

CHAPTER 3
COUTTS' COMPLICATION.

SPLASH glanced wistfully over to the other table.

Grimley and the crook seemed to be deep in conversation now that the girl had gone—and the subject of their talk would indeed have interested the newspaperman considerably.

"Listen, Balty!" Grimley was saying quietly. "I've come to give you a tip. They're tightening things up at the Yard. They're talking of forming a special narcotic squad, on the lines of that of the New York Police."

"Now, look here, Grimley," said Baltimore brusquely, "let's come down to cases. You're one of the gimme-gimme boys—and you needn't try to bluff me you ain't!"

The Yard man's face darkened. Unscrupulous though he was, this point blank accusation by the crook nettled him, but Baltimore Smith smiled imperturbably.

Grimley looked at the crook intently for a moment or two, then rose suddenly to his feet.

"Watch your step, Balty!" he said raspingly. "I'm warning you to lay off."

Balty grinned, unabashed, and watched him as he crossed the dance floor.

The Lady Melisande switched on her dazzling smile as Grimley passed unobtrusively by her table and greeted him cordially. The Yard man returned her smile with interest, and Melisande, with a murmured apology, left the table and slid a shapely arm through his.

"I'd like to speak to your ladyship privately if it's convenient," said Grimley in a whisper.

She glanced at him, startled.

"Why, certainly! There's nothing wrong, is there, my dear inspector?"

"No, of course not," he said, smiling reassuringly. "Just a little complication, you know—"

"Come in here, my dear man, and tell me all about it," said Melisande, piloting him into a little room behind the orchestra dais.

She closed the door carefully and waved him to a seat on a divan.

"Can I get you a cocktail, inspector?" she queried.

He shook his head.

"Sorry, your ladyship, I don't drink. The fact is I just dropped in to give you a friendly hint. There's nothing to be alarmed about if you go carefully, but there's a thick-headed old fool at the Yard who's liable to make trouble in the near future. He's one of the old school. You know the type, your ladyship—fussy, officious, always working by rule of thumb. If I might say so, he's not tolerant and broad-minded. Though I don't drink myself, I don't see why you young people should be deprived of an innocent evening's amusement. After all, you can afford to *pay* for it, and—"

"Exactly!" cut in the Lady Melisande sweetly, but her eyes had a hard glint in them as she noted the subtle emphasis he put on the last verb. "You are so understanding, my dear inspector! Incidentally—"

She turned and sat down at her desk. Pulling out her cheque-book and unscrewing her fountain-pen, she turned and smiled at him.

"I've forgotten the cheque for the Police Orphanage. Or is it the Sports Fund, inspector?" she asked, pen poised prettily above the pink forms. "Whom shall I make it payable to—yourself, as usual?"

Grimley's close-set eyes narrowed avariciously.

"It would be much more convenient if you could let me have it in cash, your ladyship," he said. "Er—this man, Detective-Inspector Coutts, might—er— be more amenable to common sense if he—er—"

"You mean if he got a rake-off, eh?" cut in Melisande, with a hard little laugh. "Very well, my dear inspector!"

She unlocked a drawer in the bureau and took out a solid bundle of new Bank of England notes as thick as a pack of cards. Tearing off the paper band, she peeled off ten of the notes and handed them to Grimley, who bowed his acknowledgments.

"I think that'll meet the case, your ladyship. Coutts is a stubborn old ass, but I think he'll see reason."

"Oh, I'm *sure* he will!" said Melisande. "You *will* excuse me if I fly now, won't you, dear Inspector Grimley? I've a party of guests to attend to."

"Why, certainly, ma'am!" said the Yard man, courteously opening the door and bowing.

The Lady Melisande tilted her small chin slightly as a catchy foxtrot was wafted in from the ball-room. Grimley grinned enigmatically as he watched her rejoin the group at the corner table.

"That's put a spoke into your wheel, anyway, Comrade Coutts, Esquire!" he murmured.

"THIS place gives me the jeedles, Teddie!" commented Splash Page. "Let's drink up and go. These confounded people make me sick!"

He drained his glass, and accompanied by his colleague, entered the cloakroom. He was just donning his white silk muffler, after having tipped the expectant attendant, when he glimpsed a look of alarm on the man's face. Instantly Splash Page's keen journalistic brain was alert.

He spun round, just in time to see the burly figure of Detective-Inspector Coutts, followed by four obvious plainclothes men, enter the garish entrance of the club.

Splash nudged Teddie.

"Old man Coutts on the warpath," he commented. "Oh, boy! And we nearly missed it!"

The club manager, a pasty-faced Italian, waved expostulatory palms as Coutts strode manfully past the two commissionaires.

"Excuse me, saire, but this ees a private club! Are you a member? It ees impossible to enter unless—"

"Stand out of my way, you!" snapped Coutts, shaking off the other's detaining hand as a terrier shakes off water from its coat. "I am a police-officer. I shall want to investigate your books, and I have a warrant to search the premises."

From his breast pocket he pulled out a blue official form. The manager wilted.

"Ferris—Lawton! Stand by up here!" Coutts ordered curtly. "Miller—Wills! Come down with me!"

"Wotcher, Coutts! What's this—a pinch?" queried the irrepressible Splash.

Coutts scowled as he recognised the newspaperman.

"Hallo, you!" he growled. "I might have known *you'd* be here!" He turned to the big, slow-moving Miller. "Take this feller's name!"

Splash struck an exaggerated attitude of despair and clutched wildly at Coutts' lapel.

The Yard man snorted, indignantly tore himself away, and strode, fuming, down a short flight of stairs that led to the dance floor below. Even as he did so, the strident, insistent clamour of an alarm bell rang through the building.

Quick and surprising though Coutts' raid had been, the news had flashed round, and when the Yard man entered with his stolid colleagues, waiters were frantically snatching unfinished drinks from the tables, and racing to the hatches with bottles of champagne.

Crash!

One waiter had tripped in his haste and the ice-pail was jerked from his fingers, to bounce at Coutts' feet at the very moment of the Yard man's entry.

Coutts smiled grimly and raised his hand to silence the buzz of conversation. "Keep your seats, ladies and gentlemen," he said, in his gruff, but penetrating voice. "We are police-officers."

IN the lower office the Lady Melisande turned like a tornado on the discomfited Grimley. Gone was the aristocratic veneer, the clipped intonation. In its stead was the language used by the erstwhile Rosie Gluckman.

"What the devil does this mean?" she snapped.

"My dear Lady Melisiande," began Grimley, "I assure you I am in no way responsible for this awkward complication. Coutts must have gone off his head, but if you'll leave everything in my hands I can guarantee that the whole thing will be adjusted."

"Pah! It's a put-up job!" snapped the lady. "I was a fool ever to trust you, cursed policemen! You're all the same! Just when the club was getting into its stride—"

"One moment, please!" pleaded Grimley. "I am certain I can rectify matters. If you'll only trust me to deal with it, I shall give you my word that you'll hear no more of it!"

"What do you mean?" she demanded, impressed despite herself by Grimley's earnestness.

"I mean that I can guarantee you complete immunity from any further raids—and, furthermore, the dismissal of that blundering nincompoop, Coutts, from the Force, because of his behaviour to-night!" said the Yard man vindictively. "Actually, Coutts is senior to me. Once he is removed, the whole of this district will be under my jurisdiction. That means, of course, that there will be no objection to any further ventures your ladyship cares to embark upon."

The Lady Melisande drew a deep breath.

"And if I refuse?" she queried.

"Well, I'm—er—afraid that the penalties will be rather heavy," said Grimley. "The authorities are very hot on these cases nowadays, and if the existence of gambling and—er—other activities should leak out, I'm afraid prison is inevitable."

The Lady Melisande's eyes blazed. She was no fool. She knew that Grimley was offering her the "Either —or," those terrible alternatives of the blackmailer.

There are thousands of men in the Metropolitan Police Force, and it would be very remarkable if there were not one or two crooks among them; but apart from these Scotland Yard has a record second to none for incorruptibility.

"You devil! What'll I have to do—pay again, I suppose?" she queried.

Grimley shook his head.

"No. Just let me deal with Coutts. All you have to do is to write a letter to the Commissioner of Police—and I can promise you complete indemnity and immunity."

She drew a deep breath.

Grimley whispered a few words in her ear, and as she listened she gave a slow smile of understanding.

"You're a clever devil, Grimley," she remarked, "and a dangerous man to cross."

"As Coutts will soon discover, madam," said Grimley. "But I can also be a very good friend."

He smiled significantly, and as he turned to leave:

"Don't be alarmed. I shall call tomorrow when this has blown over."

CHAPTER 4
MRS. COUTTS' COMPLICATION.

MERIDEN, Oxley Avenue, Brixton, S.W., was one of some forty suburban villas of early Edwardian architecture, the walls of which were—or had been—of a delicate fawn stucco, and the front door of which—like all the others—was flanked and surmounted by diamond shaped panes of blue and vermilion glass.

As cryptically described by the house agents, the houses in Oxley Avenue were: "Modern; s.d.; 3 bed 2 recep.; ev. mod. conven. h. and c.; dec. to choice, 3 minutes tr. and bus."

Meriden differed only from its immediate neighbours, Sandringham and Bella Vista, in its admirably kept garden, a horticultural masterpiece in miniature, with its strip of velvet lawn—about the size of a bed-room carpet—its beautifully kept flower beds, and trim privet hedges that were the pride of their owner's heart.

Meriden had been Detective-Inspector Coutts' home for over twenty years, and on a sunny morning the day after the raid on the Puce Lobster, that worthy man entered the kitchen at precisely eight o'clock after a hard hour's digging and weeding in the kitchen garden at the back. He sluiced himself at the sink, handier at the moment than the other mod. cons.

His florid face was aglow with health and soap, and he sniffed appreciatively at the appetising odour of eggs and bacon wafted to his nostrils. He was not tired, despite his short night's sleep.

"Smells good, mother!" said Coutts, sinking into a chair and opening the morning paper, propping it against the cruet.

Mrs. Coutts smiled indulgently at her spouse as she set a plateful of porridge before him.

She was a buxom, pleasant-faced lady a few years younger than Coutts himself. Her apple cheeks had not lost their country freshness after twenty years of London smoke and fog. She was a Shropshire lass, as Coutts called her in his more expansive moments, and was as much in love with her George as on the day when, as a young constable, he had wooed and won her—then a lady's maid in Meriden Hall, Salop.

"You were very late coming home last night, George dear," said his wife. "You've been working very hard lately, and you deserve your holiday."

"Huh! Working?" grunted Coutts, vigorously sugaring his porridge. "I was at the rounding-up of a lot of silly sheep. Incidentally, mother, where's young Harry been lately? He doesn't call round here so often as he used to. Too busy courting that Sellars girl, I s'pose, the young dog!" he added, with a chuckle.

He finished the porridge while Mrs. Coutts supplied details, and then pushed aside his plate and helped himself to a liberal portion of bacon and eggs.

"He's a good lad, but a bit headstrong. I'm not so sure that Molly Sellars is the right girl for him. I admit she's pretty, but she's flighty, and her skirts are far too short."

Mrs. Courts plucked nervously at the table-cloth. She had been dreading this reference to Harry Lawson, her nephew. Harry was the only son of her only sister, and when Tom had been killed, all Mrs. Coutts' maternal affection for her son was lavished on her orphaned nephew.

He was a good-looking, intelligent youth of about twenty, and had a good job as a motor mechanic at Enfield. He had made Meriden his second home for years, but of late his visits there had been more and more infrequent. She had heard several disquieting rumours of his association with Molly Sellars, a young and pretty dancing "instructress." Also, it appeared that Harry was drinking a good deal lately.

"I thought of writing and asking 'em over for dinner on Sunday," she ventured. "If it's a fine day we could go for a picnic to Boxhill or Richmond—what do you think, George?"

COUTTS grunted non-committally

"Drop him a line then—and we'll see. I've got a few words to say to young Harry—neglecting us like this!" He glanced at the clock and whistled.

"Gosh! I must hurry, mother! Gimme my hat!"

He hurriedly donned his blue reefer jacket and snatched his bowler from his wife's hand. He kissed her perfunctorily and took his leave.

When the front door had slammed behind him, Mrs. Coutts sighed. Dear, impetuous George, who beneath his gruff exterior, hid a heart of gold. She wondered fearfully what he would have said to the letter she had received that morning. With fingers that shook slightly, she drew out an envelope from the pocket of her apron. It was marked "Private." From it she withdrew the following missive:

9, Borough Street.
Wednesday.

Dear Aunt Jane,—I know you'll be surprised at not hearing from me for such a long time, but the fact is I've got myself into rather a scrape. Mollie has given me the chuck. She says she wants to go on the stage and she's running around with a fellow who says they can make lots of money as dancing partners.

Naturally, I've been feeling sore about it, and the fact is that I've been spending all my savings to try to forget her. To tell you the truth, I've been gambling pretty bad and I'm in a hole. There's a fellow named Benny Silver who's been giving me tips for the dogs. He's in with the Contrini crush and he told me that Toffee Apple was a cert and to put my shirt on him. I believed him, but as I was broke I borrowed some money from the cricket club account of which I am treasurer, and, of course, the blooming dog was nowhere.

Well, aunt, I'm in the cart all right now. There's to be an audit on Saturday, and unless I can raise £30 by then I'm ruined. Well, that's all I can say, except perhaps it's all for the best, and I'm better out of the world, anyway, now Molly's given me the go-by. Women are all the same, anyway.

I suppose it's too much to ask if you could help me. I know thirty quid is a big sum to ask for, but if you could, I swear I'd pay you back every penny. Ben says that Black Pete is a cert for the White City Cup. For goodness sake, whatever

you do don't tell Uncle George. He'd kill me for sure; besides, he's a policeman, and Benny says they ain't to be trusted nohow—relations or not.

Well, I must close, dear aunt. You've always been good to me. You are the only one I can turn to, and if you could possibly do it please write me by return, because I'm almost off my head with worry. Address it to me c/o "Floradora Club", 3a, Drury Lane, W.C.2.

Your loving nephew,
HARRY.

Mrs. Coutts removed her glasses, and her eyes filled with tears.

"The poor laddie!" she murmured. "The poor, motherless laddie!"

She did not see the selfishness, the inherent weakness in the youngster's character revealed in that naive and incoherent letter. All she felt was a passionate desire to help. But how? Thirty pounds was a great deal of money, and a police inspector's pay, since the recent cuts, was not particularly big. How could she raise the money without her husband knowing? She had never kept a secret from him in her life, but Harry had pleaded with her not to tell him—and she was afraid.

The morning sunlight streamed into the little kitchen, but Mrs. Coutts heeded it not as she buried her head in her arm, a huddled, black little figure against the whiteness of the uncleared breakfast-table.

IN his plainly furnished room at New Scotland Yard, Detective-Inspector Coutts surveyed the Thames dispassionately from his window, then went on writing.

There was a tap on the door. Grimley entered. He frowned a shade disapprovingly at Coutts' shirt-sleeves. It was a hot day, and the Yard man had hung his blue reefer on the stand, displaying braces of a particularly repulsive magenta.

"Mornin'!" grunted Coutts.

"*Good*-morning!" replied Grimley, with that aggressive, charitably amiable cheerfulness that is more offensive at times than a studied insult.

"Well, I suppose you're happy now, Coutts," said Grimley, "having raided the only decently run night club in the West End? You didn't see any gambling or cocaine orgies going on, did you?"

"No, I didn't!" snapped Coutts. "Though it doesn't prove anything—especially as you were there before me. Incidentally, that girl Cardiff Meg, who was with Baltimore Smith, was once pulled in at Liverpool for running dope."

"Really?" said Grimley. "How interesting!"

A buzzer sounded in the desk above Coutts' head. He frowned irritably.

Grimley grinned.

"The Commissioner possibly wants to congratulate you on your daring raid. Did I mention that Miss Fairfax often danced at the Puce Lobster, Coutts?" he added vindictively.

A little vein throbbed dully in Coutts' forehead—a sign of repressed anger with him. Betty Fairfax was the daughter of Sir Henry Fairfax, Commissioner of Police.

He rose to his feet and took up his notebook preparatory to the forthcoming interview.

"Let me help you on with your coat," said Grimley, with sudden amiability. He held out the blue reefer, and, with a nod of acknowledgment, Coutts covered up his magenta braces and buttoned the coat tightly across his broad chest.

Grimley watched him go and gave a low, sibilant laugh as the door closed.

Sir Henry Fairfax, a tall, elegant, middle-aged man, scanned a letter he had just received, and pulled thoughtfully at his Vandyke beard. A frown creased his forehead and he allowed his eyeglasses to drop on their silken cord as a tap sounded at the door.

"Come in!" said the Commissioner.

He looked up a trifle absently as his subordinate entered.

"Good-morning, Coutts!" he said, a trifle frigidly. "I have just received a remarkable communication by special messenger, inspector. It concerns you personally, and I may say that I view the matter with the utmost gravity. If the accusation is true—and, of course, the matter will be rigorously investigated—it reflects not only the gravest discredit upon yourself, but upon the whole Metropolitan Police Force."

Coutts' mouth went suddenly dry.

"I—I'm afraid I don't understand, Sir Henry," he said, in a queer, strained voice.

"It is only fair for you to know the accusation against you, Coutts," said the Commissioner. "You may read it. Sit down, Coutts."

Coutts murmured a word of thanks and sank dazedly into a chair.

His fingers trembled a little as he scanned the heavy cream-woven paper with its crested, embossed address.

Norfield House,
Kensington Gardens.

Dear Sir Henry Fairfax,—It is with considerable reluctance that I write you this letter, but in view of last night's utterly unwarrantable raid on the club of which I am manageress and part proprietor, I think it is only right and just that you should be in possession of the facts.

The club, as you are doubtless aware, has, since its inception, been frequented by people of the highest social standing, and I have endeavoured as far as possible to run it according to the law. I have, however, been pestered since its inception by the attention of various plain clothes officers who have hinted broadly that, in consideration of certain services, I would be immune from the usual irritating licensing restrictions. Needless to say, I indignantly refused these suggestions and threatened to report the matter to you.

I was not further troubled, however, until yesterday evening, when I received a visit from Detective-Inspector Coutts, who informed me that unless a substantial sum was looming towards what he called the Police Sports Fund, my club would be raided and struck off the register. Of course, I realised at once that it was blackmail, and consulted my partner, the Hon. Ivor Trelawney. He advised me to set a trap for the inspector. I accordingly pretended to concur in his outrageous demands and offered him a cheque for £100. He demurred at this, stating that it was too risky, and I accordingly handed him ten Bank of England notes for £10 each, the numbers of which I enclose.

He assured me that I should not be further troubled, and you can imagine my consternation when the self-same man arrived and coolly raided my premises last night.

I must therefore, in my own and the public interest, request that the whole matter should be thoroughly investigated, and am prepared to back up my statements to the hilt.

I am, sir,
Your obedient servant,
MELISANDE NOREIE.

Coutts stared speechlessly at this astounding document for a moment or two. He was literally dumbfounded. The flamboyant writing in violet ink danced fantastically before his eyes.

"Well, Coutts?" said Sir Henry sternly.

Coutts cleared his throat.

"It's a lie! A foul, damnable lie!" he ejaculated.

"I've been in the Force for twenty years, and this is the first time I—I—"

His voice broke a little. He groped in his breast-pocket mechanically for his handkerchief. Coutts pulled out his bandana with a jerk. Something fell on to the carpet with a slight thud.

It might have been a thunderbolt judging by the effect it had on Coutts. His face went a dirty grey, and Sir Henry's mouth tightened.

On the floor by the desk was a bundle of Bank of England notes.

"Hand me those notes, inspector!" snapped the Commissioner.

Coutts stooped down. A great roaring sounded in his ears. He felt that the whole world was rocking and crashing into chaos around him.

As in a dream, as if from a long distance, he heard Sir Henry's acid tones.

"How do you account for the fact the numbers of these notes coincide with the numbers supplied by Lady Melisande Norrie, Inspector?"

Coutts could say nothing. He stared like a man in a trance as Sir Henry flicked over the crisp notes and checked them with a slip of paper on his desk.

"H'm! Very well! You may go for the moment. You will, of course, hear further regarding this matter. Meantime, you will consider yourself suspended from duty!"

"Yes, Sir Henry!" said Coutts brokenly.

He turned to the door, his shoulders painfully drooped, his face the colour of death.

Suspended from duty!

CHAPTER 5
MRS. BARDELL IN A "CROESUS."

THE drowsy calm of a warm afternoon pervaded the basement parlour of Mr. Sexton Blake's house in Baker Street. It was the unwritten law that the basement of the house was the undisputed domain of Blake's housekeeper, Mrs. Martha Bardell.

On this quiet summer afternoon that worthy woman was indulging in what she described as a little "fiesta of forty blinks."

Between three-thirty and four p.m., with the kettle singing softly on the hob, with a plateful of buttered scones at her elbow, with the sunlight streaming in on her round dumpling face, Mrs. Bardell sat in her rocking chair, the embodiment of middle-aged comfort.

In her rustling dress of black bombazine, her comfortable elastic-sided boots, her lace mob-cap and shawl, she made a perfect symbol of the goddess of the hearth.

The clock on the mantelpiece ticked on with a cheerful, insistent and fussy note. Pedro dozed, his massive head between his paws, and all was calm and peaceful. Blake and Tinker had gone for a run in the Grey Panther, and Mrs. Bardell dozed.

Suddenly the front door bell rang. With a "wuff" Pedro awoke.

Mrs. Bardell rubbed her eyes and rose ponderously to her feet.

She climbed the stairs muttering, and opened the front door.

A grey-haired, matronly figure in a neat dark blue costume smiled at her on the step. She had round apple-like features almost as ruddy as Mrs. Bardel's own, but there was a careworn expression in her kindly eyes. Her shoes were dusty, and she looked tired.

"Good-afternoon, Mrs. Bardell," she said courteously. "Is Mr. Blake at home?"

"Which I'm sorry to say 'e ain't!" said the housekeeper. "Did you wish to insult 'im?" she asked with dignity.

The visitor looked startled.

"Dear me, no!" she said. "That is, yes. I mean, I wanted to consult him—er—rather urgently." She was evidently disconcerted by Mrs. Bardell's weird and wonderful use of the English language.

Mrs. Bardell never seemed to get hold of the right word; or if she did, as Tinker said, it usually meant something else.

"I'm sorry, ma'am. What name shall I say called?"

"Mrs. Coutts. I'm the wife of Detective-Inspector Coutts, of Scotland Yard. I believe you know my husband, Mrs. Bardell."

It was Mrs. Bardell's turn to look astonished.

"Why, lawks a mussy!" she exclaimed, her fat face wreathed in smiles. "This is truly entertaining angels' underwears! Come in, my dear, an' 'ave a cupper tea. You must be tired with this 'ere 'eat wave. Master Tinker's gone to 'ave a bathe in the Ludo on the Turpentine," she added.

Mrs. Coutts smiled wanly.

"Well, it's very good of you, dear Mrs. Bardell," she said. "George, that's my husband, has told me such a lot about you that I feel I've known you for years, yet this is the first time we've met."

Mrs. Bardell glowed with pleasure. She had taken instantly to this homely, pleasant woman.

"Get along, do!" she said, smiling. "Don't you believe all 'e tells you, my dear. Which I've always said as Defective-Suspector Scoots will 'ave 'is little joke, and he's got a rare gift for smattering."

"For what?" asked Mrs. Coutts, rather mystified.

"For smattering. You know, my dear—for giving a person all sorts of condiments which they don't preserve. Not but what it's pleasant to be told you are a good 'ousekeeper and all that, and I maintains, and always shall, that a good woman is worth more than boobies, as King Solomon says in the Book of Proverbs, which I sometimes used to remark to pore B. before he was took—"

She led the way to her cosy kitchen, chattering on the way without pausing. Mrs. Coutts' housewifely eyes glanced appreciatively at the apartment's spotless comfort when they entered the door.

"Sit down, do," urged Mrs. Bardell hospitably. "I'll 'ave a cupper tea ready afore you can say Jack Robertson—though why anyone should want to say Jack Robertson I never could see," she added, as she crossed over to the dresser and took down an extra cup and saucer.

Mrs. Coutts smiled wanly at Mrs. Bardell's garrulities. Despite her quaint oddities of speech there was a deal of sound commonsense in that estimable woman's character. She had realised at once that Mrs. Coutts was in some trouble and chatted volubly in an effort to put her at her ease.

She poured out two cups of tea, and passed a plate of wafer-like bread-and-butter to her guest.

"You seem very comfortable here, Mrs. Bardell," said Mrs. Coutts, with an admiring glance round the snuggery.

Mrs. Bardell smiled complacently.

"Yes, I mustn't grumble," she said. "But all the same for that, ma'am, bein' 'ousekeeper to a private sluice isn't all beer and spittles, as the saying goes. You bein' the wife of a defective-suspector well knows its disadvantages. Not, o' course, that I want to disabuse Mr. Blake, who's one of the finest gentlemen that ever I done for, and that kind and considerate, but I do maintain, as 'is 'ousekeeper for many years, that secretion is the better part of pallor, an' the least said the soonest mended."

MRS. COUTTS smiled as Mrs. Bardell concluded a trifle breathlessly.

"I'm sure the sentiments do you credit, Mrs. Bardell. My husband has often told me what a discreet person you are, and how kind you've always been to him. And as for your cooking—my, I do wish you'd give me the recipe for the steak-and-kidney pie he praises so much."

Mrs. Bardell beamed. She certainly was an incomparable cook, and any reference to her culinary art was a sure passport to her ample heart.

"Which I shall be only too delighted, my dear. 'Ave another cupper tea? You look dead tired." Mrs. Bardell noticed that, in spite of her bright chatter, her guest was looking preoccupied and careworn, and the good soul leant forward and patted her guest's hand sympathetically.

"Tell me, my dear! Are you worried about somethin'?"

Mrs. Coutts nodded. Ever since the receipt of that letter from her nephew that morning she had been troubled and distressed. Her own savings were in a joint account with her husband's, and short of pawning some of her silver and valuables, she had no means of raising the necessary sum.

Besides, she loathed the thought of pawnshops, and she knew that Coutts would soon miss the articles. She was at her wits' end when, like a flash of inspiration, had come the thought of Sexton Blake. He would help and advise her in her difficulty, as he had helped and advised others in the past. Long ago she had learned from her husband of his kindness and sympathy to those in trouble. So, taking her courage in both hands, she had sallied forth to Baker Street.

Now she had actually arrived and found Blake away from home, panic seized her. Despite Mrs. Bardell's cordiality, her heart sank. What if Coutts found out? What if Blake refused? These and other "ifs" weakened her resolve. Suddenly she became aware of the housekeeper's kindly solicitude. Nothing but sympathy and understanding was in Mrs. Bardell's blue eyes, and Mrs. Coutts melted suddenly.

"Oh, Mrs. Bardell, I'm in such dreadful trouble!" she began tremulously.

"There now, don't take it to 'eart, dear," said Mrs. B. "Nothink's so bad as it might be worse. I've lived in this vale of tears long enough to know that it's a long lane that is soonest mended. Tell me all about it. Open combustion is good for the soul, as the saying goes."

Mrs. Coutts, half laughing, half crying, pulled out her nephew's letter, and bit by bit told her trouble.

Mrs. Bardell read the letter through laboriously, and sniffed a little.

"The idea!" she said. "Getting all bothered about a little thing like that! Now, listen to me, my dear. There's no need for you to worry. This owdacious young limb of a nevvy ought to 'ave his ears boxed, that's what, gambling at 'is time o' life! I'd give 'im Toffee Apple, indeed. This 'ere girl what calls herself a dancin' destructress ain't no better than she should be, I'll warrant. A flighty young thing who is a disgrace to her sect, leading a young man on!"

"Oh, no, Mrs. Bardell dear! Molly's a good girl, only thoughtless, like Harry, at times."

Mrs. Bardell snorted.

"The pair of 'em ought to be spanked, worriting a dear, good soul like you! Now, listen to me, Mrs. Suspector, and don't speak a word till I've finished. This ain't a matter for neither Mr. Blake nor Mr. Scoots. They might be both very clever as criminal incinerators, and I'm not denying it, but they got no tack in a problem like this. Life without tack, as poor dear B. uster say, is like potatoes without salt. This is a little preposition for you and me. We don't want to drag Mr. Blake into it at all. I'll admit 'e's a great defective, and a fair marvel at comical work with microscopes, paralysing bloodstains in his idolatry, but 'e's as 'elpless as a child in 'ousehold matters. And what I says is that this 'ere's a 'ousehold matter."

She drew a deep breath, and tapped the letter.

Mrs. Coutts smiled wanly, with sudden hope.

"Yes," continued Mrs. Bardell, "we wimmin of the British Empire must stand by each other in a croesus, as dear Mr. Baldwin said on my Portugal wireless only the other night. This is what you might call a domestic financial compression, as they calls it. Now, I've put by a goodish bit o' money in my time. Mr. Blake pays me a good celery, and wot I ses is 'andsome is as 'andsome does. Mr. Baldwin, in the very same speech about perverting our War Loan, says it's a patriotic dooty. Now, I've got a few savings in the susstificates and such-like, and what's to stop me doin' a bit of perversion on me own?"

"But, dear Mrs. Bardell, I couldn't dream of—"

"Not another word, my dear. I've made up my mind. This is an investment. 'Stead of perverting thirty pounds of War Loan to three and a half per cent, I'll lend it to you at four per cent, thus being patriotic and 'elping you and myself. There now! Stop crying, and 'ave another cupper tea. We'll pop round to the post office later, and get the young lady to do the necessary perversion."

Mrs. Coutts wiped her eyes.

"But, dear Mrs. Bardell, it's most awfully kind of you, but I simply couldn't accept such a sacrifice. I mean—"

Her protests were cut short by Mrs. Bardell's significant glance.

"'Ssh! Not another word! 'Ssh! Is that the front door? Here's Master Tinker, back from the Turpentine. 'E'll be 'ollering for 'is tea in a minute. The matter's settled."

Mrs. Coutts smiled, her heart overflowing with gratitude. Mrs. B. beamed.

"I feel like one of them Boy Sprouts 'aving 'ad 'is turn for the day, Mrs. Scoots. Cheer up! Too many crooks spoil the broth. We'll leave the suspector and Mr. Blake out of it. This is part and partial of our natural economy champagne!"

Chapter 6
Coutts Butts In.

COVENT GARDEN, that strange quarter of London where night is turned into day, is a fantastically romantic district, and in a fashion fulfills the immortal Lewis Carroll's line anent cabbages and kings.

Hard by the Opera House, where, in the season, royalty foregathers, is the clamorous market itself, where, in and out of season, lorries loaded with fruit and vegetables arrive in the night hours in unceasing procession to feed London's hungry millions.

Here, where in olden days calm, level-eyed nuns once told their beads in a convent garden, is the unceasing babble and chaffing of various Cockney voices from midnight until dawn.

But in the daytime the Garden is comparatively quiet. It was shortly before noon that Detective-Inspector Coutts found himself wandering disconsolately round the district he knew so well. He had no very clear idea of how he got there, but there he found himself, a man dazed, his mental faculties numbed by the shock of that morning's interview.

"Suspended from duty."

The words echoed and re-echoed like a death knell in his ears. The stern face of the Commissioner … that monstrous, lying accusation … Grimley's mocking smile ...

He turned into the Nag's Head and ordered himself brandy and soda, striving to cope with the situation. The charge against the Puce Lobster would not come before the magistrate for at least another three weeks, so he was spared that added trouble.

The letter was a bombshell, and he groaned hollowly as he sipped his drink. It would be all over the metropolitan area by now. "Trust that grinning hound Grimley!" he reflected bitterly. And what could he do? How could he explain the possession of those notes? The Lady Melisande had lied deliberately, of course. Moreover, she had the Hon. Ivor to back her allegation. Two against one—and there were plenty of officers in the Yard who would hail Coutts' disgrace with glee.

And the missus! How could he break the news to her?

He got to his feet and stumbled unsteadily into the sunlight. His brain felt thoroughly atrophied as he turned towards Drury Lane. What, also, would his old friend and colleague, Sexton Blake, say? Blake who had shared many a perilous adventure with him in the past, the brave, loyal comrade whose friendship meant so much to Coutts. Dully he wondered how Blake would take the news of his disgrace.

Suddenly he halted as he recognised a tall, boyish-looking youngster deep in conversation with a pasty-faced fellow dressed in a loud check suit and a cap to match.

The latter seemed to be smiling as though at some unpleasant jest, but the youngster's face looked strained and set. Coutts forgot his own trouble for the moment, and watched the pair. He had recognised his nephew, young Harry Lawson.

What was he doing so deep in conversation with that notorious race gangster in the check suit, Benny Silver?

Coutts scowled. For a moment his detective training superseded his own personal troubles. Silly young ass, Harry! It was his duty to warn him against mixing with people of Benny Silver's kidney.

He quickened his pace just in time to see the pair disappear into one of the innumerable little eating-houses and coffee-shops adjoining Drury Lane.

Coutts followed quickly, and paused outside a dingy little restaurant, in the windows of which sausages sizzled slowly over a gas-ring beyond a bank of ribs of beef and pies and hot-dogs.

Over the shop window the facia declared, in faded guilt letters: "Toni Fubini Coffee House—Good Pull Up."

Coutts squared his shoulders and entered the shop. He sniffed with disgust. The atmosphere was impregnated with the odour of cabbages and a thousand bygone dinners.

Behind the counter sat an enormous Italian with graduated chins, all of which needed shaving.

"Afternoon," said Coutts. "Two friends of mine just gone in. Benny Silver was one of them."

The Italian looked at Coutts suspiciously.

"Notta down here, maybe upstairs in da club!" he said, jerking his thumb towards a curtained doorway.

Coutts grunted. There was a small, unobstrusive notice to the right, bearing the words: "Fioradora Club."

"I'll go and see!" he announced.

The massive Italian shrugged, and Coutts drew aside the plush curtain. Behind it was a sound-proof, green baize door. Coutts rapped smartly on it with his knuckles.

A hole opened suddenly in its green expanse, and an unfriendly, red-rimmed eye glowered at him suspiciously.

"Open up!" snapped Coutts. "I want to talk to Benny Silver."

"Benny's up there," volunteered the doorkeeper. "He's got a can with him."

"Has he, indeed!" said Coutts, with a scowl. He strode heavily up the stairs.

A door opened almost instantly, and he was greeted by a burly giant of a man who loomed up from a haze of blue tobacco smoke, his red head vivid against the murky background. He was well over six feet in height, and broad of shoulder; collarless, and in his shirt-sleeves. His crag-like jaw jutted out pugnaciously as he blinked suspiciously at Coutts.

"Hallo, Red!" snapped the latter. "I thought you'd given up this game?"

A look of startled recognition appeared on Red Gorman's rugged features.

"Coutts!" he ejaculated. He was somewhat slow on the uptake.

He made to slam the door, but Coutts had his foot against the bottom of it, and one hand against Red's chest.

"Not so fast, my friend! I'm coming in!"

Red Gorman stepped back, nonplussed. Coutts never lacked physical courage, and he knew it. Also, he was a police officer. Red had no further thought of stopping him as he strode into the room with his usual aggressive confidence.

IT was surprisingly large, considering the dinginess of the café downstairs. At the end was a bar, behind which a dago potman was busy polishing glasses. The walls were ornamented by a heterogeneous assortment of photographs, depicting past Derby winners, jockeys, and musical comedy stars of a bygone day.

At a corner table four men in shirt sleeves were engaged in a game of poker. Three or four other men, and one blowsy-looking girl with a raddled face and hard beady eyes, were seated over drinks in various parts of the room. The men were flashily dressed, and Coutts recognised most of them as active members of Barney Contrini's race gang. Their conversation ceased abruptly as they recognised him.

"H'm!" said Coutts. "I want a word with Master Benny."

He crossed over to the window where the ferret-faced Benny Silver was sitting at a table with his youthful companion. Harry Lawson's face flamed as he recognised his uncle. Benny kicked him under the table.

"Keep your trap shut, kid! You ain't doin' no harm!" he hissed. He turned, with a forced smile, to Coutts. "Why, inspector! Fancy seeing you here? I haven't seen you for ages," he began.

"Beat it, Benny—quick!" snarled Coutts. "Or I'll pull you in."

"But—but—I say, what have I done?" wailed Benny.

"Get out!" snapped Coutts.

Benny shot him a malevolent glance from his furtive eyes and slunk towards the door.

"What are you doing here, Harry?" demanded Coutts.

"I—I—met Benny, and he asked me to come along and have a quiet drink," mumbled the unhappy youth.

"Oh! And how long have you known Benny Silver?"

"A few weeks, uncle. He was introduced to me by our foreman down in Enfield."

"Been gambling?"

Harry Lawson hung his head. "Well, I've had a flutter or two on the dogs," he admitted.

"You're a silly fool!" snapped Coutts. "Benny Silver's a crook, a sponger, and a loafer. I'll have no relation of mine running round with him and his like—understand?"

His nephew flushed as the girl at the adjacent table giggled.

"Look here, uncle, I'm of age!" he said hotly. "I can do what I like with my own money!"

Coutts snorted.

"Yes, with your *own* money," he said with emphasis.

Harry Lawson's face went white. Had his aunt betrayed him, after all? Was everything u.p.? He felt physically sick at the thought of arrest. Coutts, however, did not appear to notice his agitation.

"It won't be your own money very long if you run around with loafers like Benny Silver. Why haven't you been round to see us lately?"

The youngster hung his head miserably.

"Well, they've been short-handed at the works lately," he began lamely,

"Pah!" snorted Coutts. "That's no reason! You'll have to watch your step, my lad. You're getting mixed up with a rotten crowd! You come with me! You're not stopping in this place!"

Harry Lawson flushed as he rose to his feet. He felt rather like a small schoolboy as he followed Coutts out to the jeering laughter of Barney Contrini and his gang.

"Wot brought him 'ere?" whispered a weasel-faced individual in a check cap several sizes too large for him. "Ol' Grimley says we're O.K. Didn't you sweeten 'im, Red?"

"Course I did," broke in Red Gorman. "But Grimley 'ates Coutts like poison. If I was you I'd tail 'im. Benny tol' me as 'ow that can's Coutts' nephew."

"Is 'e?" replied the rat-faced one. He rejoiced in the name of "Whoosis Wally," because of his frequent use of that term in his speech. He was a "nose," or informer, one of that contemptible class who perpetually hover on the outskirts of the underworld, hated by crooks and despised by the police. Fortunately, his activities as an informer were unknown to Barney and his cronies, or his shrift would have been exceedingly short.

"Gaw!" he said. "That's worth knowin', Red! I reckon I'd better tail 'em to the whoosis! So long, Red!"

He flung away a sodden cigarette and moved towards the door. He reached the end of the road just in time to see Coutts and Harry Lawson disappear into the saloon bar of the Nag's Head.

He whistled softly, then crossed over to the near-by phone box in Covent Garden Tube Station. There he called up a certain number. He waited a few minutes, and an evil grin crossed his thin lips as he recognised the clipped, incisive voice of Detective-Inspector Grimley at the other end of the wire.

"Hallo! Who's that?" demanded the Yard man.

"It's me—Wally," said the nark eagerly. "Say, Mr. Grimley, I've just left the whoosis."

"The whoosis what?" snapped Grimley.

"Red Gorman's club. Coutts's just left. 'E's up to some funny business. 'E's with 'is nephew that's bin runnin' a whoosis with Benny Silver, and 'e don't 'alf look rattled. They've just gone to the Nag's Head together naa. I'm phonin' from the station."

"Ah! Good for you, Wally."

Grimley's sigh of satisfaction sounded audibly in the diaphragm.

"Keep him tailed, Wally—you won't suffer. Report to me at the usual place at eight to-night."

"Right, boss; trust me! I'll be at the whoosis avec knobs!" said Wally.

He rang off, with a satisfied smirk.

At the other end of the wire Detective-Inspector Grimley rubbed his hands gleefully. Wally was his creature, and the information he had just received fitted in beautifully with the task he had just been assigned by Sir Henry Fairfax. He glanced at the memo form in front of him.

It was headed: *"Private and Confidential. Report on the conduct and activities of Detective-Inspector George Coutts"*

Grimley licked his lips as he wrote slowly:

From information received I learn that the subject is in the habit of frequenting a low club in Covent Garden run by an ex-convict, Red Gorman. He is frequently seen in the company of his nephew, who is a known associate of Benny Silver, notorious cardsharper, and one of the Contrini Gang.

"Hold that one, Mr. High-and-Mighty Coutts!" he muttered.

CHAPTER 7
THE SUN PARTY.

MERRICK MEWS, just off Lancaster Gate and discreetly hidden by the huge Victorian houses overlooking Hyde Park, were, until comparatively recently, inhabited by ancient cabbies who bemoaned the passing of horseflesh and the Naughty Nineties, or by disillusioned taxi-drivers and chauffeurs who bemoaned the continued existence of the aforesaid cabbies, the price of petrol, and the paucity of tips.

One day an enterprising estate agent, seeking to exploit fresh desmesnes and messuages new, discovered the habitability of Merrick Mews. After the manner of his rapacious kind, he proceeded to uproot the discontented denizens from their abodes by the simple process of raising the rent.

By judicious advertisement he convinced the smart set that it was the last word in chic to live in a mews.

The result exceeded his wildest expectations. The converted stables where once the barouches and horseless carriages of a more leisurely age were housed, were now transformed into ultra expensive flats, complete with every modern convenience, and even luxury.

Easily the most expensively, furnished and most modern flat in Merrick Mews was owned by that distinguished explorer and big game hunter, Gillie Carew. There, on a broiling summer day a week after the raid on the Puce Lobster, Fate chose to stage a drama that was to become one of the most discussed causes celebres of recent years.

Curiously enough the main actors in the drama had also played their allotted parts in the Puce Lobster comedy a week previously, and this was the way of it.

Gillie Carew had returned from the Amazon with several crates of zoological and ornithological specimens, an Indian manservant, and a fixed idea.

The name of the manservant, a silent, copper-hued individual, was Toltec. Gillie had found him in Cuzco, the ancient Inca capital of Peru, where, long before Mr. George Lansbury, the

Incas discovered the virtues of the sun as the source of life and good health.

Gillie Carew claimed, with what truth can never be known, that Toltec was the direct descendant of that Toltec who was the High Priest of the Living Sun in the days when the Inca civilisation was at its height. Anyway, Gillie thought it would be a good stunt to bring Toltec back to England with him. It would be too, too thrill-making to have as a manservant a real descendant of an Inca high priest. And, besides, Gillie really believed in sun-bathing.

His great idea was to start a new sun-bathing cult among the jaded Bright Young People, and, though the season was practically over, he planned the inevitable cocktail-party to explain his project, and introduce Toltec officially.

Gillie was certainly thorough.

The walls of his flat, an exotically furnished place, consisted in the main of Vita glass windows glass windows, in order to admit the health-giving ultra-violet rays of the sun.

The Hon. Ivor Trelawney arrived, accompanied by Monica Travers, and found the Lady Melisande already in evidence, looking ravishing in a silk sun-bathing costume. And they gathered she had lunched there with Gillie Carew.

Gillie himself looked magnificent, dressed only in a pair of khaki shorts. Beneath his golden tan the muscles of his magnificent torso rippled.

"You see, my dear Ivor, I am already converted," laughed the Lady Melisande.

"Hallo, Monica dear! You're a bit early, aren't you?" asked Gillie, with a smile. "Come on in and have a Martini."

Monica Travers bit her lip. She had noticed the growing intimacy between her lover and Melisande, and she was incensed at not being invited to lunch. She would not, however, give her rival

a chance to crow over her, and, with a smile as icy as it was polite, she linked her arm through Melisande's.

"What a charming colour!" she said, referring to the abbreviated costume. "I think pink suits you."

"And I'm certain green's your colour, darling," said Melisande, with dangerous sweetness.

The Hon. Ivor Trelawney smiled cynically at his host as the two women left the studio.

"The fair Melisande seems to be enjoying herself, Gillie," he remarked with a chuckle.

Gillie Carew's handsome face darkened.

"What the devil are you insinuating, Trelawney?" he demanded.

The Hon. Ivor shrugged. "Oh, nothing!" he said, lifting his slanting mephistophelian eyebrows. "But I understand that Monica is complaining bitterly of your neglect recently."

"And what the devil has it to do with you, anyway?" snarled Carew. "Listen, Trelawney! I don't tolerate any interference in my affairs. If you have anything to say about Melisande and myself, or even Monica for that matter, I'll—"

HE broke off suddenly as a tap sounded at the door, and a crowd of chattering people trooped into the studio.

"Hallo, hallo, hallo!" greeted Freddy Arbuthnot, a tall youth with a monocle, and butter-coloured

hair slicked back from a sloping forehead. "Where's your jolly old Aztec, Gillie?"

Gillie Carew laughed.

"All in good time!"

Trelawney turned to the newcomers trooping in.

"Hallo, Smith! How are you? Have you met our Miss Bering, the darling of the 'gods?' Babs, this is Mr. Baltmore Smith, one of those strong, silent financiers with a skin you love to touch."

"You beast, Ivor!" snapped Babs, turning to the handsome broad-shouldered man in the grey lounge suit who had who had entered with Gavin Quayle, the cubist artist, Anna Morena, the film star, and Teddie Rampling of the "Daily Radio."

Rampling glanced at Mr. Baltmore Smith, and his eyes narrowed.

What was Baltimore Smith, con man and crook, doing here?

Baltimore, blissfully unaware of the gossip man's scrutiny, turned to Babs and grinned pleasantly. It had taken a week's careful manoeuvring to gatecrash in on this crowd, but he had succeeded, and there was a chance of good pickings.

"Any of you fellows want to sun-bathe?" queried Gillie Carew, as four more guests arrived.

"I don't think I'll bother, Carew," laughed Teddie Rampling. "What's all this I hear about Archie the Aztec?"

Carew, who had been showing a newly acquired shotgun to John Mandeville, a lean, leather-faced man with a big reputation as a hunter, turned with a smile to the gossip merchant.

"Hallo, inkslinger!" he said cheerily. "It's not an Aztec, but an Inca. I suppose you'll be wanting photos?"

Teddie nodded.

"Sure! You needn't bother about flashlight. This sun is almost too strong," he added, wiping his forehead with his handkerchief.

He drew in his breath sharply as Melisande and Monica, accompanied by two more girls, entered. They were dressed in the very latest word in Lido beach costumes. He shaded his eyes at the dazzling colours.

From the tail of his eye the observant Teddie noticed Monica and their host. As the guests helped themselves to cocktails and ices from the table in the centre of the big studio, those two drew apart. Teddie guessed rather than heard that they were quarrelling. Monica's lips quivered and her eyes smouldered dangerously.

"Don't be so silly, my dear girl!" he heard Carew say. "I refuse to be tied to any woman's apron-strings!"

"You beast!" hissed Monica, an angry red flush in her cheeks.

Teddie shrugged and turned to Babs Dering.

"And how's my sea-green incorruptible?" he asked.

"Hot and thirsty!" said Babs, sinking into an enormous divan and crossing her million-dollar legs. "Tell me—"

Suddenly her question and the noise of the room with its babble of conversation, laughter, and the tinkle of glasses, was cut short by a resonant clang.

GILLIE CAREW was standing near a beautifully wrought gong of inlaid copper and silver—a trophy from Damascus. Again he raised the the stick, and at the second stroke of the gong the door on the right of the ladies' room opened.

Babs Dering gave a little shriek.

Standing on the threshold, calm, immobile as a statue in bronze, stood a queerly incongruous figure in that room of vapid worldlings.

It was Toltec, the Mayan Indian. Fully six feet in height, he was naked save for a girdle of smoke-grey feathers. The muscles of his torso bulged like live snakes beneath the copper sheen of his skin. His face was beardless, with high cheekbones, and his eyes were large and luminous. His hair was long and straight, and reached almost to his shoulders; yet there was no trace of effeminacy in that calm, sphinx-like face. On his head was a gleaming disc, and in his right hand he carried a bronze wand round which was twined a feathered serpent—god of the ancient Incas.

Gillie Carew was enjoying the situation he had created.

"Ladies and gentlemen, let me present you to Toltec, Priest of the Living Sun!" he said dramatically. "He doesn't, speak a word of English yet, but I'm sure you'd like to hear his invocation to the founder of all blessings."

Their host muttered a few words in the Mayan tongue to the statuesque Toltec, who bowed gravely. The Lady Melisande clapped her hands.

"Oh, bravo! Bravo, Gillie!" she said. "I've not had a thrill like this for years! Do, do persuade him to come to the club! He'll draw all London! We'll make enough to pay the wretched fine the first night!"

"Don't be so beastly mercenary, Melie!" snapped the Hon Ivor. "Why let your racial instincts, become apparent?"

Crack!

Gillie Carew's left shot out. So sudden was the blow that the Hon. Ivor Trelawney staggered

backward, crashed against a palm, and slumped to the floor. Gillie Carew stood over him, his nostrils dilating, his fists clenched.

"Get up, you dirty tike, and apologise! By heck, I'll ram your teeth down your throat!" he snarled.

With an oath Trelawney struggled to his feet and made a bull rush at Carew. They had both been drinking heavily. The situation looked ugly. The Lady Melisande went chalk-white. She clutched frenziedly at Carew's sleeve.

"Oh, please, please, Gillie!"

Gillie Carew laughed discordantly. He had always hated Trelawney, with his malicious wit and arrogant attitude.

"Apologise, you rat!" he snarled.

Trelawney fingered his bruised chin. There was cold hatred in his dark eyes. He turned to Melisande and bowed stiffly.

"I apologise, my dear lady. The sight of all that gold must have aroused the long dormant Gluckman blood," he said, with a sneer.

Carew ripped out an oath, and made another lunge at his tormentor.

"Stop that!" snapped Teddie Rampling, clutching him round the bare waist. "Beat it, Trelawney," he gasped, "before he kills you!"

Monica Travers, white to the lips, stood wide-eyed and trembling, watching the antagonists. The Lady Melisande smiled triumphantly, and a wave of hysteria swept over the girl.

"Kill him, Ivor!" she said vindictively. "He deserves it after the way he treated me!"

"I always exterminate vermin with Gluckman's powder!" said the Hon. Ivor viciously.

Carew struggled like a madman against the arms that tried to restrain him. He flung Teddie Rampling halfway across the studio. He was stark berserk with rage. That last taunt of Trelawney had goaded him to madness,

"Stop that, Carew!" broke in the crisp, incisive tones of John Mandeville, the explorer. His fingers closed in a vice-like grip on Gillie Carew's arm; his hard, grey eyes were compelling.

"Sorry, John, but I—I—"

Gillie Carew swayed. Someone handed him a stiff whisky. He drained it at a gulp.

"This is where we do a quiet fade-out," murmured Anna Morena.

Teddie Rampling nodded and looked at Toltec. The Indian stood there like a statue, his great dark eyes resting on Gillie Carew. Teddie shivered a little. Was it hatred or contempt that lurked in that steady, solemn glance?

The Hon. Ivor Trelawney picked up his hat and gloves.

"Coming, Monica?" he said.

The girl dashed to the adjacent dressing-room, and in an incredibly short time was dressed for the street.

"Let's go, Ivor!" she said. "This place makes me sick!"

The Lady Melisande gave a mocking little laugh as one by one, murmuring conventional excuses and apologies, the guests departed. Gillie Carew bit his lip as the last of them went. He crossed over to the sideboard in the corner and helped himself to a neat brandy. He'd been a fool to lose his temper like that! An accursed fool! But, by Heaven, that cur Trelawney deserved it.

Toltec still stood in the centre of the room—calm, immutable as Fate itself.

"Get out, you!" snarled his master.

The Indian bowed and withdrew, silent and dignified.

Melisande emerged from the dressing-room, clad once again in her ordinary clothes.

"Gillie, I think you were magnificent! Ivor is frightfully jealous of me, you know, dear," she cooed, plying her lipstick and glancing coquettishly at him beneath her provocative dark eyelashes. A sudden revulsion of feeling came over Carew. For the first time, this woman jarred on him. He wanted to be alone. His head ached abominably. Would she never stop preening herself? he wondered petulantly.

"I'm sorry it happened, Melisande," he said. "But the hound deserved a good hiding! Do you mind if I see you later? I'm—I'm not feeling too well. Stayed in the sun too long, I guess."

The Lady Melisande's carmine lips; curled scornfully; she shrugged her slim shoulders.

"Oh, well, if that's how you feel about it, my dear Gillie, you'd better sleep it off! I'll meet you at the club at 7.30."

With that she blew him a kiss that was a subtle blend of mockery and contempt, and a moment later Carew was left alone.

He punched a couple of cushions into shape and sprawled full length on the divan on the east side of the studio. His head was beginning to throb, and he closed his eyes after one look of distaste at the debris on the centre table—a litter of cocktail glasses, half-melted ices, sodden cigarette-stubs, and the like.

"Curse all women!" muttered Gillie Carew, and, breathing stertorously, fell asleep.

CHAPTER 8
THE CRIMSON STAIN.

"FORTY-SEVEN, forty-eight, forty-nine—" *Bang!*

Master Tommy Weeks, aged twelve, who was busy qualifying for the unofficial "yo-yo" championship of Lancaster Gate, paused in his solemn chanting as he negotiated that impish top for the forty-ninth time on the string. He frowned as he heard the sharp, staccato *Bang!* which echoed loudly in the quiet of Merrick Mews that sunlit afternoon.

Master Weeks was the scion of the house of Weeks, one of the original families of chauffeurs who had inhabited Merrick Mews before the Society invasion.

He had a half-holiday from school, a blessed afternoon which he was spending in the assiduous cultivation of "Over the Falls," and other "yo-yo" acrobatics.

"Noisy blighter!" said Tommy, resuming his game. Being a cab-driver's son, he put down the bang he had just heard to the back-firing of a car. Gritting his small white teeth, he began to count again monotonously.

"One, two, three, four—"

Under his grubby but skilful fingers the red-and-yellow toy slithered gracefully up and down its string. Tommy's freckled face was furrowed in concentration. He was leaning against the open door of a garage at the end of the mews—a silent, absorbed little figure in his grey flannel shorts and cricket shirt.

Suddenly he stiffened, and the "yo-yo" spun unheeded, as a shrill scream rang through the deserted mews, then a window was flung open, and a woman leaned out.

"Help! Help! Police! Murder!"

Tommy went suddenly cold. The woman's hair was dishevelled, and her face agonised and white with fear. Again she screamed. Tommy, thrusting his toy into his pocket, raced towards the window.

"Help! Quick—fetch a policeman!" gasped the woman.

A moment later her head was jerked back as if by an invisible hand. Tommy Weeks' heart pounded almost as fast as his sturdy feet on the cobbles of the mews. He dashed to the right near Lancaster Gate Tube Station, and his voice was shrill as it rose above the rumbling traffic.

"Help! Police!" he yelled, and, to the profane annoyance of the driver of a bus who missed him by inches, darted head foremost into the arms of a burly traffic policeman.

"Here, what's this?" demanded the constable.

"Come— quick!" gasped Tommy. "It's a murder in our mews!"

The policeman signalled to his mate at the corner, who hurried over.

"What's up, son?" he queried kindly.

Again Tommy told his story, simple but dramatic.

"Stand by, Bill!" said the second constable, and, taking a firm grip of the urchin's sleeve, followed the eager Tommy into the entrance of Merrick Mews.

"Where did you hear that noise?" he queried.

Master Weeks pointed a grubby forefinger to the open windows of Gillie Carew's studio. P.-c. Holbrook frowned and rubbed his stubby chin thoughtfully. He was rather sceptical, having had some experience of the genus small boy before.

"It was up there, mister!" gasped Tommy. "A lady screamin' at the top of 'er voice. 'Er face was all—"

Again the calm of that quiet backwater was shattered by a shrill, high-pitched scream. Constable Holbrook was galvanised into a heavy jog-trot. The door of the flat was ajar, and pushing it unceremoniously open, the policeman entered the hallway.

"You stay here, kid," he said sternly. "Don't you dare run away. I'll be wanting you!"

Little Tommy Weeks nodded, and glanced fearfully at the constable. Young as he was, he realised that grim tragedy was in the air.

P.-c. Holbrook, a young, fresh-complexioned man, one of the new school of policemen, bounded for his truncheon. He had just reached the first landing when a wild-eyed, distraught figure emerged from Gillie Carew's studio. It was Monica Travers.

Her face was the colour of death, and she swayed drunkenly towards him.

"Oh!" she gasped. "He's dead. He's—he's dead!"

With a piteous cry she stumbled forward into the policeman's arms.

"Now, madam!" he said, with gruff kindliness. "What's happened? Try to pull yourself together, and—"

P.-c. Holbrook broke off suddenly. The girl lay a limp and dead weight in his arms. His eyes narrowed. Down the front of her flimsy voile frock was an ominous crimson stain. The fingers of her right hand were sticky with blood.

"Gosh!" said Holbrook, and, lifting the limp burden, pushed his way into the sunlit studio. His first glimpse of that exotically furnished "glass house" as he mentally characterised it, was indelibly photographed on his memory.

Opposite him on an oval table in the centre of the room was the debris of the cocktail party. Glasses, porcelain and trays, plates of sandwiches, a half-eaten cantaloupe, melting ices, fruit, gin, whisky, and vermouth bottles; a butter-dish, a water carafe, a dish of sweets, and cigarette-boxes.

On his right were two divans of luridly hued cretonne—the one nearest was empty—and on the other lay the semi-naked figure of Gillie Carew, his gleaming brown skin stained with rapidly coagulating blood.

P.-c. Holbrook hurriedly deposited Monica Travers' unconscious form on the first divan. He crossed over to the other end, and repressing a shiver, bent over the body. One glance was sufficient to convince him that Gillie Carew was dead. Blood oozed sluggishly from a wound above his heart. His face had a peculiar leaden pallor.

On the floor between the table and divan lay a blue-barrelled sporting-gun. P.-c. Holbrook mopped his sweating forehead. He took a quick glance round the room. On the desk at the head of the dead man's divan he saw a telephone. Quickly he crossed over and lifted the receiver.

"Hallo! Police!" he said urgently, and fumed impatiently until he heard the familiar voice of the station sergeant.

"Hallo! This is Holbrook speaking, sarge," he said quickly. "A man's been shot at No. 7, Merrick Mews, and—"

"O.K., Holbrook!" said the voice calmly in reply. "The divisional-inspector's on his way—with Grimley of the Yard. A woman phoned us five minutes ago. Stand by!"

There was a click, and, a little chagrined, P.-c. Holbrook hung up.

"That's funny!" he murmured. "Looks to me as if—"

He broke off suddenly as footsteps sounded on the stairs. A moment later the door opened stealthily and a big man in a faultlessly cut grey flannel suit entered. He looked a trifle nonplussed as he saw the burly, blue-uniformed figure in the centre of the studio.

"Hallo!" said Constable Holbrook gruffly. "What do you want?"

"Why, I—er—" began the newcomer, then suddenly his face went white.

"Great heavens! What's this?" His gaze had fallen on that grim, bloodstained figure on the divan, and his hands shook. "Murder!" he gasped. "I—I say, officer, when did this awful thing happen?"

Holbrook shrugged.

"A few minutes ago. I advise you to stay where you are until my superiors arrive," he added. "Who are you?" he demanded.

"My name is Baltmore Smith," replied the visitor.

"IT'S no use, Blake, old friend, I'm finished, done for!"

Detective-Inspector Coutts shook his head mournfully and slumped dejectedly into his chair. It was the afternoon of the cocktail party at Merrick Mews (though Coutts was as yet unaware of that function), and the inspector was now paying his first visit to Sexton Blake's consulting-room in Baker Street since that catastrophic morning when he had been suspended from duty.

Sexton Blake glanced across significantly at Tinker, who was ostensibly engaged at his interminable task of indexing press cuttings. That alert young man took the hint and slid out of the room.

"Now, Coutts!" said Blake firmly. "This simply won't do, old friend! The whole thing is preposterous on the face of it. I, for one, think that Sir Henry Fairfax is not only making a grievous mistake, but what is more, has acted with perfectly unreasonable impulsiveness,"

"Bless you for that, Blake," said Coutts in a miserable voice. "I—I can't tell you how I appreciate your faith in me. I've been through hell this last week, can't sleep, can't eat, and my poor missus—"

"Help yourself to the whisky," interposed Blake. "The decanter is at your elbow."

While Coutts poured himself out a tot of whisky, Blake covertly studied the Yard man. He was shocked at the change in his old colleague. Coutts' usually florid face was pasty, and his eyes, heavily ringed, lacked lustre. His His hands shook as he squirted the soda into his glass. He looked years older. Gone was his familiar cocksure manner; even his clipped and bristly moustache was

ragged and untrimmed.

"You must pull yourself together, old man," said Sexton Blake. "Don't you worry. There's bound to be an explanation. The charge against you is absurd. Why, I've known you for over twenty years,   and we've shared perils and danger together too often for me to be mistaken in your character."

"Heaven bless you, Blake!" said Coutts huskily. "I—I wish I'd come to you sooner, but the fact is, I was ashamed, desperately ashamed. I—I didn't dare tell the missus. Of course, she's noticed that something was wrong, but she thinks I'm worried about that nephew of hers, young Harry Lawson. He's a good lad, Blake, but a bit harum-scarum, and I'm thankful to say I've managed to steer him clear of the crowd he was mixed up with."

"Good for you, Coutts!" said Sexton Blake, slowly filling his briar. "Now the point is—are you going to knuckle under tamely beneath this preposterous charge, or fight it?"

Coutts shrugged his burly shoulders helplessly.

"How can I fight it, Blake?" he queried hopelessly. "In view of that letter from Lady Norrie, backed up by her partner, to say nothing of the notes which dropped out of my pocket, who do you think's going to believe me? Yet I swear on oath I'm innocent, and—and—"

"It's perfectly obvious to me that you're a victim of a frame-up," broke in Blake calmly. "I have met this fellow Grimley on one or two occasions, and I don't like him. I am, I hope, not prone to unreasonable prejudices, but there are many things about Grimley that I dislike. He has very nice manners, speaks the King's English with a certain refinement, looks well in dress clothes, but he's a snob, and old lags dislike him."

The Yard man gave a watery smile at Blake's astute summing up.

"Yes, that's all very well, Blake, but he's got the ear of the Commissioner. And how on earth am I going to prove my innocence?"

"One moment, Coutts. You swear your first and only visit to this Puce Lobster Club was the night you raided it?"

"So help me!" said Coutts gravely.

"And Lady Melisande Norrie hardly exchanged a dozen words with you!"

Coutts nodded.

"You say that Grimley helped you on with your coat before you went in to interview the Commissioner?"

Again Coutts nodded.

"Yes. That's been sticking in my mind. I remember being surprised at it. It's my belief that he slipped the notes into my pocket then. But, of course, I haven't an atom of proof."

"It's at least probable," commented Blake. "Now, look here, old man. My advice to you is to wait until Grimley overreaches himself. I admit its deucedly unpleasant to be suspended from duty, but that is not half as bad as dismissal. Your long and faithful record of service is bound to weigh with the Commissioner. If it's any use my—"

He broke off suddenly as a tap sounded at the door.

A moment later the flushed, excited face of Splash Page peered into the room.

"I say, Blake," he said excitedly, "I've got a whale of a story for you! Monica Travers looks like being arrested for the murder of Gillie Carew, and the "Radio's" got a scoop!"

"Come in, you rude young devil," said Sexton Blake—"now that you are in" How did you get in, anyway?"

"Tinker at street door, taking dog for walk," replied the newspaperman succinctly.

"Hallo, Couttsy, old-timer! What's the matter? You look a bit peaked?" he added, as his keen eyes noted Coutts' sunken cheeks and heavy eyes.

The news of Coutts' disgrace had not yet leaked out, and Splash knew nothing of the suspension.

"Coutts has been overworking himself. He needs a holiday," explained Blake. "Now sit down and tell us all about the Carew affair."

Splash flung his hat on the table, stretched his long, thin legs luxuriously as he helped himself to a cigarette.

"Oh, boy! What a story! Incidentally, Blake, you're in on this. I've got a client for you."

"Thanks very much!" said Blake dryly.

"By the way, Coutts, why aren't you in charge of this business?" said Splash, in a puzzled tone. "I saw that pompous ass Grimley half an hour ago. He's as pleased as a dog with two tails."

"Coutts is on sick leave," Blake explained kindly.

"Hard luck!" commented the newspaperman.

Coutts craned forward eagerly in his chair.

"What's all this about murder, Splash?" he asked; and there was a pathetic note of eagerness in his voice.

"Well," responded the reporter, "Here's the low-down as far as I've got. I came on here straight from Merrick Mews after after phoning the office. You know Gillie Carew, the explorer chap? He was at the club the night you raided the Puce Lobster. Well, Gillie gave a cocktail party this afternoon. It seems he was trying to inaugurate a new cult among the Bright Young Pups. Teddie Rampling, our 'Gossip' man, was invited, that's how we got the scoop. Amongst those present were Ivor Trelawney, the well-known dilettante and blighter; Freddy Arbuthnot, the famous male impersonator; Anna Morena of the talkies; the Lady Melisande of Puce Lobster fame; Monica Travers, reported fiancee of Gillie Carew; John Mandeville, the big-game hunter, and last, but not least, Baltimore Smith."

Coutts stared.

"By Jove, that's extraordinary!" he commented.

"Gillie Carew has lately hooked up with the Lady Melisande, much to the annoyance of Monica Travers," continued Splash. "I don't blame him. She's a nice kid, and—well, you know our Rosie Gluckman, Blake?"

Sexton Blake nodded.

"Go on! Stick to facts!"

"Well the cocktail party broke up very hurriedly. The Hon. Ivor passed some uncomplimentary remarks about Melisande's ancestry. Gillie sloshed him on the jaw. Exit Ivor, breathing threats, aided and abetted by Monica, flamingly jealous of Melisande. Teddie gives a graphic description of the scene. For a young

gossip hound he's done darned well," conceded Splash generously.

"The party broke up roughly at three o'clock this afternoon. It seems that Gillie Carew was a bit tight. We now come to the climax of the drama. At precisely 3.45, the constable on duty near Merrick Mews was approached by a small boy yelling: 'Murder!'

"Sceptical, he investigates. Door of Gillie Carew's flat open. Woman in hysterics, flops into his arms. Bloodstains on her dress and hands. Lying dead on divan is Gillie Carew, half naked, shot through lungs. On the floor a sporting-gun of peculiar pattern. Constable rings up station and tries to revive the woman. Her identity— Monica Travers. She is half dazed with terror, and incoherent. She had already rung up for the police. Her story: Returned to the flat to plead with Gillie, and found him weltering in his own gore. Has confused recollection of trying to bring him round—and that's all."

"An admirable summary Splash," commented Blake, as the newspaper man lit a cigarette.

"Newspaper training, old man," chuckled Splash. Now for the trimmings. When I got there the divisional surgeon and photographers were just packing up. Grimley, thoroughly enjoying himself, was in charge. Also present: Monica Travers still hysterical, Baltimore Smith looking green about the gills, and Ivor Trelawney badly rattled."

"Grimley!" said Coutts, with a bitter smile. "How did he blow in on it?"

"He happened to be at Lancaster Gate Station when the woman's call came through," said Splash.

"He would be!" said Coutts. "He and Pearce of that division are as thick as thieves."

"What was Baltimore Smith doing in that, company?" Blake queried. Splash shrugged his shoulders. "Where do I come in on this?" asked the criminologist.

"Ivor Trelawney; by special request," replied Splash. "He begged me to see you at once, Blake. He couldn't come himself. Grimley's holding him for a statement, but he's frightfully upset about Monica. He's afraid she'll be arrested and charged with the murder. It's one holy mix-up, Blake—a case after your own heart. Trelawney's a rich man, you know, and his last words to me were: 'Try to persuade Mr. Blake to take up the case. Tell him I'll write him a blank cheque for expenses if only he'll come at once.'"

Blake smiled cynically. "I've heard of the Hon. Ivor Trelawney—and nothing to his credit," he remarked. "If I look into the matter at all it will not be on his behalf. On the surface it appears to be a sordid crime passionel, as the French call it—and that type of case doesn't interest me. However, there might be something to it, especially to see how our friend Grimley handles it. Got your Red Peril outside?"

"Sure," nodded Splash, with a grin.

"Start her up, and I'll be down with you shortly," said Blake.

"Hurrah!" said Splash. "Now we're moving! I knew you'd fall for it, Blake."

"I haven't fallen for anything yet," said Sexton Blake as the newspaperman seized his hat and left Coutts and Blake alone.

"Look here, Coutts," whispered Blake urgently. "I'm going to run along and look into this matter. Here's your chance to score off Grimley. I shall tell Trelawney that I decline to interfere, but that if he wants the matter thoroughly and scientifically sifted, he had better apply to you. I'll tell him you're on holiday, and it would be to his interests to employ you to hold a watching brief on his behalf. Leave it to me, old man. It's your big chance to reinstate yourself."

"Bless you, Blake!" said Coutts huskily. "I—I don't know how to thank you."

"Rubbish!" said Blake. "If I know anything of Grimley he's already made a prize ass of himself. Hang on here, and I'll give you a ring in half an hour's time."

He clapped Coutts' shoulder affectionately, and, hurriedly divesting himself of his tattered red dressing-gown, donned his coat and hat, and left Coutts to his meditations.

CHAPTER 9
GRIMLEY DOES HIS STUFF.

THAT suave officer, Detective-Inspector Grimley, was in his element. At last he had charge of a real Society murder. It was sheer luck that he had been present at Lancaster Gate Police Station when Monica Travers' agonised phone call came through, but Grimley was a firm believer in his lucky star.

He was seated now at the desk in the Studio of the dead man. The body had been removed to an inner room, but save for that, nothing had been disturbed. A uniformed police-sergeant stood at the door. Huddled in a deep armchair sat Monica Travers, near the dressing-room door. The Hon. Ivor Trelawney stood scowling down at Baltimore Smith, while a divisional detective-inspector sat on the edge of the first divan, a notebook on his knee.

"Now, Mr. Trelawney," said Grimley briskly, "I will read over your statement. If you have any comments to make or any additions, please let me know.

"My name is Ivor Montante Trelawney. Independent, of 17, Curristor Square, Lancaster Gate. I have known deceased for nearly ten years. We were not intimate friends, but have met frequently lately. I was Invited to the cocktail party this afternoon with others. I arrived at 2.25 with Miss Monica Travers. Deceased was quite friendly. He appeared to have had a good deal to drink."

Grimley paused and elevated his eyebrows.

"Is that correct so far?"

"Quite," said Trelawney briefly.

Grimley continued the statement, which gave a bald and accurate account of the quarrel between Gillie Carew and himself. The statement concluded:

"At 2.25 approximately, I left with Miss Travers, who was greatly distressed. I invited her round to my flat, which is close by, to have a drink. She refused, saying she preferred to be alone, and a walk in the park would do her good. I accordingly dropped her at the Lancaster Gate entrance, and returned to my flat. Roughly the time was 3.10. There I remained in my study, writing letters, until I received a call from a policeman at 4 p.m. or thereabouts. He informed me that Mr. Carew had been found shot. My valet, George Head, can vouch for my statement that I was in my flat from 3.10 until the constable's arrival."

Grimley paused.

"Anything further to add?"

"Nothing further," said Trelawney soberly.

"Very well, Mr. Trelawney. When you have signed it you may go," said the Yard man. "Remember, however, we shall subpoena you as a witness at the inquest."

"I fully realise that," said Trelawney, as he signed his statement with a characteristic flourish. "But what about Miss Travers? Surely you don't suspect her of—"

A tap sounded at the door of the studio. Trelawney broke off suddenly.

"Who's that, Craske?" demanded Grimley, as the constable opened the door.

Baltimore Smith shot a venomous glance at Grimley. To do the crook justice he was genuinely shocked at the tragic outcome of the party. The reason for his return was ostensibly to collect his malacca cane, but in reality it was to put over a shady con trick on Carew while he was fuddled. He realised at once that he had run his head into a particularly unpleasant noose, especially as Grimley was in charge of the affair.

Sergeant Craske tiptoed to Grimley, and whispered something in his ear.

"What's that?" said Grimley, and his face flushed slightly. "What the deuce does he want?" He drummed thoughtfully with his fingers on the desk for a moment or two, then with a shrug said: "Very well. Show him in, please."

A moment later Sexton Blake, accompanied by Splash Page, entered the room.

DESPITE his cocksure arrogance, Grimley stood in awe of the famous criminologist, and it was with rather a nervous smile that he greeted him.

"Good-afternoon, Mr. Blake. How do you do? This is an unexpected pleasure," he said.

"How are you, inspector?" said Blake. "Hope I'm not intruding, but I understand that Mr. Trelawney here desired my presence."

"Thank Heaven you've come, Blake!" said Trelawney fervently. "There's some dreadful mistake going on. The inspector has the absurd notion that Monica shot poor Carew."

Blake pursed his lips thoughtfully. His keen, grey eyes swept the garish studio in one swift, comprehensive glance. Grimley fidgeted uneasily with his notebook.

"Don't let me interrupt you, inspector," said Blake quietly.

Grimley smiled, regaining his self-confidence. He turned to the sergeant and whispered a few words.

"Mr. Trelawney and Mr. Smith," he said crisply, "will you be good enough to accompany Sergeant Craske to the next room for a moment."

"Monica!"

Trelawney turned to the girl, who was sobbing uncontrollably with her head in her hands. She raised her tear-stained face.

"I didn't do it—I swear I didn't do it!" she cried brokenly in a voice shaken with sobs.

"Come, madam," said Blake, with that calm courtesy which he extended to all women. "No one is accusing you of having done it! Try to be calm, and talk this matter over."

Grimley scowled resentfully. This was his affair. What right had Sexton Blake to butt in? He jerked his head towards the living-room door, and the sergeant hustled Smith and Trelawney outside.

Splash Page's keen journalistic brain noted the tense drama, and as a couple of constables entered from the landing he glanced significantly at Blake.

"Monica Eileen Travers," said Grimley in clipped, precise accents, "I arrest you on a charge of the wilful murder of Gilbert Carew, and it is my duty to warn you that anything you may say may be written down and used as evidence against you!"

Monica Travers half rose to her feet. Her face was ghastly in its pallor, her lips bloodless.

"I didn't do it!" she screamed. "I'm innocent—before Heaven, I'm innocent!"

A grey-haired woman in black emerged from behind the two stalwart policemen and took her gently by the arm.

"Come on, my dear," she said kindly. "You're overwrought. I advise you to say nothing until you've seen your solicitor."

Dazedly Monica Travers was led out of that sunlit room into a waiting taxi. Detective-Inspector Grimley squared his shoulders.

"An unpleasantly painful duty, Mr. Blake," he said, shaking his head. "It's a great tragedy, but the law must take its course."

Sexton Blake lit a cigarette. "I presume you wouldn't have arrested her unless you were reasonably certain of her guilt," he said blandly.

"Certain," laughed Grimley. "Here's her own sworn statement."

He handed a closely written page of foolscap to the detective, who scanned it narrowly.

"H'm!" commented Blake. "I see she was once engaged to Carew. She left with Trelawney at approximately three o'clock. What time was the murder committed?"

"At three-thirty-five," replied Grimley. "The lad Weeks heard a shot which he took to be the back-firing of a car. A few seconds later he heard Miss Travers scream and ran for a policeman. Constable Holbrook confirms the time. He arrived at three-forty-five, and the body was still warm."

"Ah!" said Blake, glancing at Monica Travers' statement again. "She states she left Trelawney after refusing to accompany him to his flat. She walked in the park for maybe half an hour. She was terribly upset, and decided to appeal to Carew. She came back to the mews on foot. Presumably Master Weeks did not see her arrive. That's rather a pity," Blake added.

"'I found the door ajar,' she alleges. 'I entered the studio, and at first I didn't see Gillie. I called his name, and suddenly I saw him all covered in blood. There was a gun near, or on the table. I bent over him, and saw that he was dead. I can't tell you clearly what happened next. I screamed, and must have fainted. I may have picked up the gun—I don't know. I came to, and immediately telephoned the police. The rest is blurred.'"

"Sounds pretty thin!" commented Splash.

"Thin!" said Grimley. "Why, she must have made it up as she went along! Carew was shot at a distance of approximately two feet. It was a deliberate, cold-blooded murder. The man was shot in his sleep. There was no sign of a struggle, and the wound could not have been self-inflicted."

"You are certain of that, inspector?" queried Blake.

"Certain!" said Grimley. "You may examine the body for yourself, Mr. Blake, in a few minutes. Besides, look at this." He pulled out a card from the papers on the desk. On it was a set of finger-prints, clear and distinctive. "These are Miss Travers' finger-prints," he announced triumphantly, "and this is a photo just developed by our fellows at the Yard." He handed Sexton Blake a photograph, still odorous from its methylated spirit bath. "These prints were on the stock of the gun," he declared.

Sexton Blake nodded. He saw immediately that the finger-prints were identical.

"You have certainly built up your case remarkably well and commendably quickly, inspector," he commented.

"Well," said Grimley, "I certainly don't believe in letting the grass grow under my feet, Mr. Blake. Now poor Coutts would have hemmed and hawed over the business. Just because Miss Travers is a Society woman he would have been undecided as to what action to take."

"Would he really?" asked Blake—and his eyes glittered icily. "You, of course, know how to treat—er—Society women, inspector."

Grimley flushed a little and smiled uneasily.

"I do my duty," he said stiffly.

"D'you mind if I look round a bit?" Blake queried, ignoring his tone.

"All right, Blake," said Grimley. "Perhaps you'd care to view the body. It's not a pretty sight, you know."

"Lead on," said Blake curtly, and followed the strutting Grimley into an adjoining room.

MEANWHILE, in terse but telling sentences, Splash Page gave the news of Monica Travers' arrest to the "Radio's" news editor over the phone.

"And listen," he added. "Send a special messenger round immediately to Merrick Mews with two copies of the photo Teddie Rampling took this afternoon."

Splash hung up the receiver and gazed around the sunlit studio, such an incongruous background to the tragedy that had been enacted there. On the divan there was a darkening stain. On the table the empty cocktail glasses, half-eaten sandwiches, and melting ices were strangely symbolical of the futility of the empty lives led by Gillie Carew and his set.

Suddenly Splash whistled.

"Holy Joe! What about the Inca chappie?" he murmured. "I say, Blake!"

He turned as the man from Baker Street and Grimley emerged from the death chamber.

"What about the jolly old Inca, Toltec, Blake?" he demanded. "Maybe he could throw some light on the subject."

"Possibly he could, Mr. Page," said Grimley, smiling unpleasantly. "Unfortunately, he has disappeared!"

"What's that?" gasped the newspaperman. "Toltec vanished?"

Grimley nodded.

"Yes. But he can't have got very far. I've sent an A.S. message out, and we shan't be long locating him. He's a stranger in London, and doesn't speak a word of English."

He picked up his notebook and papers, then turned to Blake.

"Well, satisfied, Mr. Blake?" he queried, with a slight sneer.

Blake shook his head.

"Far from it, inspector. May I see the gun?"

"Why, certainly," said Grimley, in the tone of one humouring a child. "Here it is."

He picked up the shotgun which Gillie Carew had shown with such pride to John Mandeville some hours before.

"H'm! Two cartridges!" said Blake, as he donned his gloves and gingerly broke the breech. "One spent and the other intact. Hallo!" He whipped out a pocket lens and carefully scrutinised the breech. "This is a somewhat new type of sports gun," he remarked. "Very curious. Very-curious! Where did you find it, inspector?"

"Here!" said Grimley, pointing to the carpet some eighteen inches between the foot of the divan and the leg of the table,

"Ah!" said Blake cryptically, as his glove rested on the table. "I wonder if Carew has such a thing as a Whitaker's Almanack?"

"A Whitaker's Almanack?" echoed Grimley in bewilderment.

"Exactly!" said Blake. "It's possibly of no importance, but I should like to call your attention, Splash, to the parsley in the butter-dish."

"The parsley in the butter-dish?" echoed Splash Page blankly. "Whitaker's Almanack? What on earth are you driving at, Blake?"

Sexton Blake did not appear to be listening. He took out a notebook and pencil and made a few rapid diagrams.

"Curious! The only thing they didn't drink was water!" he murmured, "If someone had only drunk water Gillie Carew would possibly be alive now, and that nice girl Monica Travers would not be in a prison cell."

"I'm hanged if I know what you're driving at, Mr. Blake," said Grimley. "Are you sure the sun hasn't proved too strong for you?"

"On the contrary," replied Blake blandly. "It has been exceedingly kind to me. It is really remarkable about that parsley," he added, with a whimsical smile.

Splash Page chuckled inwardly. He knew when Blake was in his most cryptic mood that some sensational disclosure was afoot.

"This is a serious business, Mr. Blake, and I consider your flippancy very ill-timed," said Grimley haughtily. "I really don't understand you!"

"Really?" said Blake, with a maddening and imperturbable smile. "You will, inspector—you will."

Detective-Inspector Grimley snorted and swung on his heel.

"Craske!" he called. "You may release Mr. Trelawney. Smith, I want you!"

Blake turned as Trelawney entered the studio, closely followed by Baltimore Smith.

"If you will call at Baker Street at eight o'clock this evening I may have some news for you, Mr. Trelawney," said Sexton Blake.

The Hon. Ivor had lost a good deal of his aplomb. He heaved a sigh.

"Thank you, Mr. Blake! Thanks!" he said. "I'm very grateful."

He bowed, and accompanied by the watchful Craske left the studio.

"Well, Balty," said Sexton Blake, "what brought you here?"

Baltimore Smith shrugged his shoulders resignedly.

"Sheer bad luck Mr. Blake," he said. "Mr. Carew was a friend of mine, and I came back to have a little friendly chat with him. When I got here I found a half-demented woman and a busy."

"So you say, Balty," interposed Grimley, with a sneer. "Can you prove it?"

"I can and all!" said Baltimore Smith. "And this is where I've got you beat, Mr. Double-Crossing Grimley! When I left here at three o'clock I went across to the barber at the corner for a shampoo and a face massage. He'll prove that I never left his chair until a quarter to four. Hold that one!"

Grimley scowled, and Balty grinned triumphantly at Sexton Blake.

"That lets me out, Mr, Blake, I guess," he said.

"Oh, no, it doesn't, Balty!" said Grimley. "What about this?" Quick as a flash his hand shot towards the crook's hip pocket, and a moment later he produced a squat blue-steel automatic. "Have you got a licence for this gun, Mr. Baltimore Smith?" he demanded, with a mocking grin.

Baltimore Smith's jaw sagged open and his fists clenched.

"You dirty, double-crossing snitch!" he snarled. "That ain't my gat! You put it there yourself, you cur! He's trying to frame me, Mr. Blake! I never carry a gat! I—I—"

"Baltimore Smith, I arrest you for contravention of the Firearms Act of 1920!" said Grimley. "You'll go down for two years for that, my lad! Now you hold that one!"

"That parsley is certainly very curious," said Sexton Blake quietly to nobody in particular.

CHAPTER 10
ENTER THE BABY.

GREAT SCOTT, Blake! If your theory is true, then he's delivered into my hands!"

Detective-Inspector Coutts bent forward in his chair, his face aglow with excitement. It was 8.30 p.m., and for the past hour Sexton Blake had been regaling the Yard man with an account of the Merrick Mews tragedy as seen from Blake's own angle. Splash had returned to Fleet Street, there to churn out a highly coloured front page special for the morrow's "Radio."

"This fellow Grimley has done it just once too often!" said Coutts savagely, after a pause. "Gosh, Blake! I can never thank you enough for all the trouble you've gone to!"

"Rubbish!" said Blake. "Now, understand, Coutts, I don't appear in this at all. I forbid you to mention my name!"

"But look here, I can't take all the credit—"

"You'll do as you're told, my dear chap!" retorted Blake. "Trelawney should be along any minute now. I'll hand him over to you and mind how you handle him. Say nothing about the parsley; and, by the way, take charge of these photos which young Rampling took. A nice set of degenerates, aren't they?" said Blake, with a curling lip, as he glanced at the photo of the cocktail party which the gossip man had taken that afternoon.

Coutts cleared his throat. His voice was husky as he pocketed the photos.

"Heaven bless you, Blake! The truest friend a man ever had—" he began.

"If you don't shut up, Coutts, I'll be seriously annoyed!" said Blake abruptly.

A tap sounded at the door, and Mrs. Bardell entered, with a visiting-card in her plump hand.

"Which there's an honourable gent named Tarpaulin as wants to insult you, sir!" she announced. "He says he's got an anointment."

"Please show him in!" said Blake.

A moment later the Hon. Ivor entered. He looked pale and ill-at-ease. His flippant manner had given place to a nervous, strained attitude.

"Here I am, Mr. Blake!" he said, with a forced smile. "It—it's most awfully good of you to take up the case! I swear to you that poor little Monica is innocent! That blundering fool Grimley will pay dearly for his mistake, mark my words!"

Blake rose to his feet.

"I'm sorry, Mr. Trelawney, but I'm afraid I cannot handle this affair on your behalf. I am exceedingly busy at the moment!"

"But, my Heaven, Mr. Blake," cut in Trelawney agitatedly, "expense is no object with me! I know your fees are considerable, but I'll pay anything—anything to—"

"Sorry!" said Blake calmly. "It is impossible! You have met Detective-Inspector Coutts before, I think?" he added, a trifle maliciously.

"How do you do?" said Trelawney distantly.

"Coutts is the man for you," said Blake. "He's on holiday at the moment, and I'm certain he would be only too glad to look into the matter on—er—conditions."

"But look here, Mr. Blake, it's—it's impossible! Coutts here raided our club, and I have reason to believe that he—"

"I shouldn't pursue that subject further, Mr. Trelawney," said Sexton Blake quietly. "My advice to you is to trust Inspector Coutts here—one of the shrewdest and most reliable police officers with whom I have ever had the pleasure of working."

Trelawney hesitated, then turned impulsively to Coutts.

"Do you think you can see any way out of this dreadful mess, inspector?" he asked anxiously.

Coutts grunted.

"Yes, I believe so, Mr. Trelawney. Perhaps you wouldn't mind if I accompanied you home. Mr. Blake, I know, is very busy at the moment, and I should be glad to hear your version of the matter."

Coutts winked slyly at Blake, and the criminologist rose and extended his hand to Trelawney.

"Good-night, Mr. Trelawney! Take my advice and entrust yourself to Inspector Coutts."

"But—but, I say," broke in the Hon. Ivor, "I—I've got a perfectly good theory to account for the murder. It's my belief that Gillie was shot by Toltec, the Indian servant. The fellow hated him—"

"Tell it to Coutts, Mr. Trelawney!" cut in Blake incisively.

Trelawney could not ignore that pointed dismissal. He swallowed hard, then, with a brief good-night, took his leave, accompanied by a jubilant Coutts, who walked with a jauntier step than he had used for many a day.

Blake slowly filled his briar as the door closed, and relaxed his limbs. He took up an open copy of Whitaker's Almanack, and scribbled a few calculations on a piece of paper. He then sketched in roughly the accompanying diagram with firm, rapid strokes, and when completed he gave a little sigh, of satisfaction.

His grey eyes grew abstracted. Curious, he reflected, how a trivial thing like a sprig of parsley should mean the difference between life and death, honour and dishonour, to a human being!

A TAP sounded at the door, and Mrs. Bardell entered again.

"Which there's a young lady, name of Baby, wishes to—"

"Insult me, I suppose!" cut in Blake wearily. "Show her in, Mrs. B.; but it's time all good babies were in bed!" he added, with a smile.

"Beggin' your pardon, she ain't no baby, Mr. Blake," said Mrs. Bardell, with dignity. "She looks to me like a fashionable young person of independent beans."

"Show her in," said Blake, with a patient smile.

Mrs. Bardell went out, to return accompanied by the young person. She was dressed in an evening wrap, and an absurd vermilion hat perched cockily on the side of her smooth, blonde head.

Blake rose to his feet, a faint flicker of surprise in his grey eyes.

"Good-evening, Miss Brady!" he said courteously. "Won't you sit down?"

"Good-evening, Mr. Blake!" said Cardiff Meg, fumbling nervously with her gloves. "Mebbe you think I've got gall calling on you like this, but I've come to put in a squeak."

"Sit down, Meg! Have a cigarette?" said Sexton Blake, proffering his case. "What's the trouble?" he inquired.

"They've pulled my man," said Cardiff Meg, her slant eyes flashing with hatred. "That double-crossing rat Grimley's framed Balty Smith for this murder, Mr. Blake!"

"Not for murder, Meg," said Blake, shaking his head. "I was there when he was arrested. The charge was being in possession of firearms."

"Balty never totes a gat, Mr. Blake," said the girl passionately. "He's been framed! But, by heck, Grimley ain't getting away with it! Listen, Mr. Blake! You're white. You ain't like these ' busies.' I'm no squeaker or nark, but now Grimley's pinched my man, I'm gonna let out a squeal that'll break him."

Sexton Blake leant back in his chair, and beneath his lowered lids, studied the girl. She was obviously genuine and sincere at that moment.

"Listen, Mr. Blake!" said Cardiff Meg. "Balty's been paying hush-money to Grimley for six months. He's the biggest twister in the Force! Melisande, of the Puce Lobster Club, has been sweetening Grimley for months."

"Go on, Meg," said Blake quietly.

"Yes," said Cardiff Meg passionately. "And that ain't all of it. The night of the raid I had a bit of a spat with Balty and Grimley. I objected to Balty paying out any more money to Grimley for laying off our racket. I left the table, and thought I'd do a little pinch on my own. That woman Melisande deserved to lose some money. I'd hidden myself in the office ready to grab it when Grimley and Melisande come in. I listened in—and I'm not ashamed of it! What do you think the dirty four-flusher did? Double-crossed Coutts, his side kick at the Yard."

"How?" demanded Blake.

"How?" echoed Meg. "I don't hold no brief for Coutts, but he's always acted straight with me. Here's the low-down, Mr. Blake, and I'm prepared to take my oath on it! Grimley suggested framing Coutts. He put the squeeze on Melisande, saying that unless she wrote a letter to the Commissioner accusing Coutts of accepting bribes, he'd ruin her!

"He said he could get Coutts fired, and that he'd plant a hundred quid in notes on him. The dirty tike told her to take the numbers, so's to have the goods on Coutts, and Melisande fell for it!"

"Meg," said Blake, with a gleam in his eyes, "I'm very grateful indeed to you for coming here."

"Don't thank me," said Cardiff Meg. "I'd like to—"

"Easy now—easy!" said Sexton Blake. "Tell me, Meg! Did they suspect they'd been overheard?"

"Not on your life, they didn't!" laughed Cardiff Meg. "And say, Mr. Blake, if you want proof that I ain't a liar, take a slant at this."

From her handbag she pulled out a slip of paper. On it was written two numbers— M.68432, and M.68442.

Sexton Blake's eyes sparkled.. Here was proof of the innocence of Inspector Coutts. For how, otherwise, could Cardiff Meg have obtained the identical numbers of the notes mentioned by Lady Melisande in her letter?

"Would you sign a statement to that effect, Miss Bradv?" said Blake quietly.

"Sure, I would!" said the girl. "And say, Mr. Blake, this'll break Grimley, I reckon. D'you think you can put in a good word for Balty?"

"I'll do my best," said Sexton Blake.

CHAPTER II
A STROKE OF THE SUN.

INSPECTOR COUTTS went home that night with a jauntier step and a lighter heart than he had had for days. Blake had confided an astonishing revelation to him, and he actually chuckled as he descended from the bus at the corner, and set out for his home.

He had listened carefully to Trelawney's story, and his circumstantial account of Grimley's handling of the the case.

It was a close, sultry night, and the sullen growl of thunder rumbled in the sky as the Yard man swung briskly towards Meriden. Not a breath of wind stirred the leaves of the trim little plane trees that flanked the avenue in an orderly row. Coutts smiled grimly as his eyes fell on a newspaper placard outside the little tobacconist shop on the corner. It bore the flaring legend:

"SOCIETY WOMAN ARRESTED FOR MURDER!"

"Go ahead, Mr. Cocksure Grimley!" he muttered.

"'Scuse me, guv'nor," whined a voice, "could you 'blige me with a light?"

Coutts turned as a shabbily dressed individual with a check cap several sizes too large for him emerged from a shadowed alleyway. He grunted an affirmative, and groped in the pocket of his blue reefer jacket for a matchbox. As he did so the other straightened suddenly, and something whizzed viciously downward, catching the unsuspecting detective a blow on the temple.

"Gotcher, you cur!" snarled a voice which Coutts heard dimly. "Quick, Barney—beat it!"

Sick and dizzy from the blow though he was, Coutts turned to grapple with his cowardly assailant. Doubling his fists, he jammed home two vicious body-blows, and heard the sudden "Ouch!" of pain as they found their mark. Blood trickled from a wound in his temple, but Coutts strove pluckily to maintain his balance. He grappled with his opponent, and, though his head sung dizzily, he managed to clutch the man's shoulder. Dimly he heard the sound of scurrying footsteps, but, tenacious as a bulldog, Coutts held on.

"Let's have a look at you, you rat!" he snarled.

The other squirmed and wriggled beneath the inspector's ham-like hand, but Coutts had a grip of iron. In the light of a street lamp he glimpsed the mean, rat-like face of his opponent. He laughed harshly as he recognised him.

With the blood flowing down his face, the Yard man frog-marched his wriggling, cursing assailant to the corner and a convenient policeman.

"I swear—" began the wretched crook again.

"I know you do—horribly!" said Coutts, with an unpleasant grin.

"Pull him in, constable, and put him in the whoosis."

Whoosis Wally went quietly.

ON his arrival at the Yard next morning Detective-Inspector Grimley, that urbane man, smiled more complacently than ever. He had spent a very pleasant hour before his arrival reading the accounts of the Merrick Mews affair in the morning papers, and as he swung into the archway of the barrack-like building he posed graciously for a Press photographer. When he reached his office he was startled to find Detective-Inspector Coutts emerging from the Commissioner's room. Coutts' head was bandaged, but his reel face was far from glum.

"Mornin', Grimley!" he said jauntily. "Getting quite a big noise lately, ain't you?"

"What do you mean?" snapped Grimley suspiciously. "I flatter myself I've handled this murder darned efficiently."

"What murder?" asked Coutts innocently.

"Why, the Merrick Mews murder!" replied Grimley with growing irritation in his voice.

Coutts burst out laughing, and leaned helplessly against the wall.

"Oh, help!" he said. "Hold me up, somebody! Our Mr. Grimley thinks it's a murder case he's handling!"

"Look here, Coutts," said Grimley, "I don't like your tone. Coming from one who has been suspended from duty."

"Wrong again, Archibald. You've only said one right thing this morning."

"What's that?" snarled Grimley.

"That you flatter yourself. The Commissioner wants you immediately. Cheerio!"

Coutts waved his hand gaily, and Grimley looked after him with a vague presentiment of impending trouble.

"WELL, that's that, my dear fellow," said Sexton Blake. "You've made a very neat job of it, Splash; and as for you, Coutts, you were magnificent and deserve all the nice headlines with which Splash has so liberally sprinkled the 'Evening Wireless.'"

It was the evening of the inquest proceedings on the unfortunate Gillie Carew. The "Evening Wireless," the "Daily Radio's" stable companion, had surpassed itself with headlines. A copy now lay on Blake's knee. There were four of them assembled in the consulting-room at Baker Street—Blake, Tinker, Splash and the beaming Inspector Coutts, head still bandaged, but looking years younger.

"Blake, old friend, you know I can never repay you," he began huskily. "I had nothing, simply nothing whatever to do with unravelling the mystery! It was only your clever idea about that—"

"George Coutts," said Sexton Blake sternly, but with a twinkle in his eye, "are you insinuating that Splash Page is a liar?" He tapped the

newspaper on his knee. "Here it is in print, so it must be true:

"'ASTOUNDING VERDICT AT CAREW INQUEST.

DETECTIVE-INSPECTOR COUTTS' BOMBSHELL.

SCOTLAND YARD VETERAN COMPLIMENTED BY CORONER,

MASTERLY AND BRILLIANT ANALYSIS.'"

"I say, guv'nor, I still don't quite understand it!" broke in Tinker, from the corner. "Everybody was staggered when the jury brought in the verdict of accidental death and Monica Travers was immediately released."

Sexton Blake thoughtfully filled his briar.

"It was the green parsley that gave Coutts his first clue, young 'un," he said modestly.

"Look here, Blake," persisted the Yard man, "you know very well that all the kudos is due to you. It was your deduction from beginning to end, and you gave me all the credit for it. You're the whitest man I know, Blake, and I can never forget what you've done for me, or thank you enough. You restored my good name with the Commissioner, saved me my job, and made my missus the happiest woman in the world."

Blake waved this aside.

"Well, actually it only goes to prove how prone everyone is to jump to false conclusions, Tinker," he began. "Grimley's handling of the ease was utterly and completely wrong from the beginning. He assumed that Carew was murdered, without sufficient verification. Now have a look at these photographs, so providentially taken by Teddie Rampling, and my—or, rather, Coutts'—sketches which Splash reproduced in his story."

Tinker craned forward eagerly as Blake traced out the elaborated diagrams in the paper.

"You'll observe first the room," he explained. "As you can see by the plan, the sun at precisely 3.30 p.m.—when the boy Weeks heard what he thought was a car backfiring—was shining through the bay window in the south-western corner of the studio."

Tinker nodded.

"Well," continued Sexton Blake, "take a look at the photo which Teddy Rampling took—the one prior to the row. You'll find that the butter-dish contains several pats of apparently firm butter; note particularly the parsley nicely in position on top of the butter, and also the position of the water-bottle."

"I see that all right, guv'nor; but what I don't see is how it proves that Carew wasn't murdered."

Blake smiled whimsically.

"Now we come to it, my lad," he announced. "When I arrived at the studio the butter had all melted, and the parsley was deeply embedded in its depths. As against that, the butter on the uneaten sandwiches, and even the ice-cream, was comparatively firm. Why, then, should the parsley be so deeply sunk into the butter so comparatively soon after Teddie Rampling took photo No. 1? I was immediately led to suppose that the butter in the butter-dish had been subjected to more heat than the other eatables on the table. That, in itself, was significant—how significant is borne out by the other photo Rampling took.

"You'll remember Gillie Carew had been showing the workings of his new sporting-gun to his colleague the explorer. Melisande apparently distracted his attention, and he laid the gun on the table—with the breech half-open.

"You'll remember Miss Travers' evidence. She picked up the gun half-hysterically when she found Carew dead; she wasn't sure where from—the floor or the table."

"Gosh! I get you now, guv'nor," said Tinker. "Here's the gun in photo No. 2, lying just between the butter-dish and the water-bottle. But even then, who pulled the trigger?"

Blake shook his head.

"That's just the point," he said quietly. "No living finger pulled the trigger. Gillie Carew was killed, if you like, by the god he affected to worship."

"Killed by the sun!" ejaculated Tinker. "I knew that Toltec chap had something to do with it."

Blake laughed.

"Now, don't jump to conclusions. Toltec was quite innocent. As a matter of fact, the poor fellow was pining for Peru, and took a trip down to the docks in order to stow away on a ship when the police found him. You see," Blake continued, "the water-bottle acted like a magnifying-glass, focusing the rays of the sun with terrific heat on the detonator of the cartridge in the open breech of the gun. It exploded, the bullet entering Carew's heart while he was in a drunken sleep."

"Gosh!" ejaculated Tinker. "What a fool he was to leave a loaded gun about like that!"

"It was criminal negligence," he answered. "But he's paid the penalty, poor devil. Don't forget, however, as the earth rotates round the sun the focal point of its rays through the water would alter every minute. After exploding the powder in the cartridge the rays moved on and melted the butter, thus allowing for the depth of the parsley, which a few minutes before was gaily festooned round the butter-pats."

"Nobody but you would have ever noticed that, Blake," said Splash.

Sexton Blake shrugged his shoulders, but there was a slight flush of pleasure at the tribute in his sallow cheeks.

"Anyway, with an almanac and a few astronomical figures the theory was easily verified, and tangible proof was provided by examination of the cartridges themselves. One was live; and the percussion cap of the spent one hadn't even been touched by the hammer, proving the trigger hadn't been pulled."

"No—curse him!" said Coutts. "And talking of Grimley, Blake, I believe he put this man Whoosis and Barney Contrini up to cosh me the other night."

"Very possibly," said Blake. "Incidentally, has he been suspended from duty yet?"

"Not on your life!" Coutts said; and chuckled. "For the next three years he'll be doing his duty as a convict."

Sexton Blake puffed slowly at his pipe,

"Thanks to Cardiff Meg," he said with characteristic modesty. "Incidentally, I hear that she and Balty Smith are definitely going straight."

"Blake, you're a reformer as well as a detective!" said Splash Page.

Sexton Blake shook his head.

"There's one type of individual I cannot reform, Splash," he said.

"What's that?" queried Splash.

"A journalist," replied the detective.

THE END

THE ADVENTURES of SEXTON BLAKE DETECTIVE.

THE GREAT BRIDGE TUNNEL MYSTERY.

Being a Dramatic Story in which Marston Hume is concerned.

"LET me see," said Bathurst, with a yawn. "It's Sunday to-morrow, isn't it ? What do you say to running across to the Henge golf-links— the other side of Salisbury? If we make an early start we could easily get in three rounds."

"All right," answered Blake, between contented puffs of his pipe. "What time do you propose to start?"

"Half past eight sharp."

The two men were enjoying a quiet after-dinner smoke in the library of Milson House, the home of Bathurst's rich old aunt, from whom he had decided expectations. A solidly-built, ugly, great, comfortable Georgian house, "miles from anywhere." as Bathurst said disgustedly, but really on the border of a small village in the heart of Wiltshire.

Bathurst, with Blake's support, was spending his annual "duty" week-end there, and was frankly bored to death.

"Beastly night!" he said, strolling across to a window, and peering into the wind-swept garden below. "Raining cats and dogs. What on earth are we going to do with ourselves till Tuesday? If this keeps on the golf-links will be under water, and motoring on these confounded roads almost impossible."

"For goodness' sake stop growling," said Blake. "A comfortable house, good cook, excellent wines— and books, tons of them. I could be happy here for the rest of my days, golf or no golf."

"Not you," snorted Bathurst. "You'd be nosing round on a 'case,' or looking for tracks of Marston Hume on Stonehenge before a week was out."

Both men laughed, Bathurst good-naturedly, Blake shortly, a hard glitter flashing into his half-closed eyes.

"I'm off to bed," he said abruptly. "Eight-thirty you said? Good-night!"

Bathurst poured himself out a final drink, crossed over to the window, and looked out once more.

Heavy lowering clouds were scudding across the sky, giving now and then a glimpse of a bright young moon and promise of finer weather.

"Fine to-morrow, thank goodness!" he remarked cheerily, turning out the light and humming himself off to bed.

Fine it was, with a cold brisk wind. The motor was spinning over the sun-dappled roads, Bathurst cheerfully conversational, and Blake, as usual, thoughtfully silent.

Halfway to Salisbury a little group of men gathered before an isolated, tall, stone house attracted Blake's attention, that, and the fact that two stolid-faced policemen were evidently on guard outside the closed hall door.

Bathurst, who was driving, at signal from Blake slowed down.

"What's up?" he asked of one of the men.

"Bloke's dead," was the laconic answer.

"Killed on the railway," supplemented another.

"Thanks," said Blake shortly. "Get on Bathurst. No, stop!"

As he spoke the hall door opened, and a plainclothes officer walked rapidly down the flight of stone steps, looked with sudden interest at the car, and advanced towards it quickly.

"Would you give me a lift to Salisbury?" he asked. "Hallo, Mr. Blake! What's brought you to this part of the world?"

"Hallo, Jenkins!" answered Blake. "I might repeat the question. Left the Yard? What's up?"

He jerked his head towards the house, the stolid policemen, and the talkative group comprehensively.

"Strikes me something in your line," answered the man, in a sudden quick undertone. "Got a bit of time to spare? Something fishy about this. If that gentleman"—indicating Bathurst—"would go on to Salisbury, and oblige me by dropping a note at the police-station, perhaps you would stop here for a bit with me and look into things. Everything points to suicide or accident," he went on hurriedly, as he looked anxiously at Blake's uninterested face; "but what stumps me is how does a man wander on to a railway line and get killed at the bottom of an eighty-foot cutting without even soiling his boots?"

Quick professional interest leapt into Blake's impassive face. He unwrapped the rug from his knees and stepped out of the car.

"Write your note, Jenkins," he said suddenly. My friend will take it on for you. Sorry," he said, turning to Bathurst. "Golf's off for the present."

"So it seems," he answered drily.

The officer scribbled a note hastily, and handed it to Bathurst. "Sorry to trouble you," he said. "Only too pleased," retorted Bathurst, with resignation. "So long, Blake!"

He started at more than twice the legal speed down the road and disappeared from sight.

Jenkins led Blake up the stone steps, and conducted him into a small ante-room at the right of the hall.

"Briefly," he said, with official importance, "this house belongs to a man called Travers—Daykin Travers. Lived here practically alone, and reported rich enough to buy up half the town, eccentric, mean almost to miserliness, and reported to keep large sums of money in the house, mostly in gold.

"Last night he dined as usual, and was writing in the library when the housekeeper went to bed. The domestic staff consists of a coachman, who sleeps over the stables, the housekeeper, and her husband, Dawes by name. Yesterday both men, who are relations by marriage, went into Salisbury for a wedding, or some such festivity, and only returned this morning. The housekeeper is a frail old woman, almost stone deaf, and sleeps on the top floor at the back of the house. All servants have been with Mr. Travers for nearly twenty years.

"This morning at six-thirty a railway servant walked along the line to inspect the new Great Bridge tunnel, which gives trouble occasionally after heavy rain. Just this side of the tunnel's mouth he found the dead body of Mr. Travers, identified by the contents of the letter-case in one of his pockets. The same man went through the tunnel after the up express at 11.30 a.m., and must have seen the body if it had been lying there then, for, of course, he had a lantern. The only train which goes through after that is the 1.20 a.m. down goods, and the engine of that must have caught the body and thrown it clear of the line, judging from the state in which it was found. How did Mr. Travers manage to get on to the line at all, even granting he wished to commit suicide? Great Bridge cutting is through solid chalk, and over seventy feet deep at that point. The top is protected by a high spiked railing, which I defy even a cat to climb over. The same fact precludes the theory of accident, yet how are we to prove murder, the only alternative left?"

Blake shook his head.

"The divisional surgeon states that he cannot fix the hour of death precisely, nor the exact cause, owing to the terrible mutilation, you understand, but he gives his opinion that it occurred somewhere about the time the goods train came along. I have made a fairly lengthy examination of things here, and I must admit that the murder theory scarcely holds water.

"In the safe, which was locked—the key was found in the dead man's pocket—is a sum of £250 in gold and notes. Also in Mr. Travers's pocket was the mangled remains of a valuable gold watch, several sovereigns, and other loose change, proving that robbery was not the motive.

"As far as I can ascertain from Dawes and his wife—the servants I spoke about—nothing is missing from the library or house. In fact, the whole thing is mysterious to a degree."

"Has the goods train been examined yet?" asked Blake.

"Yes, it has. It is on a siding at Wilton, but no bloodstains are reported on any of the wheels, another mysterious point. At the other end of the tunnel," went on the inspector, "a bridge spans the cutting. Now, if the body had been found at that end, one might suppose that Mr. Travers jumped from it on to the line, or was pushed or thrown over; but after a fall like that he wouldn't be in a condition to make his way through a dark tunnel four hundred yards

long without leaving bloodstains, and, anyhow, he could not make it without soiling his shoes. Whichever way one looks at it the thing seems to end in a blank wall."

Blake's brows were knitted together in a puzzled frown.

"No use surmising at this stage," he said slowly. "Let me see the body and the library."

Jenkins led the way across the narrow hall to a room at the far side.

"Here's the library," he went on, opening the door of a big, comfortably-shabby room.

Blake looked round critically. At each end were long windows overlooking the front and back gardens. Beneath one of the front windows was a knee-hole writing-desk, littered with papers and books. Between the other front window, and in the angle of the wall, was a massive safe.

Opposite the entrance door was another door, half-open, evidently leading to a bed-room. In the centre of the library was a circular table on which stood a tray containing an untouched breakfast.

Blake looked at it questioningly.

"Put there by the housekeeper this morning," explained Jenkins, in answer to the unspoken query. "Mr. Travers breakfasted in here at half past seven every morning. He was in the habit of getting up, uncalled, at seven, preparing his own bath in the bath-room leading out from the bed-room yonder, and breakfasting in his dressing-gown just when he pleased. Almost at the moment Mrs. Dawes brought up the tray as usual from the kitchen below this morning, her husband was opening the hall door to the men who carried the body up from the railway."

While the police-officer was speaking, Blake's eyes were travelling hawk-like round the room.

"Mr. Travers had a visitor last night after the housekeeper had gone to bed," he said slowly, after a long pause. "An unexpected visitor, I should say. See, this bottle of whisky is half empty, yet it was opened last night, to judge from these fragments of cork and the tinfoil capsule lying on the desk beside the cork-screw.

"If Mr. Travers had expected his visitor to call, and intended to offer him whisky, he would, of course, have told the housekeeper to place glasses and syphons of water ready. Yet you see he didn't, for the tumbler used belongs to the bed-room water-bottle, which is standing on the mantelpiece over there.

"I should say that he himself was a teetotaller and non-smoker. There are no evidences of any of these self-indulgences in the room where he seems to have passed the greater part of his time. The whisky-bottle, judging from the dust and faded label, has been in the house for some time—probably kept in case of sudden illness. There are no pipes, cigarette ends, tobacco-ash, or matches about, so it is safe to assume the 'non-smoker' theory. The visitor smoked, though," he added, bending down and picking up a couple of cardboard holders from among the dusty coal in the grate.

He took them over to the window and examined them for several seconds narrowly.

"The man who used these holders," he said at length, "has a sharp incisor tooth, in either the upper or lower jaw—I can't say which. See, the cardboard is bitten almost right through."

Blake probed out a brown cigarette end from one of the holders with his open knife, and squeezed the tobacco out from the paper into the palm of his hand, turning the grains over with the point of his knife.

"A particular mixture of Maryland and Cape flake," he said slowly. "Similar to a certain blend put up for a small club in London. I know it will."

He looked up, suddenly alert.

"Let's try the bed-room," he went on hastily, his eyes gleaming. He pushed open the door and entered the darkened room beyond.

On a small bed, at the far side beneath the window was something wrapped up in a tarpaulin sheet.

"We put him there," explained the inspector, in hushed tones, "pending instructions which I have sent for."

Blake pulled back the chintz window-curtains, and flooded the room with faint sunlight; then he lifted up the covering and gazed critically at the dead man beneath.

The head was frightfully bruised and battered, the face discoloured and distorted, the lips drawn back over a row of white, blunt, even teeth. The hair was matted with mud and chalk, the clothes sodden and stained. Blake bent down at the foot of the bed and examined the shoes on the twisted feet.

As Jenkins had said, they were comparatively clean, but, like the clothes, they were soaked with rain. Round the neck was a wisp of collar, soiled and stained also.

Blake lifted up the head and detached the collar, and as it came away in his hand, a broken bone stud fell from the shirtband at the back. He picked it up thoughtfully.

"Another clue," he said half-aloud, as he covered up the body again and looked around.

"There is nothing further to be gathered here," he added slowly a few minutes later, drawing the curtains once more, and crossing back into the study. "Have you the key of the safe?"

Jenkins gave it to him. Blake fitted it into the lock; it turned easily, and the heavy iron door swung back.

"Lock not tampered with in any way. If it were opened at all by the murderer, it was done with the proper key," said Blake, examining the wards closely.

The safe contained a pile of brown-paper bags, full of sovereigns, a bundle of banknotes, account-books, neat piles of receipts, bills, and private papers.

Blake glanced through them all rapidly, and seemed especially concerned with a small, leather-bound memorandum-book—half diary, half note-book—he found tucked away beneath a pile of documents.

"One thing is very evident," he said suddenly. "This sum of money has been left here as a blind."

"How do you make that out?" asked Jenkins quickly.

"By the entries in this book," answered Blake. "According to a note here, dated just three months ago, after the bills for the current quarter were paid, a sum of £2,000 was withdrawn from Mr. Travers's bank in London.

"Glancing through these notes of his, I see that for the last twenty years he has drawn £2,000 from the bank at intervals of four years, showing that his expenditure regularly amounted to about £500 a year. Unless someone helped themselves to the contents of this safe, then the disappearance of nearly four years' income in less than three months is to be accounted for—yet of

which no note is made in an otherwise concise diary.

"It strikes me," he went on, "that the balance was taken last night, and this two hundred odd left to throw any suspicious inquirers off the scent. It was a cunning move to leave this money, but a careless one to overlook the memorandum-book—a slip which may prove fatal to the man who so cleverly thought out his scheme."

"But how on earth could anyone know that the money was in the safe?" asked the inspector. "The servants are honest, simple, respectable people, and obviously know nothing of their master's private affairs. He had no friends, few acquaintances, and rarely asked anyone to come into the house at all. Yet, if what you say is correct, someone must have known a great deal about him."

Blake walked across to the window overlooking the back garden, and looked out thoughtfully at the smooth, well-kept lawn, flower-beds, and neat, box-hedged red-gravelled path.

At the end of the garden a row of untidy-looking cottages backed on to it, divided by a high brick wall covered with carefully-pruned creepers. Several of the cottages were deserted, and blatantly "To let." The whole row looked deserted and poverty-stricken, with straggling cabbage-patches divided from each other by rough chalk paths.

Blake opened the window—a long French casement—stepped out on to the lawn below, and looked at something in the grass at his feet.

Jenkins watched him tracing his way slowly to the bottom of the garden, his eyes glued to the ground. Saw him suddenly swing himself up over the wall by the aid of the thick ivy stems, and drop out of sight on the other side. A second later he came into view again, still bending low towards the ground, making his way to the back door of a cottage about the middle of the row. Then he knocked at the door.

Jenkins could see that an untidy woman opened it. After a short parley she admitted her visitor into the cottage and shut the door behind him.

Ten minutes later, Blake stepped into the library and held out an old pipe.

"That narrows things down considerably," he said quietly. "It was left in that top room of yonder cottage by an old man, who took lodgings there a fortnight ago, and went away the day before yesterday."

"Well, what do you make of it?" asked Jenkins eagerly.

"Smoked by a man with a sharp incisor tooth—upper tooth, for the top of the stem is bitten into a deep hole."

"May be a coincidence only," said the inspector reluctantly.

Blake shot out a dottle of tobacco from the bowl.

"The same blend as the cigarettes," he said. "Impossible to mistake it."

"By George, that's queer! Would you mind telling me what prompted you to go to that cottage at all?"

"If you come here to the window you can see for yourself," said Blake. "In spite of last night's rain—the first we've had for several days down here—there is a faint line of chalk, beaten well down into the short turf. Now, if you follow that line of chalk, you will see it goes down to the wall opposite. A broken twig or two of ivy seemed to me to suggest that someone climbing over from the other side might have brought that chalk on his boots. I climbed over to investigate further. Sure enough, just at the base of the wall, on the far side, there are distinct footprints, deep and blurred in the chalky soil, showing where someone had landed prettily heavily—presumably from the top of the wall—not once, but several times, for there are at least half a dozen confused prints.

"The next thing which attracted my attention was the fact that the top window of the cottage, exactly opposite these windows, was as clean as a new pin—the only one approaching anything like cleanliness in the whole row. I wondered who cleaned it—and why!

"So I knocked at the door, and inquired on behalf of an imaginary pensioner of mine, if there was a room to let in the house. There was—the top room at the back, vacated a couple of days ago by an old man who had rented it for a fortnight.

"I went up to inspect it. The lodger had left nothing behind him but that pipe, which I helped myself to from the mantelpiece, unnoticed by the woman. From the window of that room you can look straight into this, owing to the fact that the windows here are at opposite ends of the room, and there is plenty of light. I could see you walking about quite distinctly, and had a particularly good view of the safe. That view would be better still when the gas was lit at night, for there are no blinds to the back window—as you, too, have doubtless noticed—only thin lace curtains half drawn across."

"Then you think the lodger across the way watched from yonder window, saw the safe, and guessed that it contained valuables?" said the inspector.

Blake nodded.

"Also that, having had previous knowledge of the house, he took that room in the cottage purposely to watch it. Also that at night he scaled the wall and stood beneath this window, looking into this room to familiarise himself with it and Mr. Travers's movements. He probably heard through local gossip that the coachman and the housekeeper's husband would be away last night, and fixed his plans accordingly. There is not much doubt that the visitor last night and the lodger across the way were one and the same person."

"But you say he left the day before yesterday," remarked Jenkins.

"That would give him time to go to London, effect an exchange of identity, and travel down here in the guise of a long-lost friend. The whisky suggests that the man was more than a chance acquaintance, or a total stranger, for, from what I gather of Mr. Travers, he was not a man to press his hospitality on either."

"What's the next move?" asked the inspector, after a pause.

"While I was away just now," said Blake, not heeding the question, "I was able to reconstruct the murder. The broken collar-stud gave me the missing clue. Also this." He stooped down to the fireplace and picked up the poker.

"That," said the inspector incredulously. "There's nothing wrong with that."

"No," answered Blake patiently. "But it is free from dust—I noticed that as soon as I came into the room. Now, the tongs and shovel are thickly covered with dust—why not the poker?"

"Heaven knows!"

"It seemed to me feasible enough to suppose that after the visitor came in, and the two men had been talking for some time, Mr. Travers sat down at his desk for some reason. As he took up the pen, the visitor bent down, snatched the poker, and dealt him a stunning blow on the head—cracking the skull, and killing him almost instantly, with very little bloodshed. The same blow broke the collar-stud, I think."

"What happened then?" asked Jenkins, half fascinated.

"The murderer took the key of the safe, helped himself to as much money us he wanted, locked the safe, returned the keys to the dead man's pocket, and then—"

"What?" interrupted the inspector hoarsely.

"Your ordinary criminal," said Blake evenly, "would have collared all the money and cleared out, leaving the rest to chance; but a master criminal"—he jerked the words through his clenched teeth—"would not be satisfied with that. A verdict of suicide would suit his plans best, and to remove all proof of his crime, to leave the way clear for that verdict, the body, if found cut to pieces on the railway line, would tell its own tale."

"But it was found over two miles from here," said the inspector incredulously. "A man couldn't carry a dead body all that way. Besides, it was absolutely impossible for it to have been thrown on the rails at the point we found it, as I explained to you. It would be physically impossible for one man—or two—or three—to get a dead body over those high iron railings; and even if that were possible, as the bank is of chalk, the body would have dislodged lumps of it on its way down. Yet none was found on the line, and, as you yourself noticed, Mr. Travers's clothes were entirely free from chalk, and comparatively free from mud-stains."

"Granted all that," said Blake slowly. "But there is another theory which you have overlooked. Suppose the visitor last night came here in a motor-car? A car, say, driven down from London, and arranged conveniently to break down near this house. The driver could knock at the door to ask for some slight assistance—perhaps water, petrol—any excuse. Knowing the ways of the house, he would time his arrival after the house-keeper had gone to bed, so that Mr. Travers himself would have to open the door. Then recognition, and the invitation to come inside.

"The crime itself I have worked out for you. After death the murderer probably carried his victim to the car, put the money in next, carefully wiped the poker, and replaced it in the fender, turned out the lights here, closed the hall door, and cleared off somewhere about half-past twelve. I should think it was an open touring car," he went on slowly.

"Oh, how can you deduct that?" said the inspector, almost impatiently. "And the time?"

"It stopped raining at one o'clock," said Blake. "but if the journey were made before that time in an open car, it would account for the sodden condition of Mr. Travers's clothes—

"My friend," he added, with a sudden change of tone, "is getting impatient"—nodding through the window to the figure of Bathurst, sitting in the waiting motor outside. "I'm off to go to the Great Bridge tunnel. Au revoir!"

A few seconds later, Blake and Bathurst were turning down the road in the motor in the direction of Great Bridge tunnel.

"Well," queried Bathurst, "how's the case going on?"

"I told you," answered Blake, as if the words were jerked from him against his will, "that one day Marston Hume would make a slip, and I said that that day would be mine."

"Yes," said Bathurst, glancing uneasily at his companion's set face.

"I'm inclined to believe," went on Blake, "*that the day has come.*" He briefly detailed the crime, and the facts, theories, deductions, which led him to suspect Marston Hume.

"We both know," he concluded, "that Hume has a sharp incisor tooth on his upper jaw, that he always smoked that particular brand of tobacco which was supplied to the Baddeley Club at his request when he joined it, so that he would know where to obtain a constant supply. We both know that at one time he had a place down here at Wilton, for he asked us several times to spend week-ends with him. While he had that place he could have made friends with Mr. Travers, and recently, when pushed into a corner for money, he could have come down here and turned that knowledge to account."

"A fairly strong chain of circumstantial evidence," said Bathurst.

"Strong enough to hang Hume," asserted Blake quietly. " Nothing on earth can save him now. Here's the bridge. Pull up."

Blake got down from the car, and spent ten thoughtful minutes scanning the muddy sidewalk, the red brickwork of the bridge, and the line below.

He seated himself in the car again.

"Wilton goods siding, as hard as you can go!" he said hoarsely.

The goods train which ran through the tunnel at 1.20 the night before was still on the track.

Blake climbed up on to the waggons one after the other, searching with a hard glint in his eyes for something. Apparently he found it—near the end of the train—an open van, with an old, weather-worn tarpaulin-cover stretched over the top. In the sagging hollow of the cover was a tiny pool of water, dyed red, and at the near side, just clear of the edge, dull red stains round a jagged rent. Blake lifted up the corner of the cover and peered beneath. The van was packed with straw bales, splashed here and there with blood. He turned to Bathurst.

"That explains the latter part of the crime," he said quietly.

"I suppose you noticed the track of motor wheels on the sidewalk close to the bridge?" he went on. "A front grooved tyre and a back one studded with metal studs."

Bathurst shook his head.

"There for all the world to see," continued Blake. "Also the deep groove in the wall just above that track. It was made by the mudguard of

Standing in the car, the murderer dropped his victim over just as the goods train was rattling beneath the bridge.

a low, grey car, which, in scraping the brickwork, left here and there scraps of grey paint. On the top of the wall just above that mark are bloodstains. *Standing in the car, the murderer dropped his victim over just as the goods train was rattling beneath the bridge.* The body struck that van near the end, was carried along through the tunnel, and was jerked off just at the far side. If the train pulled up there the jolting would easily dislodge it from its insecure position. I must see the engine-driver next before that theory can be proved."

Half an hour later he had interviewed the man, and had proved the truth of his surmise.

From the Railway Hotel in Salisbury Blake rang up a certain number on the telephone, and spoke for half an hour to a friend of his at Scotland Yard.

Before dusk every police-station in every town and village in the South of England had been furnished with a description of Marston Hume, who was probably travelling in a low, open, grey car, the left mudguard of which might be slightly damaged.

At eight o'clock Blake received a code wire containing the information that Marston Hume was found. The grey car had been garaged for repairs at the Quay Hotel, Newhaven, at mid-day, by a man answering to Hume's description, who had booked a room there, and was supposed to be waiting to cross the Channel by the night boat. Bloodstains in the light green leather cushions were accounted for by the owner, who explained that he had picked up a cyclist unconscious on the road, bleeding from a deep wound in the head, and had conveyed him to a cottage hospital. But, by order of the authorities, he was being detained in close custody at the hotel pending further instructions and Blake's identification.

Midnight was striking as Bathurst's car turned into the deserted streets of Newhaven, and drew up outside the Quay Hotel.

Sexton Blake, joined by two Scotland Yard officials, who were waiting his arrival in the shadows of the wide stone porch, turned quickly up the steps.

Not even a miracle now could save Marston Hume.

UNION JACK

2D

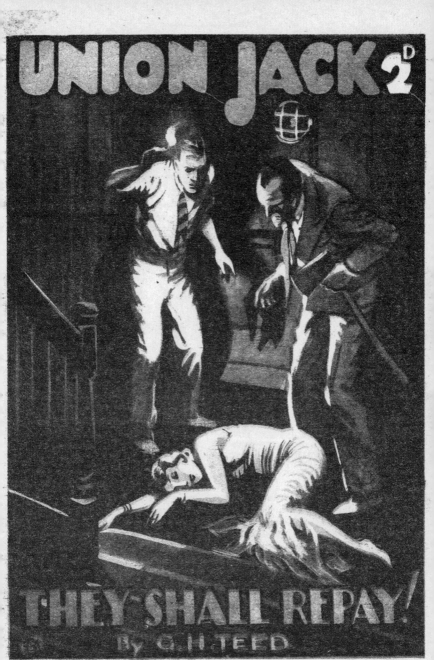

THEY SHALL REPAY!

By G. H. TEED

Introducing a new character, MADEMOISELLE ROXANE, in the first of a new SEXTON BLAKE series by the ever-popular creator of Mademoiselle Yvonne. A story of human drama and detective work, complete in this issue.

No. 1,378.   EVERY THURSDAY.   March 15th, 1930.

THEY SHALL REPAY!

𝒜 Complete Story of SEXTON BLAKE, detective.

"If we agree to sell," said Mademoiselle Roxane, "we get only one-third of what my father paid. If we refuse, we shall suffer constant pressure to force us. Is that what it boils down to? Please answer in one word."

CHAPTER I
BIRDS OF PREY.

IN the lingering caress of Indian summer, two women sat on the veranda of the spacious log camp, sewing and gazing in happy content across the mirror-like surface of the lake.

It would have been difficult to find a more perfect sylvan picture than that virgin lake set in its oval frame of silver birch and maple, the one bulwarking the other until the banks of the furthest green sloped to the dignified peak of the Sugar Loaf some fourteen miles distant.

In the soft warmth of the September afternoon there seemed no other sign of life abroad but the two women who sat rocking in the ample-armed Canadian rocking-chairs, feeling wide protection and no menace from the encircling forest.

Even a casual glance would have told one that they could only be mother and daughter. The elder was small and delicate of feature, with a pallor that caused the girl to glance at her from time to time in a way that revealed a hidden anxiety. Yet, when the faded blue eyes of the elder swept the surface of the lake or met the deeper blue eyes of the girl, she smiled happily.

Thus for more than an hour they sat, speaking only rarely, for in those surroundings speech comes with hesitancy to women as well as to men. But when the westering sun was sliding down towards the pointed tip of old Sugar Loaf, the mother allowed her sewing to fall into her lap and gave a little sigh.

"It is a nuisance that they are coming to-day, darling," she said, in tones of extraordinary sweetness.

"That sounds ungenerous and inhospitable, and I am afraid your father would wag his dear finger

By G.H.Teed

—author of
the stories
of Mademoiselle
YVONNE

Those who remember the pleasure and the appeal of our stories of the fascinating Mademoiselle Yvonne will eagerly welcome this new creation of the same author. The popularity which his masterly handling of tense human drama won for Yvonne is going to be repeated—even eclipsed, we think—by this new series concerning her even more charming successor, Mademoiselle Roxane.

at me for those sentiments. But these business men are so tiresome, and I—I do not care very much for Mr. Henley."

The girl laughed and, rising, walked across to her mother.

"Poor little mother!" she said, passing an arm affectionately about the other's shoulder. "It is only for this evening, and they will be gone tomorrow. Besides, darling, the letter seemed to hint of something important."

Mrs. Harfield became thoughtful. Slowly her gaze traversed the circumference of the lake that lay almost in the very heart of the rich timber property known as the Harfield Lumber Concession. Twenty-seven thousand acres there were in all, and in the whole of the Province of New Brunswick there was no finer stretch of hardwood timber limits than this.

Twenty-two years before, John Harfield and his bride had gone up the Tobique River valley into the remote fastnesses of the hardwood belt in Restigouche, and in those days it was no small job to attempt to get out the birch and maple which lay so far from a railway, and which could not be floated down the myriad streams to the great river basins as softwoods like spruce and fir could be.

It had been a long, uphill struggle, working with portable sawmills, cutting the logs into spoolwood, and dragging the product out to railhead on sledges. But John Harfield had stuck grimly to the task ho had set himself, optimistic to the day of his death that, eventually, Government would be forced to build a railway down through the central part of the province. There were many who thought the same as the lumberman, but the years passed and the railway was as far off as ever.

Not an election came round but the Central Railway was one of the chief planks in the platform of each party; but after, the matter was always allowed to sink into that oblivion which, receives so many election promises.

And then John Harfield died—snuffed out one drear winter's night like the flame of a candle. There were left the widow and one child, the girl Roxane; and for five years past the two had lived at Harfield Camp during most of the year, while the eight directors of the company which John Harfield had formed just six months before his death carried on desultory operations.

To those eight partners the affair was but one speculation among many in which they were interested. At half-a-crown an acre stumpage value, they had needed to put up only a small amount of money to secure a share, and, even in Montreal, it was believed that, sooner or later, the railway which had been promised for so long would be built.

Mrs. Harfield knew little of these eight associates of her late husband. The man Henley, whose name she had spoken, was the secretary of the company and the one with whom she came into most frequent contact.

Carruthers, who was accompanying him from Montreal, had been at the camp on several occasions as well, and two or three of the other directors had also appeared from time to time. But there were some on whom she had not yet laid eyes, and, had it rested with her, none of them would have found cause on any occasion to come to the camp.

A retiring, frail woman, whoso whole existence had been wrapped up in her husband and child, she flinched from the necessity to deal with the harsher things of the world. Duty had lent her courage, however, and, until Roxane grew up, she had struggled valiantly with the various details of business, because she believed it to be a duty she owed to John Harfield. In his last breath he had gasped: "It's for you and the child, Nellie—do your best!"

And she had obeyed until now, when Roxane, who had inherited her father's alertness and decision of character, had taken it upon herself to control the executive operations of the estate.

"It may be all right, Roxane," she said at last. "But I have a feeling of foreboding which

I cannot explain. If anything were to happen to the estate—if—if—Oh, perhaps I am just a little tired and foolish, darling!"

The girl laughed merrily.

"Poor little mumsie," she crooned softly. "I shall have to take you up to Montreal, to the theatre. You have been here too long this time. At any rate, we shall soon know, for, unless I am mistaken, there is the canoe just coming out of Little Bear Creek."

HER keen young eyes had not been mistaken. About a quarter of a mile away, where the lake fed Little Bear Creek, which, in turn, tumbled down into Big Bear Creek and thence into the Tobique River, a canoe had shot into view, the paddles wielded in perfect rhythm by two men; bow and stern. In the middle, the silhouettes of two other figures could be seen, and presently, as the light craft came speeding towards the beach in front of the camp, it was plain to the two women that their visitors were arriving.

"Go and tell Pierre, darling," said Mrs. Harfield, the duty of the hostess rising, for the moment, above everything else. "We shall have tea served here, on the veranda."

Roxane kissed her lightly, and, turning, entered the house by the open french windows, close to which her mother was sitting. A few moments later her voice could be heard in the back quarters, and then she once more appeared just as the two half-breeds who were driving the canoe brought the nose gently on to the beach.

The two city men who stepped out on to the strip of fine sand were entirely dissimilar in appearance. One was short and stout, swarthy of skin and oily of manner. That was Chris Henley, secretary of the Harfield Lumber Company.

The other was Harold Carruthers, a big man well over six feet in height, lean of flank, and decidedly handsome. Yet, despite this difference in their physical characteristics, the same hard, glittering, predatory look lay in the eye of each, though they were smiling and suave enough as they reached the veranda and advanced to shake hands with their hostess.

They had just bent over Mrs. Harfield's hand when Roxane appeared. Henley she had met before, but on the single occasion when Harold Carruthers had come to Harfield Camp she had been on a visit to a girl friend at St, Joseph. In the moment when Chris Henley presented Carruthers, their eyes met, and a sudden flame fired the gaze of the man as he realised the beauty of this girl who stood straight and slim as one of the saplings of the surrounding woods.

In any milieu Roxane Harfield—Mademoiselle Roxane they called her in the wide timber country among the French-Canadians—would have been beautiful. Her figure, a little over medium height, was just showing the promise of her lovely womanhood; her features were small and beautifully formed, revealing the perfection of the beauty that had been the mother's, and the decision that she had inherited from her father; her eyes were of the deepest shade of blue imaginable, like the summer sky of a Canadian midday, and the crown of her hair was russet brown and soft of sheen as the maple leaves that were turning their last caress to the Indian summer. But there was something even more devastating in her mouth when she smiled—soft red lips that curled distractingly and trembled a little, as if on the verge of tender laughter.

Harold Carruthers was a man who had travelled the wide world and had known many women, but there, on the spacious veranda of that camp, he told himself he had found such a jewel as never before. In this moment he would have swept aside all the vile plot which he and Henley and the others had formed against these two helpless women. For a brief instant in time whatever may have been decent in the man rose up above, all the hard scheming that had become the driving force of his life.

But the god of things as they ought to be sighed and flew away, and the golden moment was gone. By the time Harold Carruthers allowed the girl's hand to slip out of his, the momentary regret was past. Not that he was not already determined that this girl should come into the wide net he had cast so often in the past, but with a difference.

No mention of the business in hand was made until after tea. But then, when the two men were smoking, Mrs. Harfield broached the subject tentatively.

"Your letter did not say exactly what matter had arisen, Mr. Henley."

The stout man blew a cloud of smoke into the still autumn air and turned his suave countenance first to his hostess, then to Roxane.

"I thought it better to leave details until we came," he said in low, rather agreeable tones.

"I thought Mr. Carruthers and I could better explain verbally anything that you might not understand."

At this point Roxane drew her chair back a little, so that while neither man could gaze directly at her she could watch them.

"And the business is?" pursued Mrs. Harfield.

A swift glance passed between Henley and Carruthers. It was as if the one were saying to the other: "Shall I do it, or you?" And as if the reply was: "Go ahead. You do the talking." At any rate, Henley flicked a bit of cigar ash over the edge of the veranda and went on in those same silky tones.

"You know, of course, dear Mrs. Harfield, that your late husband always believed Government would build a railway down through this part of the province?"

A shadow came into the little woman's eyes at mention of her husband, but she mastered her emotion bravely.

"Of course. And it will come. John said so, and he knew."

The sublime faith of woman !

Henley smiled tolerantly, while Carruthers stared inscrutably across the face of the lake.

"I hope the dream will one day be realised, Mrs. Harfield, but I am afraid the prospects are somewhat vague for the present. If this Government remains in power—and they are certainly in a strong position—there is little likelihood of the work being undertaken. Election promises are one thing, fulfilment another."

"But it has been promised for years."

"Quite so! Also the St. Lawrence deep channel from the Great Lakes to the sea. But Mr. Harfield was so optimistic about this railway that when he came to Montreal a few years ago he roused in me and my associates an enthusiasm equal to his own.

"To be quite frank, dear lady, it was not the hope of any great profit from the timber operations on this estate that influenced us to invest in the company which your husband formed at that time. We are, as you probably know, men who invest for a substantial return on capital, and in this case we looked for a resale when the railway should be undertaken.

"It has been no little disappointment to us. We hoped for developments long ago, and since your husband's death we have been on the watch for a chance to sell. Of course," he added hastily, as he saw Mrs. Harfield give an impatient start, "we have been keeping you and your interests in mind as much as, if not more so, than our own."

"Liar!" thought Roxane savagely, but she held her peace.

"AT last, however, a chance has come," continued Henley. "And that is what has brought us to see you."

"Am I to understand that you have a definite offer, Mr. Henley?"

"Not exactly definite, but a tentative offer which we believe we can bring to a head. As you know, Mrs. Harfield, we could take action in this matter without your consent, for all eight directors are unanimous in the matter, and—er—we control two-thirds of the voting power of the company. But, realising your position, and out of personal regard for your husband, we have no desire to do anything without consulting you.

"It is not as good an offer as we had hoped to get, but under the circumstances, and because we are anxious to get our capital investment out in order to use the funds for other purposes, we think it best to accept."

"What—what price has been discussed?" asked Mrs. Harfield faintly.

"Five shillings per acre."

"But—but that is only what John—my husband—paid to the Government of the Province for the Crown Lands lease and stumpage rights."

"True. But during the past twenty years a good deal of timber has been taken off, you must remember. And, after all, it was the hope of a railway company coming through that gave the place its chief value as a speculation."

"I am afraid I do not quite understand. If you should accept this offer—if I should consent—what would be my share of the money received?"

Henley's body drew in a little. He had reached the point where actual figures were to be discussed, and now his mind knew exactly how to grapple with his subject

"The area of the estate is roughly twenty-seven thousand acres," he said crisply. "Of that about one-third is your interest, and two-thirds are divided among me and my fellow-directors. At five shillings a share the total purchase price would be in the neighbourhood of six thousand

seven hundred and fifty pounds. So your share would be, say, two thousand two hundred and fifty pounds."

The woman looked aghast. For a moment her eyes flashed with indignation.

"But my husband spent more—much more—than that on the place," she protested. "What could I do with such a sum as that? This is all we have, and we could not live on such a sum."

Henley spread out his hands.

"Properly invested—" he began.

But here Carruthers interposed.

"I think you should add, Henley," he said in low, deep tones, "that this phase of the matter has already been under discussion and that we agreed among us that we should place our services at Mrs. Harfield's disposal free of any charge, in order that her share should be invested to the best possible advantage. It is not a fortune, but there are some quite safe investments which would pay her eight or nine per cent, and that would yield quite a comfortable amount."

"Would you call it that, Mr. Carruthers?" came in cold, sweet tones.

The big man turned his head to look at Roxane, for it was she who had spoken. Under the direct gaze of those fearless blue eyes he flushed. For the second time the "god of things as they ought to be" was hovering over Harold Carruthers' shoulder, but once again gave a sigh and flew away.

"It is not a fortune," he said at last, "but there may be more than I suggested. I think I may assure you, Miss Harfield, that I should make it my personal care to see that your mother and you should receive enough to ensure freedom from any worry."

That soft lip which could curve so adorably could also crinkle in an expression of contempt.

"Let us cease beating about the bush, gentlemen," was the cool response. "A few questions should be sufficient—if you will answer them."

Harold Carruthers turned his eyes away. Something mocking in her eyes roused a sudden fury in him.

"I'd like the chance to teach her a lesson," he was thinking, "and I'll do it before I finish!"

But Henley had inclined his head courteously.

"I shall be most happy to answer any questions you may care to put, Miss Harfield."

"VERY well. Let us begin with the agreement you gentlemen reached among yourselves. Are we to take it that should my mother refuse the terms of sale you would still proceed?"

"As far as our own interests are concerned, I am afraid we should do so."

"To whom is it intended to sell?"

"New York financial interests have made advances."

"So if mother continues to refuse, then the position would be that, instead of our having the benefit of the advice and—er—association of you gentlemen we should have to deal with these New York financiers?"

"That is quite correct, Miss Harfield."

Both men shifted a little uncomfortably. There was a hint of something in those cool tones that got home. This interview, which they had anticipated as being a rather delicate necessity with John Harfield's widow, was not developing along the anticipated lines.

"Would we be in any worse position with these New York gentlemen than with you?" went on the relentless questioning. "Of course," and now there was sheer mockery in the voice. "we should not have the advantage of your disinterested advice, but—"

She broke off as her mother turned a helpless look towards her, but her smile reassured the other, who was learning more and more to lean on the self-reliant girl who in three short years had shown such resource in the management of the estate.

Her words, however, stirred the ruthless spirit that lay beneath Chris Henley's suavity.

"I do not believe you would find them easy to deal with, Miss Harfield," he said curtly. "Were the terms of our investment in the Harfield Lumber Company along ordinary lines, we should find it possible to make the sale on a majority vote. But out of regard for your late father and your mother we have no wish to do anything of the sort.

"These New York people have funds available which we cannot put into the business. They are prepared to put up a score or more of portable sawmills to handle the timber on the spot, to build roads from here out to the railhead, and, as a side speculation, to wait for many years for the railway to come down through the centre of the province.

"We cannot afford to do that. Therefore, since the estate is barely paying its way, and we do not believe the railway will come for many years yet, we wish to get out. If you are determined to retain your shares, I am afraid you will find the position radically different from what it has been."

"As how?"

"Well, the New York people would wish to put their own agents in this camp, and, of course, they being in control, you could not refuse them. They have intimated that they wish to purchase every share, and—well, you know how soulless financiers can be." And he laughed.

"I believe I am finding out," responded Roxane. Then: "I gather, Mr Henley, that if we did not sell you are hinting that the new directors would try to force us to do so by making things uncomfortable for us?"

"That is what I was trying to convey, Miss Harfield."

"They might even offer us less than five shillings in the end?"

"They have hinted as much."

Once more the girl mocked them, though the very soul of her was sick with apprehension.

"You seem to have travelled far in these negotiations, Mr. Henley. If we agree to sell, we get only for one-third of the estate what my father paid for the same third. We have lived, it is true. But, then, before he met you gentlemen in Montreal he owned it all. On the other hand, if we refuse, we shall suffer constant pressure to force us to do so. Is that what it boils down to? Please answer in one word."

"Yes."

"Then there seems only one answer for my mother to give, and that is to agree to the sale."

Chris Henley could hardly restrain a smile of triumph at the girl's words, for it was already plain that whatever she said would be endorsed by her mother. But somehow Harold Carruthers felt a sudden twinge of uneasiness. What it was he could not have told; to analyse it would have been impossible.

Why should those few words and that cool, sweet voice seem to hold a menace? What clairvoyant warning had swept upon him out of the future? He shook himself and rose as the girl got to her feet.

"My mother will sign whatever documents are necessary," she was saying. "How long shall we be permitted to remain here, Mr. Henley?"

"The New York people would like possession before the winter," he murmured.

"Very well; they shall have it in one month. And now, gentlemen, you will excuse us until dinner. Pierre will show you your rooms, and perhaps you will like to look about. We dine early—at half-past six."

With that Roxane gave an arm to her mother, and the two men stood watching while the pair disappeared into the house.

CHAPTER 2
TRAGEDY!

On a crisp October morning some three weeks after the visit of Chris Henley awl Harold Carruthers to the Harfield Camp on Little Bear Lake, Mrs. Harfield was sitting before an open log-fire in the big sitting-room, scanning the Montreal papers which had come in with Pierre, the breed, the evening before.

Roxane was busy in one of the bedrooms, superintending the packing of the last of the belongings which they would take away with them. But every few minutes she would steal softly to the door and peer in at her mother, sitting in the low chair by the fire, giving a sigh of relief when she saw that she appeared contented enough.

For the girl had cause to worry. Ever since the decision to sell the estate, the spirit which seemed to support that frail body had slumbered for long periods—periods that had become more and more frequent as the days went by. Anxiously the keen young eyes had watched, for she knew that her mother had taken the blow hardly—that the one thing which had held her to this world was broken.

Yet no other decision could have been made. Roxane had seen plainly enough the threat that lay beneath the suave words uttered by Chris Henley. And had she needed any confirmation, she had it when, about ten days after his visit, three men representing the New York syndicate appeared on the scene—hard-faced men, with eyes as cold as lumps of ice.

No mercy there; no pity for what made the girl and her mother cling to the camp; no soul for anything but the money the place might offer. They had inspected, had said little to Roxane or her mother, and then had taken themselves off.

And now all the Roxane wanted was to get away before other strangers should arrive. Her plans were nebulous. She would take her mother to Montreal, and when they received their share of the purchase money, perhaps it would be possible to go to some warm place in Florida for the winter. Then she would find employment of a sort, for she believed in her own brains and capacity for hard work. They would get along somehow, and she would do what lay in her power to make her mother forget the wrench of leaving the place which held for her all that was dear.

Thus she had thought and planned during those days of weary packing, while her mother had drooped more and more. Almost feverishly, the girl had worked this week to put out of sight the last single item that would keep reminding her mother, and on the morning in question she was holding a small ivory tobacco box in her hand that still contained some crumbs of the tobacco her father had smoked, when a low cry sounded in the sitting-room.

Swiftly Roxane laid the box down and flashed through the door. The moment she crossed the threshold she saw that her mother had collapsed in her chair. The paper she had help had slipped to the floor.

A sudden sharp cry of agonised concern broke from her lips, and her face went white as chalk.

"Mother— mother darling, what is it?"

She was on her knees, her strong young arms struggling to lift the frail body that drooped against the side of the chair.

"Mother! Mother! Speak to me! Oh, darling, what is it? Oh! Pierre! Pierre!"

The cry rose high, until it carried out against the trees and was echoed back.

"Pierre! Pierre!"

From the face of the lake the echo trembled, lonely and drear.

"Pierre! Pierre! Come quickly!"

Through the door leading to the back veranda sounded the soft padding of the breed's moccasined feet.

"Ma 'm'selle—"

He stopped in dismay at the sight; then the faithful fellow gave a low crooning sound, and dropped beside his young mistress.

"Yo' leave zis to Pierre!" he muttered, in sudden infinite pity. "Yo' leave zis to Pierre, ma'm'selle!"

In his great arms he lifted the drooping form as easily as if he were raising a baby, carrying her along to the bed-room, where he laid her gently on the bed. But Pierre, the breed, knew that Helen Harfield had gone at last to join the man who lay beneath the chaste silver of the birches; Pierre, the breed, knew that no machinations of man would ever take her away from the camp she had loved so well.

The dreadful truth hammered itself in upon Roxane's brain. At first the realisation stunned her. She moved about wide-eyed, tearless, scarcely knowing when people came or went. Like an automaton, she followed the coffin to the open grave that had been dug beside John Harfield's resting-place; like something that of which had ceased to beat, she went about the last duties before leaving the camp for Montreal for anywhere.

Thus it was that she knew nothing of the cause of that low cry her mother had uttered before collapsing in her chair. Not until the relief of tears came at last did her brain begin to function once more. Not until she had passed through a racking night of agony upon agony did she remember that pitiful whimper that had reached her from the chair in the sitting-room.

For the first time she began to wonder what it was that had caused that sudden collapse. Until now she had taken it for granted that her mother had just drooped and fluttered out. But as the details of that tragic morning returned to her—as she began to reconstruct in her mind each portion of the picture—she remembered the paper that had slid to the floor from her mother's nerveless fingers.

A search revealed the pile where Pierre had laid them. Dropping on to the big bearskin rug in front of the fire, she began to turn the pages. And then, scarcely had she scanned the first portion of the journal, when her eye was arrested by staring headlines.

RAILWAY EXTENSION IN PROVINCE OF NEW BRUNSWICK.

It is authoritatively reported from Ottawa that the definite arrangement with the Government of the Province of New Brunswick regarding the construction of the long promised railway through the central part of the province. The proposed line will link up with the Federal system in the Province of Quebec, and thus open up the vast timber resources of the richest stretches in the two provinces. We understand that surveys will be begun early in the coming year. This will at last bring to fruition election promises of long standing.

Three times Roxane Harfield read the brief announcement, scarcely able to believe her eyes. But at last the meaning reached her brain, and she allowed the paper to fall from her hand, while she gazed frowningly into the leaping flames.

The railway was to be built. That was all she could grasp for the moment. But presently full realisation came to her. If this report were authentic, then it meant that what her father had dreamed for so many years—what he had built on so hopefully—was at last to be realised. And it would mean that the property of the Harfield Lumber Company would immediately jump in value.

Roxane Harfield brought her keen mind to tackle the full meaning of how it would affect her. She knew it must have been this which her mother had been reading when the shock of sudden realisation killed her.

Did Chris Henley and Harold Carruthers know this when they came to the camp with the offer of the New York syndicate? Had they had this card up their sleeves when they persuaded her and her mother to sell their share for five shillings an acre? Her young eyes became hard as she began to see what might lie behind that visit. And then she moved swiftly.

She must get to Montreal—must learn the full meaning of it all. she would consult a lawyer, would discover just what the eight directors of the company had known, for she was beginning to suspect now that a vile swindle lay behind the specious words of Chris Henley and the handsome Harold Carruthers.

But Roxane had no need to go to Montreal to learn the whole contemptible plot. Two days later, just when Pierre was on the point of taking her in the canoe to the railhead at Plaster Rock, another canoe shot into Little Bear Lake, and the same two hard-faced men from New York who had visited her before got out on to the strip of beach.

This time they came, not to look and pass judgement, but to take possession. From them Roxane learned that instead of paying Carruthers and Helnley and the other six directors five shillings an acre for the property, as her mother had received, they had paid not less than three pounds an acre! Swiftly she calculated the appalling swindle of which she and her mother had been victims—the swindle that had given those city sharks nearly forty thousand pounds that should have come to the widow of John Harfield.

That afternoon Roxane stepped into the canoe which Pierre held ready while two more breeds brought her belongings in another canoe. But those belongings held small interest for her compared to the bit of paper which reposed in her handbag, for on the paper she had carefully written the names of the eight men who had been concerned in the plot which had left her motherless and to face the world with a mere fraction of the money John Harfield's long years of toil and judgement should have given her.

It wasn't the money Roxane minded, it was the brutality which had sent that gentle soul fluttering out upon its long journey. And among the noble trees of the forest she swore a vow—a vow which was to have even more far-reaching consequences than she could dream.

And the vow was that she would exact a just retribution from the eight men who—as certainly as if they had struck her down—had murdered her mother!

CHAPTER 3.
The Blow Falls.

MR. SEXTON BLAKE and his young assistant, Tinker, were engaged with the morning mail when Mrs. Bardell, their housekeeper, entered with a card on the little silver salver that was usually to be found on the old Queen Anne table in the hall.

Blake took the bit of pasteboard and read:

"MR. HAROLD CARRUTHERS,

16A, St. Francois Xavier St., Montreal, Canada."

"Show him in, please," he said briefly.

A few moments later he rose to greet a big, handsome man of some forty years of age. He was dressed in conventional morning suit, and carried silk hat, gloves, and a nearly rolled silk umbrella. He shook hands firmly with Blake, nodded curtly to Tinker, accepted the chair which Blake drew forward, and, laying his hat

on the floor, closed his knees over the silk umbrella.

"Permit me to introduce myself more fully than the name and address on my card give as particulars, Mr. Blake," he said, in deep, rich voice. "I am a member of the Montreal Stock Exchange, director in some half-dozen different Canadian companies—a promoter, if you will—and my London agents are Messrs. Brown, Forman & Co., of Crosby Square."

Blake inclined his head slightly. The name of the private banking firm of Brown, Forman & Co. was well known to him as a solid conservative establishment.

"It was Mr. Forman who suggested that I should come to you."

"What is wrong, Mr. Carruthers?"

"A good deal; I've lost my young woman secretary and sixty thousand pounds. Or, I should say, the equivalent of sixty thousand pounds in Canadian banknotes. I want you to find the girl and the money, and you can name any fee you wish."

"I haven't an idea. I'll tell you briefly just what I know. I am interested in getting control of a certain English company in order to link up the market here with on of my own corporations in Canada. Brown, Forman & Co. have been working on the thing for some time, and, about two weeks ago, cabled me that everything was ready. I realised on certain securities and sailed, bringing my secretary with me.

"We landed at Liverpool two days ago, came to London, and took quarters at the Hotel Venetia. All day yesterday I was busy at Crosby Square fixing up the details of the merger. This morning I sent for my secretary, Miss. Harrison, but she was not to be found. On further investigation I discovered that a steel dispatch-case in which the banknotes had been locked was also missing. A few questions made it plain that Miss. Harrison had left the hotel last evening and no one has seen her since."

"Is that all?"

"Not quite. While I was still investigating matters, I received an envelope by special messenger. Here it is."

He took an envelope from the inner pocket of his morning coat and laid it on the edge of Blake's desk. Before touching it the detective studied the typewritten address. It bore simply the name of "Mr. Harold Carruthers," at the Hotel Venetia,

Piccadilly, and in the upper left-hand corner the words: "By hand."

Blake drew out the single sheet of twice-folded paper it contained and spread it out. He saw at first glance that it was written in the form of a receipt, and ran as follows:

Received from Mr. Harold Carruthers, the sum of Sixty Thousand Pounds in full settlement of his

indebtedness to the undersigned.

JOHN HARFIELD.

"Who is John Harfield?"

Carruthers laid a thick, well-manicured finger against the palm of his left hand, tapping slowly.

"The only 'John Harfield' I ever knew has been dead for about fifteen years."

"You are sure of that?"

"Positive."

"Did you know his signature?"

"I have not seen it for many years, but if you mean is that signature similar I should say roughly, it is."

"But it must be a forgery."

"Of course."

"You had business dealings with this John Harfield?"

"Only in a comparatively small way. They were wound up five years ago."

"But you have just said he has been dead for fifteen years."

"I mean they were wound up with his estate. I shall explain. Harfield had some Crown lease timber land in the Province of New Brunswick, Canada. He got pushed for money, and came to Montreal to form a company. I and some friends took a two thirds interest and operated the estate after his death. It was eventually sold to a New York syndicate. That is all."

"It is odd that his name should crop up in this way."

Carrutrhers passed a finger under his collar. For the first time since entering the consulting-room he seemed a little ill at ease.

"It's more than odd—it's darned uncanny! From recollection I'd have sworn that was his signature, but it is ridiculous—the suggestion! My memory must be at fault."

"Did he leave any heirs?"

"A widow and daughter. The widow died soon after the estate was sold to the New York people; she appeared very delicate when I saw her at the time. The daughter left the place soon after, and I don't know what became of her—a very pretty girl who, I have no doubt, married."

Blake switched the subject.

"Do you definitely suspect your secretary of stealing this money?"

"She is the last person in the world I would have mistrusted. She has been with me for three years—a most reliable, level-headed young woman, I regarded her."

"Do you think it possible she has fallen into the hands of people who are hostile to you?"

"No one but she and one of my confidential clerks knew what was bringing me to London."

"Was the money in her care?"

"It was in a heavy steel dispatch case, of which she had one key and I had another. I know the money was safe on the day before we reached Liverpool, for there were some documents in the case I wanted t examine. She brought the box to my suite and we went through them together. While we were at it we checked over the money—or at least she ran through it."

"Were the notes mixed? I realise that, unlike our English system, the numbers of notes are not taken in Canada and the United States. But were they on any particular bank, or several?"

"That I can't tell you. Miss. Harrison handled the matter in Montreal, and I only regarded the notes casually as she ran through them."

"They might have been Government notes, on one bank only, or on several?"

"Yes."

"Um! That presents a difficulty, Mr. Carruthers. The documents you mention are missing too?"

"The dispatch-case with all the contents is gone."

"It looks to me as if we should try first to get some trace of the secretary. Also, while there is only a vague chance of any success, you had better have every bank in London warned, and ask them to pass the warning on to their branches."

"I have already done that, or, rather, Brown, Forman's are doing it for me. I have not yet been to the police. There are certain reasons why I don't want the newspapers to get hold of it—not until I have settled this merger."

"Pardon the question, but will this loss cripple your plans?"

The promoter flushed.

"It is going to delay matters. I have heavy commitments in Montreal, and I sold certain securities to raise this money. But I can manage all right if I can gain time. I haven't been busy as soon as I hear what you have to say."

"Well, I shall want a description of this Miss Harrison, as minute as possible."

"I can do better than that. I have a photograph which I brought along. It was taken in my office in Montreal for the 'Canadian Investors Chronicle,' and shows the girl seated at my desk in the act of taking down a letter. Here it is."

Again he thrust a big hand into the inner pocket of his coat, drawing out a sheet of glossy paper that had obviously been torn from a journal of some sort.

"She's none of your cropped flappers," he added, as he passed it over.

And Blake saw that he was right. The girl, who was sitting half-face with pencil poised over a notebook, was far more the type of the legendary women officer worker that has now disappeared.

Big, horn-rimmed spectacles disfigured the upper part of her features, and, as if to impress her features, and, as if to impress her primness upon the world, she wore her hair dragged straight back from the forehead and twisted into a plain knot at the back of the head. Her upper garment was a blouse as severely cut as that of a man, figure erect, her whole attitude one of old-maidish severity, although she didn't look more than twenty-six or twenty-seven. Allowing for the disfiguring glasses and the way her hair was done, Blake thought that three or four years might be deducted from that estimate.

"You know, Mr. Carruthers," said Blake, looking up, "you really ought to inform Scotland Yard about this matter. I don't say that I won't take the case in a private capacity, but the police net is wide. For instance, if the girl has met with an accident, they can cover the hospitals much more quickly than I. As for the Press, why—"

"No, no, no, Mr. Blake! Scotland Yard must be kept out of this. I'd rather lose the money than I have it known about this merger. The news would be cabled to Montreal, and certain people there would guess at once what was up. I want to keep the price of these shares where they are until the deal is completed."

The detective regarded him steadily.

"Is that the only reason? If I am to handle this matter, I must insist on frankness."

"Are you sure there is nothing connected with the name of this man who has been dead all these years? Can't you fathom any reason why someone should send such a document as this? It names the exact amount of your loss; it looks, on the face of it, as though it had a direct connection with the theft."

Blake's instinct told him that there was something in the mind of his client which he was unwilling to disclose. If "John Harfield," whose name was at the bottom of the receipt, had been dead for fifteen years, then how came his name to be there? What lay behind the mockery of such a document? For mockery it was, on the face of it. Carruthers seemed anxious enough to recover his money, but somehow Blake got the impression that he wished to do so without any publicity to himself. Why?

Little did he know of the uneasy feeling that was tugging at Harold Carruthers' heart. Out of the blue, so to say, had come this disaster—a blow that was far deeper than he was willing to confess to Sexton Blake. He maintained that he would be able to raise further money by cable, and, if he could keep the matter quiet, complete his deal at a profit.

But Carruthers had been deeply involved in speculations over a considerable time past. This merger which he was trying to achieve had taken almost every dollar he could raise in cash. So far, his true position was not known generally either in London or Montreal. But his state of finances was an open secret to his confidential clerk in Montreal as well as to his secretary. Miss Harrison, who had disappeared.

More than once that morning Harold Carruthers' mind had gone back five years to the time when he had swindled Roxane Harfield and her mother out of many thousands of pounds. Yet, after her mother's death, the girl dropped out sight, and, with the exception of a brief note received by him, as well as the other seven, nothing had been heard of her. This note held no threat. It had said simply:

The amount for which you sold the Harfield Lumber Company is known to me.

ROXANE HARFIELD.

For the third time since meeting the girl, Harold Carruthers felt a spasm of shame, but, as before, it had quickly passed, and with a shrug, he dismissed the whole thing.

Now this disastrous loss of the money that meant so much to him—on which all his hopes were pinned. And the name at the bottom of the mocking message which had reached him that morning. He asked himself again and again if Roxane Harfield could have had anything to do with it, and then he laughed at himself for a fool. Yet he could not bring himself to tell this cold-eyed detective the truth of that swindling deal five years before. All he wanted was his sixty thousand pounds, and he would pay the sleuth well to recover it.

"Will you take the case, and do your best for me, Mr. Blake?"

The detective was about to reply, when the telephone-bell shrilled. He lifted the receiver.

"Yes?"

"Is that Monsieur Sexton Blake?"

(in French)

"Oui."

There was a slight pause, then:

"You will be well advised, monsieur, not to lend your aid to Monsieur Carruthers. You will be treading on dangerous ground in doing so!"

Click!

That was all. Blake rehung the receiver, and turned to Carruthers.

"Did your Miss Harrison speak French?" he asked quietly.

The promoter's brows went up in surprise.

"Not to my knowledge. Why do you ask?"

"Because a very charming feminine voice has just warned me over the telephone that it will be dangerous for me to lend you my aid."

"Not to my knowledge. Why do you ask?"

"Because a very charming feminine voice has just warned me over the telephone that it will be dangerous for me to lend you my aid."

CHAPTER 4.
TWO IN A TRAP.

"A CHARMING feminine voice, and in French! Then it couldn't have been Miss Harrison. Her tones were precise, and rather harsh. Besides, I am almost sure she knew no French. Dictation in that language was always given to another girl in the office. It is absurd."

"Possibly. I only asked. At any rate, Mr.Carruthers, the purpose of your visit to me is evidently known; which is proof that interest in you and your movements has not ceased with the theft of the money. It would seem to me that there is a brain of no mean order behind this business. And twice now we have the element of the other sex in it."

For a moment Carrruthers hesitated. He was tempted to tell the detective more about that deal of five years ago, but he had beard that Sexton Blake would never touch any case that was in the least bit shady, and he guessed how he would regard that swindling of two helpless women. He was growing more frantic each hour over the loss of his money, for stark ruin was staring Harold Carruthers in the face if he failed to bring off the deal.

He shook his head

"It's got me beaten, Mr. Blake. There are some people in Montreal who are quite capable of playing a trick of this sort on me, so as to keep me out of the game until they could buy up control. But I know the secret was well kept. MacDonald, my clerk, would never sell me out, and, as I say, there is only Miss Harrison. I didn't think she was crooked, but you never can tell. She must have sold me out."

"Betraying you is one thing; lifting sixty thousand pounds in cold cash is another. However, Mr.Carruthers, I will see what can be done. I think, if you will permit me to do so, I can get Scotland Yard to make a search for Miss Harrison without the matter becoming Press copy."

"Well" —reluctantly—"if you are sure you can pull the wires."

"I think so. As for your part, I suggest you start your cables to Mont-real at once, and, if there is anyone there you can trust, make inquiries about your clerk MacDonald. We must make sure of each point as we go along. Later in the day I should like a chance to examine the girl's room at the Venetia."

The promoter rose.

"Very well, Mr. Blake, I shall be guided by you. Will you dine with me at the Venetia this evening?"

"I think I may fit that in."

Scarcely was Carruthers out of the house than Blake turned quickly to Tinker.

"Follow him, young 'un, and see just what he does. I am by no means satisfied that our client

The man jerked open the door of the occupied first taxi and vanished inside—and he did not emerge. " That's queer!" muttered Tinker.

has been quite open with us. There is something very queer about that telephone message."

Tinker caught up his hat and made for the door. On reaching the street he saw the tall, well-built figure of their late visitor standing at the edge of the kerb, in the very act of entering a taxi. The lad east about quickly for another cab, and was lucky enough to see one coming slowly along on the same side of the street. He half ran towards it and, with scarcely a glance at the driver, jerked quickly:

"Follow that other taxi, and don't let them know it."

They were off almost before he had the door closed; and leaning forward, Tinker sought for the quarry. It was just turning into another street; but when they were in Orchard Street, and almost at the corner of Oxford Street, Tinker saw it slow up for the traffic in the wider thoroughfare to clear.

At this moment something happened that puzzled him a good deal. Out from the kerb came a man, who made straight for the taxi in which Harold Carruthers was sitting.

A short, thick-set fellow the was, with a broad-brimmed black soft hat and a blue suit—neatly enough dressed, but no Londoner, as the lad quickly saw.

Without speaking to the driver, he jerked open the door of the cab and punished inside. At first Tinker thought he must be some stranger, who had believed the cab empty and had not troubled to look at the flag. But when the door was banged, and he did not emerge, the lad grew more puzzled than ever.

"That's queer!" he muttered. "He isn't the type to be pally with a man like Carruthers, and yet he got in there as if he had been waiting for that very taxi to come along. I guess the guv'nor had a presentiment all right when he told me to trail him."

As a matter of fact, Tinker was no more surprised at what had taken place than was Harold Carruthers. He had been so intent on his worries that he was scarcely aware of the opening of the taxi door until the man was half inside. Then he jerked his head round in irritation.

"Here, this taxi is engaged!" he was beginning, when the swarthy features of the intruder broke into a snarl.

Before the other could rap on the window or shout an alarm, the door was slammed, the intruder was in the seat beside him, and something hard and menacing was jammed into his side.

"You seet steel, meester, or, by gar, I blow wan beeg 'ole in you!"

Harold Carruthers had lived long enough in Eastern Canada to recognize the broken English of the "habitant"—the half-breed of the peasant class. He realized that here in London, in the midst of crowded traffic at midday, at the corner of one of the busiest thoroughfares in the whole metropolis, he was being threatened with a gun by a man from the lumber woods of Quebec or New Brunswick. And as he realized it, something cold coursed up and down his spine.

And he knew there was no bluff behind the words.

He sat as stiff as a ramrod, white to the lips. For the first time now he took notice of the driver, who seemed quite unaware of what was going on. And here, too, he sensed something sinister. A second later, when the taxi swung west in Oxford street, instead of east, he knew he had walked into a trap; the driver was part of it.

The taxi was moving now as fast as the man at the wheel dared risk. Policeman after policeman they passed, thousands upon thousands of men and women pushing along the pavements, yet Harold Carruthers was as far removed form aid as if he were being threatened in the depths of the jungle. He knew that the moment he made a break for liberty, or to call out, the man beside him would do just as he had promised—blow a hole in him.

At the Marble Arch the taxi turned down the Edgware Road until it came to a short street leading into a quiet crescent. It continued half-way round this, where the line of houses was broken by the entrance to a mews. Into this it lurched, scarcely slackening its speed, and then, at the bottom of the mews, turned sharp to the right into a deserted cul-de-sac.

At the end, a pair of heavy doors swung open, as if the cab was expected. It trundled into the dim interior so far that, from the mews outside, only a glimpse could be seen of the back. A hand came out of the gloom and turned the handle of the door. A second hand followed, another pair, and Harold Carruthers was hauled out like a sack of bran.

He stood reeling, trying to summon up courage to give a cry for help, but before he could do so something hard struck him with practiced precision on the back of the head, and he slid loosely into the arms that held him.

All the way during that chase Tinker had been sitting forward watching the quarry. He had no need to urge on his own driver, for the man kept the distance as if well used to the game. But when the leading cab turned into the crescent, Tinker began to think that it would be as well to ease back a little; and then, a little later, as the quarry disappeared into the mews, he was certain he was taking too much risk. It was in his mind that the had better do the rest of his reconnoitering on foot, so, leaning forward, he tapped smartly on the window.

His driver seemed not to hear him. Tinker gave a second rapping; but then, when his signal was still ignored, he started to press back the catch of the handle. That action was his last conscious moment for some time to come. The whole interior of the cab was suddenly flooded with a sickly odour, that sent his senses swimming, and, with one deep gasp, he slid gently to the mat.

A few moments later the second cab trundled into the dim mews behind the first.

HAROLD CARRUTHERS had been knocked out with careful calculation. Twenty minutes later, when he came to himself, he blinked confusedly at the girl who was seated opposite him.

She was beautiful. Even his still dazed senses told him that. She was beautiful from the top of her sleek little russet crowned head to the bronze shoes that covered her silken clad legs.

Some chord of memory stirred his brain. He made an effort to sit up, but found ankles and arms bound to the chair in which he had been placed; further, a heavy warning hand came on to his shoulder from behind.

He kept staring into the blue eyes that were mocking his, trying through the fog to remember where and when he had seen this girl before. Then a light laugh cleared his brain.

"Are you trying to remember me, Mr. Carruthers?" The voice was soft, with a slight drawl and huskiness that lent it extraordinary charm. "Surely you remember Roxane Harfield?"

He knew well enough now. He realized that these things he had been telling himself all morning mist be impossibilities were stark realities. What she was doing in that chair, why he was bound hand and foot before her he didn't know; but he guessed, without much mental effort, that Roxane Harfield had, somehow, come out of the past, and had lifted sixty thousand pounds of his money.

"What is the joke, mademoiselle?" he asked, with an attempt at coolness. "Of course I remember you."

True enough, but little had he dreamed that the girl of the "limber lost" would grow into such a beautiful and perfectly-poised woman of the world as this.

She still smiled mockingly at him.

"You will find no joke when you understand" she said evenly. "I have had you brought here, Mr. Carruthers, to enlighten you for the good of your soul. I might have delayed this little finish to my revenge if you had not been so foolish as to rush off and see Sexton Blake.

"Oh, yes, I know all about that and about him. But Sexton Blake is not going to interfere in my affairs. If he does, so much the worse for him. But tell me, Mr. Carruthers, do you not see any likeness at all between me and your trusted secretary, Miss Harrison?"

Carruthers stared at her in stupefaction. There was a vague something that he could not determine, but Miss Harrison— It was ridiculous that she could be the same.

"You do not believe? It doesn't matter. You will soon. You see, Mr. Carruthers, this meeting to-day is the culmination of a carefully worked out plan. It has taken me five years to do it, but I was willing to wait. A woman has more patience than a man, you know."

"You can't be the same!" he stammered.

She laughed again.

"Wait! You remember the day you and Chris Henley came to the camp and informed my mother and me that the estate must be sold." Her voice grew more husky as she spoke of her mother, but she recovered quickly. "I suspected then that we were not getting a square deal. But I did not know the truth until after. It was reading the truth in the paper that killed my mother, Harold Carruthers—the realization of what had been done to us. And, then, on the day I left, I got the proof I needed from the two men who came from New York.

"It was a cunning scheme, but a cowardly and brutal trick to play on two women. Nearly forty thousand pounds you swindled us out of, you and your seven confederates. Had it not been for that, my dear little mother would have been alive to-day. Out in those woods—clean woods, Harold Carruthers—I swore a vow of vengeance. And now the first on my list pays the price.

"For two years I played high with the little money left to me. I knew I must have plenty of resources to fight you and the others of your gang. It was all or nothing. I took a position in a stockbroker's office, and studied day and night to learn the intricacies of share speculations. You may remember the spectacular rise in Steel of Canada about three years age; and you will recall that the heaviest buying came from some mysterious source, I was that source, Harold Carruthers, and when it was over I had a million to go on with."

The man uttered some exclamation, but the girl waved it aside.

"There is more. I was ready then to begin my greater campaign. I altered my appearance to that of the 'Miss Harrison' who sought a place in your office. It took six months of patience before I got there, but it wasn't long before I became your confidential secretary. You were too strong for me, even then, but I still played the market, and I made more money even than you. Once or twice I could have rained you by giving away your secrets, but I bided my time. I wanted to get you where I could smash you beyond repair. And now that tine has come.

"For eighteen months your luck has been out. You called it your luck, but it wasn't that. You suspected someone working against you. That was true. It was I. Every time you bought, I sold, and I knew your resources so well that I knew just how heavily I must play.

"Gradually your holdings dwindled until you knew you must make one grand coup in order to regain your position. Who was it that first hinted at the possibility of bringing off such a merger as has brought you to England? Think carefully. Don't you remember?"

"My heavens! You Devil!" She laughed outright.

"So you recall that afternoon when prim little Miss Harrison laid certain figures on your desk and led you along so gently that you desk and led you along so gently that you never suspected? And she made herself so indispensable in the negotiations that you had to being her with you to England."

She lit a cigarette and blew a cloud of smoke upwards.

"I was prepared for months before you were ready to come. I had realized on all my holdings; I had agents here in London watching every move. I bought the lease of this house and staffed it with faithful habitants from the New Brunswick woods—breeds who knew Mademoiselle Roxane as a baby, and who would cheerfully kill you, Harold Carruthers, for what you did to her and her mother.

"You fell into the hands of Pierre and Napoleon to-day. Oh, they may be from the back woods, but they know their London all right, when everything was ready, when this morning was to bring the culmination of your plans, 'Miss Harrison' walked out with your dispatch-case and the sixty thousand pounds.

"You see, you can't even trace the notes, because it was I who drew them from the bank, and only I know what issues they were."

There was no bluff in these words. Harold Carruthers knew well enough now what a blind fool he had been. Yet even in this moment he kept telling himself he was suffering some mad hallucination.

It was unthinkable that the slip of a girl whom he had seen at the lumber camp five years before could have brought off that spectacular coup in steel which he remembered so well; that for three years she had had access to his every secret, had befooled him and worked the stock market against him with a hand that must win, because she had known at the start just what cards he held.

And yet—and yet, looking into those mocking, blue eyes, he realized the futility of telling himself these things. A million—several millions—she must have made in order to bring him to ruin in this way. And it was ruin—complete and utter, the stripping from him of everything. She was right; few men could have had such patience; few men could have worked side by side with an enemy for three years without making some betrayal of their purpose. Bit this girl, she had made of herself a veritable scarecrow in order to deceive him.

Harold Carruthers knew his own power over women; and now the craven in the man came to the surface, for he was afraid, almost whimpering in the fear of poverty. He would get round her, tell her that it was none of his doing, that it was Chris Henely and the others; and then when he got clear, got hold of his money again, he'd make her dance to a pretty tune!

"I don't think so, Mr.Carruthers. I can guess what you are thinking. I have seen that look in your eyes many times when you have been planning to stab someone in the back. But it's no use. I haven't worked these five years for nothing!

"My plans must be altered a little because you did just one thing I did not count on. I thought that receipt with John Harfield's name on it would make you hesitate. But you went to this detective, Sexton Blake, before I could get hold of you. But even if my plans have been altered the result will be the same. As for the detective—I have warned him already. You will know soon enough what the end is to be!"

Then, swiftly, in the French patois of the Canadian woods, she told Pierre to take him away. Carruthers made to struggle; but at a low word from Pierre Napoleon also appeared; and between them they carried out the man, chair and all, with ease. Those two husky French-Canadian lumberjacks had not been wielding the "peeve" and "cantdog" all their lives without that same fierce exercise benefiting their muscles.

WHEN they were gone Roxane Harfield sat gazing pensively through the net curtains that gave a misty view of the sunlit crescent beyond. Then her forehead wrinkled, and her round, firm chin set a little.

"It wouldn't do for him to know it," she murmured at last; "but the calling in of Sexton Blake complicates matters. I have never seen him, but I have heard enough about him. That was a mistake on my part; everything else went so perfectly. I did not anticipate that Harold Carruthers would rush off to him like that. But he must be stopped—somehow. I may be able to get something out of the lad, though how he came to start of after Harold Carruthers is a mystery to me. I'll see what he has to say."

Leaning over, she pressed a button set in the wall near the fireplace. Almost immediately Pierre appeared.

"Bring the other, Pierre, if he is conscious," she ordered.

The man bowed and withdrew; but soon after the door opened once more, and it was Tinker who was brought in, with Pierre on one side of him and Napoleon on the other. He was not tied to a chair as Carruthers had been; his ankles were free, and, willy-nilly, he was forced to walk.

A bandana was tied about his mouth, yet above this his eyes gazed truculently at Mademoiselle Roxane. The dope which had been flooded into the cab through the speaking-tube had been just enough to keep him quiet for ten minutes or so; but now his wits were perfectly clear.

Roxane looked at him closely. She was interested in this young fellow of whom she had heard and read so much. He was the sort of upstanding lad she would have liked for a younger brother,

and, for a moment, her purpose weakened. But then the memory of those live years swept over her once more, and her eyes hardened.

"You are Tinker, I suppose?" she said curtly.

Tinker was quite as much interested in her as she had been in him. He had by no means got the strength of things yet, and, after the photograph he had seen of "Miss Harrison" he couldn't quite reconcile her with the case. Yet he had seen enough be now to know that Harold Carruthers had not come to this house of his own free will; that, like himself, he had been overpowered in some way.

This lovely girl before him didn't look like a crook, but you couldn't tell anything by looks these days. Carruthers was his and Blake's client, and this girl was on the other side. Therefore, it was his duty to stand four square by the client. His only consolation just then was that it was the two hulking, swarthy brutes who held him that had caught him napping, and not this slip of a young thing whose eyes were mocking him.

He nodded his head shortly and waited.

'If I have that bandage removed, will you give me your word not to cry out? You see, it wouldn't do any good, for my men could soon stop you."

Tinker took a look towards the two long windows, reckoning his chances of leaping through if he could shake off his captors for a moment. But he soon realized the futility of that, so turning back to Roxane, he nodded again.

She made a sign to Pierre, who soon slipped off the bandana.

"Why did you follow Mr. Carruthers?" she asked, at last.

"Who said I followed him?" countered Tinker. "Maybe I just happened to leave the house after him."

She smiled and shook her head, and, despite his predicament, Tinker could not deny her prettiness.

"She's a peach," he was thinking. "What a darned shame she's a crook! But what is her game?"

"I'm going to give you a chance to tell me what passed between Mr. Carruthers and Mr.Blake. If you do—"

"Wait just a minute!" interrupted the lad. "Let me say now that you are only wasting your breath. There isn't anything that is going to make me talk about that."

She did not argue; merely lifted her hand.

"We shall see what we shall see. I have ways and means."

Then, without further ceremony he was dragged from the room.

CHAPTER 5
DOPED AND DUPED

SEXTON BLAKE was too busy that afternoon to give much thought to Tinker's movements; but when he returned to Baker Street a little before six and found no sign of the lad, as well as no message, he began to wonder.

He rang up the Hotel Venetia to try and get through to Harold Carruthers, but nothing had been seen of him since he had gone out that morning. He did not attempt to telephone to Brown, Forman & Co., for he knew the banking firm would be closed at that hour.

After attending to a few matters be changed, and then got through to the Venetia once more. Still Carruthers had not come in. Hanging up the receiver, he sat back and lit a cigarette.

"Strange," he muttered. "It was before midday that Carruthers left here, and a few moments later that Tinker followed. Carruthers was heading for the City, and Tinker was to trail him. Yet not a word. It isn't like the lad to let so much time go past without reporting. Now, I wonder what the dickens is up? I may be able to get through to Forman's home address."

Taking up the telephone directory, he turned to the "F's" until he found what he wanted. An inquiry brought the answer that Mr. Forman was at dinner, bit, on hearing Blake's name, the butler consented to take the message to him. A few minutes later Henry Forman himself was on the wire.

"I haven't seen Mr. Carruthers since I sent him to you, Mr. Blake," he answered Blake's question. "I can't understand it either, for I expected him all day. Have you tried his hotel?"

"Twice; but he hasn't returned since he left this morning."

"Do you think anything serious has happened?"

"I can't go that far yet. I shall try his hotel again. He may have sent some message. I was to dine with him, so he may turn up there before half past seven."

After a few more words Blake hung up and rose. He slipped into a light overcoat, and caught up his crush hat. Then he left the house. He walked leisurely round the corner to the garage in the lane at the back where the Grey Panther was kept ignoring the taxi that crept invitingly along the kerb.

He took the wheel of the Grey Panther himself, and drove at a moderate pace through Oxford Street to Regent Street, and thence to the Piccadilly entrance of the Venetin, where he left the ear in care of Kelly, the huge commissionaire.

Blake made light of the matter.

"I'll take a cocktail, and then, if he doesn't turn up, I'll dine in the grill room. But I should be obliged, Browning, if you will see that he is watched for. I want to see him rather importantly."

Two hours later Blake was rising from his table in the grill-room, and still no word had come regarding Carruthers. He phoned to his own number from a box on the grill-room floor, but Mrs. Bardell had seen nothing of Tinker; nor had there been any telephone message since Blake's departure.

By this time the detective was distinctly worried. From the daring with which the theft of the banknotes had been carried out he realized a cool and calculating brain was behind the affair; also he had felt from the first that Carruthers had not confided in him all he might have told.

More than that, however, he was remembering the warning he had received over the telephone while Carruthers was in the consulting-room. That alone was sufficient proof that Carruthers' movements were being watched, and if the threat had been fulfilled so swiftly, then it meant the existence of some organization behind the affair, and not merely a solitary absconding secretary.

But Why?

That was what he asked himself as he walked up the wide staircase to the lounge. If the object was to steal the money from Carruthers, why should the thief, or thieves, take further risk? If the promoter had told the truth, then the theft was a "fait accompli." Was it that the thieves had not had sufficient time to cover up their tracks and make a getaway? It certainly looked like it. And what had become of Tinker?

BLAKE idled in the lounge until nearly eleven o'clock, but without learning the tiniest item of news. Once more he put through a call to Baker Street, hoping Mrs. Bardell would not have retired. After a little delay he heard her voice,

Roxane looked at him closely. She was much interested in this young fellow whom her men had caught. "You are Tinker, I suppose?" she said curtly.

but still it seemed that Tinker had not put in an appearance.

"There's only been one message, sir," she added. "It was from Inspector Thomas, who wants to see you."

Blake rang off, nut a second later put through another call, this time to Scotland Yard. Inspector Thomas was not there, but had left a message that if Blake rang up or came to the Yard he was to go on to Bow Street Police Station.

Considerably puzzled as to why Thomas wanted to see him, and wondering if the message had anything to do with Carruthers, Blake got his coat and hat and climbed into the Grey Panther. He drove to Bow Street by way of Leicester Square, and, on entering the station, found Thomas engaged in conversation with the sergeant on duty and the divisional-inspector.

"Oh, you got my message, Blake? A queer case has been hauled in here to-night, and it seems to have something to do with you."

"Anything about Tinker?" asked Blake quickly.

"Tinker? No, nothing about Tinker. What's wrong with him?"

"Nothing, But what is this queer case?"

Blake accompanied Thomas and the divisional-inspector along the stone corridor, past the line of cells, until they came to a door at the far end. It was closed, but not locked, and when it was thrown open Blake saw Dr. Race, the divisional police surgeon, bending over a figure that lay on the cot.

The detective walked across and gazed down at the bundle of human wreckage that was receiving the doctor's attention. He saw, at first, a big man whose clothes were so ragged that no self-respecting tramp would have worn them. His face was smudged, his hands begrimed, and the soles of his boots broken away from the uppers, revealing muddy socks beneath. As woeful a picture of human descent as one could gaze upon.

He turned to Thomas.

"What about him? He looks like a common drunk."

"That's what was thought when he was brought in," rejoined Thomas, with a side look at Blake; "but, since he seemed on intimate terms with you, we thought we'd better investigate a little more closely."

"What the dickens do you mean?"

The doctor held up his hand. The lips of the man of the cot were moving, and, bending lower, Blake heard, to his amazement, his own name being mumbled over and over again.

"Se-xton Bl-ake."

Just that, thick, monotonously, then the mumbled words trailed off.

The detective moved still closer, and bent so that his face was within a few inches of the prone wretch. Then he shifted his body a little so the light fell full on the smudged features. Carefully he studied them until, suddenly, his body stiffened and he straightened quickly.

"Where did you pick him up?" he asked sharply.

"Constable Graves found him staggering about in one of the side streets near Covent Garden," answered the divisional-inspector. "We thought it was a plain drunk, but when we got him here and he began to mumble your name I thought it best to get in touch with Inspector Thomas. In the meantime we sent for Dr. Race."

"And it is no case of drunkenness," broke in the divisional-surgeon. "The man has been doped—heavily. I've given him an injection, but I can't tell yet whether he will come round or not. But he seems to have your name in his mind."

"Do you know him, Blake?" asked Thomas, who knew the detective well enough to realize that he was labouring under some unusual excitement.

"Yes. And Dr. Race is right—it is not a case of drunkenness. This man was in my consulting-room this morning, and he was dressed very differently; you couldn't have found a more neatly-clad figure in the whole of London. He has fallen into some trap, has been doped, and put into these rags. Yes, I know him."

"But who is he?"

"A Canadian company promoter. His name is Carruthers."

BLAKE could do no less than make himself responsible for Carruthers. Whatever doubts he may have had, there was no question now about the peril that overhung his client. Whether this was the end of the game he could not tell. But that it was a vendetta, he was sure.

It seemed incredible that this mumbling bit of human flotsam could be the same man who had visited him that morning. Yet this had happened to him within a few hours. And if that brief time could achieve such a terrible metamorphosis in Harold Carruthers, what about inker? Had the lad suffered a similar or worse fate?

Even while Blake talked to Thomas there was ringing in his ears the words that had come to him over the telephone that morning. They had formed no idle threat. There was danger in his association with Carruthers, and no time had been lost in showing him what could be done.

Under the circumstances, he was forced to explain matters to Thomas. He had put off informing him of the disappearance of the girl known as Miss Harrison, for, on his return to Baker Street early in the evening, his mind had been fully taken up with the puzzle of Tinker's absence.

When Carruthers had been taken to Charing Cross Hospital in a police ambulance, and Blake had phoned to Henry Forman, advising him that the Canadian had met with an accident, was lying at the hospital, and requesting him to go there in the morning, he and Thomas got into the Grey Panther.

On the way to Scotland Yard Blake gave the details, and within half an hour London was being scoured for Tinker, as well as the missing secretary. Not yet, however, did Blake say anything to Thomas about the warning that had reached him, nor of the feminine voice that had uttered it. That was his own end of the affair, and he was grimly determined to track down the speaker with the least possible delay.

"It isn't one person," he told himself, when he left Thomas and drove back to Baker Street. "No single individual could carry out all this. There is a gang, and Carruthers has been the victim. Has he been the first? That is the point.

"I can think of a few criminals at large who are capable of working a game of this sort, but most of them would have stopped when they had the money safe. There is something more behind it. If Carruthers comes out of that dope by to-morrow he may be able to tell me something of what occurred after he left me this morning. And whatever overtook him was not far away from Tinker."

He was driving at a moderate pace, busy with his thoughts and only subconsciously watching the road ahead, for, at that hour of the night, traffic was light in Baker Street.

Hence he was not prepared for the sudden appearance of a girl on the edge of the kerb only a few yards from where he would turn down to the garage, and not until he heard her utter a sharp cry and then saw her stumble to her knees did he realize he was almost running her down.

He jammed on the brakes and leaped out. A few strides brought him to where she was struggling to her feet, but before he could give her a supporting arm she was down again.

"I'm so sorry!" he said as he lifted her. "I did not see you until you were stepping off the footpath."

"I—I—It was my own fault," she gasped. "I should have waited. Oh! It's my ankle! I—I can't put any weight on it!"

"I'm terribly sorry! My house is just a few yards away. Will you let me take you there and see how badly the ankle is hurt? My housekeeper can bandage it for you, or I can get a doctor friend of mine who lives not far away to come along."

"Oh, thank you, no! It may not be so bad. I—If I could get a taxi and go home!."

BLAKE scarcely realized how closely he had been holding her. But now, as she quivered against him he looked down into her face. It was twisted a little with the pain she seemed to be suffering, but even in that light he could see that she was very lovely.

He saw, too, that her clothes had that indefinable hall mark of the best tailor, and certainly the fur that hung lightly about her shoulders could only be sable. She was obviously a young woman of some position and means; nor did it occur to him in his anxiety about her injury that it was a little odd she should be alone in Baker Street at that hour of the night.

"I was visiting a friend." She said haltingly, as if she thought this very question might enter his mind. "It is such a lovely night I thought I would walk home, and telephoned for my car not to come. It was foolish of me. But it I could find a taxi—my ankle really seems a little better now."

"Why, I'll drive you home with pleasure!" Blake hastened to say. "I should feel easier if you would come into my house first. My name is Blake—Sexton Blake—and I assure you my housekeeper is a most capable old soul."

If he had been able to peer into the eyes beneath those lids that so swiftly veiled them he would have seen an odd little gleam as he mentioned his name. But never for a moment did he guess that the quiver which again passed through the girl's little body had any genesis except the pain in her ankle. Nor did he know that she had been following him in a taxi ever since he left Baker Street that evening, had witnessed his entry to the Venetia, his exit, his visit to Bow Street, his journey with Inspector Thomas to Scotland Yard, and then had out through ahead of him in one last desperate attempt to trick him before he should enter his house.

Yet if Blake were ignorant of all this so had the girl looked for a very different person in Sexton Blake than this tall, distinguished man in faultless evening clothes.

"If you would be so kind as to drive me," she faltered.

"Why, of course!" he exclaimed heartily. "I am only too glad to be of service. Let me help you into my car."

*Blake scarcely realised how closely he had been holding her.
But now, as she quivered against him, her face was twisted a
little with the pain of her injury, but he could see she was
very lovely.*

She managed, with the assistance of his arm, to limp along to the Rools, where Blake ensconced her comfortably in the back.

"You will be more comfortable in here," he assured her as he made a cushion of the rug for her injured foot. "And now, if you will tell me where you live—"

"Twenty-six, Burford Crescent—just off the Edgware Road."

"I know the Crescent quite well. We shall be there in a few minutes."

He took the wheel and drove slowly, asking her from time to time if she were all right. She reassured him each time, and it was with a faint tinge of regret that Blake finally turned out of Edgware Road into the short street that led to Burford Crescent.

"I hope you will permit me to know how you are to-morrow," he said, over his shoulder, as he swung slowly round the Crescent, his eyes searching for No.26.

Sexton Blake was no light philanderer. But there was a "something" about this girl, a quality, if you will, that interested him as no other woman had interested him for a long time past. It was in this frame of mind he asked the question, and he was surprised at himself for the anxiety with which he awaited her answer.

"To-morrow," he heard her say, and suddenly her voice became low and appealingly husky— "to-morrow—why, yes, Monsieur Blake, I shall let you know to-morrow how much my ankle has improved."

Sexton Blake turned his head sharply. Gone from his mind was everything but the realization that he had heard that voice before; not as it had been revealed to him back in Baker Street, but as it had just come to him—low and soft, and with that husky quality. He knew now, and a sharp warning told him he was in danger. All this while his head was still turning; but before he could bring the car to a stop something sharp stabbed into the side of his neck.

Mechanically his feet went to the brakes, but already he was lurching helplessly to one side, and the last hazy recollection he had was the echo of a low, clear laugh as someone leaned over him and grasped the wheel.

CHAPTER 6
ALL AT SEA

For two days Inspector Thomas made futile search not only for Tinker, but for Sexton Blake as well.

From the moment when Blake had parted from him at the Yard, on the night when Harold Carruthers was found doped and wandering in a side street off Covent Garden, Thomas had put into action every bit of police machinery he controlled; or, rather, the whole resources of Scotland Yard were requisitioned. But both Blake and Tinker might have disappeared off the planet for all trace of them that was found.

During that time Harold Carruthers lay in Charing Cross Hospital in a state of high fever and semi-delirium. All that medical care could do for him was being done, and, during the hours when Henry Forman and Thomas sat beside his bed, they tried, between them, to piece together into a coherent whole the ramblings of the sick man. But all that stood out clear was the name of Sexton Blake.

On the third day, however, Carruthers became clear in his mind, and, although still very weak, it was certain that the effects of the drug were wearing off. Thomas was at his side when he first asked where he was, and gently led his mind along to the point where it impinged on Sexton Blake.

The mention of the detective's name seemed to do more than anything else to bring back recollection, for Carruthers was eager to talk. It was just then that Henry Forman came in, but it took all the latter's powers of persuasion to get him to reveal what he knew, for he then discovered that Thomas was from the Yard.

Yet they could learn little from what he eventually disclosed. He spoke of going to Baker Street—which confirmed what the banker had already told Thomas—and then of entering a taxi when he left. His knowledge of London was not extensive enough for him to describe how he had been driven after the cab reached Oxford Street, but he had recognized the Marble Arch.

Thomas was less interested in that for the moment than in what he had to say about the man who had entered the cab at the corner of Oxford Street and had threatened him with a pistol.

"It was the agent of some enemies," was all Carruthers would explain. "I told Sexton Blake about it, and he's the only one I'll talk to now."

"Then you'll have a long wait," returned Thomas crossly, "for Sexton Blake has disappeared. Moreover, you had better reconsider, for on the night you were found it was he who recognized you and told me a good deal about your case. You had better leave yourself in the hands of Scotland Yard, Mr. Carruthers."

"It's no crime to be robbed," snapped the promoter, who was rapidly regaining his strength. "And if I don't choose to make a complaint it's none of your business."

"Wait a minute," put in Forman, who saw that Thomas was handling his man in the wrong way. "I don't think you need fear Scotland Yard. I have explained to Inspector Thomas that you came to London on business of a very private nature, and that it is essential that you should complete it before certain business enemies learn what is going on.

"You may have been the victim of those people, or just a gang of thieves may have discovered how much currency you were carrying. But I do think it your duty to help the inspector in his search for Sexton Blake and the lad. After all, Carruthers, it was through you, it would seem, that some disaster has overtaken them."

"Well, what can I do? They 'got' me all right, but they haven't outed me. Let me get out of this place and I'll soon pull things round!"

He dared not confess, even to Forman, how desperate his position was, for he still had the gambler's hope that he would be able to make some winning turn at the last minute. He wanted to find his way to that house where Roxane Harfield had mocked him, and get his hands on her slim, white throat.

"You'll pull things round, as you put it, much more quickly if you work with us," said Thomas. "Even if you don't know London you know how you were driven. Could you take us to the place?"

Carruthers yielded. Something in Forman's eye told him that the banker was beginning to suspect the truth, though he didn't know what confidential information he had received from Montreal in the last day or two.

"All right!" he muttered sulkily. "Get me out of here, and I'll show you how I was driven; though, mind you, no publicity!"

"You needn't worry about that," Thomas assured him.

IT was evening before the doctors would permit the patient to be moved, and all that time Thomas sat fuming at the delay. But eventually he got his man in a police car, and, taking the Marble Arch as a jumping-off place, so to say, motioned for him to go ahead.

Carruthers pointed without hesitation to the Edgware Road.

"Down there—not very far."

The car crept along slowly, passing first one street then another until, suddenly, Carruthers made a gesture.

"Round this corner—I'm sure of it. I remember that bank opposite."

The driver swung into the short street leading to Burford Crescent, and the moment they began to follow the arc Carruthers lifted his arm.

"That house on the corner. There is an alley of sorts beside it. I was driven down there."

Thomas grunted, and as they approached the house scrutinized the front carefully. If there was anyone living in the place it looked as if they were out of town, for the blinds of all the front windows were drawn. Still, he figured, it wasn't likely the sort of people who had kidnapped a man in broad daylight in Oxford Street would want to advertise themselves.

At a sign from him the driver turned into the entrance to the mews. The car stopped at the right-hand turning into the mews proper, and the two plain-clothes men who sat in the back with Carruthers jumped out after the inspector.

There wasn't a sign of life about the place. The back windows of the house were obscured, as were the front, and to all their hammering on the double doors of the garage came back nothing but empty echoes.

"Get them open!" ordered Thomas.

It took but a few minutes to prise off the padlock. The doors swung open with a squeak as if they had been out of action for a long time. But the moment he stepped into the dim interior Detective-Inspector Thomas recognized the big grey Rolls that stood on the left. It was Sexton Blake's car, known as the Grey Panther.

On the right was a taxi, and in front of that again still a second taxi. In the right wall of the mews was a door, and after a preliminary examination Thomas gave the same order.

"Get it open!"

He did not even bother with making a note of the plates on the back of the taxis. He knew they would lead nowhere; it was sufficient for him that both Tinker and Sexton Blake must have passed this same way.

But more than two days! What could have happened to them in that time if Carruthers had been turned into a gibbering idiot within a few hours. Apart from the professional aspect of the matter Thomas felt a very deep concern about Blake and the lad, for they had worked together over many years and, although the edges rubbed a bit thin now and then when Thomas got choleric, the man from the Yard knew what he owed to Blake.

"If there's anything in this dump I'll find it," he muttered as he saw the door smashed open.

But Thomas was doomed to disappointment, for although he and his men combed and re-combed the place from basement to roof, they found nothing but a well-furnished house with dust covers over the furniture in the principal rooms, as if the occupant had gone away for some time.

Not a scrap of paper, not a pin, not a thread was there to show what had become of Blake and Tinker.

HAD Inspector Thomas been gifted with clairvoyant powers he would have been able to visualize a curious sight at a certain period of time when he sat at Harold Carruthers bedside, or, rather, he would have seen Sexton Blake in a curious role.

Blake's first sensation of consciousness was that of being heaved about in a way that caused him considerable discomfort. For a time he lacked the volition to open his eyes and try to discover what was happening to him, but gradually a steady, gentle throbbing sound beat so insistently on his brain that his hazy wits began to concentrate.

Then he opened his eyes. For some little time his mind refused to register the impression of his immediate surroundings. But, bit by bit, he began to realize that he was lying on a bed in a most luxuriously-fitted cabin, and that the heaving which had irritated him so was the motion of a ship. The throbbing sound, he now knew, was the grinding of the screws.

He next regarded the bed in which he lay, finding himself in pyjamas of soft silk, and under the clothes. There were no bonds to restrain him, so he sat up and pushed the bed-clothes from him; then he swung his legs over the edge.

His head ached dully, and his mouth was parched. Just opposite him was a toilet stand, in the rack of which was a bottle of water, and, beside this, a glass. He staggered a little as he walked towards it but managed the journey, and drank a glass of water thristily.

Through a big, brass-bound port he saw the tossing waves of a grey sea, but no land. On the right of the washstand was a white-painted door, which yielded to his pull, revealing a small but perfectly-fitted bath room. With another door, to the right, he was not so lucky, for it refused to budge. Beside it, however, was a light switch and a bell. He pressed the latter, then made his way back to the bed.

Sitting on the edge, he began to go back to his last conscious moments. Gradually, recollection came to him. He remembered the meeting with the girl in Baker Street, and the "accident" which had caused him to drive her to Burford Crescent; then his sudden suspicion that something was wrong, and, lastly, the sharp stabbing in his neck which had pitched him into unconsciousness. And now—this.

At this point in his cogitations there was a sound at the door. It opened a moment later, to reveal the figure of a white-jacketed steward, bearing a bundle of blue serge garments on his arm. He closed the door, and greeted Blake as respectfully and as unemotion ally as if the occasion were the first morning on any passenger ship's voyage.

"Good-morning, sir. I trust you have slept well. We had it a bit rough coming down Channel last night."

Blake regarded him sardonically, while he laid the blue suit carefully on the couch beneath the port, and proceeded to open a drawer, from which he took silk underwear, socks, a shirt, and other details of what Blake would require.

"Shall I get your bath ready now, sir, or can I bring you some tea or coffee?"

"Some coffee, please—strong—and a cigarette if it is permitted."

"Certainly, sir; at once, sir. Everything possible is to be done for your comfort."

"I am glad to hear that!' responded Blake drily.

At the door the steward paused.

"Breakfast in the small saloon at nine, sir; or would you prefer something here?"

"I'll decide when I've had my bath."

"Very good, sir."

The moment the door was closed Blake leaped across the cabin and turned the handle; but, as he half expected, it refused to yield.

"Automatic lock!" he said laconically. "Well, it looks as if I have no choice but to wait and see what follows. But someone is going to pay for this pleasantry—someone is going to pay."

APPARENTLY as unconcerned as ever, Blake looked up when the steward returned with a tray, on which reposed a silver pot of coffee and a box of cigarettes. Blake lit one, and sat on the edge of the bed, smoking and sipping the fragrant liquid while the man prepared the bath. He would have been mildly interested had he known what the other—plainly a Cockney— was thinking, for it was something like this:

"A plucked 'un he is—a rare plucked un—just like the other. But the pair of 'em don't half need watchin'."

A quarter of an hour later Blake was bathed, shaved, and dressed. He nodded grunly at himself in the mirror as he observed how well the blue serge fitted his lean frame.

"Quite a comprehensive collection of clothes this was chosen from, I should say!" he commented; and then, over his shoulder, saw that the steward had reentered.

"If you are ready, sir, I'll show you the way to the small saloon, unless you'd prefer a turn on deck first."

"When am I to have the pleasure of meeting my host?" asked Blake pleasantly.

"Not until later in the morning, sir. Her compliments, sir, and she hopes to be on deck at eleven."

"Ah! My hostess, not my host. Very well, steward, I shall breakfast first!"

Already, Blake had made up his mind that he was on board a private yacht of considerable tonnage; but not until he walked along the corridor and mounted a wide companion to be ushered into a beautiful saloon—evidently the small saloon to which the steward had referred—did he begin to appraise just how large and luxurious it was. But as he crossed the threshold he had no thoughts for anyone but the person who sat at the centre table, busily engaged in demolishing a substantial breakfast. It was Tinker, dressed in a blue flannel suit, and certainly making the best of things.

At sight of Blake his eyes goggled wide.

"My sainted aunt, guv'nor! Where did you pop up from?"

Blake smiled as he seated himself and gave his order to the man who was hovering at his elbow.

"I fancy I followed about the same course you took, my lad. I was wondering if I should see you. This is a great relief. What can you tell me?"

"Not a darned thing, guv'nor! The last I remember was being jabbed in the arm with a hypodermic needle, after I refused to tell that pretty devil what passed between you and Mr.Carruthers. The next I knew I was in bed in the yacht."

"We both seem equally in the dark, but perhaps our hostess will be good enough to enlighten us soon. So you fell for her as well, did you?"

"They got me in the taxi first. I was only obeying orders and following Mr.Carruthers. What do you suppose they have done with him, guv'nor?"

"I know that much. They doped him heavily, dressed him in rags, and set him wandering in the streets."

"But how did they get you?"

"To use your words, Tinker, I fell for the girl —stumbled into one of the oldest tricks of the game."

"But who is she guv'nor?"

"I should say she is the person who acted for some three years as Carruthers' secretary."

"Not that girl, surely whatever sort of a crook she is, she's a peach; and the secretary—well, don't you remember the picture Mr.Carruthers showed us?"

"I am forgetting nothing, nothing about that young woman, my lad," responded Blake grimly. "And before we finish I intend to know a lot more. But as we can't swim ashore at present, there is nothing to do but play a waiting game. I fancy we shall be a little wiser before the day is over."

CHAPTER 7.
ON PAROLE.

WHEN Blake and Tinker had finished breakfast, they found no hindrance to their passing up the main companion to the deck. The moment he stepped out on to the promenade, Blake looked about him with keen interest.

The first glance was enough to confirm his previous impression that they were on board a private yacht, but not until now did he realize just how splendid a craft she was. At least five hundred tons, he reckoned in swift appraisal, and couldn't have been out of the builder's hands more than a few months at most. A motor propelled vessel, she was the last word in luxury, more of a baby liner than a private ship. Her name, as he saw on the life-boats and lifebelts, was La Brise.

The after part of the top deck had been designed so that the promenade stretched the full width, and here he and the lad paced up and down discussing the extraordinary position in which they found themselves.

"But what's her game, guv'nor?" asked the lad for the tenth time. "What does she expect to gain by it? Hang it all, it is kidnapping. And what is she going to do with us?"

"I fancy the game is deeper than it appeared, my lad. If the theft from Carruthers and the personal outrage on him was the whole thing, I cannot see what object there is in hauling us off in this fashion. But—hallo, here comes a steward."

The same man who had attended Blake in his cabin paused before them and saluted respectfully.

"The owner's compliments, sir, and will you and the young gentleman attend her in the smoking saloon."

Blake nodded his head, and together they followed the steward down a short after companion that led into the smoking-room. It was a delightfully appointed apartment from which folding glass doors opened on to a glass-enclosed sun-lounge, and there, seated in a low wicker chair, they saw the girl who had duped them both so efficiently.

She smiled coolly at the pair as they stood before her, and motioned to two chairs.

"Sit down, please," she said, in the same enticingly husky tones that had caught Blake's ear at first. "You will expect an explanation, and it is possible we may come to an understanding."

Blake did not return the smile. He merely bowed, his face like chiseled stone, and dropped into a chair; Tinker followed suit.

Mlle. Roxane appeared not to notice the strain of the situation, but studied first one then the other with a little quiver playing about her lips. Whatever anger Blake felt against her, he could not deny that she was very, very lovely and, in

her smartly cut blue serge, entirely in keeping with her surroundings.

"I did not expect that the first guests should have on my yacht would be the famous detective, Sexton Blake, and his almost equally famous assistant, Tinker," she went on lightly. "Nor did I think that such guests would have come—er, shall we say unwillingly?—on this cruise. But there was no other way out. You see, Mr. Blake, I gave you plenty of warning not to interface in a certain affair, and you left me no choice."

"I am surprised if you thought melodramatic warning over the telephone would deter me from going on with a case once I had accepted it, Miss—"

"Harfield— Roxane Harfield," she supplied.

"Thank you. I guessed you were Miss Harfield, as, I take it, you are also Miss Harrison."

"So you have guessed that, have you? I do not deny it. I am very angry with you, Mr.Blake, I had planned much more regarding Harold Carruthers, but you forced my hand. Yet he is but one-eighth of the business I have to attend to, so I have no choice but to put you and your assistant out of the way until my work is complete Unless—"

"Unless what, Miss Harfield?"

"Unless you will give your word not to interfere."

"I am afraid that is out of the question."

"I expected that answer. But wait until I tell you a story."

FORTHWITH, Roxane began, and related what had happened five years before at the Harfield Lumber Camp in New Brunswick. From that she told how she had played the markets successfully, and after two years with a large fortune, had managed to secure employment with Harold Carruthers.

Followed the tale of those three years with Carruthers during which she had outplayed him at almost every turn, until he was forced into this one last desperate throw in London in an attempt to retrieve his fortunes. Then she waved her hand comprehensively.

"All this is but part of the great plan I have built up, Mr. Blake. Not a single detail have I left, and I think you will agree that it did not take me long to stop your interferences."

"If you will give me your word not to interfere with me in any way, I shall give orders at once that the yacht is to put back. It has been said of you, Mr. Blake, that you are a protector of the weak. I do not need protection, but I and my mother did need it five years age. Harold Carruthers is but one of the eight scoundrels who swindled us, and neither you nor anyone is going to interfere with my vengeance."

"I do not intend to pass opinion on the ethics of the matter, Miss Harfield," said Blake quietly. "But you over-look what is to me the chief phase of it all, I could not hold any brief for am man who treated two women as Carruthers and his associates treated you and your mother. But two wrongs do not make a right. I have only the concrete facts to go upon.

"Mr. Carruthers came to London with some sixty thousand pounds in cash which he entrusted to his secretary. He believed implicitly in her integrity. On her own confession she took that money, which is plain theft. And that is where you distort right and wrong. If I take a case, it is my duty to bring the law-breaker to justice and—theft is not permitted by English law, Miss Harfield."

"Am I to understand then that you refuse to keep out of this?"

"I know nothing about the future. But I can assure you of one thing—I shall not consider this affair closed until I have recovered the sixty thousand pounds which were taken from Mr. Carruthers."

Her lips curled, and her eyes regarded him scornfully.

"So this is the great Mr. Sexton Blake!" she flared suddenly. "Let me warn you to think well; for if you refuse, I can promise you a long sojourn in a place you will find distinctly unpleasant."

Blake shrugged.

"I am not to be intimidated by threats—least of all by those of any young woman." He rejoined.

She came to her feet, a young fury.

"You dare to mock me!" she cried. "I will show you— I will prove to you what I can do!"

Suddenly she recovered herself and became deadly calm.

"I give you one more chance. Will you keep out of this or not?"

"Will you hand over to me the money you took from Harold Carruthers and which I have undertaken to recover?"

She laughed outright.

"I didn't know one with a face so grim could posses such a delicious sense of humour. Very well; you have answered. You will discover in a few days what that answer is going to cost you. I am not alarmed that you can escape. Apart from the stewards and the men in the engine-room, there are the captain with two officers and a crew of twenty-four; and I can assure you every man is picked. Until I am ready to dispose of you I wish you to have as much freedom as possible on board, and I am willing to accept your parole. If you refuse it, it means simply that I must curtail the freedom I should otherwise be prepared to concede."

The detective allowed his gaze to wander through the windows of the sunlounge to the tossing waters that had now turned blue with the clearing away of the grey clouds that had obscured the sky a little earlier. He had cast more than one speculative glance at the course they were making.

"We're out of the Channel and heading, I should say, towards the Bay of Biscay; but after that, Heaven knows where this determinedly reckless young freebooter intends taking us. But she mustn't be allowed to walk off with us to any spot she fancies. I've got important business in London, and I want that sixty thousand pounds"

Those were his thoughts, but his cold, grey eyes showed nothing of their tenor as he turned back to her.

"For the moment, ma'm'selle," he said, with cool politeness, "I must say we are at your mercy. You hold all the cards—with the ship and the imposing crew you have at your call. Neither my assistant nor I wish to be kept cooped up on board, and I am prepared to meet you, say, half-way regarding the conditions you name. I am willing to give you my word that neither of us shall attempt to signal to any passing ship; but I must hold myself free to make a dash for freedom at any moment land is in sight,"

She smiled; and he was surprised to see that those sweetly-curved, mobile lips could appear so hard.

"That will do, Mr. Blake. I fancy when you do get your next sight of land, you won't be very anxious to reach it. I think we need say no more for the present."

It was dismissal; so Blake rose, bowed, and stalked back through the saloon, followed by Tinker.

Five days later the two prisoners of the La Brise were pacing the wide promenade deck aft. Far in the west, hull down, was a small steamer—one of many ships they had sighted since Blake had given his parole to Mademoiselle Roxane. To the east was a purplish haze that looked as if land might lie beneath its embrace.

For forty-eight hours there had been scarcely any conversation between the two. Blake had displayed a thoughtfulness of manner which the lad knew better than to break. He knew, however, that Blake's mind had scarcely ceased working during those five days to devise some means of outwitting the girl.

To consider anything so wild as to attempt to seize the yacht against the overwhelming odds they would have to contend with was, he was certain, no part of Blake's consideration. It was borne in upon them very early in the voyage that Roxane had not boasted emptily when she warned them that every manjack on board, from captain to youngest steward, was "picked," and to be trusted.

Force, therefore, was out of the question. Yet, instinctively, the lad had a feeling that Blake was planning something. It was only when the detective paused and stood gazing towards the purple bank of haze in the east that the lad broke the silence, asking the same question he had got tired of voicing, and which Blake had wearied of hearing:

"Where do you think she is taking us, guv'nor?"

"If I said I had even a vague idea I might only be putting you astray, young 'un. All I can tell you is that we have been running south ever since we came out of the Channel. Our speed has been high; I shouldn't be surprised if we had knocked off as much as twenty-seven knots at times. If I am right, then we must be south of Gib. At any rate, we haven't turned in through the straits yet. But I can't guess where we are heading for?"

"But what the dickens is she intending to do with us?"

"She has not favoured us with much of her company let alone her confidences, my lad," responded Blake drily. "I would say, on a guess, that she has it in her mind to put us in a safe place until she had carried out her purpose regarding those men."

"Good heavens, guv'nor, that might take months!"

"Or years. Don't you run away with the idea that we are going to submit without a struggle, Tinker. It would be sheer folly to make an attempt of any sort now; we might just as well hammer our heads on this teak deck— we should achieve just as much. We will lie doggo until an opportunity shows itself.

"I've got the germ of an idea in my mind; it may be worth nothing at all. But at any moment of the day or night, when I give you the word, you be ready. I fancy we shall need to do some quick moving when— Hallo; Here comes our precious steward. It isn't tea-time yet. I wonder what he wants?"

They were not long in discovering; for as the little Cockney got close he drew up and saluted.

"Beg pardon, sir; the mistress sends her compliments, and would be glad if you would attend upon her in the small saloon."

"Very well, steward; lead the way." Nothing but the ordinary intercourse of their respective positions had passed between Blake and the steward; and yet, despite the fact that they were in different camps, a mutual liking and respect had developed between them. Not that there was the slightest wavering of loyalty in the Cockney for his mistress; Blake knew without making a test that any approach in that direction would be doomed to failure. The circumstances was sufficient, however, to put a sardonic gleam in his eye as he entered the small saloon and followed the steward to the sun-veranda, where Roxane sat just as she had been on the occasion of their first interview.

When the steward was gone she motioned Blake and Tinker to chairs; but they preferred to stand. "I am sorry to inform you," she said, slow tones from which she could not eliminate the faint huskiness, "that after dinner this evening your freedom must be curtailed. I hope you will not make any difficulties that will cause me to use force."

"It would seem somewhat futile if we did, mademoiselle. Is it permitted to ask if we are, then, approaching our destination?"

She gave him a searching look, but his face told her no more than stone.

"One destination—yes; but not the place where you will ultimately spend a considerable time."

"That is interesting. Since we are quite in your power is there any reason why we shouldn't know whither we are bound?"

"Not at all, if you are curious. A little later on we shall pick up a light. That signal will be on the coast of Morocco, not far from the Spanish colony Rio del Oro. I believe you are a much-travelled man, Mr. Blake, therefore, you will appreciate just how isolated and—er—safe for my purpose is this stretch of country."

Well did Sexton Blake know that few more barren spots in all the world could be found than that inhospitable coast, nor a more savage people than the nomad tribes who roamed across it. Both in the French territory that adjoined it, as well as for several hundreds of miles along the Rio del Oro, there were only a few scattered settlements where there would be even a chance of finding succour. And it wasn't very difficult now for him to guess what she meant when she

said that the coast was not their ultimate destination.

"You have chosen your spot well," he ground out harshly. "Am I right in thinking that it is your intention to turn over to some tribe there for ransom?"

"You will be taken into the interior. There will be no question of ransom. I myself shall pay that from the sixty thousand pounds with which Mr. Carruthers so kindly provided me. It is only going to cost a trifling two thousand to ensure the hospitality of a certain tribe as long as I wish. You will be taken care of sufficiently well, Mr. Blake, and kept out of mischief. That is all. There will be no restrictions until you have finished dinner, but after that you will be asked to go to your cabin and remain there; unless, of course, you have seen the folly of the stand you took at our first interview, and are prepared to—recant, shall we say?"

Blake bowed slightly.

"You will excuse me, mademoiselle. Come, my lad!"

With that he turned away, making back for the promenade deck.

When he and Tinker were again pacing back and forth he began to speak in a low tone, emitting the words through the corner of his mouth, so that there was no perceptible movement of the lips.

"Listen carefully, young 'un! The time is come. We've got to make our move before dinner. After will be too late. I'm going to try the only plan I have been able to think of. We will go below together to change. As soon as you enter your cabin you will ring for your steward—at once, do you understand?"

"I've got that, guv'nor."

"The moment he steps inside your cabin you are to let him have it so that he will be out of action for at least a quarter of an hour. Use sufficient force, but don't crack his skull. You can find a weapon that will serve your purpose."

"You trust me for that, guv'nor. What next?"

"Leave your cabin at once and start along the cross-corridor that leads to the foot of the companion. If we time our actions properly we should meet in that corridor. I will tell you the rest then. But if we pull off what I am going to try, then we've got to get over the side in a rush. Our only chance is to swim for it. I gather they will be making shorewards now, and by that time it may be only two or three miles away. It is a big gamble, but our only chance."

"I'll be there on the dot, guv'nor. I'm glad something is going to happen. I don't fancy going in the interior. We had a dose of that once before. Besides, I hate to see her get away with this."

"She won't if I can help it," promised Blake grimly.

They kept to the deck until the first bell sounded. Then, just as they since coming aboard, they turned in an unhurried way and walked towards the entrance to the main companion by which they would descend. And, just as they had seen on those other Lights, they caught sight of their respective stewards hovering one at each end of the cross-corridor to shepherd them safely into their cabins.

Blake nodded, with a word to the lad not to be late, then strode along, with a nod to his steward in passing. Then he was at the door of his cabin and inside, with one finger on the bell as soon as the door closed. A few seconds later there was a tap.

"Enter."

There was just time for the inquiring look on the steward's face to turn to an expression of startled amazement when Blake's fist hit him behind the ear. There was terrific power and perfect precision behind that blow. There was no need for a second.

Blake eased his man to the floor and grabbed the door just before it snapped closed. Then he was out in the passage, running on rubber-soled deck shoes in the direction of the cross-corridor where he was to meet Tinker.

CHAPTER 8.
BLAKE TAKES THE CASE.

Tinker rounded the other end of the gangway at almost the same moment which revealed Blake at his end. Nearer Tinker's side of the ship than Blake's was the main gangway, leading to the saloon deck, and, as he reached this, Tinker slowed down, thinking that this was the spot that Blake meant.

But an imperative gesture started him on again, and he reached Blake, to find him standing before a big glass-fronted case that was set in the left-hand wall of the corridor. The lad had noticed it, with its five batteries of electric switches, on several occasions, but had certainly never dreamed it would play any part in Blake's desperate plans for escape.

Close at hand was a brass water-cock, with a reeled hose attached—placed there as one of several guard-points in the building of the yacht. And, just above this, also in a glass-fronted case, was a long, red-painted axe for the cutting away of burning timbers. It was this latter case that Blake hammered in with one elbow while motioning with his other hand for Tinker to get busy at the fire-cock.

"Be ready to turn it on!" he snapped. "There is bound to be a good head of water—enough to keep the passage clear for a few minutes if they rush before I finish."

By this time he had the axe free and then, standing back, he began to smash away at the case containing the batteries of switches.

Crash! The glass was sent into smithereens. Crash! The whole upper row of switches was cut clean away to the accompaniment of an appalling blue flash. Crash! The second row went with dangling wires. And with that they heard distant sounds of commotion—shouts, running feet, jangling of bells. Crash! The next row ripped away, driving asunder all connection; and with this last mutilation their own corridor was plunged into abysmal darkness.

But Blake continued, wielding the heavy axe with a will until he had ripped the case itself from the wall. Then he turned to where the lad was standing by.

"They'll soon guess what's happened. No time to lose. I'll go ahead with the axe. Better leave the hose now. Come on, up the main gangway, and right over the side. Stick close to me. Can't tell what next until we hit the water."

He moved along as quickly as he dared towards where he knew the companion to be retaining the axe as a weapon in case of need. Close behind him came Tinker, waiting for a challenge in the darkness, and then a rush.

But it was a very different sound alarm they heard, for, just as Blake was reaching out to feel the break in the wall that would indicate the opening of the companion well, there was a short, sharp cry above them, then a series of thuds as something tumbled down the stairs, and landed in a heap at Blake's feet. He bent over cautiously, one hand exploring to discover what it was. Then, suddenly, he felt the soft warmth of a human body, and next, the smooth texture of thin silk. It was no man who lay there.

He knew, of course, that Mademoiselle Roxane had brought a personal maid aboard with her as well as a stewardess, for he had caught sight of them on occasion during the preceding days. But neither of those two wore such delicate silk as the invisible woman who lay at his feet. It must be, it could only be, Roxane.

The sounds of confusion above had grown nearer. He could now hear voices, seemingly close to the head of the stairs, and he knew that it would be but a few minutes at most before lights were brought. Even yet there was a chance for him and Tinker to escape in the darkness, if they left the girl where she lay.

What was she doing so close to the head of the stairs Blake could not guess. How she had come to tumble down he did not know. But that she was unconscious, and, possibly, very dangerously hurt was obvious.

His hand against her warm body had already told him that her heart still beat, but as he knelt closer a strange pain seized him.

In that moment he made his decision. It might mean weeks, months even, of imprisonment in the camp of some Bedouin tribe—privation of the worst order—but he would never have had a soul at peace had he stepped over the body of unconscious girl to freedom.

It was Tinker's agitated whisper that sent him into action.

"What is it, guv'nor?"

"I think it is mademoiselle," came the reply. "If you have any matches get them out. I am going to carry her to the small saloon."

She was already in his arms, and the flicker of a match in Tinker's hand guided him up the stairs. Yet, before he reached the top, he saw a press of men standing in the glow of a lantern, and heard one of them saying:

"I know she was near here, sir. I saw her standing at the head of the stairs, and thought she cried out just when the lights went. I—"

"Shut up!" snapped an authoritative voice. "What is this?"

"Stand aside, Mr. Cooper," said Sexton Blake quietly, as he recognised the mate. "Your owner has fallen down the stairs, and is hurt. I don't know how badly."

"By Heaven, if you have injured her I—"

"Don't be a fool! I don't manhandle women. Get ahead with that lantern and let us see what is wrong."

There was a note in Blake's voice of stronger authority than that of the other. With a suppressed exclamation he held the lantern up so that the light fell on the girl's face that was pressed to Blake's white jacket.

On one temple was a bruise already showing, and at sight of that the mate turned and led the way to the saloon, calling out orders as he went for the maid, the stewardess, and water and bandages to be brought.

More lanterns appeared on the scene, and then, willy-nilly, Blake took command. His first care was to discover if the bruise on the head represented the extent of the major injuries. When he had assured himself that this was so, he made a more detailed examination of the mark that was growing larger each moment, after which he batched and dressed it. It was while he was engaged in this that Roxane's lids fluttered open, and her violet eyes gazed straight up into his.

"Well," she whispered, with a twisted smile, "am I badly damaged?"

Her courage was superb. He shook his head.

"You had a nasty blow on the head and it is going to be painful. You must not talk. As soon as I finish dressing it, I am going to give you some aspirin; then your maid and stewardess must get you into bed."

"You seem to be in some authority here," she mocked him.

"Be quiet! This is no time for nonsense!"

She closed her lids again, but still smiled. Then, just as he drew the bandage taut she opened them again.

"Why didn't you escape? You were going to swim, weren't you?"

"What I intended doing doesn't matter now."

"I knew you would be up to something. I have been watching you ever since I talked with you this afternoon. I knew you were making some plan and telling it to Tinker on the deck. I was going down to make sure you were both in your cabins when you began smashing the light switches. Stupid of me, that was. I must have them put in a less vulnerable place. But you can still make a dash."

"I have nothing to say," he answered quietly. "There, that is done. You will not refuse to go to bed, I am sure. I shall put your mind at ease, and give my parole for myself and Tinker that we shall not make any further attempt to escape to-night."

Suddenly her eyes became suffused, threatening to overflow; but she was still smiling up at him when she whispered:

"I give you back your parole. You are free to go. I know it was my accident that upset your plans. It was rather decent to forgo your chance."

"I don't go until I receive that sixty thousand," he said curtly. Then, before she had a chance to reply, he straightened up:

"Stewardess, get your mistress to bed at once. She needs quiet and rest. You had better give her some aspirin. Come along, Tinker!"

With that he stalked through the group of anxious men who stood waiting, and not a finger was lifted to stop him. They reached the deck just as the spare dynamo in the engine-room got into action, and a secondary circuit of lights flashed on.

From the rail of the deck they could see the stars overhead, tropically brilliant; and, from far away to the south, came the intermittent flash of a coastal light. Blake watched it for a few minutes, nothing the spacing of short flashes and long.

"San Miguel light, I think, Tinker. If so, then we have been told the truth. That point is where French territory joins the Spanish Rio del Oro.

We have made an even quicker voyage than I figured."

"What are we going to do, guv'nor? Couldn't we go ahead now, as we intended?"

"Not on my original plan, young 'un. I was ready to make a break half an hour ago and chance it. I was going to do everything possible to have ourselves taken prisoners by the same gang that she seems to have hired to look after us. Then it would have been simple case of bargaining. Our one chance was to win out on that and persuade the gang ashore to turn on the yacht. Had we attacked—well, there was a chance of getting hold of that sixty thousand.

"For the moment I am at a loss. I did not look for such a contretemps, and the officers and crew are not certain yet that we didn't knock their owner down like a couple of brutal footpads. No, I think, take it all in all, we will stick to the ship now, and await developments. I fancy that blow may have cooled our lady's blood a little. But there, did you see that? A signal light of some sort."

Tinker had caught the triple flash as well. It seemed to come from a spot almost directly opposite to where the yacht was barely keeping way. If it was on shore, then their swim would have stood a good chance of success. For the distance did not seem to be great, even allowing for the deceptiveness of night.

Suddenly they caught the flare of a light on the bridge that came and went thrice. Followed a double flash from the shore, and then a single flare on the bridge that was held for a full half-minute.

On this the screws began to revolve more perceptibly; and the yacht, that had been almost without vibration, quivered daintily under their feet. But it was not until San Miguel light began to show more and more on the port quarter that they knew they were changing course.

"What is up, guv'nor?"

"Hanged if I know, Tinker; but I'd say we were heading out into the Atlantic. Maybe we are going to hang off until daylight."

At this moment a firm tread sounded behind them; and, tuning, they saw Cooper, the mate. He saluted fridgidly.

"I am to inform you, sir that you and your companion are to return to your cabins, where you are to remain until permitted to come out. My instructions are to put you in irons if you attempt any more mischief. I have men to assist me to carry out these orders if necessary."

"They will not be called upon, Mr. Mate!" drawled Blake. "Since our swim has been postponed there is no object in our resisting."

"Then follow me, please!"

On re-entering his cabin, Blake found his Cockney steward busy making his bed ready for the night. He revealed no marks of the blow Blake had struck him, nor did he even cast a reproachful glance in his direction. He went on with his work, just as he had performed his duties on all other occasions; but when he asked if there was anything else Blake required, the detective put out his hand.

"Will you shake, Johnson? I am afraid I struck you rather hard, but at the moment I was rather pressed for time. I am sorry I had to do it."

The little steward grasped his fingers unhesistatingly; then, all of a sudden, he grinned.

"That's all right sir. I should have been on me guard like. I knew you'd need watching. It's the mistress I'm worrying of."

"She will be all right in a day or two, Johnson. She had a nasty fall down the stairs. I can assure you that neither I nor my companion were responsible other than the dousing of the lights."

" I know that sir. It's all in the game. Good-night, sir!"

All that Blake was certain of the next morning when he gazed through his porthole was that they were running under full speed and heading north. What was afoot he did not know. And he knew it would be quite useless to ask the steward.

"Sorry, sir, but horders are that you cannot go up to-day."

"Meals in the cabin here?"

"Yes, sir, hanythink you like—but not on deck or in the saloon."

Blake accepted the restriction chafingly, but with outward cheerfulness. He was one of those men who needed his full.

THE ADVENTURES of SEXTON BLAKE DETECTIVE.

FOUND GUILTY!
THE END OF MARSTON HUME.

THE manager of the Quay Hotel met Sexton Blake and the two Scotland Yard officials at the top of the hotel steps, and conducted them to a small private room on the right of the hall.

"I hope," he said, with an uneasy smile, "that there has been no mistake. The gentleman I have detained in accordance with telephoned instructions from Scotland Yard is extremely annoyed at my interference."

"There is no mistake," interrupted Blake decisively. "I hope you've taken care to keep him in close custody?"

"He's in my office at the end of the passage," answered the manager. "I asked him to accompany me there on the pretext of settling his account, and gave him in charge of two constables sent up from the police station."

"Good!" said Blake.

"A few minutes one way or the other won't make any difference," said one of the Scotland Yard officials to Blake. "Owing to the fact that we left the 'Yard' at a few moments' notice we are practically in the dark concerning the man we are to arrest. Could you explain briefly the circumstances which have led up to your charge against him?"

"The man's name is Marston Hume," answered Blake. "He is a Napoleon of crime. At one time he was one of the most brilliant barristers at the English Bar, and he has used his legal knowledge of the law as a shield to protect himself against detection of crimes which he has committed with almost diabolical cunning.

"During the last few years, he has carried out some of the most mysterious undiscovered crimes which have baffled the whole detective world, crimes of which I knew him to be guilty, but could not get a thread of real proof against him which would convict him in a court of law.

He is a murderer, forger, a thief—in fact, there is scarcely a single branch of crime which he has not thoroughly mastered."

"You don't say so!" exclaimed both officials, breathlessly.

"Hope you've got him fixed up this time, Mr. Blake," added one of the men, with an easy smile. "The charge is the Great Bridge Tunnel murder. How did you come to connect him with that?"

"For the first time in his criminal career, Marston Hume has left a trail of proof behind him," answered Blake grimly. "A faint trail, but more than enough to convict him of the murder of Mr. Daykin Travers to which you allude. He left behind in his victim's room a cigarette holder bitten in a peculiar manner, as a man with a sharp incisor tooth would bite. You will see for yourselves that Marston Hume's upper side teeth are sharp as a wolf's.

"The tobacco smoked in the holder was a special blend ordered for a club in London of which Hume was a member. In the top room of a cottage overlooking the study in which Mr. Travers kept his safe I found a pipe, the end of which was bitten in exactly the same way. The bowl half full of the particular brand of tobacco I speak of. It was left there by a man who took the room for a fortnight, and who disappeared the day before the crime was committed. Later, I was able to trace that the body of Mr. Travers was thrown over the bridge on to a goods train passing beneath, and carried through the tunnel. It was thrown from a low, open, grey motor car, with certain peculiarities in the tyres which enabled the car to be traced here to Newhaven.

"By the way," he added suddenly to the manager, "if the car is still in the garage, I should like to see it before interviewing Hume."

"The car is here," answered the manager, "Mr. Hume has given orders for it to be repaired and got ready for a journey, as he intends to leave here immediately he is released from custody—he seems to have no doubt he will be released," he added, with meaning emphasis. "If you'll come this way I'll show you the car."

He led them out across a short courtyard to a big garage at the back. Though it was well past midnight a mechanic was working on the car at the far end—a long, low grey car. Blake crossed to it quickly.

"The car won't be required," he said to the engineer, who was bending over the engine testing the magneto.

The man looked up sharply.

"Gentleman ordered it specially," he said surlily.

Blake shrugged his shoulders as the mechanic resumed his work, evidently impatient of the interruption and walked round to the side of the car, pointing to some dull red stains in the pale green leather cushions of the seat beside the driver.

"He accounted for those," explained the hotel manager, "as soon as he arrived, and asked the mechanician to have them cleared off. He says he picked up a cyclist on one of the roads, bleeding from a severe scalp wound, and took him to a cottage hospital."

"Any attempt made to verify that statement?" asked one of the officials.

"Not yet, but it can easily be traced if necessary."

"Absolutely unnecessary!" snapped Blake.

As he spoke he bent down to the floor of the car, and peered at something beneath one of the holes in the rubber matting, lifted the mat by a corner, and picked out a tiny white object.

"What's that?" asked one of the men sharply.

A curious smile gathered round the corners of Blake's thin-lipped mouth, and his eyes gleamed with sudden triumph.

"I'll explain later," he said shortly. "Now come along. Let's get the interview over."

He walked back quickly across the courtyard, and entered the hotel.

"I want you to leave Hume to me for a few minutes," said Blake.

"There are a few scores to settle between us. He has defied me for years, and I can't resist the temptation to cry quits before I hand him over," he laughed a low, hard laugh. "Both he and I have a fine sense of the dramatic," he added. "Wait about somewhere till I call you. What I have to say to him is for his ears alone."

"For Heaven's sake take care," whispered one of the men hoarsely, looking anxiously at Blake's white, set face. "Don't let there be an unexpected tragedy."

He laid a detaining hand on Blake's arm. Blake shook it off impatiently, and signed to the manager to unlock the door of the room in which Hume was detained.

"What a confounded draught," said an irritable voice from inside, as the door swung noiselessly open, giving a view of a small, circular room, with a fire burning brightly in a low grate, and a half-hidden figure sitting before it in a deep arm-chair. On each side of the chair was a constable, watchful, curious, alert.

"Confound you! Shut the door!" went on the voice. "Good-evening, Mr. Blake! What brings you down to this part of the world?" the speaker went on in a change of tone without looking round.

Blake signed to the constables to leave them.

"I came down to identify you, Marston Hume," he said quietly, as the men withdrew and left the two together.

"Really! Got a cigarette? I'm dying for a smoke."

A sudden spasm of coughing shook him for a moment. He leaned forward in his chair, and spread out his thin, iron-hard hands to the blaze of the fire.

Blake took out his case, selected a cigarette, carefully, lit it, and returned the case to his pocket.

Hume shrugged his shoulders.

"Selfish brute!" he said tonelessly. "By the way, you might do me a service. The fool of a manager here fancies that I'm someone else—a criminal of some sort, wanted by Scotland Yard for some stupid crime or other. Could you see him and tell him he has made a mistake? I want to get back to London as quickly as I can. My car must be ready by this time. I gave the engineer a fiver as a bribe to hurry things along, and promised him another as soon as the thing is finished."

"The manager, as it happens, has not made any mistake," said Blake coolly. "There are two men outside from Scotland Yard with a warrant for your arrest."

"What peculiar bee has Scotland Yard got in its bonnet now, I wonder?" said Hume meditatively, as he poked the fire into a brisker blaze.

"The warrant has been issued at my instigation," went on Blake. "You are charged with the murder of Mr. Travers near Salisbury last night—a fairly big bee," he added, with a meaning smile.

Hume sat up, sudden interest starting into his face.

"I heard some chaps talking about that in the coffee-room before dinner," he said. "Done on Saturday night, wasn't it? They were inclined to a verdict of suicide by what I could gather. You don't say you've been fool enough to connect me with it in any way! Why, I was in London on Saturday night."

"You were in Mr. Travers's house," said Blake sharply, "somewhere between midnight and one o'clock—where you murdered him, robbed his safe, and then took the body in your car to the Great Bridge Tunnel, and threw it over on to the line."

"I say I was in London," reported Hume slowly, balancing every tone of his smooth, low voice.

"I actually turned up at the Baddeley Club. Let me see! I dined there—infernally good whitebait and cutlets, and coffee excellent. Why is the Baddeley the only place in London where one can get good coffee?"

"After dinner?" said Blake, a trifle impatiently. His hands were clenched till the knuckles on the back showed dull, greyish-white, and the veins on his temples stood out like whipcords.

"Strolled into the Empire— Sure you can't spare a cigarette? Oh, never mind. Ripping good dancer there—new woman. First appearance on Saturday night. House packed, and rose at her like a bird. Never saw such an ovation. Lolita, or some such name us that—ah, here's the programme. ' Lettecia,'" he went on, looking at the name, and passing the programme across to Blake for confirmation.

Blake ignored it.

"A carefully thought out alibi," he said contemptuously, "but useless. That programme is sufficient to give you away. A man doesn't dine at the Baddeley unless he is in evening-dress. If he strolled into the Empire to see a turn almost the last on the list he doesn't, as a rule, bother about a programme; and if he does, he never takes such care of it as to be able to produce it a couple of days after from the pocket of a tweed jacket.

"Nevertheless, here it is," insisted Hume. "You must admit that."

"You got it for this particular purpose at the Empire before going to the club," said Blake. "After you dined you went to your rooms, changed, and motored down to Salisbury—a three hours' journey in that car of yours, a ninety-horse, I observed. If you left the club just before nine o'clock you would be well on your way by half-past, and somewhere after midnight you arrived at your journey's end—Mr. Travers's house. Less than half an hour would be sufficient for your plans there, and by twenty minutes past one you were at Great Bridge Tunnel with the dead body."

"Oh, well, have it your own way," said Hume, with almost childish impatience.

"There are one or two things you haven't provided for in your alibi," went on Blake. "Specks of grey paint on the bridge wall where your mudguard scraped along when you pulled up on the footpath to throw the body on to the line, to begin with. You forgot that tyre-marks there would attract attention; a groove tyre on the front wheel, and a metal studded one on the back. They correspond exactly, I need hardly say, to the tyres on your car in the garage below. Also the cushions are stained with blood."

"It's absurd to commit me on the slender evidence of motor-tyres," said Hume, a shade angrily. "That description might apply to dozens of grey cars on the road between London and Salisbury during the week-end. The bloodstained cushions might be more important—only I happen to be able to explain them in a perfectly natural way. I lunched at the Downs Hotel near Three Bridges this afternoon, and left there at two o'clock. A couple of miles out I found a man unconscious on the road at the bottom of Ray Hill with a broken bicycle beside him and a broken head jammed up against a brick wall. I took him along in my car to Ray Cottage Hospital. He was a sailor—name, Dickinson. You can easily verify my statement. The condition of his head rather spoilt my new cushions, I'm afraid." he added regretfully.

"I know you well enough, Marston Hume, to be able to reconstruct that part of your story," answered Blake grimly. "In order to account satisfactorily for those stains you would think nothing of deliberately running down a cyclist on that lonely road, and killing him, if necessary, to support your case should those stains be questioned. You have taken infinite trouble to anticipate every point of danger and provide against it. But you overlooked one thing. I grant you, but for that, the prosecution might have a difficulty to prove the case against you—though it would have been proved. But this one clue gives absolute and conclusive evidence of your guilt."

He took an envelope out of his letter-case, shook out a small round white object from it into the palm of his hand, "I found that a few minutes ago on the floor of your car beneath the rubber mat," he went on slowly. "The head of a bone collar-stud stained with blood. *The other half of it was found in the back of the collar of the dead man who was found on the railway line.* Here, none of that!" he flashed, with a quick change of tone, whipping out his revolver.

Hume started from his chair, and fell back into it again, his face suddenly grey and distorted, a scream of agony bitten back in his throat. A horrible twisting and writhing of his limbs—then deathlike stillness, every muscle rigid.

Blake laughed a hard, contemptuous laugh.

"No, my man! You've tricked me once too often," he laid roughly. "Here, sit up," he struck Hume sharply on the shoulder; then shook him, jerking the stiff head up from the chair. It bumped back into its position again against the cushion helplessly, a white froth greying the blue, clenched lips.

Blake rang the bell at the side of the fireplace.

"Arrest him!" he said curtly to the police-officers who came hurrying in. "Don't be alarmed," he added quickly. "He's playing one of his old tricks. A second ago the man was as well as you and I. Handcuff him and take him away."

The men looked doubtfully at the still, rigid figure.

"He looks mortal bad—not to say death-like," said one, in a low, frightened voice. "Hasn't taken poison or anything, sir, has he?"

"No," snapped Blake. "It's a trick, I tell you. Arrest him—it's a ruse to slip through our fingers. He had no intention of committing suicide when he bribed the mechanician with the promise of ten pounds to have his car ready to-night. He meant to get away then. He means to get away now, somehow."

The still face was growing greyer, tiny globules of froth bubbled through the stiff lips, and trailed over the discoloured chin.

"More like death than anything I've seen for some time," said the other officer stubbornly.

"Nonsense!" said Blake quickly. He bent down and felt the pulse in the rigid wrist. "Bring me a candle," he said sharply. "Quick!"

The manager lit one on the mantelpiece and carried it across to Blake.

If Hume was feigning unconsciousness he did it remarkably well. The conviction forced itself on Blake against his better judgment as he pushed open first one, then the other eyelid, and passed the candle flame backwards and forwards before the fixed glassy pupils, which gave no answering sign.

"Get a doctor," he said dully. "It's a heart seizure of some sort. Send quickly. There's no time to lose."

The minutes ticked on slowly, no sound in the room save a hissing of painful breath through the discoloured lips.

The doctor, who happened to be slaying in the hotel, came running in at last, a dressing-gown flung on hastily over his pyjamas, and a pair of bed-room slippers on bis naked feet.

Blake eyed him shrewdly, every suspicion keenly alert. The concern on his face was genuine enough. Behind the professional mask was alarm and uncertainly. Swiftly he put the unconscious man through the tests which Blake had employed a few minutes earlier, with equally negative results.

"Lay him out on the floor," he said sharply. "Get hot-water bottles, brandy, open the windows, and give him plenty of fresh air. I must go back to my room for certain drugs which I happen to have with me, and a hypodermic syringe."

He hurried out of the room as the men set about his bidding.

Blake opened the window and looked out, a curious, unconvinced light in his eyes. The room was on the ground floor, a few yards away from the back door of the motor garage, in which a light was still burning.

He glanced round the room suddenly. Hume's unconscious body was stretched out on the floor, his face now white almost as marble, and the blue lips dry, for the doctor had wiped away the bubbling foam. Blake gazed at the blue lips for a second, and then darted out of the room and slipped silently upstairs, all his suspicions suddenly alive.

At the far end of the corridor he heard a door close, and as he drew into the shadow of a big urn on the landing, the doctor came running past him with a small black bag in his hand. Blake stood for a second, a deep frown on his face; then slipped out of his hiding-place, and ran lightly down the corridor to the doctor's room.

The door was shut—locked—and the key gone.

Blake's reasoning powers were strung up to the highest pitch. What motive had actuated him to lock the door and take the key!

Blake darted to the next door. That, too, was locked, and the key on the inside. He tried the next and the next, angrily conscious that precious minutes were being wasted. At last he found an open door—evidently an empty bedroom—snatched the key from the lock inside and ran back to the doctor's door.

There was just a chance that the key would fit. He had tried the same experiment in various hotels before, and nine times out of ten had found the locks were duplicates. He slipped in the key, with firm pressure of his eager hand it turned in the lock. He pushed the door open and entered the room.

Two seconds later he was out again and running down the stairs two at a time, his face dark with anger and disgust. Round the door of the little room where Hume was lying, a group of silent figures were clustered together.

"The doctor told us to wait here," explained one of the officials hurriedly. "He thought it better for us to be out of sight when Mr. Hume regained consciousness.'"

Blake swept the man aside and turned the handle of the door. It was locked on the inside.

"It's a trick," he said furiously, "to which the doctor in some way has been made a party."

He was shaking the door impatiently, and calling to the doctor loudly.

Inside the room there was dead silence, broken at last by a low groan, and a faint call for help—the doctor's voice.

"Break open the door!" cried one of the officials, helplessly beating on the door with his hands. "What does that cry mean?"

"It means that Marston Hume has gone," said Blake grimly, through his set teeth. From somewhere outside came the faint whir of a starting engine. Blake ran across the hall to a waiting-room, and shook his friend Bathurst, who was dozing before a dull fire, roughly.

"Quick!" he panted. "Where's your motor? Hume's gone! Quick, man, I say! He's got away in his car!" He pushed Bathurst before him into the hall and down the front steps.

The motor was standing there where Bathurst had left it an hour or so before, with tail and headlamps alight.

Blake set the engine racing with a few quick turns of the starting-crank, flung himself into the driving-seat, and the cars out out into the road almost before Bathurst had time to climb up beside him, turned at a reckless angle up a narrow, dark street at the left, round to the back of the hotel.

The doors of the garage stood gaping wide. Blake steered close up to it, slowed down and peered in. His head-lamps threw a long shaft of light into the darkness, showing him that the grey car was no longer on its stand.

Obedient to his will the car sprang forward and climbed up the dark, cobbled, hilly street. At the top it halted for a second, then, with a fierce twist of the steering-wheel, swerved abruptly to the right. Half a mile or so ahead, at the end of the straight coast road, a tiny speck of red glowed, disappeared, came into view again, and then snapped out.

Blake stopped the car, got down, and searched the road narrowly for tracks of the tyres he knew so well.

"That's his car ahead right enough," he said jerkily, as he started out once more in hot pursuit.

"How on earth did you let him give you the slip?" said Bathurst, looking uneasily at Blake's white face and blazing eyes.

"Fooled me," he answered bitterly. "Managed somehow to get into collusion with a doctor staying at the hotel, feigned a sudden attack of angina, and while the doctor was attending to him managed to escape through the open window, after laying out the medical man with a real or pretended blow, and locking the door on

It was a silent, grim fight for life, Blake losing ground as the almost superhuman arms of Marston Hume wound round him, forcing him to the cliff-edge.

the inside—ah! There he is!" The red light had come into view again as Blake's car swooped over the crest of a steep hill. "We're gaining on him—fast."

"Look out!" ejaculated Bathurst as the car lurched heavily in the deep ruts of the road. "You'll upset us."

Blake held steadily on, and laughed defiantly.

"Hallo! What's happened! He's slowing down."

The red light was waving drunkenly across the narrow cliff-track, the booming sea pounding on the high chalk cliffs separated only by a stretch of thick down turf.

"By gad! The light's out!" Blake forged ahead down the steep incline, pulled up with a grinding of brakes a few feet from a low grey obstruction across the road.

Towards the sea, a tall dark figure was running swift as a hare. Blake flung himself off the car and bounded after it.

Closer and closer came the roar of the sea, only a short fifty yards now to the edge of the cliff. The running figure ahead stumbled and went down headlong as one of its feet caught in a rabbit-hole.

The next second Blake had flung himself on the prostrate man, and the two rolled over together, locked tightly in a death-like grip.

It was a silent, grim fight—a fight for life in the darkness, close to the angry sea. Inch by inch Hume struggled closer and closer to the cliff-edge, inch by inch Blake held him back, only to lose ground again, as the almost superhuman arms wound round him and edged him closer yet.

Big lumps of chalk dislodged beneath their weight and hurtled down into the leaping waves. Both men had struggled to their feet, slipping, stumbling, panting—another inch—then another tearing of grass and chalk, a hastily flung up arm, a flash, two loud reports, and a convulsive leap over the cliff-side into the water below.

Bathurst, a horrified spectator of the grim scene, was stumbling blindly across the turf, a motor-lamp swinging low at his side. Heedless of the danger, he flung himself down and peered over the cliff's edge, swinging his light down. Far below him was stretched a lifeless figure with a disfigured face, the water pounding it to and fro.

From below on the left, where a sharp edge jutted out, came a faint shout. Bathurst turned the lamp round sharply as if electrified into action.

"That you, old man?" came up Blake's voice weakly. "A close shave that! Could you lend me a hand? I must get up somehow. Gently, man! My arm's broken."

Bathurst pulled him up slowly, horrified at the stained, bruised face, as it came up over the cliff-edge, and the limp, hanging arm. Blake rolled over on to the turf, breathing heavily.

"Quits at last," he said jerkily, wiping the blood from his face.

"He meant to murder you when he fired his revolver," said Bathurst slowly.

Blake nodded.

"My arm saved me," he said, as the pain of it twisted his face. "I'm afraid it won't be much good again for some time. His second shot found a truer mark." He shuddered as the recollection of that final act swept over him. "Get me back to the hotel. My arm must be attended to as soon as possible. Bind it up tightly, and let's get off. I've still one score to settle—the doctor's."

Bathurst got up from his knees after binding the arm, picked up the lamp, and turned it for the last time down to the edge of the sea.

What was left of Marston Hume had gone out with the tide.

§

Up to a certain point the doctor's explanation was simple enough. He was positive, he said to Blake, that the patient he attended was suffering from angina pectoris in an advanced form. When called out of bed he had locked his door from sheer force of habit as he always did in strange hotels.

No, he could not possibly account for the patient's sudden return to consciousness, or the still more sudden blow which knocked him—the doctor—senseless. He knew nothing more about it—absolutely nothing. He would stake his professional reputation on the fact that the case was a genuine one. It would be absolutely impossible for him to be deceived.

Blake took a crumpled handkerchief from his pocket.

"I found this in your room," he said slowly. "You used it to wipe the froth from your patient's lips. I think."

The doctor nodded.

"Well, what about it?" he asked testily.

"That froth is merely discoloured gelatine," answered Blake quietly. "You can see there are still a few grains of red powder in it. Your patient had a deep knowledge of obscure drugs, and his attack might have been a simulated one, aided by a carefully-prepared capsule. I was speaking to him just before it came on, and took my eyes off his face just for one second while I looked for something in my letter-case. During that second he might have placed the capsule—kept at hand ready for some such emergencies—in his mouth—"

"Nonsense—impossible!" interrupted the doctor. "No obscure drug could have that effect, and pass off so quickly. The idea is medically absurd. No! I've given my opinion, and I'll stick to it." He went out of the room, banging the door loudly after him.

"*Knowing Marston Hume,*" said Blake slowly to Bathurst, "*I stick to mine!*"

2

HERE—
NOW—

begins
the most
interesting
Serial
in U.J.
history !

The N E X T

By - - - - - - - Robert Murray, Anthony Skene,— - - - -

With, as referee of the match—

G. H. TEED

G. H. TEED
LEADS OFF

WITH THE FIRST INSTALMENT OF THIS
UNIQUE STORY. IT'S A MYSTERY-STORY FULL
OF MYSTERIES THAT MYSTIFY EVEN THE
AUTHORS. NOBODY KNOWS WHAT'S COMING
NEXT ... NOT EVEN THE EDITOR. THE
AUTHORS DON'T KNOW WHAT PROBLEMS
CONFRONT THEM TILL THEY'VE SEEN THE
PREVIOUS INSTALMENT, LEARNED OF THE
PUZZLES LEFT THEM TO UNRAVEL. THEIR
NAMES CAME OUT OF A HAT, AND IN TURN
EACH MAN WILL TAKE UP THE YARN FROM
WHERE THE ONE BEFORE LEFT IT OFF. THERE
WILL BE THREE ROUNDS; EACH AUTHOR WILL
WRITE THREE INSTALMENTS, CHALLENGING
THE OTHERS' INGENUITY ALL THE TIME. IS
IT GOING TO BE INTERESTING? WELL, READ
THIS OPENING! FORECAST IF YOU CAN
THE NEXT MOVE

MOVE

FOUR AUTHORS

(each a
star)
take
up the
others'
challenge !

⎣G. H. Teed, and – – – – – – – – – – Gwyn Evans.

– – – – – – – – – The Editor

CHAPTER I
THE WAKEFUL RAY.

GILSON was literally shocked into wakeful-ness.

Tap, tap, tap!

Steadily, insistently, the tiny flat metal hammer beat against the inside of his wrist.

Tap, tap, tap!

Three beats to the second. But Gilson was wide awake before the first three had been counted off.

He sat up in the darkness and, using his right hand, unbuckled the band of metal and leather from his left wrist. Carefully he allowed the band to sink to the extent of its connecting flex so that it hung beside the night table.

Next he thrust a hand beneath his pillow and took out a loaded automatic pistol. Then, pushing back the clothes, he swung his legs out of bed, thrust his feet into the soft morocco slip-pers that stood waiting, found a small flashlight that lay on the night table, and stood up.

Someone had passed across or through the in-visible ray that guarded the front stairs, breaking the connection, and thus bringing into play the little contrivance that had been attached to his wrist in anticipation of just such a happening.

The ray had been fixed parallel with the third step and at the height of the banisters. No house-prowling cat or dog could have broken its con-tinuity, even had there been one to prowl—the height precluded that. It had been fixed so that any human being, crouching or erect, who at-tempted to pass the invisible barrier after it was switched on must break it. And that interrup-tion would bring into immediate action the tiny hammer that was strapped to Gilson's wrist.

He knew just what he had to do to reach the upper hall quickly. Every step of the way had been traversed by him scores of times. He had measured and timed his paces in every possible condition of light and gloom, of haste and de-liberation.

There was only one closed door with well-oiled hinges to pass. Then a thickly carpeted hall, and he would command the head of the stairs.

Nor had he any fear that any unauthorised person, having passed the barrier of the invisible ray, would gain the top of the stairs before he could reach a oposition to command them. The fifth and sixth steps from the top formed a double trap. If an intruder stepped over one he could scarcely miss the other, for they had been built with the precautionary thought that one mounting might be taking them two at a time.

From his dark bed-room Gilson stepped into the equally dark upper hall. But that impenetrable curtain of gloom was rent asunder when he raised his left hand and pressed the switch of the flashlight.

The beam, intensely brilliant, stabbed straight through the banisters, revealing the upper half of the staircase. And, sprawled across the upper six steps, his head chinning the very top, fingers gripped in rods of the banisters, was a man. The trap had not failed.

Hidden behind the flash, Gilson studied his catch at leisure. The man was big of frame, his fleshy body effectively covering the stairs across which he lay. His face, held up by the pressure of the chin against the edge of the landing, was broad and round, with a short, flattish nose and high cheekbones.

His clothes were of some dark material. A broad-brimmed black soft hat had fallen from his head and rolled across the carpet until it struck the wall. About a foot from the full stretch of his hand, had he reached out, was an automatic pistol with a clumsy bulk at the muzzle. A silencer had been affixed.

Gilson reached out and pressed a wall switch that flooded the upper hall with brilliant light. He dowsed the now ineffective torch and dropped it into the breast pocket of his pyjama coat. Then he moved forward until he stood in front of his prisoner.

In the baggy pyjamas Gilson's lithe figure did not show in outline. Just over middle height, he looked clumsy, but when he moved, his heels left the carpet with a natural spring that told of immense vitality. The hard light in his grey eyes reflected the same energy of body and mind. About thirty, one would say, but with a mouth hardened to greater years through some terrific experience that had seared him through and through.

He retrieved the pistol on the floor, and, with his own, laid it on a chair. He did not speak. Nor did the man who sprawled in the grip of the stair-case trap. Scarcely did their eyes meet. Gilson acted as if he might be dealing with a dummy.

A panel in the wall at the head of the stairs yielded to his touch on a secret spring. From the cavity beyond he took a coil of rope, a pair of handcuffs, a pear-shaped expanding gag, and two lengths of thick black cloth.

The other had not offered to make any outcry, yet Gilson gave his first attention to the gag. Swiftly and brutally he forced the gag between the prisoner's teeth, securing it with one of the lengths of black cloth. Next he hauled both arms round behind the other's back and snapped on the handcuffs.

It took but a few moments to tie the second length of black cloth over the eyes and to secure it at the back by short tapes that had been sewn on for that purpose. Then Gilson rose, picked up his own pistol and, stepping over the helpless man on the stairs, descended to the lower hall.

He did not even glance at the front door. He was satisfied that the intruder had not gained access that way. Nor the window. There was just one means by which one could force an entry without too much trouble, and that had been left as a weak spot deliberately.

Gilson continued into the basement, and went along the short passage there to the area door. Here, as he thought, the intruder had got in. The door was even slightly ajar, in readiness for a quick getaway, if necessary.

Gilson switched on his flashlight again, but just as he was about to swing the door farther open he paused to listen to Big Ben striking in the near distance.

When the chimes had finished he counted the strokes of the hour.

One—two—

No more. Two o'clock.

Then he stepped out into the area— a wide space and deep from street to wall of house, for the building had been built back in the sixteenth century, and still stood between the blank walls of two modern erections, recessed as it were.

Gilson turned on to the iron steps and mounted to the street, regardless of his attire. At the top, close beside a curved iron rail that guarded the old steps that led up to the front door, he paused and looked up and down the short street. Not a soul was in sight. Not a footfall broke the stillness of the summer night.

CHAPTER 2

THE WATERWAY.

HE retired to the area and re-entered the house, closing the door and locking it after him; though he knew full well that others would find it easy enough to force that lock if they came.

Now his movements underwent a quick change. Where had moved with leisurely restraint he passed back along the passage with a brisk stride.

He mounted the basement stairs and ran lightly up those from the front hall, giving no more than a glance at his prisoner as he stepped over him.

In his bed-room he dressed quickly. When he had finished, there was little beyond the disarranged bed and a few toilet articles to indicate that it was being used.

When he emerged he knelt beside the man on the stairs and, thrusting a hand into the step trap, released it, dragging the victim's leg loose as he did so. With the release, the step came back into place smoothly, leaving no indication of its hidden purpose.

Standing a couple of steps below his prisoner, Gilson bent down, and, getting his hands under him, heaved him on to his shoulders with no very perceptible effort, despite the other's bulk. He performed the action with the motions of one who has been used to shouldering heavy bales or sacks.

Descending the stairs, he pressed his elbow against a switch on the wall of the lower hall, a two-way switch that extinguished the light above. But complete darkness did not seem to bother Gilson, for he carried his burden along without stumbling or colliding with anything, and swinging the bend at the end of the hall, went down the basement stairs and along the passage until he came to a closed door on the right.

He opened the door and stepped into darkness. Easing his burden to the floor he switched on the light, revealing a room furnished as a kitchen, and with wooden shutters closed tightly over the windows.

At one end was a wide, deep old fireplace, which was, apparently, no longer used as originally intended, for in the embrasure stood a modern electric cooking range. On the left-hand side of the range were the wires and switchboard controlling the power. On the right, a narrow space unused. Behind it a wide expanse of blackened stone, surviving, it would seem, from the long-ago days when great logs had burned against it and old iron spits had turned above the flames.

Gilson stood just within the door, listening. A clock on the mantel-piece was the only thing that broke the stillness. Then he strode to the electric range, and opening the oven door, reached high up into one corner where he found a concealed switch.

He pressed this. Immediately a startling thing happened. The range swung outwards and around to the left, leaving the whole embrasure of the ancient fireplace quite empty. But that was not all. At the same time, the smooth black stone also began to move, sliding along to the left as if in a greased groove and not stopping until there was revealed an opening some four feet long by five feet high.

Gilson stepped into the alcove, and taking out his flashlight, pushed the torch into the opening. The beam of light fell on a flight of very narrow steps that descended steeply. A brief inspection seemed to satisfy him, for he switched off the torch, turned, and made his way back to the man who lay on the floor.

Again he revealed that easy strength as he hoisted the burden and hung it over one shoulder. Then he re-entered the fireplace alcove, and with some little difficulty, passed through the opening to the top step.

He paused here only long enough to press a switch that caused the panel to slide back into place, and, had one been in the kitchen on the other side, one would have seen that the electric range swung round into normal position, and then, as it ceased its swing, the light automatically went out.

On the other side of the panel a bulb now lit up the stone stairs, going both up and down. Gilson descended, still carrying his burden. About a dozen steps down, the staircase turned into a spiral that wound round and round and round, descending a great distance and confined to a space of relatively small diameter.

Here and there other bulbs gave sufficient illumination for the man's descent, and, after a time, the stone sides oozed moisture.

Then, suddenly, the stone steps ended in a stone-flagged passage along which Gilson walked a few yards until he came to a heavy oaken door that was closed.

It was only held by a simple wooden latch which yielded readily enough. Then Gilson passed through into a wide, vaulted, cavern-like place that, despite its depth below the level of the street above, smelled sweet enough, though damp to the nostrils.

IT was, in fact, a link in the amazing and all but forgotten subterranean streams of London, and through the middle of the place ran a stream of water. Here and there beneath parts of old Westminster may still be found parts of the watercourses that used to run open to the air in the Middle Ages just as others flow in secret places beneath the great houses that lie between Paddington and Park Lane, beneath the great office mammoths in Holborn and Farringdon Street.

It emerged through an arched opening in the wall and disappeared through a similar arch in the opposite wall. Never had its existence been suspected when the more recent building had been carried out above.

But Morgan Gilson was, apparently, well acquainted with its course and possibilities, for tied to a short stake in the mid bank was a small punt. And in the punt he deposited his burden.

Getting in, he cast off and seized a pole. Gently he pushed the punt along until it was almost entering the arched tunnel through which the stream flowed on its course, either to the greater creek that forms the lake of St. James' Park, or into the Thames itself.

He held the punt back by pressing one hand against the top of the arch. Then he dropped the pole at his feet, reached out and pressed a switch, which plunged the place into darkness, dropped to his knees, and crawled forward, where he pressed another switch that controlled a powerful electric torch that had been fixed in the front end of the craft.

By now the punt was being carried along at a fairly good pace, bumping against the sides of the tunnel as the current sent it along. Gilson corrected the movement as much as possible with his hands against the old brickwork, but he sprang back to the pole when the miniature searchlight revealed another opening in the tunnel.

Almost immediately the punt slid into a cave-like place similar to the one he had left, but here, where wall and tunnel began again, there was a thick iron grid that effectively stopped the further passage of the boat.

But this seemed not to worry Gilson, for he poled into the bank and got out, fastening the craft to a rusty old ring-bolt that hung close to the grid.

At the top of the sloping muddy bank, and built against the wall, were two small rooms or cellars. One was door-less, but the other had been fitted with a clumsy affair of rough wood, and this, in turn, showed a shiny bit of steel under the stabbing beam of Gilson's torch where a lock had been sunk. In the lock was a key.

Gilson climbed to this door and unlocked it. The light revealed an interior that was floored with scattered straw. There was nothing in the way of furniture except a new galvanised iron bucket.

When he had filled this at the stream and placed it in one corner of the cell, Gilson returned to the punt and once more shouldered his prisoner. Dumping him on to the straw he reached down and removed his gag and eye bandage. Then he indicated the pail of water.

"You can drink," he said tonelessly, "if you can manage to push your face into the pail without upsetting it. You can yell your head off if you want to try. You won't be heard."

With that he stepped out of the cell, closed the door, turned the key, and, removing it, slipped it into his pocket. Next he passed round the end of the cell and climbed to the very top of the bank until he stood just beneath a hole in the brick about three feet wide by a foot or so deep.

It had possibly been built originally to allow for the overflow of flood water. But, at some time or other, it had been used for other purposes, for when he had climbed through Gilson found it possible to get his feet on the rungs of an iron ladder that had been fixed to the brick.

He began to climb, going up and up and up until, at last, his reaching hand came into contact with a round iron trap. He got his shoulders against this and heaved with his great strength until the trap lifted.

A quick hand checked it before it could clang backwards, and Gilson emerged into a small cobbled courtyard that seemed to be enclosed on three tides with a high blank wall, and on the fourth by the wall of a small building containing one window and a door.

He lowered the trap into place and made for the door. When he had unlocked it and stepped inside he brought his torch into play once more.

The light revealed a curious thing. The hall was not more than six feet long, with a door on his right, and one at the other end. There were no stairs, but when Gilson opened the door on his right the light showed a tiny room that was quite bare of any furnishings, with the exception of a window that was covered by a blind and curtains.

Here, too, there was a short wooden ladder that gave to a trap in the ceiling, and had one climbed this one would have found an exactly similar room, or miniature room, unfurnished but for blind and curtains over the window. It was like a big doll's house.

Apparently satisfied with his brief scrutiny, Gilson closed the door and went along the short hall to the door at the end. This was secured by an ordinary Yale spring lock, which, after dowsing the torch, he turned.

Then he opened the door and stepped once more into the warm summer night, just as Big Ben chimed the three-quarters.

CHAPTER 3
THE DEAD MONKEY.

GILSON walked out of the impasse of which the dummy house formed the end, into an alley which brought him into the thoroughfare just off Victoria Street, which, is known as Petty France.

From here he made his way to Victoria Street and along to an all-night taxi rank, where he found a cab. At ten minutes past three he was standing on the steps of Sexton Blake's house in Baker Street pressing the bell-push.

Within the dark house a deep, ominous baying was the first answer to his ringing. Then the man at the door saw a gleam in the fanlight, above the door, and a moment later a sleepy youth in a vivid crimson dressing-gown was staring at him suspiciously.

"It's Morgan Gilson, Tinker."

"Oh, come in, Mr. Gilson. I couldn't see at first. I'm half asleep, I guess. What's up?"

"I must see Mr. Blake at once."

Tinker spoke sharply to Pedro, the big bloodhound, whose bloodshot eyes were fixed somewhat ominously on the late caller. Then:

"Come along to the consulting-room, Mr. Gilson. But I warn you, the guv'nor isn't going to be any too pleased at being hauled out at this hour of the night. He had the dickens of a hard day, and didn't turn in till two."

"I'm sorry; but you know what he said—to wait until something happened, and then get in touch with him at once."

"And has something happened?"

"It certainly has. Will you tell him?"

But there was no need. As they entered the consulting-room by one door Sexton Blake, in his famous worn old dressing-gown, came in at another. He was frowning irritably, for Pedro's deep bark had awakened them. But the frown passed when he recognised his visitor. He eyed him keenly as he crossed the room.

"So it has come, Gilson?"

The visitor nodded.

"Just as I anticipated."

"When did it happen?"

"As near two o'clock as may be."

"Any warning?"

"Only that at midnight, when I tried to use my telephone instrument, I found it dead."

"Well, you appear unharmed. Are you sure it is what you expected?"

"Dead sure. Only one got as far as my trap, but I've trussed him up safely."

"Tell me just what occurred."

Blake sank into his desk chair and lit a cigarette. He smoked without interrupting the other's tale. When it had finished, however, he shook his head.

"It's a pity about that telephone. I wish you could have got word to me without leaving your house."

"But no one saw me. I made sure of that. As I told you, I came through the dummy cottage in the blind alley."

"I'm not thinking of whether you were seen or not. I'm thinking of what may be happening while you are away from the place. It is easy enough for others to get in by that area door."

"I couldn't do anything else. The phone was dead. I couldn't call a constable. Nor did I dare risk sending a message by a taxi driver. I might have gone to a public telephone at Victoria

Station, but that would have taken about as much time as coming myself."

"Quite true. I think we had better go back as quietly as possible. If the thing has happened that you have been expecting, then it looks as if the game was starting. And we've got to be on hand for the next move."

"I was hoping you'd come back."

"I will."

Blake turned to Tinker. "Get into some duds, my lad. Then get the car. I'll dress. Help yourself to cigarettes, Gilson. And perhaps you'd like a drink?"

With the efficiency of long practice, both Blake and Tinker were dressed and ready in short time enough to please even the impatient Gilson. While Blake examined pistols and loaded a couple for himself and the lad, Tinker went for the Grey Panther, which was kept ready at all times in a mews garage at the back of the house.

With no traffic and no speed limit to restrain him, Tinker burned the asphalt as he cut across town on his way to Westminster.

HE reached Petty France by a series of short, winding streets from Buckingham Palace Road, then he slid into the alley off Petty France and brought the big car to a stop in front of the dummy house in the blind alley.

He waited only long enough to turn the patent lock of the magneto, then he followed Blake and Gilson into the little place that the uninitiated believed to be a real house with real rooms, and, because of the curtains at the windows, real occupants.

Gilson waited to close the door after him. Blake had already opened the other door that led into the cobbled yard, and by the time Tinker and Gilson reached him, had managed to lift the iron trap.

But Gilson went first down the ladder. Tinker followed, with Blake bringing tip the rear, his powerful shoulders easing the iron trap into place just before he began to descend.

He found Gilson and Tinker waiting on the other side of the hole in the wall. When he had dropped beside them, all three moved down the gradually sloping mud bank that hadn't seen the sun for more than four hundred years.

No words were spoken. They knew what to expect, and the two detectives allowed Gilson to go first while he held the torch in one hand and felt for the key with the other.

But the moment they turned the corner of the cell and were in sight of the door, they knew that the key would be useless. For the door which had been locked was now lying back on one hinge, the lock smashed as if a heavy sledge had demolished it. And it was only a perfunctory glance they gave inside. They knew already that the prisoner was gone.

Upon the realisation of this, Gilson stumbled and raised a hand as if in baffled despair. Sexton Blake reached out quickly and caught his shoulder.

"The story is plain to read," he said quickly. "We've got to move quickly. How could they get here?"

"Only through the tunnel."

"But—a boat?"

"They could wade. It isn't more than three feet deep."

Blake jerked out his own torch and flashed it towards the water. He could see the punt still tied to the ring-bolt as Gilson had left it.

"Then they've gone either up through the dummy cottage or back into your house."

"Not the cottage," responded Gilson wearily. "They would return to the house. They are probably searching now for the—"

"Come on!"

At Blake's crisp command Gilson pulled himself together. They ran down the bank to the punt.

Tinker cast off and took the pole. Under his short, steady strokes the punt made good headway against the easy current of the stream, though it was difficult work pushing through when they were in the arched tunnel.

But the lad brought them into the other cavern beneath Gilson's house, and was tying the punt to the stake while Blake and Gilson were already running along the stone-flagged passage.

Tinker overtook them on the staircase and kept at their heels during the long climb to the top.

There was a pause while Gilson found and pressed the switch that permitted them to enter the fireplace alcove in the basement kitchen.

And then, as they emerged into the room, all three drew up in dumbfounded amazement. What they saw here was even more of a shock and a puzzle than the discovery that the prisoner had vanished.

On the floor, almost in the very centre of the room, was a small, dead monkey, clad in a little ridiculous red coat, blue tights, and tiny peaked blue cap, with gold braid about it—the sort of little, fantastically dressed monkey one sees sometimes on the shoulder of an Italian organ-grinder.

How it had come there, how it had died, were questions which Blake did not pause then to attempt to answer. With his automatic in his hand, he leaped for the door and into the passage. As he wheeled towards the stairs that led to the floor above he noticed that the area door was closed.

But he did not wait to discover if it was locked. Up the stairs he went, two at a time, until he reached the hall. He did not need his torch here, for the place was brightly lighted, and as he swung round the newel post of the main stairs he called over his shoulder:

"Guns, you fellows! There's something on the stairs!"

Gilson and Tinker followed him up, but were brought to a stop as Blake bent over the figure that lay huddled against the topmost steps.

It was the figure of a girl, whose russet hair gleamed like red gold against the mahogany that, in its turn, was in sharp contrast to the green silk of the flimsy evening dress she wore.

It was Roxane Harfield, better known as Mademoiselle Roxane, the beautiful and wealthy young Canadian girl with whom Bake had trodden the adventure trail in the past in various parts of the world.

"Roxane!" he exclaimed. "What does this mean?"

But before he could find any answer the door leading to Gilson's bed-room flew open and the place was filled with the staccato racketing of automatics!

THE MAN ON THE STAIRS—THE SECRET UNDERGROUND STREAM—THE APPEARANCE OF ROXANE AND, OF ALL THINGS, THE DEAD MONKEY! WHAT'S IT ALL ABOUT? WHAT'S GOING TO HAPPEN NEXT? WELL, WE DON'T KNOW. NOBODY KNOWS; NOT EVEN GWYN EVANS, WHOSE JOB IS TO CONTINUE FROM HERE. IT'S UP TO HIM; IT'S HIS NEXT MOVE! AND HE'LL HAVE THE ANSWER READY AND WAITING FOR YOU IN NEXT THURSDAY'S UNION JACK; AND SO WILL THE OTHERS, TURN AND TURN ABOUT. IN ALL CONFIDENCE OF MANY WEEKS OF REALLY THRILLING READING TO COME, YOU CAN CHEERFULLY PLACE THAT STANDING ORDER!

THE NEXT MOVE

GWYN EVANS—

GWYN EVANS CARRIES ON FROM THE POINT AT WHICH G. H. TEED, THE FIRST OF OUR TEAM OF FOUR STAR AUTHORS, LEFT THIS LATEST IDEA IN SERIALS IN LAST

WEEK'S UNION JACK. THE PRESENT INSTALMENT WILL BE FOLLOWED BY ONE FROM THE HAND OF ROBERT MURRAY WHO WILL BE FOLLOWED IN TURN BY ANTHONY SKENE. THEN THE FIRST MAN WILL TAKE IT UP AGAIN, AND SO ON THROUGH ITS EXCITING, UNEXPECTED DEVELOPMENTS TO THE END. EACH WRITER IS CONFRONTED BY THE PREVIOUS ONE'S PROBLEMS, HAS TO INVENT HIS OWN WAY OUT, AND PREPARE FRESH COMPLEXITIES FOR THE NEXT.

THIS STORY IS GOING TO BE INTENSELY INTERESTING AND EXCITING—OBVIOUSLY! ALREADY IT'S WELL INTO ITS STRIDE. KEEP IN TOUCH WEEK BY WEEK!

PREVIOUS MOVES

G. H. TEED, IN THE FIRST PART OF THIS SUPER-SERIAL LAST WEEK, BEGAN THE STORY WHICH GWYN EVANS NOW CONTINUES BELOW. THIS IS A SUMMARY OF HIS INSTALMENT:

THE STORY OPENED IN THE THOROUGHFARE KNOWN AS PETTY FRANCE, WHICH LIES BETWEEN VICTORIA STREET AND ST. JAMES' PARK, LONDON. THE TIME WAS TWO IN THE MORNING.

MORGAN GILSON, THE OCCUPANT OF ONE OF THE OLD HOUSES IN THAT QUIET BACKWATER, WAS WAKENED AS HE LAY IN BED BY THE BEATING OF A TINY ELECTRIC HAMMER ON HIS WRIST. IT WAS A NOISELESS ALARM WHICH TOLD HIM THAT SOMEONE HAD ENTERED THE HOUSE AND PASSED THROUGH THE INVISIBLE RAY WHICH GUARDED THE LOWER STAIRS.

UNHURRIEDLY HE GOT OUT OF BED AND WENT TO THE STAIRHEAD. THERE HE SAW A MAN LYING SPREADEAGLED ON THE STAIRS, CAUGHT IN A TRAP FORMED IN THE FIFTH AND SIXTH STEPS FROM THE TOP. WITH THE DELIBERATION WHICH CHARACTERISED ALL HIS ACTIONS AT THIS TIME HE HANDCUFFED, GAGGED, AND BLINDFOLDED THE MAN. THEN, HAVING DRESSED HIMSELF, HE CARRIED HIS CAPTIVE DOWN TO THE BASEMENT.

HERE GILSON OPENED THE OVEN AND PRESSED A CONCEALED SWITCH. THE WHOLE RANGE SWUNG ASIDE, REVEALING AN OPENING IN THE WALL BEHIND AND A STONE STAIRWAY LEADING BOTH UP AND DOWN. GILSON WENT DOWN, STILL CARRYING HIS PRISONER. AT THE BOTTOM HE HAD TO TRAVERSE A LONG TUNNEL, WHICH BROUGHT HIM TO THE BANK OF AN UNDERGROUND STREAM.

A PUNT WAS MOORED HERE, AND IN IT GILSON LAID THE PRISONER. THEN HE STEERED THE PUNT ON ITS SUBTERRANEAN COURSE UNTIL HE REACHED A CAVERN-LIKE OPENING, IN THE SIDE OF WHICH WERE TWO CELLARS BUILT IN THE WELL. IN ONE OF THESE GILSON DEPOSITED HIS MAN.

HE DID NOT RETURN ALONG THE STREAM. CLIMBING THROUGH AN OVERFLOW HOLE, HE REACHED A SHAFT, AND AN IRON LADDER WHICH WENT UP ITS SHEER SIDES. THIS BROUGHT HIM TO A COURTYARD, ENCLOSED ON THREE SIDES BY BLANK WALLS, AND ON THE FOURTH BY THE BACK OF A HOUSE. GILSON HAD A KEY TO THE DOOR, WHICH GAVE HIM ACCESS TO THE HOUSE—A BIG DOLLS' HOUSE, MEASURING ONLY SIX FEET FROM BACK TO FRONT. THE PLACE WAS EMPTY, BUT THERE WERE CURTAINS AT THE WINDOWS.

EMERGING BY THE FRONT DOOR OF THIS DUMMY HOUSE, GILSON FOUND HIMSELF IN THE STREET. FROM THE NEAR-BY HOUSE OF COMMONS BIG—BEN WAS STRIKING THREE. GILSON JOURNEYED FORTHWITH TO BAKER STREET.

"SO IT HAS COME, GILSON!" SAID SEXTON BLAKE WHEN HIS VISITOR HAD ROUSED HIM. "JUST AS I ANTICIPATED."

GILSON, TOO, AS HIS PREPAREDNESS HAD PROVED, HAD EXPECTED SOMETHING. BUT WHEN HE, BLAKE, AND TINKER RETURNED TO PETTY FRANCE IT WAS THE UNEXPECTED THAT HAPPENED.

GILSON'S PINIONED PRISONER HAD VANISHED FROM THE CELLAR. HE AND HIS RESCUERS, IF ANY, COULD NOT HAVE PASSED THROUGH THE DUMMY HOUSE, SO THE THREE RETURNED TO GILSON'S PLACE ALONG THE STREAM. IN THE BASEMENT KITCHEN, NEAR THE KITCHEN RANGE, A DEAD MONKEY LAY ON THE FLOOR. IT WAS DRESSED IN A RED COAT AND BLUE TIGHTS.

THERE WAS NO TIME TO INVESTIGATE THIS. THEY RAN TO THE MAIN STAIRS. HUDDLED AGAINST THE TOP STEPS WAS A FRIEND OF SEXTON BLAKE'S—MADEMOISELLE ROXANE HARFIELD. WITH THE RECOGNITION CAME THE THROWING OPEN OF GILSON'S BED-ROOM DOOR, AND THE RACKET OF AN AUTOMATIC PISTOL VOLLEY AS SHOTS BURST AMONG THE THREE AT THE BOTTOM.

GWYN EVANS NOW TAKES UP THE TALE.

EXIT ANASTASIA

CRACK!

A bullet phutted into the wall above Blake's head as he bent over Roxane. He turned suddenly, and his gesture was instinctive as he slid his hand into his shoulder holster. Blake was far too wary a bird to carry his gun on his hip.

"They're after you, Blake!" cried Gilson. "They've got your number!"

Blake signalled to Tinker, and stood there, gun poised, back to the wall.

Crack!

Another automatic spoke.

Blake's gun spat flame, and then, with a rush, he dived forward up the stairs.

There came the scurrying of hurried footsteps as the detective followed. In the gloom beyond he could make out two shadowy forms.

"Stop, or I fire!" roared Blake, his voice reverberating through the passage.

The flying figures did not pause. Blake emptied his gun over their heads as they ran.

He had an instinctive dislike of shooting even an enemy in the back, and the two figures disappeared round the corner of the passage and up the next stairway.

He halted for an infinitesimal moment.

Why should he follow these assailants of Gilson? It was Gilson's own affair. His was the next move, and yet—

Blake's mouth tightened. He realised the thought was unworthy of him—that the reason which had prompted it was the girl on the stairs.

Down below was Roxane. She had shared many an adventurous trail with him in the past. It was her helplessness, the mute appeal of her prostrate figure and painful attitude, that— *Crack!*

Blake felt a tearing, searing pain in his left shoulder. He clasped it instinctively. A thin, warm, sticky stream oozed through his fingers. Gritting his teeth, he dashed up the stairs, firing as he ran.

"Half a sec, guv'nor! I'm here!" called a boyish voice.

And Tinker appeared just as Blake staggered on the stairs.

"Quick, Tinker! Get 'em! I'm hit! I think— Roxane—is she all right?"

The detective slumped forward and collapsed, his knees sagging under him like wet cardboard.

Crack!

Tinker's gun spoke, and there was a loud clang of a shutting door.

"Guv'nor!" said the boy brokenly, and dropped down on one knee as he saw the wan, white face of the detective.

Two instincts rebelled in Tinker's youthful breast. One was loyalty to the man he reverenced most of all in the world; the other was devotion to duty.

"I'll get 'em yet!" he announced, between set teeth. "It was that fool Gilson who—"

Sexton Blake opened his eyes, and a faint smile played about his pallid lips.

"It's O.K., youngster!" he murmured. "I shall be all right! Try to get that number! It will solve—everything!"

"But, guv'nor—"

Tinker's voice was urgent.

"Stiletti! I'm certain it was he, and—"

He did not finish his sentence, for Blake dropped limply into the lad's arms.

"Blake!"

Gilson's voice reverberated hollowly through the passage.

"They've come, I tell you! At last they've got me!"

Up the steps came staggering the wild-eyed figure of Gilson— a very different Gilson from the calm, quiet man who had taken his enemy so quietly and unawares.

"Gilson," whispered Tinker earnestly, finger to lips, "the guv'nor's hit!"

Gilson stared down at the recumbent form of the detective, and his mouth tightened.

"Holy mackerel!" he ejaculated. "There's this woman downstairs, and now—Blake—of all people! Both of them! Tinker boy, we're flummoxed! What's the next move?"

Tinker laughed shortly.

"The next move, you idiot," he said, "is to call the police! Ring up Scotland Yard and get Coutts, and, while you are about it, you'd better get an ambulance!"

Morgan Gilson's face paled suddenly.

"The police!" he snapped out, "No, never, in *this* house!"

THERE—there—is no necessity for police!" said Sexton Blake in a faint whisper.

"I am here, Gilson. Tell me—Tinker—how is Roxane?"

"Guv'nor!" The boy's voice rose joyously. "Are you O.K.?" he asked.

"Perfectly!" replied Sexton Blake.

He grabbed hold of the balustrade to steady himself.

"What happened to Stiletti?" hoe added quickly.

"But, guv'nor," broke in Tinker, "I thought you were wounded. Can't I get a doctor—or—something?"

Blake smiled.

"Maybe I am wounded," he remarked. "But, meantime, where is Roxane and—"

Even as he spoke a shrill burst of hag's laughter echoed and re-echoed through the cavernous under-depths of Gilson's house.

"Ha, ha!" shrieked the laughter. "Ha, ha, ha! I'll teach you to leave a dead monkey about my house! Ha, ha, ha! Just like a child, it is, in its tiny coat and its little hat. But what about Anastasia? She lived longer than any monkey over did."

Tinker stiffened.

At the foot of the stairs, framed against the single solitary lamp that illumined the hallway, stood an extraordinary apparition. It was an old woman, garbed in a shapeless garment of rusty black.

Her long hair was white and matted and hung over her shoulders; her face was bleak and cadaverous. In one gnarled and talonous hand she held an enamelled candlestick. Her eyes were as black and beady as boot-buttons, as she stared at the trio on the top of the stairway.

Blake steadied himself with an effort, one lean, sinewy hand gripping the banister.

"Forgive me, madam!" he said. "But, unfortunately, Mr. Brank—"

"Brank!" shrilled the woman. "Who be you? Curse ye, to use the name of Brank in this house of all houses! I tell you that—"

"Ma dear, why don't you go to bed!" Morgan Gilson spoke soothingly, as he descended the stairs. "You know perfectly well that I'm seeing to things. They've done their best, but they won't beat me yet!"

The old woman mumbled incoherently and cast a malevolent look at Sexton Blake.

"I don't like yon tall fellow!" she cried shrilly. "He reminds me of the police, curse 'em!"

And, so saying, she shuffled off, her felt slippers whispering eerily through the strange house of Morgan Gilson.

"I'm all right, youngster."

Blake leaned heavily on the shoulder of his young assistant as he descended the stairs.

"I think it is only a flesh wound. I have been working rather hard lately, and it has rather got me groggy."

Slowly the three descended towards the room which Gilson had evacuated.

"Where is Roxane?" queried Blake anxiously.

Gilson gasped.

"But I carried her from the foot of the stairs," he said blankly, "and put her on the divan in my room."

He glanced around the small but commodious bed-room, with an air of bewilderment. There was no sign of Roxane.

Blake drew in his breath sharply.

"What's all this nonsense, Gilson?" he demanded sternly. "Where is Roxane?"

His voice was urgent.

"Before Heaven, I don't know, Blake!" A wild cry burst from his lips. He dashed towards the corner of the room. "Look!" he screamed. "It's gone! My number's up!"

He stabbed a finger towards the plain mahogany table.

"Anastasia's gone!" he burst out wildly. "She's gone, and with her my combinations!"

VERY DEAD

SPLASH Page, the "star" crime reporter of that go-ahead newspaper, the "Daily Radio," was bored, and admitted it frankly to his colleague, the night news editor, Julius Jones.

"What you want, Splash, is to to go in for an Eisteddfod of 'ens. You can learn a lot from poultry, look you. Do you know, there's very few men that can look an 'en in the face and not feel he's a biped like themselves and not 'arf as clever!

Splash Page laughed. He was seated in his usual negligent attitude on the edge of the news editor's desk, his long legs dangled over the wastepaper-basket, a cigarette hung pendulous from his lips.

"You darned old Welshman!" he chuckled. "Next to a nice murder, I don't think anything interests you except poultry and your local Welsh Baptist chapel."

"Editor of Eggs, I was for years in Manchester," said Julius Jones, reminiscently. "A nice paper it was, but unfortunately it got addlepated with the 'Chicken World' and I joined Fleet Street."

Splash Page laughed.

Known as Splash Page because of his marvellous knack of obtaining a front page of feature story, the youngster had shared with Sexton Blake many a perilous task on the adventure trail.

He was very fond of Julius Jones, that hard-bitten Welshman who was the night news editor of the "Daily Radio."

Julius enjoyed his job so much that even now, so early as three o'clock in the afternoon, he was immersed in "flimsies," telephone messages, and radiograms from all parts of the world.

The door of the news-room catapulted open, and with it came the clatter of typewriters, tick-tock of the tape machines, and the insistent burr of telephone bells, mingled with the slow, low rumble of the rotary machines in the basement of the building.

An inky-faced printer's devil entered with two telegrams in one hand and a parcel in the other.

"Parcel for you, Mr. Page," he squeaked, depositing the orange-hued envelopes on the news editor's desk.

Splash took the parcel, which was wrapped in brown paper, and looked at it curiously. It was addressed to himself in typewritten characters. The size of the parcel was that of a small shoe-box, and he rubbed his chin thoughtfully. It wasn't his birthday, and it was nowhere near Christmas. He leant over the desk negligently, and borrowed Julius Jones' bone-handled knife with which he cut the strings.

"Rum business, this, Julius!" he remarked.

"Eh?" said Julius, deeply immersed in a telegram from Pontypridd announcing the birth of quadruplets to a miner's wife.

"What do you say?" he added abstractedly.

"I've had a parcel, addressed to the office," continued Splash, unwrapping the parcel.

He lifted the lid of the box, then, gave vent to an exclamation of amazement.

Nestling against a background of soft tissue paper lay the body of a parrot, a grey parrot, and it did not need Julius Jones' ostentatious sniff to comment on the fact that the parrot was very dead.

"Well, I be—er—bothered!" ejaculated Splash Page. "What's the big idea? Here, Julius, here's a bit of poultry for you."

He picked hold of the bird by its neck, and noticed for the first time that there was a label attached, on which was written in blood-red letters: "Sorry, Miss, wrong number."

Splash Page burst out laughing. It was so utterly fantastic that he, the "star" crime man of the "Radio" should receive such a senseless gift.

"Hold this one, Julius!" he remarked, flinging the dead parrot on to the editor's desk.

Julius blinked through his horn-rimmed spectacles.

"Indeet to goodness!" he began, gruffly.

Splash pinched his nostrils delicately.

"Indeet to badness, I should think," he remarked. "What's the big idea, do you think, Julius?"

The night news editor shrugged his shoulders.

"I don't know. It's obviously a South American bird."

Splash picked up the small, feathered body and glanced at it closely, then turned again to the box.

"Durn me if there isn't a good story in this," he remarked. "It's the sort of thing that would interest my pal, Sexton Blake."

An Old Character Turns Up.

SEXTON BLAKE, the celebrated criminal investigator, of Baker Street, leant back somewhat wearily in his saddlebag chair.

"My dear Coutts," he said, "I tell you that I have utterly no information about the man Brank; and as for Gilson, I admire and respect him."

Detective-Inspector Coutts of Scotland Yard snorted, "That's all very well, Blake," he began, "but you're shielding somebody, and I know mighty well that Mademoiselle Roxane is implicated in this."

"In what?"

Blake's eyebrows elevated interrogatively.

"Well—in this business of you being shot in the shoulder at Gilson's place in Westminster."

Blake touched the left sleeve of his dressing-gown and winced slightly.

"You'll pardon me, Coutts, old man," he answered, "but I have made no formal complaint to the police. My information to you was entirely unofficial."

Coutts grunted again. He leant back in his chair and crossed one pudgy leg over the other, and his cigar—one of Blake's Carotins—look an upward and belligerent angle.

"hat I can't understand, Blake," he said aggressively, "is why you associate with a man like this Gilson. I mean to say, hang it all, we've mixed up with some queer fish in our lives, but this chap Gilson—"

A tap sounded at the door. Mrs. Bardell entered, breathing heavily.

"If you'll excuse me, Mr. Blake, there's a gentleman here named Gilson as wants to insult you proficiently, and he says as 'ow if there's any Scotland Yard suspectors about he'll call again."

Blake chuckled. Mrs. Bardell's English was weird and wonderful.

Coutts reddened with indignation.

Mrs. Bardell bridled a little.

"I'm sorry Suspector Scoots!" she remarked. "I forgot as 'ow you belonged to the Criminal Incineration Department. But the gentleman downstairs was most partickler."

"That's all right my good woman!" broke in Coutts, "I must be going."

He turned to Blake as he rose from his chair.

Blake shrugged his shoulders slightly.

"I am afraid, my dear fellow, that is about all the information I can give you. You're barking up the wrong tree if you think that Gilson is in the slightest way connected with the Bond Street affair."

Coutts donned his bowler-hat and cocked it aggressively over one eyebrow.

"All right, Blake," he said gruffly. "But I warn you that you won't be too well in with the Yard if you associate with a man like Gilson. What I mean to say is—"

What Inspector Coutts meant to say was never revealed, for at that moment the door of the consulting-room opened and Tinker entered, breathless with excitement.

"Guv'nor," he said, "I've found the monkey's master!"

"Stiletti, I suppose?" said Blake, lighting his pipe. Then, turning to Coutts, remarked, with a formality that was unusual between Coutts and himself: "See you later, Coutts."

Coutts buttoned his blue reefer overcoat about his ample frame.

"Good-bye, Blake!" he remarked gruffly. "Mind you, I've warned you!" he added, as he turned on his heel in the wake of the voluble Mrs. Bardell.

Tinker flung his cap down on the divan; his boyish face was flushed and excited.

"I say, guv'nor," he began, "the net's closing in, and I think we've got a clue to Roxane."

Blake leant back in his chair, and pulled reflectively at his favourite briar.

There was a humorous quirk at the corner of his lips as he heard the front door slam.

"Gilson will be here in a moment," he remarked. "Coutts does not seem to like our friendship."

Tinker grinned.

"Don't suppose he does, guv'nor, considering the sort of man Brank must have been."

A tap sounded at the door, and a moment later Morgan Gilson entered. He was clad in a well-fitting suit of plus-fours which set off his sturdy frame to advantage.

He advanced, with outstretched hands, towards Blake.

"My dear fellow, how are you? How is your shoulder?" he began. "I shall never forgive myself for Tuesday night; but, you see, all my nerves were over-wrought, and when I saw the young lady at the foot of the stairs I—"

"I'm quite all right, thanks," said Sexton Blake. "It was a mere flesh wound, and it is healing nicely. The big point is this"—he leant forward suddenly, and stabbed the stem of his pipe towards Gilson—"what about Anastasia?"

Gilson shrugged his shoulders impotently, and slumped into a chair.

"I tell you, Blake, I'm puzzled—frankly puzzled." he confessed. "When Stutz came I was expecting him, naturally, and I kept him as per instructions. But what, in Heaven's name, was the meaning of the monkey on the floor?"

SEXTON BLAKE stretched out a long, lean hand towards the tobacco jar.

"My dear fellow, surely it is perfectly obvious," he began, slowly refilling his pipe. "Stutz is no fool, neither is Stiletti. They both knew the secret of Petty France, and that you were keen on radio and electricity generally. You yourself boasted that no human being could ever pass the Wakefield Ray on the stairs. Stiletti is clever. He is also Italian, and it was easy enough for him to train a little monkey to open the doors which led to your inner room. Don't forget that the money usually walks on all-fours, and at such a height—roughly, twenty inches—he would be able to pass underneath the selenium ray of your photo-electric cell. You arranged it, you say, to catch a man either walking or crouching. But not a small monkey."

"By Jove, I never thought of that!" broke in Gibson. "The cunning devils! They knew perfectly well they couldn't get me by fair means—"

"So they tried monkey tricks!" interposed Tinker, with a chuckle.

Bang!

Morgan Gilson leapt to his feet, and his hands darted to his hip pocket.

"What the—" he began, grey eyes blazing. His whole body was tense with excitement.

Tinker crossed to the window and glanced down towards the traffic-laden Baker Street.

"It's that idiot Splash!" he remarked. "He's just arrived in his Red Peril.'"

Splash Page was a fairly frequent visitor to Baker Street, but he had a disconcerting habit of announcing his arrival with three loud bangs on the exhaust of his vermilion roadster, which Tinker had humorously nicknamed the Red Peril.

"That's all right, my dear fellow. I know your nerves are on edge," said Blake soothingly, noting Gilson's distraught air.

"This is only a young colleague of mine. Page, of the 'Radio.' You've probably heard of him."

Footsteps sounded on the stairs, and a moment later Splash Page entered in his usual breezy fashion.

"Wotcher, Blake, old-timer!" he began. "Got a drink?"

He glanced significantly towards the side-board.

Blake smiled.

"Don't be so tempestuous, young fellow!" he remarked, "Meet my friend, Mr. Gilson!"

Splash turned suddenly, and for a moment or two the young newspaper man and Morgan Gilson were face to face.

Gilson's face went the colour of death, and even Splash Page, used as he was to control his emotion, drew an involuntary breath.

"Good lor', you!" he gasped. Then, recovering: "I beg your pardon! I am delighted to meet any friend of Mr. Blake!"

The famous detective had risen to his feet. He stood with his back to the mantelpiece, one long, lean hand caressing the well-polished bowl of his pipe.

"What's the trouble, Splash?" he demanded.

"Trouble?" said Splash. "There's no trouble, my dear Blake. But what do you think of this?"

From under his arm he pulled out a small card-board box and opened it.

"This arrived to-day at my office," he re-marked.

With that he removed the lid of the box, dis-closing the dead parrot.

Gilson's face went ashen,

"It's Anastasia!" he gasped. "But where—and how—"

"Oh, is that the bird's name?" broke in Splash Page. "She seems like anaesthesia to me! Blake, frankly"—he turned to the detective—"what do you think's the idea of sending this blooming dead parrot to me, with a note around its neck apologising for a wrong number?"

"Sorry you've been troubled!" said a deep voice from the doorway. "Don't move, gentlemen! That bird's secret belongs to me! *And this gun spits death!*

The four spun round. Framed in the threshold was a tall, imposing figure. He was clad in a sheepskin coat, wearing a strange shapeless hat of untanned goat's hide on his head. His face was bearded and swarthy. In his lean, muscular hand he gripped a forty-live Derringer automatic.

"Give me my parrot!"! he said in a curiously husky voice. "I am Robinson Crusoe!"

"ROBINSON CRUSOE!" SAYS ROBERT MURRAY. "H'M! WHERE THE DEVIL DO I GO FROM HERE? ... O.K., GWYN, I'VE GOT IT! AND NOW TO SEE WHAT WE CAN FIX UP FOR FRIEND SKENE! I'LL BE ALL SET FOR HIM NEXT WEEK—AND HERE'S MY GUARANTEE IN ADVANCE TO HOLD THE 'U.J.'s' READERS' INTEREST IN MY INSTALMENT NEXT THURSDAY!"

ROBERT MURRAY

THE NEXT MOVE

EACH AUTHOR IN TURN WRITES ONE INSTALMENT OF THIS UNIQUE SERIAL, TRYING TO BAFFLE THOSE WHO FOLLOW WITH THE PROBLEM OF EXPLAINING THE PUZZLING SITUATIONS HE SETS THEM. THE FIRST TWO MOVES HAVE BEEN MADE BY TEED AND EVANS, AND NOW IT'S THE TURN OF—ROBERT MURRAY

PREVIOUS MOVES

INSTALMENT I. BY G. H. TEED:

AT TWO IN THE MORNING, AN ELECTRIC ALARM AROUSED MORGAN GILSON FROM SLEEP, WARNED HIM THAT AN INTRUDER WAS ON THE STAIRS OF HIS HOUSE IN PETTY FRANCE, WESTMINSTER.

GILSON WAS EXPECTING THIS RAID. THE INTRUDER WAS CAUGHT IN A TRAP AT THE TOP OF THE STAIRS. WITHOUT A WORD. GILSON GAGGED AND HANDCUFFED HIM AND CARRIED HIM DOWN A FLIGHT OF STEPS CONCEALED BEHIND THE RANGE IN THE BASEMENT.

A TUNNEL BROUGHT GILSON TO THE BANK OF AN UNDERGROUND STREAM. DUMPING HIS PRISONER IN A PUNT, GILSON STEERED FOR A CAVERN-LIKE OPENING AND LEFT THE BOUND MAN IN A CELLAR BUILT IN THE TUNNEL WALL. GILSON HIMSELF CLIMBED A WELL-LIKE SHAFT WHICH BROUGHT HIM OUT INTO A COURTYARD AT THE BACK OF A HOUSE.

THIS WAS BUT A SHELL OF A BUILDING, MEASURING SIX FEET FROM FRONT TO BACK. PASSING THROUGH THIS DUMMY HOUSE, GILSON GAINED THE STREET AND HURRIED TO BAKER STREET AND SEXTON BLAKE. LIKE GILSON, THE DETECTIVE HAD ALSO BEEN EXPECTING THE RAID. AT GILSON'S NEWS, BLAKE AND TINKER FOLLOWED HIM AT ONCE TO THE DUMMY HOUSE, DOWN THE SHAFT TO THE CELLAR. BUT THE PRISONER HAD GONE.

THE THREE MADE THEIR WAY UP THE STREAM AND INTO GILSON'S HOUSE. IN THE KITCHEN THEY FOUND A DEAD MONKEY. ON THE STAIRS LAY MLLE. ROXANE, BUT

BEFORE BLAKE COULD SEE TO HER, HE WAS
MET WITH A BURST OF SHOT FROM A BED-
ROOM.

INSTALMENT 2. BY GWYN EVANS:
BLAKE WAS HIT. WHOEVER FIRED GOT
AWAY, AND IN THE GENERAL MELEE
ROXANE DISAPPEARED. TINKER WANTED
TO CALL THE POLICE, BUT GILSON, AND
A STRANGE OLD HAG OF A HOUSEKEEPER,
WOULD NOT HEAR OF IT. THEN GILSON WAS
DUMBFOUNDED TO DISCOVER THAT HIS
PARROT ANASTASIA HAD BEEN TAKEN, AND
WITH HER "HIS COMBINATIONS."
MEANTIME, SPLASH PAGE RECEIVED A DEAD
PARROT BEARING A LABEL: "SORRY, MISS,
WRONG NUMBER!" INTRIGUED, HE TOOK
IT ROUND TO BLAKE WHOM HE FOUND IN
SESSION WITH GILSON. THE REPORTER
AND GILSON RECOGNISED EACH OTHER—
GILSON WITH ALARM—BUT NEITHER
SAID ANYTHING TO BLAKE, WHO WAS BUSY
EXAMINING THE BIRD.
SUDDENLY A STRANGE FIGURE APPEARED IN
THE DOORWAY.
"GIVE ME BACK MY PARROT!" HE SAID. "I AM
ROBINSON CRUSOE!"

NOW FOR THE NEXT MOVE! IT'S UP TO
ROBERT MURRAY.

IN A PLAIN VAN

THE lighted match in Blake's hand went unerringly to the cigar he had just placed between
his lips. He gave no more than a cursory glance
to the strange figure of the man in the doorway
who had announced himself as Robinson
Crusoe.

"Give Dolland the bird, Splash," he said,
with an unperturbed smile. "Speaking in the
vernacular of the stage, he deserves it for attempting such a weak piece of acting. You have
been making free with my dressing-room and
make-up box, Dolland.

"That sheepskin coat is a memento of the Great
War. I sometimes wear it when motoring. The
Derringer automatic—which you took from the
cupboard by the fireplace—is also a memento.
It belonged to a gangster named the Spider, who
has, fortunately, no further use for it."

Gilson and Splash Page gaped in astonishment
as Dirk Dolland, an ex-criminal better known as
the Bat, stripped off his crude disguise—coat,
hat, and false beard, and smoothed his sleek,
yellow hair.

"Useless trying to bluff you, Blake, old man,"
he drawled, screwing a monocle in one eye, and
giving Tinker a sly wink. "Sorry to intrude, but
I couldn't help overhearing your conversation.
There is a method in my madness."

He shot a shrewd glance at Morgan Gilson as
he spoke. The man winced, and turned his head
away.

"Great cats, it really is the Bat!" exclaimed
Splash Page, surveying the famous ex-cracksman with a comical lift of his eyebrows. "What
the dickens is he doing here, Blake?"

"Dolland has been my guest for several days,"
answered the detective. "He finds the atmosphere more congenial and more restful than that
of his chambers in Jermyn Street. Besides, it is
safer here."

"Safer?" echoed Splash Page, scenting further
mystery, "What d'you mean by that?"

"Someone is after my scalp," smiled the Bat,
helping himself to a cigarette, "There have been
three attempts on my life within the past week.
Blake knows all about it. That is why he suggested I lock up my chambers and stay here with
him for a while. He knows I am likely to be more
useful alive than dead."

"Spill the beans, Blake," urged Splash pathetically. "What's it all about? Why should anyone
want to put Dolland on the spot?"

"I'll answer that question myself," said the Bat
quickly. "The answer is quite simple. I happen to
have a very good idea who the mysterious Mr.
Brank actually is, and what connection he has
with a certain house in Petty France."

Crash!

Gilson's face was ashen-white as he stared
in dismay at the splintered remains of the cut-
glass tumbler that had dropped from his shaking
hand.

"You—you know who Brank is?" he exclaimed
hoarsely, studying Dirk Dolland with a vague
fear in his eyes. "It's impossible! You wouldn't
be alive if you did! Name him—name the man!"

Dolland shook his head.

"Not on your life!" he said grimly. "But if
you doubt my word, you may be interested to
know that the name of the man I suspect has

been written on a sheet of paper, and sealed in an envelope, which is now locked in the safe in Blake's bed-room."

Gilson's eyes flickered towards the door loading to the room where the detective slept. The motion did not escape Blake's attention.

Splash Page flipped his cigarette end into the fireplace. There was a determined look on his face as he seized the defunct parrot between finger and thumb and dangled it at arm's length.

"Now, what about this dead fowl— Amnesia, or whatever it is your friend, Mr.—er—Gilson calls it?" he demanded suspiciously.

"Anastasia," corrected Gilson dully.

Splash shrugged impatiently.

"Well, what's the idea? What's the mystery of this darned parrot?"

"Gilson can best answer that question," said Blake.

"But he won't!" snapped the man defiantly. "Not unless Mr. Dolland cares to tell me a certain name he has locked away in Mr. Blake's safe."

"I prefer to go on living for a little while longer," was Dirk Dolland's prompt reply. "When I name the man it will be in the presence of Brank himself."

"It strikes me the whole bunch of you are crazy," remarked Splash Page bluntly. "Perhaps someone can at least enlighten me as to the meaning of this label that's attached to the bird, 'Sorry, Miss, wrong number.' Is there any sense in that? If it refers to a telephone call—"

"It has nothing to do with a telephone call," remarked Blake. "Have a look at that bird's right leg, Splash."

The reporter obeyed. He uttered a gasp of surprise as he stared at a small metal band that was clipped firmly around the right leg of the dead parrot. On the band was engraved the number "7."

Gilson uttered a hoarse cry of dismay.

"Then, by jinks, you're right, Blake!" he exclaimed bitterly. "I've been wasting my time. My combinations were all wrong. That isn't the Eight parrot!"

"You are not alone in your error," smiled Blake. "Stutz & Co. fell into the same mistake."

"Curse it all!" exploded Splash violently. "I don't care a hoot who made a mistake! What I want to know is, why was this fatheaded feathered biped sent to me ? Was that a mistake?"

"Certainly not," assured Blake soothingly. "Take your mind back a couple of years, Splash. Do you remember a big scoop you made for your paper over a case that was headlined as 'The Mystery of the Stolen Parrots'?"

Splash grinned proudly.

"I certainly do. You mean that fellow Hamright, who keeps a livestock shop in Charing Cross Road. His place was broken into half a dozen times, if I recollect rightly, and on each occasion nothing was stolen except a number of parrots. The police were baffled. The mystery was never solved."

"But you featured the story?"

Splash nodded.

"Half of it guesswork."

"Pretty good guesswork," said Blake. "Maybe that is why the dead parrot was sent to you."

The detective turned quickly towards Morgan Gilson, whom he had been watching out of the corner of his eye.

"Where did you get Anastasia, Gilson?" he demanded. "How did the bird come into your possession?"

Gilson was silent for a moment, his eyes evasive, his fingers plucking nervously at the brim of his hat.

"The parrot came from Hamright's, in Charing Cross Road," he admitted at length.

Blake nodded. All eyes were turned on Splash Page, who had suddenly grabbed the telephone, and was striving desperately to get connection with a certain number.

"No use!" he groaned disgustedly, slamming the receiver back on its hook. "I've been ringing Hamright's shop, but I can't get any reply. Blake, we've got to get along there at once, before it's too late."

"You're right," agreed the detective, jumping to his feet. "And Gilson's coming with us."

"Gilson! Where is Gilson?" gasped Tinker. "He's gone!"

IT was true. Morgan Gilson was gone. Seizing his opportunity during the momentary distraction about the telephone, he had sidled from the room. The slamming of the street door announced he had hurriedly left the house.

Blake swore under his breath.

"That settles it!" he muttered. "We've got to get to Hamright's—and quickly! Dolland!" He laid a firm hand on the ex-cracksman's shoulder. "What was your idea in pulling that Robinson Crusoe stuff just now?"

"I recognised Gilson's voice," answered the Bat coolly. "When I knew him, several years ago, he had a peculiar nickname. He was called Robinson Crusoe."

"Holy cats! Why?" asked Tinker, curiously.

"Because he came from a certain island," informed Dirk Dolland. "Gilson is an escaped convict from the French penal settlement at Devil's Island."

"That's right," agreed Splash Page, lighting a fresh cigarette. "I recognised the blighter as soon as I entered, the room."

"Well, it's no secret," said Blake, stripping off his dressing-gown. "But Gilson happens to be a victim of circumstance. He isn't so black as he's painted. What the devil's that?"

The clamour of a bell resounded through the house. Gruff voices and a stamping of feet could be heard in the hall below, mingled with Mrs. Bardell's shrill, indignant protests.

Bang!

Again the front door slammed shut. Tinker darted to the window just in time to see a covered van drive away from the house and disappear amid the traffic. He was swift to notice that no name or other lettering was painted on it.

"Mr. Blake! Mr. Blake! Lawks-a-mussy-me! What does this mean, sir?"

Sexton Blake jammed on his hat and shot from the room, with Tinker, Dirk Dolland, and Splash Page close at his heels. Mrs. Bardell was seated on the bottom step of the stairs, staring in tearful indignation at a sinister-looking object that had been dumped in the middle of the hall.

"Holy halibuts! A coffin!" gasped Splash Page.

A coffin, it was—a six-foot, polished oak burial casket, with a brass plate set in the lid, and brass handles on either side.

"The meaning of it, Mrs. Bardell!" exclaimed Blake. "I'm sure I don't know. I was going to ask you the same question. Don't you know? Where did this thing come from? Who brought it here? Didn't they say?"

"There was two men brought it in a van, sir," gabbled the distracted housekeeper. "I told them there must be some mistake, but they hinsisted

hon bringing it in and leaving it in the 'all. They wouldn't wait for me to call you."

"I'm not surprised at that," muttered the detective grimly. "It's a poor kind of a joke—"

"Not much of a joke about it," said Dirk Dolland, with a wry smile. "Or else there's something wrong with my sense of humour."

He pointed to the brass plate set in the lid of the coffin. Engraved in it was the inscription:

"DIRK DOLLAND,
alias
The Bat.
RIP."

"Gad, that's a nice cheerful sort of present!" said Splash, with a wry grin. "But a bit premature so far as your requirements are concerned, Dolland."

"I don't even feel ill at the moment, let alone on the verge of death," announced the ex-cracksman, seizing one of the brass handles and giving the coffin a tentative tug. "By gosh, there's something in the darned thing! It's as heavy as lead!"

Blake's teeth came together with a snap as he forced off the lid of the wooden casket with a putter which he snatched from amongst the golf clubs in a bag hanging on the hall stand. The lid was nailed down only lightly.

Crammed inside was the body of a man with glazed, staring eyes and a livid bullet-hole in the centre of his forehead. He was a big, fleshy man, with high cheekbones and a short, flattish nose.

"By heavens, it's Stutz!" said Blake in a low, strained voice. "The man who escaped from Gilson's house last night. He's been punished for the mistake he made."

"Mistake? What mistake, guv'nor?" jerked Tinker, turning his eyes away from the ugly sight.

"His mistake in getting hold of the wrong parrot," answered the detective promptly. "It seems to me that the mysterious Mr. Brank is a hard taskmaster."

"Sending the body here is evidently intended as a polite hint to me," remarked Dirk Dolland. But his hand was as steady as a rock as he coolly tapped a cigarette on the coffin-lid. "I suppose I'm the next on the list."

Splash Page fidgeted impatiently.

"Blake, this is a bad break, but we ought to be getting on our way. Hamright—"

The detective wheeled on Dolland, his eyes steely, his lips set in a hard line.

"Dolland, I'll leave you to attend to this business," he said grimly. "Send for the police, but don't tell them any more than you have to. And watch your step. Your life's in graver danger than you realise. I'll be back in half an hour.

THE FIVE-FINGERED MAN

THE three of them piled into the vivid vermilion roadster that was parked outside the house. Splash Page was at the wheel, Blake and Tinker crushed together in the rear seat.

The Red Peril shot away from the kerb with a roar like a thousand gatling guns, streaking through the traffic with the sinuous speed of an eel on a skating rink.

"Step on the gas, Splash," encouraged Blake, giving the high-sign to an astounded constable on traffic duty. "I'm afraid things have been happening. I should feel easier in my mind if Gilson were here."

Splash swerved between two buses, grazed the fender of a private limousine, and just missed a lamp-standard. His roaring red roadster was a familiar sight to the traffic policeman of London. How he managed to retain his driving license was something to marvel at.

Blake sat back and crushed his hat down on his head.

"Now that we've got a couple of minutes to spare," he said calmly, turning to Tinker, "let's hear all that you've discovered to-day. You claim that you've found the monkey's master?"

Tinker nodded.

"Mistress," he corrected. "The dead monkey belonged to a woman named Madame Casanova, who keeps a private dressmaking place next door to Gilson's house in Petty France."

Blake digested this piece of information in silence.

"Madame Casanova. Obviously an Italian," he said simply. "That brings Stiletti into it, as I suspected in the first place. This woman admits the ownership of the monkey?"

"She burst into tears, and started tearing her hair out by the roots when she heard it was dead," informed Tinker. "Said she'd had it for years, and that it must have escaped through an open window last night, and found its way into the next house."

"A plausible story," grunted the detective dryly. "And what of Roxane?"

There was no time to discuss the missing Roxane. Splash Page had performed a miracle in speed. With a jarring shock that almost shot its occupants on the pavement, the Red Peril came to a squealing standstill outside a dingy-looking, old-fashioned shop in Charing Cross Road.

On the facia were painted the words:

"C. Hamright—Livestock Dealer."

Blake and his companions tumbled out of the car. The detective was the first across the pavement, to push open the door, and step into an atmosphere of queer smells and discordant noises.

Parrots screeched as the front-door bell shrilled; monkeys chattered, and dogs set up a furious barking. A gorgeous-hued macaw, with a sweeping red-and-crimson tail, and a cruel, hooked beak, bent down from a swinging ring-perch and dexterously relieved Splash Page of his hat.

"Mr. Brank!" it screeched. "Mr. Brank! Turn off the water, Mr. Brank!"

BLAKE and Tinker glanced meaningly at one another.

Splash let rip a lurid oath, and shook a furious fist at the screaming bird.

"New yesterday!" he groaned, watching the utter annihilation of his hat. "I'll make Hamright pay for that! Where is the old scoundrel?"

Blake closed the door, thus stopping the noisy clamour of the electric bell at the back of the premises. The shop was packed with crates and cages. Dogs snarled and barked from beds of straw. Monkeys and lemurs capered and gibbered. Live but sleepy tortoises were piled on the floor. Goldfish in a tank goggled foolishly at the visitors.

"Gosh, what an infernal row!" muttered Tinker, clapping his hands to his ears.

Gradually the tumult subsided at last, lapsing into comparative silence. Only the macaw chattered jubilantly as it ripped Splash Page's headgear to ribbons in its pincer-like beak.

Blake banged his foot impatiently on the floor.

"Shop!" he called loudly. "Anybody at home?"

There was no reply—no stir or movement in the dim recesses at the rear of the premises.

"Perhaps he's out in the backyard, feeding the silkworms?" suggested Tinker brightly. "Or else he's stone deaf."

"Deaf? Old Hamright's got the ears of a cat!" declared Splash. He opened the door, allowing the bell to ring for a while before closing it again.

There was something sinister about the silence now. It seemed to muffle and stifle the roar of the traffic in the street.

"Hamright!"

Only the echoes of Blake's own voice came hollowly back to him. There was no sign or sound of the old man who owned the shop.

Blake walked quickly back to the far end of the room, threading his way through the stacks of crates and cages. Two doors confronted him. One was open, giving a clear view of a stone-paved yard at the back of the shop. The yard was deserted.

The second door was closed. The glow of an electric bulb was visible through the frosted-glass panel,

"Hamright's office," informed Splash, an uneasy note creeping into his voice. "The old boy must be inside."

The detective seized the handle, and flung open the door.

Carlos Hamright was inside the shabbily furnished, musty-smelling room. The reason of his strange silence was only too clear. He was bound tightly to a wooden chair, with his head lolling back, and a gag stuffed in his mouth.

He was stone dead, with a wound in his stringy throat.

"By heavens, we're too late!" breathed Bake. "They've got him!"

TINKER'S face turned white with horror. Splash Page, ever the journalist, fumbled mechanically for his notebook and pencil.

Blake uttered an exclamation of astonishment as he stopped farther into the room. The spectacle that was fully revealed to him literally took his breath away.

The floor was strewn with the dead bodies of a dozen or more parrots. The neck of each had been callously wrung. One or two downy feathers were still settling slowly towards the dusty floor.

On the plain wooden table in the centre of the room stood a portable gramophone. The record turntable was still revolving, but slowly. The spring-motor was about run down.

"Holy catfish!" exclaimed Splash, in an awed voice, as he surveyed the litter of dead parrots. "For the love of Pete, what's the meaning of this, Blake?"

The detective crossed to the huddled figure of Hamright, and touched his hand. It was limp, and still warm.

"He's been dead for no longer than ten minutes," he said definitely. "His murderer was here when we first entered the shop. Must have escaped through the backyard."

The telephone stood on a battered roll-top desk. Blake lifted it, and set it down with a shrug of his shoulders.

"Wires cut! No wonder you couldn't get any answer to your calls, Splash. Well, this is a beastly business."

"A beastly business!" echoed the reporter. "It's like a nightmare! The whole thing's so senseless! The dead parrots— And look at that gramophone! It's still running. What type of a man would amuse himself by playing a gramophone within a few minutes of committing a cold-blooded murder?"

"He couldn't have been playing the gramophone!" declared Tinker shrewdly. "Look, there are no records!"

The lad was right. There was not a record to be seen.

"There was only one record," said Sexton Blake suddenly. "The murderer brought it with him—and took it away with him. That is quite clear."

"Clear!" exclaimed Splash, running his fingers frenziedly through his hair. "If it's clear to you, then I must be half-witted. I suppose you want me to believe that the murderer was using that gramophone to try to teach dead birds to talk?"

"Oh, no! The reverse, in fact," answered the detective enigmatically.

"Well, there's one thing that's clear to me," vowed Splash. "I know who murdered old Hamright. It was Morgan Gilson!"

Tinker gasped.

Blake shook his head.

"I thought you would jump to that conclusion," he said quietly. "But you are wrong. The murderer left his handwriting on the wall!"

He pointed to the crimson imprint of a human hand, a foot to one side of the door.

It was still damp. And it had been made by no ordinary hand. This one possessed a thumb and five fingers, instead of the usual four!

THE HAND OF
ROXANE

IT was only to be expected that there would be considerable delay before Sexton Blake was free to return to Baker Street.

It was over an hour later when the police allowed the detective and his companions to leave the little shop where Carlos Hamright had been done to death.

"When you want me again you know where to find me," said Blake to the inspector in charge of the case, as he took his seat in Splash Page's Red Peril. "It is possible that I may be able to supply you with more information within the next few hours."

It was this vague promise that clinched Splash Page's determination to keep in close touch with the Baker Street detective. Already the reporter had phoned the "Radio" office, and given details of the brutal crime that had been committed in the Charing Cross Road. A "write-up" man would do the rest. Again the star crime reporter of Fleet Street was first with the news; but so close was he to the affair and so personally perplexed that he had acted more from habit than otherwise.

"I've got a hunch that I'm on the verge of a big scoop!" mused Splash, as he sent his red roadster hurtling back to Baker Street. "I'm going to stick closer to Blake than his own shadow."

The first thing Blake noticed when he let himself into the house was the fact that the coffin, with its gruesome contents, had been removed from the hall.

Next he was struck by the strange silence that reigned over the place.

Ringing for Mrs. Bardell, the only response he received was the mournful baying of Pedro, the bloodhound, who was penned in the back yard.

"The old girl must have gone shopping," suggested Tinker, as they ascended the stairs. "But where's Dirk Dolland? He must be somewhere about the place."

The sitting-room was in darkness. Blake switched on the lights as he entered the door. A figure was huddled in the armchair before the dying fire.

"Wake up, Dolland!" said the detective briskly. "I've got some fresh news for you!"

There was no answer. Blake was across the room in an instant. The figure was not that of Dirk Dolland. Wedged in the chair was the stiffened corpse of the man Stutz!

Blake's alert brain leaped to grapple with this fresh problem. The coffin had been removed, but the body of the dead man had been left behind—had been carried upstairs, and placed conspicuously in the chair before the fire.

The police would not have removed the one without the other. It was becoming increasingly obvious that the police had not been near the house. Yet Dirk Dolland was supposed to have sent for them at once!

"Dolland—Dolland! Where are you, man?"

"He can't be here, guv'nor!" exclaimed Tinker shakily. "Apparently neither he nor Mrs. Bardell are in the house."

With a sharp cry of alarm Blake wrenched open a door, and stepped into the room beyond. His eyes went to the steel safe that stood in the recess by the fireplace. It gaped wide open. The combination lock had been wrenched clean away with some powerful safe-breaking instrument.

Lying just inside the steel box was the sealed envelope that Dirk Dolland had placed there two days previously. It was no longer intact. The seals had been broken and the envelope slit from end to end.

The slip of paper on which Dolland had written the mysterious name was gone.

Blake's eyes blazed with excitement as he stared at the empty envelope. He understood the challenge it conveyed. But Dirk Dolland knew also the name that he had written on the stolen slip of paper.

"Guv'nor, there's only one man could have opened that safe and stolen that paper!" declared Tinker tensely. "He was here in this house a couple of hours ago. You know who I mean—Morgan Gilson!"

"That goes for me as well," agreed Splash Page. "I was watching Gilson's face when Dolland mentioned that sealed envelope, and—"

The noisy ringing of the telephone dinned through the room. Blake grabbed the instrument. It was the voice of Morgan Gilson that came faintly over the wires.

"Blake, they've got me! They're here in the house. I'm trapped. For Heaven's sake come at once! I can't—"

The man's voice trailed off in a harsh scream of fear and despair. These was a confused banging, and then silence.

Blake's eyes were blazing as he slammed the dead receiver in place.

"That was Gilson. He's in a bad way. They've got him trapped," he jerked, hustling his companions towards the stairs. "Brank has stolen a march on us again. Tinker, fetch Pedro! I fancy we may need him this journey. How are your nerves, Splash? I'll give you just five minutes to get us to Petty France."

"O.K.," said the reporter laconically. "Five minutes it is!"

SPLASH PAGE was as good as his word. He completed the journey with seconds to spare. Big Ben was booming the hour as the red roadster swept along Victoria Street and turned into Petty France.

All was quiet in the narrow, sheltered thoroughfare where Morgan Gilson's quaint, old-fashioned house was situated. The house front seemed as quietly dignified as any of the others, and it was difficult to conceive any sinister happenings there, or, indeed, anywhere in such a prim, sedate neighbourhood.

Yet Pedro's actions were strange and disquieting. He was out of the car in a flash, growling deep in his throat as he bounded up the steps, to fling himself savagely against the oak door.

"There's someone in there the dog knows," snapped Blake, "and it certainly isn't Gilson."

There was a light in the hall, but his tugs at the bell-pull and hammerings with the heavy brass knocker brought no response. He twisted the handle, to find, to his surprise, that the door was unlocked.

It swung back on its hinges. The silence of the house struck muffled, pulsing echoes in the

detective's ears—the quickened beating of his own heart.

Pedro plunged past him, almost knocking him off his legs. The huge hound halted midway along the dimly lit hall, to stand protectively over the limp figure of a man that lay sprawled crookedly at the foot of the stairs leading to the first floor.

"It's Gilson!" blurted Tinker huskily. "We're too late! They've got the poor beggar!"

BUT it was not. Tinker's first glance had been too hasty. The man who lay senseless, with an ugly contusion dangerously close to his right temple and a trickle of blood running down his face, was Detective-Inspector Coutts.

"He's not dead; but somebody's been giving him a nasty smash on the head," breathed Blake, as he knelt beside the C.I.D. man. "I might have known—"

The detective broke off with a violent start. Clutched firmly between Coutts' rigid fingers was a tattered fragment of crumpled green silk.

It was a piece torn from the flimsy evening gown that Roxane Harfield had been wearing on the night she had mysteriously disappeared from this same house in Petty France.

"That's Roxane's colour. A piece of her dress!" muttered Blake incredulously. "Surely it was never she who laid poor Coutts out like this?"

The next instant he had whipped out his automatic and was bounding up the stairs, drawn by the savage baying of the bloodhound that had already gained the first landing, and disappeared through the doorway leading to Gilson's bed-room.

The light was on, but the room was empty. There was no sign of Gilson, nor was there sign of Pedro. The animal seemed to have vanished.

Blake stared around in amazement. Then he crouched, his finger tightening on the trigger of his automatic as he observed for the first time a black, oblong space in the wall beside the fireplace, where a section of the oak panelling had been slid to one side. Blake guessed, and correctly as he found afterwards, that it communicated with the steps that led down behind the kitchen to the underground river.

"Be careful, guv'nor!" warned Tinker, his voice sharp with anxiety. "There's something, or someone, moving in there!"

There was a sound of deep panting, and a patter of clawed feet. In the narrow opening loomed the tawny shape of the missing bloodhound.

Gripped in his pendulous jowls they glimpsed a woman's hand. On one slender finger gleamed a strangely carved ring, set with a flashing emerald.

"Roxane's ring!" was the horrifying realisation that flashed through Blake's brain. He could not be certain, when he came to try to picture the scene again in calmer circumstances afterwards, whether the hand was attached to an arm, or whether, as he imagined in that first glimpse, it was severed. At that moment, however, a light snapped out, plunging the room into pitch darkness. A blood-curdling shriek of crazy laughter echoed through the silent house.

"WELL," SAYS ANTHONY SKENE, "THIS FELLOW MURRAY HAS GOT ME GUESSING. FOR THE MOMENT, ANYWAY … H'M! ROXANE'S HAND IN PEDRO'S JAWS … WELL, WELL! I'LL SEE WHAT CAN BE DONE ABOUT IT. I'LL MEET YOU HERE NEXT WEEK WITH A SATISFYING EXPLANATION, OR BUST!"

THE NEXT MOVE

BY ROBERT MURRAY, ANTHONY SKENE, G. H. TEED AND GWYN EVANS. WITH, AS REFEREE OF THE MATCH … THE EDITOR.

EACH AUTHOR IN TURN WRITES ONE INSTALMENT OF THIS UNIQUE SERIAL, TRYING TO BAFFLE THOSE WHO FOLLOW WITH THE PROBLEM OF EXPLAINING THE PUZZLING SITUATIONS HE SETS THEM. THE FIRST MOVES HAVE BEEN MADE, AND NOW IT'S THE TURN OF—ANTHONY SKENE.

PREVIOUS MOVES IN "THE NEXT MOVE"

G. H. TEED'S (INSTALMENT 1):

MORGAN GILSON, occupier of a house in Petty France, Westminster, is awakened in the night by an intruder who is caught in a trap on the stairs. He carries the man to a cellar alongside an underground stream which, together with an intricate tunnel system, runs beneath the house, and then seeks the aid of Sexton Blake.

Returning from Baker Street, Blake, Tinker, and Gilson find the prisoner has vanished from the cellar and that the house itself has been freshly invaded.

On the floor of the basement kitchen is lying a dead monkey, and on the stairs is Mlle. Roxane Harfield. Before Blake can see to her he is met with a burst of shot from a bed-room.

GWYN EVANS' (INSTALMENT 2):

Blake is wounded, and in the melee Roxane mysteriously vanishes. Gilson is further consternated to find his parrot, Anastasia, has been stolen, and with it his "combinations."

Meantime, Splash Page, reporter of the "Radio," has received at his office a dead parrot. Mystified, he takes it to Baker Street, where he finds Blake in session with Gilson.

The two recognise each other, but neither says anything, and Gilson seems scared.

ROBERT MURRAY'S (INSTALMENT 3):

Dirk Dolland is staying at Blake's house because his knowledge of the identity of a mysterious Mr. Brank has caused attempts on his life. He also recognises Gilson, revealing he is an escaped convict from Devil's Island.

When conversation about Page's dead parrot suggests that the burglars at Gilson's had stolen the wrong bird, Gilson slips out of the room. The others follow him, but find in the hall a coffin containing the body of Stutz, the man who escaped from Gilson's cellar. Leaving Dolland in charge of this, they pursue Gilson to Hamright's, a livestock shop.

They find Hamright himself murdered and, alongside him, a recordless gramophone still running. On the wall is the bloodprint of a hand with five fingers.

Returning later to Baker Street, they find the coffin and Dolland gone, but the body of Stutz had been left propped up in a chair. Also disappeared is a paper Dolland had put in Blake's safe, giving the real name of Brank.

G. H. TEED

An urgent phone call from Gilson sends them to Petty France hotfoot. They find Inspector Coutts lying stunned in the hall. Pedro, who is with them, leaps into an open secret panel and reappears momentarily holding in his mouth what seems to be the hand of Roxane. At that moment a shriek of crazy laughter echoes through the house.

NOW FOR ANTHONY SKENE'S NEXT MOVE:

THE NEXT MOVE
INSTALMENT 4

WAS IT BRANK?

WHEN, the moment after they had seen Roxane's hand in the jaws of Pedro, the light snapped out, and crazy laughter filled Gilson's house, Blake, Splash Page, and Tinker instinctively drew together in the darkness.

"Ho, ho, ho, ho! Ho, ho, ho, ho!" came the laughter again, and then a voice.

The laughter, crazy as it was, seemed charged with evil meaning. And presently, when it merged into words, its malevolence was, if anything, intensified.

"This house lacked one thing to be utterly accursed. It lacks nothing now. To think that of all the devils in Hades—"

"It's Ma Gilson," breathed Tinker. "Ma Gilson, and she's batty, if ever a woman was!"

"Not astonishing if she is," breathed Blake. "She could—"

He checked himself. A voice had cut across the old woman's invective. And if her malevolent laughter had brought a shudder to the men who listened, this voice, of itself—independently of its words—brought to them a coldness about the heart.

"Be quiet!" said the voice. And then, with a singular lack of inflection: "It would be as well if you were quiet."

If the voice is the index of the soul, then the owner of this voice had the soul of a fiend, for there was in it nothing of humanity, no lovable weakness, not a trace of humour. Only a transcendental and diabolical egotism.

Blake said: "That voice!" with horror, and Tinker felt him move in the darkness towards the head of the stairs.

Blake was deserting Roxane. He did not even know whether she was dead or alive, but he was so moved by instinctive hatred and antagonism that he reacted almost without thought.

Pistol in one hand, and powerful electric torch in the other, he gained the head of the stairs.

Tinker and Splash Page, who were behind him, saw the cone of white light from the lens of the torch focus with theatrical effect upon a man who stood in the middle of the tesselated floor below.

The man was wearing a cloak of some black material, sleeveless, and gathered in at the throat, so that it concealed the whole of his body, even to his shoes. A helmeted black mask, similar to what was worn by medieval headsmen, covered his face from brow to chin. Around the mouth itself there was a grotesque bulge, which was more than the evidence of an outthrust jaw.

There was no doubt that this was the owner of the terrible voice which they had heard. Indeed, Ma Gilson stood there looking at him. In her own black garment, with her matted grey hair spread out like a ruffle around her neck, bent double, and with her skinny hands plucking at her throat, the old woman was an effective contrast to the statuesque immobility of the other.

At the coming of the light she began to laugh again.

"Ho, ho! They have found you. Well, then, kill or be killed. Let death loose. I never thought that I should live to see this night."

"Death," said the Unknown reflectively. "You smell death. You are right there, in that at least I have death here ready to my hand. Death for you, and death for these others at the head of the stairs."

The voice of Sexton Blake cut across his monologue.

"Put your hands up!"

The stranger did not move. Remained standing there perfectly still, utterly composed. His attitude expressed a conscious mastery of the situation.

A growl came from behind Sexton Blake, and, without moving his head, the detective gave Tinker orders.

"Hold the hound, Tinker, don't let him go down the stairs."

Splash Page started forward.

"Why not? I—"

Blake swung round the hand containing his pistol so as to bar the newspaperman's way.

"Not if you value your life!"

Page hesitated; but he did not like the restraint.

"Why not?" he said. "I've rushed a gun before now."

Blake said:

"He's got worse than a gun down there. Get back. Get out if you can. Find a telephone. Tell the police to come here."

"The police," said the stranger, "will be too late. You, Sexton Blake, you have discovered more than a man may discover and still live. It is you that I have come for. There are three who know the secret. Morgan Gilson is one. Dirk Dolland is another. You are the third."

"You are wrong there," replied the detective. "There are four. You have forgotten the parrot."

The Unknown bit off a laugh.

"The parrot!" he said, with a slight movement of his shoulders. "Who is going to take notice of a parrot after you three are dead? Stiletti will find the parrot; or, if he should fail, it will be

found by a stray cat, and that will be just as effectual.

"And now," said the Unknown, "I leave you, or rather"—he corrected himself, with a laugh—"you leave me."

His cloak opened, revealing in his hand a glass flask about the size of a cricket ball.

He swung it.

Bang!

BLAKE had fired when the Unknown was in the very act of hurling the glass sphere towards the head of the stairs. Tinker and Splash Page were astonished to see the flask explode into small pieces, while the tumblerful of colourless liquid which it contained splashed upon the floor.

Ma Gilson clutched her hands to her face and toppled forward.

The stranger made a rapid movement sideways.

Blake fired again; and this time he fired at the man.

The torch swept over the floor of the hall to the extreme of its range.

The place was now empty.

Splash Page made another movement to rush forward.

Blake caught him by the collar and jerked him backwards.

"You fool, Splash, haven't I told you that it is death?"

"Death! What do you mean!"

"Prussic acid gas, Didn't you see that he was wearing a gas-mask?"

"But the woman?" gasped Splash. "And Inspector Coutts?"

Blake said:

"Stay here!" He drew several deep breaths, and then went down the stairs at a run.

The hall was lighted by his torch. The insensible body of Inspector Coutts still lay spread-eagled upon the tiles. Ma Gilson had crumpled up and lay in a heap, looking more like a bundle of rags than a woman.

Splash Page and Tinker saw the detective bend and drag the inspector away beyond the range of their vision.

The lights went up. The detective had found the switch.

Then the detective appeared again, bending to drag Ma Gilson away in the same direction, out of range of the poisonous fumes left by the glass bomb.

"Holding his breath," said Splash. "What lungs the man must have!"

In something over a minute the detective was back beside them.

"I've dragged Coutts clear," he said. "I think he's living. The woman's dead. She was right, Splash, only too right. Death was abroad. It came to her."

"And that murderous brute in the black cloak—aren't you going to follow him?"

Blake shook his head.

"No, Splash, I want to live for a little longer. When you know as much about that individual in the black cloak as I do—which for the sake of your peace of mind I hope that you never will—you will realise that he lays his plans for defeat. That door will be covered by a machine-gun at this moment. I may as well tell you, Splash, in case you want to feature this affair on the front page—which very likely you do—that he is the master-criminal of fiction in real life. Probably insane: certainly abnormal. But with a brain, Splash. A calculating and logical brain. We have got to meet his subtlety by subtlety of our own. It's the only way."

Again descending the stairs, the detective threw open the front door of the house. Opened window after window. Then, very cautiously, he ventured upon a breath in the middle of the hall.

"Not so bad now," he said. "You can come down. Look after Coutts. Artificial respiration. Do something for the woman—if you think it possible to bring her back to life."

"O.K., chief!" said Splash.

Despite the tragedy which they had witnessed, he was again his alert self.

"For my part," Blake went on, "I have got another matter to attend to—the hand and the ring that we saw."

He referred, of course, to the hand which Pedro had brought into their view in a dumb appeal for the assistance of the beautiful girl whose body he had discovered.

Blake went back to the wall behind the fireplace. Bent, and passed through the aperture. The place there was empty. In front was the well which went downwards, with its steep, narrow steps descending out of sight.

Was it possible that Roxane, who must have been insensible at the moment when Pedro found her, could have recovered sufficiently far during the last; few minutes to descend the steps towards the depths of the subterranean river? It seemed impossible.

Blake leaned over the well, shone his torch down into the depths, and called the girl.

"Roxane! Roxane!"

His voice echoed from the brickwork which formed the shaft. There was no other reply.

HE returned to the interior of the house, and began to search there. Out of the room which concealed the entrance to the shaft there were other rooms opening one from the other.

Blake went through the hall. Roxane was not there. There was no trace that she had ever been there.

He lighted his pipe and stood in the middle of the floor just outside the shaft space, smoking and looking out of sightless eyes at the floor beneath his feet. He was so deep in thought that his senses—sight, hearing, and the rest of it—were temporarily unused. He had a vital problem to solve.

Roxane! How did she come into the thing? Was she for ever to evade his understanding? Furnishing no reply to his questions concerning her, save her own imperious and sufficient beauty? Was she with the masked dealer of death, or was she against him? Was she, for that matter, with or against Blake and the police? Where was Gilson? What had been the meaning of that telephone appeal? Had it been real or spurious? Merely a trap, perhaps, to decoy the detective and his companions to that place, so that they might meet death from that glass bomb which the Unknown had brought.

The detective called Pedro at length, and the bloodhound came pattering up the stairs to his feet.

Blake had taken the fragment of material from the fingers of Inspector Coutts, and now he gave it to the hound to sniff.

"Seek, Pedro!"

The bloodhound went back instantly to the cavity behind the fireplace. It was clear that the scent remained strong there.

Blake watched the animal with impatience.

"Well, go on! Seek!"

The bloodhound seemed to understand what was required of him, and began to cast about in the rooms which Blake himself had traversed.

Blake literally dragged the hound out on to the landing; but again he returned to those rooms, and from them to the head of the narrow steps.

"All right!" said Blake, with a shrug of the shoulders. "You've told me what I wanted to know. It is unexpected; but I've got to believe you."

He returned to the head of the stairs, and called out to ask news of Coutts and Ma Gilson. Tinker called back that Coutts was living, but still insensible.

"The woman," added the lad, "is undoubtedly dead."

Despite their efforts, he and Splash Page had failed to bring her back to life.

Blake nodded grimly as he listened.

"All right, my lad, that is what I expected. Inform the police what has happened, and get an ambulance here for the inspector. I expect to be back at Baker Street in an hour or so."

He returned to the cavity behind the fireplace, and began to descend. On the way down the spiral which formed the lower part of the secret staircase, he was looking very carefully for traces of Roxane, but there were none.

The stone-flagged passage at the bottom was also deserted.

He passed through the oak door at the end into the groined cavern, and searched both sides of the stream which ran there.

It was there, on the soft mud which had been deposited by the water, that he discovered the first proof that another had preceded him. He found many traces of the same feet coming and going. He knew whose they were—Gilson's. Search as he might, he could not find the imprint of that small shoe with its French heel which he knew so well.

Again he stood still in perplexity. Then, as a further question occurred to his mind, went over the footprints again, and this time he found what he wanted. Some of Gilson's footprints were deeper than others. There was one series which crossed the cavern and went down to the water's edge, which were deep without having any reason to be deep, unless Gilson had been carrying a burden.

The punt had disappeared. At the point where, as Blake knew, it was Gilson's custom to enter the vessel, the man's foot had slipped; and near to the spot there were two circular indentations which might have been made by the toes of a woman's shoe, as if part of her weight had been supported for a moment against the mud.

Blake shrugged his shoulders, and a grim smile flickered across his lips.

"I expect it's deuced cold!" he said to himself, and stepped into the water.

He was right about it being cold. Before he had reached the tunnel the dark water was swirling at the height of his waist, and his legs had already lost all feeling.

He went on grimly, enduring the discomforts following the subterranean stream, terribly alone in the bowels of the earth.

THE SPRING SONG.

"GILSON, I want to speak to you."

The man who had said these words was Sexton Blake. There was in his voice a hard quality which Morgan Gilson had never heard before.

Gilson swung round with a jerk.

"Certainly, Mr. Blake. Any time you like."

"The time I like," said Blake grimly, "is now."

He walked across the hall of Gilson's house in Petty France—that hall where, only an hour earlier, he had seen an old woman crumple up in death, and heard a black-cloaked man speak with the voice of doom—and pushed open a door.

"This room," he said, "will do as well as any other."

He waited until Gilson had entered; then closed the door carefully.

"Listen, Gilson. We came here to-day because we got an S O S over the telephone which appeared to come from you. You say that it did not come from you?"

Gilson was lighting a cigarette. He did not speak, but merely nodded his confirmation.

"We found," Blake continued, "Inspector Coutts in the hall, coshed, insensible. Later an individual appeared whom I believed to be Brank. He tried to asphyxiate Page, Tinker, and myself by means of a gas-bomb. I shot the bomb out of his hand, and the woman, who called herself Ma Gilson, died as the result of it. The Man of Doom survived, because he was wearing a filter pad across his mouth. Inspector Coutts escaped, because the poisonous gases set free from the bomb were inclined to ascend; and the fact that he was prone, enabled him to continue breathing pure air."

"Ma Gilson," said the other, "was nothing to me."

"I know," snapped Blake. "I have heard you tell the police that she was a woman who kept house for you; and that her real name was Symes. I don't care who she was, or what her name was."

"Anyway," said Gilson, "I'd be glad, Mr. Blake, if you would try not to look at me as you are looking now. I've faced desperadoes and killers all over the world; but the look in your eyes—"

There was reason for his plea. Blake's face was white. His eyes were flashing steel-grey. The muscles of his face were hard; his mouth relentless. He looked a man in whom tremendous passions had been aroused; but one who could control them to perfection by the supreme effort of an iron will.

He took no notice of Gilson's words.

"Upstairs," he said, "before the arrival of the man in black, we had seen the hand of Roxane. Pedro had found her. She was lying in the secret doorway behind the electric stove. When the trouble was over, I went back to find her. She had disappeared. The movements of Pedro led me to believe that, impossible as it seemed, Mademoiselle Roxane had descended the stone steps which led to the underground river. I followed. I found imprints of your feet. You had been carrying a weight. I found what I took to be traces left by Roxane herself. I waded through the underground stream and came up the iron ladder into the dummy house. As there was still no trace, either of you or of Roxane herself, I came back here.

"I find, as I expected, that the house is in the possession of the police, and that you are here, offering an account of your movements within the last hour or so, which does not include any reference to the waterway."

Blake walked over to the window, then back again to face Gilson. He was cramming tobacco into his briar pipe.

"Now," he went on, "you lied to the police, but you're not going to lie to me. Was it you who carried Mademoiselle Roxane down the stone steps and took her away in a boat? Oblige me by an answer to that question."

Gilson forced himself to look Blake in the eyes.

"It was not I," he said slowly.

"You know nothing of Mademoiselle Roxane?"

"I haven't seen her since this morning!"

"You don't know where she is now?"

"No."

"You lie, Gilson!"

GILSON held out his two hands as if to ward off a blow.

"Blake," he said desperately, "Blake, I swear to you—"

"You swear what?"

"That I told the police the truth."

Blake stepped forward. His fists were clenched, and every muscle in his body seemed to be rigid.

Gilson shrank back.

"No, wait! I didn't tell them the truth. I told them that I had been to the Blue Café off St. Martin's Lane. I told them that because I knew the people there would alibi me. I warned them that I might need it."

Blake spoke between his clenched teeth.

"Where have you been, Gilson? You had better speak the truth this time, because—"

"Mr. Blake, you've been a good friend to me. I'm playing the game by you. I'm also playing a game of my own; but it isn't against you, or likely to be."

"Where had you been?"

"I'd been to Hamright's."

"Hamright's. And what had you been there for?"

Gilson looked stubborn.

"I've told you that I'm playing a game of my own."

"Just for once," Blake ground out, "you're going to let me in on it!"

"Who says I'm going to?"

Blake took one more pace forward. He was now within easy hitting distance of Gilson. He looked like hitting, too, and looked as if his uppercut would not be a nice thing to stop.

Gilson stared into Blake's face with fascination, not daring to move, as if any attempt at avoiding the detective might precipitate action.

"I went there," he said, dragging the words out one by one, "to find a—gramophone record."

"And you found it?"

Gilson slipped his left hand beneath his coat and brought out a black ten-inch record broken in three pieces.

Blake took it out of his hands with an exclamation of satisfaction.

"I want this!" he said.

"But, blow it, Blake, it's my property."

"I want it, Gilson. I want every weapon that I can get against Brank, the Man of Doom; and this may be a weapon which puts paid in full to his account."

Gilson jerked his head up as if he were astonished.

"Exactly how much do you know?"

"I should like to ask you the same question," said Blake. "As neither of us would answer it, it is fruitless."

He put the broken pieces of the record upon a table in the room, and from his pocket-book took a roll of surgical tape, using it to join the record together again, by strapping the tape round the circumference of the record.

"Have you got a gramophone?" he said.

Gilson went out of the room, and Blake followed him. A police-constable in uniform who was standing in the hall, watched them cross the floor.

Inside the room which Gilson now entered was a cabinet electrical gramophone, one of the few luxuries which the house contained.

They placed the assembled record upon the turntable and started the instrument. The needle tripped over the cracks with a succession of clicks; then a violinist began to play one of Chopin's nocturnes.

The constant clicking of the needle over the gaping joins robbed the transmission of any beauty which it might have had; but Blake and his companion each listened attentively until the thing was finished.

The policeman in the hall outside was shrugging his shoulders in contempt for people who could start a gramophone in a place where an old woman was lying dead.

Blake reversed the record, and the first notes of Mendelssohn's Spring Song became audible.

Again Blake waited until the end; then, to Gilson's surprise, played about half of the record over again.

TINKER and Splash Page had entered the room, and were listening with astonishment.

Blake carried the record carefully to the window and inspected it by means of a watchmaker's monocle which he took from his pocket.

"So," he said at length, "this was the record which had been played in the place where Hamright was killed, and because of which a dozen parrots also met their deaths."

Gilson was looking at the detective with a strange expression.

"You know the meaning of the mystery?"

Blake swung round on him.

"Yes; do you?"

"I am not sure."

"I remember," said Tinker, "that when we asked you whether the instrument had been used to try to teach the birds to talk, you said: 'No; the reverse.'"

Sexton Blake's face did not relax into a smile.

"I was not altogether right there," he admitted. "It hadn't been used to teach a bird to talk; but had been used to induce a bird to talk."

He turned to Gilson.

"You understand what I mean, don't you?"

Gilson nodded.

"Yes, Mr. Blake."

"And," Blake went on, "I don't think that I am making Gilson a present of information when I tell him, and you, that the part which had been so used was the first twenty bars, or thereabouts. All the rest of this record is utterly new, so far as its capacity for producing is concerned. The first twenty bars of the Spring Song are worn by repeated playing. I was aware of that aurally when I tried it over, and visually when I examined it just now by means of the glass."

"There's some bird," guessed Tinker, "which is known to respond to that music."

"Gilson," said Blake, "will tell you if your guess is correct."

The man indicated jerked to his feet.

"Gilson will tell you nothing!" he snapped.

"That," said Blake, "is an answer in the affirmative, and the bird in question is the parrot Anastasia."

Splash Page had been silent for what was, for him, an unusually long time.

"But what is there that a bird could be taught to say which would be so important?"

"We will take the gramophone record," said Blake, "to Hamright's shop, and try it over there.

Where the killer of Hamright failed, we may by chance succeed."

The four of them packed themselves into Page's vermilion roadster and returned to the shop in Charing Cross Road. On the way, Blake stopped at a music-shop and bought a duplicate of the damaged record, marking it with chalk at a certain point which he ascertained by examining the broken one through his lens.

Hamright's shop was closed, and appeared to be deserted. Blake knocked again and again, but there was no reply.

"That's a pity," said Gilson. "We can't get in."

Blake smiled very grimly.

"Yes, we can. You shall open the door yourself."

Gilson said: "How?" and tried to look surprised.

Blake stared him in the face for a long moment.

"You've been here before, you know."

Gilson shrugged his shoulders and forced a laugh; then he took a key from his waistcoat pocket and opened the door.

All of them went in. The blinds had been drawn, and in the darkened shop most of the livestock were silent.

Blake moved to the inner compartment where the dead Hamright had been found, started the portable gramophone, and placed the needle upon the beginning of the Spring Song.

Only a few notes had been played when from above their heads came a deep, throaty, voice, uttering a jumble of apparently meaningless words as a sort of accompaniment to the music.

All of them looked up. A large grey parrot was perched upon the electric light fitting in the middle of the ceiling, swinging by the cord which held it, looking down towards them with its neck twisted in an unnatural fashion.

"We have found," said Blake, with triumph, "what Brank and a lot of other people have been seeking for days past and weeks past—the parrot Anastasia. We will play the Spring Song again."

He moved the needle back to the beginning of the record.

Again the sugary melody filled the air and again the parrot began to gabble that string of meaningless words.

Before it had half finished, the report of a pistol rang out with deafening loudness.

The parrot fell to the floor an inanimate bunch of feathers.

The Spring Song went on.

THE NEXT MOVE

PREVIOUS MOVES IN THE NEXT MOVE.

INSTALMENT 1 (BY G. H. TEED),
IN HIS HOUSE IN PETTY FRANCE,
WESTMINSTER, MORGAN GILSON TRAPS
AN INTRUDER IN THE EARLY HOURS OF
THE MORNING, AND CARRIES THE MAN TO
A CELLAR ALONGSIDE AN UNDERGROUND
STREAM, WHICH, WITH AN INTRICATE
TUNNEL SYSTEM, RUNS BENEATH THE
HOUSE. HE THEN SEEKS THE AID OF SEXTON
BLAKE.
GILSON AND THE DETECTIVE ARE LATER
SURPRISED, FIRST, BY THE DISAPPEARANCE
OF THE PRISONER, SECONDLY BY FINDING IN
THE PETTY FRANCE HOUSE, MLLE. ROXANE.
BEFORE THEY CAN QUESTION HER, CROOKS
OPEN FIRE ON THEM FROM ONE OF THE
ROOMS.

INSTALMENT 2 (BY GWYN EVANS).
BLAKE IS WOUNDED. THE CROOKS GET AWAY.
ROXANE, WHO SEEMS TO BE WORKING SOLO,
DISAPPEARS. GILSON'S CHIEF CONCERN IS
BECAUSE A PARROT, ANASTASIA, HAS BEEN
STOLEN.
THE RECEIPT OF A DEAD PARROT BRINGS

SPLASH PAGE INTO THE MYSTERY, AND HE CALLS ON BLAKE, FINDING HIM IN SESSION WITH GILSON, WHOM SPLASH RECOGNISES TO BE AN ESCAPED CONVICT FROM DEVIL'S ISLAND.

INSTALMENT 3 (BY ROBERT MURRAY). DIRK DOLLAND IS STAYING AT BLAKE'S PLACE TO ESCAPE THE MURDEROUS ATTENTIONS OF A MR. BRANK, THE SAME MYSTERIOUS INDIVIDUAL WHO IS MENACING GILSON.

STUTZ, GILSON'S ESCAPED PRISONER, IS DELIVERED IN A COFFIN, DEAD. A GRIM WARNING FROM BRANK. THAT IS STUTZ'S PUNISHMENT FOR BLUNDERING.

SUSPECTING THAT GILSON IS CONCEALING SOMETHING, BLAKE, SPLASH, AND TINKER FOLLOW HIM TO HAMRIGHT'S, A LIVESTOCK SHOP. THEY MISS GILSON, BUT FIND HAMRIGHT DEAD. BESIDE HIM IS A RECORDLESS GRAMOPHONE, STILL RUNNING. ON THE WALL IS THE IMPRINT OF A HAND WITH A THUMB AND FIVE FINGERS.

ANOTHER ALARM TAKES THEM BACK TO GILSON'S HOUSE. COUTTS IS UNCONSCIOUS IN THE HALL. THROUGH A SECRET PANEL THEY GET A GLIMPSE OF A DISAPPEARING FIGURE WHICH SEEMS TO BE ROXANE. A SHRIEK OF FEAR SENDS BLAKE AND CO. BACK TO THE STAIRHEAD.

INSTALMENT 4 (BY ANTHONY SKENE). IN THE HALL BELOW IS BRANK, THE DOOMSMAN, AND MA SYMES, GILSON'S HOUSEKEEPER. BRANK IS ABOUT TO THROW A GLASS BOMB. BLAKE FIRES; THE FLASK CRASHES, RELEASING POISONOUS GAS. BRANK GETS AWAY. THE GAS KILLS MA SYMES, BUT BLAKE SAVES COUTTS.

BLAKE TAKES GILSON TO TASK, GETS FROM HIM A BROKEN GRAMOPHONE RECORD WHICH GILSON TOOK FROM HAMRIGHT'S. IT IS THE "SPRING SONG." THE FIRST BARS ARE WORN AND SCRATCHED. BLAKE BELIEVES THAT A BIRD, PROBABLY ANASTASIA, HAS BEEN TRAINED TO SPEAK AT THE SOUND OF THE MUSIC.

THEY GO BACK TO HAMRIGHT'S TO TRY THE RECORD. A PARROT STARTS TO GABBLE MEANINGLESS WORDS. THEN A SHOT RINGS OUT. THE BIRD FALLS DEAD.

G. H. TEED STARTS ROUND 2.

"CARVED NICELY."

SEXTON BLAKE was the first to whirl round and see the head and shoulders of the man who stood on the other side of an open panel. Beyond him could be seen the brick wall and cages in the back-yard.

Through the aperture an arm had been thrust, and in the fingers was grasped the automatic pistol that had sped the parrot's life.

So suddenly did the whole thing occur that, for a moment, Blake, as well as Splash Page and Tinker, was held frozen in his tracks. Then Blake and his assistant went for their guns. Page dived towards the desk and grabbed a heavy inkstand.

Bang! Bang! Bang!

Three shots rang out as one. Blake felt the concussion against his eardrum and heard the unmistakable "crack!" that means a closely-passing bullet. A minor crash, followed by a sharp curse, came as an echo. The bullet that had just missed Blake smashed Page's glass inkstand to smithereens, ricochetted, and sent Gilson reeling against the wall. He staggered away out of range, groaning.

Bang-bang!

Blake and Tinker fired again, almost together. Their bullets only passed through empty air and into one of the cages. The man in the aperture was gone.

Blake dived for the door.

"Come on! Quick! Stiletti!"

He plunged through the door into the shop, wheeled and skidded through the other door that led to the back-yard. Tinker and Splash Page were close on his heels.

All three collided to a stop on the brick-paved court, gazing at each other in stupid amazement. The place was absolutely empty of any human being.

On each side was a high wall, unrelieved by any window. Against these were the tiers of cases and cages where the defunct Hamright had kept his collection of smaller birds, small mammals, and snakes.

At the end was another high wall, with a blank face except for a tiny window high up. They could see it was begrimed with the dirt of years, and utterly inaccessible to anyone unless provided with a long ladder. Even if Stiletti had had a ladder ready in position he could not have gone up it more than a dozen rungs before the three reached the yard.

Behind them was the shop into which they knew Stiletti had not gone. But Stiletti was gone—vanished into thin air.

Blake doubtfully started forward, not knowing quite what to do next. Behind him, in the shop, shrill screaming broke out.

"Whee, whee, whee! Mr. Brank! Turn the water off, Mr Brank! Whee-eh!"

Splash Page jumped forward and grasped Blake's arm. His usually jovial face was angry and flushed.

"That devilish macaw, Blake! The same words! I'm going to fix it once and for all. The cursed thing!"

Before Blake could stop him he was racing towards the shop.

THE macaw was chained to a tall, wooden stand near the front door. It stopped screaming after that solitary outburst, and so dim was the interior to Page's eyes that he could not see the watchfulness of the macaw's wicked little beady eyes as, with head cocked on one side, it watched his approach.

Filled with anger at the recollection of how the bird had ruined his new hat on a previous visit, and nerves on edge from its screaming after the amazing swiftness of Stiletti's attack and disappearance, the newspaperman was deaf to Blake's shouts to stop. Straight at the bird he sprang, catching the shaft of the wooden stand in one hand, while he sought to reach the creature's neck with the other.

So impetuous was Splash, and so determined to finish off the bird, that he was altogether forgetful of its own powers; he was heedless of that amazing hard and thick scimitar-like beak, that could cut through the iron-like pith of an alligator pear as easily as a knife slices cheese.

At that moment when the newspaper-man's fingers were about to slide through the glossy neck feathers, the bird turned into a miniature cyclone. Screaming, flapping its powerful wings, with one incredibly swift squirm, it made a savage gash at the man's throat.

Page flung himself aside just in time. The violence of his action dragged both wooden stand and bird with him. Together they went to the floor. Like some unreal nightmare fury the bird flapped madly upon Splash Page's chest, screaming, striving again and again to get that terrible curved beak into his eyes or throat.

At this moment Blake and Tinker were rushing along the shop. With one arm across his throat and the other fighting off the macaw, Splash could only utter smothered cries for help. Blake and Tinker had their guns in their hands, but neither dared shoot. As they came along the shop Blake snatched up a small sack with the intention of throwing it over the blur of vivid colour and shrill sound that represented the fighting macaw.

But for the second time the bird outwitted them. Whether it knew that at the first crash the slim chain which secured it to the perch had been broken close to the leg-band, one cannot say. But, as Blake leaped forward, swinging the sacking as a matador would wield his cloak, the macaw uttered one last harsh scream, and, rising on wide, flapping pinions, soared above their heads.

It dipped swiftly towards the oblong of light that showed where the door gave into the backyard, was revealed in the full light there in all its flashing wonderful colour for a photographic instant, and then shot upwards and disappeared. Tinker, who had raced after it at top speed, pistol ready to take a pot shot, reached the door just in time to see it vanish over the roof of the tall building that backed on the yard.

Inside the shop Blake was assisting Splash Page to his feet. Page's right hand was bleeding in a dozen places where the macaw had savaged him deeply with his beak. For once in his life his jaunty manner had deserted him. His eyes were almost comically tragic as he watched Blake using his handkerchief to stem the flow of blood.

"What the devil is that thing, anyway?" he asked shakily.

"There are several varieties of macaw, Splash," said Blake conversationally, "and that particular breed of the genus Ara is about the most vicious of the lot. Still, you don't want a radio talk about it. If you had listened to my warning this wouldn't have happened."

"That's all right, old cockalorum, but I've had it in for that devil ever since it nabbed my hat."

"I know. But it would have been better to stalk it with more care. I have an idea it might be worth while to know where it learned to use Brank's name, and what it meant by telling him to turn off the water."

Splash looked contrite.

"I'm dashed sorry, Blake. You are dead right. I made a bloomer there. But who could have imagined the chain would break?"

"I'm thinking it was a good thing, for you it did," was Blake's response.

"Where do you think the devil has gone, guv'nor?" put in Tinker.

"Possibly put to its friends, the other macaws, in the Zoo, or possibly to find Brank, young 'un."

"Do you think it knew what Anastasia is supposed to have learned, guv'nor?"

Blake glanced at the lad shrewdly.

"What if that macaw was Anastasia?" he countered.

"But Anastasia is a grey parrot, Blake," protested Splash.

Blake finished tying his handkerchief about the other's hand.

"Well, I've always thought so," he confessed, "but I'm hanged if I am prepared to say now whether that macaw that has just got away is or isn't the bird we really needed to find. Anastasia may have been only a blind. And one thing is certain—it has certainly been under Brank's influence at some time or other."

Sexton Blake lifted his head with a jerk.

"Gilson—where's Gilson?" Both Tinker and Splash Page looked blank.

"Why, the poor devil—that bullet of Stiletti's got him," exclaimed Page. "I was so mad at that macaw, I'd forgotten all about him."

"Go and see, young 'un," ordered Blake swiftly. "I'll finish this in a moment; then we'll see to him."

But before Blake had quite finished tying the knot, Tinker was running back from the private room.

"He's gone, guv'nor! He's gone!"

Blake stared at him incredulously.

"Gone? Impossible! Wasn't he wounded?"

"Well, he's not there."

Blake went into the private room to make doubly sure. He examined the back-yard for the second time. Then he came thoughtfully along the shop.

"He could have managed it at only one moment," he was muttering, half to himself and half to the other two, "when we were in the back-yard, looking for Stiletti. But why? What did he clear out for?"

BLAKE, Tinker, and Splash Page arrived back at Baker Street to find Detective-Inspector Thomas, of Scotland Yard, sitting in one of the comfortable consulting-room saddlebag chairs, enjoying one of Blake's partagas cigars.

Thomas, like his official colleague, Coutts, was of a heavily built type, and possessed almost the same shade of florid complexion. His eyes, too, were of a bluish tint, but his moustache lacked the bristly aggressiveness of Coutts'. Also, he wore a soft felt hat, as a rule, and not a hard bowler, and, unlike Coutts again, had remembered to remove it, which his "half-section," as he called him, sometimes did not.

"Been waiting here for half an hour!" he grumbled, ignoring Blake's sardonic glance in the direction of the cigar. "Coutts is in Westminster Hospital. I'm carrying on. He told me something of this crazy business. I've come to hear the rest from you."

"Yes?" was Blake's pleasant response. "Well, I'm sorry about Coutts, but he can't say he wasn't warned. I'm afraid that I can't be of much assistance to you, Thomas. What do you want to know, anyway?"

"All you can tell me about this follow Gilson."

"That wouldn't be much."

"Well, cough it up. I'll hear it, anyway."

"I think not."

Thomas removed the cigar from between his teeth and stared at Blake with marble-like blue eyes.

"Wha'd'ya mean?"

"I spoke distinctly."

"But, hang it all, Blake, we are interested in this fellow Gilson at the Yard. He's up to some hanky-panky, and you know what it is. It's your duty."

"You wait a moment, Thomas. I told Coutts a few things in confidence. If he chose to make use of them and risk being shot, he was at liberty to do so. But he had no authority to repeat my confidences to you or anyone else at the Yard. So that's that!"

Thomas leaned forward, his pugnacious jaw thrust out.

"So that's that, is it?" he mimicked, in heavy sarcasm. "Maybe you'll tell me who plugged you in the shoulder?"

"Maybe I will. But actually, I won't."

"Well, if you won't tell me anything I'll tell you something. I'll tell you who laid out Coutts. It was your protege, Gilson. And I'll tell you another thing that Coutts didn't spill. Maybe you know something about a bit of green rag he had in his hand. That came from a dress worn by your friend, Mademoiselle Harfield. She was in the house. Coutts would have got her, at any rate, if Gilson hadn't caught him from behind. So what have you to say to that?"

"Nothing, except that Mademoiselle Roxane seems to have given you the slip."

"Maybe you won't be so cocky when we have her in the dock beside Gilson."

"Just what have you against Gilson, Thomas?" asked Blake quietly.

"Coutts came here and babbled a lot of hot air, but didn't get down to cases. What is it?"

"You come through with all you know, and maybe I'll talk."

"Then you'll stay dumb, my friend."

Thomas was about to make some heated reply, which might have led to a first-class quarrel between friends. But a sudden interruption came from Tinker. While the talk had been going on, and while Splash Page had been leaning against the mantelpiece enjoying the whole business hugely and wondering how he could fit this little breeze into his next front-page news story, Tinker had made a quiet exit from the consulting-room.

He was somewhat concerned with a fact which did not seem to be worrying either Blake or Splash Page; when they had left the house to go to Gilson's place in Petty France in response to that imperative phone call which led them to believe that Gilson was in difficulties, the body of the man Stutz had been left in the sitting-room. As that was not a place which, in Tinker's opinion, was most suitable for it, his intention was to move it to the laboratory until Blake could make the necessary arrangements about notifying the appropriate officials.

Now he burst open the door of the consulting-room and excitedly confronted the group.

"Guv'nor," he exclaimed, "the body—that man Stutz—it's gone! I've searched all the other rooms; it's not in any of them."

"Gone?" echoed Blake and Splash together.

Inspector Thomas stared blankly.

"Then who—" began Blake. But the shrill insistence of the telephone bell, ringing more loudly and longer than usual, it seemed, cut short his question.

Frowning with annoyance, Blake crossed to the instrument and lifted the receiver.

"Hallo!" he snapped. "Who are you?"

"Superintendent Ray of W Division. I've been through to Scotland Yard, and they told me I'd probably find Inspector Thomas at your house. Is he there?"

"Yes; I'll call him."

Blake motioned to Thomas, and passed over the receiver. He was filling his pipe while, the inspector talked, but as Thomas slammed the receiver on the hook and flung round he paused in the operation.

"What will you have to say now?" he heard Thomas roaring.

"Well, what is it?" Blake's voice was as cool as green ice.

"Dolland—Dirk Dolland! Wasn't he lying low here with you?"

"If Coutts told you that it must be so. What about it?"

"A coffin has been found in an old warehouse not a hundred yards from the police station in W Division. The lid was screwed down, and the body of your friend Dolland was inside. And on the lid was Dolland's name, all carved nicely."

BLAKE leaped forward and grasped the inspector's arm.

"Dolland—in the coffin—was he found dead?"

"Well, if he isn't a stiff now I'll eat my hat!"

Splash Page had come away from the mantelpiece as if an invisible foot had propelled him. His lacerated hand was entirely forgotten. His amusement at the altercation between Blake and Thomas had vanished in the presence of this fresh and more sensational news-item that had come his way. The scent of a front-page story dominated everything else. And he was thinking swiftly:

"Coffin—why, that must be the same coffin in which Stutz was sent here."

He pushed in between Blake and the inspector.

"Let's go, Blake!" he said eagerly. "That's why those guys took the coffin a—"

A sudden and painful kick on the ankle caused him to break off so suddenly as to bite his tongue. Thomas was staring from him to Blake suspiciously.

"So-o!" he said slowly. "What's this about a coffin?"

"Just what you've been telling us," responded Page urbanely.

"I'd like to know why you are butting in on this, and just what you meant," went on the inspector stubbornly. "You meant something. You'd better come across, Blake! Dolland didn't kill himself, so that means someone bumped him off—and perhaps your pal Gilson can tell us something about that!"

No one answered him. The phone message of the finding of Dolland's body had completely bewildered and upset them. Tinker, more emotional than Blake and Page, turned away towards the window to master the feelings that the news had evoked in him. Suddenly he stiffened. A taxi had swerved into the pavement and stopped just outside Blake's house, and from it alighted none other than—Dirk Dolland!

The Bat glanced up and caught Tinker's face, staring wide-eyed down at him. Dirk grinned broadly up at him, then gave a prodigious wink. Still baffled as to how Dolland could turn up after the news of the finding of his body in the coffin, Tinker realised, though, that Dirk would not want to see Inspector Thomas. He grimaced down at Dolland, and, with his back turned to the others in the room, gestured to him to go away. The Bat understood. Tinker saw him hurry along Baker Street and disappear round a corner.

"Well," cut in Thomas' voice again, "you won't speak, any of you, eh? All right—that's your funeral, but don't say you didn't get official warning!"

He jammed on his hat, and with a curt "Good-morning!" stamped down the stairs.

Tinker waited for the front door to slam; then he turned round to the others.

"Dirk's not dead! I've just seen him! I don't know what his game is—but he's alive!"

AN individual whose blue serge suit was almost entirely hidden by a long raglan waterproof coat, and whose face was partially concealed by the low-drawn brim of a soft grey hat, walked up the steps of Madame Casanova's private dressmaking establishment in Petty France and rang the bell.

The door was opened with remarkable promptitude by a tall, very striking-looking woman whose dark eyes flashed at the sight of the visitor.

"I was afraid," she said in Italian. "Come in—quickly!"

The visitor smiled and entered.

"You should not have worried, signora."

The voice was somewhat husky and treble for one of such masculine apparel and bearing, and as soon as the door was closed the Italian woman's actions would have seemed decidedly affectionate, for she grasped the visitor by the shoulder and stared anxiously.

"Oh, my dear, you are safe—you are all right?"

The other laughed a tinkling laugh and threw the hat aside.

"Perfectly! And here is the dress. It must be attended to at once."

All this time the caller had been holding a cardboard box under one arm, a long, flattish affair such as frocks are packed in. The Italian woman shuddered as she gazed at it, but at once drew the other into a small room off the hall. It had been fitted up as a reception-room for clients, and on the rather ornate buhl table in the centre Madame Casanova's visitor laid the box. Then hat and coat were removed, revealing the charming features and lithe figure of Mademoiselle Roxane.

"I was so distraught, mademoiselle," went on the older woman. "There was a young man here with the body of the monkey. I told him anything to get rid of him. And your maid, Anna, who went into the other house to make a search. Gilson brought her back through the tunnel. It was your green dress. That's what misled him—luckily for Anna. But you—where have you been?"

"To the shop of a livestock dealer in Tottenham Court Road."

"But—why?"

"I'll show you."

Turning to the table, Roxane quickly untied the cord that secured the box, and, lifting the cover, disclosed at first only a padded layer of tissue paper. But when that was removed there lay revealed the dead body of a large grey parrot.

The Italian woman uttered a gasp of incredulity.

"Anastasia!"

Roxane pursed her lips.

"I'm not absolutely certain. But if it isn't Anastasia, then it is a parrot that learned the secret that was confided to Anastasia."

"How do you know? Oh, tell me what happened!"

Roxane lit a cigarette.

"It will only take a few moments, and there is no hurry about the bird."

What this meant was obscure to the other, but before she could ask further questions Roxane went on:

"As soon as I got away from Gilson's house, while the others were fighting upstairs, I knew that I must make for Hamright's as quickly as possible. Everything was in a state of confusion at Gilson's. There was that old Ma Symes to complicate matters."

Madame Casanova held up a bejewelled hand.

"That woman is dead."

"Dead? Good heavens, signora! What do you mean?"

"When Gilson brought Anna back he told me. There was a raid. First that man Coutts, from Scotland Yard, forced his way into the house, and that is why Anna had no time to discover anything. He caught sight of Anna just as she was coming along the hall. He caught hold of her, but she tore herself free, leaving a strip of her frock in his hand."

"I'm sorry about her," interposed Roxane quickly. "It was my frock—one I gave her. Sexton Blake knows that frock. He will suspect."

"Well, Gilson came in just as Anna flew up the stairs. He had a fight with Coutts and struck him unconscious. Then others came—Sexton Blake, that newspaper fellow, Splash Page, and, of course, the lad Tinker, and the bloodhound. Another man, too."

Roxane smiled fleetingly.

"I wonder where he thinks I am, and what he suspects I am doing in this affair," she murmured dreamily. Then, incisively:

"But go on, signora. What about Ma Symes?"

"It happened after. As you know, Anna was hidden in the secret hole behind the fireplace, trying to overhear anything that might be said by the police or anyone else that came in. The dog found her, in fact, and caught her by the hand.

"You didn't expect that, or that Sexton Blake would be on the scene. Therefore, the disguise of your frock and the wearing of your ring didn't help a bit. Indeed, the dog caught her hand so hard that the ring cut her finger. But it served better than might have been expected, for she is sure that Sexton Blake thought it was you. He said something. Then, before the dog actually dragged her out, the lights vanished and it was called off."

"I'll wager he did that to give me a chance," muttered Roxane.

"I don't know. It seems that something was happening in the lower hall, and Gilson says it was—"

She paused and passed the tip of her tongue across her shapely lips.

"Yes, yes," snapped Roxane impatiently.

"Brank!"

"So he was there—faced them like that!" Roxane muttered, "He's got his nerve with him. What happened?"

"He and Ma Symes were in the lower hall where Coutts was lying unconscious on the floor. The others were at the top of the stairs. He threatened them with a gas bomb of some kind. Gilson says that Sexton Blake shot the bomb out of his hand, and that the gas spread, killing Ma Symes, and that he escaped."

"He would. Was—was Mr. Blake all right?"

"Yes."

"Where is Gilson?"

"He went away with Mr. Blake. There are police in the house now."

"I suppose that is why I saw a constable loitering outside. This is beginning to look complicated. I'll have to decide something quick. But now let us attend to this bird."

"But—it is dead."

"I hope not. I only doped it lightly."

"But how did you get it?"

"I told you—at Hamright's. I got the old man in his private room, and managed to gas him in his chair. Then I found a portable gramophone with a record on it. I told you old Hamright had been seeking the secret for a long time. I started the machine going, and, almost at once, several parrots flew in and perched about the room.

"The record was playing Mendelssohn's 'Spring Song,' and at a certain bar near the beginning one of the parrots began to speak, I couldn't hear distinctly, but I am certain it uttered one of the words of the phrase that holds the key—'Sorry, miss; wrong number.' You remember. Well, I am positive I caught the word 'number.' Then I gave it a shot of dope and put it into this box.

"I took the record off the machine and started to make my getaway, when someone burst in through the front door. I'm not certain, but I think it was Stiletti. I fled, but in doing so dropped the record and it broke. However, that doesn't matter very much, because I know the song that was used to prime the bird, and as it is a popular record it will be easy enough to get a duplicate.

"Now I'm going to resuscitate Polly, and then we'll get one of those records. But I'm worried about Brank. He's getting too close for my peace of mind. And Stiletti?"

"Stiletti has tried to kill Anastasia. He got me. Nearly got Sexton Blake. Stutz is dead. And Dirk Dolland is running with Sexton Blake—Dolland, whom I knew on Devil's Island and who knew me as Robinson Crusoe."

The words were spoken in slow, heavy tones that did not come from Madame Casanova. They were uttered by Morgan Gilson. He stood in the door, his soaking trousers oozing water on to the pile of the delicately shaded carpet.

Even as they watched he staggered forward, recovered himself, then lurched again wildly, and fell prone with a crash.

Roxane rushed forward and knelt beside him. She got his head on her arm and tried to lift him. But as she heard mumbled words coming from between his white lips, she remained, motionless, listening.

"Stiletti—Anastasia—the macaw—just as I came way—Brank—Turn off— water."

"Came away—from where, from where?" urged Roxane desperately.

But Gilson had collapsed like a dead man.

Now what has Gwyn Evans got to say? This is his second round also, and if he's as resourceful in that as he was in the first, it's going to be a good

instalment. And, between ourselves, it certainly is! You'll see that the riot of plot and counterplot hitherto is going to be straightened out in a very ingenious way next Thursday—our Christmas Number, and a Gwyn Evans number at that.

Continuing:

The Next Move

Our Fascinating, Novel, Four-Author Serial.
G. H. TEED. Gwyn EVANS. Robert MURRAY. Anthony SKENE.

Foreword

EACH of the four authors above contributes an instalment of this unique serial in turn, setting puzzles for the others to solve. None of them knows what will be the Next Man's Move!

Famous "U.J." characters in the story are Sexton Blake, Tinker, Coutts, Splash Page, Dirk Dolland, and Mlle. Roxane.

The story opened with a night raid on the house of Morgan Gilson in Petty France, Westminster. Back of that raid was a mysterious criminal known as Mr. Brank. He and his agents were after the combination of a hidden safe. The secret of the combination had been learned by six talking parrots, one of which, named Anastasia, knew the whole formula. On the night of the raid, Anastasia disappeared.

Immediately after the raid, Gilson sought the aid of Sexton Blake. Blake knew that Gilson was an escaped convict from Devil's Island, but allied himself with Gilson against Brank.

Blake's interest in the case was increased by learning that Mlle. Roxane was mixed up in it; also by knowing that Dirk Dolland had been

MENACED BY MR. BRANK.
FOLLOWING GILSON, WHOM HE BELIEVED
STILL TO BE KEEPING SOMETHING FROM
HIM, BLAKE WENT TO HAMRIGHT'S, A
LIVESTOCK SHOP. GILSON DODGED HIM,
BUT IN THE SHOP LAY OLD HAMRIGHT,
MURDERED. BY HIM WAS A GRAMOPHONE,
RUNNING. ON THE WALL WAS THE IMPRINT
OF A FIVE-FINGERED HAND.
ROXANE HAD SECURED ANASTASIA. IN
THE HOUSE OF HER FRIEND, MADAME
CASANOVA, SHE WAS ABOUT TO TEST THE
BIRD WITH A RECORD OF THE "SPRING
SONG," THE PIECE WHICH HAD BEEN USED
TO INDUCE THE PARROTS TO TALK, WHEN
GILSON STAGGERED IN, EXHAUSTED WITH
HIS JOURNEY THROUGH THE UNDERGROUND
STREAM AND TUNNELS THAT CONNECTED
HIS PLACE IN PETTY FRANCE WITH A
"DUMMY" HOUSE WHICH OFFERED A SECRET
ENTRANCE AND EXIT, SOME DISTANCE AWAY.
GWYN EVANS NOW CARRIES ON.

INQUEST

"I THINK," said Sexton Blake, slowly filling his briar pipe and gazing round at the occupants of Madame Casanova's flat, "I think the time has come for an inquest."

An hour had elapsed since Blake had sent the irate Inspector Thomas fuming back to Scotland Yard with what Tinker inelegantly termed "a flea in his ear." There were now five men in Madame Casanova's boudoir—Blake, Dolland, Slash Page, and Tinker, who had come in response to an urgent telephone call from Roxane.

Gilson lay, a wan, white-faced figure, on the divan in the corner. He had recovered consciousness, and his sunken eyes were unnaturally bright.

Blake had taken his stand at the mantelpiece, and now surveyed the oddly assorted little group with something of the impartial but judicial air of a magistrate.

He turned to Dirk Dolland.

"Now, Dirk," he said quietly, "I think it's about time you put your cards on the table. Exactly what happened when we left for Hamright's?"

The Bat shrugged his shoulders.

"Blake, you know the reason I've been lying low at Baker Street for the past few days. Brank

is clever and cunning, but I am certain he is a maniac. That idea of sending the coffin with my name inscribed on it, is simply an example of his colossal vanity. He knew that in the old days I was what Splash Page and his newshound pals of Fleet Street would call a master crook."

He grinned across at the newspaper-man.

Splash Page chuckled.

"Go on, Bat, rub it in! But let's have the low-down on this business, otherwise I believe I shall go crackers."

"I should say," Dolland continued, lighting a cigarette, "that Brank is probably suffering from the Al Capone complex, and possibly thought that an inscribed casket would meet the case; hence coffin."

"Yes, that's all very well," cut in Sexton Blake. "But what happened to Stutz? My consulting-room is not, strictly speaking, a private mortuary, and I'm glad for that reason that his body has vanished. But it's rather disturbing, all the same."

"That is exactly what I thought," drawled the Bat. "It looked to me rather untidy to have corpses cluttering the place, so I sent Mrs. Bardell out to do some shopping, then rang up for the nearest undertaker. I explained the circumstances to him and told him that you would be responsible if any inquiry arose. He agreed to remove Stutz with speed and dispatch, and I must say that, for an undertaker, Mr. Simon Tapp did his stuff."

"Well, so far so good," broke in Splash Page. "But here have I had my hand clawed to bits by an infuriated macaw at Hamright's; here's Dirk Dolland emerged from a coffin; Morgan Gilson, the man from Devil's Island, popping in and out; and Anastasia, the parrot, and—"

Sexton Blake's eyes were alive with amusement.

"You will understand better, my dear Splash, in ten minutes," he remarked.

The Bat chuckled.

"Well," he continued, "after I had seen the late lamented Mr. Stutz disposed of I came back to Baker Street. As I turned the corner I saw our esteemed friend Detective-Inspector Thomas, of Scotland Yard, going into your place.

"I was rather peeved, I don't mind admitting. I cursed Thomas in fifty-seven varieties of curses for butting in. The affair was quite complicated enough without that. However, I got a bright idea. I went to a phone box and rang up your number, and did my celebrated impersonation of a policeman conveying the sad news about myself being found in a coffin somewhere in North London, and asked him to come along and join in the fun."

"It got him out of the way all right," grinned Tinker.

"Yes. Then I took a taxi back, in case he saw me in the road. I nearly barged into him. Luckily, Tinker spotted me through the window, and gave me a warning."

Splash Page passed a hand wearily over his forehead.

"Yes, but who is Brank? Who the devil is Stutz?"

Dirk Dolland chuckled.

"I think Gilson here can answer that question best," he said. "But I know perfectly well what Brank wants, and that's what Roxane here has got, if I'm not mistaken."

"But *what* does he want?" gasped an exasperated Splash.

"Anastasia's combinations," replied the Bat imperturbably.

The newspaperman snorted. Blake turned to Gilson.

"Tell the truth now, Gilson!" he ordered; and his voice was stern.

The weary man propped himself up on one elbow.

"Give me a cigarette, Blake, and I'll give you the story," he said.

Tinker proffered his case, and the man from Devil's Island took a cigarette and inhaled gratefully.

"If it hadn't been for you, Miss Harfield," he began, with a glance at the girl, who was seated with her arms clasped round her knees, her beautiful face alive with interest, "if it hadn't been for you," continued Gilson, "and the fact that I gave my word to Frimley—"

Splash Page cleared his throat.

"Look here, Gilson, have a heart. Begin at the beginning, and then let us down lightly, coming to the complications of the combinations gently, in one-syllable words, capable of apprehension by the most turgid intelligence. Don't forget this business about parrots and wrong numbers and the mystery man, Brank, is a trifle mixed. After all, I've got to explain it to readers of the 'Radio' one of these times, perhaps."

A FAINT, satiric smile played round the lips of Morgan Gilson.

"All right," he said. "You know I am an escaped convict from Devil's Island. They used to call me Robinson Crusoe, and—"

A shrill scream rang out suddenly above his low-spoken monotone.

"Ha, ha, ha! Turn off the water, Mr. Brank. Eight—six—five—four—three—two!"

Morgan Gilson leapt to his feet, eyes ablaze with excitement. Roxane smiled.

"That," she said quietly, "is Anastasia."

She crossed over to the corner of the room, and removed a silken shawl, revealing a brass cage in which was a grey parrot, whose knowing eyes blinked beadily at the assembled company.

Gilson pointed to the parrot.

"You heard that?" he exclaimed. "That's Anastasia's combinations.

"It might be absurd to you, Splash," he went on, more calmly, "but there's money in this. And, what's more—honour! I am Morgan Gilson, sentenced to Devil's Island for complicity in the Cravetti Bank frauds. Blake, here, knows that I am innocent."

The detective nodded.

"If I did not know it, my dear fellow, I certainly should not have aided and abetted you in your fantastic escapades."

"But who the devil's Brank?" interposed Splash Page.

Gilson smiled grimly.

"Ever hear of Frimley?" he inquired.

The newspaperman looked interested.

"You mean the big sharepusher?"

Dirk Dolland put in a word.

"Yes, I thought I was a clever crook in the old days, but Frimley and Brank, his partner, were Napoleons of crime. So far as profit-making was concerned, anyway."

Sexton Blake nodded.

"I agree with you, Dolland. If you want the story in a nutshell, Splash, here it is. I have known Gilson for years; he was sentenced—in my opinion unjustly—to Devil's Island, where he met Dolland. His connection with Franklyn Frimley and Brank, Gilson will reveal later. Franklyn Frimley and Brank were partners in one of the most audacious swindles ever put over on the Continent. They amassed nearly two million pounds as a result of their sharepushing frauds. But, in the end, Frimley lost his nerve.

To save his own skin, he gave evidence against Brank, Stiletti, and the late Mr Stutz. Stutz and Brank were sentenced to Devil's Island, but Stiletti was lucky. Frimley himself did not reveal to the authorities where he had hidden the loot."

"Gosh!" ejaculated Splash. "I remember that fellow Frimley now. Looked like a bishop, wandered about with a pontifical air, a disarming smile, and—"

"Two million pounds of other people's money," broke in Blake quietly. "Frimley was a genius in his way. So, for that matter, is Brank. The main difference between them is that one is dead and the other, I regret to say, is very much alive. Gilson can tell how Frimley died."

Gilson coughed, and into his dark, brooding eyes there came a far-away look.

"Yes, I'll tell you how Frimley died," he began slowly. "He died because he was false to his trust. He paid the penalty of Judas; while I, Heaven help me, gave my word and plunged you all, unwittingly, into this morass. Listen!"

DEAD silence fell on the group, while Morgan Gilson described in quick, nervous sentences the strange secrets of his life that had led to the climax of his occupation of the house in Petty France.

He described the horrors of the penal settlement in Cayenne; the blazing sun; the sweating convicts; the death of Franklyn Frimley, and the vengeance of Brank, the Doomsman.

As Gilson talked the whole mystery clarified; the fantastic events of the past few hours pieced together like a jigsaw puzzle.

Dirk Dolland, who had met Gilson on that hell on earth beneath the tropic sun of Cayenne, was silent. His cigarette had gone out, and his usually jocular face was very grave.

"I first met Frimley two years ago on Devil's Island," said Gilson. "We had been labouring all day, clearing the jungle for a new road, half-dead from the heat of the sun and the brutal driving of our gaolers. The heat was terrific. I was almost fainting, and even the guards, tough as they were, saw that it was useless to goad us any further. Men dropped where they stood in their tracks, Frimley, old and broken, was the first to collapse. I was rather friendly with our gaoler; I had done him a good turn once, and he ordered me to carry poor Frimley to a hut

where they kept the tools, built in a space in the jungle.

"He was a decent fellow, that gaoler, despite his seeming harshness, for he muttered to me that it would be as well for me to stay with Frimley till he died. The poor wretch was obviously booked, but I don't mind admitting I thought less of that than how welcome the shade was. I carried Frimley inside. The others gazed dully after us; they envied me the job, but were too far gone to show it."

Gilson laughed harshly.

"It was in that hut that Frimley told me who he was, and all about his two-million-pound secret. He told me he went in deadly fear of Brank, whom he called the Doomsman. Brank and Stutz had already been on Devil's Island for three years, but, fortunately for Frimley, they were quartered in a different part of the settlement; otherwise, they would have murdered him for his treachery. Frimley little expected, when he had betrayed his colleagues, that Stiletti would in turn betray him as he had done."

"Oh, it was Stiletti who turned informer against Frimley?" interposed Blake.

Gilson nodded.

"Yes, he received only a minor sentence, you remember. When Frimley thought he had got rid of Brank and Stutz for ever, he came to England. It was he who built the house in Petty France. You must remember that his nerve was gone. Always over him loomed the shadow of the Doomsman's vengeance, I learnt all about it in that jungle hut from Frimley's dying lips. For a year he lived in London, terrified of the gang's vengeance for his treachery He was responsible for the subterranean passages. He was too terrified to use the loot, in case one of the gang got to hear of it. His brain must have been sapped in those last years. He was no match for Brank in cunning, and he told me that he was afraid even to trust his memory."

"Ah!" interposed Splash Page. "Now I'm beginning to see where Anastasia comes in."

Gilson smiled wryly.

"Anastasia holds the secret to a fortune."

THE COMBINATION

"GO on, Gilson," said Blake quietly.

"Well," said Morgan Gilson, "I won't weary you with the details, but Frimley caused a great iron safe to be constructed and fitted with a combination lock. He was afraid to trust his memory, afraid even to let any other living soul into his secret. But one day he had a brilliant idea. He struck up a queer friendship with the man Hamright. From him he bought half a dozen grey parrots. He was a lonely recluse, and in time grew quite fond of the birds; especially of Anastasia, the best talker. This is the secret of the parrot. He had six birds, as I say, to each one of which he taught three pairs of numbers only, which he had trained them to repeat when he played the "Spring Song" on the gramophone."

"Well, I'm dashed!" ejaculated Splash Page. "Why, it's as clear as daylight now."

Roxane laughed.

"Yes. Mr. Gilson told me all this, and that is why—"

She blushed a little as Blake's grey eyes turned and held hers for the moment.

"I wondered what brought you into this, Roxane," he said. "You are a wilful child at times."

The girl shrugged her slim shoulders.

"Well," she said apologetically, "you see, Morgan was a friend of daddy's in the old Canadian days, and when he told me of his trouble one night when we met by accident in London, I offered to help him."

Blake smiled. It was utterly characteristic of Roxane, in her quixotic fashion, to lend her aid to the hunted ex-convict from Devil's Island.

Morgan Gilson cleared his throat.

"And now it seems that Miss Harfield has beaten us all and found Anastasia. The one bird in the world that knows the three pairs of numbers."

"Ha, ha, ha!" screamed the parrot in the cage. "Turn off the water, Mr. Brank."

Its raucous voice was so startling that Tinker jumped.

Blake turned to Roxane.

"I see you have a gramophone and another record, my dear. May I hazard a suggestion that it is one of Mendelssohn's?"

Roxane laughed

"Your deduction is perfectly correct, sir," she replied primly.

"Go on, Gilson," said Blake, his eyes twinkling. "And I will take up the story when you leave off."

"Well," continued Gilson, "scoundrel though he was, I felt sorry for that poor devil Frimley, dying in the jungle hut. I was with him for two hours before the end, while he boasted at times of his money, and then whimpered like a child, terrified by the shadow of the Doomsman. He told me of his friendship with old Hamright, the parrot dealer, and of how he had tantalised him by telling him that when he was dead the birds would be worth millions."

"Oh, so that explains Hamright's interest in the matter, does it?" commented Splash Page thoughtfully. "Who's this guy Stiletti, anyway?"

"It isn't Stiletti you've got to fear so much as La Rocque," replied Gilson. "It's curious," he continued, "how in that lonely hut by listening to the babblings of a dying man, I should have obtained proof of my innocence. In one of his lucid moments Frimley mentioned the Cravatti frauds, and boasted of how he and Brank had framed an Englishman named Gilson. You can imagine how my heart leapt when I learned that. He didn't know me, you see. We were known to each other by our numbers, or by nicknames.

"As the heat of the noonday sun began to fade Frimley's strength became weaker, and he was suddenly seized with terror at the thought of his approaching death. It was then I told him who I was. I shall never forget the scene. He clutched my arm until his nails bit into the flesh. 'You're Gilson,' he said; and queer biblical phrases rose to his lips."

Morgan Gilson paused, and Blake nodded.

"Yes, I believe that in one period of his career Frimley held Holy Orders," he remarked.

"He suddenly began praying," continued Gilson. "And then his brain seemed to get control for a bit. He told me all about this house in Petty France; of the parrots, each one of which knew two numbers—and two numbers only—of the combination lock. But Anastasia, she knew the whole lot, and the code word, too. He told me also that the safe was hidden under water in one of the passages. Within that safe—"

Gilson paused impressively, and a faint sigh escaped his lips.

"Within that safe, gentlemen, are two million pounds, and the proofs of my innocence. Now do you wonder why I have stopped at nothing to find Anastasia?"

"But where does Ma Gilson come in?" queried Splash Page.

The man from Devil's Island laughed shortly.

"She was Frimley's housekeeper," he said. "When I escaped from the island shortly after Frimley's death I found her installed in the house in Petty France. She was half crazy, and knew in a vague sort of way about the parrot. I learned from her that old Hamright, learning of Frimley's death, had tried to buy back the parrots from her. She parted with them all, except Anastasia. It was she, by the way, who gave me the key of his shop, but I don't know how she got it. Must have stolen it, I should think."

"But where do you come into this, Blake?" inquired Splash in a puzzled voice.

"Let Gilson tell you," said Blake laconically. "Morgan Gilson is an honest man, and is trying to keep the oath he made to Frimley on Devil's Island."

Gilson flushed a little.

"Thank you for that, Blake," he said huskily.

He turned with a half apologetic smile to Roxane.

"I promised Frimley before he died that I would go, if I could get clear, to Petty France, open the steel safe, and restore the two million pounds to the people from whom he had stolen it. I gave him my word of honour—that's all," he said simply.

Splash Page drew a deep breath, and rose to his feet and shook Gilson's calloused hand.

"Gilson, I'm with you," he said quietly.

"Count on me, too, my dear fellow," drawled the Bat. "As a matter of fact," he added, "I haven't explained yet where I come in on this. It's really got to do with that cunning devil, La Rocque."

"Who is La Rocque?" interposed Splash.

But Gilson supplied the answer.

"La Rocque," he explained, "was a fellow-convict with me, and incidentally he was the man who burgled your safe, Blake, and pinched the paper Dolland put in there. I little dreamt that when Frimley died in my arms that La Rocque had listened in to every word that had been said. He was a friend of Brank's, and when Brank and Stutz staged their getaway, they took La Rocque with them."

SPLASH PAGE interposed.

"Then in a nutshell the situation is this, Brank, Stiletti and La Rocque know all about the secret of the safe, and are after Anastasia and the combinations?"

"Exactly!" said Gilson. "But, fortunately, they don't know which of the birds knows the word and the full number. They don't know which is Anastasia."

Splash Page chuckled.

"And that explains the cryptic reference to 'Sorry, miss, wrong number.'"

Sexton Blake lit his pipe.

"The situation having been cleared up a bit," he remarked, with a twinkle, "I propose that we have a little music."

He glanced across at Roxane.

She smiled, and went over to the gramophone in the corner.

"I wonder what 'turn off the water, Mr. Brank' means?" asked Tinker. "I suppose it's something to do with the safe."

Blake nodded.

"It is quite evident that if the safe is hidden under water the water must be turned off before we get to it."

Dolland laughed.

"As a matter of fact, Gilson, I'll tell you where I come in on the scene. When I came back to London, La Rocque approached me to lend him my skill as a cracksman to help him open the safe, once they had found it, in case it was too much for him. It was a stiff proposition, he thought; much stiffer than yours, Blake. He thought I was still a crook, but I did not like Monsieur La Rocque, nor his story. He introduced me to Brank; at least, I presume it was Brank. The name he used when I met him was Rushton, Dr. Rex Rushton.

"I suspected at once that there was something fishy about the pair of them; but, of course, could not be sure that Rushton was actually Brank until I had more proof. That is the name I wrote and placed in the envelope. Anything else you want to know, Splash?"

Splash Page chuckled, and shook his head.

"Not for a moment, my dear fellow. My head's whirling as it is. It's one of the greatest stories I have ever heard. Good luck to you, Gilson. We're allies from now on."

Gilson smiled his twisted smile.

"Thanks, Splash; but you seem to forget that I am still an ex-convict, and liable at any moment to be arrested and extradited back to Devil's Island. Now you see why I am not too keen on

Coutts and Thomas being drawn into the matter. Once I have found the safe with Blake's help, then I can carry out my promise to Frimley."

Roxane turned and smiled, and a moment later the room was filled with the mellow music of Mendelssohn's "Spring Song."

"Ha, ha, ha!"

The shrill, raucous voice of the parrot stabbed with harsh discord the haunting melody.

"Ha, ha, ha! Turn off the water, Mr. Brank!"

Gilson craned forward eagerly, his eyes ablaze.

"Frim!" screamed the parrot. "Frim!" And then, in a rapid gabble, blurted out: "855432."

"That's it," said Gilson. "At last we're on the track! Hear that—the code word, too!"

Roxane smiled.

"Make a note of it, somebody, quick!" she said. "Otherwise—"

"I've made a note of it," said Splash Page, with a grin. "We've got the combination and the word all right. The next thing to do is to find the safe."

GILSON passed a hand wearily over his brow. "I've searched until I'm nearly dead for that safe. The hours I've spent in those dank, slimy sewers with the rats!"

He shuddered.

"And now the whole cursed house is alive with policemen."

Roxane turned off the gramophone.

"Don't worry," she said. "You have staunch allies now. I think we're a match for Brank and Stiletti, now that Stutz is dead."

"Incidentally, I wonder why Stutz was killed?" broke in Splash Page.

Sexton Blake shrugged his shoulders.

"Simply because he blundered, even as Hamright blundered. The Doomsman apparently does not tolerate failures."

Splash Page was busy. In rapid shorthand he was putting down the salient points of Morgan Gilson's strange narrative.

A few moments later he and Tinker both took their departure; the one bound for the office of his newspaper in Fleet Street, the other hastening to Baker Street to attend any matters that might have cropped up during Sexton Blake's absence.

Madame Casanova, who had hitherto been a silent, but keenly interested listener to the strange narrative which Gilson had unfolded, now rose to her feet.

"If you gentlemen, who are all friends of my dear Roxane's here, would care to stay for a little refreshment, I will be both charmed and honoured.

"Roxane, my dear," she said, in her deep, husky tone, "will you mix the cocktails? These poor dears must be ravenously hungry."

From the adjoining room came the tuneful tinkle of a cocktail shaker deftly-wielded by Roxane's slim but capable hands.

"Come on, Dolland, make yourself useful!" she called out. "Help me with the glasses."

The Bat sprang forward gallantly.

It was at that moment that there came a thunderous rat-tat-tat at the door.

Gilson's face went the colour of death.

"Blake, who's that?" he gasped hoarsely. And a sudden silence fell.

NEXT, ROBERT MURRAY WILL MAKE HIS NEXT MOVE IN THIS FASCINATING GAME OF WITS BETWEEN OUR TEAM OF STAR AUTHORS.

THE NEXT MOVE

OUR FASCINATING, NOVEL, FOUR-AUTHOR SERIAL.
G. H. TEED. GWYN EVANS. ROBERT MURRAY. ANTHONY SKENE.

MOVE 7—BY ROBERT MURRAY

FOREWORD

THIS SERIAL NOT ONLY INTRODUCES SIX FAMOUS UNION JACK CHARACTERS— BLAKE, TINKER, COUTTS, DIRK DOLLAND, SPLASH PAGE, MLLE. ROXANE—BUT IS A CONTEST OF SKILL BETWEEN THE ABOVE FOUR AUTHORS. THEY ARE WRITING THE INSTALMENTS IN TURN, EACH MAN SETTING PUZZLES FOR THE OTHERS TO SOLVE.

HERE ARE THE MAIN EVENTS OF THE STORY
SO FAR:

MORGAN GILSON, AN ESCAPED CONVICT
FROM DEVIL'S ISLAND, HAS SOUGHT
THE AID OF SEXTON BLAKE TO PROTECT
HIM FROM A CRIMINAL LEADER, KNOWN
AS MR. BRANK. BRANK IS OUT TO GET
FROM GILSON THE COMBINATION AND
WHEREABOUTS OF A SAFE IN WHICH ARE
HIDDEN THE PROCEEDS OF A COLOSSAL
BANK FRAUD CARRIED OUT BY BRANK'S
GANG, BUT FOR WHICH GILSON WAS
WRONGFULLY IMPRISONED.

FRIMLEY, A MEMBER OF THE GANG WHO HAD
TRIED TO DOUBLE-CROSS BRANK BY HIDING
THE MONEY, MADE A DYING CONFESSION
TO GILSON ON DEVIL'S ISLAND, TELLING
HIM THE SAFE WAS SOMEWHERE IN A
HOUSE IN PETTY FRANCE, LONDON, AND
THAT THE LETTERS AND NUMBERS OF THE
COMBINATION HAVE BEEN LEARNED BY A
PARROT, ANASTASIA. MOREOVER, IN THE
SAFE ARE PROOFS OF GILSON'S INNOCENCE
IN THE FRAUDS.

BRANK AND HIS AGENTS—STILETTI,
STUTZ, AND LA ROCQUE—HAVE FOLLOWED
GILSON TO LONDON, HAVING OVERHEARD
FRIMLEY'S STATEMENT, AND RAID THE
PETTY FRANCE HOUSE, WHICH GILSON
TAKES OVER FROM FRIMLEY'S OLD
HOUSEKEEPER. MEANTIME, THEY HAVE
APPROACHED DIRK DOLLAND TO ENLIST
HIS AID IN OPENING THE SAFE SHOULD
THEY LOCATE IT. THE BAT REFUSES, AND TO
AVOID REPRISALS, LODGES TEMPORARILY
WITH BLAKE.

THE BAT AND SPLASH PAGE THROW IN
THEIR LOT WITH BLAKE ON GILSON'S
SIDE AGAINST MR. BRANK. ALREADY
MLLE. ROXANE HAS ALLIED HERSELF
WITH GILSON, AND DURING THE RAID BY
BRANK'S MEN ON THE HOUSE HAS SECURED
ANASTASIA. THE PARROT REVEALS ITS
SECRET—THE COMBINATION. THE NEXT
STEP FOR THE FRIENDS IS TO LOCATE THE
SAFE.

SEATED IN THE HOUSE OF MADAME
CASANOVA, A FRIEND OF ROXANE WHO IS
IN THEIR CONFIDENCE THEY ARE STARTLED
BY A THUNDEROUS KNOCKING ANNOUNCING
THE ARRIVAL OF THE POLICE, WHOM BOTH
GILSON AND THE BAT WISH TO AVOID.
ROBERT MURRAY NOW CARRIES ON.

THE VANISHING TRICK

THE cocktail-shaker in Roxane's white hands
jerked with added violence as the thunderous rat-
a-tat at the door echoed through the house.

Dirk Dolland coolly relieved her of the silver
receptacle, and distributed its contents in the
various glasses.

"Not that one needs a steady hand for shaking
cocktails," he said jokingly. "That sounds like a
telegraph-boy at the door. Anyone expecting a
wire?"

Madame Casanova shook her head and pressed
a warning finger to her lips.

"I had better make certain who it is," she said
uneasily. "I can see through the landing window.
If you will wait here a moment—"

She vanished through the door. Morgan Gilson
wiped his damp forehead, his lips twitching, his
eyes flickering uncertainly.

Sexton Blake threw a sympathetic glance at
the man. He knew that Gilson was haunted by
visions of the past, and dread possibilities of the
future.

"It's the police!"

Madame Casanova swept back into the room,
her eyes wide with alarm.

"It is the police," she repeated shakily. "That
insufferable Detective-Inspector Thomas is at
the door in company with two men. They are
in plain clothes, but they are policemen without
doubt."

Dirk Dolland uttered a low whistle of consternation.

"Looks like a pinch," he said shortly. "May be
after me."

" More likely I am the person they wish to
see?" suggested Roxane, her pretty face clouding
as she glanced appealingly at Sexton Blake.

"You're both wrong. Ten to one I'm the man
they're after," declared Gilson harshly. "I've
been expecting something like this. Thomas is a
hard man to shake off."

"He may be after all three of you," remarked
Blake, jumping to his feet and walking quickly

to the window and back. "This is a devilish awkward situation! I'll see that Thomas doesn't interfere with Mademoiselle Roxane; but it would be better if Gilson and Dolland could discreetly disappear. Is there no back way out of this place?"

Madame Casanova shook her head.

"But there is a cellar—filled with rubbish and empty boxes," she suggested hopefully. "If they could hide down there—"

"We'll have to risk it," decided Blake. "We bluffed Thomas once before; perhaps we can bluff him again. Away you go, you fellows."

Rat-tat-tat-tat! *Bang!*

The persistent Thomas was becoming impatient. Madame Casanova scurried along the passage towards the back of the house, hustling Dirk Dolland and Morgan Gilson before her. A minute later she composedly opened the front door to the waiting C.I.D. men.

Inspector Thomas and his two assistants tramped into the room to find Sexton Blake and Mademoiselle Roxane seated together, chatting, smoking, and sipping cocktails from long slender glasses.

The inspector scowled as he glared around suspiciously.

"Where's Gilson?" he demanded truculently.

"Gilson?" Blake raised his eyebrows in mild surprise. "Surely you have come to the wrong house, Thomas!" he said quietly.

Thomas crimsoned and levelled a blunt, accusing finger at the detective.

"Don't play the fool with me, Blake!" he snapped angrily. "You'll soon find that obstructing an officer in the execution of his duty is a serious offence."

" Obstruction!" Blake blinked puzzledly at the end of his cigar. "You talk in riddles, Thomas. I am neither obstructing you nor assisting you. I don't even know what duty you happen to be performing. And I don't like threats."

The inspector snorted; fidgeting beneath Roxane's cool, bland stare.

"Morgan Gilson was seen to enter this place nearly an hour ago," he challenged harshly. "One of my men on duty in the next house saw him."

"Nearly an hour ago," mused Blake. "He may not have stayed long. Perhaps your observant assistant also saw him leave?"

"He did not!" snapped the inspector grimly. "That's the point. Gilson is still on the premises."

"Well, he certainly is not here!" said the Baker Street detective, with an easy gesture that swept the whole room. "And you are interrupting a private conversation between Mademoiselle Harfield and myself."

Madame Casanova took up the cudgels, her dark eyes flashing indignantly.

"Parbleu!" she exclaimed angrily. "By what right do you force your way into my house demanding to see M'sieu Gilson? Even if he were here, it is no concern of yours."

"Can't see that it is," agreed Blake, extracting the crimson cherry from the remains of his cocktail. "What's the big idea, Thomas?"

A nasty smile spread across the inspector's heavy face as he tucked his thumbs into his waistcoat, and rocked on his thick, muscular legs.

"I hold a warrant for Morgan Gilson's arrest," he announced, with great relish. "It has been issued on the application of the French authorities. They demand his extradition as an escaped convict, from Devil's Island."

Sexton Blake started. The slender stem of the fragile cocktail glass snapped between his fingers. He uttered a smiling apology to Madame Casanova; but his heart was heavy.

"Huh! I thought that would give you a jolt!" chuckled Inspector Thomas. "You've been playing with fire, Blake, and you're going to burn your fingers if you're not careful. Better get clear of this affair while you've got the chance. Where's Gilson?"

Blake made no reply until he had lighted a fresh cigar, and placed the burned match carefully in an ashtray.

It certainly was bad news. The blow that Gilson had feared had fallen. His liberty was threatened, whilst the proofs of his innocence were still beyond his reach.

"I do not propose to discuss Gilson," he said quietly. "I know that he is innocent of the crime for which he was committed to Devil's Island, and in due course I shall prove such to be the case. Gilson is guilty of no crime against the laws of this country; therefore, I do not feel disposed to lend the French authorities any assistance in their persecution of the man."

Thomas rubbed his chin doubtfully. He was not certain of his ground in relation to the argument the detective had advanced. But he knew that he had a warrant to execute. His duty was clear.

"Where's Gilson?" he demanded of Madame Casanova, thinking to find the woman an easier victim. "He was seen to enter this house. You are committing an offence by harbouring a wanted criminal."

Madame Casanova tossed her head spiritedly.

"I harbour nobody," she defied. "This is my house, and M'sieu Gilson—a friend of mine—is free to come and go as he pleases. Yes, he has been here. Now, perhaps, he has gone. It is no concern of mine."

"Or of mine," said Roxane coolly. "I am sorry you have been subjected to this interruption, Mr. Blake. Perhaps we can continue our conversation when these men have gone."

Thomas scowled, squared his shoulders, and stared thoughtfully at his two assistants.

"We'll handle this business in our own way," he said grimly. "I'm darned certain that Gilson is still on the premises. We'll search the house from top to bottom."

MADAME CASANOVA uttered an exclamation of protest. Blake stiffened in his chair as he sensed the calamity that must arise should the inspector adhere to his threat.

"Keep within your rights, Thomas," he said curtly. "Do you hold a warrant to search these premises?"

"What the devil has that got to do with you?" snapped the inspector recklessly. "Warrant or no warrant, I'm going to search this house for Morgan Gilson. If I'm in error, this woman has her remedy. But if I find Gilson, I'm going to rope her in as well."

Madame Casanova and Roxane stared at one another in silent dismay. The situation was fraught with unpleasant possibilities. It was scarcely likely that the inspector and his men would overlook the cellar. Gilson's arrest seemed imminent and certain.

Sexton Blake clung to a shred of hope, though he could think of no eventuality that might prevent discovery of the two men in hiding.

"Go ahead, at your own risk, Thomas," he said, with assumed indifference. "If you are going to search the house, I will accompany you, to see that there is no breach of the peace."

The inspector grinned sourly as he left one man in the hall, while he and the other detective first visited the upper part of the house. They went from room to room, wrenching open cupboards and wardrobes, peering under beds, tapping the walls.

They would have ascended to the roof, but for the fact that the trapdoor was sealed with cobwebs and the bolt rusted in place, proving that no one had passed that way.

Finally they made their way to the basement, followed by Madame Casanova and Roxane. The lower rooms were searched without result. Inspector Thomas scowled, and glowered suspiciously at Blake and the two women as he looked in at the door.

"If Gilson has got away, you people must have helped him to escape," he growled.

"My dear fellow, but why?" asked the detective pleasantly. "We did not anticipate this visit, and we certainly had no idea that you held a warrant for Gilson's arrest. If he has gone, he has done so in a perfectly natural manner, and without need of evasion or secrecy."

"You can't bluff me with that sort of talk," sneered the inspector. "You're riding for a fall, Blake. You're mixed up in an affair that might well land you in gaol."

He moved surlily towards the stairs. Madame Casanova heaved a sigh of relief. But the next instant a look of despair flashed across her face.

"Wait a moment, inspector. What's this door here under the stairs?" exclaimed Thomas' assistant excitedly. "It's locked. Where's the key?"

"Yeah, where's the key?" demanded the C.I.D. man, rattling the door that led to the cellar. "What's this place, eh?"

Sexton Blake shrugged his shoulders, and threw a resigned glance at Madame Casanova. The game was up. Morgan Gilson was booked for a cell, with little hope of bail.

"That door? It leads to an old cellar that is never used," answered the woman bravely. "It is full of rubbish, and old, empty packing-cases."

"Make a nice little hiding-place, eh?" taunted Thomas, wrenching the door open with a mighty tug that shattered the rusty lock and revealed a short flight of wooden steps. "Now then, Gilson," he bellowed, "come out of there. You're under arrest."

There was no response. The inspector found an electric switch, and pressed it, flooding the cellar with yellow light. Blake gave a start of amazement as he peered over the man's broad shoulder.

The cellar below seemed empty, save for dirt, dust, cobwebs, and a stack of empty packing-cases.

And when the inspector searched it they found it was, in fact, empty.

BLAKE glanced questioningly behind his back at Madame Casanova. She shook her head.

It was obvious that she was just as bewildered as he.

Inspector Thomas scowled disgustedly as he descended the steps, and ranged around the cellar, kicking the heaps of lumber, and toppling over the pile of crates that were stacked against one wall. They concealed nothing. Gilson and Dolland had completely disappeared. There was no place for a cat to hide, let alone two full-grown men.

Crimson with chagrin, the detective returned, chewing viciously at his heavy moustache, and blind to the blank expressions on the faces of Blake and the two women,

"I'll have that door repaired," he growled sheepishly. "But don't think you've got me bluffed; Gilson's been here, and you know it! You know where he's gone, too!"

Blake stared the man straight in the eyes.

"Thomas," he said solemnly and truthfully, "I've suffered enough of these rash accusations. I give you my word of honour that I haven't the vaguest idea what has become of Morgan Gilson. And nor have these two ladies."

The inspector looked reluctantly apologetic. It was the first time Sexton Blake had offered a definite statement, and he knew that he could rely on it.

"Mebbe I've made a mistake," he said grudgingly, as he led the way up the stairs to the ground floor. "But you've admitted you're in sympathy with Gilson, and I've darned good reason to—"

Inspector Thomas recoiled with a sharp, startled cry, colliding with Sexton Blake, and almost knocking him off his feet.

"Hey! What's happened here?"

Roxane uttered a gasp of horror. Sprawled on the floor in the centre of the hall was the limp, senseless figure of the plain-clothes man whom the inspector had left to guard the upper part of the house.

His white face was marred by an ugly, blue bruise on the forehead. His hat lay some distance away. He had been struck down with vicious, murderous force.

Thomas face was black with rage as he knelt beside the unconscious man, fumbling clumsily for his pulse.

"By thunder, this is some of Gilson's work!" he vowed thickly. "I'll see that he gets ten years for attempted murder, if it's the last case I ever handle!"

"Gilson!" Blake reddened as he stared incredulously at the man. He would never believe that it was Morgan Gilson, or Dirk Dolland, either, who was guilty of the assault.

"Stop that woman!" roared Thomas.

Roxane had suddenly turned, quick as a fawn, as she darted across the hall, and through the door into the sitting-room. Her cry of dismay reached Blake's ears an instant later.

"Anastasia! She's gone! She's been stolen!"

It was true. The parrot's cage was empty!

Brank the Doomsman had struck again!

The parrot, that had held the secret to Frimley's fortune, had been daringly stolen during their brief visit to the lower part of the house!

THE BLACK POOL.

ALONE in the damp cellar, dimly lit by one barred and dusty window at ground level, Morgan Gilson and Dirk Dolland seated themselves on an empty packing-case, and stared whimsically at one another.

"Like rats in a drain!" chuckled Dolland. "Better not smoke," he added, as Gilson fumbled for his cigarette-case. "We don't want that old terrier, Thomas, to smell us out."

"He'll probably do that, in any case," said the other man, with a moody shrug of his shoulders. "It's me he's after, Dolland. I'm convinced of that. At this stage in the game, Brank would not hesitate to slip word to the French authorities that an escaped convict from Devil's Island has found refuge in England."

The Bat whistled a mournful tune on his empty cigarette-holder.

"You're getting a lot of tough breaks, Gilson," he said sympathetically. "But I reckon you can rely on Blake to see you through."

"He's the only man who can," agreed Gilson. "But he'll have his work cut out to get rid of Thomas once he sets foot in the house."

"To blazes with Thomas!" exclaimed Dolland disrespectfully. "He's like a bull in a china shop, barging in and upsetting all our plans. But, even if he nabs you, he won't stop us finding that underwater safe, proving your innocence, and putting the skids under that murdering rat Brank. It's he who'll go back to Devil's Island in the end!"

Gilson shuddered to a rush of nightmarish memories.

"I don't like to think of anyone going back to that hellish hole," he said bluntly. "We're going to have a job finding Frimley's safe, Dolland," he went on, hurriedly changing the subject. "There's an absolute maze of passages under these old houses in Petty France, and some of them have been blocked up for years. And if the safe's under water, that's going to make matters a thousand times worse."

The Bat nodded as he glanced speculatively around their foul-atmosphered hiding-place, his eyes and ears on the alert, as he tried to imagine what was happening overhead.

Faint sounds were audible vibrating through the old building—slamming of doors and tramping of feet.

"Thomas and his men are searching the house!" he declared. "I don't think there's much chance for us, Gilson. They're not likely to overlook this cellar."

Gilson frowned as he surveyed the heap of boxes and crates stacked against the far wall of the underground chamber.

"Might be better if we crowded under that pile of lumber," he suggested. "Thomas may not trouble to remove the whole lot."

"Any idea's better than none," agreed Dolland brightly. "Walk on those loose boards. We don't want to leave any footprints for the eagle-eyed sleuths."

By moving several of the crates they were able to make a roomy recess right at the back of the stack of wooden cases. Squatting down, with their backs propped against the damp stone wall, they replaced the boxes, forming a roof that entirely concealed them from view.

"Only prolonging the agony, I'm afraid," muttered Gilson gloomily.

"Agony's right!" growled Dolland, reaching behind him, to place one hand, like a cushion, over a rusty metal projection jutting from the wall that was digging painfully into the small of his back. "The beggars are getting closer. Hide and seek never was a favourite game of mine."

Footsteps echoed hollowly on the floor directly overhead. Voices could now clearly be heard, and there was no mistaking the gruff, aggressive tones of Inspector Thomas.

There came a sound that wrenched a groan of dismay from Morgan Gilson—the rattle of the knob on the door at the head of the stairs leading to their hiding-place.

More voices, raised in triumph, and then a reverberating crash as the impatient Thomas applied his shoulder to the door, wrenching the rusty lock from its fastenings.

Startled, Dirk Dolland's hand suddenly bore down on the projection that had been rasping against his spine. There was a sharp click. He uttered a muffled cry of dismay as a section of the wall behind him swung open, and he pitched backwards down two stone steps, into musty-smelling darkness.

Involuntarily he clutched at Morgan Gilson's arm. Together they fell through the aperture, to sprawl side by side on the ground, just as the electric light in the cellar was switched on.

Slowly, and without a sound the segment of stone wall swung shut again, plunging them into utter blackness. It had evidently been hung on a slightly sloping doorpost, so that it shut of its own weight.

Dirk Dolland sat up, rubbed the back of his head, and swore explosively. The beam of Morgan Gilson's pocket flash lamp cut the darkness.

"Shut up, Dolland!" he whispered, his voice tense with excitement. "By James, this is a stroke of luck! We've landed in one of the catacombs under Petty France. There's a secret entrance to Madame Casanova's house, the same as there is to mine."

The Bat blinked wonderingly at the narrow stone-walled passage that ran to right and left as far as the ray of the torch could reach. It was impossible to distinguish the aperture through which they had tumbled, so snugly did the slabs of stone fit together. Not a vestige of sound reached them from the cellar on the other side of the seemingly solid wall, where even now

Thomas was pursuing his search for Morgan Gilson.

"Well, for the love of Pete," whispered Dolland, clambering to his feet, "we'd better make a move, in case Thomas hits on that hole in the wall. Lead on, Gilson. I take it you know where we are, and how to get out of the darned place?"

"I'm hanged if I do," declared Morgan Gilson candidly. "I know my own, but this is a new one on me. Wherever I went, from beneath my house, I left chalk-marks on the walls to guide me back in case I got lost. There are none here."

"Well, we're bound to get somewhere if we follow our noses," said the Bat cheerfully. "Probably strike a familiar passage later on. It's pretty obvious Madame Casanova didn't know of that secret door, else she'd have put us wise to it."

"Few people know the secrets of Petty France," declared Gilson, as he turned to the right, flashing the beam of his torch before him. Frimley knew them as well as anybody, but he didn't live long enough to draw me a complete map of this labyrinth. Watch your step."

In places part of the roof had fallen in. They progressed steadily, clambering over heaps of rubble and loose stones, and keeping always to the right whenever the tunnel branched or forked. As Gilson explained, if it became necessary for them to retrace their steps to their starting-point, they had only to reverse and stick to all left-hand turnings on the return journey.

The Bat frowned, and lit a cigarette,

"This place is just like a confounded maze," he jerked uneasily. "And it strikes me it's going to be just as difficult to find a way out. Too much like being buried alive for my liking. Queer to think we're burrowing under the streets of London like a couple of human moles!"

Morgan Gilson suddenly halted. The narrow passage had suddenly opened into a spacious underground chamber, roughly circular in shape, with arched roof, and two other tunnels leading out from it.

But what first caught his eyes was a gleam of black, still water in the centre of the floor. It looked like a sunken pond, about six feet square, and bordered with a low parapet of stone. The whole place was strange to Morgan Gilson. It was the first time he had visited this part of the catacombs beneath Petty France.

"Queer sort of dive this!" exclaimed the Bat, peering around. "What's that in the middle—a well?"

Gilson started, and almost dropped his torch. How the idea came to flash into his mind he did not know, but instinctively he knew that he had advanced another step towards the solution of Frimley's secret. His hands were trembling with excitement as he turned to his companion.

"Dolland, supposing Frimley's safe is hidden down there?" he said huskily, pointing to the rectangle of black water. "The pool is artificial. What useful purpose can it serve? Why was it made in the first place? The concrete edging—do you see?"

Dirk Dolland started, dropped to his knees, and peered into the depths of the water.

"By thunder, I believe you're right, Gilson!" he exclaimed, in an awed voice. "I can see steps under the surface. And what's this gadget here?"

Projecting upwards, in one corner of the pool, was a rusty metal bar, topped with a stout ring. Grasping it with both hands, the Bat gave a violent tug. At first there was no movement, but at a second mighty heave the steel lever came gradually towards him.

BEFORE their astonished eyes the level of the water in the pond sank. Slowly but indubitably it sank. One by one a series of slimy stone steps came into view. With weird, discordant gurglings and groanings the black water drained away through an unseen outlet somewhere into the bowels of the earth, into one of the many sewers or streams which formed the maze under this mysterious place.

But what was more interesting than that was the doorway which was also revealed as the water level descended. When the swirling water, now beginning to form itself into a whirlpool, like that of an emptying bath-tub, was no more than five feet from the bottom of the stone tank, an obvious cavity began to appear above the surface. As the level became still lower, this cavity was disclosed as a square opening or doorway in the middle of the pool wall opposite where the watchers stood.

It was about two feet wide by five in height— just enough for a man to pass through, and the whirlpool at length separated itself into two as the water was sucked into a pair of gratings on floor level in the tank on either side of the doorway.

As the last of the water drained away with a final gulp and gurgle, leaving the bottom dry, except for a few puddles and a thin, slimy deposit of black mud, Dolland and Gilson stared at each other dumbly. It was a momentous discovery.

The mind of each asked the same question.

And then, after that tense pause, Dolland spoke what they both were thinking.

"What is it?" he asked, in a sibilant, strained tone.

Gilson merely shook his head, just as mystified as Dirk himself. He had spent many, many hours in exploring the subterranean labyrinth under the house in Petty France, but he knew that even he had not even begun to suspect all their surprises.

"Let's see!" said Dolland.

And with the gleam of Gilson's torch wavering before him in that eerie place of silence and darkness, he descended the fourteen slimy steps that gave access to the bottom of the pool.

Gilson followed, and they picked their way across the few feet of space to the opening in the farther wall. With the torchlight directed in front of them they came to a halt at the entrance and peered in.

The chamber was small—Dolland judged it to be about six feet square and about the same in height—and, unlike the pool, roofed in. They bent through the narrow opening, and passed inside. The walls were of solid stone or concrete, with no visible break, and the floor appeared to be the same, although it was covered by a similar thin deposit of ooze to that of the pool outside. There was no sign of the safe in which Frimley had hidden his hoard of two million pounds of stolen money.

"This is just a sort of stone box," said Gilson, the look of expectation dying out of his eyes as he followed the ray of the flash-light with his eyes. "No sign of the safe!"

"May be embedded in the wall somewhere and cemented over," suggested Dolland. "Or perhaps in the floor. If we could scrape away this muck—I can't help thinking we're on the right track—this place wasn't built for nothing."

"How about the roof?"

Gilson jerked the torch-ray overhead and explored the ceiling. "Visible at once was a rectangular seating of a trap-door, which was in place. Like the rest of the chamber, it was stone.

"Hallo! We're getting warm!" exclaimed Dolland.

He lifted his hands, and, with the immense leverage he had because of its lowness, he strained upwards with his whole body, thrusting against the underside of the stone.

"Phew! It's heavy!" he gasped, desisting. "But I shifted it a bit. Give me a hand, Gilson I think the two of us—"

But Gilson had already placed the flash-light on the floor, with its light directed upwards. Together the two of them renewed the attack on the trap, and this time, with a grunt and a combined heave, had the satisfaction of lifting it clear and toppling it over. It fell with a dull crash on the upper side of the stones which formed the ceiling of the chamber. Apparently there was a tunnel overhead.

"That's that!" said Dolland, dusting his hands. "And now—"

They both froze into motionless attitudes as they stood.

A hollow chuckle had echoed down the place. Unmistakably it was human; they had not imagined it. It seemed to come from outside the narrow entrance.

Coming to life, they both made a simultaneous dash for the doorway, colliding in the entrance, conscious at the same instant of a rasping of metal against metal and a clang.

The iron bar by which they had let the water out made that sound.

And on the realisation came a mighty roar as a cascade of black water swept down the stone steps facing them, entering from some inlet they had not noticed. It surged forward in a two-foot wave, knocked their feet from under them.

Together they went down, swept back into the chamber of the swirling, ever-rising torrent.

The torch went out in the first onrush, and the pair fought for air as they were tumbled dizzily about that stone death-trap in the darkness, their ears filled with the sound of falling waters.

DEADLOCK.

INSPECTOR THOMAS' assistant—Sergeant Hales—could offer little explanation of the mysterious assault that had left him senseless in Madame Casanova's hallway.

"Darned if I know much about it!" he declared bluntly, as he sat in the little sitting-room, with his head bandaged, and a stiff brandy-and-soda clutched in one hand. "I was standing in the hall, watching the stairs, when I suddenly sensed that I wasn't alone. As I swung round, I just caught a glimpse of a man, with a black handkerchief plastered over his face. Then I stopped this crack on the head—and that's all I can remember."

Thomas clenched and unclenched his big fists, breathing heavily through his nose.

"We found the front door unlatched," he snapped. "And there isn't the slightest doubt it was Gilson who laid you out."

"Of course it wasn't Mr. Gilson!" said Roxane, with cold scorn. "Why should he steal Anastasia?"

"Anastasia?" gulped Thomas. "What the—"

"My parrot," explained Roxane blandly.

"A parrot?" echoed the inspector. "Are you telling me that some crazy fool crept in here and smashed Hales on the head just to steal a confounded parrot? In the name of blazes, why?"

The girl hesitated for a moment. "It was a very valuable parrot," she answered at length. "There have been many attempts to steal it," she added truthfully, but would add nothing further to her explanation.

Blake nodded approvingly. He knew that it was Brank, or one of his accomplices, who had managed to enter the house and get away with the bird that held the secret to Frimley's hidden hoard. But it was impossible to take Inspector Thomas into their confidence.

Blake wasn't worrying so much about the missing parrot. He was wondering what the devil had become of Dirk Dolland and Morgan Gilson. And it was impossible for him to make, any investigation while Thomas and his men remained in the house.

"Roxane, I'm going to Baker Street for half an hour," decided Blake, drawing the girl to one side. "There's just a chance that Holland or Gilson may phone me there, if they've managed to get away from here. In any case, we can't discuss anything while that detective is here, listening and watching; and there are many things to be discussed. Meet me at Victoria Station at seven-thirty, No. 10 Platform entrance."

It was already dark when the detective left the house in Petty France. Roxane waited until a quarter-past seven before she put on her hat and coat and went to keep her appointment.

The street was deserted. She was oblivious of the sleek, dark, saloon car that came swiftly and silently from the other end of Petty France, flashed past her, slowed down, and came to a stop.

Deep in thought, Roxane did not give the vehicle a second glance as she walked by. Silent as shadows, two dark figures slipped through the door and closed in on the girl. A stifling cloth was flung over her head. Muscular hands gripped her, whisking her off her feet, and passing her swiftly into the dark interior of the car.

Mr. Brank chuckled softly as he lounged back in his seat and surveyed the helpless figure of his latest victim.

"If the cursed parrot will not speak the girl shall be made to!" he murmured, rubbing his long white hands.

NOW COMES THE TURN OF ANTHONY SKENE. THE EVENTS OF THIS FASCINATING YARN HAVE NOW BECOME SORTED OUT A BIT, BUT WHERE DO WE GO FROM HERE? LEAVE THE AUTHOR TO PUZZLE THAT OUT! YOUR JOB IS MERELY TO MAKE CERTAIN OF NEXT WEEK'S SPECIAL NUMBER BY HAVING YOUR COPY ALREADY ORDERED.

MOVE 8—BY ANTHONY SKENE

By Robert Murray, Anthony Skene, G.H. Teed and Gwyn Evans

With, as referee of the match, ...The Editor

FOREWORD.

THIS story is a contest of skill between the four authors who are contributing the instalments in turn, setting puzzles for each other to solve.

Featured in the story are the following UNION JACK characters: Blake, Tinker, Coutts, Splash Page, Dirk Dolland, Mlle. Roxane. Here are the main events, so far:

On Devil's Island, Morgan Gilson, wrongly sentenced for being concerned in the Cravetti bank frauds, hears the dying confession of a crook, Frimley.

Frimley relates that proofs of Gilson's innocence, together with the proceeds of the frauds, are in London, where he concealed them in an attempt to double-cross Brank, the leader of the gang which carried through the crime.

Gilson escapes, comes to London, and takes over Frimley's house in Petty France. He knows that somewhere in the tunnels which run underneath the place is the safe. The combination has been taught to a parrot, Anastasia. But before Gilson can do anything to locate the safe, Brank and his followers, who know of Frimley's confession, start a campaign of terror to get the safe first.

Although he can't appeal to the police, Gilson has powerful allies in Blake and Tinker, Splash Page, Dirk Dolland, and Mlle. Roxane. Roxane secures the parrot and gets the combination. Brank quickly retaliates. His agents steal the parrot, trap Gilson and Dolland in a stone chamber underground, which they flood with water, while Brank, himself, trails Roxane and kidnaps her as she is en route to meet Blake.

Anthony Skene now continues.

UNDER THE KNIFE

DIRECTLY Mademoiselle Roxane had been kidnapped by Brank and his friends she had been given a whiff of chloroform. During the short time that she remained in the car the chloroform pad was pressed to her nostrils several times; so that, although she never became insensible, she remained drowsy and unable either to help herself or to take note of her surroundings.

She had a hazy impression of being removed from the car outside a big house, and of being assisted to climb steps by two men who held her arms. She remembered that one of the two men was addressed respectfully as Dr. Something-or-Other, and from that moment things became clearer. The effects of the drug wore off.

She found herself seated in a large and handsome room with French windows, and a stone balustrade beyond them. The room appeared to be on one of the upper floors.

A tall, singular man was standing in front of her, looking down with an expression of mocking solitude, and with the palms of his hands close together on his breast.

The high-spirited girl made an effort to rise, and would have fallen but that the tall man steadied her with a courteous gesture.

"Please don't try to rise; you might hurt yourself, and then we should be heartbroken."

The girl's lips curled in scorn.

"You, Brank! You have no heart to be broken!"

Brank smiled; lifted an appealing hand.

"What charming frankness! But I am sure you are mistaken. I am sure that a charming lady like yourself might find me a very sympathetic person. For instance, there is the matter of two million pounds that we know about. Out of the generosity of my nature I am disposed to bestow a fortune upon you. What shall we say—a hundred thousand? Or would that be insufficient? Name your own price, mademoiselle."

Roxanne was astonished. Brank had got the parrot; his own words had proved that. From the parrot he could get as much information as he could from herself. Yet, here he was offering her a share of the treasure.

"You want me to help you?" she questioned.

Brank smiled.

"Exactly! We merely want you to tell us where the safe is—that safe, I mean, which contains Frimley's millions—and the formula by which it can be opened. A small thing, mademoiselle— just a few words. And yet, think of it, —a hundred thousand pounds! More, perhaps!"

The evil face of Brank came still closer.

"Just whisper it in my ear."

Roxane drew herself away.

"I assure you," she said, "with perfect truth, that I don't know the answer to your question; and that if I did, nothing that you could offer would buy the secret from me."

Brank washed his hands in the air.

He was crouching over the girl, smiling his loathsome smile, watching her every movement with his large protuberant eyes. When the girl had uttered her contemptuous refusal he actually clapped his hands in mocking applause.

"You don't know," he repeated; and if you did, you wouldn't tell me! That is heroic!"

He turned to the man who stood somewhat behind him.

"Did you hear that, Stiletti?" he chuckled. "She doesn't know; and if she did, she wouldn't tell me. Isn't that beautiful? Yes" —he jerked round to stare at the girl again—"and indignation gives your beauty just that final touch of—what shall we say? —vivacity which it needs to reach perfection."

He made a mocking bow.

"I must congratulate you, mademoiselle, on your beauty. I have remarked upon it before."

Here Brank turned again to his satellite.

"You have heard me—haven't you, Stiletti? You have heard me say what an admiration I have for mademoiselle? It is not the first time that we have desired your company, my child. Many times I have said, 'Mademoiselle Roxane is peerless, unique!'

"Believe me," Brank continued, "if it should be necessary for me to destroy that peerless beauty of which mademoiselle is the fortunate possessor, it would cause me the cruellest grief. Mademoiselle has no idea how I would suffer!"

The man was still hanging over Roxane where she sat in the chair. He looked like an evil bird of prey about to flesh his talons.

The girl had whitened slightly at the threat which he had hinted, but she was still staring at him as if he were something unclean. Another man would have become angry or abashed before that look of utter disdain, but Brank seemed unaware of it.

"You know," he said conversationally—" you know, my dear child, that beauty is to a woman a most valued possession. She will do much to keep her beauty. There was a woman once of whom I had to ask questions. She was like you, very like you; not quite so beautiful, perhaps, but still a lovely creature—and she was obstinate. It was such a pity! She was obstinate. But she answered my questions in the end; and then, alas! it was too late to give her back her beauty. You may have seen her. Molly Symes she was in the days that I speak of. Later she became a housekeeper. You may have known her as Ma Gilson."

"Ma Gilson!"

The words came from Roxane's lips in frozen horror. It was impossible to believe that that terrible woman had once been beautiful.

Brank read her thoughts.

"Yes, she was beautiful once. And then she was obstinate. Such a pity for a woman to be obstinate when she is beautiful!"

Brank pointed to a small table which stood not far from Roxane's chair. It was a surgeon's table, made of plated steel, and with a plate-glass top and glass shelves. Laid out upon it were a number of surgical knives and a lighted spirit-lamp.

"Yes, she sat in front of me just as you are sitting now, my dear child; and I had these detestable forceps and probes and scalpels there ready to my hand, just as I have them now. And I questioned her just as I am questioning you. She did not answer, mademoiselle, until it was too late. She was brave, of course, but foolish. But you will not be so foolish as that, will you? It would be such a pity! And, of course, you will tell in the end, you know. But what use when your beauty is gone? Remember Ma Gilson. How old do you think she was—sixty, seventy? Ah, you don't answer! But I'll tell you. She was just over forty-five years old when she died."

"Forty-give?"

"Yes. Sad, isn't it? And just because she was obstinate. Would not answer questions. But you—you will answer my questions; I am sure you will. Just in case you have forgotten, I will ask you again what I want to know. *Where is the safe which contains Franklin Frimley's millions? And what is the combination that will open it?"*

"I have told you," said Roxanne, "I don't know."

ONE rather astonishing fact which was becoming clear to her was that although Brank appeared to have become possessed of the parrot, he did not seem to have learned the formula which the parrot had been taught to recite. She began to suspect that while Brank was aware that the parrot possessed the secret, he did not know how to make it speak.

She was determined that she would never tell him. If by threats, or even by torture, Brank had forced her to betray the formula, she felt that she would never again be able to look into the eyes of Sexton Blake. She would be afraid of seeing just a shade of contempt, instead of the admiration she had become accustomed to.

The man Stiletti, who had accompanied Brank, had remained in the background, listening to his leader, and watching the face of Roxane with a wolfish grin.

The girl noticed his expression with a sinking heart. This man and his master were mad to get at the stolen millions. They would let nothing stand in their way.

Brank was speaking again.

"We shall not use an anaesthetic," he said. "And, of course, the operation will be painful; dreadfully painful. It cuts me to the heart to have to do it. Stiletti, come here. Take Miss Harfield's wrists."

Roxane tried to rise, but Brank thrust her back again, and the powerful Stiletti seized her wrists from behind so that she was incapable of movement.

Brank sterilised the knife by passing it through the flame of the lamp.

"I don't know," he said, looking at Roxane thoughtfully. "I don't know exactly whre to begin. The nose, perhaps, or the ear?"

"I know," he said, after a moment, almost jovially, " we will start with the ear. Then if Miss Harfield changes her mind—even although the ear is gone—she will be able to dress her hair differently, and so conceal the fact. You will remember that that is what Molly Symes did; but her disfigurement, of course, was too extreme at the finish. It will be a pity if the beautiful Roxane were to age by twenty years, and become somebody's housekeeper. That would be a pity. Such a pity—"

And so he went on , mumbling his hypocrisy, and smiling his fatuous smile as he pressed Roxane's head cruelly sideways and chose a place for the first touch of the knife point.

A wave of heat passed over the girl's body. She was fainting with terror. To be turned, in a space of minutes, into and old and repulsive woman. What a fate! Yet there was no escape. She feared Blake's contempt more than she feared the knife. She would not tell.

The point of the knife bit into her flesh. It began to move—slowly—slowly—Then:

Brank stopped. Jerked his head round.

"What's that?"

Roxanne's heart leaped. There had been a loud knocking upon the door of the room.

"Sexton Blake!" she said to herself.

But it was not he who entered in response to Brank's invitation. The individual who had knocked was as unlike Blake as could possibly be. Undersized and misshapen, with a pallid face, and hair as black and as glossy almost as patent leather.

When he saw the girl twisted in the chair, and the saturnine Brank poising a knife, his huge mouth opened in a fiendish grin.

"You've got the girl?" he questioned.

Brank held up an admonitory finder.

"Be more respectful, my good La Rocque. Miss Harfield to you."

The newcomer laughed.

"Anything you say. But listen, boss, I've got news for you. Gilson's been a nuisance, hasn't he? Dirk Dolland's been a nuisance, hasn't he? Well, they won't be a nuisance any more, either of them."

Brank did not alter his expression or voice. He seemed to be always the same, mocking and hypocritical.

He said: "What's this that you are telling us, La Rocque?"

The little man capered about, smacking his thighs in enjoyment.

"After I had beaned that policeman and hooked the parrot for you, I went underground. Caught Dolland and Gilson looking at the well in the lower pool, I did. Opened the sluices. You should have seen the water come through. Wow! It was like Niagara!"

Brank tossed back to the table the knife which he had been holding. He face became white with rage.

"What's this?" he said hoarsely. "What's this?"

"What's the matter?" questioned La Rocque. "You wanted Gilson and Dolland out of your way; and now they're drowned. Just like rats. Ain't you satisfied? Ain't you happy?"

"You filled that cavern with water?"

"That's right, boss. Filled it to the top. What about it?"

Brank snarled in reply.

"You fool!"

Brank's attention had been half-diverted from Roxane. The possibility of escape came into her mind; and, instinctively, she looked down at the hands which gripped her wrists. Then she sickened. Each of those huge and hairy hands had five fingers and a thumb!

Five fingers! Roxane remembered that ominous imprint on the wall of Hamright's shop. The malformed hand outlined in blood. She was in the grasp of a murderer!

Brank had given way to a paroxysm of rage. Crouching like a beast about to spring, he was following the diminutive La Rocque across the floor.

La Rocque was protesting.

"But I didn't know! How could I know?"

"No," said Brank, "you're quite right, you couldn't know. You hadn't the brain to see that the sluice was put there for a purpose. That when you filled the lower cavern you necessarily emptied the waterways at a higher level. Did you go back and search those waterways after you'd opened the sluices? Of course you didn't! If you had you would have found something— Franklin Frimley's safe. That is what you would have found."

"The safe, boss? I didn't know."

"Of course you didn't know."

Brank's hands were working convulsively.

"And soon you won't know anything—ever— any—more."

The effect of that threat was to give La Rocque the courage of a cornered rat. He whipped out a knife from somewhere near the top of his waistcoat.

"Lay a hand on me," he rasped, "and I'll cut you open!"

He hurled himself forward.

Stiletti released Roxane's hands and went to Brank's assistance.

Roxane herself stood erect and looked around her. Escape! Just a chance of escape. Which way? The door was impossible. The windows then!

By their quarrelling among themselves the attention of the men who held her prisoner had been distracted. The quick intelligence of the girl suggested a further distraction.

She picked the lighted spirit-lamp from the table, and rolled it across the floor into the window curtains. Then she swung the table itself and smashed the French doors open. She had already perceived that outside the window there was a balcony. If this balcony went round the house, as it seemed to do, she would perhaps be able to enter another room.

The strong wind which was blowing lifted the curtains up into the air. They were already afire; the flames leapt and writhed in the draught.

Roxanne dashed out on to the balcony, and found that she was no less trapped than in the room itself. The balustrade, certainly, passed across the whole front of the house; but, except where it widened in front of the two windows,

its coping was only twelve inches clear of the brickwork.

She glanced backward. Brank, Stiletti, and La Rocque were struggling together. She still held the small surgical table in her hands; and now, in the hope of attracting attention, she hurled it from the balcony, hoping it would crash down upon the pavement. But the front garden was of some breadth, and the table fell short, dropping silently among the evergreens.

Roxanne shouted for help, but, except for a taxicab in the distance, the long road was empty.

Seeing the ape-like Stiletti was crossing the floor towards her, she climbed to the coping of the balustrade. The wind caught her skirts and almost swept her from her precarious foothold. But, with slow and careful steps at first, and then a longer and more determined stride, she walked away from the window.

Thirty feet below her there was a concrete area. Beyond that the gardens, but no bush which she could use to break her fall. No tree which she could jump into as a means of reaching the ground in safety. Only the sheer and wind-swept wall.

She went forward for half a dozen yards.

Stiletti appeared at the window which she had just left. There was a heavy automatic pistol in his hand—a pistol fitted with a silencer.

"Here you," he said, "come back, or I shoot!"

The girl checked and turned.

"You had better ask Brank before you do that."

The man was evidently impressed by her earnestness, for he asked what she meant.

"I mean that I have a secret which Brank wants to get. If you shoot I am not likely to live to tell the secret."

"What does that matter? We've got the safe."

"Yes; but you don't know how to open it, and you never will know."

Roxane hoped that this was true, but she knew that although the parrot had been taught to recite the formula when prompted by the music of the "Spring Song," it would, occasionally, do so without prompting. If Brank had only known it, he had no need of her.

"For another thing," the girl supplemented, " you are being watched."

She pointed away beyond Stiletti's back.

Roxane's acting was so good that the man swung round, expecting to see a stranger in the street or garden. Roxane took half a dozen swift and reckless paces to reach the embrasure of another window. She jumped backwards, and Stiletti fired, his bullet richochetting from the brickwork, and passing away with a high-pitched whine.

Roxane was now against another French window; but, like the first, it was bolted on the inside. She stripped off her coat, rolled it around her arm, and pounded at the glass. In ten seconds she was inside the room beyond.

She rushed across the floor and tore the door open.

Stiletti was outside it.

As the girl slammed the door shut again, his hand was actually upon the panels. Fortunately there was a key, and it was on the inner side.

The girl turned it; then, panting with excitement and exhaustion, dragged a heavy armchair across to reinforce the door. She was safe for perhaps five minutes—the length of time which it would take Stiletti and his friends to break the door down.

The girl waited, expecting every moment to hear the blows of a hammer or an axe upon the woodwork.

Nothing of the sort happened.

Presently another doubt entered her mind. The window! What about the window?

She turned with a scream to see a hairy, five-fingered hand hook itself around the woodwork of the shattered casement.

FIRE AND FRUSTRATION

SEXTON BLAKE compared his wrist-watch with the clock at Victoria Station. It was not like Roxane to be late. Yet the hour was 7.45, and the time of his rendezvous with her had been 7.30.

At first the detective's impatience had been solely due to the thrill which he always felt at meeting with the beautiful Canadian girl; but now other doubts began to enter his mind. In the dangerous game which they were playing anything was possible.

He went to a telephone kiosk and called Madame Casanova. He learned that Roxane had left the house in Petty France in plenty of time to keep her appointment with him. He knew that no ordinary circumstances would have delayed the girl.

Another five minutes, a last thorough inspection of the neighbourhood of Platform 10, and Blake was in a taxi-cab, and in a hurry.

On reaching Petty France he sprang out of the taxi and snapped; "I may want you again," and walked straight up to a pavement artist who, for several days past, had adopted that somewhat unprofitable spot to display his art.

Blake knew him for a plain-clothes' man working under Inspector Thomas. Both Thomas and his underling had supposed that they were deceiving Sexton Blake. The detective had allowed them to go on thinking just that; but he had realised the meaning of the man's presence from the first hour. More than that, Sexton Blake —who never forgot a face, and was even more certain when he remembered the shapes of ears, which are unchangeable—could seldom be imposed upon by disguise. Also, he was acquainted with the identity of the man in question.

"Look here, Collins," he rapped out, "sorry to break the rule, but something serious has happened. Miss Harfield left this place at seven-fifteen to keep an appointment with me. She has not turned up. Know anything?"

For all his urgency, Blake had spoken quietly; and now he fumbled in his pocket for a copper to drop into the pavement artist's cap. To a casual observer he would have appeared to be passing the time of day with the man; but Collins had every reason to believe that Blake was deadly earnest.

He made no pretence of being anything but a policeman.

"Saw her come out," he said. "Blue Daimler picked her up—XN 7531. Anything wrong?"

"Couldn't be worse," Blake said, and went back to the taxi.

"Scotland Yard!" he said to the driver. "Hell for leather!"

He was at the headquarters of the Metropolitan Police within five minutes. He repeated the same formula, "May want you again," and rushed up the stone steps, going in at a door labelled "Registry."

"XN 7531," he said. In case he should be unknown to the policeman in uniform on duty at the desk, he passed across his visiting-card, and added: "Urgent—desperately urgent!"

The policeman disappeared. In thirty seconds he was back with a slip of paper.

Blake looked at it.

"Dr. Rex Rushton, 179a Finchley Road."

Another word of thanks and he was back in the taxicab.

"Finchley Road," he said, "and step on the gas. I pay double fare."

Twice the taxi ran into a traffic block, and twice, to the driver's astonishment, he was waved through. If he had seen the high sign which passed between Blake and the policeman on point duty he might have been less surprised.

When the taxi reached Finchley Road there was further delay in discovering the whereabouts of 179a. As they went towards the direction which had been given, they were passed by a fire engine. Two minutes later Blake observed a cloud of smoke issuing from a distant building fronted by trees.

"Looks like a fire," said the driver, turning with a cheerful grin.

"Yes, step on it!" Blake said, without responding to the driver's cheerfulness. He had a foreboding which grew stronger as he counted the numbers of the houses which they were passing.

The driver of Blake's taxi turned again, and this time his face was more serious.

"Looks to me, sir, as if this was the number you were after—the fire, I mean."

It did look like that. Blake was out of the taxi before it reached the edges of the crowd, which had already assembled. Firemen were unrolling a hose. A couple of policemen were trying to keep the crowd back.

A large residence, with stone balustrade and tiled roof, was burning fiercely. Flames streamed upwards out of the window openings of the upper floors. The windows themselves had disappeared. The timbers of the roof were crackling fiercely.

A policeman put his arm across Blake's chest. "Stand back, if you please!"

Blake gave his name, and the policeman saluted.

"Sorry, sir; I didn't recognise you."

After that Blake was allowed to go through on to the cleared space where the firemen were working.

He stood for a moment with his hands deep in his jacket pockets, staring up at the blaze; then he approached the building; ignoring the shouts of firemen and police, and skirted the flank of it, coming out in the rear. There he smashed a window and entered.

Roxane, the beautiful Roxane, had disappeared in a car, and the owner of the car was the man whose name appeared on the doorplate of this expensive house—Dr. Rex Rushton.

Blake had come there and found the place on fire. He concluded, therefore, that the fire had something to do with Roxane. He was aware that he might be wrong, but he wanted to make sure about that.

Where he was, in the rear portion of the ground-floor, he could easily have convinced himself that he had imagined the conflagration. There was very little smoke, only the smell and the sounds of burning gave evidence of what was happening.

He walked through the house very coolly and ascended the stairs. At the head of the stairs the smoke was much denser and smouldering woodwork showed that the fire was burning downwards.

He shouted on the off-chance that Roxane might be within hearing; but there was no reply. He went into one room after another. In the large front room, where the fire was fiercest, and whence came a continuous hissing of stream as the water from the hoses trickled through on the charred embers, he tripped over something soft and yielding—a body.

A sudden terrible fear flashed through his mind, then left him when he saw that it was the body of a man. He bent and saw that the man was undersized, with plastered black hair and a sallow face.

He thought at first that, impossible as it seemed, this individual had been a victim to the fumes of the fire. His own eyes were smarting so that he could hardly see. It was more by touch than by sight that he discovered the hilt of a dagger driven deep into the man's breast.

HE bent and gathered the little man in his arms and moved towards the head of the stairs.

The little man groaned.

"Don't worry yourself," he said, "whoever you are. You can't do anything for me—I'm for it—I'm booked! I want to make a statement."

Blake was astonished to hear the man speak. It had seemed impossible, after the evidence of that knife-thrust that he should be alive at all.

"Where is Miss Harfield?" he questioned. "Do you know anything about her?"

"Yes," replied the other, "I know all about her. But I've got other things to say, and I haven't much time to talk."

Blake had got the little man to the head of the stairs. Now he laid him down on the landing.

"Well," he said, "what is it? I'm Mr. Blake."

Desperately wounded as he was, the stricken man succeeded in raising himself upon his elbow.

"Blake!" he echoed. "That's fine!" I want to tell you things, Mr. Blake. I'm La Rocque. You may not know me, but that doesn't matter. First thing I want to tell you is about Brank—Rex Rushton, as he calls himself—he stuck this knife in me. He killed Stutz and Ma Gibson. He's wanted by the French police; but I want the British police to get him. He escaped from Devil's Island, but he will never escape from Wandsworth Gaol, and that's where I want him to be. I should like to be outside the gates at nine o'clock when the black flag goes up. Perhaps I shall be."

Blake asked again the question he had asked before:

"Where is Miss Harfield?"

But the dying man did not seem to hear.

"Dollant and Gibson are dead," he said—"drowned. I drowned 'em—opened a sluice and filled up the cavern where they were. Brank thinks that when this empties the upper waterways it will expose the safe. You know the safe I mean—Frimley's safe, with two million pounds in it. I expect he's gone there now with Stiletti. You know Stiletti, don't you?"

Blake nodded. He had known Stiletti for many years. Even before that individual had fallen foul of the French police, and gone to Devil's Island, Blake had known his as a crook.

He did not speak, because it was no use speaking. This man, who was dying, evidently did not hear. He was rambling a little now, but no less loquacious.

"Oh, no, Brank! You've found the safe, have you? But you can't open it because you don't know the combination! I know the combination, but I'm not going to tell you! Oh, no, Brank!

I want that two millions all for myself! Two million pounds! Mine—all mine!"

Blake actually shook the dying man by the shoulder in a last effort to get some news of Roxane.

"Miss Harfield!" he shouted. "Where is Miss Harfield?"

There was no answer.

Blake shouted the question again, and then realised that there never would now be an answer. Brank's victim had passed out.

Once more he took the body of the little man in his arms, and this time he went down the stairs.

He had hardly reached the bottom when the roof fell in. Embers and sparks rained upon him. A falling beam grazed his left shoulder, sending him staggering.

Singed by flames and blinded by smoke, he staggered with his burden to the front door and threw it open. A confused murmur went up from the crowd at the side of him. The number of police on the spot had been increased. Several came forward. The foremost was a sergeant in uniform.

"I understand that you are Mr. Blake, of Baker Street," he said. And then: "What's this? What's happened here?"

Blake walked forward until he could dispose of his tragic burden behind the front fence, beyond the reach of the fire.

"Murder," he said. "This man has just informed me that he was murdered by Brank, alias Dr. Rex Rushton."

"And what were you doing in there, if I may ask?"

"I was looking for a lady whom I suspected to be a prisoner here."

"Did you find her?"

"No, I didn't; but I'm going to look for her again!"

"You can't go into that house," said the sergeant.

Blake laughed harshly.

"Can't I?" You watch me do it!"

By now the whole of the lower parts of the premises was shrouded in heavy smoke. The hoses were no longer playing directly upon Rushton's premises, but were directed to saving the houses on either side.

Despite the heat and the dense smoke, he searched the ground floor pretty thoroughly, then he went out to the garage, looking for the blue Daimler.

The garage was empty. At which Blake heaved a sigh of relief.

It was terrible that Roxane should be in the power of Brank, but even that was better than her having been left a prisoner in a blazing building, as he had feared that she might be.

He made inquiries, but could not discover that anybody had seen the departure of the Daimler.

He went to a local telephone kiosk and asked for an "All Stations" call.

The privilege of getting an "All Stations" call upon request was on which had been given to Sexton Blake in consideration of his otherwise unpaid services to his country; but it was a privilege which Blake used as little as possible. This time, however, he felt that it was justified. His only chance of finding Roxane appeared to lie in finding that blue Daimler.

Having arranged that every policeman in Greater London should be on the lookout for Brank's car, he informed the Commissioner of Police that he could be found in Gibson's house in Petty France and went there as rapidly as the taxi could take him.

He was sure of one thing—whatever the reason for Brank's abduction of Roxane—and this in itself was a matter which puzzled Blake considerably—the most important thing to Brank and Stiletti was the acquisition of that two millions which Frimley had concealed.

La Rocque had told him before he died that the opening of the sluices in the lower cavern was expected to have exposed the safe where the treasure was deposited, and the theory sounded plausible to Blake himself, although he did not know just where either was situated. He knew that Brank and Stiletti would be seeking them.

He was back in Petty France in an incredibly short time, but doubted, even so, whether he had beaten Brank to it. He suspected that Brank and his friends had means of access to those subterranean waterways beneath Westminster which he himself had not yet discovered. He was about to test that theory now.

He went straight to Gilson's house and hammered on the knocker.

Of the tragic news which had been given him by the dying man that Gilson and Dirk Dolland were dead, and of his own discovery that Roxane had been abducted by Brank, he was not allowing himself to think. Sorrow for these things and retribution for them would come later. Just now he was a man with a fixed idea—to get to that safe, to prove Gilson's innocence, and to return to some at least of Frimley's victims the wealth of which they had been plundered. If Brank stood in the way, so much the worse—and so much the better.

Blake hammered again.

The door was opened by Gilson. Behind Gilson's elbow was Dirk Dolland himself!

And so ends Round 2! Bang goes the bell next week, and G.H. Teed will follow up with the ninth instalment to open Round 3. This brilliant four-author serial with its six favourite 'U.J' characters, and Brank the Doomsman, will repay with 100 per cent entertainment interest the precaution of an order in advance. Go to it!

The NEXT MOVE

G.H.TEED STARTS ROUND 3

Foreword.

THIS UNIQUE SERIAL IS A CONTEST OF SKILL
BETWEEN THE ABOVE FOUR AUTHORS, WHO
ARE WRITING THE INSTALLMENTS IN TURN.
FEATURED IN THE STORY ARE SIX FAMOUS
UNION JACK CHARACTERS—BLAKE,
TINKER, COUTTS, DIRK DOLLAND, SPLASH
PAGE AND MLLE. ROXANE, PREVIOUS MOVES
IN THE STORY ARE:

ON DEVIL'S ISLAND, MORGAN GILSON,
WRONGLY SENTENCED FOR GUILT IN THE
CRAVETTI BANK FRAUDS, HEARS THE DYING
CONFESSION OF A FELLOW-CONVICT NAMED
FRIMLEY. GILSON LEARNS THAT PROOFS OF
HIS INNOCENCE, TOGETHER WITH A STOLEN
FORTUNE, ARE IN A SAFE IN LONDON,
WHERE FRIMLEY HID THEM, HOPING TO
DOUBLE-CROSS HIS CHIEF, MR.BRANK.
GILSON ESCAPES FROM THE ISLAND, COMES
TO LONDON, AND TAKES OVER FRIMLEY'S
HOUSE IN PETTY FRANCE. HE KNOWS
THAT SOMEWHERE IN THE CATACOMBS
UNDER THE HOUSE THE SAFE IS HIDDEN.
THE COMBINATION HAS BEEN TAUGHT TO
A PARROT NAMED ANASTASIA. BUT BEFORE
GILSON CAN DO ANYTHING TO LOCATE THE
SAFE, BRANK AND HIS FOLLOWERS OPEN
THEIR CAMPAIGN OF TERROR TO SECURE
THE SAFE AND CONTENTS FOR THEMSELVES.
BEING WANTED BY THE POLICE, GILSON
GOES TO BLAKE FOR HELP. KNOWING HIM
TO BE INNOCENT, BLAKE AGREES AND
BRINGS IN AS ALLIES DIRK DOLLAND,
SPLASH PAGE, AND TINKER. AN OLD FRIEND
OF GILSON'S, MLLE. ROXANE, IS ALREADY
WORKING ON HIS SIDE, AND HAS SECURED
THE PARROT AND GET THE COMBINATION.
THE SAFE HAS YET TO BE FOUND.
BRANK RETALIATES. HE KIDNAPS ROXANE
AND TAKES HER TO THE HOUSE HE USES
AS "DR. REX RUSHTON." HE BELIEVES
THAT ROXANE NOT ONLY KNOWS THE
COMBINATION OF THE SAFE, BUT ALSO
KNOWS WHERE THE SAFE IS HIDDEN. HE IS
ABOUT TO TORTURE HER, BUT IS PREVENTED
BY A QUARREL BETWEEN HIMSELF AND ONE
OF HIS GANG, LA ROCQUE. WHILST THEY
ARE FIGHTING, ROXANE, IN DESPERATION,
HAS SET FIRE TO THE PLACE.
WHEN BLAKE, WHO IS TRAILING BRANK'S
CAR, ARRIVES, HE FINDS THE PLACE IN
FLAMES, AND EMPTY SAVE FOR LA ROCQUE,
WHO HAS BEEN STABBED TO DEATH BY
BRANK. BLAKE HURRIES BACK TO THE
PETTY FRANCE HOUSE. AS BRANK IS AFTER
THE SAFE, HE MAY HAVE TAKEN ROXANE
THERE. BUT IT IS DOLLAND AND GILSON
WHO OPEN THE DOOR TO HIM. THEY ARE
BOTH DRIPPING WET, HAVING ESCAPED
FROM A WATER-FILLED CHAMBER WHERE, LA
ROCQUE HAD LEFT THEM TO DIE.

G.H.TEED NOW CARRIES ON.

In the Blind Alley.

Tinker and Splash Page raced up the steps while
Blake was still staring at Dolland and Gilson.

All three pushed into the hall, and Gilson
closed the door.

"The police have gone," he announced. "Come
along into the front room."

All five entered the room on the left. Blake,
Tinker, and Splash were staring critically at the
soaking garments worn by the other two. On the
hardwood floor in the hall were dark patches
where water had dripped from the ends of coats
and trousers.

Despite Dolland's cocky air, it was plain that
he had been through some-thing very tough.
Gilson looked more washed out than ever.

Blake turned to Dolland.

"Well, what about it, Dirk? What's happened?
How did you and Gilson get out of that cellar?
And where have you been since?"

Dolland explained what had happened; how,
when he and Gilson had hidden from Inspector
Thomas behind a pile of packing-cases in the
cellar of Madame Casanova's house, his hand
had accidentally come into contact with a catch

or spring built into the wall, which released a concealed door and tumbled them both into the catacombs beneath.

"And then? But the pair of you are soaking wet. Perhaps you'd better change first."

Gilson dropped into a chair.

"You tell him, Dirk. I'm all in."

"We'll change in a moment, Blake," said Dirk. "There isn't really much to tell."

He related what had happened to him and Gilson from the time they had pitched through the concealed door in the cellar of Madame Casanova's house until they were caught by the terrific down rush of water in the underground chamber.

"When that came," he went on, "Gilson and I were caught like rats in a trap—or, rather, we thought so. It was fighting a miniature Niagara. In fact, we couldn't fight it. But it was the very violence of the rush that saved us. It droves up, naturally, and that was our only hope of getting air. And it did something else. It enabled us to reach the trap which we had found, and then crawl through.

"We were on a higher level then, of course. Gilson has mapped a good many of the levels and passages down there, but this one he didn't know. We started in the first direction that we saw, and eventually came out to a part that Gilson thought he recognised. We found an iron ladder and went down it. It brought us to what looked like the remains of an ancient sewer, and then we found a wall that us straight into the tunnel that leads from this house. It was easy enough then. We hadn't been back for more than five minutes when you arrived."

"That fits in with what La Roeque told me before he died," Blake muttered more to himself than the others. "So he did speak the truth, only he made a mistake in thinking he had drowned the pair of you."

"La Roeque—dead! What do you mean?"

It was Gilson who was speaking. The other three were staring at Blake in amazement.

"Just what I say. La Roeque was the one who swung the lever and caused the water to engulf you. He's dead now—died in my arms while the house was burning. Brank knifed him."

"Say, Blake, what on earth are you driving at?" demanded Splash. "You keep on babbling about fires and houses and La Roeque and knif-

ings. Don't forget I've got to keep my notes in order."

He had taken out his notebook and pencil, and was either making pretence of writhing or was actually adding to the voluminous notes he had already jotted down since being pitch forked into this amazing case.

"More than that," went on Blake quietly, "you can add that Brank has got Mademoiselle Roxane, and both he and Stiletti are still loose. La Roeque made a mistake. That's why he died. Just the same fate as Stutz. I'll tell you what has happened."

Briefly he related what had occurred from the moment when, at the meeting place at Victoria, he began to feel uneasy about Roxane. He skimmed over his own heroic efforts to find the girl in the burning house, but those others knew him well enough to guess what he must have gone through.

"I didn't find Roxane," he said gravely, "but I did find La Roeque. If you're still anxious about the police, Gilson, you'd better be on guard, because I've told the commissioner some of the facts about Brank, and informed him that I can be found here. There is an all-stations call out for Brank's car. But my opinion is that they will dish that as soon as possible.

"Things are moving so swiftly to a climax that I believe Brank and Stiletti will strain every effort to reach the safe tonight. Brank must know that the fire has unmasked 'Dr.Rushton.' Heaven knows what he will do to Roxane if she refuses to tell him what she knows. So I came here as swiftly as I could.

"I should not be surprised if Brank and Stiletti were even now somewhere beneath our feet searching for that safe. La Roeque told me just before he died that Brank said he had emptied the level where the safe is concealed when he turned that stream on to you two. If so, then it is exposed, and all Brank and Stiletti have to do is to blow it open. But you may know something new about those water levels."

Suddenly Blake came to life.

"Dirk, you and Gilson get off and change. Don't be longer than you can help. Tinker, you go next door and see if Madame Casanova is in. that pair may have gone through her house. Roxane may be—but go and ask."

The lad was out of the door before Dirk and Gilson reached it. When they had disappeared as well, Splash, who had been busily writing all this time, looked up.

"I say Blake, old man—"

"What is it, Splash?"

"I'm trying to get things fitted into this account of mine. I know this is a bad moment to worry you, but I wish you'd answer me one or two questions before the others get back."

"Fire away."

"You recall the first night when Gilson got you over here—the night he caught Stutz in the stair case trap?"

"Yes. What about it?"

"Stutz didn't put up any yell at the time. Why not? Why did he just lie there until Gilson bagged him?"

"That's easy. Stutz was working for Brank. He didn't want to attract the attention of the police any more than Gilson did. Besides, he knew what Brank does to those who fail him. He would rather have let Gilson trap him and count on making a getaway later, than mess things up for Brank. Of course, we know now that Brank killed him eventually for letting himself be caught."

"What a chief to work for! And why did Gilson blindfold Stutz?"

"Gilson told me why. I asked the same question. It was because he had found the catacombs far more expensive than he had imagined. He's done a lot of exploring down there on the quiet, as you heard Dirk say. He didn't think Stutz knew everything about the one that connects this house with the dummy cottage in the blind alley, and he didn't want to learn."

"So that was it. Now, another thing, Blake. Why did Gilson do a bunk from Hamright's shop when the macaw attacked me, and you came to my rescue?"

"It was because he knew the police would be on the spot within a few minutes, and he didn't want to be there to be caught. You know how jumpy he is of the Scotland Yard folks."

"I certainly do. I'll bet too, he wanted to find Stiletti or Brank. He probably figured they were somewhere underneath this house by then."

"That's just what he did figure."

"But the police were on the job. How did he get through?"

"Do you remember Roxane saying he arrived at Madame Casanova's soaking wet just before he collapsed?"

"Yes."

"He told me while he lay on the couch that he had got through the dummy cottage. Down in the stream had a fainting spell and nearly drowned. The poor devil has been through a lot you know, Splash. He looks about all in, as he says."

"He does, and he'll go through a lot more before we finish if we don't find Brank."

"He will—we all will!" agreed Blake grimly.

"Just one more, old man. How did Stiletti do that sudden disappearing act at Hamright's?"

"I'm not dead certain about that Splash, but I think I know. That place is a regular warren. Hamright took in two or three other places adjoining as his business grew, and you know what a messy old beggar he was—just knock out a wall or partition and shove a cage into the hole. My opinion is that Stilotti just dived in behind one of those cages in the back-yard and found a way out by another door. I'm going to check up on that one of these days."

Splash closed his notebook and got up. He walked across to Blake and laid a hand on his arm.

"You're anxious about Roxane, old man. What do you think can have happened?"

"I don't know, Splash. I am worried. I don't understand—Good glory! Why didn't I think of that before?"

"Of what?"

Blake did not reply. To the amazement of Splash page he turned and dashed out of the room. Splash could hear him shouting up the stairs for Dirk and Gilson to make haste.

Then he heard the front door open and, rushing to the window, saw him half way down the steps, looking towards Madame Casanova's house.

Splash saw Tinker come running along the pavement, saw him pause and speak with Blake. Then the pair came leaping up the steps into the house.

Splash made for the hall.

"What is it, Blake?"

"The dummy cottage in the blind alley. They could reach the subterranean passer-by would ever see Brank's car if it were left there."

"And Roxane?"

"They could leave her in one of the fake rooms of the dummy cottage, or take her with them. Here are Dirk and Gilson. Have you got the key of the cottage, Gilson?"

"Yes."

"Then come on, all of you!"

With that Blake rushed through the front door and down the steps, leaving the others to follow as they might.

TURNED OFF.

It took only a few minutes to reach the dummy cottage in the impasse.

The moment Sexton Blake swung the corner he knew that he was right. At the very end, with its bonnet almost touching the door, was Brank's car.

He broke into a run and peered inside the vehicle. No sign of Roxane or the two criminals.

By this time the others were close at his heels and Gilson was busy with the key. But there was no need. They had only to press the door for it to swing open.

Blake pushed past Gilson and strode to the door that gave into the tiny front room. It was as bare as ever. Only the blind and curtains at the window giving the outside world the impression that someone lived inside.

He went up the ladder to the trap in the ceiling. He threw the trap back with a slam and thrust head and shoulders through.

But there was no sign of Roxare.

There was nothing to do now but carry straight on. They made for the back yard where Blake flung back the manhole cover. Beneath. The iron ladder could be seen descending into the depths.

Blake swung his leg over the edge, but paused before begging the descent.

"Better look to your guns, fellows."

Then he was gone.

They followed him, Tinker, Splash, Dirk and Gilson. In that order. Down they went until those above heard Blake give a low word of warning.

He had swung himself across the top of the iron ladder and the wider space where the stream passed under Gilson's house—that same stream along which he had brought stutz on the first night this amazing affair began.

When the others were beside him on the wall. Blake waved his arm towards the invisible depths beyond the foot of the ladder.

"Is that the way you and Gilson got back?" he asked Dirk.

"Yes. But Gilson knows better than I do. What about it, old man?"

"This was the way. It isn't much of a drop from here to the bottom."

"Wait until I put the torch on it."

It was Tinker who spoke, and they waited until he had switched on his flashlight. They could see nothing else but wet stones beneath and brick walls dripping with moisture.

"You go to the right, and then the left," Gilson was continuing. "There are steps, lots of them, taking you to a higher level all the time. I can find the way alright."

"What we want to find is Brank and Stiletti," said Blake. "We want the level where the safe is situated. That's where we"ll find that pair."

"If it was under water before, Brank may be able to flood it again," put in Splash.

"I'm thinking of that," Blake assured him. "If he is able to do so, then I should say there must be a control that will switch the water from that level to the place where Dirk and Gilson were trapped, and vice versa. We'll have to keep that in mind. And, anyway, before we finish with this job, we may have to use a diving-suit. You lead the way, Gilson."

They dropped from the wall, one after the other. Gilson also had a flashlight, and this he used in the lead, while Tinker brought up the rear with his.

It was only a short distance to the point where they turned right into a much wider, vaulted tunnel, and then, after a matter of ten or twelve yards, they turned abruptly left, leaving the stream behind then, and finding a flight of very roughly cut and laid stone steps ahead. No one could say how many centuries ago or for what purpose those steps had been built; or, possibly, they had once been right out in the open, serving the bank of the stream where gallants took their ladies a-boating.

But just now the place was a fetid sewer. Big water-rats, the first they had seen, went dashing away, with startled squeaks, though they didn't go far; for, if one turned, one could see their vicious, little, beady eyes watching hopefully.

Up and up and up the five climbed until it seemed to Blake that they must surely be reaching something like ground level. But he was not allowing for the fact that, ever since leaving the end of the iron ladder, they had been going deeper with each step.

The steps ended abruptly in a narrow passage which gave almost immediately into a wider passage. And here Gilson paused, pointing straight ahead.

"That's the way we came," he whispered. "Shall I carry on to the point where Dolland and I came through the trap?"

"The trap—the trap—the t-r-a-p !"

All five stood frozen in their tracks as the words boomed back upon them sepulchrally. It sounded like the deep, mocking voice of the Doomsman. Was it Brank, or was it an echo playing them this sinister trick?

With one accord Tinker and Gilson had doused their torches. It was now as dark as the pit of Toped. Not a single glimmer came from any direction. So intense was the blackness, indeed, that their staring pupils began to ache with the strain.

Then out of that terrible blackness came another booming sound—horrible, sinister, mirthless laughter.

It was worse than the crazy screaming of Ma Gilson. Hard bitten though those five were, they felt a shiver at the eerie sound.

And then all doubt vanished, for someone began to speak, and they knew it was Brank.

"I've been waiting, my beauties!" he boomed from the darkness beyond. "I've been waiting to receive you ! I knew that fool Gilson would lead you here! So we prepared, Stiletti and I!"

He broke off with another unearthly cackle. Then Blake, who was now in advance, put out his arms quickly, and made as if to sweep the others back into the narrow passage out of which they had stepped.

But too late!

Even as he made the movement, the darkness was split asunder by a rapid succession of flashes, accompanied by the almost continuous racketing of automatic pistols.

With bullets spattering into the stones at their feet and into the wall beside them, they surged as one man into the branch passage.

But only for a moment did they hold this cover. Following Blake's flashing on of his own torch, each one drew his gun; and then at Blake's heels, rushed back into the wider passage and straight along towards the spot from which the shooting came.

Blake knew it could only be Brank and Stiletti. But was it only those two? Or were they dragging Roxane along with them?

His cogitations were knocked out of him as he crashed with violence into a part of the stone wall that jutted out. At the same moment came that crazy, mocking laugh once more.

"Ha, ha, ha!"

There were flashes in a direction entirely different from that which Blake had expected. He seemed, too, to see a thin line of crimson formed by the explosion of the powder as the bullet left the weapon.

The noise was appalling for the acoustics of the place were of such a nature that every sound was magnified, and echoed and re-echoed in most confusing way.

Then suddenly, as if the intense darkness has completely over whelmed them. Brank and Stiletti were heard no more.

YET, had Blake been able to pierce the blackness, he would have seen that they had their hands full with another problem.

Blake's sudden arrival had been unexpected by Brank, despite his boast. He had figured on having plenty of time to complete his fiendish work before Blake could possibly track him down.

And this work was fiendish enough in all truth. For he had hauled Roxane along and he was determined that the work he had began at the house which was now in ashes should be completed here in the safe darkness of these catacombs.

Until this moment Roxane had been helpless. Her legs had been left free, but she had been gagged and her wrists practically carried along by Brank and Stiletto for Brank believed that she knew where the hidden safe was situated and, despite her denials back at the house, that she knew how to open it.

And there, in the concealment of a short and tunnel, which the searchers might pass and repass a dozen times without seeing the opening, he slammed the girl against the wall and dragged off the gag.

"Now, you, listen!" she heard him snarl. "I'm not going to waste any time. You've got just one chance of life. And you've got to make things snappy. Where is that safe? I'm not going to ask twice. Unless you give me the truth within ten seconds I'm going to pitch you into a pool of light from which nothing will get you out. Hurry up—I'm waiting."

"I can't tell you."

Her words came painfully and thickly, for the gag had caused her tongue to swell. But Brank heard her and scarcely had the last word fallen from her bruised lips than he struck her across the face with brutal strength.

She screamed in a sudden outburst of pain and panic. It was that scream echoing and re-echoing among the catacombs that reached Sexton Blake, who at the moment was rushing along another passage trying desperately to locate Brank and Stiletti.

Roxane got no second chance to scream. The same hand that had smashed her so brutally now gripped her throat, and another hand—the thumb and five fingers of Stiletti—forced the gag back between her teeth.

Roxane went suddenly limp in their hands. She slid towards the ground, and all Brank's brutal dragging did not make her stand upright.

He released her in order to get at his torch. Stiletti had drawn back a step. And then, with wrists still bound and gagged though she was, Roxane rushed blindly into the darkness.

She could not know where she was going. She crashed again and again into the jagged stone of the walls, brushing her face and once causing her brain to reel with the force of the collision. But she was numb to this physical pain. She was driven by one overwhelming desire—to find Sexton Blake.

But Brank and Stiletti were after her like weasels after a rabbit. Before she could stumble into a wider passage they had caught her, and while her body shook with terrible sobs of hopelessness they dragged her back once more.

In the meantime, Blake and his party had got farther and farther away. Blake had risked switching on his torch, expecting each moment that Brank and Stiletti would begin a fresh fusilade from the darkness.

But nothing happened. Not a sound had come since that one eerie scream of Roxane's. Passages seemed to break off in all directions. It was becoming more and more of a maze, and when Blake consulted with Gilson he found that it was all as unknown to Gilson as to himself.

Still Blake advanced, desperately hoping that at any moment his light would uncover the pair of scoundrels he sought. But now a new sound

came to him, the quick rush of water that grew louder and louder as they pushed ahead.

All at once the probing spear of light from the torch fell on what looked like a miniature waterfall. It was at the very end of the passage they were following, and as they drew still nearer they could see that it was indeed a small rushing torrent racing through a sort of open culvert.

They could go no farther. The rushing water cut their passage completely in two.

The volume was piling into an open channel that was carrying it off, some where into the unknown darkness. Blake was still standing, staring at this new barrier when he heard Tinker say:

"If we could turn that stream off we might get past or work our way round it."

"Turn it off!"

The phrase caught Blake's ear, and he stiffened.

"Turn it off!"

What was it the parrot had said?

"Turn off the water, Mr. Brank."

Wheeling suddenly, Blake passed his torch to Tinker, and then, while the others watched in amazement, he moved closer to the pushing water and plunged his arm in almost up to the shoulder.

He worked his hand this way and that for some moments, until all at once he found an obstruction. Catching hold of this, he gave a turn, and another and another until the cock would turn no more.

But already the flow of water was lessening. Smaller and smaller grew that miniature Niagara until only a thin short of water was sliding down over the stone behind. Then that shrank to no more than a trickle and when Blake took the torch from Tinker and threw the glare full on the stone, several sharp gasps rose in the confines of that tunnel.

For there before them, plainly visible behind a thin sheet of cement that had flaked away in spots, was what could not be mistaken for anything else but the steel door of a safe.

Move 10 by Gwyn Evans

Foreword.

This unique serial is a contest of skill between the above four authors, who are writing the installments in turn. Featured in the story are six famous UNION JACK characters—Blake, Tinker, Coutts, Dirk Dolland, Splash Page and Mlle. Roxane. Previous moves in the story are:

On Devil's Island, Morgan Gilson, wrongly sentenced for guilt in the Cravetti bank frauds, hears the dying confession of a fellow-convict named Frimley. Gilson learns that proofs of his innocence, together with a stolen fortune, are in a safe in London, where Frimley hid them, hoping to double-cross his chief, Mr. Brank. Gilson escapes from the island, comes to London, and takes over Frimley's house in Petty France. He knows that somewhere in the catacombs under the house the safe is hidden. The combination has been taught to a parrot named Anastasia. But before Gilson can do anything to locate the safe, Brank and his followers open their campaign of terror to secure the safe and contents for themselves. Gilson goes to Blake for help. Knowing him to be innocent, Blake agrees and brings in as allies Dirk Dolland, Splash Page, and Tinker. Mlle. Roxane, is already working on his side, and has secured the parrot and gets the combination. The safe has yet to be found. Brank and his agent, Stiletti, kidnap Roxane to torture her into telling them the combination and where abouts of the safe, which they mistakenly believe she knows. Blake is trailing then and knows that Brank will make for the catacombs under Petty France. He picks up Tinker, Page, Dolland, and Gilson, and the five of then enter the catacombs via a "dummy house" which camouflages one of the entrances into the tunnels. For a second they glimpse Brank, Stiletti, and the captive Roxane, but, after a fusillade of shots, Brank eludes them and their quarry escape into the dark labyrinth of subterranean passes. Anxious over the fate of Roxane, Blake and his party continue the pursuit. They suddenly come to a rushing torrent which, pouring from a culvert, bars their way. Then Blake discovers a lever under the water. He pulls it and slowly the torrent thins to a trickle and in the light of Blake's torch the friends see revealed the steel door of Frimley's hidden safe!

(Gwyn Evans now carries on)

To save Roxane.

"Holy Joe!" gasped Splash Page. "The Frimley millions at last!"

Sexton Blake's lips tightened as he clambered back up the slimy bank and shook the water from his dripping sleeves.

"I think our quest is ended from Gilson's point of view," he remarked quietly.

Gilson swayed dizzily. His face was bloodless, but his eyes gleamed with feverish excitement. Dirk Dolland gripped him by the arm to steady him.

"Hold hard, old lad," he said. "Easy does it!"

"And now what, Blake?" asked Splash. He gazed eagerly at the chipped and flaking skin of cement behind which was hidden the safe door. And in that safe were the Frimley millions, the tainted money that had brought death and disaster to so many lives.

Sexton Blake's lips set in a grim, hard line.

The dramatic discovery of the safe after the nightmare events of the past few hours meant far less to him than to the others. At the moment he was not thinking of Gilson, or of Gilson's quixotic promise to the dying Frimley in the jungle, but of that despairing scream of Mademoiselle

Roxane. The discovery of the safe behind the concealing layer of cement had been an accident and incidental to search for Roxane during their explorations of the labyrinthine passages under the house in Petty France, while trying to track her and her captors down.

He knew too well the ruthless ferocity of Brank; knew that, in the desperation and urgency of his search for the safe before anyone else could find it, he would unhesitatingly go to any lengths in the torture or maltreatment of the girl.

Blake turned to Splash Page and Tinker.

"This is the safe, obviously," he said, "but the question is whether we out to try to find—"

He broke off suddenly as a stifled groan came from Gilson. Blake flashed his torch on the man's face. Gilson looked ghastly; his lips were ashen, little flecks of foam frothed round the corners of his mouth.

Blake glanced significantly at Dolland.

"He's all in I guess." said the Bat.

Gilson's eyes blazed feverishly, and his voice broke on a harsh, hysterical note.

"Let me get at it! Let me get at it!" he gasped. "I promised Frimley! Curse Brank! We've beaten him, Blake we've beaten him!"

"Stop that, man!" Blake rapped out sternly. "Pull yourself together! The safe can wait."

"Look here, Blake," broke in Dolland. "Don't you think it would simplify matters if I took Gilson back to Baker Street? He's on the verge of collapse. The last place in the world that Thomas will look for him will be your place."

Sexton Blake nodded.

His momentary quandary whether to investigate the safe further—perhaps even to try to open it—or to go in search of Roxane, was decided.

Once more he plunged into the culvert and seized the rusty stop cock.

"What are you doing, guv'nor?" gasped Tinker, in astonishment.

Blake smiled.

"Turning the water on," he said.

"We can find this place again, and we don't want Brank to locate it in the meantime. The falling water hides the safe, you see."

The original closing of the stop cock had evidently had the effect of diverting the stream down some alternative pipe, for the water which had fallen over the face of the cement covered safe door—the cliff of a miniature Niagara, as it were—was not dammed or held up.

It flowed away somewhere from the upper level unseen; and the bed of the stream, along which it had formerly found its outlet, was now dry—if the mud and ooze that squelched around Blake's boots could be called dry. Apparently turning the stopcock closed one exit and opened another, for as Blake turned the wheel the suddenly released water surged along the upper watercourse with a rushing sound towards the artificial precipice of the safe-top, in constantly increasing volume.

Blake, having turned the stopcock to its limit, scrambled up the bank once more, out of the way.

In the light of their torches the party gazed for a moment at the curtain of falling water that again hid Frimley's hoard from the world.

"Well," said Blake, "we'd better do something and quickly at that."

He glanced at his right, where the newly released stream tumbled and frothed away from the orbit of their illumination into the darkness of another vaulted tunnel.

THEY stood, as it were, at the crossroads. The tunnel along which they had come apparently continued on the far side of the shallow watercourse, which crossed it at right angles. The waterfall was on their left at the junction of the roads, and the tunnel on the right possessed a sort of narrow, eighteen-inch-wide path by the side of the stream, something like a miniature towing-path. This was all Blake could distinguish in the darkness, for the watercourse tunnel took a right hand curve, and what was beyond was mere conjecture.

He was looking at this, and wondering whether it was worth while to spend precious moments in exploring it, when suddenly a vivid beam of light cut a yellow swathe through the gloom round the curve of the path.

Blake was half blinded by its momentary glare. It came from the foot path by the watercourse. Whoever was carrying the light had just rounded the curve—and inevitably had seen them.

Crack !

A tongue of flame spat from the darkness. The noise of the shot reverberated thunderously through the dark, echoing tunnels.

"Gosh!" gasped Splash Page, jerking out his gun. "It's Brank!"

Instinctively the four men flattened themselves against the dank, slime encrusted brickwork of the tunnel, sheltering behind the wall which formed the angle of the crossroads.

The harsh laugh of the Doomsman sounded, rising above the rushing and tumbling of the stream.

Blake's lips tightened. There was no doubt about the situation. They had found Brank—or, rather, Brank had found them! It would have to be a fight to the finish!

Brank's torch snapped out. Before the others could so much as blink in the sudden darkness, Brank flashed on his own powerful light. Revealed with the clarity of a cinema film, in the oval glare they saw Brank. His face was distorted with hatred, and in his hand was a heavy automatic. Behind him stood Stiletti, balancing on the narrow cat walk with the semi-conscious Roxane flung like a sack of coals over his shoulder.

They had evidently come in single file along the narrow ledge beside the stream. So far as the strategic advantage of the position was concerned, Blake realized it was exactly fifty-fifty. Brank could retreat beyond the curve and take a pot-shot at any one who advanced; and Blake's party could retreat behind the angle of the walk and do like wise.

Only one man could pass along the cat-walk at a time, and he would virtually be committing suicide. It was hopeless to try to take Brank and Stiletti in the rear, because nobody knew how to approach them. The passages were a perfect labyrinth, and even Gilson confessed his ignorance in reply to Blake's question.

"Speak up, curse you!" rasped Brank's voice through the darkness. Evidentally he had heard the whispering. There was a mutual pause, and then he shouted:

"We've got you, Blake! Got you where we want you !"

Still Blake remained silent. He was seized with a sudden doubt. When he had turned the water off—had Brank heard anything of their talk? Perhaps—and perhaps not. But he had certainly noticed the water begin flowing. Probably he knew of the parrot's cry: "Turn the water off, Mr. Brank!" If so, would he suspect anything? But there was no answer to that; and, meantime, over the concealed safe and along the water-

course the underground stream frothed and foamed like a millrace.

Crack, crack, crack!

Splash Page darted out of cover and fired blindly into the gloom ahead.

"Surrender, Blake," snarled Brank, "or I'll put a bullet through this girl's head!"

Blake's brain worked rapidly.

To advance along the narrow path-way was impossible. The only way to reach Brank and take him by surprise was through the icy stream.

"Listen, Brank!" he said. "We're four to two. If you harm a hair of Roxane's head I'll strangle you with my own hands!"

"Come and do it!" jeered Brank, from the darkness beyond the curve.

"I'll give you ten seconds to surrender; otherwise I shoot the woman!"

"You filthy rat!" snapped Tinker, whitefaced. The lad's nerve were near to breaking-point.

"One—two—three—four—"

The hardsh metallic voice of rank boomed mockingly through the passageway.

Sexton Blake turned to Splash Page and gripped him by the arm.

"Splash," he said, "I'm going to take a chance!"

"Stop, Blake, you fool," hissed the newspaperman. "It's sudden death."

"Seven—eight—nine—"

Blake, with the automatic in his right hand, leapt from the shelter of the brickwork and plunged straight into the rushing water.

Bang!

A shot sounded from the gloom to Blake's right along the stream.

"By Heaven, he's done it!" gasped Tinker, sick with horror.

"That ends the woman!" shouted Brank. "Now you, Blake!"

Sexton Blake said nothing; did not trouble to try to avoid the bullet as he allowed himself to be carried along to the thrust of the water. It was almost up to his armpits, but he held his gun well above the flood.

Several times he was almost flung off his feet. He concentrated on maintaining an upright position and making sure of his foothold as he was pushed forward towards the spot where he knew the two men and Roxane to be.

He sensed, rather than saw, the presence of Brank and Stiletti standing on the narrow path beside the stream. He dared not fire yet. The water swayed his body as he balanced himself on the toes and he had to aim accurately or not at all. Besides, there was a chance that Brank was only bluffing in his threat to shoot the girl.

She alone—as far as Brank knew—possessed the secret of the safe combination. And, Blake argued, as he advanced through the swirling eddies of that malodorous, mud-churning water, Brank would hardly be such a fool to kill her until he had learnt the secret.

Brank's exultant laugh again rang through the tunnel. Apparently, in the darkness, relieved only by the glow of the torches of either party, Brank had not yet seen him.

"Back farther round the curve." Blake heard him say. "If they attempt to rush us they can only come one at a time."

Stiletti grunted.

"It's a risky business, boss," he said. "The water's rising."

"Quick!" hissed Brank. "Do as I tell you, you fool!"

Stiletti backed hastily away.

Crack!

Brank's gun spoke again. He was going at random towards the rushing sound of the waterfall, where, behind the corner, the other members of Blake's party were under cover.

Sexton Blake's lips drew back in a mirthless smile, for the tell-tale flash of flame had given him Brank's location.

Edging in towards the side, the one to the bank, Brank's first realization of danger was when he felt two hands closed about his windpipe.

He staggered back, his eyes bulged and his tongue protruded beneath that vice-like grip. Instinctively his finger tightened on the trigger of his gun, and a bullet, ricocheting from the brick roof, went whining down the tunnel.

Blake drew back his left fist and crashed it full into the Doomsman's face.

"What have you done with Roxane?" he snarled.

Desperately Brank strove to maintain his balance, but that paralyzing blow had sent a numbing shock through his body. His automatic fell with a clatter.

Brank gurgled out some unintelligible, meaningless sound, and as Blake shook him as a terrier would a rat he felt himself hurled against the shiny walls of the tunnel with a ferocity that beat the remaining breath out of him.

Sick from the shock, Brank slid to the ground. For a wild moment, he thrashed mechanically with failing fists at his enemy's face as Blake sprawled on top of him; but the blows fell vainly, and though he kicked and hacked savagely at Blake's shins, the detective's relentless pressure on his windpipe never relaxed.

Brank was far from being a weakling, but against the cold savage fury that was Sexton Blake he no chance.

Slowly but surely, Brank felt himself thrust over the edge as they struggled on the brink of the underground stream.

Suddenly Brank felt the ground vanish from beneath his back. He was poised above the racing water. He was dimly conscious of the trickle of blood from his broken nose. He struggled feebly, a roaring sound reverberating in his tortured ears.

Then something hit the back of his head. His senses left him, and he fell through space, it seemed, into the blankness of complete oblivion.

What had actually happened was that the two of them, struggling on the edge, had fallen in together. Blake had gone under for a moment, and been in danger of losing his footing, but had recovered himself in time to see Brank's figure floating away.

Sexton Blake laughed grimly in that tense moment as he watched the figure of Brank borne away on the torrent. He was in no mood for rescue. "Let him look after himself," was his decision then. He could not forget the man's treatment of Roxane, or the girl's present danger.

"Come on you fellows!" he called in a curiously strained voice.

"Where are you, guv'nor? Where are you?" came the voice of Tinker.

Blake staggered breathlessly against the rush of water.

"Flash your torch!" he called out. "I've got Brank; I'm here."

Instantly a probing beam of light slashed through the darkness and Blake was able to obtain a glimpse of his surroundings.

The narrow path at the edge of the water where the two men had been was empty. Of Stiletti and Roxane there was now no sign. With an effort Blake waded towards the path, and clutched a rusty iron staple in the wall. For a moment he stood there recovering his wind, then drew himself up.

"Roxane! Roxane!" he called. His voice echoed eerily down the corridor.

Silence, save for the babbling and gurgling of the black water as it gushed along its underground, stygian course.

"We're coming, guv'nor!" called Tinker from the direction of the waterfall.

Blake drew in his breath in deep gulps. Whether Brank was alive or dead, he neither knew nor cared. His one object now was to find Roxane.

Tinker's stumbling footsteps sounded nearer, and a moment later the lad, with Splash Page at his heels, came along the narrow path on which Blake was standing.

"Gosh, guv'nor! Are you all right?"

Blake laughed softly.

"I'm all right, young 'un!" he said. "Give me that torch."

"Where's Brank?" queried Splash.

Blake pointed to the swirling waters.

"In there," he said. "That fellow Stiletti—"

He broke off suddenly. A scream sounded some distance ahead.

Keyed up as they were to the events that had just happened in that catacomb, the shrill, heartrending sound that echoed through the passages literally made their flesh crawl with the horror of it.

"Roxane!" said Splash Page.

Sexton Blake gritted his teeth.

"Come on, you two!" he said grimly. "She's alive!"

The Bat was usually a nonchalant individual in moments of crisis. In fact, the greater the crisis, the more coolly did his brain work. But even Dirk Dolland was beginning to feel the strain of the past few hours.

Gilson was all in, and the Bat saw that it would be hopeless to try to make him walk down the labyrinthine passages that led under Frimley's house.

When Splash and Tinker had gone in response to Blake's urgent summons, he gripped Gilson by the sleeve.

"Listen, Morgan! I'll give you a fireman's lift. Relax your body, and we'll get through quicker that way!"

Gilson swayed.

"Thanks, Dolland!" he said faintly. "Sorry to be such a nuisance, but —"

His voice trailed away into silence. His over-wrought nerves had given way. Gritting his teeth, Dirk Dolland hoisted him over his shoulder.

He gasped with the effort of carrying his burden. The air underground was humid and close. He had no very clear sense of direction, but from the gleam to the right, where Splash Page and Tinker proceeded, he was able to make a rough conjecture regarding the way to the exit into the dummy cottage; and Gilson, who knew some of the passages, was able to guide him with a word now and again.

Panting with his load, Dolland struggled on until finally he was cheered by the sight of the pale beam of light that indicated the manhole, so cunningly hidden from the casual passers-by in Petty France.

Slowly, and with infinite caution he mounted the rungs of the steel ladder. Perspiration trickled through the skin on his forehead. His mouth was dry and parched, and Gilson was a dead weight about his shoulders.

The climb seemed to be interminable, but suddenly he drew in a grateful gasp of air and emerged into a semi-twilight, which after the gloom of the sewers was almost dazzling by contrast.

The Bat emerged into the open air. He took out a handkerchief from his breast-pocket and wiped his steaming forehead.

"Gosh, I'll be glad to get back to Baker Street!" he murmured. "This game's getting too hot for me!"

He entered the dummy cottage by the rear and pulled back the curtain.

Brank's car was still outside. The Bat grinned.

"For this relief, much thanks!" he murmured, and opened the front door.

"Kind of Mr. Brank to leave us his car!" he said, with a breathless chuckle. "It'll save taxi fares!"

He pulled the door of the dummy cottage cautiously shut behind him, then halted suddenly.

"What are you doing here?" a familiar voice said sharply.

Dirk Dolland's jaw sagged open.

In the dim light of an adjacent street lamp, he glimpsed the burly, aggressive figure of his old enemy, Detective-Inspector Thomas, of the

C.I.D. Behind the Yard man loomed four blue-uniformed constables.

The Bat hesitated. He was caught in a cleft stick, handicapped as he was by his unconscious burden. For once, his imperturbability failed. Detective-Inspector Thomas started as he recognised the Bat.

"I've got you, Dolland!" said Thomas, with an ugly grin. "Are you coming quietly?"

THE NEXT MOVE

OUR FASCINATING, NOVEL, FOUR— AUTHOR SERIAL BY –
G.H. TEED.
GWYN EVANS.
ROBERT MURRAY.
ANTHONY SKENE.

FOREWORD:

THE ABOVE FOUR AUTHORS ARE CONTRIBUTING THE INSTALMENTS OF THIS UNIQUE SERIAL IN TURN, COMPETING WITH EACH BY SETTING PUZZLES FOR THE NEXT MAN TO SOLVE. HERE ARE THE MAIN EVENTS OF THE STORY SO FAR:

MORGAN GILSON ESCAPES FROM DEVIL'S ISLAND AFTER HAVING HEARD THE DYING CONFESSION OF A CONVICT NAMED FRIMLEY THAT THE PROCEEDS OF A BANK FRAUD, FOR WHICH GILSON HAS BEEN WRONGFULLY SENTENCED TOGETHER WITH PROOFS OF GILSON'S INNOCENCE, ARE HIDDEN IN A SAFE IN PETTY FRANCE, LONDON. FRIMLEY WAS A MEMBER OF THE GANG, HEADED BY A MASTER CROOK NAMED BRANK, WHICH CARRIED OUT THE FRAUDS. IN HIDING THE LOOT, FRIMLEY HOPED TO DOUBLE-CROSS HIS CHIEF.

GILSON COMES TO LONDON, TAKES OVER FRIMLEY'S OLD HOUSE IN PETTY FRANCE, AND SETS ABOUT SEARCHING FOR THE SAFE WHICH IS HIDDEN IN THE CATACOMBS UNDER THE HOUSE. THE COMBINATION TO OPEN IT IS KNOWN ONLY BY A PARROT. BRANK HAS FOLLOWED GILSON AND BECAUSE OF THE CROOK'S TERRORISTIC METHODS, GILSON SEEKS THE AID OF SEXTON BLAKE. BLAKE AGREES TO HELP HIM AND BRINGS IN AS ALLIES HIS ASSISTANT TINKER, DIRK DOLLAND, AND SPLASH PAGE. MLLE.ROXANE IS ALREADY ON GILSON'S SIDE AND HAS DISCOVERED THE PARROT'S SECRET.

BRANK RETALIATES BY KIDNAPPING ROXANE AND TAKES HER INTO THE CATACOMBS WITH THE IDEA OF TORTURING HER TO REVEAL THE WHEREABOUTS AND COMBINATION OF THE SAFE. BLAKE AND THE OTHERS ARE HOT IN PURSUIT TO SAVE ROXANE. BY ACCIDENT, BLAKE HAS DISCOVERED THE SAFE WHICH IS UNSEALED BEHIND AN ARTIFICIAL WATERFALL IN AN UNDERGROUND STREAM THAT RUNS THROUGH THE CATACOMBS. BLAKE CATCHES UP WITH BRANK. THERE IS A STRUGGLE BETWEEN THE TWO IN WHICH BRANK IS KNOCKED OUT AND CARRIED OFF BY THE STREAM. BUT ROXANE IS STILL A PRISONER IN THE HANDS OF BRANK'S MURDEROUS HENCHMAN, STILETTI. MEANTIME, DOLLAND HAS CARRIED GILSON, WHO IS ON THE POINT OF COLLAPSE, BACK TO GROUND LEVEL. AS THEY EMERGE FROM THE MANHOLE EXIT THEY ARE SEIZED BY INSPECTOR THOMAS AND ARRESTED. (ROBERT MURRAY NOW CARRIES ON.)

INSPECTOR THOMAS FALLS IN.

Dirk Dolland knew that he must present a sorry figure as he stood in the entrance to the dummy cottage, his boots and clothes plastered with the foul mud of the catacombs, the limp figure of Gilson draped awkwardly over one shoulder.

His brain raced as he strove to grapple with the situation. He could see no loophole of escape. Inspector Thomas loomed formidably before him, with his subordinates hanging vigilantly in the background.

"Who have you got there?" snapped Thomas, stepping closer. "By James, it's Gilson! What's the matter with the man? Is he dead?"

"Hush! He's asleep," answered the Bat gravely, still fighting for time. "Please save him the shock of awakening to find half the force of Scotland Yard gathered around him!"

"That'll do, Dolland! I don't want any wise-cracks from you!" warned the inspector testily. "You've been playing a pretty game with me, and now we're going to have a show-down. Where's Blake? Where's that girl Roxane?"

The Bat carefully lowered Gilson to the ground, propping him firmly against the closed door. Deliberately he lit a cigarette, his blue eyes gleaming defiantly in the flicker of the match-flame.

"Thomas, you ask the most stupid, futile questions!" he drawled. "The whereabouts of Blake and Mademoiselle Roxane is of no paramount importance, so far as you are concerned. They are pursuing a duty that you are neglecting."

"What the devil do you mean?"

"I mean," proceeded Dolland measuredly, "that you and your men should be devoting all your efforts to the capture of Brank, the Dooms-man, instead of butting in on Blake's attempts to bring a dangerous criminal to justice, and, at the same time, to remedy the wrong that Gilson has suffered."

"You're talking like a fool!" said Thomas unpleasantly.

There was a flash of steel as he dexterously clipped handcuffs on the Bat's wrists.

"You are behaving like one!" was the ex-cracksman's blunt reply. "You haven't got a thing on me, Thomas. What's the charge?

"Obstruction—anything you like!" sneered the C.I.D man. "I'm not taking any risks with a man possessing a record like yours. As for Gilson—"

He bent over the still senseless man, propped against the door to the dummy cottage; felt Gilson's pulse, flashed the beam of his lantern into his white face, lifted an eyelid with an ungentle thumb.

"Humph! He's not foxing!" he grunted unsympathetically, "out to the wide !"

"He's in a bad way," said Dolland seriously. "He needs medical attention, and if he doesn't get it I shall hold you responsible."

"Don't try to teach me my duty!" blared Thomas. "He'll get all he's entitled to where I'm going to send him! Take him away, you men! Take him to Cannon Row, and hold him on the French extradition warrant. Whom does this car belong to?"

"The Chinese Ambassador," answered Dolland gravely.

The inspector glared, and bit his lip.

"Take the car!" he ordered recklessly. "It's causing an obstruction, and is showing no lights. You can find the owner later on, when Gilson is safe in a cell."

The Bat smiled faintly. It was evident that Thomas had jumped to the conclusion that the car was his property. He had no objection to its removal, seeing that it belonged to Brank, whom he hoped would have no further use for it.

Two of the constables lifted Gilson unceremoniously into the saloon. A third seated himself at the wheel and switched on the lights. The fourth man lingered on the pavement, glancing questioningly at the scowling inspector.

"Get back on your beat ! I shan't need you ! snapped Thomas. "You can leave this fellow to me. I'm quite capable of dealing with him."

The car started, gathered speed, and roared away into the night. Dolland and Thomas were alone outside the dummy cottage. There was a momentary silence while the inspector tilted his bowler on the back of his head, jammed his hands in his pockets, and favoured his prisoner with a less truculent stare.

"Let's get down to brass tacks, Dolland," he suggested bluntly. "I want to get to the bottom of this business, and I don't wish to do Gilson or anyone else an injustice."

"An injustice! What about these?" came back the Bat, jingling the hand cuffs on his wrists.

To his surprise, the inspector produced the key, unfastened the manacles, and slipped them back in his pocket.

"It's time we all got together instead of working at cross purposes," he said briskly. "Gilson is under arrest, and I was only doing my duty in apprehending him. If he is the victim of an injustice—as you say Blake is trying to prove—he will have the opportunity to oppose extradition. In the meantime, let's get busy, Dolland."

The Bat frowned puzzledly,

"What," he asked, "exactly do you mean?"

"I mean that I want you to take me to Blake and the others," announced the inspector impatiently. "I know that they are down below in those infernal catacombs. And it is pretty obvious by your appearance that you and Gilson have just come from there."

Dolland was silent for as long as it took him to make a swift review of the entire situation. Thomas was behaving more like a human being, and he could see no reason why he should not be allowed to share in the final scenes of the drama that was staged around the missing Frimley millions.

Gilson was temporarily out of the picture. There was no further necessity to oppose Thomas in that direction. The hiding place of the safe had been discovered, and it only remained to probe its secrets, and, incidentally, to rescue Roxane and put an end to the menace of Brank, the Doomsman, and his evil henchman, Stiletti.

In all these tasks Inspector Thomas might prove an able and useful assistant. The altered circumstances merited his co-operation. After all, he represented the law, and the law would have the final say with Brank.

"O.K., Thomas! I'm your man!" snapped the Bat, flinging the end of his cigarette to the pavement. "That is Brank's car you grabbed just now. Brank is down below, and so is Blake. If you're game to take the risk of stopping a bullet or getting chewed to pieces by sewer rats, say the word!"

The inspector merely nodded, and tested the battery of his electric lamp. It was fully charged.

"I take it we go this way?" he asked, clutching the knob of the door to the dummy cottage and flinging it open.

There was the dull sound of a smashing blow as a dark figure loomed beyond the threshold. Thomas's knee buckled. Without a sound, he pitched limply to the ground, his lamp shattering to darkness, his bowler-hat rolling crazily across the pavement.

The beam of a torch stabbed full in Dirk Dolland's astounded face. The blunt muzzle of an automatic pistol came from nowhere, to clamp itself firmly in the centre of his forehead.

"Step inside, Mr. Dolland," invited the jeering voice of Brank, "unless you prefer to be dragged in by the heels, with a bullet in your fool's head!"

Dolland had no choice in the matter. He knew death when he met it, and he was not anxious to become the Doomsman's latest victim. Mechanically he stepped forward, as if drawn magnetically by torch and pistol.

The moment after Roxane had uttered that shrill scream of terror which had brought Blake dashing down one of the tunnels to see her held

in the grasp of Brank and Stiletti on the narrow ledge that skirted the black waters of the underground stream, she was struck dumb by a paralyzing sense of fear.

Everything swooned into confusion in her terror racked brain as she was swung supine over Stiletti's shoulder; the crook's rough careless hands bruising the delicate flesh of her slender limbs.

She was not conscious of having screamed. She knew that Sexton Blake was somewhere close at hand. She had heard his voice—had heard the vicious bark of automatics awakening a thousand echoes in the hollow cata-combs.

"Surrender, Blake, or I'll put a bullet through the girl's head."

Now it was the Doomsman's snarling voice, and she could feel the muzzle of his pistol, cold as a slug, gliding searchingly up her cheek.

Something had snapped in Roxane's brain. She knew nothing of what occurred during those next fateful moments when Sexton Blake plunged desperately into the rushing waters, to come to grips with Brank, and drag him from his perch.

Stiletti uttered a squeal of dismay as he dimly saw the detective and his quarry swaying on the edge of the ledge, locked together in rigid embrace. Even as he fumbled for his automatic the two men lost their footing and toppled head long into the foaming torrent.

The loss of Brank's leadership left Stiletti without courage or resource. For a matter of moments he crouched back against the dripping wall still gripping Roxane's limp figure, while his bulging eyes probed the darkness below.

"Brank—Brank!" His voice was an inaudible croak. Roxane stirred and moaned. From the enveloping gloom came splashing and flounderings, and then a hail that jerked Stiletti to action.

"Come on, you follows!" cried Blake. "I've got Brank—I'm here!"

It was not perfectly true. The detective was there, but the Doomsman had been swept away in the raging waters.

Whimpering with terror, Stiletti commenced to sidle away along the narrow ledge.

He cursed viciously as the reviving Roxane suddenly uttered the shrill, heart-rending cry that notified Blake and his companions that she was still alive.

Stiletti groped for the girl's face, clasping his free hand brutally over her mouth, as he carried her farther and farther into the depths of the catacombs.

The voices of his pursuers faded in the distance, and now, faint above the roar of waters, came another sound—another voice—pitched in acute distress and appeal.

"Stiletti! Stiletti!"

It was the voice of Brank, coming eerily from the darkness. Stiletti halted—shuffled another few steps, hampered by his limp burden. He ventured a husky call.

"Brank, where are you? Where are you, boss?"

"Farther on," came the gasping response. "Switch on your torch, you fool ! I'm almost all in!"

Guided by the voice of his leader, Stiletti continued to advance, stabbing the darkness with a searching beam of light.

"Stop! Down below, man!"

Brank's white face gleamed amid the swift, black torrent, directly underneath the ledge where Stiletti crouched. He was clinging to the wall of the tunnel, his straining fingers wound around a jutting spur of rock.

"Hurry yourself, you cursed fool!" he gasped. "Lend me a hand. I can't hold on much longer. I shall have to let go in a moment."

Stiletti hesitated, blinking and gaping.

"What about the girl? What shall I do with her? he croaked.

"Curse the girl!" snarled the Doomsman. "Knock her on the head, if she's conscious. Dump her on the ledge."

The gunman dropped Roxane sprawling at his feet. Her eyes were closed. She lay limp and unresisting. Stiletti was not to know that she was feigning insensibility—that she was struggling with her weary senses to get a grasp of situation to control her quivering nerves.

The man clenched his fist, poising it for a stunning blow. Muttering, he changed his mind, transferring his attentions to his helpless leader. He knelt down, placing his lighted torch on the edge of the ledge while he prepared to bend over to grip hold of Brank's wrists and hoist him to safety.

"Quick, you gaping fool! My fingers are slipping!"

Roxane opened her eyes and cautiously raised her head. Stiletti's kneeling form bulked black before her, silhouetted by the reflected beam of his flashlight.

The girl realized her chance—her only chance. Swiftly, deliberately, lying on her back, she flexed her legs, raising them bent from the ground.

She straightened them again with all the strength and force at her command. Her projected feet caught the unsuspecting Stiletti squarely in the centre of the back.

The man uttered a hideous yell of voice as he lost his balance and plunged at the ledge, landing right on top of the clinging Brank. The latter's hold was broken. In an instant the fierce current swept both men swiftly away into the blackness of the tunnel.

Gasping, trembling, Roxane scrambled to her feet. The fear of Brank still gripped her. She could think only of escape. Her thoughts were confused as she snatched up Stiletti's torch and fled frantically in the opposite direction to where she would have found safety with Sexton Blake and his companions.

It was a tragic error, and one that was destined to be fraught with disastrous consequences. The girl's nerves were shattered by the terrors she had undergone. She neither knew nor cared which way she went.

Blindly she pushed along the narrow ledge, tripping and stumping, to a point where the torrent below branched off in one direction, and the mouth of another tunnel opened black before her.

OPEN AND SHUT

The door of the dummy-house slammed shut behind Dolland. Facing him was Brank, revolver in hand. Stiletti was already stooping over the senseless figure of Inspector Thomas, manacling him with his own handcuffs, binding his ankles, and forcing a brutal gag between his clamped jaws.

Brank chuckled softly as he patted the Bat's pockets, and under the arms, to assure himself that he carried no weapons.

"This is quite a pleasure, Mr. Dolland!" he taunted. "It means that I have one enemy less to deal with down below. How fortunate that Stiletti and I returned here to assure ourselves that an way of escape was still open to us."

Dolland made no reply. He noted that the Doomsman and his hireling were in wet clothes. There was no sign of Mademoiselle Roxane. And it was evident that Brank intended returning to the catacombs, to have a final settlement with Sexton Blake.

The Bat was whirled round, this wrists clutched, and lashed painfully together. Branks's automatic, now boring into his back, urged him towards the manhole, leading to the dark, winding passage beneath Petty France.

"Now that cursed woman Roxane has slipped through our fingers, you shall have the pleasure of guiding us to Frimley's safe," rasped the Doomsman, his voice suddenly ugly with menace. "And I would advise you not to pretend that you don't know where it is. I could shoot you like a rat at any time, Dolland—and I shall certainly do so unless you obey my instructions."

"Go to the devil!" muttered the Bat under his breath.

Inwardly he was rejoicing to learn in Branks's own words that Roxane had succeeded in escaping from the arch criminal's clutches.

It was not unlikely that she had fallen in with Sexton Blake, Tinker, and Splash Page. But it was equally probable that she was wandering helplessly in the pitch darkness of the maze of tunnels that honeycombed the catacombs.

"And after you have guided us to the safe," proceeded Brank, grinding his pistol brutally against the Bat's spine, "it won't take us long to find somebody who can show us how to open it."

Dolland was not so certain on that point. Roxane alone knew by heart the combination that would open the steel vault behind the spraying waterfall and so far she had defined Brank's efforts to wrest the secret from her.

Sandwiched between the two desperate men, he once again found himself in the dank passage beneath the manhole in Petty France.

"Which way?" snarled the Doomsman.

"To the right," prompted the Bat, though he was certain that he and was certain that he and Gilson had come from the left-hand branch of the tunnel. He had no intention of betraying the position of the safe if he could help it. As a matter of fact, he very much doubted his ability to do so. The maze of passages was too confusing for him to remember the exact route to take.

He was not to realize, until later, that any branch they might follow would eventually lead them in the cavern of the waterfall.

Dolland was now in the van, denied any hope of a sudden break for freedom by the pistol that rested warningly in the small of his back, a constant remainder that he was walking with death at his heels.

"How much farther ?" rasped Brank, after ten minutes steady plodding through the rank sluice of constant drippings from the dank walls. "I've warned you, Dolland. If you play me false I'll plug you in the stomach, break both your legs, and leave you to the rats!"

The ghastly threat lifted the hair on the Bat's scalp.

"You've got to give me time," he said desperately. "I'm not certain of the way, and that's the truth. I think we're heading in the right direction."

"I trust we are for your sake," was the ominous answer. "I am becoming impatient, Dolland. Unless your memory revives, it will soon cease to operate."

"Cheerful little fellow!" mused the Bat, wondering how it would all end.

Haphazardly he stumbled on, guided by the beam of Brank's powerful flashlight. His ears were alert for any sound of running water that would betray the near presence of Frimley's hidden safe.

But all was silent, save for their laboured breathing in the foul atmosphere and the squelch of the mud underfoot.

Then Brank suddenly stopped, snapping off the light, and digging his pistol warningly into the Dolland's back.

"What's that?" he breathed. "Do you hear it, Stiletti?"

Stiletti, who was carrying a submachine-gun tucked under one arm, cocked his ugly head on one side.

Clink, clink, clink!

The sound came faintly but sharply to their ears from somewhere close at hand. It held a ring of metal, like a workman's pick chipping at a concrete road.

Dolland's teeth snapped together as the truth flashed into his mind. Unintentionally he had guided his captors to the cave of the waterfall. It was directly ahead.

The water was turned off. And the noise they heard was that of somebody chipping the friable cement from the face of Frimley's cunningly concealed safe !

Dolland opened his mouth to shout a warning, believing it must be Blake and the others who were working on the safe round the bend in the passage. But Brank's muscular hand closed around his windpipe like a steel vice.

A few more paces, and they came in sight of the safe door. In that moment Dolland saw that the safe door was open and that the figure before it was not Blake, but Roxane. The next moment something happened that chilled Dirk's blood with horror.

ANKLE-DEEP in mud, her flimsy gown torn to ribbons, Roxane pursued her panic stricken flight into the bowels of the catacombs.

It was like being buried alive. The silence weighed down on her till she could have screamed if only to hear the sound of her own voice.

But gradually she recovered her self control; the dauntless courage that had supported her in so many perilous predicaments reasserted itself. She was heartened by the knowledge that Sexton Blake was somewhere within this maze of tunnels.

She had heard his voice only a few minutes ago. Or was in hours—or years? She had lost all sense of time. Every second seemed an eternity as she walked on, thankful for the powerful beam of Stiletti's torch.

It was with startling suddenness that the girl found herself confronted with the blank wall of baked, mouldering cement, that had once entirely concealed Frimley's cunningly hidden safe.

Now the covering had fallen away in patches. The rust-proof metal door beneath was clearly visible; but it was several moments before Roxane realized the magnitude of her discovery.

Here was journey's end—the finish of the long search for Frimley's missing millions, and the proofs of Morgan Gilson's innocence.

Her eyes sparkled, and her hand trembled as she stretched out to rap her knuckles against the massive door to the treasure-vault. Obviously, it had not been opened since the coat of cement was first applied.

Roxane could not guess that it was only by a fluke that she had found the water turned off, that Blake had turned the stopcock only a few minutes before her arrival in the waterfall cavern.

Roxane's heart was throbbing with excitement as she glanced eagerly around, to discover something that had somehow managed to escape Blake's sharp eyes. In one corner, half covered with the dust of years, lay a rusty iron crowbar.

Instinctively she picked it up, and commenced to chip away the thin wall of flaking cement.

Clink! Clink! Clink!

Metal rang against metal. She did her labours until she had uncovered the entire door that now gleamed dully in the light of her torch.

She alone knew the combination that would open the safe. A few turns of the knob and the secrets of Frimley's criminal past would be revealed.

Roxane was a woman, possessed of a woman's natural curiosity. Her hand went to the combination lock. The safe was as well preserved as when it was first built. Without a sound the massive door swung open on its hinges.

It was sheer instinct that caused the girl to turn her head at that thrilling moment. A scream of terror escaped her lips as the white beam of the torch revealed three figures standing within a few yards of her.

Brank's evil face stood out like veined marble. Behind him leered Stiletti, the blunt muzzle of a sub-machine-gun jutting from under one arm. To one side Dirk Dolland stood dejectedly, a look of helpless despair and dismay in his eyes.

What happened next Roxane was never able to quite explain. She took a backward step that carried her through the entrance to the huge safe. Her hand may have brushed against the door. Perfectly balanced on its hinges, it swung shut with a clang like the clashing gates of doom.

She was in darkness locked in the safe of evil secrets.

And she alone knew the combination that would open the massive door!

Fate had baffled Brank, but Roxane's life was at stake. She was sealed in a living tomb, where she could not hope to breathe for any length of time.

"HOLD on a minute, guv'nor! We don't want to take any chances!"

It was Tinker who spoke, immediately following the shrill heart-rending scream that told Sexton Blake and his companions that Roxane was still alive, despite Brank's ghastly threat.

Blake turned on the narrow ledge above the foaming torrent; his hands busily engaged slipping a fresh clip of cartridges into his automatic.

"Stiletti has got the drop on us," explained Tinker plausibly. "We can only proceed in single file along this narrow ledge. Stiletti is a murderer, and a desperate man. He'll probably lurk around some corner and pick us off like flies."

"That's unpleasantly true," agreed Splash Page. "But what's to be done about it? We can't leave Roxane in that brute's clutches without making some attempt to rescue her."

"There's only one thing to be done," declared Tinker. "Turn off the water and creep along the floor of the tunnel in the darkness. If Stiletti flashes his torch or fires a shot we shall know his exact position."

Blake gave his assistant an approving slap on the shoulder.

"Stout fellow," he smiled. "Any one of us might have thought of that, but we didn't."

Hurriedly they retraced their steps along the ledge where Blake once again reversed the submerged water cock that stopped the swift torrent, revealed Frimley's hidden safe, and emptied the passage through which the water had coursed.

In extended order, with lights extinguished, and pistols ready, the little party of three crept cautiously into the depths of the darkened tunnel.

The wet floor was slippery beneath their feet. It was an unpleasant experience. At any moment they could expect a hail of bullets from Stiletti's ready gun that might lay one of them low.

But nothing happened. There was no sound save their own stealthy movements and the constant, irritating dripping of water.

"The beggar's beat it," said Splash Page.

His whisper boomed across the silence like the bellow of a bull. But there was still no shot from Brank's gunman.

Blake ventured to switch on his powerful flashlight. The narrow ledge stretched empty as far as the eye could reach. And they were almost at the end of the tunnel. Twenty yards ahead it finished abruptly in a blank wall.

Of Stiletti and Roxane there was no sign.

"Holy Moses!" exclaimed Splash Page. "If this is the end of the tunnel, how the dickens did all that water escape?"

"It's difficult to say," muttered Blake, "but I should imagine that this big stone that seals the end of the passage at present automatically rises when the water is turned on, and closes again when it is turned off and the tunnel is dry. More of Frimley's crazy ingenuity! Ah, what have we here?"

Directing his torch to the ledge above, the detective had suddenly spotted the mouth of the passage through which Roxane had made her escape. Actively he clambered up to the ledge, bent down, and uttered a sound of excitement that brought his companions hurrying to join him.

"Roxane has gone this way," jerked Blake, pointing to the muddy floor of the tunnel. "There are her footprints. And she went alone. There is only the one trail."

"Then what's happened to Stiletti?" blurted Tinker.

Blake shrugged his shoulders.

"It may be," he said hopefully and, as it happened to be, accurately, "that she was granted an opportunity to push him off the ledge into the stream. In that event he and Brank have gone the same way here."

They had no difficulty in following the trail of feminine footprints that led them onwards through the winding passage. They came to the spot where the girl had paused to rest, and then continued her journey.

"Roxane—Roxane!"

Only the echoes his own voice came back to Blake's ears.

"She can't be far ahead," he muttered pressing on impatiently.

"I dunno about that," said Tinker. "We were a good half-hour or more sneaking along that watercourse, and—Suffering Pete!"

A sudden bend in the tunnel had brought them back to where they had started from. They were in the cavern of the waterfall with the exposed door to Frimley's safe glowing dully in the glare of their torches.

"Someone's been trying to open the safe!" exclaimed Blake grimly. "See all the cement has been dropped away and —"

"Stick up your paws or I'll plug the lot of you."

It was Stiletti's voice. The man was standing in the mouth of the empty watercourse, swinging the muzzle of his deadly machine-gun in a steady, threatening arc.

Beside him was Brank the Doomsman, leering like a gargoyle. The powerful torch which Brank had just switched on held then all in its beam. There was no chance of avoiding either the fierce light or the threat of the gun.

"A most propitious arrival, Blake," chuckled Brank. "You can now oblige me by opening that safe."

"I think not," said the detective quietly.

"I think you will," smiled the Doomsman, "especially when I inform you the Mademoiselle Roxane is locked inside the vault. She has been there several minutes. The supply of air must be almost exhausted. No doubt she is suffering extreme discomfort."

Blake's face paled. He threw a quick questioning glance at Dolland. The latter nodded his head gravely.

"It's true, Blake," he said huskily. "Roxane is locked inside the safe, and she alone knows the combination that will open it."

THE NEXT MOVE
OUR FASCINATING, NOVEL, FOUR—
AUTHOR SERIAL BY –
G.H. TEED.
GWYN EVANS.
ROBERT MURRAY.
ANTHONY SKENE.

FOREWORD
THE ABOVE FOUR AUTHORS ARE CONTRIBUTING THE INSTALMENTS OF THIS UNIQUE SERIAL IN TURN, SETTING PUZZLES FRO THE NEXT MAN TO SOLVE. THE MAIN EVENTS OF THE STORY SO FAR ARE AS FOLLOWS:

IN A LABYRINTH OF SUBTERRANEAN TUNNELS THAT RUN UNDER THE DISTRICT OF PETTY FRANCE, LONDON, A TITANIC DUEL IS BEING FOUGHT OUT BETWEEN A MASTER CRIMINAL, NAMED BRANK, AND A GROUP OF FRIENDS ACTING UNDER THE LEADERSHIP OF SEXTON BLAKE.

CONCEALED IN THE CATACOMBS IS A SAFE WHICH CONTAINS, NOT ONLY THE PROCEEDS OF THE CRAVETTI BANK FRAUDS, AMOUNTING TO TWO MILLION POUNDS, BUT ALSO PROOFS OF THE INNOCENCE OF MORGAN GILSON, WHO WAS WRONGFULLY SENTENCED TO DEVIL'S ISLAND FOR THE CRIME.

IT WAS GILSON WHO, HAVING ESCAPED FROM THE ISLAND, CAME TO BLAKE AND ENLISTED HIS AID AND THAT OF TINKER, SPLASH PAGE, AND DIRK DOLLAND, AGAINST BRANK AND HIS MURDEROUS GANG.

MLLE. ROXANE IS ALSO AN ALLY OF GILSON'S, AND DISCOVERED THE SECRET OF THE SAFE'S COMBINATION WHICH HAD BEEN TAUGHT TO A PARROT.

TO PREVENT THE OTHERS GETTING THE CONTENTS OF THE SAFE, BRANK KIDNAPS ROXANE, TAKES HER DOWN INTO THE CATACOMBS TO TORTURE HER INTO REVEALING THE SAFE AND ITS COMBINATION.

HOT IN PURSUIT GO BLAKE AND THE OTHERS. ACCIDENTALLY THEY DISCOVER THE SAFE, WHICH IS HIDDEN BEHIND THE CASCADE OF AN ARTIFICIAL WATERFALL BUILT ACROSS A STREAM THAT RUNS THROUGH THE TUNNELS.

THEY RUN INTO BRANK AND HIS MURDEROUS HENCHMAN, STILETTI, WHO HOLDS ROXANE. BLAKE MAKES A RUSH FOR BRANK. THE TWO TOPPLE INTO THE STREAM, BUT BRANK GETS AWAY. ROXANE FREES HERSELF FROM STILETTI, BUT WANDERS FRANTICALLY SEARCHING FOR HER FRIENDS WHOM SHE HAS LOST IN THE MAZE OF TUNNELS.

SHE COMES SUDDENLY TO THE SAFE. KNOWING THE COMBINATION, SHE OPENS IT. AT THAT MOMENT SHE IS SURPRISED BY BRANK AND STILETTI, WHO HAVE REJOINED FORCES AND WHO HAVE THIS TIME DIRK DOLLAND AS THEIR PRISONER. WITH AN INSTINCTIVE MOVEMENT OF FEAR, ROXANE STEPS INTO THE SAFE. THE DOOR CLANGS SHUT UPON HER.

BLAKE, TINKER, AND PAGE ARRIVE. THEY, TOO, ARE MET BY BRANK'S GUN. AND LOCKED IN THE SAFE IS ROXANE WITHOUT THEIR BEING ABLE TO SAVE HER.

Three Out Of Four.

When Dirk Dolland informed Sexton Blake that Roxane had been locked in the safe which also contained Frimley's stolen millions, and the proofs of Morgan Gilson's innocence, the detective stood perfectly still for a few moments as if the violence of the blow had robbed him even of the power of thought.

The small party stood in a groined junction of passages. On either side of them, and behind, tunnels, varying from the size of a subway to that of the smallest mine gallery, disappeared into blackness. Here and there a patch of ancient brickwork or masonry was visible. Everything wet and of an unrelieved mud colour, as if the men who stood about in front of the safe which contained Roxane were a concourse of rats disputing the possession of a sewer. Their attitudes added the comparison, for all of them were tense, watchful, keyed up to a savage recklessness.

On the other side was Blake, with Splash Page and Tinker on either side of him; and, facing them, Stiletti, with his finger upon the trigger of the sub-machine-gun; the odious, leering Brank; and Dolland, his hands manacled behind his back, his face troubled, full of sympathy for Sexton Blake.

The terrible and tragic tension of the moment was broken by a burst of harsh laughter.

It was the Doomsman. The nearness of his triumph seemed to have affected his brain. His eyes glittered strangely in the light of the torches.

"You're wrong, Dolland," he declared. "Roxane isn't the only one who knows the combination. Blake knows it. And we have a splendid argument—ha, ha!—yes, a wonderful argument, to persuade him to use his knowledge. It will save the life of Mademoiselle Roxane. And we all know —"

Blake spoke.

"I thought I knew it," he said bitterly, "and the others, too. I'll give you the secret, Brank—if it's any use to you. The combination was "Frim 865432'; Anastasia the parrot's authentic information. But—" here he gestured hopelessly towards the safe door—"those combination dials of that lock haven't got a single letter on them; they're all figures. You can try the figures if you like, but I don't think it's much use."

"No; you do it," ordered Brank. "And no tricks. Remember the guns are on you!"

"Oh, I'm not bothering about the guns!' replied Blake wearily. "I want to open the safe as much as you do."

And he stepped forward and spun the concentric dials this way and that, following every arrangement of the vital 865432 he could think of. Even the suspicious Brank saw that he was in earnest. He dragged Blake away with a snarling laugh.

"That's very amusing," he said. He turned towards Dirk Dolland. "What a fortunate thing that we have with us the cleverest safe breaker in the world! Dirk Dolland shall get to work. If he succeeds in opening the safe, perhaps I shall allow him to live. I may even give him a thousand pounds; a thousand pounds will then be nothing to me."

Blake turned his haggard face towards his friend.

"Could you do it, Dolland?"

"I don't know," said Dirk, in a husky voice. "Take these confounded handcuffs off," he added to Brank, "and let me have a look at the thing."

Brank took a key from his pocket and removed the handcuffs from Dolland's wrists.

"If you make an attempt to escape—" he said.

Dolland turned on him with cold fury.

"What kind of a dirty dog do you think I am? I am not opening the safe for you; I am opening it for Mr. Blake."

He thrust Brank aside.

"Get out of my way!" he said, walking across to the safe.

With his long, sensitive fingers he spun the dials.

"No," he added at length, "I can't do it. I should require tools."

Blake stepped across and clutched him by the shoulder.

"How long will it take, Dolland? Where are the tools? Could you get them now?"

Dolland reflected for a moment.

"I could have them here in fifteen minutes."

"And then," questioned Blake, "how long?"

"Before I opened the safe? I can't say; but my drills would be through, one every ten minutes. Each tiny hole would give a chance for air to get in."

"You mean that no air could get in at present?"

"Not with this type, Blake," said Dolland sadly. "They are so wonderfully machined that they could maintain a vacuum. Deeply sorry for you, old friend, and for Roxane, but I am afraid—"

Blake's hand, gripping on Dolland's shoulder, tightened until it crushed into the bone.

"Dolland, if you can get a drill through before twenty minutes is over, there might be a chance."

"I'll do it," said Dolland.

He swung round to go.

Surprising as it may seem, in the intensity of his fear for Roxane, he had, for the moment, forgotten the threat of Stiletti's machine-gun. He was recalled to consciousness of his own danger by a harsh word from Stiletti.

"Stop or I fix you!"

The muzzle of the gun had jerked round in Dolland's direction. Stiletti's finger was upon the trigger.

Blake tensed to rush, but Dolland held him back.

"Steady, Blake; you can't rush a machine-gun. We've got to live—for her.

"Look here, Brank," he went on, "I'll open that can for you; and, so far as I am concerned, you may have all the valuables which it contains. You can't get anybody else to do it. I tell you that, and I know what I am talking about. There are only three men in the world who could open that safe for you. I am one of them, and you don't know the others. I am your only hope; but—put this in your pipe and smoke it—if I am not allowed to do this my own way, I won't do it at all. In other words you've got to release me to get my tools."

"Dear me!" sneered Brank. "You have a very poor idea of my abilities if you think that I can't fathom a scheme like that. How long would it be before you had the police here?"

"I give you my word," said Dolland, with contempt, "that I will not inform the police."

Brank's face was distorted into a grin.

"Oh, yeah! Well, we're not having any. You stay here. We'll get your tools, and you can wait until we get them."

"Then," said Dolland, "for the love in Heaven get going! Here—" He took a notebook from his pocket and scribbled. "There's my old and secret address. My kit is there; it's packed in a brown leather bag. You won't need a key, but if anybody tries to stop you, show him this note which I am writing."

He tore out the leaf on which he had written, and held it out to Brank.

"Now," he said, "get going, and go quickly or you will never get your safe opened."

Curiously enough, despite the machine-gun, Dolland was the master of the situation, and everybody knew it.

"Better go," said Stiletti. "Better do it, Brank; he's got us."

Brank stood with the fragment of paper clipped between his fingers, looking from face to face. His eyes were narrowed in suspicion. One could almost read the thoughts which were passing through his mind.

"Are these people trying to get me out of the way so that they can have my millions?"

"All right," he said suddenly; and turned away.

They heard his feet slip slopping along the mud of the tunnel; then he was gone.

THE irrepressible Splash Page addressed words to Stiletti.

"You are the prize mug," he said "what do you think you're going to get out of this business?"

Stiletti threatened with the gun.

"You shut up!"

But you couldn't quell Splash Page by that means.

"You think," the reporter went on, "that when Brank opens that safe and gets his hands on a couple of pounds' worth of negotiable securities he is going to give you a half of what he finds? Aren't you the prize mug?"

"What do you mean?" said Stiletti.

"Think I don't know? There were four of you in this at first—Stutz, La Rocque, Stiletti and Brank. How many are there now?"

"You know as well as I do. There's Brank and myself."

"That's right. What happened to the others?"

"Brank killed them."

"I expect he explained to you, when the time came for Stutz to go, that a third share was bigger than a fourth. Then when La Rocque got his, he pointed out that a half-share was bigger than a third. Well some men seem to have mud inside their skulls. Stutz was number one; La Rocque was number two. Who do you think is going to be number three?"

Stiletti scowled, drawing back his lips from his yellow teeth.

"I can look after myself and Brank knows it."

Splash Page grinned derisively.

"That's the very reason that Brank will never give you a chance to look after yourself.

"Listen, Stiletti," he went on, "I'll tell you what Brank intends." He pointed towards the safe. "Behind that door is Frimley's confession. It implicates you, and you know it; but it doesn't implicate Brank. That confession will not be part of your share. He'll use it to blackmail you —that is, if you live long enough to be black-mailed."

Blake and Tinker had at first been shocked on hearing Splash Page's banter of Stiletti. They thought that it showed the young reporter's in-difference to the terrible peril of Mademoiselle Roxane; but they realized as he went on, the deep game which Splash Page was playing. He was setting Stiletti against Brank, preparing in advance for the moment when the safe should be opened.

Brank and Stiletti had spared their lives until now, because the use of the machine gun could only be followed by a mishap in which Dolland, who was their one hope, might stop a bullet. Directly the safe was opened, however, they would have that door no longer. They would be anxious, instead, that Dolland should be one of the last to go under. But if, in the meantime, Splash Page could get Stilleto against Brank, the situation would become complicated in a way which they might turn to their own advantage.

And Stiletto was thinking the way that Splash Page wanted him to think. The ideas which the reporter was placing into Stiletto's head had suf-ficient facts behind them to carry conviction.

The probability that Brank would try to put a bullet through his head, when the time came for the big shoot out, was one which must have oc-curred to Stiletto already. But Splash Page was showing them that it was not only a possibility,

but almost a certainty, and he did not like the idea at all.

"After all," said Stiletto, almost to himself, "when once Brank gets back with that kit of tools—"

He did not complete his sentence, but every-one there knew what the finish of it was. "When Brank gets back here with that kit of tools, I shall be no further use to him. It's him or me." That's what Stiletto was going to say.

Down there, in the bowels of the earth, the rat-tat-tat of the machine-gun would be inaudible to none but themselves; and they knew that if one of them tried to edge away, the murderous Stilet-to would shoot him down without compunction.

The rush of one or all of them would be equally unsuccessful. They could only wait until, for a moment, Stiletto's attention was distracted, and then there was just a chance of downing him.

He knew what they were thinking.

"If any of you tried to use a gun," he threat-ened, "Dolland goes first."

He knew that that was a threat which would be most effective to stop any hostile action, for if Dolland died no power on earth would save Roxane. Those who atched him, uner the threat of his terrible weapon, were occupied by thoughts of the unhappy girl who was in such a terrible plight, so near them and yet so far away. Even then she might be struggling against suf-focation, pumping the stagnant air in and out of her lungs in a last effort to draw from it one life-giving atom of oxygen.

They imagined horrors in plenty, but knew nothing. The door of the steel safe revealed no secrets. The beautiful Roxane might soon be crumpled upon the floor, insensible or dead. They did not know.

Blake, who was better able than the rest to work out the girl's chance of life, calculated that there was still ten or fifteen minutes in which they might hope to save her.

Time passed with terrible quickness. At short intervals Blake would look at his wristwatch. His movements were nervous, his features expressed the strain of a terrible anxiety.

The address which Dolland had given to Brank was not so far away that a taxi might not reach there in five minutes from the house in Petty France.

According to Dolland, there would be no hitch in Brank's obtaining the burglar's kit. The fact is that the tools were matters of pride to Dolland and were the product of many hours of research and experiment. In his eyes they were beyond price; they could not be duplicated.

"Brank ought to be back soon," gasped Blake.

Stiletto still facing them, with the torch slipped beneath his are, jerked his head round to listen. He was standing in a line with the passage might be expected to return, and he had a better chance of hearing sounds in that passage than had the others who faced him.

The small party held their breaths. The time was coming for them to rush Stiletto and seize that terrible weapon which he carried.

The four men whom he had been threatening took a silent breath, then another, then another. They tensed to rush like sprinters about to begin a hundred yards race; and Stiletto did not see.

The small party saw him crouch and began their forward rush. Then they stopped with one accord, appalled at what had happened to the man.

Death is always terrible. Murder is doubly and trebly terrible. And Stiletto had been murdered. He was gradually crumpling up with a bullet-hole just above one of his eyes.

The sound of Brank's shot echoed and re-echoed in the unexplored catacombs around. Brank had fired from a point at a bend in the tunnel. He must have watched Stiletto for some movement.

Stiletti sank down very slowly. He had reached his knees when a sudden twitch shook him from head to foot.

AT that moment, while Blake and his friends were still spellbound with with horror, Brank showed himself. He had Dolland covered. Carefully he drew nearer and took the machine gun from Stiletto's limp grip. The quickness of the man amazed them. He had seemed afflicted by a heavy sloth, terribly deliberate. Now he moved with lightning speed. The gun was in his hands, and he was facing them before they could move.

He was laughing.

"Ha, ha, ha! This is where Brank comes into his own. The Doomsman, eh? A very good name.

"Go on, Dolland," he went on, "there are your tools, back there in the tunnel. Get to work, man,

and keep on working, for when you stop your life stops, and the lives of your friends. Don't forget, Dolland, Mademoiselle Moxane is in that safe. Your drills bring life to her—life to Roxane and millions to me."

The man's laughter was insane; the nearness of wealth had evidently unhinged his mind; but the muzzle of the machine gun was steady and his eyes more watchful even than those of a sane man.

Dolland walked over and picked up the bag which Brank had dropped to the ground. Then, with feverish speed, he began to clamp to the safe the apparatus which he had brought.

Blake was standing beside him, ready to be of assistance if needed, but Dolland waved him away.

Dirk Dolland had always been a lone wolf, and he worked quicker by himself.

The oiled gear of the drill buzzed and buzzed; steel bit into steel. Steam went up from where soapy water was being used as lubrication.

Dolland's hands were trembling; his brow was beaded by perspiration. He was working as he had never worked before. Once or twice, as the minutes passed, he turned towards Sexton Blake with a shake of the head.

"Not yet, Blake."

Then a drill went through. Instantly he had it out and moved it to a new point.

"One," he said.

Blake knew something about safe breaking; and could see that Dolland was working, not so much to open the door as to give Roxane air.

In less than half an hour there were four holes drilled clean through the hardened steel door of the safe; and Blake had the satisfaction of knowing that if Roxane had survived the first period she would now have an excellent chance of survival.

Brank came nearer.

"You aren't getting on very rapidly," he said, with his characteristic suspicion.

"Well, it is difficult," said Dolland, almost apologetically. "Look here."

Interested, despite himself, Brank came nearer, bringing himself almost into Sexton Blake's reach.

This was the effect which Dolland had calculated upon, and Blake took instant advantage of it. He let his knees go, fell sideways then straightened, diving at the machine gun.

At the moment when Brank pressed the trigger, Blake's palm struck the barrel sideways.

Rat-tat-tat-tat tat!

A stream of bullets was lost in the walls of the tunnel.

Blake hurled himself forward, and Brank gave way before him.

The machine gun still vomited lead. In the confined space of the tunnels the sound hammered back upon the ears in a confused roar.

The racketing of the gun must have continued for many seconds before its sound was first eclipsed and then swept out of existence by the thunder of an avalanche.

Tons of earth and masonry came down upon them all. The sade and the man who stood before it disappeared under a wet and crumbling mass of soil and stones.

BLAKE had rushed Brank backwards, and those two inveterate enemies now found themselves isolated.

The machine gun had disappeared, but Brank's powerful torch lay at their feet, and its light showed them something of the appalling tragedy which had taken place. From the floor to the crown of the arch it was choked by a mass of loose debris. But for the violence of Blake's rush he and Brank must have perished beneath it.

Blake looked with fascinated horror at that mound of earth. He had forgotten Brank; but Brank had not forgotten him. Brank's attempts to murder Blake had been dictated, not so much by self-preservation as by personal hatred. That hatred had survived his narrow escape from a terrible death. He did not forget it for one moment.

Blake turned to meet his attack, and crashed in terrible blows with both hands.

The detective had gone berserk. The fall of earth had destroyed his friends and had wiped out any hope which Mademoiselle Roxane might have had of ever again leaving that safe where Frimley's millions lay.

Never again would he enjoy the comradeship of Tinker or of Dolland; the sparkling jollity of Splash Page. Never more would he look into the eyes of Roxane or hear her pleasant laughter. And all this was owing to Brank, the man who faced him and fought him.

Some fragment of the fallen roof had laid open Blake's brow; a bead of blood was trickling to his eye. His face was terrible. It might be that his own escape was cut off. It might be that when he had killed Brank—as he was undoubtedly setting himself to do—he also would meet death, lying on that muddy floor until starvation or the rats made an end to him.

He did not think of these things; did not really think coherently at all. His whole brain was filled with hatred of Brank. And Brank returned his with interest.

As blow after blow crashed home, both men weakened. They reeled away from each other, only to stagger in and start hitting again. Their faces were bruised and covered with blood; they were hardly strong enough to stand. Yet each devoted the little strength which he had to the destruction of the other.

At length Brank was beaten to his knees; and Blake lurched forward to fall upon him.

They fell full length and struggled side by side, clutching at each other's throats.

Then another fall of earth took place. The ground disappeared from beneath them. They were falling, and cold, black water closed over their heads.

By the fortune of war it was, at that moment, Blake who squeezed Brank's throat and Brank who struggled to get Blake's hands away.

They went deeply under water into darkness. When they broke surface again the glow of the electric torch was dim and distant.

Brank was choking. He clutched at Blake's arms; and the two men, still fighting, went down for the time. A current was carrying them along. They came to the surface once more in a place where there was no light whatever.

Blake said to himself, "This is the end!"

He might have saved his own life by releasing a grip upon Brank's throat. But he would not do so—it did not seem to matter. Without Roxane, without Tinker and others, life was valueless to him.

He gulped weakly at the fetid air of the water ways and went under for a third time. Suffocation and darkness, the sensation of one buried alive, who recovers consciousness to die horribly within the bowels of the earth. Then nothing— just a lapse of consciousness, an infinity of darkness!

The Next Move

Our Fascinating, Novel, Four—Author Serial By –
G.H. Teed.
Gwyn Evans.
Robert Murray.
Anthony Skene.
The 13th Final Round

THE FINAL ROUND BY G.H. TEED NOW FOLLOWS.

Foreword:

LOCKED IN A SAFE TO WHICH SHE ALONE KNOWS THE COMBINATION, IS MLLE. ROXANE. GROUPED ROUND THE OUTSIDE OF THE SAFE WHICH IS SITUATED IN THE CATACOMBS BENEATH PETTY FRANCE, LONDON, ARE SEXTON BLAKE, TINKER, SPLASH PAGE AND DIRK DOLLAND.

THESE FOUR ARE JOINT ALLIES WITH HER OF MORGAN GILSON, ESCAPED FROM DEVIL'S ISLAND, WHOSE INNOCENCE CAN ONLY BE PROVED BY DOCUMENTS IN THE SAFE. THE FOUR ARE IN THE POWER OF THE MASTER CRIMINAL BRANK, WITH WHOM THEY HAVE BEEN FIGHTING A RUTHLESS CAMPAIGN FOR POSSESSION OF THE SAFE AND ITS CONTENTS.

BRANK, TOO WANTS THE SAFE OPEN. INSIDE ARE THE PROCEEDS OF HIS COLOSSAL BANK FRAUDS. UNDER THE THREAT OF BRANK'S GUN, AND KNOWING THAT TO SAVE ROXANE THE SAFE MUST BE OPENED, DOLLAND STARTS TO WORK ON THE STEEL DOOR WITH HIS OLD CRACKSMAN'S TOOLS.

BLAKE SEIZES A CHANGE TO THROW HIMSELF ON BRANK. WHILST THE TWO ARE FIGHTING THE TUNNEL COLLAPSES, AND THE TWO ARE CUT OFF FROM THE REST, BUT THEY CONTINUE TO FIGHT FRENZIEDLY UNTIL THEY BOTH FALL INTO AN UNDERGROUND STREAM,

THE FALL OF THE TUNNEL ROOF NOT ONLY ISOLATES TINKER, SPLASH PAGE AND DIRK DOLLAND FROM THE STRUGGLING CROOK AND DETECTIVE, BUT BURIES THEM IN A CASCADE OF EARTH AND DEBRIS.

AFTER THE CATASTROPHE, DARKNESS AND SINISTER SILENCE FALL ON THE CATACOMBS AND THE SAFE IN WHICH ROXANE IS STILL A PRISONER.

Back From The Shadows

Darkness!

Complete, impenetrable darkness, and ominous silence, but for the intermittent roll of loose stones and earth that soon died away as the last dislodged fragments trickled their way to a resting place.

There was something terribly awesome in the swiftness with which everything had been blotted out in that catastrophic fall of the roof in the tunnels under the old houses in Petty France. The struggling Blake and Brank, the anxious Tinker and Splash Page, and the toiling Dirk Dolland—who throughout the battle at his back had grimly stuck to his job of drilling the safe with the sweat pouring from him as he strove to get the drill point through the steel door and admit air to the suffocating Roxane before it was too late—all alike were appalled and momentarily stunned by the crash of the world collapsing, as it seemed, into chaos.

It was an eternity of time before there was any movement in the place, except that faint pattering of stone and earth sliding from top to bottom of the roof-fall, but actually it was only a space of less than a minute before a voice came from somewhere indefinite and unlocatable in that blackness—a faint and feeble groan.

From another direction came, at first, an indistinct scuffing sound, a fresh pattering of falling earth-clods, and one or two dragging footsteps.

"Is that you, Tinker?"

"Yes. Is it you, Splash?"

"Yes; you all right?"

"I——I think so." But the voice obviously indicated pain or difficulty in breathing. "Held by the legs. Wait a minute. Got to crawl out. What's happened? Where are the others?"

"I'm here." It was Dirk Dolland's voice.

"Where's the guv'nor? Guv'nor? Guv'nor? Where are you? Guv'nor?"

Tinker had dragged himself to his knees, and as he called to Blake in the solid blackness his voice echoed and re-echoed within the confines of the narrow, vaulted passage.

But no Blake answered.

The three of them, Tinker, Dirk Dolland and Splash Page—groped and guided each other by voice and hand towards the bottom of the heap of debris, and, halting there, held hurried consultation.

"Who's got a light?"

"What's become of Blake? And Brank—where's Brank?"

"What's happened, anyway? The roof —"

"Roxane! Gosh, she's still in that safe!"

"The way's blocked. We —"

"A light! Who's got matches? Quick, somebody—"

The exclamations came tumbling from and another of them, jerked out with anxious, urgent concern, as they stood gripping each other's arms or shoulders with an intensity that each was quite unaware of in the tension of the moment.

"Not a torch amongst us!" snapped Splash. "Where's the torch Blake had before Brank started shooting?"

"Under this cursed heap of dirt!" growled Dirk Dolland.

The ominous words struck a chill to the hearts of everyone, and even of Dolland himself, when he realized their significance; that if the torch was buried under that mass, Sexton Blake was, too.

"Here, I've got a match!"

There was a quaver of hope, of anxiety, or both in Tinker's voice as he exclaimed the words. Then came the scrape of a match-head and a burst of brilliance that made them screw up their dirt-rimmed, staring eyes. It was only a feeble match flame, but after that darkness the light was almost overpowering in the first second or so.

But before it burned out they saw what had happened. The pile of fallen earth and stones completely blocked the floor of the tunnel, and, so far as they could see, reached up to the roof. There was no sign of Blake or Brank—no hand sticking up out of the heap, or visible portion of any clothing.

The light flickered out.

"My gosh; I —I—"

Tinker's exclamation trailed away into an uncomfortable silence as his heart almost stood still with a, wrench of cold fear for his beloved master.

"Blake!" yelled Splash. "Blake!"

Silence. Each could hear his own heart throbbing is his throat.

Another of Tinker's matches flared up.

"Only two more in the box," he said, as he held it up and they stared at the grim, immovable barrier before them.

Splash page scrambled up the sloping front of it, wedged himself in the narrow space by the roof, groped about feverishly, tossing lumps of clay and stone behind him down the slope.

"Pretty solid up here!" he gasped. "No way through that I can see."

The light faded a little as the match burned down. Tinker reversed it in his fingers, held the hot, dead end while the flame, taking a final lease of life, brightened as it consumed the last bit of wood on the stick. Then the match went out.

For some moments more stones and then clods came rolling down. Splash himself followed, and stumbled to his feet at the bottom in the darkness.

"Can't find a way through!" he muttered. "Gosh, if we only had spades and lights."

"Can't one of us go back—"

"No, it's all hands on deck! By the time we could get things here he'd be— we've got to dig with our hands in the dark! Come on. No time for anything now !"

"Hey!"

It was Dirk Dolland's voice that made that sudden exclamation. They heard his footsteps stumbling back towards the safe.

"Carry on, you two!' he called back. ``I'll be there in a minute, I think—"

The newspaperman and Tinker began to scrabble at the heap of dirt without stopping to ask what he was doing. But in less than half a minute Dirk Holland had groped his way back to them.

"Where's your matches, Tinker?" he demanded. "Quick, now! Let me get close to you. I've got a bit of candle."

"Candle!" they both exclaimed, with a burst of relief.

"Yes. Suddenly thought of it. In my tool kit. I use it for lead-soldering sometimes." Tinker felt his arm gripped as he tugged the matchbox out of his pocket, then Dirk Holland's fingers on his hand as the ex-cracks-man steered the candle to where the light would be.

"Two matches left!" was the thought in Tinker's mind as his flingers groped in the box.

"Ready," he said aloud.

"Yes.' Here's the candle. The wick's probably squashed down a bit. Been knocking about loose in the tool-bag."

Tinker scraped the match on the box.

Nothing happened.

"Wrong end!" he muttered, and reversed it. The same thing again. He felt it carefully. There was no head to the match. It was one of those duds that often intrude into a box of matches.

His heart sank as he realized how much depended on the other—the last match. Supposing that were a dud, too?

But that flared up noisily and brightly without fail, its effect exaggerated by their intensity upon it. Even Splash had stopped clawing at the heap of rubble to look on, and their faces were illumined in Rembrandtesque relief as they surrounded the feeble light that began to sputter from the candle wick and then burned up steadily in a clearly fame.

Dirk Dolland bedded the candle safely on a lump of soft clay that had rolled to the floor, and by its light they set about their colossal and perhaps hopeless task against time. Only a bare inch of candle was between them and the onset of darkness once more. If they did not find Blake by the time it went out...

DURING these few crowded minutes they had almost forgotten the peril of Roxane, immured in the airtight safe, and whose safety depended on Dirk Dorland's boring a hole through the tough steel in time to admit air.

"I'll keep on at the safe!" ejaculated Dolland, as the thought of the girl came back to him. "You two carry on here! No time to lose!" But already the other two had thrown themselves at the roof-fall. They needed no urging.

Tinker set a pace that even the agile Splash found difficult to follow. Driven by frantic dread for Blake, the lad tore at the rubble, caring nothing for broken nails or bleeding hands.

So short a time before, he had seen Blake on that very spot, locked in desperate struggle with Brank. New he had been wiped out just as if an invisible hand had sweat him out of existence, and in his place was this barrier of dead earth and stone.

Could it be possible that Sexton Blake, the one who had been everything in the world to him, had been blotted out in this manner?

The thought drove Tinker nearly mad. Splash guessed what the lad was thinking—easily enough. He turned his head to speak a word of comfort.

"Steady on, old son. If he's here we'll get him!"

Something that sounded like a sob broke in Tinker's throat.

"Here—under—this" he panted.

Then he went at the heap again with a fury that was amazing. Splash said no more. He, too, held a deep affection for Blake, and it galled him to the soul to think that are had to pass out under such circumstances. Yet, in his heart of hearts, he could not tell Tinker that he thought there was little hope. He could only keep the lad company in his frantic endeavours until they uncovered—what?

In front of the safe, Dirk Dolland was drilling as never before. He had some faint hope that the holes he had already pierced through the heavy steel would admit sufficient air to keep Roxane alive, though those holes looked woefully small for such a purpose.

Never in his palmiest days as the slickest safe-cracker at large had Dolland worked with greater will. Never did safeguarded prize urge him to energy as did the prisoner who lay behind that door of battleship steel—dead or alive, none could tell.

Those three strove with no thought of self. There was something more than heroic in the way in which each had tackled his allotted job and was giving everything he had to it.

And all the time the bit of candle end was growing smaller and smaller. Dirk, who could watch it out of the corner of his eye, was first to see a tell-tale flicker.

He said nothing to the other two. It might hold out for a minute or so yet, and every second was precious.

He kept on grinding away at the drill, the sweat dripping in great beads from his forehead.

The sputtering became almost constant now, and caught the attention of Splash. But he said nothing to Tinker. The lad was almost up to the top of the pile of debris, clawing away close to the vaulted roof of the tunnel, tearing at the rubble as if he would drag the whole heap away bodily.

There seemed to be a silent conspiracy between Splash and Dirk not to tell him what was threatening. But it served only for a few moments. For, after a violent sputtering that caused the flame to grow brighter for a few seconds, the wick of the candle subsided into the pool of its own grease and, with a wet sizzle, vanished.

IT was a cry from Tinker that broke the silent chagrin that seized Splash and Dirk. From where they were they could not understand what caused the excitement in the lad's voice. They believed that it was only angry disappointment at the loss of the light. But when he shouted a second time, Splash went scrambling up the heap of debris until his hands came in contact with Tinker's legs.

"A light. A light!"

Tinker's voice was muffed, for his head and shoulders were thrust through an opening he had clawed between the top of the heap of rubble and the broken roof of the tunnel—an opening that Splash Page himself would have made had the glimmer of Tinker's first matches lasted a little longer.

Splash was trying to get higher, and now he could see a gleam of light over Tinker's shoulder..

"A light, I tell you!" came back Tinker's voice. "I believe it's the torch. Guv'nor! Guv'nor! Give me a push through, Splash!"

Splash was quite as excited as Tinker now. Getting under the lad's buttocks, he gave a heave that sent Tinker slithering through the opening, carrying a heap of small rubble with him as he went.

He vanished from Splash's ken, but there came a confusion of sound as he rolled down the other side of the heap.

Then Splash could see through the hole, and caught sight of the sight that had attracted Tinker's attention, He waited only long enough to withdraw his head and shout down to Dirk.

"Can you work in the dark, old man?"

"You bet I can! I'll stick to this. You go with Tinker!"

Splash scrambled through and rolled down the slope to fetch up with a thud at the bottom. Tinker was already on his feet racing towards the light. Splash came up and followed him. He found Tinker with torch in his hand—the same, he knew, that had been there when Blake and Brank were fighting.

But where were Blake and Brank?

Now, with the aid of the torch, they could see where the ground of the tunnel had caved in but it still seemed that the first fall must have smothered the two struggling antagonists.

Tinker swung the light this way and that. The glare fell on water close to them, a pool that lay at the bottom of a slope revealed by the cave-in.

Then they both saw something at the same moment, something that caused Tinker to give a great cry and Splash to spit out a sharp imprecation—a human face almost submerged by the black water.

Reckless of his footing, Tinker slithered down the slope to the edge of the water. From this point he could throw the light right on to the edge of the water. There could be no mistake of the features of Sexton Blake—pallid, dead-looking.

Splash caught at the lad's arm, but he was already plunging into the water. Holding the torch in one hand, he began swimming towards that white mask that floated ahead.

Splash followed. Together they reached the spot, and now Tinker sobbed audibly and unashamedly as Splash got his arms under Blake's shoulders.

Only then did they see that something else was more submerged beside Blake. They knew it for Brank. But, in that moment of terrible dread, they had no time for anyone but Blake.

Somehow they got him to the edge and up the bank. It was useless to go back after Brank now. He was beyond aid, beyond paying any penalty in this world for the long, cold-blooded string of crimes he had committed.

But Tinker had even forgotten his existence. It was Blake, only Blake, that filled his whole consciousness.

Leaving the torch on the ground, they went to work. Both had had plenty of experience in reviving persons who were apparently drowned, and now they had cause to bless the fact.

Every possible thing was done. Slowly, patiently, steadily, they applied artificial respiration, pausing only long enough to try and discover if even a tiny spark of life still remained in that still form.

Never in his life had Splash Page looked as grim as now. Gone was all his laughing, carefree insouciance. He was as racked with dread as Tinker, and only his own admonition, spoken aloud, kept him from becoming feverishly impetuous.

"Mustn't panic, old son, mustn't panic !" he kept saying, and Tinker rent nodding dumbly.

But at the end of many minutes they could not keep their eyes from meeting. Each read the same dread in those of the other. It was hopeless.

"I tell you it can't be, it can't be!" Tinker groaned at last. "The guv'nor can't go under this way ! We've got to try something else. There must be something! You haven't any brandy, I suppose?"

"Good grief, old son, if I had I'd have got it out long ago ! This is awful. He can't be gone. I can't think of a thing. If I could get out of here to get a doctor."

"No time for that. We've got to think of something! Got to, do you hear me, Splash?"

They were at work again, but suddenly Tinker paused and grabbed Splash's arm until it hurt.

"Listen, Splash? You know that gag of Dirk's?"

Yes. What about it?"

"He carried a full kit of safe breaking stuff. He might have some nitro-glycerine. I'll keep on here. Be quick, Splash! Take the torch."

Splash looked at the lad as if he had suddenly gone mad. But he did not pause to ask or argue. Rising, he made a dive for the heap of debris and scrambled up.

He crawled through the hole and tumbled down to the bottom. Dirk was still sweating at the door of the safe, the circle of holes being almost perfect, so delicate was his touch and so true his sense of distance.

Quickly Splash told him what had happened, and what they wanted. Dirk grabbed the kitbag.

"I don't know what he wants it for, but her is a small bottle of the stuff. I use it for jolting open safe doors. For the love of Mike, handle it carefully, Splash! What the devil does he want it for, though ?"

"Dunno. Do you think there is any hope here?"

"I don't know, but I'll cut this combination clean out before I finish."

"Good luck to you! I'll tell you about Blake when I come back."

He was gone again scrambling up the heap. When he was back beside Tinker, he thrust forward the phial of explosive.

"What are you going to do with it, Tinker?"

"Listen, Splash! I remember the guv'nor once telling me about nitro-glycerine being a powerful heart stimulant. He told me about a case where he had seen it used; but that was in the form of a syringe, and I don't know how it would act if we gave a few drops internally. But I've got a plan."

"Yes—yes?"

Splash was growing more and more excited.

"I'm going to make an incision in the guv'nors arm and start a few drops into his blood stream. We'll massage after that and watch. It's the only hope left, Splash. It's his life at stake."

"Tinker, it's a terrible risk, but if you think—"

"I do think, Splash: The guv'nor would wish it. He wouldn't flinch if he knew."

"That's enough for me, old son."

They worked fast, then. Splash got out his knife, and they opened a vein, for, if the blood stream was moving at all, the vein must take it coursing back to the heart.

Then, very gently, with his own hands, Tinker forced a few drops of the nitro-glycerine into the cut. It was a rough-and-ready operation at best, but it vas a forlorn hope.

They bound the wound hastily, and set to work once more. Minute after minute went by, and still that form lay dank and dead; still those pallid features were like chalk.

Then suddenly Tinker gave a great cry. He bent lower and worked more feverishly than ever. A second cry broke out, but this time it was Splash.

"His eyelids, Tinker! They moved!"

It was true. Slowly—ever so slowly a faint tinge of colour came into the waxen cheeks. The lips that had been blue turned pink again: The lids fluttered once more, and then the eyes opened wide.

Sexton Blake had come back from the very depths of the Valley of the Shadow.

IT was many more minutes before Blake was sitting up.

But, when he did, his first words were for Roxane. Tinker and Splash glanced furtively at each other. They did not want to tell Blake their dread while he was in such a weak state.

But the man's will was dominating even this great weakness that had seized upon him. Somehow he managed to force his mind to sort out the confusion of ideas until he remembered what had happened up to that terrible moment when he had been flung headlong in the midst of a roar of falling roof.

He insisted on scrambling to his feet and then, supported by the two of them, staggered towards the heap of debris.

At the bottom he paused. For the first time lie seemed to remember Brank.

"Brank," he muttered. "Where's Brank?"

"Gone, guv'nor; gone for good! He's finished. We'll attend to him presently."

"I remember. Nev' mind now. Mus' get' Roxane."

The same indomitable will carried him over that heap of rubble and down the other side.

He swayed as Tinker flashed the light on Dirk, who was still grinding away at the drill. He took one look at Blake, and seemed to understand all that had happened.

"Hallo, Blake," he said. "Glad you pulled through. "This won't be long now. We'll be through in another quarter of an hour."

Blake frowned, and pushed forward.

"What're you doin'?" he asked, in the same thick tones.

"Getting through to Roxane," returned Dirk patiently.

"Crazy—crazy fellow! You've got holes, haven't you?"

All three were now looking at Blake. Dirk was turning back to go on with his drilling, when Blake lurched forward and grasped his arm.

"Use your voice," he said, in tones that were more his own. "if she's alive she'll hear you now."

"My sainted aunt!"

The exclamation burst from Dirk, "Of all the chuckle-headed idiots, I'm the prize goat!"

He dropped the drill, and, putting his mouth close to the steel door, began to shout Roxane's name.

Quite as excited, Tinker grabbed up the drill and began to hammer on the steel. The pair of them continued to shout and listen, and then Blake's last remnant of haziness vanished as, seemingly from a great distance, they heard a faint answer.

The excitement grew more and more intense as Dirk shouted once more, and this time they heard Roxana's answer, faint but perfectly clear.

Tinker was jumping up and down like, one gone mad.

"She's alive! She's alive, guv'nor. The air that was going in must have revived her!"

"I'll tear that combination off bodily!" snapped Dirk, but again Blake gave him pause.

"Tear nothing! Don't be a fool, man!" exclaimed Blake. "We can hear her, so she can hear us. Shout through the holes; ask her to give you the correct numbers."

For a moment Dolland looked almost sheepish. The obvious had just not occurred to him. Next second, though, his lips were within an inch or two of the clustering drill-holes.

THE NEXT MOVE
OUR FASCINATING FOUR-AUTHOR SERIAL
BY-

G.H.TEED
GWYN EVANS
ROBERT MURRAY
ANTONY SKENE

"ROXANE—Roxane!" Dirk shouted, enunciating each word distinctly. "Tell—us—the—combination. We—will—let—you—out."

Then he clapped his ear to the holes and stood listening while the others held their breath in the silence. After a pause, they could just faintly hear a far-away-voice, dimmed in a distant whispering by the airtight wails of the vault, pierced as it was only by the circle of tiny holes.

Dirk Dolland looked up.

"She refuses," he said. "She won't say!"

Tinker almost laughed at the look of comical dismay on his face. This refusal, coining one top of his frenzied labour and all the perils they had none through to reach her, had knocked Dolland endways, as Tinker inelegantly put it later.

"Here—let me come," said Blake. "She naturally thinks you may be one of Brank's crowd. Doesn't recognise your voice, Dolland. Perhaps she may mine."

The detective took his place at the ring of holes and, by repeating the question, and by assuring her that it was indeed her friends who wished to release her, was able to convince Roxane that she was not being tricked. Otherwise the courageous girl would have sacrificed her life rather than allow the Doomsman to snatch the spoils of his killing at the eleventh hour.

Blake was for what seemed an unnecessary length of time with his ear at the holes after he had got his message through, and as he turned to the others there was a smile of enlightenment on his strained and anxious face.

"No wonder those numbers wouldn't open it!" he exclaimed. "Roxane's a smart girl all right. 'Frim 865432' was merely a code for the right combination, and she has somehow managed to work it out by turning the wording of the parrot 'Turn off the water, Mr. Rank,' into figures."

"My gosh!" breathed Tinker. "And we thought that only referred to the actual water over the safe!"

"Let's get down to it, Blake!" broke in Dollard, stepping forward to the safe door "Let me do this—after all I started the job."

"Quick, then!" agreed Blake. "I'm none too energetic at the moment; I haven't got over that ducking yet."

And while the ex-cracksman began his operations Blake sat down on the stone floor and watched, leaning back against the wall.

"Right away, Roxane," he called.

I'll give you turns and numbers." came the girl's voice faintly. "Ready?"

"All ready!" yelled Dirk.

"Four right; stop sixty."

Dirk seized the nickelled knot at the combination in his long sensitive fingers; and turned the dial a full four times, to the right, pausing at the division marked 60.

"Yes," he yelled.

"Three left, forty-five."

He swung the dial spun three full turns to left and paused at 45.

"Yes."

"Two right, ninety."

Again the dial spun for two repositions, and then stopped at 90.

"One left, twenty-five. Make haste, I am—"

Her voice ceased, and Blake, Tinker and Splash bent forward anxiously, while Dirk spun the dial back one turn and brought it to rest at 25.

Then he grasped the handle and pressed back. But, tug though he would, the handle refused to budge.

"Something wrong," he muttered, "and yet I did just as she said."

Blake pushed him aside.

"Roxane! Roxane!"

No answer. Not even that faint, distant reply

Again and again he shouted. They all took up the call, and once more Tinker hammered desperately with steel too! But everything was throwback upon there; the inside of the safe was as silent as a tomb.

"Try it again, Dirk." said Blake curtly. "I remember what she said. Four to the right and stop at sixty."

"It won't do any good, Blake, but I'll try."

Once more the knob spun.

"Now to the left and stop at forty five."

Drik obeyed.

"Now two to the right and stop ninety."

The knob whirled.

"Now, one to the left, but don't stop at twenty-five. Stop at twenty-nine. We may have heard wrongly. Five and nine are a bit alike."

They watched tensely while Dirk twisted the knob once more. Then they literally held breath while he once more grasped the handle and turned.

And this time it went back smoothly, and, dragging the heavy door, Dirk Dolland at last revealed the interior of the site that had cost so many lives.

There wasn't much to be seen, after all.

In one corner were some steel dispatches cases which they found later were packed with bearer bonds running into thousands. But the thing that held their attention then was the prone figure of Roxane who lay unconscious as close to the door as she could crawl.

IT was the end; the final goal of their long fight and their strenuous seeking.

The frustrations and difficulties, ties and puzzlement and perils they had gone through to uncover the secret of Frimley's hoard had no disillusionments in the last. There was no anticlimax about the store of wealth which the man from Devil's Island had hidden with such effective cunning behind the cement-fronted safe in the subterranean waterways under his house in Petty France.

It amounted, in paper-values, to two millions sterling and more, but this was to some extent discounted by the serious drop in value of many of the undertakings whose bonds were represented there, by the fallen values of various currencies since the bonds were originally made, and by the fact also that some of the concerns were either bankrupt or in receivership or had had their capital largely written down as a result of serious financial swindles.

But, even at that there was a phenomenal sun now waiting disposal as the result of Blake's campaign against Brank, a sum which its owners had give up for lost.

Frimley had been not only a chief mover, but the treasurer and book keeper of the gang, and it was a curious bent of his character that had caused him to account meticulously not only for all the gang's expenses, but for its income as well—the records of robberies that formed a black-and-white indictment written in his own hand. No wonder, thought Blake as he later examined this record of almost forgotten crimes, that Frimley had devised such a safe hiding-place for his gang's books.

Morgan Gilson had, it appeared, had temporary contact with the gang at one time in a way which, although legally innocent was decidedly risky inasmuch as his customers were crooks. Possibly he had known or suspected this, and possibly not. In any event, Blake reflected, he had paid bitterly for any guilty knowledge. He had been a papermaker in a small way, and had supplied the gang with some of the special paper on which French banknotes are printed.

The outcome of this paper transaction was the historic Cravetti bank frauds, for, complicity in which Gilson had been sent to Devil's island. He had, in effect, been trained, and was innocent in every way except technically of any part in them.

Hence his anxiety, since his escape, in acting on the information which the dying Frimley had given him in Devil's Island; and hence also the complications and difficulties that had arisen, for Brank; alias the Doomsman, had overheard Frimley's words and had so implacably sought the safe also.

But now Brank was dead, both he and his underlings whom he had ruthlessly swept aside as he neared his goal and their usefulness to him loosened—Gilson—with Blake's aid—had triumphed.

It was a somewhat-crestfallen Inspector Thomas, and an at first-doubting Coutts, who were confronted with the proofs of Gilson's innocence in time shape of the meticulous record, in the dead convict's handwriting of the transactions in the paper deal—proofs that were amply substantiated from later entries. But both Coutts and Thomas saw the justice of his case, and promised to be as zealous in setting the wheels in motion on Morgan Gilson's behalf as they had been in carrying out their instructions to arrest him.

As for Gilson himself, the money represented by the stored wealth in Frimley's subterranean safe was a secondary matter to him. He cheerfully handed the whole lot over to Sexton Blake's care; and Blake, just as promptly, apportioned the documents to the various French and Continental banks concerned with them.

"Which is a good riddance, I should say," remarked Tinker, on the day that six of them foregathered at Baker Street to wind up the affair.

"Well, it's good for a couple of columns in the 'Radio,' anyway," said Splash Page, "and maybe a turn over to an inside page as well".

"Illustrated with pictures of the fair Roxane," added Dirk Dolland, bowing with exaggerated courtliness towards the person he named.

Mademoiselle Roxane might have blushed had she belonged to an earlier epoch—or had she been un-used to seeing her picture so often in the "Society Beauties" sections of the illustrated papers. Instead of blushing she replied, with assumed hauteur, "In which case my agents will charge the full reproduction fee, Mr. Dolland or, seeing that it's that sensation-seeking 'Daily Radio', perhaps double."

"Well talking about profile," broke in Blake, "I have told you the bonds and other securities have been handled over as Mr. Gilson desired; but from what I know they cannot all be claimed. Which means that as finder he is going to be entitled to a sum in a few months which ought to set him up for life."

"Or enable him to give us the treat of ours," put in Tinker cheerily. "A couple of Rolls-Royces apiece—"

"What does it feel like to be rich, Gilson, old man?" asked Splash. "What are you going to do with all that money?"

Gilson grinned for a moment as he sought for a reply.

"I'm going to pay to have those tunnels under Petty France bricked up," he said.

THE END

The Christmas Cavalier

A Special Yuletide Detective PLAY by Gwyn Evans

DRAMATIS PERSONÆ

Sexton Blake, the famous Baker Street detective.
Tinker, his assistant.
Mrs. Bardell, his housekeeper.
Det. Inspector Coutts, of Scotland Yard.
John Slade, a Press Photographer.
Miss Sadie K. Bell, of the "Chicago Trumpet".
The Christmas Cavalier, a crook with a sense of humour.

A Special Yuletide Detective PLAY by Gwyn Evans

The Christmas Cavalier

IT is the night of December 18th, at Baker Street.

A cheerful fire crackles in the consulting-room grate. The usually austere atmosphere has been lightened by TINKER'S handiwork until it has an air of festive gaiety.

Festoons of holly ornament the picture-rails and book-cases. Over the door (C) hangs a bunch of mistletoe, while coloured paper-chains run diagonally from the electrolier to each corner. A door (L) leads to BLAKE'S laboratory, irreverently referred to by Tinker as the "Stink Shop."

The mantelpiece has a clock, two or three early Christmas cards from overseas' admirers, and, prominently displayed, a large jade and silver tobacco jar, a gift to the detective from the Rajah of Samarkand. There is also a loud-speaker conveniently placed. The curtain rises disclosing MRS. BARDELL busily engaged in sweeping up a woeful amount of cigar and tobacco ash from the hearthrug into a dustpan. She is humming "Good King Wenceslas" very much out of tune. She is dressed in her favourite *black bombazine dress, and as she straightens after finishing her task, empties the dustpan into the grate.*

MRS. BARDELL: Being 'ousekeeper to a famous criminal incinerator ain't all 'oney. If I've tidied this 'earth once to-day, I've done it twenty times. Wot with the hash on the carpet and the smoke' in the curtains (*she crosses to window, L. C, and gives them a vigorous shake*) it's a wonder I ain't dead from seccotine poisoning.

(*The phone bell rings on desk, R. She coughs and lifts the receiver.*)

Hello! Yes, Nicely thanks, suspector. Yes, I believe Mr. Blake's in. He's carrying out a chimerical impediment—paralysing 'uman blood. (*Pause.*) I'll call 'im if you 'ang on. 'Ere's wishing you the condiments of the season an' a preposterous Noo Year an' many of 'em, suspector.

(*The door of the laboratory opens and the familiar figure of BLAKE, clad in his tattered red dressing-gown enters.*)

MRS. BARDELL (*hand on mouthpiece*): Defective suspector Coutts wants to insult you, sir.

BLAKE (*smiling*): Thank you, Mrs Bardell. (*He takes the receiver. Exit MRS. BARDELL.*) Blake speaking. What's the trouble, Coutts? No. I haven't been out all day or had a chance to see the evening papers. Rather a ticklish experiment, old man. If the stain reacts to Wasser's test, Tooler is guilty and will hang. If it doesn't, then he's due for a happy Christmas. It's an open and shut case. (*Pause.*) Oh, nonsense! It's Splash Page's stunt. Ridiculous! Come round and have a cigar and a night-cap. In the circumstances I shan't go to bed before midnight. I'd like to meet this Christmas Cavalier. (*Pause.*) In half an hour, then. Good-bye!

He replaces the receiver and thoughtfully refills his pipe from the jade jar.

Enter TINKER. He is clad in a warm muffler and heavy overcoat, the shoulders of which are powdered with snow. He shakes his cap and crosses to fireplace.

TINKER: Gosh! It's perishin' cold, guv'nor. (*Stretches hand towards fire.*)

BLAKE: Enjoy yourself, young 'un?

TINKER (*removing outer garments and sinking into a chair*): Rather! You ought to have seen Beery as Long John Silver socking the other pirates. (*He grins reminiscently and sings.*) "Fifteen men on a dead man's chest. Yo ho! and a bottle of rum."

(*Suddenly his face becomes grave.*) By the way, guv'nor, what's all this in the evening papers? I caught a glimpse of the placards as I dropped off the bus. "Challenge to Sexton Blake." What's it all about?

BLAKE (*shrugging*): Coutts has just been ringing me on the same subject. Some newspaper stunt or other. Read it out to me, young 'un. My eyes are a bit tired. I've been in the lab most of the evening.

TINKER (*picking up a copy of the "Evening Wireless" then glancing at the other*): You don't look yourself, to-night, guv'nor. You've been overdoing it on this Tooler case. Never mind. Christmas is coming and—Hello!

(*He leans forward excitedly.*) Great Scott! Guv'nor look this (*pointing to headlines and reading.*) "AUDACIOUS CHALLENGE TO SEXTON BLAKE. THIEF'S THREAT TO FAMOUS DETECTIVE. WHO IS THE CHRISTMAS CAVALIER?"

BLAKE: H'm, that's what our friend Coutts wanted to know. Go on, read it, young 'un.

TINKER (*reading*): "The 'Evening Wireless' is not in the habit of publishing anonymous letters, but in the special circumstances it prints the following amazing missive received late this evening signed by that elusive criminal, the Christmas Cavalier. This audacious crook whose recent exploits in the West-End include the theft of the famous Margrave emeralds, the robbery of the London Bullion Bank, etc," (*looking up*). One in the eye for old Coutts, guv'nor, eh? (*Resuming.*) "It will be recalled that the one clue, which the police have been able to discover after each of his daring robberies is a gilt-edged visiting card engraved with the words MANY THANKS, and signed THE CHRISTMAS CAVALIER,"

BLAKE: An engaging rascal, Tinker. I can't say I sympathise much with the victims. Margrave is a poisonous fellow, and should have been inside years ago. AS for the banks—they seem a bit too impersonal to excite my sympathy just now.

TINKER (*relighting his pipe*): But look at this, guv'nor. The blighter's had the cheek to challenge you.

(*Reading.*)

"To the Editor of the 'Evening Wireless':

"Dear Sir,

In his recent article on Modern Criminology in your paper, Sexton Blake states that the majority of criminals are of limited intelligence and almost totally devoid of a sense of humour and sportsmanship.

"I beg to protest against this slur on the profession to which I have the honour to belong, and will prove that one criminal, at least, has sufficient humour and sportsmanship to challenge him.

"Between the hours of 10 p.m. and midnight on Wednesday, December 18th"—(*TINKER lowers his paper and his voice.*) That's to-night, guv'nor! Where were we? December 18th—"I propose to steal his favourite jade tobacco jar from his consulting room. It was, I believe, a gift from the Rajah of Samarkand, and is a treasured possession. Mr. Blake is at liberty to take any precaution he likes, my sole stipulation being that he leaves the jar in its accustomed place on the mantelshelf."

(*TINKER lowers paper again.*) How the dickens does he know that, guv'nor?

BLAKE: We have had many queer clients here in the past, young'un.

TINKER:The blessed cheek of the man! (*Continuing.*) "This is a sporting challenge to Mr. Blake, to whose great detective abilities I hasten to pay tribute. If I succeed in stealing the jar before midnight, I shall expect him to donate the sum of one thousand pounds to St. Stephen's Hospital. If, on the other hand, I fail, I shall denote a similar sum to any charity Mr. Blake cares to designate.

"The money, I hasten to add, is my own, and not nefariously acquired."

BLAKE (*laughing*): Most admirable scruples, my dear Tinker.

TINKER: "In the circumstances, I regret that this letter must be anonymous, but trust to your indulgence to print it in return for the exclusive rights.

"Wishing you the compliments of the season,
"I subscribe myself,
"THE CHRISTMAS CAVALIER."

TINKER (*tossing aside the paper*): The fellow must be crazy, guv'nor. How the deuce does he think he'll get away with it? (*The phone bell rings and TINKER crosses over to the receiver.*) Hello! Yes! Tinker speaking. (*Pause, then*): That you, Splash? Sure I've seen the letter. Cheek, I call it. He hasn't an earthly. Who? The guv'nor? He's not worrying. More

amused than anything—What? Hang on a sec. 'I'll ask him. (*Turns to BLAKE.*) It's Splash of the "Daily Radio," guv'nor. Wants an interview and wants to know if you'd object to a Press photographer taking a picture of the tobacco jar and consulting-room.

BLAKE (*reaches out for the receiver*): 'Evening, Splash. Yes. Very amusing. No, don't make a stilted interview. I'm looking forward to the Cavalier's visit. Certainly I accept his challenge. No, no special precautions. He's welcome to try. (*Pause*) Well, if you can guarantee him, of course I've no objection to a photographer. What's his name? Slade? All right, send him over. Certainly, my dear fellow, I'll phone you at once. Immediately after midnight, win or lose.

How long will it take the photographer to get here? Fine, I'll expect him. Good-bye. (*He hangs up.*) Splash seems excited. He's going to feature the story complete with photographs. Better wash and brush up, young 'un, to look your best for the front page. Slade will be here in ten minutes with the camera

TINKER (*glances at himself in the mantelpiece mirror and combs his rebellious hair*) Seriously, guv'nor. What are you going to do about this Cavalier, chap? They say he's a marvel at disguising himself, and Splash Page has a theory that he is a woman.

(*A knock sounds. Enter MRS. BARDELL.*)

TINKER (*with a chuckle*): The Laughing Cavalier.

MRS. BARDELL (*placing a tray of hot coffee and sandwiches on the table*): And would you be wishful of any more service afore I expires, sir?

BLAKE: No, thanks, Mrs. B. You trot along to bed. I'll deal with any visitors. You've had a busy day. Good-night.

MRS. BARDELL: Good-night, sir. You'll find your clean laundry in the wardrobe, Mr. Tinker. I suppose you want breakfast at the usual time?

TINKER: Thanks, Mrs. B. Good-night—don't forget mushrooms in the morning. (*Exit MRS. BARDELL.*)

TINKER (*helps himself to a sandwich and pours out two cups of coffee*): We look like having one exciting night, guv'nor—or do you think this Cavalier chap's bluffing?

BLAKE: No, young 'un, I don't. His last two efforts were faultlessly planned and executed. He is that dangerous variety—a crook with a sense of humour. But, like all criminals, he suffers from a touch of megalomania which will undoubtedly prove his undoing.

(*The front-door bell rings. TINKER hurriedly gulps down his coffee and starts for the door*)

TINKER: Look out for the jade jar, guv'nor. This may be him.

BLAKE: (*rising to his feet and pointing to a narrow strand of flex running from behind the jade jar to a plug in the wall*): I have taken some elementary precautions, young 'un. Whoever touches this jar before midnight is likely to get a nasty shock.

TINKER (*chuckling*): Good old guv'nor. We ought to have some fun before the night's out. (*Exit.*)

(*BLAKE readjusts the flex unobtrusively and relights his pipe. Enter TINKER, accompanied by JOHN SLADE, a stoop-shouldered man with horn-rimmed spectacles, a drooping moustache and a Press camera slung from his shoulders.*)

TINKER: Mr. Slade of the "Radio," guv'nor.

BLAKE: Come in, Mr. Slade. Wretchedly cold night, isn't it? Care for a whisky-and-soda?

SLADE (*unslipping his camera*): Thanks very much, sir, the wind's in the East and I reckon we'll have snow before morning.

(*TINKER crosses to sideboard and mixes two drinks, while Slade busies himself with camera and flashlight gun.*)

SLADE: Mr. Page said you would not mind posing for a couple of photos. I shan't keep you long. Nice of you to receive me like this.

(*TINKER places a glass of whisky on the table and offers one to Blake.*)

SLADE (*raising his glass*): Good health and a Merry Christmas, gentlemen. (*Turning curiously to the mantelpiece*) Is that the er—tobacco jar, sir?

BLAKE: Yes. Fine piece of jade, isn't it? Our friend the Cavalier is evidently a connoisseur. Let me know when you are ready.

SLADE: If you'd stand just as you are, sir, the head a bit more to the right—that's it, sir.

(*BLAKE obligingly takes required pose. Business with camera.*)

TINKER (*hovering anxiously near SLADE as he loads the magnesium flare (sotto voce)*): Watch out for the jar, guv'nor. You never know—

SLADE: One moment, please. Ready?

(*He presses the trigger of the flashgun. There is a blinding flash and a dull report.*)

TINKER: Look out for the jar, guv'nor. Quick! Before he grabs it.

(*The magnesium smoke clears and BLAKE frowns.*)

BLAKE: Don't be silly, Tinker. The jar's safe enough. Thank you, Mr. Slade.

SLADE (*with a grin*): They call me mug-snatcher in the office, Mr. Blake, but believe me I've no intention of snatching *that* mug. (*Points to jar.*) Leastways not when you're around. Talk about putting one's head in the lion's mouth—this Cavalier fellow's got a nerve. (*He packs his paraphernalia*) Must be getting back, sir. The rag's waiting. Very many thanks, and if this Cavalier chap turns up please give us a ring. A scoop like this would be a nice Christmas box for the Street.

BLAKE: All right, Slade. I shan't forget. Good-night.

(*Exit SLADE.*)

TINKER: Phew! Guv'nor. That flashgun gave me a nasty turn. For a moment I thought Slade was the Cavalier. It would have been easy enough to snatch it when our eyes were dazzled.

BLAKE: Nonsense, my lad. Where are your eyes! Slade is genuine enough. Didn't you notice the brown hypo stains on his finger nails, distinct from nicotine stains of a smoker!

TINKER: Sorry, guv'nor, but I got a bit rattled. After all, nobody knows what this Cavalier is like. As Splash says, it may be a woman and in that case—

(*There is a thunderous rat-tat-tat at the door.*)

TINKER (*starting*): Gosh! That must be Coutts, guv'nor. Wonder what he'll have to say. (*Exit.*)

(*BLAKE takes a further look at the wire flex and sinks into his favourite chair.*)

(*Enter COUTTS, clad in his familiar overcoat, bowler hat, cocked aggressively as usual on his bullet head. He does not remove it for some moments after his entry.*)

BLAKE: Hallo, Coutts! Come in. You'll find the cigars at your elbow. Help yourself. Whisky?

COUTTS (*plunging himself into a chair and hoisting one pudgy leg over the other and not till then removing his bowler*): Thanks, Blake. Jove! It's cold. (*He warms his hands at the crackling fire.*) What *is* all this nonsense in to-night's paper? I'm not so sure the Editor isn't committing a public mischief printing a letter like that.

BLAKE: Try pulling him in as accessory before the fact, Coutts; He'd revel in the publicity.

COUTTS (*snorting*): These newspapermen! They're all the same, Blake. I'm surprised you have any use for them. Nothing but a lot of armchair theorists. Take this chap the Christmas Cavalier, for instance. He's nothing but a cheap crook out for a bit of notoriety. There's nothing clever or original in his methods. He's probably a 'Varsity man who's been seeing too many crook films. (*He snuggles deeper into his chair and lights a cigar.*) In fact I've got a theory about him—

TINKER: An armchair theory in fact, eh, Couttsy?

COUTTS (*coughing aggressively*): Never you mind, my lad. The point is, Blake, what are you going to do about it? It's after eleven o'clock now and I don't mind telling you I'll keep you company until the time's up. If he will, which I very much doubt.

BLAKE: Nice of you, old man, but I'm quite capable of looking after myself I think.

COUTTS: But hang it all, man. You must take some precautions. I'll admit this Cavalier is clever enough in his way. If by any chance he succeeded in pinching the jar, you'd be the laughing stock of London. Be sensible, Blake. If you like, I'll get half a dozen plain clothes men to surround the house, and if he tries any funny business—

BLAKE: Thanks for the offer, Coutts, but this is a duel between the Christmas Cavalier and Sexton Blake. I've accepted his challenge in a sporting spirit, I hope. Besides, a lot of plain-clothes men cluttering the up the place would confuse the issue. Can you vouch for your own detectives even?

COUTTS: What the devil are you insinuating, Blake?

BLAKE: Nothing. But with the Cavalier I cannot afford to take chances. Don't forget it is *my* reputation that is at stake, Coutts. I happen to know that the Cavalier is a past master at disguising himself. In the Bullion Bank affair his make-up as an old charwoman deceived everybody, and his escape from the Hotel Rochester in the role of a policeman was a touch of genius. The Cavalier is no ordinary crook, Coutts. You underestimate his intelligence.

COUTTS: Nonsense. By the way, if that's the jar all the fuss is about, why don't you put it in a safer place. It's tempting Providence. (*He rises and stretches out a hand towards the jade jar.*)

BLAKE: Stop! Put up your hands! (*Rises suddenly and produces an automatic.*)

COUTTS (*amazed*): What the devil's the matter with you, Blake?

BLAKE: I can afford to take no chances, my dear fellow. My reputation is at stake. If the Cavalier can fool the Flying Squad by disguising himself as a policeman, you won't fool me by disguising yourself as a plain clothes inspector.

TINKER: Great Scott, guv'nor! Then, you mean—

BLAKE: Keep your hands, well up, my friend (*as COUTTS makes a half-threatening movement*) Tinker! Turn down his left sleeve.

COUTTS (*spluttering*): Good heavens, Blake, are you crazy? Don't, you know me, you fool! I tell you—

BLAKE (*he turns to his assistant*): Tinker, see if there is a red and blue tattoo mark of a swallow-tailed butterfly on the inside of his forearm with the initials H.A.C. above it.

COUTTS (*wrathfully*): I protest. This is an outrage, Blake. I shall report this to the Commissioner.

(*TINKER, in response to Blake's gesture, turns down the foaming Yard man's sleeve.*)

BLAKE: I am taking no chance. It is always fatal to underestimate one's opponent.

(*COUTTS struggles a little bit is cowed by the menacing round O of Blake's automatic.*)

TINKER: Yes, guv'nor. The butterfly's here all right. *And* the initials.

BLAKE: Good! Dip your handkerchief in Coutts' whisky and rub the tattoo mark. I knew a tattooed lady once who earned a fortune by sticking cigarette picture transfers on her shapely limbs. You never can tell.

(*TINKER grins and, dipping his handkerchief, proceeds to rub COUTTS' forearm.*)

COUTTS: You'll hear more of this outrage, Blake. Mark my words!

BLAKE: Are there any marks on the handkerchief young 'un?

TINKER (*flourishing handkerchief*): No marks, guv'nor. Good! Sorry to appear so high-handed, Coutts, but I can't afford to take risks to-night. You've come off with, shall we say, flying colours, or no marks.

COUTTS: This is an assault, Blake. Holding up a police officer in the execution of his duty. By Heaven, you'll hear more of this, or I'm a Dutchman. I've never been so insulted in my life.

BLAKE (*pocketing his pistol*): I apologise, Coutts, but as you yourself said, my reputation is at stake. It's lucky I remembered where you had that tattooing done when we were in Ceylon together.

COUTTS (*angrily*): Pah! You can stew in your own juice now for all I care. If your precious tobacco jar is pinched, don't come to the Yard for assistance. I'm through.

(*He crams his bowler on his head and—exit—slamming the door.*)

TINKER (*maliciously singing*):

"Oh, where the spicey breezes
Blow soft o'er Ceylon's isle
And every prospect pleases
And only Coutts is vile."

BLAKE (*musingly, as he relights his pipe*): No chances, Tinker. Coutts was right. My reputation is definitely at stake to-night. (*He sinks wearily into a chair.*)

TINKER: You look all in, guv'nor. You've been working too hard. Dash it, you haven't been to bed for forty-eight hours.

BLAKE: Perhaps you're right, young 'un. My nerves are a little frayed! I'm sorry I upset Coutts. However, he'll get over it. (*Yawning. The clock on the mantelpiece chimes the half-hour.*) Eleven-thirty, young 'un. Half an hour to go.

TINKER: Let me mix you your cordial, guv'nor. It'll buck you up. You'll need all your wits for the next half-hour.

(*He crosses to door of Laboratory L exit.*) *Blake yawns again. Stirs up the fire in the grate and half closes his eyes as he relaxes in his chair. A muffled crash is heard in the lab. (off).* (*Enter TINKER; carrying a glass of fizzing green drink and stirring it with a glass rod.*)

TINKER: Here you are, guv'nor. Quinine tonic for tired tissues. Drink it up.

BLAKE (*jumping to his feet and producing his automatic*): Stop where you are !

TINKER: But, great Scott, guv'nor, what's the matter?

BLAKE: I am taking no chances. *How do I know you are Tinker?*

TINKER: But good Lor', guv'nor, don't be silly! I've been with you all the evening and—

BLAKE (*with a grim smile*): How do I know that the Tinker who left here five minutes ago is the one here now? The Cavalier is a master of disguise. What was that crash in there?

TINKER (*confused*): Why-er-nothing, guv'nor. I knocked over a bottle as I switched out the light. Surely you're not suggesting I am the Christmas Cavalier?

BLAKE (*tensely*): How do I know that the drink is not drugged. I am taking no chances. If the contents of that glass are harmless, prove it! (*He raises his gun threateningly.*) I give you ten seconds to drink. One—two—three—

TINKER: But, guv'nor, don't be absurd. What's come over you tonight? You're as nervous as a cat on hot bricks. It's ridiculous.

BLAKE (*inexorably*): Six—seven—eight—

TINKER (*pulling a wry face*): O.K. if you want proof. Here goes. (*He drains the glass with a grimace*) *Tense silence for a few moments.*

BLAKE (*lowering his gun*): Sorry, young 'un. (*He pats Tinker,s shoulder affectionately.*) You're right. My nerves are ragged tonight. I've been doing too much lately.

TINKER (*thawing at once*): O.K. guv'nor. After all, I can't blame you. I'm a bit keyed up myself.

The clock chimes again.

TINKER: Quarter to midnight, guv'nor. Do you think he'll come?

The phone bell shrills violently. Tinker makes to answer it but Blake restrains him.

BLAKE: Let me. (*Lifting receiver*). Hallo! Yes. Blake speaking. Who's that? .... Good .... you're on your way, eh? Very well, I am expecting you .... Splendid. Au revoir .... (*He replaces the receiver.*)

TINKER: Who was that, guv'nor?

BLAKE: That, young 'un, was the Christmas Cavalier. He rang up to say that he was on his way and would be here before midnight.

TINKER: Great Scott! Guv'nor, he's got the nerve of the devil.

BLAKE: Or a *she*-devil, Tinker. The voice at the other end of the wire was the voice of a woman!

TINKER: A woman, guv'nor! Then Splash Page was right after all.

BLAKE: We shall see—what we shall see, young 'un.

(*A wild, unearthly scream bubbling with terror rings out and is followed by a heavy thud outside the consulting room door.*)

TINKER: Gosh! Guv'nor, what's that? It can't be—

BLAKE: Go and see, Tinker. I'm ready if it is our friend The Cavalier.

(*He takes his stand with his back to the fire and his hand closes over his gun in the pocket of his dressing gown. Exit TINKER.*)

Blake once more arranges the wire flex and murmurs:

BLAKE: Yes, quite ready.

(*Enter TINKER in alarm.*)

TINKER: Quick, guv'nor. There's a woman huddled on the floor of the landing. She's been murdered—stabbed. What'll we do?

(*BLAKE dashes out door. His feet are heard as he runs half-way down the stairs that lead to the hall.*)

(*TINKER crosses over to armchair and arranges cushions, etc.*)

(*Enter BLAKE. In his arms he carries the limp figure of a woman in black. She is heavily veiled and is moaning feebly.*)

(*He places her on the armchair, and pressing his handkerchief to the woman's breast, shows it stained an ominous crimson.*)

(**BLAKE**, *glancing keenly at the handkerchief, slowly lights his pipe. The girl moans, rises feebly on one elbow then gasps.*)

GIRL: Save me! For Heaven's sake save me! That awful man! The Man with the Green Mask.

(*She shudders convulsively.*)

BLAKE (*harshly*): Who are you? How did you get here?

GIRL: Oh, save me from him, Mr. Blake! Hide me before he comes. I'm—I'm terrified. That ghastly green mask!

BLAKE: How did you get here?

GIRL: I—I walked; or rather ran all the way from Baker Street Station. Please, please, don't let Green Mask get me!

BLAKE (*with a grim smile*): He won't get you, young lady. Sit up! Don't lie to me!

(*He covers her with his automatic.*)

TINKER (*horrified*): Guv'nor. Can't you see she's wounded? She may be dying.

BLAKE (*tensely*): Nonsense. Red ink never has nor never will look like blood. Look at her shoes, spotless. So you ran all the way through the sleet and slush of Baker Street, eh? Remarkable.

GIRL (*sitting up and with a hard metallic laugh*): O.K., Mr. Blake. The laff's on you, I guess. You're too slick for me, but I just had to get here before midnight.

TINKER (*in blank astonishment*): My stars! The Christmas Cavalier.

GIRL (*laughing*): That's it, I reckon. Don't

be too hard on me, Mr. Blake. I admit I'm an impostor, but I just had to get into your consulting room to-night. You see, I'm an American journalist My name's Sadie K. Bell of the "Chicago Trumpet" and I wanted to interview the great British Sleuth exclusively for my paper. I read the Christmas Cavalier's letter in the noos to-night, and I reckoned it would make a peach of a story if I got your views. Tell me, has he been here yet? (*crossing over to fireplace*). And say, is that the Jade Jar?

BLAKE (*grimly*): I should advise you not to touch it, young lady, or you'll be badly burned. There are nearly a thousand volts of electricity in that jar.

GIRL: Say, you ain't so dumb, Mr. Blake! I reckon it'll be one wise guy that puts one over on you.

BLAKE: Good-night, Miss Bell. I'm sorry I cannot grant you an interview. You'll be able to read all about it in the "Daily Radio" to-morrow. I've promised them an exclusive story.

GIRL: Waal! Say if that ain't too bad, and I've ruined a good frock, too. Guess I'll charge it up to the office.

BLAKE: Show Miss Bell out, Tinker. Good-night, young lady.

GIRL: Good-night, and a merry Christmas, Mr. Blake. I reckon you're cute. Anyways I got my story!

(*TINKER ushers her to the door and exit GIRL.*)

TINKER: Five minutes to go and then zero hour. Do you think he'll come?

BLAKE: Yes, he'll come, young 'un. The Cavalier always keeps his word. That's why I'm taking no chances.

TINKER (*fidgeting aimlessly suddenly crosses over to the window*): Let's have a spot of music. This is getting on my nerves, guv'nor.

(*For a few moments the strains of a waltz tune are heard. The wind rattles the window-panes, and there is a tense hush of expectancy about the cosy consulting room. Suddenly the music fades out, and the familiar booming notes of Big Ben begin to chime. DING-DONG—DING-DONG*).

TINKER: Time, guv'nor! Zero hour! The Christmas Cavalier has funked it! (*Pause*).

(*Then, as the sonorous strokes begin to strike TINKER counts softly.*) ONE—TWO—THREE—FOUR—FIVE—SIX. You've won, guv'nor. You've won!

BLAKE (*leisurely rising to his feet*): Yes, I've won, Tinker. Stick up your hands! This gun spits death, and I'm in a nasty mood to-night!

TINKER (*retreating a step beneath the menace of the automatic*): But, guv'nor, have you gone mad? You've acted so strangely to-night that—

THE OTHER: I am not your guv'nor, Tinker. (*With that he removes a well-fitting iron-grey wig. The lean face alters suddenly, and a stranger with dancing grey eyes and fair curly hair is revealed*).

TINKER: Holy Mike! The Christmas Cavalier!

CAVALIER: At your service. Tell Mr. Sexton Blake I shall expect his cheque in the morning to be made payable to the hospital.

TINKER: But look here, you scoundrel! What have yon done with the guv'nor?

CAVALIER: Oh, he's quite safe. You see, I came in half an hour before your arrival. I'm afraid Blake didn't expect me. He was so keen on what Mrs. Bardell calls chemical paralysis that it was easy enough. Beyond a nasty headache he'll be all right in the morning, I guess.

You'll find him gagged and bound in the process room of the laboratory.

(*There is a tap at the door.*)

CAVALIER: Not a word. Remember I have you covered, and I shoot to kill.

(*He dons wig and pockets gun, keeping TINKER covered with it through dressing-gown pocket.*)

CAVALIER: Yes. Who is that?

VOICE OFF: Oh, it's only me, Mr. Blake. I've got the pallerpitations that bad. I 'eard a dreadful scream and wondered if everythink was orlright. My pore 'eart is a flutterin' like a bird in a gilded cage, an' I'm tremblin' like an aspirin. If I only 'ad a drop o' brandy.

CAVALIER (*aside to Tinker*): Not a word or I'll plug you. (*Aloud*): Come in Mrs. B.

(*Enter a familiar figure clad in flannel dressing-gown and an aureole of curl papers.*)

MRS. BARDELL: O me pore 'eart, sir. I 'ates disturbin' yer in your sluicin' and seductions, but the pallerpitations are that bad. (*Sinks into a chair.*)

CAVALIER: That's all right, Mrs. B. Tinker, pour Mrs. B. out a drop of brandy from the decanter. And mind—I'm watching you. (*His finger on the trigger suggestively.*)

(TINKER, *crossing to sideboard, pours out brandy into glass*).

(CAVALIER, *crosses to Jade Jar on mantelshelf and lifts it carefully.*)

TINKER: Say when Mrs. B. (*He has a siphon in his hand.*)

MRS. BARDELL (*rising suddenly to full height and producing a heavy colt revolver*): When! Hands up, my laughing cavalier!

CAVALIER (*spins round*); His hand starts too late for his dressing-gown pocket.

(*MRS. BARDELL snatches off a grotesque wig with his left hand and reveals the iron-grey hair and features of SEXTON BLAKE.*)

(*The stumpy figure straightens, and the CAVALIER slowly lifts his hands above his head.*)

TINKER: Guv'nor! By all that's wonderful. How on earth—

SEXTON BLAKE: You should have paid more attention to your knots, my friend. My jar, I think!

(*BLAKE picks up the jar with one hand a smiles benignly on the other.*)

Just write me out cheque for a thousand pounds, will you, and we'll call it a day.

CAVALIER: Gosh! Blake! You're a sportsman! (*Seats himself at desk and draws out a cheque-book.*) What charity shall I make it payable to, Blake?

BLAKE (*smiling*): Oh, make it payable to Mrs Maria Bardell. She deserves it. Charity begins at home at Christmas-time.

CURTAIN

BIBLIOGRAPHY

THE STORIES INCLUDED IN THIS ANTHOLOGY PREVIOUSLY APPEARED IN THE FOLLOWING
PUBLICATIONS:

THE PENNY PICTORIAL

Issue 545	Well Matched!	1909
Issue 546	The Bara Diamond	1909
Issue 547	Parried!	1909
Issue 548	Quits!	1909
Issue 549	The Removal of Mr. Soames	1909
Issue 550	The Case of the Louis Quinz Snuff-Box	1909
Issue 551	Abducted!	1909
Issue 552	Blake Scores!	1909
Issue 603	A Mysterious Disappearance	1910
Issue 604	Trapped!	1910
Issue 606	The Great Bridge Tunnel Mystery	1911
Issue 707	Found Guilty!	1911

UNION JACK

Issue 473	The Great Bank Fraud	1912
Issue 525	Tinker's Terrible Test	1913
Issue 529	The Sacred Sphere	1913
Issue 554	The Boundary Raiders	1914
Issue 672	The Inari Treasure	1916
Issue 794	Waldo the Wonder-Man	1918
Issue 837	A Duel to the Death	1919
Issue 1182	A Mystery in Motley	1926
Issue 1206	Lord of the Ape-Men	1926
Issue 1362	The Gnomid	1929
Issue 1378	They Shall Repay!	1930
Issue 1519	Suspended From Duty	1932

The Next Move was serialised weekly in Union Jack issues 1516-1529, from 1932 to 1933.

DETECTIVE WEEKLY

| Issue 95 | The Christmas Cavalier | 1934 |